100
INDIAN STORIES

100 INDIAN STORIES

A FEAST OF REMARKABLE SHORT FICTION
FROM THE 19TH, 20TH, AND 21ST CENTURIES

FOREWORD BY RUSKIN BOND

~

EDITED BY A. J. THOMAS

ALEPH BOOK COMPANY
An independent publishing firm
promoted by *Rupa Publications India*

First published in India in 2025
by Aleph Book Company
7/16 Ansari Road, Daryaganj
New Delhi 110 002

This edition copyright © Aleph Book Company 2025.
Copyright in the individual stories vests in the respective
authors/translators/proprietors.
Foreword copyright © Ruskin Bond 2025.
'The Indian Short Story' copyright © A. J. Thomas 2025.

The notes and acknowledgements on p. 812 constitute an
extension of the copyright page.

All rights reserved.

This is a work of fiction. Names, characters, places,
and incidents are either the product of the authors'
imagination or are used fictitiously and any resemblance
to any actual persons, living or dead, events, or locales is
entirely coincidental.

No part of this publication may be reproduced,
transmitted, or stored in a retrieval system, in any form
or by any means, without permission in writing from
Aleph Book Company.

For sale in the Indian subcontinent only.

ISBN: 978-81-19635-84-9

1 3 5 7 9 10 8 6 4 2

Printed in India.

This book is sold subject to the condition that it shall
not, by way of trade or otherwise, be lent, resold, hired
out, or otherwise circulated without the publisher's prior
consent in any form of binding or cover other than that
in which it is published.

CONTENTS

Foreword — xiii
RUSKIN BOND

The Indian Short Story — xv
A. J. THOMAS

1. **REBATI** — 1
   FAKIR MOHAN SENAPATI
   Translated from the Odia by Leelawati Mohapatra, Paul St-Pierre, and K. K. Mohapatra

2. **THE KABULIWALLAH** — 10
   RABINDRANATH TAGORE
   Translated from the Bengali by Arunava Sinha

3. **THE OFFERING** — 16
   PRAMATHA CHAUDHURI
   Translated from the Bengali by Arunava Sinha

4. **MAHESH** — 25
   SARAT CHANDRA CHATTOPADHYAY
   Translated from the Bengali by Arunava Sinha

5. **THE SHROUD** — 33
   MUNSHI PREMCHAND
   Translated from the Urdu by Muhammad Umar Memon

6. **THE STORY OF A CROW LEARNING PROSODY** — 40
   SUBRAMANIA BHARATI
   Translated from the Tamil by P. Raja

7. **A LETTER** — 43
   K. M. MUNSHI
   Translated from the Gujarati by Rita Kothari

8. **THE ACHARYA'S WIFE** — 46
   MASTI VENKATESHA IYENGAR
   Translated from the Kannada by Ramachandra Sharma

9. **EINSTEIN AND INDUBALA** — 54
   BIBHUTIBHUSHAN BANDYOPADHYAY
   Translated from the Bengali by Arunava Sinha

10. **THE MADIGA GIRL** — 66
    CHALAM
    Translated from the Telugu by Dasu Krishnamoorty and Tamraparni Dasu

11. THE GOVERNOR'S VISIT 73
KALKI
Translated from the Tamil by Gowri Ramnarayan

12. DHANAVANTRI'S HEALING 78
KUVEMPU
Translated from the Kannada by Chandan Gowda

13. THE GOLD COIN 85
LAXMANRAO SARDESSAI
Translated from the Portuguese by Paul Melo e Castro

14. THE DISCOVERY OF TELENAPOTA 90
PREMENDRA MITRA
Translated from the Bengali by Arunava Sinha

15. AN ASTROLOGER'S DAY 98
R. K. NARAYAN

16. A LIFE 102
BUDDHADEVA BOSE
Translated from the Bengali by Arunava Sinha

17. THE BLUE LIGHT 119
VAIKOM MUHAMMAD BASHEER
Translated from the Malayalam by O. V. Usha

18. THE FLOOD 128
THAKAZHI SIVASANKARA PILLAI
Translated from the Malayalam by O. V. Usha

19. ON THE RIVERBANK 133
S. K. POTTEKKATT
Translated from the Malayalam by A. J. Thomas

20. THE SOLUTION 136
GOPINATH MOHANTY
Translated from the Odia by Leelawati Mohapatra, Paul St-Pierre, and K. K. Mohapatra

21. THE HOLY BANYAN 141
BAMACHARAN MITRA
Translated from the Odia by Leelawati Mohapatra, Paul St-Pierre, and K. K. Mohapatra

22. A FEAST FOR THE BOSS 149
BHISHAM SAHNI
Translated from the Hindi by Poonam Saxena

23.	OF FISTS AND RUBS ISMAT CHUGHTAI *Translated from the Urdu by Muhammad Umar Memon*	156
24.	PORTRAIT OF A LADY KHUSHWANT SINGH	164
25.	LAAJWANTI RAJINDER SINGH BEDI *Translated from the Urdu by Muhammad Umar Memon*	167
26.	REPLY-PAID CARD DINANATH NADIM *Translated from the Kashmiri by Neerja Mattoo*	177
27.	THE NIGHT OF THE FULL MOON K. S. DUGGAL *Translated from the Punjabi by Khushwant Singh*	182
28.	GOLD FROM THE GRAVES ANNA BHAU SATHE *Translated from the Marathi by Vernon Gonsalves*	187
29.	TWO MAGICIANS SATYAJIT RAY *Translated from the Bengali by Arunava Sinha*	193
30.	SAVAGE HARVEST MOHINDER SINGH SARNA *Translated from the Punjabi by Navtej Sarna*	202
31.	INSPECTOR MATADEEN ON THE MOON HARISHANKAR PARSAI *Translated from the Hindi by C. M. Naim*	209
32.	THE TIMES HAVE CHANGED KRISHNA SOBTI *Translated from the Hindi by Poonam Saxena*	217
33.	LORD OF THE RUBBLE MOHAN RAKESH *Translated from the Hindi by Poonam Saxena*	222
34.	URVASHI AND JOHNNY MAHASWETA DEVI *Translated from the Bengali by Arunava Sinha*	230
35.	COUNTLESS HITLERS VIJAYDAN DETHA *Translated from the Rajasthani by Christi A. Merrill and Kailash Kabir*	248

36. BEYOND THE FOG — 257
QURRATULAIN HYDER
Translated from the Urdu by Muhammad Umar Memon

37. KING MARUTI — 272
VYANKATESH MADGULKAR
Translated from the Marathi by Shanta Gokhale

38. MIRROR OF ILLUSION — 276
NIRMAL VERMA
Translated from the Hindi by Geeta Kapur

39. THE HANGING — 287
O. V. VIJAYAN
Translated from the Malayalam by A. J. Thomas

40. TRISHANKU — 293
MANNU BHANDARI
Translated from the Hindi by Poonam Saxena

41. NAADAR SIR — 306
SUNDARA RAMASWAMY
Translated from the Tamil by Malini Seshadri

42. THE BEGGARS AT THE DARGAH — 319
TAJ BEGUM RENZU
Translated from the Kashmiri by Neerja Mattoo

43. RATS — 324
BHABENDRA NATH SAIKIA
Translated from the Assamese by Gayatri Bhattacharyya

44. A DEATH IN DELHI — 330
KAMLESHWAR
Translated from the Hindi by Poonam Saxena

45. MOUNI — 336
U. R. ANANTHAMURTHY
Translated from the Kannada by H. Y. Sharada Prasad

46. JOB'S CHILDREN — 351
VIMALA DEVI
Translated from the Portuguese by Paul Melo e Castro

47. VISION — 360
M. T. VASUDEVAN NAIR
Translated from the Malayalam by A. J. Thomas

48. GREEN SPARROWS — 372
AJEET COUR
Translated from the Punjabi by the author

49. MRS CROCODILE 379
   MANOJ DAS
   Translated from the Odia by Leelawati Mohapatra, Paul St-Pierre, and K. K. Mohapatra

50. THE PROSPECT OF FLOWERS 386
   RUSKIN BOND

51. YAATRA 391
   TURAGA JANAKI RANI
   Translated from the Telugu by Dasu Krishnamoorty and Tamraparni Dasu

52. A BLACK HOLE 396
   JAYANT VISHNU NARLIKAR
   Translated from the Marathi by Anil Zankar

53. HOUSE NUMBER 402
   KAVANA SARMA
   Translated from the Telugu by Dasu Krishnamoorty and Tamraparni Dasu

54. LABOUR 408
   R. R. BORADE
   Translated from the Marathi by Anjali Nerlekar

55. A SHEET 411
   SALAM BIN RAZZAQ
   Translated from the Urdu by Muhammad Umar Memon

56. AND THEN IT POURED 422
   GAURI DESHPANDE
   Translated from the Marathi by Anjali Nerlekar

57. VALUES 431
   MAMONI RAISOM GOSWAMI
   Translated from the Assamese by Gayatri Bhattacharyya

58. A REVOLT OF THE GODS 445
   VILAS SARANG
   Translated from the Marathi by the author

59. JOURNEY 4 454
   AMBAI
   Translated from the Tamil by Lakshmi Holmström

60. COINSANV'S CATTLE 458
   DAMODAR MAUZO
   Translated from the Konkani by Xavier Cota

61. SALVATION   464
    PRATIBHA RAY
    Translated from the Odia by Leelawati Mohapatra, Paul St-Pierre, and K. K. Mohapatra

62. REFLECTIONS OF A HEN IN HER LAST HOUR   473
    PAUL ZACHARIA
    Translated from the Malayalam by A. J. Thomas

63. LABURNUM FOR MY HEAD   476
    TEMSULA AO

64. THE FOURTH DIRECTION   488
    WARYAM SINGH SANDHU
    Translated from the Punjabi by Nirupama Dutt

65. THE SPIRITS OF SHAH ALAM CAMP   501
    ASGHAR WAJAHAT
    Translated from the Hindi by Poonam Saxena

66. AIR AND WATER   505
    AMAR MITRA
    Translated from the Bengali by Arunava Sinha

67. THE WITCH   516
    KAMALAKANTA MOHAPATRA
    Translated from the Odia by Leelawati Mohapatra and Paul St. Pierre

68. TWO OLD KIPPERS   540
    SIDDIQ AALAM
    Translated from the Urdu by Muhammad Umar Memon

69. TIRICH   548
    UDAY PRAKASH
    Translated from the Hindi by Poonam Saxena

70. THE SMELL OF BAMBOO BLOSSOMS   563
    YESHE DORJEE THONGCHI
    Translated from the Assamese by Aruni Kashyap

71. BOKHA   571
    CYRUS MISTRY

72. THE LABYRINTH   592
    SARA RAI
    Translated from the Hindi by Poonam Saxena

73. CHARLIS AND I   601
    SHASHI THAROOR

74. PONNUTHAYI 619
   BAMA
   Translated from the Tamil by C. T. Indra
75. WINTER EVENINGS 625
   NAVTEJ SARNA
76. AND THEN LAUGHED THE HYENA 629
   SYED MUHAMMAD ASHRAF
   Translated from the Urdu by M. Asaduddin
77. THE MURMUROUS DEAD: A VERY BRIEF EXCHANGE
   WITH A SPIRIT 637
   DAVID DAVIDAR
78. PREDATORS 639
   SYED SALEEM
   *Translated from the Telugu by Dasu Krishnamoorty and
   Tamraparni Dasu*
79. SHARAVANA SERVICES 646
   VIVEK SHANBHAG
   Translated from the Kannada by Jayanth Kodkani
80. AN IDEAL MAN 655
   ADDEPALLI PRABHU
   *Translated from the Telugu by Dasu Krishnamoorty and
   Tamraparni Dasu*
81. THE COST OF HUNGER 663
   ABDUS SAMAD
   Translated from the Assamese by Aruni Kashyap
82. TALE OF A TOILET 669
   RAMNATH GAJANAN GAWADE
   Translated from the Konkani by Vidya Pai
83. ON SERNABATIM BEACH 684
   JESSICA FALEIRO
84. THE GRAVESTONE 688
   SHAHNAZ BASHIR
85. CRIPPLED WORLD 693
   VEMPALLE SHAREEF
   Translated from the Telugu by N. S. Murty and R. S. Krishna Moorthy
86. THE ADIVASI WILL NOT DANCE 697
   HANSDA SOWVENDRA SHEKHAR

87. FOR THE GREATER COMMON GOOD ARUNI KASHYAP	707
88. SWIMMER AMONG THE STARS KANISHK THAROOR	717
89. MAKING AISHWARYA SUBRAMANIAN	726
90. THE POWER TO FORGIVE AVINUO KIRE	731
91. THE DEVOURING SEA AMAL *Translated from the Malayalam by A. J. Thomas*	738
92. THE SEARCH DHEEBA NAZIR *Translated from the Kashmiri by Neerja Mattoo*	745
93. GUL SHREYA ILA ANASUYA	749
94. THE ACCOUNTS OFFICER'S WIFE LAKSHMIKANTH K. AYYAGARI	760
95. THE DEMON SAGE'S DAUGHTER VARSHA DINESH	768
96. EGGS KEEP FALLING FROM THE FOURTH FLOOR BHAVIKA GOVIL	784
97. TWENTY-FIRST TIFFIN RAAM MORI *Translated from the Gujarati by Rita Kothari*	788
98. GOBYAER SADAF WANI	794
99. THE ALLIGATOR OF ALIGARH A. M. GAUTAM	798
100. THE CURRENT CLIMATE ARAVIND JAYAN	805
NOTES AND ACKNOWLEDGEMENTS	812
NOTES ON THE AUTHORS	818
NOTES ON THE TRANSLATORS	832

FOREWORD

RUSKIN BOND

A great short story reveals a moment of truth.

Unlike the novel which lumbers along in a dedicated search for eternal truths, the short story comes upon it in a flash of sheet lightning, revealing life's verities to the reader as a fleeting vision, gone as suddenly as it appears, but embedded forever in our memories.

As I wander through this labyrinth of short, revealing fiction, I become aware of the complexity of this land, a land called India (or Bharat if you prefer), a subcontinent where hundreds of languages and dialects jostle with each other, every one of them rich in its own literature and folklore. And over the last hundred years, not hundreds but thousands of writers have sought to express themselves in the language of their own special part of the sacred earth on which they have grown to maturity.

We find ourselves overwhelmed with riches—taken from the coast, from field and forest, town and village, city and slum, hill and plain—an endless stream of stories, reflecting the joys and tragedies of endless individuals. For each man or woman or child is a unique individual, and the writer is the guardian of that individuality.

Over the years, critics and academics have tried to expostulate rules for the short story. But there are no rules for telling a story. Tell it in your own way, as the storytellers of old told various legends and folk tales.

Cultivate and cherish your own style. Be different. Be yourself. All the writers in this volume are here because they were, or are, different. There is no sameness to their work. Don't let any critic assist you with your writing. You have your own style, and your own style will serve you best.

But this collection would not exist without a host of translators. How dare we ignore them! These gifted, committed lovers of literature and language have brought us the best of short story writing from the many Indian languages that have enriched our lives and literature. They bring these moments of truth to readers everywhere—in our land, and in other lands, where little is known of our literary wealth.

Honour the writers.
Salute the translators!
Celebrate the short story.

Mussoorie
5 September 2024

THE INDIAN SHORT STORY

A. J. THOMAS

Indian short-form fiction is singular. It is also unique in world literature as it has been created across dozens of languages over the last century and a half, all within the geographical boundaries of a single nation. In *100 Indian Stories*, perhaps the most ambitious attempt to showcase Indian short stories within the covers of a single volume, the reader will find one hundred glittering stories chosen from the bulk of the twenty-four languages recognized by the Sahitya Akademi (twenty-two listed in the Eighth Schedule of the Constitution plus English and Rajasthani). The stories early in the list date back to the late nineteenth century and the early years of the twentieth century, when some of the greatest names in Indian literature were beginning to come into their own; from that point onwards, stories from practically all the major phases in Indian literature (up to the present time) are represented as are most of the 'big' literatures as I call them (not 'major' literatures, as all our national literatures are equal in status).

My love for the Indian short story is of long standing. It began several decades ago when I began to read Malayalam short stories in periodicals and various collections and anthologies beginning in the late 1960s, and English short stories in the *Illustrated Weekly of India*, *Mirror*, and other magazines in the 1970s. This interest led me to focus on the short story for my academic studies. Beyond stories in Malayalam and English, my interest in the stories of our various national literatures was kindled as a result of my association with the National Book Trust's project, *Masterpieces of Indian Literature* edited by Dr K. M. George. In the early 1990s, I was the sole copy editor of this monumental undertaking based in Thiruvananthapuram. It was then that I grew familiar with the fictional works of most of the authors represented here. Over the next decades, my involvement with Indian fiction, and the Indian short story in particular, deepened as, from end-1997 onwards, I began editing *Indian Literature*, the 200-page, bimonthly English journal of the Sahitya Akademi. Over the nearly two decades I spent at *Indian Literature*, I read and published many of the masters of this literary form. This gave me invaluable insights into the Indian short story, of which there would at least be half a dozen on an average in each issue. My knowledge and admiration for short fiction grew when I was involved in another massive literary endeavour—compiling and editing material for the two-book, four volume, 1,700-page *Best of Indian Literature*, that brought together (along with poetry, drama, and critical essays), the best short stories published in *Indian Literature* from its inception in 1957 until 2007.

It, therefore, gave me particular pleasure to be able to edit this volume of remarkable Indian short fiction for Aleph. We don't make any claims to the book being a comprehensive representation of all the great short fiction published in this country. Rather, what I have tried to do is present a wide selection of stories I have read and admired. As with all anthologies, there are stories that we have been unable to include as we were unable to track down copyright holders. Other masterpieces we were pointed to hadn't yet been translated or the translations I was able to find or commission were less than satisfactory.

What has given me great satisfaction is that almost 80 per cent of the stories in this anthology have been translated into English from various Indian languages in silken smooth translations. Many of the stories in this anthology that were originally written in English were first published in the twenty-first century, and a significant proportion of their authors are Millennials. This reflects the rise in English education, and the consequent burgeoning of English-speaking communities all over the country. There are some other aspects of the evolution of the Indian short story that I was struck by in the course of editing this anthology. The reader will find that there are only a few stories by women writers in the book from the years before Independence. After Independence there was an exponential increase in the number of Indian women writers getting published across languages as the bonds of patriarchy loosened and women gained access to education, and opportunities that had been denied to them. Today, they have made their mark in many of the languages in which fiction is created—that trend is reflected in the stories found in this volume.

Other streams of literature, that started later than 'mainstream' literature, and evolved independently, with little support from the establishment, were Dalit and tribal fiction, especially short fiction in languages such as Marathi and a few other big languages. As with women writers, stories by Dalit and tribal writers make their appearance several decades (almost a century) after the short story made its appearance in Indian literature. Differently gendered writers were the latest to be published.

The stories in this book are arranged according to the date of birth of their authors, starting with Fakir Mohan Senapati, the oldest contributor to this volume, and ending with Aravind Jayan, the youngest; this was unavoidable as we were unable to pin down exactly when many of the older stories were first published, which would have been essential to have the stories appear in chronological order, based on their dates of first publication.

Before I wrap up this brief introduction, it's worth taking a quick look at how the short story originated and developed in India. Prose settled into modernity around the mid-nineteenth century, mostly through the promotional activities of Christian missionaries; thereafter, Western fictional forms and genres like the novel and the short story found their way into Indian languages, initially through translation as in the case of Malayalam. Indian writers began to be influenced by Western forms in the fiction they were creating. The earliest such story appeared in Bengali—'Modhumati' by Purna Chandra Chattopadhya, published in 1873—followed by stories in Malayalam (1891), Assamese (1892), Odia (1898), Kannada (1900), Hindi (1901), Tamil (1905), Urdu (1908), Telugu, (1910), Sindhi (1914), Gujarati (1918), and so on.

The ideals of liberty, equality, and fraternity propagated by the French Revolution in the late eighteenth century had travelled to various parts of the country along with other trends and ideas from Europe. This was especially noticeable in Bengal in the early nineteenth century, and began to become visible in other regions a short while later. Although the ills of Western colonizers like the English and French can never be forgotten, the advent of modern European ideas did inspire people to push back against feudalism, caste discrimination, and other ugly features of Indian society; along with the part they played in social reform, Western ideas influenced the modernizing of regional literatures in their earliest stages of development. The short story, as a form, gained from this in the last quarter of the nineteenth century. A few decades later, the socialist ideals broadcast through the Russian Revolution, further built upon these earlier influences, and resulted in the Progressive Literature Movement that began in the mid-1930s, with Premchand as one of its luminaries. Stories of the poor, downtrodden, marginalized, and outcast sections of society found their way into mainstream literatures like Bengali, Malayalam, Telugu, Tamil, Kannada, Urdu, Marathi, Hindi, etc. Socialist realism was the guiding spirit in this movement.

While there isn't enough empirical evidence or plausible studies to arrive at unimpeachable conclusions about the evolution of short fiction across languages in the Indian literary tradition, certain broad trends are discernible, as delineated above. In the seventy or more years since the origins of the form in the subcontinent up until the country gained Independence, writers focused mainly on social realism, nationalistic themes, social issues, and plot-driven stories. Then, in the various avatars of realism later, modernism began to make its presence felt. In the big literatures, this became manifest since the mid-1950s and gained strength through the succeeding decades leading to what I characterize as 'after-modernism' (the Indian variant of 'post-modernism' since this concept/style as understood in the West may not have relevance in our context). Satire had made its appearance early on, but it is only in the decades since Independence that there has been an explosion in the variety of themes, subjects, and forms to be found in Indian short fiction—crime, science fiction, absurdism, magic realism, expressionism, stream of consciousness writing, and much more.

In this book, the reader will encounter some of the finest examples of the various kinds of short fiction that were written in over a century by writers from India. It is my sincere hope that this selection will whet the appetite of readers to further explore the vast treasures that Indian literature has to offer.

Kaitharam, North Paravur
7 October 2024

REBATI

FAKIR MOHAN SENAPATI

*Translated from the Odia by Leelawati Mohapatra,
Paul St-Pierre, and K. K. Mohapatra*

'But oft some shining April morn is darkened in an hour,
And blackest griefs o'er joyous home, Alas! unseen may lower.'

—Rev. J. H. Gurney

'REBATI! REBI! YOU FIRE THAT TURNS ALL TO ASHES.'
Patapur—a sleepy little village in Hariharpur subdivision, district of Cuttack. At one end stood Shyambandhu Mohanty's house: two rows of rooms, front and back, with an inner courtyard centring around a well, and a shed for husking rice behind the house, along with a vegetable patch, and a garden in front. It was in the outer room that visitors and farmers waiting to pay their taxes gathered and made themselves comfortable. Shyambandhu Mohanty, the zamindar's accountant, was responsible for collecting taxes. His salary was two rupees a month, but he could earn a little more by adjusting rent receipts and land records; all told, this added up to at least four rupees. With this he could make ends meet. And not just barely; no, to tell the truth, he was quite comfortable. His family never complained of wanting for anything. They had all they needed: two drumstick trees in the backyard, and a patch of land always full of greens and vegetables; two cows, which never went dry at the same time, so there was always a little curd and milk in the pails. Mohanty's old mother made fuel cakes from cow dung and husks, so they rarely had to buy firewood. The zamindar had given him three and a half acres of rent-free land to cultivate, and it produced just about enough to meet their needs.

Shyambandhu was a straightforward person, and the tenants respected, even liked, him. He went from door to door cajoling and coaxing them to pay their taxes; he never demanded a paisa extra from anyone. On his own initiative, and without their asking, he would slip four-finger-wide palm-leaf receipts into the underside thatch of their houses. He never let the zamindar's muscleman cast his shadow over the village; he'd pump the fellow's palm, fondle his chin, tuck two paise into the folds of his dhoti to buy a plug of tobacco, and see him off.

In his own home, Shyambandhu had four stomachs to fill—his own, his wife's, his old mother's, and his ten-year-old daughter's. The daughter's name was Rebati. In the evenings, Shyambandhu would sit on the veranda and sing 'Krupasindhu Badan' and other prayer songs; at times, he would light an oil lamp, place it on a wooden stand, and read aloud passages from the Bhagavata. Rebati always sat next to him, listening with rapt attention; soon she had learnt a few songs by heart. Her melodious voice lent them more appeal, and people would stop by to listen. There was one hymn which gave Shyambandhu the greatest joy, and every evening he would unfailingly ask Rebati to sing it:

> *Whither shall I take my prayers, Lord, If Thou turnest a blind eye? Surely shall I be finished. Be it salvation or damnation, To Thee this life a dedication, To Thee, this soul laden. Empty, empty, all the three worlds When I am without Thee. True refreshment, when I thirst, Only Thy love can be.*

Two years earlier, in the course of his visit to the countryside, the deputy inspector of schools had happened to spend a night at Patapur. At the request of the village elders he had written to the inspector of schools, Orissa Division, and an upper-primary school had been established in the village. The government paid the teacher's salary of four rupees a month to which each student contributed an additional anna.

The teacher, Basudev, a young man of twenty, had attended the teacher training course at Cuttack Normal School. Urbane and polite, he never took on superior airs. He had been orphaned at an early age and had been brought up by his uncle. True to his name, he was a fine human being. Charming and handsome—the indelible mark of a bottle's mouth on his forehead applied by his mother to treat diphtheria during childhood enhanced rather than marred his looks.

From the time he arrived in the village, Shyambandhu had taken a fancy to him: they belonged to the same caste.

Occasionally, on the day of a full moon or a Thursday, when cakes and savouries were made at home, Shyambandhu would call at the school: 'Son, come to our place this evening; your aunt has invited you.' A bond of affection had naturally developed between them after these visits. Even Rebati's mother, filled with concern, would sometimes exclaim: 'Ah, the poor orphan! What does he eat, who looks after his meals?' As the visits became regular, with Basu dropping in practically every evening, Rebati would wait at the door to announce his arrival. As soon as she spotted him at a distance she would call out to her father, 'Here comes Basubhai, here he comes!' Then she would sit beside him and sing all the prayer songs she knew. To Basu's ears, the songs were fresh and ever new.

One day, as they chatted about this and that, Shyambandhu learnt from Basu there was a school at Cuttack where girls could study and also learn crafts; instantly, the desire to give Rebati an education welled up in his heart. When he confided this to Basu, the young teacher, who had already begun to look upon him as a father, answered: 'I was about to suggest that myself.'

Rebati listened to the conversation and rushed inside. 'I'm going to study,' she announced excitedly to her mother and grandmother. 'I'm going to learn to read.'

Her mother smiled. 'Go ahead,' she said, but her grandmother's reaction was sharp: 'What good will it do you? How does book learning help a girl? It's enough to know how to cook, bake, churn butter, and make patterns on walls with rice paste.'

That night, when Shyambandhu sat down to dinner on a low wooden stool with Rebati beside him, the old lady sat opposite them, restive and itching to speak her mind: 'Serve him a little more rice, daughter-in-law, give him a second helping of dal and a pinch of salt,' and so on. Then she brought up the topic: 'Shyam, is Rebi going to study? Why should she, son? What good is that for a girl?'

'Never mind, Ma,' said Shyambandhu. 'Let her study if she wants to. Haven't you heard Jhankar Pattanaik's daughters can read the Bhagavata and *Baidehisa Bilas*?'

Rebati was furious at her grandmother. 'You silly old fool!' she snorted. Turning to her father, she begged him, 'Father, I do want to study.'

'And so you will,' said Shyambandhu.

The matter was left there.

The following afternoon Basu brought Rebati a copy of Sitanath Babu's *First Lessons*. She was so overjoyed she leafed through the book from cover to cover. The pictures of elephants, houses, and cows thrilled her no end. Kings could be happy to own elephants and horses, others perhaps derived joy from riding them, but for Rebati it was enough merely to gaze at their pictures. She could hardly wait to show them to her mother and grandmother.

The grandmother did not hide her irritation. 'Take that silly thing away from me,' she shouted.

'Silly you!' the girl retorted.

The auspicious day of Sri Panchami dawned. Rebati took an early bath, put on new clothes, and flitted in and out of the house, waiting impatiently for Basu. The usual pomp associated with beginning one's studies was played down out of fear of the grandmother. Six hours into the morning Basu arrived and taught her the alphabet: a, aa, e, ee, u, uu....

The lessons went on. Basu never missed a day.

Over the next two years Rebati studied a great deal. All the rhymes of Madhu Rao were on the tip of her tongue and she could reel them off without faltering.

At dinner one night, Shyambandhu asked his mother, as if rounding off a discussion they had been having, 'Well, Ma, what do you think?'

'Nothing could be better,' said the old lady. 'But are you certain what his caste is?'

'That's what I was trying to find out. He may be poor but he comes from a good family. And he's a pucca Karan to boot.'

'Good. Caste counts more than wealth. But will he agree to live with us?'

'Why not? After all, his only relatives are his uncle and aunt. He probably won't insist on living with them.'

What Rebati made of all this she alone knew, but a change certainly came over her. She became noticeably coy with Basu. In the evening she would hang around the front door, as though waiting for someone, which riled her grandmother no end, but when Basu arrived she would hide inside the house. It took Basu quite an effort before she would come out for her studies. Blushing and smiling for no apparent reason, she would refuse to read her lessons aloud and would answer him in monosyllables. As soon as the day's lesson was done she would rush inside, struggling to stifle her giggles.

One Sri Panchami followed another, and two years passed. Providence's designs are strange and inscrutable; no two days are alike. One fine Phalguna day, like a bolt out of the blue, a cholera epidemic struck.

Early in the morning the news of Shyambandhu coming down with cholera spread through the village. As always, the immediate response was to bolt the doors and windows, and keep out of the path of the demonic deity, as though the evil old hag was out with her basket and broom sweeping up heads.

Shyambandhu's wife and mother were soon driven out of their minds by worry and anxiety. Rebati ran in and out of the house, crying for help. When the news reached Basu, he hurried from the school and, without fear for his own life, sat at the bedside, massaging Shyambandhu's hands and legs and forcing drops of water between his parched lips.

Three hours passed.

Suddenly, Shyambandhu looked up at Basu and stammered: 'Take care of my family, I leave them to you....'

Basu could not hold back his tears.

Shyambandhu passed away that evening.

The women wailed. Rebati rolled on the floor.

How could the two grief-stricken women and the inexperienced Basu make arrangements for the cremation? Bana Sethi, the village washerman, a veteran of fifty or sixty cremations, saved the day, turning up with a towel around his waist and an axe on his shoulder. Bana was rather philosophical about it: cholera or not, if your time's up you've got to go, whether today or tomorrow, but why miss out on a set of new clothes? Shyambandhu's was the only Karan family in the village, and help was neither expected nor forthcoming; the two women and Basudev had to carry the body to the cremation grounds and perform the last rites.

The morning star was shining in the eastern sky by the time they were done. No sooner had they got home than Rebati's mother came down with cholera. By midday the news of her death had spread through the village.

Providence works in mysterious ways—while one man is blessed with a regal umbrella atop his palanquin, another receives lashes on his fettered hands. Within three months of Shyambandhu's demise, the zamindar expropriated Shyambandhu's cows—apparently he had not deposited the last tax collection. This was hard to believe, however. Shyambandhu had always regarded depositing the money as sacred and would not rest in peace until every paisa of the collection was in the zamindar's treasury. The truth was that for a long time the zamindar had had his eyes on the cows. He also took back the three and a half acres he had given Shyambandhu. There was no work for the farmhand, and he left on the full moon day of the Dola festival. The team of bullocks had already been sold off for seventeen and a half rupees; with what remained after the funeral expenses, the grandmother and Rebati hung on for a month. In the month following they began to pawn household items—a brass bowl one day, a plate the next.

Basu visited them every evening and stayed until bedtime. He offered them money, but they would not touch it. Once or twice he pressed some on them, but the coins lay idle on the shelf. He had no choice but to accept the couple of paise the old woman produced every eight or ten days to buy them provisions. The house was falling apart, the straw roof had worn thin, but try as he might Basu couldn't get it rethatched; the bales of hay he bought with two rupees of his own money rotted in the backyard.

The grandmother no longer cried day and night; she now confined her wailing to the evenings. But she put so much of herself into it that it left her slumped in a heap on the floor for the night. Rebati, convulsing in sobs, would lie down next to her. The old woman's vision had declined and she had a wild look about her. She no longer cried as much and took to heaping curses and abuse on Rebati: the wretched girl was at the root of all her misery and misfortune; her education had caused it all—first, her son had died, then her daughter-in-law; the bullocks had been sold off; the farmhand had left; the cows had been taken by the zamindar; and now her eyes had gone bad. Rebati was the evil eye, the she-devil, the ill-omened.

The moment the curses started coming thick and fast, Rebati would shrink from her grandmother and hide in a corner of the house or the backyard, tears streaming down her cheeks.

The grandmother held Basu equally to blame. If he had not been so eager to teach the girl, she could not possibly have gone and taught herself! But the grandmother could not take Basu to task, because she couldn't do without him. The zamindar kept seeking flimsy clarifications, and almost every second day a messenger came asking for this account or that. Basu alone could fish them out from the clutter of papers Shyambandhu had left behind. Yet, behind Basu's back, the old woman sometimes gave vent to her feelings.

Rebati's presence no longer filled the house; gone were the days when she would be heard mourning loudly. Nobody heard her voice, nobody saw her out of doors. Her large brooding eyes, awash with silent tears, looked like blue lilies floating in water. Her heart and mind broken, day and night were alike to her. The sun brought her no light, the night no darkness; the world was an aching void. The memories of her parents overwhelmed her, their faces hung before her glazed eyes. She could not bring herself to believe they were truly dead and gone. Hunger no longer stirred her stomach; slumber no longer closed her eyes. She went through the pretence of eating only out of fear of her grandmother; she grew thin and emaciated, her skin hung loose on her bones, and she could barely lift herself off the floor where she lay day and night. The only time she revived a little was when Basu visited them. She would sit up and fasten her gaze on him, lowering her eyes with a sigh when their glances met. But the next moment she'd feverishly stare at him again. For those brief hours of the day when he was around, Basu completely possessed her eyes, her mind, and her heart.

Roughly five months had passed. On a hot Jaistha Saturday afternoon, Basu knocked on their door. Never before had he ever called at such an unusual hour. The old woman was full of foreboding as she let him in.

'Grandmother,' said Basu. 'The deputy inspector of schools will be camping at the Hariharpur police station and giving the students an oral test. All the schools have been informed; I received the order today. Tomorrow morning I'll have to start off and be away for about five days.'

Listening to the conversation from behind the door, Rebati felt her legs give way. Her hold on the door was barely tight enough to stop herself from falling.

Basu bought them enough rice, oil, salt, and vegetables for five days, and bade them goodbye.

'Son,' said the old woman with a sigh. 'Don't walk about in the sun for too long. Take care of yourself; eat your meals on time.'

Rebati could not take her eyes off him. Before, she would look away when their eyes met, but today she stared unblinkingly, unabashedly into his eyes. A change seemed to have come over Basu, too. For a long time he had contented himself with stolen glances, but today he did not turn away. They stared deeply into each other's eyes.

Evening came; darkness filled the house and covered the earth. Rebati remained rooted to the ground until her grandmother's piercing screams jolted her to her senses. Basu had left much earlier.

Rebati counted the days.

On the morning of the sixth she even rushed a couple of times to the front door, which she had avoided since her parents' death. Six hours had passed when the schoolboys arrived back from Hariharpur, bringing the news of Basu's death. He had succumbed to cholera under the big banyan tree near Gopalpur on his return journey. The village folk mourned; the women and children shed copious tears. 'What a handsome fellow!' said one. 'So polite,' said another. 'Never hurt a fly,' remarked yet another.

The grandmother cried so much she choked. 'Poor boy!' she repeated between sobs. 'You only brought it on yourself!' Implying that he had perished in his prime because he had been foolish enough to want to teach Rebati.

Rebati sank to the floor and lay there without a whine or a whimper.

The grandmother woke up the following morning without Rebati beside her and shouted out in anger: 'Rebati! Rebi! You fire that turns all to ashes.' She worked herself into a froth, and passers-by heard these terrible words repeated all morning long.

Half-blind and angry, she groped her way through the entire house. When she finally found the girl, she was shocked. Rebati, burning with fever, was unconscious. Worry and fear gnawed at the old woman's heart. She couldn't decide what to do, who to turn to for help. Exasperated, out of breath, and without hope, she tartly commented: 'What medicine can there be for an illness of one's own making!' Rebati had brought the fever on herself by daring to study.

One, two, three, four, five days passed. Rebati remained glued to the ground, her eyes and lips shut. On the sixth morning she let out a whimper or two. The old woman ran her hand over the girl's body. It was cool to the touch; perhaps the fever had left. She called out to her, and Rebati mumbled a reply, then asked for water, stared wildly around, and broke into incoherent babble. One quick look and even a country doctor could have quoted from his text: 'Thirst, fever, delirium; of imminent collapse these are the symptoms.' But the poor grandmother was overcome with a sense of relief. The fever had left, the girl was able to open her eyes and speak two words, to ask for water. A little gruel was all she needed to regain her strength and get back on her feet.

'Don't get up,' the grandmother said. 'Stay where you are. I'm going to cook you a bit of food.' She left the room and rummaged in vain among the earthen pots for a handful of rice. Her head became clouded with despair and she sat down with a sigh. If only her eyesight had been better she would have realized the provisions meant for five days had already lasted for ten.

But there was a flicker of hope in her yet. She picked up the only object of value left—an old brass bowl with a hole in the bottom—and set out for Hari Sa's store. The so-called store was in Hari's residence, in the middle of the village, and he kept a paltry stock of rice, salt, lentils, and oil to sell to travellers passing by.

Hari saw the old woman with the bowl. He understood immediately, but let her first make her plea. He then took the bowl and examined it minutely, turning it from side to side. 'There's no rice,' he said, handing it back. 'Who's going to give you anything for a bowl like this?' Of course, he had both rice and the inclination to sell it, but getting the brass bowl for a song was what interested him the most. The grandmother staggered at his words, as though lightning had hit her. What would she do if she didn't get any rice, what would she cook for Rebati, how would the girl fight her weakness? She sat there for hours, depressed and silent, still as a log, casting imploring glances at the shopkeeper.

The day wore on. Realizing she had left the sick girl alone for a long time, fear stirred her old heart. 'Time I got back home,' she mumbled to herself, picking up the bowl. 'God knows how that girl of mine is doing.'

'Never mind,' said Hari grudgingly. 'Give me the bowl. Let's see if I can scrape up a little something for you.' He gave her four measures of rice, half a measure of lentils, and a handful of salt. The old woman hobbled back home, resting every four steps or so to catch her breath. She hadn't even washed her face since morning, and her mind was in a whirl.

She reached home hoping Rebati was better. She thought she'd ask the girl to draw water from the well. The rice wouldn't take long to cook. She called out to Rebati once, twice, three times, but got no response. Then she yelled at the top of her voice: 'Rebati! Rebi! You fire that turns all to ashes.'

By now, Rebati was sinking fast. Her body, already feeble from spasms of excruciating pain, had turned ice-cold. Her thirst was so terrible she felt as if her tongue was being sucked back into her throat. She found the room unbearably hot and crawled out to the inner courtyard. Even that brought no relief. She rolled out to the veranda at the back and propped herself up against the wall.

Dusk had fallen and a gentle breeze was blowing. A bunch of bananas hung from the tree her father had planted before his death. The guava sapling her mother had planted two years ago had grown to a considerable height and was covered with blossoms. Rebati remembered how she had drawn water from the well in a small jug and tended the sapling. This brought back a rush of memories of her mother. Her head was in a whirl, her thoughts jumbled, but the image of her mother clung to her.

Night slowly descended. Darkness stole out from the boughs of the trees and shrouded the garden. Rebati tilted her head back and watched the sky. The lone evening star was gleaming brightly. She could not take her eyes off it; and it grew and grew and grew, bigger and brighter, invading the whole sky, and behold! Her loving mother sat in the heart of it, her face glowing with love and kindness, her arms extended towards Rebati in invitation. Rebati was overwhelmed. Two shafts of light pierced her eyes and moved down to her heart. Her breathing, heavy and laboured, rose and fell, breaking the stillness of the night. She wheezed, choked, and cried out to her mother twice. Then there was silence.

The grandmother crawled around the house, going from the living room to the courtyard to the rice-husking shed, but Rebati was nowhere to be found. Then it occurred to the old woman that with the fever abating the girl might be taking a stroll in the garden at the back.

'Rebati!' she screamed. 'Rebi! You fire that turns all to ashes.'

She crawled out to the narrow veranda, which was only one hand wide and two high, and bumped into the girl. 'Death to you!' she cried. 'Sitting here, are you?' She wanted to shake her, but she could sense something was amiss.

She ran her hand over the length of the girl's body and then held a finger close to her nostrils. The night's silence was rent by her eerie wail. Two bodies fell from the veranda and thudded to the ground.

That was the end of Shyambandhu Mohanty's family.

The last words which had emanated from his house were: 'Rebati! Rebi! You fire that turns all to ashes.'

2

THE KABULIWALLAH

RABINDRANATH TAGORE

Translated from the Bengali by Arunava Sinha

MY FIVE-YEAR-OLD DAUGHTER TALKED ALL THE TIME. IT HAD TAKEN her a year after her birth to master the language, and since then she has not wasted a second of her waking hours in silence. Although her mother often hushed her, this was beyond me. A silent Mini was so unnatural a being that I could not bear it for long. So I always encouraged her to prattle on.

I had barely started the seventeenth chapter of my novel that morning when Mini appeared by my side and began chattering at once, 'Ramdayal, the doorman, calls the crow kauwa instead of kaak, Baba, he just doesn't know anything, does he?'

Before I could talk about linguistic diversity, she had moved to another subject. 'Baba, Bhola says it rains because elephants spray water with their trunks from the sky. He talks such rubbish, my God. He keeps talking, talks all the time.'

Without pausing for my opinion, Mini suddenly asked, 'What relation is Ma to you, Baba?'

'Shaali,' I answered to myself. To Mini I said, 'Go play with Bhola, Mini. I'm busy.'

Flopping down by my feet, next to the desk, she began to play a game involving her knees and hands, accompanied by a rhyme uttered at express velocity. In the seventeenth chapter of my novel, Pratap Singh was about to leap with Kanchanmala in his arms from the high window of the prison into the river flowing below.

My room looked out on the street. Mini abruptly stopped her game to rush to the window and began to shout, 'Kabuliwallah, Kabuliwallah.'

A tall Kabuliwallah—one of those hawkers of dry fruits who came all the way from Afghanistan to make a living in Calcutta—was walking slowly up the road, a turban on his head, a bag slung over his shoulder, holding two or three boxes of grapes. It was difficult to say what emotions he aroused in my daughter, but she continued to call out to him breathlessly. I was afraid that if the wily peddler, with a bag of things to sell, came into my room, I could bid goodbye to any prospect of finishing chapter seventeen that day.

The Kabuliwallah turned and smiled at Mini's shouts and began walking towards our house. Her courage gave way and she ran from the room at great speed, vanishing into the house. She was convinced that if the Kabuliwallah's bag was opened and examined it would reveal three or four children, just like her.

Meanwhile, the man himself appeared, offering me a smiling salute. Although Pratap Singh and Kanchanmala were in dire straits, I reflected that it would be discourteous to invite him into the house and buy nothing.

I bought a few things and we began chatting. We exchanged notes on frontier policies involving Abdur Rahman, the Russians, and the English.

When he was about to leave, the Kabuliwallah finally asked, 'Where did your daughter go, Babu?'

I sent for Mini in order to dispel her fears. Pressing herself to me, Mini cast suspicious glances at the Kabuliwallah and his large bag. He offered her some raisins and dry fruit, but she simply wouldn't accept them, holding my knee tightly. And there the first meeting between them ended.

A few days later, as I was about to leave the house on an errand, I discovered my daughter seated on the bench next to the front door, chattering away to the Kabuliwallah who sat at her feet, listening smilingly, and occasionally saying something in broken Bengali. Mini had never encountered such an attentive listener in the five years of her life, besides her father. I even found nuts and raisins bundled into the aanchal of her tiny sari. 'Why have you given her all this?' I asked the Kabuliwallah. 'Don't do it again.' Taking an eight-anna coin out of my pocket, I handed it to him. He accepted it without demur, putting it in his bag.

I returned home to find the eight-anna coin at the heart of a hundred rupees worth of trouble.

Holding a circular, silvery object in her hand, Mini's mother was asking her daughter disapprovingly, 'Where did you get this?'

'The Kabuliwallah gave it to me,' Mini told her.

'Why did you have to take it from him?' Mini's mother enquired.

'I didn't want to, he gave it on his own,' Mini said, on the verge of tears.

I rescued Mini from imminent danger and took her outside.

There I learnt that it wasn't as though this was only Mini's second meeting with Rahmat, the Kabuliwallah. He had been coming to see her almost every day, bribing her with almonds and raisins to conquer her tiny, greedy five-year-old heart.

I observed that the two friends had established an easy familiarity between themselves, sharing private jokes and quips. For instance, on spotting Rahmat, my daughter would ask, laughing, 'What's in that bag of yours, Kabuliwallah?'

In an exaggeratedly nasal tone Rahmat would answer, also laughing, 'An elephant.'

The joke could not be termed particularly subtle, but nevertheless it kept both in splits—and the artless laughter of a middle-aged man and a child on an autumn morning brought me some joy, too.

They had another ritual exchange. Rahmat would tell Mini, 'Khnokhi, tomi sasurbaari kakhanu jaabena. Little girl, you must never get married and go to your father-in-law's house.'

Most girls from traditional Bengali families would be familiar with the word shoshurbaari almost from the time they were born, but because we were somewhat modern, we hadn't taught our daughter the meaning of the term. So, she did not know what to make of Rahmat's request, but because it was against her nature to be silent and unresponsive, she would fire a counter-question. 'Will you go there?'

Rahmat would brandish his enormous fist against an imaginary father-in-law, and say, 'I will kill the sasur first.'

Imagining the terrible fate awaiting this unknown creature, Mini would laugh her head off.

It was the clear season of autumn. In ancient times, this was when kings set off to conquer other lands. I had never been anywhere outside Calcutta, but precisely for that reason my mind wandered all over the world. In the quiet corner of my room, I was like an eternal traveller, pining for places around the globe. My heart began to race as soon as another country was mentioned, the sight of a foreigner conjured up a vision of a cottage amidst rivers and mountains and forests, and thoughts of a joyful, free way of life captured my imagination.

But I was so retiring by nature that the very notion of abandoning my corner and stepping out into the world made me have visions of the sky crashing down on my head. That was why my conversations with this man from Kabul, this Kabuliwallah, every morning by the desk in my tiny room served the purpose of travel for me. Rugged and inaccessible, the scorched, red-hued mountain ranges rose high on either side of the road, a laden caravan of camels winding along the narrow trail between them; turbaned traders and travellers, some of them on the backs of camels, some on foot, some with spears, others with old-fashioned flint guns...with a voice like the rumbling of clouds, the Kabuliwallah would recount tales from his homeland in broken Bengali, and these images would float past my eyes.

Mini's mother was perpetually jumpy, her mind alive with imaginary fears. The slightest noise on the streets would lead her to believe that all the inebriated individuals in the world were rushing towards our house, bent on making mischief. Despite all the years (not too many actually) she had lived on earth, she had still not rid herself of the conviction that the universe was populated only by thieves and robbers and drunkards and snakes and tigers and malaria and earthworms and cockroaches and white men all intent on striking terror into her heart.

She was not entirely free of doubt about Rahmat, the Kabuliwallah, requesting me repeatedly to keep an eye on him. When I attempted to laugh away her suspicions, she would ask me probing questions. 'Aren't children ever kidnapped? Don't they have slaves in Afghanistan? Is it entirely impossible for a gigantic Kabuliwallah to kidnap a small child?'

I had to acknowledge that it was not entirely impossible but unlikely. The capacity for trust was not the same in everyone, which was why my wife remained suspicious of the Kabuliwallah. But I could not stop Rahmat from visiting our house for no fault of his.

Rahmat usually went home around the end of January every year. He would be very busy collecting his dues at this time. He had to go from house to house, but still he made it a point to visit Mini once a day. There did seem to be a conspiracy between them. If he could not visit in the morning, he made his way to our house in the evening. It was true that I experienced a sudden surge of fear at the sight of the large man in his loose shalwar and kurta, standing in a dark corner of the room with his bags. But when a laughing Mini ran up to him, saying, 'Kabuliwallah, Kabuliwallah,' and the simple banter of old was resumed between the two friends of unequal age, my heart was filled with delight once more.

I was correcting proofs one day in my tiny room. The cold had grown sharper; as winter was about to bid farewell, there was a severe chill. The morning sunshine filtering through the window warmed my feet; it was a most pleasant sensation. It was about eight o'clock—most of those who had ventured out for their morning constitutionals, their heads and throats wrapped in mufflers, were already back home. Suddenly, there was an uproar in the street.

Looking out of the window I saw two policemen frogmarching our Rahmat, bound with ropes, up the road, followed by a group of curious urchins. Rahmat's clothes were bloodstained, and one of the policemen held a dagger dripping with blood. Going out, I stopped the policemen to enquire what the matter was.

The story was related partly by a policeman and partly by Rahmat himself. One of our neighbours owed Rahmat some money for a shawl from Rampur. When he disclaimed the debt, an altercation broke out, in the course of which Rahmat had stabbed him with his dagger.

The Kabuliwallah was showering expletives on the liar when Mini emerged from the house, calling out, 'Kabuliwallah, Kabuliwallah.'

Rahmat's expression changed in an instant to a cheerful smile. Since there was no bag slung from his shoulder today, they could not have their usual discussion about its magical contents. Mini asked him directly, 'Will you go to your father-in-law's house?'

'That's exactly where I am going,' Rahmat smiled back at her.

When he saw Mini wasn't amused, he showed her his arms bound with rope. 'I would have killed the sasur, but my hands are tied.'

Rahmat was in jail for several years for causing grievous bodily harm.

We forgot him, more or less. Going about our everyday routines it didn't even occur to us how difficult it must be for a man used to roaming free in the mountains to cope with years of imprisonment.

Even Mini's father had to accept that his fickle-hearted daughter's behaviour was truly shameful. She effortlessly forgot her old friend, and struck up a new friendship with Nabi, who groomed horses. Then, as she grew older, male friends were replaced by girls her age. Now, we seldom saw each other any more.

Many years passed. Another autumn arrived. My Mini's wedding had been arranged. She would be married during the Durga Puja holidays. Along with the goddess from Kailash, the joy of my house would also depart for her husband's home, robbing her father's house of its light.

A beautiful morning had dawned. After the monsoon, the freshly-rinsed autumn sunlight had taken on the colour of pure, molten gold. Its glow washed over the crumbling houses of exposed brick in the neighbourhood, making them exquisitely beautiful.

The shehnai had begun playing in my house before the night had ended. Its notes were like the sound of my heart weeping. The plaintive melody of Bhairavi was spreading the imminent pain of parting all over the world. My Mini was to be married today.

There had been a great to-do since the morning, with crowds of people going in and out of the house. In the courtyard a marquee was being set up with bamboo posts; the clinking of chandeliers being hung up in the rooms and the veranda could be heard. It was very noisy.

I was going over the accounts in my room when Rahmat appeared and saluted me. I did not recognize him at first. He had neither his bags nor his long hair—his body was not as strapping as it once used to be. It was his smile that eventually told me who he was.

'Why, it's Rahmat,' I said. 'When did you get back?'

'I was released from jail last evening,' he answered.

His reply made me uncomfortable. Until now, I had never seen a murderer in the flesh, his presence here made me shrink back. On this auspicious day, I wished he would go away.

I told him, 'There's something important going on at home, I am busy. You'd better go today.'

At this he made ready to leave at once, but when he had reached the door, he said hesitantly, 'Can't I meet Khnokhi?'

He probably thought that Mini had not changed. Perhaps he expected her to come running up as before, chanting Kabuliwallah, Kabuliwallah as she always had. To honour the old friendship he had even gone to the trouble of collecting a box of grapes and some nuts and raisins wrapped in paper from a fellow Afghan as he no longer had his own sack of goods to sell.

'There are some ceremonies at home today,' I told him, 'meeting Mini is impossible.'

He looked very disappointed. He looked at me wordlessly for a few moments, then said, 'Salaam, Babu,' and left.

No sooner had he left than I felt bad and was considering calling him back when I found him returning of his own accord.

Coming up to me, he said, 'I have some grapes and nuts and raisins for Khnokhi, please give them to her.'

As I was about to pay for them, he caught hold of my hand firmly and said, 'Please don't pay me. You have always been so kind, I will never forget your kindness....

'I have a daughter back home just like yours, Babu. It was thinking of her that I brought some fruit for Khnokhi, this isn't business.'

Putting his hand inside his long, loose shalwar, he pulled out a dirty piece of paper. Unfolding it carefully, he spread it out on my desk for me. It had the print of a tiny pair of hands. Not a photograph, not an oil painting, just some lampblack smeared on the palms to make a print on paper. Rahmat travelled to Calcutta's streets every year to sell his dry fruits, holding this remembrance of his daughter close to his breast—as though the touch of those tiny tender hands comforted the heart inside his broad chest, a heart wracked by the pain of separation.

Tears sprang to my eyes. I forgot that he was a seller of dry fruits from Kabul and I, a member of a Kulin Bengali family. I realized that he was a father, just as I was. The handprint of his little Parbati from his home in the mountains reminded me of Mini.

I sent for my daughter at once. They raised objections in the ladies' chambers, but I paid no attention. Mini appeared shyly in my room, dressed as a bride in her red wedding garb.

The Kabuliwallah was taken aback when he saw her. Unable to revive their old banter, he said nothing for a while. Finally, he said with a smile, 'Khnokhi, tomi sasurbaari jaabis?'

Mini knew now what the words meant; she could not respond as before. Blushing at Rahmat's question, she stood with her face averted. I remembered the day Mini and the Kabuliwallah had met for the first time and felt a twinge of sadness.

After Mini left, Rahmat slumped to the floor with a sigh. He had suddenly realized that his own daughter must have grown up and that he would have to get to know her all over again—she would no longer be the way he remembered her. Who knew what might have happened to her over these past eight years? The shehnai kept playing in the calming sunlight of the autumn morning, but inside a house in a Calcutta lane all that Rahmat could see were the mountains and cold deserts of Afghanistan.

I gave him some money. 'Go back home to your daughter, Rahmat,' I told him. 'Let the happiness of your reunion with her be a blessing for my Mini.'

Giving Rahmat the money meant pruning one or two things from the celebrations. The electric lights display was not as lavish as I had wanted it to be, nor were the musical arrangements as elaborate as planned. The ladies as usual objected strongly but, for me, the festivities were brightened by the benediction of a father's love.

THE OFFERING

PRAMATHA CHAUDHURI

Translated from the Bengali by Arunava Sinha

EUROPEAN CIVILIZATION HAD NOT YET THRUST ITS HORNS INTO OUR village; in other words, the railway line had bypassed us. So, to visit home from Calcutta, we still had to use traditional means of transport part of the way: the boat in the monsoon and the palanquin during summer and winter for the most part.

The road and the river ran in opposite directions. I always took the boat home, so for a long time I did not explore the land route. Then, in the year that I cleared my BA examinations, I had to go home in May to take care of some unfinished business. Today, I shall tell you of the strange incident that took place on that journey.

Getting off the train at six in the morning, I found the palanquin-bearers waiting for me. I cannot claim that the appearance of the litter was encouraging. I estimated it to be some three feet wide and less than five feet long. Then, I was transfixed by the appearance of the bearers. Cadavers such as these could probably be seen only in hospitals in other countries. Almost all of them had protruding ribs and withered flesh on their limbs.

To be carried by these fellow humans for twenty miles had at first seemed rather an unpalatable proposition. Inflicting my weight upon these spindly, half-dead unfortunates seemed exceedingly cruel. Observing my hesitation, the servant who had accompanied them from my ancestral home smiled and said, 'Get in, sir, you shall not find it uncomfortable. If you delay any more you will not arrive at your destination before four o'clock.'

Being told that travelling twenty miles would take ten hours did not boost my enthusiasm in the least. Still, I crawled into the palanquin after muttering a prayer, since there was no alternative.

At first, the glow and the breeze that filtered in from the east cheered me; the draught felt as wonderful to the skin as the radiance to the eye. My eyes as well as my heart were reborn along with the birth of the new day. I looked outside. There were fields stretching in every direction. No houses, no trees, only fields—endless fields—flat and identical, infinite and empty like the sky. Having escaped the concrete pigeonholes of Calcutta into this infinite expanse of nature, my soul experienced the bliss of deliverance. My mind shook off all worries and took on the clear, satisfied appearance of the sky with a faint red glow of joy.

But this happiness proved short-lived, for with the progress of the day the potency of the sun increased, as though nature was running a fever—the temperature rose to 105 degrees. By nine o'clock, one could no longer look out, for the sun was blinding. My eyes were thirsty for a shade of green—a search over the horizon only yielded an emaciated acacia or two. They barely quenched my thirst, for whatever other quality this tree might have possessed, it offered no green loveliness, no soothing shadow. Caught between this plain on which there was no green, no leaves, no shade, and the sunlight-stricken sky bereft of clouds, I felt a great fatigue growing. Unable to stand this dull appearance of nature any longer, I opened a book. I'd brought George Meredith's *The Egoist* with me—I had the last chapter to finish. Having read three or four pages, I realized I had paid no attention—not a word made sense. I shut the book and requested the bearers to speed up a little, promising them extra money.

This worked. We reached the halfway point at ten-thirty—half an hour early. I cannot claim this village amidst the desert was a lovely and pleasing example of an oasis. A shallow tank in the middle, eleven or twelve thatched huts on its bank, which was as high as a single-storeyed building, and a fig tree on one side. Setting the palanquin down under a tree, the bearers ran to the tank, took a dip in it, and sat down to their meal in their wet clothes. We set off again half an hour later.

The palanquin moved rather slowly now, for lunch had made the bearers slower than a pregnant woman. In the meantime, my body, mind, and senses had become so weary that I shut my eyes and tried to sleep. The afternoon sun and the rocking of the palanquin brought on slumber, but that slumber was not sleep. Just as my body had adopted a posture midway between lying down and sitting up, my mind had also occupied a position somewhere between sleep and wakefulness. A couple of hours passed this way. I was suddenly awakened by a tremendous jolt, so powerful that it penetrated my body and struck at the very seat of the soul.

Looking out, I realized that the bearers had deposited their passenger with a thud beneath an enormous banyan tree and disappeared. When I asked why, the servant said, 'They've gone for a smoke.' I took the opportunity to escape painfully from the palanquin and stretch my limbs. A little further away I found the bearers huddled together, making a great noise. At first I was apprehensive, wondering whether they were conspiring to go on strike against me, for many excited speeches were being delivered. But almost at once I realized that there was a different reason for all the shouting. What they were smoking was not tobacco—it was 'king tobacco', as was evident from the smell. Their enthusiasm, their cheerfulness, their leaps and cries made it obvious why cannabis is universally referred to in Bengali as 'quickjoy'.

At first it was amusing to watch them smoke, but gradually I became irritated. The cannabis disappeared rapidly, but none of them showed the slightest inclination to get up. When I asked how much longer they would be, the servant said, 'They won't get up, sir, unless you force them to—there's danger ahead, so they're trying to smoke up some courage.'

I said, 'What danger?'

He answered, 'It must not be mentioned, sir. You'll see for yourself soon.' I became so curious that I decided to rouse the bearers myself. Their eyes had turned red under the influence of the drug. I had to pull each one physically to his feet, which forced me to inhale some of the smoke. Entering by way of my nostrils, it went straight to my head. I was overcome by nausea at once, my head spun, my eyes felt heavy—I hastily took shelter in the palanquin. It started moving again. This time I didn't feel in the least uncomfortable—for my body seemed to belong to someone else.

After some time—how long I could not say—the bearers started shouting in unison, at the top of their voices. I had already found evidence that their vocal strength was more than their physical one, but for the first time I realized the extent of that strength. The one thing that could be heard amidst the babble was 'Ram naam'—now the leader also added his voice to the chorus, chanting, 'Ram naam sat hai, Ram naam sat hai' continuously. It made me think I had died, and that spirits were taking me to their realm in their palanquin.

Whether the cannabis had anything to do with this impression, I cannot say. I felt a great curiosity about where they were taking me. Looking out, I saw that the sky looked as though the village were on fire, but the accompanying signs of a blaze—loud screams renting the air—were not to be heard. It was so desolate, so silent, that the unbreakable peace of death seemed to have enveloped the world.

A little further on, what lay before us was a wilderness—not of sand, but of scorched earth; this earth was like a fragment of brown pottery, without a single blade of grass. There was no human habitation now on this scorched land, but numerous signs remained to show that there once had been one. This was a kingdom of bricks, as far as the eye could see there were bricks and more bricks, some stacked together, some scattered on the ground, there were bricks in the thousands; and the bricks were so red that they seemed to be bleeding. What pushed upwards from this collapsed world were trees. But none of them was leafy, they were all barren, all dry, all dead. These skeletal trees stood in clumps at some places, and singly at others. And the bricks and the timber, the earth and the sky, all seemed to have gone up in blood-red flames.

It was hardly surprising that simple people like my bearers should be frightened at this sight, for I felt a bit shaken myself. A little later, the faint sound of sobs penetrated the silence and came to my ears. The tone was so soft, so pathetic, so distressed that generations of human agony appear to have been collected and distilled in it. It filled me with compassion. In an instant, I sensed the pain of all humankind.

Suddenly, a storm came up, the wind raged from all directions. The fire in the sky swirled madly, tormented by the wind. A typhoon seemed to rise above the sea of blood, flaming waves spreading in all directions. And in that fiery deluge I saw thousands of people flailing and writhing. At this sight the elements clapped their hands in glee and shouted aloud. Gradually all these sounds coalesced into one universal laugh—its merciless, grotesque noise dispatched waves of turbulence to the horizon. Then it diminished gradually, being transformed into the same soft, pathetic, distressed sobs I had heard earlier. The conflict between the grotesque laughter and the tragic sobs brought out in me old memories of this abandoned place—whether the memories were from this life or a previous one, I cannot tell.

Someone within me seemed to say, here is the history of this village.... This brick-and-wood wilderness was the ruin of Rudrapur. The Roys of Rudrapur had once been the principal zamindars of the area. The founder of the clan, Rudranarayan, had received his title by virtue of working for the nawab, and along with it he had earned ownership rights to three divisions of land. People said the family had in its possession a deed, signed by the emperor of Delhi himself, which gave them the power to execute anyone.

Whether they were empowered by the deed or not, there was no doubt that they did carry out executions. Legend had it that there had never been such indomitable zamindars in the land before. The strong and the weak alike bowed before them. Those who earned their wrath lost both their property and their lives. The number of people whose homes and lands they had captured was beyond count. There wasn't anyone within twenty miles who dared to disobey the Roys' commands. Under their iron rule there was not the faintest trace of crime in the area, for all who could use sticks, spears, or swords were enlisted in the army.

Just like their boundless ruthlessness, their benevolence was limitless too. Providing food and clothes to the poor and medicines to the sick was an everyday affair. Countless people lived gratefully under their patronage. All the priests in the area had become rich landowners on the strength of the rights that the Roys had granted to Brahmins. And they spent unstintingly on festivals and rituals—Holi, Durga Puja, and the like. In Rudrapur, the sky would turn crimson with abir during Holi—and the earth with blood during Durga Puja.

In the guest houses, there were arrangements to feed a hundred guests daily. No Brahmin saddled with a dead father or mother, or a marriageable daughter, ever went back empty-handed from the Roys. They would say that the Brahmin's wealth is not for amassing but for spending on good causes. So, if money for such philanthropy ever ran short, the masters did not shrink from looting traders and moneylenders. In brief, they did good and evil according to their own fancies, for under the reign of the nawab, no one ruled over them. Consequently, common people respected them as much as they feared them, for they neither feared nor respected the people. As a result of such untrammelled tyranny, their estimation of their own excellence increased tremendously. Ingrained in them was the pride of race, of wealth, of power, of appearance. All the males in the Roy family were fair, tall, and strong, and the fame of the beauty of their womenfolk had spread countrywide. Because of all this, it had become next to impossible for them to think of anyone else as a human being.

But, even before the advent of the English, the fortunes of the family had started falling apart, and later, in the era of the East India Company, they were ruined. Those factions which had become penniless, because of the division of property over successive generations, found their lines dying out, for in their eyes it was contemptible to earn a living by one's own toil. On top of that were the disputes over the sharing of property. The Roy family worshipped the goddess Shakti—so much so that in Rudrapur young boys and old men alike were regular drinkers. Not even the women objected, for they believed that drinking was masculine. When the lords assembled after paying their respects to the family goddess and got down to drinking, the prominent sandalwood-and-blood marks on their foreheads and their bloodshot eyes gave them the appearance of Shiva with his inflamed third eye.

During this phase no task was too daunting for them. They would order their stick-wielding soldiers to plunder grains from one subject and to rape the wife of another. Bloodshed followed. This family rivalry took them forward along the road to extinction. Whatever property and assets remained were transferred by virtue of the ten-year settlement (under which the government granted the Roys ownership of the land for ten years provided they fulfilled certain conditions). It never occurred to them that unless the last instalment was paid by the due date they would become permanently bankrupt. Because they were not used to doing it, they never managed to pay the revenue owed to the Company on time. As a result most of their property had to be auctioned off.

With time the clan of the Roys was almost obliterated. Where they had once occupied almost a hundred houses, only six branches remained about a hundred years ago. The property and assets of those six branches gradually passed into Dhananjay Sarkar's hands. This was because Dhananjay followed English law as carefully as he knew it. The various tricks of making money with the help of the law, while staying within it, were at his fingertips. He had earned a great deal of money from practising as an attorney at the district court. Channelled into moneylending, these funds had accumulated a massive amount of interest, swelling his fortune greatly.

Public opinion held that he had earned ten lakh rupees in about ten years. Even if it wasn't quite as much, there was no doubt that he had earned three or four lakh rupees easily. After making all this money, he wanted to be a zamindar, and so he started buying the Roys' property bit by bit—for he knew every acre of the estate like the back of his hand. His family had always worked for the Roys, and in his younger days, he too, had worked six or seven years for the head of the oldest branch, Triloknarayan. But, despite buying up the entire property and even the homes of every branch of the family, he had not dared to visit Rudrapur, for Ugranarayan, the son of his former master, was still alive. Ugranarayan had sworn by his sacred thread, placing his hand on the family idol, that if Dhananjay ever set foot within the borders of Rudrapur in Ugranarayan's lifetime, he would not return in one piece.

Dhananjay had no doubt in his mind that Ugranarayan would fulfil his oath to the letter. For he knew that no one as fearsome and courageous as Ugranarayan had ever been born into the Roy family. Some weeks after Ugranarayan's death, Dhananjay went to Rudrapur and occupied the Roys' ancestral home. Not a single male from the Roy family was present in the village, so he could have taken possession of every house had he so wanted; yet he made no attempt to turn Ugranarayan's only daughter, Ratnamayee, who was a widow, out of her ancestral home.

For one thing, the subjects of Pathanpara, the village adjacent to Rudrapur, were determined to protect Ratnamayee's rights and ownership. The village comprised generations of people adept at fighting with sticks; Dhananjay knew that if he tried to evict Ratnamayee, injury or death was inevitable. He wasn't about to face such a fate, for there wasn't another person in Bengal as timid as he.

Second, Dhananjay harboured a modicum of fear and respect, arising from superstition, for the family that had provided sustenance to his own. Because of all this, Dhananjay left Ugranarayan's portion alone, occupying the rest of the Roys' family home—though only nominally. For Dhananjay's family consisted only of his daughter, Rangini, and her husband, Ratilal Dey.

After he had moved house, Dhananjay underwent a distinct change. While he had been making money, his desire for wealth had taken him over so completely that greed was all he harboured. In the grip of this desire, he had blindly gathered riches by any means whatsoever—it had never occurred to him to find out for whom or for what. But after he installed himself as the zamindar in Rudrapur, he woke up to the fact that he had made money simply for the sake of making money, not for anything else, not for anyone else.

He recalled that when his seven sons had died one after the other, he had not been perturbed even for a day, he had not neglected his business pursuits. The excessive love for money that he had harboured for a lifetime was now transformed into excessive possessiveness. He spent sleepless nights wondering how his amassed wealth could be preserved for posterity. Rudrapur itself was visible proof that even unlimited wealth could be lost over the ages. Gradually an idea took root in his mind—that man could accumulate riches by his own effort, but without the help of the gods those riches couldn't be preserved.

Although he knew the laws of the English by heart, Dhananjay was essentially uneducated. He had never outgrown his rustic origins, the education he had received had had no effect in this regard. His mind was ruled by every superstition and blind belief that a lower-caste person could be expected to subscribe to. He had heard in his childhood that if a Brahmin child were locked up with riches in a room and died of starvation, the child would be transformed into a spirit and guard the wealth forever. He was so obsessed with preserving his amassed wealth in this manner that he became convinced that doing this was his most important duty. In matters where Dhananjay had no doubts, he was used to getting his way in the face of every opposition. But in this case a great obstacle did arise. Hearing that Dhananjay meant to sacrifice a Brahmin child, Rangini gave up food and sleep. Consequently, it became impossible for Dhananjay to fulfil his heart's desire.

If Dhananjay loved anything in the world besides money, it was his daughter. Just as a tree might take root even amidst brick and mortar, this weakness for his daughter had taken root in a crevice somewhere in Dhananjay's hard heart. Though Dhananjay did not take the initiative himself, a certain turn of events fulfilled the last wish of his life.

Ratnamayee had a three-year-old son. His name was Kiritchandra. She lived alone with her son, never meeting anyone. No one was allowed into her inner sanctum. The people of Rudrapur would actually have forgotten her existence had she not visited the family goddess's temple every day, after her bath, precisely at noon—guarded by two of Pathanpara's stick-wielding citizens. Ratnamayee was twenty or twenty-one at the time. Women as wondrously beautiful as she were extremely rare in the land. She resembled the family goddess. Her eyes slanted upwards like those of the idol's—and, just like those eyes, hers too were still, immobile. People said her lashes never closed. What burnt brightly in them was her total contempt for the men and women around her. Ratnamayee had inherited the ancestral arrogance accumulated over three centuries by her family. Needless to say, she also nurtured a fierce pride in her own beauty. To her, this beauty was clear proof of her nobility. In Ratnamayee's view, the purpose of beauty was not to attract people, but to slight them. When she went to the temple people on the road stepped aside, for her very posture told them, in the silent language of her complexion and figure, 'Go away. Even stepping on your shadow would mean having to cleanse myself.' She never glanced to the left or the right, with her eyes cast downwards she lit up the path on her way to and from the temple.

Behind closed shutters, Rangini watched Ratnamayee, and her mind and her body grew rigid with the poison of envy—for however much her possessions might be, beauty was not one of them. And this deficiency pained her a great deal, for her husband Ratilal was extremely handsome. Rangini loved her husband the way Dhananjay loved money—in other words, this love was nothing more than a terrible hunger, and this hunger, just like physical hunger, was blind and ruthless. What relationship it had with the heart was difficult to say, for the hearts of creatures like Dhananjay and Rangini are not external to the body, but included within it.

Like Dhananjay, Rangini treated the object of her love as her personal property. The very thought that someone might set hands on it made her ruthless, and there was no act in the world too cruel to preserve her property. A completely unfounded suspicion had risen in Rangini's mind—that Ratilal had been entranced by Ratnamayee's beauty; that suspicion was gradually transformed into certainty. Rangini suddenly discovered that Ratilal went to Ugranarayan's house secretly, loitering there for hours. The real attraction was drinking bhang with the Brahmin who lived under Ratnamayee's patronage. And then, the childless Ratilal had developed such a weakness for Ratnamayee's son that he couldn't pass a single day without setting eyes on Kiritchandra.

Needless to say, Ratnamayee and Ratilal had never even exchanged glances, for the inhabitants of Pathanpara guarded her inner sanctum. But Rangini became convinced that Ratnamayee had decided to steal her handsome husband from her. To take revenge for this, and to satisfy her innate enviousness, Rangini decided to use Ratnamayee's son to fulfil her father's wish. She let Dhananjay know that not only did she have no objection to his plan, but she would look for a suitable young boy.

This sort of thing had to be conducted with much stealth, however. So, after much discussion, father and daughter decided to use the room next to Rangini's bedroom to carry out their plot. In three or four days all the doors and windows of this room were sealed with bricks. Then, very furtively, all the gold and silver coins Dhananjay had amassed were put into large copper pitchers and arranged in rows inside the room. When all Dhananjay's wealth had been put in there, Rangini told Ratilal that Ratnamayee's son was so lovely she desperately wanted to hold him in her arms—and that he would somehow have to bring Kiritchandra to her. Ratilal answered that it was impossible, if Ratnamayee's bodyguards got to know they would smash his head. But Rangini became so insistent that Ratilal soon managed to wheedle Kiritchandra into accompanying him to meet Rangini.

As soon as Kiritchandra arrived, Rangini took him in her arms and smothered him with kisses. Then she dressed him in red, put a garland around his neck, a red sandalwood-and-vermilion mark on his forehead and two gold bangles on his wrists. Seeing him dressed up like this, Ratilal's face lit up with pleasure. Then Rangini took Kiritchandra by the hand, pushed him into the sealed chamber and locked the door. Pushing against the door, Ratilal realized that Rangini had locked him in too, alone in his bedroom.

Although Ratilal tried to push, kick, and hammer his way out of the bedroom and into the sealed chamber, he realized his efforts were futile. The door was so heavy and so solid that it would be difficult to break it down even with an axe. Shut inside that pitch-dark room, Kiritchandra started sobbing at first, and then called out to Ratilal, 'Dada, Dada.' Two or three hours later, his sobs could no longer be heard. Ratilal realized that he had cried himself to sleep.

Locked up in his room for three days and three nights, Ratilal could hear Kiritchandra—now banging his head against the bedroom door, now sobbing, now silent. At his wits' end, Ratilal attacked the door a thousand times over those three days, but he couldn't budge it even an inch. Every time he heard sobs he ran to the door to say, 'Don't weep so, Baba, don't be afraid, I'm here.' Hearing his voice the boy would cry out even more loudly, bang his head against the door of the sealed chamber even more often; Ratilal covered his ears with his hands and ran away to the other end of the room, screaming out to Rangini and Dhananjay at the top of his voice, calling them whatever names came to his mind.

He had become so unhinged by this fiendish business that it never occurred to him that there could be some other way of rescuing Kiritchandra—his entire attention was drawn by those sobs from the boy trapped inside that sealed chamber. After three days, the child's sobs grew gradually weaker, fainter, and stopped altogether on the fifth day. Ratilal realized that Kiritchandra's little heart had stopped beating. He parted the iron rods on the window with his hands, jumped out and ran directly to Ratnamayee's house.

That day there were no guards at the door, for all the people of Pathanpara were out looking for the missing boy. Taking this opportunity Ratilal appeared before Ratnamayee and narrated everything to her. For three years no one had seen Ratnamayee smile. Hearing of the cruel murder of her son, her face and eyes lit up, she seemed to be smiling. Ratilal found this so peculiar that he fled from her presence and disappeared. Then, in the middle of the night, while everyone was asleep, Ratnamayee set fire to her room.

The houses adjoined one another. Within an hour the fire spread like the wrathful flames of the gods and attacked Dhananjay's house. Dhananjay and Rangini tried to escape, but at the front gate they saw Ratnamayee, surrounded by almost a hundred of Pathanpara's inhabitants armed with swords, spears, and shields. At Ratnamayee's command they plunged their spears into the father and the daughter until they were covered with blood from head to foot, and threw them into the flames. Ratnamayee burst into laughter, and her attendants realized she had gone mad.

Then the people of Pathanpara went berserk. Dhananjay's servants, maids, employees, guards, doormen—whoever they found were skewered by their swords and spears, and the ancestral home of the Roy family was overrun by a river of fire above and of blood below. Then came a storm and an earthquake. When everything was burnt to smithereens, Ratnamayee jumped into the flames. Everything in Rudrapur stands in ruins today. Only Kiritchandra's sobs and Ratnamayee's insane laughter still rise up to the skies.

4

MAHESH

SARAT CHANDRA CHATTOPADHYAY

Translated from the Bengali by Arunava Sinha

I

THE VILLAGE WAS NAMED KASHIPUR. AN INSIGNIFICANT VILLAGE, WITH an even more insignificant zamindar, but such was his authority that his subjects were in awe of him.

It was the birthday of the zamindar's youngest son. Having performed the holy rituals, Tarkaratna, the priest, was on his way home in the afternoon. The month of Boishakh was drawing to a close, but there was not even a trace of clouds anywhere, the searing sky seemingly pouring fire on everything below. The field stretching to the horizon before him was parched and cracked, with the blood in the veins of the earth escaping constantly through the crevices in the form of vapour. Gazing at it coiling upwards like flames made the head reel with drunkenness.

Gafoor Jolha lived on the edge of this field. The earthen wall surrounding his house had collapsed, merging his yard with the road. The privacy of the inner chambers had all but surrendered itself to the mercy of the passer-by.

Pausing in the shade of a white teak tree, Tarkaratna called out loudly, 'Are you home, Gafra?'

Gafoor's ten-year-old daughter came to the door. 'What do you need Baba for? He's got a fever.'

'Fever! Call the swine! Monster! Godless creature!'

The screaming and shouting brought Gafoor Mian to the door, shivering with fever. An ancient acacia stood next to the broken wall, with a bull tethered to it. Pointing to it, Tarkaratna said, 'What's all this? Have you forgotten this is a Hindu village with a Brahmin zamindar?' Red with rage and the heat, his words were fiery, but Gafoor, unable to understand the reason for the outburst, could only stare at him.

'When I passed this way in the morning he was tethered there,' said Tarkaratna, 'and now on my way back he's still tethered the same way. Karta will bury you alive if you kill a bull. He's a devout Brahmin.'

'What can I do, Baba Thakur, I have no choice. I've had this fever for several days now. I collapse every time I try to take him to graze.'

'Then turn him loose, he'll find food on his own.'

'Where can I turn him loose, Baba Thakur? The winnowing isn't done, the grain is still lying in the fields. The hay hasn't been sorted, the earth is burning, there's not a blade of grass anywhere. What if he eats someone's grains or hay—how can I turn him loose, Baba Thakur?'

Softening, Tarkaratna said, 'If you can't let him loose at least give him some straw. Hasn't your daughter made any rice? Give him a bowl of starch and water.'

Gafoor did not answer, only looked at Tarkaratna helplessly and sighed.

Tarkaratna said, 'No rice either? What did you do with the hay? Did you sell your entire share without keeping anything for your beast? You butcher!'

Gafoor seemed to lose his power of speech at this cruel accusation. A little later he said haltingly, 'I did get some hay this year, but Karta Moshai took it away to pay for taxes left over from last year. I fell at his feet, I said, "Babu Moshai, you're the supreme authority, where will I go if I leave your kingdom, give me at least a little hay. There's no straw for the roof, we have just the one room for father and daughter, we can still manage with palm leaves this monsoon, but my Mahesh will die of starvation."'

With a mocking smile, Tarkaratna said, 'Really! What a loving name, Mahesh. I'll die laughing.'

Paying no attention to the taunt, Gafoor continued, 'But the lord had no mercy on me. He allowed me some rice to feed us for two months, but all my hay was confiscated and the poor thing got nothing at all.' His voice grew moist with tears. But this evoked no compassion in Tarkaratna, who said, 'What a man you are. You've eaten up everything but don't want to pay your dues. Do you expect the zamindar to feed you? You people live in a perfect kingdom, still you bad-mouth him, you're such wretches.'

An embarrassed Gafoor said, 'Why should we bad-mouth him, Baba Thakur, we don't do that. But how do I pay my taxes? I sharecrop four bighas, but there's been a famine two years in a row—the grains have all dried up. My daughter and I don't even get two meals a day. Look at the house, when it rains we spend the night in a corner, there's not even enough space to stretch our legs. Look at Mahesh, Thakur Moshai, you can count his ribs. Lend me a little hay, Thakur Moshai, let the creature feed to his heart's content for a few days.' Still speaking, he flung himself to the ground near the Brahmin's feet. Leaping backwards hastily, Tarkaratna exclaimed, 'My God, are you going to touch me?'

'No, Baba Thakur, I'm not going to touch you or anything. But give me some hay. I saw your four huge haystacks the other day, you won't even know if a little of it is gone. I don't care if we starve to death, but this poor creature cannot talk, he only stares and weeps.'

Tarkaratna said, 'And how do you propose to repay the loan?'

A hopeful Gafoor said, 'I'll find a way to repay it somehow, Baba Thakur, I won't cheat you.'

Snorting, Tarkaratna mimicked Gafoor, 'I won't cheat you! I'll find a way to return it somehow! What a comedian! Get out of my way. I should be getting home, it's late.' Chuckling, he took a step forward only to retreat several steps in fear. Angrily he said, 'Oh god, he's waving his horns, is he going to gore me now?'

Gafoor rose to his feet. Pointing to the bundle of fruit and moistened rice in the priest's hand, he said, 'He's smelt food, he wants to eat....'

'Wants to eat? Of course. Both master and bull are well-matched. Can't get hay to eat, and now you want fruit. Get him out of my way. Those horns, someone will be killed by them.' Tarkaratna hurried away.

Gafoor turned towards Mahesh, gazing at him in silence for a few moments. There was suffering and hunger in the bull's deep black eyes. Gafoor said, 'He wouldn't give you any, would he? They have so much, but still they won't. Never mind.' He choked, and tears began to roll down from his eyes. Going up to the animal, he stroked his back and neck, whispering, 'You are my son, Mahesh, you've grown old looking after us for eight years, I can't even give you enough to eat, but you know how much I love you.'

Mahesh responded by stretching his neck and closing his eyes in pleasure. Wiping his tears off the bull's back, Gafoor murmured, 'The zamindar took away your food, leased out the grazing ground near the crematorium just for money. How will I save your life in this year of starvation? If I turn you loose, you'll eat other people's hay, you'll spoil their trees—what do I do with you! You have no strength left, people tell me to sell you off.' No sooner had Gafoor said this in his head than his tears began to roll down again. Wiping them with his hand, he looked around surreptitiously before fetching some discoloured straw from behind his dilapidated house and placing them near Mahesh's mouth, saying, 'Eat up quickly, if not there'll be....'

'Baba?'

'Yes, Ma?'

'Come and eat,' said Amina, appearing at the door. After a glance she said, 'You're giving Mahesh straw from the roof again, Baba?'

This was just what he was afraid of. Reddening, he said, 'Old rotten straw, Ma, it was falling off anyway....'

'I heard you pulling it out, Baba.'

'No, Ma, not exactly pulling it out....'

'But the wall will collapse, Baba....'

Gafoor was silent. The house was all they had left, and no one knew better than him that if he continued this way it wouldn't survive the next monsoon. But how long could they go on?

His daughter said, 'Wash your hands and come, Baba, I've served the food.'

Gafoor said, 'Bring the starch out, Ma, let me feed Mahesh first.'

'No starch left today, Baba, it dried in the pot.'

No starch? Gafoor stood in silence. His ten-year-old daughter knew that when the times were bad even this could not be wasted. He washed his hands and went in. His daughter served him rice and vegetables on a brass plate, taking some for herself on an earthen plate. Gafoor said softly, 'I'm feeling cold again, Amina, is it safe to eat with a fever?'

Amina asked anxiously, 'But didn't you say you were hungry?'

'Maybe I didn't have a fever then, Ma.'

'Then let me put it away, you can have it in the evening.'

Shaking his head, Gafoor said, 'Eating cold food will make things worse.'

'What should I do then?' asked Amina.

Gafoor pretended to think before solving the problem. He said, 'Why don't you give it to Mahesh, Ma? You can make me some fresh rice at night, can't you?'

Amina looked at him in silence for a few moments before lowering her eyes, nodding, and saying, 'Yes, Baba, I can.'

Gafoor reddened. Besides the two actors, only someone up there observed this little charade between father and daughter.

II

Five or six days later, Gafoor was seated outside his front door with an anxious expression on his face. Mahesh had not been home since yesterday morning. He himself was too weak to move, so his daughter Amina had searched high and low for the bull. Returning home in the late afternoon, she said, 'Have you heard, Baba, Manik Ghosh's family has taken our Mahesh to the police station?'

'What nonsense,' said Gafoor.

'It's true, Baba. Their servant said, "Tell your father to look for him in the Dariapur pen."'

'What did he do?'

'He got into their garden and destroyed their trees, Baba.'

Gafoor sat in silence. He had imagined all manner of mishaps that might have befallen Mahesh, but had not anticipated this. He was as harmless as he was poor, which was why he had no apprehensions of being punished so severely by any of his neighbours—Manik Ghosh, in particular, for his respect for cows was legendary.

His daughter said, 'It's getting late, Baba, aren't you going to bring Mahesh home?'

'No,' answered Gafoor.

'But they said the police will sell him in the cattle market after three days.'

'Let them sell him,' said Gafoor.

Amina did not know what exactly a cattle market was, but she had noticed her father becoming agitated whenever it was mentioned with reference to Mahesh. She left without another word.

Under cover of the night Gafoor went to Bansi's shop, and said, 'Khuro, I need a rupee,' and deposited his brass plate beneath the raised platform on which Bansi sat. Bansi was familiar with the exact weight and other details of this object. It had been pawned some five times in the past two years, for a rupee each time. So, he did not object this time either.

Mahesh was seen in his usual place the next day. Beneath the same tree, tethered to the same stake with the same rope, the same empty bowl with no food in front of him, the same questioning look in the moist, hungry black eyes. An elderly Muslim man was examining him closely. Gafoor Mian sat nearby, his knees drawn up to his chin. When the examination was over, the man extracted a ten-rupee note from the knot in his dhoti and, smoothening it repeatedly, went up to Gafoor, saying, 'I don't need change, take the whole thing—here.'

Holding his hand out for the money, Gafoor remained sitting in silence. But just as the old Muslim's companions were about to untie the bull, he suddenly jumped to his feet, saying belligerently, 'Don't you dare touch that rope, I'm warning you.'

They were startled. The old man said in surprise, 'Why not?'

Still furious, Gafoor said, 'What do you mean, why not? It's mine to sell or not. And I'm not selling.' He threw the ten-rupee note on the ground.

They said, 'But you took an advance yesterday.'

'Here's your advance.' Retrieving two rupees from the knot in his dhoti, he flung the coins at them, and they fell with a clatter. Realizing that a quarrel was imminent, the old man said gently with a smile, 'You're putting pressure on us for two rupees more, aren't you? Go on, give his daughter two rupees more. That's what you wanted, isn't it?'

'No.'

'Are you aware that no one will give you a better price?'

'No,' said Gafoor, shaking his head vehemently.

The old man said in annoyance, 'What do you think? Only the skin is worth selling. There's nothing else in there.'

'Tauba! Tauba!' A terrible expletive suddenly escaped Gafoor's lips, and the very next moment he ran into his house threatening to have them thrashed within an inch of their lives by the zamindar's guards unless they left the village at once.

The possibility of trouble made them leave, but soon Gafoor received a summons from the zamindar's court. He realized that word had reached the landowner.

There were people both refined and unrefined in court. Glaring at Gafoor, Shibu Babu said, 'I don't know how to punish you, Gafra. Do you know where you live?'

Bowing, Gafoor said, 'I do. We're starving, or else I would have paid whatever fine you think fit.'

Everyone present was astonished. They had always considered him an obstinate and bad-tempered man. And here he was on the verge of tears, saying, 'I'll never do it again, Karta.' He proceeded to box his own ears, rubbed his nose into the ground from one end of the court to the other, and then stood up.

Shibu Babu said indulgently, 'All right, enough. Don't do all this again.'

Everyone was shocked when they heard the details. They were certain that only the grace of the zamindar and the fear of punishment had prevented the abject sinner from committing worse transgressions. Tarkaratna was present, and provided the scriptural analysis of the word 'go' for cow, enlightening everyone as to why it was forbidden to allow this godless race of heathens to live within village limits.

Gafoor did not respond to any of this, humbly accepting all the humiliation and vilification and returning home cheerfully. Borrowing the starch from the rice pots of neighbours, he gave it to Mahesh to eat, murmuring many endearments as he stroked the bull's back and horns.

III

The month of Joishtho was drawing to a close. The sun was still harsh and severe in the sky. There was no trace of mercy anywhere. People were afraid to even hope for change, hope that the skies could again be moist and pleasurable with the weight of rain-bearing clouds. It seemed that there would be no cessation to the flames burning constantly across the entire fiery earth—that they would not die down till they had consumed everything.

Gafoor returned home on such an afternoon. He was not used to working as a labourer on someone else's fields, and it had been only four or five days since the fever had subsided. He was as weak as he was exhausted. Still, he had gone out in search of work, but all he had got was the unforgiving heat and sun overhead. He could barely see for hunger and thirst. Standing at the door, he called out, 'Amina, is the food ready?'

His daughter emerged slowly and stood grasping the post without an answer.

Gafoor shouted, 'Not ready? Why not?'

'No rice at home, Baba.'

'No rice? Why didn't you tell me in the morning?'

'But I told you last night.'

Contorting his face and mocking her, Gafoor said, 'Told you last night! How can anyone remember if you tell them at night?' The harsh tone he was using stoked his anger. Contorting his face even further, he said, 'How will there be any rice? Whether the sick father gets any or not, the grown-up daughter will eat five times a day. I'm going to lock up the rice from now on. Give me some water, I'm dying of thirst. Now tell me we have no water either.'

Amina remained standing with her eyes downcast. When Gafoor realized after waiting a few moments that there was not even any water to drink at home, he could control himself no longer. Striding up to his daughter, he slapped her resoundingly, saying, 'Haramjaadi, what do you do all day? Why can't you die?'

Without a word his daughter picked up the empty pitcher and went out in the heat, wiping her eyes. Gafoor felt heartbroken as soon as she was out of sight. He alone knew how he had brought up his daughter after her mother's death. He remembered that it was not the dutiful and affectionate girl's fault. Ever since they had run out of the paltry amount of rice he had received for his work in the fields, they had not had two meals a day. On some days, just one—or not even that. His accusation that Amina was eating five times a day was as impossible as it was untrue. Nor was he unaware of the reasons for the lack of water to drink. The two or three tanks in the village were all dry. The little water there was in the pond behind Shibcharan Babu's house was not available to ordinary people. The water that could be collected by digging a hole or two in the middle of the tanks was fought over by a crowd of people.

Being a Muslim, the young girl was not even allowed near that water. She had to wait for hours, pleading for some water, and only if someone took pity on her, and poured her a little could she bring it home. He knew all this. Perhaps there had been no water that day, or no one had had the time to take pity on his daughter during the battle. Realizing that something like this must have taken place, Gafoor found his own eyes filling with tears. At that moment the zamindar's footman appeared like a messenger of death, screaming, 'Gafra, are you home?'

Gafoor answered bitterly, 'I am. Why?'

'Babu Moshai has sent for you. Come along.'

Gafoor said, 'I haven't eaten yet. I'll come later.'

Unable to tolerate such audacity, the footman swore and said, 'The Babu has ordered me to flog you and force you to come.'

Gafoor forgot himself a second time, uttering an unprintable word in retaliation, and said, 'No one is a slave in the kingdom of the empress. I pay my taxes, I won't go.'

But for such a small man to give such a big reason was not just futile but also dangerous. Fortunately, such an insignificant voice would not reach the ears of the important man it was meant for—or else he would have lost both his home and his livelihood. There is no need for an elaborate account of what ensued, but when he returned from the zamindar's court an hour later and lay down in silence, his face and eyes were swollen. The primary cause of such severe punishment was Mahesh. After Gafoor had gone out, Mahesh had broken free from the post, entered the zamindar's yard, eaten his flowers, spoilt the paddy put out in the sun, and, when about to be caught, had made his escape after knocking the zamindar's youngest daughter to the ground. This was not the first time it had happened, but Gafoor had been pardoned earlier on the grounds of being poor. He might have been pardoned this time too had he begged and pleaded as in the past, but what he had said—that he paid his taxes and was no one's servant—was the kind of arrogance from a subject that Shibcharan Babu, being a zamindar, could not tolerate. Gafoor had not protested in the slightest against the thrashing and the humiliation, bearing it all in silence. Back home, too, he sat coiled up in silence. He had no awareness of hunger or thirst, but his heart was burning just like the noonday sky outside. However, when he heard his daughter's stricken cry from the yard, he leapt to his feet and ran outside to find Amina lying on the ground and Mahesh lapping up the water trickling out of the shattered pitcher. Gafoor lost his mind. Picking up the plough-head he had brought home yesterday to repair, he smashed Mahesh's head with it repeatedly.

Mahesh tried to lift his head just once, then his starving, skinny body slumped to the ground. A few tears rolled down his eyes, along with a few drops of blood from his ears. His entire body trembled once or twice, after which, stretching out his front and hind legs, Mahesh died.

Amina sobbed, 'What have you done, Baba, our Mahesh is dead.'

Gafoor had turned to stone, neither moving nor speaking, only staring at a pair of unblinking, bottomless dark eyes.

Within an hour or two, a group of cobblers from one end of the village arrived, and slinging Mahesh up on a pole took him to the dumping ground. Gafoor trembled when he saw their shining knives, but closing his eyes, he didn't say a word.

The neighbours said that the zamindar had sent someone to Tarkaratna to find out what should be done next, 'You may have to sell your house as penance.'

Gafoor did not reply to any of this, burying his face in his knees and not moving.

Late that night he woke his daughter up, saying, 'Amina, we must go.'

She had fallen asleep outside the front door. Rubbing her eyes and sitting up, she said, 'Where will we go, Baba?'

Gafoor said, 'To work at the jute mill in Phulbere.'

His daughter looked at him in astonishment. Despite all their troubles her father had never been willing to work at the jute mill. She had often heard him say that it was impossible to maintain one's faith there, that women had neither honour nor protection.

Gafoor said, 'Hurry up, Ma, we have to walk a long way.'

Amina was about to take the tumbler and the brass plate her father ate from, but Gafoor stopped her. 'Leave them here, Ma, they will pay for my penance for Mahesh.'

He left in the dead of night, holding his daughter's hand. He had no family in this village, no one to inform. Crossing the yard, he stopped abruptly beneath the familiar tree and suddenly burst into tears. Raising his eyes to the star-studded black sky, he said, 'Allah! Punish me as you will, but my Mahesh died with a thirst. There was no land he could graze on. Do not forgive the sin of whoever it was who did not let him eat the grass you gave us, or quench his thirst with the water you gave us.'

THE SHROUD

MUNSHI PREMCHAND

Translated from the Urdu by Muhammad Umar Memon

OUTSIDE THE HUT, FATHER AND SON SAT IN SILENCE IN FRONT OF A FIRE that had died down. Inside, Budhya, the son's young wife, kept thrashing about in labour, intermittently sending forth piercing cries of pain that momentarily froze the hearts of the two men. It was a cold wintry night. It was very still. The entire village was engulfed in darkness.

'Doesn't look like she'll make it,' said Ghisu. 'She's been writhing in agony all day long. Perhaps you should go in and have a look at her.'

Madhu replied in a mournful voice, 'If die she must, why linger on. What's there for me to look at, anyway?'

'You are a heartless man.... So unfeeling towards the woman who gave you every comfort of life for an entire year!'

'I just can't bear the sight of her flailing about in utter agony.'

Theirs was a family of Chamars, and none too liked for its ways throughout the village. Ghisu worked one day and took rest for the next three. Madhu shirked work if he could help it. And even if he did work for an hour, he spent an equal amount smoking his chillum. That's why no one felt like hiring these layabouts. If the house had a fistful of grain, well, that was as good a reason as any not to work at all. However, they would run out of food every now and again and then Ghisu would climb a tree and break off some branches for firewood which Madhu would take to the bazaar to sell. For the time the money lasted, they idled away the hours without a care, until the next bout of starvation overtook them, and the earlier routine of gathering firewood or looking for work kicked in again. It wasn't like there was shortage of work in this village of farmers. Hundreds of jobs were ready for the taking for any hardworking man. People took them on only when necessity drove them to hire two men to do the job of one. Had the two been sadhus, they would have had no need to seek contentment and trust in God through ascetic self-denial, for these were their innate attributes. It was a strange life; they owned nothing beyond a few clay pots, torn rags to clothe their nakedness—free of worldly deceptions, weighed down by heavy debts, the butt of people's insults and scorn, and yet not a worry to speak of. Despite their abject poverty, people still lent them something, fully aware that none of it was ever coming back. At harvest time, they would steal green peas or dig up potatoes from other people's fields, bake them and have their fill, or pick a few stalks of sugar cane to suck at night. Ghisu had lived through all his sixty years in such ascetic frugality, and Madhu, every bit his father's son, was following in his footsteps; if anything, he had put a gloss on his old man's fame. Ghisu's wife had died a while back. Madhu had married just a year ago. Ever since her arrival, this woman had put a measure of order and civility in their family. She would do chores for others; grind grain or cut grass to earn a little and buy some flour to fill the stomachs of these shameless bums. Her presence had made them even more indolent and slothful. If anyone offered a job, they audaciously asked for double wages, as if they couldn't care less. And now the same woman was writhing in deathly labour since the morning, while the two men were perhaps waiting for her to die so that they could finally get some peaceful sleep.

The two men had been roasting some potatoes they had pilfered in the embers of the fire that had died out. Ghisu yanked out the potatoes from the ashes, started peeling them, and told Madhu, 'Come on now, go inside and see how she's doing. Looks like some evil spirit has possessed her—yes, evil spirit, a witch. Here, even an exorcist asks for a rupee. Who's going to give it to us?'

Afraid that if he went inside Ghisu would polish off most of the potatoes himself, Madhu said, 'I'm scared.'

'Scared—scared of what? I'm right here.'

'Well then, go yourself and see.'

'When my woman lay dying, I didn't leave her side for three days. Wouldn't Budhya be embarrassed seeing me? I've never seen her face without her veil on. If she sees me in her senseless state, she wouldn't be able to thrash freely out of modesty.'

'Say, what if she did give birth to a child? Ginger, raw sugar, oil—we have got nothing in the house.'

'Oh, we'll get everything. First, let Bhagwan give us a child. The very people who are averse to giving us a penny now will rush in to provide. Nine boys were born to us and we were flat broke, but each time things worked out swimmingly.'

The emergence of such a mindset was not surprising, indeed it was inevitable in a social milieu where the general condition of those toiling away day and night was not much better than that of Ghisu and Madhu and where carefree existence was the privilege of only those who took advantage of the dismal circumstances of the peasantry. One would even venture to say that Ghisu reflected a keener sense of reality and discernment than the peasants in joining the ranks of the rogues and the rabble-rousers rather than those of the dim-witted community of farm workers. What he sorely lacked, though, was the ability to stick to the rules and the ways of the rogues. So, while others of his ilk became wielders of power and authority in the village, he remained the object of everyone's scorn. But there was comfort in the thought that as bad as his situation was at least he didn't have to work his backside off like the farmers, that his simple-mindedness and unassuming manner were his greatest assets against anyone taking advantage of him.

Both men started ravenously eating the searing hot potatoes. They hadn't had a morsel to eat since the day before and could hardly wait for the potatoes to cool. As a result, they repeatedly singed their tongues. The outer part of a peeled potato didn't feel overly hot, but the instant the teeth dug into its insides, the burning pulp scalded their tongues, their palates, and their throats. It was better to quickly swallow the live ember than chew on it. It would be cooled once it had plopped into their stomachs anyway. They hurriedly swallowed the hot potatoes; however, the effort caused their eyes to water profusely.

As they gobbled the potatoes, Ghisu remembered the day when, twenty years ago, he was part of the Thakur's wedding procession. He had eaten so much and so well at the banquet that day that it became the most memorable event of his life. Its memory was still vividly alive in his mind. He said, 'Would I ever forget that fabulous meal! I haven't had anything quite like it ever since. It was out of this world. I could eat as much as I wanted. The bride's family served fried puris. Big shots and nobodies, all—and I mean all—ate puris and satpanis made from pure ghee, raita, three types of dried leaf vegetable dishes, another kind of vegetable dish, yogurt, chutney, and sweetmeats! I cannot begin to tell you how fantastic the food tasted. You could eat as much as you wanted, ask for anything, and eat until you could no more. People ate so much, they had no room left for a drink of water. But those serving the food kept piling up our plates with piping hot and perfectly round fragrant kachoris, regardless of how much we asked them not to or shielded our plates with our hands. They just didn't know how to stop. When the guests had rinsed their mouths and washed their hands, they were each offered a cone of paan. But I had no mind to chew paan. I could hardly stand up. I made it to my blanket and splayed out on it as fast as I could. Such was the generosity of the Thakur! It knew no bounds!'

Madhu, savouring these flavourful delicacies in his imagination, exclaimed, 'If only someone served us such a meal now!'

'Who will? Not a chance. That was a different time. Now people tend to be tight-fisted. They say, "Don't spend too much on weddings! Don't spend too much on funerals!" Just ask them, "So what are you going to do with what all you have been squeezing out of the poor?" Squeezing never stops, frugality kicks in only when it comes to spending.'

'You must have eaten twenty puris, I guess?'

'More than twenty.'

'I would have gobbled fifty.'

'I wouldn't have eaten less than fifty. I was a strapping youth back then. You are not even half as strong.'

After eating the potatoes, they drank some water, covered themselves with their dhotis, and dozed off near the firepit, curling their legs in foetal position, like two enormous coiled snakes. Meanwhile, Budhya kept groaning in labour.

Come morning, Madhu went inside the hut and found that his wife's body had turned cold. Flies were buzzing around her mouth. Her stony eyes were turned upwards in a frozen stare and her body was smeared with dirt and grime. The child had died in her womb.

He rushed out to Ghisu. Both men broke out into loud wailing and started beating their chests. The neighbours came running when they heard their doleful cries. According to the age-old custom, they expressed their sympathy and tried to console them.

However, there wasn't time for much wailing and chest-beating. They had to worry about a shroud for the dead body and wood for the pyre. The money in the house had disappeared like carrion in a buzzard's nest.

Father and son went wailing to the village zamindar, who hated the very sight of the two and often had occasion to beat them up for pilfering, for not showing up for work despite promising to do so. Anyway, he asked, 'What is the matter, Ghisu? Why are you crying? You've become so scarce these days. You aren't thinking of leaving the village, are you?'

Ghisu pressed his forehead on the ground and, with tears in his eyes, said, 'Sarkar, a terrible calamity has struck me. Madhu's wife passed away last night. She kept writhing in pain all day long. Both of us stayed by her side half the night. Medicine, drugs, you name it—we tried everything, but she left us all the same. Who would feed us now? Master, we are ruined. The house is desolate. I am your slave. There is only you to help with her cremation. Whatever little we had was spent on medicine and drugs. Her funeral rites will be performed only through your benevolence. At whose door should I go begging if not yours?'

Zamindar Sahib was a gentle soul, but showing mercy to Ghisu was like trying to dye a jet-black fabric a variety of colours. He felt like telling him off: 'Get the hell out of here! Keep the corpse in the house and let it rot! When I call you for work, you put on airs and don't show up. Today, when you're in need, you come flattering me—you freeloading son of a bitch! Rascal!'

But this was hardly the time to get angry or seek revenge. Zamindar Sahib willy-nilly took out two rupees and disdainfully threw it at him, without a word of commiseration. He didn't bother to even look at him, as if he just wanted to get this weight off his chest and get it off pretty quick.

Once the zamindar had dished out two rupees, how dare the Banias and moneylenders of the village refuse him? He went around announcing loudly that the zamindar had donated two rupees. People gave, some two annas, some four. Within an hour Ghisu had bagged a tidy sum of five rupees. Some offered grain, some others wood. Around noon both men set out for the bazaar to buy a shroud, and others started to chop bamboo stalks to fashion a bier for the corpse.

The tender-hearted womenfolk of the village came to look at Budhya's dead body, shed a few tears for the hapless woman, and left.

After they had made it to the bazaar, Ghisu said, 'We've got enough wood for the pyre, Madhu, what do you say?'

'Oh yes, plenty,' Madhu replied. 'All we need now is the shroud.'

'Well then, let's get a cheap one.'

'Of course, a cheap one. By the time the corpse is carried off for cremation, it will be night. No one would care to look at the shroud in the dark.'

'What a lousy custom! Someone who could not get a tattered rag to cover her body while living must have a new shroud now when she dies.'

'A shroud burns up with the corpse.'

'What else! If we had the same five rupees earlier, we could have spent the money on her treatment.'

Both understood what the other was implying. They meandered through the bazaar until evening shadows began to deepen. Whether by accident or by design they found themselves standing right across from a tavern. They walked in, as though driven by some tacit agreement, and stood there hesitating for a bit. Then Ghisu bought a bottle of country liquor and some flats of gajak to go with the drink. They sat on the veranda and began drinking.

A few glasses down their throats in quick succession and both men's heads began to swim.

'What good is a shroud for? It would have burnt to ashes anyway. Bahu wouldn't have carried it with her.'

Madhu looked at the sky, as if trying to prove his innocence to the angels, and said, 'Such are the ways of the world. Why do these moneybags give away thousands of rupees to the Brahmins? Who can tell whether they would get any recompense for it in the next world.'

'The big shots have plenty to burn, so let them. What have we got to burn.'

'But what will we say to the people? Won't they ask, "Where is the shroud?"'

Ghisu cackled. 'We'll say the money slipped off our waists. We looked and looked but couldn't find it.'

Madhu cackled too. At this unexpected good fortune and on outsmarting fate, he said, 'Poor woman, she was so good to us. Even in death she's made sure that we are well fed.'

By now they had been through more than half the bottle. Ghisu sent Madhu for two sers of puris, a dish of curried meat, spicy roasted liver, and fried fish. The shop was straight across from the tavern. Madhu returned in no time at all, bringing everything on two leaf platters. It cost them one rupee and a half. They were left with a little bit of change now.

They sat eating with the majestic air of a tiger feasting on his prey, without a care about having to answer for their actions, or haunted by any thought of the coming disgrace. They had overcome such scruples a long time ago. Ghisu said philosophically, 'If our souls are content, wouldn't she get some reward for it!'

Madhu bowed his head with overabundant reverence and agreed, 'Of course she will, no doubt about it. Bhagwan, You are all-knowing! Give her a place in heaven. We pray for her with all our hearts. Never in our life did we taste such delicious food as we did today.'

A split second later Madhu was assailed by doubt. 'Well, Dada, we too will have to go there some day.'

Ghisu brushed aside this childish thought and looked at Madhu reproachfully.

'What if she asks us up there, "Why did you people not give my body a shroud?" What will you say?'

'Pipe down.'

'But she will be sure to ask us.'

'How do you know that she won't get her shroud? You think I'm a wretched person or something? I haven't been dawdling all my sixty years. She will get her shroud all right, and she will get a very nice one, much better than what we could have ever given her.'

Madhu, who didn't believe him, said, 'Who is going to give it? You've spent all the money.'

'I said that she will get a shroud,' Ghisu said in a huff. 'Why don't you believe me?'

'But why won't you tell me who'll give it?'

'The same people who gave this time, except the money won't come into our hands. And if somehow it did, we will again be sitting here drinking away. And we will get a shroud a third time.'

As darkness fell and the stars began to shine brightly, the tavern took on an air of exuberance. People broke into song, made merry, hugged their companions, raised wine cups to their friends' lips. The atmosphere was shot through with inebriated gaiety, the air gently intoxicating. It took just a few sips for many to get drunk. People came here for a taste of forgetfulness. Their enjoyment came more from the tavern's ambience than from liquor. Worldly cares had dragged them here—a place where they could forget for a while whether they were alive or dead, or living-dead.

And here they were, father and son, guzzling their drinks with a feeling of immense light-heartedness. Everyone's gaze was glued to them: lucky guys, an entire bottle to share between them!

After they were done eating, Madhu picked up the platter of the leftover puris and gave it to a beggar who had been standing nearby, casting greedy looks at them. For the first time in his life Madhu felt the swagger, the elation, the joy that comes from giving.

'Here...take it. Eat your fill,' said Ghisu. 'Give your blessings. The woman who earned this is no more, but your blessings will certainly reach her. Let every pore of your body bless her. It was hard-earned money.'

Madhu looked at the sky again and said, 'Dada, she will surely go to heaven, won't she? She'll become the queen of heaven.'

Ghisu stood up and, as if awash in the tide of happiness, said, 'Yes son, she *will*. She will go to heaven. She troubled no one, harmed no one, and even as she lay dying fulfilled the most ardent wish of our life. If she doesn't go to heaven, then will it be these moneybags who rob poor folk with both hands and make offerings of holy water at temples and take a dip in the Ganga to wash away their sins?'

The aura of joyful trust in providence brought on by their inebriated state soon gave way to a bout of despair and sorrow.

'But Dada,' Madhu said, 'she suffered a lot in her life, and not least even when she lay dying.' He covered his eyes with his hands and broke into sobs.

Ghisu tried to comfort him. 'Son, why do you cry? Be glad instead. At least she is rid of the web of earthly illusions, free of worldly cares and anxieties. She was lucky to break free of the bonds of moh and maya so soon.'

Both stood up and started singing at the spot:

Enchantress, why do you entice us with your flashing eyes, Enchantress!

The entire tavern watched the two tipplers in breathless amazement, who were singing away with abandon, oblivious of everything. Then they started dancing. They skipped and hopped. They stumbled and fell. Swayed their hips seductively. At last, overcome by the stupor brought on by alcohol, they crumpled to the ground.

6

THE STORY OF A CROW LEARNING PROSODY

SUBRAMANIA BHARATI

Translated from the Tamil by P. Raja

QUITE CLOSE TO KUTRAALAM A MASSIVE BANYAN TREE STOOD ON A HILL. One evening, a sad crow was sitting on one of the branches. The crow's wife moved a little closer to her husband and asked in an affectionate tone: 'What's worrying you, my dear?'

'This morning I ate too much. Now I don't feel the need to hunt for food. But I can't afford to sit still. My friends have not yet returned from their search for food. If they were here, it would be easy for me to while away the time by chatting with them. I thought of wandering in the sky and enjoying the scenes below...but my wings, legs, body, and head are heavy and painful. I'm sure I have a fever. My throat too is hoarse and unbearably painful. I have a severe cold. Both yesterday and the day before I didn't get enough to eat in the woods nearby. And so, I had to fly east for a long distance into areas populated by humans, all for the sake of food. Yet, until sunset, there wasn't enough to fill even half my stomach. It rained night and day without a break. It was summer rain and I was drenched to the bone. This may be the reason for my ill health. I also had indigestion this morning. And I don't know how to kill time. This is why I am sad.'

The crow's wife said, 'Years ago when you married me you cooed to me that nothing on earth was more pleasurable than speaking to me intimately. You said that the time you spent with me was very stimulating. I recall that you said so over and over again. But now, even when I am beside you, you say you find it difficult to pass the time. By saying this you are insulting me. Every day I look at my image in the water in the spring. My face looks more beautiful than when we married. I asked my friends about this. They agree that I'm more beautiful now than before. I don't know why you have turned away from me.'

'Who said you are more beautiful than before? Was it your girlfriends? Or your boyfriends?' asked the crow.

'My dear friends are the ones who told me. I don't have "boy" friends,' replied the crow's wife.

The crow reacted by fluffing his wings. He took off from the branch of the tree and started flying southwards. 'Caw...caw....' The crow heard cawing from behind him. He turned his head and saw it was his wife. 'Why are you following me?' he asked.

'You are not well...yet you are going all alone. If your head reels in pain, you may fall. If I am there with you, I'll be able save you from falling. This is why I am following you.'

'Oh! I see! So you are here to keep me safe, aren't you?' asked the crow.

'Yes! Of course,' replied the wife.

'If that is so, you don't have to go with me. I am fine now. All my ailments are gone. I will neither feel giddy nor fall to the earth and become food for a fox. So you don't have to escort me. Please go home.'

'Where are you going?'

'Nearby...Vikrama Singha Puram.'

'Huh! Vikrama Singha Puram? It is near Papanasam.... Quite a distance.'

'But I can cover the distance in a jiffy. You don't have to worry. Go home now,' instructed the crow.

'Why are you going there? Tell me,' said the wife.

'I know of a man named Veera Maagaala Pulavar who lives in Vikrama Singha Puram. He is a king of poets. He chooses this time to teach his children the art of Tamil prosody. And you know that I understand the spoken language of man, even though I can't speak it. So I will go there, perch on the roof of his house, and learn from him all the nuances of the language. I will then apply them to our crow language to formulate our own prosody. My main purpose is to compose songs and epics in our language. Is it appropriate to call a crow a crow if it has no love for its native land and tongue? It can only be called a little living black carcass. No wood in the world is as clean and fertile as our wood in Kutraalam. It is deathless. No other language is as great as our crow language. As I am born in this wood, I should contribute my share to the growth of this wood and my language. If I happen to die before my desire is fulfilled, I will have to die with regret. Hence, I have decided to work on our crow language and develop its potential for poetry.'

'What?' retorted the wife, 'just a few seconds ago you said no other language is as great as our language. But now, you say you want to adapt the nuances of the Tamil language to our own language in order to compose songs. So you support the view that our language is inferior to Tamil?'

'Tamil is the language of human beings. Don't be so stupid as to compare our bird language with that! What I meant was our crow language is superior to all other non-human languages. All right, it is getting late. I should leave now. You go home,' said the crow.

The wife tried another argument 'You don't have to go all the way to Vikrama Singha Puram for this! Let us go home. I will teach you, because I know.'

'What do you know?' demanded the crow.

'All the rules for composing poetry.'

'Where did you learn them?' asked the crow in astonishment.

'You may think you were the first to whom such an idea occurred. Not so! My father too nurtured such an idea. He sat on the roof of a master-poet's house and learnt the nuances when the master taught his students every day. He never missed a single one of the classes which ran for six months. At the end of the course, my father had mastered Tamil poetics and prosody. Following those rules of grammar, he formulated several strict rules for composing a thousand variations of poetry. Unfortunately, he did not live to present his work for acceptance in the learned assembly hall of the crow king. And so, the new theory of poetry in our language languished in our home. I am my father's only daughter. He had no other child, male or female. Our law forbids the female from presenting this new theory before the learned assembly and giving a new outlook to our language. But I am ready to teach *you* the theory. You can learn it from me and then present it to the assembly. You will be rewarded for that in the king's court. You will become world famous. So come home and I will teach you for two hours every day. In two months you will receive the highest honours from our crow king,' said the wife.

'I am a supporter of the Republic Party. I do not care for the honours and awards of the king,' said the crow curtly.

'So let it be...' replied the wife, 'as you said earlier you can contribute to the growth of our language and you will be remembered even after your death. For the sake of that at least, come with me. I will teach you the art of writing poetry.'

As the crow couple flew back home, that is to say, towards their nest, Manmadhan was moving in the sky, a little distance away from them. It was drizzling on the Western Ghats, a command from nature to compel the male and the female to unite in love.

In such weather and in such a place, the god of love was extremely busy. And so, he had already spent most of the arrows from his quiver and was rushing to his own world to unite in love with his beloved Rathi Devi. There were only two arrows left in his quiver. He drew out both of them and shot the love darts at the crow couple, one for each.

Before the crow couple could reach their nest, they began fondling and kissing each other. No sooner did they enter the nest than they, unable to control their passion, began to make love. The very thought of learning the art of poesy left the crow's mind. They were so deeply immersed in their passion that they were awake till daybreak. Then they slept like logs and woke up only the next morning. Before the thought of hunting for food flashed across the minds of the crow couple Manmadhan passed that way again. All that had happened in the nest a day earlier began to repeat itself. Several days passed in this manner.

The male crow completely forgot about learning prosody in the crow language. He did not study the art of poesy. He began, instead, to study the art of love.

A LETTER

K. M. MUNSHI

Translated from the Gujarati by Rita Kothari

MY LORD, MY MASTER! I WISH TO LAY MY HEAD IN YOUR LAP ONCE again, while I am on my deathbed. I had considered not writing this letter. Thousands of my heart-rending entreaties amounted to nothing, why would this one have any effect now? I have no doubt that nothing is going to change. But voicing my thoughts, my experiences, will liberate me from pain. Also, if your future wife turns out to be lucky because you finally grow wiser, she will be spared the suffering I went through, and not wither away before blossoming.

In my lifetime of sixteen years, there's so much I have gone through. God alone knows who might be responsible for my miseries, but I do need to say this at least once—abandoning shame, or the maryada of the older generation—if at all there was one person responsible for my suffering, and one person who could have alleviated it—then that person was you, my master, my lord. The world handed you an inexperienced, delicate little girl, but you didn't even think about her. This is what happened to me. I am about to lose my life, my very breath is ebbing away from me.

Do you remember the time I came into your house as your wife? Despite being the adored child of loving parents, it was you I sought and pined for. Even when I went to school before we were married, just looking at you made me feel things I hadn't felt before, and I couldn't wait to meet you. I couldn't wait to serve you and feel fulfilled. Later, you found many faults with me; you even laid the cruel charge of my being indifferent to you. How could that even be possible? In a Hindu universe, the lordship of the husband is considered greater than that of even God.

Little girls start worshipping their husbands even before they meet them. The difference, however, is this: that this husband, lord of the lords, has even more pretensions than God and much less affection for his devotees.

When I came into your home, how small I was! A month before that, I was going to school and prancing about like a deer in a forest. A mother-in-law's rage and slavery to the husband were unknown concepts to me. I did not have the foggiest notion that in six months' time I was going to feel muffled and lacerated. No matter what I said or did, it became an unnecessary opportunity to accuse my parents. Why? If I did not know certain things, it was Sasuji's duty to teach me. I was hardly a demoness who refused to learn. If a man is expected to have regard for his parents, should a girl not have any towards those who gave birth to her, raised and nurtured her? If someone were to say to you, 'Your mother and your father and your kind', you would slap that person. But an innocent young girl listens to all the aspersions cast on her parents and merely suffers in silence.

After a few months, when I finally braced myself to endure these comments, a new thing began. Dear one, what kind of strength did you expect from the body of a thirteen-year-old? How did you expect a naive child to know what the customs of your house were? Just as your sister was dear to your mother, so was I to mine. Your sister, however, was simply not bothered about my fragility. Are you saying that a twenty-year-old sister would be damaged by work while I, a thirteen-year-old, would not?

Does Hindu culture not teach the mother-in-law and husband to have any sense of fairness? I, too, was a body, not a log of wood. And after a day's arduous labour, what care did I receive from my husband? None, right?

I have endured all my life, but I shall speak today. Did you not know that I was also a young, foolish, and fragile child? That I slogged like a beast of burden every day? That I could neither sleep nor sit? You played cricket and went to office. Do you think people like us sleep at home? We worked every minute, endured abuse, filled our stomachs with leftovers, spent our lives longing for more. At the end of a hard day, when I came to you expecting a word of affection, you couldn't manage any. I was immediately made responsible for fetching every small thing you needed. A moment's delay and you began yelling. Your strong, manly feet ached from sitting in one place in your office, and you needed my weak hands to press them. If you perspired at night, I had to fan you with my small, trembling hands. Did you not think at that time, even for a moment, how was this young girl to withstand such burden? But why would you? I was a slave, wasn't I?

A daughter-in-law is like a mere cat in the house. But a cat gets to sleep and eat twice a day. What do you men know of what we go through? There were so many days when after back-breaking work I could barely sit; I also had to be deprived of sleep. Yet, I served you even during such times. Silently, I would occasionally take a brief nap, only to be reprimanded, threatened, and even slapped. But shedding tears was also a crime.

Forbidden from going to my natal home, victimized by a perpetually enraged mother-in-law, you lording over me, cruel and heartless. You made a fifteen-year-old go through all this? I did what thousands of my kind do.

I inadvertently blurted out something to my mother one day. She sent word to your mother, who exaggerated everything and instigated you to do something. That night, you beat me up. Do you remember? I sobbed into the pillow and asked for death. Let those women of earlier days—who filled pots with water from the river and carried them on their heads, or those dumb, thick-headed women who helplessly went through life—suffer if they will. But how could a delicate, young, educated girl have to go through this?

Had you shown affection, some concern for the courtesan who entertained you, the slave that fed you—some sense of fairness—then I would have made you the sovereign of my soul, not merely my husband, the owner of my body. I would have sprinkled your path with flowers and made you experience heaven. But all that remained unspoken and undone. I did not find justice, affection, nor happiness with you. I withered and wilted inside—so did my body. Finally, your words and actions managed to murder me.

At least for a day you could have talked to me about something other than your concerns. For one moment, couldn't you have allowed me to taste genuine love? At least after your meal you could have asked me, 'Is there food left for you, or mere crumbs?' At least for a day you could have exposed me to some aesthetic pleasure or a higher plane of being. But what was I expecting? Why would you care beyond gorging on food and fattening yourself? Those ideal women, the satis, prayed to have the same husband in their next birth. I could pray, too, but have you proven yourself worthy of that prayer? Those pious women had husbands who were worthy of their sacrifice. I am done with you in this birth. May God never bring us together.

Do tell Sasuji not to bring an educated daughter-in-law into her home again.

The Unfortunate Woman.

8

THE ACHARYA'S WIFE

MASTI VENKATESHA IYENGAR

Translated from the Kannada by Ramachandra Sharma

THERE IS A PLACE CALLED SALIGRAMA NEAR MIRLE BHERYA IN MYSORE district. It must have been a big village in the past. It is not all that small even now. But is it possible to see again the glory it had when the Hoysala kings reigned in Dwarasamudra? Now it looks as if the village does not realize its rundown state, lost as it is in memories of its bygone glory. It stands there dumb, a schoolboy who has forgotten his lesson, wondering who that great woman Sali could be, from whom it got its name. A gentle, eight-hundred-year-old light enfolds the village, its tank, its fields, houses, streets, its temple, and the pond with the mandapa by its side.

Eight hundred years ago, Ramanujacharya, the founder of the Vishishtadvaita school, lived here incognito, for a few years. He was born in Perumbudur, grew up in Kanchipura, and in Sriranga, and he became an ascetic and propounder of Sri Vaishnava dharma. When there was a threat to his life from his enemies, at the insistence of his disciples, he escaped into the land of the Hoysalas and lived there. Hallowed ground, it had once offered refuge to a group of mendicants, who had to flee their homes in the north when famine struck. Because of the abundant generosity of the land, the group survived and prospered. When the king in the southern region became a tyrant, those people who believed in dharma sought sanctuary here, like children who hide behind the uncle when their father is angry. The idol of Narasimhamurthy that the Acharya worshipped is still there in the temple, an object of devotion. In one of the mandirs of the temple complex, there is a statue of the Acharya. So true to life is it, that you get the impression he himself is sitting there. In front is a pond. The people point to it and tell you the Acharya used to wash here, and bathe here. As we listen to them and look at these precincts, it seems as if the wheels of time have slipped back eight hundred years, and we are now face to face with life in the age of the Hoysalas. There, look! An ascetic has stepped into the water. It is Ramanuja!

Ten years ago, I had gone to Saligrama. As I walked around the temple, I recalled the story of the Acharya. A wonderful tale. Of a boy who was brought up in a poor family, who had extraordinary intelligence, had learnt about the Bhagavata dharma from five different gurus, and who went on to become the founder of a new school of thought. He earned the respect of the king and by it, the souls of thousands were saved. I felt a sense of pride when I thought about the Acharya's life.

But one aspect of it troubled my mind. History tells us that it was mainly his wife's thoughtless behaviour that led him to renounce the world. Once, the Acharya had wanted to honour his guru. His wife served the guru and then took a bath because the guest was of a lower caste. Again, when there was an argument near the well, she spoke very rudely about the guru's family. Another time, she was lying in bed asleep, when the Acharya reached home late in the evening. This is why the Acharya decided to become an ascetic, they say. Perhaps what the Acharya did was right. But wasn't the punishment too great for her lapses?

The Acharya was full of learning and of his mission to serve dharma. Should he not have been a little more understanding and given the foolish woman some advice? Who knows what she was like! That is life. What had happened to her after her husband left her to become an ascetic and she had gone back to her parents?

I sat there, under the tree, reflecting. As I was watching a crane fly in to rest at the edge of the pond, a story was born.

After leaving the Chola land, Ramanujacharya reached the highlands of Mysore via Satyamangala. When they took one look at him, his disciples knew his enemies were at his heels. They did not allow him to wear his saffron robes and insisted that he should dress in white, while one of the disciples wore saffron. When the enemy king had sent for the Acharya a few days earlier, a disciple had gone to him, disguised as Ramanuja. The others had then led Ramanuja away to a place of safety in the north. There was some fear that he would be caught during the journey, so another of the disciples had dressed up as Ramanuja and was determined to surrender himself if someone came for the guru. When they entered the Hoysala kingdom, the disciples started looking for a place that was suitable for an ascetic. When they came to Saligrama, they decided that it was the ideal place for the Acharya to settle. Some of the disciples lived as sanyasis in distant villages and came to meet their guru now and then. One of them stayed with the Acharya during the first fortnight. Later, he found a man and his family in the village who would serve the master with devotion. So he handed over the task of taking care of the guru to them and went away. There was no trace of the enemy from the south for over a year, so the fears of the Acharya's disciples gradually decreased. Two of them stayed behind in nearby Thondanuru. Others left for their home towns with the understanding that news from those areas would be frequently dispatched to the guru.

One who stayed behind in Saligrama to serve the Acharya is known in history as Vadaganambi, which means a devotee from the north. Vadaganambi was a Brahmin of the Bhagavata tradition. As was the custom in those days, he had learnt Sanskrit, studied Vedanta, visited Kanchipura and Sriranga, and had become a recognized scholar. The privilege of worshipping the god Narasimha belonged exclusively to his family. When

Vadaganambi heard that an ascetic had arrived there, he naturally wanted to be of service to him. He knew that the ascetic was old, but there were no signs of age either on his face or in his behaviour. And even though his body showed no signs of his years, there was no doubt that the knowledge he had was too great to be acquired in a single lifetime. Vadaganambi attended on the guru for three days. By then it was clear that the master belonged to the same Bhagavata tradition, so he asked the guru to accept him as a disciple. The Acharya agreed.

Vadaganambi's efforts to find out more about his guru came to nothing. He could not possibly ask the guru. A disciple he asked would not tell him anything either. So he did not pursue the matter. Besides, what was to be gained by knowing the details? The guru commanded respect, and that was enough. The Acharya was pleased with the rare humility that Vadaganambi displayed. This quality led Vadaganambi to enter the service of the guru in a remarkably short time. Vadaganambi's wonder grew day by day as he watched his guru's life. During a casual conversation, the guru had said he was eighty years old. For a man of eighty to be like this was astonishing, thought Vadaganambi. Even after he had spent all his time with the Acharya, for many days, he did not know when the guru retired for the night. Or when he woke up, since he would be up before Vadaganambi came to attend to his needs.

The guru did most things himself, rarely expecting any help. He would accept a little food the disciple had prepared as bhiksha in the presence of God and eat it at noon. At night he would be content with a glass of milk. The rest of the time he kept himself busy, either in meditation or in the service of God, or in reciting the texts he had studied. Vadaganambi was about forty years old. He had a wife, and a son who was six years old. He thought it was his good fortune that he had found a guru like the Acharya. So Vadaganambi asked his guru to let his wife and son serve him too. It was thus that Shamalambe and Ramachandra also became the Acharya's ardent disciples.

Two years passed in this manner.

In the meanwhile, Vadaganambi and his wife had come to know that the person they were looking after, their guru, was Ramanujacharya himself. Within a few days of their entering his service, the Acharya had told his disciples that these two, Shamalambe and Vadaganambi, who were taking such great care of him, must have been his daughter and son-in-law in a previous birth. Otherwise they would not be looking after him as they did. He ordered his disciples to take the couple into their confidence and tell them everything. That was how the husband and wife came to know about the guru. Talking about the master's decision to take sanyasa, the disciples said that all women were not like Shamalambe, doing what their husbands wished them to. The Acharya's wife did not understand him, nor did she have any desire to. If he asked her to follow one path, she went along another, and upset him, they explained. So he left her to do whatever she wanted and decided to take sanyasa and devote his life to dharma.

Vadaganambi and his wife already considered the guru a great man, but after they heard this, their affection and respect for him increased. It was difficult to measure the extent of their devotion.

One afternoon, nearly two years after they had started looking after him, the Acharya was bathing in the pond. On one side of it there was a peepul tree. As he stood up after a dip, chanting some mantras, he glanced towards the tree. He felt that there was a woman peeping at him from behind it. As soon as his eyes turned in her direction, she hid herself. He wondered why any woman would behave in such a strange manner. He had not been able to see her face clearly. Perhaps it was someone who had come to the pond, either to wash her clothes or carry water from it, and was waiting for him to finish his bath, he thought. She must be someone from outside the village. The people of Saligrama had no such inhibition about the Acharya, as they knew his routine. The Acharya finished his bath and went into the temple.

That night, while talking to the guru about the day's happenings in the village, his disciple told him that a lady from the south had come there with an old companion. When they had asked who she was, she had told them that her husband had a problem and she had undertaken a pilgrimage to the north, hoping to find a cure for it. Her companion had taken ill, so the lady had requested Shamalambe to let them stay with her for a couple of days. Shamalambe had agreed. She made place for them in one part of the house and gave them all that they needed. The Acharya listened to this as he usually did to all other matters. Then a discussion of Vedanta followed.

The next day, the Acharya received news that both the disciples in Thondanuru were ill. A strange epidemic had spread across the country that year. The guru immediately went to see them. The day he returned from there, he too had a fever. Despite this, there was no change in his routine of three baths in the pond, a single meal at noon, and milk at night. This went on for three days. His body rebelled against it and the fever raged. The disciple and his wife stayed by his bedside throughout and attended to his needs.

The worst thing about the fever was the severe pain in his body. When the guru sat up, leaning against the wall, and complained of the pain in his legs, Shamalambe quickly began to massage them. He pulled them back saying, 'Don't, my child.'

'Why? Is it wrong for your son-in-law and daughter to press your legs?' asked the disciple. 'Let our lives become fulfilled by serving you,' he added.

Thus, one of them, the disciple Shamalambe or Ramachandra, was constantly beside him, to press his legs.

There was no change in his condition the next day and the pain in his body was as intense as before. Shamalambe spent all her time in the temple except when she went home to prepare food. Her husband went out only when he had to boil the milk or have his bath and his meal. The rest of the time he spent praying for his guru's recovery. During the day, Ramachandra and Shamalambe took turns to massage the Acharya's legs, but the boy could not do it at night. He was young and would fall asleep. So Shamalambe divided her night between sitting close to the guru and keeping vigil, and resting in the yard behind the sanctum sanctorum....

It was midnight. Shamalambe, lying down a little distance away from the Acharya's bed, had just dozed off. She woke up with a start when she heard the Acharya call, 'Who's that?' She quickly went to his side. Though her gaze was fixed on him, in the dim light of the lamp, she thought she saw someone walking away from his bedside. By the time she made the flame bigger and looked, there was no one there. She was a little frightened, but she could not brood on it. She was anxious to make sure the guru was all right. 'What is it, Appaji?' she asked. 'It's you, isn't it?' he asked. 'Yes,' she replied. The Acharya fell silent.

She took the lamp and went outside the temple but found nobody there. She spoke to her husband about the incident. 'Why did you lie down so far away? You should have been by his bedside,' he scolded.

'Who could have come so close to his bed? I'm frightened,' said Shamalambe.

'Who would dare to go to his bedside here, in the temple of Narasimha? Must be a god or a devi or an alwar, come to look after our guru. There are many who will take care of him even if we don't.' Shamalambe did not mind that her husband had scolded her. In fact, she was reassured to know that there was nothing to be afraid of. At that moment, she had thought it was the evil spirit of the fever which had come there to make the guru's condition worse. And she had seen it walk away. Because of her great affection for her guru, it had not occurred to her that such a thing was impossible in that holy place. Her husband's words had made her realize this, and satisfied, she returned to the Acharya's bedside.

By the grace of God, the guru's temperature came down the next morning, and he even accepted some food that was given to him. The disciple and his wife were relieved. Shamalambe did not say so to her husband, but the thought occurred to her again that what she had seen was the spirit of the fever the previous night.

Though the Acharya's health improved, the task of nursing the sick continued for Shamalambe. When she went home, she found that the lady from the south had taken ill. Shamalambe gave her a kashaya of medicinal herbs, provided her with all that she needed for her meal, then went back to the temple. The guru was telling Vadaganambi about a dream he had had the previous night.... He was in bed with fever. There was a severe pain in his legs. He was aware that Shamalambe had come to his bedside a number of times to press them. Sometime during the night, he had dozed off. That is when he felt someone else come up to him and massage his leg. It was a very different touch. Shamalambe's hands were those of a daughter. These were the hands of a married woman. He had felt his breath catch in his throat. He woke up with a start and asked who it was. He knew that someone was walking away from his bedside just as Shamalambe was coming towards him.... While the guru spoke of his dream, the disciple recalled what his wife had told him that night. Shamalambe confirmed what the guru had said, but held back her impression that someone had walked away even as she came in. Or that the spirit of the fever must have done something with his leg as it left. How could she talk about such a typically feminine intuition to either her husband or the guru?

For a while, the disciple sat there wondering what the significance of the guru's experience was. But what was the use of continuing a discussion about something which eluded his grasp? Besides, the Acharya was still not well enough. The matter could wait for a few days.

By some miracle, the guru went back to his routine the very next day. It became possible for both the disciple and Shamalambe to pay a little more attention to their own work. A couple of days later, the disciple told the Acharya that the condition of the lady from the south had worsened. Shamalambe had said the same thing when she sought permission to go back home earlier than usual. The next day, the disciple was late. He explained to the Acharya that the lady had died that morning. Before she died, she had requested Shamalambe to ask her husband to perform the obsequies for her. He had agreed because he believed that it was his duty as a Brahmin to do it. That is why he was late.

'She came from some distant place and passed away here,' said the Acharya, a little sadly, and then went back to his daily worship.

Shamalambe came to the guru in the evening. She did a namaskara to him and to her husband and sat down. It was obvious that she had been crying. For a long time, she did not say a word. After a while, the Acharya himself spoke. 'Look, child, one shouldn't mourn excessively even the death of a near one. She came to you seeking shelter. You took care of her. She passed away. Your husband performed the last rites as if he was her son. So why do you grieve?'

Shamalambe tried to say something, but the intensity of her grief choked her. No words came out, only sobs. She fell at the Acharya's feet, weeping bitterly. After a few moments she did say something, but her words were so indistinct that he could not understand anything. The guru consoled her and told the disciple, 'She is very distressed. Take her home.'

The disciple came the next morning. From his appearance, it was apparent that he, too, had been crying. 'Should you grieve so much?' the Acharya asked him.

The disciple controlled his grief and said, 'Your daughter will tell you everything today.'

When Shamalambe came that evening, she was calm and there were no signs of anguish on her face. She touched the guru's feet and sat down beside him. Her husband asked her to speak. She looked at the Acharya for a moment, then said, 'I don't know how to begin....' After a pause, she continued, 'I thought the lady who died yesterday was a stranger. I found out before she died that she was, in fact, very close to all of us.'

The Acharya sat there silently, listening to her.

'That is why I agreed that my husband would perform the last rites for her. She whispered to me about your relationship with her. She was our Acharya's wife before he renounced the world.'

There was no change in the expression on the Acharya's face. All he said was, 'Narayana.'

After a moment, Shamalambe spoke. 'She told me that there was something for which she wanted to seek your pardon. I promised to speak to you about it. You must forgive her.'

'It is only till the moment before one attains God's feet that all relationships, courtesies, and pardons—in short, the dharma of this world is valid. There is nothing for me to forgive in a life that has already reached His presence.'

'I must tell you something on her behalf. She thought that there would be no salvation for her even in heaven if you were to get angry on hearing it. If you say that you have forgiven her, I will tell you.'

'Go on, child. I have forgiven her,' the Acharya replied.

'It seems the Acharya's wife had behaved in this thoughtless manner because she had not understood his greatness. She was young and inexperienced. She knew nothing of life. Her husband was twenty-five years older than her. Besides, she came from a very orthodox family. Because of all this, her behaviour was so graceless. The Acharya was unhappy with her, and so she had to be a widow, even though her husband was alive. She was terribly distressed by the whole thing.'

'It was God's will. No one was responsible for what happened. Where's the question of forgiveness in this?'

'When she was at her mother's place, she heard you had come this way after you left the Chola land. She was very troubled about it. She reached here by asking people for directions to this place, with only one desire—to steal a sight of you. She watched from her hideout and made sure that the ascetic here was no one else but you. She intended to leave that day but didn't. On the one hand was her companion's illness, on the other was the desire to see you once more. She extended her stay by a couple of days but by that time you were taken ill. She didn't want to leave before your condition improved. She got daily reports from us about your condition and suffered greatly when your fever raged and you were in pain. I didn't understand her concern then, but I do now.'

'Forty years ago, I renounced all my bonds with the family. What's the message that's being conveyed to me today through all this?'

'This was a prelude to what I have to say now. When you were seriously ill, your wife prayed to God asking Him to spare you and give your illness to her. You remember that night when your fever was really high? I stayed here for a while and then went away to rest in the yard. She came to your bedside in my absence and by touching your leg, drew your fever to herself.'

'What?' the Acharya exclaimed.

'As she touched your feet, she was overwhelmed by memories of the day she married you and couldn't help massaging your leg. That was when you woke up and asked who was there. And I came in. She took to her bed the very next day. She wanted me to ask you to forgive her for having desecrated your body with her touch, a body to which she had lost her claim long ago, and thus lowered the quality of your tapas.'

The Acharya did not say anything.

Shamalambe continued, 'The Acharya's wife gave us these three things along with her blessings,' and showed him some jewels.

After a while, the guru said, 'The path of every life is preordained. Each one takes its own course to reach the destination. Mine had to be this. May yours be happy.'

Ramachandra was playing outside. The Acharya called him in and said, 'Annayya, let's have the stotra: Lakshminarasimha mamadehi karavalambam.' The boy's rendering of the stotra was sweet and they all enjoyed listening to him.

The companion of the Acharya's wife came to the Acharya the next day, took his blessings and left for her home town.

I was slightly depressed as the story unfolded in my mind. I looked around to see where I was. I was under the peepul tree beside the pond. My gaze rested on the temple, the pond, the village. The light from the setting sun was a protective cover over the history of many centuries, like the wings of a bird sitting on its eggs to hatch them, like the waves of an ocean engulfing a million lives within it. My mind was in the grip of a wordless pain and a wordless yearning. An ascetic and his wife...a disciple, his wife, and their son....

Trying to visualize all of them, I walked away from that place.

EINSTEIN AND INDUBALA

BIBHUTIBHUSHAN BANDYOPADHYAY

Translated from the Bengali by Arunava Sinha

I CAN'T TELL YOU WHY EINSTEIN GOT OFF THE TRAIN AT RANAGHAT ON HIS way to Darjeeling, nor can I say why he wanted to deliver a lecture 'On...etc. etc.' at the municipal hall there. I was not present at that precise moment. Therefore, I am unable to provide you with an eyewitness account, but I can recount the story as I heard it from others.

The fact of the matter is that Einstein was possibly under some financial constraints following his exile from Nazi Germany. The objective behind his visit to India was to augment his income by delivering lectures. As everyone is aware, he had indeed embarked on a lecture tour in the country. I shall not repeat this.

Rai Bahadur Neelambar Chattopadhyay, professor of mathematics at Krishnagar College, was a worthy man. Einstein's extraordinary talk entitled 'On the Unity and Universality of Forces' at the Senate Hall had overwhelmed him, as it had all the other intellectuals present. He was extremely keen that Einstein deliver a lecture at his college, but the principal appeared opposed to the idea.

'No, Rai Bahadur,' he declared, 'I have no other objection, but a German at the present juncture....'

Growing agitated (as he was wont to in the event of dissent from anyone present during the evening reading of the Bhagavad Gita at the lawyer Rammohan Babu's drawing room), the Rai Bahadur said, 'What do you mean, sir? German? What is German? Is Einstein German? Do supermen like him, sages and scientists like him, belong to particular countries? Are they to be limited by nationality? In my view....'

'I am not claiming that such is the case,' interjected the principal.

'But considering the situation today....' A bitter argument ensued between the two experienced teachers.

Proficient in philosophy, the principal cited the example of the most important preceptor of medieval scholastic philosophy, John Scotus. Despite being born in Ireland, he was so persecuted by the fundamentalists of the ninth century that he was compelled to seek sanctuary in France. He never returned to Ireland. No one cared about the real person, they only valued his viewpoint.

Eventually, as the principal refused to back down, the Rai Bahadur had no choice but to desist in his attempts. Meanwhile, he was informed that Einstein would travel to Darjeeling soon. Kept too busy by his lectures at different places in India to have set eyes on the Himalaya, Einstein was determined to visit Darjeeling, now that he was close to it.

'Why not have Einstein break his journey at Ranaghat en route to Darjeeling and deliver a lecture?' the Rai Bahadur asked himself.

He sought an audience with Einstein at the Grand Hotel in Calcutta. 'Enlighten me about Indian philosophy,' Einstein told him.

The Rai Bahadur was panic-stricken. A professor of mathematics, he knew nothing about philosophy, especially Indian philosophy. Fortunately, he had read the Gita occasionally, which enabled him to make one or two points. 'Vasamsi jirnani, etc.' Just as a person puts on new garments and so on.

Einstein said, 'Reading Max Mueller on the philosophy of the Vedanta had at one time inspired me to learn Sanskrit. In philosophy I am an intellectual disciple of Spinoza. His philosophical arguments are presented in mathematical form. Spinoza's mind is that of a mathematician's, which attracted me to him. But reading Max Mueller's essay on the Vedanta unveiled a new world to me. Spinoza's is a purely materialistic intellect, like Euclid's, where even sophistry follows predetermined paths. But at heart I am prone to imagination....'

The Rai Bahadur looked upon Einstein in wonder. 'You and imagination!' he exclaimed.

Smiling, Einstein said, 'Do you not consider my unification of space and time as having been cast in the mould of the imagination?'

The Rai Bahadur was even more astonished. 'You have brought us intelligence of a new dimension,' he stammered. 'After Newton, you are the discoverer of a new universe. To term you as someone prone to imagination....'

But when the Rai Bahadur glanced at the scientist's long hair and exquisitely dreamy eyes, his words did not escape his lips. Perhaps it was impossible to be a great scientist without a powerful imagination. He was about to speak when Einstein took a box of cigars from the small table beside him and offered it to the Rai Bahadur. Taking a thick cigar from the box and snipping the tip off with a penknife, he handed it to the Rai Bahadur. The professor's Bengali sensibilities made him shrink back. How could an insignificant mathematics teacher light up a cigar in the presence of such a great scientist? Besides, he had to consider the fact that Einstein was white-skinned. White-skinned people were of the race of meat-eating gods. Accepting the cigar, the Rai Bahadur said, 'What about you?'

'Thank you, I do not smoke.'

'I see.'

'I've been wondering....'

'What?'

'Do you think we will have an audience in Ranaghat? What kind of place is it?'

'It is a splendid city. There will indeed be an audience.'

'I need some money at once. I left behind whatever I had in Germany. They did not let me withdraw a single mark from my bank. I am more or less destitute.'

'I am making special efforts in Ranaghat, sir.'

'Will a commodious theatre be available?'

'Not exactly. But there is a municipal hall which is not too bad, it will do.'

The Rai Bahadur sought to leave soon afterwards, feeling that he had no right to make undue demands on the great man's time.

Einstein said, 'Take some pamphlets and handbills for my talks. I will inform you of the subject of my lecture in due course. How much should the tickets be?'

'Not very high—shall we say....'

'Three marks, which is ten shillings?'

'If you please, sir, no. That would be calamitous. We are a poor country. Ten shillings would amount to almost ten rupees. There is no one here who can afford tickets at that price, sir.'

'Five shillings, then?'

'Very well. One shilling for students.'

Einstein smiled. 'University students need not buy tickets. I am a schoolmaster myself. They have a claim on me. It was the same at Bombay University and at Banaras Hindu University. Students won't have to pay. Here are the handbills and pamphlets....'

Trying to read the handbill he was holding, the Rai Bahadur said glumly, 'But, sir, this is in French.'

'But, of course, it is. I had them printed when giving my talks in Paris. Don't people here have any French? I was told they teach French at the university here.'

'No, sir, they don't. One or two people might have some French. It is not taught widely. English is the preferred language here. No one will understand this, sir.'

'That's true. Will you please have it translated into English and printed at a press here?'

'Er...um...all right...sir.'

The Rai Bahadur said to himself, 'I'd better take Binod's help. He knows French quite well. How many times am I going to say I don't know to such a great man?'

Binod Chowdhury was his eldest brother-in-law. A learned man who had several languages. Translating the handbills into English and Bengali with great enthusiasm, he said, 'Chatujjey Moshai, I'll go to Ranaghat that day. Of course, my acquaintance with the theory of relativity is only through that popular book of Lyndon Bolton's.'

'Still, I consider Einstein a sage of our times. A genuine visionary sage who has been indoctrinated by those who discover truth. I may not be able to understand or solve equations the length of a train, but when it comes to understanding the worth of a person....'

The Rai Bahadur realized that his sly brother-in-law was mocking him. Laughing, he said, 'You must have determined my worth too, Binod Babu? Excellent.'

'God forbid! How can I say such a thing, Chatujjey Moshai?'

'You cannot?'

'Trapped in the illusion of the space-time continuum, can one swear as to what one has said, Chatujjey Moshai? Aren't you going to have lunch with us?'

'I can't. I have a great deal to do. I have to ensure that he can make some money. I shall try to prevail upon the chairman and vice-chairman of the municipality. Cunning foxes, all of them. If I can get the hall....'

'What are you saying, Chatujjey Moshai! How can anyone not let the hall be used by Einstein? It's tragic—imagine such a great scientist having to deliver lectures for money in his old age. The world does not know its greatest....'

'You are still a child, Binod. Your last statement is right, however. It will need a lot of lobbying. I'd better take the 5.40.'

The Rai Bahadur was kept extremely busy during the next few days. Meeting the chairman and the vice-chairman of the Ranaghat municipality, the headmaster of the school, barristers and attorneys, government employees and businessmen, he told everyone the entire story. To his joy, he discovered that all of them appeared pleased at the prospect of Einstein lecturing in their town. As though a god himself had come down to earth.

Abhay Babu, an attorney of advanced years, said, 'What did you say the sahib's name is, Moshai? Aai...what?... Eenstain? I see. Yes, a famous person. These are renowned personalities—of course I have heard of him.'

Shaking with rage, the Rai Bahadur said to himself, 'My left foot, you have heard of him, you damned old idiot. Do you think this is cloth merchant Shamchand Pal? Famous indeed! Three new generations will have to be born before you will have heard of him. First, you ruin your chances of salvation by teaching people to give false witness, and now you think you can call Einstein famous! There must be limits to idiocy.'

On the appointed day, the Rai Bahadur, accompanied by several students from Krishnagar College, got off the morning train at Ranaghat. His brother-in-law, Binod Chowdhury, had written an anguished letter, stating that he had been detained by unforeseen circumstances, not everyone could have the good fortune of attending Einstein's lecture but, etc. The Rai Bahadur did feel a pang of regret, for the young man was indeed knowledgeable, and it was most unfortunate that he could not be present. Such was fate.

Emerging from the station, the Rai Bahadur came to an abrupt halt on catching sight of the wall of a house across the street. What was all this! A giant notice, in one-two-three colours, was stuck on the wall. It said:

Bani Cinema Hall (blue)

Coming! Coming!! (black)
Coming!!! (black)
Who is coming? (black)
When is she coming? (black)
Renowned filmstar Indubala Debi (red)
Today, Sunday, the 27th of Kartik, 5 p.m. (blue)
She will greet the audience!! (black)
Entrance Rs 5, 3, 2, and 1 (black)
Ladies Rs 5 and 2 (black)
Do not waste this opportunity! (red)

Disaster! Even on that winter morning, towards the end of Kartik, the Rai Bahadur had to wipe the perspiration off his forehead. He checked the date carefully once more. No doubt about it. Today, Sunday, the 27th.

Proceeding on his way distractedly, he noticed another handbill. Wherever he went, there were notices advertising the movie star's imminent arrival in three colours. He saw as many as thirty-six such advertisements at various places on the way to the house of the vice-chairman of the municipality.

Srigopal Babu, the vice-chairman, was seated on the little veranda that looked out on to his garden, dressed only in the dhoti he wore when he oiled his body. On seeing the Rai Bahadur, he adjusted his attire so he looked a bit more presentable. Smiling, he said, 'And to what do I owe this good fortune? Good morning.'

'Good morning. Were you about to go for a bath? So early, too, on a holiday.'

'Well, yes, I always bathe early.'

'At home?'

'No, I go down to the river. If I don't take a dip in the Churni... childhood habit, you see. But do sit down. Now that you are here, you must take your afternoon meal with....'

'Please do not trouble yourself. No formalities. My cousin Niren will be furious if I do not visit him. I could not call on him the last time I visited.'

'A cup of tea in that case?'

'I don't mind. All in good time. Now to get down to business—what is this new act I see? Indubala Debi at Bani Cinema today....'

'Yes, I noticed.'

'Today of all days?'

'Indeed. That's what I was thinking too. There will be a clash.'

'Now we cannot change our date. All the arrangements have been made. Our handbills and notices have been distributed too. Einstein is coming on the Darjeeling Mail.'

'It occurred to me too. Yes, indeed.... But you know what I think?

Those who will go to the cinema for Indubala are not the ones who will come for the sahib's lecture. Those who have decided to attend the sahib's talk will certainly do so.'

The Rai Bahadur was enraged at Einstein's being referred to as 'sahib'. And this was the place to which he was bringing the world's greatest scientist! Was he a jute mill manager or a railway inspector? Why refer to him as 'sahib' then? But he said none of this. All he said was, 'That is true.'

Srigopal Babu was renowned in Ranaghat for being a generous host. The tea arrived, accompanied by a plate of snacks. When he had finished his cup of tea, the Rai Bahadur left with a view to strolling around the town. He had to meet a number of people and make several arrangements.

As he was leaving, he said, 'The keys to the municipal hall....'

Srigopal Babu said, 'At once. I'm sending Rajnidhi, the servant at the hall. My servant here will go with him. They will unlock the hall and set everything up. There's a free reading room there, people will be coming to read the newspapers. It's Sunday. I'll take the help of the younger people to arrange the chairs and benches. Don't worry.'

As soon as Srigopal Babu returned after his bath, his eldest daughter (Srigopal Babu had been a widower for three years now, and his elder daughter had moved from her husband's house to run the household) said, 'Get us five tickets, Baba.'

'Tickets to what?'

'Don't you know, Indubala is coming to Bani Cinema this evening— she'll dance and sing. Everyone here is going.'

'Who's going?'

'Everyone. Ranu, Alaka, Tempi, Jatin Kaka's daughter, Dhyanrosh.... They're getting a box—if you get a box for ladies it's two and a half rupees per ticket. Get a box for us.'

Srigopal Babu sounded irked. 'A box! Am I a rich man? I've been carrying this burden since 1903, I haven't been able to lay it down. All you want is money....'

Opening his drawer with an unhappy expression, he took out a ten-rupee note and some coins and handed them to his daughter.

A little later his neighbour, Radhacharan Nag, peeped into his drawing room. 'What's going on, Srigopal Babu?'

'Please come in, doctor. I hope you're going this evening.'

'Yes, that's what I came to ask. Are you?'

'Of course. Has Ranaghat ever been so fortunate? We must go.'

'That's what I was telling them at home. The expenditure...but no matter. An opportunity such as this...they were very keen at home, so I gave them ten rupees. I am nearly fifty-six, after all, who knows when I might die, at least once before that....'

'Of course. How many people have such a rare opportunity? We the citizens of Ranaghat are extremely fortunate that such a personality....'

'That's what I was telling them at home. I'm getting older, it's time to experience a few things, never mind if I have to spend some money.'

'And, besides, someone so famous....'

'Beyond a doubt. Everywhere you look, you see Indubala Debi. In advertisements, be it for soaps, perfumed oil or saris, it's all Indubala. How fortunate to see her in person, that too in a village like Ranaghat... most definitely we are fortunate.'

Srigopal Babu gaped at Radhacharan Babu unable to say a word at first. A full two minutes later he said hesitantly, 'But I wasn't talking about her. I was talking of the sahib's lecture, at the municipal hall.'

'Which sahib?' asked Radhacharan Babu, frowning.

'You don't know? Einstein—Mr Einstein.'

'Oh, that German or is he Italian?' said Radhacharan Babu disinterestedly, as though he had only just remembered. 'Yes, my son-in-law did mention it. What is it that he's going to lecture on? But all this at our age...I haven't looked at a textbook in years. Let all those schoolboys and college students go...Hah!'

Srigopal Babu was about to protest when Radhacharan Babu continued, 'And what do you propose to do?'

'The girls are going to the cinema. But, I simply must go to the lecture. Rai Bahadur Nilambar Babu was pleading with us....'

'Who is this Rai Bahadur? Who might this Nilambar Babu be?'

'A professor at Krishnagar College. He has taken the initiative. He specially asked me....'

Radhacharan Babu winked. 'Let me tell you something, my dear fellow. Let us go, just this once. There's a world of difference between Indubala on the screen and Indubala in the flesh. It will be the experience of a lifetime. We've seen enough of these sahibs. All you have to do is stand on the platform when the Darjeeling Mail passes twice a day. There'll be no dearth of sahibs to set your eyes on. But an opportunity like this... don't you see?'

Srigopal Babu said absently, 'Um...er...but I've given my word to the Rai Bahadur, what will he think....'

Contorting his face, Radhacharan Babu almost snarled, 'Hah! Given your word to the Rai Bahadur! Who is this Rai Bahadur! What obligation do you have, for heaven's sake! You can tell him that the girls insisted. What could you have done? And it isn't entirely untrue either.'

Srigopal Babu answered, still distracted, 'Er...yes...that is true. I must admit....'

Radhacharan Babu told him, 'That's what you can tell the Rai Bahadur when he comes. Why not request him to come along to Bani Cinema too?'

'Are you leaving?'

'I am. I'll be here on time in the evening.'

The Rai Bahadur was discussing the arrangements for the lecture at the house of the local zamindar, Niren Chatterjee.

Niren Babu was the Rai Bahadur's cousin and a lawyer. He may not have been formidable professionally, but the majority of the residents of Ranaghat could not match up to his earnings as a landlord and his inherited wealth. He was well-educated, too.

The Rai Bahadur had just finished a sumptuous lunch. The afternoon meal was taken very seriously in his wealthy cousin's household. He had all but succumbed to the attractions of sleep once or twice, but a sense of duty had kept him from giving in.

Niren Babu said, 'What will the lecture be about, Dada?'

'I'm not sure. On the unity of forces—that's the subject. Imagine the rest.'

'He has humiliated space, has he not?'

'What do you mean?'

'He says space is finite. Space is no longer endless and infinite as it once was.'

'Did you study mathematics for your MSc? Have you read Geometry of Hyperspaces?'

'Complex mathematics. I am aware of what you are referring to.'

'I am delighted to see that you are not just a zamindar, Niren, that you keep yourself informed of the important issues of the world. It may not be a great deal, but even the very little you know is unknown to many.'

'Is he leaving today, Dada?'

'Possibly. He said he was going to Darjeeling, and that he will get off on the way. We must pay special attention to ensure that he makes some money today.'

'Can't you bring him over to my house after the lecture, Dada? I can put him up for the night. There's no train to Darjeeling in the evening. Let him stay the night here. I'll ensure that he is comfortable.'

'Very well, I shall tell him.'

'Make sure that he stays. I'll have a report published in the newspapers tomorrow. *Free Press* and *Anandabazar* both have reporters here.'

The Rai Bahadur realized where his cousin's interest lay. But it was futile to talk of all this, for he had to ensure the success of the endeavour somehow. He would be relieved once the meeting ended.

Niren Babu's daughter Mina came into the room to say, 'Tell Baba to give us the money for the tickets, Jetha Moshai.'

'Go now, don't bother us,' scolded Niren Babu. 'We're busy.'

'Tickets for what, Minu?' asked the Rai Bahadur.

Mina said, 'Where has your mind wandered off to? Sabita next door studies in your college, she says you solve mathematics problems while walking on the road. Is that true, Jetha Moshai?'

Niren Babu rebuked her once more. 'Such a brash girl. Go now.'

'What a nuisance. Do you know what tickets she is talking about, Dada? Apparently, that Indubala is coming to our Bani Cinema tonight, there will be a performance, she will even deliver a lecture, the entire town is queuing up. The girls have been pestering me since morning.'

'Let them go then. They're not likely to attend Einstein's lecture in any case. But they would have had an experience to remember all their lives. Well, Minu, which one would you rather go to?'

'We'd better go to the cinema, Jetha Moshai. Ever since we saw Indubala in *Milon* we've been dying to see her in the flesh. Someone like her coming to Ranaghat....'

'...is beyond our wildest dreams.' The Rai Bahadur completed her sentence. 'Isn't that so, Minu? Give her the money for the ticket, Niren.'

Emboldened, Mina said, 'Baba and you must take us. We won't take no for an answer. Baba wants to, Jetha Moshai. It's only because he's afraid of you that....'

'What a naughty girl!' Niren Babu chided her.

Mina disappeared, laughing.

Before she left, she said, 'You have to take us, Baba. You can't get off so easily.'

It was time for the Darjeeling Mail to arrive. 5.30 p.m.

Along with several students, the Rai Bahadur, Niren Babu, and Srigopal Babu were at the station. But...what was all this? Why was there such a big crowd? All these young students, so many people, gathered on the platform. Had everyone here woken up to Einstein's presence, then? Had they all come here to welcome him as he stepped off the train? It was certainly a reception worthy of the great scientist. The platform was bursting with people. What a gathering! The Rai Bahadur was elated. The train arrived with a roar.

A long-haired, almond-eyed Einstein disembarked from a second-class compartment with a small suitcase. At the same time a lovely young lady, dressed in an expensive voile sari, her feet shod in embroidered sandals from Kashmir, a vanity bag slung over her arm, got off from the first-class carriage next to it. Two other young women accompanying her, both dark in complexion, and two menservants, busied themselves unloading her luggage.

Someone said, 'There she is. There's Indubala Debi!'

The crowd broke in her direction. The Rai Bahadur escorted Einstein through the multitude towards the exit with great difficulty.

Einstein had not realized the real reason for the turnout. He assumed the crowds were there to catch a glimpse of him. He asked the Rai Bahadur, 'Are all of them students at the local university? Are you not going to introduce me to them, Mr Mukherjee?'

The Rai Bahadur made no attempt to disabuse the simple-hearted missionary of science of his notion.

A university at Ranaghat! Alas, he had not identified this country for what it was. This was no Europe.

Niren Babu had requested the wealthy and well-known local businessman Gopal Pal for the use of his 1917 model automobile. As they got into the car, they could see large numbers of people still rushing towards the station. Someone was saying, 'The train's arrived already, there, it's standing at the platform. Run.' Another voice from the crowd said, 'She'll pass this way, no need to go in there. So crowded. We all know what she looks like, she'll be easy to spot. We've seen her so many times, just the other day in *Milon*....'

An amused Einstein said, 'These people are running to the station too? And they don't know that the person they want to see is getting into a car under their very noses. Most amusing. Which way is the university, Mr Mukherjee?'

Fortunately, a man from the crowd plunged into the path of the car and was about to be run over, whereupon the screeching of brakes and shouts from passers-by drowned the question. Once they had left the crowds behind, and reached the end of the road, Srigopal Babu and Niren Babu got out of the car. 'I hope you'll be there soon,' said the Rai Bahadur.

Srigopal Babu's response was inaudible. Niren Babu said, 'I'll be there as soon as I've taken them to the cinema. There's no one else at home to escort the ladies. With all that money spent on the tickets....'

The municipal hall was directly in front of them now. Not far from the station. But what was this? The scheduled time of the lecture was five-thirty, it was a quarter to six now, but no one had arrived. Not a soul. Only Jeebon Bhadhuri, the municipality clerk, sat behind a small table piled high with tickets, waiting for the audience.

The car drew up in front of the hall, and the Rai Bahadur helped Einstein out. Trying to summon a smile to his face, he said, 'Welcome, O Supreme Scientist. May the everlasting history of your setting foot on the soil of Ranaghat be written in letters of gold. We, the residents of Ranaghat, are blessed today.'

Simultaneously, he cast a fleeting, worried glance at the empty hall. Where were the people? Where were the other representatives of Ranaghat society?

Staring in astonishment at the desolate hall, Einstein said, 'No one has arrived yet? They're all gathered at the station. I'll need a blackboard, Mr Mukherjee. I'll have to draw on it during the lecture.'

What use was a blackboard? The Rai Bahadur was a local. He had his finger on the pulse of the town. He looked around vacantly, without hope.

Coming up to him, Jeebon Bhadhuri whispered, 'Only sold three rupees worth of tickets. They've not even paid for them yet. What should I do, sir? Tell me how long I have to be here. I have to take the children to Bani Cinema. Indubala from Calcutta is here, they're badgering me at home. Just thirty-five rupees a month...but then what I say is, never mind, hardships will always be there. But people like them won't be coming from Calcutta every day. What harm will it do to spend five rupees? You'll have to let me go, sir. Who is this sahib? No one will come for his lecture, sir—who will come here today, after all!'

So saying, Jeebon Bhadhuri disappeared. Only two creatures could be seen in the unpopulated forest of chairs and benches—Einstein and the Rai Bahadur.

Einstein was busy arranging things from his bag on the table, he would need them during the lecture. The Rai Bahadur took the opportunity to go out on the pavement and cast worried glances up and down the street.

People were passing, well-dressed women went by in carriages, those on foot were running. All of them had the same destination—Bani Cinema.

A lawyer whom the Rai Bahadur knew was following the crowd swiftly, a cane in his hand. Spotting the Rai Bahadur, he said, 'Here you are. Is the sahib here? Unfortunately, his lecture has clashed with the other thing. On any other day...no, I simply cannot...the ladies are all here, no one to escort them. I have no choice but to...you see....'

'Yes, with utmost reluctance,' the Rai Bahadur said to himself.

Half an hour passed. Six thirty. Quarter to seven. Seven.

Not a soul.

Bani Cinema was bursting with people. With the tickets sold out, hundreds were gathered outside. A group of people had tried in vain to force their way in. The balconies for ladies were so packed that there was a real fear of them collapsing. The curtains had gone up. Indubala, the film star, was singing—songs from her film *Milon*, renowned across the land, heard on the lips of the young and the old: 'The Swampy Wind is Startling', 'O Caged Bird from an Unknown Land', 'The King's Winged Horse', etc.

Pushing his way through the crowd, Rai Bahadur Neelambar Chattopadhyay entered the cinema hall, only to be astonished at the sight of Srigopal Babu. Niren Babu was sitting nearby. 'Oh, you here too?' he said.

Looking extremely guilty, Srigopal Babu said, 'I didn't really want to, what to do, the girls...had to bring them...er...how did the sahib's lecture go? No crowd?'

'How could there be? All of you are here. Who's going to listen to him?'

'Where's the sahib? Has he left?'

'Here he is.'

Einstein himself was standing behind the Rai Bahadur.

Jumping to his feet, Srigopal Babu took Einstein's hand and tenderly deposited him in his own seat.

I have saved a newspaper clipping on the events of the day. It is reproduced here.

> The price of potatoes is on the rise. Paddy is cheaper. Malaria has made an appearance. The attention of health department officials has been drawn to it, thanks to the efforts of the worthy subdivisional officer.
>
> The renowned film star Indubala Debi made an appearance at the Bani Cinema this past week. She conquered all hearts with her prowess at dancing and her heavenly singing talent. The display of high art visible in her performance of the Black Bat Dance shall never be forgotten by the residents of Ranaghat. There was an unprecedented gathering of people on the occasion at the aforementioned cinema house—a majestic spectacle in its own right. The large gathering damaged the beams beneath the ladies' balcony, the timely discovery of which saved everyone present from an accident.
>
> The famous German scientist Einstein had stopped at Ranaghat on his way to Darjeeling in order to deliver a lecture at the Municipal Hall. He too was among the audience at Bani Cinema House during Indubala's dance performance.

10

THE MADIGA GIRL

CHALAM

Translated from the Telugu by Dasu Krishnamoorty and Tamraparni Dasu

It was December vacation when, without telling anyone, I travelled to my wife's village to see how she was doing after I'd impregnated her for the sixth time in the eight years of our marriage. People in the village give the impression that they have nothing more to do on earth other than wait for their end. The fragrance of dew-drenched hay, the greenness of the crop, the freshness of grass underneath, and the music of the carefree birds hold you in thrall, like the memories of your ancestors who've left you behind.

I spent a sleepless night, ruing the thirty-five years I'd wasted, cooped up in wobbly office chairs or lounging in the sagging string cot in my wife's village. A village that seems to have an unfair share of glossy-skinned beauties bursting with life. Those girls, the village belles, with sinewy muscles undulating under their ebony skin! When I see them, unable to rein in their voluptuous charms behind their flimsy saris, I'm tempted to prostrate and pay obeisance, ignoring the risk of being flattened by an oncoming lorry, or the call of pending files, or the shrivelled visage of my supervisor.

Just as you can't help but caress a cool, smooth marble surface, or the mane of a freshly groomed thoroughbred, or the hackles of swan-like doves, I've an irresistible longing to stroke the nubile bodies of the village damsels. No matter that they're not beautiful, or decked in gold, or draped in snow-white Uppada or gossamer Banaras saris, or that their hair is undone, or that they have rustic forms, or that they lack the delicate complexion of their sophisticated counterparts. What man wouldn't give his life to get lost in those mesmerizing curves? And to gawk at the gait that animates their hourglass waists and the pure sheen of their bodies?

They don't flee at the sight of a stranger, or peep from behind doors, or shy away mumbling inaudible invective when you greet them. They laugh all the time, their pearly teeth gleaming pure white, like the perfectly set seeds in a tender pomegranate. They are not laughing at you. I think it is the sheer joy of living that courses through their bodies, the thrill of enjoying the God-given light and air. It is difficult to say whether the caprice in their eyes is the glint of the setting sun or the burden of the grace of their bosom.

My very first evening in my wife's village revived an acute desire that had been killed by kitchen smells, wailing kids, remonstrating supervisors, and visitors baiting me with bribes. It is not the mundane desire that familiarity and a home-cooked meal arouse in you. Nor is it the hurried act and the stealthy exit after a promiscuous rendezvous that make you vow never to see the face of the wayward bitch again. It is the call of the cowherd beckoning the straggling herd home, the tingling when the cool breeze scatters her hair and caresses the back of her neck. Then I want my love to sit by my side, smile, and, pressing her young bosom into my flesh, look into my eyes.

Such a desire is natural in any living, breathing human being; I could never conquer it despite my best efforts. I'm timid. In my village, such thoughts would never cross my mind. Toiling, eating, going to bed, making love, and loafing about with fellow clerks are the things that make me happy. But the breeze here, in my wife's village, is so intoxicating that I can't rein in unruly thoughts. Even God, my creator, couldn't have suppressed them. Not even those worthies who invented morality to deny men and women their due could accomplish this.

You've seen the coastal highway, haven't you? The road runs sandwiched between the canal and the plantations. The sun fills the canal waters with twinkling images of swaying orchards. It was on this road that one day my heart skipped a beat at the sound of a giggle that had the melody of a gurgling stream. I stood in the middle of the road, enchanted by words falling to the ground like rose petals. A song filled the air. 'Does she, the source of this music, have a care in this world?' I wondered. That laughter merged magically with the morning light, the limpid water, and the birds' love songs. 'Did this same laughter stir the flowers, the air, and the coconut fronds?'

Fifteen minutes later, she appeared before me like a nymph, emerging from inside the orchards, talking to an old Muslim man and singing. She was in her early twenties and wore a red sari. She approached the canal, hitched up her petticoat and stepped into the water to wade through. My searing scrutiny failed to dent her equanimity. I'd never seen such a resplendent complexion. She wore no blouse. Her sari covered her bosom. One glimpse of her velvety body conjured up a new moon in a sky lit up by stars; all those poetic descriptions you read in the epics fail to do justice to the radiance of her body. A speck of dust has no choice but to slide off her marble-smooth skin. The sun played hide-and-seek on her shoulders. The mere thought of the curves of her shoulders...oh my lord, ignited the body with desire. The dark thighs radiated a blinding light under the hoisted hem of her petticoat.

My wife, with her distended abdomen, reedy arms, and the elongated neck of a stork, greeted me when I returned home from that visit to paradise.

'Where did you go, so early in the morning?'

I ignored the question and fled inside, afraid to meet her eyes. By all accounts, my wife is a beautiful woman. She has all the attributes of beauty mentioned in the ancient scriptures. She has an hourglass middle when she is not pregnant. She is fidelity personified. I think she would spit at the nymph, were she to see her. But my infatuation with the rustic damsel was such that I'd have readily strangled my wife that night. If I had to choose between the damsel and the office of a governor, I'd be the first to sign a document relinquishing the office.

Restless, I ventured out again that afternoon. The rain had spoilt the day but the evening after the rain was magnificent. The roads were puddled. The trees and birds were busy flicking off raindrops. The breeze romped with joy. The desire to see her had become acute, like a school-going child wanting to skip classes. 'What more would I want in life, once I have her friendship? How about caressing her hand, her curves!' My thoughts hit a low. In my mind, I could see the water flow under the fickle shade of the coconut palms, the grass flanking the cool, moving waters, and a strong wind fluttering her sari. The furtive glances of her love-filled eyes intoxicated me.

If this dream comes true, does it matter if I slave as a clerk for the rest of my life, or face an abusive supervisor? I would ask everyone, 'Miserable fellows, what do you know about the sensual pleasures of rasa and happiness?'

I arrived at the orchard and settled down for a long wait. No trace of life. Half an hour later, I saw my swaying beauty returning from some unknown rendezvous. It didn't take long to start a conversation with the simple girl. We start trading pleasantries.

'It's slushy here. Let's find a better spot,' she said, and guided me to the veranda of a factory next to the orchard. We stood there chatting. I was happy to stand close to her, close enough to read the thoughts that animated her face. Isn't it enough for me if her eyes meet my gaze, enough to look at her as she stealthily watches the road for fear of detection, pulling back the inconstant sari onto her shoulder?

'What will the passers-by think of us? They are foul-mouthed. Come stand here,' she said and pulled me aside.

'I first mistook you for the mailman. He often passes this way like Brahma,' she giggled.

That laughter erased my jealous thoughts about the mailman and disarmed me. What was I to do? Could I be content with appropriating that laughter, kissing those smiling lips, touching her tremulous neck, and pressing against her swaying bosom? Why is this silly mailman spoiling the fun? Should I slaughter him, burn him, or simply trample him?

'Why are you chatting with me for so long...don't you have important matters to take care of?' she asked me.

'Because I have a crush on you.'

'What a joke! We're poor folk. No nice clothes or ornaments. Only darkness and crudeness,' she said and stretched her arms forward. A raging desire to grab her hands and taunt her to free herself swept over me, but I held back, afraid of scaring her away. In those ten minutes, I longed several times to touch her but fear stood in my way.

An inner voice told me to act fast before someone showed up and time ran out. But courage failed me. A passer-by might notice!

To prolong the conversation, I asked her if the orchard belonged to her family.

'Oh, you want to see the orchard? Come,' she said and led the way.

I trailed her, watching her swaying behind. Ah, the curves. I realized what I'd missed until now and rued my barren life.

'Watch for carpenter ants, come this side,' she said and pulled me aside. Was it intentional? I was not sure.

We stood behind the dense hibiscus growth. She plucked two flowers and tucked them into her serpentine braid. That tug lifted her bosom and chased my fears and reticence away. I clasped her hands. The firm flesh of her arms resisted my touch. Such delight! Such warmth and smoothness! How different from the married ones who give in too readily, and then act coy. Depressing, my God!

What a contrast those five minutes were! How can I explain my delightful plight? The more she tried to free herself the tighter I held her. But my hands kept slipping. My strength ebbed. The natural scent of her body was making me feel faint—the perfumes arrayed in the attar vendor's shop are no match! Neither is the fragrant rosemary that homeless urchins sell on passenger trains. Her presence exuded a feral scent, a commingling of the scent of the scorched earth after rain and of the fragrance of the musk deer. I would gladly spurn divinity and immortality in exchange for these few moments.

She pushed me away and in mock anger said, 'Please, don't touch me.' Then she ran off to the riverbank, laughing. Was she amused by my shock and disappointment?

I followed her, admiring her loping gait, like a heifer. Letting me move closer, she leant in towards me.

'I'm not that type,' she said, and laughed in an odd way.

My head began to reel. I was having difficulty keeping my eyes open. Her eyes, her entire body were mocking me now.

'The sun barely sets before couples sneak into those rooms.' She laughed again pointing to some shacks not far from us. 'They've no shame, nothing,' she said.

I was intrigued. Who is this woman? Is this a charade or genuine innocence?

'Men like you think I'm that type. We're respectable folks. Now, hands off...no more mischief. Who do you think I am?'

What does she see in my eyes, despair or resignation? As I stare stupidly, she comes close to me. She nudges my shoulder with her bosom and passes her hand across my pocket.

'There's no rice for the night. If you can give me....'

I averted my face; I couldn't look her in the eye. That statement shattered my dreams. My heart bled at the loss of the beauty and romance I'd imagined. I couldn't believe that she was of the same ilk as the jewellery-crazed, mansion-inhabiting city vampires. But I was not ready to shun her. Perhaps she really needed money for the night meal. Before I could answer, an old woman spotted us.

She asked the girl, 'Who is this fellow? What are you doing here?'

Oh my God, would she complain that I was trying to molest her? Or, is she just playing with me? I regretted having met her. I began imagining terrible things—public humiliation, my in-laws discovering their son-in-law messing around with a Madiga girl.

'Nothing, he wanted to see the garden,' the girl said.

'What business do you have with these men? Go home, girl! Ha, wanted to see the garden!' the old woman scoffed.

The girl hesitated.

'Why aren't you leaving? Do you want me to tell your father to thrash you?'

'Don't be angry. This man is a gentleman, don't you see? You're angry for no reason.'

'Hmm, everyone is a gentleman. There is no rice for the night. Go get some. Will chatting with gentlemen fill your stomach?' the old woman barked and left.

'My mother,' the girl said.

'Do you really have no food? Whose orchard is this, then?'

'We leased it, but it is always losing money. This year is no different.'

I pulled out a five-rupee note.

'Come inside,' she said.

'Not now, I have to go.'

'Not now? Then when?'

'I won't come again.'

'Why?'

'I have nothing to do here.'

'Then why did you come today?'

The question rattled me.

'I never thought you were this type.'

'What type do you think I am?'

'You'll do anything for money.'

She bit her lip and looked at me with tear-filled eyes.

'Why did you pay me, then?' Her voice shook.

'Because you need something to eat.'

She stood silently as two tears rolled down her chest. A cuckoo warbled incessantly. A humid breeze floated in. The dying rays of the sun kissed her hands. Stray strands of hair fell over the flowers in her braid. Her beauty beckoned me again. Spontaneously, my lips brushed her tear-filled eyes. I was happy to be with her but the matter of money still irked me. I made a move to leave.

'You may go but listen to me for a moment,' she pleaded.
'I'm listening,' I said, rooted to the spot.
'Will you come inside that room with me?'
'All right, let's go,' I said.

She steered me into the room and bolted the door. In one corner of the room were a cot covered with a cotton mat, a soiled pillow, and many bidi stubs on the floor.

'What?' I asked her, confused.

She let her sari drop down deftly and placed my hand on her bare bosom. Would I have pulled my hand back were it not for the smelly room, the dirty bed, and the bidi stubs? Would I not feast on that body? Would I not greedily take in that neck, that belly button? Just their sight gave me all the bliss I needed in this birth.

'No,' I said, retrieving my hand with some effort.

'Why did you touch me a while ago when we were in the garden?' she said combatively, adding, 'I'm not as cheap as you think.'

Her eyes filled again, her lip trembled, and she drew back. I did not know what to do.

She stretched out her hand and pressed the five-rupee note into my palm and closed it.

'Where will you find food for the night?' I asked her.

The look she gave me would have reduced any mortal to ashes.

'Are you angry with me?' I asked.

'What does it matter? The anger of lowly people like us does not count.'

'Look, you're angry.'

'Not at all. You may go now.'

'Please accept this,' I said stretching out the note.

'Not if it is charity.'

'Is it worse than the way you make money?'

Silence.

'I'm your friend. This is a gift; I can't see you go hungry. Please accept.'

I touched her cheek with affection and gazed at her. She slumped onto the bed, covered her eyes with her palms, and cried. I knew this would happen. I wiped the tears and kissed her eyes and sat by her side.

'Why do you cry?' I asked.

She did not reply, but I knew she wanted to tell me something. I waited.

'You think I asked you for money for myself? But it has become my job, my living, whether I like it or not. We've always lived beyond our means. I guess my mother used to raise extra money in this manner. One day, she gifted me to Venkayya, a man of our caste.

'We owed him a few hundred rupees. He tried to take me when I was asleep. I shouted for help but Mother had already left. My father too.

'I ran all over the orchard and hid behind a jujube bush, gasping. It was a full moon night. He found me and threw me down. I fought him till my strength failed. I collapsed. I closed my eyes and awaited the worst.

But I don't know what came over him. He bashed my head against the ground, spat, and left, cursing my parents. I was lying there like a corpse when my mother came and began beating me and complaining that I hadn't pleased him. I told her I wasn't going to allow him to enter me. That angered her more and another round of thrashing followed. "Who'll repay the debts; your husband?" she yelled.'

'What happened then?' I asked.

'Oh, what a night that was! He returned the next day. "I'll kill you if you touch me,"' I told him. My mother threw me out again.'

'There was no one to help me. My husband, whom I had never seen after I came of age, had migrated to Rangoon.'

'You must have been in quite a difficult spot,' I said.

'I was. There was hardly a man who didn't ogle me whenever I stepped out. I was too innocent and didn't understand the meaning of those looks. Over time, I began to fear my beauty. I realized why Muslim women wore the burqa. The lecherous looks of these men bothered me more than their touch or illicit caress. I wanted to spit in their faces.'

'Then?' I asked her.

'One day, the owner of the factory asked me to report for the night shift. I refused. "You won't get any wages, then," he said. How do we repay our mounting debt? So, I reported for the night shift. There was no one else in the factory. He grabbed my hand. I told him not to touch me. "I'm a Madiga and you're a Brahmin. It doesn't befit you," I told him. I managed to slip out and ran to his house, not far from the factory, and fell at the feet of his mother and wife. "Don't touch us, you Madiga," they shouted. "What about your son who is stalking a Madiga?" I asked them.'

She paused for a minute to catch her breath.

'They hurled a sickle at me. The owner came and tried to molest me regardless of the presence of his wife and mother. I picked up the sickle and threw it at his face and fled. Soon, the police caught me and locked me up in jail. A constable came by and said he could get me out if I agreed to sleep with him. I didn't. He beat me till I became unconscious. Then he had me. Then others followed.'

She sighed.

'That was it. After I'd lost my chastity, there was no point in virtue, I thought. I agreed to become Venkayya's concubine. He gave me good clothes, jewellery, good food. When he died, I was back on the streets again. This is the only way I know to save my family from starvation. Tell me, is there any other way?'

I had no answer.

11

THE GOVERNOR'S VISIT

KALKI

Translated from the Tamil by Gowri Ramnarayan

SRIMAN SIVAGURUNATHAN CHETTIAR RELAXED ON HIS EASY CHAIR AFTER lunch as usual and picked up the newspaper. As he scanned the headlines he was startled by the announcement, 'Poikai Dam: Governor to lay foundation stone'.

Chettiar had goosebumps all over. His heart began to race. Controlling himself with some effort, he read on. The report gave details of the Governor's arrival at the railway station on the 20th at 7 a.m. He was to take a car to the site of the dam.

Chettiar at once summoned his clerk, Jayarama Iyer, and asked him, 'Have you heard the news?'

'No, sir, anything special?'

'How is it that you always seem to know nothing? Haven't I told you again and again to read the papers? Why do we spend 250 rupees every year on their subscriptions? What would have happened if I hadn't followed the news carefully?'

'Sir, please give me the news.'

'The Governor is visiting our town on the 20th.'

The clerk gaped in wonder. He was too astonished to do anything except break into incoherent exclamations.

'All right, what do we do next?'

'We must get everything organized.'

'I must be at the railway station on the morning of the 20th. Make sure our car is shining and spotless.'

'Didn't I insist you should buy a motor car? Wasn't it an excellent suggestion?'

'My good man, it is that foresight which makes you so valuable to me.... Well, shouldn't we get our house decorated for the occasion?'

'Why, is the Governor going past our home?'

'I'm not sure. He may go straight to the site from the station. I must persuade the Collector to take him through our street.'

'It doesn't matter. In any case, the fact that our house is being decorated will be reported in the papers.'

'True enough. But will the news of the Governor's arrival escape the eyes of Kurmavataram Iyengar? Doesn't he read the papers as keenly as I do?'

'Don't worry. Even if he gets to know, there is nothing much he can do about it. First of all, he has no motor car, only an old-fashioned coach. Don't you remember how the whole durbar burst into laughter when Iyengar accepted the Rao Bahadur title from the Collector, dressed like a clown and bowing as if he would never stop? The same thing will happen again.'

Chettiar chuckled as he recalled that scene. 'Still, he must not know our plans. Keep everything ready and put up the festoons on the night of the 19th after 10 p.m. Let Iyengar get up and blink in the morning.'

Chettiar and Iyer held long discussions about the necessary preparations. Finally, they were struck by a bright idea. Chettiar sent a message to the president of the town council saying that at their next meeting he would propose the presentation of a citation to the Governor. After that the clerk went about his usual business.

Sivagurunathan Chettiar was a prosperous businessman. He owned the only three-storeyed mansion in his little town. He had started life as a poor clerk in a hardware store. But soon the goddess Lakshmi glanced at him from the corner of her eye, and Chettiar opened his own shop and business. His wealth increased day by day. His large pre-war stock of iron doubled and tripled in value during the World War. Chettiar became a millionaire overnight.

He began to crave social recognition. His next-door neighbour, the advocate Kurmavataram Iyengar, became his role model in social graces and sartorial style. Chettiar engaged a tutor to teach him English. He adopted all the ostentations of high living. He threw frequent parties for government officers. He squandered an enormous sum to become town councillor. Presently, his entire ambition was focused on obtaining the Rao Bahadur title.

A sneaking fear plagued him. What if Iyengar became Dewan Bahadur before that? He intended to overtake Iyengar by hook or by crook in securing the Governor's favour. That was the reason the advocate figured repeatedly in his conversations with his clerk.

The next day Chettiar attended the council meeting with a beaming face. His well-prepared proposal to present a citation to the Governor was tucked into his shirt pocket.

His speech was divided into three parts. Part one described the benefits of British rule in India. Part two traced details of the Governor's ancestry, family history, character traits, and individual merits. The third part listed all the contributions of the Governor, real and imaginary, to the welfare of the state.

At the end of his peroration, Chettiar drew the kind attention of the esteemed Governor to the single regrettable act of omission in his regime. Loyal subjects of the Crown were not given sufficient recognition or reward. He humbly prayed that the Governor show discrimination in the conferment of titles on deserving persons.

The clerk sent copies of the proposal to all reporters with the assurance that Chettiar would bear the cost of telegraphing the whole speech to their respective headquarters. The reporters were also invited to Chettiar's home the day after the Governor's visit.

But alas! The moment he took his seat in the council Chettiar's joy turned to grief and anger. He came to know that Rao Bahadur Iyengar had sent his claim to make a similar proposal before Chettiar had. He would therefore get precedence in the matter. But Chettiar was not a man to be stumped by reversals. Life had taught him that determined effort achieved results. He successfully manoeuvred the right to second Iyengar's proposal. After that it was but an easy step to read the entire speech in the guise of seconding the proposal. Poor man, how could he know Iyengar had made arrangements to prevent his speech from reaching the newsrooms?

As Chettiar cursed God and man, his clerk brought him information which consoled him a little.

'The Governor arrives at the station at 7 a.m. He has to travel fifty miles to be at the river Poikai by 9 a.m. to lay the dam's foundation stone. He has no time to receive the citation at the town council or at the railway station. This message came just now from the Governor's personal secretary.... Good thing you did not propose the citation. You have been spared a loss of face.'

Chettiar was very glad. 'Ah, Kurmavataram Iyengar got what he deserved. Didn't he try to steal a march over me?'

'All the same, shouldn't you be at the station on the 20th morning?'

'Of course. All our other plans stand as before.'

At last, the appointed day arrived. Chettiar was up at dawn. After his bath and breakfast, he stood before the mirror for a good half-hour finishing his toilette. His beloved wife was beside him, smoothening the folds in his garments and polishing his ornaments. As soon as he was ready, he sent the clerk to fetch the car from the garage. Chettiar's wife took a look at the street outside to check if the signs favoured her husband's trip. When the omens and the time were deemed auspicious, Chettiar stepped out of the house and entered his car. A big flapping Union Jack graced the car's bonnet.

Chettiar felt a pang when he saw his neighbour's house. Iyengar too had played a waiting game through the previous day and had put up flags and festoons in the dark. The car began to move and there was little time for more speculation.

It took five minutes to reach the station. Chettiar saw that Iyengar was there before him, ready for action. Their fierce competitiveness remained strictly hidden. To the world they were the best of friends.

'What brings you here so early?' Chettiar enquired.

'A small errand. I heard you were leaving for Madras. Is that why you are here?' Iyengar asked mischievously.

'Never mind. But tell me, your house has been festooned with decorations overnight. Any special occasion?'

'I saw festoons in your house too. Is it true that you are celebrating your sixtieth birthday?' Iyengar's query had a sarcastic ring to it.

Chettiar wished to give him a severe setback but suddenly the station was filled with people. There were members of the town council, taluk, and zila board; graduates and those who were struggling to become graduates; advocates, officers, members of the security force; volunteers who had come to stage a political protest and watch the fun at the same time; representatives of the secret police who shadowed the volunteers. All of them stood cheek by jowl, their eyes straining to remain unblinkingly fixed on the railway track.

Finally, the Governor's special train arrived. Police officers strode up and down to establish peace. The honourable Governor disembarked. A path was cleared for him. All those who had come with manifold dreams stood breathless in adoration—with pounding hearts and earnest eyes. They trembled lest the honourable Governor leave without a single glance at them. Later it was learnt that an ardent soul among the multitude had fainted in rapture, but so great was his loyalty to the Crown that, determined to cause no disturbance, he stood upright even in such an extreme condition, clutching the pillar which hid him.

Meanwhile, the Governor took off his hat as a mark of civility and held it in his hand. His sweeping glance surveyed the crowd from one end to the other. Everyone present knew it was the moment of fulfilment of their lifetime ambition.

Petrified by the thought that the Governor might miss their salute at the precise moment his eye rested on them, they continued to salute him until he left the station. For five whole minutes their hands kept touching their foreheads and dropping down, like forest branches swaying incessantly in the west wind.

Having brought everyone under his royal glance, the Governor swiftly strode out and got into the waiting car. And those who had come to be exalted by the 'gracious sight' returned to their respective homes.

Sriman Sivagurunathan Chettiar reached home safe and sound. He was immediately surrounded by an excited group of wife, children, clerk, and staff. Chettiar was a kind man. He did not wish to disappoint so many eager souls.

'We must call the priest to arrange a special thanksgiving puja to the temple deity. Things went very well today.'

'Did the Governor speak to you? What did you say to him? What actually happened?' Everyone wanted to know every detail.

'As soon as he got off the train, the Governor spoke to one or two officials like the zila collector and came straight to me,' Chettiar told them. 'Do you think I felt the slightest fear? Not at all! He shook my hand and said, "Chettiar, I have heard a lot about you. How do you do?

Are your friends and relatives doing well?" You know me. Once I start talking I cannot stop. I said, "Your Excellency, under your rule we have no complaints. But I am forced to express my discontent over the fact that your government shows no discrimination in awarding titles."'

'Ayyayyo! That was quite severe! Didn't the Governor get angry?' the clerk asked with concern.

The words gushed forth from Chettiar's lips. 'Angry? What do you mean? As soon as I said this, the Governor shook my hand again and said, "Chettiar, thank you very much for bringing this to my attention. I will take steps to rectify the matter." The crowd broke into applause. But you should have seen our Rao Bahadur Iyengar. He was dumbstruck. He was standing in an obscure corner. No one took the slightest notice of him.'

At that very instant, if anyone had eavesdropped on the women's quarters at Rao Bahadur Kurmavataram Iyengar's house, he would have heard Iyengar say to his beloved spouse, 'But the Governor did not waste a single glance on Sivagurunathan Chettiar. Poor thing! He stood in an obscure corner and slunk away quite unnoticed.'

DHANAVANTRI'S HEALING

KUVEMPU

Translated from the Kannada by Chandan Gowda

IN THE CORNER OF NANDANAVANA FOREST, THE SAGE VISHWAMITRA paced back and forth in the shade of an unknown tree that stood at a distance from the wish-fulfilling Kalpavriksha tree. Although he had mastered his senses, he knew from experience that standing beneath a tree that instantly granted one's wishes was hazardous. Imagine if every desire darting through one's mind—good, bad, advantageous, disadvantageous— were fulfilled? Despite his elevation from being a rajarshi to brahmarshi, he wasn't arrogant enough to have full faith in the purity of his mind.

In a mood of deep contemplation, Vishwamitra was also incensed. He looked up in anger when the celestial gods and goddesses immersed in pleasure pursuits far away laughed loudly. He frowned and bit his lip. Like a million rainbows dancing together in love, Indra and the other gods were swaying their heads in the light breeze, and singing and dancing with Ramba, Urvashi, Tilottama, Ghritachi, Menaka, and other nymphs amidst trees bursting with fragrant flowers. This spectacle enraged the restrained and detached Vishwamitra. His fury was probably tinged with resentment. In particular, the sight of Menaka infuriated him greatly: she had humiliated him in front of the whole universe. Still, he did not curse anyone. Abhorring the celestial beings who were drunk on nectar and crossing all limits of modesty, he bent his head and began pacing back and forth again.

'What kind of heaven is this? It is worse than a liquor shop! The dignity of suffering can at least be found in hell. The superficiality in heaven, though, has simply no limit. Feasting endlessly, spoiling the penance of sages, and seeking refuge in Brahma, Vishnu, and Maheshwara after losing to the demons—their lives will pass away in great deeds like these. Wait, how can immortal beings ever pass away?'

As these thoughts drew a pitying smile from the sage, a long, heart-piercing cry of anguish rose above the dance of the nymphs, above the sounds of their celestial music, as if tearing apart the forest floor.

Trembling, as if struck by thunder, the sage stood open-mouthed in fear: 'Again? The same groan!'

The merry-making gods didn't hear the groan at all. Their shameless drunken revelry continued undisturbed.

The loud groan had been following Vishwamitra for several days. Wherever he might be, whichever hour of day, whatever he might be doing, it reached his ears without fail, and disturbed his equanimity. He had heard it during a visit to Kailasa. And during his visits to Vaikunta and Satyaloka too. Even while he passed by hell, he had heard it above its din of lament—the mysterious groan of distress.

His attempts to find the source of that groan had not succeeded. When he enquired with Vashishtha in Vaikunta, the latter said he hadn't heard it ever. Attributing it to Vishwamitra's delusion, he advised him to perform a yajna to cure himself of it. Since Vishwamitra had ceased to believe in superstitions, he didn't take Vashishtha's idle advice.

The pensive Vishwamitra noticed Parashurama approaching him. The son of Renuka seemed to be gloomy. He hurried to him.

Placing his right arm around Vishwamitra's shoulders, Parashurama asked, 'Son of Kushika, did you hear a groan just now?'

Vishwamitra told Parashurama about his recent experiences. Admitting that he had shared the same experiences, Parashurama said that he had set off to travel the three worlds to get to the bottom of it all.

While they were still talking, the bloodcurdling groan that yet again drowned the merry music of the gods and nymphs was heard. Utterly bewildered, both the sages stood trembling. Imagine someone placed on a bed of thorns, and a boulder placed on his chest for a long time, and struck repeatedly with a heavy hammer, crying out in pain. The terrifying groan seemed like that!

Vishwamitra and Parashurama were shaking in fear. At this time, Narada, who was on his way to Vaikunta, ambled by, singing praises of Vishnu. Both the sages hurried towards the traveller of the three worlds and told him about what they had experienced. A delicate smile flickered on Narada's face. Tears also flowed from his eyes. While Vishwamitra and Parashurama were puzzling over these contrary reactions, Narada said, 'I've known that sorrowful groan for a long time! My heart trembles whenever I hear it. My soul feels squeezed. Even I don't fully understand the matter. But I know clearly that the groan arises from the earth.' The sage of the gods continued on his way, singing the praises of his Lord. Both the brahmarshis made their way swiftly towards the earth.

Vishwamitra and Parashurama were both stupefied when they neared the earth. The earth was transformed beyond recognition: civilization and culture now existed alongside barbarous forces that could instantly destroy the former, life-protecting medical knowledge existed along with terrible health habits, prosperity beside poverty. Noticing the trains, motor cars, planes, postal services, electricity, guns, bombs, paper, printing machines, and so on, admiring some of them and criticizing some others, they landed in human guise in a big city.

The movement of motor vehicles, the hustle and bustle of humans, the chaos of trade, the rush inside restaurants, the weave of electric wires and the throng of poles, the display of strange advertisements, a toddy shop that existed behind an office for preventing alcohol abuse, a gambling den in the upper storey of a house behind a police station, the unbearable stench emanating from under a hoarding that asked that the street be kept clean, the factories, the schools, the art institutes, etc.: observing all of these with surprise, curiosity, loathing, and delight, Vishwamitra and Parashurama went in search of the root cause of the sorrowful groan.

Their search led them to a temple. Seeing the priest extract money from the temple worshippers in the full awareness that there was no God in the shrine, and the commercial-mindedness of the devotees made the two sages laugh.

Turning towards Parashurama, Vishwamitra said, 'Did you see, son of Renuka? The priests have remained just as they were back then! The world has changed so much, but they remain the same.'

Parashurama replied, 'Poor things. What can the priests do? The priests in olden times suited the rulers of their time. The priests today are playing to the present-day rulers.' He shifted the blame to the Kshatriyas.

The crowds outside another temple drew the sages' attention. A storytelling session was going on there. The storyteller spoke about God's compassion in words that drew tears from the listeners. The two sages stood listening for a while. Just then, holding forth on the virtues of penance, the storyteller began narrating the stories of Parashurama and Vishwamitra. The two sages stood gaping as they heard completely new stories about themselves. They had no idea about their own powers!

'Which Vishwamitra is the storyteller talking about, oh son of Kushika?' Parashurama asked smiling.

Vishwamitra said, 'That storyteller isn't talking about you or I. He is making up stories.'

A large assembly had gathered elsewhere near a building. At the entrance stood soldiers in colourful uniforms, with swords in their hands. People dressed variously in embroidered turbans, hats, caps, boots, and long and short upper garments were moving in that direction. The two sages disguised themselves to look like the people around them and went inside. After the finely dressed, contented, and smiling people gathered inside had shaken hands in mutual congratulation and taken their seats, a dancer came onto the stage and started prancing around. Both the sages made up some excuses and came outside.

Wherever they went, none spoke about the sorrowful groan. None seemed to have even heard it. In some places the situation was such that the sages almost forgot the purpose of their visit to earth.

After they had looked and looked everywhere in vain, the tired sages left the city. As the great sound of the city's arrogant laughter receded, the terrifying groan was clearly heard again. Shivering in fear, they continued to walk. As they moved along, the groan sounded closer. They came upon a forest and entered it. It was a desolate forest without a sign of human habitation anywhere. The forest became denser the deeper they went. It had grown thickly on the slopes of a mountain. When they reached the mountaintop, the sound of great anguish appeared to emanate from the valley below. The terrified sages held on to each other as they descended towards the valley.

On reaching the valley, a thatched hut standing at the corner of a small field met their eyes. The terrible groan of anguish that soared above Satyaloka, Kailasa, Vaikunta, and spread across the cosmos was emerging from that hut. The sages walked towards it in the guise of ordinary men.

There was no one outside the hut. A skinny dog, which lay on a mound of ash, whimpered a couple of times before becoming still from exhaustion. A hen was scratching around in the dirt with her chicks. On all sides, boundless forests spread over a sky-caressing mountain range, deepening the silence and solitariness. The sun was raining fire. In the silence, the groan from inside sounded frightening. Vishwamitra peeked inside through a hole in the bamboo wall of the hut and motioned to Parashurama to do the same.

Inside, the hut was enveloped in a dim darkness. Sooty cobwebs hung everywhere. A crowbar, an axe, a chest, a basket, a pot, a plough, a sickle, and other farm implements, were scattered around in disorder. Dead dirt as well as living flies seemed to have earned total freedom of the place. A peasant, who was naked save for his dirty dhoti, lay on his back on a woollen blanket spread in the middle of the hut. He was pressing both hands to his chest and groaning frighteningly. The hellish suffering made his blackened body and head writhe in pain, like a snake trapped under a rock. While the sages looked on, blood poured from his mouth and soaked the floor. Beside the peasant sat his emaciated wife in a ragged, dirty sari that just about protected her honour. She was shedding tears, her head resting on her hands. Behind this woman lay as if unconscious a scruffy-haired little girl with a shrivelled body and a bloated belly.

The hearts of the sages melted. Hot tears started flowing down their cheeks. And they became especially enraged when the scenes of enjoyment they had seen in the big city came to mind. Gently pushing the thatched door open, they bent down to avoid hitting their heads and went inside.

Although they were dressed as ordinary men, the peasant's wife screamed at the sight of them. Folding her palms, she lamented: 'I beg you! I'll fall at your feet. I don't have any money now. After his disease is cured, my husband will repay you even if that means taking out a loan. For my child's sake, at least, please show mercy!'

After the sages convinced her that they were not tax officials, marauders, or the landlord's loan recovery men but visitors from abroad, the woman fell at their feet and shared her woes.

'What disease does your husband suffer from?'

'God only knows.'

'How long has he had it?'

'For a long time. Sometimes it gets better, sometimes worse. No one has been able to identify the disease. Suddenly he feels as if someone has climbed on his chest to hold him down. Blood frequently flows from his mouth. Doctors, astrologers, gods, small time deities—we have tried everyone. Even God has forsaken us, sir.' The woman wept inconsolably.

'No, God hasn't forsaken you. Be calm. We'll do what we can.' Both the sages examined the diseased man.

They thoroughly examined the heart, lungs, stomach, intestines, brain, and other vital organs. Not even the slightest defect or sign of disease was found. The patient was in no position to answer questions. But when a hand was placed on his chest, he winced and moaned with pain, as if a blister had been touched.

The sages felt helpless. The peasant's affliction was more mysterious than Ultimate Knowledge! Taking a chance, they brought over a doctor from a government hospital in a nearby town. Although he had refused to visit a village which his car couldn't reach, the gold coins of the sages made him follow them obediently, like a bull with a cord through its nose.

But, as soon as the doctor came near him, the heaviness in the patient's chest got worse, and his groaning and vomiting of blood increased. The doctor examined him hurriedly. Although he could tell nothing from the symptoms, he mentioned a disease with a long Latin name and left after giving the patient some coloured water as medicine. As the doctor moved further and further away, the patient was restored to his former condition.

The woman had no faith in the doctor. She suggested that a priest be summoned. Because she was certain that a ghost's mischief was behind her husband's disease.

While Vishwamitra demurred, Parashurama summoned a priest saying, 'Let's try it out.' Although clueless about the cause of the disease, the priest mentioned a ghost and claimed that he had blocked it through magic rituals. He collected his fee in gold coins and went away a pleased man.

Vishwamitra turned to Parashurama: 'The priests are all the same! Plunder!! Plunder!!! This priest is plundering in the same way Vashishtha did back then! He stuck to the Raghu clan like a bad omen! Ikshvaku, Raghu, Dileepa, Dasharatha, Rama—he harassed them no end with his priestly work! Didn't I ask you not to get a priest?'

The two sages stayed back in the hut and tried to find the cause of the peasant's mysterious disease and the cure for it. Their efforts were fruitless.

With word getting out that the visitors in the hut generously gave gold coins, the concern for the peasant's health went up among the officials and the people in the nearby villages. Those who had never set foot near the hut now kept dropping by to enquire about his health.

When the officials came over, the chest pain of the peasant doubled, just as it had happened with the doctor and priest.

A few days later, an idea struck Vishwamitra: Dhanavantri, the physician of the gods, was the only one who could understand the mystery of the disease! Parashurama agreed. They sent for him. Dhanavantri soon came, disguised as an ordinary physician.

The pitiable condition of the peasant's chest pain and bloodcurdling groans left Dhanavantri totally perplexed. Reminding himself quickly that he was a doctor, he gathered courage and got down to examining the patient's body.

Like the peasant's wife, Vishwamitra and Parashurama stood watching anxiously without saying a word. After a lengthy examination, Dhanavantri cast an ironic glance at the sages. Noticing despair in it, the peasant's wife began to weep silently.

To the peasant's wife, Dhanavantri appeared only to be glancing at the sages, but the divine physician and the sages were actually having a conversation.

Dhanavantri said, 'This isn't a disease of the body.'

Parashurama asked, 'Is it of the soul?'

Dhanavantri shook his head. 'It isn't even that.'

Vishwamitra was surprised. 'What is it then?'

Dhanavantri explained: 'If it were a bodily disease, it could have been spotted easily. But I've examined the body thoroughly. I found nothing. If the disease afflicted the soul, it would have appeared in the form of sin. But this disease is yet to touch this peasant who leads a simple, ordinary life.' Taking out a divine instrument from his pocket and showing it to them—it was invisible to the peasant's wife—he continued, 'If examined with this, any possible mystery can be revealed.' He stood at a distance from the patient and began his inspection with the divine instrument.

As Vishwamitra and Parashurama looked on, Dhanavantri's face reddened. He started breathing rapidly, his chest heaving up and down. Tears sprang from his eyes and flowed down his cheeks and soaked the floor.

'You sinners!' Dhanavantri roared, like an elephant. But the peasant's wife, who was only a human, felt that he had only coughed.

The bewildered sages rushed towards Dhanavantri. 'What is it? What is it? What happened? What happened?'

Without saying a word, Dhanavantri handed them the divine instrument. Both the sages peered through it intently. They were taken aback by what they saw!

The entire country stood imperiously on the peasant's chest in the form of a great mountain. The capital city that the sages had visited stood resplendent at the peak! Putting all their weight on the peasant's chest, the temples, places of learning, sports complexes, recreational parks, office buildings, factories, and stately mansions of the city were flaunting themselves in the name of culture and civilization.

'Alas, alas, alas!' Parushurama cried. 'It's a miracle that the peasant survived this long! Even Krishna, who lifted up the Govardhan mountain, would have shattered to bits under the weight of this country.'

Vishwamitra gnashed his teeth in rage. 'Jamadagni, your lifelong effort to propagate equality after you destroyed all the rulers back then has proved futile!'

'Didn't you also devote your life to remove distinctions of high and low? Even that has been in vain.' Parashurama then turned towards Dhanavantri. 'Tell us quickly, Dhanavantri. How can the peasant be saved?'

'He'll be cured when the weight of the country on his chest is lifted,' replied Dhanavantri.

'Won't the world fall into anarchy without any rules?'

Slightly angered, his eyes reddening, Dhanvantari rebuked him: 'Can't you understand? Let the disease get cured first. The peasant will then regain his strong body and, instead of being forced to carry the country's weight on his chest, he'll carry it on his shoulders, and take on the weighty responsibility of its administration.'

Immediately, Vishwamitra snorted, like a bull. It brought forth terrifying revolutionary spirits who stood in line with bowed heads and folded arms and begged to be commanded.

'Go ahead, lift the weight off that peasant's chest,' roared Vishwamitra with a wave of his arm.

Thunder, rains, storms, and earthquakes immediately broke out across the country and caused a calamity. The country's façade came off. The towers of the temples came crashing down loudly....

The peasant's suffering seemed to come down gradually. The functioning of his lungs was restored. The light of happiness flashed in his eyes...and within a short while, to everyone's surprise, he rose up smiling and greeted the sages with folded hands.

13

THE GOLD COIN

LAXMANRAO SARDESSAI

Translated from the Portuguese by Paul Melo e Castro

FIFTY YEARS AGO
Before leaving home, Narain Rao stepped into the deva kood, knelt before an image of the goddess, Shantadurga, and began to pray. Lakshmibai, his wife, joined him in his devotions and implored with pious fervour: 'Shantadurga Devi! At least this time allow us to succeed. Give us the strength not to give in....'

After their prayers, Narain Rao opened a cupboard and retrieved the mohar, the family coin, from a jewellery box. With great reverence he held it up to the light. It had belonged to his glorious ancestors, who had inherited that gold coin, the symbol of a magnanimous tradition sanctified by hundreds of blessed hands.

His father, before breathing his last, had summoned him to his bedside. Placing the gold coin in Narain Rao's hand, he murmured solemnly: 'Here is the family Lakshmi. No emergency will ever deprive you of it.' These were the venerable old man's final words.

As Narain Rao crossed the threshold of their home he cast a compassionate glance behind him at his dear wife, the only ray of light in the murk surrounding him.

It was at her urging that Narain Rao had decided to visit the noble Purxottam-bab, estimable representative of the Quencró family, whose son he coveted as a son-in-law.

That same day, at dawn, Lakshmibai had whispered in his ear, 'Last night our goddess appeared in my dreams and gave this advice: go to Purxottam-bab and your wish will be granted.'

IN SEARCH OF A GROOM
Moved by the iron faith of his wife, Narain Rao yielded to her entreaties. He knew that his task was not an easy one. Over the previous four months, he had called upon a dozen noble families. Each had rejected him. Their excuses were varied, but behind them all lay his poverty. Twenty-five years earlier, the maidens of his house had been sought in marriage by all the wealthy men of the district. Today, his fate was to wander from house to house in search of a groom for his gracious daughter, Tulsi. But where would he find the dowry? Nothing remained of their past opulence but the thick walls of their house. Yet his family's traditional nobility had set thorns in his path. His household received many visitors and guests and

often he and his family went without in order to feed them. That was the order of the day. In honour of the meritorious past of his forebears, no one left dissatisfied. And this was enough for Narain Rao to offer up thanks to his patron goddess.

Purxottam-bab was held to be a singular man, for whom the material things of life counted less than humanity. His generous hands had silently eased the pain of many people. This trait was a beacon of hope to the desolate Narain Rao.

Just then Tulsi approached her father. What a lovely creature she was! Her eyes like altar lamps, her brow so gentle and innocent. Only twelve springs old but shimmering with life. It glowed through her simple dress. Yet, for this tiny, precious being, how many difficulties must her father surmount? Her appearance alone dispelled the shadows, infused the very light with new splendour, sparked endless bliss, lent purity to glory itself. How anxious he was to offer this precious girl's hand to a noble and worthy young man. But the prestige of a family is measured by its wealth. No sooner does poverty peek out than scandal flourishes. Were another year to pass without his daughter's marriage, ill-intentioned tongues would begin to wag.

But how had they ended up in this woeful situation? Neither they nor their forebears had been libertines, sinners, or reprobates. Yet the noble character of the family had led, little by little, to their material decline.

Before leaving the house, Narain Rao caressed his daughter's cheek and asked, 'My dear! Do you also want to leave this house?' Then he trudged down the steps with a pained heart.

Lakshmibai looked on in sad silence at the rapidly departing figure of her husband. She recalled times now past when her father-in-law would leave the house on a palanquin flanked by servants. At this memory her eyes brimmed with tears.

When Narain Rao arrived at his destination after a journey of some hours, he was informed that Purxottam-bab had left for Manguexi, where he was to stay for several days, and that he had been accompanied by his youngest son. Nonetheless, Narain Rao was cordially welcomed.

After dinner he went to rest in the guest room. He was not quite asleep when he heard an uproar amongst the children playing in the corner of the front room. He got up immediately to investigate. The children told him that Purxottam-bab's grandson had just lost the gold coin with which he was playing. Taken aback by this unexpected news, Narain Rao reached down with his left hand to pat the coin he had wedged into the waistband of his dhoti. Shortly after, the house servants and members of the family rushed to the scene to begin searching for the lost coin.

VICTIM OF HONESTY

Narain Rao was in despair. He had seen the precious coin, as had the people of the house, but just as the mohar went missing he had been alone with the children in the front room. To the bystanders Narain Rao appeared to be a man in desperate straits. The search turned up nothing. How could a three-year-old explain what he had done with the coin?

Narain Rao noticed the servants glancing at him suspiciously, saw them whisper to one another and gesture knowingly. The idea that he was under suspicion was unbearable. God had seen fit to take away his wealth—now he was stripping away the good name of his family. A great tribulation? His forebears had protected their honour with such zeal; was he going to let it be stained? He recalled his dying father's solemn words. Over the centuries had his family not striven for honour over wealth? This question pierced his mind like a bullet.

The huddle dispersed. With a tremulous hand Narain Rao removed his coin and hid it beneath a broom, his heart torn to shreds. He didn't tarry, or even reveal to the family of the house the reason for his visit. Instead, under the malicious gaze of the servants, he walked crestfallen out of the room.

Two days later, Purxottam-bab returned home and was informed of the incident. He took little heed, as, according to the members of his household, the coin had been found a day later in the corner of the front room. What did disturb his peace of mind was the sudden visit and abrupt departure of Narain Rao. Why had he come? To ask some favour? But he knew Narain Rao and his noble family well. His pride would certainly not have allowed him to make such a petition. For a long while these doubts plagued the soul of Purxottam-bab, a man too caught up in his own business affairs to take note of those, like Narain Rao, who scrupulously avoided revealing their indigence.

Another matter occupied his mind during those days: he sought a bride for his son, Vishnu. It was a vexed issue, as it was no easy thing to find a maiden who met his requirements. For his son he wanted a girl who had abundant affection for all, who took delight in compassion, who was hardworking and cheery yet resolute, who, in sum, would continue the glorious tradition of their family. How was he to find such a bride in an environment so full of egotism, vanity, and dissimulation?

As Purxottam-bab had no time to call upon Narain Rao, he decided to write him a letter asking for the reasons behind his unexpected visit. He wrote it out with his own hand. In those days it was customary to dry the ink with a sprinkling of sand. Purxottam-bab groped for some inside the clay pot that stood on the table. What a shock it was when his fingers felt the cold touch of the coin!

MYSTERY UNRAVELLED

Where could this coin have come from, if the one his grandson had lost had already been found? The treasurer was summoned and an investigation was launched straight away. It proved that the coin buried in the sand of the pot had been stuck there by the little grandson of Purxottam-bab.

Another doubt emerged. Where could the coin found in the corner of the room have come from since it was not his? The investigations shed light on this conundrum. The staff of the house, confusedly and haltingly, revealed that the only stranger present in the room had been Narain Rao.

Thus, the enigma was resolved. Purxottam-bab could guess what torments the virtuous Narain-bab had suffered. The idea of this pure and innocent man beset by moments of great anguish, through no fault of his own, filled Purxottam-bab's soul with pain. He decided to leave his house immediately, to find and embrace that great man, Narain Rao.

Purxottam-bab ordered his treasurer to fetch a beautiful jewel case studded with pearls and rubies. He placed within it, reverently, that rare artefact which symbolized the glorious tradition of a noble family. With no further delay, accompanied by his retinue, he departed by palanquin for the village. The announcement of Purxottam-bab's visit left Narain Rao in a fluster. Had his secret been revealed? He hurried to the patio where the old philanthropist awaited. Without uttering a word Purxottam-bab embraced him. Both struggled to contain their emotions.

They entered the house in silence. The illustrious visitor was shown to the parlour he knew so well from his youth. Looking around, the old man saw only evidence of decline. Even the Kashmiri rug that had once borne witness to opulence had been reduced to tatters.

Seated on that rug, unable to hold back his emotions, Purxottam-bab tightly embraced the virtuous man, as a bird takes its young under its wing. Narain Rao, magnetized by the curious touch of those strong arms, began to sob.

VIRTUE REWARDED

The men then looked one another in the eye. In an instant Narain Rao realized that the slightest place in this man's affection would ensure life and prosperity for his family.

A few moments passed. Purxottam-bab removed the scintillating jewellery box from one of his pockets, opened it, and spoke thus as he presented Narain Rao the coin: 'Here it is, the Lakshmi of your house! The excellence of your family! You made a grave sacrifice to save your honour. You are, without doubt, a blessed man!'

The emotions he felt at that moment were so intense that Narain Rao was unable to utter a word. His mind was awhirl. He bowed his head and, with great difficulty, replied, 'Please do not embarrass me with these words. I am not worthy of such great honour.'

At that precise moment his daughter Tulsi appeared in the doorway. Her loving father said, 'Come here, my daughter, and ask Purxottam-bab for his blessing.'

And so Tulsi, maiden and modest, twelve years old, sincere and splendid, the image of virtue and modesty, of beauty and gentleness, stepped gracefully forward. She bowed before the venerable figure of Purxottam-bab and pressed her hands together in homage.

Purxottam-bab gazed at her. He felt he had just found what for months he had sought in vain.

He drew her to him affectionately. Running his fingers through her hair, he exclaimed, 'You shall be happy, my child.'

Purxottam-bab offered her a precious necklace of pearls from Hormuz, then turned to her poor father and, in a pleading voice, said, 'In truth, you are great. I wish my house to match yours in nobility. Thus, I beseech you to give your daughter's hand in marriage for my Vishnu.'

The eyes of Lakshmibai filled with delighted tears as she watched on from a window. Her mother's heart, weary of so much suffering, leapt for joy.

Deeply touched, Narain Rao pronounced these words: 'Purxottam-bab, I respect and honour your will. Our Tulsi shall be your daughter-in-law.'

As he spoke, Narain Rao opened the jewellery box and gazed with reverence at the ancient coin. In it he saw reflected the virtue and generosity of twenty generations. Two tears ran from his eyes and fell upon the shining gold piece.

14

THE DISCOVERY OF TELENAPOTA

PREMENDRA MITRA

Translated from the Bengali by Arunava Sinha

IF SATURN AND MARS—IT MUST BE MARS—ARE IN CONJUNCTION, YOU, TOO, can discover Telenapota someday.

In other words, if a day or two of leave can be obtained unexpectedly, just when you are gasping from work and multitudes of people, and if someone tempts you with the information that in a lake of miracles somewhere, the most simple-minded fish in the world are waiting eagerly to have their hearts impaled on a hook at the end of a rod for the first time in their lives, and if you have never had the good fortune of extracting anything but small fry from the water, then you too might unexpectedly discover Telenapota one day.

To discover Telenapota you must board a bus packed with people and their possessions in the waning sunlight one afternoon, suffer jabs from other passengers' elbows every time there is a bump on the road, and then, in the August heat, drag your sweaty, dust-caked body off the bus without warning, somewhere along the road. In front of you, you will see the road running over a low swamp like a bridge. After the bus passes along it with an eccentric rumble and disappears around a bend, you will notice that although the sun has not set yet, darkness has descended on the thick jungle all around you. You will not see a soul anywhere. The birds, too, will seem to have forsaken this place. You will become aware of the damp, sultry weather. A cruel, coiled source of venom will rise up slowly from the swamp, its invisible hood poised to strike.

You will have to step off the highway, walk down to the swamp, and wait next to it. It will seem as though someone has dug a muddy canal running through the dense jungle stretching out before you. But even its line has petered out in the distance amidst the bamboo groves and tall, shaggy trees on both sides. You should have two companions for your discovery of Telenapota. They may not be drawn to fishing as you are, and yet they have come with you on this journey—no one knows why.

The three of you will gaze eagerly at the canal in front of you. From time to time, you will stamp your feet to prevent the mosquitoes from getting too intimate, while you exchange questioning glances.

A little later, you will no longer be able to see one another's faces in the gathering darkness. The chorus of the mosquitoes will grow sharper. Just as you are wondering whether to return to the highway and wait for a return bus, you will suddenly hear an exquisite sound, wondrous to your senses, from the point where the muddy canal has vanished into the jungle. Someone will seem to force even the silent forest to emit unworldly sobs.

The sound will make your wait restless. But be patient, and your patience will not be in vain. You will see, first, a pinpoint of light swaying in the darkness, and then a bullock cart will emerge slowly from the jungle, rolling from side to side as it moves along the canal.

The cart will match the bullocks—it will seem as though this minuscule version of the bullock cart has come from an underground land of the dwarves.

Without wasting words, the three of you will squeeze yourself beneath the hood on the cart, somehow solving the problem posed by three pairs of arms and legs and three heads—how to place the largest of objects in the smallest of spaces.

The bullock cart will then return the way it came, along the canal. In utter wonderment, you will see how the dense and dark jungle reveals the way forward little by little, like a narrow tunnel. At every moment, the wall of darkness will seem impenetrable, but the cart will move ahead slowly, unperturbed, as though clearing a path with its wheels.

For some time, you will be uncomfortable and discomposed as you try to position your arms, legs, and head suitably. At every moment, there will be inadvertent collisions with your friends, and then you will gradually realize that the last island of consciousness has been submerged in the dense darkness surrounding you. You will feel as though you have left the familiar world somewhere far behind. There is another one here, shrouded in fog, devoid of sensation, where the current of time is stilled, silent.

With time standing still, you will not know how long you have been sunk in this mist. Woken up suddenly by a cacophonous music, you will realize that the stars are visible from beneath the hood, and the driver is beating a tin canister at intervals with great enthusiasm.

Curious, you will ask why, whereupon the driver will inform you indifferently, 'To get rid of the damned wild animals.'

Once you have grasped this properly, the driver will reassure you before you can ask, your voice trembling, whether beating a canister is sufficient to keep tigers at bay, that he is referring to leopards, and unless the beast is famished, this sound will be enough to keep it at a distance.

While you wonder how a place infested by leopards can exist a mere thirty miles from the metropolis, the bullock cart will cross an enormous field. The delayed waning moon will have risen in the sky by then. Dimly, silently, a succession of giant men on guard will appear to pass slowly on either side of the cart. The ruins of ancient palaces—here a pillar, there the arch of a gate, elsewhere a fragment of a temple will be standing with the futile hope of offering their testimony to eternity.

Sitting as upright as you can in the circumstances, you will feel a shiver run down your body. Something will make you feel you have gone beyond the living world to enter a murky realm of memories from the past.

You won't know what time of night it is, but it will seem the night never ends here. Everything will be sunk in a deep silence without beginning or end, just like carcasses preserved in formaldehyde at the museum.

After two or three bends in the road, the bullock cart will finally stop. Reclaiming your limbs with great effort from the different places you have deposited them, you and your friends will disembark stiffly, one by one, like wooden marionettes. A foul stench will have been welcoming you for some time. You will realize it is the stink from rotting leaves in a pond. Just such a small lake will catch your eye by the light of the half moon. Next to it there will be a decrepit palace, standing like the ramparts of a fort with a crumbling roof, collapsed walls, and shutterless windows like empty eye sockets.

It is in a relatively habitable part of this ruin that all of you will have to make arrangements to stay. The driver of the cart will fetch a cracked lantern and set it in the room. With it, a pitcher of water. When you enter, you will realize that you are the first representatives of the human race to set foot in this room in a long, long time. Maybe someone has made a vain attempt to clear the cobwebs and the dust and the grime. A slightly musty smell will be evidence of the fact that the resident spirit of the room is unhappy. The slightest movement will cause the worn-out plaster to flake off the walls and ceiling, falling on you like the curses of an angry soul. Two or three bats will fight with you all night for possession of the room.

To discover Telenapota, one of your two friends must be partial to the bottle, and the other, a soulmate of Rip Van Winkle. The moment you enter the room, no sooner will a sheet be laid out on the floor than one of them will stretch himself out on it and proceed to snore, while the other will immerse himself in a glass of whisky.

The hours will go by. The glass chimney of the cracked lantern will get progressively blacker with soot and eventually go blind. Having been informed by a mysterious wireless message, each and every adult mosquito in the neighbourhood will arrive to welcome the newcomers and establish a blood relationship with them. If you are wise, you will surmise from their manner of perching on the wall and on your body that they are the most aristocratic among mosquitoes—the one and only mount for Lady Malaria, the anopheles. Your companions will by then be unconscious to the world, each for his own specific reason. Therefore, you will abandon your bed slowly to rise to your feet, and then, in a bid to get some relief from the humidity, you will try to climb up the ruined stairs to the roof by the light of a torch.

The danger of plummeting to the ground at any moment, in case a brick or a tile loosens itself beneath your feet, will thwart you for a moment, but some irresistible attraction will make it impossible not to ascend to the terrace.

Up on the roof, you will discover that the railing has crumbled to dust in most places, and the fifth column of the forest has conspired to plant its roots in the cracks to make considerable progress on the task of demolishing this edifice. And yet, everything will appear mesmerizing by the faint light of the waning moon. If you gaze at all this for a while, you will sense that, in a secret cell somewhere in this enchanted palace under the pall of the sleep of death, an imprisoned princess is sunk in the deepest and longest of slumbers with magic wands of gold and silver at her side. At that very moment, you may see a thin line of light through the window of what had originally appeared to be a ruin across the narrow street. An enigmatic, shadowy figure will appear between you and the light. You will wonder about the identity of this woman at the window at the dead of night, and why she is not asleep, but the answer will elude you. A little later you will think it was a mistake, for the figure will have disappeared, and the light will no longer be there. You will conclude that a dream had momentarily bubbled up to the surface from the depths of the sleep of this ruined palace, appearing fleetingly in the living world before exploding.

You will return downstairs gingerly. And you won't know when you will make space for yourself next to your two friends and fall asleep.

When you awake, you will be surprised to see that even in this land of the night morning does appear, and the call of birds can be heard everywhere.

Surely, you will not have forgotten the objective of your visit. Sometime later, having made complete arrangements for your act of worshipping the fish, you will settle down at one corner of the moss-covered, dilapidated flight of shallow stairs leading into the lake and lower your hook, complete with suitable divine offerings, into the green water.

The sun will climb higher in the sky. From the tip of a bamboo stalk leaning low over the water on the opposite bank, a kingfisher will repeatedly dive into the lake with an iridescent flash of colours, as though to mock you, and will return to its perch euphoric with its successful hunt to taunt you in an unintelligible tongue. To terrorize you, a long and plump snake will slither out of a crack in the flight of stairs to swim across the lake at a leisurely pace and climb up the bank on the other side. Beating their thin, glassy wings, a pair of dragonflies will compete to alight on the float of your fishing rod, while your mind wanders every now and then at the wistful cry of a dove.

Then, a sound in the water will break your spell. There will be waves in the still water, and your float will bob up and down gently on them. Turning your head, you will see a young woman pushing aside the hyacinth to fill her shiny brass pitcher with clear water. There is curiosity in her eyes, but no bashfulness or stiffness in her movements. She will look at you directly, observe the float on your fishing rod, and then look away before balancing her pitcher against her hip.

You will be unable to gauge her age. The serenity and compassion in her expression will suggest that her journey through life has been long and cruel, but her lean, tall, and undernourished frame will give the impression that her passage from adolescence to youth has been postponed.

As she leaves with her pitcher, she will suddenly turn back towards you to say—'What are you waiting for? Reel it in.'

Her voice will be so steady, sweet, and composed that it will not seem remotely abnormal that she is spontaneously talking to a stranger. Only, your sudden surprise will make you forget to reel in the line. When the submerged float rises to the surface, you will discover that the bait is no longer on the hook. You will have no choice but to throw her a rueful glance. She will turn away and leave with measured footsteps, but it will seem to you that in that instant before she turned away, her serene, compassionate face had glowed briefly with the hint of a smile.

Your solitude will not be disturbed any more. Unable to embarrass you, the kingfisher on the opposite bank will have abandoned its efforts and flown away. Probably full of contempt at your abilities, the fish will not be desirous of another round of competition. The recent incident will seem unreal to you. You will be unable to accept that there really can be a woman like her in this desolate place.

Eventually, you will have to pack up your equipment and leave. When you return you may discover that your prowess at fishing has somehow become known to your friends. Upset at their derision, when you ask who told them this story, your tippler friend may say—'Who do you think! Yamini, of course, who saw it for herself.'

You will have no choice but to ask in curiosity who Yamini is. Perhaps you will discover that the unreal woman with tragic eyes at the lake is a relation of sorts of your friend who loves his whisky. You will also learn that arrangements for lunch have been made at this woman's house.

Seen in daylight, the hideous decrepitude of the ruined building, where the fleeting appearance of a shadowy form had given you cause for wonderment last night, will pain you considerably. You would not have imagined that the retreat of the enchanted veil of night would make its bare, dilapidated form so very ugly.

You will be surprised when told that this is where Yamini and her family live. Arrangements for your meal have probably been made in one of the rooms in there. A frugal repast, perhaps Yamini herself will serve all of you. You have already observed that there is no superfluous reserve or awkwardness about her, but her tragic quietude will be even more conspicuous. The unarticulated anguish of this derelict, forgotten, and abandoned locality will be reflected on her face. Even though she has seen everything, her eyes are submerged in the depths of exhaustion. As though she too will disappear within these ruins one day.

Still, you will see her looking uneasy and anxious once or twice while serving the three of you. Someone will be calling faintly from a room upstairs. Yamini will hurry out. Every time she returns, the agony on her face will seem a little deeper—and, with it, a helpless, distracted look in her eyes.

Perhaps, you will take a short rest after your meal. Hesitating near the door, Yamini will finally say in desperation, 'Just a minute, Manida.'

Manida is the tippler friend of yours. The conversation that will ensue when he goes up to the door will not be in voices low enough to prevent you from hearing.

You will hear Yamini say in a stricken, imperilled tone, 'Ma simply refuses to listen. I can't tell you how restless she has become since she heard you're here.'

'Still the same thing?' Mani will ask in irritation. 'She thinks Niranjan is here?'

'Yes, she keeps saying, "I'm sure he's here. Just that he's too embarrassed to see me. I know. You must be hiding it from me." I don't know what to do. She's become so impatient since she went blind that she refuses to understand anything I tell her. She flies into a rage and creates such a scene that sometimes I think she'll die.'

'This really has become a problem. If she could at least see she would know for herself that neither of them is Niranjan.'

Now all of you will be able to hear the faint but sharp, angry call from upstairs. A distressed Yamini will plead, 'Come with me, Manida, maybe you can explain things to her and calm her down.'

'Very well, you go along, I'll come in a while.' Re-entering the room, Mani will mutter to himself, 'Such an annoyance. She's blind and practically paralysed, but she's vowed not to die.'

Perhaps you will now ask, 'What's going on?' An irked Mani will reply, 'What do you suppose? When Yamini was still a child, her mother had arranged her marriage to a distant nephew of hers named Niranjan. Four years ago, the fellow had turned up to tell her that he would marry Yamini when he returned from his job abroad. Since then the old woman has been sitting here, in this godforsaken house, counting the days.'

You will not be able to stop yourself from asking, 'Has Niranjan not returned from his job abroad?'

'He would have had to go abroad first. He lied to her only because the old woman was so insistent. Why should he be interested in rescuing a pauper's daughter? He's long been married. But who's going to tell her? She won't believe it, and if she does, she'll die on the spot. Who wants to carry a burden of sin?'

'Does Yamini know about Niranjan?'

'Of course she does. But she can't tell her mother. Let me go pay for my sins.' Mani will proceed towards the staircase.

At that moment, you will also rise to your feet, not entirely of your own volition. Perhaps you will say, 'I'll come too.'

'You!' Mani will look at you in surprise.

'Yes, do you mind?'

'No, why should I?' A perplexed Mani will lead the way.

The room you will reach after climbing the narrow, dark, and broken-down staircase will appear to be situated in an underground tunnel rather than on an upper floor. Just the one window, and closed, at that. Coming in from broad daylight, everything will appear blurred at first. Then you will become aware of an emaciated, skeletal figure lying on a dilapidated cot, wrapped in a torn quilt. Yamini will be standing by the bed, turned to stone.

Your footsteps will stir the cadaverous figure into showing signs of animation. 'Is that Niranjan? You've finally remembered your unfortunate aunt. My heart's been in my mouth waiting for you all this time. I couldn't even die in peace. You won't run away again, will you?'

Mani will be about to say something, but you will interrupt him to say, 'No, I won't run away again.'

Even without raising your eyes you will sense Mani's bewilderment and the shock and astonishment on the face of the young woman standing like a statue. You will be staring at the sightless eyes, holding your breath. Two black flames will appear to emerge from the empty eye sockets to lick at your body enquiringly. You will feel the stilled moments falling like dewdrops on the ocean of time. Then you will hear: 'I know you couldn't have stayed away. That's why I have been guarding this haunted house and counting my days.' The old woman will begin gasping for breath after this long speech. Flashing a glance at Yamini, you will wonder whether something is melting slowly behind her hard mask. It will not be long before the foundations of her stern vow against destiny and existence, fired by hopelessness, begin to crumble.

The old woman will continue, 'You will be happy with Yamini. It's not because she's my daughter, but there isn't another girl like her. My sorrows and suffering and illness and old age have made me a mad woman, I make her suffer endlessly with my constant nagging—I know only too well I do, but she doesn't say a word. This is a land of the dead, you'll have to scour a dozen homes to find a single man, only corpses like me live here, gasping for life and clinging to the ruins, and yet there's nothing she leaves undone, she's man and woman rolled into one.'

Despite an ardent desire, you will not have the courage to lift your eyes for a single glance. For then you will no longer be able to conceal the tears in your eyes.

With a small sigh, the old woman will say, 'You will take Yamini, won't you? Unless you give me your word, I will have no peace even in death.'

All you will be able to say hoarsely is, 'I promise you. Nothing can shake my resolve.'

Then the bullock cart will draw up at the door again that afternoon. The three of you will get in, one by one. Yamini will come up to you as you are about to leave, raise her wistful eyes to your face and say, 'You forgot your fishing rod.'

Smiling, you will say, 'Let it remain here. I may not have been successful this time, but the fish of Telenapota cannot elude me forever.'

Yamini will not look away. Not from her lips, the grateful smile will come from her eyes, floating like white autumnal clouds across the horizon of your heart, gracing it with their beauty.

The cart will begin to roll. A hundred or a hundred and fifty years ago, the first malaria epidemic here had swept Telenapota away like an irresistible flood to this forgotten extremity of life, abandoning it there—perhaps this will be the subject of your friends' discussion. All this will not penetrate your hearing. The constricted space in the cart will no longer trouble you, the monotonous whining of its wheels will not sound harsh to your ears any more. Only a single phrase will resonate in time with your heartbeat—'I shall return, I shall return.'

When you reach the crowded, brightly-lit avenues of the metropolis, the memory of Telenapota will still be burning bright in your heart. The days will pass, punctuated by minor obstacles. You will not be aware of whether a fog is gathering in your head or not. Then, the day that you will have overcome all hindrances to prepare to return to Telenapota, you will have to burrow under a quilt because of a sudden headache, shivers, and chills. The thermometer will signal one hundred and five degrees, the doctor will ask, 'Where did you get malaria?' You will sink into a feverish haze.

Much later, when you drag your weakened body into the sunlight on tottering steps, you will find a good deal of your mind and body wiped clean, unknown to yourself. Like a star that has set, the memory of Telenapota will appear to you as a blurred dream. It will seem as though there isn't really a place named Telenapota anywhere in the world. With her stern, serious expression and her distant, pensive eyes, the young woman, just like the derelict building, will feel like nothing but a misty figment of your imagination, conjured up in an idle moment of vulnerability.

Having been discovered for a fleeting moment, Telenapota will once again become submerged in the depths of eternal night.

AN ASTROLOGER'S DAY

R. K. NARAYAN

PUNCTUALLY AT MIDDAY HE OPENED HIS BAG AND SPREAD OUT HIS professional equipment, which consisted of a dozen cowrie shells, a square piece of cloth with obscure mystic charts on it, a notebook, and a bundle of palmyra writing. His forehead was resplendent with sacred ash and vermilion, and his eyes sparkled with a sharp abnormal gleam which was really an outcome of a continual searching look for customers, but which his simple clients took to be a prophetic light and felt comforted. The power of his eyes was considerably enhanced by their position—placed as they were between the painted forehead and the dark whiskers which streamed down his cheeks: even a half-wit's eyes would sparkle in such a setting. To crown the effect he wound a saffron-coloured turban around his head. This colour scheme never failed. People were attracted to him as bees are attracted to cosmos or dahlia stalks. He sat under the boughs of a spreading tamarind tree which flanked a path running through the Town Hall Park. It was a remarkable place in many ways: a surging crowd was always moving up and down this narrow road morning till night. A variety of trades and occupations was represented all along its way: medicine-sellers, sellers of stolen hardware and junk, magicians and, above all, an auctioneer of cheap cloth, who created enough din all day to attract the whole town. Next to him in vociferousness came a vendor of fried groundnuts, who gave his ware a fancy name each day, calling it Bombay Ice Cream one day, and on the next Delhi Almond, and on the third Raja's Delicacy, and so on and so forth, and people flocked to him. A considerable portion of this crowd dallied before the astrologer too. The astrologer transacted his business by the light of a flare which crackled and smoked up above the groundnut heap nearby. Half the enchantment of the place was due to the fact that it did not have the benefit of municipal lighting. The place was lit up by shop lights. One or two had hissing gaslights, some had naked flares stuck on poles, some were lit up by old cycle lamps and one or two, like the astrologer's, managed without lights of their own. It was a bewildering criss-cross of light rays and moving shadows. This suited the astrologer very well, for the simple reason that he had not in the least intended to be an astrologer when he began life; and he knew no more of what was going to happen to others than he knew what was going to happen to himself next minute. He was as much a stranger to the stars as were his innocent customers. Yet he said things which pleased and astonished everyone: that was more a matter of study, practice, and shrewd guesswork. All the same, it was as much an honest man's labour as any other, and he deserved the wages he carried home at the end of a day.

He had left his village without any previous thought or plan. If he had continued there he would have carried on the work of his forefathers—namely, tilling the land, living, marrying, and ripening in his cornfield and ancestral home. But that was not to be. He had to leave home without telling anyone, and he could not rest till he left it behind a couple of hundred miles. To a villager it is a great deal, as if an ocean flowed between.

He had a working analysis of mankind's troubles: marriage, money, and the tangles of human ties. Long practice had sharpened his perception. Within five minutes he understood what was wrong. He charged three pies per question and never opened his mouth till the other had spoken for at least ten minutes, which provided him enough stuff for a dozen answers and advice. When he told the person before him, gazing at his palm, 'In many ways you are not getting the fullest results for your efforts,' nine out of ten were disposed to agree with him. Or he questioned: 'Is there any woman in your family, maybe even a distant relative, who is not well disposed towards you?' Or he gave an analysis of character: 'Most of your troubles are due to your nature. How can you be otherwise with Saturn where he is? You have an impetuous nature and a rough exterior.' This endeared him to their hearts immediately, for even the mildest of us loves to think that he has a forbidding exterior.

The nuts vendor blew out his flare and rose to go home. This was a signal for the astrologer to bundle up too, since it left him in darkness except for a little shaft of green light which strayed in from somewhere and touched the ground before him. He picked up his cowrie shells and paraphernalia and was putting them back into his bag when the green shaft of light was blotted out; he looked up and saw a man standing before him. He sensed a possible client and said: 'You look so careworn. It will do you good to sit down for a while and chat with me.' The other grumbled some vague reply. The astrologer pressed his invitation; whereupon the other thrust his palm under his nose, saying: 'You call yourself an astrologer?' The astrologer felt challenged and said, tilting the other's palm towards the green shaft of light: 'Yours is a nature....'

'Oh, stop that,' the other said. 'Tell me something worthwhile....'

Our friend felt piqued. 'I charge only three pies per question, and what you get ought to be good enough for your money....' At this the other withdrew his arm, took out an anna and flung it out to him, saying, 'I have some questions to ask. If I prove you are bluffing, you must return that anna to me with interest.'

'If you find my answers satisfactory, will you give me five rupees?'

'No.'

'Or will you give me eight annas?'

'All right, provided you give me twice as much if you are wrong,' said the stranger. This pact was accepted after a little further argument.

The astrologer sent up a prayer to heaven as the other lit a cheroot. The astrologer caught a glimpse of his face by the matchlight. There was a pause as cars hooted on the road, jutka drivers swore at their horses and the babble of the crowd agitated the semi-darkness of the park. The other sat down, sucking his cheroot, puffing out, sat there ruthlessly. The astrologer felt very uncomfortable. 'Here, take your anna back. I am not used to such challenges. It is late for me today....' He made preparations to bundle up. The other held his wrist and said, 'You can't get out of it now. You dragged me in while I was passing.' The astrologer shivered in his grip; and his voice shook and became faint. 'Leave me today. I will speak to you tomorrow.' The other thrust his palm in his face and said, 'Challenge is challenge. Go on.' The astrologer proceeded with his throat drying up. 'There is a woman....'

'Stop,' said the other. 'I don't want all that. Shall I succeed in my present search or not? Answer this and go. Otherwise I will not let you go till you disgorge all your coins.' The astrologer muttered a few incantations and replied, 'All right. I will speak. But will you give me a rupee if what I say is convincing? Otherwise I will not open my mouth, and you may do what you like.' After a good deal of haggling the other agreed. The astrologer said, 'You were left for dead. Am I right?'

'Ah, tell me more.'

'A knife has passed through you once?' said the astrologer.

'Good fellow!' He bared his chest to show the scar. 'What else?'

'And then you were pushed into a well nearby in the field. You were left for dead.'

'I should have been dead if some passer-by had not chanced to peep into the well,' exclaimed the other, overwhelmed by enthusiasm. 'When shall I get at him?' he asked, clenching his fist.

'In the next world,' answered the astrologer. 'He died four months ago in a far-off town. You will never see any more of him.' The other groaned on hearing it. The astrologer proceeded.

'Guru Nayak—'

'You know my name!' the other said, taken aback.

'As I know all other things. Guru Nayak, listen carefully to what I have to say. Your village is two days' journey due north of this town. Take the next train and be gone. I see once again great danger to your life if you go from home.' He took out a pinch of sacred ash and held it out to him. 'Rub it on your forehead and go home. Never travel southward again, and you will live to be a hundred.'

'Why should I leave home again?' the other said reflectively. 'I was only going away now and then to look for him and to choke out his life if I met him.' He shook his head regretfully. 'He has escaped my hands. I hope at least he died as he deserved.'

'Yes,' said the astrologer. 'He was crushed under a lorry.' The other looked gratified to hear it.

The place was deserted by the time the astrologer picked up his articles and put them into his bag. The green shaft was also gone, leaving the place in darkness and silence. The stranger had gone off into the night, after giving the astrologer a handful of coins.

It was nearly midnight when the astrologer reached home. His wife was waiting for him at the door and demanded an explanation. He flung the coins at her and said, 'Count them. One man gave all that.'

'Twelve and a half annas,' she said, counting. She was overjoyed. 'I can buy some jaggery and coconut tomorrow. The child has been asking for sweets for so many days now. I will prepare some nice stuff for her.'

'The swine has cheated me! He promised me a rupee,' said the astrologer. She looked up at him. 'You look worried. What is wrong?'

'Nothing.'

After dinner, sitting on the pyol, he told her, 'Do you know a great load is gone from me today? I thought I had the blood of a man on my hands all these years. That was the reason why I ran away from home, settled here and married you. He is alive.'

She gasped. 'You tried to kill!'

'Yes, in our village, when I was a silly youngster. We drank, gambled, and quarrelled badly one day—why think of it now? Time to sleep,' he said, yawning, and stretched himself on the pyol.

A LIFE

BUDDHADEVA BOSE

Translated from the Bengali by Arunava Sinha

GURUDAS BHATTACHARYA, VACHASPATI, THE MOST SENIOR TEACHER OF Sanskrit at Khulna's Jagattarini School, was brought up short by a word while teaching Bengali literature to Class IX students.

'Amaar projagawn amaar cheye tahare bawro kori mane....' The pandit found a word in the sentence confusing. Cheye? Did that refer to the Bengali word for glance? Or for desire? After some thought, he explained the sentence as, 'The king says his subjects want him, they desire his sanctuary, but they respect the King of Kaushal more. Grammar has been distorted a little here.' The boys on the first bench exchanged glances. Then one of them stood up to say, 'It's fine, sir. The word "cheye" in this case is used for comparison, in the sense of "than". My subjects consider him more noble than me. See, it says a little later, "Are you so bold as to imagine you can be more pious than me?"'

'If only I were an Arab Bedouin rather than this,' the boy next to him recited.

Gurudas did not respond. Accepting the correction made by his students, he continued teaching the poem. The bell rang.

It was the last period. Collecting their umbrellas and books, the other teachers left for their homes, while Gurudas made his way to the school library. The library was nothing but three cupboards full of books in one corner of the staff room—most of them textbooks obtained as free samples. Among the more valuable volumes were several hardbound sets of the Bengali literary magazine *Probashi*, a Philips atlas of twenty years' vintage, a Chambers Dictionary, and three Bengali and English-to-Bengali dictionaries used by students. Clearing his throat, Gurudas said, 'Can you unlock this cupboard, Nabakeshto?'

Not even the servants at school paid much attention to the Sanskrit teacher. And Nabakeshto donned the mantle of bearer, doorman, and gardener single-handedly. 'The library is closed, sir,' he answered with a touch of insolence.

'Never mind, just unlock it. I need some books.'

'But I have to leave for Rasoolpur right away—my daughter's in-laws have invited us....'

'That's all right, you can go. Leave the keys with me.'

'All right then. Don't forget to give them back to me before eleven tomorrow. You know how strict the new headmaster is. And lock the door of the room before you go...here's the padlock, see?'

Unlocking the cupboard, Gurudas planted himself in front of it; with a glance at his back, Nabakeshto gathered his bundle, wrapped in a gamcha, from its place beneath the table—he was taking a bunch of grapefruits from the tree in the schoolyard as a gift for his son-in-law.

No one was allowed to take the dictionaries home; Gurudas spent a good deal of time leafing through the two Bengali dictionaries. The light grew dim, the silence of a provincial evening thickened inside the room. He forgot to sit down, forgot his hunger, his internal senses seemed to soak up the rows of letters. Today's incident had wounded him—he had not been able to capture the meaning of a word which millions of adults and children used every single day without a thought. How could he—he was a teacher of Sanskrit. He had learnt Sanskrit, but not Bengali. But he was a Bengali—that was the language he spoke. He seemed to realize for the first time that the Bengali language was not Sanskrit, not even a corrupt form—it was a complete, living, changing, evolving, independent language, the spoken language of seventy million people, their mother tongue. 'A living language, the mother tongue'—he repeated the words in his head several times. But prowess in one's mother tongue was not automatic, it needed nurture.

Gurudas noticed that none of the dictionaries included the word he had tripped over that morning. He was reminded of other words used in similar fashion—'thekey', the Bengali word used for 'from' or 'since', or 'dyakha', used for 'seeing' or 'meeting' or 'looking after'. This was how the Bengali language perfumed the Sanskrit verb ending. None of this was in the dictionary. There were mistakes—mistaken explanations, even mistaken spelling. How were the students to learn? And I—how am I to learn?

It was late evening by the time Gurudas returned home. His wife Harimohini asked, 'So late?' Gurudas did not answer. He ate his dinner in silence. 'Are you ill? You aren't eating.'

'I am not ill.' He went to bed early that night.

Jagattarini School began at eleven in the morning, and the district school, at ten-thirty. Gurudas went to the district school around a quarter past eleven the next morning, spending half an hour in the library before breathlessly entering his own class in the nick of time. It was Saturday the next day—from the school he went to the only college in Khulna. He had a nodding acquaintance with the Sanskrit teacher there (here, too, it was he who taught Bengali). They conversed for some time, and he flipped through three or four books in the library—but his restlessness did not leave him.

No, he had not found it—he had not found what he was looking for anywhere. Could there not be a complete Bengali dictionary, which had room for every single word (both Sanskrit and vernacular) in the language, which included every combination, every application, every colloquial usage, which would enable the Bengali language to be learnt, its nature to be understood, its unique creative spirit to be appreciated? The college professor had said there was not a single such book. There were a few good ones among those he examined, but in a workmanlike way—where was the dictionary that one could use for real scholarship?

The biggest bookshop in town was Victoria Library. In the evening Gurudas asked to see a major Bengali dictionary and the Oxford English Dictionary. Having leafed through them for a few minutes, he said softly, 'There's something I want to discuss, Rebati Babu.'

In a small town, everyone knew everyone else. The owner looked at Gurudas over the rims of his glasses.

'It's Saturday—may I take these two books home? I'll return them to you first thing Monday morning.'

'Take them home?'

'I'll handle them very carefully—won't soil them, won't crease them—I'll look after them. I need them urgently, you see.'

'Someone's already ordered those books, Pandit Mashai.'

'I see.' Gurudas's fair, lean face reddened. A little later he said, 'Then I'd better buy them.' He had to wage a terrible war against himself, but... he had spoken, he couldn't take his words back now.

'Pack these books for Pandit Mashai...' Rebati Babu made no further reference to the books having been ordered.

'But I can only pay next month.'

'Hmm...' Gurudas sent up a silent prayer, 'Let him not agree, O Lord.' But Rebati Babu's mouth softened.

'Very well. But on the first of the month, don't forget. We run a very small business, you know...sign here, please.'

He had got them at a discount by virtue of being a teacher. Thirteen rupees and fourteen annas—nearly a third of his salary.

Gurudas browsed through the two books late into that night by the glow of a lantern. His grasp of English was poor, but he had no difficulty in realizing the difference in the presentation of the two books. And yet this was just a condensed version, he had heard that Oxford had a giant dictionary too.

Before going to sleep he mused over Panini, considered the sheer extent of the Sanskrit dictionary *Shabdakalpadruma*, and recollected Vidyasagar. An extraordinary talent for grammar, unbeatable enthusiasm for analysis, bottomless vocabulary. He used to have them all. What had happened to them?

Harimohini had planted flowers in a fenced-in corner of the small yard. She was watering them with her daughter on Sunday morning when Gurudas came up to them, smiling.

'Shibani, go check if Nidhu's ma has brought the milk.'

'Later. Listen to me first.'

Harimohini paused and looked at him.

'I'm about to start something new.'

A ray of hope flashed across Harimohini's face. Had the match for Shibani been finalized with the Chatterjees of Nimtala, then? Their elder daughter Bhabani had been married into a high-born family—this was the other daughter. She had turned fifteen, if she didn't get married now, then when?

'Have they sent word?'

'Who?'

'The Nimtala Chatterjees.'

'No, that's not it. I am going to write a dictionary of the Bengali language. I made up my mind last night.'

There was no flicker of expression on Harimohini's face.

'You know what a dictionary is, don't you? A collection of words. The meaning of words in the Bengali language, similar words, usage of words, and so on. There isn't a book like this at the moment.'

'Not a single one? You're going to write it?' Harimohini felt a burst of pride. 'Will it say anything about gods and goddesses?'

'Everything.'

Yes, everything. Unknown to Gurudas, a smile spread across his face. He had fallen asleep the previous night as soon as he had come to this decision—a deep sleep. And when he awoke this morning, he discovered his mind was calm, his heart, cheerful, and his body, healed and rested, while support for his endeavour radiated from the branching rays of the sun in the sky. As though nature had been waiting these last few days only for his resolve to do this: as soon as he accepted it, satisfaction spread across the heavens, and the movements in his body acquired an easy rhythm. Gods and goddesses—of course he would have to include them. But all the gods? All their names? He would have to determine which of them belonged to an encyclopaedia and which to a dictionary. Which of the Sanskrit words could be considered Bengali? What to do with Brajabuli? What were the indications that a word was part of the Bengali language? Would he have to add words which were not in circulation but might be required? There was so much to think about. So much to think—but even Harimohini's flowering plants were urging him to start at once.

Gurudas had been to Puri once as a student, he was reminded now of his visit. He could see just such an ocean stretching ahead of him—a succession of waves, hollows, whirlpools, effort...the horizon in the distance. On this ocean his raft would have to float, this was the sea he would have to cross. For a moment Gurudas felt his skin prickle.

After lunch he brought the subject up again with his wife.

'I was thinking of the dictionary.'

'Yes, what?'

'The thing is, I need some material. Books and things.'

'Very well.'

'Very expensive books. I was thinking, Chakraborty Mashai had made an offer for that acre of land back home....'

'You'll sell it?' A shadow fell across Harimohini's face. 'We have nothing else, and the girl's growing up too.'

'We can survive on what we have.' Gurudas could not inject too much confidence into this assertion, so he tried to compensate with a gentle smile.

'That is to say, I will survive, and once your son's grown up you'll have nothing to worry about.'

'The things you say! I think only about myself all the time, don't I? But I shan't let Nobu be a teacher like you. You know Netai, my nephew? He's passed his matriculation examination and joined the Railways. Sixty rupees a month already—and extra earnings on top of that.'

Gurudas did not approve of the final statement, but swallowing his criticism, he returned to the original subject.

'Just the railways? Nobu might even become a deputy magistrate like my brother,' said Gurudas, throwing a sidelong look at his wife. It was a calculated ploy—he was fully aware of Harimohini's reverence for his stepbrother's status as a deputy magistrate.

'Do you suppose I could ever be so lucky? But then, everything is possible if the gods smile on us, isn't that right? That reminds me, I'd sent you sweets after Lakshmi Puja the other day, but Shibani said you didn't eat them.'

'I touched my forehead with them—that's better than eating them. Listen, I'm giving the land to Chakraborty Mashai then, all right?'

'Giving it? We hardly have anything anyway—and there's not only the girl who has to be married off but also the boy whom we must leave something to.'

'Everything will be done. But I cannot turn back now.'

'Cannot turn back—what do you mean?'

'Wealth is by nature temporary, but....' The pandit groped for the right word, and then turned helplessly to emotional appeal. 'I have made up my mind—are you going to stop me now?'

The land they owned was in Nandigram, about an hour away by steamer. Gurudas paid a visit during the Janmashtami holidays. A house, fruit-bearing trees, a small pond, some farmland. Some? It was about seventy acres in his grandfather's time. After being divided up, about eight acres had come to Gurudas. He had had to sell nearly two acres for his elder daughter's wedding, and now another acre. Never mind, at least he was getting a hundred and fifty rupees. Rummaging through the books at home, he even found an old Sanskrit dictionary printed in Bombay—it had belonged to his father—and, how fortunate, the Sanskrit grammar that he had borrowed from a schoolmate and forgotten to return. The first thing he did on returning to Khulna was to buy two reams of the cheapest paper, which Shibani laced into a notebook.

On the first day of the Puja holidays at school, Gurudas travelled to Calcutta, where he had to put up for three days at a boarding house in Sealdah. Two more Bengali dictionaries; Suniti Chatterji's book on linguistics; an ancient (but excellent) Sanskrit-to-Bengali dictionary found after scouring the pavements of College Street and Chitpur; a Bengali grammar written by an Englishman; Tekchand's novel, and *Hutom Pyanchar Naksha* published by Basumati; and Kaliprasanna Sinha's *Mahabharata* published by Hitabadi. He didn't dare ignore Rabindranath Tagore's 'The Theory of Words' when it caught his eye—poets were the creators of language, might as well find out what he had to say. All this accounted for nearly fifty rupees. Then there were the new clothes for Durga Puja, a pair of shankhas each for Harimohini and Bhabani, a dhoti for his son-in-law, a pair of rubber slippers for Nobu costing a rupee and thirteen annas. He had to spend eight annas on his way back on a porter to carry all the books—that really pinched.

They had a wonderful time back home that year during Durga Puja. Harimohini stayed back with the children, while Gurudas returned to Khulna the day after Lakshmi Puja. He cooked his own meals, and read all day. He found the English difficult, but managed to make sense of it, and it grew easier the more he read. On the day before Kali Puja, in one of the notebooks made by Shibani, he wrote the first letter of the Bengali alphabet, 'Aw', in a bold hand. Fifty words were written that day. The school opened three days later, the family returned, and his leisure hours shrank.

Gurudas set himself a routine. He woke up at five in the morning to write for two hours, and then drank his share of milk, went out to take private tuition, bought the day's provisions, and returned. This gave him a little time before his bath. He had to take private classes in the evening too—the exams were approaching—but he didn't go to bed until he had put in a couple of hours of writing. Gurudas was making smooth progress.

Winter came. There was no light before six in the morning, and this was when the pressure of checking annual exam papers intensified. But the Christmas holidays were approaching.

He had to visit Calcutta again during Christmas vacation. The subject was like Draupadi's sari—unfolding constantly, an unending mystery, one whose depths you kept sinking into. How would he prove equal to this task—he, a mere Gurudas Bhattacharya, a minor Sanskrit scholar? He did not know his way on this road, had no clear idea of where he would find the bricks and cement needed to build this structure. In Calcutta he laid siege to the Imperial Library: the days passed navigating his way through the dense jungle of comparative linguistics. Many of the books were written in German, with an abundance of Greek letters and a thick growth of Latin, Gothic, and Persian references, as though the immense vegetation of the Aryan languages had stretched up to the sky, spreading its branches far and wide. Sanskrit alone had never given him this feeling of kinship with the West, with the entire world. For the first time he set eyes on the Monier-Williams Sanskrit dictionary, he discovered Skeat's etymological dictionary too. Ten days passed cramming his notebooks with jottings.

When he was about to set off for Calcutta again during the summer holidays, Harimohini could not keep herself from objecting mildly.

'Why must you go to Calcutta again?'

'Do you need me here?'

'I was thinking of the expenses. The boarding house costs money too.'

Gurudas had thought about this as well. The examination season was in the past, and not many studied Sanskrit these days, he had no private tuitions. Thanks to a supply of food from the land back home they managed to survive on forty-five rupees—but barely. They could afford coarse rice and dal, and their clothes—anything more was virtually impossible. But... he simply had to go.

'Doesn't your mother's brother live in Calcutta?' said Harimohini. 'You could always....'

'Of course not, how can I stay a month at someone else's house? And he's only my mother's cousin—I haven't met him in years...it's impossible. But I'll manage—don't worry.'

'It's all very well for you to say that, but I spend sleepless nights.'

'But why?'

'Have you decided that Shibani will remain a spinster?'

That was true. He had to accept that his daughter was showing signs of womanhood. It was time for her to be married. But...how?

'Why so anxious? She's not even fifteen yet. Many people don't even think of marriage till eighteen these days.'

'You, of all people, are saying this? Your family, the Brahmin pandits of Nandigram didn't allow their daughters to pass the age of ten.'

'Why shouldn't I? Didn't Rammohan Roy speak up against idol worship? Didn't Vidyasagar introduce widow remarriage? They were Brahmin pandits too.'

'Those who get their daughters married at eighteen also give them the chance to go to school and college, right? They don't let them rot at home and turn into liabilities. Do you have it in you to educate her?'

Gurudas's lean, fair face grew pale. She was right. He had no response. He must try to arrange a match.

From the matchmaker he learnt that Rameshwar Banerjee of Hatkhola in Calcutta was looking for a bride for his third son. Rameshwar had been a professor at Sanskrit College during the single year that Gurudas had read there. He decided to plead with Rameshwar in Calcutta to provide a safe passage for his daughter.

In Calcutta Gurudas rented a 'seat' in the cheapest room in a boarding house he was familiar with. His meals were at a 'pice hotel' (which he had discovered on his previous visit; for four paise you could eat so much that you didn't need a second meal). His days were spent at the Imperial Library, at the university library, wandering among second-hand bookshops, and seeking audiences with renowned professors. He had sensed a new requirement: instructions, advice, discussions—he had brought along all the pages in his notebook, in case anyone had any constructive comments to offer. It wasn't easy to meet professors—some had gone to Darjeeling, others were busy. Only two deigned to meet him. Leafing through the notebooks apprehensively, both of them said, 'Excellent, it's coming along very well, you must complete it.' When he enquired whether a detailed discussion was possible, he learnt that both were engaged as chief examiners for the BA exams, and did not have the leisure even to die at present.

One day he overheard a young man at a bookshop on College Street. The buyer was looking for a book on the history of Bengali literature; turning over the pages of two or three, the words he uttered were clearly weighed down with nausea. 'Dead! All dead! Rotting and infested with worms which this swarm of professors is picking out to eat. They collapse when they see living literature. Rabindranath was born in vain.' The young man disappeared, his sandals flapping.

Chuckling, the shopkeeper said, 'Subrata Sen speaks as forcefully as he writes.'

'Who was that?' Gurudas stepped forward. 'What did you say his name is?'

'Subrata Sen. You haven't read him? Very powerful.'

At the boarding house he normally drank a large glass of water and went to bed—his exhaustion taking him beyond the hot weather, the stench, and his hunger in an instant. But sleep eluded him that night, the young man's statement ringing in his ears constantly. And you, Gurudas Bhattacharya, engaged in composing a dictionary of the Bengali language—what do you know of Bengali literature? Ishwar Gupta, Bankim, Michael—and that was it. The young man had named Rabindranath—some people said he had injected new life into the Bengali language, but you know nothing about him, you haven't read him at all. And these new writers—take Subrata Sen, for example—language lived through transformation in every era. It would die if it were to lose this power. And if a dictionary could not provide a portrait of this evolution, what use was it?

He had to think of the whole thing afresh. A dictionary was not a compendium of explanations for students, not a list or collection, not an immovable, static, ponderous object. Its essence lay in the flow, in movement, in showing the path to the future—to move ahead it had to gather sustenance from the creative work that writers were engaged in constantly. It would have to be replete with hints, allusions, advice, even imagination—just like a flowing waterfall glinting under the light. He would have to read literature—living works, current, changing literature—all that was being written, read, said, heard in the Bengali language—all these were his ingredients.

He came back home bathed in a new glow. Within five minutes of his return Harimohini asked, 'Did you meet Rameshwar Banerjee?'

'I did.'

'What did he say?'

'In a minute.' Gurudas sat down on a mat, leaning back against a post. 'They have many demands. They're well-off, you see.'

'Who'll marry your daughter on the strength of her appearance alone?'

'A thousand rupees in cash. Twenty-five bhori gold. All expenses. Provided they like the girl. But...can we afford all this? I'd better make some more enquiries....'

Sighing, Harimohini went away. Evening fell.

This time Gurudas had brought a ream of foolscap paper from Calcutta. It was cheaper there, and available at even lower prices if bought by the ream. He had nearly exhausted his older notebooks. He had to scribble copiously—scratch out bits, make changes, there was new information every day. And yet he wasn't even done with the first letter, 'Aw'.

Gurudas got down to work calmly. Some of it involved reading. He had avoided reading the newspapers all this time, but now he had to scan a couple of Bengali dailies every evening at the public library. And he left no Bengali book he could get hold of untouched. Happening to read Rabindranath's *Ghare Baire*, he was astounded. Could the Bengali language actually be used in this way? This was not Hutom, this was Kalidasa. Not even Kalidasa, something else altogether.

His notebook and pencil were always in his pocket. He took voluminous notes. Most of them would not prove useful, but who could predict what would?

The Bengalis' forms of self-expression became the subject of his discoveries, something he paid careful attention to. He listened closely when his wife, son or daughter spoke; with so much interest that he often did not grasp the content, and forgot to answer when they asked him a question. What he wanted to know was not what they were saying but how they were saying it. When the younger students raised an uproar during lunch break at school, he lurked unobserved behind them. At the market he kept his ears peeled for rural dialects. When he went home on holidays, he sought out Muslim peasants and made unnecessary conversation with them—they had a special way of speaking, which he wanted to grasp.

And he had to go to Calcutta during the longer vacations. He learnt the Greek alphabet, took help from a priest at St Xavier's School to understand the rules of Latin grammar, even had to visit madrasas for Arabic and Persian. Hardly any books were available in the provinces—for this too he had to visit Calcutta.

How did he afford all this? Cheap boarding houses and pice hotels, but still. Gurudas had made arrangements, getting rid of another acre of land, this time without telling his wife. He didn't know anyone in Calcutta particularly well, feeling beleaguered if he had to speak in English. Nor did his soiled clothes evoke respect from anyone. He had to discover everything he needed all by himself, with the help of that eternal quality, effort, the capital that God endowed every human being with. Effort, endeavour, waiting, patience. It took him four hours to do an hour's work—he was lighting rows of fireflies and pushing through the darkness. But there were lights at every street corner—like signals for trains in the blackness of night.

Summer holidays once more, the monsoon once more. The rains were torrential that year. Earthworms burst through the kitchen floor in July. Leeches in the front yard. Snakes here and there. On some nights water streamed through gaps in the tin roof—having found dry spots for the children to sleep, the parents stayed up all night. After seven days of incessant rain, Gurudas opened his safe one day to get the shock of his life. Instead of his best books, what he saw were millions of termites wriggling about. Fifty pages of Suniti Chatterji's book were missing, the third volume of the Mahabharata was in shreds, the Sanskrit dictionary from his father's time crumbled in his hands when he picked it up. The day passed battling the termites—he poured in four annas worth of kerosene.

Immediately after this accident there was a bit of hope; Shibani's marriage suddenly seemed a possibility. The groom was from Barishal, recently posted here at the Khulna steamer station. The groom's family approved of the bride, and made no demand for dowry—only the cost of the wedding, and shankha and sindoor for the bride. This was no cause for concern—Harimohini still had some ornaments.

The wedding would not take place before March, but Bhabani was overcome with joy when she heard. At long last she would be able to visit her mother. She lived in a large family, surrounded by her in-laws, at Madaripur—she didn't even have the chance to visit her own family during Durga Puja.

Shibani came down with a fever after the rains. When the fever didn't go down even after a week, Gurudas sent for the kaviraj. He prescribed plenty of red and black pills—but to no avail.

On the twenty-first day the official assistant surgeon turned up. His fees were four rupees, and he stomped about in boots. Typhoid, he said, after examining the patient. Give her nothing but glucose. Pour water over her head morning and evening. Here are the medicines. Note down the temperature at four-hour intervals. Inform me after three days.

The medicines were bought with borrowed money. The doctor came once a week—paying his fees was a near-impossible task. Milk and fish were stopped; Harimohini's deity was given a quarter of her regular rations.

Shibani lost weight, the fat disappeared from her cheeks, her discoloured teeth grew bigger and uglier. Then came the day when her hair had to be cut on the doctor's orders. Her scalp needed water, the more the better. Harimohini poured water over her daughter's head every hour, but Shibani was delirious.

At the time of her death, her limbs had withered away to resemble sticks, her chest was like that of a seven-year-old boy's. And this girl was sixteen, and had been healthy, full of grace. The ornaments put aside to pay for the wedding were used to clear the debt to the doctor.

Gurudas returned home at ten at night after the cremation. It was the end of February; winter was on its way out. He felt rather cold—wrapping a shawl around himself, he sat down next to his wife, who was slumped on the floor. The night passed in the same position.

A long night, but the sun rose finally. Harimohini had fallen asleep, while Nobu was curled on the floor in the cold. Covering his son with the shawl, Gurudas carefully slipped a pillow beneath Harimohini's head. Then he went out, spread a mat and sat down with his notebook. This last one had also been made by Shibani. For a moment, all the letters blurred. Wiping his eyes on the end of his dhoti, he set down more letters next to the blurred ones.

Five more years passed, the dictionary was in its seventh year. He was done with twenty-four letters, up to 'Thaw'.

The words no longer flowed. What had started as an extraordinary, thrilling joy had now turned into work. Work, duty, responsibility, compulsion. The madness of discovery was gone, the excitement of gathering material had dissipated. He had an enormous quantity of information at his disposal now, the roads were familiar. It was time to work, it was time for nothing but work. Daily work, weekly work, monthly, annual, continuous. No likes, no dislikes, no reluctance either. This was an immaculately conceptualized world, where individuality was dead.

That year saw the fruition of a long drawn-out effort of the Jagattarini School—the government finally approved grants. Teachers' salaries were increased; Gurudas's monthly earning leapt to fifty-five rupees—it could even get to seventy or seventy-five eventually. In that same year Nobu, or Nabendu, vaulted over the hurdle of the matriculation examination. Not just that, he got a job almost immediately. A job with the railways, as his mother had hoped.

A few months later there was tragic news: Bhabani had become a widow. And within two months she appeared in her father's yard with close-cropped hair, dressed in a widow's garb and holding three children by the hand. Her late husband's parents were no longer willing to shoulder the burden of their daughter-in-law, without whom they couldn't survive a moment at one time. 'They are not as well-off as before, my brothers-in-law have several children, and he didn't leave anything for us, Baba.'

Her father said, 'Don't worry. Nobu has a job now. I'll look after all of you.'

Gurudas went to Calcutta during the summer holidays that year—after a gap of two years. He couldn't postpone things any more, it was time to find a publisher.

In his canvas shoes, holding a dusty umbrella, he scoured the summer pavements from Goldighi to Hedua with his manuscript stuffed into a tin trunk. Finally, he came across Bharat Press in a lane off Sukia Street. They published old Sanskrit and Bengali books, and were inclined towards dictionaries. But the proprietor Bipin Babu said, 'We cannot judge how good your dictionary is. If you can get a recommendation from someone worthwhile, we'll think about it.'

'Such as? Whose....' Gurudas was too embarrassed to utter the word recommendation.

Bipin Babu mentioned three or four people. The very first one was that of the vice-chancellor of the university.

Gurudas arrived at this gentleman's house the next day. About a dozen people were waiting in a small room. As the day progressed, a crowd of people waiting for an audience filled the open space in front of the house. Dhotis, Western suits, Madrasis, Punjabis, even saffron. Some paced up and down, some leaned against the railing, some peeped over the swing door before ducking behind it. Young men, old men, women, helpless faces, grave expressions—but all of them similarly afflicted by the need for recommendations. The clacking of typewriters, the ringing of telephones, the bustle of orderlies and clerks—it was impossible to tell who had got an audience and who was waiting in despair. From seven the clock moved on to eleven—there was no hope of a meeting today.

Gurudas slipped while getting off the tram on the way back, hurting himself. Putting tincture of iodine on his bruises, he rested on a plank in the boarding house all day. When he awoke the next morning, his hips were aching. But still he got into the second-class coach of the tram with his trunk.

No luck that day either—four hours passed, alternately sitting and standing. Four successive days went by this way.

On the fifth day he arrived even earlier, in case he could get in before anyone else. He discovered there were only two people already there. A man of dignified appearance walking across the yard stopped suddenly on seeing him.

'What's the matter? Here again?'

'I had to come again, because....'

'You haven't met him yet? Haven't I been seeing you every day? Well, what do you need?'

'I have composed a dictionary of Bengali. It's about this dictionary....'

'Oh, a dictionary? Of Bengali?' The man surveyed Gurudas from head to toe, not omitting his tin trunk. 'You've actually brought your manuscript?'

'Just...in case he wants a look...if he has the time.'

'Very well, sit down. Go straight in as soon as he arrives. Through this door here—there's nothing to be afraid of.'

He really did get an audience, along with a slip of paper with the words, 'I endorse this book for publication' along with a signature.

Five hundred copies each of several slim volumes would be published, each costing one rupee. The books would not be bound. Half of whatever was left over after paying for costs would go to the author, but if expenses were not recovered within a year, the writer would recompense the publisher.

These were the terms of the contract. Bipin Babu kept the manuscripts for the first four letters, 'Aw' through 'Dirgho-ee', and Gurudas received the proofs within a week of returning to Khulna.

Six volumes were published in a year; the vowels were done. But Bipin Babu welcomed him sombrely the next summer. 'The books aren't selling at all. There they are—see for yourself. An entire dictionary is available at ten rupees, who's going to pay six for just the vowels? And who cares for so many details? I couldn't cover my costs, but I know you cannot recompense me. I can absorb this loss, but if you want to publish further you'll have to pay half the costs. If the books sell, I'll recover my costs first, plus 30 per cent commission. The rest will be yours.'

'Half the costs? How much?'

'It takes between two hundred and two-fifty to print each volume. You'll get bills.'

Gurudas left another six volumes of his manuscript with the printer. For each volume that was printed, he sold half an acre of land. Eventually nothing but the homestead was left, and then that was sold too.

By then ten more years had passed. Gurudas was almost through with 'Baw'; all the letters up to 'Dontyo-naw' had been published. Meanwhile his hair had greyed, he wore thick lenses in nickel-framed glasses—but despite the spectacles everything seemed blurred at night. Harimohini was suffering from arthritis, she couldn't do the household tasks any more. The entire family was under the care of the lean, indefatigable Bhabani. She paid a little extra attention to her father, offering him whatever she could—a little milk or fruit, or some juice. When she had a few moments to spare, she leafed through his dictionary. Gurudas had taught her, the first child of his youth, a little Sanskrit and Bengali. She knew her grammar, and had even picked up proofreading skills. There were times—perhaps on the morning of a holiday—when Gurudas sat outside the house, writing, while Bhabani sat at his side, turning over the pages of books, not talking. They never spoke—but they were happy, both of them.

Nabendu now had a salary of seventy-five rupees. He lived in Calcutta, his job was to check tickets on trains leaving from Sealdah Station. His days passed travelling on trains, but he rushed home whenever he could, and he handed over a decent sum of money to Gurudas every month. It was thanks to him that they survived—even with three growing children. Gurudas could afford to go to Calcutta from time to time, and Harimohini did not come to know that they didn't own any land any more, that they actually had to buy all their provisions now.

Harimohini busied herself in finding a match for her twenty-seven-year-old son. Nabendu wasn't willing, he said he was trying to get the post of stationmaster—it would be better to marry after he had settled down. Actually, it was the state of the family that had made him reluctant to add to his financial burden. But Harimohini insisted, and he was married in May.

Along with new quilts and sheets, a painted box of toiletries, and the fragrance of Vaseline and scent, the new bride brought a wave of joy into the house. A beautiful girl of fifteen. A little pain was unavoidable too; reminded of Shibani, Harimohini wiped her eyes covertly.

Nine months after his wedding, Nabendu slipped while trying to climb into a moving train and fell on the tracks. By the time he was pulled out, his heart was still beating in his mangled body, but not long enough to make it to the hospital.

His wife was seven months pregnant at the time. She fell unconscious when informed, and delivered a premature, dead baby four hours later. She never succeeded in getting back on her feet; overcome by 'childbed' fever, suffering for six months, she finally vanished into the shadows like an insubstantial shadow herself.

Gurudas received one thousand five hundred rupees from Nabendu's provident fund, and another two thousand rupees as 'compensation'. And a few months later, just before Durga Puja, the war between Germany and England broke out.

From 'panchambahini'—fifth column—to 'anubidaran'—splitting the atom—Gurudas collected many new words during the six years of the war. These would have to be added to the appendix. But his work didn't progress significantly during this period, he only got as far as the Bengali letter 'Law'. Nor could he publish beyond the Bengali letter 'Raw'; printing had become four times as expensive, and paper was hard to come by. Meanwhile, the landlord suddenly demanded seventeen rupees as rent for the house for which Gurudas had been paying seven and a half rupees all this time; the price of rice vaulted from four rupees per maund to forty; kerosene became too expensive for lanterns. And his eyes began to trouble him. The doctor said he had developed a cataract in one of them, and that surgery was necessary. This meant a trip to Calcutta and a cost of about a hundred and fifty rupees. He dismissed the proposition as soon as he heard it—it was more important to remain alive, even if on only one square meal a day.

They survived on Nabendu's three and a half thousand rupees. He dipped into it to pay for Bhabani's daughter's wedding, which cost about five hundred. Despite controlling his expenditure strictly, the rest melted during the war years like ice put out in the sun. He had returned his daughter-in-law's jewellery to her father.

It was during the war that Harimohini learnt that they no longer owned a home of their own. But she was not perturbed—she had lost that ability. She had turned inert after her son's death—indeed, she was not quite right in the head. She seldom spoke, just ate her meals and stayed in bed most of the time, suffering from arthritis. Her teeth had fallen out, she was an old woman now.

Bhabani stood like a pillar, resilient. Her sons Amal and Bimal were in school. The elder one passed his matriculation examination and joined Khulna College, where Gurudas interceded with the principal to ensure that he would not have to pay any fees. Bimal gave up his studies suddenly and, applying his own judgement, got a job at the ration shop, where he learnt to pilfer. When the sixteen-year-old's mother found out, she used a piece of wood to take the skin off his back.

Gurudas was penniless when the war ended. His salary and allowance at the school amounted to sixty-three rupees, but because of his age the authorities were pleading with him to retire. After much begging, he secured an extension of two years—he would have to leave after that.

But suddenly the problem of employment became a trivial one. Rivers of blood began to flow as the country's independence approached. After Independence, Khulna was allotted to Pakistan. After waiting and watching developments for a while, Gurudas decided to go to India with his family.

It's best not to talk about how the journey was made. Partly on foot, partly by train, occasionally on a boat across a river. Their belongings (such as they were) were left behind; they took only absolutely essential clothes, a few utensils, and his case of books. The published copies, handwritten notes, and...and virtually nothing else. All those books he had collected with so much effort since childhood had to be left behind.

Although they were unencumbered, the journey was not an easy one. He had grown old, his vision was dimmed. His wife hobbled. Amal and Bimal actually had to carry their grandmother at times—but how far can you walk bearing the weight of a heavy old woman? They had to pause for rest beneath trees, while Harimohini shrieked with arthritic pain. Rain. Sun. Dust. Droppings. Flies. And hordes of helpless people. Two babies were crushed to death by the crowd at Ranaghat Station.

It took ten days to get to Calcutta. They passed a week at Sealdah Station, eating nothing but muri, and were then transferred on a lorry to a camp at Bongaon, where they were served a lump of rice and dal at two every afternoon. Gurudas recovered a little on this diet, but there was no respite from Harimohini's cries of pain.

Finally, the Lord took pity on her. Cholera broke out in the camp, and her heart gave way after she had emptied her stomach out several times. They could not cremate her themselves; government officials gathered bodies wholesale and took them away in a black vehicle.

Two months later, they were given shelter at a refugee colony near Kanchrapara. Rows of one-room bamboo shanties with a little space to cook in. A pond nearby, a tubewell for fresh water at a slight distance. Still, Bhabani set up a household despite the limitations. Amal got a job at a nearby mill, which helped them survive somehow. Bimal began to lead a dissolute life, spending all his time outside the house, smoking and watching films, though no one knew how he got the money for it.

Gurudas pulled out his notebooks again. One eye was clouded over with cataract, the other had dimmed too. Every moment of daylight was priceless. He went outside as soon as the sun rose, while Bhabani brought him a cup of tea and a little muri. Bhabani had to have her tea with her father—he insisted on it. Gurudas had discovered tea towards the end of the war. It really provided energy, and suppressed hunger too. Starting with the first light of day, he worked till the last rays of the sun faded. He sat cross-legged, his notebooks on a small stool, and just two or three books open around him—whatever he had been able to salvage from Khulna. When his back ached, he placed a book beneath the small of his back and lay down for a few minutes. It brought relief.

The next month Bhabani made him a bolster. And that same day he wrote a postcard to Bipin Babu at Bharat Press.

The reply came two days later. Bipin Babu had asked after him, expressing pleasure at hearing from him after such a long time. Demand had picked up for his dictionary recently, the previous editions had almost sold out. It was necessary to publish the subsequent volumes now. The money realized from the sales of the earlier volumes would be enough to publish the new ones—Gurudas would not have to pay any more money. Bipin Babu wrote that he would be obliged if Gurudas could inform him when the new manuscripts would be available.

After a few more letters had been exchanged, Bipin babu agreed to provide a monthly 'assistance' of fifteen rupees. Gurudas saved some of it to get some new books all over again. Several volumes were published in succession over the next two years; he got as far as the letter 'Dontyoshaw' meanwhile.

The following year Gurudas finished his dictionary; it took another two years to publish all the volumes. He had to read everything in print once more: the corrigenda, the appendices, everything. The *Great Bengal Dictionary* was completed in fifty-two volumes. It had taken him thirty years. He had been a young man of forty when he began—now the hair on his head was white, his back was bent, his cheeks were like crevices, his veins protruded on his skin. He was blind in one eye, and had marginal vision in the other.

Gurudas took to his bed a few days later. The task for which he had conserved the last drops of his energy had been completed, he no longer needed it. He recalled Shibani, Nobu, Nobu's wife. He recalled his wife. 'Don't perform my last rites, Bhabani,' he told his daughter. 'I don't believe in any of it.'

But he simply suffered in bed. Death wasn't at his beck and call.

Meanwhile, there were murmurs in Calcutta about his dictionary. One Gurudas Bhattacharya had apparently composed a dictionary—an outstanding achievement. It was talked about in the university, at literary gatherings, and newspaper offices. Those who bought the dictionary praised it, those who didn't praised it even more.

Eventually, a young journalist appeared in a jeep one day, accompanied by Bipin Babu from Bharat Press. Gurudas did not speak much—he had no strength. Covering her face, Bhabani answered all their questions in a soft tone. A sensational report appeared in the next day's paper, peppered with magnificent words like sacrifice, dedication, and devotion.

And so Gurudas became famous.

It was the fifth year after Independence. The government had announced literary awards. Someone on the committee proposed Gurudas for an award. Gurudas Bhattacharya? Oh, the dictionary. Well…well, one has to admit he has accomplished a mammoth task, written thousands of pages. And, we hear he's in financial difficulties, eking out an existence in a refugee colony—it would be a splendid gesture. Something to capture the popular imagination with. You've seen how *Swadeshi Bazaar* has praised him, haven't you?

Gurudas was chosen to receive the award.

In reply to the official communication, Bhabani wrote that her father was ill and unable to visit Calcutta in any circumstances.

One of the younger ministers said, 'Very well, let us go to him. People will approve.'

As a result, an enormous car drew up at the Kanchrapara refugee colony at ten o'clock one morning, escorted by a jeep. A minister of the state emerged from the car, accompanied by two high officials, and two orderlies in shining red uniforms. The young journalist who had written the report, a government clerk, and a photographer with a camera jumped out of the jeep. The car could not come all the way to the door. As children and women stared, the visitors walked along the narrow path between rows of shanties to Gurudas's hut. The tiny space was suddenly filled with people.

There was no room to sit—the ceremonies were conducted with everyone standing. The minister said a few words. A silk shawl, a bouquet of flowers, and one-hundred-rupee notes tied with a silk ribbon, amounting to five thousand rupees, were placed on Gurudas's bed. The cameras clicked, Gurudas's weak eyes blinked as the flashbulbs went off.

He lay still on his back, his hands gathered at his chest. His expression did not betray whether he was aware of what was going on. But when the guests had moved away from his bed, their demeanour suggesting they wanted to depart but were staying back only because they were embarrassed to be leaving so quickly, Gurudas spoke clearly but faintly, 'Turn me on my side, Bhabani. This is very funny, but if I laugh I will be insulting all these people. Make me face the other way.' The eye with cataracts was still, but laughter flashed in the other eye for an instant. Bhabani turned him over on his side carefully.

He died the same afternoon. His grandsons and the young men from the neighbourhood took him to the crematorium draped in the same silk shawl and covered with the same flowers.

He had made a single statement before dying. 'Keep the money, Bhabani, it'll prove useful to you.'

THE BLUE LIGHT

VAIKOM MUHAMMAD BASHEER

Translated from the Malayalam by O. V. Usha

THIS STORY IS ABOUT AN EXTRAORDINARY, NO, MIRACULOUS EVENT IN my life. That I call it miraculous...well, what else can I say?

This is what happened.

No need for the date, month, or year.

I was on the lookout for a house. Nothing new about that. Those days I was always looking for a house. I never came across a house or even a room to my liking. As far as the place, which called itself a hotel, where I stayed, a hundred flaws, more, had come to light there. But to whom to complain? Leave? And go where?

And so it went, hating where I stayed, constantly looking for a place and finding only those that I hated even more. I lost count of the number of houses I looked at and disliked. And, as is the way with rented houses, someone who liked them took them.

Still, it was a time when there was a dearth of houses for rent. What could be had at one time for ten rupees was not available now for even sixty.

So, I spent my days, roaming the town daily, until, suddenly, one forenoon, there it stood—a house, no, my house! It was a small, two-storeyed building. 'Bhargavinilayam'. Far from the bustle and noise of the town. Yet, close to the municipality border. A decrepit board on the gate said 'For rent'.

I liked the place instantly. It was an old house. There was something strange about it even at first glance. Didn't matter; it was perfect for me. Two rooms and an open veranda upstairs. Four rooms downstairs. Also, there was a bathroom, a kitchen, and a pipe with running water. The only thing missing was electricity.

In front of the kitchen there was an ancient well with a stone wall around it. A small way off, in a corner of the walled compound around the house, stood a toilet. Trees in abundance. The public road ran right before the property.

I was surprised and delighted! Why had no one snapped up this house yet? A lady of great beauty she was. Ah! She shouldn't be seen by anyone. Should hide her behind purdah! Such unusual thoughts and feelings that old house evoked in me. I was in a happy daze; I was entranced.

I quickly made whatever arrangements needed to be made, borrowed money from various friends, paid the two months' advance rent, and got the keys in my hand. Wasting not a moment, I moved into the upstairs of the old house. I bought a hurricane lamp and kerosene. I swept the rooms myself, upstairs and downstairs, kitchen, bathroom and all. I ritually cleansed the place, sprinkling water. There was a good deal of accumulated waste; there was plenty of dust. After the sweeping, I thoroughly washed all the rooms until they were spotless. I saw one room downstairs that was locked. I did not try to open it.

I had a bath, and felt a great sense of relief and well-being. I came out and perched myself on the wall around the antique well. Such bliss! One could sit and daydream here, or walk or run or whatever in complete privacy inside the walled compound around the house.

There should be a garden in the front yard, I thought, mainly of beds of roses. Jasmine too. A cook? No, that would be a bother. I could fill the thermos with tea from the tea shop when I went for breakfast after my morning bath. Lunch could be arranged from the old hotel. Hopefully, they would send me dinner as well.

The postman had to be informed about the change of address, and tipped not to reveal my whereabouts to anyone. Nights of lovely solitude; days of lovely solitude: I would be able to write a lot! Borne along by these and other happy thoughts, I peered down into the well. The tangle of plants growing across its mouth and from its walls made it impossible to see if it had any water. I threw a pebble into the well.

'Bhllllum!' it rang after a moment. There was water.

All this by eleven in the morning.

The previous night I hadn't slept a wink. I settled my account with the hotel. I met the houseowner. I folded the canvas cot and secured it. Gramophone, records—all neatly packed. Boxes, papers, armchair, shelf, everything—all my assets had been set in order. At the crack of dawn, I set out with my luggage loaded on to a pair of pushcarts. The men who brought my luggage left it outside the gate...as if they were frightened to come into the place.

Arriving at my new residence, I brought my possessions in myself, then, elated, locked the house, walked humming to the gate, fastened it, and went out on to the road with a fine new sense of pride, walking on air.

As I went along, I wondered: with whose song should the new house be inaugurated? I had more than a hundred records in my possession. English, Arabic, Hindi, Urdu, Tamil, Bengali. Nothing in Malayalam. There are talented singers. They have cut records. But the music direction and finish of all of them is poor. But good directors and singers are coming up. Yes, I must buy some Malayalam records.

Whose song should I play first today, I wondered. Pankaj Mullick, Dilipkumar Roy, Saigal, Bing Crosby, Paul Robeson, Abdul Karim Khan, Kanan Devi, Kumari Manju Dasgupta, Khursheed, Juthika Roy, M. S. Subbulakshmi...some twenty names passed through my mind. Finally, I decided: there is a song which says that someone from a distant land is here. It begins with, *Door desh ka rehne wala aaya*. Whose voice was it? Male or female? I could not remember. I would find it when I got back home.

Thus, I went on my way, happily. First of all, I met the postman. Talked to him. When I told him which house I had moved into, he looked unnerved.

'Ayyo, sir! There was an unnatural death in that house. That's why it's been lying empty for so long. No one will stay there.'

An unnatural death? I was a little flustered. I asked, 'What unnatural death?'

'Did you see the well in the backyard? Someone jumped into it and died. After that there is no peace in that house. Many tenants came but none stayed. At night doors would bang shut on their own. Taps would open by themselves and water would gush out.'

Doors banging shut on their own. Taps opening by themselves. Startling indeed. I'd seen that both taps were secured with locks. Travellers scaled the compound wall and bathed at the taps, that was why they were locked—that was the houseowner's version. But what was the need for a lock on the bathroom tap inside the house—it did not occur to me to ask.

The postman continued, 'Some invisible thing or person would try to choke anyone sleeping inside that house! Did no one tell you, sir?'

I thought, oh, good! And I've paid two months' rent in advance. Putting a brave face on it, I said, 'All that doesn't matter. The whole thing will just take a mantra to settle. Whatever it is, bring my letters and other mail there.'

Though I spoke evenly, I did feel a ripple of anxiety, as any other man might. Call me a coward, if you will. My pace on the road slackened. What could I do? I do not usually court eerie experiences. But if they happen anyway, what does one do? But what could really happen?

I went to the hotel and drank some tea. I did not feel hungry. It was as if a strange fire had been lit in my gut, driving out my appetite. I spoke to the man in the hotel about sending regular meals to my house.

When I told him where I was living, he said, 'I can arrange to send you food during the day. At night none of the boys will come there. A woman killed herself by jumping into the old well in the yard. She still hangs around the place. Aren't you afraid of ghosts, sir?'

It was a woman; half my fear melted away.

I said, 'Oh, nothing to all that. Moreover, there's the mantra.'

I had no idea what the mantra was. But it was a woman...some softness there. I walked into the bank nearby. I had a few friends among the clerks there. I talked to them. They were furious with me: 'How foolish could you be?! It's a haunted house and it's mostly men that are harmed.'

She hated men! That was nice to know.

One of my friends said, 'Couldn't you have told us you were planning to take Bhargavinilayam on rent?'

I said, 'Who knew it was like this? Let me ask you a question—why did that woman jump into the well?'

'Love!' said another friend. 'Her name was Bhargavi. She was twenty-one. She passed her BA. Before that she was in love with someone. Big love. Then the fellow married another woman. And Bhargavi jumped into the well and died.'

Most of my fear was gone. So this is why she hated men.

I said, 'Bhargavi will not harm me.'

'And why is that?'

I smiled, 'Mantra! Mantra!'

'We'll see about that. You're going to howl in your bed at night.'

I did not say anything more.

I went back to the house. Opened doors and windows. Went downstairs and walked to the well.

'Bhargavikutty!' I called softly. 'We don't know each other. I have come to stay in this house. I believe that I am a good man. I've been celibate all my life, you know? I have already heard many rumours about you, Bhargavikutty. That you do not allow anyone to live here. That you open the taps at night. That you bang the doors shut. That you strangle men, especially, with invisible hands. Yes, I've heard a lot. What do I do now?

'I've already paid two months' rent as advance, and I have very little money. Also I like this house, this house that belongs to you, Bhargavikutty, I like it so much! It's named for you, isn't it? Bhargavinilayam!

'I need to stay here and work. I must write some stories. Bhargavikutty, do you like stories? If you do, I'll read everything that I write to you. I have absolutely no quarrel with you, Bhargavikutty. No cause for that either, is there? A while ago I did drop a pebble into the well. I did it without thinking. Nothing like that from me in future, I promise.

'Listen, Bhargavikutty, I have a first-rate gramophone. Some two hundred excellent songs, too. Are you fond of music?'

I fell quiet after saying that much. Who was I talking to? To the well, ready with its mouth open to swallow anything? To whom—the trees, the house, the air, the universe? Was it to the disturbance in my mind? I was talking to an idea, an abstraction—Bhargavi! I had not seen her. A young woman of twenty-one. Deeply in love with a man. She dreamt of a life as his wife, his life partner. But that dream...yes, it passed as a dream. Despair gripped her, and shame, disgrace, and betrayal, too.

'Bhargavikutty!' I said, 'you needn't have done what you did. Don't think I am blaming you. The man you were fond of did not love you enough. He loved another woman more.

'Life turned bitter for you. That much is true. However, all of life is not full of bitterness. Forget about it! And, for you, now history will not repeat itself.

'Bhargavikutty, don't think for a moment I am blaming you. Was it really for love that you died? Love is only the golden dawn of eternal life. Silly girl! You didn't know a thing about it. That's what your hatred of men proves. Consider that you knew just one man. Also, let's accept, for argument's sake, that he wronged you grievously. But is it right to view all men through the tinted glass of that one experience? Had you lived instead of killing yourself, you would have known through experience that your extreme reaction was not right. There would have been someone to love you, to adore you, to call you "my goddess!" Now, didn't I say for you history will not repeat itself? Bhargavikutty, how can I get to know your whole life story?

'Whatever it is, don't harm me, I beg you. No one will question you if you were to choke me to death tonight. Not that it's anyone's business to question you. All I mean is that there is no one to do it. You know why? I have no one.

'Now you know how things stand. We, you and I, are living here. That is, I mean to live here. Having paid rent, legally, the house, well, and everything else is mine. But let that be. You use the well and the four rooms downstairs. We share the kitchen and the bathroom equally. What do you say? Do you like my idea?'

Night fell. I came back with a tea-filled thermos after having eaten dinner at the hotel. By the light of my electric torch, I lit the hurricane lamp. The room was flooded in yellow light.

I went downstairs with the torch. I stood still in pitch darkness for some time. My intention was to turn the taps off tightly. I opened all the windows wide. I approached the kitchen, near the well. Suddenly, I had the strong feeling that I must not tighten the taps.

I closed the doors, climbed the stairs, and had some tea. After that I lit a bidi and sat in my armchair. I was just beginning to write, when I had the feeling that Bhargavi was behind my chair.

I said uneasily, 'I don't like anyone watching while I write.'

I turned my head; no one there.

I'm not sure why, but I didn't want to write any more. I drew up another chair in front of mine.

'Sit down in this, Bhargavikutty.'

The chair stayed empty. I got up and began strolling through the two rooms. No breeze. The leaves of the trees outside didn't stir. I looked down through the window: a light!

Blue, red, or yellow—I couldn't tell. It was gone in a second.

Just my imagination, I told myself. I can't swear that I saw that light. Still, how could one think one sees without actually seeing? Was it a glow-worm perhaps?

I spent a long time pacing the rooms. I spent a long time standing at the windows. There was nothing unusual. I tried to read something but couldn't concentrate. The chair remained empty.

Let me go to sleep early, I thought. I made my bed and turned off the lamp. Then I wanted to play a song! I lit the lamp again. Opened the gramophone. Fitted a new needle into the playing arm, and then I wound up the machine.

Whose song should I play? The world was still and silent. Then, an uncanny whooshing filled both my ears! Like the wind, like the sea. And then absolute quiet again. Fear seized me. I must shatter this ominous silence into a thousand pieces. Whose song would best serve that purpose?

I looked through my collection, and chose a record of the black American singer Paul Robeson. The gramophone began playing. A man's voice rich and majestic:

Joshua fit the battle of Jericho....

That song ended. Pankaj Mullick was next:

Tu dar naa zaraa bhi....

You don't be afraid at all!

The next was a sweet, soft, and alluring voice:

Kaatrinile varum geetam....

The song that arrives on the breeze....

And in time, M. S. Subbulakshmi finished that song.

Somehow, after these three songs, I was at peace. I sat quietly, for quite a while. Finally, I invited Saigal in. He sang in his languid voice, full of melancholy and sweetness:

So jaa raajkumaari, so jaa....

Go to sleep, princess; may beautiful dreams visit your sleep.

That also ended.

'That's all for now, the rest tomorrow,' I said aloud, and lowering the lid of the gramophone, lit a bidi, turned off the lamp, and went to bed. Next to me I had the torch, a watch, and a dagger. Also the empty chair.

I closed the doors to the veranda before getting into bed. It must have turned ten now. I lay alert, my ears strained to the night.

There was no sound other than the tik-tik of the watch. Minutes passed, and hours. There was no fear in my mind. What there was...was a cold wakefulness. This was not new to me. I'd had some unusual experiences in my life over the years, in many lands, many places, during my lonely life of twenty years, none of which I could find the meaning of. Because of this, my attention constantly shifted between the past and the present.

Would there be a knock at the door? Would there be the sound of water flowing from the taps? Would I be throttled in my sleep? I stayed awake and vigilant till three in the morning.

I heard nothing, felt nothing. Finally, I fell into a deep and tranquil sleep. I did not have a single dream. I woke up at nine the next morning.

Nothing had happened.

'Good morning, Bhargavikutty, thank you so much! I have understood one thing for certain—people are spreading false rumours about you. Let them talk, no? Who cares?'

My days and nights passed in this manner. I would think of Bhargavikutty...her mother, father, siblings, there must be so many unknown stories.

I wrote most nights. When I got tired, I played records. I would announce the singer, the content, the mood, and so on, before the song began. I would say, 'Here, Pankaj Mullick, the great Bengali singer. The song is filled with sadness, and invokes memories. These are bygone times, you know. Listen carefully.'

Guzar gayaa voh zamaana kaisa, kaisa....

How wonderful were those days that are now gone.

Or else I would say: 'And now Bing Crosby. *In the moonlight*—it means.... Oh, I beg your pardon, you must know, you're a graduate!'

I would talk like this, to myself. Two and a half months passed. I planted a garden. When flowers appeared, I said: 'All the flowers are for Bhargavikutty!'

In the meantime, I finished writing a short novel. Many of my friends visited me. At times, some stayed overnight. Before going to bed, I would go downstairs without their knowing it. And I would look into the darkness and whisper, 'Bhargavikutty, listen! Some friends of mine are here. Don't strangle them. If you do, the police will arrest me. Be careful. Good night!'

Usually before going out, I would say: 'Bhargavikutty, take care of the house. If any thieves get in, you can strangle them. Don't leave the bodies here, though. Dump them some miles away, or we will be in trouble.'

When I returned from the cinema after a late show, I would announce, 'It's me!'

All this I said in the newness of the first days. As time passed, I forgot Bhargavi. Well, my long chats to her stopped. I would still remember her occasionally, but that was all.

I will tell you what sort of remembering that was. Millions have died since human life began in this world...haven't countless men and women died? All of them have mingled with this earth as smoke or dust. We know this. Bhargavi was reduced to a memory of that kind.

Then, as life went by without any great event, something happened. That's what I am going to tell you about now.

One night. It was ten o' clock. From around nine I had been writing a story. It was emotionally charged and I was developing it briskly. I became aware that the light was getting dim.

I lifted the lamp and shook it gently to check the oil. There was no kerosene. Still, I thought, let me write one more page. I was entirely absorbed by the story I was writing, and in the meanwhile the light had faded. What could one do at a time like that? Check if there was oil in the lamp. That was what I did. I raised the wick a little; I continued writing. After a while, the light faded further. I raised the wick again, resumed my writing. The light dimmed again; again, I raised the wick. Eventually, the wick turned into a smoking red ember four inches long.

I turned on my torchlight and lowered the wick completely. The lamp was snuffed out.

I said to myself, 'How can I get some light?'

I needed kerosene. I could borrow some kerosene from the bank clerks' stove.

I locked the door and went out with my torch and kerosene bottle. I went down and out of the house, locking the front door behind me. I went down the path and out of the gate, latching it. I walked along the deserted road. A faint moon lit my way. There were heavy clouds above, too, so I strode along quickly.

I came to the bank building and, from the street, called out the name of one of the bank clerks. I called twice or thrice before one of them came down and opened the side gate. We went up using the staircase behind the building. I found that the three of them were playing a game of cards.

When I talked about kerosene, one of them asked with a laugh, 'Couldn't you have asked your girlfriend to get you kerosene? Have you finished writing her life story?'

I didn't say anything. Must write, I thought. As one of them was pouring kerosene into the bottle, it began to pour outside.

I said, 'Give me an umbrella also.'

They said, 'One? There is not even a quarter of one. Let's play cards for a while. You can go when the rain lets up.'

So we played cards. My partner and I did three rounds of salaam. Mostly because my mind was on my story and I was distracted while playing. The rain stopped at about one. I got up and picked up the torch and kerosene bottle. By now, my friends were also ready to sleep. After I went down to the street they switched off their light.

There was neither movement nor light in the street as I walked back home. When I took the turning towards my house the world lay immersed in mist and hazy moonlight. I didn't remember what thoughts ran through my mind then. Perhaps I was not thinking at all. I continued walking along the dark road, empty and silent, flashing my torch. No living thing stirred anywhere.

I reached my house, opened the gate, shut it, and then opened the front door. I entered the house and latched the door from inside. I had no cause to think that anything unusual would have happened upstairs. But something had.

For no reason whatever, a vast sorrow abruptly filled my heart and I felt like crying. I can laugh easily but never shed a tear. Tears just don't come to me. When sorrow overwhelms me, a divine exaltation takes hold of me, as it did now—a great compassion!

In that state of mind, I climbed the stairs. And what I saw when I arrived on the upper floor was extraordinary, no, it was miraculous.

When I locked my room and left, you remember, there was no oil left in the lamp; the flame had gone out and I had withdrawn the wick into the base of the lamp. Darkness had filled the room. Later, while I was out, it had rained and some hours had passed. Now, I saw light shining through the chink below my door. Well, my eyes saw the light but my mind did not yet register or believe what I saw.

Out of sheer habit, I took out my key and flashed the torchlight on the lock. The lock shone like silver; why, it seemed to smile.

I opened the door and went in. And now, what I saw before me struck me with full force. An indescribable sensation surged through every atom of my being. No, I did not quake with fright. Rather, as I stood transfixed, my mind was flooded by a tide of tenderness.

Blue light!

White walls, the whole room, drenched in ethereal blue light. That light came from the lamp in which a blue flame blazed.

Who had lit this blue light in Bhargavinilayam?

18

THE FLOOD

THAKAZHI SIVASANKARA PILLAI

Translated from the Malayalam by O. V. Usha

THE TEMPLE STOOD ON A RISE, THE HIGHEST GROUND FOR MILES around. Despite this, its deity was submerged in water up to its neck. There was water everywhere you looked. In the three-roomed uppermost storey of the building, sixty-seven children, three hundred and fifty-seven adults, and assorted dogs, cats, goats, and fowl had taken refuge from the floodwaters.

Most of the locals had fled their homes, and made their way to dry land. If the family owned a boat, one of them would remain behind to guard their house and their possessions.

Chennan, the pariah, had been standing in water an entire night and day. It had been three days since his master had escaped to safety. Chennan did not own a rowboat so inside his hut he had built an elevated platform out of coconut fronds and twigs that jutted above the level of the floodwaters. The family spent two days in this primitive loft, hoping the floodwaters would recede soon. Chennan was concerned that if they left the hut, his five banana trees that were heavy with fruit and his hayrick would be stolen. The waters continued to rise. Chennan was now knee-deep in water as he stood on his platform. A couple of rows of thatch on the roof slipped under water. Chennan shouted for help, but who was there to hear him? He was convinced that he and his dependents—his pregnant wife, four children, a cat, and a dog—would die within the next twelve hours, as, by then, the waters would have risen above the roof. The downpour, which had started three days ago, showed no signs of abating.

Undoing a portion of the thatch from inside the hut, Chennan somehow scrambled on to the roof and looked around. He saw a big boat moving north. He yelled to the men in the boat for help. They heard him, and began rowing towards his hut. Chennan pulled out his children, his wife, the dog, and the cat through the opening he had made in the roof. When the boat came alongside the hut, the children began climbing into it. Just then they heard a voice.

'Chennacho... Poohay...!'

It was Matiyathara Kunheippan, calling out from the roof of his house.

Chennan hastily helped his wife into the boat. The cat also jumped in. No one remembered the dog. It was sniffing at something on the western edge of the roof when the boat began to move away from the house.

When the dog eventually returned to the spot on the roof from which the family had made its escape, the boat was far away. The animal began to run around frantically on the roof, sniffing here and there, whining all the while. A frog which had been sitting on the roof was alarmed by the commotion the dog was creating and jumped into the flood as the dog drew close. The movement frightened the dog; it reared back, then stared intently at the ripples caused by the frog when it had dived into the water.

The dog was hungry now, and began sniffing around for food. It disturbed another frog, which urinated on its nose, before jumping into the water. The dog sneezed and snorted, shook its head violently, began cleaning its face with its forepaws.

The rain which had stopped for a while, began lashing down again, and the dog crouched down miserably under its onslaught. Meanwhile, its master and family had got to safety in Ambalappuzha.

Night fell. An enormous crocodile, half submerged in the water, drifted by the hut. The dog put its tail between its legs in terror, and howled, but the crocodile paid no attention to it and was soon out of sight.

Starving, terrified, tired, and without any protection from the driving rain, the dog crouched on the roof of the hut. It howled piteously and the gusting wind carried its cries of distress across great distances. The few people who remained in that flooded wilderness guarding their huts probably felt sorry for the dog when they heard its anguished howls.

Its master was probably eating his dinner. He was probably rolling a ball of rice for the dog between his fingers, as was his practice at the end of a meal. The dog's howls began to weaken, then died away. It pricked up its ears when it heard a man reciting the Ramayana. It remained silent for a while, almost as if it was listening to the chanting of the verse, and then began barking again as loudly as it could manage. The melodious chanting of the Ramayana rose clear and strong into the still night. The rain had stopped. The dog listened intently to the sound of that human voice. The voice died away into the cold air. Now there was no sound except that of the gusting of the wind, and the lapping of waves against the hut.

The dog lay down on the roof. It snuffled miserably. A fish splashed in the dark water. A frog jumped. The dog barked once or twice, then fell quiet.

When the sun came up, the dog began a low howling, almost as if it were keening. Rows of frogs, lined up on the roof of the house, would eye the dog, and if it made a move, would jump into the water. The dog looked at the thatched roofs poking out of the floodwater in the vicinity, hoping that they would contain food; but there was no food to be had. It began nuzzling at its fur, feeding on the fleas it found there; it scratched the flea bites with its hind legs, and then it briefly fell asleep in the feeble warmth of the sun.

Dark clouds enveloped the sun. The wind rose, and with it the waves. The carcasses of drowned animals floated past the hut. The dog looked longingly at them, and barked once or twice.

Every now and again small rowboats would come into view and the dog would look at them hopefully. One of them went past in the distance and disappeared behind a thick clump of ketaki shrubs. It began to drizzle again. Sitting on the roof, the dog presented a picture of utter helplessness.

The rain stopped. A small boat appeared in the distance and steadily drew closer. It moored under a coconut tree close to the hut. The dog wagged its tail, stretched, yawned, growled under its breath. The man in the boat climbed the tree, lopped off a coconut, sliced it open, drank its contents, and then rowed away.

A crow flew down and landed on the huge, rotting carcass of a dead buffalo that was floating by, and began to rip and tear at the flesh. Chennan's dog barked longingly at the prospect of a meal. The crow ate its fill and flew away. A green bird landed on a banana trunk and chirped. An ant's nest that had become dislodged from somewhere upriver snagged on the eaves of the hut. Thinking that it was something it could eat, the dog nosed at the nest, and got bitten for its pains. It jumped away, snorting and sneezing, its tender nose flushed and swollen.

That afternoon, a small rowboat drifted by, with two men in it. The dog began barking joyfully, jumping up and down in its happiness. Its demeanour, the way it was trying to express itself, seemed almost human. It went down to the water's edge, ready to jump into the boat.

'Look, a dog,' one of the men said. The dog began to whimper in a peculiar key—it was almost as though it was responding to the compassion in the man's voice.

'Let it be,' said the second man.

The dog whimpered, opened and closed its mouth, it seemed as though it was praying to the men to rescue it. It tried twice to jump into the boat, and was rebuffed both times. The boat began to move away from the house. The dog howled. It was heart-rending. One of the men looked back.

'Ayyooo....' The sound wasn't from either of the men but the dog. 'Ayyooo....' It was an exhausted, pitiful sound. It was almost as if the animal was bidding goodbye to the world.

The men did not look back again. The boat drew steadily away, and the dog remained where it was on the roof, watching it go. Its moaning and the expression on its face seemed to say that it would love human beings no more. The boat disappeared from sight.

The dog lapped up some water, looked at some birds flying overhead. A water snake was borne along by the flood at great speed towards the hut. Startled, the dog retreated along the roof. The snake slipped into the opening in the thatch through which Chennan and his family had made their escape. The dog peered into the opening and began to bark furiously.

The barking gradually tapered away into a whimpering. It was a sound of lament, full of the hunger the animal hadn't been able to sate, its despair at the hopelessness of its situation, and its fear that it might not survive.

What it was trying to express would have been clear to anyone—even to a man from Mars.

With nightfall, a storm picked up. The roof of the hut began to shake as waves battered against it. The dog nearly fell off—twice. A long, sinister head rose out of the dark water. The dog began to bark frantically when it saw the crocodile. From somewhere close by came the sound of chickens squawking.

Another boat came into view, heavily loaded with coconuts and bunches of bananas. It stopped beside a banana tree close to the hut.

'Where is that barking coming from? Hasn't the hut been vacated?' one of the men in the boat asked.

The dog turned towards the sound of the men's voices and began barking. As one of the men began to climb the banana tree, the dog's barking grew in fury and menace.

'Better watch out, that dog sounds really angry, it might bite you,' the man who had remained in the boat warned his companion who had climbed the tree. No sooner had he spoken than the dog leapt at the thief who was trying to steal Chennan's bananas. The man tumbled down into the water, the dog with him. The thief's companion pulled him into the boat, while the dog swam back to the rooftop. It clambered back on, and shook the water off its coat, barking furiously all the while. The thieves lopped all the bananas off the trees, and loaded them on to the boat.

The men goaded the angry animal on to even greater rage. 'Just you wait, we've got something to show you,' they said grimly.

They transferred as much hay as they could from Chennan's hayrick on to their boat. Then one of the men got on to the roof and advanced threateningly towards the dog. It attacked him immediately, and sank its teeth into his leg. Howling in agony, the man jumped back into the boat, while his companion took hold of an oar and brought it crashing down on the dog's head. The animal yelped, and retreated.

The man who had been bitten lay in the bottom of the boat tossing and turning in agony. As the boat receded into the distance, the dog sent it on its way with a volley of barks. It was close to midnight by then. An enormous bloated carcass of a cow drifted up to the house, and snagged on the roof. The dog kept an eye on the carcass. After a while, pushed by the current, the carcass began to move away slowly. Galvanized into activity, its tail wagging, grunting, the dog rushed down the roof to where the carcass was still within reach, and began tearing at the flesh, sating its terrible hunger. Just then, with a loud cracking noise, the entire carcass was dislodged from the roof, and the dog, which was eating from it, went with it. The carcass rolled over in the current, and the dog disappeared from view. Now one could only hear the sound of the gushing wind, the cacophony of frogs, and the sibilant whisper of the waves. There was no other sound.

Those who still stood guard in some of the flooded homes could no longer hear the dog's piteous whining, or heart-rending moaning. Every so often, another bloated carcass of some drowned animal would float by on the flood. Crows fed on some of them. Everywhere you looked there was nothing but desolation. And the only people who thrived in this wilderness of water and destruction were thieves and looters.

The hut collapsed after a while, and sank out of sight. And the loyal animal, which had stood guard over its master's property for as long as it could, was gone as well. The crocodiles had it now. It was all over, the waters covered everything.

The flood receded slowly. One day, Chennan swam across to the spot where his hut had once stood, looking for his dog. Under one of the coconut trees, he saw the corpse of a dog, gently rocking in the eddies of the shallow water. Chennan turned it over with his foot to check if it was his dog, he thought it might be. One of the animal's ears was missing. You couldn't even tell what colour the dog was, for its skin had rotted and sloughed away.

19

ON THE RIVERBANK

S. K. POTTEKKATT

Translated from the Malayalam by A. J. Thomas

A SMALL RIVER SNAKES ITS WAY ALONG THE BASE OF A ROUNDED HILL. The riverbank is almost hidden by the low, overhanging branches of a variety of ancient trees, especially thickets of strychnine trees and a dense outgrowth of creepers.

Even during the daytime, the place is shadowy and dark. In the middle of the river is a deep pool. A rock lies partially submerged in the pool. Old-timers call it thalavettippaara—the beheading rock. It is believed criminals were beheaded on this rock. No one bathes there. The water has a different colour near the rock.

Near the hill there is a stunted sago palm. On the top of the palm, there is a flower that blazes like a fire. The intoxicating fragrance from it wafts all around. Near the sago palm, there is a Barbados nut bush, half of it withered. On one of its branches hang five or six bundles wrapped in old screwpine mats whose reflection can be seen in the still waters of the river. These are the placentas of cows and goats placed there by locals. Other vegetation catches the eye—the thick red taproot of some tree exposed by soil erosion, a crooked pulakkalli tree bereft of all its leaves, wild aloe vera plants looking like snakes with their hoods open.

Towering over the other shrubs and trees on the riverbank is a gigantic wild jack tree reaching straight to the sky. Below the pool, a thin trickle of a brook joins the river—it's a place that is used as a ford.

It is midday. The sand on the riverbank scorches in the fire-like sun of Kanni, the months between mid-September to mid-October. Madhavi Amma has just bathed her son, dried him off, brushed his hair with her fingers, wiped his face, and dressed him in a silk loincloth. Having done so, she sends him off to the riverbank. At first, the six-year-old boy sits on a rock in the shade of a tree, his legs spread out. A few minutes later, his limbs begin to move.

Childhood is like a drop of mercury. No one can make it keep still. The boy's eyes flit around here and there. He begins to count his fingers, to check if all ten digits are there. He measures the length of his brow, his chin, and his nose, using his index finger. Then he presses down on one of his nostrils with a finger, breathing out through the other, and making a humming sound. For some time, he plays the fiddle in that fashion; then, he stops it. He presses his upper eyelids down with one of his fingers and is entertained by the way the trees and bushes in his line of vision become distorted. Suddenly, an idea flashes through his mind.

'Mother! May I build a dam across the brook?'

'No, no! Don't play in the mud, Unni! Sit still. See you don't lose that ring!'

Unni picks up a ring that he has balanced on his thigh. A gold ring with a red stone. His mother entrusted it to his care until she had finished her bath.

Unni begins to play with the ring. First, he tries it on all his fingers, before he finally puts it on the thumb of his right hand. Then he shuts his eyes tight, crosses his hands on his chest, and wonders what to do next. When he opens his eyes, he tries to touch his nose with the tip of his tongue. Then he fills his mouth with air and hisses like a snake.

'I'm hot, Mother. The sun has moved, and there's no shade. Can I move over to the clump of bamboo?'

'Hmm,' Madhavi Amma says absentmindedly.

Pretending to be lame, the child walks over to the bamboo clump. Now his mother can no longer see him.

The brook is next to the bamboo clump. In one of the puddles, it has formed, the blazing midday sun can be seen. A dragonfly is frolicking over the puddle, rising suddenly in the air above the water's surface, diving quickly, touching the water and then rising again, hovering.

It attracts Unni's attention. Turning his neck, then looking at it sideways, he gets up slowly.

It is a pretty dragonfly, wearing a red loincloth like his. There's a game he likes to play, catching hold of dragonflies and making them carry tiny pebbles tied to their legs. But as he approaches the red dragonfly, it darts away and perches on a nearby jungle geranium shrub.

The boy creeps towards it, the thumb and forefinger of his right hand stretched out before him to catch the insect. Just as he reaches the plant, the dragonfly flashes away. Unni doesn't give up. Resolutely, he follows the dragonfly.

It pauses on a lantana bush. Just as he creeps inside the bush and reaches for the dragonfly, it flits away and lands on the Barbados nut bush. And then it's gone again. It descends lightly on an aloe vera leaf.

Cursing the waywardness of the dragonfly, Unni, without lowering his raised right hand, bites his lips, and waits quietly for the dragonfly to come to rest somewhere. It lifts off from the aloe vera bush and settles on the Barbados nut bush, its wings flat.

Close to where the boy is chasing the dragonfly, the rays of the midday sun have penetrated the foliage of the large jack tree, drawing a chiaroscuro of light on the ground.

There is movement in a hole in the ground at the base of the jack tree. The dry leaves rustle. A king cobra comes out and circles itself around the base of the rough, peeling trunk of the tree.

The dragonfly continues to sit on the branch of the Barbados nut bush.

Next to the bush are the sago palm and the pulakkalli tree. Unni's hands inch towards the dragonfly. He is completely focused on that branch. The dragonfly's red tail is the only thing he can see in the whole world now.

The sunshine, like molten silver, falls on his fingers. The red stone embedded in the ring on Unni's thumb flashes in the light and attracts the attention of the snake which has been drawing in the fragrance of the sago palm flower. It raises its head further, flashes its eyes, inflates its hood, and begins to rise.

The dragonfly doesn't move. Unni's hands move imperceptibly towards it.

Suddenly, the dragonfly moves a little from its perch and begins to beat its wings. It hovers near the branch on which it was sitting, describing small circles before settling back on the branch. It appears reluctant to move away from the sunlight on the branch of the shrub.

The king cobra is standing immobile, staring at the shining stone on the ring. The fingers of Unni's hand are formed in the shape of pliers, one frozen in mid-air. Unni's fingers begin to make minute movements. This time, they do not descend directly on the insect but in childish cunning, they approach the dragonfly from the right, a manoeuvre that brings him perilously close to where the king cobra is. Following the tiniest movements of Unni's fingers and the flashing of the stone on the ring, the serpent turns its hood. As the red light advances further and further, the serpent turns its hood back as if poised to strike.

The dragonfly is dozing off in the intoxicating sunshine. The fingers approaching the dragonfly have now reduced the distance between them to that of a mustard seed. A moment frozen. Unni closes in with his fingers like eyelids shutting. The dragonfly's tail is in his grip. The instant the dragonfly beats its wings and squirms about, Unni twists his body once like lightning, lets out a shout, and races across the riverbank, disappearing from sight.

Perplexed, the king cobra turns around. Then, as if having lost face, it slowly shrinks its hood, drops to the ground, flicks its forked tongue, sniffs one of the dangling screwpine bundles on the Barbados nut bush, coils briefly around the exposed bare root, then slithers past the pulakkalli tree and makes its way through the wild aloe vera plants, before vanishing from view.

THE SOLUTION

GOPINATH MOHANTY

*Translated from the Odia by Leelawati Mohapatra,
Paul St-Pierre, and K. K. Mohapatra*

DADHIBAMAN STARED OFF INTO THE DARKENING HORIZON, EYES dilated, face crushed by humiliation as he recalled the turbulent day at the office. He felt angry, hot, tired, and worried. Night was falling and he had just got home. A dog's day, toiling from ten to five, practically the whole time, unrelenting pressure at work, file upon file, no end in sight. And on top of all that, calls for explanations, reprimands, insults.

All for a measly salary of seventy-five rupees a month—not even the cost of three large sacks of rice in these hard times. Out of that, the house rent, the doctor's fees.... Laundry alone came to seven rupees, and firewood to fifteen, and so much else too. It was tough to make ends meet. Delicious food was only a dream; patched rags worn at home; skimp and save, skimp and save. How he and his family managed to hang on was a mystery. Ten years in the job, yet nothing more to show for it. His debts had only grown larger and the sheer pressure of work was nearly splitting his skull. The insults, the reprimands, the threats were only the final straw.

There—that was his life. Looking at the sahada tree at the back of the house he mulled things over. What more was there than work and reprimands? The future seemed as bleak as the past. They were his life; nothing more.

'Mein...mein...mein....' A tug at the hem of the rag wrapped around his waist and Dadhibaman came out of his reverie. His pet goat was demanding attention, producing a sound closely resembling 'I' in the national language: 'Mein...mein...mein....'

Dadhibaman bent over and patted the animal on the back. The soothing contact reduced his bitterness by half. His voice dripped with affection as he murmured his name: 'Betu! Betu!' Betu twitched his tail, raised himself up on his forelegs, shoved his nose into his master's face, and expressed himself in his native tongue. Then he moved away and scampered around a bit, the bells around his neck tinkling. He circled Dadhibaman, rubbed against him, and bleated: 'Mein...mein...mein....'

Just one year old, but how he had grown! Dadhibaman hadn't been able to put off his young son when he had asked for a kid goat as a pet. In the twelve months since then, Betu had grown a goatee, while Dadhibaman wondered whether or not to have him castrated.

Dadhibaman touched the goat. He ought to get a she-goat so they could raise some kids. The price of goat meat had soared; already three rupees a seer! Meat—curried, roasted, fried! The intimate relationship between the eater and the eaten always came to Dadhibaman as a revelation, increasing his desire to stroke the goat.

Dadhibaman continued to pet him.

As Dadhibaman's three young children came bounding out of the house, Betu began to prance around again, his bells tinkling. 'Betu!' The children chanted. 'Betu!'

Dadhibaman stood watching his life's main achievements. He had stuck to his damned job for the sake of his children. Why else would he have done it? Even a cobbler made five rupees a day, and a rickshaw puller, three—the coolie carrying sand and bricks made a rupee and a half. If he had had a paan shop he could have built a house for himself! Feyda Mian, who had just a bicycle repair shop, had managed to buy four houses in just twelve years, with still enough money to lend out at a high interest rate. Couldn't Dadhibaman have done the same?

He was afraid on account of his children, he realized, as he watched them. What if a business took two years to take off? How would he manage during that time? How would he earn at least a steady seventy-five a month? And if he didn't, what then?

No friend in the future, and none in the past! If he were about to starve to death, no one would come to his rescue. This is what made him hesitant. Shutting the unfulfilled dreams out of his mind, he sighed—business wasn't for him, it was not his destiny! Though those who succeeded in business weren't necessarily better than him. Many a time he had been about to give up his job, only to back out at the last moment—what would his children live on the first few years?

If not for this fear he'd gladly have left his bloody job—today, this very moment. The insults, reprimands, and jibes were becoming intolerable. Just today the big boss had clucked and tut-tutted for an hour, as if Dadhibaman had set fire to his house or something. And as if that weren't enough, the boss had then demanded a written explanation why Dadhibaman hadn't attended to such-and-such files.

Dadhibaman fished the boss's letter out of his pocket. The overpowering urge to read it yet again was like trying to find out if a wound had healed by picking its scab. He had almost learned the words by heart. What thundering language—demeaning, insulting, soul-killing! How would he reply? What reply would work? The pressure of work? No one would buy that. That he didn't get two square meals a day? That he didn't get enough sleep on account of his children constantly falling ill? No one would buy these either. If Lord Brahma had to work as hard as Dadhibaman, even he would make mistakes! Would anyone accept such an explanation? No one was willing to recognize the truth, but the same people would be content with clever lies! But what clever lies could Dadhibaman cook up? He was sadly lacking in imagination.

Dadhibaman smoothed the boss's letter out on the ground and went through it once again. Tears welled up in his eyes. What a life, what a wretched life!

'Mein...mein...mein....'

Dadhibaman lowered his head and gently pressed his eyelids to Betu's lips. The goat turned away, shook his ears, rubbed his head against his master's knees, and looked up at him in bewilderment.

A goat's life was fine, Dadhibaman reflected. Everyone's life was fine. Everyone's except his.

All of a sudden Betu snatched the letter from Dadhibaman's hand, and the folds of skin over his jaws started moving up and down furiously. Before Dadhibaman could stop him, the piece of paper was already inside his tummy.

'What—you gobbled it up, Betu? Now what explanation will I give?'

'Mein...mein...mein....' bleated Betu, shaking his beard. 'Don't worry,' he seemed to be reassuring him. 'I'm here for you.'

All this took some time to sink in, but when it did Dadhibaman was dumbstruck. This was the last straw. Instead of providing an explanation he would have to ask the head clerk for another copy of the boss's letter—an unpleasant prospect, at the very least. He thought he knew the letter verbatim, but now that it was gone, so was his memory of it.

The words seemed to have faded into oblivion, even as he wondered what is remembered and what is quickly forgotten.

Damn it, what's gone is gone! Suddenly resolute, Dadhibaman stood up. Betu's round eyes seemed to have become bloodshot. Dadhibaman suddenly remembered the enormity of the problem, and smoke seemed to come out of his eyes. When people had made up their minds not to be convinced by a genuine explanation, why provide any? No, he wouldn't bother; let them do as they pleased. Dadhibaman's self-control had crumbled. He was on fire.

He strode inside, Betu in tow. Heaped on the table were some office files. Picking up Betu he brought him near the table. Betu seemed to show great interest. All worked up, Dadhibaman pushed a file towards Betu's mouth. The goat wagged its short tail and gratefully fell on the task of disposing of the file at hand. The taste of the local newspapers and the papers the children did their homework on was familiar, but office work clearly had a distinct flavour! He placed his forelegs on the edge of the table and propped himself up. 'These files are so delicious,' he bleated from time to time, 'but there's so little to sate my hunger.'

Dadhibaman gently nudged another fat file towards Betu.

The next day, at around ten o'clock, the office watchman saw Dadhibaman coming from his house, just a stone's throw from the office, followed by a goat. There was a red ribbon with bells tied around the animal's neck. The bells were tinkling.

'Shoo! Scram! Beat it!' the watchman yelled at the goat. 'Look at the damned goat, it's trying to get in!'

'Stop, don't do that,' Dadhibaman said. 'He's a pet; he won't do any harm: he's just like a person.' Dadhibaman turned to the goat. 'Come on, Betu. Follow me.' Betu did, most obediently.

'So well-trained!' commented the watchman.

'Yes, just like a human; understands everything. Goats are like that. Haven't you seen how well they perform in circuses?'

In the office, Betu was introduced around.

'Well, well, a damn healthy specimen,' commented Ram. 'About ten seers of quality meat, don't you think?'

'But what's the use?' remarked Gopal. 'The meat would have a god-awful stink. Pity, Betu wasn't castrated when he was a kid.'

'Mein?' bleated Betu, looking askance.

'There'd be no foul smell to the meat, I tell you,' said Feyda Mian, 'if, as I do, you knew the secret of how to slit its throat!'

A lively discussion ensued about various meat dishes and their preparation. Betu took a leisurely stroll around the office and came back to his master. Butting his feet with his head, he seemed to ask, 'Mein?'

Dadhibaman turned over the wastepaper basket for Betu. The goat settled down at his feet and set about disposing of the scraps of paper.

Betu went about his job at a lively pace. Hour after hour passed. Done with all the wastepaper baskets, Betu turned his attention to the files sitting on the shelves. It didn't take him long to go through one. Once he'd caught hold of it, he was finished in minutes. Sometimes he pulled down eight or ten at a time. After a little rest, he'd reach for someone else's. It was a feast day.

Finally he reached the head clerk's table, loaded with piles of papers and files all marked 'urgent'. The head clerk had gone to see the big boss, and Betu set to lightening the poor fellow's load. After a bit of good work he ambled off, but not before depositing by the table a few precious droppings—a particularly good fertilizer.

'Betu,' Dadhibaman called out.

The goat came running back, his bells ringing.

'Come, lie down here.'

Betu wedged himself between Dadhibaman's legs.

The head clerk returned. 'You all have so many pending files that the boss is boiling. Now, tell me frankly—and I want your word on this—are you going to dispose of the files before the end of the day? What about you, Dadhibaman?'

'All done, sir.'

'Really? That's very good.'

'Mein?' Betu bleated, getting up. 'Mein?'

'Hey look, look, a bloody goat has strayed inside,' the head clerk shouted. 'Watchman!'

'The goat's my pet, sir,' Dadhibaman said. 'He's followed me to the office. He's no nuisance, sir; just let him be. The smell of a goat fights tuberculosis, you must know that, sir. At least that's what doctors say. And considering the dark, dingy halls in which we work....'

'Oh yes,' answered the head clerk, seeming to think out loud, his eyes riveted on the goat. 'Could easily make eight or ten seers of lovely meat. But why on earth didn't you get it castrated, Dadhibaman?'

'Mein!' Betu shook his beard, nimbly stepping up to the head clerk's table, with a large stack of 'urgent' files still on it. Betu's work was far from finished: there were plenty of disposals pending.

21

THE HOLY BANYAN

BAMACHARAN MITRA

*Translated from the Odia by Leelawati Mohapatra,
Paul St-Pierre, and K. K. Mohapatra*

IF YOU'VE EVER PASSED THROUGH NARIPUR, YOU WOULD'VE SAT AND rested for a while in the shade of the holy banyan. (The tree is no longer around, alas; bedevilled by humans, it gave up the ghost leaf by leaf—branches, roots and all.)

For a long time, the holy banyan was a well-known landmark. Spreading well over an acre, it once stood at the edge of the village; its hanging roots had become mighty trunks. The ground underneath it was clean, polished like a cement floor. The roads connecting Naripur to the surrounding villages—Dihasahi, Daitapur, Dhanua, and Gamara to the east, and Nuagaon, Nuapatna, and Ahmedpur to the west—all passed the tree.

To the north lay the village cremation grounds, littered with human skulls big and small, discarded torn mats, mattresses, and pillows of the dead. It resounded now and then with cries of Haribol, and the sobbing and wailing of women. They threw their clay cooking pots and pans into the growing heap of rubbish, took a dip in the pond, and returned home. The blazing cremation fires died down, silence and darkness surged back in again. After the period of mourning, everything returned to normal; life went on as before. But the dead remained dead, their flesh and bones enriching the soil, nourishing the grass and the weeds. What became of their souls? Christians believe they wait until Judgement Day and then, according to their karma, are sent either to heaven or to hell. Hindus believe in rebirth, the day after someone dies or two hundred years later. Atheists, of course, dismiss everything: once dead and turned to ashes, all is over! But doesn't the Bhagavad Gita say the soul endures forever? But no matter what the pandits say, the people of Naripur believed—and had reason to believe—that when a rebirth was delayed, many a soul, unable to get over their attachment to their former homes and families, chose to take shelter under the holy banyan. Even those who'd normally have found a place in heaven. Only the other day, Anta, a robust young man in the prime of life, passed away after an attack of cholera. His young widow cried so bitterly she fainted on the cremation ground. As Anta's relatives were returning home after the cremation, a fat branch of the holy banyan broke off and crashed to the ground. No whiff of a breeze, let alone of a hurricane or whirlwind. Unable to get over his love for his young wife, Anta's ghost had obviously settled in the big tree. No matter that within a month the young widow eloped with Ram Pradhan to Calcutta. This led to tongues wagging, and it came to light the young woman had poisoned her husband at the instigation of her lover. Anta's ghost was often sighted; it never left the tree.

No one could keep count of all the ghosts inhabiting it. Not only those of Naripur but the ghosts of several surrounding villages had chosen the tree as their nesting place. People claimed to have seen them climbing up and down the tree and roaming the roads.

Not a drop of rain nor a ray of sunshine could penetrate the holy tree's foliage. The ground beneath it stayed warm in winter, like a mother's lap, and dry in the monsoons. When it threatened to rain, cowherds would shelter their cattle, goats, and sheep under it. The animals would sprawl on the smooth surface and chew their cud in peace. The boys would climb up and prance about on branches as wide as roads, while some stretched out on their backs belting out snatches of a song: *Tell me, oh sweet damsel, whose daughter or wife are you, and who has reduced you to tears?* Others swung from the hanging roots.

A weary traveller, longing for a short rest on a hot summer day, would choose the shade of the mighty tree. Some said it gave forth a cool breeze to welcome visitors as soon as they came near. The traveller would take off his turban, wipe away his sweat, and lean back against the trunk to catch his breath. A while later he'd swig a bellyful of cool rice water, delicious with salt and crushed chillies, lie at the foot of the tree, and pass into deep, contented sleep. He'd awaken by late afternoon, when the shadows had grown long and, with a reverential bow to the tree, resume his journey. In winter, merchants would stop there for the night, accompanied by thirty or forty bullock carts piled high with merchandise. With the bullocks fed after being unyoked and tethered to the hanging roots, dinner cooked and eaten, everyone would drop off to sleep. The place, snug and warm as if under a blanket, kept the biting cold at bay. In the morning, after paying their respects to His Holiness, they'd go on their way.

The holy banyan had been planted by Banabehari some four generations ago. A quiet, honest, and truthful man, he felt disturbed by the bad blood between the two villages and went away to the high Himalaya to pray and meditate. In those days, community leaders did not have recourse to politics to solve problems; no, they considered all discord their personal failure and would undertake fasts and meditations, after which they would try with redoubled ardour to establish the rule of virtue. Quite unlike the leaders of today who advocate the rejection of religion and spirituality. There's apparently no place in modern, scientific society for such concepts, considered figments of the imagination. The only true aim of life these days is making money, creating wealth, through industry, through commerce; money alone matters. Well, time will tell who is right. Maybe imagination makes a god out of a human being, while science turns him into a demon.

After a year of penance and meditation in the Himalaya, Banabehari returned with a tiny banyan sapling and planted it at the edge of the village in a ceremony enthusiastically attended by people from nearly twenty-five nearby villages. The feasting went on for seven long days.

The sapling grew into a gigantic tree. Burying their differences, the villagers met and mingled in peace, harmony, and brotherhood under its vast canopy.

When Banabehari died, his ghost settled on its branches, instead of pushing off to heaven. Until recently, generations of his descendants had distributed rice water to thirsty passers-by under the tree during the summer. Whenever Batasundar, a descendant of Banabehari, recited the Sivastaka or the Siva-tandav Stotra by Ravana, not only the temple in which the mantras were chanted but the mighty tree, too, seemed to vibrate. Batasundar could not get over his attachment to Naripur, and when his mortal remains returned to the dust of the cremation ground, his ghost, too, decided to nest in the holy tree.

Every year, on the occasion of Dwitiya Osha, the tree was given a ceremonial bath. This was an important occasion, marked by the sound of drums, conch shells, and ululation. The tree was draped in new clothes, the main and the larger trunks were dabbed with vermilion. Incense sticks were lighted, their fragrance enveloping the place, and the feasting began. The Hindus from twenty-five villages even sat and ate with the Muslims of Ahmedpur. Shops sprung up, folk opera and pala troupes performed day and night.

Apart from this great annual celebration, there were smaller functions all round the year: offerings made when a wish came true—whether it was a child begotten, or that child getting a job. The tree had brought together people over a vast area. For four generations, it had been the centre of their existence.

The village of Haldia was to the north, bordering the Naripur cremation grounds. A large village, its inhabitants were richer and more educated. The children of Naripur went to work in the fields from an early age, minded cattle and picked up swear words instead of learning nursery rhymes like, *There goes Kanhai, the dark-complexioned, with Rohini's son....* No wonder the Naripur upper-primary school never grew into a middle school, while the middle school of Haldia had long since blossomed into a high school, and was all set to become a college. Haldia villagers were in business and government service, quite a few in high positions, too; the local MLA came from the village, as did the panchayat chairman. While Naripur was full of dingy little houses—its cowsheds bigger than its living rooms—Haldia had many brick-and-mortar buildings.

But Naripur's greatest pride was its mighty banyan tree, before which, no matter how big or important the other villages were, all had to bow their heads. It was the Kalpataru, the wish-fulfilling tree, a living god.

But times began to change. The Panchayati Raj came to stay. More and more people became educated. The economy changed. Like Bhagiratha bringing the Ganga to earth from the heavens, the architects of the country's destiny got funds from abroad, which then flowed from the centre to the states to the panchayats. These modern-day Bhagirathas even tried to direct the flow directly to their own states. Some funds disappeared in transit, just as the waters of the Ganga had—a crafty Lord Shiva or a Jahnu Muni could reroute the stream in their matted locks! But that made little difference. As long as the torrents jetted in full force, a little stealing here, a little pilfering there made no difference, did it? Well, who cared!

But the trouble started when those who had been deprived awoke and suddenly turned patriotic. Their attire changed overnight: white cap on the head, cloth bag slung from the shoulder, and coarse white dhoti down to the knees.

Naripur's Batakrishna was seen dressed like this one fine day. He had been working in a jute mill in Calcutta, but once he got the scent of what was cooking in the village he rushed there like a vulture to a carcass. It took him less than a moment to figure out how to divert the flow of funds from Haldia. The first thing he did was set up the Divine Banyan Development Committee and call for a meeting. People from the twenty-five villages attended. They decided that, henceforth, every village would contribute an anna a month to the development committee. Individuals wanting special services would have to cough up two rupees. The washerwomen could no longer carry away for free the mountains of dry leaves and twigs they swept up from under the tree; they'd have to pay a paisa for every bundle; and so on and so forth.

Batakrishna became the secretary of the committee. Funds were collected, and quite a handsome amount they added up to. Around the principal trunk of the tree a huge cement platform was built; smaller platforms came up around lesser trunks. A brick ashram was put up for Batakrishna, and he came up with ever new ideas to increase collections.

He recognized a brilliant opportunity in the poetic excellence of Jaan Mohammed of Ahmedpur. Jaan, a popular bard, wrote slim books of verses on subjects like 'The Quarrel between Mother and Daughter-in-law' and 'The City-smart Daughter-in-law from Cuttack' and sold them out of his bag, trudging from village to village. It was he who had earlier versified the story of Anta's wife poisoning him and then eloping with Ram Pradhan to Calcutta. That book had done quite well; the village women had snapped up copies. Batakrishna commissioned Jaan to pen *Miracles of His Holiness the Sacred Banyan*. When the book was ready, the name of Batakrishna appeared as its humble author. The stories of miracles spread, the number of pilgrims grew. Not only did the fame of the holy tree grow, but so did Batakrishna's too. More and more money flowed into the committee's coffers, and some of it found its way into Batakrishna's.

Batakrishna then made a foray into the village panchayat committee, becoming an ordinary member. Shortly afterwards a rumour began to circulate that a no-confidence motion against the president of the panchayat committee—Batuk from Haldia—was in the offing.

The roof on Batuk's second floor remained to be cast. He saw trouble approaching, but he wasn't one to take it lying down. A compulsive litigant, he always wreaked vengeance through the law courts. On his payroll could be found a phalanx of witnesses swearing to speak nothing but the truth and then proceeding to speak anything but. For just two rupees and a free meal, they could casually tell the most outrageous lies, even as they tripped miserably during cross-examination. Poor judge! What could he be thinking while reading the transcripts? The truth completely eclipsed by lies, like the moon by dark clouds.

Batuk was naturally much feared. Before the panchayat meeting convened to push through the no-confidence motion against him, he slapped four or five false cases on Batakrishna, with charges ranging from molestation and rape to cheating and committing burglary—involving all the important sections of the Indian Penal Code.

Batakrishna appealed to His Holiness and went on a fast, stepping up the sales of *Miracles of His Holiness the Sacred Banyan*. The cases were fought using the banyan's funds, the false witnesses were bought off. Batuk lost the presidency. Batakrishna took his place, but he claimed it was a victory for His Holiness, not for himself.

As the flames of fights between Naripur and Haldia leaped higher, the cracks between Naripur and the other villages surfaced too.

But Batuk became more determined than ever, hatching plans to bring a no-confidence motion against Batakrishna. He bribed the members, piled them into a truck and drove them to Bhubaneswar, where they were made to swear their loyalty and allegiance not only in the presence of the minister but before Lord Lingaraj in his temple over consecrated mahaprasad, before returning to their homes. All this before the night was over. The whole operation was carried out as stealthily as the silent movements of the sly murrel fish; not even their next-door neighbours got whiff of it.

But Lord Lingaraj's influence apparently did not extend as far as Naripur, which was under only the fiat of the holy banyan. Groups of pala singers, daskathia and jatra troupes, in addition to Jaan Mohammed, fanned out to the villages to spread the gospel of His Holiness and, in the process, the stories of Batakrishna's greatness. Neither Lord Lingaraj nor the minister was enough to pierce the wall of propaganda. Batakrishna eyed the position of the chairman of the panchayat, and seemed to inch closer to his goal by the day. He adopted the banyan tree as his election symbol.

It was then that it struck Batuk that the myth of the sacred banyan had to be shattered once and for all.

A couple of days afterwards, an ascetic was found in the cremation grounds of Haldia deep in meditation. His name was Batia Baba. The news eddied around that he was a worshipper of Goddess Kali, that he honed his spiritual powers on corpses at the dead of every new moon night. He had harnessed evil spirits and could destroy anyone by letting them loose, or just as easily could rid anyone of a chronic disease, or dogged ill luck, with a pinch of ash from his sacrificial firepit. Like lightning the news spread and soon there started an unending stream of people to the baba.

A few days later, a new panic gripped the villagers all around: their homes were being bombarded with stones and excrement at midnight. No one could figure out what was happening. Terrified, people went to Batia Baba to find out the cause and the cure. So Batia Baba went into a trance, and what he revealed after his puja stunned everybody. The issue was the ghosts of all twenty-five villages, who until now had lived in perfect peace and harmony in the branches of the sacred banyan, like the members of a large joint family, were having problems. The ghosts of Naripur, cussed as always, were suddenly trying to evict all others to have full run of the tree, and their evil designs were being supported by the Muslim ghosts of Ahmedpur. So, naturally, the homeless ghosts of the other villages were up to all sorts of mischief, including pelting homes with stones and faeces. What was the remedy? Let every village plant a banyan tree of its own to shelter its own ghostly population. A bright idea, it appealed to all. Dhulia, the chief of Batuk's lackeys, accosted him in private and suggested: 'Sir, why not slap the Naripur ghosts with Sections 17, 447, 426, 323, 500, 504, 325, 354, and 379 of the Indian Penal Code? We have a doctor who can issue medical certificates to order, though his graphic account of bruises can be misleading. And witnesses? Not only am I myself available, I can easily round up several others.' For once, Batuk was supposed to have lost his cool and told the lackey to bugger off.

The decision was taken that Batia Baba would plant the first banyan sapling in the Haldia cremation grounds and name it His Majesty the Mighty Banyan. The preparations afoot, Batuk left for Gaya to bring back a sapling of an ancient holy tree.

Batakrishna caught on to Batuk's plans and swung into action. It didn't take a lot of work. He caught hold of Naripur's Widow Bati. Although no great beauty, she had felled many a mighty man, just as she had saved some from doing time. She did not tolerate any opposition, if she was properly cajoled and appealed to.

Three or four days after she paid nocturnal visits to Batia Baba's ashram, the baba left Haldia to set up an ashram in Naripur.

When Batuk returned from Gaya, he found his wits deserting him. He had been outsmarted and was left gnashing his teeth. Asked why he had returned empty-handed, he spoke of the dream he had on the way. It was revealed to him that if the new banyan trees were not the offshoots of the holy banyan, the homeless ghosts would refuse to roost in them. Every village had equal rights over the banyan, and was free to break off branches and grow them into new trees. 'Besides,' he added, 'to tell the truth, the holy banyan is really my property. I own the land he stands on; I bought it from Sapani for five hundred rupees. I have paid the land rent for the last five years and have the receipts to show for it. But I'm donating the holy tree to the people of all twenty-five villages. You all are welcome to cut a branch, take it to your village, and grow your own holy banyan trees to save yourselves from the menace of your brood of ghosts.' Batuk Pradhan's generosity surprised everyone; they were in a hurry to act upon his suggestion. But the whole thing was kept under wraps for some time.

One day, at midnight or thereabouts, Batakrishna awoke to the sound of axes falling on the banyan tree. People from Haldia and a few from other villages were hacking off branches. It took minutes for the news to swirl through Naripur. Armed with knives, axes, sickles, spears, and sticks, its denizens came rushing out. A mighty branch came crashing down. It echoed eerily in the temple of Bateswar, sounding like the last gasp of Time Eternal.

The two sides promptly came to blows. The holy tree trembled. Volleys of deafening laughter issued from the temple. Doomsday had arrived. Into the fray jumped the Muslims of Ahmedpur, brandishing swords. Batuk had kept them on standby. The Muslims had borne a grudge against Naripur people, ever since Batakrishna had banished them from the communal worship of the holy tree.

The combatants scattered at the sight of the naked swords. Before running for his life, Dhulia buried, as instructed by Batuk, a large quantity of the deadliest poison under the main trunk of the sacred banyan.

The next morning the bodies of eight men and fifteen severely wounded were found at the foot of His Holiness. The ones who had sustained minor injuries had managed to crawl away.

The police arrived on the scene. Section 144 was imposed on and around the holy banyan. About a hundred arrests were made. Both Batuk and Batakrishna were handcuffed and taken into custody. All the sections of the IPC Dhulia had once suggested using against the ghosts were now cited against the two, with Section 302 for murder thrown in for good measure. Just as vultures and dogs arrive in droves to clean up carrion, touts and lawyers descended upon the villagers to make money. The wealth Batuk and Batakrishna had amassed seemed to vanish in a bonfire.

A few days afterwards, the holy banyan began to droop and wilt. The mighty tree seemed sunk in sorrowful meditation. Thinking about the past? Worrying about the future? Lord Shiva, the embodiment of eternal time, had swallowed poison during the churning of the oceans to save mankind. Perhaps the sacred tree had decided to give up the ghost to save the people of Naripur?

But, of course, it was a plain case of murder. But could a tree file a case against its assassins under Section 302? If you are a tree you have no recourse, and nobody laments your passing.

The government auctioned off the wood. The people of Naripur and Haldia, their resources burnt up in court cases, didn't have money enough to bid. The ones who did were the Muslims of Ahmedpur. They logged away the big trunks and branches. The Naripur folks bribed them to leave a little something behind—the smaller branches and twigs. In two days flat, the holy tree had completely vanished; not a vestige remained.

A civilization had come to an end. Another had begun. Nothing to worry about of course. Nothing remained forever, except eternal time.

Even to this day many people swear to have seen the ghost of Banabehari wandering about, lost, and to have heard the sound of his sighs and his wooden clogs slapping against the ground.

22

A FEAST FOR THE BOSS

BHISHAM SAHNI

Translated from the Hindi by Poonam Saxena

THERE WAS A FEAST FOR THE BOSS IN MR SHAMNATH'S HOUSE TODAY. Shamnath and his wife didn't have a moment to even wipe away their perspiration. The wife, in a dressing gown, tangled hair scraped back into a bun, unmindful of the powder and rouge spread all over her face, and Mr Shamnath, smoking cigarette after cigarette, holding a checklist in his hand, were going in and out of rooms.

Finally, by five o'clock, the preparations started falling into place. Chairs, tables, stools, napkins, flowers, everything had been moved to the veranda. The drinks had been arranged in the sitting room. Now all the useless household things were being hidden behind the almirahs and under the beds. That's when an obstacle presented itself to Shamnath—what was to be done with Ma?

Neither he nor his accomplished housewife had given this matter any thought. Mr Shamnath turned to his wife and asked in English, 'What about Ma?'

His wife stopped her work and after thinking for a while, said, 'Send her to her friend's house, the one who stays in the house behind. She can even stay the night. She can return tomorrow.'

With his cigarette in mouth, Shamnath looked at his wife with narrowed eyes for a moment, then shook his head and said, 'No, I don't want that old woman to start visiting our house again. We stopped those visits with such difficulty in the first place. We should tell Ma to eat her dinner in the evening and then go to her room. The guests will come around eight. She should finish with everything before that.'

The suggestion was reasonable. Both liked it. Then his wife said, 'But if she falls asleep and begins snoring? The veranda where everyone will eat dinner is right next door.'

'So we'll tell her to close the door from inside. I'll put a lock on the outside. Or I'll tell Ma not to sleep when she goes in, what else?'

'And if she falls asleep, what then? Who knows how late the dinner will go on? You keep drinking till eleven o'clock in any case.'

A bit irritated, Shamnath said, 'It was all set, she was going to my brother's place. But because you wanted to appear good and noble, you had to interfere.'

'Wah! Why should I become the villain between mother and son? Do what you want!'

Mr Shamnath was silent. This was not the time for an argument. A solution had to be found. He turned to look at Ma's little room. Its door opened onto the veranda. Looking at the veranda, he said quickly, 'I've figured it out,' and went and stood outside his mother's room. Ma was sitting on a low stool close to the wall, head and face wrapped in a dupatta, fingers moving over her prayer beads. Seeing all the preparations since the morning, she had been anxious and tense too. The bada sahib from her son's office is coming home, everything should go off satisfactorily.

'Ma, eat your dinner early today. The guests will come by seven-thirty.'

Ma slowly removed the dupatta from her mouth and, looking at her son, said, 'I'm not going to eat today. You know, beta, whenever meat or fish is cooked in the house, I don't eat anything.'

'Whatever it is, wrap up your routine early.'

'All right, beta.'

'And, Ma, we will first be in the sitting room. During that time, you stay in the veranda. Then when we leave, you go into the sitting room through the bathroom.'

Ma looked at her son, at a loss for words. Then she said slowly, 'All right, beta.'

'And, Ma, don't fall asleep early today. The sound of your snoring can be heard from far away.'

Shamefaced, she said, 'What can I do, beta? It's not in my control. Ever since I recovered from my illness, I can't breathe through my nose.'

Mr Shamnath had figured out the solution all right, but despite that, his dilemma persisted. What if the boss suddenly decided to come to this side of the house? There would be eight to ten guests, desi officers, and their wives. Anyone could go towards the bathroom. Anger and agitation sparked off his irritation all over again. Picking up a chair, he placed it in front of her room in the veranda and said, 'Come on, Ma, just sit here for a moment.'

Adjusting her pallu, carefully holding on to her beads, Ma got up, slowly went to the chair and sat down.

'Not like this, Ma, don't put your feet up. This is not a cot.'

Ma put her legs down.

'And, for God's sake, don't wander around with bare feet, and don't wear those wooden clogs. One day I'm going to throw them away.'

Ma kept quiet.

'What will you wear, Ma?'

'Whatever I have, beta. I'll wear whatever you tell me to wear.'

Cigarette in his mouth, Mr Shamnath looked at his mother through half-closed eyes and began to consider her clothes. He wanted everything to be just so. The supervision of the entire house was in his hands. Where should the wall pegs be placed in the rooms, where should the beds be placed, what should the colour of the curtains be, which sari his wife should wear, what the size of the table should be.... Shamnath wanted to be sure that if Ma were to appear before the boss, he, Shamnath, shouldn't be embarrassed. Looking at his mother from head to toe, he said, 'Wear a white salwar and white kameez, Ma. Go put it on now, let me see.'

Ma got up slowly and went to her room to wear the clothes.

'This problem with Ma isn't going anywhere,' he said to his wife in English. 'If it was some reasonable issue, then one could do something about it, but this.... If something were to go wrong and upset the boss, then everything will be spoilt.'

Ma came out wearing a white kameez and salwar. With her tiny, shrivelled-up body wrapped in white clothes, eyes dim and cloudy, half of her sparse hair covered by her pallu, she looked only a little less unsightly than before.

'Well, it's all right. If you have any bangles, put them on too. There's no problem.'

'Where will I bring bangles from, beta? You know very well that all my jewellery was sold to pay for your education.'

This sentence pierced Shamnath like an arrow. Flaring up, he said, 'Why are you raking up this topic, Ma? Just say you don't have jewellery, that's all. What is the connection with education-veducation? The jewellery may have been sold, but I've made something of myself. I haven't come out a useless fellow. You can take back double of what you gave.'

'May my tongue burn, beta, will I take jewellery from you? It just slipped out. If I had any bangles, I'd wear them thousands of times.'

It was already five-thirty. Mr Shamnath had yet to bathe and get ready. His wife had gone to her room long ago. Before leaving, Shamnath gave instructions to his mother once again, 'Ma, don't sit all silent and lost like you do every day. If sahib happens to come this way and asks you something, answer his question properly.'

'I'm not literate, beta, I'm not educated, what will I say to him? You tell him that my mother is illiterate, she doesn't know or understand anything. He won't ask me anything then.'

As seven o'clock approached, Ma's heart started beating fast. If the boss came to her and asked her something, what would she say in reply? She panics when she sees an Englishman even from a distance, this man is an American. Who knows what he may ask her? What will she say? Ma wanted to quietly slip away to her widowed friend's house at the back. But how could she go against her son's diktat. Silently, legs dangling, she sat on the chair.

A successful party is one where the drinks flow. Shamnath's party was kissing the pinnacle of success. Conversation flowed in an unbroken stream, with the same fluidity with which the glasses were getting replenished. There were no stoppages, no obstructions. The sahib had liked the whisky. The memsahib had liked the curtains, the design of the sofa cover, and the décor of the room. What more could one ask for? The sahib had started recounting humorous stories and anecdotes during the second round of drinks itself. He was as friendly here as he was intimidating in the office. And his wife, dressed in a black gown, a string of pearls around her neck, awash with the fragrance of scent and powder, had become the object of worship for all the desi women sitting in the room. She would laugh and shake her head at every comment and she chatted away with Shamnath's wife as if they were old friends.

And with all this conviviality and drinking, it was suddenly ten-thirty. No one realized where the time had flown.

Finally, everyone drained their glasses, got up for dinner, and walked out of the sitting room. Shamnath was leading the way, followed by the boss and the other guests.

As they reached the veranda, Shamnath suddenly stopped. The sight that met his eyes caused his legs to totter and, in a flash, all his alcohol-induced intoxication began to evaporate. In the veranda in front of her room, Ma was sitting as she had been, but both her feet were resting on the seat of the chair, her head was rolling from side to side, and loud snores were emanating from her mouth. As and when her head stopped rolling for a bit, the snores would become louder. And when her sleep would break for a moment, her head would once again start rolling from right to left. Her pallu had slipped from her head and her scanty hair lay disordered over her balding scalp.

As soon as he saw her, Shamnath became enraged. He felt like pushing her awake and shoving her into her room, but it was not possible to do this. The boss and the other guests were standing just there.

Seeing Ma, some of the wives of the desi officers tittered but the boss said softly, 'Poor dear.'

Ma woke up with a start. Seeing so many people standing in front of her, she got so panicky that she couldn't say a word. Quickly covering her head with her pallu, she stood up and stared at the ground. Her feet felt unsteady and the fingers of her hands trembled and shook.

'Ma, go and sleep, why are you awake so late?' Shamnath looked at the boss with mortification.

There was a smile on the boss's face. Standing there, he said, 'Namaste.'

Timidly, shrinking within herself, Ma put her hands together but one hand was inside the dupatta, holding her beads, the other outside. She couldn't do a proper namaste. Shamnath got even more annoyed at this.

By then the boss had extended his right hand. Ma became more nervous.

'Ma, shake his hand.'

But how could she shake hands? Her right hand was clasped around her beads. In her nervousness, Ma placed her left hand in sahib's right hand. Shamnath burned inside. The desi women giggled.

'Not like this, Ma! You know you have to shake hands with the right hand. Do it with your right hand.'

But by then, the chief, repeatedly pumping her left hand, said, 'How do you do?'

'Say that I'm all right, Ma, say I'm doing well.'
Ma mumbled something.
'Ma says she's fine. Say how do you do, Ma.'
Slowly, hesitantly, Ma said, 'How do do....'
Once again, there was a loud burst of laughter.

The mood lightened. Sahib had saved the moment. People had started laughing and talking. Shamnath's agitation subsided a little.

Sahib was still holding Ma's hand in his own, and she was shrinking further into herself. She could smell the alcohol on sahib's breath.

Shamnath said in English, 'My mother is from the village. She's lived all her life in the village. That's why she's so shy in front of you.'

Sahib appeared pleased at this. He said, 'Really? I like people from villages very much. Your mother must surely know some village songs and dances?' Shaking his head with delight, the boss was gazing raptly at Ma.

'Ma, sahib is saying, sing him a song. Any old song, you must know so many.'

Ma whispered, 'What can I sing, beta? When have I ever sung?'

'Wah, Ma! Can one turn down a guest's request? Sahib has asked you so eagerly; if you don't sing he'll feel bad.'

'What can I sing, beta, what do I know?'

'Wah! Why don't you sing a nice tappa? *Do pattar anaaran de....*'

The desi officers and their wives clapped their hands at this suggestion. Ma looked miserably first at her son's face and then at the face of her daughter-in-law, who was standing nearby.

And the son, in a voice that brooked no disobedience, said, 'Ma.'

After this, there was no question of a yes or no. Ma sat down and in a weak, trembling voice, began singing an old wedding song:

Hariya ni maaye, harya nimainde
Hariya tain bhaagi bhariya hai!

Oh mother of Hariya, sisters of Hariya
Hariya is blessed!

The desi women started giggling. After singing three lines, Ma fell silent.

The veranda resounded with the sound of applause. The sahib wouldn't stop clapping. Shamnath's vexation morphed into pride and pleasure. Ma had introduced a new mood into the party.

When the applause stopped, the sahib said, 'What is the craftsmanship in the villages of Punjab?'

Shamnath almost swayed with pleasure. He said, 'Oh, many things, sahib! I'll gift you with a set of all the things. You'll be thrilled when you see them.'

But the sahib shook his head and again asked in English, 'No, I don't want things from shops. What is made in the homes of Punjabis, what do the women make with their own hands?'

Shamnath thought for a while and said, 'Young girls make dolls, the women make phulkaris.'

'What is a phulkari?'

After an unsuccessful attempt to explain what phulkari was, Shamnath said to his mother, 'Ma, is there any old phulkari in the house?'

Ma went inside and came out carrying her phulkari.

The sahib looked at it with great interest. It was an old phulkari. The threads had come loose in many places and the cloth had started fraying. Noticing the sahib's look of interest, Shamnath said, 'This one is torn, sahib, I'll get a new one made for you. Ma will make it. Ma, sahib really liked the phulkari, you'll make one just like this for him, won't you?'

Ma was silent. Then, she said, her voice low and fearful, 'My eyes are not what they used to be, beta! What can these old eyes see now?'

But interrupting Ma midway, Shamnath said to the sahib, 'She'll definitely make it. You'll really like it.'

The sahib nodded, said thank you and then, lurching ever so slightly, moved towards the dining table. The other guests followed him.

When all the guests had sat down and their gaze had been averted from Ma, she slowly got up from the chair and, hiding from everyone's eyes, went into her room.

She had barely sat down in her room when the tears started flowing from her eyes. She wiped them with her dupatta, but they kept gushing out, as if they had burst through a dam that had held them in check for years. Ma tried again and again to calm her heart, she folded her hands, called out to God, prayed for her son's long life, but the tears, like the monsoon rain, would not be contained.

It was midnight. The guests had eaten and left. Sitting close to the wall, Ma kept staring at it with wide-open eyes. The tension in the house had lifted a little by now. The stillness in the rest of the neighbourhood had settled on Shamnath's house too. The only sounds, of plates clanking against each other, came from the kitchen. That's when the door to Ma's room started rattling loudly.

'Ma, open the door.'

Ma's heart sank. She got up in a panic. Did I make some other mistake? Ma had been cursing herself—why did she fall asleep, why had she started feeling drowsy? Had her son still not forgiven her? Ma got up and opened the door with trembling hands.

As soon as the door opened Shamnath swayed forward and caught her in an embrace. 'Oh, Ammi! You really set the mood today. Sahib was so happy with you that I don't know what to say! Oh, Ammi! Oh, Ammi!'

Ma's tiny form was lost in her son's embrace. Ma's eyes filled with tears again. Wiping them, she said hesitantly, 'Beta, send me to Haridwar. I've been telling you for so long.'

Shamnath's swaying stopped at once. His brow became furrowed with tension again. His hands fell from his mother's body.

'What did you say, Ma? What is this old story you've started again?' Shamnath's anger was rising, he said, 'You want to ruin my reputation so that the whole world can say that a son can't keep his mother with him.'

'No, beta, you can stay with your wife the way you would like to. I have lived my life. Now what will I do here? I will take God's name in the remaining days of my life. Send me to Haridwar!'

'If you go, who will make the phulkari? I agreed to give sahib the phulkari in front of you.'

'My eyes are not what they used to be, beta, that I can make phulkari. You can get it made somewhere else. Get a readymade one.'

'Ma, will you let me down and just go away like this? You'll ruin something that's working out so well for me? Don't you know, if the sahib is happy with me, I will get a promotion.'

Ma fell silent. Then, looking at her son's face, she said, 'Will you get promoted? Will your sahib give you a promotion? Has he said anything?'

'He hasn't said anything, but didn't you see how he went away so happy. He said, when your mother starts making the phulkari, I'll come and see how she makes it. If the sahib is pleased, I can get a bigger job than this one, I can become an important officer.'

The expression on Ma's face began changing. Gradually, her wrinkled face brightened, her eyes started shining with a gentle light.

'So you will get a promotion, beta.'

'Will I be promoted just like that? I'll have to please the sahib, only then will he do something, otherwise there's no dearth of people eager to please him.'

'Then I'll make it, beta, however I can, I'll make it.'

And in her heart, Ma once again began praying for her son's bright future. And Mr Shamnath, stumbling a little, said to his mother, 'Now go to sleep, Ma,' and left the room.

OF FISTS AND RUBS

ISMAT CHUGHTAI

Translated from the Urdu by Muhammad Umar Memon

THERE WAS QUITE A CRUSH OF PEOPLE AT THE POLLING STATION, AS IF IT was the premiere of some movie. A long line stretched out to infinity. Five years ago, too, we'd formed such endless lines, as if we'd come to buy cheap grain, not to cast a vote. Wisps of hope flitted across our faces: regardless of how long the lines, our turn was bound to come sometime. And then you just watch, we'll be raking in piles and piles of money. He's our trusted man; the reins of good fortune will be in the hands of one of our own. All our miseries will vanish.

'Bai, oh Bai! How are you?' The woman wrapped in a dirty-looking kashta bared her filthy yellow teeth and grabbed my hand.

'Oh, it's you, Ganga Bai....'

'No, Ratti Bai. Ganga Bai was the other one. She died, poor woman.'

'What a pity! Poor woman....' And my mind zoomed back five years. 'Rubs or fists?' I asked.

'Rubs,' Ratti Bai winked. 'I kept telling her not to, but why would she listen, the blasted woman. Who are you voting for, Bai?'

'And you, who for?' we asked each other casually.

'Our caste-wallah, of course. He comes from our area.'

'Five years ago, too, you voted for a man of your own caste, didn't you?'

'Yes, Bai. But he turned out to be a real scrap. He did nothing for us,' she said, making a long face.

'And this one, he's also from your caste?'

'But he's really first class. Yes, Bai. You'll see, he'll get us our farmland.'

'And then you'll go back to your village and thresh rice.'

'Yes, Bai,' her eyes flashed.

Five years ago, when I was in the hospital giving birth to my Munni, Ratti Bai said that she was on her way to the polling station to vote for her caste-man. He'd made a solemn promise before a crowd of tens of thousands gathered at Chowpatty that the second he came into power he would change everything. Milk would flow in rivers, life would become as sweet as honey. Today, five years later, Ratti Bai's sari was even shabbier, her hair even more grey, and her eyes twice as dazed. Hobbling on the crutches of promises made again today at Chowpatty, she'd come to cast her vote.

'Bai, why do you talk to that slut so much?' Ratti Bai opened her bundle of exhortations and advice as she pushed the bedpan under my cot.

'Why? What's the harm?' I asked, acting as though I didn't know.

'Haven't I told you? She's a very bad woman. Downright wicked, a slut.'

Before Ratti Bai came on her rounds, Ganga Bai had used exactly the same words to let me know her opinion of the former: 'Ratti Bai's a first-rate tramp.' The two hospital workers were always at loggerheads. Now and then they didn't even hesitate before coming to blows. I heartily enjoyed talking to them.

'That bum Shankar, he's not her brother.' Ganga Bai told me. 'He's her lover. Why, she sleeps with him!'

Ratti Bai's husband lived in a village near Sholapur. He had a small piece of land and was stuck to it. The entire yield was sucked up by debt and interest payments. Just a little bit was left; before long it too would be paid up. Then she would go and live with her children, happily ever after threshing rice to separate it from the husk. Both women dreamed with such longing of living happily pounding rice in their homes, the way a person dreams of Paris.

'But, Ratti Bai, why did you come to Bombay to earn money? It would have made more sense to have your husband come instead.'

'Oh, Bai, how could he? He works in the field. I couldn't have managed farming.'

'And who looks after the children?'

'Oh, there's a slut,' she said, calling her every bad name in the book.

'He hasn't married another woman, has he?'

'The bastard, he hasn't got the guts. No, she's a keep.'

'What if she becomes the mistress of the house in your absence?'

'How could she? Wouldn't I beat her hollow and stuff her with hay?'

'Once we've repaid the debt, I'll go back.'

It turned out that Ratti Bai had herself chosen the poor helpless woman left to care for her husband and children. Once the field became theirs, she would return home as a proper housewife and thresh rice. And what would become of the keep? Oh, she would find another man whose wife has gone to Bombay to earn money and who had no one to look after the kids.

'Doesn't she have a husband?' I asked.

'Why, of course.'

'So why doesn't she live with him?'

'The little land he had owned was gobbled up. He works as a farm labourer, but for eight months of the year he steals and pilfers, or wanders into big cities and supports himself panhandling all day long.'

'Does she have children?'

'Of course, she does. Four, at least she used to. One was lost right here in Bombay. Nobody ever found out what became of him. The two girls ran away and the youngest boy lives with him.'

'How much money do you send back to the village?'

'The full forty-one.'

'How do you get by?'

'My brother supports me.' The same brother Ganga Bai had said was her lover.

'Doesn't your brother have a family of his own?'

'Of course, he does.'

'Where do they live? In the village?'

'Yes. It's a place near Poona. His elder brother takes care of the farming.'

'You mean *your* elder brother,' I said just to tease her.

'Come on now. Stop it! Why would he be *my* brother? Oh, Bai, do you really take me for that kind of woman? I'm not like Ganga Bai. Do you know, hardly four days go by in a month that she doesn't receive a beating. Bai, if you've got any old, worn-out clothes, don't give them to that vile woman. Give them to me instead. Okay?'

'Ratti Bai.'

'Yes, Bai.'

'Does your "brother" whack you?'

'That tart Ganga Bai, she must have told you that. No, Bai, not very much. Just sometimes, when he's had too much to drink. But then he also shows affection.'

'He shows affection, too?'

'Why wouldn't he?'

'But, Ratti Bai, why do you call that scoundrel a brother?'

She started to laugh. 'Bai, that's just how we talk.'

'But Ratti Bai, when you earn forty rupees, why whore around?'

'How else would I manage? Three rupees for renting the kholi, the rathole where I live, and then I have to pay five to Lala.'

'To Lala, whatever for?'

'All the chawli women have to, otherwise he would throw us out.'

'Because you carry on this business?'

'Yes, Bai,' she seemed somewhat embarrassed.

'And your "brother", what does he do?'

'Bai, really I shouldn't say, but selling drugs is a nasty business. If someone doesn't bribe the police, they chase him out.'

'You mean throw him out of Bombay?'

'Yes, Bai.'

Meanwhile a nurse barged in and scolded her, 'What are you doing here jabbering away. Go, the bedpan needs to be removed in No. 10.' Ratti Bai promptly left the room, grinning, flashing her yellowed teeth.

'What's with you, you spend hours talking to these loose women. You need rest, otherwise you'll start bleeding all over again.' The nurse picked up my baby girl from the hammock and left the room.

Ganga Bai was on duty in the evening. She walked into my room without bothering to ring the bell first.

'Bai, I've come for the bedpan.'

'Oh no, Ganga Bai. Sit.'
'The sister will start hollering. The slut. What was she telling you?'
'Sister? Oh, she was telling me to rest.'
'No, not the sister. I mean that Ratti Bai.'
'Just that Popat Lal beats Ganga Bai black and blue,' I teased her.
'That son of a bitch, forget it. He wouldn't dare.' Ganga Bai started pounding slowly on my legs with her fists.
'Bai, you promised to give me your old chappals.'
'Okay, take them. But tell me whether you got a letter from your husband.'
'Of course.' Ganga Bai promptly pounced on the chappals. 'If that whore of a sister saw it, she would kick up a ruckus. She makes too much fuss.'
'Ganga Bai.'
'Yes, Bai.'
'When will you return to your village?'
Ganga's shining black eyes drifted off to the lush green haze of fields far away. She took a deep breath and said softly, 'May Ram give us an abundant crop this time. And then, Bai, I will go back. Last year the flood ruined all our rice paddy.'
'Ganga Bai, does your husband know about your "friends"?' I probed.
'What are you saying, Bai?' She became deathly quiet. I sensed she was feeling somewhat embarrassed. She immediately tried to change the subject, 'Bai, you had two girls in a row. The seth will be mighty angry, won't he?'
'Seth—who?' I asked, confused.
'Your husband. What if he got himself another wife?'
'If he did, I would also find myself another husband.'
'Your people do that? Bai, I thought you come from a high caste.' I couldn't help feeling that she was making fun of high-caste people. I tried my best to make her understand, but she firmly believed that by giving birth to a second girl I really would be thrashed. If my seth didn't beat me black and blue, then he must be an absolutely third-class seth.

Staying in a hospital is nothing less than solitary confinement. Friends and acquaintances visited me for two hours in the evening, the rest of the time I spent chatting and gossiping with Ganga Bai and Ratti Bai. Had it not been for them, I would probably have died long before then from boredom. A little bribe was all it took to get them to spill all kinds of things about each other, whether true or false. One day I asked Ratti Bai, 'You used to work in a mill, so why did you give that up?'
'Oh Bai, the blasted mill was a racket.'
'Racket?'
'Oh Bai, for one thing, it was awfully hard work. Still that would've been bearable, but the bastards kicked you out after a couple of months.'
'How so?'
'They would hire other bai log.'

'Why would they do that?'

'Why? Because if a person stayed for six full months, the Factory Law kicked in.'

'Oh, now I get it.'

In other words, the entire staff changed every few months. If any worker stayed longer in her job, she would be entitled to sick leave, maternity leave, the works, to comply with the Factory Law. So they kept switching workers every couple of months. That way a worker was employed for hardly four months a year. In between, women often returned to their villages. Those who couldn't afford to would run around to other factories looking for work. Some would roost along the sidewalks selling piles of rotten old vegetables. Swearing matches and fights broke out over turf. And since they carried on without a licence, they had to cough up some cash to 'feed' the policeman at the corner. Still, when an unfamiliar officer wandered that way now and then, there would be a veritable stampede. Some would quickly bag their merchandise and slither into a side street; some would get caught and start crying and wailing. But the police kept dragging them to the station. When the situation cleared up, they would swarm back, spread their tattered pieces of cloth and put their wares on display. The clever ones threw a few limes and ears of corn into a shoulder bag and walked along pretending to be shoppers themselves. When someone passed by, they would utter softly, 'Hey, brother, buy some corn. Just one anna a piece.' Buying vegetables from one of them was to practically invite cholera.

The totally wretched ones resorted to begging, and if the opportunity presented itself they weren't above a quickie on the run. Perfectly primped, at least in their opinion, with a wad of paan stuffed in their mouths, they strolled up and down in the dimly lit area by the railway station. A customer walked in, glances were exchanged, and the deal was struck. The customers were mostly milkmen from Uttar Pradesh, or homeless labourers with wives back in villages, or eternal bachelors who only had these squalid streets and sidewalks to call home.

One morning a brawl broke out between the two bais on the veranda. Ratti Bai plucked out Ganga Bai's topknot. In return, Ganga Bai broke Ratti Bai's mangalsutra—her marriage necklace of black glass beads—an assurance that her husband was still alive. The poor woman started sobbing inconsolably as if she'd been widowed. The cause of the fight was the cotton pads that were used for cleaning wounds or for pregnant women and then discarded. According to the city ordinance, they had to be carefully burned, but it turned out that the two bais would remove the soiled cotton from the containers, wash it clean, roll it into a bundle, and take it home. Since their relationship had become quite tense lately, Ganga Bai snitched about it to the supervisor. Ratti Bai started swearing at her, which quickly turned into fisticuffs. Both of them would have been fired but they whined and pleaded so much that the supervisor kept the matter under wraps.

Ratti Bai was a bit flabby and older. Ganga had really let her have it. When she came in to return the bedpan with a swollen nose, I asked, 'What do you do with the dirty cotton, Ratti Bai?'

'Wash it and dry it. It's perfectly clean.'

'And then?'

'Then we sell it to the cotton merchant.'

'Who would buy such germ-filled cotton from him?'

'The mattress man—the one who makes cushions for rich people's furniture.'

'Oh my God!' I bristled with revulsion. I remembered that when I had the cotton removed from a wicker sofa so that it could be re-fluffed, it had turned out to be completely dark. Oh no, was it the same cotton that was used for cleaning and dressing wounds! Is my daughter's mattress made from that too? My daughter, as delicate and fair as a flower, and this pile of germs! God curse you, Ganga Bai! God take you away, Ratti Bai!

Because they had gone after each other with their shoes today, Ratti Bai was writhing inside. And since Ganga was relatively younger, Ratti Bai considered her a greater sinner than herself. To add more fuel to the fire, a few days ago she'd managed to snatch Ratti Bai's standing customer. All those abortions Ganga Bai had had over time, and the live baby she had dumped in the gutter that still kept breathing even after she stuffed the umbilical cord in its mouth! A whole crowd had gathered near it. If Ratti Bai had wanted to, she could easily have spilled the beans and got her caught, but she buried the secret in her chest. And look at the cheek of that vile woman, the way she sits on the sidewalk selling piles of unripe jujube and guava, as though nothing had happened.

'Friendship is one thing, but what if something went wrong, Ratti Bai? Isn't it better to go to the hospital?'

'Why should we? We've got plenty of bais among us who are as good as any doctor. Absolutely first class.'

'Do they give you medicine to get rid of the foetus?'

'Of course they do. What did you think? Then there is this fists method, but rubs work best.'

'What is this "fists", "rubs"?'

'Bai, you won't understand.' Ratti Bai blushed a little and started to laugh. She had been eyeing my powder case for some days now. Whenever she dusted me with it, she would put a pinch on her palm and rub it on her own cheeks. I thought the box would be enough to get her to talk. When I offered it to her, she took fright.

'No, Bai, the sister would kill me.'

'No, she won't. I'll tell her I didn't like the smell of the powder.'

'Why it smells fine, very fine. Oh Bai, you're crazy in the head.'

After a good deal of prodding, she described the details of 'rubs' and 'fists'.

'Rubs' work perfectly during early pregnancy—like a doctor, absolutely first class. The bai makes the woman lie down flat on the floor, then holding herself with a rope suspended from the ceiling or to a club, she stands on the woman's stomach and works it with her feet real well, until the 'operation' is performed. Or she makes the woman stand against the wall and after combing her own hair she ties it tightly into a topknot. Then, after dousing it with a fistful of mustard oil, she bangs it against the woman's legs like a ram. Certain young women, used to hard labour, don't respond to this. Then it's time for 'fists'. After dipping her unscrubbed hands with their grimy nails in oil, she just pulls out the throbbing life from the womb.

Most of the time the operation goes off without a hitch on the very first assault. If the performing bai happens to be a novice, sometimes one of the hands is broken off, or the neck comes out dangling, or even a part of the woman's own body that needed to stay inside spills out.

Not too many die from the 'rubs', but the woman generally falls prey to all kinds of disease. Different parts of her body swell up. Permanent wounds form and never heal, and if her time's up, she dies. 'Fists' are used sparingly—only when everything else fails. Those who survive aren't able to walk. Some drag on for a few years and then die.

I threw up. Ratti Bai, who was describing all this with relish, panicked and ran off. I felt overwhelmed in the dreary silence of the hospital. Oh God, such a dreadful punishment for bringing life into this world—I thought, drifting off into a haze.

My throat was stinging from pure horror. My imagination began colouring in the pictures Ratti Bai had drawn for me and then breathed life into them. The shadow of the window curtain was trembling on the wall. Soon it began to flail like a blood-soaked corpse on which Ganga Bai had applied her 'rubs'. A horrific iron clamp in the shape of a fist with filthy nails sank its teeth deep into my brain. Tiny fingers, a drooping neck, in a sea of blood—the prize of the first assault. My heart sank, my mind felt dazed! I tried to scream, to call someone, anyone, but my throat jammed. I tried to reach for the bell, but my hand wouldn't move. Silent cries were stifled inside my breast.

It was as if the screams of someone murdered suddenly shot up in the impenetrable silence of the hospital. They rose from my own room, but I was unable to hear them, unable to hear anything that was spilling from my own mouth unconsciously.

'You must have had a dreadful nightmare,' said the nurse as she stabbed me with the syringe of morphine. I tried to tell her, 'Sister, please, don't. Look, there, the dead body covered with blood from Ganga Bai's rubs is writhing on the cross. Its cries are piercing my heart like a poker. The feeble sobs of the child dying in some gutter far away are pounding in my brain like a hammer. Don't give me morphine to dull my senses. Ratti Bai has to go to the polling booth. The newly elected minister is her caste-man. Her debt will be paid up with interest now. Ganga Bai will happily thresh rice. Please lift this mantle of sleep from my mind. Let me be awake. The spots left by Ganga Bai's blood are swelling on the white sheet. Let me be awake.'

I woke up when the man sitting behind the desk looking like a clerk stamped one of the fingers of my left hand with blue ink.

'Vote for *our* caste-man, okay,' Ratti Bai admonished me.

The ballot box of Ratti Bai's caste-man rose like a massive fist and came down with all its awesome power on my heart and mind. I didn't drop my vote into that box.

PORTRAIT OF A LADY

KHUSHWANT SINGH

My grandmother, like everybody's grandmother, was an old woman. She had been old and wrinkled for the twenty years that I had known her. People said that she had once been young and pretty and had even had a husband, but that was hard to believe. My grandfather's portrait hung above the mantelpiece in the drawing room. He wore a big turban, and loose-fitting clothes. His long white beard covered the best part of his chest and he looked at least a hundred years old. He did not look the sort of person who would have a wife or children. He looked as if he could only have lots and lots of grandchildren. As for my grandmother being young and pretty, the thought was almost revolting. She often told us of the games she used to play as a child. That seemed quite absurd and undignified on her part and we treated them like the fables of the prophets she used to tell us.

She had always been short and fat and slightly bent. Her face was a criss-cross of wrinkles running from everywhere to everywhere. No, we were certain she had always been as we had known her. Old, so terribly old that she could not have grown older, and had stayed at the same age for twenty years. She could never have been pretty; but she was always beautiful. She hobbled about the house in spotless white, with one hand resting on her waist to balance her stoop and the other telling the beads of her rosary. Her silver locks were scattered untidily over her pale, puckered face, and her lips constantly moved in inaudible prayer. Yes, she was beautiful. She was like the winter landscape in the mountains, an expanse of pure white serenity breathing peace and contentment.

My grandmother and I were good friends. My parents left me with her when they went to live in the city and we were constantly together. She used to wake me up in the morning and get me ready for school.

She said her morning prayer in a monotonous sing-song while she bathed and dressed me in the hope that I would listen and get to know it by heart. I listened because I loved her voice but never bothered to learn it. Then she would fetch my wooden slate which she had already washed and plastered with yellow chalk, a tiny earthen ink pot, and a reed pen, tie them all in a bundle and hand it to me. After a breakfast of a thick, stale chapatti with a little butter and sugar spread on it, we went to school. She carried several stale chapattis with her for the village dogs.

My grandmother always went to school with me because the school was attached to the temple. The priest taught us the alphabet and the morning prayer. While the children sat in rows on either side of the veranda singing the alphabet, or the prayer in a chorus, my grandmother sat inside reading the scriptures. When we had both finished, we would walk back together. This time the village dogs would meet us at the temple door. They followed us to our home, growling and fighting each other for the chapattis we threw to them.

When my parents were comfortably settled in the city, they sent for us. That was a turning point in our friendship. Although we shared the same room, my grandmother no longer came to school with me. I used to go to an English school in a motor bus. There were no dogs in the streets and she took to feeding sparrows in the courtyard of our city house.

As the years rolled by, we saw less of each other. For some time, she continued to wake me up and get me ready for school. When I came back, she would ask me what the teacher had taught me. I would tell her English words and little things of Western science and learning, the law of gravity, Archimedes' principle, the world being round, etc. This made her unhappy. She could not help me with my lessons. She did not believe in the things they taught at the English school and was distressed that there was no teaching about God and the scriptures. One day I announced that we were being given music lessons. She was very disturbed. To her music had lewd associations. It was the monopoly of harlots and beggars and not meant for gentlefolk. She rarely talked to me after that.

When I went to university, I was given a room of my own. The common link of friendship was snapped. My grandmother accepted her seclusion with resignation. She rarely left her spinning wheel to talk to anyone. From sunrise to sunset she sat by her wheel, spinning and reciting prayers. Only in the afternoon she relaxed for a while to feed the sparrows.

While she sat in the veranda breaking the bread into little bits, hundreds of little birds collected around her, creating a veritable bedlam of chirrupings. Some came and perched on her legs, others on her shoulders. Some even sat on her head. She smiled but never shooed them away. It used to be the happiest half-hour of the day for her.

When I decided to go abroad for further studies, I was sure my grandmother would be upset. I would be away for five years, and at her age one could never tell. But my grandmother could. She was not even sentimental. She came to leave me at the railway station but did not talk or show any emotion. Her lips moved in prayer, her mind was lost in prayer. Her fingers were busy telling the beads of her rosary. Silently she kissed my forehead, and when I left I cherished the moist imprint as perhaps the last sign of physical contact between us.

But that was not so. After five years I came back home and was met by her at the station. She did not look a day older. She still had no time for words, and while she clasped me in her arms I could hear her reciting her prayer. Even on the first day of my arrival, her happiest moments were with her sparrows, whom she fed longer and with frivolous rebukes.

In the evening a change came over her. She did not pray. She collected the women of the neighbourhood, got an old drum, and started to sing. For several hours she thumped the sagging skins of the dilapidated drum and sang of the homecoming of warriors. We had to persuade her to stop to avoid overstraining. That was the first time since I had known her that she did not pray.

The next morning she was taken ill. It was a mild fever and the doctor told us that it would go. But my grandmother thought differently. She told us that her end was near. She said that since only a few hours before the close of the last chapter of her life she had omitted to pray, she was not going to waste any more time talking to us.

We protested. But she ignored our protests. She lay peacefully in bed, praying and telling her beads. Even before we could suspect, her lips stopped moving and the rosary fell from her lifeless fingers. A peaceful pallor spread on her face and we knew that she was dead.

We lifted her off the bed and, as is customary, laid her on the ground and covered her with a red shroud. After a few hours of mourning we left her alone to make arrangements for her funeral.

In the evening we went to her room with a crude stretcher to take her to be cremated. The sun was setting and had lit her room and veranda with a blaze of golden light. We stopped halfway in the courtyard. All over the veranda and in her room right up to where she lay dead and stiff, wrapped in the red shroud, thousands of sparrows sat scattered on the floor. There was no chirping. We felt sorry for the birds and my mother fetched some bread for them. She broke it into little crumbs, the way my grandmother used to, and threw it to them. The sparrows took no notice of the bread. When we carried my grandmother's corpse off, they flew away quietly. Next morning the sweeper swept the breadcrumbs into the dustbin.

LAAJWANTI

RAJINDER SINGH BEDI

Translated from the Urdu by Muhammad Umar Memon

TOUCH THE LEAVES OF THE LAAJWANTI, THEY CURL AND WITHER AWAY. After Partition, when countless wounded people had finally cleaned the gore from their bodies, they turned their attention to those who had not suffered bodily but had been wounded in their hearts.

Rehabilitation committees were formed in every neighbourhood and side street and the campaign to help the victims acquire business, land, and homes for themselves got underway with much enthusiasm. There was one programme, though, which seemed to have escaped notice. It concerned the rehabilitation of abducted women. Its rallying cry was 'Rehabilitate them in your hearts!' It was bitterly opposed by Narain Bawa's temple and the conservatives who lived in and around it.

A committee was formed in the Mulla Shakur neighbourhood near the temple to get the programme off the ground. Babu Sundar Lal was elected its secretary by a majority of eleven votes and the Vakil Sahib its president. It was the opinion of the old petition writer of the Chauki Kalan district—in which other well-regarded individuals of the neighbourhood concurred with him—that no one could be expected to work more passionately for the cause than Sundar Lal, because his own wife, Laaju—Laajwanti—too had been abducted.

Early in the morning when Babu Sundar Lal and his companions Rasaloo and Neki Ram used to make their rounds through the streets singing in unison, *Touch the leaves of the laajwanti, they curl and wither away*! Sundar Lal's voice would fade. Walking along in silence he would think about Laajwanti—who knows where she might be? In what condition? What would she be thinking of him? Would she ever come back?—and his feet would falter on the cobblestone pavement.

But by now things had reached a point where he had stopped even thinking about Laajwanti. His pain was no longer just his; it had become part of the world's anguish. And to spare himself its devastation he had thrown himself headlong into serving the people. All the same, every time he joined his companions in that song, he couldn't help wondering at how delicate the human heart is. The slightest thing could hurt it. Exactly like the laajwanti plant, whose leaves curl up at the barest touch. Well, that may be. But for his own part, he had never spared any effort in treating his own Laajwanti as badly as possible. He would beat her on the flimsiest pretext, taking exception to the way she got up, the way she sat down, the way she cooked food—anything and everything.

Laaju was a slender and agile village girl. Too much sun had turned her skin quite dark, and a nervous energy informed her movements, which brought to mind the fluid grace of a dewdrop rolling like mercury on a leaf: now to one side, now to the other. Her slim build, which was more a sign of health than its absence, worried Sundar Lal at first, but when he observed how well she could take all manner of adversity, including even physical abuse, he progressively increased his mistreatment of her, quite forgetting that past a certain limit anyone's patience is sure to run out. Laajwanti, too, had contributed her share in obscuring the perception of such a limit. She wasn't, by nature, one to dwell on her anguish for too long. A simple smile from Sundar Lal following the worst fight, and she was unable to stop her giggles: 'If you beat me ever again, I'll never speak to you!'

It was obvious she had already forgotten all about the fights and beatings. That's how husbands treat their wives—she knew this truth as well as any other village girl. If a woman showed the slightest independence, the girls themselves would be the first to disapprove. 'Ha, what kind of man is he? Can't even keep his wife in line!' The physical abuse men subjected their wives to had even made it into the women's songs. Laaju herself used to sing:

Marry a city boy?—No sir, not me. Look at his boots, and my waist is so narrow.

Nonetheless, at the very first opportunity she had fallen in love with just such a city boy, Sundar Lal, who had first come to her village as part of a wedding party and had whispered into the groom's ear, 'Your sister-in-law is pretty sexy, yaar! Your wife must be quite hot too!'

Laajwanti had overheard him. She took no notice at all of his large, heavy boots, and forgot all about her own narrow waist.

Such were the memories that Sundar Lal recalled during his early morning rounds with his companions. He would say to himself, 'If I could get another chance, just one more chance, I'd rehabilitate Laaju in my heart. I'd show the people that these poor women are hardly to blame for their abduction, their victimization by lecherous rioters. A society which is unable to accept and rehabilitate these innocent women is rotten to the core, fit only to be destroyed.'

Sundar Lal would plead with the people to take these women under their roofs and give them the same status which any woman, any mother, daughter, sister, or wife enjoyed. He would urge the families never to mention, even to hint at the things the poor women had to suffer, because their hearts were already wounded, already fragile, like the leaves of the touch-me-not plant, ready to curl up at the merest touch.

The Mulla Shakur Rehabilitation of Hearts Committee took out many early morning processions to put its programme into effect. The early hours of the morning were the most feasible time for their activity: no human noise, no traffic snarls. Even the dogs, after an exhausting, night-long watch, would be asleep at this hour, as they lay curled up inside the tandoors long since gone cold. And people, huddled in their beds, would wake up to mumble drowsily, 'Oh, that group again!'

People listened to Sundar Lal Babu's propaganda, sometimes with patience, sometimes with irritation. Women who had made it safely to this side of the border lay relaxed in their beds, while their husbands, lying stiff beside them, mumbled protests against the noise kicked up by the morning rally, or a child somewhere opened its eyes for a moment and fell back to sleep, taking the doleful petition of 'Rehabilitate them in your hearts' for a lullaby.

Words which enter the ear so early in the morning rarely fail to produce an effect. They reverberate in the mind the entire day, and even if their underlying meaning is not plain, one nonetheless finds oneself repeating them. So, thanks to this effect, when Miss Mridula Sara Bai secured the exchange of abducted women between India and Pakistan, some people in the Mulla Shakur neighbourhood willingly took their women back. They went to receive them outside the city at Chauki Kalan. For a while the abducted women and their relatives faced each other in awkward silence. Then, with their heads bent low, they returned to pick up the pieces of their lives and rebuild their homes. Meanwhile Rasaloo, Neki Ram, and Sundar Lal encouraged them with slogans, now of 'Long Live Mahendar Singh!', now of 'Long Live Sohan Lal!' They kept it up until their throats went dry.

But there were some abducted women whose husbands, parents, or siblings refused even to recognize them. As far as their families were concerned, they should have killed themselves. They should have taken poison to save their virtue. Or jumped into a well. Cowards—to cling to life so tenaciously!

Hundreds, indeed thousands, of women had in fact killed themselves to save their honour. But what could they know of the courage it took just to live on? What could they know of the icy stares it took for the survivors to look death in the face, in a world where even their husbands refused to recognize them? One or another of the abducted repeats her name to herself: 'Suhagwanti'—she who has suhag, the affection of her husband. She spots her brother in the crowd and says only this one final time, 'Even you, Bihari, refuse to recognize me! I took you in my lap and fed you when you were small.' Bihari wants to slip away, but he looks at his parents and freezes, who steel their hearts and look expectantly at Narain Bawa, who in turn looks in utter helplessness at the sky—which has no reality, which is merely an optical illusion, the limit beyond which our eyes do not reach.

Laaju, however, was not among the abducted women Miss Sara Bai brought back in the exchange. Sundar Lal, balanced precariously between hope and despair, saw the last girl come down from the military truck. Subsequently, with quiet determination, he redoubled his efforts in advancing the work of his committee. No longer only in the mornings, the committee took out an evening rally as well, and now and then also held meetings at which the old barrister Kalka Parshad Sufi, the committee's president, held forth in his raspy, asthmatic voice, with Rasaloo always tending his duties beside him, holding the spittoon. Strange sounds would pour out from the loudspeaker: 'kha-ba-ba-ba, kha-kha....' Next, Neki Ram, the petition writer of the Chauki, would get up to say something. But whatever he said or quoted from the Shastras or Puranas served only to contradict his point. Just then Sundar Lal would move in to salvage the situation. But he couldn't manage more than a couple of sentences. His voice would become progressively hoarser and tears would roll down his cheeks. He would give up and sit down. A strange silence would sweep over the audience. Sundar Lal Babu's two sentences, which sprang from the depths of his heart, affected them more than all the eloquence of the old barrister Kalka Parshad Sufi. But the people shed a few tears then and there, which eased their hearts, and returned home, as empty-headed as ever.

One day the committee-wallahs started out on their preaching mission early in the evening and ended up in an area long known to be a conservative stronghold. Seated on a cement platform around a peepul tree outside the temple, the faithful were listening to stories from the Ramayana. Narain Bawa was narrating the episode in which a washerman had thrown his wife out of the house saying, 'I'm no Raja Ramchandar, who would take Sita back after she had spent so many years with Ravan.' Which led Ramchandarji to order the virtuous Sita out of the house even though she was with child.

'Can you find a better example of Ram Raj?' asked Narain Bawa. 'True Ram Raj is one in which a washerman's words too receive the utmost consideration.'

The rally had by now reached the temple and it stopped to listen to the Ramayana story and pious hymns. Sundar Lal caught the last few words and retorted, 'We don't want Ram Raj, Bawa.'

Angry voices shot up from the throng of the faithful:

'Be quiet!'

'Who do you think you are?'

'Shut up!'

But Sundar Lal, undaunted, moved forward. 'Nobody can stop me from speaking!' he shouted back.

To which he received a fresh volley of equally angry words—'Quiet!' 'We won't let you speak!'—and from a corner, even the threat, 'We'll kill you!'

Narain Bawa said to him gently, 'Sundar Lal, my dear man, you don't understand the rules and regulations of the Shastras.'

'But I do understand one thing, Bawa. And it is that even a washerman could be heard in Ram Raj, while its champions today won't even listen to Sundar Lal.'

The very people who a minute ago had got up determined to put him in his place quickly sat down, sweeping away the peepul fruit which had meanwhile fallen on their seats, and said, 'All right, let's hear him out.'

Both Rasaloo and Neki Ram spurred Sundar Lal on, who said, 'No doubt Shri Ram was our great leader. But why is it, Bawaji, that he believed the washerman but not his own wife, the greatest maharani ever?'

Narain Bawa explained, putting a novel spin on it. 'Sita was his own wife. It would appear, Sundar Lal, that you have not realized the importance of this fact.'

'Yes, Bawa,' Sundar Lal Babu said, 'there are many things in this world that I don't understand. But as I look at it, under true Ram Raj, man wouldn't be able to oppress even himself. Injustice against oneself is as great a sin as injustice against another. Today, Lord Ram has again thrown Sita out of his house, just because she was compelled to live with Ravan for some time. But was she to blame for it? Wasn't she a victim of deceit and trickery, like our numberless mothers and sisters today? Was it a question of Sita's truth or falsehood? Or of the stark beastliness of the demon Ravan, who has ten human heads, but also has another, bigger one, that of a donkey. Today our Sita has been expelled once again, totally without fault, our Sita...Laajwanti....' He broke down and wept.

Rasaloo and Neki Ram raised the red banners on which the schoolchildren had that very day skilfully cut out and pasted different slogans for them, and the procession got going once again, all shouting 'Long Live Sundar Lal Babu!' in unison. Then someone yelled 'Long Live Sita—the Queen of Virtue!' and someone else 'Shri Ramchandar....'

'Silence! Silence!' a joint cry went up. Within seconds, months of Narain Bawa's labour was wasted, as a good portion of his congregation got up and joined the procession, led by barrister Kalka Parshad and Hukm Singh, the petition writer at Chauki Kalan, both triumphantly tapping their old walking sticks on the ground. Sundar Lal walked along with them. Tears were still streaming down his cheeks. His heart had been hurt very badly today. The people were shouting with great gusto:

Touch the leaves of the laajwanti, they curl and wither away.

The song was still reverberating in the ears of the people. The sun had not yet risen and the widow in house number 414 in Mulla Shakur was still tossing restlessly in her bed. Just then Lal Chand, who was from Sundar Lal's village and whom the latter and Kalka Parshad, using their influence, had helped to set up a ration shop, rushed over to Sundar Lal's. He offered his hand from under his thick, coarse shawl and said, 'Congratulations, Sundar Lal!'

'Congratulations for what, Lal Chand?' Sundar Lal asked, putting some molasses-sweetened tobacco in his chillum.

'I just saw Laaju Bhabhi.'

The chillum fell from Sundar Lal's hand and the tobacco scattered on the floor. 'Where!?' he asked, grabbing Lal Chand by the shoulder, and shaking him hard when he didn't answer quickly enough.

'At the Wagah border.'

He abruptly let go of Lal Chand's shoulder. 'Must be someone else.'

'No, bhaiya, it really was Laaju,' Lal Chand tried to convince him. 'She was Laaju all right.'

'Do you even know her?' Sundar Lal asked as he gathered the tobacco and ground it between his palms. 'Well then,' he said, removing the chillum from Rasaloo's hookah, 'tell me, what are her distinguishing marks?'

'A tattoo on her chin, another on her cheek.'

'Yes, yes, yes!' Sundar Lal himself completed the description. 'And a third one on her forehead.' He didn't want there to be any doubt.

Suddenly he recalled all those tattoos on Laajwanti's body he had known so well, tattoos she had got as a little girl, which resembled the light green spots on the touch-me-not plant and caused it to curl up its leaves at the slightest hint of an approaching hand. Exactly the same way, Laajwanti would curl up from modesty the instant anyone pointed at her tattoos. She would withdraw into herself and disappear, afraid that all her secrets had been let out, that she had been made poor by the plunder of a hidden treasure. And Sundar Lal's entire body began to burn with an unknown fear, with an unknown spirit and its purified fire. He grabbed Lal Chand by the shoulder once again and asked, 'How did Laaju get to Wagah?'

'There was an exchange of abducted women between India and Pakistan,' Lal Chand said.

'What happened then?' Sundar Lal asked, as he squatted down on the floor. 'Tell me, what happened then?'

Rasaloo too sat up in his cot and asked, coughing as only smokers do, 'Is it really true? Laajwanti Bhabhi's returned?'

Lal Chand continued. 'At the Wagah border, Pakistan handed over sixteen women and received sixteen in exchange. But an altercation developed. Our volunteers objected that there were too many middle-aged, old, and useless women in the contingent Pakistan was handing over. A crowd quickly gathered on the scene. Just then, volunteers from the other side pointed at Laaju Bhabhi and said, "Here, you call her old? Have a look. None of the girls you have returned can match her." Meanwhile Laaju Bhabhi was frantically trying to hide her tattoos from the people's probing eyes. The argument got more heated. Each side decided to take back their "goods". I cried out, "Laaju! Laaju Bhabhi!" But our own military guards beat us up and drove us away for making a racket.'

Lal Chand bared his elbow to show where he had been struck by a lathi. Rasaloo and Neki Ram remained silent, while Sundar Lal gazed far away into space. Perhaps he was thinking about Laaju, who had returned, but then again had not. He looked like someone who had just crossed the scorching sands of Bikaner and now sat panting under the shade of a tree, his parched tongue hanging out, too exhausted even to ask for water.

The realization struck him that the violence of the pre-Partition days still continued even after Partition, only in a different form. Today, people didn't even feel sympathy for the victims. If you asked someone about, say, Lahna Singh and his sister-in-law, Bantu, who used to live in Sambharwala, quick and curt would come the answer: 'Dead!' and the fellow would move on, unaware of death and the difference it made.

Worse still, there were cold-blooded people who traded in human merchandise, in human flesh. Just as at cattle fairs prospective buyers pull back the snout of a cow or a water buffalo to assess its age by examining its teeth, these human traders now put up for public display the beauty of a young woman, her blossoming charm, her most intimate secrets, her beauty spots, her tattoos. This sort of violence had sunk right down to their very bones. In former times, at least, deals were struck at fairs under the protective cover of a handkerchief. Fingers met, negotiated, and concluded the deal in secrecy. Today, however, even that screen had been lifted. Everybody was bargaining shamelessly in the open, with no regard for decorum. This transaction, this peddling, recalled an episode straight out of Boccaccio—a narrative depicting the uninhibited trafficking of women: countless women stand lined up, baring themselves before the Uzbek procurer, who pokes and prods them with his finger. It leaves a pink indentation where it touches the body, a pale circle forms around it, and the pink and the pale rush to meet. The Uzbek moves on, and the rejected woman, crushed by humiliation and shame, sobs uncontrollably, holding the waist cord of her loosened lower garment with one hand, hiding her face from the public's gaze with the other. Later, even the feeling of shame departs. Thus she walks nude through the bazaars of Alexandria.

Sundar Lal was getting ready to go to the border town of Amritsar when the news of Laaju's arrival overtook him. Its suddenness unnerved him. He hurriedly took a step towards the door but, just as swiftly, stepped back. A sudden feeling to give in to his unhappiness overwhelmed him. He felt he wanted to spread all the placards, all the banners of his rehabilitation committee out on the floor, and sit on them and cry his heart out. But the situation was hardly proper for such an expression of emotion. He bravely fought back the turmoil raging inside him and picked his way slowly towards Chauki Kalan, the venue for the delivery of the abducted women.

Laaju stood straight in front of him, shaking with fear. If anyone knew Sundar Lal, it was she. She had forgotten nothing of how badly he had treated her before, and now that she was returning after living with another man, there was no telling what he might do. Sundar Lal looked at Laaju. She had draped the upper half of her body in a black dupatta, one of its ends thrown over her left shoulder in the typical Muslim fashion, but only out of habit. Perhaps it made it easier to socialize with the Muslim ladies and finally to make her escape from her captor. Then again, she had been thinking of Sundar Lal so much and was so mortally afraid of him that she scarcely had the mind to change into different clothes or even to worry about draping herself with the dupatta in the right fashion. As it was, she was unable to distinguish the basic difference between Hindu and Muslim cultures—whether the dupatta went over the right or left shoulder. Right now, she stood before Sundar Lal, trembling, balanced between hope and fear.

Sundar Lal was shocked. He noticed that Laajwanti looked fairer and healthier than before; indeed she looked plump. Whatever he had imagined about her turned out to be wrong. He had thought that grief would have wasted her, that she'd be too weak even to speak. The thought that she had been happy in Pakistan wounded him, but he said nothing to her, for he had sworn not to quiz her about such matters. All the same, he couldn't help wondering: why had she chosen to return if she lived a happier life there? Perhaps the Indian government had forced her to, against her wishes.

But he was quite unable to see the pallor on Laajwanti's tawny face, or to fathom that it was suffering, and suffering alone, that made her firm flesh loosen and sag from her bones, making her look heavy. She had become heavy with an excess of grief, though superficially she appeared healthy. Hers was the kind of plumpness which made one pant for breath after taking only a few steps.

Sundar Lal's first glimpse of his abducted wife unsettled him. But he fought all his thoughts back with great manliness. Many other people were also present and one of them shouted, 'We're not about to take back these Muslim leavings!'

But the slogans of Rasaloo, Neki Ram, the old petition writer of Chauki Kalan drowned out the man's voice. Above them all rose the loud, cracking voice of Kalka Parshad, who somehow managed to speak and cough at the same time. He was absolutely convinced of this new reality, this new purity. It seemed he had learnt a new Veda, a new Purana, a new Shastra, which he desperately wanted to share with others. And surrounded by all these people and voices, Laaju and Sundar Lal returned home. It seemed that after a protracted moral exile, the Ramchandar and Sita of an age long past were entering Ayodhya, while the people both celebrated their return by lighting lamps of joy and, at the same time, showed regret for having put the couple through such incredible misery.

Sundar Lal continued his 'Rehabilitation of Hearts' campaign with the same ardour even after Laajwanti's return. He had lived up to it both in word and deed. People who had earlier taken his involvement for just so much sentimental idealism were now convinced of his sincerity. Some were truly happy at this, but most felt disappointed and sad, and many women of the Mulla Shakur neighbourhood, except for the widow, still felt uncomfortable crossing Sundar Lal's threshold.

To Sundar Lal, however, it made no difference at all whether people recognized or ignored his work. The queen of his heart had returned and the yawning emptiness in his chest had been filled. He had installed the golden image of Laaju in the temple of his heart and diligently stood guard at its doorway. Laaju, who used to be so afraid of him, now began slowly to relax under his unexpectedly gentle and caring regard.

Sundar Lal no longer called her Laaju, but Devi, which made her go mad with indescribable joy. How much she wanted to tell him what she had been through, and cry so profusely that the tears would wash away all her 'sins', but Sundar Lal deftly avoided listening to her. And so she still carried a trace of apprehension in her newfound ease. After he had fallen asleep, she would simply gaze at him. If he caught her watching him and asked for a reason, she wouldn't know what to say beyond 'Nothing' or 'I don't know'. Sundar Lal, exhausted from the day's gruelling work, would go back to sleep. Once, though, in the beginning, he did ask Laajwanti about her 'dark days'. 'Who was he?'

'His name was Jumma,' she said, with downcast eyes. Then, fixing her eyes on his face, she wanted to say something more, but faltered. He was looking at her in a strange way, as his hands caressed her hair. She lowered her eyes again. Sundar Lal asked, 'Was he good to you?'

'Yes.'

'He didn't beat you?'

'No,' Laajwanti said, dropping her head on Sundar Lal's chest. 'He never hurt me. And yet I was very afraid of him. You used to beat me, but I never felt scared of you. You won't beat me again, ever, will you?'

Tears welled up in Sundar Lal's eyes. He said, feeling deep shame and regret, 'No, never again, Devi.'

'Devi!' Laajwanti thought, and she too broke down in tears.

She felt overwhelmed by a desire to tell him all, holding back nothing, but Sundar Lal stopped her saying, 'Let's just forget the past. You were hardly to blame for what happened. Society is at fault for its lack of respect for goddesses like you. In that it doesn't harm you a bit, only itself.'

And Laajwanti couldn't get it all out. It remained buried inside her. She withdrew into herself and stared at her body for the longest time, a body which, after the Partition of the country, was no longer hers, but that of a goddess. Yes, she was happy, indeed very happy, but it was a happiness marred by a nagging doubt, a misgiving. She would sit up in bed with a start, like someone surrounded by a surfeit of happiness who suddenly hears an approaching sound and looks apprehensively in its direction, waiting.

Ultimately, the nagging doubt replaced happiness with a chilling finality. And not because Sundar Lal Babu had again started mistreating her, but because he had started treating her with exceeding gentleness. She didn't expect that from him. She wanted to be the same old Laaju once again, the one who would quarrel over trifles and then make up in no time at all. Now, though, there was no possibility of even a quarrel. Sundar Lal had convinced her that she was in fact a laajwanti, a glass object too fragile to withstand the merest touch. Laaju would look at herself in the mirror, and after thinking long and hard would feel that she could be many things, but could never hope to be the old Laaju ever again. Yes, she had been rehabilitated, but she had also been ruined. Sundar Lal, on his part, had neither the eyes to see her tears, nor the ears to hear her painful groans. How fragile the human heart can be—this escaped even the most ardent reformer of the Mulla Shakur neighbourhood. The early-morning processions continued and, like a robot, he joined in the refrain with Rasaloo and Neki Ram:

Touch the leaves of the laajwanti, they curl and wither away.

REPLY-PAID CARD

DINANATH NADIM

Translated from the Kashmiri by Neerja Mattoo

I

'ZOON DED! ZOON DED! AREN'T YOU UP YET?' ANNOUNCING HIS arrival loudly, Jamal Mir walked in and sat down on the doorstep. He pulled out a snuffbox from a pocket somewhere in the folds of his tattered pheran and, taking a large pinch from it, rubbed it all over his teeth and gums. There was a little stick in his hand and with it he began to draw shapes in the dust. After about fifteen minutes had passed, there was a creaking sound to his left. He was startled and looked towards the noise. It was the door to the barn, which had begun to open, revealing the figure of Zoon Ded. Seeing her standing there, he felt as if he had sighted the full moon and his lips parted in a broad grin. He then gave a full-throated laugh.

'Oh, you slime, it's you, is it? I wondered who it could be so early in the morning! How loudly you shouted!' Zoon Ded said with a smile.

Zoon Ded, grandmother to everyone in the village and mother to the whole world, her hair white as snow, with deep eyes, full as brimming cups of wine, a high, commanding nose, long arms, dressed in a spotless white under-pheran, standing at the door like a queen from the wild forests.

'Why, Ded, the sun has risen so high and you still seem reluctant to give up your sleep?' said Jamal Mir through a mouthful of snuff-stained saliva.

'When will you learn some manners? I don't know what to say to you,' said Zoon Ded. 'Didn't you see me coming out of the barn? How could I be sleeping?'

Jamal Mir looked a bit sheepish, but still went on, 'No, Ded, I thought maybe because of Gula Sahib, perhaps....'

This brought a thoughtful look to Zoon Ded's brow. Jamal Mir ate the rest of his words. For a while, they both kept their eyes on the ground. Then Zoon Ded said with a sigh, 'You are right in a way, but I have actually been spending most of my time attending to Badri since dawn. She neither touches grass nor her feed.'

Meanwhile, some others had turned up and as usual a regular circle formed around Zoon Ded and everyone began chattering away.

Who was Zoon Ded? Where had she come from? How old was she? No one in the village knew the answer to any of these questions. Even the oldest among them did not remember her looking any different from what she looked like today. But Zoon Ded was everything to them—she ruled the village, she was judge, maulvi, police officer, nambardar, chowkidar, patwari. In fact, all authority rested with her. She was counsellor to the old and a friend to the young, a listener to mothers-in-law, and a repository of daughters-in-law's secrets. When the panchayat met, it was Zoon Ded who delivered the verdict. If somebody had to be sent for forced labour, it was Zoon Ded who decided whether to send him or not. When marriages had to be fixed, Zoon Ded was the one to act as a go-between. When someone fell ill, Zoon Ded provided medical assistance. The whole area knew that what Zoon Ded declared must prevail, her word was law and could not be challenged. Not even the viceroy could change her writ. That is why Zoon Ded's home was open to all villagers—they treated it as their own grandmother's place. Whenever they were in any trouble, even if it was merely a thorn that had pricked them, they would rush to her for comfort.

II

Bonapore is known as Kaav Maalyun or Kawpore, the home of crows, among the people here. The reason is that all the crows in the area spend their nights here among the high branches of the chinars, where many of them have built their nests. Today, too, the crows had started making a huge racket at sunset, so much so that even the rumble of the mountain stream had been drowned in it. Suddenly, there was the sound of a gunshot and all the crows flew away from their perches in the chinars, cawing loudly in panic. Who could have fired the shot? There, look, see that soldier advancing—it must be his doing, the crows thought, perched on the branches of fruit trees, turning their necks this way and that. A jawan, well built, with a broad chest, well-rounded shoulders, handsome face, imposing stride, looking like an officer from a foreign army. How he swaggers along without a care in the world!

As soon as he reached the village, all the children gathered around him, some hugging his legs, some putting their hands in his pockets, some scratching his gun with their nails and all of them setting up a shout of welcome, 'Gula Sahib! It is Gula Sahib. Zoon Dedi, it is Gula Sahib. He has come home to you...it is our own Captain Gula Sahib!' Singing this refrain, the procession of children reached Zoon Ded's doorstep. Throwing her door open with a bang, Zoon Ded came out. Her eyes were smiling, though she tried to keep a serious expression on her face. 'Oh yes, "Gula Chaab" indeed! A captain, did you say? A cockatoo sahib, I say...if they make fools like him a captain, I don't know what they will do next!' But even as she said this the mother and son were hugging each other.

How was Gula Sahib related to Zoon Ded? Nobody knew for certain—there are always as many stories as there are mouths to tell them. Some said he was her sister-in-law's daughter's son, some declared that he was her own grandson, while some others were sure he had been found by her on the stairs to the shrine of Makhdoom Sahib. But why are we concerned about their real relationship? The fact was obvious to everyone that Gula Sahib was her life, Zoon Ded lived for him. Since he had joined the army, his name was always on her lips, she would talk of nothing else. His name figured in all her conversations.

'Did you hear, Vaasa? I received a letter from Gula today. He says that he killed seventeen tribal raiders in one single day!'

'Do you know, Sonamali? Gula Sahib, may God bless him, has sent me a reply-paid postcard! It is beautiful, as though not words, but pearls have been studded on this paper.'

'Jamal Mir, our seven generations have been blessed, such glory has been brought by a son like Gula! Today he is defending the honour of the whole of Kashmir.'

III

The day Gula Sahib left for the frontline, the whole village was on its feet. At the first light of day, their kitchen hearths had been lit and by the time the sun rose they were all—men and women, the elderly, and the young—at Zoon Ded's door. Some carried sanctified food from holy places, some brought talismans with powerful spells in them. Ordinary peasant women came with gifts of little packets of pickles or chutney tied to the ends of their veils. Some even brought bundles of dried vegetables like turnips and haak leaves with them. As soon as Zoon Ded opened her door, they all rushed in, jostling for space, each visitor eager to be the first to give their gift.

'Here, Zoon Ded, take this bunch of dried turnips. These grew from pure farm seeds,' said Rahti, the milkmaid, shyly holding out her gift. 'I had saved it for Gula Sahib all these days.'

'Take this bunch of dried greens too, they are from the famous kohlrabi produce of Khashipore,' said Ramzu Begari.

'Tell Gula Sahib that finding such stuff is not possible in the city!'

'Would you please take this little portion of pickle, too, Ded? Tell him it is from genuine Kashmiri kohlrabi of Bonapore.'

'Zoon Ded! Please call Gula Sahib. Why doesn't he come out? Is he still in his nightcap?' said Vaasa Bhat, hesitantly.

'Didn't I say that you had become senile? Would he be still sleeping at this hour? He has gone to the stream to wash himself. He must be on his way here now. Why, are you getting late for something?' said Zoon Ded jokingly.

'How you dote on him! It is just that I got this powerful talisman for him with potent mantras from Kanth Guruji and I wanted him to wear it in my presence,' responded Vaasa Bhat.

As soon as Gula Sahib walked in after his ablutions at the stream, they all crowded around him, some hugging him, some kissing his forehead. When he came out dressed in his uniform and picked up his gun, their hearts swelled with pride. The women showered blessings on him, 'God be with you, Gula! May you reach even greater heights, may good fortune follow your steps!' The whole village walked along with him for many miles into his journey. They only retraced their steps when they lost sight of him behind the trees.

IV

The sky had been hazy since the day dawned. Before the sun could show itself, clouds had enveloped the whole sky. The cloud cover was so thick that it reached down from the high crags to the foothills. Blinding forks of lightning accompanied by loud, terrifying thunder came from the east. It looked like there was about to be a huge downpour. Generally, on a day like this, the villagers preferred to stay indoors. But today they were all gathered in groups by the stream, talking in whispers. No one seemed to be their normal self. A little distance from the groups of men, the cluster of women seemed to be silently writhing in agony. Bare-headed, half-dressed, and breathless, Vaasa Bhat ran up to them, clenching his fists as though to control his emotions, and burst into a loud wail. 'What is this I hear, Karim Joo? Oh God, what calamity is this? A disaster...disaster....' he lost his voice.

'Quiet! Be silent,' Karim Kral put his hand on his lips, 'this won't do. Take heart. Think of Zoon Ded. For her sake we have to be brave. We have to think of how we should inform her.'

'But how did it happen? Who brought the news? Who could have wished for it! Oh no....' Vaasa Bhat said through sobs.

'Who could wish it? Only our wretched luck! Last night Jabbar Postman came and handed this card from Gula Sahib to me—it was blank, just as it was when Zoon Ded had sent it from here. He must have...on the battlefront....' Karim Kral fell silent.

V

Broken in spirit and body, one after another they all reached Zoon Ded's house. Today, too, as usual, she was in the barn giving her cow her feed and talking to her. 'You have lost your mind, you have! Do you expect him to stay at your bedside all the time? Since he went to the front to fight, you seem to have been struck by paralysis! This won't do at all, don't you realize?' Then she heard a suppressed cough. 'Is it you, Vaasa? How come so early in the morning?' she said as she came out of the barn.

'You know this Badri has been ruined by Gula.... But, no, something has happened...is all well?' Seeing the crowd gathered before her, she was taken aback and asked, 'Have you all fought over something? Tell me, why don't you speak to me?' They all stood there, mute, choked into silence, unable even to give vent to a sigh. 'Go on, say something, why don't you? Has a mouse stolen your tongue?' she asked, but the colour seemed to be draining from her face. 'What has happened? Has something happened to me?'

At last, his face averted, Vaasa spoke in a low, hesitant voice, 'Zoon Dedi, we would die for you....' He couldn't go on, his voice broke and he wept loudly. Everyone sobbed, tears streaming down their cheeks, overcome by uncontrollable grief. Zoon Ded stood still, uncomprehending and began to speak as though to herself, 'Is my Gula all right? Of course, he is all right. Doesn't he know, with how many sacrifices, in exchange for how many...?'

Vaasa Bhat took courage and handed her the reply-paid postcard, 'It came yesterday, this postcard. It is a reply-paid one, but it is blank. I don't know....'

Zoon Ded seemed paralysed, but she stood there erect like a rock. The postcard, having been touched and handled by so many of them, was crumpled. She spread it out carefully and began to scrutinize it, back and front. Silence once again fell on the scene, a deathly silence. Not a sound was heard except for the murmur of the stream, which sounded like somebody was mourning a dear one at his graveside on Eid.

Within a few minutes, it seemed that Zoon Ded's face was covered in as fine a dust as rises when one winnows rice. All the wrinkles on it suddenly became visible. Tears appeared in her eyes, but were drawn back before they could fall.

'Hahahaha!' Zoon Ded laughed. They were all dumbfounded.

'Didn't I tell you Vaasa that you have become senile? If you had any brains, wouldn't you have been a tehsildar by now?' Zoon addressed them all. 'See, it is all written here clearly. Have you all lost your sight, too?' She spread out the card. The creases on it did look like pencilled writing from a distance. 'See, what my Gula has written to me. He asks me to go and join the women's militia,' Zoon Ded declared with great authority.

The day Zoon Ded left, a wooden gun in hand, dressed in her white underpheran tied with a sash, a pall of gloom fell over the whole village. No child made a sound, nor did a single crow caw in the trees of Kawpore that day.

THE NIGHT OF THE FULL MOON

K. S. DUGGAL

Translated from the Punjabi by Khushwant Singh

NO ONE BELIEVED THAT MALAN AND MINNIE WERE MOTHER AND daughter; they looked like sisters—Minnie was quite a bit taller than her mother. People said, 'Malan, your daughter has grown into a lovely woman!' They never stopped gaping at the girl. She was like a pearl and as charming as she was comely.

When Malan looked at her daughter she felt as if she was looking at herself. She too had been as young and as beautiful. She hadn't aged much either. And there was somebody who was willing to go to the ends of the earth for her even now.

Why had her mind wandered to this man? He must be a dealer in pearls because every time she thought of him pearls dropped from her eyes! Her daughter was now a woman; it was unbecoming of her to think of a man. She had restrained herself all these years; why did her mind begin to waver? She must hold herself in check. Her daughter was due to wed in another week; she must not entertain such evil thoughts—never! Never!

'My very own, my dearest,' he had written only yesterday, 'do not forget me.' But every time he came to the village she sent him away without any encouragement. She shut her eyes as fast as she shut her door against him. He had refused to give her up. She was his life; without her he found no peace. He had spent many years waiting for her, pleading with her, suffering the pangs of love and passion. An age had passed and now the afternoon shadows had lengthened across life's courtyard.

Malan knew in her heart that he would come that night. Every full moonlit night he knocked on her door. And tonight the moon would be full. The night would be cold, frosty, and still. She had never unlatched her door for him. Would she tonight? She recalled a cold, moonlit night of many years ago. She was dancing in the mango grove when her dupatta had got caught in his hand. She had come to him bare-headed with the moonlight flecking her face with jasmine petals. He had put the dupatta across her shoulders—exactly the way it lay across her shoulders now. A shiver ran down Malan's spine.

Minnie came down the lane, tall and as slender as a cypress. Fair and fragile, she looked as if the touch of a human hand would leave a stain on her. Modestly, she had her dupatta wrapped around her face, and her eyes lowered.

Minnie was returning from the temple. She had prayed to the gods, she said softly to her mother, to grant her wish. She had prayed to the gods to grant everybody all their wishes.

Malan smiled. Something stirred her fancy. If her wish could be granted, she thought to herself, what would she ask for?

'Father has not returned!' complained Minnie.

'He is not expected back today; it will be a thousand blessings if he gets back by tomorrow. He has a lot of things to buy. At weddings and feasts it's better to have a little more than to run short,' explained Malan.

Minnie took off her sequinned dupatta and spread it on her mother's shoulders. She took her mother's plain dupatta instead, and went into the kitchen.

The light of the full moon came through the branches and sprinkled itself on Malan's face. The full moon always did something to her. It made her feel like one drunk. In another four days women would come to her courtyard to sing wedding songs. They would put henna on the palms and the soles of her daughter's feet. They would help her with her bridal clothes; load her with ornaments. How would her daughter look in bright red silk? And then the groom would come on horseback and take her to his own home and make love to her. He would kiss the henna away from the girl's palms and the soles of her feet.

It wasn't so very long ago that all this had happened to her, Malan. But Minnie's father had not once kissed the soles of her feet, nor ever pressed her palms against his eyes. He always came home tired; he ate his meal and fell fast asleep. Only the desire to have a son would occasionally arouse him at midnight. And then it was over so quickly that Malan had to spend hours counting the stars to cool down and get back to sleep. These midnight efforts had produced a daughter every year. The girls came to the world uninvited and departed without leave. Only one, Minnie, remained. She was a replica of her mother; like the fruit of a tree that bears only one. Minnie had large gazelle eyes—the eyes of Malan. Her long black hair fell down to her waist. And she had a full-bosomed wantonness that often made Malan think that all her frustrated passions had been rekindled in her daughter's body.

Minnie scrubbed the kitchen utensils, bolted the door of the courtyard, and went to bed in her own room. Malan was left alone.

It was late. The moon was so dazzlingly bright that it seemed to be focusing all its light in that one courtyard. Was it cold? Not really. Just pleasantly cool. Malan asked herself why she sat alone in the courtyard under the night of the full moon. Was she expecting someone? Minnie had gone to bed and her father had gone away to the city. Why was he away on a night like this? On full moon nights she used to keep herself indoors, away from temptation. But tonight she had her daughter's sequinned dupatta wrapped about her face. The sequins glistened in the silvery moonlight; it seemed as if the stars were entangled in her hair; they twinkled on her eyelashes, on her face, and on her shoulders. A nightjar called from the mango grove: *uk, uk, uk*. It would call like that all through the night: *uk, uk, uk*.

Her thoughts carried her with them. Her daughter would be married in a week's time. Then she would be left alone—all alone in the huge courtyard. A shiver ran through her body. The empty courtyard would terrify her. She would have to learn to live by herself. Her husband was too occupied with the pursuit of money; his moneylending and debt-collecting. He came back late in the evening only to collapse on his charpai. She had often asked him why he involved himself in so many affairs, but it had not made any difference.

Malan went indoors and saw her daughter fast asleep—dead to the world as only the young can be. Her red bangles lay beside her pillow. Silly girl! She had only to turn in her sleep and they would be crushed. Malan picked them up to put them on the mantelpiece. Before she knew it, she had slipped them on to her own arms; six on one, six on the other. They glistened even in the dark. They were new; her daughter had only bought them the day before from the bangle seller.

Malan came out into the moonlit courtyard—the sequinned dupatta on her head and her arms a-jingle-jangle with bright red glass bangles. She felt like a bride—warm, lusty. Blood surged in her veins.

There was a gentle knock on the door. It was he. It was the same knock—a nervous, hesitant knock. He was there as he had written in his letter he would be: 'On the full, moonlit night of December, I will knock at your door. If you are willing, open the door; if you are not willing, let it be. I will continue to knock at your door as I have always done.'

Knock, knock, knock—very soft, very sweet, a very inviting knock. Who could it be but he! The prowler on moonlit nights. Suddenly, the moon went behind a cloud and it was absolutely dark.

In a moment, Malan's feet took her across the dark courtyard. With trembling hands she undid the latch. Another moment and she was in his arms. Their lips met; their teeth ground against each other. Passion that had been held in check for over twenty years burst its banks and carried them on the flood.

Malan did not know how they went to the bo tree outside the village. She did not remember how they went into the field beside the bo tree—nor how long they stayed there. She was woken by the train that passed by the village in the early hours of the dawn. She extricated herself from her lover's embrace, covered her face with her dupatta, and hurried back to her home.

She slipped off the bangles from her arms and put them back beside her daughter's pillow. She folded her daughter's sequinned dupatta, took her own back and went to her charpai. She fell asleep at once and slept as she had never slept before—almost as if she were making up for a lifetime of sleeplessness.

When she woke, the sun was streaming into the courtyard.

'How you slept, like a little babe!' teased Minnie. Minnie had swept the rooms and the courtyard and cooked the morning meal. She had bathed and was ready to go to the temple. She had tied jasmine flowers in her dupatta to offer to the gods.

As soon as Minnie left, Malan stretched herself lazily on a charpai in the courtyard. She was filled with sleep and her head was filled with dreams.

A soft breeze began to blow. Warm sunshine spread in the courtyard. Malan felt like a bowl of milk, full to the brim—with a few petals of jasmine floating on it. It was a strange, heady intoxication. Her eyes would close, open, and then close again.

'O Malan! Where's that slut?' cried a voice suddenly. Malan felt as if someone had slapped her face.

'Never heard of such goings-on!' said another voice, 'and only four days to her wedding!'

'What has my daughter done?' shrieked Malan, rising up in anger. 'She is as innocent as a calf.'

There were derisive exclamations. Then someone sneered, 'Your little calf has been on the dung heap all night.'

Malan's body went cold, her lifeblood draining from her veins; a deathly pallor spread over her face.

Lajo, her neighbour, was speaking. 'It was barely dark when the bitch walked off with a stranger. I had got up to relieve myself when I saw them go away into the fields, with their arms entwined around each other's waists. I didn't get a wink of sleep. We have to watch the interests of our daughters. I've never heard of anyone blacken the faces of her parents in this way.'

Malan sat still as if turned to stone. She did not seem to hear what was being said.

The village watchman took up Lajo's story.

'Sister-in-law Malan,' he said, trying to attract her attention.

'What is it, Jumma?' Her voice seemed to come out of the depths of a deep well.

'Bhabhi, this is not the sort of thing one can talk about easily. An awful thing happened in the village last night. My hair has gone grey with the years I've been watchman of the village, but never have I known such a scandal. Your daughter blackened her face with someone under the bo tree. Twice I passed within ten paces of them. There they were locked together, limb joined to limb; oblivious of all but each other. I kept guard over your house. I said to myself, "The wedding is to take place in another four days; the house must be full of new dresses and ornaments and the door wide open!" I left at dawn. I don't know what time your daughter came back after whoring. If she were my child I would break every bone in her body.'

Malan gazed at the watchman, stunned.

Jumma was followed by Ratna, the zamindar. He was in a rage.

'Where is that slut?' he roared. 'Couldn't she find another field for whoring?' Ratna leapt about as he spoke. The neighbours came out of their homes to watch and listen. Ratna continued. 'I was on my way to the well when I saw her come out of the field with her face wrapped in the sequinned dupatta. I thought that the girl had come out to ease herself; but then her lover emerged from the other end of the same field. I saw them with my own eyes.'

At that moment, Minnie tore her way through the crowd. She had heard all that had been said about her. 'You are lying, uncle!' she shrieked.

'You dare call me a liar, you little trollop! You ill-starred wretch! And how did a broken red bangle happen to be in my field?' He untied the knot in his shawl, took out a piece of red bangle and slapped it on Minnie's palm. Minnie ran her eyes over her arms and counted the bangles; there were only eleven. The world swam before her eyes and then darkened.

The women exchanged glances. They had seen Minnie buy the bangles. Yes, there were ten and then two more. And she had especially asked for red ones.

The courtyard was full of babbling men and women. Minnie's fiancé's father edged his way through; his wife was behind him. They flung all the presents they had received in front of Malan: clothes, money, and rings. The crowd gaped. Women touched their ears; young girls bit their fingernails. This was drama indeed. A broken engagement was a broken life. What would Minnie do, now that she would never find a husband? It served her right, shameless harlot!

Over the sound of their angry droning, there was a loud splash. For a moment the crowd was petrified. Then someone shouted, 'The well!' and understanding dawned.

Minnie was nowhere to be seen. Gentle Minnie who never raised her voice against anyone, who was as pure as the jasmine she wove into garlands. Minnie, who never tired of praying to her gods for the happiness of everyone she knew.

Suddenly sobered, people ran to the well. Only Malan sat where she was, numb with horror, unable to move. Her courtyard was empty—emptier than it ever had been, as empty as it always would be now.

28

GOLD FROM THE GRAVES

ANNA BHAU SATHE

Translated from the Marathi by Vernon Gonsalves

HEARING THAT A POWERFUL MONEYLENDER HAD DIED IN A NEARBY village, Bhima sprang to his feet. He was exhilarated. His joy wouldn't subside. Looking in the direction of the village, he suddenly turned to glare at the sun in the sky.

The sun was setting. Rainclouds crowded the sky. They had the rough, battered look of freshly ploughed land. The retreating light, filtering through those nasty looking clouds, streamed down over Mumbai.

There was a gentle breeze. The fifty or so huts in this suburb in the jungle began to creak in the breeze. The huts were made of old tin sheets, mats, planks, and sacks. And those houses contained people. Cast-off things sheltering a cast-off people. Burnt out after the day's fight for food, they now rested. The kitchen fires were alight. White smoke loitered through the green trees. Children were playing.

Bhima sat lost in thought beneath a massive tamarind tree. He was terribly agitated. Drawn relentlessly towards that dead moneylender, his spirit was racing back and forth between that village's cemetery and the tamarind tree. He repeatedly glanced at the sun and then at that village. He needed the dark, so he was getting all fidgety. His beloved daughter Narbada, was playing close by and his wife was in the house, patting bhakars into shape. Bhima looked awe-inspiring. His Satara outfit comprised a long red turban, a yellow dhoti, and a shirt of thick, coarse cloth. He looked a proper wrestler. His massive forehead, thick neck, dark eyebrows, flamboyant moustache, and broad yet fiery features had struck fear into many a ruffian.

Bhima's village was a long way off, on the banks of the Warna. However, seeing that even his bull-like strength could not fill his stomach there, he had moved to Mumbai. He had combed the entire city in search of work. But he hadn't found any. As his many dreams of getting a job, becoming a worker, bringing home a pay packet, making his wife a coin-necklace, were shattered, Bhima had lost hope and had moved to this suburb in the jungle. Mumbai had everything, except work and shelter. So he had got upset with Mumbai. However, just after shifting to the suburb, he had found work in the quarry on a nearby hill.

On finding work and shelter, Bhima was happy. As he put all his bull-like might to work, he seemed to almost challenge the hill. He lifted his pickaxe and the hill would recoil. As his sledgehammer rose, the dark rock face would flinch. The contractor was happy with him. Bhima too was contented, as he was getting a wage.

But, within a space of just six months, the quarry closed down. When he got to work one day, he learned that the quarry had shut. Hearing that he had lost his job, Bhima was thrown into a daze. Hunger danced before his eyes. Anxiety and indecision gripped him. What was he going to do, he wondered despondently.

Clothes under his arm, Bhima turned back from the quarry. On the way, he stopped at a stream. He bathed there and prepared to make his way home, devastated beyond belief. It was then that his eyes fell on a mound of ashes. They were the ashes of a dead body. As he looked at the charred human bones Bhima grew even more despondent. Must be some jobless wretch; poor chap must have given up on life. I'll also die like this! Starvation will start in a couple of days, then Narbada will sit crying. My wife will fall into a deep depression and there'll be nothing I can do about it....

Suddenly he saw something sparkling in the heap of ashes. When he looked closely he discovered that the sparkle came from a gold ring of about a tola. Overjoyed, he grabbed hold of the ring. One tola of gold and that too from a corpse's ashes! He was delighted by his discovery—there was gold to be found in the ashes of a corpse. He had found a new means by which to live.

From the next day onwards Bhima began visiting crematoriums, and cemeteries on the banks of rivers and streams. He would sift through the ashes of bodies and pick up a fragment of gold here, an ornament there—earrings, nose rings, a gold coin, bracelet or anklet; he would find something of value every day.

Bhima's new venture began to flourish. He discovered that gold ornaments which were left on bodies that were being cremated would melt with the heat of the fire and enter the bones. So he would crush burnt bones and remove the gold. He'd break skulls. He'd crush wrists. But he'd get the gold.

In the evening he would go to Kurla, sell the gold, and collect cash. On the way home he would get dates for Narbada. Business was steady.

Bhima lived by sifting through the ashes of corpses. He soon lost sight of the difference between life and death. What he understood was that if there was gold in the ash it was the ash of the rich and if there was no gold it was that of the poor. Sometimes he would rave to whoever was within earshot—so it is the rich who should die and the rich who should live; the poor should never die. Continuing with his rant, he would loudly proclaim that the lowly lot had absolutely no right to live or to die. Happy was the man who died with a gold tola in his molars, is what he believed.

The brutal reality of unemployment had made him brutal. Night and day he hovered around cremation grounds and graveyards. Corpses had become his means of existence. His life had become one with the dead.

Before long, people began to notice that bizarre things were happening in those parts. Buried bodies were rising from their graves. The corpse of the young daughter-in-law of a moneylender had moved mysteriously from the burial ground to the riverbank. People living in the area were terrified by all this. Suspecting that somebody was digging up the bodies, the police began keeping watch. But keeping watch on corpses is no easy task.

The sun had set. Darkness covered the land. As his wife served his meal, Bhima ate in grim silence. When she realized that he was preparing to go out, she said softly, 'You're going somewhere, aren't you? I don't think what you are doing is right. You should find some other way to make a living. Corpses, corpses' ashes, gold, this existence, it's all wrong. People brand—' Bhima was upset by what his wife was saying. 'Be quiet,' he said irritably. 'How does it matter what I do? If my home fires go cold who's going to come and light them up?'

'It's not like that....' she said quietly, noticing her husband's angry face, 'It's not good to roam around like some ghoul or ghost. I'm saying whatever it is I'm saying because I'm afraid.'

'Who told you that there are ghosts in the graveyards? Listen, this Mumbai is a ghosts' bazaar. The real ghosts stay in houses and the dead ones rot in those graveyards. Ghosts take birth in the village—not in the wild,' raved Bhima.

In the face of his anger she kept her mouth shut as he made preparations to leave. He growled, 'I didn't get work even after going to Mumbai. But sifting through corpses' ashes, I've got gold. When I broke hills they gave me two rupees. But now that ash easily gives me even ten rupees....' Saying this he left the house. It was quite late by then. It was quiet and peaceful outside.

Bhima had tied a muffler around his head. Over that he had put on a hooded, cloak-like covering made of sackcloth, which he cinched at the waist. Carrying a pointed crowbar, he was walking with big strides. It was pitch-dark but he felt no fear. A sari, one petticoat and a blouse, dates in the morning was all he had on his mind. He was in a wild mood today.

There seemed to be a certain amount of tension in the air and it was getting tenser by the moment. A pack of jackals ran past him. A snake crossed the path and slithered away. An owl hooted in the distance adding to the eerie atmosphere. Nothing moved in the desolate jungle. Straining to catch every sound, Bhima drew near the village in which the moneylender had died. He sat down and surveyed the surroundings. All was silent in the village. Occasionally someone would cough. A lamp winked in a hut. When he saw that there was nothing to be worried about he slipped swiftly into the cemetery and started searching for the new grave of the moneylender. Pushing aside shattered pots and battered biers he jumped from this grave to that. He advanced from row to row looking carefully for the moneylender's grave. Clouds filled the sky. They deepened the darkness. Then abruptly lightning shone, dancing in the nooks and crannies of the clouds. It looked like it would rain. That made Bhima panic. Worried that he'd not be able to find the new grave if it rained, his search grew frenzied. He began to sweat, he felt he was losing his mind. By midnight he had searched the whole burial ground. From one end he reached the other end and slumped to the ground, distraught and confused. The wind was building up. It rattled the old poles of broken biers. It was almost as if someone were gnashing his teeth. Then a fearsome snarling erupted out of the night. Something was snarling, sobbing, and scraping at the mud. Fearfully, he moved towards the sound. It died out at once. But almost immediately he felt as if someone was dusting his hands and feet, and he got startled. He stopped abruptly. Fear ran like an electric current through his body and struck him right inside his head. For the first time in his life he was afraid.

In the next instant he got a grip on himself when he realized what was actually happening. He felt somewhat ashamed that he had been so scared. The new grave was close by. Ten to fifteen jackals were busy digging it up as they had scented the dead body. As stones had been placed on top of the grave, they had started tunnelling into it from all sides. As they scraped away the earth, they snarled and snapped at each other; each one was desperate to be the first to get at the corpse. Bhima was enraged by the sight of the jackals. He took a giant leap and landed right on top of the grave. He began lifting the stones on the grave and hurled them at the pack of jackals. In the face of this sudden onslaught the jackals retreated. Determined to dig up the grave before the jackals renewed their assault on it, Bhima began scraping away the mud. The jackals, only momentarily deterred, attacked him. In a fit of madness one of the jackals pounced on Bhima. It bit him and leaped back. Excitement and anger surged through Bhima's body. He had wrapped his hand in the sacking he had brought with him. He removed the sacking and grabbed hold of the crowbar. When the jackal that had bitten him returned to the attack, he brought the crowbar down on its body with all his tremendous strength. The jackal yelped and died. Bhima began digging up the grave once more. The remaining jackals attacked in a solid, snapping mass. A desperate fight broke out. Bhima lunged at the snarling animals with his crowbar. The jackals were coming at him from every side, and he was getting bitten all over his body. But his flailing crowbar was finding its mark as well and he was wounding the jackals every time he connected.

And so battle was joined between this modern Bhima, heir to the legacy of Kunti's son Bhima, and the jackals. He struggled with all his strength—if he was going to have a meal tomorrow he needed to get to that corpse. Nature was asleep. Mumbai was resting. The village was quiet. And in that burial ground the clash over gold and corpse was reaching its climax. Bhima was attacking and felling the jackals, who yelped in agony every time they were hit. Even as some were wounded, others dodged the blows and bit Bhima, who moaned and cursed every time a bite was taken out of his flesh. Curses, growls, screams, the sound of the crowbar making contact with the jackals—all this mayhem sent tremors through the cemetery.

After a really long time, the jackals stopped attacking and retreated into the darkness. Taking advantage of this, Bhima removed the remaining mud from the grave. He wiped the sweat from his face. He jumped into the grave. At that the jackals again charged him. He began furiously lashing out at them once more, and finally managed to drive them off. As the last of the animals scurried away, Bhima got hold of the body, shoved his hands under its armpits and scooped it out of the straw in which it had been wrapped. As the man had been dead for a while, his body was stiff and unyielding. He leaned it upright in the grave, and began examining it for loot. He found a ring on its finger and pulled it off. It had an earring in one ear, which he clawed off. There would definitely be some gold in the mouth. He tried to insert his fingers into the corpse's mouth but its jaws were clenched tight. Quickly, Bhima took the crowbar and pried open the dead man's mouth. Propping it open with the crowbar he inserted his fingers into the open jaws. Just then, the jackals, which had been skulking unseen in the darkness, began howling in unison. Their wailing and howling woke up the village dogs, which began barking, and running around. The commotion woke up the villagers. Someone yelled: 'The jackals are eating the body, come on....'

Afraid that the villagers would find him robbing the corpse, Bhima hurriedly put the ring he had stolen inside his pocket and began rooting around inside the corpse's mouth. He yanked out the crowbar that he had used to prop open the mouth, without remembering to extract his fingers first. The dead man's teeth clamped down on his fingers like a nutcracker on a betel nut. Bhima writhed in pain.

He could see the men from the village approaching with lanterns. Desperately he tried to extricate his fingers. When they wouldn't move, he became furious with the corpse. He swung the crowbar at the dead man's jaw. The blow only succeeded in jamming his hand deeper into the dead man's mouth. He felt the corpse's teeth cut into his fingers. He froze, thinking: this is a real ghost, today it will catch me and hand me over to the people who will kill me because I am desecrating this body. Or they will hand me over to the police. As all this went through his head, Bhima lost control and began to savagely attack the corpse. 'Pimp, let me go....' he began to yell, before he realized any noise would give away his position; he struggled on in silence. The villagers were drawing close. Bhima forced himself to calm down, to think. He realized what he must do. He pushed the crowbar back into the jaws of the corpse, levered them apart and slowly pulled out his fingers. They had been almost bitten through. Cradling his wounded hand with the other one, he leaped out of the grave and ran into the night.

When he reached home he had a high fever. His wife and daughter wept when they saw the state he was in. A doctor was summoned and he amputated two of Bhima's fingers. The same day, news arrived that the quarry was resuming operations. Hearing this, the elephant-like Bhima started sobbing like a small child. He had lost two of his 'hill-breaker fingers' for the sake of gold from the grave.

29

TWO MAGICIANS

SATYAJIT RAY

Translated from the Bengali by Arunava Sinha

'FIVE, SIX, SEVEN, EIGHT, NINE, TEN, ELEVEN.'
Having counted all the trunks, Surapati turned to his assistant, Anil. 'All right. Send them off to the brake van. Just twenty-five minutes to go.'

'Your compartment is ready too, sir,' Anil said. 'It's a coupé. Both berths are reserved for you. No one will disturb you.' Chuckling, he added, 'The guard's a fan too. He's been to your show at the New Empire. Ah, here he is—this way, sir.'

Biren Bakshi, the guard on the train, extended his right hand towards Surapati with a wide smile.

'If I may, sir, allow me to be honoured by shaking the hand whose tricks have given me so much pleasure.'

A single glance at any of Surapati Mondol's eleven trunks would reveal his identity. The words 'Mondol's Miracles' were stencilled in bold letters on the lids and sides of every trunk. No other explanation was necessary—for, just two months earlier, at the New Empire theatre in Calcutta, the audience had conveyed its appreciation through prolonged applause. The newspapers had been full of praise too. Mondol had been forced to promise the theatre authorities that he would perform again during the Christmas holidays.

'Please do let me know if you need anything, sir.'

The guard escorted Surapati to his compartment. Looking around, Surapati breathed a sigh of relief. It looked comfortable.

'Now if I may take leave, sir....'

'Thanks very much.'

When the guard had left, Surapati leaned back against the window and took a packet of cigarettes out of his pocket. This was probably the start of a triumphal journey. Delhi, Agra, Allahabad, Banaras, Lucknow. That was all this time around, but there were so many states yet to be covered, numerous cities and towns. And why think of India alone? There was a world beyond—a huge expanse. Being a Bengali didn't mean being unambitious. Surapati would show everyone. His fame would reach as far as America, home of the magician Houdini, reading about whom used to give him goose pimples once. He would prove to the world how far a boy from Bengal could go. Just let a few years pass. This was just the beginning.

Anil came running. 'All okay, sir. Everything.'

'Have you checked the locks?'
'Yes, sir.'
'Good.'
'I'm just two carriages away.'
'Have they cleared the line?'
'Any moment now. Will you have a cup of tea at Burdwan?'
'Not a bad idea.'
'I'll get you some.'

Anil left. Surapati lit a cigarette and looked out the window. A constant and noisy stream of porters, passengers, and vendors streamed past in both directions. As he gazed at them his mind wandered. His eyes clouded over. The hubbub on the platform died down. He went back a long way in time, to a place far away. He was thirty-three now, but then he was only seven or eight years old. A tiny village in Dinajpur district—Panchpukur. It was a quiet autumn afternoon. An old woman was seated in front of Moti the grocer's shop with a gunny bag. People old and young were thronging around her. How old was she? Could be sixty, could be ninety. Her sunken cheeks were criss-crossed with hundreds of creases, which doubled whenever she smiled. She kept up a torrent of words through her missing teeth.

'Bhanumatir khel. Magic!'

The old woman had put on a magic show. For the first and last time. But Surapati never forgot what he saw, and never would. His own grandmother was sixty-five—her entire body shook uncontrollably when she tried to thread a needle. And this old woman had so much magic in her wrinkled hands. She was making things disappear under everyone's noses, and then conjuring them from thin air the next moment—money, marbles, spinning tops, nuts, fruits. Taking a rupee from Kalu Kaka, she made it vanish, sending him into a rage. When she made it materialize again, going off into peals of laughter, Kalu Kaka's eyes turned into saucers.

Surapati had been unable to sleep for several days after this magic show. And even when he eventually did, apparently he would often cry out, 'Magic! magic!' in his sleep.

After this, whenever there was a fair in the village, Surapati would visit it in the hope of watching some more magic. But he hadn't come across anything remarkable.

At sixteen, Surapati moved to his uncle's house on Bipradas Street in Calcutta to study for his intermediate degree. Alongside college textbooks, he read books on magic. Surapati had bought them within a month or two of arriving in the city, and had taught himself all the tricks in the books soon afterwards. He had had to buy several packs of cards. He would stand in front of the mirror for hours on end, practising. Surapati would sometimes perform his magic tricks on Saraswati Puja celebrations in his college or at friends' birthday parties.

He was invited to his friend Gautam's sister's wedding during his second year in college. It was a memorable day in the history of Surapati's magic training, for this was where he met Tripura Babu for the first time. A marquee had been erected in the field behind the enormous house on Swinhoe Street, and Tripura Babu was sitting in one corner, surrounded by guests. He had appeared nondescript at first glance. He was about forty-eight years old, with wavy, parted hair, a jovial expression, and traces of paan juice at the corners of his mouth. You saw countless such people on the streets. But what was happening on the sheet in front of him forced you to change your mind. Surapati couldn't believe his own eyes at first. A silver fifty-paisa coin rolled along to a gold ring placed three feet away, and then escorted the ring back to Tripura Babu. Surapati had been so stupefied that he hadn't even been able to summon up enough strength to clap. And then, the very next moment, another extraordinary piece of magic. Absorbed in the performance, Gautam's uncle had spilled all his matchsticks from the box while trying to light his cigar. As he was about to bend over, Tripura Babu had said, 'Why put yourself to trouble, sir? Allow me.'

Piling the matchsticks in a heap on the floor, Tripura Babu had held out the matchbox in his left hand, calling, 'Come, boys, come along now....' And, just like pet dogs or cats, the matchsticks had trooped into the box, one by one.

After the wedding dinner, Surapati had gone up to Tripura Babu who was standing by himself in a corner. Tripura Babu had been astonished by Surapati's interest in magic. 'Bengalis are happy enough just to watch,' he had said, 'I don't find too many people interested in performing. I am genuinely surprised that you're interested.'

Surapati had visited Tripura Babu at home within two days. He lived in a tiny, ramshackle room in a boarding house on Mirzapur Street. Surapati had never seen anyone live in so much poverty and deprivation. Tripura Babu had told Surapati how he made a living. He charged a fee of fifty rupees for a magic show. He barely got two commissions a month. Making more of an effort might have helped, but Surapati had realized that Tripura Babu was not that kind of a man. He couldn't have imagined that such a talented person would be so lacking in ambition. When he said as much, Tripura Babu had answered, 'What's the use? Who's going to value good things in this accursed country? How many people really understand art? How many can tell the original from the counterfeit? You praised my magic so effusively at the wedding the other evening, but no one else did. As soon as they were told dinner was served, they abandoned the magic to line up to worship their bellies.'

Surapati arranged for Tripura Babu to perform on special occasions at a few friends' and relatives' houses. Partly out of gratitude, and mostly out of affection, Tripura Babu had agreed to pass on his magic skills to Surapati. He had objected vehemently when Surapati had mentioned paying him. 'Don't even bring it up,' he had said. 'What is important is that I will have an inheritor. Since you are so interested and so enthusiastic, I will teach you. But don't be in a hurry. You have to dedicate yourself. Haste will achieve nothing. If you learn properly, you will experience the joy of creation. Do not expect too much money or fame. But then you will never share my plight, because you have ambition, which I don't....'

'You'll teach me all your tricks, won't you?' Surapati had asked hesitantly. 'Even the one with the coin and the ring?'

Tripura Babu had laughed. 'One step at a time. Don't be impatient. You have to keep at it. It needs dedication. These are ancient arts. This form of magic came about at a time when man had genuine willpower and concentration. Modern man cannot take his mind to that level easily. Have you any idea what an effort I had to make?'

Something happened after about six months of training with Tripura Babu.

On his way to college one day, Surapati noticed colourful posters on every wall in Chowringhee for Chefalo the Great. Going up to a poster to read the details, Surapati learnt that Chefalo was a famous Italian magician who was coming to Calcutta to perform. He would be accompanied by his fellow magician, Madame Palermo.

At the New Empire Surapati had watched Chefalo's magic from the one-rupee seats. Incredibly eye-popping and mind-blowing acts, all of them. Surapati had only read about such magic in books. Entire humans disappeared in smoke in front of everyone's eyes, emerging again like Aladdin's genie from coils of smoke. Putting a girl inside a wooden crate, Chefalo sawed the box in half; the girl appeared from a different box within minutes, laughing, without a scratch on her. Surapati's palms had turned red with clapping.

And Chefalo himself was a source of continuous amazement for Surapati. The man was as good an actor as he was a magician. He was dressed in a shiny black suit and a top hat, with a magic wand in his hand. Was there anything Chefalo couldn't conjure out of that hat with his magic skills? On one occasion, he reached into a hat and pulled out a rabbit by its ears. The poor thing had barely finished shaking its ears when pigeons flew out—one, two, three, four. The magic pigeons flew around the hall, their wings rustling. Meanwhile, Chefalo was pulling chocolate bars out of the same hat and tossing them into the audience.

And throughout, Chefalo kept talking. Verbal fireworks. Surapati had read that this was referred to as patter. This patter was the magician's mainstay—while the audience drowned in its currents, the magician performed his sleight of hand unnoticed.

But Madame Palermo was a strange exception. She didn't utter a single word, performing her tricks like a silent robot. When did she perform her sleight of hand, then? Surapati had later found out the answer to this as well. It was possible to perform certain magic tricks on stage that required no sleight of hand. These tricks depended on machines, which were run by people behind the black curtain at the back of the stage. Cutting people into two halves and rejoining them, or making them disappear in smoke, was all a matter of machinery. If you had enough money you could buy these machines—or have them made—to put on these magic tricks. Of course, there was a certain flair and art involved in performing them with showmanship and panache, making them more attractive with glittering clothes and shiny props. Not everyone had mastered this art, which was why wealth was not enough to be a magician. After all, not everyone could....

Surapati's web of memories snapped suddenly.

The train had just left the platform with a bone-rattling jerk when the door to the compartment was flung open and the man who entered was... what! About to shout in indignation, Surapati held his tongue.

It was Tripura Babu! Tripuracharan Mullick!

Surapati had had similar experiences earlier. Someone he knew well, but hadn't met in a long time, suddenly cropped up in his thoughts or in a discussion and, the next thing you knew, the person was actually in their midst.

But still Surapati felt that Tripura Babu's sudden appearance put all those incidents in the shade. For a few moments he could not even speak. Wiping the perspiration off his forehead with the edge of his dhoti, Tripura Babu set his bundle down on the floor and sat down on the opposite end of the bench. Smiling at Surapati, he said, 'Surprised?'

Gulping, Surapati said, 'Surprised in the sense that—first, I didn't know you were alive.'

'What do you mean?'

'I visited your boarding house shortly after my BA exams. I found the door locked. The manager—I forget his name—said that you'd been run over....'

Tripura Babu burst into laughter. 'Something like that would have been wonderful. I'd have been relieved of all my worries.'

'And the second thing is,' added Surapati, 'I was thinking of you just the other day.'

'What's that?' A pall of gloom seemed to settle on Tripura Babu's expression. 'Thinking of me? You still think of me? I'm surprised to hear that.'

Surapati looked contrite. 'What are you saying, Tripura Babu! You think I can forget so easily? You introduced me to magic. I was especially reminded of the old days today. I am travelling for a show. Outside of Bengal for the first time. Did you know I'm a professional magician now?'

Tripura Babu nodded.

'I do. I know everything. And I came here to meet you today because I know everything. Everything that you have done over the past twelve years, how you have established yourself and achieved the fame you have today, is known to me. I was present at New Empire that evening, the first day. In the very last row. I saw how everyone appreciated your craft. I admit to feeling some pride. But....'

Tripura Babu paused. Surapati was silent. What could he possibly say? Tripura Babu could not be blamed for feeling disappointed. It was true that Surapati wouldn't be what he was today if Tripura Babu hadn't taught him the fundamentals. And what had Surapati done for him in return? On the contrary, his memory of Tripura Babu had faded over the past twelve years. Even his sense of gratitude had diminished.

Tripura Babu continued, 'I was proud of your success that day. But it was mixed with regret. Do you know why? The path you have chosen is not one of pure magic. A lot of what you're doing is fooling people with smoke and mirrors, tricks using machinery. It's not your own magic. Do you remember mine?'

Surapati had not forgotten. But at the same time he had felt that Tripura Babu had been hesitant about teaching Surapati his best tricks. 'Not yet,' he used to say. The time never came. Chefalo came before that. Surapati began to weave dreams, putting himself in Chefalo's place. He imagined himself travelling around the world performing shows, making a name for himself, giving pleasure to people, earning their approval and applause.

Tripura Babu was gazing out the window absently. Surapati observed him closely. He seemed to be in a bad way. His hair was almost entirely grey, the skin on his face was slack, his eyes were sunken. But had his eyes dimmed at all? It didn't seem so. He had a strangely piercing gaze.

With a sigh, Tripura Babu said, 'Mind you, I understand why you chose this path. I know you believe—and perhaps I am partly responsible for this—that purity is worthless. To perform magic on stage you need a little glitter and showmanship. Isn't that so?'

Surapati didn't deny it. He had concluded as much after watching Chefalo. But was glitter necessarily bad? Times had changed. How much could you earn performing your magic tricks at a wedding, and how many people would come to know of you? He had seen Tripura Babu's plight with his own eyes. What use was magic if performing it in all its purity couldn't even bring you two square meals a day?

Surapati told Tripura Babu about Chefalo. Was something which gave pleasure to thousands, earning their praise, not to be appreciated?

Surapati was not disparaging pure magic. But there was no future down that route. So he had chosen this one.

Tripura Babu seemed to become agitated suddenly. Hoisting his feet on to the bench they were sitting on, he leaned towards Surapati.

'Look, Surapati, if you had really understood what genuine magic is, you wouldn't have chased the fake kind. Sleight of hand is just one aspect, although there are countless kinds. Like yogic acts, you have to practise them for months and years. But there's so much more. Hypnotism. Bringing people under your control with just a look, turning them into putty in your hands. Then there's clairvoyance, telepathy, thought-reading. You will have unrestricted access to people's thoughts. You can check someone's pulse and tell them what they're thinking. Once you've really mastered the art you won't even have to touch them. Just looking at them for a minute will tell you their innermost secrets, what's in their heart. Is all this magic? These things lie at the root of the finest magic in the world. There are no levers and pulleys here. There is only dedication, devotion, concentration.'

Tripura Babu paused for breath. He had had to talk above the sound of the train, which had probably exhausted him. Now he moved closer to Surapati, saying, 'I wanted to teach you all this, but you didn't care. You couldn't wait. You were taken in by a flashy, foreign charlatan. You abandoned the real path for the one that leads to quick wealth.'

Surapati was silent. He really could not deny any of these allegations.

Placing his hand on Surapati's shoulder, Tripura Babu softened his tone. 'I have come to you with a request, Surapati. I don't know if you can tell from my appearance—but I have really fallen on hard days. I know so much magic, but the magic of making money has eluded me. The lack of ambition has been my undoing—I would hardly have had to worry about how to make a living otherwise. I have come to you out of desperation, Surapati. I have neither the strength nor the youth to establish myself now. But I do have the faith that you will help me during this difficult time, even if it means a little sacrifice. I shan't bother you after that.'

Surapati was perplexed. What did the man want?

Tripura Babu continued, 'The plan may appear somewhat drastic to you, but there is no other way. The trouble is that it isn't just money that I need. I've developed a new desire in my old age, you know. I want to demonstrate my best acts to a large audience. Perhaps, for the first and last time, but I simply cannot suppress this wish.'

Surapati's heart quaked with an unknown fear.

Tripura Babu finally got to the point.

'You're going to Lucknow for a performance. Suppose you were to fall ill at the last moment. And instead of turning back a disappointed audience, what if someone else....'

Surapati was flabbergasted. What was Tripura Babu saying! He really must be quite desperate to make such a proposal.

When he didn't speak, Tripura Babu said, 'Because of unavoidable reasons, your guru will perform instead of you—this is what you will inform them. Will people be very disappointed? I don't think so. I am certain that they will enjoy my magic. Still, I propose that you will get half of what you would have been paid for the performance. Whatever's left over will be enough for me. After which you can continue as you are doing now. I won't bother you any more. But you must give me this one opportunity, Surapati.'

Surapati was furious.

'Impossible! You don't know what you're saying, Tripura Babu. This is my first show outside Bengal. Don't you understand how much depends on the Lucknow performance? Should I begin my career with a lie? How could you even imagine such a thing?'

Tripura Babu looked steadily at Surapati for some time. Then his measured, restrained voice was heard above the clatter of the wheels.

'Are you still interested in the coin-and-ring trick?'

Surapati was startled. But there was no change in Tripura Babu's gaze. 'Why do you ask?'

Smiling, Tripura Babu said, 'I shall teach you the trick if you agree to my proposal. Right now, if you give me your word. And if not....'

A train bound for Howrah passed theirs with a grotesque shriek of its whistle. Tripura Babu's eyes glowed repeatedly in the light from the compartments of the other train. When the lights and sound had died down, Surapati said, 'And what if I don't agree?'

'The outcome will not be pleasant, Surapati. There's something you must know. If I'm in the audience, I can disrupt and humiliate any magician—I can even make them completely incapable of performing any magic.'

Taking a pair of cards from his pocket, Tripura Babu extended them to Surapati.

'Show me your sleight of hand. Nothing very difficult. Basic tricks. Bring the jack of clubs from the back to the front with a shake of your wrist.'

It had taken Surapati a mere seven days to perfect this trick in front of the mirror at the age of sixteen.

But today?

Picking up the cards, Surapati discovered his fingers turning numb. Not just his fingers, but also his wrist and elbow. All numb. His vision blurring, Surapati could only see a strange smile on Tripura Babu's lips; he was looking into Surapati's eyes in an almost inhumanly penetrating way. Surapati's forehead was covered in perspiration, and he felt himself shaking.

'You realize my power now?'

The cards slipped out of Surapati's hand. Gathering them, Tripura Babu said grimly, 'Are you willing?'

Surapati was no longer feeling incapacitated.

In a weak, exhausted voice, he asked, 'You'll teach me the trick, won't you?'

Holding the index finger of his right hand in front of Surapati's nose, Tripura Babu said, 'Because of your indisposition, your guru Tripuracharan Mullick will perform his magic skills instead of you at the first show in Lucknow. Correct?'

'Correct.'

'You will give me half the payment due to you. Correct?'

'Correct.'

'Come, then.'

Fishing a coin out of his pocket, Surapati handed it over, along with the ruby ring on his finger.

Anil arrived at his boss's compartment with some tea when the train stopped at Burdwan, only to find him fast asleep. Surapati sprang up when Anil called out to him softly after some hesitation.

'What...what is it?'

'I got you some tea. I disturbed you, please don't mind.'

'But...?' Surapati looked around frenziedly.

'What is it, sir?'

'Tripura Babu?'

'Tripura Babu?' Anil was bewildered.

'No, of course...he was killed by a bus...in 1951...but my ring?'

'Which ring, sir? The ruby's on your finger.'

'Oh yes, of course. And....'

Surapati took a coin out of his pocket. Anil noticed that his hand was shaking uncontrollably.

'Come in for a minute, Anil. Quickly. Shut the windows. Yes, watch now.'

Surapati placed the coin at one end of the bench and the ring at the other. Then, praying for all he was worth, he applied the technique acquired in his dream to cast a concentrated gaze on the ring.

Like a dutiful child the coin rolled up to the ring and escorted it back to Surapati.

The cup of tea would have slipped from Anil's hands had Surapati not taken it into his own with a miraculous sleight of hand.

When the curtain rose on the first day of the magic show in Lucknow, Surapati started by expressing his respect for his departed magic teacher Tripuracharan Mullick.

The last trick of the evening—which Surapati termed Pure Indian Magic—was the one with the coin and the ring.

SAVAGE HARVEST

MOHINDER SINGH SARNA

Translated from the Punjabi by Navtej Sarna

As HE BENT OVER THE FURNACE STUFFED WITH HARD COAL, DINA'S IRON-black body shone with the sheen of bronze; in fact, he seemed to be moulded in bronze, resembling a statue of a healthy labourer. The muscles of his well-exercised torso rippled as he swung the hammer around his head, and a great blow fell on the red-hot bits of iron.

The blows continued to fall and echo. Immersed in his work, Dina was lost to the world until the hot sun of late August, streaming in through the open window, began to lick at his very bones. With a start, he looked out. Already the sun was at its height and his work was not even half done. He shut the window to keep out the heat but then found it difficult to breathe. A clammy sweat broke out on his forehead. It had rained furiously all night, as if the skies had opened up, and then continued to drizzle all morning. But now the sun shone brightly and a suffocating humidity had built up. He threw the window open again and bent over the furnace. The sweat was flowing down his ears on to his body in little rivulets. He wiped it off his forehead with his forearm. Thick drops fell on the fire. There was a little hiss and for a split second, a piece of coal found some relief.

He seemed to be on fire with the combined heat from the sun and the furnace. This fire had dissolved into his blood and was now roasting the marrow of his bones. The sharp, roaring flames made his eyes burn. Every hair on his body had become a wick and it seemed to him that one of these wicks would catch fire any moment and blow up his body like a huge firecracker.

Suddenly he dropped his tools and went to the window. The sky was lit up by the screaming sharp sunshine. His eyes could not adjust to the brightness and he winced. When he could see, he gazed at the fields that spread far before him, and at the sandy path that cut through them and went all the way to the horizon like a straight white line. On the right of the path stood the cotton crop, and the puddles of water in the fields occasionally flashed silver. On the left, the ploughed furrows awaited the seed. The scent of the earth, wet from the recent rain, made him nostalgic and he wanted to jump out of the window. He wanted to roll in the fields and let the pores of his burning body soak in the moisture from the wet earth.

He loved the fields. During the sowing and harvesting, his blood would tingle and a strange freedom would enliven his limbs. He was the village blacksmith, but there wasn't much work for him in the village and he would spend a lot of time helping out the peasants in the fields. There wasn't a man in seven villages that could match him during the harvest or lift a larger load than him. Suddenly, his hands yearned for the feel of a sickle.

Sickles, harvests, the sugar cane swaying gently in the moonlight. The call of the golden earth and the lilt in the songs born of this earth.... He forgot, for a moment, that a hellish fire raged behind him and that for the last twenty days he had done nothing but mould metal into axes and spears. The season of sickles and scrapers had passed; this was the time of axes and spears. And it had been a strange harvest. Instead of the wheat, those who had planted it had been chopped up.

What kind of a mess had he got himself into? It was as if he was shouldering the entire responsibility of arming the warriors of the newly born Pakistan. Pakistan already existed, but to complete that reality it seemed necessary to kill all the Hindus and the Sikhs.

He did not understand this fully, but this was what everybody said, from the village heads to the imams of mosques. And this jihad would succeed only if his furnace kept raging and spitting out fierce instruments of death.

He turned again to the fire. The sharp bits of metal in the furnace were brighter than the coals. His head began to swim. A sharp, hot pain rose inside him and he gripped his side. Hunger! He hadn't taken even a drop of water since the morning. Now hunger was ravaging his insides and thirst had turned his lips to wood.

'Oh! Bashir's mother!' he shouted towards the house. 'Give me water, quick.' A woman of about forty-five brought water in a jug. She wore a nose ring and her silver earrings swayed as she walked. She stared at her husband. He was panting with thirst. She had offered him food and water three times already since the morning, but he hadn't responded and had continued to blow at his fire. What had made him think of food and water now? She looked at the torrid fire, at the bits of iron scattered all over the floor, and at the evil pile of axes and spears. Then she stared at her husband's face for a long time, as if she didn't recognize him. Dina drained the jug at a go. 'More,' he panted. She brought more water and watched him as he drank. 'That's all,' he said.

The taut veins of his body and forehead relaxed. His breathing eased. And then a shadow of discomfort crossed his face. 'Why are you staring at me like that? Why don't you talk to me? And why do you stand away from me, as if I have the plague?' She didn't reply. Instead she went into the house and brought him food. 'I'm talking to you,' Dina shouted, shaking her by the shoulders. 'Why don't you speak to me? Have you put rice to boil in your mouth that you can't speak?'

The woman remained silent. Dina tore at a roti and tried to swallow a few large mouthfuls. But the food wouldn't go down his throat. He took a few bitter gulps of water and pushed away the basket of rotis. 'Not talking to me, just staring as if I've been possessed by demons.'

'Allah forbid,' she said, 'but it does appear so to me.' Dina's mouth fell open in surprise. He had lost all hope that Bashir's mother would ever speak, that she would break the stubborn silence of so many days.

When he recovered somewhat from his surprise, he said, 'I know what's on your mind, but what can I do? Your sons won't let me be. Now Bashir wants fifty axes ready by tomorrow night. He'll be at my neck if they aren't ready. I know you think otherwise but if I don't obey them they'll cut me into pieces.'

'Are they your sons or someone else's?' she asked, a little ashamed of her own question.

'Mine,' he replied, somewhat foolishly.

'Then should they fear you, or should you fear them?'

'You talk as if you don't know your own sons, what savages they are. Can I say anything to them? As if they wouldn't skin me alive....' said Dina.

'They are my sons, too.' His wife's tone was softer now. 'You know they shout at me and curse me. But I don't go making axes for them.'

'I only make the axes,' he replied. 'I don't kill people with them.'

'It's worse than killing,' she said. 'The killer kills one or two or at most, a handful of people. Each axe made by your hands kills dozens.'

A tremor passed through Dina's spine. Then this trembling touched every pore of his body. For a long time he was silent. And then, 'You are blaming me! Why don't you talk to your sons, the great warriors who burn two villages every night!'

'Nobody listens to me.' Her tone had grown even softer now. 'How can I tell anyone what to do? Everyone will have to answer for their own sins; why should I say anything to anyone?'

For some time, both of them stared at the floor, silently. Suddenly the woman said, 'And why don't you eat your food? Do you want to starve?' She slid the basket in front of him.

A soft knock on the front door shook Dina. He stood up in fright. It must be Bashir or his companions. They had come to threaten him. He hesitated with his hand on the latch and looked around. The fire in the furnace was raging; everything was in place. He opened the door. Rusted with the season's rain, it screeched on its hinges.

He jumped back several steps in fear, just missing the furnace. His wife's face drained of blood and a scream escaped her lips. At the door stood the old wife of the Brahmin of the thakurdwar, a net of wrinkles spread across the turmeric powdered on her face. Her head of snow-white hair shook uncontrollably. Their eyes filled with fear, Dina and his wife stared at the old woman. She seemed to be alive, even though she was most certainly a ghost.

At long last, Dina's wife took courage and said, 'Aunt, you are still alive?' The old woman did not reply. Dina's wife recalled that she had been hard of hearing. Perhaps the affliction had pursued her in death too. She went closer to the old woman and, loudly, repeated her question.

Understanding flashed in the old woman's eyes and she said, 'Can't you see that I am alive? Seven days was I racked with fever. There was no one to give me even a sip of water there. Tulsi has been away for many days. I could've died in his absence.... One can go anytime.... My fever went down today. I hardly had the strength to get up but somehow I have pushed myself till here. Why are the two of you staring at me so?'

The old woman was drenched in sweat from the effort of speaking and her breath came in uneven bursts. Holding her temples she sat down on the floor on her haunches. The light seemed to be fading in her pupils and every breath came as if it were her last.

Dina and his wife exchanged looks of immense relief. She really was the Brahmin's wife and not a ghost. The fever had saved her from the fate of the rest of the village. Her deafness had prevented her from hearing of the great sorrow that had befallen the village on Thursday night. She hadn't realized that her village was now in Pakistan. She did not know that Pakistan was now in her village. That not one Hindu or Sikh was alive except for a few girls in the hands of the rioters.

Suddenly, the old woman asked, 'Dina, have you seen my goat anywhere?'

Goat, thought Dina, her goat! In these days, when the rioters had cooked and eaten even the looted cattle, this old woman was bothered about a goat?

'I don't know where she has run off to,' the old woman continued, 'and she's due. I can't even look after myself now. I can't go looking for her, and how can I catch her anyway? If you see her anywhere, tie her up, God bless you. You know she's due. I hope she doesn't give birth somewhere outside.'

Dina said, 'Old woman, your goat is not there. She has been eaten up and has been digested by now.' But the old woman heard nothing. He was about to repeat himself loudly but a glance from his wife silenced him.

'And look at this,' the old woman said, 'I found this chain near the door of the thakurdwar. I don't know how this goat managed to loosen the chain. This link, where the lock goes, has been eaten through and through. I thought I'd ask you to fix it for me.'

For some time, Dina's wife had been staring at the old woman in a strange manner. She seemed to be wrestling with something.

And then, as if everything had suddenly become clear, she said, 'Aunt, why don't you stay here? You will be alone in the thakurdwar. And your fever has just abated. Cook your food here, and bring your own utensils, since you are a Hindu. Let Tulsi return, then you can go back.'

The old woman seemed to have grown even more deaf. Maybe it was the effect of the fever. She only caught Tulsi's name.

'I'm telling you, he's gone out of the village. He's gone with Ram

Shah's daughter's betrothal party to Nawachak. On the first of next month, Preeto is to be married. I told Shah to gift me a cow. It's not every day that there are celebrations in the houses of the rich. And you know, Tulsi needs the milk and the curd for his health'.

Ignoring the old woman's talk, Dina's wife was trying to catch her husband's eye. She wanted to say something but before she could, Dina was already speaking.

'I know what's on your mind, but we can't do it. I have no objection, but where will we hide her? Soon your sons will be here, their nostrils sniffing out human flesh, and we won't be able to conceal her. They will figure it out instantly, and what will they do to us then?'

'She's old,' beseeched Dina's wife, 'the last of our village's Hindus. A God-fearing old woman. It's only a matter of a few days. Let her son return and then we will send her to some other village.'

'Which village will you send her to?' Dina was almost screaming now. 'Is there a village left where she will be safe? And her son: he'll never return. This time he has been sent to a place from where there is no return. All the Hindus of Nawachak have been killed. Not one of them is left.'

His wife's face fell. She put a trembling finger to her lips, begging him to lower his tone. 'Can't you speak softly? Or won't you be satisfied until she knows that her son has been murdered?'

Except for Dina's outburst, they'd been talking in whispers. But it was unnecessary, for even their loudest tones would not have reached the old woman through her deafness. She stared at them with her fevered eyes.

'What are you two whispering away about? And, Dina, why won't you look at me? Just repair this cursed chain. It's not that I'm asking for much.'

'Come tomorrow,' Dina shouted into the old woman's ear. 'I don't have any time today. And go home now.'

'All right,' the old woman croaked, putting her hands on her knees to steady herself as she rose. 'I'll go. If you say tomorrow, then let it be so, but keep an eye out for my goat. I've told you, just tie her up if you see her. Wretched thing. God knows where she has run away to.' And, before Dina's wife could stop her, the old woman had lurched out into the lane.

How much time this old woman had wasted, Dina fumed. He could have made five axes in that much time. And Bashir was not going to listen to any excuses; he would want his fifty.

But he could not put his heart into the work. Something began to gnaw at his heart. He could not dismiss the vision of fever-ridden eyes and snow-white hair. Those eyes were burning holes in his head like two red-hot embers. Most of all, it was her ignorance that bothered him. She knew nothing. That Tulsi was never to return, that Preeto was never to get married, that Bashir had already taken Preeto, along with her rich father's estate.

It was a rotten thing that Bashir had done. Defending the honour of the women of the village was a common burden. Everyone's daughters were just like your own. The loss of any woman's honour was a catastrophe for all.

A horrible scene appeared before his eyes—Preeto, wailing and clutching at her father's corpse; Bashir pulling her away by her hair. Imploring him, wailing and screaming, she had been dragged away. And then she had gone silent, just like a lamb in the moment before its slaughter.

And he, Bashir's father, had watched this evil sight unfold from the threshold. He had not stopped Bashir, or pulled him away by the scruff of his neck and thrown him on the ground. He had done nothing to save the honour of this daughter.

The pale, childlike face of Preeto began to swim before his eyes and her plaintive cries echoed in his ears. He was seized by a shiver, a cold and uncontrollable shiver that seemed a precursor to certain death. The shivering, he felt, could be stopped only if he picked up the red-hot iron from the fire and clasped it against his heart. But why was his head on fire? The entire blazing furnace seemed to have entered his head. He pressed his head with both hands and the fire came on to his palms.

He was going mad. He would end up doing something terrible. He must run away, far away from all this. He opened the window and jumped out. For a long time he wandered aimlessly in the fields. The afternoon had now become evening. On the horizon, someone had murdered the sun. The blood of innocents had spread across the sky and had dissolved into the waters of the streams and canals. Would anybody eat the sugar cane that had been sprayed with blood? Or wear the cotton which had been irrigated by blood? What kind of wheat would grow in this blood-drenched soil? And what kind of a harvest would it be after this bloody season? The shower of blood that had reddened everything had been caused by the axes he had fashioned. This crop of bones and flesh had been sown by spears made by his hands. And he had just finished making axes for the handful of villages that were still left. Those, too, would be gone by tomorrow night.

He was guilty. Heavily, deeply guilty. Bashir's mother had been right. At least he should not let them lay their hands on the new axes. His sins would not be wiped out even if he prevented that. But what else could he do?

And then he started running, like a man possessed, towards the village. He wanted to reach home before Bashir's men. He wanted to throw the axes in some well or canal from where they would never be found.

When he reached the village, it was dark. The indifferent light of a hazy moon threw faint shadows on to the lane. The previous night's rain had left a muddy slush everywhere. Again and again his feet caught in the thick slush, but he kept walking quickly through the lanes. Suddenly, he stopped. He could hear voices coming from a short distance away. In fact, they were coming from his house. Had they already come, then? Was he too late? He could clearly hear Bashir's vulgar laughter.

He stumbled against some heavy object near his house and fell on his face. He tried to get up, but couldn't. An icy-cold grip had clasped his feet. He tried to free them but the grip only seemed to get tighter. A terrible fear clutched at his heart and a cold sweat covered his forehead. With a strong jerk, he turned to look back. In the dim moonlight, he saw a thatch of white hair rippling in the wind. The old woman's wrinkled forehead bore a long gash from an axe. And there was a curse in the wide open, frightened eyes. He looked at his feet. They were caught in the chain that was entangled around her forearms.

He screamed once and fainted. That night he was gripped by a high fever. All night he tossed wildly on the bed; all night his delirious shouts echoed in the silence of the village. 'Don't kill me, don't kill me with those axes! Get this chain off my neck! Oh, my daughter! Don't harm my daughter! Don't harm Preeto! Oh, these chains! In Allah's name, don't use those axes! Don't kill me!'

INSPECTOR MATADEEN ON THE MOON

HARISHANKAR PARSAI

Translated from the Hindi by C. M. Naim

SCIENTISTS SAY THERE IS NO LIFE ON THE MOON. BUT THE SENIOR inspector, Matadeen, says, 'The scientists lie. There are men, just like us, on the other side of the moon.'

Science has always lost out to Inspector Matadeen. Let experts argue till they are hoarse that the prints on the dagger do not match the fingerprints of the accused, Inspector Matadeen will still manage to put his man in prison.

Matadeen says, 'These scientists, they never investigate a case thoroughly. Just because they can see only the bright side of the moon they've declared there's no life on it. I've been to the dark side. There are men living there.'

That has to be true. When it comes to dark sides, Inspector Matadeen is the recognized expert....

But, you might ask, why did he go to the moon? As a tourist? To catch a fugitive?

No. He went under the Cultural Exchange Scheme, to represent India. The Government of Moon wrote to the Government of India, 'We are an advanced civilization, but our police force is still not good enough. They often fail to catch or punish criminals. We understand you have established Ram Rajya in your country. Please send one of your police officers to give our men proper training.'

The home minister told the home secretary, 'Send an IG.'

He replied, 'Sir, we cannot send an inspector general. It's a matter of protocol. Moon is only a small satellite of Earth. We cannot send someone of too high a rank there. Let me depute some senior inspector.'

And so they chose Inspector Matadeen, the investigating officer of a thousand and one cases, and the Moon Government was asked to send an earth-ship to fetch him.

Meanwhile, the home minister sent for Inspector Matadeen. 'You're going there,' he said, 'to represent the glorious traditions of the Indian Police. Make sure you do a good job. Make the universe applaud our department, so that even the prime minister hears about us.'

On the appointed day, an earth-ship arrived from the moon. Bidding everyone goodbye, Inspector Matadeen started walking towards the ship. He was chanting a chaupai under his breath: *Pravisi nagara kijai sab kajaa, hridaya rakhi kausalpur raja....*

On reaching the ship, Inspector Matadeen suddenly called out to his clerk Munshi Abdul Ghafoor. 'Munshi!'

Abdul Ghafoor clicked his heels, saluted, and said, 'Yes, Pectsa.'

'Did you remember to pack some FIR forms?'

'Yes, Pectsa.'

'And a blank copy of the Daily Record Register?'

'Yes, Pectsa.'

Inspector Matadeen then sent for Havaldar Balbhaddar and said to him, 'When it's time for my wife to deliver, send your wife to lend a hand.'

Balbhaddar replied, 'Yes, Pectsa.'

'You needn't worry, Pectsa,' Abdul Ghafoor added, 'I'll send my wife too.'

Inspector Matadeen then turned to the pilot. 'You have your driver's licence?'

'Yes, sir.'

'And your headlights work?'

'Yes, sir.'

'They'd better,' growled Inspector Matadeen to his men, 'otherwise I'll challan the bastard mid-space.'

The pilot overheard him and said, 'In our country, we don't talk to people in this manner.'

'I know, I know,' Inspector Matadeen sneered, 'no wonder your police is so weak-kneed. But I'll kick them into shape soon enough.'

He had placed one foot inside the earth-ship's door when Havaldar Ram Sanjivan came running. 'Pectsa,' he said, 'SP Saab's wife would like you to bring her a heel-polishing stone from the moon.'

Inspector Matadeen was delighted. 'Tell Bhai Saab I'll definitely get her one.'

Finally, he climbed in and took his seat and the earth-ship took off. It had barely crossed the earth's atmosphere when Inspector Matadeen shouted to the pilot, 'Abbe, why aren't you honking?'

'There's nothing for millions of miles!' the pilot replied.

'But a rule is a rule,' Inspector Matadeen snarled. 'Keep your thumb down on the horn.'

The pilot pressed his thumb down on the horn, and kept it that way until they arrived on the moon.

Senior officers of the Moon Police had come to receive Inspector Matadeen. He swaggered out of the earth-ship and ran an eye over their shoulder-patches. None had a star on it, or even a ribbon. Inspector Matadeen decided it wasn't necessary to click his heels or salute. He also thought: after all, I'm now a special adviser, not just an inspector.

The welcome party took him to the local police lines and put him up in a fine bungalow.

After a day's rest, Inspector Matadeen decided to begin his work. First, he went out to inspect the police lines. In the evening he expressed his surprise to the host inspector general. 'There's no Hanuman temple in your police lines! In our Ram Rajya, every police lines has its Hanumanji.'

The IG asked, 'Who is Hanuman? We've never heard of him.'

Inspector Matadeen explained. 'Every policeman must have a daily darshan of Hanumanji. You see, Hanumanji was in the Special Branch in Sugriv's administration. It was he who discovered where Ma Sita was being held forcibly. It was a case of abduction—Section 362 IPC, you know. Hanumanji punished Ravan right on the spot—set fire to his entire property. The police must have that kind of right. They should be able to punish a criminal as soon as they catch him. No need to get bogged down in courts. But, sad to say, we are yet to achieve that in our Ram Rajya.

'Anyway, Bhagwan Ram was highly pleased with Hanumanji. He took him to Ayodhya and assigned him the city beat. That same Hanumanji is our patron god. Here, I brought his photograph along. Use this to get some figures cast, then have them set up in all the police lines.'

A few days later, an idol of Hanumanji was enshrined in each and every police lines on the moon.

In the meantime, Inspector Matadeen began to study how the local police worked. It seemed to him that the Moon Police was careless and lacked in enthusiasm, that it showed little concern for crime. But the reason for this attitude was not apparent.

Suddenly, a thought occurred to Inspector Matadeen. He sent for the salary register. One glance at it and everything was clear. Now he knew why the Moon Police behaved the way it did.

That evening he reported to the police minister. 'Now I know why your men are so lackadaisical. You pay them large salaries, that's why. Five hundred to a constable, seven hundred to a havaldar, and a thousand to a thanedar! What kind of foolishness is this? Why should your police try to catch any criminal? In our country, we give the constables just one hundred, and the inspectors two. That's why you see them running around catching criminals. You must immediately reduce the salaries.'

'But that would be highly unfair,' the police minister protested. 'Why would they work at all if they are not given good salaries?'

Inspector Matadeen replied, 'There's nothing unfair about it. In fact, as soon as the first reduced pay cheques are sent out, you'll see a revolutionary change in your men's attitude.'

The police minister ordered a cut in the salaries. Sure enough, in a couple of months, a drastic change was evident. The policemen suddenly became extremely zealous in their performance. There was panic in the criminal world. When the police minister sent for the records kept at the police stations, he was amazed to see that the number of registered cases was several times higher than before. He said to Inspector Matadeen, 'I must praise your keen insight. You have brought about a revolution! But do tell me how it works.'

'It's very simple,' Inspector Matadeen explained. 'If you pay an employee little money, he won't be able to live on it. No constable can support a family on just one hundred rupees a month, nor can an inspector live with dignity on two hundred. Each will have to make some extra money. And he can do that only if he starts catching criminals. Immediately, he becomes concerned about crime, and turns into an alert and dutiful policeman. That's why we have a most efficient police system in our Ram Rajya.'

The news of this miracle spread all over the moon. People began to come to look at the man who could reduce salaries and yet create efficiency. The policemen were the most happy. They said to Inspector Matadeen, 'Guru, if you hadn't come we'd have continued living on our salaries alone.' The Moon Government was also delighted, for it could now have a surplus budget.

Half the problem was taken care of in this way. The police had started catching criminals. Now only the investigative process remained to be reformed—how to get a criminal sentenced after one had caught him. Inspector Matadeen decided to wait for some major incident so that he could use it as a model to display his special methods.

One day, some people quarrelled and one of them was killed. When Inspector Matadeen heard about this, he marched to the police station, sat down at a desk, and declared, 'I shall investigate this case to show you how it's done. All of you just watch and learn. This is a murder case. And in a murder case one must have rock solid evidence against the accused.'

The station officer said, 'Before we start collecting evidence against anyone, shouldn't we first try to discover who did the killing?'

Inspector Matadeen replied, 'No, why work backwards? First, make sure of your evidence. Did you find any blood? On someone's clothes or elsewhere?'

One of the inspectors said, 'The assailants ran away as the victim lay dying on the road. A man who lives near the spot picked him up and brought him to the hospital. His clothes did have some blood on them.'

'Arrest the man immediately.'

'But, sir,' the station officer remonstrated, 'he only tried to help the dying man!'

'That may well be true,' explained Inspector Matadeen, 'but where else are you going find blood spots? You must grab the evidence which is readily available.'

The man was arrested and brought to the police station. He protested, 'But I carried the dying man to the hospital! Is that a crime?'

The local officers were visibly moved, but not Inspector Matadeen. Everyone waited to see how he would respond.

'But why did you go where the fight occurred?' Inspector Matadeen asked the man.

'I didn't go there,' he replied, 'I happen to live there. The fight took place right in front of my house.'

It was clearly a test of Inspector Matadeen's genius. He quietly responded, 'True, your house is there, but why go where a fight is taking place?'

There could be no answer to that question. The man could only repeat and go on repeating, 'I didn't go there. I live there.'

And each time Inspector Matadeen responded, 'That's true, but why go where a fight is taking place?'

This line of questioning greatly impressed the local officers. Inspector Matadeen settled back and explained his investigative principles. 'Look,' he said, 'a man's been killed. This means someone definitely killed him. Someone is the murderer. Someone has to be convicted and punished. You might ask, who is guilty? But, for the police, that's not so important. What is important is who can be proven guilty or, better still, who should be proven guilty?

'A murder has occurred. Eventually, someone will be convicted. It's not for us to worry if it is the actual killer or someone innocent. All human beings are equal. In each of them is present a bit of the same God. We don't discriminate. We're humanists.

'So the question actually is who ought to be proven guilty? That depends on two things. One, has the man been a nuisance to the police, and two, will his conviction please the men at the top?'

Inspector Matadeen was told that though the arrested man was otherwise a decent person, he was given to criticizing the police whenever they made a mistake. As for the question of pleasing the men at the top, the man belonged to the opposition party.

'This is a first-rate situation,' Inspector Matadeen declared, thumping the table. 'Rock solid evidence, plus support from the top!'

One inspector tried to protest, 'But we can't let a decent man be convicted of a crime he didn't commit!'

Inspector Matadeen explained patiently, 'Look, I've already told you that the same God resides in all of us. Whether you convict this man or the actual killer, it is *God* who will hang. Further, in this instance, you're getting blood-spattered clothes. Now where would you find bloodstains if you let him go? Go ahead, file the FIR as I tell you.'

Inspector Matadeen dictated the First Information Report leaving a few spaces blank for future needs.

Next day, the station officer came to Inspector Matadeen and said, 'Gurudev, we're in deep trouble. Numerous citizens are demanding why we are trying to frame that poor innocent man? It has never been done before. What should we say? We feel so ashamed....'

'Don't worry,' Inspector Matadeen said consolingly. 'In this job, one always feels a bit of compunction in the beginning. But later you'll feel ashamed for letting innocent people go free. Now, you should understand that every question has an answer. The next time someone comes to you to question this decision, tell him, we know the man is innocent, but what can we do? Those at the top want it so.'

'In that case they'll go to the SP.'

'Let him say, "Those at the top want it so."'

'Then they'll complain to the IG.'

'He too should say, "It's the men at the top who want it so."'

'They'll then go to the police minister.'

'So what? He should say the same thing, "Friends, what can I do? Those at the top want it so."'

'But the people won't give up. They'll go to the PM.'

'The PM should respond in the same way, "I know he's innocent, but those at the top want it so."'

'Then....'

'Then what?' Matadeen stopped him short. 'Who can they go to next? To God? But has anyone ever come back after going to God?'

The station officer remained silent. Such brilliant logic left him dumbfounded.

Inspector Matadeen continued, 'That one sentence—those at the top want it so—has always come to the rescue of our government in the last twenty-five years. You too should learn it well.'

They began to get the case ready for trial. Matadeen ordered, 'Bring me a few eyewitnesses.'

'How can we do that?' the station officer asked. 'How can there be eyewitnesses when no one saw him kill that man?'

Matadeen smacked his head in despair. 'God, what fools I have to deal with! They don't even know the ABC of this business.' Then he added angrily, 'Do you know who an eyewitness is? An eyewitness is not someone who actually sees an event take place, he's one who claims that he saw.'

'But why would someone make such a claim?' the station officer protested.

'Why not?' thundered Inspector Matadeen. 'I can't see how you people manage to run your department at all. Arre, the police must always have a ready list of eyewitnesses. When one is needed, you just pick a name from that list and present the person in court. In our country we have people who "eyewitness" hundreds of cases every year. Our courts have recognized that these men possess some divine power that lets them foresee the place where some incident is going to happen, allowing them to get there beforehand.

'I'll get you eyewitnesses. Bring me some bad characters. You know the kind—petty thieves, gamblers, goondas, bootleggers.'

The next day, half a dozen fine specimens showed up at the police station. Inspector Matadeen was delighted. It had been a long while since he had last seen such men. He had missed them. His voice melting with affection, he asked them, 'You saw that man assault the deceased, didn't you?'

They replied, 'No, sir, we didn't see a thing. We weren't even there.'

Inspector Matadeen knew it was the first time for them. He patiently continued, 'I know you weren't there. But you saw him attack with a lathi, didn't you?'

The men decided they were dealing with a lunatic. Who else would talk such nonsense? They began to laugh.

'Don't laugh!' said Inspector Matadeen sternly. 'Answer my question.'

They again replied, 'How can we say we saw it when we weren't even there?'

Inspector Matadeen lost his temper. 'I'll tell you how,' he snarled. 'I have here detailed reports on what you fellows have been up to. I can have each one of you locked up for at least ten years. Now, tell me, do you wish to stay in business or would you rather go to jail?'

Terrified, the men said, 'No, sir, we don't want to go to jail.'

'In that case, you saw that fellow beat the victim with a lathi, didn't you?'

'Yes, sir, we did. We saw him come out of his house and start hitting the man with a lathi until the poor fellow fell to the ground.'

'Good. In future too, you'll see more such incidents, won't you?' Matadeen said firmly.

'Yes, sir. We'll see what you tell us to.'

The station officer was overwhelmed by this miracle. He couldn't move for a few minutes. Then, getting up from his chair, he threw himself at Inspector Matadeen's feet.

'Here now, let go. Let me do my work,' Inspector Matadeen remonstrated, but the station officer clung to him and kept repeating, 'I want to spend the rest of my days at your feet.'

In due course, Inspector Matadeen put together the entire dossier and, in the process, taught the local police everything he knew—how to substitute FIRs, how to leave some pages blank for future use, how to change entries in the Daily Record, how to win over hostile witnesses.... The man he had arrested was sentenced to twenty years.

The Moon Police was now fully trained. Case after case was brought before the courts and, in every instance, a conviction was won. The Moon Government was delighted. The Moon Parliament passed a resolution to thank the Government of India. It noted the remarkable efficiency the Moon Police had achieved under Inspector Matadeen's guidance. Inspector Matadeen was given a civic reception. Covered with garlands, he was taken around in a procession in an open jeep. Thousands of people lined the road and shouted his praises. Inspector Matadeen responded in the style of his home minister—with folded hands, lowered eyes—full of humility. But this was his first time and he felt somewhat ill at ease. He had never even dreamt, when he had entered the service some twenty-six years ago, that one day he would be so honoured on Moon. He wished he had remembered to bring along a dhoti-kurta and a Gandhi cap.

On Earth, the Indian home minister watched the proceedings on television. 'This may be the time for me to make a goodwill visit,' he mused.

A few more months passed.

Then, suddenly one day, the Moon Parliament met in an emergency session. It was a stormy but secret meeting, and so its report was not made public. We can only offer what was faintly heard by people outside the chamber. The members seemed enraged and could be heard shouting:

'No one takes care of sick parents!'
'No one tries to rescue a drowning child!'
'No one helps if a house catches fire!'
'Men have become worse than animals!'
'The government should resign immediately!'
'Resign! Resign!'

Next day the prime minister of Moon sent for Inspector Matadeen. Inspector Matadeen could see that the prime minister had visibly aged, that he seemed not to have slept for a few nights. He looked quite disconsolate as he said, 'Matadeenji, we are extremely grateful to you and to the Government of India but you should go back tomorrow.'

'No, sir,' Matadeen replied, 'I'll return only after I've finished my term here.'

'We'll give you your full term's salary,' the prime minister said. 'Double the amount...triple, if you wish.'

Inspector Matadeen was polite but firm. 'No, sir, I'm a man of principles. My work is more dear to me than money.'

In the end, the prime minister of Moon sent a confidential letter to the prime minister of India.

Four days later, Inspector Matadeen received orders from his own IG to return immediately. Picking up a heel-polishing stone for the wife of his SP, Inspector Matadeen climbed aboard the earth-ship and bade farewell to the moon. The entire Moon Police burst into tears as the earth-ship lifted off.

What happened on the moon that he had to leave so suddenly? What did the prime minister of Moon write to the prime minister of India? These questions remained unanswered for a long time.

Then someone got hold of that confidential letter and made parts of it public.

> Thank you for lending us the services of Inspector Matadeen, but now you must recall him immediately. We had thought India was our friend, but only an enemy could have done what you did to us. We were innocent and trusting, and you deceived us. Ever since Inspector Matadeen has trained our police, things have come to a terrible pass. No one comes to the help of an assault victim for fear he might himself be accused. Sons abandon their sick parents, lest they be charged with murder. Houses catch fire and burn down, but neighbours don't help for fear they might be accused of arson. Children drown before people's eyes but no one comes to their rescue lest they be accused of drowning them. All human relations are breaking down. Your man has destroyed almost half of our civilized life. If he stays around longer he'll destroy the remaining half. Please call him back immediately to your own Ram Rajya....

32

THE TIMES HAVE CHANGED

KRISHNA SOBTI

Translated from the Hindi by Poonam Saxena

DAWN WAS BREAKING BY THE TIME SHAHNI, WRAPPED IN A THICK cotton shawl, rosary clasped in her hands, reached the banks of the river. A rosy hue was spreading far above on the curtain of the sky. Shahni took off her clothes, placed them to one side and, saying 'Shri Ram, Shri Ram', stepped into the water. She filled her cupped hands with water, saluted the sun god, splashing a little water on her sleepy eyes.

The waters of the Chenab were as cold as before, and the waves were kissing each other. Far away, in the mountains of Kashmir, the ice was melting. Bouncing, rolling waves smashed against the overhanging banks, but somehow that day, the sand that stretched far into the distance seemed silent and still! Shahni put on her clothes, looked around, there wasn't even a shadow to be seen. But below, on the sand, were countless footprints. She shivered a little with fear!

She had a sense of danger and fear in the sweet silence of dawn. She had bathed here for the last fifty years. What a long time! This was the same riverbank where she had first stepped foot as a bride. And today there was no Shahji, nor her educated son. She was alone, alone in Shahji's enormous haveli. But no! What was she thinking so early in the morning? Why was she unable to turn away from worldly matters! Shahni took a deep breath and, chanting 'Shri Ram, Shri Ram', made her way home through the bajra fields. Smoke rose from some of the whitewashed courtyards. Tann-tann rang the bells of the bullocks. Even so...even so, there was a feeling of suffocation. Even the Jammiwala well wasn't working that day. All the people here were Shahji's tenants. Shahni looked up. These fields, stretching for miles, are ours. Looking at the full, abundant, fresh harvest, Shahni was swamped with a love born out of a sense of belonging. This was all because of Shahji's blessings. Lands extending right up to far-off villages, dotted with wells—they owned all of it. Three harvests in a year, the land bequeathed gold. Shahni moved towards the well and called out, 'Shera, Shera! Hussaina, Hussaina....'

Shera recognized Shahni's voice. He would, wouldn't he! After the death of his mother, Jaina, Shera had grown up in Shahni's care. He picked up the chopper and pushed it under the pile of grass lying nearby. Holding the hookah in his hand, he said, 'Ai Hussaina, Hussaina....' How Shahni's voice affected him! He had been thinking about taking the trunks full of silver and gold lying in that dark, little room in Shahni's grand haveli....

And that's when he heard, 'Shera, Shera....' Shera was enraged. Who should he vent his anger on? On Shahni? He screamed, 'Ai, are you dead!... May God give you death....'

Hussaina put aside the platter she was using for kneading dough and hurried outside, 'Coming, coming, why are you so irritated early in the morning?'

By now Shahni had come closer. She had heard Shera's angry outburst. Lovingly she said, 'Hussaina, is this any time to quarrel? He is mad. But you should be more strong of heart.'

'Strong-hearted!' Hussaina said, her voice full of pride, 'Shahni, boys will be boys, after all. Have you asked Shera why he only curses so early in the morning?'

Shahni patted Hussaina's back fondly and said with a laugh, 'Silly girl, I like the bride more than the boy! Shera....'

'Yes, Shahni?'

'I believe those people from Kulluvaal came here at night?' Shahni said in a grave voice.

A little rattled, Shera said hesitantly, 'No, Shahni....' Without listening to Shera's answer, Shahni continued in a worried voice, 'Whatever is happening is not good. Shera, if Shahji were here today, he might have done something. But—' Shahni stopped mid-sentence. What is happening today! Shahni felt choked with emotion. Shahji had been gone many years, but—but something was melting inside her that day—perhaps memories of the past.... In an attempt to control her tears, she looked towards Hussaina and laughed gently. And Shera wondered, what was Shahni saying! No one could do anything today, not even Shahji. What had to happen would happen and why shouldn't it? Shahji could weigh his sacks of gold only because he made money from the interest he took from our brothers and friends. Shera's eyes burned with the flames of vengeance. He thought of the long-handled chopper. He looked at Shahni. No-no, in the last few days Shera had already committed thirty-forty murders. But...but he wasn't such a degenerate.... Shahni's hands floated in front of his eyes. Those winter nights.... Sometimes, after being scolded by Shahji, he would be lying in some corner of the haveli. Then, in the light of the lantern, he would see Shahni's tender hands holding a bowl of milk, 'Shera, Shera, get up, drink this.' Shera looked at Shahni's wrinkled face and found that she was smiling gently. He felt unsettled and moved. After all, what wrong had Shahni ever done to him? Whatever Shahji had done had gone with his death. He would definitely protect Shahni. But what about last night's conference! How had he agreed with what Feroz had suggested? Everything would be all right...they would distribute all the belongings!

'Come, Shahni, let me see you home.'

Shahni got up. Shera followed Shahni with firm steps as she walked ahead, deep in thought. He kept looking around uneasily. The words of his companions echoed in his ears. But what would they get from killing Shahni?

'Shahni.'

'Yes, Shera.'

He wanted to warn Shahni of the impending danger, but how?

'Shahni....'

Shahni lifted her head. The sky was full of smoke. 'Shera....'

Shera knew this fire. A fire was to be lit in Jalalpur that day, and it had been lit! Shahni was unable to say anything. All her relatives lived there.

They reached the haveli. Shahni stepped across the threshold, her mind empty. She had no idea when Shera left. Her body was frail, she was alone, without any support! She had no idea how long she lay there. Afternoon came and went. The haveli stood, its doors open. Shahni couldn't get up. As if her authority was, of its own volition, slipping away from her! The mistress of Shahji's house...but no, today, she felt no attachment. As if she had turned to stone. It was twilight but she still lay there, unable to get up. She was startled by the sound of Rasooli's voice.

'Shahni, Shahni, we've heard the trucks are coming to pick up people.'

'Trucks...?' Shahni couldn't say anything else. She clasped her hands together. In no time, the news spread all over the village. Lah Bibi said in a choked voice, 'Shahni, this has never happened before, it's never been heard of before. It's a disaster, there's darkness and violence all around.'

Shahni stood still as a statue. Said Nawab Bibi, her sorrowful voice full of love, 'Shahni, we never thought it would come to this.'

What could Shahni say. She herself had thought of this! She heard Patwari Begu and Jailldar talking below. Shahni understood that the time had come. She walked down like an automaton but couldn't cross the threshold. In a hollow, barely-there voice, she asked, 'Who? Who all are there?'

Who wasn't there that day? The whole village was there, the village that had once done her bidding unquestioningly. They included her tenants whom she had never considered any less than her close relatives. But, no, that day no one was hers, that day she was alone! The Jats of Kulluvaal were there in the huge crowd. She'd understood this in the morning itself!

Who knew what Patwari Begu and the mosque's Mulla Ismail thought. They came and stood next to Shahni. Begu couldn't bring himself to look at her. Clearing his throat softly, he said, 'Shahni, this is what God has willed.'

Shahni's feet faltered. She felt dizzy and held on to the wall. Had Shahji left her alone to see this day? Looking at the inert Shahni, Begu thought, 'See what Shahni is going through! But what can be done! The times have changed.'

Shahni's leaving the house was not an insignificant event. The entire village was there, standing at the door of the haveli, all the way up to the gate built by Shahji when his son got married. All the consultations and decisions in the village were taken here. Discussions about looting the haveli had also taken place here. It's not as if Shahni didn't know anything. She knew but pretended she didn't. She had never known enmity, never wronged anyone. But she didn't know that the times had changed....

It was getting late. Thanedar Dawood Khan stepped forward arrogantly but seeing the motionless, lifeless shadow standing at the door, he hesitated. This was the same Shahni whose Shahji had had tents set up near the river for him. This was the same Shahni who had given his fiancée flower-shaped gold earrings when she saw his bride-to-be for the first time. When he had come to see her in connection with the 'League' the other day, he had said in a high-handed manner, 'Shahni, a mosque has to be built at Bhaagovaal, you'll have to give three hundred rupees.' With her usual simplicity, Shahni had placed three hundred rupees in front of him. And today?

'Shahni!' Dawood Khan called out. He was a policeman, otherwise he might have teared up.

Shahni was lost, silent, unable to say anything.

'Shahni!' he came near the door and spoke softly, 'it's getting late, Shahni! Take something with you if you want to. Have you put away something or not? Any gold, silver....'

In a muffled voice, Shahni said, 'Gold, silver!' She paused for a moment and then said simply, 'Gold, silver! All that is for you people, child. My gold is spread out on every inch of this land.'

A shamefaced Dawood Khan said, 'Shahni, you are alone, you should keep something with you. At least keep some cash with you. Who knows what could happen at any time....'

'Time?' Shahni laughed, her eyes wet with tears. 'Dawood Khan, will I be alive to see a better time than this!' she said, her voice a mix of anguish and censure.

Dawood Khan had no answer. Gathering his courage, he said, 'Shahni...a little cash is necessary.'

'No child, this house....' Shahni's throat choked with tears, 'is more beloved to me than any money. The money that is here will stay here.'

At that moment Shera came and stood nearby. From a distance he had seen Dawood Khan next to Shahni and suspected that Dawood was probably extracting something or the other from her. 'Khan Sahib, it's getting late....'

Shahni started. Getting late.... I'm getting late in my own house! Rebellion emerged from her whirlpool of tears. I am the queen of this house made by my ancestors and these people have grown up under my care. No, this is too much. All right, it's getting late. It's getting late. That was the only thing echoing in her ears: it's getting late, but, no, Shahni would not leave her ancestral home in tears, she would leave with pride, she would cross the threshold with her head held high, the same threshold where she had once arrived and stood like a queen. Steadying her wobbling legs, Shahni wiped her eyes with her dupatta and crossed the threshold. The old women in the crowd broke down. The one who had been their friend and companion in both happy and sad times was leaving. Who could be compared to her! God had given everything, but, fortunes changed, times changed....

Shahni covered her head with her dupatta and looked at the haveli one last time, her eyes blurred with tears. Even after Shahji's death, she had looked after the legacy entrusted to her so carefully, now that legacy itself had betrayed her. Shahni folded her hands. This was the last sight, the last salutation. Shahni's eyes would never again see this great haveli. Her love made her think: why don't I walk through the entire house one more time? She was feeling disheartened, but she wouldn't let it show in front of the people before whom she had always stood tall. This was enough. Everything was done. She lowered her head. After crossing the threshold, a few tears trickled out of the eyes of the daughter-in-law of this noble house. Shahni set off, the grand mansion was left behind. Dawood Khan, Shera, Patwari, Jailldaar, children, the very old, women, men, all followed in her wake.

The trucks were full by now. Shahni dragged herself forward. The assembled villagers were moved. Shera, the bloodthirsty Shera's heart, was breaking. Dawood Khan stepped forward and opened the door of the truck. Shahni moved ahead. Ismail stepped forward and said in a heavy voice, 'Shahni, say something before leaving. Any blessing from you will come true!' And he wiped the tears from his eyes with his turban. Suppressing her sobs, her throat full of unshed tears, Shahni said, 'May God keep you well, my child, may you have joy and happiness....'

That small mass of people wept. There was not a grain of bitterness in Shahni's heart. But we—we couldn't keep Shahni with us. Shera stepped forward and touched Shahni's feet. 'Shahni, nobody could do anything, the ruling power changed....' Shahni placed a trembling hand on Shera's head and said falteringly, 'Live long, my dearest one.' Dawood Khan gestured with his hand. Some of the old women embraced Shahni and the truck set off.

It was time to move on. The haveli, the new sitting room, the high chamber, the big veranda—one by one, all of them spun in front of Shahni's eyes! She knew nothing—whether the truck was moving or whether she herself was moving. Her eyes rained tears. A shaken, unsettled Dawood Khan looked at the old Shahni. Where would she go now?

'Shahni, don't keep any bitterness in your heart. If we could have done something, wouldn't we have kept you with us? The times are what they are. The government has changed, the times have changed....'

Shahni reached the camp at night and, lying on the ground, she thought in her wounded heart, 'The government has changed...but how can money change, I've left it behind anyway, what does it matter to me....'

And Shahni's eyes filled with tears.

It rained blood that night on the villages around the green fields.

Perhaps the government was changing, the times were changing.

LORD OF THE RUBBLE

MOHAN RAKESH

Translated from the Hindi by Poonam Saxena

THEY HAD COME TO AMRITSAR FROM LAHORE AFTER SEVEN AND A HALF years. Attending the hockey match was an excuse, they were more interested in seeing those houses and bazaars that had become foreign to them seven and a half years ago. You could see groups of Muslims wandering around the different streets. They gazed at every little thing with such enthusiasm, it was as though the city was not just an ordinary city but a full-fledged 'attraction centre'.

Going through narrow bazaars, they reminded each other of all the old, familiar things—Look, Fatehdina, there are fewer sugar shops in the bazaar! Sukkhi Bhatiyarin used to have a furnace in that corner, right there where a paanwallah is sitting now...look at the salt market, Khan Sahib! Every lalain here has so much salt in her that....!

Ornate plumed turbans and red Turki caps were seen in the bazaars after a long time. Many of the Muslims who had come from Lahore had been forced to leave Amritsar during Partition. Seeing the inevitable changes that seven and a half years had wrought, their eyes either filled with astonishment or clouded with regret. Vallah! How did Katra Jaimalsingh become so wide? Did all the houses on this side burn down? Wasn't Hakim Asif Ali's shop here? Now a cobbler has usurped it?

Snatches of such conversations could also be heard—Wali, the masjid is still there, as it was! They haven't turned it into a gurdwara!

Wherever the Pakistanis went in the city, people looked at them with eager curiosity. Some fearful folk still stepped aside when they saw the Muslims walking towards them, but others went forward to embrace them. Mostly they asked the visitors questions such as: what is Lahore like these days? Is Anarkali as lively as it used to be? We've heard that the Shah Almi Gate Bazaar has been built anew? Has there been any special change in Krishan Nagar? Has the Rishwatpura there really been built from money got from bribes? They say that the burqa has completely vanished from Pakistan, is this true? There was such affection in these questions, it was as if Lahore was not a city, but a close relative of thousands of people, and they longed to hear about the well-being of that dear relation. The visitors from Lahore were the guests of the entire city for that day and people were thrilled to meet them and chat with them.

Bazaar Baansa was a derelict bazaar in Amritsar that had largely been inhabited by lower-class Muslims before Partition. It mostly had shops selling bamboo and wooden roof beams, all had been destroyed in a fire. The Bazaar Baansa fire was Amritsar's most terrifying fire and for a while there was the fear that the entire city might burn down. The fire had consumed many of Bazaar Baansa's neighbourhoods. It had eventually been brought under control, but for every Muslim home that was burnt, four to six Hindu homes had also been reduced to ashes. Now seven and a half years later, many new buildings had come up in their place, but there were still piles of rubble here and there. These little hills of debris sitting next to new buildings created a strange ambience.

But even on such a day, Bazaar Baansa saw no hustle and bustle, no excited throngs, because most of the people who lived there had perished along with their houses, and as for those who'd survived and left, perhaps none of them had the courage to return. There was only a thin, old Muslim man who ventured into the deserted bazaar that day. Looking at the new buildings and burnt houses, he felt he had strayed into a maze. When he reached the lane that turned left, he made as if to enter, but then hesitated and remained standing where he was. As if he couldn't believe that this was the lane where he wanted to go. On one side of the lane, a few children were playing and a little further, two women were screaming abuse at each other at the tops of their voices.

'Everything has changed but the way people talk hasn't changed!' said the old Muslim softly to himself. He stood where he was, leaning on his walking stick. His knees stuck out of his pyjamas.

There were three or four patches sewn on his sherwani, just above his knees. A small child came crying out of the lane. He called out to him cajolingly, 'Come here, bete! Come, I'll give you something, come.' And he put his hand inside his pocket, looking for something he could give the child. For an instant, the child stopped crying, but then he pursed his lips again and began wailing. A young girl, around sixteen or seventeen, came running out of the lane, caught the child's arm and took him back into the lane. Now the child squirmed, trying to free his arm even as he continued crying. The girl picked him up, gathered him tightly to her, kissed him and said, 'Keep quiet, khasam-khane! If you keep crying, that Muslim man will grab you and take you away! Keep quiet, I tell you!'

The old Muslim had taken out a coin to give the child, now he put it back in his pocket. He removed his cap, scratched his head a little, then tucked the cap under his arm. His throat was dry and his knees were trembling a little. Taking the support of a wooden platform of a closed shop just outside the lane, he put his cap back on his head. In front of the lane was a three-storeyed house. Once that space had been used for storing tall piles of wooden beams. On an electric wire in front sat two plump eagles, inert and unmoving. There was a patch of sun near the electric pole. For a while, he gazed at the tiny specks of dust floating in the sunshine. Then the words 'Ya malik!' escaped from his mouth.

A young man swinging a bunch of keys came towards the lane. Seeing the old man, he said, 'Why are you standing here, Mianji?'

The old man felt a faint quiver in his chest and arms. He moistened his lips with his tongue, looked at the young man carefully and said, 'Bete, your name is Manori, isn't it?'

The young man stopped twirling the bunch of keys, closed his fist around them, and asked in some astonishment, 'How do you know my name?'

'Seven and a half years ago you were this high,' said the old man, trying to smile.

'You've come from Pakistan today?'

'Yes! We used to stay in this very lane,' said the old man. 'My son, Chiragdin, was your tailor. We had built a new house here six months before Partition.'

'Oh, Ghani Mian!' Manori said, recognizing him.

'Yes, bete, I am your Ghani Mian! I can't meet Chirag, his wife, and children, but let me at least see the house once!' The old man removed his cap, rubbed his head, and controlled his tears.

'You left much before, didn't you?' said Manori, his voice full of sympathy.

'Yes, bete, it was my cursed bad luck that I left on my own much earlier. If I had stayed here, then along with him, I too....' As he spoke, he felt he should not have said this. He stopped the words from coming out of his mouth but let the tears that had gathered in his eyes flow.

'Let it be, Ghani Mian, what is the point of remembering all that?' Manori took Ghani's arm. 'Come, let me show you your house.'

The news travelled all over the lane that a Muslim standing outside had been about to grab Ramdasi's little boy. His sister reached him in the nick of time, otherwise that Muslim would have taken him away. As soon as they heard this, all the women who had been sitting on their little stools in the lane, picked them up and went inside their homes. They called out to the children playing outside and brought them indoors. When Manori entered the lane with Ghani, it was empty save for a hawker and Rakkha pehelwan, the wrestler, who was sprawled out in the shade of the peepul tree at the well, fast asleep. There were many faces peeping out from the windows and from behind doors. A soft whispering began when they saw Manori and Ghani together. Even though his beard had turned white, no one had any difficulty in recognizing Chiragdin's father, Abdul Ghani.

'That was your house,' Manori gestured towards a pile of rubble, some distance away. Ghani stumbled for a moment and looked at it with anguished eyes. He had accepted the death of Chirag and Chirag's wife and children long ago. But he was not prepared for the tremors that shook his body when he looked at the condition of his new house. His tongue dried up and his knees trembled even more violently.

'This rubble?' he asked in disbelief.

Manori saw the changed expression on his face. Holding Ghani's arm more firmly to give better support, he replied in a flat tone, 'Your house burnt down then itself.'

Leaning heavily on his walking stick, Ghani walked towards the rubble. It was mostly just mud, with bits of broken and burnt bricks peeping out here and there. Anything that had been made of iron or wood had been taken away long ago. Only a charred door frame had somehow been left behind. At the far end were two burnt almirahs, a thin film of white dust coating their blackened surfaces. Coming close to the rubble, Ghani said, 'This is what's left? This?' And it was as if his knees gave way; clutching the burnt door frame, he sat down right there. A few seconds later he rested his head on the door and a sob escaped him, 'Haye, oye, Chiragdina!'

The charred door frame had stood, head held high, for seven and a half years, but its wood had completely rotted. As Ghani's head touched it, fragments fell off all around him. Some fell on Ghani's cap and hair. Along with the shards of wood, an earthworm too fell down and started crawling on the bricks that lined the side of the open drain, just six or eight inches away from Ghani's feet. It was searching for a hole where it could hide, but finding nothing, it thumped its head on the ground a couple of times, then veered the other way.

More and more people peeped out of their windows. They whispered that something was going to happen today.... Chiragdin's father, Ghani, has come, and so the truth will come out as to what happened seven and a half years ago, everything will come out in the open. People felt that the rubble itself would narrate the whole story to Ghani....

Chirag was eating his dinner upstairs in the evening when Rakkha pehelwan called him—he asked Chirag to come down for a minute as he had something to say to him. Those days the pehelwan was the king of the lane. He had a great deal of influence among the Hindus. And Chirag was Muslim. Chirag got up in the middle of his meal, and went downstairs. His wife, Zubeida, and daughters, Kishwar and Sultana, peered down from the windows. Chirag had barely crossed the threshold when the pehelwan grabbed him by his shirt collar, pulled him close, threw him down and clambered on to his chest. Chirag caught his hand, the one that held a knife, and shouted, 'Rakkhe pehelwan, don't kill me! Hai, help me someone!' Upstairs, Zubeida, Kishwar, and Sultana screamed in terror and, still screaming, ran downstairs to the door. One of Rakkha's disciples seized Chirag's flailing arms and Rakkha, pinioning Chirag's thighs with his knees, said, 'Why are you screaming, you sister.... I'm giving you Pakistan, here is Pakistan, take it!' And by the time Zubeida, Kishwar, and Sultana reached the spot, Chirag had got Pakistan.

The windows of the nearby houses had shut by then. Those who had witnessed the scene closed their doors, to absolve themselves of any responsibility for what had happened. Even through closed doors they could hear Zubeida, Kishwar, and Sultana screaming for a long time. That night Rakkha pehelwan and his companions sent them to Pakistan too, but through another route. Their dead bodies were not found at Chirag's house, but recovered later from the canal.

For two days, Chirag's house was ransacked. After everything had been looted, someone—no one knows who—set the house on fire. Rakkha pehelwan vowed that he would bury the arsonist alive since he had decided to kill Chirag only because he wanted the house. He had even bought the necessary ingredients to purify the house. But till today, no one had discovered who lit the fire. For seven and a half years Rakkha regarded the rubble as his property and wouldn't allow anyone to tie their cows or buffaloes there or set up a stall of any kind. No one could remove a single brick from that rubble without his permission.

People hoped that Ghani would come to know what had happened just by looking at the rubble. And Ghani was scrabbling at the mud of the rubble with his nails, throwing it on himself, cradling the door frame in his arms and weeping, 'Say something, Chiragdina, say something! Where have you gone, oye? Oh Kishwar! Oh Sultana! Haye, my children, oye! Why did you leave Ghani behind, oye!'

And fragments of wood from the door frame kept falling.

Rakkha pehelwan who was sleeping under the peepul tree, woke up, either at someone's prodding or of his own accord. As soon as he came to know that Abdul Ghani was here from Pakistan and was sitting on the rubble of his house, a little phlegm bubbled up in his throat and he had to cough and spit it out on the ground near the well. He looked towards the rubble, as wheezing, laboured breaths emerged from his chest, and his lower lip stuck out.

'Ghani is sitting on his rubble,' his disciple, Lachche pehelwan, said, sitting down next to him.

'How is it his rubble? It is our rubble!' said the pehelwan, in a voice hoarse with phlegm.

'But he is sitting there,' said Lachche said, a furtive, significant look in his eyes.

'If he is sitting, let him sit. You make the chillum!' Rakkha spread his legs out a little and patted his bare thighs with his hands.

'Suppose Manori has told him something?' Lachche said in the same significant manner as he got up to fill the chillum.

'Will Manori invite trouble upon himself?'

Lachche went away.

Old peepul leaves were scattered around the base of the well. Rakkha kept picking them up and crushing them in his hands. When Lachche handed him the chillum with a cloth wrapped around its base, he took a drag and asked, 'Did Ghani talk to anyone else?'

'No.'

'Here, take this.' Coughing, he handed the chillum to Lachche. Holding Ghani's arm, Manori was coming towards them from the rubble site. Squatting on the ground, Lachche began taking deep drags of the chillum.

His gaze flitted from Rakkha's face to Ghani's.

Holding Ghani's arm, Manori was walking a step ahead of him—as if trying to ensure that Ghani would walk past the well without seeing Rakkha. But given the way Rakkha was sitting sprawled out, Ghani had spotted him from afar. As he reached the well, he spread out his arms and said, 'Rakkhe pehelwan!'

Rakkha lifted his head and looked at him with narrowed eyes. An indistinct, wheezing sound came from his throat, but he didn't say anything.

'Rakkhe pehelwan, don't you recognize me?' Ghani said, lowering his arms. 'I'm Ghani, Abdul Ghani, Chiragdin's father!'

The pehelwan examined him from top to bottom. Abdul Ghani's eyes had acquired a sort of shine on seeing him. His wrinkles smoothened out a little beneath the white beard. Rakkha's lower lip quivered. Then a heavy voice emerged from his chest, 'How are you, Ghaniya!'

Ghani again made as if to raise his arms but seeing no reaction from the pehelwan, he stopped. Taking the support of the peepul tree, he sat down on the base of the well.

The whispers from the windows above grew even more urgent now that the two men were face to face. Surely the story will come out... then maybe there will be some sort of abusive exchange between the two.... Now Rakkha can't do anything to Ghani. Times have changed now...look at him, fancying himself the owner of that rubble! Actually, that rubble is neither his, nor Ghani's. That rubble is the property of the government! That wretched man doesn't even let anyone tie their cow there! Manori is also a coward. Why didn't he tell Ghani that Rakkha was the one who killed Chirag and Chirag's wife and children? Rakkha is not a man, he's a bull! All day he wanders about the lane like a bull! Poor Ghani has become so thin! The hair on his beard has turned completely white!

Ghani sat on the stone base of the well and said, 'See Rakkhe pehelwan, see how the world changed overnight! I had left behind a complete, happy family and today I have come here, to see this mud! This is the only memory left of a once flourishing household! But to tell you the truth, I don't feel like leaving this mud and going away!' And his eyes glistened with tears again.

The pehelwan drew his legs together, picked up his towel from the parapet of the well and threw it over his shoulder. Lachche passed the chillum to him. He began taking drags.

'You tell me, Rakkhe, how did it all happen?' asked Ghani, somehow arresting the flow of his tears. 'You people were close to him. There was brotherly love between all of you. If he wanted, couldn't he have taken refuge in any of your homes? Why didn't he have that much sense?'

'That's how it was,' Rakkha himself felt that his voice had an unnatural kind of echo. Dribbles of thick saliva stuck to his lips. Sweat was trickling down from his moustache into his mouth. He felt as if his forehead were being pressed down by an unknown weight and his spine craved some support.

'How is it with all of you in Pakistan?' he asked. There was tension in the nerves of his neck. He wiped the sides of his body with his towel and spat out the phlegm clogging his throat.

'What can I tell you, Rakkhe?' said Ghani, stooped over his walking stick which he held with both his hands for support. 'Only my God knows how I'm going on. If Chirag had been with me, things would have been different.... I had told him so many times to leave with me. But he was stubborn, he kept saying he wouldn't leave the new house and go—this is our lane, there is no danger here. The innocent little dove didn't think that there may be no danger from the lane, but there could be danger from outside! All four lost their lives trying to guard the house! Rakkhe, he set great store by you. He used to say that as long as Rakkhe is there, no one can do anything to me. But when there was a threat to his life, not even Rakkhe could stop it.'

Rakkha tried to straighten himself because his spine was hurting badly. He felt a severe pressure on the joints of his waist and thighs. It was as if something deep inside his intestines was preventing him from breathing. His entire body was soaked in sweat and the soles of his feet were smarting. Blue lights, like the lights of sparklers, swam in front of his eyes and floated away. He felt a gulf between his tongue and his lips. He wiped the edges of his lips with his towel. And prayed, 'Dear God, you are the only one, you are the only one, you are the only one.'

Ghani saw that the pehelwan's lips were drying up and the circles around his eyes had deepened. He put his hand on his shoulder and said, 'What had to happen, happened, Rakhiya! No one can undo it. May God protect the wisdom of a wise man and pardon the foolishness of a fool. I came and saw all of you, and it is as if I have seen Chirag. May Allah keep you well!' And, pressing down on his stick for support, he hauled himself up. As he made to leave, he said, 'All right, Rakkhe pehelwan!'

A low sound came from Rakkha's throat. He folded his hands together, still clutching the towel. Looking around him with grief and a sense of longing, Ghani slowly made his way out of the lane.

In the windows above, the whispers continued for a while—after leaving the lane Manori must have definitely told Ghani everything.... See how Rakkha's mouth dried up in front of Ghani! How will Rakkha face people now? He'll stop a cow from being tied to the rubble, will he? Poor Zubeida! She was so good! A forsaken fellow like Rakkha with no home to call his own, what respect would he have for anyone's mother or sister?

After some time, the women came down from their houses into the lane. The children began playing gilli danda. Two girls of about twelve or thirteen started quarrelling over something.

Rakkha kept sitting at the well till late in the evening, puffing at his chillum, clearing his throat and spitting out phlegm all the while. Many passers-by asked him, 'Rakkhe Shah, we heard that Ghani had come from Pakistan today?'

'Yes, he had come,' was the reply Rakkha gave every time.

'Then?'

'Then nothing. He went away.'

At night, like every night, Rakkha went and sat down on the wooden bench in front of the shop outside, to the left of the lane.

Every day, he would call out to people he knew who happened to be walking by, ask them to sit next to him and give them advice on market speculation and tips on matters of health. But that day he sat there and gave Lachche an account of the journey he had made to Vaishno Devi fifteen years ago. Sending Lachche away, he entered the lane and found that Loku Pandit had tethered his bull near the pile of rubble and, as was his habit, he started pushing it and shooing it away, 'Tat-tat-tat...tat-tat!'

After having chased the bull away, he slumped down lethargically in front of the rubble. The lane was deserted. The municipality hadn't installed any lights, so it got dark when evening fell. Water flowed in the open drain below the rubble, making a faint sound. Cutting through the silence of the night were indistinct noises from the rubble...chiu-chiu-chiu...chik-chik-chik...kirrrr-rrrr-ririri-chirrrr.... A lone crow flew in from somewhere and perched on the door frame, causing fragments of wood to scatter. The crow's activities made a dog, lying in the corner, growl and get up and start barking loudly—bow-wow-wow! The crow sat timidly on the door frame for a while, then, flapping its wings, flew off to the peepul tree. The crow having flown away, the dog came down to where the pehelwan was sleeping and started barking at him. Trying to make him go away, the pehelwan said loudly, 'Durr, durr, durr...durre!' But the dog came closer and continued barking—bow-wow-bow-wow-bow-wow....

The pehelwan picked up a clod of mud and threw it at the dog. The dog stepped back a little but didn't stop barking. The pehelwan shouted abuse at him, then got up, slowly made his way to the well and lay down there, on the base of the well. As soon as he moved away, the dog went down the lane, turned towards the well, and continued barking. When, after barking for a long time, he couldn't spot anyone moving around in the lane, he shook his ears once, went back to the rubble, sat down in a corner, and began growling.

34

URVASHI AND JOHNNY

MAHASWETA DEVI

Translated from the Bengali by Arunava Sinha

JOHNNY WAS SITTING WITH URVASHI IN HIS LAP, FOR SHE WOULDN'T SIT anywhere else. If she was asked to sit elsewhere, she would just flop dramatically on the floor. What sort of coquetry was this? Was Urvashi going to sit in Johnny's lap in full view of the doctor? The doctor wasn't pleased at all.

Eventually, he said, 'Get up, come this way.'

Settling Urvashi in the chair carefully, Johnny got up. The doctor talked to him while keeping an eye on Urvashi. As usual, Urvashi didn't answer the doctor's question. The only person she spoke to was Johnny.

'What was the problem with the throat at first?'

'Sore throat, hoarseness.'

'And then?'

'Coughing.'

Johnny's eyes turned yellow with jealousy whenever the doctor looked at Urvashi. The doctor ignored this and said to Urvashi, 'Didn't you realize earlier? Didn't you see a doctor?'

Johnny said with a smile, 'This woman, you see, Doctor, is eating me up. You know what a bitch is like, she won't tell you when something's wrong. Look at that face, she still makes your head spin. I did go to a doctor.'

'Which doctor?'

'Kaviraj, hakim, the lot.'

'Have you brought a letter from Dr Husain? Did he check?'

'He was the one who sent me. I don't like what I'm seeing, Johnny, he said. This Urvashi is killing you. Your life will be hell because of her.'

'Did he say what's wrong?'

Johnny's face fell. As though a familiar figure—a doll or an ancient statue—had suddenly cracked and faded from constant exposure to rain and storms. Johnny said, 'You know very well, Doctor, that without Urvashi all the shows will flop. She will sing, chat, dance, sway her hips, laugh. The public will say, how are you, Urvashi? She will say, I'm so happy. I'm the queen of happiness. Johnny keeps me in such comfort.'

'Get to the point.'

Johnny whispered, 'What Dr Husain told me has scared the shit out of me, Doctor.'

'What did he say?'

'He said it'll all come to an end, Johnny. Your Urvashi will no longer laugh or sing or speak.'

'Do you know why he said that?'

'Something wrong with the throat.'

'What's wrong?'

'Something.' Johnny twisted his neck from side to side, like a sacrificial lamb who knows the blade is about to fall.

'It's throat cancer, Johnny.'

'Give us medicines, injections.'

'It's too late, Johnny. You went to the cancer hospital, too, didn't you? Didn't they tell you?'

'They did.'

Johnny's voice broke, sobs welled up. 'That's what they said, saar,' he said. 'I beg of you. If Urvashi can't sing or dance we'll starve to death.'

Johnny wept. Urvashi kept sitting without turning a hair. Suddenly the doctor felt a stab of fear. Of what, he couldn't say. He was delivering a death sentence. There were so many different kinds of death. End of life. Being killed. Ceasing to be. That object which has ceased to be is dead. Urvashi is dead, deceased, rejected. For everywhere in the throat from which Urvashi spoke and sang and laughed, the windpipe, the food pipe, the membrane, the vocal cords—cancer has claimed all of them as its kingdom. The throat was the cancer's throne. When its term ended, the cancer would take its throne and depart.

But Urvashi was detached, alluring, exquisite, her breasts arrogant, her lips reddened, her eyes still. Only Johnny wept. His despair and Urvashi's indifference chilled the young doctor to the bone. As though it was he who had died and frozen. But why the fear? After death there could be neither fear nor courage.

'Say something, Doctor.'

'Johnny, at the hospital, the cancer hospital....'

'They know nothing at the cancer hospital, Doctor, you can have stomach cancer, lung cancer, have you ever heard of throat cancer?'

'Getting admitted there might....'

'Urvashi can't be left alone.'

'This is madness, Johnny. What harm can Urvashi come to?'

'You won't understand.'

Johnny got to his feet with a sigh. Wiping his eyes, he said, 'Let's go home, Urvashi.'

'Johnny, I've known you a long time, I'm giving you good advice. You can't do at home what can be done at the hospital.'

'Will going to the hospital make Urvashi dance again, sing again, talk again?'

'No, Johnny.'

'The voice with which she sings *Kar le muhabbat Lolita*...will it be repaired?'

'No, Johnny.'

'Then why?'

Johnny lost his composure. 'All the "bastards" have signed up with that one-eyed Kani Moti,' he said. 'You want to separate me from Urvashi. Shut up, you swine, say the word hospital again and I'll stick a dagger up your arse.'

Johnny began to shout. A flood of invective, starting with bastard. The nurses and orderlies and hospital staff came running. All of them scared stiff.

'Get away, all you bastards—yes, fuck off. I'll kill the lot of you. All you motherfuckers have joined hands with Kani Moti. You think I don't know. Come on, Urvashi, I'm not letting you go. Shaala thinks he's a doctor. Wants to separate you and me.'

The doctor said, 'Let him go, he's gone mad.'

'YOU have gone mad. Weren't you staring at her all this time? If you're talking about illness, motherfucker, why were you looking at her tits? You think I don't understand?'

The doctor rose to his feet. Placing his hand on Johnny's shoulder, he said, 'Don't shout, Johnny. Not another word. Speak softly, then leave.'

'You're telling me Urvashi won't talk or sing any more, and you expect me not to shout?'

'No, you won't.'

Johnny lowered his voice fearfully. 'I won't shout?'

'No.'

Johnny began to cry. In his patched and floppy trousers, bright T-shirt, the bandanna around his neck, the oversized shoes, and the feathered cap, the old man looked like a weeping monkey. Like a sobbing clown on a poster stuck on a wall. Still weeping, he gathered up Urvashi tenderly in his arms and left.

Outside the hospital, where bottles of medicine were sold, Ramanna, the cripple, was selling tea. Johnny squatted in front of him, helping Urvashi take a seat on a packing box.

'Well, meri jaan?' said Ramanna. 'A cup of tea? A red skirt today, I notice.'

'Shut up, you cripple,' said Johnny.

'You have some, then.'

'Give me a cup.'

'Ginger?'

'Yes.'

'What did the doctor say?'

'Cancer.'

'Where?'

'Throat.'

'Huh!'

Pouring scorn into his voice, Ramanna said, 'Who gets throat cancer?

Don't show me cancer, Johnny. I've grown up with death. If it's cancer there's a rotten smell even when alive. Don't you remember that fellow? When they were lowering him from the ambulance the stench was everywhere. When he died, you know, Johnny, they doused him in perfume, still the fucker didn't stop smelling.'

'I remember.'

'When he died everyone scattered coins, the bastards.'

'You slipped when you tried to pick them up.'

'And you ran away with my money, you fucker. Two rupees sixty paise.'

'Who paid for the drinks the next day?'

'Did I say you didn't?'

Johnny drank his tea. Then he said, 'What do you think I should do?'

'Go to Lengri.'

'Why?'

'Because Kani Moti can't handle this. Lengri will tell you.'

'Why do you say that?'

Scratching his belly with his amputated arm, Ramanna said, 'I went to Lengri. She's greedy. Says, get me good cigarettes, some fries. She wanted a pillow from a dead body. The corpse of a married woman. I told her I'd get her one. So I brought her cigarettes and fries....'

'With your own money?'

'Who owns money? Whom do you belong to, money? Whoever I'm with. No, not my own money. Do you know what happened that day?'

'What?'

'Bhagirath had sold the medicines. Meant for the patient. When the patient died the family went to fetch a cot. Bhagirath disappeared with the medicines and Horlicks, everything. He paid.'

'What did Lengri say?'

Ramanna looked grave. 'You're blaming Kani for nothing, Johnny,' he said. 'She loves you.'

'Fuck off! Kani, that hag. Who wants her love?'

'No, Johnny. True love is a very good thing. She gives you food, doesn't even take rent every month. Just the other day she was sitting with me in tears. She said, "Johnny just has to ask once, I'll support him for life. But, yes, he has to leave Urvashi."'

'What did you say?'

'I said, forget it, Kani. Johnny won't leave Urvashi, talk about other things.'

'What did Lengri say?'

'She said, someone else wants Urvashi. So he's done some black magic. You can't get throat cancer otherwise. So I said, Johnny is my closest friend. I know everything about him, Lengri. Tell me.'

'What did she say?'

'She said, "Tell him to come to me tonight."'

'Should I go to her today?'

'No, it's that man's chautha today. Lengri is a boss at gathering leftovers. She'll be there with her people. So much fucking trouble everywhere. There are rules. Lengri and her people will get the leftovers from all the feasts on the left of the Lakka field, and Magandas on the right. But now these fucking beggars have abandoned all principles, you know? Lengri never goes to the right, but Magandas and his gang have begun targeting the left and creating trouble. They don't know Lengri. She's taking Badri and Hamiza with her today. If Magandas creates trouble they will fuck him all the way to hell and back.'

'Badri and Hamiza are going?'

'Bloody right, they will! They manage their own areas, no problem. Who allotted the Lake Market pavement to Badri and the Kamlavilas pavement to Hamza? Lengri, of course. Do you know how much Badri collects from the market? Meat and fish entrails, vegetables, Badri has a lot of clout. So he said, Mashi, as long as Badri is around, Magandas will not be able to collect food from your dustbins.'

'Big feast tonight, then.'

'Fuck off. It's not Bengalis doing their last rites, there's no meat or fish or anything. But then Lengri said this is a battle for our rights. I'll lose face if I give in. Lengri knows what it is to fight. Even after she's gone, her reputation as a fighter will remain. We'll fucking name a pavement for her.'

'Then I shouldn't go today?'

'Go tomorrow. Full moon, a good time.'

'Will she give medicines?'

'Of course! Lengri never goes back on her word. But don't go in the morning. She cleans taxis in the morning, in shorts. Making lots of money. Go at night. Take a bottle.'

'Kani Moti is innocent?'

'Yes, Johnny.'

'Call for a rickshaw.'

'You'll go home?'

'Yes. If I take Urvashi out in the sun she....'

'Johnny.'

'Yes?'

'Do you consider me a close friend?'

'Of course.'

'From naked butt days.'

'Of course.'

'Leave Urvashi.'

Johnny's heart froze in fear. Ramanna, Ramanna! Such an old friend of his. And here he was, saying the same thing. The icy coldness of a morgue settled in Johnny's heart. Was he to die of fear? What if he did? But what was all this fear, this terror, even after death? Surely, man went beyond fear and courage when he died? At least, he was supposed to.

'Why are you saying this, Ramanna?'

'She will eat you up.'

'I know.'

Johnny looked mournful. As though the clown on the posters stuck on the walls had decided not to show a smiling face to the city any more. Like a melancholy, aged ape he said, 'I know, Ramanna. But you know how I've spent so much of my life in joy and in sorrow with my love. I'll die if I cannot see her eyes, her face, her smile.'

'I know.'

'Would anyone survive, you tell me. You know how beautiful life is, everyone wants happiness. People ask her, how are you, Urvashi? She says, I'm very happy. People say, and how are we? She says, you're very happy too. People say, then sing a song of happiness. She laughs and sings: O *jeenewale*. Jeena. Living.'

'I know.'

Ramanna grew sorrowful too. He said, 'Urvashi is a witch, a prisoner of the devil, a djinn. She has finished everyone she's been with. She will finish you too. And no one knows who'll be next.'

Johnny said, 'I'll kill her before that.'

'You!'

'Yes, me.'

Ramanna sighed. He said, 'Go to Lengri at night. Take her something to eat and drink. She won't talk otherwise.'

'Of course, I will. Urvashi will dance, she'll sing *Bareilly ke bazaar mein jhumka gira re*. Lengri will give medicines. Or else I will plunge a dagger into my heart and in hers too.'

Ramanna clucked. 'A knife through those breasts? Fuck off then, I won't organize your chherad.'

Winking with one clouded eye, Johnny chuckled. 'That comes later, first you have to decide whether to burn me or to bury me. Do you have any idea?'

'To hell with you, as if you have any religion.'

'Bury me and burn me too.'

'Will there be two corpses, you fucker?'

'Me and Urvashi, got it? Get a band with bagpipes, get acetylene lamps, cover us with flowers, buy all the flowers in the city. Then light the pyre. And then bury the ashes. Have a grand chherad. Lengri's gang, Magandas's gang, Badri's gang, Hamiza's gang...give all of them a feast on the pavement. Get uniformed bearers from the canteen.'

'Who'll pay for all this?'

'Oh, everyone will do everything for free. Johnny's dead, Urvashi's dead, everything's free. Fuck it, Laila and Majnu are leaving us. Who will ask for money? When we're dead, you'll see, no one will fly pigeons, no one will sing. They will die too, beating their breasts and chanting, *hamein gam dil, hamein gam dil*. We'll take all the joys with us when we die, fuck everything.'

Ramanna, the cripple, and Johnny began to laugh. Still laughing, Johnny helped Urvashi into a rickshaw. He lit a bidi, taking care not to burn Urvashi's silky tresses. Winking at Ramanna, he blew out a mouthful of smoke.

The miraculous light of the moon bathed Calcutta in love. As though the moonlight was Laila herself, and the city, her lover, Majnu, filthy because he was mad with passion for the moonlight, which was why the amorous Laila had to bathe him.

It was very late at night. Hours made no difference to the night any more. No one but a few street dogs, maddened by the moon, were taking advantage of the flood of passion. Everyone else was either asleep, or wandering around in the hope of getting drunk, or searching for flesh without love after closing the windows through which the moonlight could have entered.

Under such a moon, drenched in this deluge of love, Johnny leant against a pillar, crying. He was very sad. Now he was both Laila and Majnu. *Asmaanwaale teri dunia hamein ghabra diya, saare dunia men chandni kyun mere liye badal ho gaya?*

He was plunged in despair. Even Lengri had clucked sympathetically. When Lengri realized at the age of seventy that she would have to become a warrior goddess to retain control over the footpaths, she gave up her sari and began to dress in shorts and T-shirts, swapping her flowing white hair for a bob. She kept a cloth bag tied at her waist and a mirror hanging from a black wire around her neck.

Mirror in hand, she pulled out and examined the patterns made by the nail of a newborn baby, the beak of a hornbill, the hair of one pregnant corpse, and the vermilion of another. Then she said, 'No hope, my darling. Someone has done some black magic, a demon. I no longer have the power to do any counter magic. My heart is breaking at your misfortune. If you did have to come, why couldn't it have been when the trouble had begun with Urvashi's voice?'

Johnny was crying brokenly. He was dressed in his floppy trousers, bright T-shirt, and bandanna. Oversized shoes and feathered cap. He didn't look like a man, but like a clown who had walked out of a poster stuck on a wall. Determined not to smile, or to make others smile. Rebelling, because his heart was broken. The pain of a cracked, damaged heart is unbearable. A burning in the breast. The flames of anxiety blaze stronger than the funeral pyre. Johnny was weeping, transformed into the clown on the poster. What did he have to laugh at, after all? The flood of love in the moonlight could not heal him. Where was he to go now with his broken heart? *Yeh dil kahan le jaaun?* The voice with which Urvashi— seductive like a swaying skirt, unpredictable like lightning, beautiful like dawn, always alluring, woman of the forest—sang *dukhia ziara rote naina*, sang *love me darling*, sang *tomar golay gaan chhilo, amaar golay shur*, sang *banska khirki banska duara aao banaye gharwa pyaara*, would now be stilled. The glorious moon would set—*mujhe bhi le chalo sapno ke paar*. And so Johnny was weeping. The moonlight laughed at his tears, the dogs copulated. Lengri gazed at the full moon with her clouded eyes, weeping. 'You're Ramanna's closest friend, darling. I don't have the power to stop the black magic, my son. I can't even see clearly any more. That is why I cannot see his reflection in the mirror.'

'It's not Kani Moti then?'

'No, my son. She loves you very much.'

'I'm afraid of her love.'

'Afraid of what? Leave Urvashi. Set up home with her. She will cook for you, feed you, don't forget you're getting old.'

'But how can I leave Urvashi? What will happen to her?'

'Someone will buy her.'

'Who?'

'That I couldn't see, darling. Someone who wants her has done black magic.'

'That's what I suspect. Everyone is jealous.'

'You've gone mad, my boy.'

'I wasn't mad, Mashi, she made me mad. I was young then. I travelled all over in a coach with her on my lap. Dholpur, Banda, Khani, Lalthapur, Hasirpur. What performances those were, Mashi. When she sang *ankhia milake jia bharmake chale nahin jaana*, I would say, *kabhi nahi pyare*. She would sing *jaanse na jaane doongi, jaake raasta tokh loongi, saiyan ke paiya par par jaoongi, roke kahoongi, aankhiya milake*.'

'I know everything, darling.'

'But all dead, Mashi. The throat from which her songs come—it's got cancer.'

'Not cancer, sweet, someone has done black magic.'

'Do you know anyone?'

'Know whom?'

'Someone who can stop the black magic.'

'No, my boy. There was Ansari at Tiretti Bazaar....'

'Dead.'

'Now ask for the lord's mercy.'

'Lord!'

Johnny walked off with a glance at the moon, his head bowed. Kani Moti loved him? Pyaar? Mohabbat? *Pyaar se phir kyun darta hai dil?* Because of Urvashi, because of Urvashi. Suddenly, he felt that Urvashi was alone. Kani Moti leered at Johnny and despatched Urvashi to the crematorium twice a day. Johnny began to run. And as he ran, he changed into little Johnny fleeing the orphanage.

Who had left him at the orphanage door? He didn't remember anything. The orphanage belonged to Puranchandji. Along with all the other boys, Johnny too would sing *deene daya karo* on the train to Bandel and back. It was his singing that made Dalip Singh lure him away.

'I'll show you the world,' Dalip would say.

Johnny had not realized that Dalip was another Puranchandji, who used to take away all the alms they would get, and had the children's limbs amputated. It was he who had turned Ramanna into a cripple. Johnny was spared because he could sing well.

Ramanna and Johnny had run away together. Dalip had given Ramanna a clay pot. He would use his amputated arm to hold the pot against his body and drum on it with the other hand. Johnny would sing. In train compartments.

Johnny had learnt in childhood that people loved pleasure. He could see the sheer effort made to give people pleasure. Horse-drawn coaches would pass, distributing handbills about royal astrologers, non-surgical cures to injuries, and films. Musicians played on the roof. Happy songs, all of them. The coaches would race along, happy tunes wafting from them, and young boys would run behind them, collecting the confetti that Johnny scattered in the breeze. Johnny knew that everyone loved big pleasures. Puranchandji from the orphanage used to love them too. He would distribute sweets on his parents' birthdays. Those whom he had crippled were not left out. Puranchandji would climb on to a large table and sit cross-legged. He wouldn't even drink a glass of water till he had performed his puja to Shiva; he had a permanent trident drawn on his forehead with sandalwood paste. From a huge basket he would toss the sweets to the boys, and order them, 'There! Pick them up! Eat! Laugh, sing, dance.'

Johnny and his companions would laugh and sing and dance uninhibitedly. The cripples and the one-eyed among them would laugh the loudest. Johnny had discovered that people loved pleasure. Pink handbills would turn the air of the city pink. Some of them would say that the astrologer was the storehouse of happiness. Some would say the most terrible wounds could be cured without pain. Abdalla would sit with his parrot on the pavement, distributing happiness. The movies offered 200 per cent happiness. The heroes would always get the heroines at the end.

Even when Dalip turned into another Puranchandji and took away the money that Johnny and Ramanna made from singing in trains, Johnny used to sing songs of happiness. He knew people went to the movies in search of pleasure. All these Bengali clerks, salesmen, peddlers, middlemen, shopkeepers, hawkers, all of them went to the movies for happiness. They tolerated the sad scenes and sad songs because all sorrows would ultimately be converted to joy.

So Johnny would sing a sad song, *yeh dil kahan le jaoon*, first, followed by *main ban ki chidiya*, to make everyone happy. People could become happy quite easily. Those who did not watch films because they had no money got their pleasure from the queues at the cinema halls. The penniless people who could not afford sweets got their pleasure from licking the pots thrown into the street. Legless and armless beggars who rolled on the melting tar of Chowringhee to collect money for Puranchandji got their pleasure by staring at the apple-like foreign women.

He had realized right then that he would have to escape from Dalip's reach. He would peddle happiness all by himself, all over the country.

Ramanna did not leave, staying on in Calcutta instead. Kani Moti had not become blind in one eye yet. She was the landlady's niece at the time. Ramanna and Johnny had pimped for Chandni and Reshmi and Bedana and other women for some time.

Johnny would also sell film tickets on the black market. He slept on the pavement. When he came into some money, he ate seekh kebab at Habib's. Johnny was one of those beggars who felt Calcutta was in their pocket when they had twenty-five paise to call their own. Eternally happy, independent. Which was why he ignored the landlady. Marry Moti, start a family—he didn't care for such advice. Who was going to marry Moti? Who wanted to become another Puranchandji, another Dalip, and become rich on the money earned by Chandni and Reshmi with physical labour?

Pleasure was to be found in the air in Calcutta.

Johnny had said, 'You can stay here.'

'What will you do?'

'I'll pick up pleasure from the world, phir sab ko de dega—it'll be the biggest charity, motherfucker. I'll give everyone all the pleasure they want. I'll tell them, you bastards, sleep on the pavement, eat on the pavement, dress up and leer at women. Sing, laugh. Happiness is the greatest jewel of life. I'll put the jewel in everyone's hand.'

'And am I just going to die here, you fucker?'

'Not at all. Let me find my pleasure first, then I'll take you along.'

'So you won't marry Moti?'

'Never, motherfucker.'

'She won't marry me.'

'You're a cripple.'

'My heart will break if you leave.'

'But you're my closest friend. Even if I leave I'll send for you.'

'You must go.'

'You're sure?'

'My word.'

'Ev...erything.'

'You'll take care of my chherad if I die. If you die, I'll take care of yours.'

'Sign in blood.'

'Okay then, bastard. Here.'

They had sliced their skin open with the same knife. Laughed in unison. Watched a film with their arms around each other's shoulders. Had seekh kebab at Habib's. Then Johnny had gone off to Howrah Station, climbing into the first train he could see. He hadn't bought a ticket—he had just curled up on the floor. He was in Ranchi before dawn. That was when

Johnny had planned his life. Master Johnny's One-man Show. Ranchi, Daltanganj, and then, going further north, westward through Banaras, Allahabad, Lucknow. Different lives, different performances. Like the patterns of performances, the patterns of life also varied. When the film ran, Johnny could see the pattern. At the market, on the street, at the crossroads. As Majnu he would sing *chalti hai karvan*. As Laili he would sing *aasmanwale teri dunia mujhe ghabra diya*. As the villain he would say, bachho, mere chakku se tere kalije nikal dunga. As the joker he would stuff a pillow into his pants and dance.

The coins would rain into his bowl. Those who were in the greatest need of pleasure had no money. All of them would crowd around to watch Johnny's performance. Johnny would say, 'People of the world! Pleasure is a bird in this world. It flies around. I've captured it to give it to you.' As Tansen he would sing like Saigal, *bina pankhe panchhi hoon main*. As Akbar he would say, 'Tansen! Tumne yeh gaana kyun gaaye, Tansen?' As Tansen he would say, 'Yeh gaana nahi, Shahenshah! Yeh tute huye dil ka pukara hai.'

Still as Tansen, he would lie down and say, 'Mera pyaas bujhao!' Back on his feet, he was the singer again, raising his arms to the sky and singing, *Barso re! Kaale badaria, piya par barso*.

Johnny would return to the station platform after vending pleasure to the public, and lie down by himself on a bench. Every life had its own pattern. The sahibs and memsahibs went to Simla with their dogs. He was very keen to have a street dog as a pet in this lonely life of his. He would name it Rover. Rover would walk around with him on a leash. He would tell people it was an alchechhian. Stunted because I can't afford meat.

He had many other desires. Of travelling in a coach with Phulkalia from the Nautanki troupe. Of putting up dance shows with Anar from the bazaar. Of spending the night with Panna from the tea shop.

But the pattern of life was strange. Phulkalia and Anar and Panna had heard richer people than Johnny talk of the same dreams, and spent themselves trying to fulfil them. All that the women would say was, will you marry me, make a home with me?

Johnny would say, 'Never. Free men don't become slaves. Only donkeys get married. I'm saying I'll bring you happiness from all over the world.'

The women would roll with laughter. 'You can't get happiness free, Johnny.'

'What do you mean free? I'll give you bangles, clothes, meat for dinner every day.'

'Everyone makes the same promises. Who keeps them?'

Phulkalia's aunt was a fortune teller. She said, 'You're wasting your time trying to bind him down. There's just the one Laili for him who will find him and make him her Majnu.'

The arrogance of youth made Johnny eternally free. He would laugh with joy. 'The girls aren't willing, Mausi. You come with me. Will you be my Laili?'

'Die like a dog.'

'You'll be the one to die.'

'You'll die first.'

'If I do my best friend will organize my chherad. We've sworn in blood. There will be gas lanterns all around my corpse, a band will play, all the people I've given pleasure too will beat their breasts and lament, hai! Gam-e-dil! Hai! Dunia ke khushi ki roshni bujh gailo. They will weep all the way. When you die the cleaners will take your body away.'

The old woman would try to slap him. Johnny would run away, laughing. But one day Phulkalia threw herself at his feet. 'I've fallen in love with you, Johnny. I can't think of anyone but you. I don't want you to marry me or give me a home, just take me with you.'

'Take you where?'

'Wherever you go.'

Phulkalia was a voluptuous woman. She had pockmarks on her face, her complexion was shiny, she sported a tattoo on her forehead. Her body was like a pitcher brimming over with milk, spilling as she walked.

When Johnny looked into Phulkalia's eyes he realized that a dagger had been plunged into her heart. Imagine a woman who wasn't willing even to take a coach ride with Johnny unless they were married now saying she was ready to go wherever he wanted to take her.

Was Johnny afraid? What was the woman saying? He was a vagabond, a nomad, wandering from place to place. Johnny did not dream of freedom. He had been free since birth. He knew that happiness was a bird. Its iridescent feathers flashed in the sunlight. Johnny kept capturing the bird to offer it to penniless, naked men. How was he to take responsibility for Phulkalia's full and desirable body, of her bleeding, passionate heart? Johnny had run away. Phulkalia's aunt's curse may have followed him. Why else would he have ended up in Mumbai? Why would Hamid have told him at Bhuleshwar Chowk, 'What is this one man show of Master Johnny's? Have you seen my Urvashi's performance?'

'I will if you show me.'

'Put on an amulet with the pir's blessings before you do, Johnny. Or Urvashi will make you mad for her.'

'Hmmph, I've seen hundreds of Urvashis.'

'Not like her.'

'What does she have?'

'Name the one thing she doesn't have.'

'Hah! Everyone says the same thing.'

That evening Urvashi had dressed in a peshwaz and blouse with a churni. Hair ornaments, necklace, earrings. Urvashi was singing on Hamid's lap. Talking. Her complexion was like an apple's, her breasts were like ripe pears, her eyes like lotus petals, her eyebrows flying hawks, her lips a blooming rose.... Johnny was thunderstruck. Why did people flock to his performance when there was Urvashi? She was singing huskily, speaking, telling the audience jokes.

After the show Hamid told Johnny, 'Come with me.'

'Why?'

'Urvashi will sing so sweetly.'

'Will she sit on my lap?'

'On my lap and on yours.'

It was Johnny who had added new acts to the show. He had been educated a little at the orphanage. Then, in his quest to capture the bird of pleasure, he had picked up a working knowledge of Hindi, English, Marathi, and Gujarati during his travels. He used to buy film magazines all the time. 'You bloody Hamid, there's no bichhnechh unless your invess.'

He would say, 'The show must finish with comedy. Happy ending. Look, start with the happiness of the hero and the heroine in the rain. Second part, tajidy. But if it ends in tajidy people feel sad. A comedy ending puts the bird of happiness within their reach. Comedy endings are best.'

Now, half asleep next to Urvashi, Johnny could still see Hamid. Hamid was crying. 'I sold her to you when I was drunk, Johnny. Don't take her. I'll die if I don't see her. I'll sell my tent and pay you. Don't take her.'

'Fuck off, who wants money?'

'I'll stick a dagger in your chest, Johnny. She's an enchantress, a djinn. I got her from a Lahori. Now you're taking her from me? The witch will finish me and then punish you.'

If only Johnny had known. Oh God, how beautiful she was. *Tere gore badan mein gori kaale kaale ankhiyan.*

Johnny fled Mumbai the same day with Urvashi.

Kanpur, Jhansi, Agra, Delhi, Peshawar, Lahore, Karachi, Bhopal—so many different cities. Everywhere at the crossroads and markets and on the pavements penniless, naked people wanted the bird of happiness in their hands. All of them traders in a currency of no value. When they got money they drank, they smoked hash after Johnny's performance. If they didn't have money they died on the streets without taking the world to court.

But times change. Back then, at the height of his youth, Johnny had asked Ramanna to join him. Ramanna would play his music with one hand, gripping the instrument with his amputated arm. Johnny and Urvashi would ride around the city in a coach. Johnny would throw pieces of pink paper up in the air, colouring it with the pink feathers of the bird of pleasure. By then everyone had come to know that Johnny was madly in love with Urvashi. Urvashi was the rose, and Johnny her nightingale. The penniless, pleasure-hungry boys would run behind the coach to grab the coloured sheets.

Johnny began to grow old racing along the desolate streets under the passionate moonlight. Like a gooseberry branch which had lost all its leaves in winter. Just as the leafless branch is all that's left behind when all the green has been shed, so too had the good days fallen away from Johnny's life, leaving him bereft.

The good times hadn't disappeared overnight. Gradually, Johnny's shows stopped drawing people. He had to leave the glittering big cities and start touring Bardhaman, Krishnagar, Suri, Bolpur, Baharampur, Rampurhat, and other small towns. Tattered tents, out of tune music. Johnny's floppy pants, bright T-shirt, oversized shoes, and feathered cap saw him through.

But this was a performance of love. Johnny had loved Urvashi for thirty years and become her Majnu, mad for her. The things that Laili wanted were imitation-pearl necklaces, glass bangles, satin skirts. Then to Calcutta. Come into the tent, pay nineteen paise, watch the performance. At every fair and festival in the city, wherever they were held.

Moti had sacrificed one of her eyes to the goddess, Sheetala, to become Kani Moti, one-eyed. She had fallen on bad days. Reshmi and Chandni and Bedana had been carted off the crematorium, one by one.

It was Kani Moti who settled them into a slum behind Beckbagan.

'You too?' asked Johnny sympathetically.

'Naturally.'

'Did it have to happen?'

'It did.'

With Kani Moti's help Ramanna set up a tea shop on the pavement outside the hospital. The shop was a packing crate, the bench for customers to sit on was a plank raised on bricks. Hot tea and country biscuits. Drink from your little cup, throw it away.

Kani Moti gave Johnny and Urvashi a home. Three rooms, partitioned with pieces of cardboard and rotting wooden crates. 'Pay me ten rupees as rent, Johnny,' Kani Moti told him.

A slum. Putrid living. A single hole in the ground masquerading as a toilet for twenty-two families. There were many other landladies like Moti in this slum. Little children and old men and women sat in the doorways.

The air was heavy with the stench of garbage.

Johnny's heart grew heavy. Would Urvashi have to live in a room like this? There was no reaction from Urvashi. Kani Moti had made things worse.

After the performance Johnny began to cough until he almost died.

Kani Moti brought him a concoction to drink. Medicines from a hakim, an amulet from a pir.

'Why do you do all this for me, Moti?'

Kani Moti said, 'That Urvashi's going to eat you up, Johnny. Leave her.'

'Why? What's your plan?'

'Live with me.'

'Get away from me, you witch.'

Kani Moti left, weeping. But she hadn't asked Johnny to pay his rent for the past seven years, taking it only when he offered. She brought him tea and biscuits and bread and sweets. Johnny called her a witch. Moti said, 'I'm going to set that witch on fire one day.'

Johnny wasn't afraid when Kani Moti spoke in anger. But sometimes her heart broke so much that her tears were converted to song. On those nights she sat with her legs splayed out, giving people medicines and singing. Just as Johnny's songs were old, Kani Moti's songs were ancient, primal. The heartfelt lament of all fallen men and women. She croaked, out of tune:

> *I was as beautiful*
> *As the moonlight*
> *Just like all of you*
> *At home I wore the best clothes*
> *Coaches lined up at my door*
> *The men came*
> *To love me so*
> *And to call me*
> *Darling moon*

Johnny's heart broke too at such songs. Kani had lived in Calcutta all her life. Had she not realized the need for pleasure?

Johnny came home.

A foul odour. Sunlight and moonbeams were forbidden from entering the slum. Johnny lit a lamp. Urvashi was sitting on the bed, looking at him, leaning against a pillow. Johnny alone could tell her eyes were heavy with sadness from being neglected.

'I'm back, my love.' Johnny kissed Urvashi loudly. Urvashi did not respond. Absolutely quiet.

Johnny interpreted the question in her eyes correctly.

'Lengri knows nothing. Says someone's doing black magic on you. To hell with all this nonsense. We have a show tomorrow. We'll make love tonight.'

Uncorking the bottle that Lengri had returned, Johnny raised it in Urvashi's direction. 'Cheers! Only love tonight. Love with you.'

He lit a bunch of incense sticks, and then put on his red trousers and green coat. He was emptying the bottle down his throat. The universe was spinning inside his head. Putting his cap on, Johnny winked. 'What does Lengri know? What does the doctor know? My coat and pants are old, it's been so long since I bought you a skirt to replace the torn one. How do I buy new clothes?'

Caressing Urvashi's breasts, Johnny said, 'Everything will change from tomorrow. The show you'll put up, the songs you'll sing will have everyone asking for more.'

Urvashi did not reply.

'Let's rehearse today. The whole city will be in our pocket again tomorrow, Urvashi, promise me you won't leave me.'

Urvashi was silent.

'We'll do that song tomorrow. I'll start with Urvashi ka khel. She's my Laila, I'm her Majnu. All of you are her Lakshmi. She will answer any question you ask. She will sing any song you want. She will do whatever anyone asks her.'

Urvashi was expressionless. Everything had turned misty. The universe was whirling inside Johnny's head. Puranchandji, Dalip, Ramanna, Hamid, Phulkalia, Moti, Lengri, the doctor—they were all laughing. Pointing at him and saying, 'You lost, Johnny.'

'Never,' Johnny roared. Dressed in his bright coat and trousers, his oversized shoes, and his feathered cap, Johnny said, 'Who dares defeat me. Show me. Mein Johnny hoon. Bastards, swine. Did I or did I not bring you the bird of pleasure?'

Everyone was laughing, the laughter of cynics.

Johnny said, 'Who am I anyway? Urvashi is my mistress, I'm her servant. Urvashi sings *aayega aanewala*. Don't you people know? Don't you ask her at the end of the show, how are you, Urvashi? Doesn't she answer, I'm happy? Johnny keeps me like a queen. Don't you ask, how are we, Urvashi? Doesn't she say, you're well, all of you are happy?'

They left. Suddenly, Johnny found himself alone in the room with Urvashi. He put his arms around her. He said, 'Promise me that you won't leave me? Promise me, I'll die if I don't see you.'

Urvashi was silent.

'Should I turn out the light? You can talk to me in the dark. I can hear everything. Shall I turn out the lamp?' Urvashi did not reply.

Johnny began to cry. A putrid room, filled with smoke from the lamp and the incense. Urvashi was smiling, the smile she enchanted the world with.

Johnny sobbed.

Urvashi's show. Johnny and Urvashi's show. The last show of the season.

Nineteen paise for a ticket. Buy and enter.

The curtain parted. Johnny entered and sat on a chair, with Urvashi on his lap.

Johnny had made up his face today, put fresh feathers in his cap.

Today Urvashi was dressed in a shiny silk sari, with a crown of imitation pearls on her head and wearing costume jewellery.

Johnny said, 'You've never seen the kind of show that Urvashi has for you today. Urvashi, say hello to the people.'

'Hello hello hello people. I am Urvashi. Aami Urvashi. Mein Urvashi hoon.'

'What can you do?' asked the people.

'I sing, I dance, I talk.'

'Why do you sound hoarse?'

'Because you came as my lover and got me ice cream.'

A wave of laughter.

'Will you sing a song, Urvashi?'

'Kya gaana? Ki gaan? Which song?'

'One Hindi, one Bangla, one English.'

Urvashi smiled and bowed her head. Then she tilted her neck and said something to Johnny. Johnny nodded in agreement.

Urvashi said, 'One lover got me ice cream, another got me thandai. My voice doesn't feel right. Can I sing soft and warm?'

'No, sing hard and hot.'

Urvashi sang in three languages: *Chalte chalte alvida mat bolo, Jhilimili kancher churi shohag rani go, Do re mi.*

'Listen to her. Her voice has cracked.'

'Lovers' torture.'

'Then talk instead.'

'Ask me questions.'

'Oye Urvashi! What will you do if you get a thousand rupees?'

'Johnny and I will have fun.'

'If you get a lakh?'

'Johnny and I will have fun along with all of you.'

'Ten lakh?'

Urvashi whispered, 'I'll catch all the birds of pleasure and put them in your hands.'

'What is it, why don't you answer?'

'Why don't all of you tell me instead?'

'Why so soft today? Are you shy?'

'I'm shy.'

'Why is Johnny crying?'

'Stupid, randy old man.'

'How are you, Urvashi? How are we? Tum kaise ho? Hum kaise hai? Speak up, like you used to. We've paid, do you realize we can't hear you speak?'

Urvashi was silent. Johnny had a terrified look in his eyes. Why wasn't Urvashi speaking?

'What's happened, Urvashi?'

Urvashi didn't answer.

'What is it? Is the show over?'

Urvashi forgot her usual soft and sweet tone. Suddenly, she screamed. Urvashi screamed in a discordant, harsh, tearful, desperate voice.

'I'm not well. My voice has been silenced. I won't laugh any more, I won't sing any more. I won't talk to you any more, people. The Urvashi who used to catch the birds of happiness for all of you, that Urvashi is no longer happy. Do you know why? My voice has fallen silent, there will be no sound any more. Everything has ended, people. I'm not well, I'm not happy, how will any of you be well? Your happiness has taken away my voice.'

The audience was dumbstruck.

Urvashi grated, 'My voice is gone, I am not well any more. Not well any more. Not well any more.'

'Not happy any more.' Urvashi shouted at the top of her voice. But suddenly her sobs, her screams, stopped. The curtain fell. The frightened, terrorized audience began to shove and yell. Everyone shouted, 'What is it, what's happened?'

Something behind the curtain was breaking, falling apart, loud sounds.

The bewildered, curious public rushed onto the stage, tearing away the curtain. And then all of them fell silent.

Silence, silence, silence.

In fear, the audience watched Johnny tearing his talking doll apart, sobbing loudly. Johnny's eyes and face and chest were soaked in tears. His lips kept moving. They said, 'I'm not well, because my voice has been silenced.'

But not a sound came from his throat.

COUNTLESS HITLERS

VIJAYDAN DETHA

Translated from the Rajasthani by Christi A. Merrill and Kailash Kabir

THE FIVE WERE ONLY MEN. SOME YOUNGER, SOME OLDER, ALL BETWEEN thirty and fifty. The eldest was beginning to grey here and there, but the others had heads of hair as black as bumblebees. They looked like men: eyes where eyes should be, noses where noses should be, teeth where teeth should be. Arms and legs where arms and legs should be. Copper-coloured complexions. White turbans, some old, some new. Cholas of white muslin, like their dhotis. Knotted gold earrings in their ears. Gold pendants around their necks hung from black cords. Each man spoke like a man. Each man walked like a man.

All were farmers. They worked the land and reaped the yields. The dry womb of the earth turned green with their wheat and fennel, mustard, cumin, and fenugreek. After Independence, these mighty farmers had done well. They cast seeds in the dirt with their eyes closed, and then gathered up the fruits. The five looked as if they had been born not of woman's flesh but from the earth's own womb. As if they had grown up and blossomed among the kareel, aak, khejari, and acacia trees. As if the grass, the trees, the shrubs, the flowers were their kin.

The five were brothers, cousins of near about the same stock. They were going to Jodhpur to buy a tractor. Each had bundles of rupee notes stashed in the undershirt pocket at his breast. The heat of it made their faces glow. The roots of wealth may lie deep in the heart, but the sheen of such invisible fruits shines clear for all to see.

They stepped off the bus with their hands in their pockets and headed off, their strides long and brisk, towards the tractor showroom as arranged. If it were in their power, they wouldn't have let their feet even touch that pavement black as rot. Once they reached the showroom, they recognized the owner through the window. As soon as their eyes fell on his shiny bald pate they cried, 'We're in luck! Omji himself is here today.'

A blast of ice-cold air rushed over them as soon as they pulled open the door. They walked into the shop, and one sighed, 'Here he's enjoying heaven, while we toil like beasts of burden.'

Omji smiled a thin smile and said in a delighted voice, 'If you want to exchange your farm for my shop, I wouldn't object.'

'Hah! You'd regret it!'

'That remains to be seen.'

The eldest cousin scolded them, 'We've only just walked in the door and already you're talking about regrets. Each person must follow his own fate, and do the work that suits him best.'

Sitting on those cushiony chairs felt like sitting on nothing. They poked and prodded the soft cushions two, three times to make sure the seats would hold their weight. Satisfied, they settled into the chairs, elbows on the armrests. After the perfunctory duas and salaams one of the cousins began, 'Somehow or the other our number has finally come. We need to have the tractor today. We started out this morning at an auspicious hour. We need to return to our village before the day is done. We would consider it a favour if you could arrange for it somehow.'

'Every customer I meet makes the same demand. You have waited more than two years and now you cannot even wait two more days?'

The youngest cousin said, 'Two days would be too long. At this point we cannot wait another two hours. Our women have been standing at the doors ever since we left this morning watching for our return to bless the tractor. Charge a little extra if you have to, but you must deliver it today!'

Omji smiled at their impatience, then said, 'I know how you rustics are. I made sure the tractor was ready yesterday. Take it whenever you wish.'

Their joy knew no bounds. It was as if they had suddenly been handed the whole world to rule! The middle cousin looked at Omji's head shining like the moon and said, 'How could a man with such a lucky brow ever shirk his work? May you live long.'

The cousins were familiar with Omji. One or the other would visit him from time to time to check their number on the waiting list. He became as friendly with them as business demanded. His manner was easy, his words pleasant. Every bit of him looked like it had been manufactured in a factory, like the parts of the tractor. There was a bald spot where a bald spot should be, fringed on three sides with thinning hair. A neck where a neck should be. A smile as the occasion required.

He scanned the five faces before him and said, 'You must be relieved. You've spent your whole day bouncing up and down inside a bus. Now sit back and relax, have some cold water,' and he reached for his buzzer as he continued to make polite conversation. A man came in at once. Omji asked him to bring some lassis. When the man disappeared, he began apologizing, 'I will not be able to offer anything to rival what you have in your village. The milk here is water-thin. The curds will turn your stomach. All you get in cities is cooled air, icy water, soft cushions, and bright lights. The grandiosity of the adulterated and the ostentation of the fake. You cannot find good grain and spices at any price. I am ashamed to offer you anything at all.'

One of the cousins laughed and said, 'If you really mean to offer, there are plenty of luxuries to be had around here. The envy of the gods above. Otherwise, we'll just have to cool down with a lassi instead.'

The hint was clear enough. Omji laughed loudly and said, 'No, we cannot have any of that here in the store. But if you can wait till evening, I will be able to offer you real hospitality at my home.'

'Your invitation alone is enough, Omji! Where's our tractor? Let's just take a quick peek.'

'First, have your lassis and then we'll go down and have a look.'

'The lassis aren't going to run away, are they? The sight of the tractor will cool us down. Then the lassis will taste sweeter.'

Omji went with them himself. The tractor stood ready in the workshop. A blood-red Massey Ferguson, vivid as a mound of birbahuti bugs. The sight of it made them flush in their hearts. They patted the tractor and inspected it closely. Then they all went back to the office. Their glasses of lassi were sitting on the table, carefully covered.

Omji eased himself back into his chair and began musing, 'How times have changed! There used to be just one thakur who ruled over the area. But now you big peasants have become the new thakurs. You are the ones who have really taken advantage of Independence. Where before people used to dream of having buttermilk, now they order all the luxuries as if they were water. In the old days people couldn't even afford a plough and a spade but now no one even gives a second thought to spending thousands of rupees on a tractor. Yaar, enjoy this Independence, have as much fun as you can, don't even think twice.'

The fourth cousin interrupted him. 'I wouldn't call this khak fun! Nothing to eat but grain and you barely fill your belly. We've suffered for a thousand generations. Now the one-eyed lady puts on make-up and you begrudge her airs? Thanks to Gandhi Baba we actually live like human beings now. How else would our villages have got all those motors, tractors, and radios?'

'And soon we'll have to fill our stomachs with paper notes. Before too long we won't even be able to buy grain.'

'You just keep giving us tractors and we'll keep giving you grain. Draw up a contract if you like.'

The eldest cousin spoke up. 'No one gives anything to anyone just like that. The water buffalo grazes only to fill its own belly. Everyone everywhere wracks his brain just to find a way to meet his own needs. One does it by selling a tractor, and another by buying it.' When his words reached his own ears the eldest cousin realized his talk had gone down the wrong path and he tried to steer the conversation back to better terrain by adding, 'Still, what you say is true. Due to Gandhi Baba's grace, we're better off since Independence. Heaps of grain in every home, milk and curds flowing freely....'

Omji began shaking his bald head and cut in, 'No, not in every home, that's not true. It's only a small number of you big farmers who have all you could want.'

The youngest cousin had been to college. He said, 'What do you mean *all* we could want? The best you can say is that the jaws of misery's grip have loosened a little. Just enough to give us room to breathe. But happiness is still as distant as the moon.'

Wanting to put an end to all this nonsense the middle cousin said, 'What's the use of wishing for the moon? Let's get down to business. Take the money out of your pockets to give it to Omji so we can get our goods and return. We're wasting time talking.'

Suddenly they remembered why they had come. A moment later their hands were in their pockets, pulling out rupee notes, piling them on the table. A 50-horsepower, foreign-built tractor with trolley, harrow, and plough.

A sixty-thousand-rupee transaction.

Omji got busy counting the money and putting it away in his drawer while the five cousins all stood up at the same time and went down to the garage for their merchandise. The eldest cousin sent the youngest off to the bazaar for garlands, mounds of gur, rum, and bright red gulal powder. The four cousins helped to load the plough and harrow on to the trailer. They had just caught their breath when the youngest returned. They celebrated by passing around the gur and festooning the tractor's hood with marigold garlands. Then they painted a gleaming red swastika on the front of the hood in gulal. The youngest three were able drivers.

The day had passed quickly. The sun was just about to slip behind its western veil. From the Ajmer–Jodhpur toll gate the road looked clear, smooth, and wide. The garlands fluttered in the breeze to the rhythm of the engine's roar. Sitting atop the tractor the five cousins felt as if heaven itself were gliding beneath their wheels. And the earth curving towards the horizon before them seemed punier than a coconut shell. As if the sinking sun had paused in the sky just to gaze at them. As if the thrumming wind were trying to sweep away any inauspiciousness. All the happiness in the world tossed inside their hearts. Even the long journey of the setting sun's rays seemed to be made worthwhile at the touch of the goddess sparkling in their pendants. The tractor's clanging sent birds hidden in roadside thickets and trees flying in all directions. But, to the cousins, it was their own happiness taking wing.

Suddenly, a shrill cry broke into their reverie. They looked around, startled. A hawk was swooping down, wings spread wide, on a baby hare it had spotted hiding in the brush. It seized the trembling body in its talons and soared upwards, back into the sky. The cousins smiled and looked at one another. The eldest observed, 'One's fate can never be postponed. It was destined that his death should take place in this very bush, by this very hawk, at this very moment.' They gazed into the sky until the hawk faded away. The tractor continued to roar along the road. They were approaching a small overpass. The fourth cousin urged the driver on, 'As much as we're hurrying, we're still running late. So far everything has been auspicious—there were good omens when we left the village.'

A steep slope lay just ahead. As they came over the crest they noticed a cyclist riding on the road, a few furlongs ahead. The cyclist heard the roar of the engine and turned to look behind him. A tractor coming. He turned back and began pedalling furiously. The men sitting in the tractor noticed him speed up, and watched as the gap between them widened. The youngest cousin was at the wheel. He muttered, 'Fool! Pedal as fast as you like, you'll never beat a tractor!' He gave the throttle a little tug, and it roared even louder.

The engine's roar rattled louder in the cyclist's ears. He pedalled faster, and the gap widened again. The driver couldn't stand to see the distance between them. He accelerated even more, saying, 'Little mother-lover! He'll tire out in the end, let him enjoy his little triumph while he can.' The middle cousin added, 'You never know what's going on inside the skulls of those bareheaded punks.'

The tractor was racing along by now. The garlands began flapping even more wildly. The eldest cousin agreed, 'Of course, he'll wear out. Why bother speeding up? A poor cycle can't compete with a tractor!'

A piercing shriek struck their ears as a hawk swooped down from the sky and pounced on a mouse scurrying desperately to get to his hole underground. A moment later, the shrieks faded away. The sun was half-sunken. Now the sun would also disappear for the night. Scarlet light radiated from the setting sun, red as gulal, as if reflecting the tractor's red gleam. The brothers turned from the setting sun and looked at the road ahead. Arre! He was even further ahead! The same thought pinched everyone inside: a two-hundred-rupee cycle against a sixty-thousand-rupee tractor. No match! Does a mouse dare to wrestle an elephant?

The second cousin spat out, 'If he pumps those pedals till his lungs burst, it's his family he'll be leaving behind.' The fourth cousin said, 'Ram only knows when he'll leave his family behind; all I can see is that he's leaving our tractor in the dirt.' The youngest cousin eased out the throttle a little more. The tractor was brand new. It wasn't good to race along at full throttle.

The cyclist looked back. He had quite a lead now. And his exhilaration made him pedal even faster. His feet were spinning round and round like reels. The cycle slipped down the road as easy as water down a mountainside. As if the cyclist had turned into a whirlwind, or even that he were riding a whirlwind.

All the eyes on the tractor were riveted on the cyclist. Quite a gap lay between them now. And it was only growing wider. A foreign tractor. Worth sixty thousand rupees. Festooned with marigold malas. And a two-paise cycle! A college punk. Head bare. Wearing shorts.

A sharp gust of wind snapped one of the garland threads. The garland began to flap around. Doubling up, unfurling straight. Another garland snapped. The tractor driver felt every thump of the marigold garland on the hood like a thorny cane beating against his breast. He ground his teeth together and pulled the throttle out to the limit. The tractor catapulted forward like a shot from a cannon. The sound of the revving engine echoed in the air. The sky that moments ago seemed to be falling beneath their wheels now seemed to be rising higher and higher over them.

The gap began to close. Even more. Ah, now they were really close.

The world seemed as small as a coconut, reduced to two little dots. The tractor. The bicycle. A sixty-thousand-rupee machine. And a two-paise piece of junk.

As it happened, two army trucks came bumping down the road from the other direction just at that moment and the tractor was forced to slow down. The cyclist saw his chance and slipped ahead.

The middle cousin said, 'These city punks are worthless! Taking advantage of a chance like that!' The eldest cousin said, 'If the poor fellow wants to show off for now, then let him. How long can he carry on like this? He's bound to run out of breath. Pagla, squandering his energies like this. Once his internal piping starts sagging, he won't even be able to do it with his woman. Were such drives meant to be spent on a cycle?'

Now that the road was clear the youngest cousin opened up the throttle. Like gunpowder suddenly touched with a spark. The tractor was like a dust storm trying to catch the wind. And gradually the gap began to diminish.

The cyclist heard the tractor just behind him and looked around. He snapped his head forward in a fury. And his feet began to spin like reels. They became speed itself, speed and nothing else.

Now he had begun to sweat. He was the fastest cyclist in all of Rajasthan. And, yes, he was also a man. Arms where arms should be, legs where legs should be. Breath where breath should be. Dreams where dreams should be. He had been working out on his bicycle, sixty or seventy miles a day for the past two months. If he came first in the All India Bicycle Championship next month, then he might get to go to Paris. He felt confident enough after two months of dedicated training. But today's little contest would prove it for certain. He clenched his teeth and poured all his strength into spinning the pedals.

He went to college with a young woman who had fallen in love with him the first time she saw him race and proposed to him. But he had not been able to reply with a forthright yes or no. They kept meeting and talking and spending time together, and once they had begun to know each other in their souls, it became clear what they had to do. He had promised to marry her as soon as the All India Championship was over. He had been raised in tight circumstances. And she had grown up in a house of plenty. But they lived only for one another. They ate as if with the same mouth. And on their priceless wedding night the moon would smile on their bridal bed.

Suddenly, her face appeared before his eyes. As if she had turned into the breeze to watch the race. His vigour increased tenfold. As if his feet had grown wings. What power did that lifeless tractor have compared to the shimmery image of his beloved? The cyclist pulled further and further ahead. Before long, the distance between them had doubled.

Now the tractor was at full throttle. They could do no more. Their insides started writhing. The whistling wind was being swallowed up by the roar of the engine. Their reign over the whole world had been grabbed from their hands in a dash. The new tractor shot down the road like a cannonball. It looked as if a whirlwind had taken over that bareheaded boy's feet. His beloved's face shone before his eyes. The distance grew and grew. His lungs didn't quaver, and his breath didn't break.

Half of the marigold garlands had snapped and fallen. But what could the cousins do?

No one can see what the ephemeral future holds. Suddenly the feet fast as a whirlwind were spinning emptily. The chain had come off. Still the boy didn't worry. He figured his feet could match the tractor's speed. Images of his beloved's face surrounded him. There could be no greater power than this in the world. He stopped the cycle and quickly dismounted. He leaned the bicycle on the kickstand and patiently began putting the chain back on.

Slowly the distance was decreasing. The air could not contain the tractor's roar, nor the five cousins' happiness. Well, who knows when luck will smile on you? It didn't matter how, but this sixty-thousand-rupee matter of honour was saved. If people want to deceive themselves into believing in fraudulent victories, then who would stop them?

The tractor's roar sounded closer. It was taking much too long to get the chain back on in the flurry. Before long the tractor was right there. And still he had confidence in his strength, and the power of his beloved's face before him.

The tractor roared past. All five cousins shouted out words typically human as they sped by. A flock of crows began cawing overhead as if in one voice. The voices of the humans couldn't be heard over the cawing of the crows and the roar of the engine.

The tractor was already one or two farm-lengths ahead when the cyclist got the chain back in place and started off again. Four of the cousins turned back to watch him. They thought to themselves, the bastard was just pretending his chain came off! Maybe the race was too much for him.

But the chain was back on and he had turned into a tornado again. The distance between them slowly began to decrease as he came closer and closer.

The scenery was beginning to merge with the darkness. The four cousins were straining to see the boy behind them. He was gaining ground!

Now it was an all-out race. The tractor couldn't go any faster. They gnashed their teeth. The red of the tractor began to dissolve in the fading light. The youngest cousin asked, 'Where is that haraami now?'

The fourth cousin said through clenched teeth, 'Looks like he's going to pull ahead.'

'Hah! Even his father wouldn't have dreamed of it!' As he said this, the youngest cousin started to hear first the hawk's shrieks, then the mouse's squeals, echoing in his ears in turns. After a moment the shrieks were in one ear, the squeals in the other, and wouldn't stop. It seemed as if the entire universe were about to rip apart. The tractor's roar got swallowed up in that echo.

A whole different world was glittering in the eyes of the cyclist. Everywhere he looked, images of his beloved's face were twinkling—in the soft scattering of stars, in the trees and shrubs, in the sand dunes, in the tractor's trolley up ahead. Today would be the test. If he could get ahead of the tractor, then he would get married as soon as possible. Tomorrow, if she agreed. If not, then the day after. Or the day after that. Whenever she wanted. Why wait to pass them? All the world was in the palm of his hand. The warp and woof of golden dreams was being woven in front of his eyes.

Meanwhile, the hawk's shrieks and the mouse's squeals were smothering every particle of air. The four cousins shouted through clenched teeth, 'That bare-headed fellow is making us lick the dirt off our turbans!'

Then they came up with a new plan. 'Make the tractor swerve as soon as he gets close. What will the little haraami have to say to that....' The hawk's shrieks and the mouse's squeals had now found human voices.

And meanwhile the images of his beloved's face began growing brighter and brighter. Each image became more and more distinct.

Now he had moved up, beside the trolley. The shrieks and squeals hid themselves away in the driver's head and assumed a posture of silence.

The next moment the speeding cyclist crashed into the tractor. Lightning flashed before his eyes and the lights of his beloved's faces extinguished one by one. The tractor's rear tyre passed over his bare head, mashing it into chutney. The rest of the faces were snuffed out.

A human voice hissed once more in the wind, 'Mother-lover, he had nerve trying to overtake a tractor!'

The youngest cousin had been to college. He pulled the tractor over, grabbed a bottle out of a sack and said, 'Let's give the poor guy some rum!'

Then he went over to him, walking on two legs like a man. Opened the bottle above the cyclist. Emptied half the bottle of rum into the boy's mouth. Then he broke the bottle near the boy's head and ran back to the tractor. The tractor roared as he took off. The women must be standing in the doorway waiting for them. How happy they would be to see them return!

Human laughter echoed in the wind.

A picture was left behind them on the road, waiting for expert appraisal. Brain-white smudges on a blood-red background. Shards of broken glass. A man's dead body. White shorts. Bloodied sky-blue undershirt. Mashed dreams. Streams of love. The painting wasn't bad!

But...paintings of the two World Wars, pictures of Hiroshima and Nagasaki, of Vietnam, of Bangladesh...those are the true masterpieces. Compared to this one, those are so much more refined, so much more complex and nuanced. This one doesn't compare. Still, considering it was done by a band of rustics, it wasn't so bad.

Yes, the five were only men. Each man spoke like a man. Each man walked like a man.

BEYOND THE FOG

QURRATULAIN HYDER

Translated from the Urdu by Muhammad Umar Memon

I

THROUGHOUT THE DAY ENGLISH SAHIBS, MEMSAHIBS, AND THEIR BABA log cross the bridge on mules and horses or riding in rickshaws and dandis. In the evening, the same bridge becomes the site of milling crowds of Indians. The swarm of rushing humanity going up and down the slopes huffing and puffing looks like the surge of a massive tidal wave. Movies starring Esther Williams, Joan Fontaine, Noor Jehan, and Khursheed are playing in the local cinemas. Skating continues in the rinks. In the ballroom of the Savoy the Anglo-Indian crooner and his band will soon start, *Enjoy yourself, it's later than you think*. Drums will be struck; maharaja and maharani log, nabob log, burra sahib, and burra mem log will start dancing.

At this hour, while the whole of Mussoorie is absorbed in merrymaking, a poor man stands quietly on the bridge near the bazaar—*Kabira stands in the bazaar praying for everyone's well-being*.

In his tattered khaki jacket, a cap coming down to his ears, he looks very much like a sweeper out of work. Holding a little English girl in his arms, he often wanders into the bazaar and stands there silently until dusk or sits on the low protective wall of the bridge.

Why does this sweeper Fazl Masih look so destitute and run down if he is entrusted with the care of some sahib's daughter? Strange!

And this fellow also looks a bit cuckoo. The likes of him were called holy fools in czarist Russia, and majzub in our culture. God knows whether this poor man is a majzub or was merely born an idiot. Anyway, most of the time he just stands quietly. The little girl with curly blonde hair is so incredibly pretty that she attracts the attention of passers-by who stop spontaneously to look at her. Now and then babu log will smile broadly and utter a 'Good evening, Missy Baba' to her. Even recent English arrivals in Mussoorie look at Fazl Masih with a smile, but the local English just pass by, totally indifferent to his presence. The one-and-a-half-year-old girl, nestled in Fazl Masih's lap or riding on his shoulder, laughs, cries, or becomes absorbed in her teddy bear or her lollipop. Fazl Masih gazes at the Himalaya in the distance, beyond which lies the invisible 'valley of flowers'.

When it gets dark, he hoists the girl atop his shoulders and sets out for Vincent Hill with his head hung low. Just once, when some Lukhnavi passer-by stopped briefly and asked, 'Ama, whose daughter is she?' He replied with irritation, 'My sister's, sahib.'

'What do you think, mian, that Hindustan's Anglo-Indians just dropped from the sky?' another passer-by retorted with a resounding laugh. 'Well, this is just how they came into being.'

Perhaps the sound of that laugh reverberates in Fazl Masih's ears, but he never opens his mouth. He just plods along the uphill track to Vincent Hill with his head bent low, the little girl mounted on his shoulders.

The residents of the Vincent Hill area know that Katto ayah is the real mother of the little white girl whose father was a gora, a white man who played the drum in the army band, and that she is being brought up by Miss Celia Richmond, the white landlady of Richmond Guest House. Katto, a shapely and graceful sweeper woman with a delightfully sallow complexion, originally from Gorakhpur district, whose parents had been made Christians by Miss Celia's missionary father, was now Miss Sahib's nurse. Her real name was Martha, but she was called Katto because she went up and down the neighbouring hills with the speed and agility of a squirrel. Miss Richmond received the guest house as an inheritance from her uncle. The entire Richmond family is buried here in Mussoorie's English cemetery. Miss Richmond has spent her whole life running this guest house. Circumstances have made her quite irritable, and because she makes a lot of noise, like a lapwing, the domestics and coolies of Vincent Hill have given her the nickname Chunchuniya Mem, the Rattle Ma'am. Hers is a second-class 'Europeans Only' facility where run-of-the-mill English, poor white missionaries, or fair-skinned Eurasians come to stay. With her keen, hawk-like sight, Miss Richmond can immediately see who has what percentage of English blood. If an Anglo-Indian with even the slightest trace of sallow shows up, she has Katto tell him that all the rooms are taken.

During the last days of World War II, a young Tommy came to stay at Richmond Guest House. He was in Mussoorie on two months' leave recuperating from a recent illness. (During the war, out of sheer patriotism, Miss Celia Richmond had offered her guest house to the British government for the use of soldiers.) Before the war, Corporal Arthur Bolton, the white Tommy, used to be a drummer in the orchestra of an ordinary restaurant in London. He wanted to earn himself a name among world-class musicians, but lack of better opportunities, the fate of many artists, kept him anonymous and poor. When the war broke out, he enlisted in the army as a drummer and was packed off to India. Like other soldiers in the British army, he was given instruction in romanized Urdu. But he also liked Indian music. In short, Arthur Bolton was an extraordinary Tommy, quite different from other whites of his ilk.

Because he wasn't a sahib bahadur of any consequence that would allow him to stay at the Savoy, he flopped down at poor Chunchuniya Mem's. He strolled in the hills all day long or wrote poetry. He'd have

Katto nanny sing kajris for him and keep time as she sang. When she sometimes swirled her billowing white lehenga-skirt and jingled her bunch of keys with a jiggle of her hips, singing, *Mirjaapur men oaran-thhoran Kashi hamaaro ghaat*, Arthur would become overjoyed, clap like a child, and start dancing with her. He liked Katto nanny a lot and had also struck up quite a close friendship with her crazy brother, Fazl Masih. The two would set out for the valleys at the crack of dawn to roam around and stare at the fog floating across the mountains. What lies beyond that fog?

II

When the time came for Arthur Bolton to return to the Meerut Cantonment he said, 'I'm used to speaking the truth, so I always end up losing. Our regiment will probably leave for Germany. A fierce battle is going on there. I may not be able to write to you at all, or if I do write a letter, I might not write any others. I'm pretty sloppy when it comes to correspondence. And what can a person write in a letter anyway?' But, as courtesy required, he did drop Miss Richmond a note of thanks from the Meerut Cantonment, in which he also sent his greetings to Katto and Fazl Masih and said that he was leaving for the European front in a few days.

When a daughter as white as snow and resembling Arthur Bolton in every last detail was born to poor Katto, Miss Richmond, unexpectedly, didn't grill Katto about the matter at all. She knew that Katto was not dissolute. And furthermore, she'd been born in her own house and had been a loyal domestic all along. With the birth of the child, Miss Richmond's otherwise quite dreary existence became somewhat animated and no longer felt so empty. She often wondered why on earth she was killing herself over the guest house. For whom was she piling up all this money? Now God had sent her such a lovely girl.

Miss Richmond also indulged in absurd fancies and theatrics now. And very much like her kind, ordinary middle-class English ladies, she was a perfect snob. She cooked up quite a story about the little girl to tell to the erstwhile residents of the guest house. 'Her father, Colonel Arthur Bolton, was lost in action on the Berlin front. Poor Arthur...' she would say heaving a deep sigh while serving guests their breakfast. 'Poor Arthur was my first cousin. Before coming to India he married the daughter of some Irish lord. Both of them were stationed at the Peshawar garrison. Soon after Arthur left for the front, poor Bridget died giving birth to the girl in the military hospital. Arthur had given my address as "next of kin" so the Red Cross sent the girl to me.'

Even at the girl's baptism at an English church in Mussoorie she had put down the name of the father as Colonel Arthur Bolton and crossing her heart with two fingers said under her breath, 'So help me God.'

India gained her freedom and suddenly Mussoorie began to empty of its English, except for Miss Richmond, who was not about to return to Britain to work as a dishwashing and cleaning lady. Unexpectedly, her hotel, its 'European Only' sign now removed, picked up business, because Indians took great pride in staying in an 'English guest house'. Where earlier quite ordinary English stayed there, it now became the haunt of upper-class, wealthy Indians.

Catherine Bolton, nicknamed Katy, who was now called 'little Katto' because of her frisky, wanton behaviour, went to a convent school. Here, they had started teaching Hindi and Sanskrit after Independence. The teacher was a wily young local man. Katy took Hindi lessons from him, and her fair colour left the free children of free India in a state of awe.

The English priest who had baptized Catherine left India and settled in Australia, but he kept up a correspondence with Miss Richmond. On Katy's fifteenth birthday he wrote about his concern for the girl. What kind of future would she have in India? Surely Miss Richmond didn't wish for her to marry some Hindu heathen? It would be far better if she brought the girl over to Australia.

Miss Richmond gave the matter serious thought: really, what future could such a beautiful Anglo-Indian girl have in India? Telephone operator, office secretary, or, God forbid, a call girl or cabaret dancer? Already Katy Bolton had become the talk of the town throughout Mussoorie for her geniality. The day the shifty Hindi teacher tried to get fresh with her and, when she tried to fend off his advances, outright called her 'a coquette, a mongrel', she went home in a rage and told Miss Richmond everything that had transpired. There and then on that cold evening Miss Richmond made up her mind. She spent the whole night awake in her bed. It wasn't easy to leave home for good. What might become of her in a foreign land? But Catherine's future was at stake, it took precedence over everything. Come morning, she sent for Katto and Fazl Masih. They came and stood in the doorway. Miss Celia sat by the fireplace busily knitting. Katy stood by the radiogram. In a grave tone of voice Miss Celia Richmond began, 'Katto, we're going to Australia. Katy Baba will go with us. Start packing our stuff.'

Both Katto and Fazl Masih were stunned. The two white women before them seemed to have gone off their rockers. They burst out crying. After a while, Katto sniffled and said firmly, 'Memsahib, I gave birth to Katy; I won't let her go. My brother too, this girl is his entire life, Miss Sahib. The only reason I didn't marry was the fear of how a stepfather might treat her.'

'Be quiet!' the old hag yelled. 'Don't forget your place, Katto. What proof do you have that Katy is your child? How dare you say that?'

Katto was stupefied. She never expected that. Miss Sahib had never said such a cruel thing before. Falling to the floor, she cried her heart out.

Katy went into the other room. She could hardly wait to go to Australia. The prudent and far-sighted Miss Richmond had already told her a few days ago that Colonel Arthur Bolton was an imaginary being. Corporal Bolton and Katto were her real parents. But her entire well-being lay in keeping this secret under wraps. Katy, who had an instinctive understanding of the rules of survival, had taken this advice to heart.

In an attempt to reason calmly with the distraught woman, Miss Richmond now said, 'Katto, you're crazy, altogether crazy. You really ought to think a bit...with a cool head. What will be Katy's future after I die? A smattering of Mussoorie natives still knows that she's your daughter. What if the news spreads all over? The caste system is rampant in India. Who will marry her? What is the value of an Anglo girl here after all? People regard her as no more than a tart. Do you really want your daughter to become a striptease dancer in some hotel? Or do you plan to marry her off to some municipality sweeper? Something to think about, isn't it?'

Katto was speechless.

Miss Richmond sold her establishment to a Sindhi who lost no time in expelling Jesus and Mary from the lounge, installing Guru Nanak and Shankar Parvati in their place, and replacing the 'Richmond's' sign outside with 'New Himalayas Vegetarian Hotel', but he let the old staff, Katto included, stay on. A bereft Fazl Masih and Katto came all the way to Dehradun station to say goodbye to Miss Richmond and Katy. The train left the station, leaving behind a forlorn Fazl Masih in his kantop and a light brown quilted vest staring vacantly into space, as was his wont.

III

At the Sydney airport Miss Richmond swept her glance over the place and smiled with satisfaction. She had made it to a white country...finally. (Although she was pure white on both sides, she was born in Gorakhpur. Only once in her whole life had she been to England, and for no more than a few months.) Both she and Katy waited for some coolie to rush to pick up their baggage, but no one paid any attention to them. Finally, taking their cue from other travellers, they found themselves a trolley and started to load their bags. When Miss Richmond started to push the cart, her heart suddenly broke a little.

Reverend Sigmore was waiting outside in the hall and took them to his house. He helped Miss Richmond buy a small grocery shop in the market adjacent to his church and also a flat. Within two weeks, Miss Richmond found herself sitting in her shop by the scales. She had made her entry into Sydney's working class.

Catherine was enrolled in a school. It didn't take her long to unfurl her wings. She went on 'dates' now, returning late in the evening. Miss Celia Richmond, brought up on Victorian and Indian values, would admonish and rebuke her. Heated arguments would follow. The lives of both women had become miserable. A sixty-five-year-old uprooted English spinster and a sixteen-year-old girl of mixed blood with no clear background to speak of. A tragic pair of fake aunt and niece.

In Sydney, Miss Richmond couldn't cope with either her self-imposed exile or her loneliness for very long and died while Catherine was still in her eighteenth year. Reverend Sigmore assumed guardianship of the girl. He had her admitted into the school's boarding house. Within a few months she ran away. Not even in a blue moon did she deign to drop a letter to her mother or uncle. A few months later the priest also died. Catherine's boyfriends knew she had come into a lot of money. When she attained legal maturity they started to play fast and loose with it. A ravishing beauty, her life's ambition was to become an actress, but back in those days Australia boasted neither a regular theatre scene nor a movie industry. Some rake advised her to take off for Hollywood, or if she wanted to enter London showbiz, the best place to start was the nightclubs there. She took cabaret lessons. In the meantime, she sold her grocery shop and had pretty much spent her entire inheritance. Money just slipped through her fingers like sand.

And so, wandering through Hong Kong and Singapore, she ended up on the Kuala Lumpur nightclub circuit, dancing cabaret here, working as a hostess there. But there she had to suffer the fierce competition of slant-eyed, Anglo-Chinese prostitutes, and she was not, at any rate, a call girl, but the daughter of 'Colonel Arthur Bolton'. This imaginary colonel ensured, at every step, that she maintained her dignity. At times, she remembered her overly strict, fake Aunt Celia Richmond and, on occasion, the image of her own mother and uncle sailed before her eyes. She would wipe her tears and light another cigarette wondering about all the upheavals her life had gone through. The Southeast Asia nightclub circuit had made her quite wise and equally melancholy. She had danced at the stag parties thrown by the high-living, pleasure-seeking sons of corrupt politicians and knew well enough the political and moral state of this part of the Third World. In every city in every country, she found the same Bible on the side table in the hotel suites, and found the sacred text to be utterly useless. The mysterious old Chinese hags with incredibly small feet who sat in the back rooms of Chinese restaurants amid the blue haze of incense smoke and told fortunes were never able to solve even one of her problems.

In one Jakarta Chinese restaurant she ran into a delightful Dutchman, about forty, with a toupee pasted on his head and wearing something resembling a robe over his suit. He told her that he was a Dutch Sufi and a disciple of the Paris Sufi preceptor Inayat Khan. 'I've come from Amsterdam to gain knowledge of the mysteries of Indonesian Sufism,' he told her. 'I'm one of those who are referred to as "Dutch Sensitives". We possess a heightened sixth sense.'

'Your father is alive,' he abruptly said, digging into his chop suey.

She was jolted.

'You'll certainly meet him one day. He's a great man.'

'Really? What kind of great man?'

'I can't tell you. But he *is* a great man.'

Did this mean he really was a colonel and, by now, maybe a general in the British army? The thought made her incredibly happy. Half of her miseries vanished there and then. She felt herself quite safe.

The Dutch Sufi's nearness gave her a sense of profound comfort. Swept away by Sufism, ESP, and her own desire for some sense of security in her life, she followed this mysterious man all the way to a mosque in Jakarta, where a slant-eyed, scraggly-bearded Indonesian 'Shaikh' had her recite the kalima. She was given the name Halima and she was married to the Dutch Muslim, Muhammad Moeen Koot. As she signed her name 'Catherine Halimawati, daughter of Colonel Arthur Bolton' on the marriage register, she couldn't resist feeling an immense exhilaration flooding her soul.

That new Dutch Muslim was a staunch momin. He ordered Halimawati to cease her dancing and singing forthwith. But here was the problem: if she didn't dance in the Jakarta hotel where she did her floor show she would have to pay for her room and all her bills. Since Muhammad Moeen's money orders from Amsterdam wouldn't be in for quite a while yet, Catherine Koot was once again obliged to dip into her savings.

They had been living in the hotel for a fortnight when one morning she woke up and found that her Dutch Sufi was clean gone. And gone too were the diamond rings, the genuine pearl necklace, and the earrings Celia Richmond had left for her, along with her remaining cash. The lofty Bible on the side table still remained, untouched, with an empty plastic cup on top of it. Just last night, her Dutch literature-loving spiritualist had repeated a line from some American short story writer, which went something like: 'You may wander through the whole world but a day comes when you realize that the world is full of Holiday Inns and plastic cups and that you must go back home.' So Catherine Koot, stumbling about, returned from Jakarta to her home in Sydney. She was getting along in years, her ravishing beauty dangling precariously on the edge of evanescence. All she could find there was a job as a bus conductor.

A peculiar feature of the struggle for survival is that humans never admit defeat. Distributing tickets to the bus riders, she still daydreamed. Maybe at the next stop she would find the prince of her dreams, for who knows what lies beyond the fog?

IV

Raja Sir Narendranath's great-grandfather was a poor Brahmin fortune-telling astrologer from Kannauj. Pleased by some of his auspicious predictions, Shahenshah Jahangir bestowed on him a jagir by the edge of the Kali River. The present Raja Sahib is a staunchly religious man who firmly believes in sadhus and sants. After the government abolished princely states, he moved into a gorgeous mansion in New Delhi and started a big business. It was in this connection that his eldest son (who earlier went by the name of Yuvraj Shailendranathji, but now is merely Mr S. N. Bajpai) took a business trip to Japan, Singapore, and Australia. This was the first trip out of the country for this rather naïve youth, so he was left quite dazed and fazed in Australia.

It was the Christmas season and a boisterous hustle and bustle had gripped Sydney. That day, as he was getting ready to go to the Opera House, he suddenly remembered the test match that was to take place in the afternoon between Australia and India, so he hopped aboard a bus for the cricket stadium instead and found himself a seat next to the window. The bus was a veritable portrait gallery of faces, one more beautiful than the next: Lebanese girls, Italian immigrants, round-faced Australians. When the bus conductor's hand came abreast his face, he lifted his head and his eyes were dazzled: such a lustrous face, as beautiful as the full moon. Is such beauty possible! Seeing an Indian, the fairy-face smiled with a trace of fellowship.

The Rajkumar had once heard someone say: if a white woman smiles at you, she's as good as hooked. He looked into her eyes a little less afraid and fell in love with her, heart and soul.

Those who visit a white country for the first time and fail to marry a mem within the first six months escape, otherwise not. Rajkumar Shailendra had been in Australia hardly ten days.

The conductor handed him his ticket and moved on smiling. Afterwards she gave him no more attention, but he was a man of firm resolve and nothing if not steadfast. The next day he boarded the bus at the same time. He succeeded, but only on the fourth attempt. He introduced himself: Prince Shailendranathji of India.

'Prince' did seem to make an impression on the earthly houri, because she had been watching princes and the sons of royalty all her life in Mussoorie, right from childhood, and if someone on a bus in Sydney was introducing himself as a rajkumar, her experienced cabaret dancer's eyes could easily see that he was no fake.

The magic began to work on the fairy. Appointment for the evening, candlelight dinner, ballroom dancing, a leisurely stroll, shopping, high-placed family, English girl, a colonel's daughter, granddaughter of some lord—well, what's the harm?

It was a standing practice among our nabobs and raja log that they got themselves a junior begum or a junior rani of European blood, most of whom had been mere London barmaids in their earlier incarnations. But the headline news of free India was that all the rajwaras had been folded up, harems put paid to, and the law of single marriage had been slapped on the people. All the same, the snob value that an English or an American wife still had in free India was not something that Shailendranathji was unaware of. His first wife was a princess, a rajkumari, but the poor thing died within two years of marriage.

So when he proposed to Catherine she found herself in a Sydney ashram the very next day. Her nikah had been performed at a mosque in Jakarta. Here, the pandit recited Vedic mantras. She was given the name Shailaja Devi, to accord with Shailendra—the Bengali pandit explained with a smile.

'Akhand Sobhagyawati, Yuvrani Rajyalakshmi Shailaja Deviji—may she prosper and fructify!' Her nitwit of a husband, several years her junior, shook hands with her, beaming. On the marriage register her father's name was inscribed as 'Colonel Arthur Bolton of London and Peshawar Cantonment'.

V

From Meerut Cantonment, Corporal Arthur Bolton had straightaway headed to Berlin. The war ended shortly thereafter and he played his drum in the army band to celebrate the victory in different parts of England. Later, he was let go of his temporary employment in the army.

Arthur Bolton's father, a shoeshiner who worked in Piccadilly Circus, had died during the bombardment of London. His mother had died too. Arthur found himself a job with a dance band in the West End. He didn't marry. Why get into that mess? Years passed. After paralysis disabled one of his arms, he had to give up drumming. When he got out of the hospital he started working as a doorman. By now age had caught up with him. He still wrote poetry, which never got printed. He attended church regularly—churches, that is, that had somehow escaped being turned into Sikh gurdwaras. Since he knew Urdu he was able to hit it off quite well with Pakistani and Hindustani labourers. Actually, it was a Sikh watchman friend who had got him his present job in one of the stores of a major Punjabi businessman, Mr Khosla. It was a gorgeous showroom in Knightsbridge. There, everyone liked this soft-spoken, loveable, slightly eccentric old man.

That day, after arriving at the showroom, he did his cleaning and dusting in the hall. As he was arranging the scattered periodicals on the table his eyes fell on the cover of a women's magazine published from Bombay. The face of the girl on the cover caught his attention. Inside there was a photo essay on the interior decoration of this beauty's house. Arthur Bolton plopped down on the sofa, took out his eyeglasses, and began reading it:

> Yuvrani Shailaja Deviji is English and a member of British aristocracy. Her father, Colonel Arthur Bolton, was lost in action in the last World War. Her grandfather was an Irish lord. Rajkumariji spent her childhood in Mussoorie. Later she left for Australia with her aunt, Lady Richmond, where she trained in ballet dancing, piano, and interior decoration.

Old man Arthur was dumbstruck. He closed his eyes and remained in a state of quiet immobility for some time. Then he got up, walked over to a corner, dropped down on his knees, and immersed himself in prayer.

For some strange reason he felt certain that Katto was still in Mussoorie and that if he wrote to her at the same old address, she would reply.

And so she did. When he got her letter he asked the manager of the showroom for a month's leave which was granted. He went to India House to obtain a visa. Next, he withdrew his life's savings from the bank, bought himself a return plane ticket, and spent the rest on gifts for Katto and Catherine. Carrying the heavy bag of gifts in his working hand, he would get tired, catch a brief rest in some doorway, and start walking again. With the money saved by walking, he bought a tie for his son-in-law.

Exactly a week later he found himself standing in front of the servants' quarters at the New Himalayas Vegetarian Hotel.

Katto nanny told him plainly, 'Sahib, my daughter didn't send me a letter and got herself married. What does this mean? Just one thing: she doesn't want me to ruin her new life.'

Katto was sitting on a rock outside the quarters working mustard oil into her hair. As ever, Fazl Masih sat under a pine tree staring quietly at the Himalaya. The valleys in the distance had become filled with purplish fog.

Old man Arthur lit his pipe with his working hand and pondered how incredibly peaceful this poor, illiterate, and heartbroken woman was.

'Katto, you're not angry at all?' he said, in a voice genuinely surprised.

'Angry—whatever for, sahib?' she said. 'In whatever I had to go through, I lived up to the fate assigned by Chhati Ma.'

'Chhati Ma? Who is this lady?'

'A Bohri memsahib of Bombay once came here. When she heard how angry I was, she told me, "Katto Bai, the sixth day after a child is born, Chhati Ma appears at midnight and inscribes its fate on its forehead." Here we call it the karm ke lachhann, the signs of fate.'

Arthur listened attentively. Raising his eyebrows, he rubbed his forehead and started laughing.

Katto continued, 'In the front room of these very servants' quarters, Chhati Ma came at night and inscribed on my Katy Baba's forehead that she would become a queen. Listen to me, please, sahib. Don't go to meet her.'

'Why?'

'Because I'm telling you.'

'No, Katto. Chhati Ma has also written down that both you and I will go to Delhi to visit her. I've brought so many gifts for her from England.' Arthur sat down beside her on the rock and started to open the bags with longing and eagerness.

VI

A small, nicely manicured lawn was visible at the front of the grand mansion and right across from the gate stood the window of the bedroom which was featured in that English-language women's magazine. It was a pleasant Sunday morning in early spring. Out on the lawn Raja Sahib, his middle son, and a few European men and women were immersed in listening to the discourse of a swamiji. This was some relatively new swamiji who had just recently joined the international guru circuit and was now staying at Mouriya, having returned only a few days ago from France with a slew of his millionaire French and German disciples. After breakfast with Raja Sahib, he was holding forth on sat and a-sat when a taxicab pulled in at the gate and a threesome got out: a grubby old Englishman holding a Selfridges shopping bag, a poor native woman in an ordinary sari, and a crazy-looking man in a kantop and faded quilted vest with a matted salt-and-pepper beard who cringed and huddled behind one of the columns of the gate. The shabby Englishman held the hand of the boggled, fearful woman and started walking towards the lawn.

Raja Sahib lifted his eyes and looked at the new arrivals with extreme annoyance and wondered: how in the world did his Gurkha gatekeepers ever allow this riff-raff in!

Maybe this clumsy bunch was from the horde of Jehovah's Witnesses, harmless, crazy missionaries. Early on Sunday mornings they just descend on the homes of decent people and tell them doomsday is right around the corner. Oh, how they make life miserable!

Coming near the chairs, the old Englishman stopped. When Swamiji raised a silver glass to drink some water, the Englishman said cheerfully, 'Good morning friends!' Both he and the native woman stood there for some time. Everyone remained absolutely silent. Swamiji was apparently quite irritated by this intrusion in the middle of his bhashan. In utter disgust he picked up a flower and started inhaling its sweet aroma. The maharaja signalled with his eyebrows for them to sit down, and both promptly did.

'Maharaj, please go on,' Raja Sahib, a staunch believer in sadhus and sants entreated by humbly joining his hands.

Swamiji picked up where he had left off in his discourse on sat and a-sat. Old man Arthur craned his head and started to listen carefully. After a few minutes the swamiji paused to allow his French female disciple to change the cassette.

The old Englishman addressed him, 'Mister Guru! Your thoughts about truth and nontruth have affected me greatly. I too have come from England to make manifest a truth.' Then turning to the Raja Sahib he said, 'Your Highness, I'm the father of your dear daughter-in-law, Catherine...' he took out the clipping from the women's magazine, 'Akhand Sobhagyawati Rajyalakshmi Shailaja Deviji.'

'Oh, what a pleasant surprise, Colonel!' The Raja Sahib quickly thrust his hand forward for a handshake, smiling warmly. 'Colonel Bolton! Why didn't you inform us that you were coming? Ahead of time?'

'Your Highness,' old man Arthur cleared his throat, glanced around, and said with an angelic smile, 'there hasn't been a single colonel in my family in the past seven generations. My father was a shoeshiner, my mother a cook; I joined the army as a drummer. Now I'm just a doorman.'

Everyone present had turned into statues of solid ice. Arthur threw a sweeping glance around him and shook his head regretfully. 'All my life this has been my problem. I've always spoken the truth, nothing but the truth. And when I arrive here, what do I see but that Swamiji is talking about the essence of truth. This made me very happy. I've spent my entire life's savings just to see my daughter. I'm a poor man. All the same I've brought her some things as a dowry.' He bent over, picked up the Selfridges shopping bag from the lawn and then put it back down. The people remained as frozen as before.

Arthur started again, 'I'm sure Catherine would be delighted to meet her mother, too. After all, she's been away since she was fifteen years old.'

Arthur stopped to catch his breath. Katto just looked at him, aghast, dumbfounded. Suddenly the atmosphere had turned entirely surreal. Such episodes don't happen in real life. Arthur started again, 'This foolish woman was afraid to come here. I told her, "Martha, are you afraid of the light? Don't be afraid of the light of truth. Truth is God. And we are His children. Aren't you eager to see your lovely child? So let's go to Delhi and meet our daughter. How could it be that parents and their children would hesitate to meet each other? How can they go against the law of nature? There's nothing to fear." And Your Highness, it is mentioned in your mythology that when Lord Shiva arrived at his in-laws, his arrogant and haughty father-in-law scorned him....' Arthur paused and cleared his throat, 'Forgive me, I gave the wrong example. What I meant was....'

The old coot, he's really insane, Raja Sahib thought. He was gaping at this weird stranger with wide eyes and his face was quickly changing colour, but Arthur Bolton went on with his introductory harangue with perfect calm.

'So, Your Highness, just now as I arrived at the gate I thought for a minute you might turn out to be as arrogant and haughty as Lord Shiva's father-in-law, but then your words struck my hearing. You were expressing your agreement with Mister Guru's utterance that man must speak the truth in all circumstances and have the courage to face it. Indeed it is siddhant and gyan. And Raja Sahib, you'll be pleased to know that my Saviour Jesus Christ has also said exactly the same thing. Actually, it is His truth-speaking that brought Him to the cross—quite a well-known event, you must surely have heard of it.'

The middle prince sensed that Raja Sahib, an irascible man, was just about ready to lose his temper and God knows what he might do. To smooth things over, he quickly asked, 'Would you like coffee or tea?'

Arthur looked at him with a smile. 'Martha, coffee?'

Meanwhile the swamiji had started to stroll on the grass. The middle prince poured some coffee and offered it to Katto nanny. Old man Arthur shook his head and said excitedly in Urdu, 'I'm very pleased to see that you don't practise untouchability. We are all children of God the Father. Jesus said that there is room for everyone in My Father's palace. Your Highness, my daughter's mother was never married to me. I didn't even know that Martha had given birth to Catherine. Thirty-five years later I saw her picture in a magazine. This is all God's work. Martha is a very courageous woman; she still works as a nanny in Mussoorie. She is a righteous woman, a true Christian. Her mother and father were also true

Christians, and they were also very poor. They worked as sweepers, cleaned bathrooms. Jesus said that the poor shall truly inherit the Kingdom of God. Your Mister Gandhi says the same thing too. He used to live in the Bongi colony in Delhi. My Katto is also a Bongi. She will also inherit the Kingdom of God, no doubt about it.'

Raja Sahib, who was glaring at the old man, dropped his head between his hands, and bellowed at the top of his voice. Raja Sahib was ill-tempered but no one had ever seen him shout like that before. Everyone stood up and rushed to him. He felt dizzy and closed his eyes, letting his head droop. He was beginning to faint. He had a weak heart.

VII

Catherine, standing by the bedroom window, was watching this whole scene, which looked like a stage set from that distance. Life couldn't be more unbelievable! In the morning, when she was introduced to Swamiji at breakfast, both had instantly recognized each other. Swamiji was none other than the former Hindi and Sanskrit schoolteacher at Mussoorie who had tried to get fresh with her, leading to Miss Richmond's sudden decision to leave for Australia. Just as they were about to leave, it had come to light that he had siphoned off a considerable amount of school funds and dropped out of sight with some girl from the hill country. Back then too he was quite engaging and a sweet-talker.

After breakfast, when the opportunity offered itself, he told his former student, 'Now look here, Katto Junior, it has taken me twenty long years and a lot of hard work to fashion this career for myself in the West, which is teeming with swamis nowadays and a cut-throat competition is raging among them. Even so, I've got no less than eighteen ashrams in Europe and America, not to mention disciples numbering in the thousands, so don't you go spilling the beans! In the bargain, I'll keep mum to your in-laws, conservative royal family that they are, about your being the daughter of Mussoorie's Katto nanny.' The blood had drained from Catherine's face and her colour faded when she heard those words whispered to her. She'd left right away and hidden herself in her bedroom.

Meanwhile, Swamiji had returned to the lawn and resumed his bhashan, but what had to happen, happened. A taxi stopped at the gate and she saw her mother getting out, followed by her half-crazy uncle, and an eccentric-looking English codger. They walked in and sat down on the lawn, and Catherine heard every word of this unbelievable father of hers.

One time a Delhi Begum Sahib had taught Miss Celia Richmond how to cook baoli handia—crazy dish. Life too was a crazy handia which, having simmered for some time, now suddenly came to a boil.

Shaking from sheer terror, she looked at what was in front of her. Her uncle stood like a pillar by the gate, staring into space, while on the lawn her insane father diligently went about destroying her life. How fervently and how much she had always yearned to meet him. How many stories of this man's innate goodness and innocence her mother and her aunt Celia had recounted—the man who had stayed barely two months in the guest house and left after winning everyone's heart. Perhaps God had created him just for that: wander in suddenly from somewhere, change the course of lives, and wander out just as swiftly. Unbelievable! Impossible! Are goodness and truth in their essence destructive forces?

Transfixed, she watched the players on the stage in front of her in what might well have been a scene from some comic opera had it not been so horrific: discovering that his oldest daughter-in-law was the child of a sweeper woman caused the Brahmin Raja Sahib to faint on the spot; the four Europeans, in order to escape the tentacles of the arch swindler Maya, had walked straight into the trap of the arch swindler Swami; the bogus holy man was now mouthing mantras to revive the unconscious Raja Sahib; her poor mother, who had shed tears all her life, still couldn't do anything but shed more; and her destitute father, paralysed in one arm, who had saved every penny with so much thrift to bring her something for her dowry from across the seven seas, was now looking at everyone, dumbfounded, like some foolish angel who had walked into the wrong place. A sudden wave of compassion and love washed over Catherine and she was overwhelmed by an instinctive desire to rush out and hug her half-mad, eccentric father, her suffering mother, and her dear uncle, to give up this palace, this aristocratic Brahmin family and her well-heeled husband, and leave with these loving, penniless, naive, and crazy people, because her real home was where they lived, because ultimately the world is filled with Holiday Inns and plastic cups, three-storey, Heinz-style houses with red sloping roofs, and nowhere had she found her place, her home. Was she really Akhand Sobhagyawati Rajyalakshmi Shailaja Deviji? Inside her skin she was just plain Catherine Bolton, and the conflict between Colonel Bolton and Corporal Bolton that had always left her exhausted and worn out was finally over. She would go outside and announce: Daddy, Mummy, here, I'm back. I'm coming with you.

She summoned up her courage and made for the door. Just as she was opening it, her eyes fell on her diamond bracelet. Her personal Mercedes gleamed in the sunlight up ahead in the driveway, and she suddenly recalled that she was expected at the golf club at eleven o'clock. Would all this disappear in the blink of an eye?

The sound of the shower rose from the marble bathroom and another thought crossed her mind: might her husband throw her out after this dreadful denouement? Much better if I leave honourably with these people on my own.

Her head swirled, as though she was standing on a sinking ship. She tried to grab on to the door. She must do everything to save herself. Such was the law of survival. Her nitwit husband emerged from the bathroom in his robe. 'What's all this noise outside?' he asked, walking towards the window.

Catherine heaved a deep sigh and said in a clear, firm voice, 'Darling, that magazine which had a pictorial essay about our interior decorations, remember? It seems to have created havoc. Some wicked gang has barged in to blackmail us. They're claiming to be my parents. Your father is running for election. I wonder whether this has something to do with that. Looks like your father's opponents have sent an Untouchable woman with some English geezer to say that she is my mother, just to turn the Brahmin vote against your father. The old coot might just as well be a CIA agent. You must call the police...right now.'

Rajkumar Shailendra was a moron all right, but perhaps not an absolute moron. He lifted his face and looked at his fairy-faced yuvrani somewhat suspiciously. Catherine turned pale. She was shaking from fear. Pushing her out of his way, Rajkumar Shailendra rushed to the door and out to his father who had by now regained consciousness. Catherine ran straight to the bathroom and locked the door.

Outside at the gate her crazy uncle was asking after the well-being of everyone with his hands raised in prayer.

Kabira stands wishing everyone well.

KING MARUTI

VYANKATESH MADGULKAR

Translated from the Marathi by Shanta Gokhale

ON A WET MORNING IN JUNE, A HUGE LANGUR TURNED UP IN THE village. He came alone, without friends or family. A langur is a rare sight in our parts. That is what makes him an object of wonder and respect. The last time we saw one was at least ten years ago. Who knows where this one had appeared from and why. But he came in style, waving his tufted tail as he walked through the village and went straight into the Maruti temple. He entered the sanctum sanctorum, emerged after a few minutes, and settled on the dome. His long tail waved as he soaked in the sun.

The priest Pandu Gurav's wife saw this wondrous sight, picked up her daughter, and made straight for the jungle where her husband had gone to graze his horse. He had to know what had happened. Maruti had come to the village. He had paid a visit to the temple.

The village brats who came swinging their slates and satchels to the school across from the temple sat on its steps. The school had still not opened. The teacher had still not come. He had still not had his tea. They sat in a tight row on the steps like sparrows on a wire. Their drowsy eyes were taking in the lustrous glow of the early morning sun when they spotted a creature they had never seen before sitting atop the Maruti temple. Their hearts trembled with joy, amazement, and fear. Then a bold boy rose, took a step forward and, scratching his snub nose, shouted, 'Monkey monkey chee chee, on your tail a pound of ghee.'

The others joined in the chant. The monkey turned his black face towards them and bared his teeth to scare them off. Then he got up and danced. The bold brat picked up a stone and aimed it straight at the monkey. The stone got him in the back. He jumped high in pain and fled screeching chee chee. He climbed to the topmost branches of a peepul tree and hid behind the foliage. The kids gathered under the tree. He looked down and scolded them roundly. This excited them even more. They began to throw a regular stream of stones at him. But the monkey was too high for the stones to reach him. The animal was clever enough to see this. He relaxed among the leaves, munching on the tender ones.

Meanwhile Pandu Gurav had heard the news. He rushed home, picked up the basket in which lay a quarter bhakri, and carried it to the peepul tree. He gave the kids a few whacks and drove them away. 'Where will you pay for this sin?' he shouted. 'Twelve devils from twelve homes get together and fling stones at our Marutraya! What harm did he do you?'

Driven away by Gurav, the wicked imps ran off screaming abuse at him and informing the world of his affairs with loose women.

Holding the piece of bhakri up high, Gurav began pleading with the langur. 'Come down please and have this, Hanumanta.' But the monkey did not as much as glance at Gurav and continued eating leaves.

Old Abbanana, who had halted on his way to the jungle to watch the show, thought Gurav had gone mad. Swinging his chin left and right he called out, 'Pandya you idiot, what day is it today, haan?'

'Saturday, Nana.'

'So how will Marutraya accept bhakri today, eh?'

'Then?'

'Then get him some snack, you donkey.'

Nana was a Varkari, a follower of Vitthal. Very pious. He would collect a handful of villagers together and sing bhajans. He had all the required paraphernalia at home—cymbals, mridang, this and that. He never failed to celebrate Ram's birth, Maruti's birth, and other such sacred days. The old man's word was highly respected in the village.

Gurav saw sense in what Nana said. He returned home in great haste and came back with a handful of peanuts. Once again he pleaded, 'Dear Lord, please accept these. Come down, dear Lord.'

But all the monkey did was peer down, blink his strange white eyelashes, scratch his underarms with his slender black fingers, and continue grabbing and eating leaves.

Seeing that the monkey did not heed him, Gurav called out to Nana, 'Nana, he doesn't want to eat from this sinner's hand. See if you fare better.'

Nana stepped forward, took the peanuts, and began pleading, 'Dear Lord, I have been the slave of your slaves. Please accept my offering. Don't test this old man.'

As Nana continued to plead in a variety of ways, calling the monkey by names from the scriptures, the monkey deigned to begin climbing down. By now a crowd of villagers had collected. When they saw the monkey climbing down, they became impatient.

The monkey had now reached the lowest branch of the tree and was sitting in its fork. Nana went closer and raised his hand. The monkey leaned over, reached out, and grabbed Nana's hand in his black paw. He looked around, enjoying himself. Nana said, 'Please take this. Don't be offended now.'

All of a sudden, the monkey thrust his face forward and scratched Nana's hand as one scrapes corn kernels off a corn cob. Then, hoisting his tail high, he leapt up to the top of the tree again.

Nana winced with pain and flopped to the ground. The villagers ran to him, picked him up gently, and helped him home to bed. They applied homegrown medications to his hand. When the old man's son saw his father's lacerated hand, he blenched. The old man would be of no use now with the sowing. He would have to hire help on daily wages. The thought distressed him.

The villagers began to whisper. It was probably true that the old man had a thing going with his daughter-in-law. Why else would the monkey have attacked him! After this, nobody was willing to offer peanuts to the monkey. They didn't dare. Why test poison? At the same time how could they keep God, who was visiting their village, unfed? This was unacceptable to Gurav. He handed the peanuts over to his eight-year-old daughter and pleaded with the monkey, 'My lord, this little one is innocent of sin. Please accept her offering.'

That poor innocent soul stood under the tree with peanuts in her hand. The monkey came down again and slashed at her calf. He then parked himself on the lemon tree outside the goldsmith's house. Gurav's wife beat her chest and cursed the monkey. Gurav put the child on his back and went off to the medical centre in the taluka town. The villagers whispered, 'The Gurav may be a womanizer. But his wife's no better. What's happened is their fault.'

The monkey would not accept food from anybody's hand. The village fell into deep anxiety. They abandoned their betel leaves and nuts and stood around in groups discussing the problem. In the meantime, the monkey had left the goldsmith's lemon tree for the ironsmith's jambhul tree. The ironsmith, who was quietly beating the dents from a bucket, spat out a mouthful of betel leaf juice, rose, and said to his wife who sat nursing the baby, 'Get me a handful of peanuts will you. The monkey has come to our door.'

'You mad or something? To hell with that monkey. Look after your work.'

'Woman, he's at our door, of his own will. Shouldn't we feed him?'

Without waiting for his wife, he picked up a fistful of peanut pods from the lot that had come to him by barter and walked out. Showing the handful to the monkey, he urged him to come down. Seeing that there was nobody else around, the monkey leapt down, took a large bite of the ironsmith's thigh, and ran up the tree again. With the village's only ironsmith laid low, who would make their farming tools now?

The monkey ran wild all day like a rabid dog, testing his teeth on whoever came by. It was evening. Nana's eldest son could no longer contain his rage. He picked up a handful of stones, stood under the tree, and said to the monkey, 'Raya, you've done enough harm', took aim and flung a stone. The monkey sidestepped it nimbly, bared his teeth, and ran down to charge at Nana's son. The boy, no less alert, picked up another stone and stood at the ready. The monkey leapt away lightly on all four feet into Anna Jarga's orchard.

Nana's son raced after him like Nemesis, stone in hand. Infected by his ferocity, other lusty young fellows of the village ran alongside him carrying sticks and stones. A few miles of furious chasing and the monkey was fagged out. He was too slow now to dodge the stones. A dozen or so stones hit him and he fell. Instantly, the boys surrounded him. Realizing the game was up, the shrewd monkey made pleading signs, held out his hands, turned around himself. The grocer's son, Sada, held back his hand and said to Nana's son, 'Look, he's folding his hands, touching our feet, begging us not to hit him.'

But Nana's son could not control his rage. He stepped forward and brought a stick down on the monkey with immense force. The others stoned him mercilessly. With blood bubbling from his nose and mouth, the monkey thrashed around and died. He lay still with his paws linked together, the thatch of hair on his head matted with dirt.

Nana's son was filled with pity at the sight. He said thoughtfully, 'Listen, chaps, one of you stay here. We'll go get cymbals and drums and give Maruti a right royal funeral.'

His voice had grown incredibly tender. Sada cast a compassionate look at the dead monkey and said, 'Poor chap died at our hands. Bad thing.'

Following the general view, he stayed back to keep the vultures off while the rest of the boys returned to the village. When news of the monkey's death reached the village, they joined their hands together and asked Maruti for forgiveness for the crime that had been committed in the village.

The lads returned to the jungle with the village bhajan singers. They bore the monkey respectfully to the stream, chanting Lord Rama's name, and cremated him like a human being.

Nana's heart grieved at what had happened in the village. When he recovered from his illness, he built a square stone slab on the spot where the monkey had died.

Now pious folk bow worshipfully to it as they pass by.

MIRROR OF ILLUSION

NIRMAL VERMA

Translated from the Hindi by Geeta Kapur

LAYERS OF BURNING SAND HAD SETTLED ON THE TIN ROOF. WHEN THE wind rose, a bright curtain of sand flapped around the house. The wartime barracks were being demolished, there were mounds of rubble everywhere and it looked like the dust road had developed lumpy warts.

One could see everything from the window. Coloured shadows slid across the hillocks all day long. In the distance one heard, continuously, the sound of the stone-breaking machine. Like a growling giant—grr, grr, grr.

Noises intruded upon the brittle edges of her afternoon sleep and Taran woke up with a start. She touched her forehead. Strands of hair were sticking to her brow, the powder of her bindi had trickled down to the bridge of her nose. I have been awake all this while, she thought: it seemed to her she had been thinking the same thing while she was asleep... it's always like that in the afternoon—you drift in and out of sleep.

She washed her eyes, wiped off her bindi, worked the pump, and splashed her face with water. From the bathroom window she could look out over the fields where they were pulling down the barracks. Half demolished, they stood around like broken-down skeletons. The sand was ablaze. Taran could feel it crackling between her teeth.

'See if Babu is awake, Taran. If he is, take the hookah to him,' Bua called from the room adjoining the kitchen. Even at her age Bua remembered everything. It seemed that while she did her chores, or even sat dozing by the door, her attention was tugged about by Babu's every need.

As soon as evening fell the Diwan Sahib waited for his guests impatiently. Even if he went out to the small train station for a stroll he returned hurriedly in the hope of some unexpected guest and immediately asked Bua if someone had visited them in his absence. She never said more than yes or no. After so many years she still felt an obscure dread in his presence. Even as a child she had kept her head bowed before him. When she became a widow, the Diwan had provided her with a small pension. Now, in her dotage, she lived in his house. When Taran's mother died the girl was left all alone. Had it not been for Bua she could never have endured a moment in this dismal place.

With sunset there was a regular little crowd on the Diwan's veranda. The government supervisor, Mr Das, the wealthy contractor, Meharchand, they all came after their day's work and sat together for a while. What was there to do, after all, in this wilderness; where could one enjoy an evening out? A few tribal mud huts, a couple of shacks selling paan-bidi, some wayside eateries, and over there on the hill the temple of Kali Devi. All said and done there was just Diwan Sahib's house and these men from different parts flocked to it eagerly.

'Taran, will you fill the chillum for Das Babu,' the Diwan called, turning his face to the door. Now his veneer of indifference vanished. Das Babu had arrived, the others would be coming along soon. 'How is it you got so late today, the siren went off long ago,' he said.

Das Babu's round, flabby body slumped into the chair. When he spoke his two rows of yellow teeth rattled faintly. 'I'd gone across the canal to see some land. On my way back I stopped at the new petrol pump. Now there won't be any petrol problem here Diwan Sahib.'

When Taran brought the chillum to him he shrank into himself. He was getting to be over fifty but he still felt awkward around a woman. Taran turned away and he relaxed, cleared his throat. Still, when he spoke his voice was strained: 'Why don't you make a trip to Haridwar, Rishikesh for a few days, Diwan Sahib? If nothing else it will be pleasant for your bitia. She's alone all day long, doesn't she get bored?'

Das Babu would not call Taran by her name. Had she been a little younger he would not have felt this embarrassment. Had she been older the name could have been pronounced naturally. Between these two boundaries there was a certain awkwardness. Her youth seemed to have got stuck in the marsh somewhere...how was he supposed to regard her?

Diwan Sahib sat there, saying nothing in response. He enjoyed talking to his friends, to be sure, but in his heart he always held himself aloof from them. There was a line of privacy no one was allowed to cross.

Taran stopped short on hearing Das Babu's comment, then she went back inside. Bua was sitting there mending clothes. She avoided her and went into her own room. She shut the door and stood leaning against it for some time. The thick silence of the house pressed against her, the voices from the veranda were left floating out there, detached and unfamiliar.

From one of her windows she could see the veranda. If on an evening his friends did not turn up, Babu sat there all alone with his eyes half-closed. How terribly remote he looked in his stillness! She had often thought—I should go and sit with him, talk to him about this and that. After all there are only the two of us left; we can at least share each other's memories. But she had never taken the step. She just watched him from the window.

There was a strong wind those days. Gusts of hot dust came swirling up to the house, rattled the doors and then scattered in the courtyards. Far out in the distance they were dynamiting the boulders. Every now and then there was an explosion, then a vast echo. The earth vibrated underfoot. And one could see flags fluttering a warning all over the landscape.

Taran sat dozing by the window. Then she suddenly got up, startled, as though someone had come and touched her. The twilight glow had spread across the fields and crept quietly up to her.

Bua came into the room and, seeing her sitting in the dark, admonished her: 'How many times have I told you not to sit indoors in the evening? Why don't you go out for a bit, you can take Shambhu along.'

But just then someone climbed up the stairs. Taran looked out excitedly. Engineer Babu had arrived. How strange he is, she thought, the way he comes up thumping his feet and shaking the whole house.

He had come to the township four or five months ago as a government architect, but everyone always called him Engineer Babu. He had simple, easy ways, and he talked in such a friendly manner—one would have thought he had lived in the place for years. He was not one of the regular visitors to the house. It was difficult to say if he could be called Babu's friend at all. Babu was twice his age and felt a little awkward in his company.

Taran went to the mirror and quickly tidied her hair, combing it, waving it here and there. She powdered her face and her eyes fluttered. As she raised her hand to put on a bindi, below the parting of her hair, right in the middle of her forehead, she stopped and asked herself if this wasn't some delusion. No, she did not delude herself any more. She was not attractive: this hardly even depressed her now. Years ago if someone looked her up and down in the street her whole body would start to flush and quiver. She would run back to her room and gaze at herself in the mirror for hours. What is it people notice in me...this question would tantalize her and she would think up all sorts of answers, her heart racing. Now if anyone glanced at her she only felt a wry sort of surprise; and stepping out of herself she would regard her own body with careless inquisitiveness.

'You are here, all by yourself, at this hour?'

Taran's train of thought was interrupted. Engineer Babu stood at the door.

'I was just coming out to the veranda, have you had some tea?'

'I'll have tea another time. Some day when you agree to sit with us out on the veranda. I have to hurry off now.'

But Taran insisted that he stay for a bit. 'Wait, you must have something to eat. You've just arrived,' and she started off for the kitchen.

'No, really, don't bother, please...I'm just on my way home from town and I've swallowed so much dust my stomach is all filled up.'

When he laughed, Taran always felt a little wistful. Everyone in town addressed him respectfully as Engineer Babu, yet he looked so young, even younger than herself. The first time she saw him sitting with her father's friends she was astonished. He looked like a college student among all those venerable men.

'We haven't seen you in our neighbourhood recently. Montu often asks after you.' Montu was his little servant. Every time Taran went for a walk along the railway line he would come and greet her.

'I'll come one of these days, will you be there?'

'Come next week, I have a lot of work to get through in the next four or five days.'

Before leaving he stopped, took out his handkerchief and wiped his glasses. Taran raised her eyes and looked at him timorously, and her gaze hung on the spot even when he had moved away. What a man this Engineer Babu is, she whispered to herself. When he pounds up the stairs the whole house trembles!

The dying sun had left a blood-red trail across the sky. It was beginning to get dark. She could just make out the labourers' shacks huddled in between the boulders, and further away, on top of the hill, the temple of Kali, wrapped in a cloud of smoke.

She left the window and came to her bed. A half-written letter lay under her pillow. Every time she began writing to her brother his face emerged and hovered above the grey mass of time. Not the face he had worn when he left home after clashing with Father. That was a distorted face, and even now her heart winced as she recalled it. No, not that face, but the one that had looked on, so young and so forlorn, when their mother died.... She had looked up to him for consolation, not daring to cry before Babu, and he had whispered to her, 'Don't you see, Taran, how lonely Babu is now? We must stand by him. In a few days everything will be normal again.'

And did it ever become 'normal' again? She was too young then, she had not understood why her brother had left home, why Babu had not been able to stop him. Now she knew. Mother had been the only link between Babu and the rest of them. When she died they fell apart, drifted away.

Bua came to call her for dinner. She looked at the sheet of paper in Taran's hand and asked, 'Why, was there a letter?'

'I was writing to Bhai. His letter came yesterday.'

'He's asked you to come, hasn't he?'

'Yes, he's been asking me to come and spend some time with him. Bua, tell me, should I go?'

Bua looked at her in amazement—all the way to Assam? She could not imagine Taran going so far away, and all alone. 'Ah, but if he feels so lovingly towards his sister why hasn't he come and met her in all these years? He has a quarrel with the father, but should he cut you off as well?'

Bua suffered from asthma, she could not speak for too long. She brought up a few words and the others drowned in her rising breath. Taran looked at the tears in her eyes and couldn't tell whether they were for her estranged brother or were squeezed out by the fit of coughing.

'You go along, Bua, I'm just coming,' she said casually.

A dull silence filled her room. She could hear her father's footsteps going up and down the veranda. Outside there was pale moonlight and the mounds of rubble threw long, thin shadows across the empty fields.

A hazy image formed within her. Tea plantations...lush green sprawled all over, up and down the sloping valleys.... Somewhere there, hidden inside a grove of trees, is my brother's house, she thought. They say you have to board a steamer to get there...wonder how it will feel to travel on a steamer!

Taran stood and looked at the green signal beside the railway station. The wheels of the train rumbled close by the house—the hillocks all around and the distant boulders reverberated with the sound. For a moment the frightful sound of the stone-breaking machine was drowned. The beam from the engine's headlight lit up dry shrubs along the tracks. Then again the same dense, heavy silence shrouded everything.

That night Bua came and sat in Taran's room. She kept chopping betel nut for herself. Every few minutes she would look at Taran and let out a long sigh, 'Are you asleep, Taran?' she would ask in a doubting tone.

'No, Bua, not yet.' Taran knew she was leading up to something. She lay there with her eyes closed, waiting.

'I went into your mother's room today,' Bua started slowly. 'I was so amazed, Taran. How much she had collected and preserved over the years. There was her wedding sari too, carefully folded and put away in the big trunk.'

Taran's heart stirred with curiosity. Mother too had been a bride once. How difficult it was to imagine that.

'At that time your Babu had just been appointed diwan... The wedding was such a grand affair. In the Sikh court he was the only Hindu diwan who had unbridled access to the king.'

An old, irretrievable dream floated into Bua's eyes, the betel nut chopper lay still in her hand. 'One day the English Resident of the state came to meet him. Everyone in the locality came out and looked on in awe. But your Babu was so particular about his caste, as soon as the Englishman left, he bathed and got the servants to throw away all the dishes.'

Taran sat up in bed. How many times she had heard this story from Bua! Yet every time she heard it, she felt a vague thrill, as if each time she was being led anew into a strange, illusory world.

'Bua, you've known Babu in those days, were you always so afraid of him?'

'Ah, but who wasn't afraid of your father then? It's the same fear that continues to this day. Your mother was even more timid, she would just keep gazing up at him. The day he went to court, I peeped at him through a chink in the curtains. He used to wear a dazzling white churidar, a silk achkan, and a superb pink turban...we couldn't take our eyes off him.'

Bua's hands were on the betel nut chopper, but her gaze was fixed far away on the past.

'At times I wonder if your Babu's insistence on pedigree and a noble family for your match is justified. After all it's no longer the same. What is our status now that we should demand these things? But who will ever tell him this?'

Her face clouded over with bafflement, she couldn't work out how something that was long past and altogether finished could still cling to them like a leech. There were no honours attached to the family now, their properties had been sold and all their possessions of value lost a long time ago. The house was the last remaining piece of their ancestral heritage. And, of course, the tattered, dust-laden title of diwan. You could wrap it around you, flap it about, but it was of no consequence. No one was likely to defer to it.

There was a lump in Bua's throat but a smile stuck to her face, as though she had forgotten to wipe it away. Taran did not like this part of Bua's ruminations. She liked to remember how her mother teased her, showing her what she was to take as her dowry. That used to fill her with a lovely sensation...not the thought of her wedding, not even the jewellery...it was just an unknown happiness that welled up in her—she would float in it all alone. Taran lay down again. She looked out of her window and at the signal, far out in the dark. Across the canal were the barracks. Night had sifted down upon them. Somewhere out there, she thought, in a narrow little room, Engineer Babu lives. She closed her eyes.

For a moment she became oblivious of herself. She did not know whether Bua was still talking. A sweet weariness overcame her, a long-forgotten feeling welled up inside her. She was lying in a tub full of water, her body stretched out before her, soft and naked. Nothing had happened between then and now, whatever had been gained and lost with time was all present, drifting above the water's surface.

'Have you gone to sleep, Taran?' Bua asked. Taran was startled by the question, she couldn't tell if she was on this or the other side of sleep... shadows flitted over the water and she lay underneath in limpid silence.

Then there were days when the Diwan would not emerge from his room. The veranda would be deserted. The chairs would stand around, unused and covered with dust. Bua would go to Babu's door and come back. He would ask for his food to be sent in to him. If he came out and encountered Taran, he would refuse to look at her, or if he looked at her it would be as if he had trouble recognizing her. And he would turn away abruptly.

Taran had begun to understand why he avoided her for no reason, why there was tension in the house. At first this had baffled and enraged her. But that time was past. Now a dry apathy filled her heart...why doesn't he get rid of me, she wondered. Bua had urged him many times to approach people. Letters were written, matters seemed to be taking shape. Her photograph and horoscope were sent off. But somehow things always stopped midway. Taran couldn't understand why that happened.

Even now when Taran remembered that night her body shuddered...

Bua had come to her room just before midnight. She was awake, listening to Bua's footsteps coming towards her. She held her breath and kept lying on her bed.

Bua's voice was trembling. 'Did you hear anything?'

Taran had sat up in bed. 'What is it?'

'I can't stay in this house any longer.'

'What happened, Bua?'

'Is there anything left to say, Taran?' Her voice had choked.

Numbly, Taran had stared at the shadow in the dark that was Bua. 'Did he talk to you?'

'I was sitting in my room, he came himself...I ask you, if he has something to say why doesn't he say it direct to you? You aren't a baby any more, why on earth does he drag *me* into it?'

'But what did he say?'

'I can't figure him out. He started off saying it would have been best if it had all happened in your mother's lifetime. I used the opportunity and said—who goes by the family's name these days? It's more than enough if one can find a decent fellow. As soon as he heard this he stiffened. Then he strode out of the room and slammed the door. After a while when he came back I could hardly recognize him. His hair was dishevelled and his eyes were bloodshot. That's how he looked when your mother died, as if he wouldn't ever forgive her.... He had a bundle under his arm. He came and threw it in front of me and said—here's her mother's jewellery, she can take it all and go wherever she pleases. When her brother left home I didn't perish, did I? If she leaves nothing will happen either.... I was quite bewildered. Taran, how can he talk like this about his own daughter?'

That night Bua's question hovered about her in the dark. She didn't know what her father wanted of her. He had become suspicious of her—that she would run away from him one day. Like her brother. She had never considered the possibility, but that night her father's dread became her own. She felt restless and guilty. Did she really want to live on in this house? She asked herself the question again and again, and she realized that Babu was right. She had a horror of the house, the empty rooms. She had tried deluding herself but the question wouldn't stop nagging her—do you want to go on living here?

Such a simple question and yet she wouldn't dare answer it. She would curl up all night in bed, her face hidden in the pillow, quailing before her own dreams.

Then, one day, she suddenly decided she would visit her brother for a few days. But she could not bring herself to tell Babu. She went across to his room several times but always turned back.

Finally, she asked Bua to go and tell him. Bua gazed at her doubtfully but later when she had thought it over it seemed like a good idea to let her go away for a while.

That day Babu called her to his room. She went and stood hesitantly at his door. Her breath caught in her throat, she felt stifled.

'Come in and sit here,' Babu said in a dull voice. He sat resting on a pillow against the wall, very quiet and very still. A thought flashed in her mind—there is still time, I should turn and go back to my room, quietly, just as I came in, and it will all pass away.... But her feet were suddenly glued to the floor.

'I believe you want to go away for a while?' Taran sat there, alert in her silence. She thought—he does not want to mention my brother, he never refers to him. Every time a letter came from him he would send it on to her without opening it.

'You don't feel happy here, Taran?' There was bleak curiosity in his voice, but also an innocence, as though he had thought of this possibility for the first time.

Taran looked at him and her heart began to pound with the tension she felt. Maybe Babu will ask me to stay, she thought feverishly, maybe he too feels lonely without me. She began to tremble inwardly. If only he would ask me to stay, she thought, I would immediately drop the idea of going...just let him ask me....

But Babu didn't say a word. Taran lowered her eyes.

'It's all right, if you want to go you can. Don't worry about me,' he said finally. His voice was poised, unfeeling.

Going out of the room, she faltered a little. She had hoped he would call her back, say something else. But the room was filled with a terrible silence.

That afternoon she lay in her room, willing herself to sleep. She would have liked to be able to draw sleep to herself any moment of the day, like a shroud. This compulsion to keep awake, to look around with wide-open eyes, it seemed unnecessary and false. She had begun to wonder if all her waking moments all these years had not been some delusion...they had hovered about at sleep's edge and left her untouched.

In the evening Taran came out of her room. Her body dragged because of the day's lethargy. The wind had blown all day. The sky was lined with thick yellow layers of sand. Far off, the sun glittered on the rocks. Taran noticed Babu had not come out to the veranda, his door was still shut.

Bua sat in her own room, coughing and mumbling something to herself. Every time the breeze swept through the house all the doors rattled. Taran went back to her room quickly and put on her sandals. She told Bua she was going out for a walk. But she couldn't say if Bua had heard her at all; she could hear her gurgling cough as she descended the steps.

The sand fields stretched out to the far horizon. The sun had left a mottled layer of gold on the ground. Beside the new road, rubble heaps stood about like pyramids. Taran walked along these and reached the water tank.

She was very familiar with this barren landscape, had been witness to its changing contours ever since she was a child. During wartime, when the barracks were being erected, a whole lot of military trucks would drive around, raising clouds of dust. She was there then...now, when those giant boulders were being cut down to make a new road and the barracks stood half demolished, she was still around, watching everything from her window, all day long.

But soon she was going to be rid of all this, she thought with a little tremor. And when she saw Engineer Babu coming down the road she broke into a smile. He came and stopped by the water tank. His shirtsleeves were rolled up and she could see his hairy forearms were coated with dust. There was sweat on his neck, all along the open shirt collar. His eyes were always alert behind his glasses, restless and yet extremely serious.

'How come you're standing here?'

'Oh, I'd come out for a stroll. It's so humid and still in the house, I couldn't bear it.... I saw you from a distance, Engineer Babu, though I could hardly recognize you in that sola topi.'

He laughed and Taran remembered the first time she had heard that laugh. She had hidden herself behind the door of the veranda where Babu entertained his friends and she had watched him, saying to herself—he is even younger than I am....

'Have you been to the town, Engineer Babu?'

'No, how could I?' He recounted his problems with such style, one would have thought he quite relished them. 'How could I? The lorry has not been out for three days. I can't get there on my own, nor can Montu.'

'The lorry hasn't been? But who brings the food then? There isn't even a decent restaurant here.'

'Ah, but you don't know Montu,' he laughed boyishly. 'We are both lazy about going into town to shop, so he's discovered a nice dhaba here. He gets food for us both from there.'

Taran gazed at him in wonder. What a man this Engineer Babu is, she thought. He's come all the way here, leaving behind his home and family. And there is no one here in this wilderness he can call his own, except his servant boy.

'Come, you'd set out for a stroll, let's go on.' They started walking on the rough, uneven path.

Every time the wind blew they had to swallow a mouthful of dust. In the Kali temple right above the labourers' hovels the evening lamp had been lit. A white curtain of sand fluttered around it, screening it from the last rays of the sun.

Engineer Babu stopped suddenly. 'Do you see the boulders behind those huts?' His gaze rested on them. Taran looked at him curiously. 'After the road is made all those will be razed to the ground. The land around the railway line will be prepared for cultivation. On the far side of the canal factories will come up. You'll see everything change before your very eyes.'

His voice had grown eager. The glass of his spectacles glinted in the evening sun. He always related such exciting stories. And Taran gazed at him fascinated, thinking to herself—he looks just like a college boy, yet how much he knows! But one detail always made her laugh. He spoke to her so forcefully about his plans, almost as if he was afraid she was going to thwart them!

They stopped at the gate beside the railway line. He had fallen silent now, as if the gathering dusk had hushed him and left him suddenly forlorn.

A slender moon lit the sky. The jagged cliffs which looked harsh in the daylight seemed to soften in the evening glow. They lost their aggressive bulk and huddled closer to each other.

'Engineer Babu, have you ever been to Assam?'

'Assam, no, why, what's there?'

'Nothing, I just thought of it. My brother lives there. He's about your age.'

'Oh,' he said, a little uninterested, and she felt embarrassed. The wind had fallen, it was almost night. She had to turn back.

'Perhaps you should return home now. It's getting late. Shall I send Montu with you?'

'No, I'll manage, it's hardly any distance.'

He crossed the rail tracks and started walking across the vast bare fields. Taran turned around and kept looking after his receding figure. Then she started walking back and an inexpressible happiness rose inside her.... All the worries that had been nagging at her seemed irrelevant, she could not explain to herself why she had been afraid for so long, what, after all, had made her so afraid? Look at Engineer Babu, she said to herself, here he is, so far from home, how must he feel? Walking along the dirt road she felt as if all the staleness of the past years had been washed away from her. No, now I will never return to this house, she repeated to herself, I shall live my own life, I will not let anyone drag me back into this wasteland.

Climbing the steps of her house Taran noticed the veranda was deserted; the whole house stood in absolute silence. There was light only in the kitchen and it stretched out in a faded patch up to Babu's door.

The door was slightly ajar. Taran began to feel uneasy—was Babu sitting there all by himself in the dark? As she came up to the room, she pushed open the door a little further. Now, her hands were trembling. At first she couldn't see anything in the dark. Then, suddenly, she shrank back. Yes, Babu was there, walking about in the room as if in a delirium. She watched him. He stopped suddenly in the middle of the room, as if he was trying to capture a forgotten memory.

Then, as abruptly, he turned around and walked up to a photograph that had stood for years in the little alcove. She saw him pick it up and wipe off the dust with unsure hands.... An image gleamed through the faded curtain of memories. The photograph had been taken at the silver jubilee celebrations of George V. Babu sat there, amidst other state officials, flanking the English Resident.... He stood there with the image in his hand, hypnotized to see himself there, sitting with them in such glory.

Taran came in and stood by the door, petrified. This was the first time she had seen old age so nakedly. Babu's brittle grey hair, his bony hands with the blue veins sticking out, those innumerable wrinkles which made his face so pitiful...he had grown so very old before her eyes.

'Babu,' Taran's lips quivered. She approached him in the darkness. This was perhaps the first time she had dared to go so close to him.

He raised his head and looked at her. His eyes had glazed over. 'What do you want?' he asked tremulously.

She turned and left the room, then stood for a long time on the veranda outside. A certain fear began to crawl around her mind.... Babu will never let me go, she thought, I will live here alone, bound to his shadow.... Even when he is gone his wretchedness will cling to me all my life.

The moment of courage that had come and touched her that evening had fled already. Perhaps it had never belonged to her...no, it would not come to her again.

All night she could hear Bua coughing in her room. Sometime in the middle of the night Taran went to Babu's room and stood there, leaning against the door. She felt as if her mother had died again that night and that she was weeping the tears that had remained choked within her all those years.

Then she came back to her room and stood by the open window. There was moonlight over the barren fields. A few lights glimmered beyond the railway line. Engineer Babu lives somewhere there, she thought. And suddenly she remembered what he had said to her: that in a few years everything would change. Was he right? She smiled now, a dry, wan smile.

She came away from the window and lay down on the bed. Her eyes were heavy but she could not sleep for a long time. Once she was swept by a light wave of sleep and dreamt her brother stood before her. That dear, familiar face with its lonely eyes.... It was so long ago that she had seen him, would she know him now if she ever chanced upon him all of a sudden?

And then it all came floating before her eyes.... Somewhere, very far away, hidden in the shade of a plantation, was her brother's house. They say you have to board a steamer to get there...wonder how it feels to travel on a steamer!

THE HANGING

O. V. VIJAYAN

Translated from the Malayalam by A. J. Thomas

VELLAAYIAPPAN SET OUT FOR KANNUR. AS HE BEGAN HIS JOURNEY, A wailing rose from the family members gathered in his hut, and from Ammini's hut. The fifty or so families in the village of Paazhuthara listened to the mournful sounds, and grieved along with the mourners. If they had had the funds to accompany Vellaayiappan, Ammini and the rest of the villagers would have gone with him to Kannur. But the villagers were so poverty stricken that Vellaayiappan made the journey alone.

He left the last of the huts of the village behind and took the earthen bund that led across the paddy fields. Behind him, the lament of the villagers grew faint as he walked on. The bund he was walking on led to a footpath that meandered through pasture land.

'My gods, my lords,' Vellaayiappan wept within himself.

The footpath was lined by palmyra palms on both sides. A strong wind rattled the fronds of the palms. Today, the familiar sound seemed strange, it was as if the gods and ancestors were communing with him. As he walked on, he felt the dampness of the cooked rice his wife had wrapped for him in a piece of cloth begin to soak into his arm. The tears of his wife, Kodachi, as she cooked the rice, must have seeped into the sour curd that it was mixed with, he thought; it was the wetness of tears that was dripping on his arm.

The railway station was four miles away. As he walked towards it, he saw Kuttihassan approaching. Kuttihassan reverentially stepped aside as he came up to him.

'Vellaayi,' said Kuttihassan.

'Kuttihassan,' said Vellaayiappan.

Just two words. Nothing more. Yet both the travellers could sense the strings of sentiments and unspoken sentences that lay beneath the surface.

An unvoiced conversation passed between them:

'Kuttihassan, I have yet to pay you back the fifteen rupees I borrowed from you.'

'Vellaayi, you shouldn't be thinking about this matter today.'

'Kuttihassan, it's just that I might never be able to repay you.'

'Unpaid debts are for the Creator to keep. Let it remain that way.'

'I am burning up inside. I feel my life force is being drained away.'

'May God keep you, may His beloved Prophet comfort you, may your gods and mine help you.'

Vellaayiappan continued his journey. The wind in the palmyra fronds turned dense with intense intimations of the deities. Soon, he encountered another acquaintance, Neeli, the washerwoman, carrying her bundles of freshly washed clothes. She, too, stepped aside from the path.

'Vellaayiappan.'

'Neeli.'

Just two words once again. But, as before, they contained a torrent of unsaid things.

Vellaayiappan walked on. The path widened into a dirt road that eventually came to a river. On the other side of the river was an embankment, and beyond it, the road that led to the railway station. Vellaayiappan waded into the shallows of the river. Schools of fish nibbled at his calves. He walked deeper into the waters. Memories arose within him—bathing his father's corpse, teaching his young son how to swim. The memories overwhelmed him, and once he'd crossed the river, Vellaayiappan sank down on the riverbank and wept.

Presently, he picked himself up and continued towards the station, although tears continued to trickle down his face. When he got to the station, Vellaayiappan stood in line to buy a ticket. The train fare was knotted up in a corner of his mundu. When his turn came, he said, 'Kannur' to the ticket clerk. The clerk gave him his ticket, and as he did so, Vellaayiappan thought: the first stage of my journey is over.

Carefully tying the ticket into a knot in his mundu, Vellaayiappan made his way to the platform, and sat down on a bench to wait for his train. Over the darkening palmyra trees in the distance, birds were returning to their nests. Vellaayiappan remembered how, as a little boy, his son would look in wonderment at the birds returning to their nests at dusk, as they walked through the paddy fields. Then he thought of walking with his own father in the gathering dark through the paddy fields, holding on to his hand with his little finger just as his son had done. Two pictures in his memory, and between them an ocean of unexpressed things.

An old man came to sit beside him on the bench.

'Going to Coimbatore?'

'To Kannur,' Vellaayiappan replied.

'I'm off to Coimbatore,' the other said.

'I see,' Vellaayiappan said.

'The Kannur train will arrive at ten o'clock.'

'I see,' Vellaayiappan said.

'What are going to Kannur for?'

'Nothing in particular.'

'Oh, just for fun, then.'

The stranger's conversation began to grate, his words began to wind themselves around his neck like a noose. He thought, once you leave the paddy fields of Paazhuthara behind, you enter a world of strangers, and their uncaring, impersonal conversations form countless nooses around your neck.

The Coimbatore train arrived and the old man got up and left, leaving Vellaayiappan on his own once again. He did not feel like eating the rice his wife had packed. He could feel its wetness through the cloth in which it was packed. He dozed off, and dreamed unquiet dreams. He called out in his sleep, 'O, my son, Kandunni.'

The hissing of steam and the rumbling of the tracks woke him from his sleep. His train had arrived. Vellaayiappan got up from the bench, checked that his ticket was still securely knotted into his mundu, picked up his packed rice, and walked down the platform looking for a compartment he could get into. He was turned away from the first one he tried.

'This is the first-class compartment, O elder.'

'Oh? Is that so?' He walked further down the train.

'This is a reserved compartment.'

'Oh, really.'

'Try elsewhere, O venerable one.'

The voices of strangers.

Vellaayiappan finally managed to climb into a crowded carriage. There was no space to sit but he mused to himself: 'I'll stand, I don't need to sleep. My son is certainly not going to sleep tonight.'

The train's rhythm changed from moment to moment with changes in the terrain; he noted the trackside lamps flashing past, the dim contours of the riverbank, trees, other objects vaguely glimpsed. He had travelled by train just once before, many years ago. That journey had taken place in daylight, this was a night train. They were passing through a long tunnel, on the walls of which there was fading graffiti.

It was not yet daybreak when they reached Kannur. He still hadn't opened the parcel of curd rice his wife had packed for him. Getting off the train, Vellaayiappan made his way out of the station; he handed over his ticket to the ticket collector at the gate. In the far reaches of the darkness above him, there were signs of the coming dawn. The tonga drivers clustered around the station did not pester him.

He asked one of them: 'Which way is the jail?'

Another driver laughed: 'Look at this old man enquiring about the way to the jail so early in the morning.'

A driver standing nearby sniggered and said: 'Eh, old man, just steal something. Best way to land in jail.'

The voices of these strangers wrapped themselves around his throat, and began strangling him. Vellaayiappan felt asphyxiated.

Finally, someone took pity on him and pointed him in the direction of the jail. Vellaayiappan began to walk towards it. The skies above him slowly began to lighten; the cawing of crows filled the air.

At the gates of the jail, Vellaayiappan was stopped by a sentry.

'What are you doing here so early in the morning?'

Vellaayiappan felt so helpless, he was on the point of breaking down. Then he slowly unknotted a portion of the mundu tied around his waist, and took out a crumpled, yellowing piece of paper.

'What's this?'

Vellaayiappan handed over the piece of paper to the sentry, who cast a cursory glance at it.

Vellaayiappan then said, 'My child is here.'

The sentry said gruffly: 'Who asked you to come so early? Let the office open.' The man then looked down again at the piece of paper he held in his hand, and registered what was written on it. All at once, his face softened, grew compassionate.

'It's taking place tomorrow, isn't it?'

'I don't really know,' Vellaayiappan replied. 'What's written on the paper?'

The guard looked closely at the document in his hand and then said, 'Yes, at five in the morning.'

Vellaayiappan's face filled with sorrow.

'Please sit down, sir,' the guard said, pointing to the steps leading up to the gates of the jail. Wearily, Vellaayiappan slumped on to a step looking like someone waiting for the sanctum of a temple to open and admit him.

'May I get you some tea, O elder?' the guard asked him.

'No.'

Vellaayiappan thought: 'My son would have remained sleepless all night. If he hasn't slept, how is he going to awaken, break his fast?' His hand reached down to the bundle of rice he had brought with him. 'Son, your mother packed this rice for me. I haven't eaten it. This is all I have to give you.' In the heat the rice had turned rancid.

The sky began to brighten, the day grew hotter.

The jail office opened, employees took their places behind desks. The guards took part in the morning parade. Everywhere, there was activity. Officers shouted out orders, sentries checked papers. All these voices twined together to form impersonal nooses that wound themselves around Vellaayiappan, suffocating him. The day grew even hotter. Still, he waited.

Eventually, the guard led him into the prison. Down cool corridors that had never known the heat of the sun.

'Here.'

Kandunni stood before him, behind the bars of a locked cell. His son looked at him without emotion as if he were a stranger, his mind seemed incapable of giving or receiving consolation. The guard unlocked the door and let Vellaayiappan into the cell. For some moments, father and son faced each other, motionless, without a sound. Then Vellaayiappan embraced his son. Kandunni wailed in terror and pain, a sound almost beyond the range of hearing. Weeping, Vellaayiappan said brokenly, 'My son.'

Kandunni said, 'Appa.'

Just those words. But what lay between them was the enormity of sorrow, and unexpressed words:

'Son, what did you do?'

'I don't remember, Appa.'
'Son, did you murder anyone?'
'I don't remember.'
'It's all right, son. You don't have to remember anything any more.'
'Will the guards remember?'
'No, my son.'
'Will you remember my pain, Appa?'

Again an intense keening issued from Kandunni, a wail so high-pitched and shrill, it was on the edge of auditory perception.

'Appa, don't let them hang me.'
'Time's up, sir. Please come out.'

Vellaayiappan walked out of the cell and the door clanged shut. When he looked back, he saw his son looking at him from behind the bars as a stranger might from behind the barred window of a train hurtling past.

Vellaayiappan kept walking. Just before he turned the bend in the corridor, he looked back one last time, to bid his son farewell.

For the rest of the day, he wandered listlessly around the jail compound, keeping a sort of vigil for his son. The sun rose higher and then the day began to ebb away. When night fell, Vellaayiappan wondered whether his son would sleep that night. When dawn broke, Kandunni was still alive within the walls of the jail.

Vellaayiappan heard the sound of bugles at dawn. He wasn't aware that they signalled the start of the execution. The sentry had told him that the hanging would take place at five in the morning. Vellaayiappan had no wristwatch but his peasant's instincts told him what time it was.

When the guards delivered his son's body to him, Vellaayiappan received it as a midwife would a baby.

'O elder, what funeral ceremony did you have in mind for your son?'
'I don't know.'
'Don't you want the body?'
'Masters, I have no money.'

The prison officials handed the body over to the scavengers who took care of such things and instructed them to transport the body to the public burial ground. The scavengers put the body on a trolley and began pushing it towards the cemetery. Vellaayiappan walked along with them. On the outskirts of town, a place of desolate marshes; vultures wheeled in the sky above them.

When they got to the burial ground, the scavengers dug a pit and laid the body in it. Just before they closed the grave Vellaayiappan looked at his son's face one last time. He placed his hand on his cold forehead in a final blessing.

After the scavengers had filled in the grave, Vellaayiappan walked aimlessly away from the burial ground in the intense heat of the day.

Eventually, his wanderings brought him to the seashore. He was seeing the sea for the first time. He became aware of something cold and wet in his hands, and realized he was still carrying the rice his wife had prepared for his journey. Vellaayiappan opened the bundle, and scattered the rice on the ground in remembrance of his dead son. From the gleaming sunlit dome of the sky, crows descended on the sacrificial rice—like embodied spirits of the dead come to receive the offering.

TRISHANKU

MANNU BHANDARI

Translated from the Hindi by Poonam Saxena

'THE FOUR WALLS OF A HOUSE PROVIDE SECURITY TO A PERSON BUT ALSO confine him. School-college develop a person's mind but, at the same time, in the name of rules, regulations, and discipline, his or her personality also gets blunted. The thing is, brother, everything has its opposite within itself!'

I'm not giving these examples from some book. I don't have the ability to read such weighty tomes. These are snatches of the conversations and arguments that take place in our home day and night. Our house, the wrestling ground of intellectuals. Here, in the midst of cigarette smoke and coffee cups, there is big talk, and major rhetorical revolutions come to pass. In this house there is more talk, less action. I haven't read this anywhere but, looking at my home, it certainly seemed to me that working was perhaps forbidden for intellectuals. Mother dear, after amusing herself with a light three-hour job, was free for the day. The time left after reading and writing was spent in talking and arguing or lying down. She was of the view that the mind becomes active only when the body is inactive, and so for twelve hours out of the twenty-four hours in a day, she wanted to keep her mind active. Father dear was two steps ahead! If he had his way, he would bathe at his table.

The topic that is discussed the most in our home is modernity! But, wait, don't interpret modernity in the wrong way. This modernity is not about cutting your hair or eating with a knife and fork. This modernity is the modernity of real, genuine intellectuals! What that is exactly, even I don't know for sure, but, yes, there's always a great deal of talk about abandoning established practices and customs. You should kick such customs aside, if you embrace them, you are the one who will get a kick.

Every subject in the world is the focus of discussions and arguments but there's one topic that is especially dear to everyone: marriage. Marriage, that is, ruin and destruction. Conversations that begin on a light note all of a sudden reach an intellectual plane—the institution of marriage has become utterly hollow...the husband–wife relationship has become so artificial and forced...and then marriage is made fun of with much vigour and spirit. Often, in these arguments, the women are ranged on one side and the men on the other, and things sometimes became so heated I thought some of the couples would end up divorcing. But that never happened. All the friends continued in their neat and securely organized marriages.

But, yes, the tone and manner of the arguments continue to be the same even today!

Now think about it, if they curse marriage, then it is necessary to support free love and free sex. In this, the men were the most enthusiastic and at the forefront—as if they could experience half its pleasure by just talking about it. Papa himself was a big supporter! But it so happened that when a young, quiet, and retiring distant female relative who stayed in the house and never participated in such discussions acted on these principles, all that modernity went dhummmm! It was Mummy who took care of everything in an easy, natural way, and by tying her down in a meaningless marriage, gave meaning to her life. Though this is a very old story and I heard it mentioned only in hushed tones and muted whispers.

Actually Papa–Mummy also had a love marriage. It's another matter that from the time I was old enough to understand things, I never saw them being affectionate with each other, instead I only saw them arguing constantly. Mummy had had to fight with Nana, and for a long time. Despite this, theirs was not a marriage of argument but a marriage of love and Mummy used to mention this with great pride. Pride not because of the marriage itself but because of the way she had battled Nana for it. She'd repeated the conversations between Nana and herself so often, I knew them by heart. Even today, when she talks about it, there's a flash of contentment on her face, that she did something outside of established norms.

So, this is the kind of house I'm being brought up in—in a very free, independent way. And one day, suddenly, I grew up. I didn't feel the fact of my growing up as much from the inside as from the outside. There's an entertaining incident connected with this. It so happened that right opposite our house was a barsati—a single room with a sprawling terrace.

Every year, a few students would come and stay there. They would walk up and down the terrace as they studied, but I never noticed them, perhaps because I was not of the age to have any interest in them. This time, I saw that two boys had moved in. They were just two, but in the evening a big crowd of their friends would gather, and not just their terrace, the entire neighbourhood would come alive! Fun, laughter, music, song, and the passing of sharp comments and jokes on the girls who lived nearby and happened to come into their sights. But their real focus was our house...to be clear, me. If I came out on the veranda to do anything, some remark or the other would fly and land there and I would quiver to my core. For the first time I became aware of myself...and that I was the centre of someone's attention. If I were to be honest, I found this first awareness very thrilling and I felt new in my own eyes...new and grown-up!

It was a strange situation. When they would pass those remarks, I would burn with anger, though there was nothing rude or uncouth about the remarks. They were more in the nature of light-hearted fun. But when they became busy with each other or if they were absent, I would keep waiting...and wrestling with an unknown restlessness. My attention was forever fixed in that direction and I was always hanging around outside my room, in the veranda.

But the neighbours were fed up of the boisterous, loud behaviour of these boys. Our neighbourhood was inhabited by the lalas of Hathras–Khurja. Those who had adolescent girls at home would threaten to break teeth and legs, because for them, the future of their daughters was in danger. The neighbourhood was all aflame but my parents had no idea what was going on. The fact is, they lived as though they were on an island. Away from everyone, despite living in the midst of everyone.

One day I told my mother, 'Mummy, these boys who live opposite us, they keep making remarks about me. I'm not going to stay quiet; I'll answer back.'

'Which boys?' asked Mummy in surprise!

Amazing! Mummy didn't know anything. My tone a mixture of irritation and delight, I told her everything. But there was no reaction from her.

'Tell me who these boys are....' she said calmly and went back to her reading. I didn't like her indifference to what, for me, was a scandalous matter. If it had been any other mother, she would have taken them to task with the utmost severity. But not my mother.

As the afternoon waned and the boys gathered on the terrace, I told Mummy, 'Look, these are the boys who keep looking and passing comments.' I don't know if there was something in the way I said this, but Ma kept looking at me unblinkingly, then smiled gently. After sizing up the boys on the terrace, she said, 'They look like college boys but they're like little kids.'

I felt like saying: if kids won't tease me, then who will, old people? But at that moment, Mummy said, 'We'll call them for tea tomorrow evening so you can make friends with them.'

I was speechless!

'You'll call them for tea?' I couldn't believe what Mummy was saying.

'Yes, why, what happened? Arre, all this happened in our time that boys and girls couldn't meet each other, and you had to be content with passing comments from far away. Times have changed now.'

I was ecstatic at the thought. I felt my mother really was someone very exalted. These people will come to our house and make friends with me. All at once I began feeling I was very alone and that I desperately needed to make friends. I didn't really know anyone in the neighbourhood and the only people who came home were Mummy–Papa's friends.

I went through the next day with great anxiety. Who knows if Mummy will keep her word or whether she said it impulsively? And if that were the case, then that was the end of the matter! In the evening, just to remind her, I said, 'Mummy, will you really call those boys?' These were my words, but the emotion was actually Mummy, please go and call them!

And, indeed, Mummy did go. I don't remember Mummy going to anyone's house in our neighbourhood more than three or four times. I waited for her to return with bated breath. I experienced an unfamiliar thrill in every part of my body. What if Mummy brings them with her? Suppose they behave rudely with Mummy? But, no, they didn't seem like that. Mummy returned after about an hour! Very happy!

'They were struck dumb when they saw me. They thought that until now people were sitting in their homes and threatening to come and break their arms and legs, and I had actually turned up to give them a good hiding. But the poor things looked after me so well! They are very sweet kids. They've come from outside—they couldn't get space in the hostel, so they've taken this room. We'll call them over when Papa comes home in the evening!'

I learnt for the first time how ponderously time passes when you're waiting for something. When Papa came, Mummy elatedly explained the whole story to him. Pride and gratification that she was doing something quite out of the ordinary overflowed from every word. Papa was scarcely going to hold back either. He too was delighted.

'Call the boys! Arre, let them come and have fun, let the kids enjoy themselves.' Mummy–Papa were pleased that they had got such an excellent opportunity to display their modernity.

The servant was sent to bring them over and the whole lot of them appeared in the very next instant! Mummy introduced them properly and there was an exchange of hi-hellos.

'Tanu bete, make tea for your friends!'

Oh crap! When Mummy's friends come, it is 'Tanu bete, go and make tea,' and when it's Tanu's friends, then too Tanu should make the tea! Glumly, I got up.

Everyone had tea. There was much laughter and bonhomie. They kept defending their reputation by saying that everyone in the neighbourhood was after them for no reason. They hadn't done anything to annoy anyone. Whatever they may have done was just for fun.

Papa said encouragingly, 'Arre, this is the age for all this. If we got a chance even at this age, we wouldn't hesitate.'

A wave of laughter surged from one end of the room to the other. After about two hours, they got up to leave and Mummy said, 'You should think of this as your home. Come over whenever you feel like it. Our daughter, Tanu, will have pleasant company. Sometimes she can study with you. Also, if you feel like eating anything in particular, let me know, I'll have it cooked for you.' Bowled over by Papa's openness and Mummy's warmth and affection, they went away. But they had actually been called to become friends with someone and that poor someone ended up becoming a mere spectator to the whole show.

There was a great deal of discussion about them long after they had left. Calling those very boys who had been teasing your adolescent daughter to your house for tea so that they could become friends with her, why, the whole thing was so thrilling. From the very next day, Mummy began recounting what had happened to everyone who dropped in. Mummy was an expert at making even the dullest thing seem interesting, but here, this story itself was riveting. Whoever heard it said, 'Wah, this is wonderful. You have such a healthy outlook on such matters. Otherwise, people talk big but suffocate their children and don't hesitate to spy on them if they have the slightest suspicion about them.' And Mummy would bask in the praise, and say, 'But of course. Be free and keep your children free. When we were young, there were so many restrictions on us. We were told: don't do this, don't go there. At least our children shouldn't be suffocated in this manner.'

But at that moment, Mummy's child was becoming the victim of another kind of suffocation because though she was supposed to be the heroine of the play, it was Mummy who had become the heroine.

Anyway, the outcome of the entire affair was that the behaviour of those boys changed completely. They had no choice but to live up to the mantle of decency that Mummy had thrown on them. Now when they saw Mummy–Papa on the roof, they would greet them with a namaste and when they saw me, they would throw a hi and a smile in my direction. Instead of those mocking remarks, now we actually had conversations...very open and free conversations, and there was just enough distance between our veranda and their roof that we could talk to each other if we spoke a little loudly. It was another matter that the entire neighbourhood heard our conversations and listened to them with a great deal of interest. As soon as we'd start talking, four or five pairs of ears and bodies would attach themselves to each window. It wasn't as if girls had never had romantic liaisons in the neighbourhood. There had even been incidents of girls running away from home. But all that had happened furtively and in utmost secrecy. And when the people of the neighbourhood discovered such a secret, they felt intense gratification. The men, twirling their moustaches with smug satisfaction, and the women, gesticulating dramatically with their hands, would broadcast the news, adding generous amounts of salt and spice to it. Their attitude was: we have seen the world, no one can make a fool of us. But here the situation was the opposite. Our conversations were so open that people listened by hiding behind windows but even then they couldn't find anything that would give them any inner gratification.

But things had to get out of hand and they did. What happened was that the gathering on the roof slowly started moving to my room. Every day, sometimes two, sometimes three or four boys would install themselves in my room and there would be long hours of chatting, joking, laughing about everything in the world. There would be music and singing and rounds of tea and other refreshments. When Mummy's and Papa's friends would come in the evening, one or the other of the boys would still be hanging around. When all those people who had initially praised the idea of 'be free and let others be free' saw this type of freedom, you could see the doubt in their eyes. A couple of Mummy's friends even said to her, sotto voce: 'Tanu is moving very fast.' Mummy's enthusiasm began waning and then the thrill of doing something against established norms completely dissipated. Now she had to face the naked truth that her very naive, inexperienced daughter of tender years was always surrounded by three or four boys. Mummy's situation was such that neither could she fully accept the situation, nor was she able to reject what she herself had started so eagerly.

Eventually one day she called me, made me sit next to her and said, 'Tanu bete, these people come here every day and stay for so long. After all, you have to study too. I've been noticing that your studies are getting affected. This can't go on.'

'I study at night,' I said carelessly.

'I don't think you study anything at night, how much time do you get anyway? In any case, I don't like these noisy gatherings on an everyday basis. They can drop in once in a while after every five or six days for some chit-chat, but right now, someone or the other is parked here every single day.' The tinge of displeasure in her voice became more pronounced.

I didn't like Mummy's tone, but I stayed quiet.

'You've become very friendly and frank with them, tell them they should go and study, and let you study too. And if you can't say it, I will.'

But it didn't come to that. Because of the pressure of studies and because of the lure of Delhi's other attractions, the hostel boys started coming over less and less often. But Shekhar, who lived in the room in front, would turn up every day, sometimes during the afternoon, sometimes in the evening! I hadn't noticed many things about him when he was part of the group, but those aspects of his personality came out clearly when he was alone. He spoke little, but tried to say a great deal without words and all of a sudden, I began understanding his language of silence...not just understanding it, but replying as well. Soon I realized that something like love was growing between Shekhar and me. I would probably not have realized this in the normal course but after watching Hindi films, I found no difficulty in understanding it.

As long as there was nothing to hide, everything was very open, but the moment that 'something' happened, so did the desire to hide it from everyone's eyes. When the other boys came, they would make a racket from the stairs itself, talking in loud voices. But whenever Shekhar arrived, he would slink in and we would talk in whispers. They were ordinary conversations—about school, college. But they became special because they were conducted in whispers. When love is clandestine and hush-hush, it becomes very thrilling, otherwise it's plain vanilla! But Mummy had a sixth sense that could ferret out every secret of the people in the house. Even Papa was afraid of it. She lost no time in figuring out what was going on. No matter how noiselessly Shekhar walked in and no matter which corner of the house she was in, she would instantly appear or call out from wherever she was: 'Tanu, who is in your room?'

I noticed a strange look of worry on Mummy's face at Shekhar's behaviour. That Mummy would be worried by it had never crossed my mind. In a household where there were discussions about all kinds of romantic liaisons—between unmarried youngsters, married people, love affairs of people with two or three lovers—for such a household, this should've been a very ordinary matter. When you're friendly with boys, it's possible that love can happen. Perhaps Mummy thought this whole situation would unfold like the present-day art films—of which she was an admirer and supporter—where, from beginning to end, nothing sensational ever happened.

Whatever it was, I was definitely perturbed that Mummy was worried. Mummy was not just my mother but also my friend and companion. We talked about everything under the sun, laughed and joked with each other like two close friends. I wanted her to talk to me about this business but she didn't say anything. But whenever Shekhar came, she would abandon her customary indifference and hover around my room in a vigilant manner.

One day I came downstairs, ready to go out with Mummy when I bumped into a gracious-looking woman from the neighbourhood. After the namaskars and enquiries about each other's well-being, she came to the real purpose of her visit.

'Are these boys who stay on the roof opposite your house related to you?'

'Not at all.'

'Really? They are always at your place in the evenings, so we thought they must certainly be related to you.'

'They are Tanu's friends.' Mummy threw this at her with such indifference and lack of hesitation that the woman's attempts to fire an arrow at her target failed and she had to leave, crestfallen.

She left and I felt that now Mummy would pick up the topic and scold me a little. The neighbour hadn't achieved what she set out to do but she did place a weapon in Mummy's hands which could make things difficult for me. Mummy had been grappling with some internal conflict for quite a few days now, but all she said was: 'It seems as if...is always busy poking their nose into someone else's house.'

Not only was I reassured, I took this as a green signal from Mummy and speeded things up in my life. But I made sure that of the three hours I spent with Shekhar, at least one was devoted to studying. He taught me with great earnestness and I studied very diligently too. Yes, in between, he would pass me little notes where he'd write the kind of lines that would thrill me to the core. Even after he left, those lines, the emotion behind those words, would make every vein in my body sing and I would be lost in them.

Another world, a big, full, colourful world was taking shape inside me. I didn't feel the need for anybody else. It was as if I was complete in myself. Even Mummy, always with me, was fading away and maybe that's why I'd stopped paying attention to her. Everyday conversations did happen, but just that—nothing else.

The days were passing and I was lost in myself, sinking deeper and deeper into my own world—quite oblivious to the outside world!

One day I came back from school and changed my clothes. I clamoured for my food, ate it, cribbing all the while, and when I went to my room, Mummy, who was lying down, called me: 'Tanu, come here.'

It was only when I went closer that I noticed for the first time that Mummy's face was flushed with anger. The penny dropped. She picked up a book from the side table, pulled out five or six pieces of paper from it and showed them to me. Tauba! I wanted Mummy's help with studying so I had given her this book when I left. Shekhar's notes had got left behind in the book by mistake.

'So this is how your friendship with Shekhar is going? This is the studying that happens sitting here...this is why he comes here?'

I was silent! I knew it was the height of foolishness to answer back when Mummy was angry.

'I let you be...gave you freedom, but this doesn't mean you misuse it!'

I remained silent!

'A slip of a girl but look at her exploits! The more leeway you give, the more she keeps grabbing! One slap and all this romance will vanish in two minutes....'

I suddenly flared up at this remark. I looked up at Mummy angrily—but wait, this was not my Mummy. This was not Mummy's manner, nor was the language hers. But the sentences sounded very familiar. I felt as if I'd heard all this before and it suddenly struck me like a flash of lightning—Nana! But Nana had died so many years ago, how had he suddenly come to life? And that too, inside Mummy...who had fought him ceaselessly ever since she'd begun making sense of the world...she had opposed every single thing he'd said.

Mummy's 'Nana-type' lecture continued for quite a while, but I remained completely unmoved. If there was one thing bothering me, it was this: how come Nana had installed himself inside Mummy?

And then a strange, tension-filled silence settled on the house, especially between Mummy and me. No, Mummy wasn't even in the house, it was between Nana and me. I can explain myself to Mummy, I can understand her views, but Nana? I couldn't understand this language, this attitude, so there was no question of talking or discussing anything. Yes, Papa is also my friend, but of a different kind. Playing chess, arm-wrestling, extracting favours that Mummy hadn't agreed to.... As a child, I always clambered onto his back and even today, I do the same unhesitatingly and get him to agree to whatever I want. But despite being 'my dear friend' I always confided my personal feelings only to Mummy. And there was utter silence on that front—having knocked Mummy down, Nana was fully in command of her.

I had discreetly shown Shekhar the red flag so he'd stopped coming over and the evenings stretched interminably.

Many times I thought of going to Mummy and asking her in a forthright way why she was so angry. You know about my friendship with Shekhar. I never hid anything from you. And if there is friendship, then all this is inevitable. Did you think that we'd be like brother-sister? But then the thought came.... Mummy isn't even around, so I can't go and tell her all this.

It's been four days, I haven't seen Shekhar. Just a slight indication was enough for him to stop coming to the house, indeed, stop coming to the roof altogether. Even his friends who stayed in the hostel couldn't be seen on the roof, nor did they come to the house. If one of them had come I could have at least asked after him. I knew he was emotional to the point of foolishness. He didn't even know what exactly had happened here. It seems as if the mere possibility of Mummy's anger had crushed all of them.

But since yesterday, the tension on Mummy's face had definitely relaxed a little. It was as if the sternness that had frozen over her face had melted. But I decided that Mummy should be the one to break the ice.

In the morning, bathed and fresh, I was ironing my uniform behind the door. Outside Mummy was making tea and Papa was buried behind the newspaper. Mummy didn't realize that I had finished my bath and come out. She said to Papa: 'Do you know what happened last night? I don't know, I've been feeling bad since then—I couldn't even sleep.'

Hearing the softness of Mummy's tone, my hand froze and my ears pricked up.

'I woke up to go to the bathroom in the middle of the night. In front, the roof was in pitch darkness. Suddenly, a reddish, star-like light shone. I was startled. I looked carefully and slowly made out a silhouette. Shekhar was standing on the roof smoking a cigarette. I came back quietly. I went again after two hours and saw he was still pacing the roof in the same way. Poor thing, I don't know what to think. Tanu is also so subdued these days....' Then, as if reproaching herself, she said, 'First, give them liberty, then when they move forward, pull them down. Is this fair?'

A deep sigh of relief came from within me. An indescribable sensation surged in my heart and I felt like running to Mummy and flinging my arms around her. It felt as if Mummy had returned after a long absence. But I didn't do anything. Yes, now I would speak freely. In the last four days, so many questions had been swirling about in my head. But now... now Mummy is here, and with her at least everything can be discussed.

But when I came home I was taken aback by what I saw! Shekhar was sitting in a chair, his head in his hands, and Mummy was sitting on the arm of the chair, gently stroking his forehead and his back. Seeing me she said in a very natural, normal way: 'Look at this crazy boy. He hasn't gone to college for four days. Nor has he had anything to eat or drink. Set a place for him also to eat along with you.'

And then Mummy sat next to him and very lovingly entreated him to eat. But despite pressing him to, Shekhar didn't stay on after he finished the meal. Full of gratitude towards Mummy, he went away and such a tide of emotion overflowed inside me that all the questions I'd thought of vanished inside it.

The entire situation took time to return to normal, but it did. Shekhar began coming after every couple of days and when he did, we mostly spoke about study-related things. Expressing remorse at his behaviour, he promised Mummy that he would never do anything that would give her cause to complain. On the days he didn't come I would talk to him two or three times a day, for a short while, from the veranda itself. This love story, conducted in the open, with the permission and cooperation of everyone in the house, lost its novelty for the neighbours and after cursing these dangerous times, they abandoned their interest in the matter, till such time as some scandal might emerge.

But there was one thing I did notice. Whenever Shekhar stayed a little later than usual in the evening or if he came in the afternoon as well, Nana would start stirring within Mummy and you could see that reflected on Mummy's face. Mummy would attempt with all her might not to let Nana speak, but she didn't have the power to banish him totally.

Yes, this entire business did end up becoming the subject of everyday conversations between Mummy and me. Sometimes she would joke, 'This Shekhar of yours, he's a very limp sort of fellow. Arre, at his age boys should want to loaf about, have fun. What is this constant hanging around on the roof like some lovelorn Majnu, staring in this direction?'

I would just laugh.

Sometimes she would get very emotional and say, 'Why don't you understand, bete, I have so many ambitions for you! I have so many dreams for your future.'

I would laugh and say, 'Mummy, you are too much. You dream dreams about your life and you have dreams about my life as well...leave some dreams for me!'

Sometimes she would say, as if trying to explain something to me: 'Look, Tanu, you are still very young. All your focus should be on your studies and you should banish all these unnecessary obsessions from your mind. When you're older, fall in love and get married by all means. In any case I'm not going to find a boy for you—find someone yourself, but you should have enough sense and maturity to make a proper choice.'

I understood she didn't approve of my choice right now, so I asked, 'All right, tell me, Mummy, when you chose Papa, did Nana approve of him?'

'My choice! I made a choice at the age of twenty-five, after having completed my education—intelligently, after thinking over everything, understand?'

Mummy would say this, hiding her agitation under her anger. Age and education—these are the two points on which Mummy always pins me down. I was good at studies and, as for age, I felt like saying, 'Mummy, what your generation used to do at twenty-five, my generation will do at fifteen, why can't you get this?' But I would remain quiet. Nana's name has already cropped up, what if he awakens?

The mid-term exams were coming up and I was completely focused on my studies. No more comings and goings, and all the music and singing was at a standstill. I studied so hard that Mummy was delighted. Maybe a bit reassured too. After the last exam, I felt as if a burden had lifted. Light of mind, I wanted to have some fun. I asked Mummy: 'Mummy, Shekhar and Deepak are going for a movie tomorrow, can I go with them?' I had never gone out with them but after studying so hard, I deserved at least this much freedom.

Mummy looked at my face for a few seconds, then said: 'Come here, sit! I want to talk to you.'

I went and sat down but couldn't understand what there was to talk about—either say yes or say no. But Mummy had an incurable habit of talking. Her yes-no wouldn't emerge until it had been wrapped in fifty-sixty sentences.

'Your exams are over. I myself was making a plan to go see a movie. Tell me, what movie do you want to see?'

'Why, what's the matter if I go with them?' My voice was so full of irritation that Mummy stared at me.

'Tanu, I have given you full liberty, bete, but walk only so fast that I can keep up with you.'

'Tell me plainly, will you let me go or not? This is all useless talk...I can also walk with you—where did this business of walking with you come from?'

Stroking my back, Mummy said, 'I will have to walk with you. If you fall face down, there has to be someone to pick you up, isn't it?'

I understood that Mummy was not going to let me go, but by refusing so lovingly, I couldn't even fight with her. Arguing with her meant listening to an elaborate philosophical lecture—that is, a fifty-minute class. But I couldn't understand what, after all, was the objection to going with them. Everything was a no. She always said that when they were growing up, they were scolded and told 'Don't do this, don't go there', and now she herself is doing it. I'd had enough of all this big talk. I got up and stormed off to my room. Yes, I did toss this line out before flouncing off: 'Mummy, the one who walks will fall, and the one who falls will get up and get up by themselves, they don't need anyone else.'

I don't know if my words had an effect on her or whether something nagged her from within but that evening she called Shekhar and three or four other boys who were visiting him to our place and set up a proper party in my room with plenty of hot food. The mood of the evening was such that all my resentment of the afternoon washed away.

The exams were over and the weather was pleasant. Mummy's behaviour was in accordance with it and so the whole friendship saga, which had come to a standstill, picked up again. It was as if there was no space for anything else these days. But then again, a shock.

That day when I returned from a friend's place I heard Mummy's stern voice: 'Tanu, come here!'

Her voice was enough to indicate danger. For a second, I was unnerved. When I went in, her face was hard, like before.

'Do you go to Shekhar's room?' Mummy fired a salvo at me. I understood that someone from the back alley had tattled on me.

'Since when have you been going?'

I felt like saying that the person who gave you this news would no doubt have told you everything else as well...and would've probably embellished the story too. But the way Mummy was boiling with anger, it was prudent to remain quiet. Though I couldn't understand why Mummy was angry. What was the big deal if I'd gone to Shekhar's room a few times for a short while? What sin had I committed? But everything Mummy does doesn't necessarily have a reason...bas, it all depends on her mood.

It was a peculiar problem—there was no point talking when Mummy was angry but my silence fanned her rage even more.

'Remember I had told you in the beginning itself that you should never go to their rooms. He sits here for hours at a stretch, that's not enough for you?'

The lines of distress, rage, and panic on her face kept getting deeper, and I didn't know how to explain everything to her.

'It's a good thing those people who stay in front came and told me—do you know, this head hasn't bent before anyone till today, but today I couldn't raise my eyes in front of them. I won't be able to show my face to anyone because of you. Everyone in the lane is doing thoo...thoo...to us. You've disgraced us.'

Disaster!

This time the entire neighbourhood was talking from within Mummy! It was astonishing that Mummy, who till today, had kept herself aloof from the neighbourhood, in fact, used to make fun of them—today, she was singing their tune.

Mummy's lecture was in full flow but I had switched off. When her anger cools down, when Mummy is back to being herself again, then I will explain to her—Mummy, you're unnecessarily making such a big deal of a small thing.

But I don't know what kind of dose she'd taken this time that her anger showed no signs of cooling down, and her anger started making *me* angry.

Then a strange kind of tension grew in the house and this time perhaps Mummy told Papa everything. He didn't say anything. From the beginning he had stayed out of the whole affair but now there was an unspoken tension on his face.

When a similar incident had occurred around two months ago, I'd been cowed down but this time I vowed that if Mummy was going to behave like Nana, I too would have to open a front against him just like Mummy had...and I'll do it. Let me show her that I am your daughter and I'm following your lead. You broke away from established norms, all my life you fed me this tonic, but no sooner did I take my very first steps in this direction, you began making strenuous efforts to drag me back to the line you had drawn.

I thought up a whole lot of logical points with which I would one day have a proper argument with Mummy. I'd tell her clearly: Mummy, if you had to impose all these restrictions on me, you should have raised me accordingly right from the start. Why did you talk of giving me freedom, why did you teach me about freedom if it was all going to be lies? But this time I was so upset, it was as if my heart had burnt and turned to ashes, I just stayed listlessly in my room, silent, lost in myself. If I felt too overwhelmed, I would cry! I'm usually all over the house, chattering and laughing, but now I turned absolutely silent and withdrawn. Yes, there was one sentence I kept repeating: 'Mummy, you should understand that I too will do what I please.' Though I had no clear idea of what it was I wanted to do.

I don't know what happened in these three or four days. Cut off from the world outside, shrunk inside myself, I was thinking of ways I could open a front against Mummy.

But this afternoon I couldn't believe my ears when I heard Mummy yelling from the veranda: 'Shekhar, tomorrow all of you will leave for home for your holidays, come over this evening with your friends for dinner.'

I don't know what internal struggles Mummy had to go through to arrive at this moment.

And that night, Shekhar, along with Deepak and Ravi, was busy tucking into the food at the dining table. Mummy was feeding them as lovingly as before. Papa was joking with them as openly as he always had, it was as if nothing had happened in the interim. A few heads poked out from the windows of nearby houses. Everything was as easy and natural as it had been before....

I was the only one looking at the whole situation with an objective eye and thinking that Nana was in every way Nana—a hundred per cent—and that's why it was easy for Mummy to fight him. But how can one fight with this Mummy who is Nana one second and Mummy the next?

NAADAR SIR

SUNDARA RAMASWAMY

Translated from the Tamil by Malini Seshadri

THESE DAYS I OFTEN REMEMBER NAADAR SIR. I AM GETTING TO BE QUITE old, and I have this nagging feeling that Death, which came by and snatched him up, actually brushed me too in passing and is now lurking somewhere nearby, biding its time. I have lost many loved ones over the years...relatives, friends. I have always been nagged by guilt for never visiting Naadar Sir, although he lived barely half an hour away. Yet, the thought that he was still there, living in the village, had given me some solace. Now it's just me, my loneliness, and memories of the past....

These events are from fifty years ago. I was in the tenth class in Sethu Parvathy Bai School. Our maths teacher was ERS (our nickname for him was Kaaraboondhi). That month, thirteen students, including me, scored zero in the maths test. 'Good-for-nothing idiots! After this week I'll wash my hands off you fellows! Ekambara Naadar will take my place. From now on, he is the one who will have to put up with you fellows....' shouted ERS.

We started imagining this new teacher, creating mental images of this Naadar Sir. He will be riding a bicycle, said one of the boys. The rest of us couldn't believe this. Our teachers had always arrived walking and carrying an umbrella. In fact, it seemed they were incapable of walking except under an open umbrella. True, a few of the scrawnier teachers did arrive in jutkas. And SP Sir, with a huge bandage on his leg, like someone who had recently been wounded in war, would roll up in a cart drawn by a single bullock. He would crawl onto the veranda and then clamber into a chair with a great deal of effort. Wouldn't it be beneath the dignity of a schoolteacher to be pedalling a bicycle along the road? How come Naadar Sir didn't know this?

Naadar Sir entered the classroom. His appearance was comical.

Our mental images of the new teacher bore no resemblance to the real man. We had imagined cropped hair or a tuft; some sandal paste on his forehead, or a smear of sacred ash; a coat and the traditional panchakachham dhoti, or maybe a double-length dhoti; a turban; a watch on the inner wrist, or perhaps a pocket watch on a chain. A severe expression, wounding words, refusal to be satisfied even with high test scores. And the power to make us cower under his thumb.

As it was, the whole class burst into laughter the moment Naadar Sir entered. Even the girls giggled, covering their mouths with their hands, heads bent. It was as if someone who happened to be passing by on the street had inadvertently wandered in, unaware of the reputation of the premises into which he was trespassing. The hair on his head stood up like stubble. When he placed the thumb and forefinger of his right hand on either side of his forehead and pressed upwards, the stubbly hair would stand up straighter and then ripple forward when released. He seemed totally unaware of what a comical sight he presented. The pointed ends of his twisted moustache arched upwards, and Sir would try to get a glimpse of them by squinting his eyes inwards. Khadi dhoti, khadi jibba, rough rubber sandals. His bare wrist was a curious, unsettling sight. Instead of a pen in his pocket, he sported a pencil sharpened at both ends. (How often our teachers had whacked us for breaking a classroom taboo and doing exactly this!)

'Without any warning they've thrust the maths class on me,' Naadar Sir informed us. 'I've forgotten everything. So now I have to learn it first.' And he laughed.

We laughed too.

'Take out your maths notebook, ma,' he said, holding a hand out towards Vilasini who was in the front row.

His use of 'amma' to address a student sounded bizarre to us. It set off a fresh wave of laughter.

'So, the very sight of me amuses you all so much?' remarked Naadar Sir, joining in the laughter.

He turned the pages of the maths notebook one at a time. 'Enna de, each is more frightening than the last,' he remarked.

Laughter rose in billows and crashed against the four walls. Sir stood staring at us with a bemused expression.

'It's not all that difficult, Sir. You can easily work them out with some practice,' Nagarajan reassured him.

Sir observed Nagarajan's face closely. 'How many marks do you score in maths, thambi?' he asked.

'A hundred,' said Nagarajan.

'Always?'

'Yes, always.'

'He has never got less than hundred, Sir,' shouted Thirumalai.

'Then naturally you would find it easy,' said Sir.

We were beginning to feel a strange sensation, as if the whole class was being dissolved in some strange fluid.

'How many marks did you get when you were in the tenth class, Sir?' asked Chakrapani.

Now, this Chakrapani was the most cowardly fellow in the class. And yet, here he was asking Sir a bold question like this! Did a whole yuga somehow go by in an instant? The student was questioning the teacher about the marks he secured. And that too in Sethu Parvathy Bai School, where Headmaster Rajam Iyer, ruled with an iron fist!

'Too low to announce publicly,' said Sir.

Again the students laughed.

'I don't think I will start teaching maths today. I will tell you about some games instead. Tomorrow we will get started with maths.'

'But are we allowed to talk about games in class, Sir?' Seshan wanted to know.

'Nothing wrong with that. After all, sport is also a kind of education.'

He started talking to us about football. He spoke with great involvement and passion. As he went on, he seemed to forget he was in a classroom. His hands were waving about. He headed away an imaginary ball. As though it had rolled down the stairs and into the garden, he stared into emptiness. He scored goal after imaginary goal, kicking the invisible ball through the goalposts repeatedly, while we sat watching in tension, wondering if his khadi dhoti might get ripped in the process.

We students could not contain our excitement. 'Goal! Goal!' we yelled. Sir sidled towards the classroom door like a child, and peeped around the edge cautiously.

Upstairs, at the front of the building, was an imposing structure resting on a stone foundation supported by massive pillars—the Headmaster's room—flaunting its grandeur and proclaiming its importance to the universe. On three sides, wide windows displayed sturdy curved grilles, each of them having dark green curtains. It even had a tall, wide, green bamboo screen just in front of the entrance door; placed so close to it in fact that one had to slide in sideways to enter.

Sir took in the scene outside our classroom door with a keen eye. Then he looked at us and smiled a mischievous smile.

'De, don't make such a noise. He will pluck out your eyes,' he said, pointing upwards in the direction of the Headmaster's office.

'We couldn't beat Carmel School in the football match, Sir,' said Govindankutty.

'Why, de, what's so special about them. Do they have horns growing on their heads or something?' Sir mimed the horns by holding the back of his right hand against his forehead and extending the forefinger and little finger upwards.

'What's needed is coaching. And a strong will to succeed,' he told us.

'Sir, do you think it's possible for us to defeat Carmel School?'

'De, any game requires intelligence and discipline. What do you boys have? Do you have the brains for it? Do you have physical strength? Discipline? Determination?' asked Sir.

Each of his questions fell like blows on our skulls.

'If you show us how, we will play beautifully, Sir,' said Vallinaayagam.

'You all have to get permission from above, de,' said Sir, pointing at the ceiling above which sat the Headmaster's room.

'We're scared, Sir,' shouted all the boys in one voice.

'If that's so, then go and find a game that cowards can play. Then we will see,' declared Sir.

It suddenly dawned on us that Sir was capable of anger. The bell rang. Sir waved at us and strode out briskly.

Naadar Sir had stirred our minds deeply. Time and again, we had been made to swallow humiliation. In a school full of teachers who saw red at the very mention of sports, how could we ever learn a game? We saw that we had lost all sense of pride and self-respect. That is what rankled the most in our hearts.

Every year, on the day before Christmas break began, a familiar humiliation would await us. Carmel School challenged us every year to a football match, because they had the competence and skill to play. But why did our Headmaster have to accept their invitation? That was the question for which none of us had an answer. We went to Kumaravel Sir and pleaded with him.

'Let's not accept the invitation this time, Sir. We can't stand the repeated humiliation.'

'How is that possible? Our school is the largest one in the whole of Thiruvithangur. The Rani Amma, out of affection, sends the silver cup to our school. Isn't it proper that we should present it to the winning team?' asked Kumaravel Sir.

'But does that mean we should accept and then lose dismally year after year just so that Carmel School can win the cup?'

'They play beautifully, they win the cup. You scrawny fellows...are you capable of playing at all?'

'We are not going to play this year, Sir,' we declared.

'The Headmaster has already announced your names on the noticeboard. Is there any among you who has the guts to defy him?' shouted Sir.

'We are too scared to tell him, Sir. Please tell him on our behalf,' we pleaded.

'If I do, he'll ask me "So, then will you take the silver cup home with you or what?"'

The next thing we knew, the date of the match had been announced.

'Sir, Sir, wha-a-t's this?' we protested to Kumaravel Sir.

'I will coach you fellows for three days, de. Enough?'

'But there's no ball, Sir.'

Kumaravel Sir was angry. His voice rose.

'Balls are there aplenty. But the room key is lost. The Headmaster has written to the Inspector's office in Thiruvananthapuram for permission to break the lock, but the wretched people there haven't bothered to reply. You fellows are not even smart enough to get a ball on loan from somewhere and you're standing here arguing.'

'The rival team has had five years of coaching. You're telling us you will give us three days of coaching, Sir. Year after year they come and score goal upon goal, and taunt us by shouting "One more, one more" each time they score.'

'De, I will tell you something and I want you fellows to listen carefully. Those who are good at studies cannot be good at games. And those who play sports well will be hopeless at studies. In the whole of Thiruvithangur, which school tops in academics? Our school!' declared Kumaravel.

We were stumped for a suitable response to this, so were momentarily silenced.

Kumaravel Sir continued: 'Look, I have an idea. Go stealthily to Carmel School, observe the coaching they're receiving there and learn the techniques, de. You fellows can't get anything done, but still you want to win. Hmmphh!'

The next day three of us set off on our quest. Me, Subramania Sarma, and Emanuel. The moment we entered Carmel School, we were confronted by five or six students. The very sight of them brought fear to our minds. Each of the boys was about a foot taller than any of us. We had to crane our necks to look at their faces. Their chests were so broad that their vests were in imminent danger of giving way. Big, muscled thighs like mature banana plant stems. Knees moulded in solid iron. They were wearing special boots. We had heard that the soles of these boots were studded with nails.

'Aren't you the fellows from the Keerathandu school?' demanded one of them who seemed to be their leader.

We remained silent.

'Did you come to watch our football coaching?' he asked. Sarcasm spread over his face and scorn dripped from his voice.

How did he know? Who could have revealed to this accursed fellow what was in our minds?

He cleared his throat. Then he made a pronouncement: 'I will tear you limb from limb. I will disconnect all your joints. Be wise and run away from here.'

Sarma and I looked at Emanuel. Emanuel had some acquaintance with boxing techniques. His face was flushed.

'Some day you will be at my mercy. Then you will find out what I am capable of,' retorted Emanuel.

'Oh, get lost, you son of a bitch!' responded the Carmel School fellow.

I tugged Emanuel's shirt gently. The three of us shuffled away.

The failure of our mission brought us further humiliation.

'You hopeless fellows…you can't get even the simplest task done. But you want to win the silver cup,' scolded Kumaravel Sir.

✧

There were six or seven football fields on our school grounds. They were the best in the whole of Thiruvithangur. We also had a lot of footballs.

But because the key to the storage room had been lost, we had not seen a football for a very long time.

We managed to borrow a football, and practised for three days. Even our

Sanskrit teacher turned up one day to watch us at practice. He continuously twirled the tuft on his head as he watched us, like someone trying to unscrew the lid of a ghee pot. When we ran he would shout out, 'Careful! Careful! Don't fall and break an arm or leg!' It seemed even the teachers were beginning to empathize with us. Kumaravel Sir stayed with us the entire three days. Because of his blood pressure condition, he couldn't join us on the field. But he supplied instructions and admonitions aplenty. 'Slice kick...now tap...no, no, idiot, not there, kick it into the goal...the goal!' Joseph Sir also came by. He had received football coaching at Carmel School in his student days. His football exploits and his goal count were among his favourite talking points. And—surprise of surprises—even the Headmaster watched our training session. Except that he watched from the veranda. When we had finished our practice we went up to the Headmaster.

'You all played well,' said the Headmaster in English.

Grabbing the unexpected opportunity that had presented itself, we said, 'We need a ball, Sir.'

The headmaster turned to Joseph Sir. 'Tomorrow itself we should write a reminder letter to the Inspector about the locked room. Don't forget,' he said.

We had been instructed by Kumaravel Sir that each of us should eat a nendran banana before turning up for the evening match. He explained that this input was essential to ensure that we were able to kick the ball hard and well. So we bought a whole bunch of nendran bananas and ate two each before heading for the football field. Just abutting the field was a spacious raised area of ground. The peons Arunachalam and Chokkalingam were arranging chairs on it. The Sanskrit teacher, Joseph Sir, Kumaravel Sir, Malayalam teacher Unnikrishnan Nair, ERS Veerabhadran Chettiar, Sivaramakrishna Iyer, R. L. Kesava Iyer, the Arabic teacher, Sarvottam Rao, Sivan Pillai, Pannirugai Perumal, Achamma Thomas, Kanthimathi Teacher... many of the teachers were there. Near the front gate of the school, the Carmel School team players were standing together in a bunch. They were in uniform outfits: blue shorts and yellow jerseys. As we watched them, their formidable combined strength seemed to leap across from where they stood, turning our insides to mush.

'Only ten minutes left for the game to start. Why are they still hanging around over there?' the Headmaster asked sternly.

'They will come only after Father Xavier arrives. He is their coach,' explained Kumaravel Sir.

'What a big hoo-haa,' remarked the Headmaster, frowning. A motorcycle was heard approaching. It came in through the front gate and onto the raised area, and stopped under the neem tree. From it alighted Father Xavier, the hem of his cassock billowing stylishly in the breeze. His slender frame darted rapidly towards the Headmaster. The latter was still in the process of raising his arms with the intention of greeting the visitor with folded palms, when the visitor grabbed the Headmaster's half-raised right hand

and shook it heartily. The Carmel School team fell into line and walked in. The awesome discipline that emanated from the group further impressed us.

'Please be seated, Father,' invited the Headmaster. The two sat down next to each other. We team members stood next to each of them. The student leader we had encountered during our humiliating visit to Carmel School was present, his expression full of menace. But no way would he have the courage even to lay his little finger on us with our teachers watching.

'Shall we have the first whistle now?' asked Kumaravel Sir.

'Go ahead,' said the Headmaster.

The Carmel School fellow turned towards Father Xavier and asked, 'Father, how many goals would you like us to score?'

Father Xavier lifted his head slightly and asked, 'How many did we score last year?'

'Nine,' replied the team leader.

'Then let's make it the same this time also. No more and no less,' advised Father Xavier.

We looked at the Headmaster. We looked at our teachers. The Headmaster wore a sheepish smile. His lips twitched slightly as though a mosquito had settled on them. The rest of the teachers stood with heads bowed, whispering among themselves.

Eight goals were scored against us before half-time. In the interval, the Carmel School heroes opened a large leather suitcase and took out soft freshly-laundered towels, one each, and wiped their faces and hands. They took out juice bottles, flipped open their caps, and gulped down the coloured drinks. As for us, we only had a tin bucket of water. As we dipped a tin mug into the bucket and took turns drinking water, the Carmel team captain came over to us. He said, 'We will score our last goal exactly three minutes before the final whistle. You poor weaklings, don't run around too much and kill yourselves.' He sauntered away.

One must praise his commitment towards keeping his promises. When the game was over and we looked around, the Headmaster's chair was empty. So were all the other chairs. All the teachers had left. Even Kumaravel Sir was nowhere to be seen.

'We must destroy our school, flatten it,' fumed Emanuel. 'My heart won't know any peace till it is reduced to rubble.'

⁓

One day in class, Naadar Sir showed us some photographs and certificates. Each photo featured a team he had represented in his college days; and in each photo, Sir held a trophy. One, particularly, which showed him standing next to the Rani and holding a huge cup, made us rub our eyes in disbelief. What a radiant smile on the Rani's face!

Sir said, 'This afternoon, at three o'clock, the HM has agreed to meet me. Whoever is interested in playing football, give me your names.'

'What are the requirements, Sir?' we asked him.

'Both legs should be normal, with no knock knees. You should be prepared to work hard. You should have a determination to succeed. Tell yourself, if we lose the match this year, our life is over right there and then on that field. Those of you who can do all this may submit your names.'

Sir arrived in front of the HM's front door screen at 2.45 p.m. We were already waiting. Through the side of the screen, we could see that the blades of the ceiling fan were turning hesitantly, as though expecting a reprimand any moment. On the wall hung a large clock with no pendulum, its second hand twitching as it moved around its face. None of us had ever been inside the HM's room before. Before long, our feet would tread its floor; and as we stood with hands respectfully clasped together, the full majesty of the room would disclose itself to us. The momentousness of the anticipated event evoked emotions in us that we could barely control.

At exactly three o'clock, a peremptory summons was heard: 'Ekambaram! Ekambaram!'

'Sir, sir,' said our Sir, as he inserted himself sideways through the narrow opening between screen and wall. Then, turning back to us for a moment, he warned, 'Not a word from any of you in there.'

The Headmaster said, 'Ekambaram, we must win the silver cup this year. I don't know what you will do or how you will do it, but it must be done. Money is not a constraint. I will stand behind you and support you all the way.'

'Sir, I have brought some photos and certificates to show you,' said Naadar Sir.

'I don't need to see any evidence. I know football means Ekambara Naadar and Ekambara Naadar means football. The whole of Thiruvithangur knows this.' Then, turning towards us, the Headmaster said, 'If you don't listen to Sir and play the way he tells you to, I will break your legs.'

Naadar Sir turned his gaze towards us. 'They are all very fond of football, Sir,' he said. Then, he added: 'Sir, I have a request.'

'What is it?'

'If you look up an auspicious day for us, I will start the coaching on that day.'

'Auspicious...inauspicious...no such thing. Start right now, this very minute.' The Headmaster turned to us and asked, 'What do you have in the last period, da?'

'History.'

'Who's the teacher? Sarvottam Rao, right?'

'Yes.'

'I will talk to him. You boys run to the playing field, right now. If you lose the match this year, I won't allow any of you donkeys to take the exams.'

Naadar Sir strode unhurriedly along the veranda. We followed in his wake. We descended the big staircase. Sir came to a halt at a tiny room that stood near the foot of a ladder. He tugged at the padlock. Then

Sir took a few steps back, ran forward, and delivered a mighty kick to the bottom of the door. The hasp of the latch shattered. 'Collect all the footballs and throw them out of the room, de,' said Sir. And that is what we did. Big and small, there were seventeen balls in all.

Naadar Sir's house was on the route from my home to school. Before sunrise every morning, Emanuel would come up to Saanthaan Chetty Circle and signal for me with a shrill whistle (which he managed to produce by inserting a couple of fingers in his mouth and blowing hard). Primed for his signal and raring to go, I would leap out. Sir would be standing at the door of his house in khaki shorts and a white vest. The moment he saw us approaching from a distance, he would descend his front steps and start jogging away slowly. This was our running practice. Once in a while he would turn back and look at us to see whether we were using the proper running technique he had taught us. 'Heads up!' he would shout.

By the time we reached the school playing field, seven or eight bicycles would already be parked under the neem tree. At least twenty boys would be present. Sir would join the game and play with us. Sometimes, to get a better view of our on-field performance, he would station himself at the goalmouth.

How that remarkable brain of his could itemize and codify every single movement made by every single one of us remains a mystery to which only God above holds the key. Once our practice session was over we would move over to the wide steps leading down to another field at a lower level. We would sit down on these steps in a neat row. Sir would stand in front of us and talk to us non-stop for half an hour; and during all that time he would keep tossing the ball between his hands. He explained every mistake that each of us had made, and he followed it up with instructions on how to avoid these. No scolding, no censure.

'It's not only the legs that come into play, de,' he said. 'Your whole body has to play. The eyes play, the brain plays, the ears play...everything must join in the game. And another thing. You must anticipate what will happen next. Your mind must work out the strategy...the angles, the approaches, in a split second. De, the ball is willing and ready to carry out your instructions. Finally, always keep some of your strength in reserve. Keep the opposition guessing about your capabilities.'

Solid, powerful words, flowed towards us in a stream from Naadar Sir.

From Christmas right up to the Pongal vacation we did not miss a single day of practice. Morning and evening. Plus training sessions three times during the week. Physical exercises, running. We ourselves couldn't believe how much we had improved. Our relationship with our physical selves was rapidly and noticeably growing more intimate, as was our relationship with the football itself. Sir was fond of saying that the ball was the most emotionally responsive creation of the Almighty. We were beginning to understand what he meant. But whenever we thought we had attained great heights in football, Sir would say, 'De, we have only now placed our feet on the first step. Don't become overconfident. There's still a long way to go.' As a team, we were beginning to instinctively understand one another without actually speaking, and this intimacy strengthened day by day. If one of us tackled an oncoming player and got possession of the ball, we could be sure that the appropriate person would be in place, ready to accept our pass, and take it forward to the danger zone near the goal. There another of us would be in just the right spot to send the ball into the goal with a well-directed header.

On one occasion, Seshan said, 'Sir, this game is not just a game.... It is something else, something more.' He couldn't quite explain what exactly he felt.

'A sport is like a gold mine. You can keep digging, layer after layer, deeper and deeper, and continue to take out treasure,' said Sir.

His words seemed to lend shape to our muddled thoughts.

Sir would invite several of the teachers to come and watch our evening practice sessions. The teachers were astonished at what they were witnessing. They were full of praise and encouragement for us. The Sanskrit teacher told Sir, 'Ekambaram, you have transformed these reedy fellows into the swift arrows of Lord Ram! This is truly some kind of magic.'

Because it was the twenty-fifth anniversary of the school, the Headmaster was busy with preparations for the silver anniversary celebrations. He had already decided to invite the Rani, and was going ahead with the necessary arrangements. On the auspicious occasion, our school team should receive the winner's trophy from the Rani's hands. What could give the school greater pride than reaching that pinnacle of glory?

The day of the football competition dawned! That afternoon, Naadar Sir asked us to assemble in one of the vacant classrooms, and started talking to us. We felt detached from our bodies, as though soon some spirit would possess us and we would be able to walk on fire. Sir continued to encourage us. 'Today, you are definitely going to win, de. I don't have even an iota of doubt about that,' he declared. 'Let me remind you again. Strength of mind is the most important thing. Never waver. Within five minutes of the start of the game you should score a goal. It is do or die.'

As we stepped on to the playing field, we had no worries at all about our bodies. We felt we were walking on air. Electricity was coursing through us, from the soles of our feet to the hair on our heads. If we lose, let me die here and now, said the mind.

Within three minutes of the commencement of the match, we scored our first goal. At that moment it felt as if all the things around us... trees, buildings, people, even the sky...were leaping around wildly. Father Xavier, who had been sitting in a chair, jumped up, shouted something in English, and ran around the edge of the field. Our rivals were mere broken cobwebs in our path. They tried their utmost to somehow respond with a goal of their own. But they couldn't even get the ball to our half of the field. Their frantic efforts revealed their desperation. Our hearts were like cores of steel in our chests, and the vapours that emanated from them were overpowering, enfeebling our rivals. Every time their bodies brushed against ours in the course of play, we sensed their weakness.

During the half-time break, Sir was so overcome with emotion that he couldn't utter a word. His eyes were brimming. Stammering a little, he managed to say, 'You played well, de. But you must score one more goal. They mustn't wriggle away by somehow managing to score an equalizer.'

'We are sure we can score another goal, Sir,' said Emanuel.

Sir looked at our faces. It seemed to us that he was reassured by the confidence he read in our eyes.

In the fifth minute after resumption of play, we scored another goal.

The crowd erupted with a roar. Our teachers, oblivious to decorum and dignity, were prancing around in glee. Like small children, they clambered on to chairs and cheered. The Headmaster raised both hands and waved wildly. The moment the game was over, the Headmaster and the teachers rushed onto the field. Totally unembarrassed, they embraced each of us.

'Ekambaram, the entire credit goes to you,' shouted the Headmaster in English.

'The boys played well,' replied Sir.

From wherever they stood, our school students began chanting 'Jai to Ekambaram Sir! Jai to Ekambaram Sir!' The chanting group broke up, fell into line, and approached the field in a procession. Ekambara Sir looked at the Headmaster and at the teachers. Then, in a loud voice, he shouted, 'Jai to Sethu Parvathy Bai School!' But his words did not reach the students, and they continued with their chants praising Ekambara Sir.

That week, school inspectors came from Thiruvananthapuram. Our teachers had given us two or three days of preparation ahead of their arrival. The school was clean enough already; how could we make it even cleaner? The teachers went around looking for tiny bits of dust on window grilles and in the corners of the rooms, and asked us to wipe harder. In the evenings we tidied the garden beds and removed every weed. The black paint on the wooden fence of the garden was fresh enough, but the Headmaster decided it was not an auspicious colour. So we had to paint it green instead.

Our class teacher ERS was in a state of great agitation that day. He told us that the inspectors would be visiting our class in the first period of the day, which happened to be English. But the bell rang after English class and they had not yet come. When they did come, Pannirugai Perumal's Tamil class was going on. None of the three inspectors knew any Tamil. One of them asked in English, 'Do you study Tiruvalluvar's *Tirukkural* properly?'

'Yes,' we chorused. We had exactly three kurals in our syllabus. 'Right,' said the inspectors, and walked away.

That afternoon, during Ekambara Sir's maths class, the three inspectors paid us another visit. Neither Sir nor we had anticipated that this would happen. Along with the inspectors, the Headmaster had also arrived.

'We have come to tell you a few things,' said an inspector, addressing Ekambara Sir. His tone was stern and disapproving.

'Why is it that all the students are scoring so poorly in maths?' asked the inspector.

'But that's not so, Sir,' said our teacher.

The third inspector was holding a large sheet of white paper. He placed it on the table and unfolded it. He continued to consult the contents of the paper as he spoke, 'Earlier there were seven students in this class who usually scored a centum; now there are only six.'

All three inspectors turned their gazes on Ekambara Sir. The Headmaster was staring at Ekambara Sir in total surprise.

'Earlier the average mark was fifty-four; it is now fifty-one,' added the inspector.

Sir was looking at the Headmaster, waiting for him to intercede. Nothing.

Why was the Headmaster silent? Did he have nothing to say?

'Many of the students who were scoring above ninety are now managing not more than eighty-five marks.'

Sir stood silent, head bowed.

The first inspector told Ekambara Sir, 'You must do your job more responsibly and teach better.'

Sir raised his head. Humiliation was writ large on his face. The Headmaster was still silent. Why did he have nothing to say?

'We will give you two months of grace time. You must bring the students back to their previous level,' ordered the first Inspector.

Sir nodded.

After the inspectors had left, Sir was not in a state of mind to conduct the class as usual.

'De, do you all think I don't do a good job of teaching you?' he asked us, in a pathetic tone of voice.

'No, no, Sir. You are teaching us well,' we said in unison.

Our attempt to reassure him seemed to have made him more despondent. He stood gazing at nothingness through the open window.

That whole day, Ekambara Sir was the topic of discussion among all the teachers. We heard that the Headmaster had sent for him that evening. He seems to have told our Sir, 'The inspectors have written good reports about all the teachers except you. You are the only one who has received an adverse report.'

Hearing this, Ekambara Sir apparently asked the Headmaster, 'What is your own opinion of me, Sir?'

'When the inspectors base their comments on some data, we have no choice but to accept it, Ekambaram,' was the Headmaster's response.

The school building was resplendent. Garlands of coloured lights, elaborate festoons of leaves and flowers, arches flanked by lush banana plant stems, not a speck of dust or dirt anywhere. A huge pandal had been put up on the football field. Inside, a wide dais had been erected. The Rani sat smiling in a chair on the dais. The Headmaster stood close to his chair. More than once the Rani had urged him to sit down, but still he stood, lost in his thoughts, unaware of his surroundings.

The items followed one another as per the agenda. Music competitions. Dances. Fancy dress competitions. Debates. Prize distribution to the children. Suddenly, the Rani turned to the Headmaster and asked in Malayalam, 'Where is Sri Ekambara Naadar?'

The Headmaster looked around here and there. 'Mr Ekambaram! Mr Ekambaram!' he called aloud. He spoke to the teachers seated in the front row. 'Where is Ekambaram?' he demanded sternly. The teachers looked around. Ekambara Sir was nowhere to be seen. The Headmaster spoke directly to ERS Sir. 'I want Ekambaram here in the next one minute,' he ordered. ERS Sir rushed over to where we were gathered. He told Emanuel, 'Go quickly on your cycle and fetch Sir.' When Emanuel got on his cycle, I clambered on too and sat behind him. 'Give the cycle to Sir and ask him to get here at once,' shouted ERS Sir.

We entered Sir's home. He was lying shirtless on a coir rope cot.

'Sir, what's the matter?' asked Emanuel.

'Headache. That's why I couldn't come,' said Sir.

'Who will receive the trophy, Sir?'

'HM can receive it. Nothing wrong in that.'

'Sir, the Rani asked for you,' I told him.

'Oh, so she remembers me,' remarked Sir.

Emanuel's voice was all choked up when he pleaded again: 'Sir, without you there...how...?'

'Just study hard, de, that's the most important thing,' was Sir's response.

We both studied Sir's expression. His face looked different, wrapped in gloom. It was as if he was in his own world.

'Sir, even if not for anyone else, please come for our sake,' urged Emanuel.

New shadows danced across the doorway. We turned to look. Seshan, Vallinaayagam, Govindankutty, Manikandan...all of them were there. We could see more faces through the window. Disappointment was writ large across all their faces.

Sir's wife stood leaning against the kitchen doorway.

'You toiled day and night for the sake of these boys, and now they are asking you to come,' she told her husband.

Sir made no move to get up.

'Then we won't go either,' declared Emanuel.

Sir looked into our faces, one by one.

His wife went over, removed Sir's jibba from where it was hanging from a nail on the wall, and handed it to him.

Naadar Sir rose from the cot.

THE BEGGARS AT THE DARGAH

TAJ BEGUM RENZU

Translated from the Kashmiri by Neerja Mattoo

IT WAS MORNING. A NOISE WOKE ME UP AND I LOOKED OUT. YAHOO THE Mad One was creating havoc at the gateway to the dargah as usual. With a stick in hand, he was striding up and down the lane, shouting abuse at himself and everyone else. Fear had driven some of the half-crazed beggar women to hide behind the Noorkhana Gate, while others stood under a chinar tree, watching him with terror in their eyes. He had caught two of them and was beating them mercilessly and shouting, 'Didn't I tell you not to ask for food, but money? Didn't I tell you not to sit too close together but to spread out in the lane? Didn't I tell you to sit facing the Kaaba?' Yahoo the Mad One's thundering voice sent shivers down the beggar women's spines; they could not speak a word. Even if they could, they would not dare to, lest Yahoo killed them.

Of all the deranged folks that begged at the gate of the dargah, Yahoo the Mad One was the tallest and the toughest, the most strongly built. It was only where his mind was concerned he was wanting. He had decided that he was the head of this motley group of men and women and had terrorized them into obeying his orders. When he went on his rounds in the morning, all the beggars saved a portion of their alms for him. He would come back by noon, stamping his feet, raising clouds of heat and dust and shout obscenities at everyone, not even sparing himself. He had a huge store of invectives, which he spent generously on everyone, from the governor downward to his relatives, bestowing on them the choicest terms from his repertoire. Sometimes, he would address an imaginary adversary, 'Oh father-in-law, go to the highest boss by all means! You think I care? What can he do to me? You think I am obliged to anyone? You can go to the governor and complain, you mother...!'

That was his way, and hundreds of curses would roll off his tongue in the course of the morning, filling the air of the dargah. One of his most frequently used obscenities was reserved for the governor's mythical daughter. He would repeat it constantly, like a chant—as he did so, the beggar women would cower in fear and slide closer to one another. The non-stop verbal barrage would line his lips with specks of spittle. He would put away his stick, pull off his long socks, remove his pheran, while the stream of abuse would flow on, without a break, 'The boss...his mother, why don't you go to him? And you, Sondar! Do you do any work here, or just sit around, fattening your thighs?' followed by more weighty abuses.

Sondar, equally unhinged in mind, would retaliate with, 'You overweight bull, may lightning strike you! Always present when it is time for food and showering abuse!'

'You bedmate of food! Why do you talk rubbish? Didn't you know your husband has gone for work and now must be fed?'

Sondar had a problem with her legs so she dragged herself from beggar to beggar, gathering Yahoo's share of food from them, mumbling, 'I don't know why the wretch is after me today.... The devil doesn't even die!'

'He has fallen for you...' commented a beggar woman who heard her, with a snigger.

'Shut up this minute, or I will cut you up into a hundred pieces!' Sondar was furious.

But she gathered stuff from everyone for Yahoo's meal: pieces of bread, dry rice, a little bit of vegetable curry, a green chilli or two, and set it down before him, saying, 'Here, stuff your belly, you rogue! The wretch wants to be fed but will do no work!'

'You maidservant of a nawab, there is too much salt in the curry, as usual!'

'It has been cooked by your sister today,' Sondar retorted, provoking a guffaw from all the other beggars.

∫

There are about twenty or so of these beggars, men and women, that hang around the entrance to the dargah. They are a mixed bunch, from the city as well as the villages, but those from the city consider themselves superior to the villagers. Within the dargah is a room known as the Noorkhana, meaning abode of light, where the women sleep at night. The others sleep in another room in the dargah compound, away from the Noorkhana. Their day's work begins with the muezzin's first call, when they get up and quickly take their places in a line on both sides of the approach road to the dargah. All the visitors to the dargah give them alms. They remain there till about nine o'clock and all the while it is their cries that resonate in the area.

'Give something to this helpless wretch in the name of Allah!'

'Something to this blind one, please sir, Allah will give you happiness!'

'Oh brother, spare a penny for this miserable widow, the Master will reward you with plenty!'

'Dear sister, this cripple begs of you—may all your misfortune fall on me!'

That is what goes on until nine, after which they leave their places, and, away from each other's eye, count the money they have collected, and tie them up in a rag. The male beggars wear this makeshift money pouch around their waists like a belt. Then they all go on their rounds in the mohallas close by, begging for food and money. They are back near the dargah by noon.

Strangely enough, the women do not keep their money with themselves, but hand it all to Ahad Sahib, a functionary of the dargah, for safekeeping. This is not his job, but he does it out of consideration for these poor outcastes, who trust him completely. Whatever they earn through the day is passed on to Ahad Sahib and he keeps a meticulous account. In fact, he maintains a special register for the beggar women's cash, which he brings out to the dargah compound in the evening when all of them crowd around him, each one by turn counting out her money and handing it to him. He charges two annas from everyone for his pains and they are happy to oblige. What amount Ahad Sahib writes against the name of each one is known only to him or his God. By their own counting each woman makes from sixty to eighty annas in a day, but they say that when Ahad Sahib counts them, they never add up to more than thirty or forty. If any one of them dares to complain, Ahad Sahib turns on her in a rage, 'Why, you think I am a thief? Why do you come to me if you don't trust me?' and his face turns crimson, like a red chilli. The humbled wretch immediately begs forgiveness, saying, 'Oh, I never meant it, please, I am ready to die for you, huzoorji.'

'What else was it? I don't know why do this dirty work for you. Actually, you are all nothing but scum!'

This would be enough to make the other women pounce on the complainant. Ahad Sahib would push away the register, pen, and ink with a dramatic gesture, and assume a hurt expression, prompting the poor beggar women to fall at his feet, begging him to forgive the errant one. Then he, as if with great reluctance, would agree to keep their money with him. It is said that this charitable work earns him an income of five to seven rupees per day. Once a month, or in a fortnight, a relative of one of these castaways of society turns up and she takes her money from Ahad Sahib and hands it over to her relative.

One day, one among them decided to resist. She raised the flag of revolt against Ahad Sahib's deceitful banking practices and went to the wife of the corner baker, asking her to keep her money safe with her. The baker's wife was moved by her plight and agreed to do so. When the news reached Ahad Sahib, he was furious, but he did not confront the rebel, nor did he say anything.

A few days later, a noise was heard from the Noorkhana. As the people were rushing to it, a man came out, smiling meaningfully. But when he saw the crowd, he assumed an expression of great shock and, shaking his head in horror, said, 'Anything is possible in this Kali Yuga! Nothing should surprise one any more, even the heavens cracking open and falling on our heads!'

Then the people came to know that Malo the Madwoman had been caught with a man. Two women swore that it was so, they were ready to bear witness to the fact. This Malo was the same woman who had chosen to keep her money with the corner baker's wife rather than with

Ahad Sahib. After this incident, no one saw Malo in the area ever again.

Frequent fights break out among these half-mad beggar women and the whole neighbourhood has to come out to mediate and settle the issue. The fight is a regular battle, no less fierce than the tribal raid on Kashmir. The battle lines are drawn with half of them on one side and half on the other. Some are armed with sticks, some raise a racket beating little tin drums, some jump about monkey-like, others bleat like goats. No sooner is one battle over than another begins the next day.

One morning Sondar, who is quite unhinged, woke up screaming, 'God will slit her belly open, the one who has robbed me! She will vomit her innards out, damned in hell she will be, just you wait and see!'

Mogli, sitting under a chinar, yelled at her, 'You wretched lunatic! Why are you cursing everyone? Abuse the one who has stolen from you, not us.'

'Why is your heart breaking? What should I do if not curse? After all, more than a kilo of my rice is stolen!'

'I am asking you to only curse the one who is responsible for the theft.'

'Why are you protesting, you scavenger? It makes me think that you must be the culprit.'

The next moment saw Mogli rise in a fury and fall upon Sondar, beating and scratching, pulling her hair out and dragging her on the street. Sondar cried out in pain and some of the women came to her rescue, others sided with Mogli. It was a free for all with both sides giving as much as they got. The battle raged on for some time and finally both sides decided to withdraw. Sondar and her supporters came and sat on the steps of the Noorkhana, while Mogli and her side went to sit under the chinar. The compound of the dargah, where the battle had been fought, was littered with heaps of hair, broken kangris, shattered bowls, and bits and pieces of rags and sticks. The whole neighbourhood had come out to watch. After a short period of silence. Sondar called out again, 'Rice thief, shame, shame! Look everybody, there sits the rice thief! The rice thief!'

Mogli was incensed and shrieked, 'I spit at you, you shameless creature. Look everybody, there sits Yahoo's whore! Yahoo's whore! There he comes, your pimp, see, Yahoo comes!'

The drama that followed was something worth seeing. One woman got up and wrapped a torn sheet round her waist. Then she caught hold of another woman and began to drag her away. The idea was to show what the tribal raiders had done to Mogli. The other side was not to be silenced. One of them tied a rag to a stick and, waving it around, shouted, 'Look at all the bastards born to them! Bastards! Bastards!'

These peppery dialogues and play-acting would have continued endlessly had not Yahoo suddenly appeared, silencing everyone with his obscenities, 'The governor's...! The boss's...!'

This is how the life of these beggars goes on from day to day. They seem so insensitive to each other's pain if one is ill, no one goes near her. They live, fall sick, and die like insects at the doorstep of the dargah. Looking at them, one could not tell that every one of these dregs of society had been a whole human being once. This I learnt when I called four of the most wild-looking of the women to my home, gave them tea, and drew them into conversation.

Ashmi had been married to a farmer who had died and his family had driven her away from home. There were tears in her eyes while she narrated her story, the first time in many years—perhaps she was overcome by the feeling that someone wanted to listen to her.

Another one, Fata, had been married to a sixty-year-old widower when she was fourteen. Soon she was pregnant, had a difficult delivery, and gave birth to a stillborn baby. Then, she had lost her mind. No one had any use for her thereafter and she found her way to the dargah.

The third one, Rahti, had been married thrice, but all three of her husbands had died. She had no children. When her third husband died, his brothers grabbed his property and threw her out of the house. She had gone to her brother's house where she was made to work round the clock—the drudgery and ill-treatment seemed to have no end. One day, she ran away and found refuge in the community of beggars at the dargah.

The fourth one, Raja, had been cast out because of the humiliation she brought to her husband—the tea she had made for the guest, a patwari, who was the local government accountant, was not up to the mark. Her parents were already dead and where was she to go but to the dargah and its world of beggars?

Life around the dargah goes on. Individuals may come and go but the beggar's world carries on, without any interruptions.

RATS

BHABENDRA NATH SAIKIA

Translated from the Assamese by Gayatri Bhattacharyya

ALL THE WOMEN WHO LIVED IN THE HUTS RUSHED OUT. THEY TRIED TO find out what exactly was happening. They behaved very much like a blind man resting with his cane propped up nearby does, when he suddenly hears some commotion. His first reaction is to seek out and grasp his cane, and only then does he try to find out the reason for the turmoil. Normally, these women did not bother to find out where their children were or what they were doing, their attitude being that they would turn up when hungry. So, they did not worry. But today, as soon as they became aware of the tumult and confusion, all the women ran out of their huts, frightened and anxious. They began to rush around, each one screaming out her children's names. One woman could see her son standing nearby but this did not calm her anxiety. She went up to where the boy stood, dragged him out of the crowd of onlookers, and clasped him tightly to her. Only when her son was safe in her arms did she try to find out the details of what had happened. Within two minutes more of the women had found their children, and the shrill voices that were screaming out their names stopped.

Only the voice of Moti's mother gradually got louder. And louder. Her high-pitched voice could be heard clearly over the tumultuous din created by the crowd. In the beginning, she had called out to her son, Moti, like the other mothers, and had run hither and thither looking for him. But, as time passed, and there was no sign of him, she grew more and more panicky. She started running around anxiously, calling out his name in distress.

His companions said that Moti had been with them right there.

'He was here?'

'Then where is he now?'

'Are you sure he was here?'

'Exactly where, where was he exactly?'

She went around asking every boy and every girl the questions in an agitated voice. She was hoping to hear that Moti might have strayed away without their knowing. But the children told her categorically that Moti had been right here with them—in the place that was now full of heavy sacks, two and a half maunds each.

The open place abutted a narrow lane leading to huge warehouses. The narrow road emerged from another slightly wider dirt road. A long wall of corrugated sheets, marking the compound of a soap company bordered one side of the narrow lane, and on the other side was this open space. A bit further on, this lane split up and spread out among the many large warehouses. These were the storehouses that fed thousands of people in the city. The relationship of these to the city was as vital as the relationship of a handsome youth to the horrible-looking entrails of his stomach. They were ugly, but inevitable and unavoidable. Numerous huge trucks roared into that narrow lane, carrying hundreds of tonnes of produce and food products. These they unloaded into the warehouses. Some of the empty trucks would then load up other consignments from the godowns to transport elsewhere. Most rickshaw drivers found it difficult to turn their small vehicles on this lane. The truck drivers alone knew what they had to conjure up as they manoeuvred their trucks within that cramped space. Sometimes, if one vehicle created chaos by not being driven with the requisite skill, there would be a traffic jam in the lane, and the filthy, stinking environment would be overwhelmed with the riotous shouting of drivers and their assistants.

The appearance and size of the drivers matched the size of their trucks. Indeed, it seemed as though the truck-building companies had taken the measurements of the drivers first, and then fitted the vehicles to suit their bodies! Their eyes were always red, perhaps due to driving through the night, or maybe because of something they had imbibed. As far as possible, these drivers preferred to sit comfortably and quietly in their seats and rest; it was the handymen, their assistants, who created noise and confusion. These handymen would sit on top of their loaded trucks, yelling at each other, trying to find out who was to blame for the roadblock. Sometimes, the traffic jam would continue for hours together. That narrow space would become overcrowded with trucks and vehicles lined up, one after the other, all the way up the main road. No one would agree to shift his own vehicle even a little bit to help break the jam. 'Why should I? Let them do what they like!' each driver would say. Each of them would leave his truck and go to spend his time in the tea shop nearby. Sometimes, the trucks would enter the lane at midnight, heavily loaded, but the warehouses opened their doors only in the morning. On such days, the area would become still more filthy and smelly and sometimes both drivers and handymen would sleep, like babies in their cradles, inside their trucks.

A peculiar thick, slimy green and black liquid covered about half of this open space. Originally, this was probably plain rainwater. But over time the liquid had got mixed with green moss, motor oil, and such other substances, and turned into this peculiar colour and consistency. When the small children got dirty playing, they cleaned themselves in this water.

The line of shacks built with bits of bamboo, straw, sacks, packing boxes, and so on, that stood on one side of the open space had been occupied in the past by a few daily wagers employed to load and unload the trucks. But now the owners of the warehouses employed labourers on a regular basis, and no one from these huts got those jobs. So, they had left. Now, there were women living here with their children. There were no men living here permanently, and the few men seen around, at times, were not the fathers of these children. Most of the women, except a few like Moti's mother, were old. Some of them went out in the morning to beg; two of them worked in the hotels nearby, cleaning rice and grinding spices; and one of them kept herself busy selling snacks of puffed rice mixed with salt, oil, onions, and chillies.

But it was the children who helped the women most in earning their daily bread. They spent almost the entire day on the roadside, armed with woven bamboo baskets of various sizes and shapes. When there was no serious work to be done, they spent their time playing, screaming, and crying. But when the empty trucks returned after unloading their consignments in the warehouses, and when they were held up due to a traffic jam, and were forced to stop right here, then these children immediately jumped onto the trucks. Quickly they swept the floor of the vehicles, put the sweepings into their bamboo baskets, and ran home to their mothers. When these sweepings were carefully cleaned, the women would be able to collect quite an amount of rice, lentils, and other commodities. The drivers and handymen were quite happy to let the children do the sweeping because their vehicles were cleaned in a trice. And the boys and girls were happy when there were traffic jams. If the traffic jams were long-drawn out, they were still happier, because they got time to sweep all the trucks, and every child got a chance to share in the spoils.

Each child had managed to obtain an iron rod, one end of which was sharpened. If loaded trucks happened to get held up in a traffic jam, children would jump onto the trucks and pierce the sacks with their rods. They would push their fingers through the holes made by the rods, and take out rice, lentils, sugar, and other such goods. If the handymen saw them and gave chase, they would laugh with great merriment and run away. But, after a little while, they would come scampering back again and fearlessly resume their work.

If the drivers and handymen happened to go to the tea shops, the children had a field day. They, therefore, prayed that there would be many more such jams. Whenever they saw two vehicles approaching from opposite directions, they would clap and shout, 'Come on, come on, get into a traffic jam!'

But today, there was no such big traffic snarl. What had happened was this: a truck was coming towards a godown heavily loaded with huge, plump sacks of rice. Another truck belonging to some cooperative store was leaving the godown loaded just as heavily with sacks of rice, lentils, sugar, flour, salt, and other food items. Both drivers were aware of the truck approaching from the opposite side but each hoped that the other would give way, allowing him to proceed. Therefore, neither of them stopped, and ultimately both vehicles came to a standstill facing each other. The two drivers started to quarrel and shout at each other. This went on for some time, and the children started yelling: 'Come on, come on, get into a jam!'

Normally, when only two trucks were involved, the drivers took advantage of the open space, and managed to use their skill to manoeuvre their vehicles past each other and go on their way. And indeed, after arguing for some time, the drivers did start to do just that. But they were both still rather angry, and saw no reason why they should give way to the other driver. After backing up just a little, with a huge roar and emitting a great deal of smoke, both vehicles again advanced. The children, seeing the situation, started screaming out their infernal refrain.

And the trucks did get into a jam. The trucker from the cooperative society did not give as much leeway as he could have; and the trucker carrying the sacks of rice was forced to move to his side of the road than he would have liked to. The vehicle, loaded very high with heavy sacks, slid off the road and into soft mud. It leaned dangerously to the left—and, in an instant, the tragedy had occurred. As the truck veered to the left, one by one, many of the sacks it was carrying toppled over heavily and fell to the ground. The children ran away in confusion from the scene of the accident. Moti screamed in terror, and tried to run, but a sack fell on top of him, and squashed him under it. Then another sack fell on top of that...then another and another....

A large crowd gathered to witness the accident. They started to look for Moti only after his mother had gone almost mad with anxiety and grief. One by one, the sacks were removed. At first, one of Moti's feet appeared. The foot looked quite normal and natural. But after the last sack had been removed, they all looked the other way. The only thing that could be seen was blood, a lot of blood. No one had the heart to even try to remember what the boy had looked like before the accident.

The police came. And for that day, all loading and unloading was stopped in the warehouses. It was getting darker anyway, and the trucks lined up on the main road to wait for daybreak. The women surrounded Moti's mother and consoled her while the police collected the boy's body and took it away to the police hospital.

Gradually, night fell. The two trucks that were involved in the accident were taken to the police station. The sacks of rice lay where they had fallen. A few loaded sacks had fallen from the other truck also, on the opposite side of the road, against the corrugated sheet wall. These were laden with salt and lentils.

Most of the children had become quiet and still, and were sitting despondently in the common courtyard, situated at the centre of their huddle of huts. The older ones occasionally talked quietly with each other. None of them could sleep much that night, and although they went to bed quite late, most of them woke up very early the next morning. Probably they had been awake since before dawn. The older ones came out at daybreak armed with their rods and bamboo baskets, and went up to the fallen sacks. They collected rice, salt, lentils, and sugar. But they were careful not to go near the sack covered with Moti's blood.

Later that morning, some labourers arrived, along with a few well-dressed men, and started removing the sacks under the supervision of the latter. It was not known which of these well-dressed persons took the decision, but it was noticed that two of the labourers took the blood-stained sack to Moti's mother's hut. She, who had spent the night sitting on her string cot, jumped up in distress, and cried out, 'No, no! I don't want it!' She clasped the sack, and started wailing in grief and in helplessness. The labourers leaned the blood-stained side of the sack against one of the hut's walls. When they let go of the sack, the weak wall trembled under the weight of the sack.

For quite a few days, Moti's mother continued to shout, 'Take it out, take it away. I do not want it!' The neighbouring women grieved for her, understanding her sorrow.

This woman had no parents. She had lived in her paternal uncle's house and helped with the cultivation of lentils and gram. A man had said he would marry her and had brought her here, but he was not a good man. After Moti was born, hearing of a drug smuggling operation, he had abandoned Moti and his mother and gone away to try to make some money working with drug smugglers. Moti's mother waited for a long time for him to return. The drivers and handymen who came to buy puffed rice snacks at the next hut would say to her, 'Stop hoping he will come back. He will never return. And what sort of woman are you, sitting here thinking of him, when there are so many other men here!' The others would laugh when they heard this, and Moti's mother would get angry.

True, she was a bit scared of living alone. But she was afraid, not of other people, but of herself. Indeed, sometimes the natural needs and instincts of her body and age troubled her greatly, and threatened to overwhelm her. But she had always been able to overcome these feelings by clasping Moti to her breast. If, somehow, she could manage to pass a few more years like this, she thought, she would approach the age of 'beggarhood'. She could then transform herself into a beggar by wearing dirty, torn clothes like the older beggar women. And even if she could not beg, it would not matter, as long as she had Moti with her. A son was a far more important possession than a husband! She just wanted the words, 'Ma, Ma', ringing in her ears always, that was all.

But this sudden loss, this loneliness, and the empty hut almost drove her mad. She would sit alone, staring at the heavy, full sack and quietly weep her heart out. As time passed, all she would do is sit still and silent all day, not even weeping. Some neighbour would sometimes bring her a little rice and lentils gathered from the sweepings, or from what they had got from begging. She would cook them, but leave them untouched. Sometimes, she did not even bother to cook. The handyman of the truck from which the sacks had fallen on Moti, often came to visit her. He would bring her a packet of sweets, jalebis, and other sweets, too, from the nearby tea shop. But she would never talk to him.

More time passed. Moti's mother was always hungry. Some days the neighbours would not bring rice and lentils. Gradually, she started becoming tormented by hunger pangs. She had noticed as she lay on her string cot that some rats had started making holes in the sack leaning against the wall, and every morning, the floor near it would be strewn with a few grains of rice. Sometimes, her eyes would become moist as she swept away the grains of rice. One day, after lying for a long time on her cot, hungry and desperate, she slowly got up. She brought a bamboo tray and held it against the sack. Poking her finger through the hole made by the rats, she slowly teased out a little rice. The hole was small, and it took a long time to collect enough for one meal.

The hole in the sack got bigger with the constant poking of her fingers. Or perhaps the rats themselves had made it larger. Whatever the reason, after a few days there was quite a lot of rice strewn on the floor. Moti's mother did not like the idea of rats spoiling the rice, so she folded a piece of torn cloth, and placed it over the sack, and placed her bamboo tray against the sack so that it pressed against the hole. Later, she took to getting up whenever she heard a scraping sound. Maybe the rats had made another hole in the sack?

Sometimes the handyman would come and say to her, 'How can anyone eat only rice? Let me get you some lentils or something.' But she would refuse.

In time, the sack became lighter and thinner. It was becoming difficult to bring out much rice with her fingers, even though the hole had become much wider. After some time, Moti's mother could put her entire hand through the hole. Then, after some more time had passed, she found that she could find no rice even after pushing her arm in, right up to her elbow. Whatever rice was still there had become embedded in the stitching of the sack.

One morning, Moti's mother undid the stitches at the top of the sack, and, holding it upside down on the floor, gave it a few good shakes. She was able to collect sufficient rice for the night meal. She swept up the grains, and putting the rice in her bamboo tray, cleaned it properly. She then put the sack out in the sun. The side of the sack which had been leaning for such a long time against the wall now fell flat on the ground. In the evening, she took the sack, shook it out, and placed it on her cot.

After eating her meal that night, she lay down on the cot. It had become quite chilly, and Moti's mother always felt cold at night. In past winters, Moti used to curl up to her in bed, and she had not felt the chill. Today, too, she did not feel the cold seeping in from below because of the warmth of the piece of sacking. As she lay there feeling warm and comfortable, she felt something gnawing at her. It was as if the rats were biting her. She felt at the instant that if the handyman came to her and asked if he could get her 'lentils or something', perhaps she would say, 'Yes. Bring me some.'

If not for herself, at least for the sake of the Moti who would come along in the future.

A DEATH IN DELHI

KAMLESHWAR

Translated from the Hindi by Poonam Saxena

THE FOG IS EVERYWHERE. IT IS NINE IN THE MORNING, BUT ALL OF DELHI is enveloped in mist. The streets are damp. The trees are wet. Nothing is clearly visible. You can make out the bustle of life only by the sounds. These sounds are lodged in our ears now. There are sounds coming from every section of the house. Vasvani's servant has lit the stove, like he does every day, and the hissing sound can be heard through the wall. In the room next door, Atul Mavani is polishing his shoes. Upstairs Sardarji is putting Fixo on his moustaches. The bulb outside his curtained window is glowing like an enormous pearl. All the doors are closed, all the windows have curtains, but every part of the house resonates with the clink and clatter of life. On the third floor, Vasvani has shut the bathroom door and opened the tap....

Buses are speeding through the fog. The joon-joon sound of heavy tyres comes closer and then fades away. Motor-rickshaws are speeding recklessly. Someone has just pushed down the taxi meter. The phone is ringing in the house of the doctor next door and some girls are walking to their morning shift in the lane behind.

It is bitterly cold. The streets shiver and honking cars and buses slice through the fog and hurtle away. The streets and footpaths are crowded, but each person, wrapped in the mist, looks like a restless lost spirit.

These spirits are quietly growing in the sea of mist...the buses are crowded. People are huddled on the cold seats, some are hanging in the middle of the bus, as if they have been crucified, Christ-like, arms upraised, no nails in their hands, just the shiny, frigid metal bars of the bus.

And amidst all this, from far away, comes a funeral procession.

The newspaper has a report of this funeral. I just read it. It must be news of this particular death. It's printed in the newspaper—Seth Diwanchand, a renowned and well-liked businessman from Karol Bagh, died in Irwin Hospital tonight. His body has been brought to his kothi. Tomorrow morning, his funeral procession will pass through Arya Samaj Road on its way to the Panchkuian cremation ground where it will be ritually consigned to the flames....

This must be the funeral procession coming down the street right now. Some people, wearing caps and mufflers, are quietly walking behind the bier. They are walking very slowly. I can see a little, I can't see everything, but it seems to me that there are some people behind the bier.

There is a knock on my door. I put aside the newspaper and open the door. Atul Mavani is standing outside.

'What a hassle, yaar, no ironwallah has turned up today, just give me your iron,' he says and I feel relieved. For a moment, I was scared that he might suggest joining the funeral procession. I immediately give him the iron, secure in the knowledge that Atul will now iron his pants and depart for his embassy rounds.

Ever since I had read the news of Seth Diwanchand's death, I was on tenterhooks every second: suppose someone comes and says we should join the funeral procession despite the bitter cold. Everyone in the building knew him and they're all decent, worldly people.

At that moment, Sardarji's servant comes racing down the stairs noisily and opens the door to go out. To reassure myself some more, I call out to him, 'Dharma! Where are you going?'

'To get butter for Sardarji,' he answers from the door and, taking advantage of the situation, I hand him some money to get me cigarettes.

Sardarji is getting butter for his breakfast, this means he isn't going to join the funeral procession either. I feel a little relieved. If Atul Mavani and Sardarji have no intention of going, there's no reason for me to go. Both of them and the Vasvani family were better acquainted with Seth Diwanchand than I was. I had just met him four or five times. If these people are not going to participate, there's no question of my having to go.

I spot Mrs Vasvani on the balcony. There is a strange pallor on her beautiful face, and on her lips, a faint redness from last evening's lipstick. She has come out wearing her gown and is now tying her bun. She is saying, 'Darling, just give me the paste, please....'

I feel even more relieved. This means that Mr Vasvani is not going for the funeral either.

Far away, on Arya Samaj Road, the funeral procession is moving forward, ever so slowly....

Atul Mavani comes to return the iron. I take it and want to close the door, but he walks in and says, 'Did you hear, Diwanchandji died yesterday?'

'I read it in the newspaper.' I give a direct reply, to prevent any further talk of this death. Atul Mavani's face has a white tinge, he has already shaved. He goes on, 'Diwanchand was a good man.'

Listening to him, I get the feeling that if the conversation proceeds further, there will be a moral responsibility to join the funeral procession, so I say, 'What happened to that work of yours?'

'Just waiting for the machinery, that's all. As soon as that happens,

I'll get my commission. This commission work is so crass. But what can be done? If I can get eight or ten machines passed, I will start my own business,' says Atul Mavani. 'Bhai, when I first came here, Diwanchandji helped me a lot. I got some work only because of him. People really respected him.'

My ears prick up on hearing Diwanchand's name again. At that moment, Sardarji pokes his head out of the window and asks, 'Mr Mavani! What time should we leave?'

'The time was nine o'clock, but perhaps because of the cold and fog, it might get a bit delayed,' Atul says and I guess that they're talking about the funeral procession.

Sardarji's servant, Dharma, has given me the cigarettes and is upstairs, setting the tea on the table. Just then Mrs Vasvani's voice can be heard, 'I think Premila will definitely be there, isn't it, darling?'

'She should be there...you should get ready quickly,' says Mr Vasvani, crossing the balcony.

Atul is asking me, 'Coming to the coffee house this evening?'

'I might,' I say, wrapping my blanket around me, and he goes back to his room. In just half a minute, his voice can be heard again, 'Bhai, is there electricity in your place?'

I answer, 'Yes.' I know he is heating water with an electric rod, that's why he asked.

'Polish!' The boot polish boy calls out in his usual polite manner, as he does every day, and Sardarji beckons him upstairs. The boy sits outside and begins polishing while Sardarji gives instructions to his servant: bring the lunch at one o'clock sharp, roast the papads, make the salad....

I know that Sardarji's servant is a scoundrel. He never reaches on time with the food, nor does he cook what Sardarji likes.

∽

Outside, on the street, the fog is still dense. There is no sign of the sun. Vaishnav, the kulcha-chholawallah, has put up his stall on the street. He is arranging the plates like he does every day, and their clink and clatter is audible.

Bus number 7 is leaving. Many Christs, hanging on crosses, are in the bus and the conductor is distributing tickets in advance to the people in the queue. Every time he returns change to the passengers, the tinkle of small coins can be heard till here. The black-uniformed conductor looks like the devil in the midst of the fog-enveloped, ghostly forms.

And the bier has reached a little closer by now.

∽

'Should I wear the blue sari?' asks Mrs Vasvani.

Vasvani's reply is muffled, it sounds as if he's adjusting the knot of his tie.

Sardarji's servant has cleaned his suit with a brush and draped it on a hanger. And Sardarji is standing in front of the mirror tying his turban.

Atul Mavani appears again, portfolio in hand. He's wearing the suit he got made last month. His face looks fresh and his shoes gleam. As soon as he arrives, he asks me, 'Aren't you coming?' And before I can ask him where he calls out to Sardarji, 'Come, Sardarji! It's getting late. It's already ten.'

Sardarji comes down the stairs. Vasvani looks at Mavani from upstairs and asks, 'Where did you get this suit stitched?'

'From Khan Market.'

'It's very well stitched. Give me the address of your tailor.' Then he calls out to his missus, 'Now come along, dear.... All right, I'll wait downstairs.' He walks down to where Mavani and Sardarji are standing, feels the fabric and asks, 'The lining is Indian?'

'English!'

'Excellent fitting!' he says and notes down the address of the tailor in his diary. Mrs Vasvani appears on the balcony—the damp, chilly morning is making her look even more beautiful than usual. Sardarji sends a discreet message to Mavani with his eyes and lets out a soft whistle.

∽

The bier is right below my room now. It is accompanied by a few men and a couple of slow-moving cars. People are busy talking to each other.

Mrs Vasvani comes down, fixing the flower in her bun and Sardarji starts adjusting the handkerchief in his pocket. Before they leave, Vasvani asks me, 'Aren't you coming?'

'You go ahead, I'm coming,' I say, but in the next second I wonder—where is he asking me to go? I am still standing there, thinking about this when the four of them leave the house.

The bier has moved a little further by now. A car comes up from behind and slows down as it reaches the procession. The driver has a brief conversation with one of the people walking in the funeral procession, then the car speeds ahead with a whoosh. The two cars behind the bier also streak forward.

Mrs Vasvani and the other three go towards the taxi stand. I keep watching them. Mrs Vasvani is wearing a fur collar and the Sardarji is either showing her his leather gloves or giving them to her. A taxi driver comes forward, opens the door and all four get inside. Now the taxi is heading this way and I can hear the sound of laughter from inside. Vasvani is saying something to the driver, while pointing to the procession....

I'm watching everything silently and I don't know why, but now I think that the least I could have done is participated in Diwanchand's funeral procession. I know his son quite well and at such a time, one shows sympathy even to an enemy. I couldn't bring myself to go because of the cold...but the thought that I should go keeps bothering me.

The taxi with the four of them slows down near the bier. Mavani pokes his head out and says something; then the taxi cuts across to the right and moves ahead.

I get a bit of a jolt and, putting on my overcoat and chappals, go downstairs. My feet automatically take me towards the bier and I start walking behind it silently. Four men are carrying the bier on their shoulders and seven men are walking alongside—I am the seventh. And I think, everything changes when a man dies! Last year Diwanchand got his daughter married and there were thousands of guests. There was a line of cars outside his kothi....

Walking alongside the bier, I reach Link Road. The Panchkuian cremation ground is at the next turn.

As the bier turns the corner, I see a throng of people and a line of cars. There are a few scooters, too. A group of women is standing to one side. I can hear their loud voices. Their posture, their bodies have the same suppleness you see in Connaught Place. Everyone's hair has been styled differently. Cigarette smoke is rising from the crowd of men and dissolving in the mist. The red lips and white teeth of the women talking to each other are shining and their eyes have a certain arrogance....

The bier has been placed on a raised platform outside. A hush descends on the gathering. The scattered groups of people move closer and stand around the body and the chauffeurs holding floral bouquets and garlands wait for a signal from their employers.

I happen to glance at Vasvani. He is trying to signal his missus with his eyes to go and stand closer to the body, but she is busy chatting to another woman. Sardarji and Atul Mavani are also standing there.

The face of the body has now been uncovered and the women are placing flowers and garlands around the body. The chauffeurs, their duty done, are standing near the cars smoking cigarettes.

One of the women, after placing a garland, takes out a handkerchief from her coat pocket, dabs her eyes with it, starts sniffing, and then steps back.

Now all the women take out their handkerchiefs and make sniffling sounds.

Some men have lit incense sticks and placed them near the head of the body. They stand quite still and motionless.

From the sounds it seems as if the women have suffered a more severe shock.

Atul Mavani has taken a paper from his portfolio and is showing it to Vasvani. I think it's a passport form.

Now the body is being taken into the cremation ground. The crowd is standing outside the gate, watching. The chauffeurs have either finished their cigarettes or stubbed them out and are standing, alert, next to their cars.

The body has gone inside.

The men and women who came to mourn are leaving. There is the sound of car doors opening and slamming shut. Scooters are starting and some people are moving towards the bus stop on Ring Road.

⁌

The fog is still thick. The buses are going by and Mrs Vasvani is saying, 'Premila has called us this evening, we'll go, won't we, dear? The car will come. That's all right, isn't it?'

Vasvani nods, indicating his acceptance.

The women leaving in their cars smile at each other in farewell. Some 'bye-byes' can be heard. The cars are starting and leaving.

Atul Mavani and Sardarji have moved towards the Ring Road bus stop and I stand and think, if only I'd got ready and come, I could've gone straight to work from here. But it's half past eleven now.

The pyre has been lit and four or five men have sat down on a bench under a tree. Like me, they too seem to have just come along. They must have taken leave from office, otherwise they would have got ready and come.

I can't decide whether to go home, get ready and go to work or to make this death an excuse and take the day off—after all, there has been a death and I did join the funeral procession.

MOUNI

U. R. ANANTHAMURTHY

Translated from the Kannada by H. Y. Sharada Prasad

BHAVIKERE KUPPANNA BHATTA AND SEBINAKERE APPANNA BHATTA ARE like the cobra and the mongoose. Theirs is an old enmity, its origin lost to memory. Their houses stand on two hillocks half a mile apart. A fence in the valley separates their estates. Both of them are tenants of Narasimha, the deity of the Sri Matha. Years ago both of them had come here to work on the areca plantations, with just a copper tumbler each and not a coin between them. Now both have accounts in Gopala Kamti's grocery shop six miles away.

Kuppanna Bhatta is the older of the two. His face looks like a sour dried mango, his fifty-odd years etched on it. There was a time, in fact till just two years ago, when he was known for his sharp tongue—one lash from it was enough to split anything. His short, hairy frame has been shrinking with each passing day, but the way he carries himself has not changed at all. The same shining bald head, the same pudgy nose, that curved jaw heightening the resemblance to a mango. But the small eyes, fiery once, are now milky, and look as if they are covered with a layer of ash. The banana stains on his dhoti and the dhotra thrown over his shoulder, like his debts, have stayed with him through the years. He still keeps a wad of tobacco tucked into one cheek. Earlier, when angry, he would wait with drawn lips until his adversary stopped speaking, stride to a corner of the courtyard, spit out the tobacco, and return to utter something which was like a tight slap. The other man would be left speechless. And Kuppanna Bhatta would mix another little pellet of tobacco with lime in the palm of his hand and, transferring it into his mouth, lapse into a long silence. Nowadays, his face is like a locked door. If anyone tries to pick a quarrel with him, the closed expression on his face seems to say, 'You and I have nothing to do with each other.'

Appanna Bhatta, on the other hand, has always been popular. He is a man who gets along with everyone. Words slide off his tongue as smoothly as a strand of hair drawn through freshly-churned butter. Even the Brahmins of Buklapura, the agrahara two miles away, are his friends. More so because Kuppanna Bhatta has antagonized them. Appanna Bhatta keeps a good house and his estate is pleasing to the eye. There are chrysanthemums at his doorstep, a canopy of coconut fronds shades his courtyard. Coloured mats are spread out for visitors and no one leaves his house without being offered a cup of coffee. A far cry from Kuppanna Bhatta's courtyard. Cow dung here, children's shit there, garbage and flies everywhere, and leeches which latch on to the soft flesh between the toes. Appanna Bhatta often says, 'Even the hut of Koraga the sweeper is better kept than this.'

Kuppanna Bhatta's arrears with Gopala Kamti have mounted from year to year. He must owe Kamti more than a thousand rupees. Everyone knows that a messenger from Gopala Kamti goes to Kuppanna Bhatta every few days to demand payment. Appanna Bhatta is very different. At the end of each year he clears his account to the last rupee. He is equally prompt in paying his dues to the matha from which both Kuppanna Bhatta and he have leased their areca estates. Not a single nut does he withhold. Not only that, the agent of the matha who comes to collect the dues is shown the utmost respect, and served a special meal with payasam.

As for Kuppanna Bhatta, he owes the matha some five thousand rupees. Every year he is short ten or twelve maunds of areca nut.

The matha authorities have warned him to either pay up or surrender his tenancy. The agent is also worried about Kuppanna Bhatta's neglect of the plantation. He has often said that the only way to save the areca palms is to hand the land over to Appanna Bhatta.

Before the Swamiji of the Sri Matha went to Kashi, Appanna Bhatta had invited him over to his house. Humbly, he had made an offering of fifty silver rupee coins on a silver plate and prostrated himself at the holy feet.

Even his own brother-in-law believed that Kuppanna Bhatta was to blame for his unpopularity. Little wonder then that the Brahmins of Buklapura nodded when Appanna Bhatta said, 'I can understand his resenting my shadow. But what wrong have you people done to him? Could he not have performed the upanayana of his oldest son here and invited you all to the feast? Did he have to go all the way to Agumbe by bus and spend twice as much money in the temple there?' Then he continued in a soft voice, winking, 'One should not stretch one's feet beyond one's bed, our elders have said. But, believe my words, this man has got some concealed wealth. Otherwise, how could he have afforded such a lavish show?'

Why does he sit so listlessly, wondered Kuppanna Bhatta's wife, Gowramma, who is confined by asthma to a corner of the hall. Even after the evening birds have fallen silent, the cows have come home and been milked, and his daughter Bhagirathi has lit the lamp in the puja room, he has to be reminded three or four times to sit down to his evening prayers. In the past he had never allowed the children to light the kerosene lantern for fear that they would break the glass. Now the older son wipes the glass, lights the wick, and places the lantern on the jagali.

Gowramma remembers...two years ago, her brother Subrahmanya had come to visit her. Hardly anyone comes to their house now. But never mind. At least one of her brothers is now a prosperous farmer, earning enough to live a decent life. That makes her happy. But why wasn't her husband able to do this? Appanna Bhatta too had come here in search of his fortune. He had done well and was now even able to invite the Swamiji of the matha to his house! After the meal was over, Swamiji had sent a boy to fetch Kuppanna Bhatta. But how much should her husband tolerate? How could he step into his adversary's house, over a threshold he had not crossed for thirty years? How would it have been possible for him to stand there and be humiliated by Swamiji in front of Appanna Bhatta? So he had done something he had never done before in his life. He had taken refuge in the kitchen and said to Bhagirathi, 'Tell the boy I am not at home.' Naturally, Appanna Bhatta added his own twist to the story when he narrated this to Swamiji.

It is all one's fate. Otherwise, why would he be tied down to someone like her, an invalid, racked by asthma twenty days out of thirty? Across the fence, Appanna Bhatta's palms are laden with bunches of areca nut. Here, in her husband's plot, the nuts fall off the diseased trees. No labourer stays with him. They all go to the other estate. He has antagonized everyone. There is not a single two-legged creature in the entire region he has not quarrelled with. But he has never taken advantage of people. He does not know what deceit is and has never told a lie to save his skin. But what a temper! It is all in his stars. Just as it is in mine to suffer before I die. Fate. That's all.

What was I thinking about? Ah, Subrahmanya's visit. He had not been patronizing. In fact he had shown great deference. 'Bhavayya,' he had said, 'you have no friends here. I hear the matha people too are asking you to hand over the land. Bhagirathi has come of age. How long can you keep a girl who has shot up like a banana plant in the house? When you approached those Tirthahalli people, Appanna Bhatta came in the way. He is always sharpening his knife.... I have no right to advise an elder. But frankly, this plantation does not seem to suit your horoscope. Give it up and come away with me. You know that I have some five hundred areca palms in Halasoor. You can take care of as many as you wish to. I shall look after the rest.'

No matter how humble and hesitant Subrahmanya had been when he had said all this, Kuppanna Bhatta, like Parashurama, had flown into a towering rage. 'Wait till I am dead. After that you can look after your sister and her children. Until then, mind your business,' he had said harshly, dismissing Subrahmanya.

That was two years ago. Where was all that anger now? Since the bill collector saab from Kamti's shop and that rude man from the matha had begun to pester him, he had shrunk to half his size.

Then one day, he who had never asked for anything, came to his wife and said, 'Will you give me your ornaments? I will return them to you in six months.' The note of supplication in his voice drove a dagger through her heart. All she thought of was, let my husband and my thaali, the symbol of my marriage, be safe. She opened her box, and took out the jewels which had come to her at her wedding and which she had saved for Bhagirathi's marriage—earrings, a four-strand necklace, a chain, a gold belt, an ornament for the hair. She gave them to him, taking care not to let him see the tears in her eyes. She made only one plea to God: 'Protect my husband, and let Bhagirathi get married into a good home.' She kept telling herself, 'What do I need these ornaments for? His self-respect is more important.' But who would look at a girl who had no gold? She had kept the ornaments for only one reason. Her own disease-racked frame had no use for them. Tormented by the change in her husband's manner she waited anxiously for Subrahmanya to visit them again. She could confide in him and lighten her grief.

Bhagirathi was in the kitchen trying to coax some flames from the damp firewood. Her mother could hear her coughing from the smoke in her lungs. A few minutes later, Bhagirathi came out, wiping the tears streaming down her cheeks, her hair tousled. 'Amma, there is nothing to make hooli with,' she said. Gowramma told her, 'Then make cucumber-seed saaru.'

Why couldn't her husband go to Halasoor? How long could he carry on here? Appanna Bhatta has been pursuing him like a Yamadootha. If he can build a bund to prevent his plantation from flooding, can't he build a fence to keep other people's cattle from straying in? Or at least chase them away? Why did he have them sent to the pound four miles away? Her husband had waited and waited for the cattle to come home, and when they didn't, he trudged all the way to the pound, paid the fine and had them released. Appanna Bhatta surely has his eye on their plantation.

Ganapa, who was five, and whose belly was swollen from disease, went weeping to his mother. 'Give this child some of the water you have washed the rice in,' she told Bhagirathi.

No one in the neighbourhood cares whether we are alive or dead. Not once has anybody given my daughter a string of flowers or asked her how she was. Suddenly, the memory of the jewellery brought forth all the tears she had held back when she had given it to her husband. A fit of coughing followed. Wheezing, gasping for every breath, she stared at the darkness in the house around her, too weak to move from her corner.

Kuppanna Bhatta had decided that if his wife demurred even a little he would not touch the jewels. But she had not said a word. She had just opened the box and given him the small bundle wrapped in silk and he was overwhelmed. 'This is my last chance to get rid of my debts,' he had thought as he pledged them in the bank for two thousand and five hundred rupees. He vowed to redeem the jewels in six months and restore them to his wife.

Then Kuppanna Bhatta sought out the smaller cultivators, those who had only a hundred or two hundred areca palms, and advanced them twenty-five rupees a maund, with the promise that he would pay another twenty-five after the sale. Even Appanna Bhatta had never gone beyond forty-seven or forty-eight rupees a maund, and had never paid more than fifteen in advance. So the smaller growers agreed to go along with Kuppanna

Bhatta, who was then able to transport a hundred maunds to the wholesale mandi at Shimoga. 'When the price goes up a little, I will come and conclude the sale. Let me know how the market is,' he told the traders.

All this infuriated Appanna Bhatta. His regular clients had been snatched away from him. He told the whole town that here was clear proof that his rival had come into money. Kuppanna Bhatta had failed to pay the rent, but had enough for speculating on the market.

Meanwhile Kuppanna Bhatta made a careful calculation of his liabilities. He scrutinized all the figures he had noted in the margins of the panchanga. He owed five thousand rupees to the matha, one thousand to Gopala Kamti, and three hundred for the medicines for his wife's treatment. There was the interest on the sum borrowed from the bank. And the money he needed for Bhagirathi's marriage. The first thing he had to do was to get the jewels back. He could pledge them again the following year.

Areca nut should sell at sixty this year. That would give him a clear thousand by way of profit. He would pay two hundred rupees to Kamti, fifty to the doctor, two hundred and fifty to the matha agent. He would get the gold back with the remaining amount and use it as his reserve capital. A few more such careful transactions and he would be a free man. He took the cowries from his bag, laid them out and looked for the omens.

A fly flew up from the manure-pit and sat on his nose. Mango-gnats and mosquitoes hovered around his face. As it was summer, the courtyard was dry. Every whiff of breeze brought with it the smells of the cowshed. A withered jackfruit tree stood in one corner. The child with the malarial belly was defecating a few feet away, a black cur near his feet. A grey dog dozed on the ash-heap.

Kuppanna Bhatta rose, scratching the spot on his foot where a mosquito had bitten him. He went out and came back with a twig of tube cactus which he tied to a beam in the roof to attract mango-gnats. Just then Bhagirathi came out with a pot of water and asked Ganapa, 'Have you finished?' The black cur and the grey mongrel rushed to the spot vacated by Ganapa and Kuppanna Bhatta, disturbed by their barking, shouted, 'Hacha, hacha,' to chase them off.

From a corner of the room came the sound of wood being sawed. It was Gowramma's wheezing. 'Give her some medicine, Bhagirathi,' Kuppanna Bhatta told his daughter and began pacing up and down the jagali.

The tiles will have to be re-laid before the monsoon. Or the damp walls will crawl with hairy caterpillars. There are a hundred holes in the floor where the water has dripped from the roof. It is difficult to find a dry spot for the children to sleep. And there is mildew everywhere—on the mat, in the rice container, even under the box which contains the family deities. It does not grow on people's buttocks, yet. That's all.

The flies covered the octopus-like branches of the cactus, making its green turn black in no time. Kuppanna Bhatta stood there, looking out in front of him. There was nothing in the landscape to hold his attention.

Paddy fields in front of the house and then the jungle. A hill in the distance. A cart-track cut across the jungle from left to right. Someone seemed to be walking along it.

'Who is it?' shouted Kuppanna Bhatta.

'It is me, Manja,' said the man who was carrying a large load of dried branches, without slackening his pace.

'Wait a moment. When will you come to our place to split the firewood?'

'After I have finished the work for Sebinakere ayya,' replied Manja, moving away.

Feeling utterly helpless, Kuppanna Bhatta picked up a knife and went into the garden to bring in some banana leaves. By the time he returned, the three older boys had come back from school, which was four miles away. Bhagirathi was waiting for the cattle. The sound of wood being sawn continued to be heard from Gowramma's corner. The medicine had had no effect. Ganapa sat in the corner, stuffing his mouth with dry avalakki and pieces of jaggery.

Areca nut that season went up to fifty-one, fifty-two, and, in a month, to fifty-five rupees a maund. Kuppanna Bhatta waited for it to touch sixty.

'Your money has gone down the drain,' Appanna Bhatta mocked those who had sold their stock to his adversary. They in turn gave Kuppanna Bhatta a hard time. Every day, ten to twelve people came to his doorstep and demanded immediate payment. Making excuses and holding them off exhausted Kuppanna Bhatta. With abject humility, he pleaded with them to wait for a month more. But they would not listen. So he was compelled to go to Shimoga and raise a loan of two thousand and five hundred rupees at fifteen per cent interest on his stock. He paid his suppliers ten rupees per maund and promised to pay the remaining fifteen in a month's time.

Seeing all these transactions being made by his rival, Appanna Bhatta instigated Gopala Kamti and the agent of the matha to demand a settlement of their dues. 'This is the right time for it,' he whispered to them.

Gopala Kamti's bill collector turned up one day at Kuppanna Bhatta's house and planted himself on the jagali. No amount of pleading could move even a hair on his moustache. He shouted at the top of his voice that he would not stir until he had been paid at least five hundred rupees.

If Kuppanna Bhatta had been the sort of person to weep he would have cried. As the bill collector's voice rose, Gowramma's breathing became more agonized. Like a man in the grip of a nightmare, Kuppanna Bhatta seemed incapable of any movement. Whenever someone passed by the estate, the bill collector's voice became louder.

At last, Kuppanna Bhatta went in, opened his box and brought out four one-hundred-rupee notes. The bill collector took them, mounted his bicycle, and, still muttering, rode off. On the way back, he met Appanna Bhatta, reported to him what had happened and was treated to a tumbler of coffee.

Hardly had the bill collector left when the doctor's compounder presented himself. His peace was purchased with a hundred rupees. There were still a thousand rupees left. The loan would have to be repaid now from out of the profit. It was all right, Kuppanna Bhatta reassured himself.

But early next morning, the agent of the matha turned up. Kuppanna Bhatta laid out a seat for him and asked him if he would have some coffee. The agent refused. 'I have come to you even though there is a swelling on my leg. Anybody else would have treated you roughly. You do not show your face at the matha on your own. Even when Swamiji sent for you from Appanna Bhatta's house, you did not come. He who deceives the Sri Matha Narasimha, will not prosper, Bhatt-re. You had better settle your debts,' continued the agent, as he sat there fanning himself. He had come to know that Gopala Kamti had received four hundred rupees.

The more Kuppanna Bhatta pleaded, the angrier the agent became. 'I will bring a search warrant and a notice of attachment tomorrow,' he said, preparing to leave.

Kuppanna Bhatta resigned himself to the inevitable. He counted out eight hundred rupees and handed them over to the agent. 'You must pay the remaining amount by the next date or else you will have to give up the plantation,' he warned before he left. And he hurried off to Appanna Bhatta's house for his afternoon meal.

The next day some of those who had sold areca nut to Kuppanna Bhatta besieged him. 'We are in financial difficulties, Bhatt-re. The rainy season is coming. We need to buy things for the house,' they said. The whole world seemed to know that Kuppanna Bhatta had some money!

The price of areca nut did not rise beyond fifty-five. In fact it tumbled to fifty. In dismay Kuppanna Bhatta hastened to Shimoga by bus and sold off the stock. He paid back the short-term loan to the last rupee, including the interest. He also paid his suppliers in full. Only the jewels remained in the bank.

Just before the rains set in, Subrahmanya turned up in his bullock cart and implored Kuppanna Bhatta to go with him. 'Come with me, Bhavayya,' he urged. 'I will find a groom for Bhagirathi. Gowramma's health has deteriorated and Ganapa is as thin as a stick.'

Turning to Gowramma, he said, 'Akka, my wife is pregnant. If you and Bhagirathi come and stay with us for a few months, you will do me a favour. There is no one to take care of her. Bhagirathi will be a great help. I will look for a boy for her. Don't listen to your husband. Come with me to Halasoor.... Why did you give him all your gold, Akka? He is a selfish, stubborn man. He cares only about his pride, his self-respect. His wife and family mean nothing to him. Why has he not done well like the other areca growers, tell me? I just don't understand any of this.'

Gowramma replied, 'How can I leave him in this condition....'

'I am asking you to come only for a few months, Akka. Till the confinement,' Subrahmanya persisted.

Kuppanna Bhatta did not say yes, nor did he say no. 'It's her wish,' he told Subrahmanya and left it at that. He refused to go with them. 'There is no one to look after the plantation,' he said.

Gowramma was torn between anxiety for her husband and the pull of the home of her birth. But Bhagirathi's marriage had to be thought of. And without the gold to give as dowry, finding a husband for her had become more difficult.

Kuppanna Bhatta spent the whole of the monsoon alone, cooking his own kanji. Without his wife and her wheezing, the house seemed to be swallowed up by silence. As the rain poured down, Kuppanna Bhatta spent many nights awake, his eyes wide open. And he came to a decision. He would get the gold back from the bank. He did not want to be obliged to anyone.

Where Kuppanna Bhatta had expected a hundred maunds of nuts from his own plantation, the yield that year was only fifty. Swamiji was away in Kashi at that time. Kuppanna Bhatta wrote a letter, and with great humility, asked for leniency just this once. He undertook to hand back the land the following year.

He waited for fifteen days. There was no reply. If he waited any longer, Kamti's bill collector and the agent would descend on him and carry away the crop. The ornaments in the bank would remain unredeemed.

The areca nut had to be moved to the market before the debt collectors could lay their hands on it. If he allowed the ornaments to remain in the bank, the interest would mount and he would not see them again in this lifetime.

He went to the town to enquire whether there was any lorry bound for Shimoga. There was only one, it belonged to Gopala Kamti's relation. He struck a deal, thinking, whatever has to happen will happen.

The very next day, Kamti's bill collector presented himself outside Kuppanna Bhatta's house. His heart sank. Whatever he tried to say was drowned out by the bill collector's ranting. The man insisted that Kamti had ordered him to come back with not a coin less than six hundred rupees, plus fifty rupees more by way of interest.

The argument was conducted at such a pitch that one of Appanna Bhatta's servants heard it and carried the news to his master. Appanna Bhatta yoked his bullocks to the cart and promptly proceeded to the matha.

By the afternoon, Kamti's man, who had gone back to report to his master, returned with some gunny bags and scales. 'Sell us fifteen maunds of areca nut at forty-five rupees a maund, then we will have to pay you twenty-five rupees,' he said, taking the money from his pocket.

The selling price in Shimoga was fifty rupees. Besides, Kamti's weighing scales were adjusted, so he bought at one weight and sold at another. 'Not possible,' said Kuppanna Bhatta gruffly.

The bill collector saab made bold to step into the house. For Kuppanna Bhatta, a Muslim crossing the threshold was the limit. He sprang towards the room in which the areca nut was stored and shouted, 'You will see me dead before you touch this door.'

The man was taken aback at the outburst. Wiping his face with a towel, he sat down, the scales in front of him. 'What can you do when grown men behave like children?' he muttered. Kuppanna Bhatta made no reply. He shook with emotion. His lips trembled. But he continued to sit outside the door, his arm stretched across it. The bill collector just stared at him.

Fifteen to twenty minutes had passed, when the sound of the bells of a bullock cart were heard. Kuppanna Bhatta recognized it as the cart from the matha. For a moment, his body went limp and he shut his eyes. But he quickly steadied himself. The agent of the matha walked straight in, accompanied by the shanbhog—the village accountant—the matha storekeeper, and a servant with another set of weighing scales. 'What is going on here?' asked the agent loudly. Kamti's bill collector told him.

'He is our tenant. God's dues will be paid first, the annual rent as well as arrears. The grocer's claim can only come later. Go tell your master that,' the agent said to the bill collector. But the saab was not so easily cowed. He said Kuppanna Bhatta had promised that Kamti's debt would be cleared first. This was not true. He also described how he had foiled Kuppanna Bhatta's plan to move the areca nuts secretly to Shimoga.

'So this is what you have fallen to, Kuppanna Bhatta? You think you can swallow and digest what belongs to Narasimha?' asked the agent contemptuously.

With a meekness he had never shown in all his life, Kuppanna Bhatta told him about the petition he had addressed to Swamiji at Kashi. He took his janewara between his thumb and forefinger and vowed that if he was given a reprieve this time, he would clear the dues the following year.

'Clear the dues, he says! With what face can you say it? You have money to speculate on the market, but you have no money to pay what you owe to God. You were arrogant enough to defy Swamiji and not come when he sent for you. You are eating his food, God's food! You don't bother to take care of the plantation. Look at the way you have kept this place. Thath! Anyone would think that it belonged to an outcast! Anyway, this is Swamiji's order.' He took a piece of paper from his pocket and read it out. It said that the estate should be taken away from Kuppanna Bhatta and entrusted to Appanna Bhatta for cultivation.

The shanbhog put on his reading glasses and added up Kuppanna Bhatta's dues—unpaid rent, loan and interest—and pronounced, 'Six thousand.' The agent told the storekeeper, 'Weigh the areca nuts kept in the room.'

The storekeeper had recently been employed by the matha, after having lost all his money through trading in buffaloes. He was a dark, hefty man, built like Bhima. As soon as he heard the agent's words, he scrambled up to impress him. 'Move. Move....' he bellowed.

'Hoi, fifteen maunds of it should go to Kamti.' The bill collector was persistent.

'Will you clear out of the way, or should we set you right?' the agent threatened the bill collector, looking as if he was ready to swallow him up. The bill collector hurriedly climbed onto his bicycle and left unceremoniously, wondering what excuse to give when his master scolded him.

Once again the storekeeper shouted, 'Move out of the way,' to Kuppanna Bhatta, who sat there, barring the door.

'Before you touch one areca nut in this room, you will have to go over my dead body,' said Kuppanna Bhatta, loudly and firmly.

The shanbhog and the storekeeper were speechless.

'What did you say?' the agent challenged.

'That you will see me dead before you get to the areca nuts,' Kuppanna Bhatta replied, his whole body burning with the fire of his resolve.

'You, born a Brahmin and you are descending to this, Bhatt-re!' said the agent. The shanbhog put in his bit of advice. But Kuppanna Bhatta was unmoved.

'Very well, you will see what you are in for,' the agent said, as he made ready to leave with his entourage. On the way he went to Appanna Bhatta's house, instructed him to keep an eye on Kuppanna Bhatta in case he tried to move the areca nuts at night, and went off without having any coffee.

Kuppanna Bhatta sat for a long time where he was, until his legs went dead under him. Late in the afternoon, he got up and stretched his limbs to get the blood flowing in them again. He latched the front door, bathed, and boiled some kanji for himself. When the cows came back a couple of hours later, he tied them up in the shed, gave them bran-water and milked them. He lit the lantern and sat down in the courtyard. He did not feel like cooking, so he warmed some milk, drank it and lay down right there. But sleep eluded him. After a long time he opened the door and went out. From the clearing in front of the house, he looked up at the sky. Through the still silence of the trees, he could see the silver of pre-dawn spread across the sky. He calculated the hour, then went back into the house, bolting the door behind him. His eyelids drooped with weariness.

It was only when the cowherd called his name that he woke up. After the cows were led away, he drew water from the well and poured it over his head. He put a vessel of water on to boil.

Soon he heard someone pounding on the door.

'Bhatt-re, it is me, the ameen. Open the door.'

Kuppanna Bhatta made no reply to the bailiff. He went and sat at the threshold of the room where the areca nuts were stored. After a while, there was the sound of a bicycle bell. Then came the voice of Kamti, 'Open the door, Bhatt-re. I shall pay you forty-seven per maund. You can clear my account.' Kuppanna Bhatta did not move.

Kamti's bill collector shouted, 'Will you open the door or not?'

An altercation between the ameen and Kamti ensued. The ameen hurried away, threatening to summon the agent of the matha.

Again Kamti said, 'Bhatt-re, open the door. I will pay you fifty rupees. Settle my account.'

When there was no answer even to this, he began abusing him.

'If I had known what kind of a shameless man you are, I would never have let you set foot in my shop!' he said.

Then he said to his bill collector in a loud voice, 'Budan, go to this man's brother-in-law in Halasoor and demand a settlement of our accounts. Do not move from there until you are paid the money. He cannot be as shameless as this man is.'

Just then the agent arrived. He and Kamti began to quarrel. They sounded like the raucous crows that gather around the rice balls offered to them during a shraddha.

The agent used his ultimate weapon. He told the town crier, 'Go and announce to the whole of Buklapura that Kuppanna Bhatta's movable property is going to be publicly sold.'

The man began his job right there. Kamti's protests were drowned in that noise. Gradually, the drumbeats moved farther away.

'I will go to court,' threatened Kamti.

'Why don't you?' replied the agent.

The sound of the town crier's drum faded into the forest. Silence descended on Kuppanna Bhatta's house. Outside, the noonday sun blazed.

'You have to take the next step now,' the agent told the ameen.

'Do whatever is necessary. The storekeeper will help you. If Kuppanna Bhatta gives any trouble, send for me. I shall be at Appanna Bhatta's place,' he added, before he left.

'Bhatt-re, for the last time, will you open your door, or do you want us to break it?' The storekeeper called out.

There was no answer. He picked up a crowbar and rammed the door with it. The bolt rattled.

'Open the door now at least.'

There was still no response. One more blow and the door flew open. Like Yamadootha, the ameen stood in front of Kuppanna Bhatta who looked as if he was deep in meditation. The ameen signalled to him to get up but Kuppanna Bhatta remained sitting, his eyes closed.

The storekeeper picked up Kuppanna Bhatta's shrunken body as if it were a handful of sticks and put him down outside, in the hot sun. One by one, he piled up the areca nut sacks in another corner of the courtyard. He was in high spirits. 'Are the vessels and other things to be sold too?'

The ameen pulled out a piece of paper from his pocket and read out the order, 'Everything movable and immovable is to be sold.'

The storekeeper darted into the kitchen. He brought the milk vessel into the courtyard and poured the milk on the ground. Then he brought all the goods out. A copper handi, a set of rice vessels, kadais, a set of bronze thalis, a silver jug, a copper teertha vessel (the same one that Kuppanna

Bhatta had brought with him from the plains), a sankha and a brass thali used for the puja, a number of tubs for storing water at feasts, a cradle, a collection of ladles, a torn mat and a patched blanket, a wooden bench, a dozen wooden planks, a framed silver picture of Krishna, a silk dhoti, a pair of brooms—everything except the holy box containing the family deity, the saligrama. Kuppanna Bhatta sat amidst his worldly possessions, his hand to his forehead, his eyes lowered.

'Aren't the cattle part of movable property?' the storekeeper asked.

'Of course,' said the ameen.

The town crier had finished his job and come back. 'Go, bring home the cattle grazing on the slopes of the hillock,' the ameen told him.

Then he went inside and fetched a gunny bag for the assortment of vessels. As he shook the gunny bag, four or five baby mice, newborn and still pink, fell out of it. They writhed and wriggled in the hot sun. 'Eesh,' the ameen exclaimed in disgust. 'Thath!' said the storekeeper, as a crow hopped in stealthily and, lunging suddenly, carried off one of the baby mice.

A number of people from Buklapura stood behind the trees around the house. They had ropes and sickles in their hands and pretended to be there in the course of their work. No one dared to step into the courtyard. Not one person made a bid for the goods. 'Why should we commit the sin of coveting another's belongings?' some thought. 'Cheh! Poor man,' cried several others, feeling sorry for him. One by one, they moved away from there. Only a few, who could not conquer their curiosity, stayed back to see what would happen.

The agent had the areca nut sacks loaded on to the cart. The ameen made a detailed list of all the articles they had seized. Everything except the brooms, the silver picture, and a couple of broken vessels was placed on the cart. Without looking at him, the agent admonished Kuppanna Bhatta. 'No one who misappropriates that which belongs to Narasimha can survive, let alone prosper. Understand, Bhatt-re? From today, neither the land nor the house is yours. The tenancy has been made over to Appanna Bhatta.'

As he heaved himself up into the cart, he fired a last salvo, 'Anyway, why should you worry? You have already sent your hoarded wealth with your wife to her parents' place!'

There was an old ajji in Buklapura whose name was Sitakka. No one knew how old she was. She seemed to have been living there from the beginning of time. She addressed everyone in the singular, showing no respect for anyone. Married and widowed when she was still a child, she lived all by herself in a dilapidated little hut. Sitakka had no one to call her own, not even someone to offer a ball of rice at her shraddha when she died. Every day, she begged for a handful of rice to make some kanji for herself, her only meal of the day.

Sitakka had a sharp tongue, and everyone in the agrahara was terrified of her. If the shadow of a lower caste person fell across her path, if children accidentally touched her while they were playing, if she found anyone retreating into their homes when they saw her (because she was a widow and hence a bad omen), she would pour out a stream of imprecations. It was almost as if she could not sleep if she did not spend a couple of hours a day raving and ranting at someone. Perhaps she thought that unless she picked a quarrel and invoked their forefathers for several generations and cursed these evil times, people would take her for granted. Afraid of her abuse, people gave her rice even before she asked for it! After her meal, she spent her time sitting either on the stone steps leading to the river or on the platform outside the temple, twisting cotton into wicks.

At the sound of the town crier's drum that day, Sitakka's ears perked up. Quickly, she took the mandatory three dips in the river, gulped her kanji down, and went to find out what had happened. The agrahara seemed to have been emptied of all men. None of the women would tell her anything. Finally she got the information from a farm labourer. Sitakka marched into Kuppanna Bhatta's courtyard. There she saw a couple of misshapen vessels and a few brooms strewn around. Kuppanna Bhatta sat among them, his bald head exposed to the fierce sun.

Sitakka's harsh outburst shattered the oppressive silence. 'Which son of a whore has ruined your home? May his house crumble. Let his cattle be seized by tigers. But what is the matter with you? Why are you sitting like this? Have you too begun to believe that a poor man who loses his temper loses his teeth? Where is your arrogance now? Your insolence? You never cared to talk to me, to ask whether I was dead or alive.' Kuppanna Bhatta made no reply. Sitakka was puzzled.

'Let the fire swallow your enemy....' Sitakka began again but stopped when she noticed someone standing under a nearby tree. 'Who is that lurking there like a ghost?' she asked, crossing over to him. It was a young man called Narasimha Bhatta from Buklapura. But she did not recognize him. 'Who are you? Come here, will you,' she said. The man came forward timidly.

Together the two of them took hold of Kuppanna Bhatta by the arms, picked him up and seated him in the shade of the jagali. Quietly, the young man sneaked away.

Cursing Appanna Bhatta, the agent, Kuppanna Bhatta, the other Brahmins of Buklapura and anyone else she could think of, Sitakka picked up the pots and pans scattered around and placed them on the jagali. She saw the lock on the door of the storeroom and heartily cursed the hand that had put it there. 'May a snake bite it,' she muttered. Then she hastened to her own home, but before that, she stood in front of Appanna Bhatta's house and showered curses on his heartlessness. She got together some avalakki, asked someone for some curds to mix it with, crushed a green chilli into it, added a pinch of salt and took it back to Kuppanna Bhatta. She wrapped it in a banana leaf, which she pushed in front of him and ordered, 'Eat this. Don't starve yourself like an idiot.' Then she went home, had a bath and lay down on the bare floor.

After the sun had set, Appanna Bhatta called one of his labourers and told him, 'Go and see what Kuppanna Bhatta is doing—whether he is there or has slunk away to his wife's place. Take care that you're not seen.' The servant did as he was told. In the light of the moon, he saw the still, motionless figure on the jagali, and was frightened. He rushed back to report what he had seen.

'See what a schemer he is!' Appanna Bhatta said to his wife. 'This is another one of his tricks. Do you know what a drama he put on for the benefit of the agent? I tell you, if he does not creep to his wife's home by the first light of the day, my name is not Appanna Bhatta.'

The next day dawned. The man who brought in the firewood announced, 'He is still on the jagali.' Curious to see what was happening Appanna Bhatta took the key the agent had given him and set off. As he neared Kuppanna Bhatta's house, his heart started thudding. For a while he lingered behind a large tree, pretending to cut down something.

Kuppanna Bhatta was sitting on the jagali, like a stone, his dark body leaning against the wall, his dhotra thrown over his head. Appanna Bhatta's heart missed a beat. As he went nearer, he thought to himself, 'If Kuppanna Bhatta picks a quarrel, I will give him a fitting reply. I will ask him about the wealth that he has already dispatched to his in-laws' place.' He felt reassured and stepped into the courtyard. A grey dog lay in front of Kuppanna Bhatta, gazing intently at him. A plantain leaf with a small heap of dried-up avalakki on it lay untouched. Before he realized it, Appanna Bhatta had called out, 'Bhatt-re!' There was no reply. With a shaking finger, he jabbed at the figure who continued to sit with his eyes closed.

All the blood had drained out of Kuppanna Bhatta's aged face, leaving it wan and pale. Appanna Bhatta shook him by the shoulder.

Kuppanna Bhatta opened his eyes.

'You need not have been so rough with the agent,' Appanna Bhatta stated.

There was no reaction, but Kuppanna Bhatta's eyes were open. Appanna Bhatta felt emboldened.

'What do you lack, Bhatt-re? You have carried your hatred of me this long. But I don't hold it against you. After all, you are older than me. As an elder, you should wish me well. That's what I want. You should not leave with hard feelings against me. So I have come to speak to you. I shall send you to your brother-in-law's house in my own cart. Come and eat a meal in my house before you go. Let us forget this enmity of thirty years.'

Appanna Bhatta had not meant to go so far. One word had led to another without his realizing it. Kuppanna Bhatta's continued silence had made him raise his own voice. But it appeared as though his words did not penetrate the other man's eardrums. Not a muscle on Kuppanna Bhatta's face moved. His stillness hit Appanna Bhatta with the force of a blow.

And Appanna Bhatta was speechless. After a while, he recovered. As he paced up and down the courtyard, he continued, more softly this time, 'I have not done anything to ruin you, Bhatt-re. For thirty years I have endured your resentment. But did I ever try to compete with you? It is true that I informed the agent that Narasimha's share of the produce was being diverted to Gopala Kamti's account. If I am not telling the truth, let my tongue split into two. Call the elders of Buklapura and let them adjudicate. If they find that I am in the wrong, I shall fall at your feet.'

Appanna Bhatta's voice became shrill. 'Last year you took away all those growers who used to supply areca nut to me. When you had money to trade, was it right to default on your payments of rent? Wouldn't anyone get angry at that? Aren't there some rules in such matters? Like you, I am a man with a family. Like you, I have a daughter to marry off. I also have my troubles. For the past year, I have been suffering from some ailment of the stomach. I am in constant pain. Last month, my buffalo, which used to give a bucketful of milk, suddenly died. It is all our fate, Bhatt-re. Come on. Get up and come with me. Have a meal at my place. I will get the bullock cart ready and you can start for your brother-in-law's place in the cool hours of the evening.'

The grey mongrel looked at one face, then at the other, and then at the avalakki on the plantain leaf. Kuppanna Bhatta's eyes stared vacantly past Appanna Bhatta and into the forest beyond. Appanna Bhatta felt his throat go dry in the oppressive silence. He kept repeating, 'Bhatt-re, Bhatt-re...' as if he were reciting the names of his ancestors during a shraddha. The dog rose, stretched its limbs, and lay down again. Mango-gnats hovered around. The sun blazed. Kuppanna Bhatta sat on his haunches, resting his head on his palm and his elbow on his knees, a towel over his head. Appanna Bhatta looked at him again, as if seeing him for the first time. There was a churning feeling in his stomach. The avalakki on the banana leaf was dry, though it had once been soaked in curds. Flies sat on it. And flies sat on Kuppanna Bhatta's nose. Every few seconds, he blinked.

'Bhatt-re, I don't want your property. Stay on in your house. I will let you cultivate this land as long as you live. Just pay me the rent every year. I am not a butcher. Like you I came from the coast with an empty copper vessel in my hand. All I want is that I should not drop dead on a jungle path as my father did. There was no one even to pour a few drops of water down his throat as he was dying. When I found him, lying there in the sun, the crows were pecking at him. I pray that kind of death does not come to me, that's all, Bhatt-re. Here, take your keys. Keep them,' Appanna Bhatta cried. Overcome with emotion, he blew his nose.

The man who sat there on his haunches, as if waiting for his last breath, did not react. This still, shrouded figure seemed to burn into Appanna Bhatta's mind, and his tongue, never lacking in fluency, grew silent too. Appanna Bhatta put his towel over his head and he too squatted on the jagali, opposite the silent one.

JOB'S CHILDREN

VIMALA DEVI

Translated from the Portuguese by Paul Melo e Castro

I

GIVEN A CHOICE BETWEEN THE RIVER AND THE OPEN SEA, BOSTIÃO would pick the former without hesitation. At dawn each day, he went forth in his canoe, rowing laboriously out to the stakes where he strung his nets. But river fish are measly, and yield little profit. To continue like this, at the mercy of chance, was untenable. Barely covering his daily expenses would no longer do. Life shows no mercy to the weak, nor do our fellow men. It was an old lesson which time imparted pitilessly. As a result, each year, when the mackerel returned, he braved the open sea with the others, despite his age and the great weariness of his body.

'Leave yourself be at home, man. The sea is too much for you now,' his wife would say to him.

It was true. His scrawny body, worn out by over six decades of toil, was growing weak, faltering under the strain. Yet he kept on, screwing up his courage into strength.

'Don't fret, Angelina! You know I'd rather not go. Once there was the lure of adventure...but the sea only entices the young. For old-timers like me it holds no attraction.'

After the monsoon, when the large shoals began to appear, this scene would recur each day. And each day it would end in tears and entreaties.

'Don't go, Father.... Stay in the river! Prawns fetch money too....' his daughter would plead with all the tenderness of her twenty years, remembering other fishermen who had set out one day never to return.

Bostião tried to explain every which way he could his position in Shudra society, and the duties he couldn't shirk that enslaved him. He was well aware that in the village all the girls Carminha's age were getting married. Around the neighbourhood, whispered comments passed from mouth to mouth. 'Just when will Bostião marry off his daughter?' they asked, shaking their heads sadly, filled with apprehension. Bostião knew this. Heard this. Felt this. It pained him, but what could he do? He alone knew how hard it was to make ends meet. But one thing was certain—in the words of the other fishermen was a veiled reproach. They expected him to earn enough for his daughter to marry, even though he was old and could barely row out to the stakes each morning to collect his nets. That was just the way things were, and had been down the ages, Bostião well knew. And they were right. If girls go past the age...and it wouldn't be the first time it happened! 'The body gives poor counsel, arrangements must be made as soon as girls begin to awaken,' they said, with time-honoured wisdom.

'I'll never scrape your dowry together selling prawns,' Bostião muttered. 'Do you think I can die in peace without seeing you settled? It's like a weight inside me, and I feel so old!'

'If only Sapai hadn't fallen ill....' exclaimed his wife, referring to her father-in-law. 'We spent everything we had and more besides! And even then he didn't recover from that damn malaria....'

'It wasn't malaria, Angelina! We thought it was, but the doctor said lung trouble all along. If we'd listened to him from the start, perhaps Father could have been saved.'

Their house had no clock. They measured time by the rising and setting of the sun, by the opening and closing of the shops, by the arrival and departure of the ferries and, lastly, by the bells of the village church in Penha de França.

After dinner, the family said its prayers. Bostião then went out, lighting a bidi and leaving his wife and daughter to wash the copper plates and earthen vessels.

He crouched in the doorway. It had been cemented over not too long previously, before Sapai had fallen ill, when things had been less desperate and they still had some money put aside.

He gazed out at the river before him, the tranquil, paternal river.

Bostião spent many hours here, smoking in long draws, alone with his thoughts. Sometimes he would just sit and stare, his mind a blank. Other times, he would let his thoughts roam free. But they always returned to Carminha, as they did that day. He thought of her and the little time he had left, how he had grown old. 'Who wants a girl without a dowry?' he thought. 'A girl without a dowry, who'd want her?' he repeated. He stared on, wide-eyed, immobile, until he heard Gustin's voice from the quay.

'Bostião! Hey, Bostião, let's go!'

It was a wrench to leave the comfort of his home, the protection of its palm-leaf roof, the warmth of the stove in which the coals were not quite spent, to pass the whole night at sea, locked in a struggle he no longer wanted any part of. And then, that cold, the wet night air, and the sea wind that left his whole body shivering....

Lazily he stretched out his legs, took one last drag on his bidi and then rubbed his hands. But before long he heard Vitoba: 'Hey, Bostião, let's go!'

'Just a moment....'

'We've got to leave with the tide!'

Bostião sprang to his feet, determination showing through in every movement. Carminha handed him his cambolim, cloak, with a smile. Bostião slung it around his shoulders and walked off slowly to meet his companions.

Carminha stood and watched in silence. When her father turned back towards her, she smiled again.

More than ever it was necessary to inspire courage in him. Her chances of getting married were at stake; her future prospects as a woman were in his hands. She often asked herself how long she would remain prey to the sharp eyes of neighbours, family members, and local gossips.

What's more, those burning urges she had from time to time, disturbances that left her beside herself, which made her almost shout out loud…. At heart, however, she was not so greatly troubled. Within Carminha was a natural simplicity that kept her on an even keel. Had her father not spoken with such frankness maybe she would have remained caught up in the whirl of youth and taken far longer to realize the true nature of her predicament. She was happy going to the market to sell her father's catch. This trip alone represented a small yet seductive adventure into society. At Mapusa market she could chat with the young men who came back from Bombay, or further afield, to spend their holidays in Goa. They would brag about sights seen abroad, likely exaggerating, she knew, in order to impress the locals. Carminha liked them. They were stylish. They had a different way about them, wore lots of brilliantine in their hair, and always came to market in pyjama trousers unlike the fishermen who almost only wore langotins.

In the doorway, eyes closed, Carminha breathed in the fresh breeze from the river. She recalled one by one the young men with brown faces who appeared in the village each year, their glistening hair, the wide horizons in their eyes. And, turning them over in her mind, she fell asleep on the cement floor while old Bostião, stretched to the limit, slogged his guts out at sea.

II

Next morning, very early, the women gathered anxiously on the wharf and peered out towards the mouth of the river. They placed their baskets on the ground and sat down beside them, unfazed by the already scorching sun. On the water the traffic was just getting started. Vessels ferrying people over to their jobs in Panjim crossed to and fro. The women sat and stared, motionless, hoping that the big boat would appear, the big boat with no tarpaulin cover filled with a fine catch.

Suddenly the women broke into smiles. They smiled in unison as if they were one woman. Their hearts leapt in unison, for it was their men who were returning on the big boat which now approached. At their sides stood baskets that would soon be full of silvery mackerel.

'Our men are rowing in silence today. Perhaps they didn't have any luck….' one of them murmured.

'No. Maybe you're wrong. It's the right season!' said another.

'I can't see Bostião among them!' exclaimed a third.

They stopped short, nudging one another in silence until the boat drew in. The men stooped low, lifting Bostião up in their arms.

The women shivered and turned to stare at Angelina. Her eyes widened, the hem of her capod twisted between her fingers.

Suddenly, from her very guts, she let out a raw cry of anguish and dismay.

'Oh, Deva, Deva, my Bostião! Deva!'

The other women crowded around Angelina, blocking her view, while the men carried Bostião home.

Angelina followed behind, sobbing all the way and wailing, 'Oh, Deva, Deva, look how they've brought back my Bostião!'

When the men arrived, the women moved aside so she could approach her husband who was stretched out on a mat.

'Oh, Bostião!' she cried, sinking to her knees.

But the men had already begun to act.

'Bring some kanji,' Salvador ordered, imposing silence.

To bring someone around from a faint, Gustin recommended wafting an onion soused in firewater under their nose.

'Some feni to revive him!'

Carminha was on her way back from the well with two pitchers of water. Seeing the crowd, she shuddered. One of the pitchers fell from her head, drenching the cow dung floor. 'Father!' she sobbed.

'I've already sent for the distican, faith healer,' someone said. This word alone expressed what they thought had caused Bostião's plight.

Angelina rubbed coconut oil on to her husband's chest and arms vigorously. Little by little, Bostião came to his senses. He opened his eyes and swallowed a little of the kanji a neighbour was spooning into his mouth.

'Eat, Bostião, so you get well again!' she said, refusing to take no for an answer.

At that moment the distican arrived, huffing and puffing.

A small woman around fifty years old, she was brisk and full of self-assurance. Her hair, thick with coconut oil, was tied up in a bun. She gave the patient an astute look and wrinkled her nose. Walking around to the far side of the mat, she crouched in front of Bostião and waved her hand above his face. He shut his eyes, exhausted.

'I need salt and three peppers,' the distican shouted hoarsely. Without taking her eyes off the fisherman, she began loudly and rhythmically to pray:
Satmantam Deva bapasarvhukumdar....
I believe in God, the Father Almighty.

One of the women passed her the peppers and the salt. The old woman leant over and trailed them three times across the ill man's body, repeating:
Satmantam Deva bapasarvhukumdar...Sorguincho ani samsarachorachnar....
I believe in God, the Father Almighty...Creator of heaven and earth.

Afterwards, amid the general silence, she rose to her feet and threw the peppers into the fire. A tongue of brighter flame flashed up and a crackling sound was heard.

Angelina turned to the other women: 'See? Didn't I say it was down to the evil eye?'

'It's no surprise!' Florinda chipped in. 'Lately everyone has been saying "old Bostião still has what it takes to go mackerel fishing". I knew it then. They should have called in the distican even before he set out to sea!'

'He'll be all better by Wednesday. I guarantee Wednesday's the day to lift the evil eye,' said the old woman, standing in the doorway.

Angelina reached out her hand and gave the woman four tangas, which she shoved into her pocket. Then she turned away satisfied, and set off for home.

As soon as the distican had left, people started to file out of Bostião's shack.

'Send for me if you need anything,' said Tomso.

'If you need any money...I'm not rich, but I can scrape something together,' Gustin said quietly.

'Don't cry, Carminha,' said Venctexa, who had come to buy fish and then stayed after learning what had happened. 'Go to my house. My wife will give you a root. Rub it on a stone with some water and then place it on your father's forehead. He'll get better straight away, you'll see. Up and about in no time,' he guaranteed.

III

Bent low, Dr Amoncar was having trouble checking the patient's heartbeat.

'It's always the same story, the same old story!' he grumbled. 'Why didn't you send for me before? First you call the distican, then the gaddi, sorcerer, and then me as a last resort! How many times have I told you not to take palliatives?'

Gustin, Tomso, Vitoba, Franxavier, and Savitri stood at Bostião's feet. Sharp ribs seemed to pierce through his desiccated skin. At the doctor's words, the group bowed their heads, anguish etched on every face.

Dr Amoncar had grown accustomed to expressing himself bluntly. It was part of his routine, a mechanical response. It was also true that he had become hardened and was under no illusion that the fishermen would obey. These people had their distican in whom they had great faith—to take that away would perhaps do more harm than good. To Amoncar what was more urgent was to lift them out of their ignorance, to remove their inner disdain for progress. Admittedly, when all was said and done, this ignorance allowed them a happiness of sorts, yet it was also what left them powerless, subject to each and every misfortune.

'If it's a question of your fee, Doctor....'

The doctor interrupted before Gustin could finish his sentence: 'Fee! You know I've never cared a fig about my patients' money, man. I treat the poor without receiving a paisa in return. I'm interested in the way you live your lives, don't you understand?' It pained him to speak harshly once more but he was conscious of fulfilling a duty. His main task was not to treat the patients but to exert his influence over them. He had to enter the minds of these Dravidian fishermen he knew so well and whom, in consequence, he esteemed as the true men they surely were. He knew that they allowed themselves to be governed by instinct, and that their lives were ruled by omens. So he sought, whenever possible, to impart to them the most elementary knowledge about the treatment of their ills. 'Before them, millions of men lived in ignorance,' he thought. 'These men will learn too one day.' He smiled gently, reflecting on the incalculable progress made by man, that sad yet clever ape.

He finished writing out the prescription, then hesitated before passing it to one of the men.

'You can collect some of these medicines from my house. The others you will have to buy yourselves.'

Vitoba edged meekly forward: 'Thank you, Doctor. Tell us what we have to do to help rid Bostião of this sickness.'

'He can't go on sleeping on the floor. Don't you at least have a mattress?'

'A mattress...? No, Doctor,' Carminha stammered.

By this time Dona Lavínia had come in. She had entered unseen but wasted no time in making herself noticed. She cut in, 'If it's a bed you need, I can lend you one, but without a mattress. It's got boards underneath, all you need do is put a mat on top and it'll be fine.'

The fishermen stared in surprise; her conscience must have been pricked. Despite frequent 'charity visits', Dona Lavínia was incapable of lending— much less giving—anything to anyone. Confronted with pressing misfortune, she would say, 'May God help you!' and add, 'God knows I struggle to make ends meet.' Everybody knew this to be a lie. Her husband had left her a substantial inheritance, including lands rich in coconuts and rice, and her two sons had found comfortable positions in the Persian Gulf from where they sent home a generous monthly allowance.

Gustin hadn't forgiven Dona Lavínia for refusing to lend him a handful of fine rice when his daughter had taken ill and the doctor had forbidden her to eat coarse corangute grain. Wanting to teach Dona Lavínia a lesson, he retorted, 'There's no need, Lavin-bai. Poor we may be, but we can always make do a bed.'

The others pursed their lips in smiles of approval. Angelina took advantage of events to avenge the humiliation she had felt when, during the litany of the Cross, Dona Lavínia had refused to sell her coconuts to make a sweet for her guests. She added, 'We don't want your bed, Lavin-bai. If worse comes to the worst, we can always lay a mat out across a few boards....'

'What riff-raff!' Dona Lavínia exclaimed in Portuguese to the doctor. 'Miserable ingrates, the lot of them. What arrogance!'

She didn't hide her disdain for the behaviour of the 'common herd'. The only thing that allowed her to save face, and gain a measure of revenge, was the opportunity to flaunt her Portuguese to the 'riff-raff' who spoke only Konkani.

This exchange only increased Dr Amoncar's admiration for these humble, dark-skinned Shudras. At heart, he detested this silly little woman who was so tiresome and presumptuous, a consummate hypocrite, a ruthless exploiter of her own mundcars. He replied angrily, 'You're wrong, Dona Lavínia. These people aren't riff-raff, and you'd do well not to confuse dignity with arrogance! There are so many things this invalid obviously needs and what do you do? Offer to lend him a bed. Not even give—just lend. What about the rest? Bostião needs more: medicines, injections, a good diet, tonics.... Where on earth is he going to get the money for all this? For my part, I shan't receive a single paisa for my work and will try to get him his medicines for free.'

Dona Lavínia blushed crimson, before hitting back, 'You defend the dignity of these people, yet forget mine, which is of a higher order. Like you, I too am a Brahmin. As for handouts, each of us gives what we can. Our consciences are known only to ourselves and to God, Doctor.'

Dr Amoncar shrugged indifferently. Dona Lavínia grimaced with displeasure and wiped her face with her hand. Rising abruptly from the only chair in the ill-lit room, she mouthed a pretext to rush back home.

'As a good Christian, I had to fulfil my duty to visit the patient,' she said, holding her hand out to the doctor. 'But I cannot stay, you must understand. My sons arrived back from the Gulf yesterday, and the preparations for their welcome reception are not yet complete, you must understand....'

She felt much better on the way home. 'What riff-raff!' she grumbled, regretting ever having gone there. 'Heaped up like ants in that wretched little room, with that slit of a window that hardly lets in any air. Phew! How stifling it was!'

No sooner had she arrived home than she flopped down in her Voltaire armchair and began to cool herself nervously with a fan bought at the fair of our Lady of the Immaculate Conception. This gesture signalled that she was not in a good mood. Entering the room, her eldest son Robin asked, 'Mama, are you feeling poorly?'

'I'm fine,' Dona Lavínia snapped. 'It's just that those people in the village are getting airs above their station. I've just been to that fisherman Bostião's house and those riff-raff really got my goat. The worst of it was that doctor. He's in cahoots with them all.'

Robin spotted a chance to impress his mother with the knowledge he'd acquired in far-off lands and said, 'That doctor is probably a communist!'

'Heavens above!' murmured Dona Lavínia. 'These newfangled terms are too much for me...what was that again?'

IV

At Bostião's a veritable battle was being waged between the fishermen and the doctor. Dr Amoncar was striving to explain that the patient had tuberculosis and needed to be admitted to the sanatorium. Nobody would listen.

'No, Doctor, I won't go to the hospital! Leave me be here with my people! I'd prefer to die in my own village, in my own house, surrounded by Gustin, Vitoba, Tomso, and my neighbours. No, Doctor, no hospital! Never!'

The patient's feeble words were drowned out by Angelina's shrill voice, 'Dr Amoncar, if you don't want to treat my husband just be upfront about it. We'll call in another doctor. If we must we'll even pawn our fishing nets and copperware!'

'You can count on me, Angelina,' chipped in Gustin, 'I'm not rich, but I can always find some money for Bostião somewhere!'

'You can count on me too!' added Vitoba. 'Chin up, Carminha. Your father will not leave this house!'

Dr Amoncar was on the verge of giving in. He found himself on a strange battlefield, where feelings and traditions outfought reason and where he had no hope of triumph. He decided to switch tack. He turned to the patient and said with great sincerity, 'Look Bostião, forget that I'm a doctor. Let's talk man to man, okay? Tell me something, do you remember how your father died?'

'Yes, sir, it wasn't malaria...it was lung trouble....' he turned over on to his side to face the doctor, making the boards of the improvised bed groan in the process. 'You wanted him to go to the hospital too. I remember it well, Dr Amoncar.'

'Now listen to me: you've got your father's condition. Do you get that? You need to be admitted to the hospital. If you don't go, it'll be bad for you and bad for the others—they could catch your illness. If you do go, you'll get better and be home in no time!'

Bostião stopped and stared, thinking it over. He looked the doctor straight in the eye, trying to work out whether he was telling the truth, and then nodded, finally convinced. Dr Amoncar was an honest man, and never misled anybody. He'd said the same thing about Sapai and nobody had wanted to listen. And Sapai had died. Dr Amoncar was right—Sapai had died because he hadn't gone to the hospital. He looked at the doctor, his mind made up, 'The others can catch my illness, doctor? I'll go then...I don't want to be anyone's ruin. I'll go to your hospital....'

On their Dravidian faces a mixture of guilt and admiration signalled the dignified acceptance of defeat. As for Dr Amoncar, he could consider himself the victor. Yet instead of triumph, all he felt was pain. There was a lump in his throat, and he found it hard to speak.

At that moment, and against her own wishes, Dona Lavínia entered the room which reeked of medicaments and incense. She'd decided never again to cross that threshold but her damn conscience had rounded on her and wouldn't leave her alone. She had gone to confession to regain some peace of mind, and the priest had ordered that she humble herself in penitence. 'Go back to Bostião's and take him succour. You have no right to curse or despise those people. They are Shudras. You inherited your wealth and caste from your forbears, and thus have done nothing to deserve either. Remember the words of God: it is easier for a camel to pass through the eye of a needle, than for a rich man to enter the kingdom of heaven.' So she had no choice but to go. She went unwillingly, however. One couldn't go soft on these people, or they would take advantage. Looking fixedly at Bostião, she walked to the centre of the room. And then, slowly, so that everyone could see her generosity, she took a rupee from her bag and placed it in the patient's hand. 'This is for milk!' she said, stressing the word 'milk', which those people never drank. 'May God speed your recovery. I shall pray for you,' she added and was instantly moved by her own piety.

'Thank you, Lavin-bai,' Angelina murmured. 'Pray also for Carminha, who now needs her father more than ever, and for all the fisherfolk of Orlim.'

In his head, Dr Amoncar calculated the time it would take to transfer the patient to the hospital. He couldn't let another night pass, for fear they might change their minds.

'Right, you'd better get a boat ready to transport Bostião,' he exclaimed. 'I've already spoken to the hospital. All you have to do is show them this letter.'

He took a letter from his coat pocket and handed it to Gustin, the head of the group.

'Don't forget to show this at the hospital. The rest is already taken care of.'

Venctexa made a sign for the others to follow him out. Only Gustin stayed behind, listening attentively to the doctor's instructions.

'Let's see if our boat's got stuck in the soft mud. The tide's on its way out.'

The next moment, the distican appeared. She'd run all the way from the market where she'd heard the news, and was exhausted. She squeezed her way past the women and offered her help, only there was nothing left to do. Angelina had made up a little bundle of clothes and was now crying, wiping away her tears with the hem of her capod. When the fishermen returned, their feet dark with mud, her sobbing increased until it became an animal-like keening.

'What are you waiting for? You'd better take him....' Dr Amoncar growled in a harsh voice that was not his own. Angelina, Carminha, Savitri, and Dona Lavínia wept as if there, before such pain, they were equal, no longer divided by caste until their dying day. Bostião glanced up one final time at his old village: his house with its palm-leaf roof, his wife and daughter, the friends who until the last hadn't abandoned him. In the distance, the Church of our Lady of Penha de França, mirrored in the Mandovi, rose up, an embodiment of hope.

On the wharf, nothing but the sound of oars against water. And Carminha, frozen, like a statue of resignation.

VISION

M. T. VASUDEVAN NAIR

Translated from the Malayalam by A. J. Thomas

FROM TIME TO TIME SUDHA WOULD GO HOME FROM MADRAS TO HER village to visit her mother. But she shouldn't have assumed that news of her marital woes wouldn't have reached the village. She had eaten her breakfast, and was relaxing on the veranda of the house, when Amma came over and said abruptly, 'Is what we have been hearing true, Sudhakutty?'

'What have you heard?'

'That you and Prabhakaran have separated.'

Amma was blinking hard, a nervous tic that came over her whenever she was trying to talk about difficult matters. Sudha looked at her mother severely. She decided to go on the offensive rather than try to explain herself.

'How did you hear all this? Over the radio?'

Amma said: 'Sreedevi from Narayanankutty's house had come over the day before yesterday. Her devu's husband also lives in Madras.'

Sudha's older sister was also responsible for spreading the news. 'Visalam wrote. Her letter got here yesterday.' She had no doubt her other sister Chandri too would hear about this from her older sister and write to Amma as well.

Wanting some respite from the interrogation, Sudha walked into the yard. Although it was still quite early in the day, it was already very hot. She went for a walk in the shade of the compound wall. She could hear the sound of her rubber slippers echoing off the yard as she walked.

Amma lived alone in this old house. She kept visiting not only to see her mother but also for the calm these visits brought her. No telephones ringing. No parties to dress up for. No need to wear a fixed smile when she hosted parties. No need to listen to the creepy jokes of colleagues. Her visits would have been more frequent but she didn't always get permission to go on leave. And even when they were approved, they were rarely for more than three or four days. After a brief walk, as Sudha returned to the veranda, Amma said: 'People are saying all sorts of things. What actually happened?'

She did not reply.

'From what I heard....'

Amma stopped midway.

'That's right, Amma. It was better for both of us to part ways....'

Amma looked away into the yard.

When the girl who helped in the kitchen came out to ask about something, Amma rose and went inside.

Sudha had taken fifteen days' leave from the bank to make this trip home. She needed to escape the gossip and tension at work. Her colleagues had begun alluding to her troubled marriage even though she had only really opened up to the cashier, Nirmala Sreenivasan. It was Nirmala who had arranged a room for her in the YWCA.

⸜

Amma liked to live alone. She did not encourage relatives and others to visit. She had no complaints if her children did not visit. Every month, she would write an inland letter card to all three of her offspring, whether she received replies or not. She always had a girl from the neighbourhood to help out in the kitchen. On Sudha's last visit, Amma had told her about the impending wedding of the girl who had been working in the house. She was planning to give her a gold chain worth a sovereign.

'The three of you must help out as much as you can. Send a money order in the name of Kuttiraman. It's all right even if you send it in my name.'

Her older sister, Visalam, and Chandri, the younger one, were to give three hundred rupees each. Sudha was to give four hundred, because she and her husband were working, and they did not have children.

When the girl who worked for her got married, her younger sister replaced her.

Not all her children were comfortable with Amma living alone. Visalam who lived in a huge house in Thiruvananthapuram with a number of servants was the most vocal about her concern. At one family gathering, she had said: 'There isn't even a doctor nearby if she were to fall ill suddenly.'

'I won't fall ill,' was Amma's response.

A clump of banana trees grew near the compound wall, which had crumbled here and there. Through one of these gaps, a black hen and her brood entered the courtyard, hesitantly. They cautiously began foraging for food.

'It's a junglefowl and her chicks. They come around at the same time every day,' she heard Amma say.

Sudha looked at them amusedly. The mother hen kept looking around warily, clearly nervous at being so close to human habitation. Trying not to startle her, Sudha cautiously moved a little closer to get a better look at the junglefowl. But her actions spooked the hen and she scurried away with her brood.

Amma did not bring up her marriage at lunch. That evening, Sreedharanettan arrived. The older brother of her younger sister's husband. He was a high school headmaster and a local leader.

Mentally bracing herself for questions about her marriage, outwardly Sudha remained calm. She asked after his wife and children. She spoke about the weather, how hot it was.

'How many days' leave do you have, Sudhakutty?'
'A week.'
Amma butted in, 'There isn't a drop of milk to make tea for you, Sreedharan.'
'No need.'
Sreedharan then began chatting generally about things in Madras, the blazing sun of Madras, Jayalalithaa's assets, Karunanidhi's rule, etc. Sudha sat listening. There was nothing to add. She had heard that at the time when marriage proposals were coming her way, his horoscope was also under consideration by the family. Sreedharan left after a while.

In the evening, a host of dragonflies hovered in the wind. She had heard it said in her childhood that if dragonflies flew low, it indicated the onset of rains. She wished it would rain at least once. The scorching heat of the month of Meenam here was no less than the Vaikasi sun of Madras. There were no fans inside the house, and none of them had been able to agree on who would pay to have fans installed.

'You can sleep in the room in the southern wing. You'll get some breeze there,' Amma said, as she ladled out supper.
'I'm fine anywhere.'

In Amma's room, there was an old, rusty table fan which Father had bought a long time ago. Sudha hadn't brought along anything to read, nor had she bought anything on the way. On the round table in Amma's room, Father's old books remained as they were years ago. Amma used to read at night. But there were no new books. She looked at the book that Amma had placed above *A Concise History of the World*. It was *Himagiriviharam*, a book by a guru.

Amma had made up a bed for her in a room on the south side of the house. Sudha changed into a nightie. She looked at her watch. Eight forty-five. This was when Prabhakaran would return home after playing rummy and finishing two beers.

Amma came in.
'You can bring that table fan and put it here. Though it makes a sound, it still works.'
'No need.'
Wishing that Amma would go away, she made as if to go to sleep.
'And yet....'
Amma wanted to say something.
'Go on, Amma!'
'To part ways after living together for five years....'
She didn't say anything.
'What will people think?'
She turned away. Now she could avoid seeing Amma's face.
She changed the subject.
'What does one do to make a phone call here, should the necessity arise?'

'There is a booth now in the room next to the medical store. You can make a call to any place now.'

Sudha couldn't think of anything else to say.

'What have you decided?' Amma asked.

'I am thinking about it.'

'Should I come to Madras? Have a talk with Prabhakaran?'

'No. No.' She said quickly.

Amma looked at her with pity. Sudha said, trying not to lose her temper, 'There is no need for any mediation in this matter, Amma.'

Without a word, Amma left the room. Sudha knew that Amma wouldn't raise this issue any more. Amma's nature was to suffer silently. Father had died after one and a half years of being bedridden, having suffered a paralytic stroke. Amma never complained in all that time. She refused to say anything even when people were whispering about his kept woman who had swindled them of all his savings.

In the morning, Amma said, 'Valyamma of Cholayil said she wants to meet you. Janu told Valyamma that you were expected. She met her when she went to buy milk from her neighbour.'

'I will go and meet her.'

'You said you would go during your last visit, too, but you didn't.'

'Right.'

'She is going on eighty-four. We don't know how long she'll live. Her eyesight is almost gone. But she doesn't fuss about anything.'

Valyamma of Cholayil was the older sister of their grandmother. They had called her Valyamma hearing Amma call her that. Valyamma had lived in the house as her younger sister's guest long ago. In the mornings, she would often braid and tie up Visaledatthi's hair. In the evening, she would gather the girls together to recite the evening prayer.

Grandma would sleep on the floor and leave the cot for her big sister, Valyamma. She was fond of telling stories at bedtime. Night after night, Sudhakutty was her only avid listener. Visalam would avoid getting caught in that situation and Chandri would be dozing off. Grandma listened, half-nodding, she recollected. The story of Unniyamma who shielded Palat Koman behind her thick, long hair, and the legend of Kannagi and Kovalan were imprinted on her mind. When they had visited Madurai for the first time, they recalled how Valyamma told the story of Kannagi. She would narrate it as if she had been an eyewitness to Kannagi plucking out her breast and burning the city with it.

Sudha had met Valyamma last when she had gone to get her blessings before her wedding. That was more than five years ago. Even when their grandma was alive, they were fonder of Valyamma for some reason. In the last five years, she had visited Amma seven times. Yes, seven times. Prabhakaran was with her on two of these visits. Valyamma had asked after her on all those occasions. Her house was not even three furlongs away, yet she hadn't gone to see her even once, something or the other had always cropped up. The last time around she had planned to get her something. But on the day fixed for shopping, she and Prabhakaran had quarrelled. She had ended up spending the day lying down quietly in the hotel room until it was time to catch the train.

The junglefowl family came out to the front yard again the next day. They did not seem as afraid this time. Sudha slowly walked up to the hen and her brood; their black feathers were shining in the sun.

Just then she heard someone calling out: 'Guests have arrived.' The hen and her chicks scurried away in alarm.

She turned to see Sreedevi Amma and her younger sister standing in the courtyard.

Amma invited them to sit down as was customary and asked Janu to make tea. Then, after giving Sudha a disapproving look, she went inside.

The look conveyed something like, 'Listen to a mouthful from her!'

Sreedevi Amma said: 'Sit down, Sudha. Let me talk. Don't be annoyed.'

Sudha did not sit down. She tried to smile, but failed.

'Go on,' she said.

'Why beat around the bush? I can't help but talk. If what I heard is correct, it is in bad taste.'

Sudha made as if to smile. And then, as if it were a simple matter, she replied, 'Yes, it's bad. But there's no other way.'

Sreedevi Amma's face turned dark. She glanced at her younger sister as if to prompt her to speak. The younger sister picked up from there, 'If there's something to what Narayanankutty was saying, it'll be a matter of shame for our family.'

Sudha didn't respond.

'To say that you want to separate after living together for five years....' She looked at Sreedevi Amma, 'Why don't you tell her what you were thinking?'

'Certainly, things go wrong sometimes; there may be problems but one must put up with them. That's what marriage is all about. Your Amma put up with so much, don't you know?'

Sudha tried to stay calm. The first thing she felt like blurting out was, 'O Sreedevi Amma! The fault is not Prabhakaran's, but mine!' Then she decided against speaking her mind.

They went on talking.

She had, from early childhood, developed a miraculous ability to tune out unwanted conversations. She would start to think of other things—the names she had forgotten, the characters in novels, the topography of the places she had seen in childhood, the faces of her classmates from elementary school—and the voices would go away at once.

As she was leaving, Sreedevi Amma said, 'Do you think shouting myself hoarse has been utterly useless?'

'No,' she said.

'Don't you think there's at least some sense in what I said?'

'Yes.'

Sreedevi Amma heaved a sigh of relief. 'What's your decision, then?'

'Let me think about it,' she said, laughing.

With the satisfaction of having succeeded in their mission, Sreedevi Amma and her younger sister left in good spirits.

Amma asked, 'When are you going to see Valyamma of Cholayil?'

'I'll go soon.'

Valyamma too would be waiting for her, wanting to give her advice.

At midday, Sumathi, who was her classmate in high school, visited with her three-year-old daughter. She used to wait for her at the boundary wall of the carpenter family's house every day when they went to school together. The wart below her nose looked as if it had grown bigger. She had married before she had completed Class X.

Sumathi did not sit down, although Sudha urged her to take a seat.

'How are you, Sumathi? Happy?'

'Just going on.'

She wore a shiny sari on which blue, violet, and red stood out loudly. Her husband, who worked in the Gulf, must have bought it for her. Every two years, he would visit on two months' leave. A pungent perfume encased her. Her neck and her hands were covered in gold ornaments leaving not an inch uncovered.

'I heard that you had come. Are you going to be here for a few more days?'

'Yes. For a few more days.'

Next Monday would be the house-warming of Sumathi's new house.

'Sudhakutty, you must certainly come!'

'I will, if I am around.'

Tousling the hair of the girl who stood tracing the flowers on Amma's sari, Sudha said, 'I'm sorry, I've forgotten her name.'

'Karthika.'

She tried to get hold of Karthika's hands and draw her near. The child snivelled and stood by her mother, winding her tiny hands around her body.

Sumathi whispered: 'I heard something is amiss....'

'O, did you hear it too?'

'When the wife of Sankarettan who does the mosaic work told me, I didn't believe it.'

Sudha hummed under her breath.

'Is it true, Sudhakutty?'

Sudha laughed, 'Somewhat....'

Widening her eyes in alarm, Sumathi leaned forward and said softly: 'Please don't think that I am advising someone who has more education and wisdom than me but it's better to live together whichever way you look at it.'

Sudha stroked her hand.

'Hmmm. Let me think about it.'

'Your first mistake was to decide to not have children immediately. If there are children, there wouldn't be any unwelcome thoughts in the man or woman.'

Sudha looked at Sumathi wonderingly. A local phrase she should inscribe on her mind was 'unwelcome thoughts'.

Sumathi left. Later, Janu who had gone out to buy milk, said upon her return that Valyamma of Cholayil had once again enquired after her. Amma said, 'Go and meet her once, please!'

'Hmmm. I will go tomorrow.'

'She does not need any money. Nevertheless, give her something. When Visalam went to see her, she gave her fifty rupees and the old lady wouldn't stop talking about it.'

Amma laughed. This was the first time that Sudha saw Amma's face brighten up ever since she had arrived.

Sudha thought of countering, 'I am not going to compete with Visaledatthi.'

She decided that she would return to Madras on Monday. There was no way she was going to spend all the two weeks of her vacation in the village. There has already been so much commotion within three days of her arrival.

Should she call the one in Hyderabad, she wondered. She had jotted down his mobile number in her diary. His direct number in the office, she had inscribed in her mind.

There's no one who could book a ticket for her. Never mind. She could get into the ladies' compartment. It's just a matter of a night.

He had told her to call him when she got to her ancestral home.

'If possible,' he had added.

The next day, after breakfast, she said, 'I'll go meet Valyamma now.'

'Take Janu along with you.'

'No need.'

First, she went to the newly-built house of the Asaripparambil family. Sumathi was beside herself with wonder and joy. She belonged to a lower sub-caste and had not expected Sudha to visit her at home. She was at a loss as to how to entertain her guest. Two workers were varnishing the window shutters, under the supervision of the carpenter Narayanan.

She was taken on a tour of the house.

'Both rooms have attached baths,' Sumathi said with pride.

She struggled to sidestep Sumathi's request to drink something before she left.

'My husband has written that he'll come on leave in July.'

'Ask him to take you along the next time he returns to Dubai. That way you too can see the city.'

'That's not possible. Only those with high salaries can manage that, he says.'

Yet, Sumathi was very happy.

'I'm off, Sumathi. I have to visit Valyamma of Cholayil.'

'You remember what I said, don't you?'

'Yes.'

She laughed.

On the way to Valyamma's house she passed a clump of bamboo by a dried-up stream. Earlier, there were thickets on either side of the stream. In those days, it used to be full of water in all seasons. During the monsoons, it would brim over the banks. Farther down, it would become broader and become a small tributary of the river downstream.

Valyamma's house had been built in her father's elder brother's time. There was a bamboo stile in place of the old gatehouse now. When she climbed the steps and reached the courtyard, there was no one around. Black pepper had been spread out to dry on the bamboo mat in the yard.

She stood there hesitantly. It was Thankedatthi, the cousin who lived with Valyamma, when she came out on the veranda.

'What a surprise to see you here! Grandma had mentioned you just this morning. She was worried that you'd go away without meeting her.'

Thankedatthi sat her down on a chair placed next to the woodwork railing.

She began to talk about her family. Both her boys were studying. They had returned to the hostel the previous week because they had to prepare for their practical exams. Her daughter, the youngest, was in Class IX. Thankedatthi's younger sisters had divided the property when their mother died. They had sold their shares and built houses on their husbands' land and were living there.

'This tottering, mouldering old house fell to my lot. There was no one to take my side....'

She choked on her words as she remembered the passing of her husband, as she was expected to. She went through the motions of wiping her eyes.

'Where's Valyamma?'

'In the vadakkiny, the northern wing of the house. Her eyesight is almost gone but she resents anyone holding her hand to help her. Who knows when she's going to stumble and fall!'

Just then she heard Valyamma saying: 'No one will have to face any trouble on account of me.'

When Valyamma held out her hands to feel the frame of the door opening on to the veranda, and carefully stepped on the threshold to the veranda, Sudha hurried over to her. Even at eighty-four, she stood ramrod straight. The rauka, traditional blouse, and the upper cloth she wore over it were dazzling white. The mundu with a decorative border that she had draped around her waist was stiffly starched. The luminous face that Sudha had seen in her childhood had not dimmed even a bit. She took special note of the thickness of her snow-white hair, done up in the classical style. When she had heard the tale about Komappan of the *Northern Ballads*, she would imagine it was Valyamma herself who had hidden him behind her hair, while bathing in the pond.

When Thankedatthi tried to bring a chair for her, Valyamma said, 'No, I'll sit here. Sit down, Sudhakutty!'

She extended her hand towards Sudha's.

Sudha sat next to Valyamma and leaned against the parapet of the veranda.

'Haven't you put on weight, Sudhakutty?'

She looked at her own hands. Yes, Valyamma was right. She had indeed put on weight.

'You were gasping when you walked four steps towards me? I could make out that you had put on weight just by listening to your breathing, without actually seeing your body.'

Valyamma laughed.

There were lifeless spots in her ashen eyes, but her face was smooth. Only a few folds on her neck were indicative of ageing.

'Thankam! Make some tea. Fry some jackfruit kernels too.'

'No! I don't want anything. Just half a glass of tea will do,' Sudha said.

Valyamma waited for Thankedatthi to go inside the house and then said: 'What did you decide, my child?' Valyamma's abrupt question made her flinch.

'Don't be afraid. I didn't call you here to shout at you or admonish you. Hasn't it been four or five years since I saw you last?'

She felt relieved.

'The ones around here merely grin when I speak my mind about anything. They think, "What does this old one, with both her eyes blinded with cataract, see?" But are they able to see what I see?'

She guessed that it was for the benefit of Thankedatthi in the kitchen that Valyamma raised her voice as she said this.

Valyamma lowered her voice again, 'What have you decided?'

Her breathing quickened.

'If you feel that you are through with him, get rid of him. This arrangement called marriage is for our convenience. There's no point in engaging in an act for the benefit of others.'

Valyamma sighed deeply, crossed her legs, and leaned forward.

'None of you met my first husband.'

'Amma has seen him. He was a Bhagavathar, a vocalist, wasn't he?'

'That's how the trouble started. Music classes were held at the sharathu, household of a Pisharoty, a higher sect Sannyasi Brahmin; he would eat at our house. His singing was excellent. He wore gold earrings in which red gemstones were embedded, sandal paste on his forehead, and looked so striking. I was infatuated with him.'

Valyamma laughed quietly, running her fingers through her hair.

'He went away before the year was out.'

'Amma said so.'

Valyamma whispered, 'He didn't go away on his own. I asked him to leave.'

Valyamma kept smiling, her sightless gaze fixed on nothing in particular.

'He wasn't able to provide for me. I let that be. But he had a kind of lisping affectation in his speech and coquettish gestures! Mannerisms of women. Shouldn't men be at least a bit manly and smart? I told him bluntly that he would have to leave, that our marriage was over. What else was there to do?'

Although she had heard about Valyamma's first marriage with the Bhagavathar, she didn't know much about it. She had then married Valyachchan. He was a peon in the government salt depot. The couple had three children. Valyachchan died. Then the children died too. Valyamma was left alone.

'Hadn't you seen him? Valyachchan was not that handsome or anything. Was he?'

'I saw him when I was a child. He was on his deathbed at that time.'

'There wasn't anyone like him in this entire land. He'd always be there right in front of the temple festival procession.'

Thankedatthi brought tea.

When Thankedatthi was standing nearby, Valyamma sat with a serious mien without saying anything. When she went back into the house, Valyamma began to smile, as she remembered Valyachchan.

'Those who saw only his exterior would say he was a boor. He would shout and create a ruckus most of the time. But only I knew how gentle a soul he was. Even if I so much as caught a cold, he would fuss about it.'

Valyamma suddenly laughed out aloud.

Sudha forgot about her troubles. She sat waiting with the same eagerness she'd had as a child for whatever Valyamma was going to say next.

'Everything was going smoothly, suddenly some trouble arose. It was just after I had given birth to Kuttinarayanan.'

'What?'

'Imagine.... I was attracted to another man. I told myself, "You wretch; control yourself, forget about this." So, things didn't go out of hand. Still....'

Without completing the sentence, Valyamma laughed out loud, open-mouthed. She saw that Valyamma had lost only her wisdom teeth.

'I was exactly your age, then,' Valyamma heaved a sigh.

'Is he still around, Valyamma?'

Valyamma's face clouded over.

'Gone. Everyone's gone. I am the only one left. Until I'm called, when the time comes, I'll just lie here. I can't kill myself!'

She shook her head.

'Who is the other one, Sudhakutty?'

She was startled, 'Eh?'

'You met someone. You like him. And you decided that you are going to be with him. Isn't this what has happened?'

'Who told you?'
Valyamma pulled up her legs.
'There's no need for anyone to tell me. Who is it, my dear girl?'
She tried to control her agitation.
'Is it someone who you work with?'
'No.'
She could not explain it to Valyamma. She had met him at a farewell dinner that was being given for the manager of the branch where he'd been transferred. Late in the evening the chief guest, the organizers of the party, other guests were all quite drunk. It was then that she had spotted him, standing by himself at one end of the hall. She had not heard him earlier. He held a glass of orange juice. He stood looking at her now and again and then finally moved towards her. As he walked towards her, she thought to herself in a frenzy of excitement: 'My lord! He is coming towards me. Please God, what am I going to say?'
She was so happy when he told her that he would be in Madras for ten days every month. Watching other people move towards them, he said, 'Can I call you at the bank?'
She nodded quietly.
Valyamma said, 'Does he have a wife?'
'No.'
'Does Prabhakaran know?'
Her reply was a bit delayed, 'I think he suspects.'
'Then, you must separate immediately. Prabhakaran will also get another girl. Don't bother too much about such things. Get rid of him.'
Sudha was amused. 'It's not that easy to get rid of him like in the old days, Valyamma.'
'If you don't want him, you don't want him. Doesn't it end there?'
'No, it doesn't end there. First, there needs to be a joint petition. The judge will then summon both of us after six months and ask us whether we are still bent on parting. Even if we say yes, we have to wait another six months.'
She watched agitation spreading over Valyamma's face.
'Does it need the judge's consent if two people meet, like each other, and decide to live together?'
'That's the law, Valyamma.'
Valyamma was not at all satisfied.
'If there are children, their expenses and other things have to be settled, yes. That's the proper way. But what has the judge got to do with two people who like each other living together?'
'That's the law.'
'What law...?'
Thankedatthi came over to pick up the empty glass. Valyamma mumbled something to herself. Thankedatthi said, 'Till last year, Grandma could still see things faintly. Now she's completely blind.'

Sudha said, 'She can regain her eyesight with surgery, even at such an advanced age. I can take her to Madras.'

Valyamma laughed bitterly.

'No, no. Why should I have eyesight at this stage? I'm done with all that I've seen so far!'

Sudha prepared to leave.

Thankedatthi said, 'You can leave after lunch.'

'Oh no! Amma would've prepared lunch for me.'

'The rice is cooking. When you come next, visit us, please, Sudhakutty.'

Thankedatthi went inside. Her fourteen-year-old daughter arrived at the gate just then. Valyamma looked over to the gate. Removing her chappals and leaving them below the veranda, the girl looked at Sudha and smiled. Lowering her head, she walked inside without making any noise. When she reached the door, Valyamma asked, 'Hey! Where have you been?'

The girl was startled.

'To the sharath. To get a book from Sarada.'

'Why should you wear a silk skirt to the sharath, like a vamp?'

The girl went pale and quickly escaped inside.

Valyamma turned her face towards Sudha.

'There was no book in her hands, was there?'

'Aye, no.'

'I knew that it was silk by the rustling of the skirt.'

'She is a child, Valyamma.'

'Hmm...mm. The girl is flirtatious beyond her age. I can see everything.'

'May I get going?'

Valyamma stood up.

Remembering what Amma had said, she opened the purse in her hand.

Valyamma said, 'No need. It seems you are going to give me some money. Don't. What need does this Valyamma have for money?'

She closed the purse in amazement.

'When you come...next time....'

Valyamma's voice faltered.

'...if I am around, just come and meet me. I need only that....'

She saw Valyamma's lightless eyes tear up. Her eyes, too, were brimming. She bent down, touched Valyamma's feet, paying obeisance. She remembered having done exactly the same thing five years ago.

Valyamma placed her hand softly on Sudha's head.

'Let the best happen to you, at least this time around.'

She walked out. When she reached the market, she saw the signboard of the STD booth from a distance.

She turned the two phone numbers she had memorized over in her mind. She reminded herself that she should look up her diary and confirm the mobile number. If, after making the call, she was able to reach home quickly, she would not miss the junglefowl and its brood entering the courtyard.

She quickened her steps.

GREEN SPARROWS

AJEET COUR

Translated from the Punjabi by the author

IT WAS THE MONTH OF KARTIK. THE HOT SUN BLAZED THROUGHOUT THE day. Clear and sharp, its glare was unbearable.

He wore dark sunglasses when he went out. Still, in a couple of hours, he would get a headache, his eyes would be tired and he would return and seek solace in the darkness of his room.

He had come home after almost seven years. Life in a foreign land moves along a set rhythm. The morning passed in a rush: getting up, shaving, a quick shower, pulling on one's clothes with an eye on the clock. Then, running for the subway to his office. A sandwich and coffee for lunch. Then, back home in the evening.

Sometimes, a pub. Drunken gossip with friends and then home again. Heating up something out of a can—beans mostly, or scrambled eggs, toast. And then, bed.

Only Saturday and Sunday were different. On both these days the morning alarm would be silent. His impotent irritation with the alarm would also ease. He would sleep until late. Then, he would go for a walk and meet Emma.

Sunday afternoon he would cook chicken and manh ki dal, with a garnishing of ginger and green chillies! The back door of the kitchen would remain closed so that the sharp pungent aroma of the tempering would not pervade the neighbourhood! Shopping! Groceries for the week would be bought. Then, a long and vigorous bath. Laundry. House cleaning! Watching television or listening to music!

Saturday afternoon to Sunday evening, Emma would be with him in his flat. She would go back home on Sunday evening.

Only her toothbrush, nightie, and towel would be left in his flat. Her towel would hang on the rod, drying in his bathroom, for the next two days.

Abruptly, after seven years, he was back home, and free. Free of work, and free of worries. Every day was like Saturday and Sunday for him now. He was totally idle, crowded in by a host of Saturdays and Sundays.

He had nothing to do. No rush to wake up, he slept till late in the morning.

His room was on the rooftop, a barsati, a terrace apartment. It had been his own place since childhood. When he had been young, it had been his study. Later, he had also started sleeping here.

Years ago, the family had slept on the terrace during summers. They slept indoors during winter. He had slept in his mother's room; he and his younger sister, Ashu. Bauji, his father, slept in the next room.

Biji, his mother, put the stuffed paratha and a glass of milk on the table and sat down on a chair near him....

It seemed as if she wanted to say something, but could not decide how to begin the conversation.

As he broke a morsel of paratha, he felt as if his fingers had lost some of their nimbleness.

'Are you not eating?' he asked, trying to overcome the sense of uncertainty he was feeling.

'I can't eat parathas now. Bad for the stomach....' Biji replied diffidently. She felt strange talking to her own son, who had come back home after such a long sojourn abroad.

What is it that has come between us, he asked himself. This feeling of alienation!

Perhaps it was the distance of seven years that stood between them, frozen and still like ice.

They had lived these seven years differently, fighting different battles. He and Biji. Why only Biji and him? All of them—Bauji, Kamal, and Ashu.

They had asked him to come home for Ashu's wedding! Ashu had written to him, appealing to him to come! But he couldn't. He had been studying medicine, and had to work in the library for three hours daily to pay his fees. Later on, he had got a scholarship, but the two years in between had been extremely difficult. It had meant studying for long hours, attending practicals and dissections. Then, in the evening, working in the library, on his feet for three hours, to earn a living. Life stretched out as a long journey of weariness, exhaustion, and running about. All the threads of his life seemed to be strung to the hands of a clock. And the clock was running faster than he could!

No, he had not been able to attend Ashu's wedding.

After that, he did not know how, and when, the letters from home had become cold and distant.

And now he was looking at his old life from beyond the seven years he had lived abroad. Distance had made many things hazy.

Even now, there were things, which, when seen at close quarters, pierced the heart like shards of broken glass.

He did not know why, but he was upset with himself as he ate the paratha. As if he had stolen something from his family in broad daylight. His feelings surprised him.

He thought...arre, this is your own mother! She who sits in the chair near you. Sad, but looking at you with tolerant eyes. The same mother with whom you would quarrel for four or eight annas, new socks, or a new pen. Who had looked behind your ears to see if they had been washed properly or not! Who had pulled your ears, and also smacked you—and sometimes had hidden you to save you from Bauji's beatings.

This is the same mother whose bed you would stealthily creep into at night when you felt scared!

But ever since he had come home, an awkward distance yawned between Biji, Bauji, and him.

Ashu was with her in-laws in Chandigarh. Her husband was an IAS officer and was posted there. He had forgotten whether he was with the Punjab government or Haryana government, though Bauji had told him. But what difference did that make?

The day after his arrival, Ashu's husband had called from Chandigarh. Ashu had also talked to him. After a couple of minutes, he had felt that there was hardly anything to say on either side.

'Achcha then,' he had said.

This was the same Ashu whose plaits he used to pull, wrestle with, crack jokes with, squabble with over marbles or crayons or books, or scold for cheating at cards, and with whom he fought over comics.

What had happened to him that he was no longer fit even to quarrel with anyone! Not to fight, not to be upset, and not even to have the pleasure of making up.

༄

Biji sat on one side of the table, and he on the other, trying to eat the paratha.

Finally, Biji said softly, 'Maybe you could visit Ashu for a few days....'

Visit Ashu's in-laws' home? What would he talk to them about? What would he say to anyone there? Ashu's husband! A stranger who was married to his sister! The same Ashu, his doll-like sister. Ashu, in bed with that stranger....

He was upset with himself, his own thoughts.

You cannot talk to your own mother, you sit silent reading a newspaper with your father! What will you talk about with those strangers? he reproved himself.

'We can invite Ashu here,' he suggested.

'But what will her in-laws say? Why don't you go and fetch her? Spend a day there and then come back with her and Bubbles the next day. If Kuldip can get leave from work, invite him too.'

Biji was not demanding that he do this. Request? There was no request either. It was as if she were talking to a neighbour, asking him if he was going to the bazaar, and if he was, could he get a box of matches for her.

Yet, there was, perhaps, a trace of some mild entreaty in her voice.

He stayed silent, taking refuge in sipping hot milk.

༄

After breakfast, he walked around the veranda outside, and then came back into the sitting room. Bauji was reading the newspaper. As he walked into the room, Bauji held it out and asked, 'Newspaper...?'

He took it.

The pages of the newspaper fluttered like the wings of an injured crane in the air swirling under the ceiling fan. He opened the paper and looked over the printed words, conscious of Bauji's eyes on him through his thick glasses. There was a strangely helpless and bemused look on Bauji's face. Trying hard to make sure that nothing would offend or upset his foreign-returned son.

Wasn't Bauji avoiding him these days? As if he were a special guest who could not be disturbed.

He realized that he was not reading the newspaper, but was merely trying to hide behind it. He felt dismayed to see his father, who had always had such a regal and dignified aura about him, look so vulnerable. He felt a sense of fear grip him. This fear was absolutely different from the fear he used to feel in his childhood, which had driven him and his sister to hide in their own secret haven when they heard him come into the house. At that time, it was Biji's kitchen which seemed the safest place to hide in; rather like a 'no-war zone' under UN observation.

This helplessness of Bauji's he could not bear. It was like the wretchedness of a torn quilt from which clumps of cotton wool escaped the rent fabric. But the arm that he could extend in support hesitated; it was difficult for that arm to reach his father, because a wide distance of seven years sprawled between them, frozen over, and hard like the ice of the South Pole!

A desert of snow!

A piercing ray of bright sunlight had penetrated the glass panes of the window and, peeping into the room from behind the curtains, stretched out across the worn-out old carpet.

Even otherwise, there was a naked brightness in this room. Upstairs, he had put up thick, dark-coloured bedcovers over the curtains on all the windows of his terrace barsati. Thick covers and curtains, both had combined to preserve the darkness of night inside, keeping the bright glare of the October sun out of the room.

But, here, under the brilliance of the sun, and under Bauji's eyes, he felt strangely conspicuous and exposed.

In a daze, he gave the paper back to Bauji.

'Have you read it?' Bauji asked in a manner which held no question.

'Bas!' he answered softly, tiptoeing out of the room and towards the stairs.

'What should I cook?' Biji walked out. She stood at the back door, which opened into the backyard. Actually, it opened on to a veranda, which led to the backyard. The stairs to the terrace were in the backyard.

'Whatever you like,' he replied and hurriedly went up.

He felt very safe in his room. Safe and secure.

Lighting a cigarette, he fell on the bed. Suddenly, he noticed a cobweb in the corner of the room. 'Arre! Still there?' he thought. Since the day he had come, whenever he lay on his back on the bed with a cigarette, he noticed the cobweb. Every time he thought: I will sweep it away with a long brush or broom when I get up. But, once the cigarette was done, he would turn on his side, close his eyes and fall asleep, forgetting the cobweb.

'Surely, today....' he decided.

⁌

He was eating a paratha. Bauji sat nearby, listening to the radio, and looking at him. Biji sat on a low stool, her chin resting on her palm, and head leaning on the kitchen door's jamb. The skin of her face was like dried strips of turnip—her face, her hands, and elbows too. Like a crumpled sheet of waste paper.

He thought that in these last seven years her eyes had shrunk. They had always shone brightly, like brilliant lights. Now they were shrivelled and bleary. Like small puddles of wet mud dotting the road after a heavy shower.... If you think of it, it is nothing. You hardly feel the passing of the years. Mornings, evenings...and time goes on. Till you look in the mirror and see someone else's face! You are taken aback, perplexed. Then, the realization of time gone by, clear and sharp, pierces your heart just like a shard of broken glass.

Suddenly, he thought of Emma. If he wanted to share this sensation that he just experienced—of the glittering dagger-point piercing him—with Emma, would she understand it? Did she understand him? Perhaps not. One cannot convey the intensity of one's emotion to another.

'Poor words....' he thought.

Bauji switched off the radio. The news was over. He was surprised that the room had all along been filled with the newsreader's voice, yet he had not heard anything.

Bauji said with a slight laugh, 'I am also getting parathas to eat these days—stuffed with cheese, cauliflower, radish, and methi! Otherwise, your mother doesn't cook. She just gives me a glass of milk, that is all. And boiled eggs.'

'What to cook for two people...and what not to cook!' Biji replied with a deep sigh.

He thinks: all this is not being said to Bauji. She says it to you but it is meant for me.

'When the sabziwallah comes to the lane I buy a few vegetables and cook, otherwise we make do with dal. Sometimes, I do not have the strength even for that. Bas...then we just eat some bread with milk.' Biji seemed to be in the mood to talk today. Less with him, more with her own self. Biji...who had always been so silent....

Perhaps this was her way of telling him: 'Come home. Stay!' The obvious.

He understood, yet persisted in pretending not to understand the obvious.

⸙

Every day the sparrows raised a hue and cry at the break of dawn. His first morning in Delhi—when he had got up early in the morning—he had thought that he was hearing all this clamour in his sleep. Drifting in and out of sleep, the tumult of the sparrows had seemed mysterious. As if his childhood had come back and was standing near his bed, laughing at him.

Those days, Biji would wake him up with a laugh, 'Even the sparrows are up and about, but this boy is still in bed! Get up, don't you have to go to school?'

Implying that the lesson that even the unlettered foolish sparrows had learnt—getting up when the sun is not yet out—was wasted. Why couldn't he learn that lesson?

And he would sheepishly get up.

Lying on his bed, he peeped into his childhood and smiled.

Now that he had been here for all these days, he was used to the clamour of the sparrows.

The day of his departure was also drawing closer.

After eating the paratha, he again came back to his room on the terrace.

The room wore an extremely forlorn look.

Gradually, it seemed as if the roof of the room had disappeared. The roofless room seemed desolate in the vast blue expanse of the dusty huge vacuum of space. Then, slowly and softly, even the walls of the roofless room seemed to recede. He lay on his bed, alone, in endless vastness, in eternity. Then, he did not know when even the floor from under the bed disappeared. And, it seemed to him that he was floating in the air. Like a leaf fluttering in gusts of wind...like a scrap of paper in infinite space. Who was he? Why was he? Where were his roots? And who was rooted in the soil of his mind? He did not know.

Solitary! A non-entity!

A sparrow twittered. He floated down to earth, like a rag of muslin. The bed came down. The floor under the bed came back. The walls also came back from their wanderings.

The sparrow seemed to be chirping only for him. Full of wondrous joy. When it twittered, its whole body quivered, the shiver starting at its beak and weaving through the last feather on its tail. It sang in happy abandonment, full of extraordinary intoxication.

It seemed to him as if he were a king and the sparrow his slave singing only for his pleasure.

Suddenly, an idea came to him, 'Don't these sparrows grow old?'

It startled him. He had seen dogs growing old, and also seen old cats. Horses, lions, all of them grow old. And gradually become helpless and die...like human beings...dependent, lonely, and colourless. Slowly breaking away from life. Dying bit by bit.

But these sparrows.... He had never seen an old sparrow, friendless, sitting quietly, with its beak hanging open listlessly. He had never seen a sparrow walking with halting steps, half bent. He had always seen sparrows singing and hopping about, with a flutter of wings, their bodies quivering with an eternal thirst for life. Always in a group, with other sparrows, singing—wanton and enraptured! Full of life! Intoxicated! Forever celebrating life! Evergreen sparrows!

When they die, they must be dying suddenly. Singing away, he thought to himself.

Why doesn't man die suddenly? With a song on his lips!

MRS CROCODILE

MANOJ DAS

*Translated from the Odia by Leelawati Mohapatra,
Paul St-Pierre, and K. K. Mohapatra*

MILES AND MILES OF SWAMPS; VAST STRETCHES OF SAND, MUDFLATS, and backwaters—none of this seemed to have fazed pre-eminent anthropologist Dr Batstone. He took a train, a jeep, and a bullock cart before trudging over a mile on foot to finally arrive at our village in the middle of nowhere, in the back of beyond.

A man who had lived all his life in Western cities amid high-rises, Dr Batstone's first wish when he touched down on Indian soil was to visit a truly primitive village.

In those days, when we were still in school, the gulf between towns and villages hadn't shrunk as much as now. The villages were yet to become the distorted shadows of towns. Huge red triangles, those ubiquitous symbols of the government's family planning programme, the election slogans of political parties, advertisements of small-saving schemes or brands of cigarettes had not yet made their appearance on village walls; microphones hadn't yet arrived.

'Wonderful! Amazing!' Sprawled in a wooden armchair on the veranda of our house, Dr Batstone erupted into delighted exclamations every five minutes: 'Wonderful! Amazing!'

His sense of wonder and heightened feelings was understandable. Wasn't it awe-inspiring to be able to survey, without interruption, the full horizon of the clear uncluttered sky to one's heart's content? To see a young cowherd boy controlling a large herd of perhaps a hundred head or more, across unending pastures? Watching the cattle following peaceably without breaking ranks, Dr Batstone experienced the same heady feeling he had while reading 'The Pied Piper' for the first time as a child. Wasn't it wonderful that ninety per cent of village folk could live in perfect harmony and happiness, without any regrets whatsoever, without ever having seen a train or a cinema!

But more than anything else, it was the interview with Maku Mishra, the venerable headmaster of the village lower-primary school that stoked the distinguished visitor's sense of wonder and awe. In all his forty years of imparting precious education to the village ragamuffins, Mishra hadn't heard of Darwin, Marx, Freud, Einstein, or Bernard Shaw—not even one of the illustrious five!

That a white man would one day make a trip to our village was beyond the wildest imagination of the local inhabitants. Even *Malika*, the Book of Predictions, which had unerringly predicted the devastating mid-century cyclone, the sudden collapse of the local temple, and the emergence of Mohandas Karamchand Gandhi on the political firmament of India, had remained pointedly silent about this eventuality. No wonder, then, that at any given point of time about twenty or two dozen villagers sat cross-legged around the visiting sahib, gaping and gawking.

The sahib too caught on that the villagers meant no harm, that their behaviour was driven by simple curiosity. Bemused, he told me more than once with a smile: 'Where else could I have experienced anything of this kind? If I'd known how to dance I'd have danced up a whirlwind to entertain these God's good people sitting in front of me.'

As he was getting emotionally entangled in the lives of the villagers, he once asked me, out of the blue: 'Well, my dear boy, do these people believe in ghosts and spirits?'

Over the days I had proven to be his most reliable interpreter. As soon as I translated his question for the benefit of the crowd, they all answered loudly in the negative, which made the sahib sit up straight. It was his turn to be amazed. After a long silence he turned to me: 'You know something, babu! These people are more modern and progressive than my countrymen. Believe me, more than fifty per cent of our people believe in ghosts and spirits, whether they admit it or not. Just go on and ask these good people—do they believe in God?'

I translated his question. There was an uneasy silence.

'What's the matter—aren't they sure?' asked the sahib, trying to interpret their silence. 'They're having doubts, right?' His voice was deep with respect. 'Believe me, no matter how rational the people of my country may outwardly seem, they....'

Then there was an uproar as one villager after another began to respond excitedly: 'Never trust ghosts or spirits, sahib! They've no conscience at all.'

'Would you believe it, sahib,' said another. 'My cousin—actually my father's uncle's son-in-law's own nephew—what haven't I done for him, beginning with sharing my pillow to doing his wedding shopping! What haven't I done for the bastard! Who'd believe that once dead he'd zero in on me, of all the people in this village and beyond, to scare the living daylights out of! Who doesn't know I footed half the expenses for his funeral rituals, which were observed in great style? Who doesn't know I couldn't stir out at night to my own backyard to piss or shit, until his spirit was properly appeased.'

'Sahib,' said yet another. 'You're a foreigner. You shouldn't believe in the ghosts and spirits of our country. They're so nasty that given half a chance they'll twist the neck of the exorcist who tries to keep them on a leash.'

'Of course,' added a fourth, 'there are kind and helpful spirits too—nobody can deny that. As a child I've seen the Languli Baba with my own eyes.' Turning to me, he pleaded: 'Explain to the sahib who Languli Baba is, will you? The great naked seer. When I saw him he was already over two hundred years old.' The villager turned to the white man and went on excitedly: 'The circumstances of his auspicious birth are shrouded in mystery. There was once a great epidemic of cholera sweeping the land. His mother, then pregnant with him, was taken for dead and hauled off to the cremation grounds by her relations. It was there the holy man tumbled out of his mother's womb. He lay there crying helplessly for one whole night and a day before another group of mourners reached the cremation grounds. They picked him up from between his dead mother's legs. Tell us, sahib, who looked after the mahatma during those crucial twenty-four hours?'

The compulsively argumentative villager who had asked the question inched closer to the white man and offered the answer himself. 'The spirits and ghosts, of course. No wonder the mahatma neither wore clothes nor spoke to a living being. Whenever an intense desire for conversation came over him he'd hold parleys only with those invisible souls.

'As to your question about believing in God, sahib—is he some kind of a moneylender and we his debtors, or vice versa, that the question of trusting or not would arise at all? He created everything and put us at the heart of it. Now, he might choose to get rid of us, or then again he might decide to keep us...'

The way the crowd nodded it seemed everyone wholeheartedly agreed with him.

I translated as best I could. The sahib listened intently and leaned back in the armchair. 'Fabulous!' he gurgled. 'Amazing!'

'Sahib,' said another villager. 'Do you see the cremation grounds beyond the river? That was where the great naked baba was born. If you have no faith in us, or if you disbelieve us even the tiniest bit, you can go there and check it out for yourself.'

As soon as the river was mentioned, the sahib sat bolt upright once again. 'I don't need hot water for my bath tomorrow. The river seems clean enough. So tomorrow I'll bathe in the river. I only hope there aren't any crocodiles.'

I didn't know many things about the village since I'd been away most of the time, so I asked the villagers about crocodiles. They seemed mighty insulted and protested vociferously. 'Young man, you may be well educated because you've been up to a lot of school learning, but more than anyone you should know crocodiles live in water and not on the top of mountains. Has a crocodile ever harmed a single person from this village? As long as the crocodile's wife is alive and in our midst....' The villagers all pointed their fingers in a particular direction.

I had no intention of making a full and faithful translation of all they'd said. So I simply allayed the sahib's fears: there was absolutely no reason to worry about crocodiles.

But, in the meantime, the white man had become quite eager to follow the entire conversation. The pointed fingers had piqued his curiosity too.

'Dr Batstone,' I tried to paraphrase. 'The tales are quite ridiculous for one thing. By now you must have realized that these villagers are rather simple-minded, inclined to believe anything and everything they get to hear. Anyway, it all goes back a long time. There lived a poor couple by the river. They had only one child, a daughter. She was married off when she was three years old, became a widow at the age of five, and after that lived with her parents.

'The child grew into a beautiful young woman. One day, when she went to the river to bathe, the villagers saw her being dragged into the deep waters by a crocodile. They thought that was the end of her. But miracle of miracles, she resurfaced ten years later. By then her father was long dead and her mother nearing her end, and their small hut on the riverbank dilapidated and ready to cave in.

'The girl looked after her mother as well as she could, but wasn't able to save her. When she passed away a few days later, the girl could do nothing but cry her heart out, alone in that ramshackle hut.

'Two days later, an old male crocodile was bludgeoned to death as it was trying to climb up the embankment behind the hut.

'The girl kept on crying, without uttering a word. God alone knows how a strange, jumbled story began to do the rounds of the village: after being dragged away by the crocodile the girl had lived with him as his wife all these years, and her poor husband had lost his life while trying to do what any good son-in-law would have done—look up his wife when she was visiting her parents.

'In the course of time the young woman became old. She's still alive and well, pushing ninety, and is referred to as Mrs Crocodile by everyone. It's firmly believed that, in deference to her, the entire tribe of crocodiles living in the river has not harmed the villagers. In response, the villagers have taken to providing the old woman with her morning and evening meals.'

'Wonderful!' the sahib exclaimed. 'Amazing. Fantastic. But where did she live those ten years she was gone from the village?'

'I don't know. I don't think anyone really does. Because the villagers simply swallowed a story as outlandish as this they never felt the need to cross-check it with the old woman.'

'My dear boy,' the sahib begged. 'Let's get the story of those ten years of her life. I'll regret it if I leave without knowing.'

The moonrise was some hours away; it was still very dark. I switched on the flashlight and walked in front, the sahib following behind. On the way to the old woman's hut he stumbled twice: first over a silent and self-effacing pye-dog, then over a perambulating turtle, perhaps out on a village visit. Each time he just barely managed to avoid falling. But every experience, good or bad, thrilled him no end.

The old woman was sitting by herself, her chin on her knees, beside a lamp burning weakly in her hut. She gave us a warm smile when we entered. The sahib and I poured into her stone bowl the milk, rice, and mashed bananas we'd brought with us as offerings. She rewarded us with another beaming smile.

'Grandmother,' I began. 'We're here to ask you a few questions. This gentleman you see with me—he's a true sahib from beyond the seven seas. It's his deepest wish to hear your story from your mouth.'

Not a hint of surprise or hesitation flickered across her wrinkled, weather-beaten face. She seemed to have been expecting our visit. 'Son, I'll tell you the story of a wandering prince and a fairy princess,' she promptly began.

'No, Grandmother, not just any old story. He wants your story, the story of your life. You must know everyone refers to you as Mrs Crocodile. That's plain rubbish. But it's also a matter of record you went missing for ten long years. Where were you all those years, where did you live and how? What did you do? Tell us about it.'

The old woman's hearing didn't seem impaired. Neither did she slur when she began to speak, even though she had not a tooth left in her mouth. And what a raconteur she turned out to be. After every three or four sentences, I had to stop her so I could translate word for word for the sahib. He told me not to leave out a single syllable.

'No sooner did I step into the water than a crocodile dragged me off into the deepest part of the river. God knows how deep it was, probably seven cubits or more. I don't know how...but when I....'

'No embroidery, Grandmother, just give us the hard facts. How did you escape from the jaws of the crocodile? Where did you end up when he set you free? How did life treat you....?'

All these questions didn't seem to make any impact on the old woman. She went on unperturbed: 'Son, when I regained consciousness I found myself under water seven cubits deep, with a large male crocodile in front of me, contemplating me with unblinking eyes. As he stared at me, God knows what happened, but I couldn't take my eyes off him either....'

'Grandmother, if you don't remember how you escaped from the jaws of the crocodile, at least tell us how you lived afterwards and where....'

'Son, did I ever try to escape from the crocodile's den? I told you I found it impossible to avert my eyes from him. There, in the deep waters there was no sun, no moon; it was neither day nor night. I don't know how many days or years passed.'

I thought better of interrupting the old woman once again. Not only did she herself believe her own yarn, but the sahib seemed to hang on to her every word. In the dim light of the lamp I watched our shadows fluttering on the wall. I continued to translate, but now with a certain detachment. Sometimes, when the sound of a boat pushing off the bank reached us, the old woman would pause, as if the call of the river had revived old memories.

The old woman spoke for an hour and a half, recounting the tale of a young woman setting up home with a crocodile in the awe-inspiring depths of the river eighteen miles from the village. During the first few days she hadn't the slightest desire to live with him and had every intention of running away at the first opportunity. But when she came up from the deep and began to float on the water, she found herself turned into a crocodile. When had her husband worked this magic on her? When he was dragging her to his underwater lair, or when he sat staring into her eyes? She felt utterly miserable and began to cry. The crocodile did everything he could to divert her and keep her amused, but she couldn't—and wouldn't—forget her past life. So her husband finally gave in: 'All right. Listen carefully to this mantra and learn it by heart. If you recite it you'll be able to return to your former self whenever you wish. But only not when I'm around, because, you see, no matter how hard I might try to hold back the counter-mantra—and keep you in the form of a crocodile—it'll slip out of my mouth.'

That day as he was preparing to leave his lair for his constitutional, the poor crocodile couldn't help shedding tears. 'I know you'll be gone by the time I return,' he said. 'But take care not to recite the mantra midstream—you'll turn into a human being and drown immediately. Make sure you're safely ashore before you say the mantra.'

When he returned home in the evening he found her still there. Needless to add, he was thrilled.

The young woman didn't leave the next day, nor the day after.

Weeks and months passed.

The crocodile couple began to swim together, delighting in each other's company, roaming far and wide, from one bathing ghat to another.

Once they travelled from their river to another and stopped close to a shrine. She said to her partner: 'Husband, you stay in the water. I'm going to crawl up the bank, assume my human form, and go have a darshan of the deity.' He agreed.

After this, she went on to visit a large number of temples and shrines. She'd swim to the riverbank at night, say her mantra, assume her human form and spend the whole day in pilgrimage, and at night jump back into the river, where her husband would be waiting to transform her back.

But during all this time she took great care to stay away from her own village; she had this fear that, once there, she might not feel like going back to her husband.

After ten years had passed she was seized with a deep desire to look up her parents and, with her husband's consent, returned to her village for a day. What she saw there filled her with dismay. The old way of life had been completely destroyed. Her father was dead and her mother lay dying; in fact, the old lady would die inside of a couple of days. Those two days were all the time she got to spend with her mother.

She remained in the deserted hut brooding about her life, her parents, and their love for her, and yet another day passed. Meanwhile her husband's patience was running out and he was beginning to panic. He wanted to find out what had happened to her, and so he came out of the water. While he was trying to climb up the bank he was spotted and clubbed to death.

Sixty years had passed since then. The old woman had continued to live by the river, all alone.

A pack of jackals began to howl in front of the old woman's hut. The sahib started. As we took leave of her, she gave us a big smile.

The moon had risen. The smoke swirling up from the thatched roofs of the village homes made the moon look bluer and softer than ever.

We walked back in silence. The sahib, wrapped in his thoughts, stumbled twice: first over the turtle—this time it was journeying back to the river—and then over the dog, who remained as silent and motionless as before.

He stopped on the riverbank. 'How far from here is the deepest part of the river she spoke of? Is it upstream or down?'

'What deepest part?'

'The deep waters in which the crocodile couple lived.'

'Wonderful! Amazing!' I laughed. The two words the sahib was so fond of had involuntarily slipped out of my mouth.

Dr Batstone became grave.

We walked back to the village in total silence.

∽

Some years later I received a letter from Dr Batstone. 'Even now, when I think of the time I spent in your village, I feel I metamorphosed into some other being for the entire duration of that night the old woman told us her story—just as she herself had once changed into a crocodile. And I treasure the sensation of my metamorphosis as true and real.'

THE PROSPECT OF FLOWERS

RUSKIN BOND

FERN HILL, THE OAKS, HUNTER'S LODGE, THE PARSONAGE, THE PINES, Dumbarnie, Mackinnon's Hall, and Windermere. These are the names of some of the old houses that still stand on the outskirts of one of the smaller Indian hill stations. Most of them have fallen into decay and ruin. They are very old, of course—built over a hundred years ago by Britons who sought relief from the searing heat of the plains. Today's visitors to the hill stations prefer to live near the markets and cinemas and many of the old houses, set amidst oak and maple and deodar, are inhabited by wild cats, bandicoots, owls, goats, and the occasional charcoal burner or mule driver.

But amongst these neglected mansions stands a neat, whitewashed cottage called Mulberry Lodge. And in it, up to a short time ago, lived an elderly English spinster named Miss Mackenzie.

In years Miss Mackenzie was more than 'elderly', being well over eighty. But no one would have guessed it. She was clean, sprightly, and wore old-fashioned but well-preserved dresses. Once a week, she walked the two miles to town to buy butter and jam and soap and sometimes a small bottle of eau de cologne.

She had lived in the hill station since she had been a girl in her teens, and that had been before World War I. Though she had never married, she had experienced a few love affairs and was far from being the typical frustrated spinster of fiction. Her parents had been dead thirty years; her brother and sister were also dead. She had no relatives in India and she lived on a small pension of forty rupees a month and the gift parcels that were sent out to her from New Zealand by a friend of her youth.

Like other lonely old people, she kept a pet—a large black cat with bright yellow eyes. In her small garden she grew dahlias, chrysanthemums, gladioli, and a few rare orchids. She knew a great deal about plants and about wildflowers, trees, birds, and insects. She had never made a serious study of these things, but having lived with them for so many years had developed an intimacy with all that grew and flourished around her.

She had few visitors. Occasionally, the padre from the local church called on her, and once a month the postman came with a letter from New Zealand or her pension papers. The milkman called every second day with a litre of milk for the lady and her cat. And, sometimes, she received a couple of eggs free, for the egg seller remembered a time when Miss Mackenzie, in her earlier prosperity, had bought eggs from him in large quantities. He was a sentimental man. He remembered her as a ravishing beauty in her twenties when he had gazed at her in round-eyed, nine-year-old wonder and consternation.

Now it was September, and the rains were nearly over and Miss Mackenzie's chrysanthemums were coming into their own. She hoped the coming winter wouldn't be too severe because she found it increasingly difficult to bear the cold.

One day, as she was pottering about in her garden, she saw a schoolboy plucking wildflowers on the slope above the cottage.

'Who's that?' she called. 'What are you up to, young man?'

The boy was alarmed and tried to dash up the hillside, but he slipped on pine needles and came slithering down the slope on to Miss Mackenzie's nasturtium bed.

When he found there was no escape, he gave a bright disarming smile, and said, 'Good morning, miss.'

He belonged to the local English-medium school and wore a bright red blazer and a red and black striped tie. Like most polite Indian schoolboys, he called every woman 'miss'.

'Good morning,' said Miss Mackenzie severely. 'Would you mind moving out of my flower bed?'

The boy stepped gingerly over the nasturtiums and looked up at Miss Mackenzie with dimpled cheeks and appealing eyes. It was impossible to be angry with him.

'You're trespassing,' said Miss Mackenzie.

'Yes, miss.'

'And you ought to be in school at this hour.'

'Yes, miss.'

'Then what are you doing here?'

'Picking flowers, miss.' And he held up a bunch of ferns and wildflowers.

'Oh,' Miss Mackenzie was disarmed. It was a long time since she had seen a boy taking an interest in flowers and, what was more, playing truant from school in order to gather them.

'Do you like flowers?' she asked.

'Yes, miss. I'm going to be a botan—a botantist?'

'You mean a botanist.'

'Yes, miss.'

'Well, that's unusual. Most boys at your age want to be pilots or soldiers or perhaps engineers. But you want to be a botanist. Well, well. There's still hope for the world, I see. And do you know the names of these flowers?'

'This is a bukhilo flower,' he said, showing her a small golden flower. 'That's a pahari name. It means puja or prayer. The flower is offered during prayers. But I don't know what this is....'

He held out a pale pink flower with a soft, heart-shaped leaf.

'It's a wild begonia,' said Miss Mackenzie. 'And that purple stuff is salvia, but it isn't wild. It's a plant that escaped from my garden. Don't you have any books on flowers?'

'No, miss.'

'All right, come in, and I'll show you a book.'

She led the boy into a small front room, which was crowded with furniture and books and vases and jam jars, and offered him a chair. He sat awkwardly on its edge.

The black cat immediately leapt on to his knees and settled down on them, purring loudly.

'What's your name?' asked Miss Mackenzie, as she rummaged through her books.

'Anil, miss.'

'And where do you live?'

'When school closes, I go to Delhi. My father has a business.'

'Oh, and what's that?'

'Bulbs, miss.'

'Flower bulbs?'

'No, electric bulbs.'

'Electric bulbs! You might send me a few, when you get home. Mine are always fusing and they're so expensive, like everything else these days. Ah, here we are!' She pulled a heavy volume down from the shelf and laid it on the table. '*Flora Himalayensis*, published in 1892, and probably the only copy in India. This is a very valuable book, Anil. No other naturalist has recorded so many Himalayan wildflowers. And let me tell you this, there are many flowers and plants which are still unknown to the fancy botanists who spend all their time with microscopes instead of in the mountains. But perhaps, you'll do something about that, one day.'

'Yes, miss.'

They went through the book together, and Miss Mackenzie pointed out many flowers that grew in and around the hill station while the boy made notes of their names and seasons. She lit the stove and put the kettle on for tea. And then the old English lady and the small Indian boy sat side by side over cups of hot, sweet tea, absorbed in a book on wildflowers.

'May I come again?' asked Anil, when he finally rose to go.

'If you like,' said Miss Mackenzie. 'But not during school hours. You mustn't miss your classes.'

After that, Anil visited Miss Mackenzie about once a week, and nearly always brought a wildflower for her to identify. She found herself looking forward to the boy's visits—and sometimes, when more than a week passed and he didn't come, she was disappointed and lonely and would grumble at the black cat.

Anil reminded her of her brother, when the latter had been a boy. There was no physical resemblance. Andrew had been fair-haired and blue-eyed. But it was Anil's eagerness, his alert, bright look, and the way he stood—legs apart, hands on hips, a picture of confidence—that reminded her of the boy who had shared her own youth in these same hills.

And why did Anil come to see her so often? Partly because she knew about wildflowers and he really did want to become a botanist. And partly because she smelt of freshly baked bread and that was a smell his own grandmother had possessed. And partly because she was lonely and sometimes a boy of twelve can sense loneliness better than an adult. And partly because he was a little different from other children.

By the middle of October, when there was only a fortnight left for the school to close, the first snow had fallen on the distant mountains. One peak stood high above the rest, a white pinnacle against the azure blue sky. When the sun set, this peak turned from orange to gold to pink to red.

'How high is that mountain?' asked Anil.

'It must be over twelve thousand feet,' said Miss Mackenzie. 'About thirty miles from here, as the crow flies. I always wanted to go there, but there was no proper road. At that height, there'll be flowers that you don't get here—the blue gentian and the purple columbine, the anemone, and the edelweiss.'

'I'll go there one day,' said Anil.

'I'm sure you will, if you really want to.'

The day before his school closed, Anil came to say goodbye to Miss Mackenzie.

'I don't suppose you'll be able to find many wildflowers in Delhi,' she said. 'But have a good holiday.'

'Thank you, miss.'

As he was about to leave, Miss Mackenzie, on an impulse, thrust the *Flora Himalayensis* into his hands.

'You keep it,' she said. 'It's a present for you.'

'But I'll be back next year, and I'll be able to look at it then. It's so valuable.'

'I know it's valuable and that's why I've given it to you. Otherwise, it will only fall into the hands of the junk dealers.'

'But, miss....'

'Don't argue. Besides, I may not be here next year.'

'Are you going away?'

'I'm not sure. I may go to England.'

She had no intention of going to England; she had not seen the country since she was a child, and she knew she would not fit in with the life of post-war Britain. Her home was in these hills, among the oaks and maples and deodars. It was lonely but at her age it would be lonely anywhere.

The boy tucked the book under his arm, straightened his tie, stood stiffly to attention, and said, 'Goodbye, Miss Mackenzie.' It was the first time he had spoken her name.

Winter set in early, and strong winds brought rain and sleet and soon there were no flowers in the garden or on the hillside. The cat stayed indoors, curled up at the foot of Miss Mackenzie's bed. Miss Mackenzie wrapped herself up in all her old shawls and mufflers but still she felt the cold. Her fingers grew so stiff that she took almost an hour to open a can of baked beans. And then it snowed and for several days the milkman did not come. The postman arrived with her pension papers but she felt too tired to take them up to town to the bank.

She spent most of the time in bed. It was the warmest place. She kept a hot-water bottle at her back and the cat kept her feet warm. She lay in bed, dreaming of the spring and summer months. In three months' time the primroses would be out and with the coming of spring the boy would return.

One night the hot-water bottle burst and the bedding was soaked through. As there was no sun for several days, the blanket remained damp. Miss Mackenzie caught a chill and had to keep to her cold, uncomfortable bed. She knew she had a fever but there was no thermometer with which to take her temperature. She had difficulty breathing. A strong wind sprang up one night and the window flew open and kept banging all night. Miss Mackenzie was too weak to get up and close it and the wind swept the rain and sleet into the room. The cat crept into the bed and snuggled close to its mistress's warm body. But towards morning that body had lost its warmth and the cat left the bed and started scratching about on the floor. As a shaft of sunlight streamed through the open window, the milkman arrived. He poured some milk into the cat's saucer on the doorstep and the cat leapt down from the windowsill and made for the milk.

The milkman called a greeting to Miss Mackenzie, but received no answer. Her window was open and he had always known her to be up before sunrise. So he put his head in at the window and called again. But Miss Mackenzie did not answer. She had gone away to the mountain where the blue gentian and purple columbine grew.

51

YAATRA

TURAGA JANAKI RANI

Translated from the Telugu by Dasu Krishnamoorty and Tamraparni Dasu

VENKATRAO CAME HOME, LIGHT AS A FLUFF OF COTTON ON A GENTLE breeze, wearing a jasmine-white smile. His back, which had become hunched during the five years of retirement, was unusually straight. Eswari, his wife, brought him a cup of water and knew what the big news was, even before he'd said a word. He unbuttoned his shirt to cool off from the afternoon heat and with smiling eyes said, 'Happy days are here again.'

Eswari laughed and said derisively, 'Oh, they have come ten years too soon.'

'It's no joke, madam. We'll get the benefit of the new salary scales now. Arrears will be paid from 1971. My colleagues demanded a round of coffee to celebrate the good news,' said Venkatrao.

He switched on the table fan and flopped into an easy chair, pulling it close to the fan.

'How much do you think you'll get?' asked his wife.

He wanted to tease her a little, so he triumphantly said to her, 'Guess.'

Though she hated this guessing game, she said, 'One lakh rupees?'

'How artless of her,' he thought and said, 'Only a lakh for twenty years?'

This hint that there was more in store was like a tonic and she disappeared into the kitchen to make coffee.

Joy filled Venkatrao's heart as he looked out into the street from the easy chair. He was not sure about the amount, but it couldn't be less than three or four lakh. He calculated rapidly in his mind, adding, multiplying, and subtracting. A promotion and, on top of it, a salary in the higher scale! He offered silent thanks to his colleagues for the assurance that all his accounts would be smoothed out in ten days.

Other than entering them into ledgers, he had never had to handle so many zeroes and had never seen such a large sum of money. He recalled with irony how everyone had dismissed his grandmother's prediction that the stars were in his favour. They laughed it off as a joke. A joke it remained for a long time. The property he had thought his marriage would bring him evaporated in litigation. His father had gambled away the estate he had inherited and died a slave to bad habits. Goddess Lakshmi's blessings eluded Venkatrao. With his pittance of a salary, he ran the household, fed his wife and three children, as well as his grandmother. The cupboard was always bare. He had to scrape the bottom of the barrel for every small need. When he retired, he had a past but no future.

In such a situation, the elevation of his post, and the kindness of a good samaritan in the accounts department who juggled the rules in his favour, was a dream come true. When the tribunal announced his award, the senior officers were happy that he got his dues at last. Was this not a reason to celebrate?

Eswari brought the coffee and fried vegetable bhajis.

'Didn't I tell you? God is with us. Bad days are over for us and our daughter,' she said.

Venkatrao was slightly taken aback. Eswari had already started filling her mind with expectations. He checked her fervour and asked, 'What bad days do we and our daughter have?'

'You think we are happy?' asked Eswari, irritated.

'You mean you and me? You have everything. You are a maharani,' joked Venkatrao.

'When was the last time he spoke to me so pleasantly without frowning?' she wondered. If she didn't curb his exuberance now, he might go overboard.

'Maharani indeed, changing jewellery every day of the week and staff quarters teeming with servants! Enough of your joking. Did I ever buy anything for even a thousand rupees without first thinking a hundred times?' she complained.

True, theirs had been a hand-to-mouth existence. But he didn't like his wife pointing out his incompetence.

'Fine. Take a thousand and go splurge on shopping. Will *that* see the end of our misery?'

'Our misery? Look at our children's gloomy lives. Our luckless daughter, she has never expected a cent from us. Poor girl,' Eswari said in a voice choked with maternal affection and pain.

'Her two children need money so they can go to a decent school. We owe her husband five thousand rupees, the remainder of the dowry. And the five sovereigns of gold we promised at their wedding. He now wants a colour TV and his mother needs an extra three sovereigns.... Her life will get back on track if we keep our word. It is a matter of fifty thousand rupees.'

'Don't look at me like that,' she continued. 'I'm talking about our daughter, Visala. Not yet twenty, poor girl already has two kids.'

His daughter's plight moved Venkatrao. That apart, was it right of his wife to hurriedly draft a budget for expenditure?

'We will see,' he said, hiding behind the day's newspaper.

'Tell me first, when can we hope to get the money?' Eswari asked impatiently.

He glared at her and said, 'It comes when it comes. Is there nothing but money to talk about? You...sticking to that topic like glue!'

She returned his angry stare, collected the plates and cups, and stalked off.

The family began to mentally multiply the amount that Venkatrao would get. The eldest son in Vijayawada discovered he had problems. He had a daughter and a son who had qualified for engineering and medicine programs. They needed at least sixty to seventy thousand rupees to go to a university.

'Our eldest son has written that he will pay the sum back when the children start working. He is unhappy that he and his brother only had a middling education. At least your grandchildren should get a good education, he writes,' said Eswari.

Their second son, Anil, and his wife, Rama, lived in a two-bedroom flat not far from where Rama worked. The couple visited the older couple every Sunday. Anil would often plead with his parents to live with him in a bigger house. His wife would curb his enthusiasm saying, 'They won't be able to find a house of this size to rent at a reasonable price these days. How can they come and live with us in our pigeonhole? Let them stay in the big house where the grandchildren can spend their vacation. If they vacate the house now, they can't rent it again for less than five hundred. You talk such nonsense!'

These squabbles were not new to Eswari. 'The girl is used to living with just her husband and kids. Why bother her with the responsibility of taking care of her in-laws as well? Our son doesn't mean what he says. We will not move out,' thought Eswari firmly.

Three Sundays after the news of the windfall, Anil and his wife visited his parents. Venkatrao sensed an overdose of affection in their words but soon chided himself for such unkind thoughts. Anil began cautiously, 'A builder I know has promised a flat in the complex he is building near our house.'

Rama sat near her mother-in-law helping her roll out puris.

'Yes, Ma. They are really fine two-bedroom flats. They are usually available only on the fourth floor. Your son insisted that it should be on the first floor because it is hard for mamaiyyagaru, his father, to make it to the fourth floor. Big doors and closets, and cool marble floors. So beautiful,' said Rama ecstatically.

'It's a good idea, planning for a house when you are still young. Why should you rent when both of you are earning?' said Venkatrao.

'Isn't it yours too?' said Anil, looking hurt.

'Yes, your house is mine too,' Venkatrao agreed, soothingly.

After Anil left Venkatrao realized that the flat needed an advance payment of sixty thousand rupees and another lakh and eighty thousand in six months. Anil told his mother that his wife would borrow from her office and he would borrow against his insurance policy. It would be nice if his father would help him with the advance payment of sixty thousand rupees now and another twenty-five thousand later.

Venkatrao's heart sank at the hopes his windfall had kindled in his children's hearts. Wasn't he the master of his life any more? Didn't he have the right to decide how to spend money that he had toiled for? Who were these people to decide how he spent his money?

The money came sooner than expected. He greased the palms of everyone up and down the hierarchy and accepted unscheduled cuts in the payment. In the end, a sum of three lakh, seventy-eight thousand, four hundred, and sixty-one rupees swelled his bank account. He worried that if the news leaked out people would mob him for loans.

He had never kept anything from Eswari. He sat in the chair and took out some papers from a bag and called his wife.

'Eswari, I need to tell you something. Are you ready?' he asked. She glanced at him, then signalled to him to go ahead.

'We reared our children with care, gave them a good education, and a good life. What else do we owe them, tell me?'

It took a while for her to understand what he was driving at.

'You mean...we need not give them the money they are asking for?' She was indignant.

'Don't put me on the spot. Did my father give me anything? What did your father give you? Didn't we give the children whatever we could all these days?' His anguish was audible as he searched for answers in her face.

She stopped stringing the flowers in her lap and said, 'Should we deprive our children because our parents deprived us? When you get this money, give the children what they want.'

He understood her heart now. He pushed the papers back into the bag, sad that Eswari, his wife of forty years, had reservations about his decision.

He said firmly, 'I have already made my plans. I've put two lakh in a fixed deposit, ordered a fridge, a colour TV, a VCR, a sofa set, a double cot and mattress, ceiling fans, and a dining table and chairs. You may come along with me to see them if you like. Hire a cook. Buy nice clothes for the children and their families. I have booked tickets for a railway tour of the South. You can buy jewellery for twenty-five thousand rupees.'

As he reeled off these words, she was stunned. She was furious that he had not consulted her before deciding to deny their children in this way.

'What do you say?' he said.

'What is there to say,' she thought and snipped a small part of the string of flowers. She wove it into her hair, putting the longer section around the Shiva–Parvati statuette.

'Why don't you say something?' he said.

'What kind of a father ignores the needs of his children? You can't bear to see the children happy. You think they should buy what they want for themselves. Such an inconsiderate....' Choking with grief, she broke down and went away to sit on the veranda outside.

She sat watching people and vehicles in the street until the daylight faded. She came back, cooked dinner, called him when it was ready, and served him the meal. Very soon, the sofa set, dining table, and other things he had ordered crowded the house. The house lit up with all the new things, including a sparkling chandelier he had bought. The four rooms of the house looked like a luxury hotel resort.

Anil and Rama visited and were dazzled. Accustomed to seeing the old couple in modest surroundings, Rama succumbed to a strange nausea. A fortnight later, Venkatrao and Eswari's daughter, their eldest son, and their grandchildren came and stayed for a couple of days. It was the festive season and the house shone like Goddess Lakshmi's abode, replete with children, toys, and new clothes. But there was darkness in their hearts. Though Eswari wore her new gold necklace and bangles, her face lacked lustre.

Once the children left, Venkatrao showed her the railway circular tour tickets. She remained quiet with a blank expression.

'Pack our clothes for the trip. I'm tired,' he said. What was left of his grey head of hair, strayed on to his face.

'I'll take care of the clothes. Let's eat first,' Eswari said, sighing deeply.

Venkatrao's long-awaited, much-longed-for moment had finally arrived—a dining table instead of wooden planks, a double cot with a soft mattress instead of the string cot covered with a patchy quilt. The moment of truth when he could sleep in comfort, with his arm around Eswari's waist. He wanted deliverance from a life of want and looked forward to a time when he could throw money around freely. What was wrong with such a yearning? According to Eswari, everything.

A friend dropped by to check in on Venkatrao's travel plans. 'May I have some water, please,' the friend asked. Venkatrao shouted out the request so Eswari could hear him in the kitchen. The friend was all praise for Eswari's sweets as he inhaled their fragrance. While they were talking Venkatrao's aged frame began to sweat. An ache deep inside started making its way across his chest.

'What happened?' Eswari cried anxiously as she rushed over. The friend hurriedly stepped up to him and laid Venkatrao on the new sofa and gave him a sip of water. He had a bad feeling. He told Eswari to switch on the fan and rushed out to get a doctor.

Eswari watched her husband lying on the sofa, peacefully staring at the ceiling with an enigmatic smile on his face. It was not until much later, after the doctor arrived, that she realized that Venkatrao's smile would never fade and his eyes would never close.

A BLACK HOLE

JAYANT VISHNU NARLIKAR

Translated from the Marathi by Anil Zankar

'THIS CRAZY COMPUTER IS REALLY HARASSING ME!' SAID PRAKASH AS HE stirred his coffee vigorously. 'I must have asked it at least fifty times in the last week, but it responds with the same reply!'

'What is the computer saying?' Sanjay asked him, feigning innocence. Sanjay, being a student of pure mathematics, looked down on the computer, like an artist looking down on a house painter.

'The computer is telling me that my postulations are all wrong. I thought that I'd hand over all the data received from the Prof to the computer, be done with it by the end of the day, and then go on the hike as planned. But the fact is—man proposes and the computer disposes.'

Prakash had received some new data from the Yerkes Observatory regarding the planet Jupiter and he was expected to validate it.

'Maybe you got the calculations wrong.'

Sanjay expressed a regular mathematician's belief that physicists are weak in mathematics.

'You see, if at all there is any mistake, it is not mine, but that of Newton and Einstein. Even with your limited knowledge, you know that planetary motion is decided as per their laws. Yet, the computer says that the new data does not fit into its laws. The Prof is sure that the data is accurate. So, where is the hitch?'

'I think you should keep chanting the names of the Dashavataras—the ten big incarnations—in astronomy for inspiration,' Sanjay mocked him. 'Say hail Newton, hail Halley, hail Herschel, hail Adams, hail Eddington....'

'Adams...Adams...you just said something marvellous! Wise words should always be welcomed even when uttered by a kid!' Prakash slapped him hard on the back and simply took off, leaving behind the half-finished coffee in the room.

Sanjay stood gaping after him. In this institute, the mathematicians had the monopoly on eccentricity, so he probably did not approve of Prakash's.

'Prof' meant Professor Ramesh Agrawal, a professor of astronomy who worked in the same institute. He had earned a worldwide reputation in celestial mechanics—a branch of theoretical astronomy that deals with the calculation of the motions of celestial objects such as planets. In the beginning of the twenty-first century there were very few scientists who were conducting research in this field, and whenever any incomprehensible problem arose, the scientist working in that area unfailingly sought his advice. That's why the new data regarding Jupiter had been sent to him.

Prakash Pawate was his favourite student. He had scanned the recent data and sent it to Prakash for a detailed examination. He did not need to tell him, 'Do not meet me till you have reached a definite conclusion.'

A week had passed and there had been no reply from Prakash and the Prof began to wonder about it. Just as he was thinking of contacting Prakash, Prakash himself came rushing into his room.

'Calm down! Calm down! And speak only one sentence a minute so I can follow what you are saying,' he said rather mildly.

'Sir! Around 1846, Adams observed some irregularity in the trajectory of Uranus and with the help of logical speculation and maths discovered the new planet Neptune. I am sure that a new celestial body has arrived in the vicinity of Jupiter. The replies given by the computer definitely indicate that.'

The professor had firmly embedded in the minds of his students the principle—never make a statement without a proof. Yet, this statement of Prakash was so unexpected that he decided to enter the fray himself. Over the next ten days, after employing several astronomical methods to test the hypothesis, the two of them came to the conclusion that this statement was correct.

When the renowned scientific weekly *Nature* from London published the paper written by Agrawal and Pawate, it caused a sensation in the world of astronomy. The irregularity observed in the speed and trajectory of Jupiter was caused by a new celestial body that had arrived in its vicinity was what the paper said in essence.

They had temporarily named this body X and had published the details of its weight, velocity, and trajectory in relation to Jupiter. All kinds of speculation began about the nature of X. According to some, it was a new planet that may have been formed by the fusion of stray asteroids that were in orbit around Mars and Jupiter, while others thought it could be a comet that had entered the solar system from outside. Soon there began a competition amongst the astronomy observatories of the world to physically sight X.

But no one could observe anything!

Three years passed. Although X was not sighted, scientists were convinced of its presence, hence it was decided to send a spacecraft towards X. For this was a very important issue. The future of the age-old law of gravity depended upon it. Since Indian scientists had discovered X, the launch of the spacecraft would happen from the Sriharikota base in India. Prakash Pawate had the honour of being the scientist-traveller in it and he had only one co-traveller, a Captain John Faulkner from USA. Faulkner was a very skilled engineer. This was the tenth spacecraft of the World Space Organization launched towards Jupiter from India. It was named WIJ 10. After deciding on a suitable date to launch the spacecraft, preparations began.

During these three years, Prakash Pawate and Sanjay Joshi had obtained their doctoral degrees and had continued in the institute as fellows. It had been a year since Sanjay had been married, but Prakash was still single. Their friendship had continued as before. Their chats and verbal duels continued as before. A week prior to the launch of the spacecraft, Prakash visited Sanjay's home on the occasion of the naming ceremony of Sanjay's newborn daughter. He had carried a teddy bear for her as a present.

'Vahini, what have you named your daughter?' he asked, pushing the teddy bear towards her.

'Anupama. Would you like to hold her?'

'Oh no! I'm fine. I am quite scared of holding a baby in my arms.'

'Okay, then tell us from a distance, whom does our daughter resemble?'

'She resembles both of you,' Prakash answered diplomatically. 'She is really cute. You'll see how boys will want to woo her in about eighteen, twenty years.'

'In that case, why don't you wait for another eighteen, twenty years? We will happily accept you as our son-in-law.' Anupama's mother was already on a mission to find her son-in-law. Prakash became awkward when the topic of his marriage—be it after eighteen days or be it eighteen years—was discussed. He hurriedly took his leave.

'You unnecessarily frightened that poor bachelor!' Sanjay reprimanded her.

WIJ 10 was launched as per plan. During its journey, it continued to communicate with many stations on earth. Communication remained normal and regular till WIJ 10 reached the atmosphere of Jupiter. Prakash sent the following message to the mission control room:

'I think we are now close to X, but we have not sighted anything yet. But we do see many bodies like meteorites and asteroids accelerating rapidly towards X. Had X been a luminous body, I would have said that it reminds me of the description of the moth flying into the flame in the Bhagavad Gita....'

'Okay. Enough of your poetic ideas. What are you planning to do next?' the mission control room cut him short.

'Listen, when Oppenheimer witnessed the atomic explosion, he thought of the Bhagavad Gita. What I see or don't see here is far more abnormal than the atomic explosion. If permission is granted, I wish to go closer to examine it.'

'You have permission, but if you sense any danger, retreat immediately.'

'Certainly, I'll take full care of WIJ 10.'

These were the last clear words from Prakash that were received by the mission control room.

John turned the spacecraft in the direction of X. Gradually it began to gain speed. 'Take it easy, John. We should not go too close,' Prakash warned John.

'I shut off the engine some time ago. Can't understand why the velocity is still increasing!' John said with a worried look at the speed counter; the needle inside was surging ahead.

Then it hit Prakash like lightning. He rushed to the computer inside the spacecraft, took out a programme from a drawer, and loaded it into the computer. This was a programme that had not been used till now. It was called Black Hole. He punched in the information regarding the rapid acceleration of the spacecraft and the computer answered within a few seconds. He read it and hurried towards John.

'John, John, the mystery of X is solved, but it is too late for us. X is a black hole and we are hurtling towards it.'

A black hole is a dense body formed by the extreme contraction of matter. It has such strong gravitation that even light does not pass through it. That was the reason why X could not be sighted from Earth or from WIJ 10, which was much closer to it. According to Einstein's theory of gravity, black holes can exist in the universe, but till now no black hole had been found by scientists. Very few scientists have put forth this idea and the majority has not supported it.

'So, what next?' asked John, even though he almost certainly knew the answer.

'We are most probably heading straight into the mouth of X. But there is a ray of hope. Our original trajectory is not towards its centre but around it. The computer cannot tell us accurately yet. It'll need more data on our orbit. I'll get it reactivated. Until then, you try and contact the mission control room.'

John tried to send a message, but it was futile. The mission control room was sending some messages, but they sounded garbled, as if they were spoken with extreme rapidity. Just then Prakash came back, his face was ashen.

'John, the computer has virtually predicted our death. It says we will approach X, complete a million rounds around it, and then perish by falling into it. What does the mission control room say?'

John explained the situation to him. Prakash realized that contact with the mission control room was lost for good and they had to take their own decisions.

'There is still hope for us. We will be passing the unstable circular orbit that rings the black hole. I am going to exploit the indefinite nature of the path. If we can fire a rocket at the opportune moment, the unstable conditions created around it could possibly move our spacecraft away from X. If that happens, well and good. Otherwise, we say goodbye to the world. We must put on our space suits right away.'

'What is the need for the space suits?' John asked.

'As we approach X, the tidal power of its gravitational force will be increasingly felt by us, just as the Earth feels the tidal power of the gravitational force of the Moon, resulting in a high tide at sea. Now imagine that as you are approaching X, your head is closer to X and the feet are distant. In that condition, your head will face a greater gravitational force compared to your feet. Can you imagine what could happen then?'

'My body will be stretched from head to toe?' John was beginning to think now.

'Right! And this pull will be so great that we will not be able to bear it. However, if we are in a space suit then our organs may not be affected as much,' Prakash explained.

'You keep the spacecraft in auto-pilot mode so that the computer can guide it back to Earth. If our luck holds, the people on the base will wake us up.'

After making all the preparations and before getting into the space suits, their eyes hovered over the galactic space around them. The constellations seemed brighter to them. Was that going to be their last view of the universe?

When WIJ 10 landed at the Sriharikota base, the technicians there were taken aback. Nobody remembered a spacecraft by that name. There was no announcement or notice regarding its arrival. They checked this uninvited, unknown spacecraft thoroughly, then brought out the two Kumbhakarnas sleeping inside, and straightaway sent them to the Maximum Security Medical Section (MSMS). These two people's names and faces were completely unknown to all.

'Sir, please take it easy. The doctor hasn't allowed you to move or think,' Sister Anupama from MSMS said to Prakash. 'Very soon, the chief scientist will be with you. Please tell him everything.'

'Let me at least call up a couple of my friends, just to let them know that I am back and well. This automatic watch of mine tells me that it has been three years since I left this place. They all must be worried about my whereabouts....'

'Three years?' exclaimed chief scientist Dr Ramaswamy, who was just entering the room. 'No spacecraft has left this base in the last three years. For the last five years we have been sending only unmanned spacecraft.'

'That's impossible! Do check your records,' Prakash exclaimed in great surprise. 'As per my watch, John Faulkner and I took off towards Jupiter three years and fifteen days ago. Ask John. Or contact Professor Ramesh Agrawal so that you can confirm this.'

'John is still not conscious, but Dr Agrawal, whom you mentioned, retired recently. Let me see if I can get his address,' Dr Ramaswamy told him.

Prakash felt dizzy. When he had begun the journey with WIJ 10, Prof had just turned forty. He asked quite apprehensively,

'What year is it now?'

In response, Dr Ramaswamy handed him the newspaper. Prakash almost fainted when he saw the date on the newspaper.

He had returned to Earth twenty years later.

Prakash took two weeks to regain his senses fully. Sister Anupama played a crucial role in his recovery. And it began to look like the confirmed bachelor was going to be bowled neck and crop. The doctors had warned Anupama not to refer to his space journey in any manner during their romantic conversations. She observed this to the letter.

After his recovery, Dr Ramaswamy brought Prakash and Dr Agrawal together. Dr Agrawal congratulated him on his safe return and also on having found a suitable girl for himself. After that he proceeded to explain to him the passage of time. This was the alchemic effect of the fierce gravitational force of the black hole. Prakash and John were asleep while they were in orbit around the black hole but only for a second as per the time scale of the black hole, for the gravitational force had frozen the lapse of time for them. During that time Earth had moved ahead by seventeen years. John and Prakash, still in their twenties, were living proof of Einstein's concept of relativity.

'Okay. Now, tell me, where is Sanjay? He will really be shocked to see me,' said Prakash smiling.

'Sanjay who?' asked Anupama.

'Sanjay Joshi. He is a close buddy of mine. We were both researchers at the same institute. We would often argue about.... Oh! What happened? Why are you crying?'

'He was my father. He and my mother...they both died in an aeroplane accident, leaving me an orphan....' Anupama said sobbing.

It was in this way that Anupama's mother's matchmaking efforts succeeded. Thanks to the black hole.

HOUSE NUMBER

KAVANA SARMA

Translated from the Telugu by Dasu Krishnamoorty and Tamraparni Dasu

DR APPALRAJU SURVEYED THE NEATLY APPOINTED ROOMS AND NODDED. It had taken him a week of house-hunting to find the place. He signed the lease of the two-room tenement for five hundred rupees in Dwaraka Nagar district of the Steel City. Now, all he had to do was to write home asking Her Excellency to come join him. With that, the day's to-do list would have been accomplished.

He bathed with half a bucket of water, saving the other half for any need that might arise before the next day's quota of water arrived. He wrapped a white lungi around his waist, and sat down close to the table fan to write to his wife:

Oh, my queen, my sweetness,

Found a place at last! Pack your things and ask your dad to put you on the next train; I'll receive you here. I've spruced up the rooms, though not as well as they do in America. But India is not America. When you were there you used to complain: 'There is no NTR or ANR. Every weekend, all we do is crowd into some friend's basement and see a movie. How about watching it in the comfort of cushioned seats in air-conditioned luxury for just half a dollar in a grand Indian multiplex? A city without Telugu films is a godforsaken place, my Appalraju darling. No jasmines here, only those pathetic surrogates for jasmines; no fragrance of any kind!' Well, we're back in our country. No houses to rent, no state-of-the-art kitchens or sparkling sinks. Daily power cuts for ten hours. The faucets are always dry. But, you have Simhachalam selling you sampangi flowers at your door, paan cones made of betel leaves, and bottled soda. Today's temperature here is 42°C. I've lost count of the sodas I've downed. Without you, Vizag is a bore. Hurry home to me!

After he'd signed the letter, he went out to check the house number on the front door. 48-12-15. What a quirky number! Four and eight add up to twelve, one and two add up to three. The grand total is fifteen. He wondered if there was anyone other than him who could crack such a complicated code. He was a genius, an intellectual. Anyway, self-adulation is not a virtue, he reminded himself. Srinivasa Ramanujan could decipher such cryptograms in his sleep. Who would win if he, Dr Appalraju, and Ramanujan were locked in a battle of wits? Ramanujan perhaps, he conceded. There are R and J in his name too. Like Ramanujan, he too understood the uniqueness of numbers. An unseen bond existed between him and the world of numbers—once he saw a number he never forgot it.

Well, he'd better write the house number to help his wife to write back. She might write to his office address, God forbid. That was the last thing he wanted. First, he wrote his name with the care of a calligrapher on the envelope. Then he wrote Dwaraka Nagar, Visakhapatnam. Postal code? He couldn't remember. He hadn't paid attention. Oh well, it was not the end of the world. But he'd have to write the house number. What was it? Was it 12-3-15? No, he was not sure. His genius having deserted him, he thought it better to go out again and confirm. For all you know, Srinivasa Ramanujan might have riffled through the books stealthily when Hardy was not around! No shame in taking a second look, he decided.

So, Appalraju went out and checked the door number once again. It was now clear: two ones, one two, one four, one five, one eight. Simple! 48-12-15. He scribbled the number on the envelope.

What next? Find a mailbox. It was eight o'clock. 'Enough time to go to Ooty restaurant for a meal and chuck the letter into the mailbox on the way back,' he calculated. He was not in a mood to change into pants. One could step out of the house in America wearing unpresentable clothes. No one cared. Any rag would do. No questions asked. Why should it be different in India? We just don't try. And what had happened on the one occasion he *did* try? That was the time he'd visited Kakinada to look up his wife's folks. One day, the entire household set out for a drive because it was too stuffy inside the house. He took off his shirt and drove in an undershirt. On the way, his wife, Rani, had spotted a boy selling iced sodas on the sidewalk. She pointed to the soda cart, and cooed into Appalraju's ear, 'I want one, my love.' The dutiful husband that he was, he stopped the cart and asked the soda boy to uncork four iced sodas.

He thought he'd drink one at the cart itself so that he need carry only three cold bottles back to the car. The boy stopped him mid-gulp and yelled, 'What are you doing, man! First take the sodas to your boss and the lady. What impudence! You louts from the countryside are infesting the place and bringing your boorish ways here.' Appalraju couldn't understand why the soda boy took him for a chauffeur. His brother-in-law stepped in hurriedly and said, 'Bavagaru, pass the sodas to me, please, I'll take them to my sister.'

The soda boy realized his mistake and turned his ire on Appalraju's brother-in-law, 'What sir, you couldn't buy a decent shirt for your brother-in-law? What happens to the image of our city if our sons-in-law wander the city shirtless?' he said. The vendor didn't know that not only had the young man not bothered to get a respectable shirt for his brother-in-law but had borrowed his Levi's pants instead.

After that experience, Appalraju made up his mind to change the values of this country. Stirred by such reformist zeal, he pulled out from the closet a red undershirt with a pocket but no collar. He thrust a ten-rupee note into the pocket, locked the house, and marched out. He arrived at Emporium Point and flagged down a rickshaw for Ooty restaurant. He got off near a red mailbox and gently slid in the letter to his queen.

The rickshaw driver shouted after him, 'Sir, you haven't paid the fare!'

'I'm sorry,' Appalraju said and paid him.

Appalraju bought a meal ticket at the restaurant cash register and put the change in his pocket. The food tray arrived and, eating, he slipped into a reverie. Prices in India had shot up into the stratosphere during his stay in America. By the time he'd returned to India, the Janata Party was in power. The Emergency had been lifted. 'It has restored our esteem abroad,' his friends in the US had argued, sipping whisky. Irritated, he'd asked, 'If India's prestige is so dear to you, why don't you go home and restore it?' The patriotism of these expatriates was limited to boasting about the greatness of their country. They mocked Appalraju for enjoying the comforts of the US even as he criticized the Emergency. He should return to India and protest, they said.

He had returned, but not to protest the Emergency. He wanted to share in the poverty and prosperity of the country, and act on his faith that India was great. Such noble thoughts enriched his meal. By nine o' clock, he had finished his meal, stepped outside the restaurant and bought a betel leaf cone from the paan shop. As he walked back home, monstrous wall posters warned him in large fonts, 'Naughty Krishna and Cheeky Rama. Hurry up lest you should regret later'. For good measure, at the bottom of the poster blared another admonition, 'Delay means Disappointment'.

'I should respect these posters,' he thought. 'The movie seems to have a good cast. I should give it a try. Rani said she had seen the film in Kakinada and recommended it. I don't even have to get up early. Tomorrow is Sunday, ha!'

He'd passed a theatre on his way to Ooty. His watch showed that he had fifteen minutes to get there. The film had been running for more than a hundred days. So, he had no problem getting a ticket. 'Ah, this theatre is air-conditioned,' he chuckled. But the euphoria was short-lived. The management had switched the AC off. Obviously, they'd not taken a vow at Raj Ghat in Gandhiji's holy presence to keep it running during the entire duration of the movie.

Halfway through the film, Raju got bored and stood up to leave. The audience tried to persuade him to stay, telling him about the fight scenes and dances yet to come. As Raju made his way out, he came between the women and their heroes on the screen. They bristled and cursed him. 'Why should such an impatient man come to see a movie, he should stay at home and not spoil other people's fun!' They yelled at him to sit down.

Raju scurried out of the movie hall and approached the metal gate of the compound. It was locked. The gatekeeper was engrossed in watching the fight scenes from the cheap seats closest to the screen. Raju requested him to come out and open the gate but he said he needed the permission of the manager. 'If you leave the hall in the middle what will the people at the box office think, sir?' the manager chided him.

'This is the last show,' Raju said.

'Last show? There is a morning show in a few hours. People are already lining up because tomorrow is a Sunday. Is it fair of you to leave the hall in their presence?'

Finally, the manager relented and had the gatekeeper open the gate.

Raju stumbled out and wiped the sweat off. He shredded the ticket stub and blew the pieces into the air. Despite everything, he was in a good mood and decided to walk back home. As the old saying goes, the miles go by quickly if we walk with a song on our lips and a hop in our step.

Walking with a jaunty stride, he began belting out, *Raindrops keep falling on my head...my head....*

Constable Appalsaami was on patrol. He eyed Raju with suspicion. 'Is this fellow really mad or is he a burglar pretending to be mad?'

He needed to book at least two arrests to keep up with his quota. He took a good look at Raju's flip-flops, the satchel slung across his chest, the red undershirt over a lungi secured by a belt.

'Here's a pickpocket,' he decided.

Appalsaami stopped Raju and asked with mock politeness, 'Where is it raining, sir?'

'My head...my head,' said Raju and stopped singing.

'On your head? Look at the sky and tell me where it is raining from, you drunk.'

'Sergeant, mind your language!' said Raju angrily.

'What, you think I don't know Ingilis? I'll thrash you. Where are you coming from at this late hour?'

'From the second show,' Raju said.

'Which movie?'

'*Naughty Krishna and Cheeky Rama.*'

'That show is not over yet.'

'I came away in the middle,' said Raju.

The cop laughed. This was the first time he had heard of anyone walking out from that movie in the middle. Appalsaami saw himself in the role of Naughty Krishna. I certainly look the part, he thought. Wasn't that why he'd been honoured by the theatre owners with the responsibility of being on duty on the opening night?

'Really? You walked out halfway through such a good film?'

'Of course,' said Raju.

'Where's the stub then?'

Raju looked for it in his pocket and remembered that he had thrown it away. Nice touch, the policeman thought.

'Okay, where are you going?'

'Home.'

'Where is it?'

'Dwaraka Nagar.'

'What's your house number?'

Raju smiled. He was sure he could handle this challenge without a problem, thanks to his special relationship with numbers. There are two ones, one two, one four, one five, one eight.

He thanked Ramanujan and said, '11-24-58.'

'There is no such number in Dwaraka Nagar,' snapped Appalsaami.

Raju came up with another number. '21-15-84.' He worked it out in his head. Two plus one is three. Five plus one is six. Two times three is six. That is, the sum of the second set of digits is twice the sum of the first set of digits. Now, eight plus four is twelve. Twelve is two times six, the sum of one and five. So, the rule applied to the second and third set of numbers as well. He was thrilled by his own brilliance. That had to be his house number and so he told the policeman.

'Come,' said Appalsaami.

'Where?'

'To the police station.'

'I'm allowed a phone call, according to the rules. You have to produce me before a magistrate if you take me into custody.'

'Will you follow me, or do I have to give you a taste of the baton?'

'Third degree is prohibited by law, officer.'

'Follow me quietly,' the policeman said flourishing his baton. It whipped through the air with a crack like a bullet.

Raju accompanied the policeman docilely to the station.

'What's the matter?' the writer at the station asked.

Raju was shocked that there was nothing like the statutory warning usually heard in American police precincts, the Miranda rights, which warned the suspect that whatever he said could be used against him.

'Caught him prowling around, I think he was planning to burgle a house. Let's put him inside and inform the sub-inspector.'

'I want to make a call and it is your duty to allow me,' Raju asserted his rights.

'You can receive a call, but not make it,' the writer corrected him. 'The guy is firing away in English, man,' he told the constable.

'Who doesn't speak English these days, sir?' Appalsaami said and pushed Appalraju into the lock-up.

That was the last straw.

'I'm Dr Appalraju. You'll regret your actions. There is no Emergency now. The magistrate will take you to task tomorrow. What crime have I committed?' Raju began shouting from behind bars.

'You should inform the SI,' the writer told the constable.

Appalsaami hesitated for an instant, but he walked down anyway to the SI's home, though he feared the boss might resent being disturbed at that late hour.

Luckily for Appalsaami, the SI was awake but in a bad mood. His son had sneaked out to watch a late-night film. He looked up at the cop.

'Not my fault, sir. I just did what you told me to and put the guy in the slammer. He says he will make us pay for this because there is no Emergency. Please tell me what to do.'

The SI told his wife to send his son to the station as soon as he came home from the movie and followed Appalsaami to the station.

'Where is your officer, where's the boss?' Appalraju was shouting when the SI walked in.

'You, there! I'm the boss. What's the problem?' the SI asked.

'Look at the address, sir. All wrong. There is no such number. He was singing that the rain is falling. He claims that he is going home from the theatre but he couldn't even produce the stub,' Appalsaami reeled off an account of what had happened.

'You know you shouldn't go by what a man wears. For that matter, look at what you are wearing. Let me see your ID,' Raju demanded.

The SI was taken aback by this audacity. He'd left home in a hurry, clad in a lungi and banian.

'In case he acts up,' he told the constable, 'just use the stick.'

Appalsaami made no such attempt because the bars of the lock-up grill got in the way.

'You have no right to torture me. It is for the court to punish me.... Provided I'm guilty,' Raju said.

An orderly interrupted the exchanges. He had a sixteen-year-old boy in tow.

'So, you thought you could do things behind my back and get away with it?' the SI snarled and slapped the boy hard.

The boy began to cry.

'Why is he pummelling the boy? I'll tell his father to file a case, and I'll testify with pleasure!' Appalraju yelled.

'You mean to say our boss can't thrash his own son?' asked the writer.

'Who gave him the right to do that?' Appalraju demanded and bawled out a slogan, 'Police violence!'

The boy promptly supplemented, 'Down, down!'

'Where did you find this guy? What a nuisance this bum is, throw him out on the street,' the SI barked.

Once out of the lock-up, Raju asked the SI, 'Do you remember the house number of your relatives in Hyderabad?'

As the SI struggled to answer, his son bolted.

'See, just like you, I too can't remember house numbers...but that doesn't make me a thief,' Raju said and walked out onto the street.

LABOUR

R. R. BORADE

Translated from the Marathi by Anjali Nerlekar

THE SEASON OF STEADY RAINS HAD RECEDED AND NOW AN unreasonable rain started from clouds that seemed untimely pregnant. The sky would fill up once in ten to fifteen days. Occasionally it would sprinkle the hot, steaming yard with water. Seeming to winnow the woods, the rain would splash down in a circle for a while and then the sky would grow quiet again. And then there were times when the rain would pull no punches. The sky would fill up everywhere you looked. It would become dark as night. And it would rain uncontrollably, for hours at a stretch. The rain would then retreat after having stung the doggedly ripening crops.

From where she lay, Putali kept an eye on the eastern horizon where the clouds were gathered together like guests invited to an event. Slowly, the sun hid behind the clouds and it felt as if someone was holding a shade over one's head. It looked as though it was going to rain soon. Putali shook her head vigorously to dislodge the flies from her tired eyes and wet nostrils. She stood up, just barely. Her entire body was trembling and her legs were about to collapse. Putali dug her hooves into the ground. She was scarcely able to carry the weight of her heavy belly on her shaky legs. But she felt better for having stood up.

She lifted her exhausted gaze and tried looking around. At first, everything was blurry. She felt as if someone had placed a sheer curtain in front of her eyes. But gradually her gaze settled and she was able to focus. She looked at the expanse in front of her. The other cattle had started walking briskly in the direction of the village. The dust flying from their hooves floated in the air. Putali looked around her. This wasteland that stretched in front of her was covered with thorny weeds and thistle. A little distance away, there was a stubby and thorny acacia tree. Other than that, there was no other shelter anywhere in sight. Putali glanced again at the cattle walking in the direction of home and she began to low intensely. She bellowed as if her voice were being squeezed out of her and she suddenly felt nauseous because of that effort. Lowing a second time became too difficult for her. She opened her mouth and then shut it again. She looked at the cattle disappearing into the distance again. As she stared desperately at them, her eyes filled with tears. Helplessly, she looked to her left at the stunted tree. Gauging the intervening expanse between it and her present location in her mind, she turned towards it and began walking.

Lifting one foot after the other, she started her journey. She had barely walked a few steps when she felt a sudden movement in her stomach. The bulge inside her was moving continuously now. With pleading eyes, she looked up at the sky. Each cloud seemed to be hugging the next as if a carpenter had trimmed the edges and joined them together like pieces of wood. It was getting darker and the rains looked like they were approaching fast. With an effort, she picked up her pace. She had barely walked a short distance when she felt a piercing pain in her stomach. The pain made her body go limp and every hair on her body stood up in agony. She spread her hind legs, and crouching her body, urinated profusely. She straightened up. Just then a drop of rain splashed on her back. She shivered. She raised her head and watched the darkening sky. Then, with determination, she started walking again. Again, she felt an intense pain in her stomach. The waves of pain kept coming, one after another. It was as if a mill wheel was churning in her stomach. Putali slumped to the ground. Then she hoisted herself up again with an effort. But the stomach pains were unstoppable. She lay down, got up again. After several such attempts to sit down and stand up again, she felt a new and soft sensation within her belly. Gentler, even pleasurable, this feeling; she stood there with eyes closed, experiencing this inexplicably enjoyable sensation.

Just then a balloon the colour of a shiny pebble emerged from her belly and started filling up with air fast. She felt as if a heavy burden had been tied to her. She began walking slowly. She lifted her head and looked at the tree in front of her. The balloon began to swell until it was almost as big as a large water container and then as if overfull with air, it burst. Putali was relieved. It felt like her burden had lightened.

She looked up at the sky. The black clouds were ranged in shells one atop the other. It looked like the sky had been plastered with black ink. She looked again at the acacia tree that stood a little way ahead. Again, she gauged the distance between herself and the tree and began walking. Step by step, the mill wheel in her stomach that had temporarily stopped started churning again. The bulge in her belly started moving. Pain lanced continuously through her. Putali lowered her head and let the labour pangs come.

Then she felt as if someone had touched an axe to the inside of her underbelly. She shuddered deeply. The waves of pain crashed through her one after another. As they kept coming, the hooves made an appearance, just about four fingers long, and then they stopped there. She kept heaving with pain but the hooves would not move. There was a firestorm in her belly now. Everything seemed to be tossing around wildly within her. Putali clenched the muscles of her face. She tried looking ahead but she was unable to see the tree that had seemed to be so close. It felt like a curtain of darkness was falling in front of her eyes. Putali sank to the ground and, holding her breath, she heaved again. The hooves, stuck inside her all this while, started moving out again. It seemed she would be released from this agony in a little while. She closed her eyes and kept pushing. The hooves were emerging rapidly.

Just then the sky thundered, signalling the coming rain. Putali was terrified. She stood up with a jerk and tried to start walking towards the tree. But she could not lift a foot. A strong gust of wind swirled around her. With the wind came rain. At first it was just a few drops but it soon turned into a steady downpour of heavy and large raindrops. The heavy drops started ringing on the half-emerging hooves and that sound resounded within her stomach. It was like the sound of drum sticks on a drum.

Putali felt helpless. She tossed her head and made an attempt to low. But no sound came from her throat. Just as abruptly as it had begun, the heavy downpour stopped. Putali was relieved. She looked again at the tree. She attempted to walk towards it once more. Just as she lifted one foot, she felt a big convulsion within her belly. Planting her feet determinedly on the ground, she stopped right there, shuddering again. The inner jolts kept coming after that first one. The face of the calf was emerging little by little.

Just then it thundered again. The rain came down in streams as thick as one's fingers, making a loud sound as it hit the ground. The thunder sounded like gunshots. Lightning whiplashed across the sky, so bright it shocked the eyes. Putali looked up. She tried to focus and see as far as she possibly could but visibility was down to a few feet. She could not see the tree in front of her. The pains in her stomach kept on coming. She kept feeling the convulsions in her belly. The calf was slowly moving out of her.

The rain refused to stop cascading down and the calf was struggling to come out. Putali started trying to contract her body, to hold her breath in order to try and suck the hooves inside of her again. But the hooves would not go in, and the calf would not put its face back in. The breath, which she had been trying to hold, started escaping into the atmosphere like steam. Her body loosened up and the calf began to emerge, inch by inch, even as the rain, as if stoked with some demented energy, kept pelting down. There was water wherever the eyes could see. Putali tried to contract her body again but the calf would not heed her. Instead, Putali's pangs grew stronger and faster and more of the calf began to emerge. Desperate and helpless, Putali looked all around her. Just then an enormous bolt of pain surged through her. The calf put its face completely out. Putali realized this and was confused. She began turning round and round, as if in a circus ring. Trying to suck the calf's face and body into her body, she started screaming loudly. Putali kept circling round and round as if mesmerized and the rain, as if crazed, kept falling....

A SHEET

SALAM BIN RAZZAQ

Translated from the Urdu by Muhammad Umar Memon

HE WAS STANDING BY THE WINDOW LOOKING OUT ONTO THE STREET, which one could see in the distance shimmering in the sun as if somebody had magically stopped a flowing river. It was the same street on which traffic flowed uninterrupted well into the night, where crowds of people milled about like crawling ants right up to midnight. Morning and evening, the noise from the traffic and the people gave the sidewalks the atmosphere of a carnival. But at the moment, both the street and its sidewalks were completely deserted. Not a soul anywhere, not even a sound.

His mind too was as empty as the street in front of him. Now and then, though, a whirlwind of some inarticulate anxiety or fear did sweep over him. Dread and despair had begun to thicken around him, and he felt smothered. He picked up a packet of cigarettes from the table near him, lit up, drew a deep breath, and exhaled the smoke out the window. There was no wind at all. The smoke dissolved slowly, like life ebbing away from a dying patient. He longed for home. The image of his beautiful wife, Salma, the innocent pranks of his sons, Sajid and Majid, and the deep affection in the eyes of his old, paralytic mother flashed before his eyes. Salma had told him as he was leaving, 'It doesn't look good at all in Bombay. I'm worried.'

But he had tried to allay her fears. 'Riots are common in big cities like Bombay. Nothing to get so worked up about. They usually don't affect business there at all.'

'But you said you were going to Dadar. Dadar is one of the places affected by riots. The newspaper said so.'

'Oh, come now. After all, Vidyacharan also lives there. I'll go to his house first. I'll meet the party with him.'

'What if you waited a few days?'

'You don't understand. Vidya told me that these people are absolutely genuine. The supermarket under construction there in Bhawani Peth belongs to them. Two or three local interior decorators are bending over backwards to clinch the deal for themselves, but Vidya wants me to get the contract. He's the chief engineer. It's a big contract, worth several lakhs. Such an opportunity's not likely to come my way again in a long time. I'll take the bus straight from Dadar after the deal and be back home in Pune by the evening. Don't you worry.'

Salma hadn't said anything further, but the cloud of worry hadn't quite left her face.

His conversation with her running through his mind, he tossed the cigarette butt out through the window, stepped back and half-stretched out on the sofa. The ceiling fan was whirring away, making a muffled sound, like someone trying to let something out but held back by a nagging fear. Even though he was perfectly safe here, he still could feel fear surge up in him like a wave. Vidya, Vidya's father, Vidya's mother—they all tried to keep his spirits up with reassuring words. Vidyacharan's wife, Sushma, and his sister, Aarti, kept piling more puris and servings of vegetable on his plate, and Vidyacharan's younger brother Shyam kept inviting him to games of carom. In short, the entire household was doing its best to draw his heart away from the thoughts that troubled him; still, anxiety weighed even more heavily with every passing moment.

It had been around one o'clock in the afternoon when he got down from the Ashiyad bus at the Dadar terminal. He strode over to the sidewalk and stood there, his smallish briefcase in hand, looking for a taxi. But he spotted none. There was very little traffic on the street. Most of the stores had their shutters pulled down. The sidewalk had only a few pedestrians, who walked on swiftly with a purposeful gait, looking cautiously around, as though they were in a big rush to get somewhere. There was a strange but palpable tension in the air. He suddenly remembered what Salma had told him in the morning as he was leaving. An anxious thought reared up inside him, which he quickly shrugged off. Just then he saw a taxi approach from the right, carrying no fare. He stepped down from the sidewalk and waved, but the taxi just zoomed past him without stopping. The driver didn't so much as look at him. He was sitting behind the steering wheel like a statue, his hands frozen on the wheel. Afterwards a couple more taxis came along, but not one stopped. 'Okay,' he thought. 'I can just walk. Vidyacharan's house isn't all that far anyway. It'll take ten minutes at most to get there.'

He had set out, briefcase in hand. After crossing the main street, he entered an underpass, and felt even more acutely the sense of gravity in the air. The entire passageway was infused with an eerie silence, and the sound of his footfalls was making his blood freeze in his veins. The passageway ended in a series of buildings, but most had their gates closed. Some four or five young men stood in a group in front of one of the buildings, heatedly discussing something or the other. Seeing him approach, one of the young men said something to his companions. They all fell silent and looked over their shoulders at him. He lowered his eyes and took long strides past them. He didn't turn around to look at them, but he could hear that they had resumed talking. He entered the gate of Building 11 and took the stairs to the third floor, where he pressed the bell to Vidyacharan's apartment.

Vidyacharan himself opened the door. The moment he saw him, he said, 'Arre, Anwar! Come on in. We were waiting for you.'

Inside, Vidyacharan's father was sitting in a wooden swing-seat poring over a fat tome. He closed the book as soon as he saw him and said, 'We were quite worried about you, son! You didn't have any problem on the way, did you?'

'No, Uncle. But I did feel a strange tension in the air. The streets are deserted, shops are closed, and I couldn't get a single taxi to stop.'

'Yes, it's been like this for the last two or three days. Today, though, the atmosphere appears to be even more grim.'

'I called your house this morning,' Vidyacharan said. 'Bhabhi said that you'd already left about an hour earlier. If I'd caught you on the phone, I'd have told you not to come today.'

'What's the matter? Is it really serious?'

'Seems that way. Police cars are out patrolling. And there are rumours everywhere. About a hundred huts were torched last night in Dharavi. We could see the smoke even from here in the morning. I just heard on the telephone that several chawls have been set on fire in Jogeshwari as well.'

Now his heart began to sink even deeper, like a heavy stone in water. He could feel a faint restlessness squirm inside him. His silence prompted Vidyacharan to comfort him, 'There's no reason for you to worry. Everything is okay. Here, give me your briefcase.'

Vidyacharan took the briefcase from him and he sat down on the sofa. Meanwhile, Sushma appeared with a glass and jug of water. After greeting him, she set the glass and the jug on the tea table, smiled and asked, 'How are Bhabhi and the children?'

'They're fine,' he responded, smiling formally.

In the meantime, both Vidyacharan's mother and sister walked in. 'Vidya!' the old lady said to her son, 'Take Anwar to wash his hands. Lunch is ready.'

Shortly thereafter low wooden stools were set on the floor and everybody took their seats. Thalis were placed in front of everyone, and Sushma and Aarti dutifully served the food. He took a look around and said, 'I don't see Shyam. Where is he?'

'He's gone to college. He'll be back soon.'

After the meal he picked up a piece of betel nut from the saucer and put it in his mouth. Then he said, 'Vidya, shouldn't we go now and take care of the job? I'll take the bus home right after.'

'But the office is closed today...because of the riots. I called you this morning to tell you just that.'

'Oh.' Anxiety deepened in the lines on his forehead. 'In that case, allow me to leave. I should return right away. Otherwise Salma and Mother will start worrying.'

'All right. But I think you should take the train instead. Let me walk you to the station.'

'Uncle, I'm leaving now,' he looked at Vidyacharan's father.

'Okay, son. Given the situation, we can't even ask you to stay over. But be careful. Give us a call as soon as you've arrived in Pune.' His voice was full of concern.

Just then the bell rang. Vidyacharan opened the door and in walked Shyam. The minute he saw him, he said, 'Arre, Anwar Bhaiya! When did you arrive?' He then came over and sat down right next to him.

'About an hour ago. Tell me, how are your studies?'

'Perfect. And I mean perfect....'

'How is it outside?' Vidyacharan enquired.

'Bhaiya, it isn't good. Somebody was knifed outside the railway station just a little while ago. Police cars are patrolling everywhere. A curfew's been declared in the area around the station.'

Abruptly everyone fell silent. He looked up, only to see that everyone else was looking at him. Vidyacharan cleared his throat and said, 'Let me call Inspector Rana and find out.'

Vidyacharan got up and dialled the number. He talked with someone briefly, hung up and returned to the sofa.

'What did the inspector say?' he asked, feeling impatient.

'He said that the trains are running all right, but the situation isn't at all good. A curfew is expected in the entire area any time. News has just come that a terrible riot's broken out in Mahim as well.'

'But, Vidya, I have to return today. If I don't, they'll be worried sick.'

Once again everybody fell silent. After a while, Vidyacharan's father said, 'Anwar, son, listen to me and stay here tonight. You can go back tomorrow after the work is done. Likely the situation will have become normal by tomorrow. Call Bahu and let her know that you'll be staying here tonight.'

'But, Uncle, if I start right away, I can make it to Pune by evening. If the situation doesn't improve by tomorrow....'

Just then a police siren blared outside. The police van was announcing the curfew.

'There, they've imposed the curfew. Didn't I say that they would, pretty soon?' Shyam said, suppressing his excitement. Then he got up, walked over to the window, and peered outside.

Vidya's father chided him: 'Shyam, shut the window and sit down quietly.' Then he ordered his elder son, 'Vidya, see to it that the windows in all the rooms are securely shut.'

Vidya got up and started to close the windows like a dutiful son, while his mother, Sushma, and Aarti stood quietly inside the inner room.

Vidya's father got up and started to pace aimlessly. Shyam, somewhat miffed, went over to the sofa and plopped down on it. The room became dark with the closing of the windows. Vidya's seven-year-old boy, Pappu, asked his grandmother, 'Dadi, Dadi, what is a curfew?'

But nobody gave him a reply. In the semi-dark room they looked like so many quiet, immobile shadows. The only movement came from Vidya's father, who was still walking restlessly with his hands folded behind his back. He was bare-chested above the waist. The sacred thread hung over his shoulder. His head was clean-shaven except for a tuft of hair that hung over his back like a squirrel's tail. He had vibhuti painted between his eyebrows, and he was clad in a white dhoti.

Anwar had often seen him in just this garb. In fact, he had seen him like this for many, many years. A devout, religious man, he was nevertheless quite secular in his thinking. He was well read, not just in his own religion, but also in many others. Anwar respected him a lot, and the old man always treated Anwar with affection. Every time he met him, every time he spoke to him, he had the feeling of sitting in the shade of some ancient peepul and listening to an old, dreadlocked sadhu expound on the meaning of contemplative life.

Today, however, he appeared to be an altogether different man. A stranger, who never had anything to do with him at all, and not just the old man alone—even Vidya's mother, Sushma, Aarti, Vidya himself, and Shyam, seemed strangers to him.

Anwar felt he would suffocate. His throat went dry and he longed for water. But, at this moment, asking for water would have amounted to an admission of his weakness. So he satisfied himself by running his tongue over his parched lips.

The darkness intensified the heaviness inside the room. Why didn't anyone turn on the light? Just then Vidyacharan, as if sensing his friend's wish in some occult way, got up and did just that. The moment the room lit up, a current of animation swept through it. Vidya's father resumed his place on the swing-seat, which began to sway gently like a houseboat. Shyam got up and turned on the TV. Pappu ran up to the rocking swing-seat and stood on it, clutching the bar for support. Sushma and Aarti retreated to the inner room. Vidya's mother edged up to Anwar and said softly, 'Son, think of this as your own house. And don't let yourself worry too much. Nobody's going to harm you here. Now get up and call Bahu. She must be out of her wits with worry. Give her a few words of assurance. Tomorrow, as soon as the situation improves, you can return.'

He peered into the old lady's eyes: empathy and motherly affection was all he could see there. The unknown fear that had taken hold of his mind relaxed somewhat, and the feeling of being in the midst of strangers that had tormented him a while ago slowly began to disappear. Fear had raised a wall of suspicion. As the fear itself lessened, the wall too crumbled away. He took out his handkerchief from his pocket, wiped the sweat off his forehead, got up and went over to the phone. Sure enough, it was Salma who answered. The moment she heard his voice, she was overcome with emotion, on the verge of tears. 'How are you?' she enquired. 'Vidyacharan Bhai called right after you left. Where are you calling from? Come home quickly, please. I feel terribly afraid.' She said it all at one go, without seeming to take even a breath. Fighting back his own emotion, he tried to say in as normal a voice as he could possibly muster, 'Don't worry, Salma. I'll be back tomorrow. I'm calling you from Vidyacharan's house. Ordinary skirmishes, that's all. Nothing big. It'll all return to normal by tomorrow.'

'But why do you want to stay on overnight? Why not return this evening, if your work's finished?'

'That's just it. The work isn't finished. The office of the people we want to meet is closed today. I'll take care of the paperwork first thing tomorrow morning. I'll be back in Pune by the afternoon. Tell Mother not to worry. Vidyacharan is here with me. Kiss Sajid and Majid for me.'

'Give your mother my namaskar,' Vidya's mother instructed him in a loud voice.

'Aunt is sending Mother her greetings. I'll call you back again in the evening. And now I'll hang up. Khuda hafiz!'

Salma, too, from the other end said in a drained voice, 'Fi amani 'l-Lah!'

'It's good that you didn't tell Bhabhi about the curfew,' Vidya said.

'All the same, she'll find out. Tomorrow. In the papers. She'll know everything. And she will feel miserable....'

He wiped the sweat off his forehead once again and sat down on the sofa. Then Vidyacharan grabbed his hand and brought him into the other room, with a bed, a couple of couches, a writing table, and a few books. 'This is my room,' Vidyacharan said as he opened the window and slid the curtain to one side. 'I had it built only recently. You can rest here.'

He didn't reply.

'Pitaji worries too much. But really there's no need to close the window. You keep it open. Nothing will happen.'

He peered down from the window. It opened onto the main street. But the street was completely deserted at the moment.

'The bathroom's over there. Take a shower if you like. You'll feel fresh. But just rest now. We'll meet again over tea at four o'clock.'

He then stepped forward and put his hand on Anwar's shoulder. 'Don't think that I don't know what you're going through. But don't you worry. Everything will turn out okay. You'll get back to Pune in one piece—I promise.'

He looked at Vidya with a wan smile and stretched out on the sofa. 'I'm okay, Vidya. Don't worry about me.'

'Just yell if you need anything.' Vidyacharan left the room.

The evening news on TV showed a few glimpses of the riots in the city. The dreadful scenes left no doubt that rioting had spread through the entire city, and a curfew had been imposed in several areas. Towards the tail end of the news, the police commissioner was shown repeating the same asinine assurance: 'But the situation is under control.'

His restlessness grew worse. Even before the news had ended, he quickly got up and dialled his number at Pune, but couldn't get through. He tried again and again. Perhaps there was a problem with the line itself. A bit irritated, he returned to his seat.

'What happened?' Vidya's father asked.

'Looks like the line is out of order.'

Later, Vidyacharan himself tried a few times but had no luck. They'd already had their supper and were now commenting on the news.

Vidya's father said: 'What's got into people that they are slaughtering others just like them as though they were goats and sheep? I can't understand how a man can hate another so much.'

'God knows where these riots will take the country,' Vidyacharan wondered in a voice full of anxiety.

Vidya's mother joined both her hands against her forehead and said, 'May Ishwar protect us all.'

Suddenly they were all looking at him. He too wanted to say something, but just couldn't get it out. Not a single word. Thoughts were swirling in his mind like a whirlwind, but the corresponding words, before they so much as reached his tongue, perished like bubbles on the surface of water. The feeling that he had been caught in thorny brambles took hold of him. If he stirred even slightly, countless sharp needles would prick him all over his body. Never before had he felt himself so helpless. Just then Shyam got up, brought the carom board over, and said, 'Anwar Bhai, how about a game or two?'

A sense of relief washed over him, as if somebody had pulled him from the water just as he was drowning. He agreed right away.

The board was laid out. Aarti and Vidyacharan sat opposite each other as partners, with Shyam and he as partners against them. The game began.

The round black and white pieces were arranged in the circle in the middle of the board and were then hit with the striker, which scattered them all over the board. For a long time, the striker kept hitting the pieces, sending them into the corner pockets.

He was playing well enough, but his thoughts were elsewhere, as scenes of the rioting played over in his mind—houses going up in flames, women running out screaming and crying, children weeping bitterly, old men stumbling along, young men brandishing swords and spears, and rising above them all the loud, body-shaking cries of 'Allahu Akbar!' and 'Har Har Mahadev!'

'What are you thinking about, Anwar Bhai?' Shyam alerted him. 'Take the queen! It's just within reach!'

'Where is it?' he asked, with a start.

The queen was within easy reach of him. He hit it with the striker. The piece banged against the edge and bounced back, fluttering on the board for a while before dropping dead.

∫

Once, seven or eight years ago on Bakri Eid, he had sacrificed the goat with his own hands. But before the knife had completely slit the throat, the animal thrashed violently and got away from him, blood gushing from the gaping wound. People ran after it and grabbed it. But he was unable to finish the job. Somebody else had to do it for him. Never again since that day was he able to slaughter an animal for sacrifice. Looking at the queen, now, as it wobbled on the board, he suddenly recalled that goat with its throat only half-slit.

'Come on, Anwar Bhai, what's this? You could've pocketed the piece so easily,' Shyam said, showing his regret.

'I'm sorry, Shyam. I'm just tired.' He leaned back in his chair and closed his eyes.

'Shyam, you play with Aarti. Let Anwar rest.' Vidyacharan then grabbed Anwar's hand and made him get up.

'Let's try to call again,' Anwar said.

'Yes, sure.' Vidya dialled the number. He dialled again. And again. He shook his head in disappointment and said, 'I don't think it'll work. Looks like the line's dead.'

He quietly went into the other room and lay on the bed face down. His heart was sinking. If only he had got some news of Salma and the children, perhaps it would have helped ease his worry. The thought of his helplessness hit him hard. He felt like breaking down in tears, crying his heart out. But even crying wasn't easy. What will these people think—people who were doing their best to comfort him? If he cried, not only would he humiliate himself, but he'd also hurt their confidence. Perhaps the limit of helplessness is the inability to cry when tears alone might help. Just then he heard a click and the light was turned off in his room. He turned over with a start.

'Nothing! It's just me. Go to sleep!' Vidyacharan said, closing the door gently behind him on his way out.

After his departure a deathly stillness swept over the room. Not even the sound of a dog barking anywhere. Perhaps even the dogs had withdrawn to their shelters, cringing with fear. Only the sound of some policeman's whistle rose now and then, or that of a siren. Meanwhile, he fell asleep.

God knows what hour of the night it was when a sound woke him. The same darkness and stillness was around him once again. But no, small cracks had begun to appear in the wall of silence. He heard the muffled screams of hundreds, no, thousands of people coming from afar. He got up from the bed, quietly opened the window and peered out. The street lay just as quiet and deserted as it had been earlier during the day. But he did see what he thought was smoke rising somewhere far off on the western horizon. The sky, too, looked reddish. Perhaps there had been an immense conflagration there. The noise too seemed to be coming from there. Just then he heard the rumble of a lorry on the street. It too was coming from the same direction. He couldn't see clearly because of the darkness, but could make out several people huddled inside the lorry with weapons flashing in the hands of at least a few of them. A tremor shot through his entire body. Just then he heard a faint clatter outside his room, which set his heart pounding. An unknown fear reared up in his mind like the hood of a cobra. God only knew what was about to happen! Could it be that the neighbours had found out that Vidya's family was harbouring an enemy, and so now were insisting, even this late at night, that they hand him over to them? He imagined himself being dragged out by a group of young men with saffron headbands. He would be gagged and, try hard as he might, just wouldn't be able to get a sound out. He groped for the light switch and turned it on. The room brightened. Shortly thereafter the door opened and Vidyacharan entered.

'You turned on the light—what's the matter?'

'Nothing. I just woke up suddenly.'

Vidyacharan stared and then said as he sat down on the sofa, 'I peeked in earlier, but you were sleeping.'

'How come you aren't in bed?'

'I can't fall asleep.'

'Why not?'

'I keep thinking that you don't feel safe here.'

'No, it isn't like that at all. You wouldn't let me be harmed in any way—I know that, Vidya. But given the conditions, it's hard not to feel at least a little bit alarmed.'

'I understand. But remember this: no matter how volatile it may be all around, all it'll take is a phone call, and a whole battalion of policemen will show up. The police commissioner is my friend. If you'd like to talk to him, I can arrange that right away.'

'No, no. There's no need. Vidya, please don't misunderstand me. I trust you completely.'

After a brief silence, Vidya abruptly asked, 'Want some coffee?'

'I suppose I could use a cup.'

'Wait. I'll go and make some.'

The entire household came together again in the morning at breakfast. The situation outside remained unchanged. The curfew, though, was lifted for two hours. It was back in effect at ten o'clock.

Vidya called the railway station, police station, S.T. bus depot, Ashiyad bus terminal, taxi-stand—just about everywhere to get some idea of the situation. Everywhere he got the same answer: 'The situation doesn't look good. Better not travel.'

The telephone line to Pune was still dead. Enquiries were made at the telephone exchange, but no satisfactory explanation was offered. His anxiety was growing worse by the minute. But deftly hiding what was eating away at him inside, he kept talking to Vidya, his father, his mother, Shyam, and Aarti as normally as he possibly could. He had Pappu recite two poems for him, and told him the story of the triple-horned demon, in which the prince hacks off each of the three horns one after another with his sword. Pappu was extremely pleased. He clapped and laughed for a long time. For his own part, though, he wondered: how could a six-foot-tall prince possibly exterminate a giant six times his size? But children are so gullible. How easily they believe everything in a story. It's only when they grow up that they sink into the quagmire of doubt, suspicion, scepticism, and lack of trust. Seeing Pappu clap so joyously, he remembered his sons Sajid and Majid. He quickly bent over Pappu and kissed him on the forehead. Once again he started to feel anxiety tug at his heart. He got up and returned to his room.

Standing at the window he gazed into the desolate street for the longest time. All looked clear in the direction where he had seen that terrible smoke rising last night. A few young men stood talking inside the compound wall of the building directly in front. A police van drove in, moving at a snail's pace, and slowly inched further and further away. Suddenly a noise erupted to his left. He poked his head out to see. A scrawny young man ran out of a narrow alley. His wrists were bound behind him and his clothes were on fire. 'Help! Help!' he was shouting. 'Water! Water!' Perhaps his clothes had been doused with kerosene, because the fire was spreading very fast. His screams prompted the windows of the buildings around to open one by one. A few people craned their necks to look at him. The emaciated young man was jerking his head, all the while screaming for help. 'Untie my hands! What will you get by killing me? Water!...Water!'

He ran towards the compound where the group of young men stood talking. But the moment he came near the gate, they quickly closed it. The man kept begging them for water. But they turned around and went inside the building.

By now the flames had completely enveloped the youth, who looked like a single flame in motion. Running, he fell, and started to roll in the middle of the street, still screaming in sheer torment.

The tied hands finally broke free. All at once, charged with a sudden surge of energy, he got up and started madly to tear off his burning clothes from his body. But once again he stumbled and fell down, and began to writhe and thrash on the ground. His screams subsided into moans, his convulsions getting progressively weaker. His clothes had turned to ashes that stuck to his body, which had itself become as charred as a piece of charcoal. His moans too subsided.

Only one or another part of his body twitched as the fire began to die down.

Anwar gazed at the scene like it was a frightening nightmare, his hands clutching the frame of the window. His temples pounded as though he had been stuffed into the belly of an endlessly beaten kettledrum. He was shaking...slowly.

Down below, the body of the youth had by now become completely charred. The fire too had died down, giving off a few stray curls of smoke. Just then a police siren blared. People peering out quickly shut their windows, though some were left open just a crack through which they could peek. He too backed up and closed the window with his tremulous hands, leaving just a chink open through which he looked at what was going on. The police van stopped a little distance from the charred body. Four or five constables got down from the van, and the inspector from the front seat. The inspector walked over to the body with perfect composure. He had covered his mouth and nose with his handkerchief. The constables too held their noses between their thumbs and index fingers and followed him. They stood around the body. The corpse was now naked and had been rendered grotesque by the fire. The inspector said something, and one of the constables, still holding his nose, bent over and poked the corpse with his long stick. Then, shaking his head 'No,' he stood up straight. The inspector lifted his head and gave a sweeping look at the neighbouring buildings. Heads peering from behind the slim openings in the windows instantaneously withdrew like turtles.

The inspector thundered: 'Who burnt him? Tell me, who burnt him? Answer me!'

The openings in the windows further narrowed. Waving his stick the inspector walked to the corner of the alley on the left, peered into it, and then walked back to the corpse. Once again he raised his head to the windows and yelled, 'At least throw down a cloth to cover the body. Have you lost all sense of humanity?'

A painful silence swept over the scene for a while. Then a window on the first floor of the building in front opened and an old man, leaning halfway out, tossed a white bedsheet down to the street. Then another window opened. A woman poked her head out and she too threw a folded white bedsheet down to the street. And then another window opened, and then another. Seven sparkling white bedsheets were tossed out within a few minutes. The inspector shouted, 'That's enough charity! Now stop it!'

Two constables stepped forward. Picking up one of the sheets, they unfolded it and spread it over the corpse.

Anwar closed his window and sat down on the bed. Suddenly he felt the whirlwind of dread starting to subside in his mind, replaced by a terrible emptiness. Astonishingly, all at once, he had risen above every fear, every apprehension.

AND THEN IT POURED *

GAURI DESHPANDE

Translated from the Marathi by Anjali Nerlekar

AMMI IS MY MOTHER, NOT BY BIRTH, MY STEPMOTHER. BUT YOU shouldn't conclude that this is a typical story of a stepmother abusing her stepdaughter. Forget about raising her voice at me, Ammi rarely even lifted her gaze to meet anyone's eyes. As for her raising her hand to spank me, even those who knew her couldn't have imagined anything like it in their wildest dreams, let alone she herself. If anyone was abused at all, it was her by me. She was so meek that she almost invited such exploitation. But if you think I will follow in the footsteps of many revered gurus and teachers and hang the story of a virtuous mother around your neck, then you are certainly wrong. This is Ammi's story, and in my view, remarkable enough as is. But since it is I who will tell the story, of course, I will bend it to my own will here. And since I am not at all virtuous or exemplary, if there is even the slightest moral to this tale, then attribute it to your own love of literary writing.

Anyway, when Appa married Ammi, I must have been thirteen or fourteen years old. I never felt the need for a mother as a kid. In fact, in my class, another girl and I were the 'poor girls without mothers'. The other girl would start crying uncontrollably whenever anyone started singing 'Aai Mhanoni Koni'** (and since that poem was in the school textbooks, such occasions arose frequently). I would always be amazed at that. Not wanting to be mocked by the other girls, I also pretended to cry at those times. But later, when such dramatic situations started happening three or four times a year, I gave up the pretence of weeping. But people pitied me despite that. Appa had a travelling job and he earned a lot of money from it. At home we always had a throng of servants and maids, secretaries, cooks, and chauffeurs. I didn't have the time to feel lonely or neglected. Why Appa should get married thirteen or fourteen years after his first wife passed away, at the age of forty, that I can understand very easily. But I never figured out why the twenty-year-old, good-looking woman married him, not until she died. One day Appa returned from his trip to Mangalore

---
*The Marathi title 'Paus Ala Motha' is a line from the popular children's rhyme, 'Ye re ye re pausa/ Tula deto paisa/ Paisa jhala khota/ Paus ala motha (rain, rain please do come/ I will give you a paisa/ the paisa turned out fake/ and then it poured).
**'Aai Mhanoni Koni' is a famous Marathi poem by the poet Yashwant. This was also featured in an equally famous film, *Shyamchi Aai* (1953). It is seen as a tear-jerking, sentimental poem about the loss of a mother.

with Ammi in tow. A simple, everyday sari, nothing else on her except the mangalsutra around her neck, smudged kunku on her forehead the size of a ten paisa coin, scrawny and pale presence, and wisdom beyond her years on her face.

In his usual manner, Appa said, 'This is Amala, my wife. And this is Savitri, my daughter. This, the house. Savi will explain all. It's your house.' And with noisy shoes, he started walking towards the office room. I didn't really mind any of this. Children are generally self-absorbed. I said to myself, *So she is Appa's wife, what's it to me? There are so many people in the house, what's one more.* I said, 'I want to go to my friend's house,' and escaped from there. I don't know what Ammi did after that.

She did not join us when the two of us sat down to have dinner. As usual, Appa was reading some documents, and I, a comic book. As I turned a page, I asked, 'How should I address her?'

Appa said, 'Hmmm.'

I asked again, upon which, he frowned and asked, 'Who?'

'Your wife?'

'Her relatives called her Ammi.'

I said, 'Um-hmm.'

After dinner, each one of us retired to our own room. The next day at chai time, during breakfast, I saw Ammi again. She occupied herself with my schoolbooks and asked me some superficial questions about school. I told her, 'Feel free to take any book to read if you like.'

She looked down and said haltingly, 'I cannot read or write.'

I found this extremely strange. Until then, I hadn't met anyone who could not read or write. I think that was the first time I expressed some interest in someone else. I asked, 'What will you do the entire day?'

'I will manage,' she said and changed the subject. But what exactly she would do the whole day, I never found out. After all, she had entered a well-established home as the mother of an adolescent girl. She had hardly any work to do. Now when I think back, I don't remember her spending time talking to the servants nor do I remember seeing her walking in the garden. If I returned home unexpectedly, I would find her lying on the divan in the balcony upstairs, watching the world go back and forth on the street. The house was run impeccably as always, and within it, we behaved as before, trying as much as possible not to get entangled in each other's life. These were the last years of my school life. Visiting girlfriends, movies, theatre…it went on endlessly. I had to return home by six, other than that Appa had not imposed any other rule on me. Once he had laid down the rule, he assumed that I returned home on time. And at least until then it had not occurred to me that I needed to break this rule either. But sometimes, because I was lost in chatting with friends, or because there were play rehearsals and one could not just get up and walk away in the middle of it, if it turned out six o'clock became six-thirty or seven, there was no reason for him to know about it. So, one day, as I returned carefree at six-thirty and climbed the stairwell outside and stepped into the living room, I unexpectedly faced the early arrival of Appa.

'You are late.'

'Yes, but....'

'Starting tomorrow, every day I want a phone call to my office informing me that you have returned home straight after school.'

'But Appa, the drama rehearsal....'

'No excuses.'

'Am I a child to be treated like....'

'Savitri, you cannot speak to me in that tone!'

'Then you shouldn't in that tone either....'

'Shut your mouth! Get out!'

'You say get out? I refuse to listen to you. If you yell at me like this, I will yell back ten times louder. To be utterly stifled in this manner, and then handed such an overbearing judgement, have I committed burglary or murder? Do I tell you what to do when....'

A sharply delivered slap to the face cut out the rest of the statement. Before Appa's other hand could slap my other cheek, someone dragged me to my room and locked the door on the other side. Outside, Appa's voice was shaking in anger.

'Amala, you should not interfere here. She is a rude and feckless brat and she must be disciplined and brought into line.'

Ammi's tone was subdued and fearful.

'You slap your daughter, a fifteen-year-old girl who has been raised by you, in front of the servants! Really? Even if she has abandoned all shame, surely you aren't juvenile like her.'

Ammi was actually talking back to him and in that tone! My anger had long since melted in the surprise of it all. I silently put my ear to the door. But there was some murmuring outside and then both of them went away. The next day, the door was unlocked, and at breakfast Appa tried to pretend as if nothing had happened. While leaving, he shoved his chair back and said to me, 'Don't you forget the rule—come home straight after school.'

I bit my tongue.

I was home at four-thirty every day. Time to chit-chat with Ammi. There was an age difference of a mere six or seven years between us. She must have felt much closer to me than to Appa. But in that forced friendship of some six months to a year, she never said a word about herself, something I realized only many years later. Mostly she sat on my bed mending clothes, and I used to read out things to her, while reading something myself, or doing schoolwork, or browsing through a magazine as I lay on my back on the carpet. If he returned home early, Appa used to go straight to his room, and she wouldn't bother to go to his room to serve him tea or snacks either. Wasn't there the butler or the servant-boy?

Once the heat of the sun had clearly diminished, we used to take walks in the garden around the house. Ammi used to make long garlands of rubber plant flowers and gulbakshi flowers and wrap them around the trees. Her first reaction would be to laugh at anything I told her. She was amazed by everything. Once I told her that a girl in my class was named Maharukh. That was the first time, I think, that she could not control her peals of laughter even in front of Appa. After that, for many days, I just had to say the word Maharukh and Ammi would start laughing helplessly. In my case, she would praise every little thing I did, that even though I was no longer a child I wore frocks, that I had a boyish haircut, that I spoke English fluently, that I acted in plays, that I swam, that I played, nothing was left unappreciated. Frequently, I would ask her in frustration, 'You didn't live on the moon or some other planet before this, did you? How are you so rustic?' Then she would shut right up. Just as he was with others, Appa was distant and curt with her as well. He never called out to her, never told her anything, at least not in my presence, except for that one incident outside my closed door. In fact, given the minimal talk happening in our home, she would have felt as if she were in a school for the deaf-mute if I hadn't been there. Also, Appa had gathered around him servants who spoke as little as he did, and my friends never visited me at home. Before Ammi joined us, even if someone did come over, because of the deathly silence pervading the home, there was little possibility that they would ever return. I did not mind this because I was used to it from the beginning. On the contrary, upon listening to the commotion in others' houses I used to prefer my own home.

That year in June I applied to go to college and the frail relations between Ammi and I descended into less than nothing. New friends, new issues, conferences, and meetings, debating and drama societies, picnics, play, all of this meant that I was hardly at home any more. That I came home to eat lunch was itself a feat. Because of this and many other reasons, it was a constant battle between Appa and I. It was he who had brought me up so I was equally reckless, scornful, and brash. I did not let a single accusation from anyone pass me by, nor did I hesitate to say anything for fear of how it would be taken. Ammi was at her wits' end. Appa never again raised his hand to hit me, but that was more than compensated for by his words. Appa yelled more at me in those four years of college than he had ever spoken to me in his entire life. I used to bring my friends home when he was not around. And very pointedly I would introduce Ammi to them, 'This is my stepmother.' How strange and provincial she was, that was the topic of our conversation. This easily lasted all of four years. I found the 'weird' relationship between Ammi-Appa very useful to show how I had led a different life from that of others. Later, when I studied psychology, I would discuss seriously with my gang of friends how Appa must have had a complex because he married such an extremely young girl when he was so much older himself, or how Ammi must have had a father fixation. Now, I regard a man in his fifties as mature, in his prime, etc., but as a twenty-year-old, I saw a man of forty-five as being almost in the jaws of death. Unless he suffered from some kind of a complex, why would he enter the world of married life that is rightfully the space for the young? That was the logic. And that he should constantly quarrel with me, or behave churlishly, that seemed quite significant.

I had applied to all kinds of educational institutions in my last year of college. I was successful and got admission in an institution in Mumbai to continue to study further. Of course, that meant facing another quarrel. 'I am not saying you shouldn't study further, but why must you leave home and go to Mumbai for that?'

My intention in studying further, at that time at least, was precisely in order to leave home, hence there was no sense to this argument. I decided I would go for the win in this battle and I reached for the heart of the matter.

'But, Appa, you are not going to provide for me my entire life. Once I become a specialist in this topic, high-paying jobs will be aplenty. Then you need not worry about me at all.'

'But, Savitri, it isn't like they are piling the wood on my funeral pyre just yet.'

'But don't they say nowadays that the years between forty-five and fifty-five are the most dangerous?'

Ammi said under her breath, 'Savitri!'

Appa was a little uneasy. But he persisted and asked, 'Don't you want to get married at all? You have so many friends who are boys, anyone special among them?'

I was slack-jawed and stared in disbelief. He too must have felt awkward, but still he waited for a response. I laughed with derision and tossed the standard reply at him, 'I don't want to get married at all.'

'It is good to get such things done in time, Savi.'

His sweet tone only enraged me.

'What did you do in time for me? John Butler was with me when I got braces for my teeth. Information about periods and so on I got from the family doctor, your steno went to buy bras for me. I got the "facts of life" from the stealthily-read *Samajswasthya*, while hiding it inside my desk, and *Time* magazine informed me about the pill. Where was there any connection between your life and mine?'

Performing the typical father's role, Appa jumped into my trap:

'Savitri!' he thundered. 'Why do you need information about the pill? Do you dare to tell me....'

'Don't be medieval, Appa!'

Of course our quarrel took the predictable route:

'Go to hell, do whatever you like, do not come back to show me your face.' Saying this, Appa walked away fuming.

At night, as I was packing to go, Ammi came to enquire what had happened. The quarrel about 'the pill', etc. had taken place in English so she hadn't understood anything. Appa had left his dinner uneaten and was walking up and down angrily, muttering to himself, she said.

I laughed out loud. 'Serves him right!'

'But, Savi, why won't you get married? You have such lovely men friends!'

'Yeah, right! Your very happy conjugal life should absolutely inspire me to get married, yes?'

Ammi had been holding a pile of clothes in her hand. She set it down slowly. Weighing each and every word of hers, she retorted angrily, for the first and last time in her life, I think: 'Savitri, what faults you find in your father, what you say to him, I have not interfered in that until now, and will not in the future. But how he should behave with me, whether it is appropriate or not, that is our issue—you do not have the right to speak about that! Do not talk about this with me again ever.'

She was about to turn and leave. I was mortified. As soon as I had uttered it, my churlish tongue itself had minded it. But a leopard and its spots. Gathering some nerve, I said: 'Then you don't have any right to meddle in my affairs either! Don't come to me asking any more questions.'

I had thought she would be hurt. But turning, she smiled and said, 'It's true, my mistake', and walked away.

I left for Mumbai in the morning. Of course, in those two years I never returned home nor did I write any letters to them. On his work travels, if Appa was ever in Mumbai, he would call me. How are you, I am fine, was the type of conversations we had. As I had predicted, I got a well-paying job in Mumbai after finishing my studies, and I settled down there. This topic of my study, my knowledge of it, its use, all of this became really interesting to me now, so the days, full and busy, passed by quickly.

It must have been the second or third year of my job when Ammi suddenly appeared in my doorway, bag in hand. It had been four or five years since I had last seen her. I didn't even recognize her initially. I was getting ready to go out to eat somewhere.

'What is this? How come you are here?'

'I have come to stay with you. At your place.'

She had come in by then. Then I noticed the absence of the ten-paise coin size kunku on her forehead.

'Ammi....'

'Yes. Your father passed away a fortnight ago. Heart attack.'

I felt like an idiot, I could find no way to respond. I said, 'Didn't I always say that it's a dangerous age?'

Ammi said, 'Yes.'

I sat down. And what came to my mind first and foremost? That now there's no point in going out to eat. Then I thought, many years ago I would have had to pretend to cry when they played the song 'Aai Mhanoni Koni'...it's a similar situation now. I lifted the phone and stated, 'Sorry.

I will not be able to come. I just heard that my father has passed away.' But then I stopped. How do I tell them he died a fortnight ago but that I only came to know just now? Putting the phone down, I screamed at Ammi, 'Why didn't you call me? A phone call, a telegram—'

She actually smiled a little and said, 'He forbade me.'

I hit my forehead with my palm.

I called some people in the office, told them I wouldn't be coming for two or three days. Listening to their shocked condolences, I kept staring at Ammi. Watching me and listening to my sad voice, she continued to smile. I slammed the phone down and said, 'Ammi, this is the limit! How am I supposed to face people now? My own father died and I didn't even know of it for an entire fortnight! So, okay, Appa forbade you to contact me while alive. But you could have contacted me as soon as he died. Some acknowledgement of custom, of tradition....'

My voice died down in the face of her silent laughter. She responded in a quiet, calm voice: 'The will leaves the entire estate to you, the only condition is that you take care of me in your home as if I was your own mother, with love. A few shares or some such have been placed in my name and their interest comes to me. Before I die, I will turn them over to you.'

I didn't understand. 'So you will stay here with me? Forever?'

'Yes,' she smiled again.

I kept staring at her face. Slowly, I realized that Ammi had no one else now. Her husband had died. I might have felt bad about losing a father, but for her....

I got up shamefacedly and rubbed her back to console her. She spoke in a nonchalant manner and asked, 'It won't be a problem for you, will it? I will take care of your home.'

We didn't talk much after that.

Ammi settled down. So much so that one could wonder how I managed before she arrived. But our behaviour with each other was the same as before. She must have got used to the eccentric nature of our 'family'. She never spoke unless specifically called or addressed. It was I who used to think how strange she is. Two people live in the same house and yet not more than four sentences are exchanged between them, and she feels nothing about it. If at times I felt embarrassed about always spending time outside, I would ask, 'Want to join me at the cinema? Want to go out shopping?' She would say, 'No, I don't understand those things.' Only when friends visited home did we talk with each other a little more in front of them. With hesitation, I would introduce her: 'This is Ammi, my mother.' Then turning towards those who were listening, she would add with a smile, 'Her stepmother.' To which, embarrassed, I would add, 'Yeah, she has harassed me no end!' and at this standard joke everyone would laugh dutifully.

Ammi fell ill six months after she came to my home. Something quite simple, a cold or cough, or something. But she insisted, 'Take me to the hospital.'

Though I was a little irritated, there we were at the hospital. When it was time to go inside to consult the doctor, and I got up to accompany her, she said, 'You wait here.' Frowning, I sat there for half an hour when the nurse came out and said, 'The doctor wants to see you.'

I stepped inside and he said, 'Do sit.' Ammi was nowhere to be seen. I sat down. He said nothing. I pointedly looked at my watch. He cleared his throat and fumbling with his stethoscope, said: 'Miss Raghavan, your... your....'

I added, 'Mother?'

'Mother. Well, your mother has....' he inhaled sharply and blurted out, 'Your mother has leukaemia. She doesn't have too long to live.'

My eyes turned as wide as saucers and seeing the extreme shock on my face he got up hurriedly and came towards me and, patting me on the back, said 'There, there' or 'Now, now' or something like that. The nurse came there and said, 'Come this way, please.' Stumbling, feeling as if I were dead, I went where she took me. To Ammi's room. She was lying on a bed. There was a bottle of blood attached to a drip in her arm. She saw me and said, 'Sit down.'

I sat down and the two of us stared at each other. Finally, I stood up abruptly and in a cutting tone asked, 'So, you knew about this all along?'

'Yes.'

'And Appa?'

'Yes.'

'How long have you been ill?'

'Since I was nineteen or twenty. The doctor had said then, even if you get four or five years more, that would be a stretch. Now the time has come.'

I stayed silent for a long time. Then again, I blurted out, 'But why not tell me? Either you or Appa? How is one supposed to know that....'

'What difference would it have made? Would you have changed anything just because I was going to die at any moment?'

Again we were silent. Then I thought of something else.

'Did Appa know this before the wedding?'

'Yes.'

'Then....'

'My father was his classmate. On his travels, Appa used to visit us from time to time. Once when he visited us, it was when my father had just passed away from typhoid. I had no one else. Like you, my mother also died when I was very young. Thinking that you and I could be company and support for each other, he brought me home.'

She started panting a little. I was silent again. The nurse came in and said, 'You should go. She tires easily. Come back again in the evening.'

I got up and mumbled 'Ammi, Ammi....'

She smiled a little. Then said, 'Sometimes we don't realize the story we are in, Savitri. You still have a lot of your life ahead of you. You go now.'

That was the last thing Ammi said to me. She died sometime that night. I was sitting in the waiting room outside when the nurse came and told me.

The death of the mother never-seen forced me to face again the old quandary of crying at 'Aai Mhanoni Koni'.

When my own father died, all that my mind had mustered was, 'Today's dinner date is cancelled.'

But now with a lifelong sorrow that could never be assuaged, I wept bitterly.

VALUES

MAMONI RAISOM GOSWAMI

Translated from the Assamese by Gayatri Bhattacharyya

PITAMBOR MAHAJAN, THE MERCHANT, SAT DEJECTEDLY ON A TREE STUMP in front of his house. He had still not taken off his muddy shoes. At one time, Pitambor had been a fit and well-built man. Now he was about sixty years old and although that was not an age that could be said to be old for a man, all kinds of worries and discontentment had taken their toll on him. His face sagged and he had a haggard look about him. His head always hung low; he could never look directly at the person he was talking to. The way he held his head, it seemed as though he was scrutinizing the ground, searching intently for something.

A big teak tree had recently been cut down, and Pitambor sat on its stump looking at the children with their improvised fishing rods, trying their luck in the gutters that lined both sides of the road. The incessant rains of the last few days had made the entire village muddy and slushy. The sides of the dirt road had become covered with all kinds of vegetation, both edible and useless, and the frogs were having a great time jumping from one ditch to the other.

Pitambor was looking intently at one particular boy who was trying to untangle his fishing line from an arum plant, when a deep voice suddenly caught his attention. He looked up to see the priest, Krishnakanta, standing near him. 'Pitambor,' said the priest, 'you have been sitting there looking at those children for a long time. You were sitting exactly like this when I passed by some time ago, and you are still sitting in the same place in exactly the same way, staring intently, and with a peculiar longing, at those children. Is it because you do not have any children of your own? "Whose beloved child is being chased to the waters? Call out and bring him back so that I can kiss him!"—is that what you are thinking? By the way, is your wife any better? Is she able to leave her bed and do some work now?'

'No. How can she move about when her hands and feet have become swollen? I have already taken her to the hospital in Guwahati at least twenty times, but she is no better.'

'There seems to be no chance of your ever having any children of your own, then? So your family will become extinct,' said the mischievous and malicious priest.

Pitambor sighed dejectedly. What else could he do?

Krishnakanta stood there silently for a while. He was dressed in an old knee-length dhoti, a tattered and worn-out kurta, and an equally old endi sador. His cheeks were hollowed out as he had only two front teeth left—all the others had fallen out—so that when he spoke, his face took on an odd and twisted shape. His eyes had a malicious glint, and a sly look, and his balding pate only intensified his cunning look. He leaned close to Pitambor and whispered, 'Have you given any thought to what you will do if something happens to your wife? Have you thought about marrying again?'

Pitambor was about to answer when he happened to look up, and his eyes fell on Damayanti. She was the widow of the priest, Shambhu, who had died not too long ago. Everyone knew that she was a dissolute woman, and after her husband died she had become the centre of attraction for all the young men of the village.

Krishnakanta called out to her, 'Where are you coming from, Damayanti?' he asked.

'Where do you think I am coming from?' she replied. 'Don't you see the endi silkworms in my hands?'

'So, you have started hobnobbing with that Marwari businessman, have you?'

Damayanti did not reply and instead started to squeeze out the water from the bottom of her sopping wet mekhela. As she bent down to do so, her blouse rode up, exposing her slim, soft, and fair waist. Neither man could resist looking at this attractive spectacle, but the priest quickly averted his gaze. After she had squeezed out the water from her clothes, she calmly walked away, without even bothering to look towards the two men.

'They say that she has no inhibitions and even eats fish and meat,' said Pitambor.

'Yes, I've heard that too,' replied Krishnakanta. 'She has put all the Brahmins to shame. She does and eats whatever she likes, and does not care for any traditions or rules. In the beginning, after Shambhu died, when she cooked fish for her two daughters, she used to go down to the river and bathe and then cook separately for herself. But now, I am told, she does not bother and even sits with the girls and eats the fish.'

'Yes,' replied Pitambor. 'I have seen her taking fish from the fishmonger in exchange for paddy.'

'Dear me!' exclaimed Krishnakanta. 'What is the world coming to! A widow buying fish in exchange for some paddy!'

'Softly, Purohit, softly,' said Pitambor. 'You do not need to publicize the fact that a Brahmin widow is eating fish. Such things are common these days, even in orthodox places like Dakhinpaar and Uttarpaar. And I do not really think it is such a sin. These old rules should be abolished.'

Staring at the departing figure, Pitambor asked, 'Bapu, what is the condition of your clients these days? Has it changed at all?'

'What a surprising question, Pitambor! You know everything and yet pretend not to know! Don't you know that it is because of the quarrel between my brother and myself over our clients that I am in this poverty-stricken condition?'

'It is mainly because your brother went around telling everyone that you do not know how to read Sanskrit,' replied Pitambor.

Krishnakanta said angrily. 'Tell me,' he shouted, 'how many priests are there these days who can recite the mantras as clearly and correctly as Narahari Bhagabati? He and I studied at the tol, the school for priests, together. He was the one who got the caning, not me. No, no. The main reason for our poverty-stricken condition is the attitude of the clients—of those people who ask us to go and conduct their pujas for them. We priests who know how to conduct the rituals and pujas should not be in such an impoverished condition. In the olden days, there was no problem getting at least one sacred thread, a pair of dhotis, and some money from each of our clients every month. But nowadays everything is different. People want to perform the rites and pujas, but are unwilling to pay the priests. Only the other day, instead of utilizing our services, Mahikanta Sarma, one of your oldest clients, took his two sons to the Kamakhya temple for their upanayan, the sacred thread ceremony. One of my clients in Maisanpur, Surja Sarma, held the shraddha ceremonies of his mother and father together on the same day. People are gradually starting to ignore the Nandimukh shraddha, the shraddha ceremony of nine ancestors which is such an essential part of the wedding ceremony. And, of course, the smaller rituals and pujas, like the naming ceremony, house blessing puja, Basanti puja, purifying a house by holding a hom, organizing a purifying and sanctifying holy fire if a vulture happened to roost on the house...these have become things of the past. Time was when a man had to undergo a purifying ritual if he lost his sacred thread. But how many Brahmin boys today even chant the Gayatri mantra!'

Pitambor had been listening to the priest's rant without saying a word.

His mind was still on Damayanti, and her lovely, silky-smooth back which had been exposed when she bent down to squeeze the water from her mekhela. He thought that he had never seen such a beautiful woman's waist or back. And it was not as though he had not seen or touched a woman's body. He had married his second wife just two months after his first wife had died, mainly because his first wife had died childless. But this second wife was a sick woman. Soon, she became almost completely bedridden due to acute rheumatism. Pitambor had taken her to doctors in Guwahati many times, but to no avail. Ultimately, the woman had become thin, more like a skeleton than a living woman. She lay in her bed all day, quietly watching her husband's behaviour. The man seemed to have almost lost his mind, longing for a son to carry on his family name. People said that he was waiting impatiently for his sick wife to die. After a few years, he had given up going to the hospitals in Guwahati, and had given up all hope for a son and heir. The priest continued to lament his lot in life, but Pitambor hardly heard him. His wife had signalled to one of the servants to give the priest a mora to sit on, but Pitambor was not even aware of the coming and going of the servant!

'You are so absent-minded, thinking all the time only of the fact that you don't have a son and heir. In fact, many people belonging to our satra (an Assamese socio-religious institution) have started saying that you are becoming unbalanced, that you are on the verge of insanity,' said Krishnakanta. 'There are hundreds of people in the world who do not have children. It is nothing so terrible. And why don't you think of what our gurus have said—that families, sons, and so on are, after all, transitory things, and hence valueless—simply manifestations of maya.'

Pitambor simply lowered his head in dejection. The priest noticed that his hair was greying, that his eyes were circled with small, cobweb-like wrinkles. The man had become completely unmindful of how he dressed and his shoes were caked with layers of mud.

Krishnakanta was overwhelmed by a sense of pity and compassion for Pitambor. Just a few years ago, many of the older villagers had called him the 'gora soldier', he was so well-built, fair, and fit. Now, even though there was no dearth of money or means, the poor man had no peace of mind. His granary was full, but there was no one to enjoy it.

Then, Krishnakanta said something quite shocking. Before saying it he looked all around to ensure that there was no one nearby. But the door of Pitambor's bedroom was wide open, and he could see the skeletal body of Pitambor's wife lying on the bed. Her sharp eyes, he noticed, were shining with a peculiar brightness—as though she was trying to find out what the priest was saying to her husband. Krishnakanta was astonished to see that a single glance, even from a distance, could be so keen, and could express such heartfelt sadness. Even so, he whispered to Pitambor, 'If you think that you can help me with some money, I too will help you to get what you so desire.'

'How?' asked Pitambor. 'How will you arrange things?'

'Don't worry about the arrangements. There will be no problems,' said the priest.

'What do you mean?' Pitambor asked curiously.

'What I mean is that I will arrange matters so that when you meet her, there will be no question of her not conceiving. I have found out that she has aborted and buried the results of her illicit and guilty pregnancies four times!' Krishnakanta said with confidence.

Pitambor almost shouted, 'Bapu, are you talking about Damayanti?'

'Yes, yes. I am talking about Damayanti,' replied the priest. 'Our Brahmin girls have started going across the Dhanasri River to marry Shudra boys. Don't you know that the Gosain of Mukteswar Satra's son has gone and married a Muslim girl? It seems that our Gandhi Maharaj has shown this path—that caste and community do not matter. That is why I am thinking about Damayanti for you.'

Pitambor jumped up in excitement. 'What are you talking about?'

'If you so desire, you can make Damayanti your own woman.' Krishnakanta glanced towards the open bedroom door again. The eyes of the woman lying on the bed were wide open and it seemed as though they were burning with a fierce fire. She was staring at Krishnakanta.

Pitambor got up and tried to clutch the priest's hands, but the latter hastily stepped away. He had just bathed and was on his way to the Adhikaar's house. He had been asked to bathe the image of Murulidhar in the Adhikaar's temple, because the regular priest there had gone to Guwahati. It was a very important duty and he had to be clean and untouched by any other person, particularly one who was not a Brahmin. But the priest's words had opened an unthinkable world for Pitambor and he did not know how to thank the man.

'So, Pitambor,' said Krishnakanta, 'it seems that you have been thinking about this for some time.'

A happy smile played over Pitambor's lips. Once again, Krishnakanta glanced towards the bedroom. The woman's eyes were now shut, but it seemed as though she was undergoing some terrible suffering and pain. Touching the priest's feet, Pitambor spoke humbly and pleaded, 'Bapu, do this for me. Everyone knows that she goes out at night to bury the things she aborts. I know it too. But she is a Brahmin woman and I am a Shudra. If she comes to me, I will place her on a pedestal and worship her.'

A sly smile spread across Krishnakanta's toothless mouth. 'It will not be easy. I will have to negotiate, I will have to get the two girls to agree to it, and for that I will have to bribe them with sweets.'

Pitambor got up hurriedly and went inside. The eyes of the woman lying on the bed flew open. She had probably just shut her eyes and was not asleep. She saw her husband go to the small wooden box that was placed on top of a stool and open it; she also saw him going out to Krishnakanta again after a while.

'You will let me know everything soon, won't you?' he said to the priest.

Taking the twenty rupees from the merchant, the wily priest went away with a mischievous smile....

Seven days passed without any word from Krishnakanta, while Pitambor waited eagerly every day for him. He had seen Damayanti a number of times; making her way to and from the Adhikaar's house to deliver the sacred threads she spun from the finest cotton. It was only now that he began looking at her properly that he thought he had never seen a woman as beautiful as her. Her mother, they said, was from the village of Routa situated on the banks of the Dhanasri. After seeing Damayanti now, Pitambor came to the conclusion that the Brahmin girls from near the Dhanasri must be among the most beautiful women in the whole country. Her father, the priest Purnananda, had once lost a couple of his ploughing bullocks. At that time he had had many clients in comparatively distant places like Maisanpur, Gargora, and so on. Searching for his precious bullocks, Purnananda had gone to the village of Routa by the Dhanasri riverbank. No one seemed to know why he had had to go so far to find his cows. But it was then that he had seen and married the beautiful daughter of Bhagawati of Routa. No priest of the area had ever before married a girl from so far away....

It was the month of June, and the rivers and wetlands were overflowing with water. Both sides of the dirt road were full of shrubs and climbing plants that invariably came with the season. The road running in front of Pitambor's house was now covered with mud and slush. One day in spite of the mud and slush on the road, Pitambor saw Damayanti walking along, plucking the edible greens such as the tasty kolmou or water spinach which grew in abundance on the roadsides during wet weather. She had lifted her mekhela up to her knees, and was accompanied by her six-year-old daughter, who was completely naked. Damayanti's legs and hands were soft and shiny, and healthy, like a new mango plant. Her hair, which cascaded down her back, was a reddish bronze colour, very much like the colour of rusted cannons, he thought. Oh, yes, the exact tinge of an old, rusted iron cannon! Pitambor remembered the huge iron cannon that was found when they were digging a well. It was said that the Burmese soldiers had left it behind when they had to retreat. He remembered that a group of students had come after some time and hauled it away.

After looking at her for a while, Pitambor plucked up the courage to speak to her. 'You will get sick if you walk about in this foul weather, on this dirty, muddy road,' he said. She turned and looked at him, her face and eyes expressing a surprised curiosity. But, as earlier, she did not utter a word in reply. 'If you had only asked me I would have sent my servant to get you all....' But before he could complete his sentence, she turned to look back at him again. Her eyes were blazing. Pitambor felt her fiery look would burn him to ashes. He walked rapidly away and sat down on his usual seat on the stump of the teak tree. He glanced towards his house and saw that his wife had taken to her bed again. She had tried to get up that morning after a long time. Her wasted limbs creaked with a ghastly sound when she tried to lift herself up, and she felt dizzy, so she had to take to her bed again. Now she lay there staring at her husband. Pitambor gazed at her with a heartless and, at the same time, somewhat embarrassed look. It was time for him to go and give her one of her medicines, and he was quite aware of it. But he did not get up—he simply sat where he was, looking down, contemplating his shoes. There were only four people in their satra who wore shoes—the clerk of the satra office, the two sons of the Adhikaar, and he himself. He bent down and tried to clean his mud-caked shoes with his handkerchief, and then again looked up at the road to see if Krishnakanta had arrived. But there was still no sign of him. As he sat waiting impatiently, a bullock cart came creaking into his compound. His tenant farmers were bringing his share of the paddy they cultivated. On any other day, Pitambor would have rushed over enthusiastically and counted the baskets of paddy. But today, seeing that his master was absent-minded and indifferent, the servant came and counted the baskets and stored them inside the granary. After some time, having rested and eaten some refreshments, the tenants came up to Pitambor to take their leave. As always, they had some complaints about Pitambor's tight-fisted attitude. But nothing moved him today; he sat where he was, silent and indifferent.

Glancing towards the bedroom of his house, he saw that his wife was lying with her eyes open. He noticed that someone had replaced a tumbler of water near her, and he remembered that the time for her medicine was past. But he got up anyway and was about to go and give it to her when he heard Krishnakanta's voice. Forgetting about his wife's medicine, he hurried to the gateway where the priest was waiting for him.

His wife's eyes, he noticed, seemed to be unusually weak—the fire that normally gleamed in her eyes whenever she looked towards him seemed to be slowly dying out. 'Mahajan,' the priest called out.

'Yes, Bapu. Tell me, have you any news?' asked Pitambor.

'You will have to go to meet her on the coming full moon night in the dhekal,' he said. 'It's located behind her house.' A dhekal is a room containing the dheki, a wooden instrument used for pounding and cleaning rice. The priest looked furtively all around, and continued, 'I have found out that she is not pregnant at the moment. Her daughter told me this after I had bribed her with sweets. It seems that it hasn't even been a month since she terminated her last pregnancy. The girl is too young to understand these things. It seems that she had helped her mother by holding an oil lamp while the woman finished her job. She also told me that on this occasion her mother had used a spade belonging to a Brahmin boy from Chataraguri. This boy used to come cycling from his home to study in the college near here. He is a boy from a well-to-do family, but of loose character. Instead of going to college, he hid his books inside a basket of rice in Damayanti's hut and spent his time with her. He would spend the money for his college fees buying things for Damayanti. The foetus she buried this time was this Brahmin boy's....

'Listen, Mahajan,' the priest continued, 'I have spoken to her about you. At first she was quite angry, "That Shudra man," she said. "How dare he even think about such a thing! Does he not know that I am the daughter of a good Brahmin priest?" I replied that everyone knew that she was a Brahmin woman. But now that she had taken the sinful path, there could be no difference between castes. I also told her that no Brahmin would stoop to marry her now. They would simply exploit her body and then cast her aside like the useless husks of sugar cane stalks. I told her that you would marry her with all due rituals, as soon as your ailing wife died, that your wife is even now as good as dead. After you marry her, she would live a good and prosperous life, I told her. Do you know, Mahajan, when she heard all this, she went into her hut and cried her heart out, I do not understand why.... She came out after some time, wiping her tears and said, "I do not keep well these days, and it would be a relief if I could lean on someone's shoulders." I replied that it was not surprising that she did not feel well, after having had no less than five or six abortions within a short time; that if her case happened to come up in a panchayat meeting, no one would even consider going near her, because anyone found to be giving her even a tumbler of water would be fined a sum of twenty rupees!

'"What other option did I have?" she wept. "My daughters were starving. The Adhikaar's wife used to ask me to do small jobs for her in the kitchen. But now she says that I am not fit to work in her kitchen, that whatever I touch will become impure and contaminated. Before I used to be asked to spin and make the laguns—sacred threads. But now the Brahmin families of this area will not allow me to make the laguns. They say that I am corrupted. The tenant farmers know that I am all alone with no one to look after me or my interests. So they too have started behaving like monsters. What do they care that I am a lonely Brahmin widow with two small daughters? How can I fight them? I own some acres of farmland in Satpakhila, but I have not been given my share of five maunds of paddy ever since my husband died. I have not been able to pay the revenue tax for that land for three years, and the land could be auctioned off any day now. What was I to do? I had to think of feeding my two daughters...."'

Pitambor was getting more and more impatient. He almost yelled, 'Yes, yes, I understand all that. But what about me, my case?'

'Yes, I am coming to that,' replied the sly priest.

'She said, "He is a Shudra belonging to the fourth caste. Having relations with him...." But finally, she told me that she would meet you on the full moon night in the dhekal behind her house.'

Pitambor could hardly contain his joy. And taking advantage of that Krishnakanta said, 'But you will have to give me about one hundred rupees.... Damayanti says that she needs a mosquito net, and the two girls will have to be given sweets from Bhola's shop....'

Pitambor hurried into his house and went to his bedroom. He walked up to the small wooden box he kept in a corner of the room. His sick wife opened her eyes and followed his every move. Suddenly he shouted at her, 'What are you staring at? One day I will come and pluck your eyes out!'

From where he sat outside the house, Krishnakanta could hear everything that was being said in the bedroom. He was a sly fox. When Pitambor came out and handed him one hundred rupees, he whispered, 'If necessary, give your wife a small pill of opium that night. She lies on that bed listening to everything, and understands everything. It is better to be careful.' And laughing meaningfully, the sly Brahmin priest left. The woman on the bed simply shut her eyes.

Moments later, Krishnakanta returned, 'Damayanti is very keen on money. She acts like a tigress where money is concerned.... Never mind, you will be able to hold her hands intimately.'

The Mahajan felt rather guilty, and looked at his wife. No, she had heard nothing. She was asleep. But her forehead glistened with perspiration.

⁓

It was the full moon night of the monsoon month of Ashaar. Pitambor wore an endi kurta and a fine Santipuri dhoti. Across his shoulders he had thrown a sador of fine cotton. After a long time he had brought out the mirror with the wooden frame and scrutinized his face. He had shaved that morning, and now out in the sunlight, he could see fine wrinkles covering his face, and he was somewhat disturbed. It seemed to him that the wrinkles were a net and he was the fish trapped in it.

At the appointed hour, he walked towards Damayanti's house. It was located near the bridge on the Singra River, beyond the forest of teak trees. Very few people of the satra lived here, and it occurred to Pitambor that Damayanti was able to live as she did only because she lived in an almost deserted area. He looked up to see some mushroom-coloured clouds floating in the sky, looking for all the world like cannons. And that round moon! As though it was a deer shorn of its skin. A skinned deer—her meat shaking uncontrollably without the skin to bind it in place! Lovely fresh vigorous meat! This skinned deer suddenly transformed into Damayanti. A completely nude Damayanti! There were her lovely breasts—shaped like a pregnant goat's stomach. Her body was the colour of tender bamboo stalks, and her lips? They were soft and lovely like freshly-cut mangoes oozing sweet nectar.... Pitambor could not stand there any longer looking up at the sky, weaving fantasies about the woman. It was deathly quiet and completely deserted. It was the night of the annual bhaona performance, and the entire village had gone to see it, which was why she had chosen this night for their first assignation.

He heard some jackals howling from the thorny shrubs nearby, as he walked rapidly to Damayanti's hut. He took off his shoes and sat on the plinth. A heady fragrance of champa flowers floated in the air. Damayanti lay with her younger daughter on a small cot set between a basket meant to store rice and a heap of ripe jackfruit. The girl was drowsily writing the letters of the alphabet on a slate in the light of a dirty old lamp with a broken chimney. From where she lay, Damayanti was watching the man. After a while, she beckoned to him to come inside, and sit on a mora. A small earthen lamp filled to the brim with mustard oil burned nearby. For some reason, Pitambor was afraid to look at her body in the pale light of the lamp—he had a peculiar feeling that everything might be over if he did.... It was all a land of illusion, he felt. Was this Brahmin widow in front of him a real woman?

'Have you brought any money with you?' Pitambor was startled into reality. He had not expected her first question to be so very materialistic.

'Whatever I have is yours,' he replied and handed her a cotton bag. She took the small bag and put it inside a cane basket that was hanging on one of the posts of her dheki ghar. In the meantime, the girl who was writing the alphabet went and lay down with her sister and instantly fell asleep. There was a very low cot in one of the rooms that was used to store baskets of rice. Damayanti's dead husband, a priest, had been given those baskets during the shraddha of the Adhikaar's brother.

Pitambor followed Damayanti and sat down on that cot. After a while, she came to him....

Two months passed by. One day, after the Mahajan had left her, Krishnakanta happened to see Damayanti bathing in the river, and made fun of her, 'Why Damayanti, I never saw you coming to the river to bathe after you spent the nights with the Brahmin boys of Dudhnoi Bongora!'

Damayanti did not reply. But the sly priest was not put off. 'I suppose it is because this one is a Shudra....?'

Again she did not reply, but she suddenly jumped up out of the water and began to vomit violently on the riverside.

For some moments, the priest stood where he was, dumbfounded. Then he said, 'This must be Pitambor Mahajan's child then?'

Again she was silent. But Krishnakanta continued, 'That is very good news. Poor Pitambor will be very happy; he was almost going mad at not having any children! Then I will go and give him the good news.' After a pause he said, 'Listen, you must not worry or feel bad. Our Gandhi Maharaj did not believe in all this business of caste. He said that all men are equal and the same. Just you wait and see, Pitambor will marry you with all the proper rituals as soon as his wife is dead. I am sure that you are aware that the villagers were getting fed up of your way of life, and were thinking of having a panchayat meeting about it. I don't think you know that some time back one of the things you aborted and buried beneath the clump of bamboos was dragged out by a jackal and deposited in the courtyard of one of the priests. Have you any idea how much that poor man had to spend to get himself purified—and for no fault of his own!'

Damayanti started vomiting again.

'Be careful, Damayanti,' warned Krishnakanta. 'Do not do anything this time. Even after knowing all about you and your repeated abortions, Pitambor is willing to accept you. If you do anything this time to damage the child within you, I tell you, you will go straight to hell. No one and nothing can save you.'

Krishnakanta then went to give the Mahajan the best news he had ever heard. 'Pitambor, if she does not go and abort this child, you can be sure that she will not be unwilling to marry you.'

As usual, Pitambor was sitting on the stump of his favourite tree.

He had not even bothered to take off his mud-caked shoes. Hearing the priest's words he started trembling in sheer excitement. He would be a father! Could it be true? Would he really be a father at long last? But of course it must be true. The Brahmin priest himself had told him so.

He stood up, deeply agitated, and started walking about aimlessly.

Krishnakanta said, 'What is the matter with you! Why are you walking up and down like a monkey! But of course you have more than enough reason to be happy and excited! It is not a small matter to become a father after thirty years of waiting! Great good fortune indeed!'

Suddenly, Pitambor came and knelt down in front of the other man. 'Bapu,' he pleaded, 'please see that she does nothing to frustrate the dearest desire of my life. You well know what kind of men my father and grandfather were. Only a sufferer can understand the despair of a childless man! Besides, she is a Brahmin woman from a priest's family and now she holds my life in her hands! What will I do, Bapu, what will I do?'

Krishnakanta lifted one hand as if in blessing and said, 'I will keep track of her and what she does, like a vulture keeping track of a corpse. Do not worry. I will also warn the old woman who helps in these dreadful things. But I will need some money to bribe her too.'

This time Pitambor did not have to go to his small box to get the money. That morning he had sold all the fruits from his seven jackfruit trees, and the proceeds were still in his pocket. He took out the entire bundle of notes and handed it to the priest. Extremely pleased at the way his plans were going, Krishnakanta put his hands on Pitambor's head and blessed him.

Later, when Pitambor went to the bedroom, his eyes met his sick wife's eyes. And in spite of himself, their sad and desolate expression moved him to compassion. But the next moment he regained his composure and forced himself to anger. 'Oh, you sick and barren woman! How dare you stare at me like that?' And he yelled out to his servants, 'Come, come! Lift this bed. Take it to the small room next to the dhekal. Come, hurry up!' Along with four of his servants, Pitambor carried the bed with his wife still lying on it, and put it inside a small, dark room without any sort of ventilation, near the room where the paddy and the dheki were placed.

Since his affair with Damayanti, Pitambor seemed to have almost forgotten that his wife needed at least some looking after, and had to be given medicines regularly. She was just skin and bones now, and seeing that their master did not bother about her, the servants too had started to neglect her. They were even careless about bringing her food on time, and often did not bother to bring her a glass of water with her meals let alone give her the required medicines on time. The poor woman's throat would often become parched and dry with thirst, but she would not utter a word of protest. People said that she looked more like a corpse than a living woman. Even now, when her husband brought her to this small, dark room and left her there, she kept quiet. But surprisingly, even in the dank darkness, her eyes shone brightly, and it seemed as though she saw, and understood, everything that was going on, more clearly than if she was out in the open.

The very thought of fathering a child made Pitambor delirious with joy. He lived in a world of joyful imaginings—the child in Damayanti's womb seemed to him to be already a boy, then a young man. In Pitambor's imagination, the boy walked along the banks of the Dhanasri, holding his father's hand! The ever joyous and sparkling golden thread that binds fathers to sons seemed to stretch far into the distant horizon, where all was sheer happiness, where the ties and traditions of family were an unbroken celebration of joy....

Pitambor got a couple of his trusted servants to bring down an old wooden box from its perch near the roof of his room. When he was sure that he was alone, he opened the box and took out a bundle tied in an old gamosa. In the bundle were a few pieces of ashthi—half-burnt bones—of his long dead father, and entwined in the dried-up bones was a chain of the precious poal or coral beads that were so much a part of the traditions of Assam. Pitambor remembered how his father, as he lay on his deathbed, almost choking with the effort to speak, had said, 'Keep this chain of my poal beads carefully. Your son will wear it, and then his son, and then his son's son, and so on. It will be the living symbol, the everlasting flag of our clan....' The old man died before he could complete the sentence. Pitambor took out this chain now, then wrapped the pieces of ashthi in the gamosa again, and put the bundle back in the old box. Finally, he called his servants and had the box put back in its place on the shelf.

Days turned into weeks, and weeks into months, and Pitambor became more and more impatient to hear some news. He had heard that a foetus that was five months old could not be aborted and he calculated that it was now three months since Damayanti had conceived. As he waited each day without any news, the tension grew more and more unbearable. Each passing day loomed in front of him like a mountain he had to cross in order to gain access to his happiness, and survive.

Almost every moment he seemed to hear the Brahmin woman's footsteps approaching him, and he imagined that she was whispering to him, 'Mahajan, hurry up and prepare the wedding rituals. I can no longer hide my condition. Do you not see how big my stomach is? Hurry up. Get the wedding preparations ready.'

Again, 'All those things about Brahmins and Shudras, about Hindus and Muslims, are just a lot of nonsense. We are all human beings, and you will find that the same red blood flows inside all of us.... Get the rituals for the wedding ready.'

She seemed to walk with ghungroos tied to her feet and she came to him with tinkling feet. He imagined her lovely, fair, and slim legs.... 'Mahajan,' she seemed to whisper, 'nowadays I do not bother to go and bathe in the river after I sleep with you. Go, get ready for our wedding....'

Three months passed by uneventfully, and the Mahajan still dreamt of walking along the Dhanasri riverbank with his hands on the shoulders of a handsome youth—his son!

It was the late monsoon month of Bhadra and violent storms often lashed the villages. A storm had been steadily gaining force since that afternoon. Going inside to shut the door of his wife's room, he noticed that her eyes today burned more brightly, more malevolently than usual. As the storm raged, the lamps were blown out, and all other sounds were drowned out by its sheer ferocity. Pitambor shouted for his servants, but no one could hear him. The only sounds to be heard were the rumblings and thundering of the storm and of trees being felled, either by being struck by lightning, or being uprooted by fierce winds.

There, another tree had crashed down. Which tree was it, Pitambor wondered. Somewhere in the distance, he saw a streak of lightning that had definitely struck another tree! He could hear the frightening sounds of the tree being split down the middle and crashing to the ground. He went outside to see which tree had fallen and how much damage this terrifying storm had caused.

In a corner of the grounds, the fruits of seven of his coconut trees had been heaped up waiting to be sold. Now he saw his servants running about trying to salvage them and store them inside the dheki ghar. Some of the fruits which were still on the trees thudded to the ground, having been blown down by the wind. No one could hear anyone else, but gradually the storm began to calm down, the rumblings and thunder died down, and a heavy rain lashed the village. Lighting a lantern, Pitambor could now see the heavy raindrops; he imagined he could hear the tinkling sounds of Damayanti's anklets as her feet came towards him....

Suddenly amidst the rain, Pitambor heard someone calling him by name. Picking up the lantern, he hurried outside, and saw the priest coming towards him, completely drenched and shivering. Pitambor was frightened. Only some emergency could have prompted the man to come out in this terrible weather. Krishnakanta held an umbrella over his head, but it had so many holes that it afforded no protection whatsoever. His dhoti had been drawn up to his knees, and only a thin sador that was dripping wet covered his bare body.

Holding up the lantern, Pitambor shouted, 'Bapu! What brings you out in this foul weather, so late in the night?'

Krishnakanta sat down on the plinth of the house. Leaning the torn umbrella against a post, he took off his sador and tried to wring it dry, and wiped his wet face with it. Then, pointing a shaking finger at Pitambor, he said in a choking voice, 'Pitambor, when your first wife died, were there three inauspicious stars in the ascendant, three puhkars. Three or four?'

'I do not remember,' replied the Mahajan. 'Why?'

'When three puhkars are found at the time of death of a person in the house, even the dubari grass dries up and dies. When your first wife died, there were three puhkars. And, as a result, the ill effects are still there. Everything is dead and gone!'

'What has happened, Bapu? What is wrong?'

'She has destroyed it, Mahajan, she has aborted! She refused to carry the seed of a Shudra man! She belongs to the highest Brahmin clan, a woman from the Sandilya gotra! She has spoiled your seed, Pitambor, she has terminated her pregnancy!'

As these words crashed into him, the boy holding Pitambor's hand let go and fell into the depths of the Dhanasri River. Who was it who had fallen? Was it Pitambor, or the youth? Dear God, who was it that tumbled and fell headlong into the deep waters of the river!

∽

Soon after this encounter between the priest and Pitambor, Damayanti heard a sound near her house in the dead of night. Someone was digging up something beneath the clump of bamboos behind her dekhal. She shouted, 'Who is it? Who is there?' and woke up her elder daughter. The six-year-old girl and her mother stood near the window, listening. The sounds of digging came from the same place where the two of them had gone in the dead of night two days ago and buried that thing the woman had ruined. Mother and daughter had gone out that night and dug a hole with the spade the Brahmin boy from Chataraguri had given them. The young girl had shivered in fright when she heard the jackals howling nearby. And today, the unmistakable sound of digging came from that very same place. Thud, thud! Thump, thump! Standing near the window, the two of them saw a lantern burning on the spot. In the light of the lantern they saw the figure of a man, a strong, well-built man digging away at the very spot where Damayanti had dug just two days ago. Indeed, he was digging up the same hole!

Damayanti's entire body and soul trembled at the sight. The man was Pitambor Mahajan. He had hung his lantern on a bamboo pole, and was digging away furiously. The man had assumed a terrifying aspect and he was hacking at the earth like a madman. She trembled in fear and terror. Should she shout? Yes, of course she must. Such a terrible thing was happening outside her own house—of course she must shout!

'Mahajan! Mahajan!' she shouted. But there was absolutely no response. He simply kept on digging.

'Mahajan, why are you digging up my ground?'

Pitambor looked up towards the window, but did not utter a word.

Damayanti said in a state of great agitation. 'Yes, I buried it. But what will you find there now? It was just an unformed lump of flesh.'

Pitambor lifted his head and looked at her. 'It was my child! I will at least feel the flesh of my flesh! I will feel my child, my son and heir, with my own two hands!'

A REVOLT OF THE GODS

VILAS SARANG

Translated from the Marathi by the author

I

It was the time of the Ganesh festival. In the evening I had to go out to photograph one of the numerous festival shows that were being staged all over Bombay. It took me longer than I expected, and the next morning I rose late. Dalvi was already at the studio when I arrived and was busy developing negatives in the darkroom. We had been getting a lot of extra business during the festival, having been called in to photograph several shows. Amateur singers and actors were particularly eager to be photographed on stage. While Dalvi handled such jobs expertly, I was much happier doing portraits in the studio. During the festival, however, there were often two assignments on the same evening, and then I had to go out too. Dalvi enjoyed these stints; I hated making my way among the noisy crowds, toting a camera and other paraphernalia, and moving from one end of the stage to the other in search of a better angle, often crouching awkwardly in order to catch someone in a good pose. It's different in the studio: an elegant curtain in the background, lights placed at strategic points, and in their midst the customer seated silently and meekly, if somewhat uncomfortably. This was the last day of the Ganesh festival, and I was relieved that there would be no more spells of working late. There was still a lot to do in the studio, of course—making prints, enlargements, and so on.

I set about touching up some passport photos. Touching up—that's my forte. It's mostly Dalvi who looks after developing and printing; he's better at it than I am. We've set up our studio in partnership, relying largely upon Dalvi's technical skill; I take care of things like touching up, cutting prints, and keeping the accounts.

A young man who looked like someone in search of a job came in to have some passport photos taken. I asked him if he wanted to wear a tie, and he said yes. Inspecting the tie I handed him, he remarked that it seemed old-fashioned and asked if we had another one he could use. We only had one tie, I said curtly. I was annoyed. If he was so particular, he should've come with his own tie, I thought. He couldn't even manage a decent knot, and had probably seldom worn a tie before. I had to tie it for him.

I found it difficult to keep working until one o'clock, and my eyes were heavy from lack of sleep. Just as we were about to close down, a blind man walked up, tap-tapping his cane and asked if his pictures were ready. Four days ago he had come in, feeling each step with his cane before climbing it, had stood at the counter for a few moments taking in my presence, and then asked, 'Is this the Gajanan Photo Studio?' Apparently some institution was sending him to the US to study music, and he needed pictures for a passport. He was talkative, as all blind persons seem to be, and was excited about his prospective journey. He told me that the blind had a difficult time in India, and how a blind person could hope to develop his abilities in Western countries. I listened absent-mindedly as I led him to the seat. It occurred to me that I was taking a blind man's picture for the first time. I switched on the lights; he stared with eyes wide open. Usually, people blink in the glare, or turn their heads away. The blind man sat motionless, with his sightless eyes shining defiantly under the violent lights.

I had told him that he could pick up the pictures today; I searched but couldn't find them. They must be lying somewhere amidst the heaps of festival pictures, I thought. 'I'm sorry, could you come back in two days?' I said. He went away, tap-tapping his stick. I locked the studio and went home. I was glad that the studio was closed for the day. That evening Dalvi had to go to witness the immersion of his household Ganesh.

I slept for an hour after lunch before being awakened by the noise of kids in the courtyard below. The members of the festival committee for our building were getting things ready for the Ganesh immersion. Like countless other buildings in Bombay, ours too had its Ganesh, with shows every evening for eleven days, the whole affair financed by donations from each tenant. I got out of bed and made myself a cup of tea. Refreshed, I went out for a stroll. I thought I'd catch up with the procession bearing our building's Ganesh somewhere along the way.

The evening shadows were lengthening. I walked, looking at the shadows of buildings, of electric poles, and of men and women. I like observing shadows more than watching things and human beings. Buildings and poles and men remain the same for years, or change very little, very slowly. On the other hand, the shapes and angles of shadows change minute by minute. They are sometimes clearly etched, and at other times like badly focused photographs. Men, stolid and heavy, merely dream of transfigurations, while shadows change endlessly. A man is nothing compared to his shadow. Without shadows, life would have been far duller.

The main street was crowded. Small groups of people went by with their household clay figures of Ganesh. One man carried upon his head a small figure on a wooden platform, and the rest walked behind him singing hymns. The large civic figures were brought down later in the evening. I sat in an Irani restaurant on the way to the seashore. After some time I observed people from our building approaching with the clay image. I got up and merged into the tail end of the procession.

As always at the yearly immersion, the beach was swarming with people. Amid the sea of human beings milling about one could spot here and there the colourful figure of the elephant-headed god. The civic images, perched comfortably upon handcarts and trucks, were in greater evidence. The figure from our building was medium-sized. Members of the festival committee had complained that the collection was unusually small this year. I was sure, though, that they had managed to pocket their usual share of the money. Anyway, I didn't take much interest in their dealings.

The roads had become so congested that all the processions had more or less ground to a halt. The sea was only a short distance away, but it would take a long while to reach the water's edge.

Then I noticed a disturbance at the head of our procession. Being at the tail end, I didn't know what was wrong at first. I craned my neck, but couldn't see our Ganesh figure and wondered if it had fallen off the handcart. Then someone said that the Ganesh had jumped off. Naturally, I thought he was joking. But the commotion seemed to be spreading. Indeed the figures in the different processions had begun to disappear, apparently deserting their seats on the wooden platforms and handcarts and trucks. In the melee I couldn't quite see what was happening, but I did observe a huge civic figure jumping down from a truck. I saw a man fall to the ground at a blow from its trunk.

Here and there one glimpsed clay images that had come to life, as it were, and were sprinting away. But scarcely anyone possessed the composure to watch this miraculous spectacle. Confused and terrified, everyone ran back towards the city. Even the traffic cops had abandoned their positions and were running with the rest. Knocked about in that disorderly retreat, I lost one of my slippers. For a while I ran with one slipper, but then realized that there was no point in returning that way. I cast it off too and ran barefoot.

When I reached the building, I noticed that almost everyone else was already there. People gathered in the courtyard and discussed the event in excited tones. Since everyone was talking at the same time it was hard to understand what was being said. The women, many of whom chanted prayers breathlessly, looked particularly frightened. Children cried.

After some time the clamour became more intelligible. An attempt was made to discover the significance of the supernatural event. At first everyone seemed to be convinced that it was a manifestation of divine wrath.

Mr Kini—who was an accountant in a government office, and was commonly known as Accountant Kini—appeared even more excited than the rest. 'Look,' he said in a cracked voice. 'For a long time I've had the feeling that sooner or later something of this sort was going to happen. True, Lord Ganesha is called Lambodara—pot-bellied—but how many sins can you expect him to swallow? I bet now he won't return to heaven without giving a good lesson to all the black marketeers, smugglers, food adulterators, and politicians. They're the ones who've brought this on.'

'But all these images that have come to life—just what are they going to do now?' Akshikar, who lived on the third floor, asked. 'How will they punish the guilty?'

It was something to think about.

'Well, who can tell what the gods will do?' someone said. 'We just have to face up to whatever happens next without complaining.'

Professor Matkari had a different view. He said, 'I see no reason for being so frightened. You must have seen that the gods just jumped off their seats and went away. It didn't seem as if they were lashing about at people, or wanted to hurt anyone.'

'That's right,' Subodh, who was studying physics in college, said. He was on the festival committee in our building. 'I see no point in talking about sin and the like. The gods have not arisen to dispense punishment. They could've done that without resorting to miracles. They're gods, after all. I think they were simply outraged by the whole spectacle—the sweaty crowds, the hurly-burly, and the disorder. Why should the gods put up with it? When they couldn't stand it any longer they just got up and walked away.'

The discussion continued. I slipped away and went upstairs to my apartment. I stretched out in bed. The excitement and the exertion had made me tired.

II

The next day there was a great stir in the city. People wondered if the absconding gods had vanished completely, or were still prowling about. At first it seemed that they had disappeared, but then fleeting glimpses of them were caught here and there. The elephant-headed god's trunk would appear around a corner, or, climbing a flight of stairs, one would suddenly become aware of a shadowy figure disappearing ahead. A lonely passer-by might receive a blow on the head from a god's trunk. No one was hurt seriously, but some people were sent into a state of shock for a few hours. They would behave strangely for a while, say unintelligible things, and then gradually return to normalcy. That was all the gods did. They didn't unleash any terrifying forces, or throw the daily life of the city out of gear. In a few days people calmed down and went about their business. And of course the people of Bombay have a reputation for not being thrown off balance or surprised by anything. Still, people tended to return home earlier in the evening, and avoided walking through isolated areas. There was no telling when one might receive a blow on the head.

The day after the revolt of the gods I didn't go to the studio. Like everyone else, I thought I'd see how things turned out first. Then we went back to business as usual. For a week or so, there were very few customers. But we had plenty of work at the studio. Dalvi spent most of his time in the darkroom. I had taken pictures at the show in the Makarand Housing Society, and they had all come out poorly. The entire roll of film had been exposed at the wrong speed. Dalvi wasn't happy about it. I told him not to worry; I'd touch up all the pictures and set them straight.

One day the blind man returned. I had forgotten about his pictures in the meantime. I searched for them again without success. I didn't know what to do. I didn't feel I should make a blind man come back time and again. For a moment I thought of handing him someone else's pictures: after all, he couldn't see them. I said, 'Please come back in four days; I'll definitely have them ready.' He seemed upset and went away, tap-tapping his cane noisily.

Another day Accountant Kini came to my room with a roll of film. Photography is his hobby and that has made us friends. He comes in often to talk over technical matters. Some of his pictures of flowers and the like have appeared in the Sunday newspapers, so he feels he is an artist.

While leaving Kini said, 'For the last two or three days we've been bothered by mice. We've never had them in our apartment before. These must have come in recently. Last night I set a trap; in the morning I found two. Then it suddenly occurred to me—when the Ganeshas arose and left, the mice that had invaded my house were the same ones on whose backs the gods are supposed to ride.'

'What did you do then?' I asked.

'Well, I didn't know what to do,' Kini said. 'I was appalled at the idea that the mice I was going to kill might belong to the gods.'

'You could've taken the cage with the trapped mice to the sea and drowned them,' I said. 'As it is, don't we immerse the mice along with the Ganeshas?'

'Oh, no,' Kini said. 'It's one thing to carry Lord Ganesha and his mouse reverently to the sea for immersion, and quite another to drown mice.'

I saw no difference, but didn't have enough interest in the matter to argue about it.

Touching up the pictures I had taken at the Makarand Housing Society show turned out to be an exhausting job. It wasn't the same as touching up a studio portrait. There were often a number of persons in a single picture, with faces much smaller than in a portrait. Touching up each little face was tedious. Then one day their man came and picked up the pictures. The next morning he was back at the studio. 'Are these our pictures, or someone else's?' he asked. 'We can hardly recognize a single face.' I shrugged. 'What's so special about a face?' I said. 'We won't come back next year,' he said.

Then I spent an entire morning looking for the blind man's pictures, again without success. I was exasperated. I decided that I'd take his picture again, free of charge of course. He was supposed to come in the next day. The next morning I waited for the sound of his cane, but he didn't turn up.

As I was getting ready to go to bed that evening there was a knock at the door. My first thought was of the blind man. Then I laughed, realizing how absurd the idea was. He didn't know where I lived; besides, photographers aren't called at night like doctors. I wondered who it could be. Opening the door, I saw Accountant Kini. I thought he had come to ask about the roll of film he had given me the other day. I said I hadn't been able to develop it, what with all the work on the festival pictures. But he stayed on, making small talk. I saw that his mind wasn't on the conversation, but on something else he wasn't mentioning. He kept fidgeting.

Then the conversation faltered; I deliberately remained silent. Kini looked around aimlessly at the calendar on the wall, at my books, at the curtains. Then he looked at me and said, 'There's something I wanted to talk to you about.'

'Go ahead,' I said.

'I've never mentioned this to anyone until now. My wife is the only person who knows about it,' Kini said. 'In the last few years I've developed a strange habit—that of cursing the gods.'

Kini paused and stared at the foot of my bed. I remained silent.

'In our family we worship Lord Ganesha,' Kini continued without raising his head. 'I've known the hymn to Ganesh by heart since childhood. Yet, instead of hymns and prayers, what comes into my mind are curses. Unspeakable, abominable curses. I was brought up well as a matter of fact. Never learned bad words as a child. Even today I wouldn't say something like damn. And yet when I think of God my mind literally spews out curses. At first I was shocked to discover that I knew so many.'

There was a knock at the door. 'Papa, papa,' little Sushma shouted. 'What a nuisance,' Kini said, and rose to open the door. 'What do you want?' he asked his daughter.

'Mummy's calling you,' Sushma said. Then she seemed to want to get in. But Kini pushed her away. 'I'll be back in a few minutes,' he told her.

'And don't you come knocking again.'

He bolted the door and returned to his seat.

'So that's my story. Usually, the cursing goes on silently in my mind. Often, when I'm at home, I mutter to myself. On a few occasions, when my wife and Sushma have gone out, I've shut the doors and windows and, standing in front of the images of the gods, shouted curses until I was hoarse, I found it nauseating to my own ears, but my mouth wouldn't stop.'

Kini paused. He suddenly looked tired.

'At first I tried to control my mind, but without success. Then I tried different kinds of charms and amulets. I made offerings to many deities. Nothing worked.'

'Perhaps it's due to something nagging at your mind,' I said. 'Deep in your mind there may be resentment at some injustice, or some disappointment. Perhaps it comes to the surface in this way.'

'Oh, no,' Kini said. 'I'm as happy in life as anyone could be. My only son—a bright boy, and well-behaved—is studying to be an engineer. We're all in good health and there's no great worry on my mind. Oh yes, I've been happy. And yet, there's this horrible thing that won't go away.'

'Have you been to a psychiatrist, then?' I asked.

'I don't believe in that sort of thing. This isn't a matter of mere chemicals, or of nerves. Scientific mumbo-jumbo would be of no use. It's only God who can save me.'

From Kini's apartment came the sound of his wife shouting, and then of Sushma crying. Kini listened for a moment and then ignored it.

'Then this thing happened the other day,' he said. 'The gods became angry. Since that day, I've been thinking—did that happen because of my dreadful habit? I had a feeling that something of this sort would happen one day. Sins must bear fruit, sooner or later.'

For a few minutes I didn't speak. Then I said, 'Look, Mr Kini, what you've said doesn't make much sense. Think about it—hundreds of Ganesh images in Bombay got up and went away. That couldn't be the fruit of one person's sins. I mean, there'd be too large a gap between cause and effect. God doesn't watch you alone. His eye is on everyone, you know.'

I lit a cigarette and continued, 'But I don't find it strange that such an idea came into your head. When a shattering public event like this occurs, everyone begins to see his own life in its light. I'm sure thousands of persons in Bombay at this moment have similar ideas. On the other hand, your petty sins may not count for much in God's account books.'

Kini remained silent. My words seemed to have made some sense to him, but I doubted that he would change his mind.

Lying in bed, I thought for a long while about what Kini had told me. It was past midnight when I fell asleep, but I woke up almost immediately. I was wondering what had awakened me, when I heard small noises coming from the kitchen. I listened. Mice, I thought. I hadn't had mice in my apartment before. Then I remembered that Kini, too, had spoken about mice the other day. Mice must be invading the whole building, probably because of the squalor in the new shanty town growing up behind it.

The noise of the mice made it hard to get back to sleep. Sounds in the dark are particularly irritating. As long as things are visible, noise recedes into the background. But once things have become invisible, noises—be they loud or small—begin to rule. I got out of bed, went into the kitchen and knocked a knife-handle upon the kitchen table. I went back to bed. Things were quiet for a few minutes. Then the noises began again. Suddenly I remembered Kini's notion: these were Lord Ganesha's mice. Sacred mice. I smiled.

Listening to the sound of mice in the dark, it seemed to me as though someone were scratching words that I couldn't decipher upon a black slate with a rough slate-pencil. It occurred to me that I had some rat poison in the house, and I thought of scattering some on the kitchen floor. But instead of getting out of bed I lay in the dark with my eyes wide open. Perhaps someone was photographing me under powerful lights, although I was unable to see them. Then the photographer, with a black cloth still over his head, began to help me knot a tie around my neck. I pulled away the tie with both hands and jumped out of bed. I switched on the light and splashed cold water on my face. Then I dressed and went out.

III

The streets were deserted. I felt like roaming about, and thought of going to the beach. I often went to the beach at night. In the evenings the beach is crowded. It's nice at night, with few people around and the sea babbling in sleep. Once in a while a plane passes overhead, blinking red and green lights.

It was different now, though. It wasn't safe to wander around alone at night any more. You didn't know when you might be struck by an elephant's trunk. I thought it over for a minute or two and decided to go to the beach all the same. I didn't care. Perhaps somewhere inside I wanted that blow on the head.

I arrived at the beach and sat on the huge pipe that pours sewage water into the sea. I could see a few forms wrapped in blankets sleeping by the beach wall. The sea shimmered under the moonlight. It was midway between high and low tide, and a cool breeze was blowing in over the calm water towards the beach.

After an hour or so I saw two or three figures walking towards the beach. Some sleepless wanderers like me, I thought. The figures were short, and I wondered if they were children. What were children doing out by themselves at this hour? Then I saw something waving like a tail, and thought they were dogs. The figures came forward, and walked out on to the sand. Then I realized in amazement that they were Ganesha images.

More figures began to arrive. The ones that had come first reached the water and went straight in. I watched them disappear under the surface, legs first, then belly and shoulders, and then the elephant head. One after the other the images came down to the beach and entered the sea. Their sleek bodies shone in the moonlight. They walked with such an air of freedom, with such grace! As each entered the sea, the water seemed to make way for the god, compliantly breaking into ripples. Some of the gods, as they entered the water, playfully waved their trunks in the air. All was quiet, and the gods were disappearing noiselessly one by one into the sea.

Spellbound, I watched the unearthly sight. The gods were quietly going home, spurning all rituals. They had come down the beach in a wave of pure joy; their clay figures melted into the sea like lumps of sugar. I thought their melting figures would make the salt sea sweet.

Somewhere in my mind questions were fluttering. Why were the gods leaving so suddenly? Had they accomplished their mission? Why had they risen up? Were they returning because they had failed to achieve some objective? Perhaps they had decided to leave the affairs of men to men themselves. Perhaps they had undertaken this experiment to undo some divine entanglement of their own which had nothing to do with the world of men. Or they had staged the uprising for fun, and now, having tired of the game, they were departing. I remembered the tale of the Pied Piper and the rats. I thought that a Pied Piper who can lure away the gods must be very powerful indeed.

But such questions and ideas didn't linger long in my mind. They appeared pointless, entranced as I was by the sight before me. I watched for a long time. Then the number of figures coming down to the sea grew smaller. In the end a very small god came skipping down and threw himself into the water with abandon. Then the beach was deserted; the water shimmered quiescently. I fell asleep without realizing it.

The sun was up when I awoke. Slum dwellers were coming down to the edge of the sea to defecate. The sea was low. I felt stiff. I stretched myself and started for home.

I pondered over the previous night's spectacle as I walked. I wondered if it had really happened, or whether it was just a dream. Who was I to be blessed among all men with the sight of such a vision? I thought I could find out the truth when I got back to the city. If the gods had truly left, people couldn't have failed to have noticed it. Also, on other beaches of the city a few people must have seen the gods leaving. But then I didn't really care if what I had seen was real or the play of my imagination. To have seen it was enough.

I recalled an incident from my childhood. In the village where I grew up there lived an old astrologer who was something of a crank. One day he made some calculations and declared that on a certain day there would be great floods and storms and everything would be washed away. He began to warn the villagers, telling them to leave their huts and go to the top of a mountain on the appointed day. Everyone laughed at him.

The astrologer became increasingly frantic, running about to save the villagers from what he believed was their folly. On the day before the world was to end, he packed a few of his belongings and, warning the people for one last time, climbed up to the top of the mountain behind our village. It was a hard climb, and the old man must have been half dead with exhaustion when he reached the summit. That night there arose by chance a great storm; sheets of rain poured down for hours, and trees fell. In the morning, when the sky had cleared, a small band of villagers climbed the mountain. They found the astrologer's stiffened body.

When I was small I hadn't realized it, but many years later it struck me: braving the violent winds and the rain, the old man must have died in the conviction that he was indeed witnessing the end of the world. That was the truth as he saw it; and, in the final analysis, what other truth is there?

I reached the building where I lived. Climbing up to my room, I stopped and knocked on Accountant Kini's door. Kini opened the door, and looked at me with sleepy eyes.

'Mr Kini,' I shouted. 'They've gone. The gods have left.'

'What, the gods have left?' Kini muttered, rubbing his eyes 'How? And when? Why did they leave?' And, with half-shut eyes, he began to mumble curses as though he were reciting prayers.

JOURNEY 4

AMBAI

Translated from the Tamil by Lakshmi Holmström

THERE WAS STILL SOME TIME BEFORE THE BUS WOULD START. SHE HAD already demolished a paper packet of peanuts, following it with a ginger murabba, just to aid the digestion. Still no sign of the driver. Next to her, a pregnant woman, on a seat meant for three passengers. She looked as if she were five or six months gone. Wrists covered in bangles: red, yellow, green, and dark blue. Around her neck, chains, thaali, mango-patterned necklace, etc. The middle-aged woman beside her—possibly her mother—kept blotting the sweat off her forehead, shoulders, and neck with a small towel. She touched the younger woman as gently as she would a bird. 'How it's pouring off you! At least when the bus starts there will be a bit of a breeze,' she said, fanning the girl with the newspaper she held in her hand. The pregnant girl accepted all her mother's attentions with quiet pride. At the same time, she was mindful of the young man who stood outside, beneath the window. He, for his part, continued to hand her, one after the other, a tender coconut, gram sweets, murukku, bananas, and so on.

'Come back soon. Don't stay on there,' he said, standing solidly there. Firmly moulded arms and legs. A body like a rock.

'I've told Bakkiyamanni to send you your meals. Eat properly. And don't go about in the heat, Ayya. It's not good for you,' she told him, again and again.

The same conversation might have been repeated ten times over, without change of tone. Yet it seemed to contain different meanings each time. The expressions on the speakers' faces kept changing too, showing in turn elation, fond reproof, playfulness, laughter, tenderness, yearning, and sadness at parting.

Now and then the mother intervened to say, 'Why don't you let Thambi go home? He shouldn't have to stand there in the sun.'

The driver jumped in and sat down. Noises preparatory to starting the journey ensued. All at once, the man standing beneath the window began to cry.

'Go and return safely. I'll be yearning for you,' he said, sobbing hugely, and crying aloud. The girl was shaken. Greatly anxious, she said, 'Don't cry. I'll be back. I'll be back very soon.' He wept the more. Broken words came from him, 'The house, so lonely....'

The girl rose to her feet. 'Ayya, should I just stay here? Will you go on your own?' she asked piteously, wiping her tears.

'No, no. It's a wedding in your relative's house. You must go. But come back quickly,' he said.

The bus began to move slowly. The girl leaned forward and stretched out her hands to reach him. He touched her fingers, then laid her hands against his cheeks. 'Go safely, Kamalam,' he said, breaking down yet again.

The bus began to pick up speed. The words 'careful', 'heat', and 'food' mingled with the wind and were lost. As the bus left the station and turned into the main street, when they looked back, they could see him standing in exactly the same place; his whole self shaken, his shoulders rising and falling soundlessly. The girl must have caught sight of him.

'He's still crying,' she announced. 'He's like an innocent child. He won't even realize when he's hungry,' she said.

'Oh, really. It's not a year since you married. Did he stay hungry before that? He's his father's only son. After the woman of the house died, his father brought him up, didn't he? What are you talking about?' The mother snapped at her.

'You don't know anything, Ayya. Within four months of arranging his son's marriage, my father-in-law went off on his countrywide pilgrimage. No, he'll be all alone at home. Only a wife knows what goes on inside a house.' The girl's eyes filled with tears.

'As if he's the most fantastic husband around town! I've borne four children, remember? Are you trying to teach me?'

'Let's say he is a fantastic man. He's certainly better than the bridegroom you wanted to tie me to—the one who demanded another half sovereign's worth of gold and a motorcycle before he would put a thaali on me.'

'Why do you want to rake up that old story now? You just go to sleep,' the mother consoled her, laying the girl's head against her shoulder.

The girl laid her head on her mother's shoulder and went to sleep, her handloom sari of green with yellow checks tucked conveniently at her waist, her stomach slightly raised, her bangles jingling each time she moved.

When the bus stopped at Nagercoil, several people had arrived to meet mother and daughter. A small girl in a rose-coloured pavadai skirt, who wore butterfly-shaped slides studded with brightly coloured stones in her hair, hugged the young woman, calling her Athe. A young boy who looked as if he had just begun to wear long trousers came and stood next to her. Love, sympathy, and contentment on all their faces.

∽

When she had finished her work, her friend told her she must not leave Nagercoil without going to Kanyakumari. At Kanyakumari, waves like shoals of whales. Yet as they touched the feet they were as gentle as a kitten's tongue. The sun, smeared in liquid orange. When she turned her head to take in the full sweep of the sea, the girl came within her orbit. The pregnant girl on the bus. She was standing by the waves, at a little distance from her relatives. A round vessel with a lid in her hand. There was a tenderness in her expression as she gazed at the sea. Like a mother looking at her child. A softness played on her face, reminiscent of Balasaraswati when she mimed gazing at the Baby Krishna in his cradle, as she danced to the song *Jagadhodharana aadisathalu Yashoda* (Yashoda played with the saviour of the universe). Was she looking at the sea, or at some illusory form? Even as she gazed at her, the young woman turned sharply towards her, returned her look for a second, and recognized her. She came forward, smiling.

'Watching the sea?'

'Yes, I've never seen it before. How the waves beat against the shore! I want to watch it forever.'

'Did the wedding go off well?'

'Mmm. All of us are here together. We'll be leaving soon.'

'You'll go back home soon, won't you? Your husband was in tears, wasn't he, poor man!'

She smiled. 'Yes, he wept. He's got a heart as soft as cotton wool, Akka.' She stopped, then repeated, 'A heart as soft as cotton wool.' She looked at the sea.

'My family looked for a different bridegroom for me. That man worked in a government office. He seemed all right. But when we were about to buy the wedding clothes, he cut in, "So you are going to spend two thousand rupees on her sari, but only eight hundred on my vetti? In that case I must have two vettis." People in our town laughed amongst themselves, "What's this! He's talking like a child!" But gradually the whole story changed. Before he would tie the thaali, he claimed that the wedding jewellery was short by half a sovereign's worth, and demanded that it should be made good immediately, besides a promise of a motor bike within the month. It turned into quite a fracas. My sister held my brother-in-law's chin and pleaded, "Let me give her the chain I'm wearing around my neck." Something like a frenzy came over me, at that time, Akka. I rose to my feet and rushed outside. I said, "I don't want this bridegroom. I will not marry him. If there is a man here who is willing to marry me as I am, then let him come forward." My voice was trembling. The base of my throat was hurting. Everyone was stunned. Their party said, "How brazen of her to say all this!" My family worried, "She's gone and thrown it all away by speaking out." Our townsfolk meanwhile, were wondering, "Who will marry her now, when she does this at such a tender age?" But then, his father came forward, bringing his son, his hand on his shoulder. His face was as innocent as milk. His body well set and sturdy. He was smiling slightly.

'The older man said, "This is my son. He is educated. He supervises my lands. There is no woman in our house; I have brought him up myself. He is willing to marry the girl. Ask her what she wishes." I stood there in shock. I looked at my father and nodded assent. I bowed to the departing bridegroom's people and said, "Stay and eat before you leave."

'And that's how this thaali came to me, Akka. He has such a good heart. A child-like heart.'

She stopped and looked at the sea. Then she continued, as if she were speaking to the sea. 'He dotes on children. All the children in our town come to him if they need anything. To fly kites, play ball, produce a play, to be taken to cricket matches. But a senior doctor has said that he of all people can't have children. It seems he wasn't looked after properly when he had mumps as a child, and became infertile as a result. He doesn't know this. He would die if he knew.'

Because of a short bus journey together, she was willing to take her entire life apart, and to share it. Responding to the glance on her slightly raised stomach, she said, 'This belongs to his family, absolutely.'

An image flashed through her mind of an older man on pilgrimage, dipping into and rising from many temple tanks.

'He's never seen the sea. If I catch the waves in this vessel, will they still be tossing when I show him, Akka?'

She imagined a wave rising and falling within the small circular vessel. In the evening light, the pregnant girl who stood by the shore seemed one with the sea.

She could only touch her gently and say, 'No, you cannot capture the rise and fall of the sea's waves.'

COINSANV'S CATTLE

DAMODAR MAUZO

Translated from the Konkani by Xavier Cota

DRIVING HIS CATTLE BEFORE HIM, INAS HERDED THEM INTO THE SHED where he tethered them for the night before entering the house through the back door. Bent over the fireplace, Coinsanv was coaxing the fire to life by patiently blowing on the embers. Hearing Inas come in, she asked in surprise, 'Haven't you tied up the cattle yet, Inas?'

'I've just come in after tying them up,' mumbled Inas, sitting down on the box by the wall. Retrieving the butt of the viddi stuck above his ear, he struck a match to it and drew in the smoke, deeply.

'Strange! Then, why aren't they lowing today?' Coinsanv asked in wonder. Invariably, the cattle would set off a continuous mooing after being tied up in the shed. And here was Inas, back in the house after tying them up and they were still silent!

'They dare not open their mouths!'

'Why? What happened?' Coinsanv asked with a stab of apprehension. 'Did they enter someone's garden or....'

'Not in anybody's garden. They got into Paulu Bhatkar's coconut grove. They chewed up some of his saplings, it seems. He threatened to impound them unless I paid him fifteen rupees. Only after I pleaded with him and promised to work on his plot did he let them go.'

Coinsanv heard him out in silence. Warming the tea that she'd brewed in the afternoon, she poured out a mug and placed it in front of Inas. The cattle were still quiet.

'Bitter...like poison!' muttered Inas, grimacing distastefully after taking a sip of the smoky, stale black tea.

But Coinsanv was too preoccupied to pay attention to his grumbling. Why are the cattle still not mooing? How could they still not be hungry!

'Did the cattle destroy many coconut saplings?'

'Nonsense! Not a single one! I doubt that they even touched a single leaf!' In that case.... In a trice Coinsanv realized what had happened. 'Inas, did you by chance vent your anger with the landlord on the cows?'

Inas's sullen silence was answer enough.

Leaving whatever she was doing, Coinsanv rushed to the cowshed. Both the cow and the bull were standing mutely. Normally, they would both lick her with their sandpaper-like tongues as soon as she walked into the shed. Today, they made no such move. For a moment, Coinsanv imagined that they were averting their gaze from her! Could they be angry? Coinsanv laid both her hands on each of their backs. Immediately, they both started trembling. The cow started mooing first, followed immediately by the bull. Coinsanv started stroking the cow's neck with one hand and, with the other, she gently scratched the bull's forehead. The cow responded by licking her hand. Coinsanv's glance roved over the animals minutely. Though there were no definite welts on their bodies, Coinsanv's experienced eyes could tell exactly where each stroke of the lash had landed. The animals were now continuously lowing in unison. They were famished. Patting them, Coinsanv coaxed them gently, 'Okay, okay, quiet now.' She then went to the house. Inas was outside readying the coconut fronds for thatching.

'Inas, is there any oil cake in the house?'

Inas maintained a stoic silence. In any case, what could he do? Whose stomach was he supposed to fill? Three children. With their precarious hand-to-mouth existence, all they could think about was getting through each day. As long as the cow was yielding milk, they could afford to buy oil cake. Last year they had a pair of bullocks which they used for ploughing. But at Christmas, the black bull had died. Had it not died, they would have earned something from ploughing. Now, how could they afford oil cake for a cow gone dry and an idle bull?

'There's a little bran in the house, Inas. I'll go and collect some dhonn. Don't go out.'

By the time she made the rounds of their four Hindu neighbours, collecting the slop that they kept for her, the Angelus bells were ringing. She had barely entered the house, balancing the earthen pot on her head, when the cattle set off an insistent bellowing.

Lowering the pot, Coinsanv put her hand in a bag and drew out some bran that she'd saved. She distributed the bran equally between two kodhim. Pouring the slop into both the earthen vessels, she stirred it with her hand till the bran was soaked.

The cattle were still lowing ceaselessly. Inas came out. Flicking the butt of his viddi, he got to work. Taking an old broom, he quickly cleared away the area in front of the cattle. As soon as Coinsanv had finished stirring, he lifted the feed containers and placed them in front of the cattle. They began to feed greedily. Coinsanv went to the well and drew a pitcher of water. By this time, the cattle had licked the containers dry. Pouring water into them, Coinsanv went inside. Outside, the children could be heard raising a ruckus. The pot was bubbling on the fire. Inas must have kept the rice water to boil while she'd gone to collect the slop. Mentally thanking him for his thoughtfulness, Coinsanv resumed her interrupted chores.

She roasted some dried sardines on the embers. After removing them from the coals, she sprinkled the last few drops of coconut oil from the bottle. The aroma that wafted up was appetizing.

'O, Inas!' somebody from outside called out.

'Coming!' Inas replied from the back as Pedru made himself comfortable on the balcão. Catching a whiff of the roasted salt fish, he joked, 'Coinsanv,

I'm inviting myself to dinner tonight!'

'Please join us! We have excellent fish today!' retorted Coinsanv.

'That's obvious from the aroma!' Pedru laughed, lighting up a viddi. By then Inas came out.

'Where are the cattle, Inas?' Pedru's question made Coinsanv's heart skip a beat. What now? Had their cattle got into somebody else's compound too? Pedru's next remark allayed the fear.

'Day after tomorrow is the Purument fest in Margao. I'll be taking my buffalo heifer to sell at the fair. I've come to see if you're planning to go too.'

After a moment's hesitation, Inas replied, 'No. You carry on.'

His logic was telling him to sell the cattle. A single bull was useless for ploughing and a cow that yielded no milk was expensive to look after. But his prudence was warning him not to do anything without consulting Coinsanv. She loved the animals dearly.

'Don't be foolish! Your bull is getting old. What will you do if he too dies?' asked Pedru, exhaling smoke.

Inas remained quiet. Inside, Coinsanv listened intently. Pedru continued, 'I'm selling my heifer. If I get a good crop this year, I may buy another one next year. You decide about yours. But do remember that you'll get the best price only at this fair. In my opinion, you'd better sell both the cow and the bull. You can always buy one later.'

Pedru left, yet Inas did not go back in. Coinsanv must have heard every word that Pedru spoke. But he did not dare broach the subject with her. Coinsanv called the children in to eat. She served them bits of the roasted salt fish along with the kanji.

'Coinsanv, I'll be back soon,' said Inas.

Coinsanv knew exactly where Inas had gone.

Reflecting on what Pedru had said, Coinsanv squatted in front of the fireplace. One cow and a pair of bulls. How Coinsanv had doted on them! There was nothing that both she and Inas wouldn't do for them. They had even deprived themselves to feed the cattle. Despite this, one bull had died of snakebite exactly on Christmas day. During Carnival, the cow had stopped yielding milk. And now....

When fending for three children and two adults was itself an overwhelming task, can one afford to be emotional about animals? The spiralling prices.... They were already in the last days of May and had not even thought about the transplanting of paddy which had to be done before the monsoon broke out in June. Others had already germinated their seedlings. Some had already been transplanted, hoping for early rains. Both Coinsanv's paddy plots were still fallow.

The neighbours kept asking her, 'When will you be sowing?' But where would she get so much money from? Seedlings, fertilizer, weeding—for all this she needed...yes. It was essential that they sowed their field. It was only because they had cultivated last year that their children could at least have kanji this year. Otherwise they would...! They must sow...the rains were nearing...day after tomorrow was the Pentecost fair where one had to stock up on provisions for the rainy season!

Inas trooped in after a tot at the taverna. Coinsanv served Inas some kanji. Inas glanced into the kanji buddkulo. As Coinsanv readied to ladle out some more for him, Inas said he'd had enough. Coinsanv guessed that he'd said that because there was very little kanji left in the pot. But Coinsanv was not hungry and said, 'I've already eaten, Inas. You eat well. You have to work tomorrow.'

'Don't lie to me. Have that kanji!' said Inas, getting up.

Coinsanv sipped her rice gruel and got up. She cleaned up the fireplace and came out of the kitchen. The kids were fast asleep. Inas had squatted on the box and was puffing away.

'Inas, day after tomorrow is the Purument fest.'

Inas dragged on the viddi and exhaled, but remained silent. He was bothered by the same thoughts.

'You're taking the cattle, aren't you?'

Inas stiffened. Was Coinsanv goading him? Testing him? Inas shook his head vigorously.

'What do you mean by no? Are you mad?' She was speaking to Inas but was obviously trying to convince herself. 'How will we manage if we don't sell the cattle? Don't we have to sow the fields? Where will the money for the fertilizer, the seedlings, come from? From your father?'

Inas heard Coinsanv out in wonder. He had been thinking along the same lines but hadn't said anything because of Coinsanv's feelings. Now Coinsanv was herself telling him this!

'Are you serious?' Inas croaked in disbelief.

'Is this the time for jokes? There's only tomorrow. On the day after, you take them at dawn. Do you want me to come along?'

'There's no need.' Inas was relieved. All along, he'd been hesitating to broach the subject but now Coinsanv was herself urging him to sell the cattle. He slept soundly. After Coinsanv blew out the light and went to bed, Inas wasn't awake to hear her sobbing bitterly.

Getting through the next day was hell. Early in the morning, Mari Santan called out, 'Coinsanv, have you seen the sky? It looks like the monsoon is coming soon!'

'Maybe.'

'Aren't you transplanting?'

'We're transplanting after the fest.'

'You'd better hurry up! The rains are around the corner! Some people have already transplanted. And haven't you heard, people are queuing up for fertilizer? You better reserve yours fast!'

If in the morning it was Mari Santan, Caitan came by at noon. 'Have you bought your paddy seedlings?'

'Not yet.'

'Do you want some?' Caitan asked.

'Do you have stock?'

'Not me. But Bebdo Santan, the drunkard, has some for sale. If you need it, you better tell him now.'

'I'll speak to Inas about it.'

The cattle had not been put out to pasture that morning. Coinsanv herself took them to graze in the evening. Taking out some money that she'd saved, she bought a kilo of oil cake. Earlier, with one rupee you could get a kilo of oil cake and a small tablet of bathing soap besides. Now soap has become precious and a rupee would not even buy a kilo of oil cake! Mentally cursing the greedy shopkeeper, Coinsanv soaked the cake in water. Asking Inas to remain in the house, she went to the houses of the neighbouring Hindus. At each house, she collected the slop and, barely controlling the tears welling up in her eyes, she told them, 'From tomorrow, we won't need the slop. We are selling the cattle in the morning!'

Ladling out a generous portion of feed for the cattle, Inas and Coinsanv went in. Both were heavy-hearted. They had brought up these two dumb animals like their own children. And now they had to sell them for the sake of their own stomachs.

It was a terrible night, full of turmoil for them both.

Coinsanv got up at the crack of dawn. She lit the fire and put the kettle on for tea. She went into the cowshed and sitting with the animals, she cried her heart out. She got up when she sensed that Inas had woken up. Coinsanv poured out the tea and both of them sipped it in silence by the fireplace. Outside, the world was stirring. Filip, Hari, and Pedru were supposed to be taking their cattle to the fair. As he was putting on his shirt, Inas told her, 'Coinsanv, go to our field and straighten out the ridges. And send a message to Bebdo Santan that we'll need his seedlings. If it rains tomorrow, we can transplant the day after.' But Coinsanv was hardly listening. Her other ear was in the cowshed.

Pedru arrived noisily. 'Hoi there, Inas!'

Inas went out through the back door, untied the animals, and herded them out of the shed. Coinsanv couldn't restrain herself. Rushing out of the house, she hugged the cow. The bull came up to her and started licking her calves. With that, the dam burst and Coinsanv cried a flood of tears.

'You get inside now!' muttered Inas gruffly.

Her leaden feet would not move and Coinsanv remained rooted to the spot she was standing on. Inas tugged at the cattle. Since Pedru was almost out of sight, he stepped up his pace, straining at the ropes. Coinsanv sensed that the cow's feet had become heavy and the cattle didn't want to go. Inas was actually having to drag them away. What Coinsanv wanted to say was, 'No, Inas! Don't take them!' but the words did not come. What broke out instead were uncontrollable sobs. She sank down to the ground and squatted on her heels.

As the sun came out brightly, Coinsanv got a grip on herself. It was over. She served breakfast to the children and went to the fields. With a hoe, she softened the soil and levelled it. She then straightened the ridges. Having spent half a day there, she went home. After lunch, she went to Santan's and booked some seedlings. She next went to the fertilizer shop and found out which was ideal. 'I'll collect it tomorrow, keep some for me,' she told the shopkeeper. When she reached home again, she remembered her cattle. She became uneasy. Her feet took her to the cowshed. She entered the shed; its emptiness oppressed her. Such wonderful animals! We should never have sold them. Where did we get this awful idea? Our cattle were so loving, so gentle. If that stupid Pedru weren't to come that day, we wouldn't even have thought of it! Hurling two curses at Pedru, a couple at Inas, and cursing herself, too, Coinsanv got up. She then put rice in the pot boiling on the fire for kanji. As she put it in, she consoled herself. Never mind; let the cattle go! At least we won't go hungry next year. The sun had set and the lengthening shadows of darkness were casting their gloom in the house. Misgivings started assailing Coinsanv once again. It was this same cow's milk that nourished my children. By selling her milk, we could manage to buy provisions. This very bull helped maintain our household with his ploughing. And today we have decided to sell them! Our lovely cattle! God help us! I hope nobody buys our cow! I hope our bull comes back! Coinsanv consoled herself with these fervent pleas.

It was past Angelus, time for Inas to be back. But Coinsanv did not allow herself to go out and sit. Without even lighting a lamp, she squatted inside in the dark.

Quite often, many cattle come back unsold. But those cattle are quite different. Our animals are so loving; anybody will grab them. We should never have sent them! As she sat there with these thoughts tormenting her, she heard the distant tinkling of cowbells. Coinsanv stepped out.

Pedru was in front. Inas was trailing him. In the darkness she felt she could make out Pedru returning with his buffalo. But she had forgotten that Pedru's buffalo did not have a bell. Surmising that Coinsanv would be pleased even if the cattle were not sold, Inas was coming back with them with a spring in his step.

A stunned Coinsanv was motionless for a moment. That fallow field, those seedlings, that fertilizer—everything began swimming before her eyes. The cow had barely started licking her hand affectionately when Coinsanv began screaming and flailing her arms at the two dumb animals. 'You whore! You wretched animals! How the hell are we to manage now? How are we to sow the field? What are we going to eat next year? Go—and die!'

SALVATION

PRATIBHA RAY

Translated from the Odia by Leelawati Mohapatra, Paul St-Pierre, and K. K. Mohapatra

FOR FORTY LONG YEARS THE MAN AND THE WOMAN HAD LIVED UNDER one roof, sharing joys and sorrows, delight and despair. Yet never once had they stolen a glance at each other, never once had they exchanged a word or a casual touch.

Since becoming part of her household, the very first time Nuri Das had a chance to look upon the face of his wife's elder sister was when her body was lying on the funeral pyre, and his wastrel of a son, Satya, was about to set fire to it. Her face was enveloped in a haze. Or maybe he couldn't see too well because of his cataracts. He was all of fifty-nine, and the dead woman, Soshi, was eleven years his junior.

When Satya bent down to light the pyre, Nuri Das felt as if someone from up above had slipped the boy a sliver of flame. What did Soshi really look like? Nuri couldn't be sure. How could he? A blurry impression was all he had, which was just as well. Didn't society decree that he should not look upon the face of his elder sister-in-law?

Home after the cremation, Nuri found the emptiness of the house overwhelming. It was hard to step into the courtyard, where he had seen Soshi's two little feet flitting about all these years. He couldn't bring himself to sit on the veranda, where Soshi had always served him his meals. So he went and sat under the mango tree in the backyard, as stiff as a log. Why did the home feel so deserted, so empty without Soshi?

Whenever he had seen her feet approaching, he had backed away; whenever he had seen her arms dropping down in front of him to serve him food, he had shrunk back. When he needed to communicate with her, he'd beam his words at the walls, and Soshi would reply not so much in words as in action. She seemed to anticipate every move of his; there was no room for words. At first light he wanted his black tea, sweetened with jaggery, and rice puffs, followed by four paans. After breakfast, he headed to the vegetable patch, and he'd find all the tools neatly laid out on the veranda—shovel, spade, pots, and baskets. Sometimes in the middle of his labour Nuri would catch a whiff of the curry being prepared. When the sun climbed to the middle of the sky, and it was time for his bath, he'd find a bottle of oil sitting on the veranda, so he wouldn't have to enter the house. He'd give himself an oil massage and proceed to the pond at the end of the backyard for a dip. On his return, he'd find the prayer mat and rudraksha beads laid out on the inside veranda. He'd sit cross-legged and proceed to draw lines of sandal paste across his arms and chest, and on his forehead down to the bridge of his nose. Between the twin lines across his forehead, he'd draw a large dot the size of a four-anna coin. Then he'd launch full tilt into the whole routine—japa, tapa, pranam, prayer, meditation, and obeisance. By the time he had taken his last bow to the deities, steaming bowls of food would be laid out on the veranda, and, like an obedient child, he'd tuck in, never ever finding fault with the dishes. He never commented if the curry was salty or without salt, if it was too spicy or too bland. Nor did Soshi ask; she'd find out for herself when she ate after him.

But she did cook for him with genuine love and affection. He ate without a word, perhaps purely out of hunger, never letting on if he was upset or angry. Of all persons under the sun it was she, Soshi, who alone knew what a straight and narrow path the poor man trod, the razor's edge he lived on.

If Soshi's appearance remained hidden for Nuri beneath her layers of clothing, or behind the end of the sari veiling her face at all times, she was fully aware how handsome he was. A superb specimen of a man, he hadn't aged much, neither losing nor gaining weight. Though a little stooped, his features hadn't coarsened. In his twilight years he looked almost as good as in his younger days. He always dressed simply, just a clean white dhoti reaching his knees when at home. He added a short white shirt when he went to the market or elsewhere. And of course he was never without the sandal paste marks on his forehead, nose, arms, and earlobes, the two strands of tulsi beads around his neck, and a towel on his shoulder. Full five hands in height—tall by village standards—his complexion was as fair as his appearance was pleasing: his nose was straight, forehead wide, small eyes bright and piercing, chest wide as a door panel, shoulders strong enough to carry mountains, straight and long like a ploughshare, a flat belly that seemed to touch his back.

The family did not have much land. Their backyard contained a mango tree, and a couple of drumstick and banana trees. There was also a small vegetable patch, where Nuri grew whatever seasonal herbs and greens he could, which he sold in the market to buy rice and other things that were needed. During the mango months their income went up. He did not know where the mango sapling had come from or when it had been planted, but its fruit was a marvel: fully round like a zero, tapering a little towards the stem, fleshy and full of juice, the skin quite thin, its pulp quivering like aloe vera. With hardly any fibre, it was best served in thin slices. The aroma alone could set the body tingling from the belly to the brain. Buyers snapped up the mangoes. Prices shot up at the end of the season; Nuri demanded fancy prices, according to size.

This patch of green was the mainstay of the family of three. The pond at the back was tiny, but it served quite well for bathing and cleaning; it was also used to water the vegetables the year round. But at the height of summer it went dry, and a deep hole had to be dug in the middle to tap the water underground. Just as stars sprouted in the sky, fish, big and small, sprouted in the pond—kerandi, dandikiri, crayfish, eels, creols, and sheuls—but they were of no use to Nuri, a devout Vaishnav and strict vegetarian. No fish or meat ever entered his kitchen. For him the fish polluted the water of the pond, and he encouraged his neighbours to rid him of them, for free. But while generous with the fish, he wouldn't let anyone spirit away a single chilli from his garden.

Summer was a trying time: the aubergines dried up before they grew to full size, the chillies shrivelled up too; he could only dream of growing gourds, pumpkins, and cucumbers. But while in other homes greens were lacking, in Nuri's there was not enough rice. How did he manage the summer ordeal year after year?

He did have another resource, although not a regular one. Once a hobby, it had now become a means to keep the wolves of hunger from the door. Sometimes the pickings were too good to be true. He played the mridanga in the kirtan troupes whenever they were called upon to perform—at birth, death, or religious ceremonies—and for his labour he received rice, rice flakes, coconuts, sweets, a little cash, and a dhoti and a towel. He had always loved singing kirtans, and now it had become a love affair—since God knows when. From the evening until dinner was ready, he'd sit on the outside veranda drumming his mridanga, eyes shut in the dark. Sometimes he'd go on until midnight. The evening tempo was slow, soft, unhurried; the midnight beats were fast, furious, obviously matching the rumblings of a belly without food.

Hunger on God's good earth has many facets with different tastes—sweet, sour, pungent, salty, and bitter. But the four major hungers—of the flesh, belly, mind, and soul—were primal, and held all human beings in their thrall. And the hapless victim—so went one of the lines of a kirtan that Nuri sang—was swept up by a stream of lies and deceit. But he himself recognized only two: the hunger of the belly, and the hunger of the soul. The first had to be sated with food, the second with the singing of kirtans. Hare Krishna, Hare Krishna, Krishna, Krishna, Hare, Hare.... All other forms of hunger could be ignored.

What kind of hunger did Soshi have? Everything seemed buried behind her covered face. Nuri saw only a pair of hurrying feet and busy hands. She slaved from morning to night: she scooped the dung from the cowshed, made fuel cakes and put them out in the sun to dry, swept the rooms and cleaned the floor, raked dry leaves and twigs, and gathered fuelwood, cooked and washed the utensils...not all of it to quench the hunger of her belly. But she had learnt to trample all other hungers underfoot as she stamped on cow dung to make patties before laying them out to dry, as she swabbed the floor with water and fresh cow dung, as she fed leaves and twigs to the fire over which the food was cooked. Who knew whether the hunger of her soul ever yearned to join the rhythm of her brother-in-law's mridanga.

When she was younger, her pale white feet were like steamed rice cakes, puffed up in the middle. But that was just due to the filarial fevers she came down with month after month. She also had a flower tattooed in the middle of each foot. Her hands were slim and shapely, like the succulent centre of a snake gourd, and her palms were soft and as wafer-thin as pancakes. Nuri caught an occasional glimpse of her arms when she served him food—arms covered with intricate blue tattoos. Sometimes there were flashes of her face from behind her veil—a part of her nose resembling the petal of an upside-down kaner flower, with a tiny shining nose ring. Nobody had ever seen the end of her sari slip off when Nuri was around, nor for that matter did Nuri's gaze stray in her direction. They outdid each other in their respect for what society required. Bound by custom and tradition, all restrictions were carefully observed.

Had Sashi, her younger sister, not died at childbirth, Soshi wouldn't have veiled her face for the rest of her life in her own home. Sashi's son was born in her father's home, as she and her husband, Nuri, both lived there. Nuri had nowhere else to go. Adopted by his maternal uncle and aunt when they were childless, he fell out of favour once their three sons were born. His aunt turned openly hostile. But where could poor Nuri go? Poverty had driven his own father to give him to his maternal uncle; what was due to him had already passed on to his four brothers.

It was around this time that his would-be wife's family was looking for a son-in-law who'd move in with them. Soshi, the elder daughter, was a child widow, and there was no male heir to keep the family line going. Indeed, both the old man and Soshi were in danger of not having a male family member to perform their death rites. So Nuri, who was welcome neither in his own home nor in his uncle's, came to live with his wife's family after marriage.

Everything went all right until Sashi died giving birth to a boy. The grandfather was able to see the newborn and died soon after, a happy man. It was left to Soshi, the widowed aunt, to cut the umbilical cord and raise the child as her own.

So now they were three in the family: twenty-nine-year-old widower Nuri Das; his newborn son, Satya, motherless from the moment of his birth; and widowed aunt Soshi, who was only eighteen.

Despite the gap of eleven years between them—his wife, after all, had been even younger—Nuri could have married Soshi, but only if she had been his wife's younger sister.

The relationship between a man and his wife's elder sister is the most sacred—holy like the water of the Ganga. Even one and a half times more sacrosanct than that with his mother-in-law. Not only can they not look at or touch each other, they cannot speak to one another, let alone joke and laugh. A little slip and the cost is damnation—an eternal sojourn in Hell.

After her sister died, Soshi let Nuri know through a neighbour that he was free to go wherever he liked, marry a second time, have children, and settle down. Society didn't ordain that a young man must remain a widower. But she'd keep her nephew; he was needed to perform rites on the anniversary of her death. And, in addition to that, she'd never let even the shadow of a stepmother fall on the child. Nuri was free to come and see him as often as he wished, but he shouldn't dream of taking the boy away.

Nuri didn't relish the prospect of spending the rest of his life without a wife, but he found the idea of leaving his son behind with his aunt utterly unbearable. Besides, he didn't have a home of his own. Soshi was still a helpless young widow, and the child no more than a waif; he couldn't leave them to their fate and make a fresh beginning elsewhere. It wouldn't have been proper for a good man to do so.

'I'm only interested in my son,' Nuri had it conveyed back to Soshi. 'Not in the property of this family or anything else. And do not ever again broach the subject of my remarrying.'

That same evening he took the mridanga off the wall, where he had hung it from a peg. This was his only possession when he had moved in. He had drummed it while practising kirtans with his uncle when he had lived with him, but hadn't touched it since his wedding. Tonight, it seemed his sole companion—true and intimate. He drummed on it late into the night. From then on he played it for an hour or two every evening without fail, wondering how he could have given it up for the past few years.

A cat will do, so goes the saying, if there's no tiger. In the same way, an aunt could fill the role of a mother. Satya hadn't seen a tiger, nor had he seen a mother. Maybe he'd get to see a tiger once he grew up—in the circus or in the wild, but a mother he'd never see. His aunt loved him more than would have a mother, but he didn't know the difference between an aunt's love and a mother's; he hadn't seen his mother, he didn't even have a picture of her. He grew up to be a rogue—wicked, wayward, obstinate as a mule, and a liar to the marrow of his bones.

And he couldn't stand his father. When his old man affectionately called him 'mother-killer', he would retaliate by angrily calling his father 'wife-killer'—an expression he had picked up from the neighbours, who didn't miss a chance to castigate Nuri: 'That man is definitely a wife-killer. What else can explain a healthy sixteen-year-old perishing in childbirth, when girls as young as thirteen or fourteen deliver children without a problem?' Apparently, in Nuri's horoscope, death was the ruling planet in his wife's house. But that came to light only after she had passed away.

A well-known high school, established by the British, was right next door—Nuri's walls practically touched it—and Satya could eat at home and rinse his mouth in the school courtyard. Nuri hoped the motherless boy would seize the chance to get a decent education, pass his matriculation, and find himself a government job, so he wouldn't have to eke out as miserable an existence as his father's: banking on mangoes in season and, out of season, on sweet rice puffs at the end of a long kirtan performance.

But Satya turned out to be a disappointment—he stayed as shy of school as a goat does of water. Maybe because he had no love for his father—his father's 'yes' was the son's 'no'; they argued all the time—and he played truant from school. Once in a while a teacher would bring it to the father's notice, and Nuri would take the boy to task. He'd throw him into a room, tie him to a piece of furniture with a rope, and lock the door from outside. 'It's either me,' he'd say as he read the riot act, 'or him. No one should untie him or give him food. Not until he promises to mend his ways, promises not to cut classes and to concentrate on his studies.' The warning was obviously addressed to Soshi. Who else was there who could set the boy free, wipe away his tears, and give him food?

Soshi wouldn't butt in right away. A father had every right to discipline his son. It was even his duty to do so. But the aunt also had a duty towards her nephew, and no one could stop her from doing what she thought was right. So, as soon as Nuri left home, she'd open the room, free the boy from the leg of the cot to which he'd been tied, dry his tears, coax and cajole him to eat. When Nuri returned from wherever he'd gone, he'd find the boy on the veranda poring over a book, the picture of a perfect student. Of course, he knew who was behind it all. But by putting a book into the boy's hands she couldn't make a student out of him!

This happened not just once but more than a few times every month. The boy spent two—sometimes three—years in every class. But that didn't worry his aunt. If the boy sat for the exams but didn't pass, she thought the fault lay with the teachers. What good were they if only the better students got through?

Nuri blamed the boy, Soshi blamed the teachers, the boy blamed his father. Satya was determined to take it out on his father. He was intelligent enough to pass his exams, but he wouldn't grant his father that pleasure.

Meanwhile, time flew by imperceptibly, regardless of the daily worries the boy caused his father and aunt. Then, one fine day, when he was eighteen, he upped and left, got himself a small-time job in town, where he got married and lived with his wife, determined to keep away from the village.

That left only two people at home. Soshi, fair and plump, was still very much a young woman, and Nuri, quite a strong and virile man; both in good health, neither of them sick or in decline. Their only worry was where the next meal would come from. If they had any other thoughts in their minds, it didn't show, drowned out by Nuri's mridanga drumming, absorbed in the darkness under Soshi's veil.

Meanwhile, all kinds of scandals broke out around them—in the colonies of milkmen and of washermen, and in the more respectable Mohanty homes. There was no end to the transgressions: affairs between a young woman and her husband's younger brother, between a man and his wife's younger sister, between a man and a woman sworn before God as brother and sister, between a widowed aunt and her nephew. Sometimes affairs took place between daughters-in-law in rich and aristocratic families and their farmhands. Where were the country and society headed?

But these brought a measure of excitement to village life. Townsfolk could get theirs from the cinema, theatre, and folk opera performances, but villagers had nothing but gossip to fall back on. And so they gossiped wherever they could, from the bathing ghats to the panchayat office. The stories got embroidered, enlarged, exaggerated in the telling, like a large fruit emerging from a tiny seed. Reputations were sullied, dragged through the mud. All this led to the imposition of fines, social boycott, ostracism, fights, murders, suicides, and black magic to cast an evil eye, a hex, or a spell.

But Nuri's house—strange how nobody ever referred to it as Soshi's—remained untouched. When Satya lived there the villagers' curiosity had centred on his latest scrapes or acts of mischief. But once he left, the house was as silent as a temple that had permanently shut down. No one could find even the smallest misdemeanour, one the size of a mustard seed. What would the gossips do when there wasn't even a kernel to start with? Not that the villagers were full of praise for Nuri and Soshi. They wondered if the two would have been as self-controlled in a different situation. What if instead of the wife's revered elder sister she had been the approachable younger sister? Only then would they have truly been tested: was he indeed a man with absolute self-discipline and she a woman of impeccable virtue and integrity?

Weighed down by the weight of what was expected from them, Nuri and Soshi grew old. Nuri became asthmatic, and Soshi's legs swelled up from her all too frequent bouts of filaria. There was no one to look after them when they were sick, care for them when they took to their beds. Soshi clucked her tongue in despair when Nuri couldn't breathe during an attack of asthma; Nuri took to drumming his mridanga relentlessly when Soshi came down with a fever. Sometimes they both railed against the unjust social system: even when dying, the elder sister of a man's wife couldn't pour a drop of water through his lips. A man could be pardoned for having a child with his wife's younger sister, but he could not run a hand over the pain-wracked body of the elder one.

As years passed and they both became old and gnarled, they loved and cared for each other more and more. The pain of one badly affected the other. They began to fondly refer to each other as 'old man' and 'old woman'. Before her female companions, Soshi would say: 'The old man's having it bad because of his asthma. There's no one at home to massage a drop of mustard oil on the soles of his feet. What high hopes he had pinned on that son of his! Indeed, the man stayed on at his in-laws' only because of the boy. But the boy chose to move away. As long as I'm alive, I'll drag myself around, no matter how ill I am, and cook for the old man.

But what will happen when I'm gone? How on earth will he manage? And yet he's not willing to swallow his pride and get in touch with his boy and ask him to come home. But I know how much he's missing him. They share the same blood, after all. I can read his mind as clear as daylight.' And before the menfolk Nuri would think aloud: 'The filarial fevers will be the death of the old woman. Six days a month she goes down and lies like a corpse. No one at home to put a drop of water in her mouth when she most needs it. She showered all her love on the nephew, loved him more than a mother would have, but the ungrateful boy never treated her as anything other than an aunt. Who knows whether he'll turn up to light her funeral pyre? That's the old woman's last wish. She might not say so in so many words, but don't I know what's on her mind?'

No one wanted to know just how they knew each other's mind without exchanging a word. But words have a way about them; they might remain unspoken, but they're never unknown. Even legs and hands speak. People betray their feelings through the slightest gestures: how a person walks says volumes about whether he or she likes or dislikes somebody, how food is served shows whether she cares or not. The way a man beats his mridanga reveals whether he's laughing or crying. Forty years of life under the same roof, seasoned by sorrows, hunger, depression, and deprivation, worries and anxieties, regrets and anger, understanding and blaming one another had given them insight into each other's minds and hearts, although their lips were sealed, although they behaved as if the other person didn't exist. Words were unnecessary, redundant. Their understanding was as palpable as the fragrance of a flower spreading on the breeze, like the seeping of water into the parched earth, like the notes of the mridanga rising to the moon.

So when Soshi had a particularly terrible attack of fever, Nuri swallowed his pride and wrote to his son: 'Satyananda, may you live long. Your aunt is dying. Although she's not asking for you, her last wish is to see you. And she thinks her soul will have no salvation if you don't light her pyre. Come as soon as you can. Hurry. Treat this letter as a telegram. This will be the last time I will be making a request of you. And you will not have to come home ever again. Ever with good wishes for you, Nuri Das.'

Satya knew his father, proud as ever, had written for the sake of his dying aunt. He hadn't signed the letter 'your father'. Still he made haste to reach home with his wife and children. The salvation of his aunt's soul was more important than the tone and tenor of his father's request.

Soshi had stopped talking by the time Satya arrived; she couldn't move her lips even a little. Her eyes were half open, unblinking. She was breathing, but just barely. Did it register that her nephew had come at last?

But it struck Satya that the old woman had been waiting only for him; she passed away at dawn.

Back from the cremation grounds after Soshi's body had been consumed by the funeral fire, Nuri sat on the veranda into the gathering gloom of the evening, gently drumming his mridanga, softly repeating a kirtan refrain: 'Hare Krishna, Hare Krishna, Krishna, Krishna, Hare, Hare....'

Inside, Satya's wife was loudly sobbing and wailing: 'Where have you gone, Aunt, leaving us forsaken....' The loud wailing was supposedly for the satisfaction of the departed soul.

Satya sat by the oven, in which the fire had long ago died, calling out to his aunt, torrents of tears streaming from his eyes. The tears were for real. Would that help the soul find salvation?

Nuri drummed his mridanga all through the night to mourn the passing of his dead wife's elder sister. His fingers, bruised and bleeding, worked up a delirious beat for the salvation of Soshi's soul.

REFLECTIONS OF A HEN IN HER LAST HOUR

PAUL ZACHARIA

Translated from the Malayalam by A. J. Thomas

OH, MY DEAR JACKAL, PLEASE DON'T LOOK AT ME LIKE THIS. THRILLS RUN up and down my body. My eyes grow dim. In this darkness smeared with the fragrance of coffee blossoms, I am already feeling intoxicated. I can't bear this gaze of yours. Even though I'm hesitant to look in your direction, I am aware that you are gazing at me. I am aware that, amid the shadows, beneath this coffee tree, your look is fixed upon me. When I think of that, I want to look into the glowing embers of your eyes. But because of my fear, it is to the sky that I look instead, sitting on this coffee tree bough. But as I gaze upon a sky lit by the light of star clusters that are like bunches of coffee flowers, I want to lower my head and look into the steady gaze of your eyes. Please don't perplex me in this way. Can you see me in this darkness? What am I to you? A throbbing heart in the bough high above? A rustle of feathers? Doesn't my dim figure escape from the hold of your eyes and vanish into the foliage and dark clouds?

Don't trouble me so. Am I not a mere hen, a female? Where do I get the strength to suppress so much excitement? My feathers are standing on end again. Why do you vex me like this, as a secret wooer, an unseen fear, a thrill? Isn't that the reason I began to like you although I am afraid of you? Oh, voyeur, do you know how much I want to see you? Still, I can't gather enough courage to look at you! What is this fear that is seated deep inside me and weighs me down? With what fear did I flee, raising a shower of dry leaves all around me, when the dog rushed at me from behind a tree draped in pepper vines. The fool, the idiot! Will I let him touch me? The slave who spends half his life on a chain! Is there any meaning to his sudden lunge towards me? But your arrival, braving sticks, stones, guns, and crackers, is warm, defiant, and captivating. Even if you manage to seize me.... What will you do to me if you get hold of me? What will you do with me before you eat me? Is it merely to eat me that you keep looking at me thus, risking your own life? Is a hen so tasty? I wish I could look into your eyes and ask all these questions. But I am afraid.

Today you didn't howl at all. I've been straining my ears since dusk. When you howl from your lair which I shall never look at nor walk into, what dreams I am immersed in! How dark and remote is your world! It is your amazing howls that rise at odd hours from the land of the night, more than the cock's crowing at the beginning of light, that give me an urge to dream, and my mind dances with excitement. More than the crowing of cuddling roosters, your howls exhilarate me. Will you take me to your lair? When I sit at its edge waiting for your pleasure, will you howl just once for me? Let the moon rise early, to give your howl a sheen as it rises into the sky; let the moon climb the sky along with it. As you carry me, I'll gaze into your face and eyes without a trace of fear. I know that any lingering fear will dissolve the instant you catch me. Weren't you the rustle and movement I sometimes detected at dusk through the fading vistas of the grove? Weren't you the commotion that sometimes came towards this courtyard, climbing stone walls, rubbing against the base of trees and shaking thickets? I recall a moment from my time in the coop when an unsettling presence in the dark wind caught our attention. Startled and shivering, we quickly gathered and huddled together. Wasn't it you who came flowing in the wind? During nights illuminated by the moon, I've observed while sitting on this bough, a figure prowling through the periwinkle thickets on the banks of the pond in the southern compound. Where were your journeys to, then? Why didn't you come and stand beneath my coffee tree back then and look at me with your blazing eyes? Didn't you know that every day I would hide myself without getting into the coop and perch alone atop this coffee bough? It isn't as suffocating here as in the coop. And there are no coxcombs to force themselves on me. There isn't that long wait in the morning, for the coop to be opened. I enjoy myself sitting here, listening to the rhythmic beat of the dewdrops that fall from the leaves, the rumble of rain that draws near, and watch as the lightning flashes and fades from the far limits of the sky. I also enjoy the excitement and trepidation your impending arrival creates in me. When your howls seek me out through the silence among the trees, excitement courses through my entire being. I have pecked at this bough, holding firmly on to it. I have pecked at it again and again. My head reels when I think that you are actually looking at me, sitting in the grass at the base of this coffee tree. I feel as if the stars have clustered together to blaze forth. Treetops quiver and part right in front of my eyes. Will I fall down even before getting your invitation? If so, will you accept me?

Didn't you look at me from the tall grass in the grove, when I was feeding in the tilled earth in the western farm field? Your gaze touched the base of my every feather like sharp points. I stood there with lowered head, still and quiet, without the strength to gaze back at you and with the feeling that you filled the entire clump of grass and thicket. I stood there for a long time for you to come to me. I started up and hastily retreated only upon hearing the piercing cries of the kites soaring in the sky. Did you think I wasn't beautiful when you saw me in the sunlight? Didn't you like me in the daylight?

How many days did I hide my eggs in the heaps of dry leaves in the banana grove for your pleasure! Haven't you seen the members of the family coming in search of them? Wasn't it you who ate all of them? Or was it that damned dog or that rat snake which hisses from the hole in the stone wall? Those were the eggs I specifically laid for you, with great joy and satisfaction. I offered them to you, overlooking my own desire to hatch them. Yesterday and the day before I had let fall through the dusk a feather to let you know of my vigil on this coffee bough. You know I can't help flying up to this bough to await you. I can meditate on you in peace only when sitting at this height. Because I am also afraid. Yet I can't help waiting for you. I can't help feeling your gaze. Here comes another feather as a sign of my presence. I want to gaze into your eyes when it lands near you, but I find I'm unable to do so. Here's yet another, as a sign of my love, yearning, and fear. Let me lower my eyes along with the falling feather. Oh, my jackal, here I come. Here I come, saturated with the fragrance of coffee blossoms and love. I fall into your eyes. Do not go away thinking that it's a bunch of flowers that has broken off and fallen down. I am indeed your hen. Here I am, coming down. Please support me. Please hold me.

LABURNUM FOR MY HEAD

TEMSULA AO

EVERY MAY, SOMETHING EXTRAORDINARY HAPPENS IN THE NEW cemetery of the sleepy little town. Standing beyond the southernmost corner of the vast expanse of the old cemetery—dotted with concrete vanities, both ornate and simple—the humble Indian laburnum tree erupts in glory, with its blossoms of yellow mellow beauty. The first time it happened, some years ago, surprised visitors to the concrete memorials assumed that it was an accident of nature. But each year as the tree grew taller and the blossoms more plentiful, the phenomenon stood out as a magnificent incongruity, in the space where man tries to cling to a make-believe permanence, wrenched from him by death. His inheritors try to preserve his presence in concrete structures, erected in his homage, vying to outdo each other in size and style. This consecrated ground has thus become choked with the specimens of human conceit. More recently, photographs of the dead have begun to adorn the marble and granite headstones.

But nature has a way of upstaging even the hardest rock and granite edifices fabricated by man. Weeds and obstinate brambles sprout from every inch of soil uncovered by sand and cement. So every Easter week, the community comes together to spruce up headstones and get rid of the intruding natural growth. The names on individual gravesites are lovingly wiped clean of dust and bird shit by loved ones; occasional strangers read them as incidental pastime.

But the laburnum tree will not or cannot reveal readily who or what lies beneath its drooping branches during its annual show of yellow splendour. That particular spot displays nothing that man has improvised; only nature, who does not possess any script, abides there: only she owns the seasons. And the seasons play out a pantomime of beauty and baldness on the tree standing on the edge of the lifeless opulence, spread over the remains of the assorted dead: rich and poor, young and old, and mourned and unmourned. The headstones in the old cemetery bear mute testimony to duties performed by willing and unwilling offspring and relatives. The laburnum tree on the other hand is alive and ever unchanging in its seasonal cycles: it is resplendent in May; by summer end the stalks holding its yellow blossoms turn into brown pods; by winter it begins to look scraggly and shorn. Springtime brings back pale green shoots and by May it is wearing its yellow wreaths again, to outdo all the vainglorious specimens erected in marble and granite.

But the story is running ahead of itself and must be told from the beginning. It all started with a woman named Lentina and her desire to have some laburnum plants in her garden. She had always admired these yellow flowers for what she thought was their femininity; they were not brazen like the gulmohars with their orange and dark pink blossoms. The way the laburnum flowers hung their heads earthward appealed to her because she attributed humility to the gesture. So she decided to grow a couple of these trees in her own garden which, though not big, could accommodate them if they were planted in the corners, without affecting the growth and health of the other plants. She purchased saplings from a nursery and had them planted at the edge of her boundary wall. She followed the instructions faithfully and hoped that within two years, as the nursery man assured her, the plants would flower.

That first year, her new gardener pulled out the small saplings along with the weeds growing around them. After loud recriminations, Lentina bought some more saplings and this time, planted three of them in three corners of the garden. She hoped that at least one of them would survive. But it was not to be. One day she heard loud barking and cows mooing very close to her compound. When she came out to investigate, she found that some stray cows on being pursued by her neighbour's dogs and finding her gate slightly ajar, had rushed into her garden and were blissfully munching on the plants they found there, including her precious laburnum saplings. She began to wonder about these accidents in her garden ever since she had planted the laburnum saplings. Nevertheless, she did not give up and the third year too, she planted some more saplings of her favourite flowering tree. Almost miraculously they survived the first few months and began to thrive.

Lentina was thrilled and could not wait to see them bear the magnificent yellow blooms she so admired. But before her wish could come true, another disaster struck. One day, a worker from the health department came while she was out visiting a friend, and sprayed a deadly DDT concoction on the edges of the garden. As ill luck would have it, it rained heavily that night flooding the entire garden. Except the full-grown trees, all her flowers, including the laburnums, withered and died. Lentina was devastated and began to think that her efforts at bringing the strange beauty into her garden would never be successful. But whenever she saw these flowers in bloom, on highways and in gardens, the intense yearning to have them closer home began to overpower her. Her husband and children were convinced that she was developing an unhealthy fetish for the laburnum and began to talk openly about this in close family gatherings. She could not understand their concern and was inwardly hurt by their seeming insensitivity to beauty around them. But she never gave up her hope of having a full-grown laburnum tree in her garden some day.

Lentina did not mention laburnums to anyone any more; nor did she attempt to plant the tree she so ardently admired and wished to have in her garden. Meanwhile, her husband began to show signs of a strange disease and before any proper diagnosis could be made, he passed away quietly one night in his sleep. The funeral services were long and elaborate because the deceased was a respected and prominent member of society. On the burial day, while the hearse was about to leave for the cemetery, Lentina surprised everyone, including herself, by announcing that she was going to accompany her husband on his last journey. Usually it is men who take part in the last rites at the gravesite and stay on to supervise the erection of the temporary fence around the fresh grave. But when Lentina saw the group, including her sons and her own brothers, stepping out of the house behind the hearse, some impulse urged her to join them. Her words were met with silence, because no one was prepared to voice dissent at such a moment. So the party departed, and in the graveyard while the last prayers droned on, Lentina stood among the assortment of headstones and began ruminating on man's puny attempts to defy death; as if erecting these memorials would bring the dead back to life.

Lentina decided that she did not want any such attempt at immortality when her time came, and at that thought she experienced an epiphanic sensation: why not have a laburnum tree planted on her grave, one which would live on over her remains instead of a silly headstone? This way, even her lifelong wish to have such a tree close to her would be fulfilled. In spite of the sombre occasion, she began to smile but when a relative saw her, she quickly went back to looking appropriately bereaved. But the sense of elation she felt could not be hidden for long. So she looked around for her driver and, gesturing to him to follow her, made her way home.

That night she could not sleep from excitement: it was as if a big problem had solved itself; but how was she going to accomplish it? It was clear that she could not confide in her relatives or children; so she had to find someone who would understand her deep-seated longing for the yellow wonders. She turned her attention to her servants: whom among them could she trust? Not the cook or the gardener, they had families, and secrets in families are never sacrosanct. Suddenly, her mind turned to the driver who had been in their employment for more years than she could remember. He was a widower. She decided to make him her confidant. She would take him for a drive the next day to the cemetery and would explain to him what she wanted for a headstone when she died, and why. But there would be one condition: she had to see the tree bloom during her lifetime. The driver's name was Mapu but everyone called him Babu because Lentina's grandson called him by that name, unable to pronounce Mapu at first. The name stuck and Mapu good-naturedly did not object even when the older people began calling him Babu.

The next morning, she sent for Babu and they took the road to the cemetery. This in itself would not appear strange: a widow paying a visit to the grave of her husband. But Lentina's intention was different; she wanted to survey the still-empty sites and to reserve a spot where she would be buried. It had to be a spot which would not be disturbed in a long while and would not pose any problem for others. When they reached the cemetery, instead of heading towards her husband's grave, Lentina marched to the extreme corners of the ground, as if looking for a lost treasure. After what seemed to be an arduous trek, she settled on a spot in the southernmost tip of the cemetery and began to nod her head, as if she had found what she was looking for. Babu was puzzled and was almost beginning to see what his young masters had said about madam losing her mind. When she gestured to him to approach, he went hesitantly. Motioning to him to walk faster, she pointed to the spot where she was standing and said loudly, 'This is my spot, I want to be buried here when my time comes.'

Babu was taken aback and began to protest, 'But, madam, your place is already earmarked beside my master!'

'Nonsense, it can go to whichever son goes first. My place is here and you are going to see that the town committee gives a written commitment on this. But mind you, no one at home is to be told.' She knew that Babu's son-in-law was a petty officer in that office. 'Arrange it with your son-in-law. I'll pay whatever amount it costs. And also swear him to secrecy just as you are going to do now. Will you keep my secret?'

Babu, seeing the fire and intensity in her eyes, answered, 'Yes, madam, I will keep your secret and I will see to it that my son-in-law does the same.' Lentina added, 'He is not to tell even his wife.' Babu nodded and said, 'Yes, madam.' Having made this momentous decision, she stretched her hand to him and with her leaning on him, they made their way to the car parked outside the gate and came home. The old woman looked exhausted and went straight to bed. No one thought it strange, because the funeral activities had taken a lot out of everyone and even the young women of the household were looking forward to an early night. But lying in bed, Lentina was wide awake and planning her next move: she wanted to plant a laburnum tree on her gravesite while she was still alive to ensure that all this trouble of securing the plot and keeping everything quiet had the desired results. She *had* to see the tree bloom before she breathed her last. Even for this task she had to enlist the help of her faithful Babu. But unfortunately, it was almost winter and they had to wait till the next spring.

In the meantime, Babu began the preliminary discussions with his son-in-law about reserving a plot in the cemetery. At first the young man was puzzled; why was his father-in-law talking of such a morbid subject? Was he suffering from some terminal disease that he had kept secret from his own family? But he kept his thoughts to himself. From him Babu learnt that most people wanted the front rows in the cemetery and there was always some dispute or the other about such issues among the more prominent people of the town. Babu's request surprised his son-in-law because it was for the most insignificant plot in the cemetery. He assured his father-in-law that as far as the location went, he could foresee no trouble at all. But, he told him that there had to be an official request; only then could the committee take appropriate action.

Babu informed his mistress about this and once again Lentina was faced with a dilemma. Should she sign on the application form or devise another ploy to keep the identity of the applicant secret? The latter seemed to be a better idea but how was she going to achieve it? As she pondered, she remembered a conversation she had with her husband long ago. They were discussing the prospects of real estate and he had said, 'If you want to gain from investments in land, go for inconspicuous plots, but ones which have future prospects. That way no one will pay attention when you buy it, and when the town expands, your holdings will appreciate in value many times over.'

Taking a cue from this, she abandoned her original idea of buying a plot in the already congested cemetery and went for another visit there the next day. This time she invited Babu to walk with her around the perimeter of the wall, and told him to examine the direction in which the cemetery would expand. Babu at once caught on and asking her to rest a while did a quick survey of the surrounding area and came to a conclusion. He helped her to the car and after they were seated comfortably, he said, 'Madam, the land adjoining the southern boundary will be the best, though I do not fully understand why you want to do this when a small plot of land would serve your purpose.' She looked at him with a glint in her eyes and replied, 'Be patient Babu, time will answer your question.' With that enigmatic reply she dismissed him and they drove home in silence.

Once again, Lentina withdrew to her bedroom and began to worry about the prospects of acquiring the adjacent plot of land. The only person she could rely upon to accomplish this was Babu; she decided to entrust him with the job. But before she could talk to him, fate intervened and an opportunity presented itself to her in the person of a man from a neighbouring village who was the son of her late husband's friend. The friend himself was dead and the son, named Khalong, had been away at the time of her husband's death. When he heard about it he came to pay his condolences. Lentina noticed a certain dejection in Khalong's demeanour and when she pressed for a reason he blurted out how bad his financial situation had become as a result of the father's prolonged illness and many hospitalizations outside the state. He sighed, 'If only I could sell our land! But unfortunately now that the cemetery has expanded, people only laugh at me when I talk of selling our land adjoining it. They even joke about it and say, turn it into another cemetery and charge rent! Aunty, I do not know what is going to happen to us.' The poor man was on the verge of tears but Lentina, instead of sympathizing, appeared to become excited about his outburst.

After what he considered to be a period of rude silence, Lentina turned to him and began to ask for the details of his land. Khalong thought that it was simply her way of expressing concern. But what came next completely floored him. 'Will you sell that piece of land to me?' she asked in an excited manner. He could not answer immediately because he was debating with himself whether it would be right to sell her a piece of unsuitable land just because she felt sorry for him. It would amount to taking advantage of her sympathy and would certainly be unethical. Reading his mind correctly, the old woman said, in a gentle voice, 'I know what you are thinking, but let me assure you that it is not merely out of my concern for you that I am doing this. I have a selfish motive. For quite some time now I have been looking for a suitable plot where I want to be buried. And before you say anything, let me add that I do not wish to be buried among the ridiculous stone monuments of the big cemetery. I need a place where there will be nothing but beautiful trees over my grave. So, tell me now, will you sell your land to me?' Khalong was convinced that Lentina meant business and uttered a feeble yes. But the woman was not done yet; she continued in the same serious tone, 'Listen, I will buy the land only on one condition: you are to tell nobody about the transaction yet, not even your wife. If you agree to this condition, tell me how much you want and come tomorrow with the documents and we will finalize the deal.'

Khalong was so overcome by the unexpected turn of fortune that he stated an amount beyond his expectation. He was even more shocked to hear her say, 'Okay, come tomorrow at eleven.' He did not wait for any formal dismissal after she gave her instructions, hurrying out of the house in a daze, still wondering whether all that had transpired was actually real. Lentina knew that had she bargained a bit, the price would have been reduced but she felt that heaven's gifts should be accepted without any murmur, and simply proceeded to put together the amount needed for the next day's transaction. Once again she enlisted the help of Babu who was to be a witness to the deal. When Babu reminded her about the negotiation with the town committee and that he would have to explain the abrupt halt to his son-in-law, Lentina smiled and told him, 'Let him think that it was a wild scheme thought up by someone going senile.'

As instructed by Lentina, Khalong came with the thumbprint of a relative on a paper where the agreement was inscribed. The deal was accomplished without a hitch and Lentina became the proud owner of a plot of land right next to the south wall of the old cemetery. Lentina ordered Babu to engage some labourers to erect a temporary boundary fence. It was only when the fence was almost complete that her sons came to know about their mother's 'crazy' plan. They remonstrated with her, they sulked at having been left out of the deliberations, and even threatened to move out of the compound if their mother treated them like rank outsiders; they were upset that a mere driver had usurped their rightful place in her schemes. But even then, they were not aware of the full extent of her designs for the new cemetery. She tried to pacify them by saying that she did not want to burden them with tasks which she and Babu were perfectly able to handle. The sons kept quiet but the elder daughter-in-law wanted to assert herself and began to accuse Lentina of putting too much trust in a servant and this, she said, amounted to insulting them. Lentina, smarting from the unfairness of the charge, blurted out something which she overheard during her husband's funeral and had decided to keep it a secret. It was an argument between the two daughters-in-law about who was to pay for the funeral expenses. The elder one had said, 'It is not fair that we alone should bear the costs, you and your husband should pay half of it.' To this the younger one had replied, 'How can I say anything? Tell that husband of mine, if you feel like it. But I am not going to give a rupee towards this unnecessary show.' Everyone knew that the younger daughter-in-law had money of her own and that gave her an edge over the other. She continued, 'And if you think that we are going to waste money on some grandiose headstone for the old man, think again. Such pretensions this family has!'

Lentina had kept this knowledge to herself and had resolved that she would never divulge this to anyone. But, being goaded into speech by interference from her family on a matter she thought did not directly involve them, she decided to speak out. She addressed the two ladies, 'Why are you all worked up about such a trivial matter? After all, I have not spent anyone else's money. And another thing: you need not worry about any headstone for me. I want none.' The two ladies were completely taken aback; they had assumed that they were alone in the room when the altercation had taken place. The deft and crafty manipulation of her knowledge helped Lentina put an end to all opposition. When the husbands learnt how their mother 'took care' of their wives, they merely chuckled and muttered, 'That's mother for you. Hope you've learnt your lesson.'

News about Lentina's acquisition of the plot of land adjacent to the cemetery soon became public knowledge, and she knew that sooner than later she would be visited by members of the town committee and the issue about 'ownership' would be raised, because all such grounds were to be only in the custody of either the church or other religious organizations, with due permission from the committee. Anticipating their move, she had already drawn up a legal document with the help of her nephew who had just started practising law in the district court. In the document she had declared that she would donate the piece of land to the town committee, and not to the church, if, and only if, they gave a written undertaking that it would be managed according to her terms:

1. The new plot of land could be dedicated as the new cemetery and would be available to all on fulfilling the condition that only flowering trees and not headstones would be erected on the gravesites.
2. Lentina, as the donor, should be the first to choose a plot for herself.
3. Plots would be designated by numbers only and records of names against plot numbers would be maintained in the committee register.

4. The terms were to be widely publicized and the town committee would ensure that they were adhered to strictly.

As expected, the members came one day and were ushered into the big drawing room where they seated themselves with obvious ceremony, stressing their eminent status in society. Lentina greeted them amiably and expressed surprise at their 'official' visit. The chairman cleared his throat and began first by expressing the committee's collective sympathy for the bereaved family. Lentina replied in a befitting manner and enquired to what she owed the honoured visit. The chairman looked at his colleagues and launched into his rehearsed speech about ownership of sacred grounds and what the town's administrators had to say about it. Gently but firmly, Lentina interrupted him and said, 'Thank you Mr Chairman, I want to assure you that I am aware of your responsibility regarding the matter and I have taken the initiative to seek your cooperation by drawing up this legal document for your consideration. Kindly discuss this with your colleagues and let me know as soon as possible if the terms are acceptable to you.'

The chairman gave her a sharp look but refrained from saying anything, though it was clear to all that he resented being cut off in the middle of his speech. He turned to an elderly member and asked, 'What do you say, brother? Shall we discuss this here or take it back with us and discuss it in the office?' The other read the document and said in a voice more authoritative than that of the chairman, 'We can do it here; it seems the terms are quite simple. I see no harm in accepting them because the town is getting a substantial plot of land, the need for which has long been felt. The kind lady has indeed come to our rescue, she must be congratulated.' After this emphatic endorsement by an important member, there was no need for further discussion of the terms. Through another deed drawn up a few days later, the new cemetery with its unusual stipulations came into the possession of the town committee. On the day the legal formalities were concluded, this time in the presence of her sons and their wives, Lentina said, almost like an afterthought, 'By the way, can I choose my plot now?' Everyone in the room was struck by the ingenuity of this seemingly innocuous request. It was as if she were asking for a candy, and not for a place where she would eventually be buried. The entire transaction was of a somewhat morbid nature but she took the sting out of it by what she added next, 'You see I want to plant something there.' No one could say anything to this and as the visitors departed, the faint voice of the chairman could be heard, 'After all, she being the donor, it is only right that she should be given the first choice.'

Lentina and Babu made frequent visits to the new ground. Then one day Babu drove up with the gardener carrying laburnum saplings which he planted on the prepared ground. Lentina discontinued her visits to the cemetery because she was beginning to feel the fatigue that comes after a sustained effort and achieving a long-cherished dream. How that plot of land came into her possession was still a mystery to her when all she had craved was a spot to be buried where a laburnum tree would bloom every May. Ah, the laburnum tree! Would the saplings survive this time, she speculated? Would they really bloom and would she live long enough to actually see the trees with flower? Before one knew it, another May with laburnum blossoms everywhere had come and gone. A small consolation for the frail woman was that her plants out 'there' were doing fine. Babu, the ever-faithful friend, for this is how she thought of him now, brought news about many things including that of her treasured plants.

Once in a while she would tell Babu that she wanted to see them herself to which he would say, 'Soon, madam, but not today.' Her days were now threatening to blur into dusk. Sometimes they would find her roaming in the garden barefoot and without a shawl. That winter Lentina caught a bad cold and fell seriously ill. Everyone thought that she would not last the winter. Even her doctor, usually a jolly person, began to show signs of strain after every visit to her room. Only Babu remained calm and steadfast during the crisis. When relatives and close friends were allowed brief visits, it was Babu who stood guard outside the door to see that they did not stay too long. Sometimes Lentina would pretend to be sleeping when noisy and nosy relatives came to visit; Babu then had the perfect excuse to shoo them out quickly. During the day Babu would disappear for some time and when he returned, he would make straight for Lentina's room. He would tiptoe in and she would turn her eyes towards the door and as their eyes met he would give a faint nod and withdraw. This was a message that he had just visited the trees and that they were doing well. This seemed to provide her with the will to live where food and medicines seemed to have failed.

To every one's astonishment, Lentina survived the fierce winter and one clear February morning she rang her bell peremptorily. The maid went in to find her searching for her gown and bedroom slippers. She offered to bring her tea to the room but Lentina ordered her to take her to the drawing room. She sat by the fireside where her tea was brought and she sipped the hot brew as though she were tasting it for the first time. From that day on, she began to move about the house and resume her old routine of supervising the activities in it. When her daughters-in-law visited, she was warm and amiable with them; occasionally she would even give them pieces of jewellery: a ring, ear tops, and necklaces. The sons too, sensing a new spirit in their mother, began to ask for her advice on business and family matters, something which had never happened during their father's lifetime. They were pleasantly surprised to find how sharp her mind still was. They also discovered how uncannily like their father she sounded sometimes! There was a visible easing of tension among them and it became apparent that not only Lentina, but the entire family, was heading towards a healing that was more than physical.

That year, the year of Lentina's recovery, something happened in the new cemetery that only Babu saw; he kept the knowledge to himself. Of the two laburnum trees planted on Lentina's plot, one languished and died. But the surviving one had flourished and, wonder of wonders, even produced a tiny sprig bearing a few yellow blossoms. One could not see this from the road because the plant was still small and the flowers sparse. But Babu frequently visited the site and discovered the shy showing one fine May morning. He was tempted to tell Lentina but decided against it because the excitement might have been too much for her. And, if the plant did not develop as hoped for, the disappointment might have a devastating effect on his mistress, weakened by her recent illness. He was both happy and afraid: happy because the long-cherished desire of his mistress to see a laburnum bloom had been fulfilled; afraid, because he instinctively knew that as soon as Lentina laid eyes on the blossoms next May, she would conclude that the right moment to leave the world had arrived. Not that she would do anything drastic like taking her own life, but she would let everything slide and simply bow out of life, with a contented sigh.

But, for all his apprehensions about the future, Babu knew that he could not hold back the force of nature that had accomplished the small miracle of the first showing that May. By next year, the bush would be taller and the flowers more plentiful; it would become visible to all who passed by that lonely road to the new cemetery. He had to tell his mistress about this, but when? He thought about it for many nights and finally decided that the best time would be the next season's flowering and hoped that she would be alive to hear the good news from him. If Lentina now thought of him as her friend, Babu was also beginning to reassess his relationship with her. Till the time of her husband's death, though she had treated Babu with civility and kindness, she had always maintained a discreet distance as befitting a master–servant relationship. But she gradually broke down the barriers by showing her dependence on him, first by only extracting 'dutiful service'; then imperceptibly as a friend; and, finally, a confidant. Outwardly, the protocol demanded by their positions was never breached or altered, but it soon became apparent to everybody how much Lentina relied on the old driver for things she wanted done. And, surprisingly, this was accepted by her sons and their wives—it relieved them from the onerous duty of being on call for their frail and aged mother. A strong-willed woman and her faithful servant were thus drawn into an unusual bond of common humanity, based on trust and loyalty.

By the time the New Year came, Lentina showed signs of fatigue brought on by old age. Her family watched her keenly all through the winter months and she was never left alone. When March came and the weather became warmer, she wanted to be taken out in the car. Her wish was at first just ignored but when she refused to eat unless she was taken out for a ride, the family decided to accede. And so a routine was established: twice a week, weather permitting, Lentina would go out in the car accompanied by her maid. Lentina did not object to this arrangement and came back from these outings a much happier person. She ate well and some colour returned to her pale face. But during these jaunts, she sat quietly, without uttering a word, and even when Babu or the maid commented on something new or strange they had seen in the town, she did not respond. On return, she would head straight to her room and remain there until dinnertime.

And then another May was upon them and every one noticed a visible change in Lentina; she wanted to go out more frequently. But the doctor put his foot down and the twice-a-week routine continued. Seeing her agitation, Babu approached her door one day and sought permission to speak. He assured her that he was keeping a close watch on the plants and that he was confident that they would bloom this season. He still did not tell her about what had happened the previous year. He promised to give her reports on the days she was forced to stay indoors. But during the outings now, the first thing she wanted was to drive by the new cemetery, to see if the laburnum trees were showing signs of producing flowers. She had seen other trees in town with their gorgeous display of cascading yellow flowers. Her disappointment was acute and after a few times, she refused to go out at all.

And then one day, late into the month, on his daily excursion to the cemetery Babu discovered the miracle that they had been praying for: the little laburnum tree was awash with buttery yellow blossoms! The unflappable driver gave a shout of joy and darted away, heading to his mistress with the wonderful news. On his way, he rehearsed how he was going to break the news to her. He cautioned himself that he should do it gently, so that his dear mistress would not get too excited. When he reached the house, he walked slowly to the lady's room and knocked gently. To his surprise, he heard a sharp command, 'Come in Babu, I've been waiting for you.' He entered and started to speak but she cut him off, 'I know what you are going to tell me; I felt it in my bones.' He saw that Lentina was dressed as if for a grand occasion and standing by her side was the maid, also dressed. The old lady fumbled for her walking stick and said impatiently, 'Let's go, what are you waiting for?'

The bewildered driver and the slightly dazed maid followed the old lady who suddenly seemed to have a spring in her walk, and proceeded on their apparently routine outing. But only Lentina and Babu knew what this phenomenon signified. Once they reached the site, Lentina withdrew into a more sombre mood, as did Babu; only the maid exclaimed at the sight of the luxuriant blossoms on so small a tree. Lentina gazed at the flowers for a long time and, sighing deeply, told Babu to drive to the park, located about four kilometres from the town and was the highest point from where the entire town could be seen. It was a popular picnic spot and was full of people at weekends. When they reached the park they found that not many people were around because it was a weekday. Choosing a quiet corner, Lentina and the maid sat down to rest. The maid had packed some biscuits and a flask of tea, which the three of them shared. After about half an hour they drove back home. As she entered her room, Lentina turned to her maid and Babu and shook their hands, murmuring, 'Thank you and God bless you.'

Lentina stayed in her room for most of the week. She turned down suggestions of any further outing and busied herself with tidying up her room even refusing help from the maid. On the fifth day of this self-imposed isolation, she called the maid and asked her to help her with her bath and to dress her in her favourite outfit. Having done that, she ordered the maid to bring her some food as she wanted an early dinner. The maid did as she was told and bade her mistress an early goodnight before retiring to her own quarters.

The next morning when she knocked on Lentina's door with the morning tea, there was no answer. She knocked again but only silence greeted her. She entered the room and found Lentina stretched on the bed; she seemed to be sleeping soundly. Putting the tray on the bedside table, the maid said gently, 'Madam, I've brought tea.' She went and drew the curtains as usual but when she came near the bed, she noticed a certain stiffness in the body and an unusual pallor on the old lady's face. Distinctly alarmed, she went out and urgently called the others, the sons, their wives, and all the servants. They all came rushing, except Babu, who stood near a post, crying like a baby. They entered the room and the elder son bent closer to determine if his mother was breathing. He straightened up with a sharply drawn breath and shook his head. When the doctor came, he pronounced that Lentina, the mistress of the house, had died in her sleep.

So ends the story of the undramatic life of an ordinary woman who cherished one single passionate wish that a humble laburnum tree should bloom once a year on her crown.

And every May, this extraordinary wish is fulfilled when the laburnum tree, planted on her gravesite in the new cemetery of the sleepy little town, bursts forth in all its glory of buttery yellow splendour. And if you can tear your eyes away from this display and survey the rest of the ground, you will notice that in the entire expanse, there is not a single stone monument. Instead, flowering bushes take root, blooming in their own seasons on the little mounds dotting the landscape. Hibiscus, gardenia, bottlebrush, camellia, oleander, and croton bushes of all hues comprise the variety of flowering plants, and at one or two spots you can see some jacaranda trees trying to keep up with the others. A lone banyan and a few ashoka trees standing on the far edges also seem to be doing quite well. And if you observe carefully, you will be amazed to see that in the entire terrain, there is so far, only one laburnum tree bedecked in its seasonal glory, standing tall over all the other plants, flourishing in perfect coexistence, in an environment liberated from all human pretensions to immortality.

So every May, something extraordinary.

THE FOURTH DIRECTION

WARYAM SINGH SANDHU

Translated from the Punjabi by Nirupama Dutt

MY HEART WAS KEEPING PACE WITH THE SUNSET. JUST AS THE ORANGE ball of light in the far west sank beyond the tall trees, my heart too began to descend into darkness and fear.

My thoughts darted from the ticking of my watch, to the driver and the slow speed of the bus, to the dusk spreading outside. I glanced at my friend, Jugal Kishore, seated next to me, to see if there were signs of fear and worry on his face but he laughed and said, 'This driver is a slowcoach if ever there was one. He slows down the moment he sees just about any vehicle approaching. It's as though he is saying, "Sir, you go first, please. If you want, I will stop by the side." Wretched son of a motherless goat!'

He shook his head in irritation.

Instead of continuing the conversation, I started counting the heads in the bus to see how many were turbaned and how many short-haired. To my dismay, the turbaned heads outnumbered the others two to one. I wondered if I had messed up in my haste. So I started counting all over again. This time the two kinds of passengers were equal in number. Heaving a sigh of relief, I relaxed and taking out a small pocket comb, ran it through my hair.

I put the comb back in my pocket and looked out of the window. The momentary relief I had experienced was inked out by the darkness outside. Travelling in a bus in this place after sunset was like walking with death—and the direction we were heading in, which took us deeper into this terrible place, made things even more frightening.

Last week my cousin, my father's sister's son, wrote to me declining an invitation to a family wedding in Amritsar saying, 'I really want to attend Sheela's wedding but, my brother, the truth is that I feel scared to visit Punjab and more so Amritsar. I am reminded of the story our nani used to tell us of taking the fourth direction. You surely remember because she was your granny too although a dadi. Do you recall how many times we must have heard it together, sitting on her bed, wrapped in the warmth of her quilt as well as her words? I was in the fourth standard and staying with all of you in Amritsar for three months. I had a constant low fever and when I recovered Nani took me to the Golden Temple to give thanks for my recovery. She bathed me in the pool and we then bowed our heads to the Dukh Bhanjani Beri. Tending to me all day she would keep muttering praises to the glory of Guru Ramdas, the fourth Sikh guru, who had founded the city of Amritsar. I would so like to see her pious face again for she is frail and may soon be gone. However, nothing but fear keeps me away. I am sending you a draft for five hundred rupees, do buy our dear sister a gift from me. Do ask my mama and mami to forgive me for being not able to make it for this auspicious occasion. No matter how old one may be it is always a joy to visit one's maternal home, but....'

This letter reminded me of the story of a prince or a rajkumar that our grandmother used to tell us. Once, at a crossroads, a prince was told that he was free to take three routes but was forbidden the fourth direction because it was perilous and he might face danger and not return alive. But the curiosity and courage of the prince took him in the fourth direction.

Battling grave dangers, not only did he return safely home but brought back with him something priceless—what it was, whether wealth or wisdom, or something that gave him joy or courage is anybody's guess.

Well, I too could claim to be a prince of sorts for I was named Rajkumar. But in no manner was I the prince of the story. I was a mere clerk in a remote government school close to the Indo-Pak border in Amritsar district who rushed every evening to Jalandhar to catch the last train to Amritsar on working days. What should I know of courage? Well, in the time I am speaking of, it did require courage to go and work in villages if one was clean-shaven and short-haired. What use was courage anyway when an anonymous bullet might fly from the left or the right and kill just about anyone? No one knew the enemy's true capability, his intent or the time the bullet would be fired. Really—no one knew anything.

Just then the bulb right above my seat lit up and I read the notice written by its side: *Passengers will be responsible for their luggage.*

I read the line and repeated it to Jugal with a smile saying, 'They should also write that passengers will be responsible for their own lives.'

At this Jugal laughed and pointed to another line on the side that said: *Do not put your head or arm out of the window.* Then he pretended to be a gunman and said menacingly, 'Don't bother to put your head or arm out of the window for we will be at your service right inside the bus.'

We tried to laugh at our own dark humour but a streak of dread accompanied our laughter. Jugal had some work to take care of at the office of the Director of Public Instruction at Chandigarh and I had gone along with him. After we had finished our work we hastened to the bus stand only to see the last bus to Amritsar speeding away. The departure of the last bus placed people like us in danger for there were few safe places to stay in the city.

It was necessary to reach Amritsar by nightfall. We had assured our families that we would be home on time. If we didn't get back two families would spend the entire night in fear as though hung on the cross of anxiety. But for marriages or mourning, I rarely think of going out at night. At sunset one enters the house and firmly shuts the doors and windows. Another reason I was anxious to get back was because my colleague Master Harcharan's daughter was getting married in the morning. Harcharan was a good man and had lent me ten thousand rupees at the time of my sister Sheela's wedding. I still owed him that money. I would also borrow oil, basmati rice, molasses, and sugar cane from him as and when I needed them. In return I would try and help him with clerical matters that he needed attended to without charging him a fee. If I was unable to reach the wedding ceremony he would wonder. I was keen to go and bless his daughter with a small gift. On top of all these reasons to get back to Amritsar, where did clerks like us have the resources to stay in a safe hotel in Chandigarh?

'Raju! Do you recall those days when we would come to Chandigarh on work and after we had finished have a drink, watch a film, and then take a late-night bus from Chandigarh and reach Amritsar in the morning. We would take a short nap and then get ready to go to work.'

As I listened to Jugal I felt that the Punjab he was reminiscing about belonged to an era long past. We had left it far behind.

After having missed the last bus to Amritsar, as we were trying to figure out what to do, someone suggested that we take the bus to Jalandhar that was just about to leave; from there we could catch a train to Amritsar. That was how we came to be sitting on this bus. As we drove along my heart beat faster even than the speed of the bus. I kept looking at my watch, trying to calculate whether we would make it on time to Jalandhar to catch the last train to Amritsar. The bus seemed to be arriving at each of the towns en route—Kharar, Ropar, Nawanshahr, Banga, Phagwara—behind schedule. I felt the distance between me and the last train increasing with each passing minute. I grew more and more uneasy as I thought about what would happen if we didn't get to Jalandhar on time.

Then I told myself that instead of worrying if we would reach Jalandhar on time, I should be more concerned about reaching it safely. It seemed to me that any moment someone would hold a gun to the driver's head and ask him to divert the bus to a side road leading to some village while at the same moment the turbaned sardar seated behind me would open his score for the evening by shooting me dead.

Jugal once again started mourning the days gone by. It seems unimaginable that there were times when if someone missed a bus, he would put his arm under his head and sleep by the roadside. How different things were then?'

I kept nodding. Then something he said set off questions in my mind. 'What have they done?' I found myself wondering 'Who had changed Punjab so much?' My thoughts were interrupted by the loud voice of the very pious Sikh physical education (PE) instructor of my school. He was saying, 'The Brahmins, who else?' He would never say Hindu but

Brahmin, a word that he would grind angrily with his teeth before uttering it. Then he would say, 'A treacherous, blood-sucking community that can never be relied upon...first, they asked us to stay with them...let us gain freedom, they said, and then we will share its bounties...but what was our share—burning tyres flung around our necks? And now they wish to compromise...and when the Sikhs ask for freedom they make such a din... the entire country goes on high alert.'

The truth, however, is that we Brahmins never fought back, we would meekly agree with whatever was being said. None of the staff members stood up to the insults of the PE teacher. Everyone chose to ignore his words because to speak out would be to invite death. One of the boys from our school had joined the other side. Only four months ago he, along with two others, had marched into a neighbouring village and killed three schoolteachers in broad daylight.

The bus halted with a jolt. We had reached Jalandhar cantonment. We decided to get down there as there would be less of a rush and we could save time by boarding the train there. We rushed up the stairs into the station but were told by a bystander that the train had already departed. He said, 'Why don't you take a three-wheeler to the main station and catch the train that has just left?'

Cursing the slowcoach of a bus driver, we hurriedly caught a three-wheeler and reached the main Jalandhar Railway Station only to find that the train had departed from there too.

I slapped my head in disappointment.

'What now?'

I had no real answer to Jugal's frightened question.

'All that can be done now is to get some magic carpet out of a fairy tale or charter a plane and reach Amritsar by air.'

Sitting on a wooden bench on the platform, I felt that my reply had a tinge of irritation to it. Instead of saying anything to me, Jugal started cursing the government for first stopping late-night buses and then late-night trains to Amritsar. After sometime a train from Ludhiana arrived and halted at the platform. I got up from the bench hopefully. Passengers were getting off the train. Before I could do anything, Jugal asked one of them, 'Is this train going to Amritsar?'

'No, I think Jalandhar is the last halt,' the passenger said, extinguishing the last ray of hope in our hearts. Soon all the passengers left the station. We were the only ones remaining on the platform disappointed, sad, and anxious.

Some security personnel, including members of the Railway Police and the Central Reserve Police got onto the train and began checking it for stowaways. They were also shutting the doors and windows of the train.

A middle-aged Sikh carrying a suitcase came up to us and asked, 'Do you have to go to Amritsar?' He had heard us enquiring about a train to Amritsar.

I looked the man up and down. The truth is that I was suspicious of him. But soon I realized that he was just another passenger like us.

'I too have to go to Amritsar but I am late. Actually this train is going to Amritsar. But it does not take passengers. If we were to plead our case to them, they might take us.'

He was a Sikh, a man from the other side but our shared helplessness made us allies in the moment.

'Whom should we ask?' I said.

'Let's ask one of the policemen in the accompanying coach. Who knows—some kind man may agree,' he said.

Outside one of the coaches of the stationary train stood a havaldar of the Punjab Police. He was shouting orders to a constable inside, 'Come on, young man, look under and above the seats carefully.'

We decided to talk to the havaldar. Jugal and I trailed two steps behind as we'd decided it would be better for a Sikh to speak to the policeman.

'Sardar Bahadur, the three of us have to get to Amritsar. Do help us. We will give what we can in return.'

I felt that the Sardar had couched his request correctly but I was wrong.

'No, my brother,' said the havaldar, 'the Punjab Police has already acquired a bad reputation...now people will say we take money and carry passengers illegally.' Then taking his eyes off us he asked the constable who was alighting from the train, 'Everything in order inside?'

'It is, sir, all is F-I-T FIT,' joked the younger man and laughing they moved on to talk to another constable standing some distance away.

The three of us just stood there looking at each other, not knowing what to do next.

'I will go and find out....' Jugal said and made his way to a Railway Police official. He returned laughing and said in his usual colourful way, 'Pimps all of them, not one of them gave any sign of hope.'

The havaldar came up to us and this time I pleaded with him, 'Sardarji, please help us out.' He seemed a bit irritated but as he was moving away, he turned and said, 'Check with the guard and see....'

Filled with hope, we started walking towards the guard's coach. He was standing outside talking to someone. We stood a few steps away waiting for him to be free but the conversation he was having seemed to go on and on. We were anxious that while we were waiting the train might leave.

'Why don't you talk to the guard?' our Sikh companion said to me, perhaps because the guard was clean-shaven too.

I approached the guard hesitantly, 'Sir! We are stranded. We took a bus from Chandigarh to Jalandhar in the hope of catching the last train to Amritsar from here but we missed it. We would be very grateful if you could get us to Amritsar. Who else can we ask for help? We will travel standing in your coach.'

From his looks, the guard seemed to be a gentle person I thought he would say yes.

'Mister, have you no idea of the times we are going through. Allowing unauthorized people into the guard's compartment would put my job in danger. It could even put my life in danger. How can one trust anyone these days? If all was well why would we be operating an empty train? There must have been some reason for the authorities to have made these new rules. I understand your predicament and I sympathize with you but I cannot take the responsibility of taking you along...it is all because of the times we are passing through, I am really sorry.' Having said this, the guard boarded the train.

'Wretched spokesmen of the times!' Jugal said laughing and then started talking like Pandit Ram Chand, who lived down our lane, and could be heard complaining all the time about the wretched times we were living in. 'The times we are passing through are very hard.... Anything can happen anytime. It is difficult for a thinking person to live through all this. Gone are the days when people would embrace one another like brothers and be ready to help if required. These politicians hungry for power have poisoned society. No one trusts anyone else. Everything has changed.'

The people had nicknamed him the 'Pandit of Hard Times' and would tease him: 'Pandit Hard Timesji, when will things change?'

Jugal said, 'Now where has this Guard of Hard Times come from?'

The havaldar came up to the guard and announced, 'Okay, sir...we're ready!'

'Have all your people boarded?'

'Yes-yes,' the havaldar replied raising his hand in a customary salute.

The guard gave the green signal from the window of his compartment, the whistle blew and the train jerked forward.

What was to be done now?

I quickly put my hand on the window. The guard said, 'What are you doing? Please step back.'

I walked two steps beside the moving train and pleaded with him, 'Sir, please...we are your Hindu brothers...if you will not help us then who will...have mercy on us?'

I noticed that he had softened a bit. I put my foot on the step of the guard's compartment and climbed in. The guard spoke to Jugal who had followed me in. 'What are you two doing...have some sense and get down at once.'

The train continued to move slowly forward. The middle-aged Sikh with us had folded his hands and was begging the guard to let him in too. The guard had blocked the door.

'Nothing doing, Sardarji!'

'I beg you in the name of God...the train can easily accommodate me.... May the Almighty bless your children with a long life.'

I was quiet fearing that the guard might ask us to get down too but then my heart went out to the Sardarji who had befriended us.

'Please let him in, he is known to us,' I said. I felt that now that I was on the train it gave me some right to intercede on his behalf.

'If you have so much sympathy for him then why don't you two also get down,' said the guard angrily.

By then the Sardarji had ducked under the arm with which the guard was blocking the entryway and had entered the compartment. Helpless, the guard mumbled, 'Really this is too much.... This is no way to behave. What on earth are you trying to do?'

By now the train had left the platform.

'The best thing for me to do would be to stop the train at a station like Butari and throw you three out. You seem to have no concern for yourselves or others. I allowed one and two more climbed in. There is no point in being kind to anyone. Let me see what needs to be done.'

The words, 'Let me see what needs to be done', filled us with dread. I thought for a moment that he might stop the train by the Beas River and throw us out into the wilderness on the banks of the river, a notorious hideout for terrorists. There were many stories of terrorists escaping from the police on the pretext of relieving themselves, only to vanish into the rushes that fringed the river.

'Don't fret, brother, all will be well,' Jugal said, touching the knees of the guard.

The guard shook his head despairingly.

As the tension slowly receded, and I began to feel a bit more relaxed, I glanced around the small compartment. There were four other persons inside. Two were crouching on the luggage carrier and two were seated on a wooden crate. Not one of them had spoken during the entire exchange between the guard and us. Perhaps they were in the same predicament as us but their silence seemed to amount to indifference.

Although I was rather less tense now, my mind was still numb with all the fear and pain I had been experiencing. I looked carefully at those travelling with us. The two Hindus seated on the luggage rack with their heads down seemed to be railway employees. This was evident from their exchanges with the guard. A little further away, on the wooden crate, two Sikh men were sitting close to each other. The slim boy had just sprouted hair on his chin. He had on a smart maroon turban wound in a style popular with college students. The other one seemed five or seven years older. He was well built and wore a blue turban and had a thick, flowing beard. They sat quietly.

To me their silence seemed conspiratorial. Such silent operators waited tensely like a tiger and pounced on their prey at the right moment. The older one looked like the physical education instructor of our school. He was glaring at me. At least it seemed so to me.

A glance at his expression and I braced myself for the familiar tone and words I expected to hear: 'So now we have captured the progeny of

Gangu Brahmin, who betrayed our tenth guru. Now there is no getting away for you...the words heard at Harmandar? were still troubling my soul... "No one can win a battle against the Sikhs...."'

For a moment I shivered when the same man whom I was dreading began to speak to me, 'Listen....'

I meekly raised my head like a child being addressed by an authority figure.

'One of you can come and sit with us. We will manage somehow. The journey will take over an hour. You will get tired standing all the way. The other two can sit on the trunk next to you,' he said.

I felt ashamed of my suspicion. It was my own fear that was making me so insecure. However, I still did not feel like sitting next to him. I asked the middle-aged Sikh to go and sit with them.

'May you live long...may you live long...thanks,' the Sikh said patting the young man's back.

I signalled to Jugal to sit on the trunk next to us and he in turn pointed to the guard who was staring out the window at the deepening darkness and some lights flickering in the distance. Giving Jugal a reassuring wink both of us sat down on the trunk. Just then one of the railway employees spoke up, 'Be careful that you don't break the trunk with your weight.'

The trunk seemed quite sturdy. There was little chance of it breaking. The man probably just wanted to needle us because we had pushed our way in. The guard turned to look at us and said, 'Break it...break it... You are up to no good.'

Just as students stand up on being reprimanded by an angry teacher, I got up from where I was sitting with alacrity.

'Oh, sit down...sit down now,' the guard muttered and I sat down once again on the trunk like a trained pet. I felt like a wound-up toy, I seemed to have no will of my own.

∽

Till now I had seen few nights as frightening as the one we were travelling through. The only uncertain night that I was able to recall was from about ten years ago when I had accompanied my wife and son to her home in Rampur on the occasion of her sister's wedding. It was payday and I had gone with the headmaster to withdraw money. Disbursing it among the staff, took a long time. By the time I reached home, picked up my wife and young son, Neetu, and got into the bus, the winter sun was already setting. Those times were not as bad as now. When we got off at the bus stand it was dark. The road to Rampur was a mile away and wound its way through another village. The other route we could take passed through the fields of this village—after walking some distance we could then take the dust track to Rampur. Since the second option was shorter, I picked up Neetu and asked my wife to follow and started walking through the fields.

It was a dark night. Somehow finding our way through the dust we walked on. My wife was grumbling about the delay in setting off. She was wearing her jewellery and I was carrying money with me. If we ran into the wrong sort of person, it could be dangerous. I reassured her by saying I could see a light; the dirt track to the village was just beyond the light.

But, when we reached the light, I found that I was mistaken. I had expected to find the light shining from a house but there was no house just a tubewell shed. I had lost my way. I could hear people talking inside. In the dim light of the bulb, I could see clouds of grey smoke. The smell of country-brewed liquor was in the air. What had I done? I was unarmed, had my wife and son with me, and here I was in the dead of night in the midst of a group of drunken louts. Anything could happen. I trembled in fear.

I put my finger on my wife's lips. I could see two lights at some distance. One was on the right and one on the left. Probably we had to go that way. I estimated that the track we were looking for would be by the light on the left. We stumbled towards it. We were quite scared. Neetu had woken up and was sobbing. My wife had broken a strap of her sandals and her feet were covered with slush. She was on the verge of tears.

'Tonight will be the end of me,' she sobbed. I tried to comfort her even though I was dejected and afraid.

'I can see a house and I can see some cattle. Let's ask for help,' I suggested but my wife shrank back fearfully.

'All right. You hold Neetu and I will go and enquire,' I said.

I reached the house, called out, and a dog barked from inside followed by a voice asking, 'Who is it?'

A man in his thirties came to the door.

'Brother, I have to go to Rampur to the home of Pandit Ram Nath. I am his son-in-law. I decided to take a shortcut through the fields but have lost my way.'

'You took the wrong direction. You have to go the other way.'

'Who is it, Surjit beta?' A woman's voice called from inside.

The young man explained and a middle-aged woman came out to the courtyard.

'Bring him in. If he is a relative of Pandit Ram Nath then he is no stranger to us. We belong to the same village but since our fields were here we built our home here. Are you married to the older girl, Dulari?'

'No, I am married to Parvati, the younger one, and we live in the city.'

'Just come inside,' she said and turned to her son, 'why are you blocking his way? Move aside.'

Surjit laughed and made way for me. Seeing as there was no danger I asked Parvati to go in first.

'Oh! My dear Paro, this is your uncle's home. Come in, why you are standing outside?' she said moving forward to pat Parvati's head.

Quickly Aunt Kartar Kaur seated us on cots, and washed Parvati's feet according to the fine gesture bestowed on travellers on foot in some northern parts of the country.

'You silly girl! It is unwise to set off from home late in the evening. Is this the way to attend your sister's wedding? Girls come a few days earlier to help their mother out. But now you too have become a city girl....'

Next, our hostess ordered her daughter-in-law to warm milk for us. After we had drunk the milk she asked Surjit to guide us to our destination. She said, 'You could have stayed here tonight but Parvati's family will be concerned. Today is the day for all relatives to get together. Just guide them to the village, Surjit.'

Surjit picked up a staff and a torch and said to my wife, 'Sister, let me carry my nephew.'

But Neetu got scared and buried his head in his mother's shoulder.

'Don't worry, I will carry him,' Parvati said.

'You crybaby, I am not holding a stick to scare you but...' Surjit did not complete the sentence.

He then led us out of the house. Lighting the way with his torch, he got us safely to the outskirts of the village.

The train moved over the bridge on the Beas, making a din.

'You made a big mistake forcing your way into the train,' the guard said sternly, 'what if I throw you off the train and get you arrested?'

'Sir, forgive us, please. We had no other way. That is why we got into the train.'

'You could only think of your compulsions, what about ours? What if I am caught? Won't I lose my job? The times are bad...the whole atmosphere is poisoned.... Who knows who you people are? If some mishap were to happen how would I explain it?'

In a way, the guard was right. I looked at the young man whose face resembled that of the PE instructor from my school. What if he was one of them?

Seeing me looking at the Sikh boys, the guard felt that I was being suspicious of them and questioning the guard's decision to let them board the train.

'Now these boys told me about their plight and I could not refuse them. One or two people may be all right but a whole bunch of them....' the guard said, then lapsed into silence.

'Thank you for your kindness. We are indebted to you....' I said.

After this there was silence. As the train lurched along, I started wondering about the circumstances of the boys. What story did they tell the guard?

The guard was gazing outside and the worldly wise, middle-aged Sikh gentleman addressed us, making sure the guard would hear what he had to say, 'We should offer something to the guard sahib—at least pay the fare.'

He glanced at the boys sitting next to him and then at Jugal and me before taking out a ten-rupee note from his pocket. Jugal and I also gave a ten-rupee note apiece and the two boys a twenty-rupee note to the Sikh.

The guard was now looking at us. Seeing the boys give a share, he said, 'Not from the boys. Return the twenty-rupee note.'

The Sikh got up to hand the money to the guard but the latter called out to one of the two railway employees and said, 'Murari, you take the money.'

When Murari pocketed the thirty rupees, I felt relieved for a moment. I shut my eyes and tried to relax. But suspicion was plaguing me. Was the guard afraid of the two boys?

I felt the face of the older Sikh boy merging into the face of the PE instructor who would torment me at school. The face seemed to be spreading out over the whole coach. I could hear the teacher shouting, 'Our days are at hand!'

Harcharan and the other masters at the school rarely said anything to anyone in public. Perhaps, when they were with the others of their community, they might have indulged in such talk but never at the common table. The talk there would embrace all. No one spoke like the menacing instructor who had vented the other day, 'Now they are killing our young Sikh boys in false encounters just like the butcher Mir Mannu of the eighteenth century. But never mind no matter how many they kill many more come forward.... Where are the courts now? It is police rule all the way.... The police are the law.... They are the witness.... They are the judiciary.... They are the killers and such is the story of our democracy!'

On hearing him, the maths teacher, Naresh, took me aside and said, 'What are they wailing for? They are out to kill everyone, be they policemen, witnesses, judges. No court is going to try or punish them.... As for their day...it has always been their day.... Whichever party rules the state, the chief minister has to be a Sikh. The country's president is a Sikh too.... Important ministries are with them.... They have high ranks in the police and the army.... Just compare the percentage of their numbers to the posts they hold... What, then, is their problem?'

To cut him short for he was just not stopping, I laughed and said, 'It certainly is their day! They shoot one here and another there....'

The two boys sitting on the crate were completely silent. The younger one had just uttered a word or two the entire journey. It seemed to me that my fears about them were unfounded.

But fear of another kind returned when the guard said, just as the train passed the Manowal station, 'It is not possible to drop you at Amritsar station. When we get there we will be questioned and so will all of you. The police may even round you up.'

The train slowed down on entering Amritsar. Just as it reached the twin gates of the railway crossing next to the Golden Avenue it slowed down even further.

'Okay, everyone, time to get off. The exit is at ground level,' the guard announced. Although the light of the moon was quite bright, the guard flashed his torch on the track ballast sliding past the open door and ordered us to jump out.

'Hurry! Move out!' he said.

I was closest to the exit. I put my feet on the steps and carefully got down on the rail track. In seconds, Jugal also stepped down. The others too got down at short intervals. We did not look back, although we felt uneasy walking along the rail track at this hour. If we were caught, we could have been accused of anything. 'Are you tampering with the tracks? Is it your intention to derail the train?'

I turned to Jugal, 'Let's leave the track and head to Dande Teende settlement.'

We started walking briskly. The truth was that I was still afraid of the two Sikh boys who had travelled with us. Who knew who they were? There was something mysterious about them and their silence seemed ominous.

I turned around and saw that the two were following us. Our middle-aged Sikh companion seemed to have headed off in a different direction. When I noticed the Sikh boys were behind us I began to panic. I told Jugal, 'Let's walk faster. These boys look dangerous....'

Just then I overheard the boys talking to each other. One said, 'Let's run and catch up with them.' It was the voice of the younger boy. I thought they would catch up with us and fire their pistols bang-bang. The bullets would pierce our backs and pass through our chests. I strained my ears to hear what they were saying, 'Let's call out to them....' It was the older boy's voice.

Afraid, Jugal and I walked on without exchanging a word. The two boys were walking so fast that they had almost caught up with us. I was just about to tell Jugal that we should make a run for it when I heard them call out, 'Babuji....' I was so terrified that my legs refused to move. Jugal stopped as well.

'You moved away so fast without taking us along,' the older boy said, 'Actually, my aunt, this boy's mother, passed away at about three in the afternoon. We explained our situation to the guard and he let us travel in his compartment.'

When I heard this, words failed me, but I was still afraid.

The younger boy said, 'Come on, let's keep moving.'

I just stood there fear-struck. Seeing me stand motionless, the older boy explained, 'We are afraid of walking to the city on our own lest the CRPF or the police shoot us down because we are Sikh. These are trigger-happy times. No one stops to ask before firing. If you are with us, we will be safe.'

As he spoke the shadows of fear surrounding me started fading away. The blood that had frozen in my veins thawed and started flowing again.

Now unafraid, I began walking and asked them to relax and follow me.

～

As I walked on I felt that I was Surjit who had led the way for my wife, son, and I many years ago in the dark when we had to reach my wife's village for her sister's wedding. I imagined that I was carrying a staff in one hand and a flashlight in the other.

I felt I was living up to my name, Rajkumar, and walking fearlessly in the forbidden fourth direction.

THE SPIRITS OF SHAH ALAM CAMP

ASGHAR WAJAHAT

Translated from the Hindi by Poonam Saxena

I

THE DAYS SOMEHOW PASS IN SHAH ALAM CAMP BUT THE NIGHTS ARE THE worst. There is such anguish all around that only Allah can help. There are so many voices in the camp that even a whisper in the ear can't be heard. Such yelling-shouting, noise-clamour, weeping-screaming, sighs-sobs....

At night, the spirits come to meet their children. The spirits stroke the heads of their orphaned children, look into their empty, silent eyes with their own vacant eyes and speak to them. They clasp the children to their breasts. Their heart-rending screams before they were burnt alive keep reverberating in the background.

When the entire camp goes to sleep, the children wake up. They wait to see their mothers...to eat a meal with their fathers.

'How are you, Siraj?' Amma's spirit asks, gently caressing his head.

'How are you, Amma?'

His mother looks happy. She says, 'Siraj...now...I am a spirit...now no one can set me on fire.'

'Amma...can I too become like you?'

II

After midnight the flustered, agitated spirit of a woman came to Shah Alam camp searching for her child. The child was not in that other world, nor was he in the camp. The child's mother felt her chest would burst. The spirits of the other women started helping the woman look for her child. Together they searched every corner of the camp. They went to her old neighbourhood. The houses are still burning there...ghoon-ghoon. Because they were spirits, they could enter the burning houses...they looked in every nook and cranny but couldn't find the child.

Eventually the spirits of the women went to the rioters—they were preparing petrol bombs for the next day, cleaning their guns, polishing their weapons.

When the mother of the child asked them about her son, they laughed and said, 'Oh, you crazy woman, when ten-twenty people are burnt all at once, who keeps track of one child? He is sure to be lying in a heap of ash somewhere.'

The mother said, 'No, no, I have looked everywhere...I couldn't find him anywhere.'

Then one of the rioters said, 'Arre, is she the mother of the boy we hoisted on our trishul?'

III

The spirits come to Shah Alam camp after midnight. They bring food from heaven, they bring water, they bring medicines, and they give them to their children. This is why no child in Shah Alam camp is without clothes, or hungry, or sick. This is also why the Shah Alam camp has become so famous. It is well known in far-off countries.

When an important politician from Delhi came on a tour of Shah Alam camp, he was delighted and said: 'This is an excellent place...all the Muslim children in the country should be sent here.'

IV

The spirits come to Shah Alam camp after midnight. They stay with the children all night, watch over them intently...think about their future.

'Siraj, now you should go home,' his mother's spirit said to him.

'Home?' Siraj shrank with fear. Shadows of death started dancing on his face.

'Yes, how long will you stay here? I'll come to see you every night.'

'No, I won't go home...never...never....' Smoke, fire, screams, clamour.

'Amma, I will stay with you and Abbu.'

'How can we stay with you, Sikku?'

'Bhaijan and Aapa also stay with you, don't they?'

'They burnt them along with us, didn't they?'

'Then...then I will...go home, Amma.'

V

The spirit of a little boy comes to Shah Alam camp after midnight...the child looks like a shining firefly at night...he flits around here and there...runs all over the camp...leaps and jumps about...does a bit of mischief...doesn't lisp...speaks clearly...clings to his mother's clothes...holds on to his father's finger.

Unlike the other children in the Shah Alam camp, this child always looks very happy.

'Why are you so happy, child?'

'You don't know...everybody knows.'

'What?'

'That I am proof.'

'Proof? Proof of what?'

'Proof of bravery.'

'Whose bravery are you proof of?'

'Of those who ripped open my mother's stomach and took me out and cut me into two pieces.'

VI

The spirits come to Shah Alam camp after midnight. The spirit of a young boy's mother came to see him. The boy was surprised to see her.

'Ma, why are you so happy today?'

'Siraj, today I met your grandfather in heaven. He introduced me to his father…and he in turn introduced me to his grandfather and great-grandfather. I met your great-great-great-grandfather.' His mother's voice was bursting with happiness.

'Siraj, your great-great-great-grandfather was a Hindu…Hindu… understand? Siraj, tell everyone this. Understand?'

VII

The spirits come to Shah Alam camp after midnight. A sister's spirit came one night. The spirit was looking for her brother. While searching, the spirit saw her brother sitting on the steps. The sister's spirit became happy. She leapt towards her brother and said, 'Bhaiya…' The boy pretended he had not heard. He kept sitting like a statue.

The sister again said, 'Listen, Bhaiya.'

The brother still didn't respond. Nor did he look at his sister.

'Why aren't you listening to me, Bhaiya?' asked the sister loudly and the brother's face flushed red like fire. His eyes boiled over with emotion…he jumped up and began beating his sister savagely. People collected around them. Someone asked the girl what she had said that her brother had begun thrashing her. The sister said, 'I just called him Bhaiya.' An elderly person said, 'No, Salima, no; why did you make such a big mistake.' The old man started weeping bitterly and the brother began hitting his head against the wall.

VIII

The spirits come to Shah Alam camp after midnight. One day, an old man's spirit came with all the other spirits to Shah Alam camp. The old man was bare-chested, his dhoti tied high, chappals on his feet, and he had a bamboo staff in his hand. He had a watch tucked inside his dhoti somewhere.

The spirits asked the old man, 'Do you have a relative in the camp too?'

The old man said, 'Yes and no.'

The spirits thought he was crazy and left him and he began circling the camp.

Someone asked the old man, 'Baba, who are you searching for?'

The old man said, 'I am looking for people who can murder me.'

'Why?'

'Fifty years ago I was killed by a bullet. Now I want the rioters to burn me alive and murder me.'

'Why do you want this, Baba?'

'Only to tell the world that I didn't die when they killed me with a bullet, nor will I die if they burn me alive.'

IX

A political leader asked a spirit in Shah Alam camp, 'Do you have a mother and father?'

'They were killed.'

'Brothers and sisters?'

'None.'

'Anyone?'

'No.'

'Are you comfortable here?'

'Yes, I am.'

'You get food etc.'

'Yes, I do.'

'Do you have clothes etc.?'

'Yes, I do.'

'Do you need anything?'

'Nothing.'

'Nothing?'

'Nothing.'

The political leader was happy. He thought: this boy is sensible. He's not like other Muslims.

X

The spirits come to Shah Alam camp after midnight. One day the Devil's spirit came with the other spirits. Looking around him, the Devil was ashamed and embarrassed. He couldn't meet people's eyes. He tried his best to avoid them. Keeping his head down, he tried to find a place where he wouldn't see anyone. Eventually the people cornered him. In truth, he was ashamed and said, 'I had no hand in what happened. I swear by Allah, I had no hand in it.'

The people said, 'Yes...yes. We know. You couldn't do something like this. You have a standard to maintain, after all.'

Sighing with relief, the Devil said, 'A burden has been lifted from my heart...all of you know the truth.'

The people said, 'A few days ago Allah Mian had come and He said the same thing.'

AIR AND WATER

AMAR MITRA

Translated from the Bengali by Arunava Sinha

I

TALAPATRA BABU MAY NOT HAVE BELONGED TO PASANDPUR, BUT fourteen months of living in this market town had turned him into a local. A food department inspector who accepted bribes energetically and lacked the benevolence to spare anyone from kickbacks, Ramshankar Talapatra was transferred from Sonarpur in 24 Parganas to our Pasandpur on the border between Bankura and Purulia after falling foul of the authorities. No story about Pasandpur is complete without him, because it seems that Pasandpur, with its rough terrain and rocks and hillocks and vanishing jungles and red soil, had charmed Talapatra Babu. It had captured his heart. He used to assert with conviction that he had never been posted to such a wonderful place in his career of thirty-five years—where he could breathe deeply and easily, and accept both official and unofficial payments with equal ease, without anyone asking questions or sending anonymous applications to the higher authorities; a place where one could work happily for a hundred years.

Let me tell you about Pasandpur. Call it a market town or even a city, but the fact remains that outsiders have never cared for Pasandpur despite the pasand in its name. No local ever gets a job here—outsiders work at the offices and courts in this town. And from the moment they arrive, they count the days to freedom from this sentence of exile. Tarapada Babu, the high school teacher, openly says that once the remaining five years of his working life are done, he'll move to Durgapur or Burnpur, buy some land, and live his life out there. 'What attractions does Pasandpur hold for me?'

We don't exactly know what attractions Pasandpur holds for people, but what we have seen is that because of the offices and courts and the narrow-gauge railway line, we are never deprived of new faces. Clerks or vagabonds, those who arrive never stay on. We don't see why they should. What does Pasandpur have to offer besides the unpolluted air here? The tiny toy train loses its novelty quickly. We cannot persuade the people who come here to stay, even if we want to. They leave. If they can't, they grow old criticizing Pasandpur. Inspector of Food Talapatra Babu, and a few vagabonds are the only exceptions. Their faces are wreathed in smiles as they try to pronounce the name of the town. As Talapatra Babu himself acknowledged, even those with whom he played cards in the evening paid him his bribes during the day, saying softly, 'Here you are, sir, five hundred it is.' The Food Babu had never seen anything like this in his life.

When he heard this, Rabilochan Babu, the headmaster of the high school, said, 'But this is your legitimate due, how can my nephew expect to run a business without paying you off?'

Examining his cards, Talapatra Babu said, 'Not everyone understands, you know, they think all that is needed is a smile to get things done. For heaven's sake, if the doctor or priest or teacher aren't paid....'

Talapatra Babu paused halfway, seeking his fellow players' support. The headmaster was the first to nod in assent, 'Of course, of course....'

The headmaster's nephew had a kerosene oil dealership. He had been entreating the inspector to increase his quota of oil—could he not make a recommendation to headquarters? And, yes, he did sell the oil on the black market at inflated prices instead of giving it to ration cardholders, but then how was he to expand his business? Talapatra Babu had found him out, and had promptly held out his palm under the table. He had haggled intensely with the nephew, making off for the card session as soon as he had pocketed the payment. The headmaster's nephew's wife served tea and chanachur.

Sipping his tea, Talapatra said, 'There can be no relationship between work and leisure, you know, the other thing is a matter of the day job....'

'Of course, of course.' The innocent headmaster smiled at the inspector. 'Thank goodness you take bribes, that's how things get done. The previous inspector had got my nephew into all kinds of trouble. He was almost arrested, saved himself only by paying off the police.'

Talapatra Babu didn't spend a single night outside Pasandpur during his fourteen months here. The place had offered him sanctuary, he would say, given him relief during his last days at work, so he would not leave.

'Why should you go, you must help my nephew establish himself first, sir,' the headmaster had told the inspector deferentially, 'you're not exactly without friends here.'

Pasandpur offers sanctuary to people. Vagrants take shelter here. Besides those who are transferred on work, the rest of the visitors are all wanderers. Some on their way in, others on their way out. Some of them are empty-headed, while others are brimming with intelligence, holding on to their ponderous heads and grey matter and brain cells carefully as they climb out of the palanquin-like bogies on the narrow-gauge railway. It's this train with two bogeys that brings people with jobs as well as drifters to Pasandpur from time to time. It had brought Ramshankar Talapatra too.

A befuddled Talapatra Babu, halfway to old age, had got off the evening train one day with his suitcase and bedding. His skin blackened by the smoke from the coal engine, his drooping white moustache, blackened too, a faded, ancient pair of Terylene trousers hanging loosely around his waist, dressed in a khaki, full-sleeved sweater, his feet shod in an old, patched pair of strapped sandals, his greying hair untouched by oil for months. People had mistaken him for a vagrant, eyeing him suspiciously, trying to size him up—was he half mad or entirely mad, cunning or simple, a stayer or a traveller? But when the man had said, looking around him as he got off the train, 'What a nice place,' their suspicion had ebbed. He had not got off at Pasandpur only to declare it napasand.

No one knows when Pasandpur became a pilgrimage site for eccentric vagabonds. Probably it was from the time the narrow-gauge railway was set up. The toy-like train would frequently deposit an empty-headed or brainy drifter on the platform in the afternoon or evening and whistle its way along to the next station. There is a station here, it's true, but that's just an empty field, with neither an office nor any railway employees. There is no stationmaster, no pointsman, no tickets. There's no fixed schedule for the train either. It might not show up for two days before arriving unexpectedly one evening, whistling. It might then stay here all night, periodically snorting and emitting smoke. The headmaster cannot sleep on those nights because of the sound made by the engine's exhalations. He isn't married, lives with his nephew and nephew's wife instead. One of his nephews is established, but not the other one. One of his nieces isn't married yet. Worry has made him a light sleeper. Rabilochan Babu, the headmaster, doesn't care for the train or the engine or its bogies. Once, a rather manly drifter had got off the train and had almost torn asunder one of his nieces after dragging her into the jungle. Such a commotion! Pasandpur's people had decided to beat him to death. But, fearing charges of murder, the headmaster had said, 'Never mind, put him back on the train, are the people of Pasandpur really capable of killing a fellow human being?'

It had certainly caused a furore. The people of Pasandpur still talk about it whenever the subject comes up. What else do we have here, after all, besides the train and the outsiders? Even the hailstorms are not as severe as they used to be. There was a hailstorm once, a long time ago. A twenty-kilo block of ice fell into the jungle from the sky. The cowherds saw it and told everyone. Apparently, the ice took seventy-two hours to melt. Just that one time. And the other time was what the terribly beautiful and rather manly vagabond had gone and done. Forcing him onto the train had not proved easy, either. The guard and driver had refused to take charge of the man, asking, 'Where should we take him?'

'Wherever you like, he's a criminal.'

'No,' the guard had flared up, 'I won't do anything ugly like that.'

'Then hand him over to the police,' the railway people had said.

Word would get out in that case, with his niece becoming involved, scandal would follow, which was why the headmaster had not taken that route. He had said, 'The man came by your train, we're returning him.'

But the drifter hadn't wanted to leave, saying with a strange smile, 'I shall be back, no one can love the way the woman I met here was able to, oh how exquisite her eyes, how bewitching her smile, how silken her breasts. There's meaning to this town.'

The headmaster had turned red. 'What meaning?' he had muttered.

'There's a meaning to all this—why the sun here is so hot, where the winds swirl in from, why the girls here are so lovely inside.'

The headmaster had felt overcome. He was told that the drifter had not forced his niece into the jungle—on the contrary, it was she who had ensnared him. She was not particularly beautiful, but her eyes held the magic of water. It was the height of summer. Their joy had made flowers blossom on the palash trees in the forest. They had touched each other the way the breeze touches the flowers and the leaves. When a cowherd saw them, everyone came to know, and then the trouble started. People had raced to the spot to find the young woman with her arms around the vagabond's unclothed, rock-solid body, covering his rough chest with kisses. The sound of kisses spread through the jungle like the splashing of rain in Pasandpur. The smell of damp earth rose from the scorched clay of summer. Much more would have taken place had the cowherd not seen them. The headmaster would have had to tackle everything. The girl is now a mother of two children, living in Burnpur. She has not been to Pasandpur in a long time. Because, when she visits, she has no inclination to return, forgetting her husband and family and home.

Now the headmaster became Talapatra Babu's companion. No one except that drifter and this Food Babu had ever loved Pasandpur.

Sometimes, the headmaster mentioned the vagabond in passing, 'He said this spirited sunshine, balmy breeze, a woman with a beautiful heart, her eyes like a limpid pool—none of this has ever happened before, and I don't even know why they have now. Can you tell me, where is the real home of the wind that swirls about in Pasandpur?'

Talapatra said, 'I've come here from Sonarpur, but that's not where my home is. My home is in Midnapore, it's been such a long time since I've been there.'

'Won't you go home?'

'I'll stay here as long as I'm happy—after all, no one's filed a petition accusing me of taking bribes or stealing, so I'm not likely to be transferred again.'

II

One evening, the headmaster, Rabilochan Babu, turned to Talapatra, 'Will you do me a favour?'

The food inspector's experienced eye had discerned that the headmaster was in trouble, that he really needed help. 'Come to my office tomorrow afternoon,' he said sternly.

'No, this isn't for my nephew.'

Dropping the cards in his hand, Talapatra said, 'I know, I have my eye on your nephew. I know he's selling kerosene at six rupees in the open market instead of two and a half as he should.'

Looking troubled, the headmaster responded, 'What can I do, he's so obsessed with money that he simply won't listen.'

'If he listened he would be a kerosene dealer all his life. Did you know he's selling cement too?'

The headmaster said, 'He has no choice—he didn't even finish school. Do you think I enjoy listening to people saying that my nephew hasn't even passed his higher secondary exams? The other teachers taunt me.'

Talapatra chuckled, 'It's all out of envy—do they have any idea that out of the twenty-six dealers in this area your nephew pays me the largest amount?'

The headmaster summoned his nephew's wife, 'Can you make us another cup of tea, Lalita, my dear, Inspector Babu will be here for a while.'

'No tea,' said Talapatra, 'I'm off now, Rabi Babu, we'll talk tomorrow afternoon.'

The headmaster wouldn't relent. He followed Talapatra, catching up with him. 'That's not it, I just wanted to talk about my niece's wedding.'

'Tomorrow afternoon, then.'

They did talk the next afternoon. Not that Talapatra Babu charged a fee for listening. But he said, 'Pay me for matchmaking, it won't amount to a bribe.' The headmaster would have to pay, for he had made a match with one of the dealers. The groom lived in Rangamati, close to Pasandpur, young, of marriageable age. Could Talapatra finalize the match, on condition that the dowry would have to be reduced?

'Is that all? It'll be done. I have him under my thumb,' Talapatra Babu had said with a smile. 'He sells the entire quota of rice and wheat meant for the ration shop in the open market. Just watch what I do to him.'

The headmaster had told his intimate associates everything afterwards. The match would not have been finalized if Talapatra Babu hadn't intervened. The groom could not ignore the inspector. The headmaster was relieved after the marriage. Like her sister, this girl too had started frequenting the station and the jungle of palash trees. He wouldn't have been able to take it if something untoward were to happen.

Talapatra Babu was a double beneficiary, extracting a fat fee for matchmaking and remaining in the headmaster's good books. He would claim he needed money desperately, that there was no way to survive without money. And yet, he cooked for himself, slept on a khatia, put on a freshly washed shirt just once a week, and freshly laundered trousers just once in two months. Someone used to visit him from Midnapore at the beginning of every month—his son, possibly. He would leave by the evening train with money. In addition, Talapatra also sent a money order around the middle of every month. He had no bank account here. He would be anxious at the beginning of the month, looking relieved only after his son had arrived and he had handed over the money. He would keep track through the month of the ways in which his twenty-six dealers were breaking the law. Using this information, he would corner them, 'Two hundred won't do this month, Parimal, add another hundred, I can't bear to look at what you've done with the sugar.'

He had got hold of a ramshackle cycle from the headmaster, promising to return it when he left. He would patrol Pasandpur, Rangamati, Shaltora, Naw Pahari, and all the other areas on this cycle. When one of the tyres was punctured, he got the headmaster's nephew to pay for a new one. 'The people of Pasandpur are the finest of all,' he would say.

One day he observed, 'It's amazing—when I got off the train last winter, my hair was so grey, and my skin sagged, but just look at the change in me over this past one year, Headmaster Moshai.'

'Really!' The headmaster was astonished.

'Oh yes. Check for yourself.'

He was right. The inspector had indeed arrived with a head full of grey hair and a stoop. Looked like a vagrant. But you wouldn't know that now when you looked at him.

'What hair oil do you use?' asked the headmaster.

'I don't use hair oil.'

'Then how?'

'It's the air and the water here, I've never encountered such fresh air anywhere, not even such water, all the grime in my inner machinery has been washed away.'

The headmaster was pleased. As a long-time inhabitant of Pasandpur, he couldn't stand criticism of his town. Something happened to him in his happiness, and he asked, 'What was that you were saying about the air?'

'Not just the air, the sunshine too, one is warm all the time, very useful.'

The sunshine too! The headmaster began to mutter, 'Do you know what this air and sunshine mean?'

Talapatra Babu guffawed. 'What do you mean, how can they mean anything?'

'Where do they come from?'

Talapatra Babu laughed uproariously again. 'Where on earth will they come from? What are you talking about? By the way, my days here are drawing to an end, a month and a half to go.'

'A month and a half! And then?'

'I'm retiring, got my letter already. Tell your nephew to increase my payment this month, all right?'

The headmaster asked, 'And after retirement?'

'I'll go home.' A note of mourning entered Talapatra Babu's voice.

'You'll get a pension, won't you?'

'It's a pittance. The salary's a joke, you know, my real earnings come from the dealers. The salary is just evidence of having a job. What I earn is from bribes. Can you imagine how much I have to cycle around for it? No one lets go of money easily—neither your nephew, nor anyone else. But, yes, extracting bribes in Pasandpur is easy. Let's say I buy a packet of cigarettes and tell the shopkeeper that so-and-so dealer will pay, he doesn't object. My son takes away toiletries too every month, besides the money.'

The headmaster said, 'It's all thanks to the air here, don't you think?'

As he left, the inspector said, 'Remind your nephew to double the payment this month....'

'I will,' nodded the headmaster.

III

Talapatra Babu arrived panting a fortnight later, 'Didn't you tell him, Master Moshai?'

'Of course I did.'

The inspector had become thinner in a mere fortnight. He seemed to be combing the area on his cycle all day, returning home late at night, and becoming irregular at the card sessions. The nephew had said, 'Inspector Babu is desperate for money, but now that he's about to retire, why should people pay him more?'

'But he's been here so long.'

The nephew had chided his uncle, the headmaster, 'Don't you speak up for him now.'

The headmaster gave up his seat to the inspector. 'Let it go, it's only a matter of a few days more.'

Talapatra muttered, 'I wrote home saying I'm retiring next month—so my wife wrote back, "Bring money".'

'You have your provident fund, gratuity....'

Talapatra Babu shook his head. 'I've already withdrawn my provident fund, only the last few months' money is in there now, a couple of thousand at best.'

'And the gratuity?'

'No knowing when I'll get it, and they'll deduct most of it anyway. I embezzled government money once for my eldest son to start his own business. The business failed, I've been ruined too—no increments for four years, they'll take away most of the gratuity, and my salary isn't high enough for a fat pension.'

Talapatra's hair suddenly appeared greyer to the headmaster. For the first time he realized that the inspector used dentures, for in his agitation Talapatra had forgotten to put them on. So he was looking very old, his cheeks sunken, eyes clouded over. He had aged a great deal in a fortnight. He stuttered when he tried to speak.

The headmaster couldn't make any promises. The inspector disappeared for the next few days. One evening the nephew said, 'The man is sniffing around like a dog, he's even harassing dealers at home in the middle of the night.'

The headmaster said, 'He's in trouble, before he leaves you'd better....'

The nephew said, 'We'll give him a farewell.'

But what farewell? With ten days to go before his retirement, the inspector said, 'I'm getting an extension.'

'Wonderful, six months more in that case, right?' The headmaster inspected Talapatra closely. The man had acquired a stoop, his shoulders seemed bent. He had not shaved for at least a week, and even his eyebrows seemed to have greyed suddenly. He looked like the man who had got off the train on a winter evening. His hands shook as he picked up a cup of tea.

Sipping his tea, Talapatra said, 'I don't need cordiality—my rates have increased, I need my payment at once.'

'Why are you telling me all this?' The headmaster seemed irked.

'No, not you, but please tell your nephew.' The man suddenly fell silent. Then he said in a low voice, 'There's no place like Pasandpur, Master Moshai. Nor people like the ones here. Moreover, you're my friend.'

'Yes,' said the headmaster inaudibly.

'Then let me tell you that my wife has written that she will only let me enter the house if I hand over whatever money I have to her and my two sons. How much money do you suppose that is? I informed them, but they don't believe me.'

IV

'But the house is yours, what do they mean they won't let you in?'

'No, sir, my wife is the official owner. My sons have written, "If you're retiring, you won't have any money to give us—so better look for work." What do I do?'

The headmaster was silent, experiencing a significant lack of ability to offer advice.

The next day the headmaster was told by his nephew, 'All lies, how can he get an extension—his corruption is legendary, the dealers in Sonarpur even beat him up, they know everything at headquarters.'

'Never mind, he's leaving.'

'That's why we aren't saying anything, but he's making unfair demands. If we'd known he would do this we'd also have beaten him up and thrown him out. But then how could we have done that—the previous inspector got us into deep trouble, that's why this one was spared.'

The headmaster said, 'Give him a proper farewell at least, find out what he wants, a TV set if possible, he probably doesn't have one at home.'

'He doesn't want any of that, he wants cash—we had thought of using last month's payments for a grand farewell. Pasandpur would have earned a name for itself.'

The inspector arrived again on the day before his retirement. Floppy trousers, khaki sweater, uncombed hair, sunken cheeks, trembling on his feet, 'Yes, I admit I lied, everyone knows there was no chance of an extension, I had tried to collect three months' extra payment in advance, but everyone's come to know, I'm a thief after all, how can I get an extension?'

He was raving, thought the headmaster.

'When I saw how rich some of my relations were I began to take bribes in Ranaghat, then it got to be a habit. I even smuggled rice myself when I was in Murshidabad, it's all a matter of habit, during the food movement I took government-supplied rice home, all out of habit, terrible. And not just me, my family has become used to it too. When I wrote that I would go home penniless after retirement, they replied, fend for yourself in that case, you can't get away with lies....'

'Forget it, forget the whole thing, would you like some coffee?'

Talapatra Babu shook his head. 'I took money from you too, although it was put to good use, but what do I do now, I'm in such a hole, let me see how much I can take with me, Pasandpur's air and sunshine are lovely....'

Talapatra Babu didn't budge even after retiring on the thirty-first of the month. Never mind the farewell, he hadn't even received his allowance for the final month. His successor had warned all the dealers to stop bribing Talapatra Babu. 'He's a thief, don't any of you give him any money. Why should you have to pay if you're running a clean business? And if you must pay, give it to me, I'm the inspector of food at Pasandpur now.'

The headmaster asked, 'Why did you have to lie?'

Talapatra Babu grimaced at the headmaster's question. 'I was forced to lie so that I could make a little extra money.'

Talapatra couldn't extract any money. Nothing at all. He spent his final days wandering from one shop to another, from one godown to the next, from one house to another, returning despondently each time. Everyone promised to pay the next day, or the day after. Eventually they didn't even invite him in any more. Even when they invited him in they didn't talk to him. Even when they talked to him it was just small talk, 'When are you going home?', and so on. No one offered him a cup of tea. No farewell. People who used to genuflect before him twice a day averted their eyes now.

He kept saying, 'Make the payment, I need the money desperately, I'm retiring.'

No one paid any attention. Eventually, he spent his days alone at a tea shop, sitting on a bench, facing the road. Winter had left, but its last bite was still to come. A bitterly cold north wind blew every morning. It raised each of the grey hairs on his head. His head drooped, his body trembled. He looked exactly like a sick, infirm tiger, its teeth fallen out, but its greed for flesh intact. He kept hailing passers-by, 'Just a minute, Saha Babu; here, Netai; I believe you're planning to increase your wheat quota, Mandal Babu....'

The ration shop owner strode past without heeding him. Only the headmaster noticed him on his way back from school. Stopping, he said, 'Not here, Talapatra Babu, come home with me for a cup of tea.'

The inspector got to his feet with a wan smile, 'Not today, Gobindo Saha is about to return, the dealer from Shaltora, owes me three months' payment, I'm lying in wait for him.'

'How can you, just send word, he'll send your money to you.'

'He won't, the treacherous miser that he is. I have no choice, I can't go back empty-handed, can I?'

The headmaster said, 'The people of Pasandpur aren't traitors—all right, I shall send for him, his son goes to my school.'

'Yes, I had always thought the people of Pasandpur wouldn't turn out this way. I'll be leaving soon, Master Moshai, I'll just sit here till then to feel the sunshine and the air, why don't you go home? Ah—even breathing is such a joy here. There's meaning to this town, don't you think?'

The headmaster was reminded of the drifter. He had said something similar when he was being hustled out of Pasandpur. The inspector had been caught in the same web.

That evening the headmaster told his nephew, 'All of you should give Talapatra Babu something, it doesn't feel good to see him sitting there all day.'

The nephew shook his head. 'He doesn't want a TV, he wants money, the dealers aren't interested any more, they're all chasing the new inspector.'

'Ask them once more.'

'Everyone's avoiding him. They think there's no point throwing money at him now that he's retired—he took quite a lot during these twelve months, after all.'

The headmaster couldn't accept this. He realized that his nephew was also avoiding Talapatra. But there were other people in Pasandpur. When they heard, they said, 'This can't go on, the man just sits there breathing in the dirt and grime, he's aged visibly, we can't bear to see this. No one in Pasandpur can be allowed to be unhappy. Those of us who are long-time residents of Pasandpur said, how much does he want, we'll take up a collection, let him go back home.'

Talapatra shook his head at this, 'No, the dealers must pay, why should you, I didn't do anything for you.'

'That doesn't matter, you've lived in Pasandpur for over a year, we shall give you a farewell so that you can go back home.'

Talapatra Babu kept shaking his head, mumbling, 'Who will I go back to? They know money, but they don't know me. I made a big mistake—if I had come to Pasandpur earlier, thirty-five years ago, I wouldn't have developed this habit of taking bribes. The air and sunlight here mean something, don't you think, that's why I cut down on the bribes here, I used to earn a lot more at Sonarpur....'

Talapatra Babu kept repeating the same thing for several days, there on the roadside. The man began to change visibly. If he had come here thirty-five years earlier, he might have never taken bribes, he rued. The bribes had done him no good. He had just become a slave to his wife, sons, and money. 'Ah! What a lovely place Pasandpur is, even my grey hair had turned black.'

Then Inspector Talapatra disappeared suddenly. That is to say, he boarded the train without being observed by anyone. The next day we confronted the guard and the driver, 'Have you taken the inspector back?'

The aged driver, covered in coal dust, and the aged guard both began to chortle, 'Yes, we took him back, the last time all of you had forced a vagabond on us, this time we took him back of our own volition. "Get in, Talapatra," we told him, "why spend any more time here?"'

'He got in?'

'He did, but he has promised to return, he won't abandon this place—just as it is easy to take bribes here, it's also possible to live here happily without taking bribes, here grey hair turns black, teeth stop wobbling and set themselves firmly back in the gums, sagging skin turns taut, eyesight improves, apparently there's meaning to living here, there's....' The guard and the driver, two aged men, chattered on.

The headmaster's eyes misted over. Talapatra won't return.

A month and a half later, Ramshankar Talapatra's sons came instead, two demons in search of their ungrateful father. They began to scream, 'The swine has escaped. Where does he think he can hide, we'll find him and get our money.'

The people of Pasandpur beat them up and forced them back onto the train. Boarding, they said they would take revenge on their father, or on Pasandpur. Sonarpur was much better, even though their father had been beaten up there he had made lots more money, Pasandpur had corrupted him.

Now the headmaster of Pasandpur gazes at the railway lines all day long. He has retired, after all. The lines are clearly visible from his veranda. I wonder what he stares at. Even though he cannot recognize people a couple of feet away, now and then he calls out to his nephew's wife, 'Isn't that a drifter there, bent over and covered in coal dust? Could it be Talapatra Babu? Or is it the beautiful man who had come earlier... Inspector Babu...he-e-e-e-re....'

The dust blows across the empty road. The summer winds are encroaching on Pasandpur, a little at a time. The nephew's wife's eyes mist over too. She covers her mouth with the end of her sari.

THE WITCH

KAMALAKANTA MOHAPATRA

Translated from the Odia by Leelawati Mohapatra and Paul St. Pierre

I

WE WERE OUT ON THE HOSTEL TERRACE THE EVENING FOLLOWING THE full moon night of Dola, drinking a bottle of local rotgut about as safe as rat poison. We did have a pitcher of water, but preferred our drinks neat. The oil-soaked paper bags were empty: omelettes, diced onions, spicy gram, and fried chips had all been eaten. There was only a finger of drink left in the bottle. We lit a cigarette—just one, so we could pass it around.

Ramesh finished his story with the burp of satisfaction rustics reserve for a hearty meal. 'So there,' he said. 'Big pricks and tiny pricks, can someone please sum up the moral of the story?'

Before anyone could speak up, he added, 'The moral of the story, if there's one, is this: don't trust the police any more than you would thieves, or even less. Although several years have passed since the incident, my arse hots up when I think of it. Therefore, ladies and ledas, eunuchs and double-pricks, the finger of rotgut in the bottle is rightfully mine—something to cool my scorched arse with; nobody else has a stronger claim, let me tell you. And in the meanwhile the morning is a long way off.'

When the half-smoked cigarette reached me, I held it up against the moon. 'Who the hell sucked on it as if his life depended on it? The damn stick's almost down to the filter before even one full round. Go easy, boys. There aren't many left. This is the last but one, and when we've had the last there'll be nothing left to smoke but your pricks. And what baby prick Ramesh said about the police is really true—they bugger you so hard the pain lasts for seven generations.'

'You too had some experience, huh?' Siva said, tenderly cradling the bottle against his breast as if it were a baby.

I could have shot back something smart-alecky but didn't.

'Listen, Sasank,' Siva continued. 'I don't know where you'll get it, but you have to find me fifteen rupees tomorrow morning. I've got to go home. A second letter from my mother arrived two days ago, but I didn't breathe a word to anyone 'cause I didn't want to miss out on the binge tonight.'

'What did she have to say? How come you've sat on it for two days without letting us know? If this is how you behave, what should we expect from outsiders and strangers?' we teased in unison.

'Quit joking, boys,' Siva said with a long sigh. 'It's bloody serious business. Ma writes that for the last fortnight my younger brother seems to be possessed by a witch. He's fine during the day—plays about, eats, screams, and fights like any young child—but come evening he starts bawling for no earthly reason. It goes on and on for hours on end until he drops off to sleep, tired out and hungry. Ma says he's become as thin as a stick, you can see all his ribs. He's been seen by local doctors and quacks of all kinds, but to no avail. Then somebody told Ma it could be the evil eye, and an exorcist was roped in. He did his bit but nothing's helped. Then somebody told Ma that it couldn't be a simple case of possession by a witch, but that it must be a virgin witch who's just reached puberty. In such cases, it seems, even the witch herself doesn't realize she has someone in her thrall. Dangerous witches, these; if they even look at you sideways they can wreak havoc. The only cure is a consecrated wood apple leaf from the temple of Lord Lingaraj. That's what I'll do tomorrow morning—collect a leaf and catch the first bus home. Though how I'll identify the new witch among all the pubescent girls in the village remains to be seen. Anyway, that's not my problem. So give me fifteen rupees, someone, and I give you my solemn word: once I finish college and find a job, the first thing I'll do is repay the loan, even if it takes ten years or fifteen.'

'Wait, wait,' said Gandharb. 'I'm dying to pee. Don't say another word, anyone, until I'm done. Meanwhile, anyone up for a gulp of hot water?' He walked to the edge of the terrace and peed on the peepul tree growing out of a crack in the parapet. 'The tree must be wondering why hot rain is falling from a cloudless, clear sky.'

'Move away from the peepul, you dimwit,' I warned him. 'It's a nesting place for witches and spirits—attracts them in droves, like iron to a magnet.'

A round-bellied moon hung perilously in the sky. The stray clouds looked anaemic. A covey of birds flew by overhead, their wings almost motionless, like an aeroplane's.

'Ghosts and witches!' guffawed Ramesh, getting to his feet to pee. 'Tall tales.'

'Tall tales, you say,' I retorted, munching on a peanut which the dew had turned soggy. 'You mean ghosts and witches don't exist. Is that what you're implying? Ah, you little bugger, you've lived all your life in a town, so what would you know about witches? They don't crowd towns, mind you. They don't like din and bustle, well-lit roads and markets, fast moving cars and trucks, arid and treeless spaces. Why, towns don't even have a decent cremation ground. The little patch that passes for one is so tiny that pyres have to be lit on top of each other. No mango or polang groves, of course, not even a big, wide field with a few trees for taking a shit outdoors. Besides....' My voice was sounding like my father's—deep, heavy, and thick from chewing paan, '...you city slickers, you don't have the pure, unadulterated blood witches love to suck. Flies, mosquitoes, bedbugs, disease, politics, and corruption have turned your blood so black and bitter that if a witch sucks your blood she'll die before you do.'

'Shut up, Sasank Mishra,' said Ramesh. 'It's not for nothing you're known as foolish prick. Spare us, for heaven's sake. Spare us a lecture on the wonders of village life and the crooked ways of the town. We've heard it all before. And let me tell you: last year I went to my uncle's village after a long time, hoping to see some lusty-busty village belles, who, as literature would have us believe, grow like wildflowers in such an idyllic environment, their beautiful breasts bared for all the world to marvel at. My bloody prick, I didn't come across a single girl who wasn't wearing a goddamn blouse. So much for your idyll of rural innocence! And now you're telling us villages are teeming with witches.'

'How dare you run down villages,' I said, warming up. 'Wait a sec. Let me wet the wall and then I'll ask all you poor little city pricks to open your stuffed arses and ears wide and listen to what I have to say. It's a two-in-one tale. You'll have the police and the witch in a single story.'

A dog howled in the distance. A train whistled. Someone farted. We covered our heads with our handkerchiefs to protect ourselves from the dew. Someone filled the rum bottle with water and our glasses were replenished for one last round. A quarrel sprang up between Arun and Gandharb over the empty bottle, but we all scolded Gandharb. It was always up to Arun to rub the empty bottle against his thigh to warm it up. He was always the one to strike a match and drop it into the bottle. The thin blue ribbon of light that swirled out with a sigh was a sacred ritual of our drinking binges. Ramesh collected the cigarette butts lying around and said, 'See why I insist on cigarettes without filters? Then there'd be something to fall back on!'

We opened the dinner packets—bread, baked potatoes, and boiled eggs wrapped in large thick lotus leaves, but none of us had much of an appetite.

'Get on with your story,' Siva said, turning to me.

'Yes, start,' said the rest. 'But don't go overboard.'

'Not a single word is an exaggeration, let me tell you,' I assured them. 'Here goes.'

II

I sat on the cement bench at the police station cooling my arse. It was past eight in the morning, and there was no policeman in sight. Two deodars and a few mango trees, their branches hacked off, stood like sad, servile sentries. Not a whiff of a breeze, but there was a chill in the air. The dew was still on the grass. The red-pebbled road from the doorsteps of the police station to the canal bank lay like a line of dried blood. There were just two people ahead of me, but the crowd thickened afterwards. And we all waited. Occasional coughing, betel-spitting, throat-clearing, arse-shifting, but mostly silence.

Around ten, along came the inspector, bare-bodied, a blue silk lungi knotted around his bulging waist. People who knew him sprang to their feet. He swept a smiling glance over us all, spat a thick jet of blood-red betel juice down the veranda and shouted: 'Eh! Where are you—Pitambar, Nityanand, Nabaghan, et cetera, et cetera? Have you all died and gone to the cremation ground? Bring me water, someone. Quick. A bird's chosen to drop its precious shit on my bald head. What is that—good or bad? Who knows how the day will go!' He looked around at us, his captive audience. 'Ladies and gents, what do the Shastras, scriptures, holy books have to say about this? Is having a bird shit on your head on your way to the office a good omen?'

A sleepy constable came out with a bucket of water. The inspector became even more theatrical. 'Why, Agani! My dear man, you're still here? I thought you'd hurried off after last night. Did you know the fish you brought me last evening was so bitter I couldn't eat it? The bile sac must have burst as the fish was being chopped to pieces. Did you get it for free? Or did you discover the fish was bad and decide you'd better palm it off on the son of a bitch of an inspector so he'd drop dead the moment he ate it?'

I was watching the dark-skinned, squat, balding man standing beside me. A fat pink ant was crawling about on the collar of his sweat-stained off-white shirt. The way the ant was scurrying about from one end of the collar to the other made me doubt its sanity; I was just waiting to see if it'd bite the poor man on the neck. All I had to do was just raise a finger and flick the ant away, but I had lost any inclination to be a good scout since early morning.

The inspector splashed water on his scalp and removed the flecks of bird shit. He washed his face and rinsed his mouth. Every jet of water he sprayed down the veranda produced a fleeting little rainbow. I took a good look at him: middle-aged, maybe around fifty, tall, full-bodied, dark-skinned, a flat nose, small ears glued to the sides of the head, a thick moustache with flecks of grey, thick lips, red from betel chewing. 'All right, no ladies, all gents,' he began solemnly. 'Now rattle off your precious complaints. Anyone here whose village is being ravaged by tigers, bears, snakes, frogs, grasshoppers, thieves, dacoits, thugs, burglars, house-breakers, tunnel-diggers, spirits, or demons? Anyone with a missing cow or goat or wife or daughter, or the same raped, assaulted, molested, obscenely gestured at? Anyone whose fish pond has been emptied? Anyone who's had a cucumber stolen from his patch of green? Now, my good folks, make it snappy. Tell you what, let me chant aloud the sections of the Indian Penal Code and you stop me at whichever one applies. Good God, what miserable times we're living in! People think nothing of rushing to the police station if they step on a thorn, or if a monkey bares its teeth at them; people enjoy reporting their neighbours for a coconut frond blown by the wind. Everyone's so eager to file an FIR these days. And they want us to write down every damn word that drops from their eager lips. They treat the police station like their uncle's home! In the good old days, when the whites ruled over us, even flies and mosquitoes, not to mention human beings, would think twice before venturing anywhere near!'

We all remained silent. This was the inspector's show.

'Agani!' he hollered. 'Where're you, you son of a police stick? Bring out the paraphernalia—chair, table, register, pen, ink bottle, and whatever else. We'll have an outdoors office today. Surely our friends here can't have a problem with that?'

Something seemed to hold Agani back.

'Are you dead, Agani, you bastard?' the inspector screamed. 'Gone for a shit or what? Got the runs from eating bitter fish last night?'

Another constable, thin as a stick and as brittle, hauled out a chair. The inspector sat down, and eyed the constable quizzically. 'By God, Nityanand, you seem to have put on weight overnight! What did you have for dinner last night, man? Never mind. Have you asked this grand gathering here whether anyone has come not to file a complaint but to invite us to a feast? Isn't anyone celebrating a son's or a daughter's wedding? No one's holding his son's sacred thread ceremony? When did we last get an invitation? No wonder you're so thin, Nityanand!'

Nityanand dragged out a table. Its top looked like the map of a hitherto unknown territory, stained as it was with ink and blotches of unknown antiquity. On it he placed a register, a pen, and a ruler.

'Now then,' the inspector barked. 'Enough horseplay. Let's get down to business. Tell me who's at the head of the queue.'

The two men in front of me looked at each other.

'File your complaint,' said the first to the second. 'Mine will take time.'

'You're first in line,' protested the second man. 'File yours first.'

The inspector guffawed good-humouredly. 'Listen here, keep one thing in mind: at the police station and the doctor's it's the same. The moment you go there you have to jump the queue.'

Silence.

'Will either of you begin, or shall I call the third fellow?' The inspector was enjoying himself.

'My complaint's a trifle,' said the first man.

'If it's a trifle why are you here? Is the police station your uncle's home or what?'

Silence.

'What's your name?'

'Arjun.'

'Arjun what?'

'Arjun Das.'

'Your village?'

'Khandipara.'

'Hey, how's Madan Santra? How's he doing? Tell him I remember him. And what shape's his fish pond in? No one has been poisoning the water to kill off the fish, I hope! All right, tell me what brings you here.'

'How can I, sir, in the presence of so many people? I came with the hope of whispering into sir's ears.'

'Anything embarrassing?'

'Oh no, nothing of the sort.'

Pretending to be annoyed, the inspector rolled his eyes as he got up and walked into his chamber.

The first man and the inspector remained closeted for ten to fifteen minutes. When they came out, both looked cheerful and satisfied. The inspector said, 'Don't worry. Go back home. I'm sending some constables right away. See how precarious my position is! Such a huge area to police and so few constables. From the river Devi in the east to Balikuda in the west, from Nanigaon in the south to Goddess Sarala's temple at Jhankad in the north—it's unmanageable. So huge. Listen, Das, don't go and shout from the rooftops you've filed a police complaint. Another thing: everyone talks highly of the bananas from Khandipara. Send us along a big bunch, will you? The test of the pudding is in the eating, they say, don't they, eh, Das?'

The first man, whose name we all now knew, bowed down from his waist and took leave of the inspector, walking backwards. The whole thing was so theatrical and absurd, it took a great effort not to laugh.

Before the second man's turn, there was a tea break. A little imp of a boy from the nearby tea stall turned up with a moss-green glass of tea in a wire-tray. His loose, flapping khaki shorts, criss-crossed with patches, reached his heels. They were obviously a gift from a kindly constable. A thread from the hem of a sari fastened them at the waist.

'How dare you come to the police station in a state of partial undress, boy!' said the inspector. 'What for—to show off your impressive physique? One of these days I'm going to put you in jail. That'll teach you.'

The boy laughed, his bright white eyes shining. He was obviously used to the banter.

The inspector raised the glass to his lips and stopped. 'Hey, there's a dead ant floating in the tea.'

'You expected an elephant?' replied the boy, jumping off the veranda.

The audience tittered. The inspector roared with laughter. I waited for the hot tea to splash from his shaking glass and stain his lungi.

But nothing of the sort happened, and the fellow put the glass on the table. He threw back his head and laughed for a long time.

'What do you want to be when you grow up?' the inspector asked the boy.

'Police.'

'So you can have free fish?'

'And also free oil to fry it.'

'Wait until I catch you. I'll have the hide off your back.'

'I'll file a complaint with the police.'

'Oh, my God, in that case I'll invite you to play dice.'

There was a familiar, practised ring to the exchange. Had I heard it before?

The inspector raised his ruler and made as if to fling it at the boy. The little scamp took to his heels.

'The little devil!' the inspector said. 'He's so quick. Not even the governor can match him when it comes to repartee.' He swept an imperious glance over us. 'Back to business. Hurry up! The sun's getting hotter. Very soon I'll be thirsty. A new fresh fruit juice shop has opened in Balikuda. Who's going to stand us the first drink of the day?'

The second man had his complaint recorded. It turned out to be a case of a missing cow. The poor little beast had been gone four days, and he had looked for her everywhere. A black cow that had calved only twice so far. She gave a litre of thick, sweet, creamy milk twice daily, and had a white spot the shape of a crescent moon on her head. She was extremely gentle—didn't even shake her horns or swish her tail to whisk off a fly.

The inspector joked with the complainant even as he jotted down the details. 'What's today—Tuesday? Isn't today the Jagatsinghpur cattle market day? My hunch is you'll find your black cow there. If I bring back your cow, will you send me a litre of milk and paneer every other Sunday for a year?'

Then it was my turn. The inspector fixed me with a detective-like stare. Maybe he thought he was Sherlock goddamn Holmes or something. 'My guess is you're in college,' he said.

'What else?' I retorted in a devil-may-care way.

He gave me a hard look. Then he burst into a guffaw. 'You've been holding your pee for a long time.'

'Really?'

'Oh, yes! Why else would a young man like you sit tucking his legs in like a woman?'

Truth be told, I badly wanted to pee. 'Go on.'

'No, you go on. Out with your name and address. For the record state your father's name. Make it quick, we don't have all day. Keep the long queue in mind. Oh God, what am I to do—sit here and take down first information reports or go and make on-the-spot enquiries? The station writer's on long leave and I, the inspector, have to do both!'

After I mentioned my father's name, the inspector put his pen down and stood up. 'Our former magistrate's son? Guess what. From the moment I saw you I've been trying to think where I have seen this face before, why it looks so familiar? Dear boy, I'm truly angry with you. Why didn't you tell me who you were the moment I arrived? You didn't have to sit here on this chipped cement bench waiting for me! My residence is right behind the office, not some six or seven miles away, and you could've gone straight there. Who told you to wait here?'

He wiped his face with the corner of his lungi and hollered: 'Agani, Nityanand, where are you bastards? Bring another chair. Quick. This is our former magistrate's son!' He looked at me. 'The eldest or the middle? I can't believe that any of our ex-magistrate's sons has grown so big.'

A constable dragged out a chair with a broken arm.

'So, does the sahib come home sometimes?' the inspector continued. 'Or does he stick to his office in Koraput? I've never seen anyone so keen about his job, and I've seen quite a few in my time, mind you. Certainly, no other magistrate with so little vanity! Whenever he saw me he'd pat me on the back and ask after my children.' He turned to the constable. 'Nabaghan, run along to the tea shop and bring our guest a glass of tea. Make it special tea. And ask the chap to add cardamom and ginger. And yes, if there're any freshly fried potato chops, pick up half a dozen or more. Hurry.'

I was beginning to feel uncomfortable with this fuss. It was all going too far; I didn't want to be entertained like a cherished guest or something. All I wanted was have my complaint recorded and return home and sleep.

'Someone's stealing our firewood regularly,' I began.

'Stealing firewood? What thief could be that petty?'

'It's been going on for quite some time. When the pile started going down fast, we decided to keep watch. Last night....'

'Did you catch the thief red-handed?'

'No. Yes.'

'A man or a woman?'

'A woman most likely.'

'Could you place her?'

'She ran away before I could reach her.'

'Of course she'd run away. What did you expect—wait for you to catch her so she could put her arms around you and thank you?' The inspector gave a croak of a laugh and bit his tongue. 'This tongue of mine is my own worst enemy. Always quick with the wisecracks. Someday it'll land me in deep shit. Won't be surprised if I say something outrageous in the presence of a superior and he takes my job away. Never mind, continue with your complaint. Where were we? Yes, you saw the thief from a distance. Where were you when you saw the thief?'

'I was on the veranda covered in a blanket. Our garden is huge and the cowshed is some hundred yards from the gate. Late in the night—I'm not sure about the exact time—a woman opened the gate and entered the garden. The cowshed is never locked—just a bamboo trellis door. She pushed it open and went inside. After a while she came out with a bunch of firewood on her head.'

'And you saw it all?'

'Yes. I'd forgotten to keep a stick handy.'

'A stick to beat the thief with? Go on.'

'When she was in the middle of the garden I ran towards her, flailing my upraised arms. She threw the firewood on the ground the moment she saw me and broke into a run. But instead of heading for the front gate she made for our backyard.'

'And you chased her?'

'I did. But I was scared too.'

'Go on.'

'She stumbled and fell. Perhaps she tore her sari; perhaps she broke one or two bangles. But before I could pounce on her she leaped up and bolted away.'

'If only you had laid a finger on her when she was down. She'd have remained curled up like a centipede until eternity and a day. What a missed chance! Did you collect bits of her broken bangles? Or a bit of her torn sari? Very necessary for identification.'

I shook my head. 'I was shaking all over.'

'Naturally.'

'I was frightened out of my wits.'

'Frightened, why? You knew the thief was a woman. Never mind, tell me, did you see her face?'

Just as I was wondering what to say and how much to reveal, someone got off his bicycle and salaamed the inspector. I looked at him. A thin, unsteady man, with a sunken face and protruding cheekbones, bloodshot eyes, grey stubble that seemed like a coat of ash on the face. The red police turban sat askew on his head and his khaki uniform was wrinkled like crumpled paper.

'Bholi!' the inspector bawled. 'Bloody Bholi, son of a gun, Guntayat! Where were you?'

Bholi Guntayat leaned his bicycle against the veranda and freed something wrapped in straw from the carrier.

'First, tell me who was buggering you and where. Imagine a constable missing from the station for two whole days and the inspector none the wiser.'

Bholi unwrapped the straw and took out a fish. A big fish, a rohu.

'Fuck the fish,' the inspector screamed. 'Don't show me the tail of a fish as if you've brought me a whale. I'm sure this rohu weighs less than three kilos. Bholi, you can shove it up your arse. No self-respecting police inspector would touch a fish this size with the long end of his baton.'

'Sir!' Bholi hung his head down, drawing lines on the ground with the tip of his worn boots. 'Sir, the thing is, sir...how do I put it, sir... forget it, sir, I have never been in worse trouble, sir, see sir, I'm boxing my ears and taking a vow in your presence, sir...I'm ready for whatever punishment you hand me....'

'Enough sir-siring. Don't think I don't see through your trick. Are you taking me for the son of a donkey? I'm going to put the screws on you one of these days. Unless I do, you won't remember that my name's Haradhan Pradhan, son of late Somnath Pradhan, grandson of late Sanatan Pradhan. Go. Take the fish to my residence and then run along with this young gentleman here to his village, Nuagaon. Make full enquiries about the theft and get back here before sundown. Make sure you bring the thief in tow, too. I don't care if it's a man or a woman or a bird or a frog or a ghost—I want to see the culprit handcuffed, with a rope around the waist.'

The inspector looked at me and beamed. 'I'm sending this man with you. All you've got to do is point out the suspect to him, that's all. The rest is his job. Most of my constables might be thin, but they're efficient. At least none is scared of a woman. How could anyone be scared of a woman?'

III

As I waited for Bholi Guntayat I mulled over the inspector's last words. The incident of the previous night was still vivid in my mind.

The fat, pot-bellied moon had climbed up to the middle of the sky, surrounded by a halo of white haze. Fluffy clouds, as white as soap bubbles, were scattered about the heavens. The moonlight made everything seem magical and mysterious: the spindly, one-legged coconut palms, their drooping fronds flapping like dogs' ears; the tamarind tree with its dark, impenetrable foliage, brooding like a temperamental child; the chakunda raintree, free and frivolous, its leaves folded for the night; flocks of night birds criss-crossing the sky, their wings not disturbing the stillness of the night. Far away, a wakeful dog howled. The night suddenly seemed to have many voices: the sound of something slithering over a bed of dry leaves; the keening of bamboos brushing against one another; the sharp, agitated call of a solitary bird separated from its flock.

A blanket over my head, I took in the magical night. I began to get aroused as I thought of girls. What would they be doing now? Fast asleep, lips and eyes shut tight, or getting aroused thinking of boys? Their breasts swollen like the earth after rain and their skins glowing. I once ran full tilt into a girl just as she was hurrying out of her class; the sensation of softness lingered for seven days. And because of the teasing of my friends I continued to blush for two whole days. My friend Ghana said, 'Sasank, you're damn timid; had I been in your place I'd have hugged and kissed that little thing no matter what the consequences.' Gazing into the heart of the thick moonlight I began to blame God for not making me as daring as Ghana. Why had he made me someone whose throat went dry, who stammered, whose heart thudded violently and who broke into a sweat at the sight of a girl?

I must have dozed off. The creaking of the bamboo door of the cowshed jolted me awake and I thought I saw a yellow ball rolling into its cavernous darkness. I started; my heart began to beat wildly. Throwing aside the blanket, I rubbed my eyes. I could not make out whether the cowshed door was open or shut. The moon had ducked behind a cloud. As if sucked into the vortex of a great silence, the world seemed to stand still. I felt light and bodiless—as when in the throes of great joy a moment seems like an aeon, or an aeon like a moment. Only when a trickle of steaming perspiration slid down my neck did I come up for air, breathless and chilled to the bone.

I stood up, listening intently.

Not a sound.

I climbed down from the veranda and headed for the cowshed. Halfway there, I saw someone coming out carrying a headload of firewood. Obviously a woman, in a yellow sari, but I couldn't make out her face.

With a weak cough I pressed on, despite my fear.

The moon came out from behind the cloud. The woman's bare arms twined around the load seemed to burn like molten gold.

The thief stopped short the moment she heard me. Instead of running away she stood still. What did she think—that she'd become invisible or could blend into the landscape like a chameleon?

A whiff of breeze would have felled me. I was light in the head, my legs wobbled; I couldn't take a step forward or back. My body was drenched but my throat was so dry it hurt to swallow.

'Who're you?' I asked, my voice breaking. It came out like gibberish, which even I couldn't make out.

She lowered the load of firewood and stood covering her arms.

'Tell me,' I croaked. 'Who're you?' This time I spoke slowly and clearly.

No answer.

I took a step forward.

A breeze sprang up. The end of her sari twirled up like an elephant's trunk. She raised her right hand. I thought she was going to brush it aside and reveal her face. Instead, she undraped the garment from her shoulders.

I began to tremble with fear, excitement, and God knows what else. This was the first time I was seeing a young woman's breasts up close. Not in broad daylight, true, but the full moon had never been brighter than on that night. It was bright enough to read.

'Who?' I asked again, but my voice was so weak I couldn't hear it myself. Or maybe, I hadn't spoken at all but simply imagined it. Who knew?

She ran a hand across her breasts.

I took another step.

Her breasts seemed to stare at me like round lidless eyes.

'Answer me while I'm still being polite,' I said in a hoarse whisper.

In reply, she covered her breasts and pulled up the hem of her sari to her belly.

It was dark and dangerous where her thighs met. Moonlight fell between her legs.

'Are you a human or a ghost?' I had already noticed she cast a shadow. 'Answer me or I'll scream.'

'Scream,' she said, stepping up to me, uncovering her face. Her eyes gleamed like red-hot embers.

I flinched.

She took another step towards me.

'You!' I couldn't believe my eyes.

Koili was grinning, her white teeth shining. I stared at her like a drowning dimwit.

Let me tell you who or what Koili was, otherwise you won't understand why I was so startled.

Five or six houses down from ours is the village weaver Pahala's house. He was by no means well off. Four days a week he didn't work his loom. Handwoven towels were costlier than mill-made ones, their colours not fast enough, and so his clientele had fallen. He had very few customers. Poor chap, he was forced to resort to a bit of stealing. A wrinkled old fellow, at fifty-five he looked eighty, with thin arms and thinner legs and poor eyesight. But barely six months after his first wife's death he had married again, this time to a very young thing. She was as thin as a stick when she first came to the village, but the wedding waters did wonders for her and in just a couple of months she metamorphosed into a beauty who made people stop and stare. Once she had put on the right amount of weight, in the right places, she looked like a ripe, juicy mango, ready to be plucked. Although the regrettable fashion of young women wearing blouses had caught on in the village, not every young woman, from eight to eighty, sported that stupid piece of attire. So, many people in the village had a chance to glimpse Koili's back or breasts, particularly when she leaned over the mouth of a well to draw water. These sightings only drove them even madder with lust. How could the shrivelled old weaver satisfy a young wench like her, was what boys and young men asked each other. Although I never took part in these discussions and treated them with a show of utter indifference, I was probably more heated up than the rest. In that state, I'd have sooner than later gone and grabbed her breasts or buttocks or done something as shameful. Mercifully, a rumour began to spread that Koili was a witch. After dark her light blue eyes became like the burning eyes of a wild cat. The colour of her tongue, pink during the day but pitch black at night, was like a snake coiled up inside her mouth. She went out in the dead of night to gorge on shit. Three or four villagers swore to having seen her at it. Apparently, she would take off all her clothes on the canal bank and walk upside down, head to the ground, feet in the air, and slurp up slop like a pig. Grass withered where she peed, and a hole would open up that reached down to the navel of the earth. Three young children had perished since she came to the village and a fourth was hovering between life and death. The well she drew water from had dried up earlier than others, or else its water turned bitter. Her husband aged twenty years in six months; she must have sucked his blood through a straw. She was an ugly duckling when she married but had become, in just six months' time, a striking beauty who could fell even a confirmed misogynist. No ordinary witch, this one. She could suck anyone's life out with just a sideways glance. If you met her face to face on a moonless night, you'd perish in an instant; on a full moon night she'd make love to you so fiercely that she'd steal all your semen and have you run around her like an impotent dog for the rest of your life—which wouldn't be more than a week, anyway.

That was the woman who now stood smiling at me in the moonlight. She began to run her long, tapered, witch-fingers across her breasts. I shivered so uncontrollably that I feared I'd fall into a swoon. Strange things were happening to me. One moment I wished I were dead, the next I felt I was roasting over a cold fire of sexual excitement I didn't want to ever end.

'How can you be sure I'm a ghost or a human unless you touch me?' Koili said in a breathy whisper.

She loosened the knot of her sari at the waist. My eyes were riveted on her breasts.

With a smile she started walking towards our back garden, her sari trailing behind her. The dust, stones, and dew on the grass were of no consequence to her.

I followed her like a mesmerized sheep. She stopped in the middle of the garden, turned, and faced the moon and me. I stopped two or three steps from her. She dropped her sari; all she had on was the black thread around her waist, her glass bangles, and a dot of vermilion the size of a quarter-rupee on her forehead.

The moon overhead became fierce, casting its white light on the garden. The place seemed to catch fire. The breeze became warmer. I started to sweat again.

She moved towards me.

I stood as if turned to stone.

Our bodies touched. The heat from her body seemed to singe me. My sweat turned to blue smoke and clouds floated up into the sky. Her breasts were round and firm like chitou cakes; and the nipples, jutting out like spikes, pricked me.

Her icy left hand caressed my thighs and I shivered like a patient in the grip of malarial fever. She placed her right hand on my shoulder and lifted my dead left hand and placed it on her left breast. I don't think I had ever touched anything as soft and as spongy. As I leaned against her, trembling like a leaf in a storm, she undid the buttons of my damp shirt; her nails seemed to scratch and draw blood from my chest.

The bamboo clumps started swaying even though there was no breeze. A crow began to caw. Blood rushed to my brain and my head felt so heavy that I thought my neck would break. Koili's scent overwhelmed my senses: her body seemed to give off several odours and fragrances all at once, a unique blend of sweat, unwashed clothes, sun-baked earth, coconut oil, overripe jackfruit, yellow kaniar flowers—sharp, fruity, intimate, fleshy—a smell that would make the lame scale mountains, the wingless fly, non-swimmers cross the seven seas. It suddenly struck me that if I made love to her I'd be burnt to cinders, and that I'd explode if I didn't; one moment

I was a ball of fire, the next, a block of ice.

The moon went behind a cloud again. Koili did not seem human.

'Are you really a witch?' I asked.

She smiled silently, but I felt the earth shake. Perhaps like the bat's her voice was too high-pitched to be heard by humans. The world went oddly silent as I watched her smile widen.

'I eat people alive,' she whispered. 'Tell me which part I should start with.'

She held me so tight I thought she had become part of me. I was choking with desire. 'Witch, witch, witch,' I repeated like a dull student trying to learn a difficult word.

'I'm going to chew you up and you're going to enjoy it too.'

And I was ready for it.

She folded her sari in four and spread it on the ground between the dew-drenched grass and the moon. It was as if a gossamer yellow bed was floating in the void. Pressing a finger against my chest, she lowered me to the magic bed. The sky seemed so blue that it hurt my eyes. There were just a few popcorn stars scattered here and there. Koili's long black tresses were outlined in the moonlight. Her shadow fell on me, covering my entire body, as if swallowing me whole. I fought not to faint.

Just as she was lowering herself onto me I sat up suddenly. For no reason the bamboos began beating against each other, as if a school of monkeys were jumping about in the clump. Birds of all kinds began calling. A tomcat started mewling. A thick, dark cloud blotted out the moon and in the dim light hundreds of snakes—of all colours, shapes, and sizes—slithered out of their holes entwined around each other. Some coiled around Koili and their hoods swayed, coming out from her hands, breasts, and thighs. Was this all a dream? Some kind of furry animal—difficult to say what, mouse or puppy—brushed past me.

Someone started coughing and couldn't stop. Doors and windows started banging. The snakes sneaked off to their lairs, the bamboo clump became still, the birds suddenly fell silent. Koili pulled her sari out from under me, her face split in a grin that was more a grimace, her teeth gleaming blood red in the moonlight. She seemed to have fangs, her canine teeth appeared needle-sharp, her long tongue twirled out and swayed, like a snake's split in two—wet, red, ravenous. And before she ran off she spoke under her breath: 'You're damn lucky, you Brahmin boy. Damn lucky. Another moment and you'd have been my dog for life. But don't worry, you won't escape me. I'll come again under the pretext of stealing firewood from your cowshed. I'll come soon. Be ready.'

A strong beam of light dazzled my eyes and I felt I was hurtling down from a great height. I screamed—an endless, silent, blood-soaked scream of fright, longing, and loathing.

Someone splashed cool water on my face. When I came to I found myself surrounded by my mother and younger brothers. They were armed to the teeth—stick, knife, axe, and sickle. I was making a weird guttural sound and had wet my pants. To this day, I don't know whether I had come in my pants or just peed.

I was carried to the veranda. My mother went to inspect the cowshed. When she came back she asked, 'Were you not able to recognize the thief?'

I nodded my head: Yes, no, yes, no....

'Who was it?'

I continued to nod my head.

'A man or a woman?'

'Don't know,' I croaked, my voice hoarse.

IV

'So you didn't know!' Constable Bholi Guntayat mocked.

Bholi had wormed out of me what I had kept from everyone—from my mother, my brothers, the police inspector. But I tried to throw him off: the thief simply resembled Koili, it could easily have been someone else, my suspicion was entirely unfounded, my eyes could have played a trick on me.

We weren't more than a mile from the police station when Bholi's bicycle had a flat tyre—it exploded like a firecracker. Leaving it in the custody of a roadside grocer he sat on the crossbar of my cycle. He wanted to sit on the carrier at the back, but I told him I wouldn't be able to keep control over the two-wheeler. He said the crossbar would eat into his bum, which would ache for a fortnight and need hot mustard oil with salt rubbed into the sore spot. Every fifteen minutes he wanted me to stop so he could get down to ease his pain. I made faces at his red turban and deposited droplets of spit on its crest.

'So how's this Koili of yours to look at—an eyeful?' Bholi suddenly asked.

'What do you mean?'

'Is she dark or fair, short or tall, slim or fat, sweet or sour? You get my point?'

'No, I don't.'

Bholi turned his head a hundred and eighty degrees and gave me a broad wink. 'What are you trying to keep from me?'

'Look, I don't suspect her at all. Her name simply slipped from my lips.'

'All right, this bitch Koili isn't a thief. Fair enough. But tell me, what does she look like?'

'Like any other witch.'

'Thick black lips, protruding teeth, black tongue, large forehead, spiky hair, duck feet, thick thighs jutting from a slim waist, breasts as big as pumpkins?'

'Didn't care to note all that.'

Bholi dragged his left foot along the ground and forced me to stop. He patted his sore bottom and lit a bidi. 'Sir,' he said. 'I can't conduct this enquiry. I'm scared shitless of witches. If someone tells me there's a witch in some village, I skirt past it. To tell you the truth, I'm scared to go to my own village, Nadeigarh, east of Sahdevpur. People make fun of the name. Until a year ago there was a witch in this village. She's since been neutralized, unmasked. Fisherman Madhua's daughter-in-law, she came to our village when she was sixteen, maybe seventeen. She had two miscarriages in the first two years of marriage. That was when an ugly rumour raised its head that this beautiful young thing—Nitei was her name—was sucking her father-in-law's blood. Madhua was around fifty-five, broad as a sal tree from casting the fishing net, his arms thick as maces and as hard, his skin light, with a shock of curly black hair hanging down over his eyes. He played the part of Lakshman in the village Ram Navami performances. He was handsome enough to appear as Ram—look here, don't mind my saying this because you're a Brahmin—but the whore-fucking Brahmins of our village would never let a fisherman play that role. So Dharmu Rath, that stick of a mean Brahmin bastard played the part of Ram, but the women in the audience only had eyes for Lakshman. When Madhua began shrivelling up, with a malady of an unknown kind, naturally people started talking. His son was a peon at the government printing press in Cuttack, and over and above his regular salary he made a fair amount on the side by selling stolen paper and ink. Plus, he had free meals at his boss's place, where he doubled up as a cook. He didn't have to spend a rupee on himself and was rolling in money, as you can imagine. He took his father to the town hospital and showed him to the best doctors. Madhua returned to the village with a big bundle of medicines, but his health continued to deteriorate. He began to avoid company, took to hiding from everybody. By day he didn't stir out. He would only take a pee or a shit long after nightfall, rushing through them like a newly married young woman. That bull of a man shrank to a twig in just a few months. Some said he came face to face with the water goddess, others said his hopeless condition was brought on by eating the liver of some poisonous fish. When medicines failed, quacks and witch doctors were called in. He was treated for the evil eye. Nothing worked. One day a sadhu arrived in the village. Six feet tall and as much in width, skin like liquid gold, his white beard reaching his navel. He had a pair of brass tongs that weighed not less than seven kilograms. The villagers came to him with their problems. In the end they mentioned Madhua's plight. The sadhu asked them several questions and finally wanted to see the man. As soon as he reached Madhua's house he began to bellow: "Arre salaa behenchod, this is the den of a blood-sucking witch!" The villagers couldn't believe their ears. The news crackled around the village that a witch was sucking Madhua's blood and that she was none other than his own daughter-in-law, his own son's wife. The sadhu asked her to come out, but she wouldn't. "Bitch," screamed the sadhu. "I'm going to break your poison tooth today." After many a threat she shuffled out. A tall, strapping female, in full bloom—you know what I mean? All high hills and deep valleys. An undulating landscape. And her complexion? Ripe wheat. Nobody would ever have suspected she was a witch—just didn't look like one, you know. Not to ordinary eyes, not to yours or mine. But the sadhu's were something else. He could sniff out a witch from a mile away. He asked Nitei to stick out her tongue. After much hesitation she did. It was pink like everybody else's, but the sadhu noticed six black spots. He asked her to show him her nails and when she did they seemed no different than ours, but the sadhu said he found horizontal cracks and black spots on them too. He asked to see her feet. To us they looked all right—five toes and all in front, and not too crooked either—not webbed like a duck's. But the sadhu let out blood-curdling screams: "The bitch has mastered the art of covering her tracks. We have to see her hidden parts." Madhua sat in a stupor throughout all this. The sadhu pulled him to his feet and herded him and his daughter-in-law into a room he locked from inside. They stayed there almost an hour and when they emerged the daughter-in-law, tears streaming down her cheeks, admitted to sucking her father-in-law's blood.'

V

'You know what,' said Gandharb, rolling the empty bottle across the terrace.

I stopped.

We were silent for a while.

'Sucking the father-in-law's blood is all bunkum,' Gandharb continued. 'The young woman was sleeping with him. It was an acute sense of guilt that was doing the man in.'

'Don't think this didn't occur to me while Bholi Guntayat was telling the story,' I said. 'Brother, I learnt the ins and outs of sex three seconds after I was born, if not earlier, and have been chasing girls ever since. I told Bholi the same thing but he wouldn't buy it. He said he had suspected that too. But in his village attractive young girls were not exactly in short supply and where Madhua was concerned any young thing would gladly have parted her legs for a handsome hunk like him. So, he had no good reason for bedding his daughter-in-law.'

Then Bholi told me another story: 'There was another witch in the neighbouring village. I've forgotten her name. She was already very old when we were children. She was so dark we called her Night. And what a vocabulary of swear words she had. Sometimes we'd provoke her just to hear them. She didn't spare her own husband and sucked his blood. The poor man suddenly began to lose weight and shrivel up without any kind of visible ailment. "What's wrong with me?" he wondered. "Why am I drying up for no reason?" The more concerned he became the less he slept well. One night he lay sleepless, eyes shut, when he heard his wife stirring restlessly. He opened his eyes a crack to see what was the matter and would you believe what he saw? The woman took a piece of straw from under her pillow, stuck one end between her lips and the other to his neck and began to suck his blood. The man got the shock of his life. He pretended to thrash about in his sleep and gave the woman a mighty push, sending her sprawling. Then he sprang up and pinned her down, sitting on her chest. The night passed and when the morning came he drove her out of the house. She went mad. Shortly afterwards he married a young thing. Some people said the crummy old bastard wanted to marry a second time so he turned the old woman out, branding her a witch. Who knows the truth! Truth is the hardest thing in this world to know. I sometimes think there's nothing called absolute truth.'

VI

'Wait a sec,' Ramesh said. 'I'm dying to pee.'

'I've got a bad taste in the mouth,' complained Arun, 'from not having a smoke in a long time.'

We laughed.

A meteor streaked across the night sky. Before I could alert the others it was gone.

Gandharb began to sing an old Hindi film song, which we all loved to death, and his voice was suddenly so tremulous that Siva said, 'Be careful. You might wake up the young girls in the neighbourhood, and they'll come rushing here.'

The breeze dropped. Swarms of mosquitoes descended on us.

Siva put a brick under his head. 'A hard pillow heightens one's wisdom.'

Ramesh leaned over the terrace parapet and peed.

'Be careful,' Siva warned. 'Piss like a bull—in spurts, so no witch can climb up the line of your pee.'

'Don't worry,' Ramesh reassured him. 'I'll stop when she's just a hand away. She'll crash to her death. I love peeing from heights, that's what I always do. You remember how I peed on the policemen when there was a strike on campus last summer?'

I picked up a small stone and threw it at him, missing, of course.

'If you look up at the moon while peeing,' Gandharb commented gravely, 'you lose your power.'

'What power?'

'Your sexual power.'

Arun sighed deeply. 'I badly need a couple of beautiful young witches to drain mine. I have so much I might burst.'

'Spill your seed thrice a week. That'll help you until the witches take pity on you.'

Siva took a crooked cigarette from his shirt pocket; it had no fewer than eight bends. He looked for the matchbox, and we all searched our pockets. Finally, we found it under a leaf plate, but there were no sticks. We got very upset with Arun for having wasted seven or eight matchsticks.

'Don't worry,' he said. 'I'll sing Raga Deepak and invoke fire.'

Ramesh came back and lay down. 'Go ahead, Sasank.'

'Where was I?'

'On the canal bank road. You and Bholi Guntayat were on your way to your village.'

VII

Oh yes. Bholi Guntayat, that snake of a constable. Don't underestimate him, he was a policeman to the marrow of his bones: he had managed to extract from me every bit of information about Koili—her age, looks, husband's age and profession, their relationship with the villagers. Twice, he made me stop on the way and treat him to tea. After all, he was coming to conduct an enquiry into our case, so he had to be kept in good humour. He continued to prattle on. He had lots of problems: last year's cyclone had completely destroyed his crops; his eldest boy became a failure because of his mother's pampering—he had flunked class eight three times already; his wife never felt she had enough jewellery and was always demanding more. Police Inspector Haradhan Pradhan might talk and act like a clown but was an ace investigator, the only problem with such a competent boss being that he'd pocket everything himself and leave the constables only the crumbs. A young superintendent who was honest to the bone had been posted to the district and came on inspection twice a month. He suspended two inspectors and four constables for dereliction of duty. The police force was the butt of jokes; no one was prepared to accept that policemen were ordinary human beings underneath their khaki uniforms and red turbans.

From time to time he'd assure me: 'Wait until I lay my hands on that Koili. I'll make her sorry she's a witch. I'm going to put a rope around her waist and drag her all the way to the police station. If I don't rid her of her witchcraft I'll change my name and ask you to name your pet dog Bholi Guntayat! Just you wait, you bloody witch. I'm coming to straighten out every bend in your body. Choose what you want to be—a witch or a thief. You can't be both. I'm going to take the sari off your arse and horsewhip you.'

Our village was just half a kilometre away when he got off the bicycle. 'It won't look good if we reach the spot together. Jump on your bicycle and be off. I'll follow you on foot. Look here, sir, I'm dying of hunger. Tell your mother to give me some lunch right away. Hot rice with dal and vegetables will be enough. I shouldn't expect fish at short notice. Don't worry, I'll find my way to your house. It must be the only two-storey building in the whole village.'

It was half past one by the time I reached home. My tummy was growling with hunger, my throat was dry, my mouth stank like dank mud, and my body was caked with sweat and dust. My younger brothers were overcome with excitement; avid readers of the detective novels churned out by Kanduri Das and Yogendra Mohanty, they wanted to follow the police investigation up close.

After Bholi Guntayat reached our place the villagers gathered there too. Bholi, however, shooed them off: 'Get a move on, go run your errands for now, I'll call and question you one by one once I've had a moment to myself to catch my breath. I'll ask each one all sorts of questions, but all in my own sweet time. Anyone who disturbs or distracts me or doesn't cooperate with me will have the bloodthirsty Haradhan Pradhan to contend with. Is that clear? Now, off with you.'

I took a bath and kept Bholi company at lunch. He ate like it was his last meal, praising Ma's prawn curry with spinach to the heavens. Then he took a nap.

I was so tired my eyes closed before lunch was over. I slept so soundly and so long that when I woke up it was twilight, and I couldn't make out whether it was day or night. I looked for a twig to brush my teeth, and my younger brothers tittered. The youngest was whining: Bholi Guntayat had made off with his magnifying glass—he had borrowed it and conveniently forgotten to return it. Ma was angry with him: 'Serves you right. Who asked you to lend it to that monkey face of a constable? One look at him and I knew he'd be the last person to catch the thief.'

I washed my face and decided to take a walk to the bazaar. On the way I saw Koili come out of her house with a lighted wick, which she placed at the foot of the sacred basil plant in front of her house with a deep bow. Our eyes met and her mouth widened in a grin that set the three worlds quivering.

'Did she brush her sari off her shoulder and show you her breasts again?' Gandharb asked. Before I could answer, he added, 'If I'd been you I'd have grabbed her the way a male frog grabs a female, even if it landed me in the clink!'

'Don't brag,' said Siva. 'Save it for strangers. We know you through and through.'

A white cloud sailed by. 'What if it rains wine now?' asked Ramesh.

'I'll keep my mouth wide open,' I answered.

'Then you'd better finish your story before it rains.'

'I don't think I will. You people have interrupted me once too often.' I was tired, my mouth dry.

So my friends begged me to continue, showering me with outlandish promises they had no intention of keeping if only I would finish—ten movie shows, five dinners in the city's best restaurants, a trip to Puri, virgins from Kashmir and what not.

I groaned, I farted, I sighed. With a great show of reluctance I told them the rest of my tale.

VIII

I didn't find out the details about the investigation—how it got underway, whom Bholi Guntayat questioned, whom he threatened, whose homes and barns he inspected—because early next morning I went to my uncle's place, where I promptly fell ill and was bedridden for two weeks. Only on the last two days of my convalescence did I feel cheerful enough to sit up and play cards in the afternoon. A sweet young thing, my uncle's neighbour's daughter, dropped in on both afternoons but I could make no great headway with her. Only once did I brush my hand against her left breast. The results of the matriculation exams were out and I had to apply for a college seat. Naturally, I had forgotten all about Bholi Guntayat. Besides, firewood no longer went missing from our cowshed. At least for the time being. I was after Ma to buy me a pair of terry-cotton trousers and bush shirts, but my brother played the spoilsport, demanding the same treat. Father hadn't sent money home for the last three months, and Ma stayed away from spending like a monkey from water.

A couple of days later I went to the bazaar to drink tea and have a smoke on the sly. It was then that I ran into Bholi Guntayat. He seemed to be in a tearing hurry, the way he was pushing on the pedals of his bicycle. I called out to him. 'Hello, there! Where're you headed this evening?'

'Oh!' Bholi stopped when he saw me. 'So?'

'So?'

'How are you?'

'How are you? What happened to the enquiry?'

'Going on.'

'How long will it go on?'

'Let's see.'

'And how are *you*?'

Bholi looked up at me. For some inexplicable reason I gave him a broad wink.

Bholi leaned his bicycle on a slender custard apple tree by the roadside; the sapling bent backwards. Bholi couldn't have cared less. He gripped my arm and dragged me to the tea shop, ordering special tea with a lot of cream on top.

'Want a cigarette?' he asked. 'Have you started smoking?'

When I turned down his offer, he took a bidi from his breast pocket. 'In that case let me make do with a khaki cigarette,' he said with a croak of a laugh. With a pair of tongs he picked an ember out of the fire and lit his bidi. He took two hefty drags and, linking his fingers in mine, gently dragged me out of earshot.

'So what's new?' he asked.

'You tell me.'

'What's there to tell! I'm swamped with work and haven't a moment to breathe in peace. Crime seems to be multiplying faster than human beings: a theft here, a murder there, and a rape somewhere else—no end in sight. What can the police do? We're too few and completely stretched. But don't think I won't figure out the case of the mysterious theft of firewood from your cowshed. I'm determined to catch the thief.'

'We heard the police had already reached an understanding with the culprit!' It was a shot in the dark, but it seemed to hit home. Bholi Guntayat winced.

'Is that the talk in the village?'

'Of course!'

'Who can stop people from talking? Every time there's a little delay in an investigation, this is what they come out with.'

'Yes, professional hazard.'

'You said it.'

'So you don't suspect Koili any longer?'

Bholi winced again. An inch of ash fell from his bidi straight into his bulging breast pocket.

I stared at him, surprised.

'Who's Koili?' he stammered.

So Bholi had forgotten about Koili, I thought with delight. Good.

'Oh, are you talking about the old weaver's young wife? You were absolutely right when you insisted she wasn't the one who stole firewood from your cowshed. You know something, I scared the daylights out of her. I told her I'd drag her to jail and keep her there for seven days without a drop of water or a morsel of food, but her behaviour didn't give me the slightest cause to suspect her. You know, you can't fool us police fellows. We catch on to a twitch, a batting of an eyelid, a puckering of the lips—nothing escapes our notice; we can sniff out a criminal from five miles away. The job has given us some kind of a sixth sense. But don't think I didn't keep my eyes on that girl! I did, but the more I saw her the more I was inclined to agree with you. She was simply incapable of stealing even a piece of straw, let alone firewood. But that doesn't mean I've cleared her entirely. I'm still investigating her. I still make surprise visits and inspections. We policemen have our methods.'

I smiled.

God knows why it rattled him, he began to babble. 'You know something, sir. She might not be a thief but she's no saint either. She's full of crap.'

'How did you find out?'

'Like I said, we can sniff.'

'Her shit?'

'The woman.'

'You sniffed her?'

'Just an expression, sir. Are you thinking I buried my nose into her or something?'

He looked around and fished out another bidi from his pocket. His hands trembled when he lit the match; the horse head label stuck on the matchbox wobbled. He took off his red turban. Without it he looked helpless and vulnerable.

'You ill or something?' I asked.

'No, why?'

'You seem run down.'

'Do I?' He looked around as if afraid someone might be eavesdropping. 'The thing is...' His voice trailed off. He puffed at his bidi thoughtfully. 'The thing is....'

The smoke stung my eyes and I stepped back. A swarm of insects descended on us, and I waved my arms frantically to fight them off.

'The thing is,' Bholi tried again, his voice a hoarse whisper. 'Is this what the villagers are gossiping about?'

'About what?'

'The police enquiry and all, and my frequent visits to the village.'

'I don't know. I've been away from the village for over a fortnight. Returned only recently.'

'Good you were gone from the village.'

His face looked different, unlike his own. He sounded so unlike himself too.

'Tell me, do you believe in witches and spells and all that mumbo-jumbo?'

'Why bring that up?'

Bholi started a third time. Clutching his head, he sighed. 'My brain's completely addled. Conducting enquiries and investigations day in and day out has done me in. I'm going completely mad. If Haradhan Pradhan hears of this he'll twist my neck. There's a rumour he might be transferred. I hope to God he will, and soon.'

'By the way, did you take my brother's magnifying glass by mistake?' I asked, suddenly remembering.

'Magnifying glass? Whatever's that?'

Bholi Guntayat seemed to have regained his composure. He was back to playing the insensitive buffoon. He wouldn't let me pay for the tea. He promised to wrap up the investigation within eight days, nab the thief, and drag him to the police station, a rope around his neck.

I reminded him the thief was a woman.

'Thieves dress up as females to mislead the police,' he said.

'What do female thieves dress up as—males?'

'Fairies.' Bholi Guntayat laughed as he took his bicycle.

I returned home.

The following night a stack of firewood was stolen from our cowshed.

'It's started again,' Ma said.

'Don't ask me to go to the police station a second time,' I said. 'I'm off to Bhubaneswar this afternoon to collect college admission forms.' *An Evening in Paris* was showing at Ravi Talkies, and word had it that the heroine wore a bikini and flaunted a goodly amount of her golden skin.

'What will I do when there's no more firewood left—shove my legs into the oven and burn them?' Ma wanted to know. I kept quiet. A wisecrack would have been disastrous. Ma would have slapped me, and if I got away she'd have slapped herself, which would have been worse.

'Ma,' I said. 'Last evening, I ran into Bholi Guntayat. He said he'd complete his investigation in the next eight days and arrest the thief.'

'To hell with Bholi Guntayat.'

I had never heard Ma swear before.

'Don't ever mention his name in my presence,' she fumed.

'Why, Ma? What's the matter? What can he do? He's trying his best.'

'Trying his best, my foot.'

'How can you say he isn't trying? He said he's been coming to our village every two or three days.'

'That's just it! Why does he come every two or three days? What does he do here? Who is he investigating?'

'So what is it he does here?'

'What do I know?'

'Tell me, Ma. You seem to be keeping something from me.'

'Forget it.' Ma walked off.

IX

Gandharb yawned, cracking his knuckles. Arun seemed to have fallen asleep. Ramesh and Siva, covered from head to foot to keep away the mosquitoes, were quiet, difficult to say if they were still awake. The night too seemed asleep. Not a sound.

I looked up at the sky. An aeroplane seemed to be flying at a great height, its red tail light blinking. A night bird flew by. Who was it looking for—parents, children, wife, husband, lover, mistress, witch, who?

'You never met Bholi Guntayat again?' Siva asked suddenly, his voice hoarse with phlegm.

That startled me; my heart gave a lurch. I spat on my chest to calm myself down.

'So it was constable Bholi Guntayat's great good fortune,' said Ramesh, 'to enjoy that delicious witch of yours!'

'God knows who enjoyed whom—the constable the witch, or vice versa.' I said. 'Do you guys remember a piece of news in the papers around four years ago? A small news item in a box: Constable Missing. That was just about a week before my college admission. The news crackled around the village that Koili the witch had vanished. Her old husband looked for her everywhere—in the bushes of the cremation ground, in the waters of the village wells, in ponds, ditches, and rivers, everywhere. That went on for five days and only afterwards did he go to the police station to file a report. It was there that he learnt that Constable Bholi Guntayat too was missing. The man had left behind his red turban, his tiffin box, and his bicycle. Why a middle-aged man with a wife and children and landed property had chosen to disappear nobody could say, nor with whom.'

TWO OLD KIPPERS

SIDDIQ AALAM

Translated from the Urdu by Muhammad Umar Memon

'...sleeping as quiet as death, side by wrinkled side, toothless, salt and brown, like two old kippers in a box.'

—Dylan Thomas, *Under Milk Wood*

RECENTLY TWO PENSIONED OLD MEN IN CALCUTTA MET BY CHANCE IN A public park. Six years ago, but on different dates, they had both retired from government service. Ever since, providence had been preparing for the day when they would be found sitting side by side on a single bench. Apparently, they had each lived their lives and were now trying to invest their remaining days in something useful. Having arrived at this point, they were still poles apart.

Since retirement, one of them could be seen every evening without fail—every evening, that is, unless he was out of town—on one of the wooden or concrete benches at the edge of the grassy patch in the park. He spoke very little, and when he settled down on a bench, he stuck his umbrella vertically between his legs and rested his chin on its handle. Usually, he preferred a bench that was remote and empty, but sometimes, when all of the benches were taken, he deigned to choose the one that had the least number of people and sat crouching in a corner so that if anyone tried to accost him, he could pick up his umbrella and leave without wasting a second. During these six years he had had surgery on his right eye, and most of his brows had turned grey. The crown of his head was bald, and in the last light of the evening he often looked like a corpse that had escaped from the morgue of the nearby medical college and crossed the street to come here. All in all, his face seemed to be that of the ideal government pensioner who'd left everything that was his inside the walls of his office building.

The other old geezer, because he'd retired from the railway service, was able to get two free travel passes, which he used to visit places within the country. His addiction to gambling, acquired in his youth, had nearly ruined him. But now, at the tail end of his life, he mostly went to see religious sites, such as those at Varanasi, Puri, Tarkeshwar, etc. He'd also bought a little hut in a hermitage at Puri so he could spend his last days in peace. But mentally he wasn't yet ready for that, so, instead, he spent his days leafing through newspapers, or sitting idly and dozing on the terrace outside his building, or going to the public park. Now and then while dozing, he unconsciously found himself standing on the Antipodes with the waves of the Pacific swelling up around him. But all he could see, even on the waves, were racehorses swimming, or playing-card jokers rowing boats, or whirlpools circling around him like a roulette. These Antipodes had stuck in his mind since his school days when his geography teacher had resorted to using a globe to explain the true shape of the earth.

One evening, when a tired sun was breathing its last on the kadamb and karanj trees planted outside the park's perimeter wall, a chubby-cheeked boy was seen crossing the grassy patch escorted by his nanny. Noticing the two old coots sitting side by side, the boy, for some strange reason, began laughing and kept on laughing for quite a while as he repeatedly turned around to look at them. The first old man was still trying to figure out what might have made the boy laugh when he heard the sound of another laugh. Without thinking he turned sideways to look. It was another man, about his own age, perched on the other end of the bench.

'Why was the kid laughing?' he asked the other man in spite of himself, although it was the laugh of his own peer that was bothering him more than the boy's.

'Perhaps because he thought we're so old,' the other replied and started to laugh again.

'Well now, that's not so strange that you should laugh about it. At his age, I'd have laughed too.' He came to the boy's defence for no reason at all. 'And anyway what are old-timers for?' He was pleasantly surprised at his own magnanimity.

'What for? To burn in the Nimtala crematory—what else!' The second man tittered heartily. Then he stopped, leaned towards the first, and asked, 'Tell me a secret: would you allow them to perform an autopsy on you when you're dead?'

'What kind of question is that? And if they did, would I be there to stop them?'

'But you can. You can tell them in your will, I mean, if you die a normal death.'

To get off the subject the first man said, 'Oh well. We'll worry about it when we cross that bridge,' but deep inside the question had rattled him. For a while, he gazed at the immense field where giant tents and canopies were set up during the winter for the circus. The buildings outside the park rose high into the air like so many cardboard boxes, which some tiny hand might reach up and send crumbling to the ground any instant.

'But why was the kid laughing—really?' he wondered to himself.

Later, he was surprised to realize he'd blurted out a whole lot of things to that stranger—that didn't jibe at all with his reticent nature. Then, in quite a mysterious way, the two old men ran into each other the next evening, and again the following evening, and then every evening. Neither had asked for the other's name. They also avoided talking about personal matters, which was good; it helps prevent discussing many painful subjects.

One day, the second old man asked, 'Why do you always have an umbrella? Especially now when the weather is perfectly fine?'

'I feel defenceless without it,' the other replied unpleasantly. 'I've been lugging it around all my life. I can't give it up now. Impossible!'

'What kind of protection do you expect from an umbrella?'

'Why?' the other said irritably. 'There are many advantages, not counting the sun and rain. Suppose we're sitting on this bench and a snake slithers out of the grass right between our legs. We can at least defend ourselves with the umbrella. Or suppose you're late getting home one night and you take the Carmichael Hospital route where you find a body on the pavement. You can at least poke it with the umbrella tip to see whether it's alive or dead. And to tell you the truth, I can't even remember how many times I've used it to fend off attacks from stray dogs.'

'Wow! But you're forgetting one other advantage.' The other old coot was having a hard time suppressing his laughter. 'Say you're sitting on a bench and you're afraid you might have to face this man you really don't want to see, so you snap your umbrella open and hide comfortably behind it. Isn't that something? Ha-ha-ha!' He was laughing heartily, as usual.

'Have you ever been a circus clown?'

'No. But I've wallowed enough in the Hooghly mud to be a turtle,' the old man retorted.

There was a fence on three sides of the area of the park earmarked for the circus, and a row of dense and not-so-dense almond, kadamb, ashoka, chatiyan, and karanj trees ran along it. Beneath the trees, at suitable intervals, wooden or concrete benches had been placed haphazardly. Around this huge area a blacktop path had been laid out for strollers. When the lights came on in the buildings outside the park, the area was submerged in a kind of semi-darkness in spite of a few halogen lamps installed by the city. Many couples came here to take advantage of the semi-darkness. They sat on the thick carpet of grass and spent time enjoying the nice, cool breeze. The two old coots just looked at them indifferently, as if they had no interest in whatever strange acrobatics were going on in that darkened spot. They had stopped holding forth critically on society's many different ills a long time ago anyway.

'Life's an awfully tiring game,' the second old man said philosophically one day. 'That fellow above,' he pointed at the sky, 'is a mighty dangerous scorekeeper. No matter how many goals you score, he cancels them out in the end and you're left with a big zero.'

'Have you started thinking about dying?'

'What good would dying do? Even if a tree stops flowering or bearing fruit, even if no leaves sprout on it, it's still better that it stays put. If nothing else, at least snakes and squirrels can find refuge in it.'

In the fading daylight their eyeglasses would light up as if somebody had carried off two mannequins from the show window at the Grand Hotel and set them down next to each other. The first old man was used to wearing a dhoti and kurta, so he appeared much older than his companion, who wore old-fashioned pants and a shirt.

'Judging by your clothes, you still look quite fit. Perhaps you'll live longer than me.'

'Don't curse me,' said the second man. 'My grandfather was already bedridden at fifty, but he dragged on for another thirty years. The old coot made life miserable for everyone. So, it's kind of difficult to say.'

Then he came up with an idea: 'Why don't we toss a coin? Heads you'll live longer, tails I will.'

Before the first old man could say anything, the other had pulled out a five-rupee coin and was holding it between his thumb and index finger, looking at him expectantly.

For a moment, the first old man stared at the other. His pupils didn't move and he appeared to be immersed in thought. Suddenly he leaned towards his companion and said, 'You take heads and leave the tails for me.'

A derisive grin splashed across the lips of the second man. He tossed the coin in the air. It went up, spiralled down in front of the bench, rolled, and then disappeared into the tall grass. They both got up from the bench and started looking for it. The second man stretched his hand out under the bench and ran his fingers through the grass. The first one thought it was his duty to provide moral support and joined in. They went on searching under the bench, behind it, and on either side, but the grass was so thick and the daylight penetrating that thickness so weak it seemed impossible to ever find the coin. Even so, the two old codgers went on rummaging through the grass until their fingers became soiled. Strollers passing by gawked at the two with wonder and amusement. Some even stopped to watch a while.

'Looks like those old geezers have lost their dentures,' a teenager mockingly commented. The two stopped searching and quickly sat up. They were holding on to the edge of the bench, panting as if they had travelled a long distance. Suddenly, their eyes met and they both realized the disappearance of the coin was in perfect accord with their wishes. Suppose they *had* found it? At least they were happy now.

But the second old man wasn't satisfied. 'We can think of some other way, can't we?' he said.

'For instance?'

'You see that fellow coming toward us. We can ask him his name. If he turns out to be a Muslim you'll live long, and if he's a Hindu I will.'

'What if he's a Christian? Quite a few of them live in this part of town.'

The second old man shook his head, disappointed.

'In that case, we'll need a third party to play this game. But what's the use. This world is so divided on every issue there aren't enough coins in it to suffice.'

In spite of himself, the first oldster had started to take an interest in this game, all the while conscious that what was happening didn't sit right with him. But their meeting every second day had acquired the force of destiny. Every time he traversed the distance from his home to the park, supporting himself on his weak, spindly legs and his umbrella, he was always overwhelmed by a compelling desire to go back, but some invisible force kept pushing him to the other man and that familiar corner in the park.

'Do you realize,' the second old man brought it up again, 'we can still do a lot to make our remaining time meaningful.'

'What do you want me to do? Start working again? Or join some social movement?'

'Of course not!' the second man smiled. 'Old men like us aren't good for anything. We have to stay the way we are. I do feel, though, that a hermit's life, the fourth state in which old men live in the wilderness and practise renunciation, is about right for us. This will cure the world of many ills. The new world will belong to new people. What do you think? I've gone so far as to buy a small hut in a hermitage. All it needs is a bathroom, which will be built soon. It's right on the edge of the sea.'

'I lost my faith during the Hindu–Muslim riots of 1947, or rather, I threw it into the fire.'

'That's strange.'

'Isn't it, though?'

'And you think this will bring peace to your soul?'

'Well, at least it's made me rise above these filthy events and look at them dispassionately.'

For some reason the second old man started grinning again.

'You know what?' he whispered. 'We should try again. Maybe this time we'll succeed.'

'What difference would that make? Whoever dies first, it will be the same for the other. Sooner or later we'll all be on our pyres. But if you insist, all right....'

'Oh no, I wasn't joking. I'm quite serious. All right, let's just let it hang for a while. God knows I occasionally begin to fear you.'

Sometime during the afternoon it had rained and the smog had been cleared from the sky over Calcutta. The stars appeared large and bright in the sky. The second old man shifted uneasily on the bench. Perhaps he'd arrived at a fresh decision. He lifted his finger and pointed towards the Pole Star that had risen with the sunset.

'You see it, don't you, shining right between the two almond trees? It's my guess that in half an hour it'll be over the top of the tree on the right. Let's walk around the grounds once. If the star doesn't reach there by then, you'll live longer.'

'Who wants to live longer? Even so, if you must insist....'

The two old-timers started to walk along the edge of the blacktop path. The first man was intentionally walking fast, followed by the other, who was plodding along slowly on his long, spindly legs.

'You're walking fast,' the second old man said from behind laughing. 'Looks like you're hell-bent on living long.'

'That's nonsense,' said the first old man, slowing down because his heart was beating quite fast, which made it hard to breathe. 'This nonsense is not likely to alter the course of nature.'

'Then why are you practically running? You'll ruin your heart. Remember your age.'

'You're really a pest,' said the first old man as he continued walking. 'You should have been in politics. That kind of work suits your kind of dirty people.'

Without bothering to look behind him, he kept walking and covered half the distance in the dim light. The second old man had been left far behind and was shaking his head meaningfully. The first one stopped to catch his breath.

'If you walk so slowly, you'll miss the Pole Star.'

He heard the other shoot back from behind, 'Shut up! Can't you stop blabbering? Your mouth stinks, dirty old man.'

He started off again, but with each step his heart pumped so hard he felt as though a hefty hammer was pounding away inside his ribcage. Time and again he would stare up at the sky. He felt as though all the stars were rushing forward, as if they too were hell-bent on defeating him. He started to walk even faster, so fast that cold beads of sweat started to sprout on his skull. He could also feel traces of muted pain in his chest which quickly grew so intense that he promptly sat down on the ground, clutching his umbrella tightly. As he drew quick, deep breaths he felt as though the people and lights around him were fusing together in the cool atmosphere pervading the area.

The second old man was standing in front of him, grinning.

'If you run so fast, this is what you have to expect. It's not good for your health. So greedy and at such an age!'

Rubbing his chest, he ignored his interlocutor. His chest pain was beginning to subside a bit. He got up, took a few steps on his wobbly legs and stopped again. The pain had returned.

'Let's drop this foolishness,' said the second old man, gently rubbing the other's back. 'Where in the world have you heard of a star moving? Why would it inch its way to the top of a tree? It's the earth that moves and gives this mistaken impression.'

The first old man was pissed off. Grabbing his umbrella, he pointed the tip at the other man, making a gesture, and mumbled something.

'Don't get mad,' the second old man said. 'Looks like you're not feeling well. Shall I take you to your house?'

'Go to hell!' the first one pushed the other's hand aside rudely. 'I don't need your help to get home. But I do feel we should rethink our acquaintance. Perhaps we're not meant for each other.'

And tap-tapping his umbrella, he started walking in the dim light of the field towards the park's southern gate. The second old man shook his head in disappointment.

'Strange! Why should it be my fault if the stars don't move?'

The next day he arrived at the park somewhat early, wondering how his companion was doing. But the old coot couldn't be seen anywhere. And he didn't appear for the next two weeks either, although the second old man went about methodically looking at every bench. A feeling of guilt began to stir in his heart: maybe the joke wasn't suitable for a man his age, he thought. One day, he simply couldn't stand it any more and set out to look for him. He'd always seen him come into the park through the southern gate, so he went out that gate and started walking along a fairly big street. He wandered in and out of the many small streets and alleys that branched off from it. He stared at the windows and balconies of buildings hoping to spot him somewhere, until night descended on Calcutta. Suddenly, a dog materialized from somewhere, lifted one of its hind legs and started to pee on his shoes. By the time he realized what was happening, it was too late. The dog was already gone. Vanquished and unsuccessful he returned home with wet feet. He washed his socks and hung them to dry on the line in the balcony.

'Oh Lord, could he have died?' he wondered, pressing his eyes.

Three days later, he suddenly saw him, but on a different bench and in a different corner. He leapt towards him, but before he could reach him the first old man snapped open his umbrella and hid himself behind it. Stopping in front of the umbrella, he smiled, cleared his throat, and said, 'I'm sorry for what happened that day.'

The umbrella didn't reply.

'Yesterday, I tried to look for you. But perhaps that was a foolish thing to do. To tell you the truth, I don't even know where you live, your street or your house number.'

The umbrella remained silent. The second old man gave a long, cold sigh.

'I've decided to go to the hermitage. That's all I'm good for now. I can give you the address if you like. It's a nice place. You would like it. You can stay as my guest for a week or two.'

The silence continued. Finally, he admitted defeat, turned around, and left the park.

Three years later, he returned to Calcutta. It was two o'clock and the park was deserted. On the grounds in front of him, a little boy was playing with a rubber ball under an almond tree. As soon as the second old man entered the park his feet carried him to the same old bench that stood in its place, somewhat skewed, as if it had all happened yesterday. He sat quietly on the bench for a long time. The trees' shadows grew longer, stretching across the field. It seemed as if the circus had just left a few days ago because potholes could be seen everywhere and there were animal droppings here and there. Remembering his old companion, the man smiled. Who knows, he might meet him again on this very bench. And if he did, he would tell him about life in the hermitage, about the tranquillity and peace he had found there. He would tell him how nice it felt to walk along the edge of the sea, with the land behind and nature's azure secret stretched out in front of his eyes. The sea from which Brahma and his progeny had emerged, from which every living creature had crawled like a fledgling just hatched from an egg. Look, old fellow, if you're listening to me, if you want to live long, if you truly believe in living, you must consider abandoning the cares and noise of the city. The city's demands gnaw a man completely hollow from the inside. I wouldn't be surprised at all if one day people began withdrawing inside themselves. God knows what kind of ribs keep them from deflating or what strings help them walk.

He remembered all the wagers he'd put to the other man. And how, despite appearing indifferent on the outside, deep inside they were both anxious to win, as if their whole life depended on some insignificant coin or the movement of the Pole Star. What if his companion *had* won! The sky wouldn't have fallen. If one really takes stock of a man's entire life objectively, would it be so wrong to say that he has nothing to lose or gain?

His reverie broke to find the little boy standing before him.

'You want something? What are you looking for?'

'My ball,' the boy said hesitantly, pointing with his finger under the bench. The old man turned his head and looked behind the bench where a pink ball was waiting to be rescued from the small jungle of green grass. The man stretched out his hand to pick it up when something suddenly glittered on the wet ground beneath the grass.

'Good God!' Handing the ball to the boy, he stood his frail body up on its legs, went behind the bench, and squatted in front of that shining object. It was a coin, a five-rupee coin, its Ashoka column side facing up. Wet from a recent shower, the coin was sending a shaft of cool, dim light towards him.

'Heads!' he screamed. His mind raced back to the time three years ago when the first old man had bet with him one evening about living a long life. 'So, *I* won the bet that day. What a miracle! How strange, this coin's been lying here all this time!'

He pried the coin from the wet dirt, returned to his place on the bench and started rubbing it between his thumb and index finger. The boy was kicking his ball under the almond tree. The jagged edges of tree shadows had advanced quite far and were touching the fence around the field. He realized time had flown by and he raised his slumped shoulders.

'Curse me! The one who said that in the end it's a man's character that counts was right. I'll probably remain a worthless old man till the day I die.'

He got up, wiping tears from his wrinkled face, and walked over to the grass behind the bench. He stuck the coin back in the wet dirt under the grass with its tail side pointing up.

TIRICH

UDAY PRAKASH

Translated from the Hindi by Poonam Saxena

This incident is connected with Pitaji. And with my dream and also with the city. And with my inborn fear of the city.

Pitaji had turned fifty-five. He was thin, his hair was absolutely white like the down on an ear of corn. It was as if his head was covered with cotton wool. He used to think a lot—far more than he spoke. When he did speak, we would be relieved, as if breath that had been held for long finally escaped. At the same time we would also be afraid. It was a big mystery for us children. We knew that the vault containing all the knowledge of the world was with Pitaji. We knew that he could speak all the languages of the world. The world knew him and, like us, gave him respect even as it feared him.

We were proud to be his offspring.

Sometimes, though this would happen only a couple of times in many years, he would take us with him when he went for an evening walk. Before setting off, he would fill his mouth with tobacco. Because of the tobacco, he would be unable to say anything. We would find this silence very grave, splendid, wondrous, and solemn. If, along the way, my younger sister tried to ask him something, I would immediately try and reply, so that Pitaji wouldn't have to speak.

Actually, this task was difficult and fraught with risk. Because I knew that if my answer was wrong then Pitaji would have to speak. That would be difficult for him. For one, he would have to get rid of the tobacco juice, and then, because he lived in another world, it would be hard for him to come out of that world and travel from there to here. Though there was nothing special about my sister's questions. For instance, what do you call that bird sitting on the dry branch of the tree in front of us? And since I knew all the birds I could tell her that that was a blue jay and it was important to see it on Dussehra day. I tried to ensure that Pitaji would not be disturbed and left free to continue with his contemplations.

My mother's and my own wholehearted effort was to see that my father lived in his own world happily and peacefully. He should not be forced out of there. It was a very mysterious world for us, but Pitaji solved many problems about our home and our lives while remaining there. Like the time the question of my fees arose—at that time all the glasses had vanished from our house and everyone was drinking water from a lota. For two days Pitaji was completely quiet. Ma too wondered if he had forgotten about the fees or whether the solution to this problem was beyond him. But early in the morning on the third day, Pitaji gave me a letter in an envelope and sent me to Dr Pant in the city. I was very astonished when the doctor gave me sherbet to drink, took me inside the house, introduced me to his son, and gave me three hundred-rupee notes.

We were proud of our father, we loved him, we feared him and having him with us, being with him, made us feel as if we lived in a fortress. A fortress that had deep moats dug around it, with high turrets, whose walls were made of hard red rock, a fortress that was impregnable from any outside attack.

Pitaji was an extremely strong fortress. Inside, in that enclosed space, we forgot everything and would run around and play. And I would sleep soundly at night.

But that day, in the evening, when Pitaji came back from his stroll, there was a bandage tied around his ankle. After a while, quite a few people from the village arrived. It turned out that Pitaji had been bitten by a tirich, a poisonous lizard, in the jungle.

All of us knew that no man could survive the bite of the tirich. At night, in the hazy and dusty light of the lantern, many people from the village gathered in our courtyard. Pitaji sat in the middle, on the ground. Then Chuttua, the barber from the neighbouring village, also turned up. He was known for drawing out poison with leaves from the castor oil tree and ash from dried dung.

I had seen a tirich once.

There was a crack in one of the rocks among the pile of enormous rocks near the pond. These rocks became very hot in the afternoon. I saw the tirich come out of that crack and go to the pond to drink water.

Thanu was with me. He told me that this was a tirich, it had a hundred times more venom than a black cobra. He was the one who told me that a snake bites you only if you step on it accidentally or tease it deliberately. But a tirich charges the moment you look into its eyes. It comes after you. You should never run straight if you want to escape from it. You should run in a zigzag fashion, or in circles, round and round.

Actually, when a man runs, he doesn't merely leave the imprints of his feet on the ground, he also leaves his own scent in the dust. The tirich chases this scent. Thanu told me that to trick the tirich, a person should first run fast for a short distance, taking small steps, feet close together, and then leap forward in four or five long jumps. Sniffing all the while, the tirich will come running, it will speed up when it comes to the marks of the feet that are close together, but it will get confused when it comes to the point where the person took long jumps. It will keep wandering, lost, till it locates the next set of footprints with the scent trapped in them.

We knew two other things about the tirich. One, the moment it bites someone, it runs away and urinates somewhere and then rolls about in its own urine. If the tirich does this, the person it has bitten cannot survive.

If he has to survive, he must—before the tirich wallows in its own urine—take a dip in a river, well, or pond or kill the tirich.

The second thing is that the tirich rushes to bite you only if you have looked into its eyes. If you happen to see a tirich, you must never look into its eyes. The instant that happens, it recognizes your scent and goes after you. After that, you may circle the whole earth, but the tirich will never stop chasing you.

Like many of the other children, I too was very afraid of the tirich. The two deadliest characters in my nightmares were the elephant and the tirich. The elephant would at least get tired after running for a while and I would escape by climbing a tree, or flying into the air but with the tirich I'd get caught in a web of sorcery. If I was going somewhere in my dream, I would suddenly come across the tirich, there was no fixed spot where this would happen. It wasn't as if I would only see it in the crack of a rock or behind old monuments or near some bush—it would appear in the bazaar, cinema hall, shop, or even in my own room.

In my dream I would try not to look into its eyes but it would gaze at me with such familiarity I wouldn't be able to stop myself and that was it, the moment my eyes would meet its eyes, its gaze would change—it would start running and I would take flight.

I would run in circles, take quick, small steps, suddenly jump long distances, try and fly, climb up to some high point, but despite a thousand attempts, it never fell for any of my tricks. It seemed very cunning, clever, wily, and dangerous to me. I felt as if it knew me very well. That familiarity shone in its eyes and looking at that glow I sensed that this was one enemy that was aware of every thought that entered my head.

This was my most terrifying, tormenting, fearful, disquieting dream. My body would be exhausted with all that running, my lungs would inflate, I would be drenched in sweat, become breathless, and a frightening, numbing kind of death would creep even closer. I would scream, start crying. I would call out to Pitaji, Thanu, or my mother and then I would know it was a dream. Despite knowing this, I also knew very well that I could not escape this particular death. Not death—murder by the tirich—and that's why I would try my best to wake up from my dream. I would exert my full strength, open my eyes wide inside my dream, try to see the light and say something out loud, forcefully. Many times I did succeed in waking up at the last minute.

Ma told me that I had a habit of talking and screaming while dreaming. Often she would find me crying in my sleep. She should have woken me up in such situations, but she would gently stroke my forehead, cover me with a quilt, and I would be left alone in that terrifying world. In my feeble attempt to escape my death—or rather, my murder—I would run, flee, scream.

But slowly, with experience, I worked out that making a sound in such situations was my only weapon to escape the tirich. Unfortunately, every time I would remember this weapon at absolutely the last minute, when it was *this* close to getting me. I could feel the breath of my impending murder actually touch me, I would be engulfed by a lifeless yet frightening darkness full of the intoxication of death, I would feel as if there was nothing solid beneath my feet—I was in the air and then that moment would arrive when the end of my life was near. At that point, in that infinitesimal and fragile moment, I would remember this weapon of mine and I would start speaking very loudly and I would come out of the dream. I would wake up.

Many times Ma would ask what had happened to me. At that time I didn't have enough command over the language to tell her the whole story, to narrate every single thing the way it happened. I was well aware of this inability of mine and that's why I would be filled with a strange kind of tension, disquiet, and helplessness. In the end, defeated, all I could say was, 'It was a very frightening dream.'

⸻

I don't know why I had this fear that the tirich that bit Pitaji was the same one that appeared in my dreams and whom I recognized.

But the one good thing was that the instant the tirich bit Pitaji and ran, he followed it, and killed it. If he hadn't killed it immediately, the tirich would have urinated and then rolled about in its own urine. Then Pitaji could not have survived in any circumstance. That's why I was not overly worried about him. Instead, I felt relief and happiness because of that. One reason was that Pitaji had killed the tirich instantly and the second was that my oldest, most dangerous, foe had finally died. It had been slaughtered and now I could go anywhere I wanted in my dream, carefree, whistling, without any fear.

That night, the crowd stayed till late in our courtyard. Charms, incantations, invocations were going on to cure Pitaji of the bite. The wound had been torn open and the blood drained out, it had then been filled with the red medicine (potassium permanganate) that was put inside wells. I was not worried.

The next morning Pitaji had to go to the city. He had to appear in court. There was a summons in his name. Buses travelled to the city on the road that skirted our village by around two kilometres. There were barely two or three of them in a day. Luckily, as soon as Pitaji arrived at the road, he saw a tractor going to the city from a nearby village. The people sitting inside were known to him. The tractor would reach the city in two to two and a half hours. That is, much before the court was to open.

On the way, the matter of the tirich came up. Pitaji showed those people his ankle. Pandit Ram Avatar was also in the tractor. He explained that a specialty of the tirich's poison was that sometimes it would begin having an effect after twenty-four hours, exactly at the time the tirich had bitten the person the previous day. That's why Pitaji should not be entirely relaxed. The people in the tractor drew Pitaji's attention to another big mistake. According to them, Pitaji had done the right thing by killing the tirich immediately, but after that, the tirich shouldn't have been left like that. At the very least it should have been set on fire.

These people claimed that many insects and living things came alive again at night in the light of the moon. The dew and chill present in moonlight contains nectar and it has often been noticed that a snake left for dead and thrown away carelessly in the night becomes wet with the coolness of the moon, comes to life again, and slithers away. After that, it is always on the lookout for revenge.

The people in the tractor were worried that the tirich, after coming to life again at night, would urinate and roll about in its urine. If that happened, then twenty-four hours later, at exactly that moment, the tirich's fatal venom would start taking its effect on Pitaji. Their advice was that Pitaji should go back at once and, if he found the body of the tirich where he had left it, he should burn it thoroughly and reduce it to ashes. But Pitaji told them it was important for him to appear in court. This was the third summons and if he did not appear this time, there was the possibility that a non-bailable warrant would be issued. The appearance in court was to do with the house in which our family lived. He had not been able to pay the lawyer his fee on two previous occasions and if the lawyer displayed the slightest carelessness and the judge decided to be whimsical, he could declare us bankrupt.

It was a peculiar situation—if Pitaji got off the tractor to go back to the village to burn the tirich's body, then he could be arrested on a non-bailable warrant and our house would be taken away from us. The court would turn against us.

But Pandit Ram Avatar was also a vaid. Apart from the astrological almanac, he had a deep knowledge of roots and herbs. He suggested that there was a way by which Pitaji could appear in court as well as save himself from the tirich's poison. He said that the essence of Charak was the formula that venom itself is the medication for venom. If he could get the seeds of a datura plant he could prepare the medicine needed to cut the tirich's poison.

The tractor stopped at the next village, Samatpur, and a datura plant was finally found in the fields of an oil merchant. The medicinal extract was prepared by grinding the datura seeds and then boiling them along with an old copper coin. The extract was highly bitter so it was mixed in some tea and Pitaji was made to drink that tea. After that everyone was relaxed and reassured. The idea was to protect Pitaji from grave danger.

Actually, I knew a third fact about the tirich, which I suddenly remembered some hours after Pitaji had left. It was similar to that fact about snakes because of which the camera was invented.

It is believed that when a man kills a snake, the snake takes a proper, close look at the face of its killer before dying. As the man kills him, the snake looks at him fixedly, registering every minute detail of his face in the retina of its eyes. Once it's dead the man's picture is clearly imprinted on the snake's retina.

Afterwards, when the man has gone, a second snake, the partner of the dead one, peers into the latter's eyes and is thus able to recognize the killer. All the snakes start recognizing him. He can go anywhere after that, but they will forever be ready and waiting to take their revenge on him. Every snake becomes his enemy.

I was worried that Pitaji's face had been imprinted on the retina of the dead tirich. Some other tirich could come and peer into the eyes of the dead one and recognize Pitaji. I began feeling uneasy. Why had Pitaji not been more alert to this possibility? After killing the tirich, he should have taken a stone and smashed both its eyes. But what could be done now? Pitaji had left for the city and I was faced with the problem of finding the exact spot—in that vast, spread-out jungle near the village—where he had left the tirich after killing it.

Along with Thanu, and with a bottle of kerosene, matches, and a big stick, I stumbled around in the jungle looking for the tirich. I recognized it well. Very well. Thanu didn't have much hope that we would find it.

Then, all of a sudden, I sensed that I knew this jungle intimately. Every single tree looked familiar. This was the place where I ran in my dreams to escape the tirich. I looked around carefully—it was the very same place. I told Thanu about the narrow canal that flowed south a little distance from here. Above the canal, there were big rocks and an old keekar tree with massive beehives on it. They looked as if they were several centuries old. I knew that particular brown-coloured rock, which was half submerged in the stream throughout the monsoon, but could be seen fully after the rains, when mud and slush filled its cracks, and strange, weird-looking vegetation grew out of those cracks. The rock was covered with a layer of congealed moss. The tirich lived in the topmost crack of this rock. Thanu thought I had imagined all this.

But very soon we found the stream. And the aged keekar tree with its beehives, as well as the rock. The dead tirich was lying flat on its back on the grassy ground a little away from the rock. This was the very same tirich. A thrilling sensation of violence, excitement, and a kind of joy ran through me.

Thanu and I gathered dry leaves and sticks, poured a whole lot of oil on it and set it on fire. The tirich began burning in that fire. The smell of its burning flesh spread in the air. I felt like shouting at the top of my voice but I was scared I might wake up and all this might turn out to be a dream. I looked at Thanu. He was crying. He was a good friend of mine.

This was the place from where the tirich would emerge and chase me many times in my dream. I was surprised that I had known where it lived for so long, but I had never tried to come there during the day and finish it off.

Today, I was recklessly happy.

Pandit Ram Avatar told us that the tractor passed the toll tax booth in the city at around quarter to ten. They had to wait for a bit while the toll tax was being paid. Pitaji got off the tractor to relieve himself. When he came back he said his head was swimming a little, by then it had been about an hour and a half since he had drunk the medicinal extract of the datura. The tractor dropped Pitaji off in the city at five or six minutes after ten. According to Master Nandlal of Palra village, who was also travelling in the tractor, when Pitaji was dropped off at the crossing near Minerva Talkies in the city, he complained that his throat was feeling dry. He was slightly worried because he didn't know the way to the court and he disliked asking people for directions.

That was the problem with Pitaji—he remembered all the little paths in the village or jungle, but he would forget the streets in the city. He rarely went to the city. When he had to go, he would keep postponing the date of his departure until he could not delay it any longer. Many times it so happened that Pitaji left for the city with his luggage, but came back from the bus terminus itself. The excuse was that he missed the bus. Whereas we knew that nothing of the sort had happened. Having seen the bus, Pitaji would have gone and sat somewhere—gone for a pee or to eat a paan. Then he would have seen the bus leaving. He would have waited a little longer. When the bus picked up speed—he would have run behind it for a short distance. Then his feet would have slowed and he would return, expressing annoyance and disappointment. By doing so, he would actually believe that he had missed the bus. We, who had assumed that he had left for the city, would be astonished to find him back home.

There is only a hazy picture of everything that happened to Pitaji in the city from seven minutes past ten when he got off at the crossing near Minerva Talkies, bang opposite Singh Watch Company, till six in the evening. This information was also pieced together after talking to people and making enquiries. You get such information after somebody's death, especially if that death has occurred in a very unexpected, unnatural manner. An accurate and detailed account of where Pitaji went and what happened to him on that day, Wednesday, 17 May 1972, from seven past ten till six in the evening, a period of about seven hours forty-five minutes, is hard to get. A rough idea of the events that happened can be gleaned from the information and reports that came in later.

Like Master Nandlal from Palra village saying that Pitaji complained of a dry throat from the point when he got off the tractor. Before this, near the toll tax booth, when he had come back after taking a leak, he had mentioned that he was feeling dizzy. That is, the medicinal extract from the datura was already having an effect on Pitaji. In any case, by the time he reached the city, it had been two hours since he had drunk it. I am guessing Pitaji would have been extremely thirsty by then. He would have gone towards some hotel or dhaba so that he could moisten his throat but, knowing his nature, he would have stood there for a while, unable to make the decision to ask for a glass of water or not. Once he had recounted how, a few years ago in the summer, when he had asked for water in a hotel, one of the servants working there had abused him. Pitaji was very sensitive, that's why he must have suppressed his thirst and left.

There was no information forthcoming from anywhere as to where he went between about ten and eleven o'clock, a period of around forty-five minutes. Nothing out of the ordinary happened in this period that anybody could say. It was difficult to find out whether any passers-by on the street saw him or noticed him. My guess is that during this time he would have asked a few people for directions to the court and thought that once he reached there, he would ask his lawyer, S. N. Aggarwal, for some water. But either people didn't reply to his queries and walked past quickly or they replied so irately, and in such a rush, that he would have been humiliated, upset, and distressed. This is usual in cities.

In these forty-five minutes, I suspect the effect of the medicinal extract would have become more pronounced. The hot May sun and his thirst would have made the effect worse. He would have stumbled a little and it is possible that during this time, he would have felt dizzy too.

At eleven o'clock, Pitaji entered the State Bank of India's branch in the city's Deshbandhu Marg. It is not clear why he went there. Ramesh Dutt from our village is a clerk in the city's Bhoomi Vikas Sahkari Bank. Maybe Pitaji just had 'bank' in his mind when he was walking by, so when he saw the words State Bank, he turned in there. He hadn't drunk water till then, so he probably thought that he would ask Ramesh Dutt for water, ask him the way to the court, tell him that his head was spinning, and also that last evening he had been bitten by a tirich. According to the State Bank cashier, Agnihotri, he was checking the cash registry at the time. There were bundles of approximately 28,000 rupees on his table. It was about two or three minutes past eleven when Pitaji arrived. His face was dusty and he looked ghastly and then he said something abruptly in a loud voice. Agnihotri said he got quite scared. Normally, such people don't manage to reach the cashier's table, which is set quite far inside the bank. Agnihotri also said that if he had seen Pitaji coming towards him a couple of minutes before, perhaps he wouldn't have got so scared. But what happened was that he was completely immersed in the accounts in the cash register when he suddenly heard Pitaji's voice, he looked up and, seeing him, got frightened and screamed. He also rang the bell.

As stated by the bank's peons, two watchmen, and other bank workers, they were all startled by the cashier's sudden scream and ringing of the bell and ran towards him. By then the Nepali watchman, Thapa, had grabbed

Pitaji and taken him towards the common room, hitting him all the while. Ramkishore, a peon, who was around forty-five years old, said that he thought some drunkard or madman had entered the office and because his duty was at the bank's main door, the branch manager could have charge-sheeted him. But what transpired was that while Pitaji was being beaten, he started saying something in English. This made the peons even more suspicious. In the midst of all this, the assistant branch manager, Mehta, perhaps said that this man should be thoroughly searched before he was allowed to leave. Ramkishore, the peon, said that Pitaji looked frightening, in a bizarre kind of way. On top of that, he was covered in dust and smelt of vomit. The bank peons denied that they had beaten him up badly, but outside, right next to the bank, was a paan shop and Bunnu the paanwallah said that when Pitaji emerged from the bank at about eleven-thirty, his clothes were torn and his lower lip was cut and bleeding. The skin below his eyes was swollen and blotchy. Such marks turn purple and blue later.

After this, that is between eleven-thirty and one o'clock, there is no information to be had about where Pitaji went. Yes, the paanwallah Bunnu did say something, though he was not totally clear, or it could be that he was afraid of the State Bank employees and so avoided recounting everything clearly. Bunnu stated that after coming out of the State Bank, maybe (he stressed the word 'maybe') Pitaji had said that the bank peons had snatched his money and papers. But Bunnu was of the opinion that Pitaji could have said something else too, because he was unable to speak properly, his lower lip was badly cut, there was saliva dribbling from his mouth and he didn't seem to be in his right mind.

My own guess is that by this time, the effect of the medicinal extract had become quite pronounced. Though Pandit Ram Avatar doesn't think so. He pointed out that datura seeds are ground with bhang on Holi as well, but it never happens that a person takes leave of his senses. Pandit Ram Avatar believes that the tirich's venom had started making its presence felt in Pitaji's body and its disorienting effect had reached his brain. Or it is possible that when the watchman Thapa and the State Bank peons were beating him up, he might have suffered an injury to the back of his head which caused him to lose his mind. But I feel that till then Pitaji still had some degree of awareness and he was making every effort to somehow get out of the city. It could be that since his court papers and his money had been seized from him in the bank, he thought there was no point in him staying on there. Perhaps he thought he should go back to the State Bank and at least retrieve his papers. But he may not have had the courage to go back there. He must have been afraid. This was the first time in his life he had been beaten like this, that's why he hadn't been able to think clearly. He was very thin and since childhood, he had been troubled by appendicitis. It's also possible that at that time, the effect of the medicinal extract was so overpowering that he was unable to concentrate on any one thing and, in the grip of thoughts that erupted every second like tiny bubbles in his brain, or because of the recent shocks to his system, he kept stumbling about. But I do know, I can feel it very distinctly, that the thought of leaving the city and coming home must have definitely been on his mind—a constant thought, emerging out of the darkness again and again, even if weak and muddled.

Pitaji reached the police station at around fifteen minutes past one. It is situated on the outer edge of the city, near the Victory Pillar that stands close to the Circuit House. The astonishing thing is that the court is barely a kilometre away from the police station. If Pitaji wanted, he could have reached the court in ten minutes. What we don't know is that though Pitaji had managed to reach there, was he still thinking about going to court? He didn't have his court papers with him.

The SHO of the police station, Raghavendra Pratap Singh, said that it was fifteen minutes past one at that time. He had opened the tiffin he had got from home and was about to have lunch. There was bitter gourd with parathas in his tiffin. He didn't like bitter gourd and he was irritatedly trying to decide what to do. That's when Pitaji arrived. He didn't have a shirt on and his trousers were torn. It seemed as if he had fallen somewhere or had been hit by a vehicle. At that time there was only one constable at the station, Gajadhar Prasad Sharma. He says that he thought some beggar had entered the police station. He even called out to him but by then Pitaji had reached the SHO Raghavendra Pratap Singh's table. The SHO said that he was anyway in a bad mood because of the bitter gourd. Despite thirteen years of married life, his wife still didn't know the things he disliked heartily, disliked so much that he positively loathed them. By the time he put a morsel of food in his mouth, Pitaji had got very close to him. There was vomit on his face and below his shoulders, which gave off a strong stench. The SHO asked him what the matter was. Whatever Pitaji said in response was very difficult to understand. Later SHO Raghavendra Singh was full of repentance. If he had known that this man was the pradhan of Bakeli village and a former teacher, he would have made him sit in the police station for at least two or four hours. He wouldn't have let him go out. But at that time he felt that this was some madman who had come in because he saw him eating, and that's why he angrily called out to Constable Gajadhar Sharma. The constable dragged Pitaji outside. According to Gajadhar Sharma, he wasn't violent with Pitaji and he noticed that when Pitaji had arrived at the police station, he had a cut on his lower lip. There were scratch marks on his chin, as if he had fallen and scraped it against something, and the skin on his elbows was broken. He had definitely fallen somewhere.

No one knows where Pitaji wandered for about one and a half hours after he left the police station. It was difficult to know whether he had even had any water from the time he entered the city and got off the tractor at the crossing near Minerva Talkies at seven minutes past ten in the morning. It seems unlikely. It could be that by then his mind was in no condition to even register thirst. But if he managed to reach the police station, there must have been a thought in his head despite the intoxication, no matter how feeble and drowned in darkness, that he could ask the way home, or the whereabouts of the tractor, or lodge a report about his money and court papers being snatched from him. It is deeply distressing to think that at this time, Pitaji was not just fighting against the venom of the tirich and the intoxication of the datura, but even in this state of groggy inebriation, he was worried about saving our house. Perhaps by then he had begun feeling that whatever was happening to him was nothing more than a dream, and he must have kept trying to wake up from the dream.

At about fifteen minutes past two, Pitaji was spotted stumbling around the northern limit of the city, in its most prosperous colony—Itvari Colony. This was a colony of jewellers from the commercial and money markets, big PWD contractors, and retired bureaucrats. A few well-off journalist-poets also lived there. This colony was always peaceful and incident-free. Those people who saw Pitaji here said that by this time all that was left on his body was his striped underwear, and since its drawstring was probably torn, he kept trying to hold it up with his left hand. Whosoever saw him thought he was a madman. Some people said that every now and then he would stand and shout words of abuse. Later, a resident of the colony, retired tehsildar Soni Sahib, and a special correspondent and poet of the city's biggest newspaper, Satyendra Thapliyal, said that they had heard Pitaji clearly and, in fact, he was not shouting abuse but he was repeating the words—'I am Ramsvarth Prasad, ex-school headmaster…and village head of…village Bakeli….!' The journalist-poet Thapliyal expressed his anguish. Actually, at that time he was going to a special party at the US embassy in Delhi to listen to music, he was in a hurry, so he left. Yes, the tehsildar, Soni Sahib, said that he 'felt very sorry for that man and scolded the boys too. But two or three boys said that this man was about to assault Ramratan Saraf's wife and sister-in-law'. The tehsildar said that after hearing this, he too felt that perhaps this man was actually a hoodlum who was just playacting. The boys were harassing him and in the midst of all this, Pitaji kept saying, 'I'm Ramsvarth Prasad…ex-school headmaster….'

If you were to calculate, from the crossing near Minerva Talkies where Pitaji got off the tractor at seven minutes past ten in the morning to the State Bank on Deshbandhu Marg, then the police station near the Victory Pillar and Itvari Colony on the northern tip of the city, all in all, Pitaji had wandered for approximately thirty, thirty-five kilometres. All these places are not in the same direction. This meant that Pitaji's mental state was such that he couldn't think things through clearly and would start walking in any direction. As for the matter of him going to assault Saraf's wife and sister-in-law, which Thapliyal Sahib thought to be true, my own assessment is that he had gone to them either to ask for water or to enquire about the road to Bakeli village. Pitaji must have been in his senses for that one moment. But they must have become frightened and started screaming, seeing a man with this sort of appearance coming so close to them. He got the injury to his brow, from which blood was trickling into his eye, at Itvari Colony itself, because later some people said that those boys began throwing stones at him.

The place where Pitaji received the most injuries is not too far from Itvari Colony. Pitaji was surrounded in an open space in front of a cheap dhaba called National Restaurant. The throng of boys from Itvari Colony that had started following Pitaji now included some older boys as well. Satte, a servant who worked at National Restaurant, said that the mistake Pitaji made was that on one occasion, he lost his temper and began throwing stones at the crowd. Probably one of the bigger stones that he threw hit a seven, eight-year-old boy Vicky Agarwal, who had to get many stitches. Satte said that the crowd became menacing after that. They were creating an uproar and pelting stones at Pitaji from all directions. The dhaba owner Satnam Singh said that at that time Pitaji was wearing only his striped underwear, you could see the bones on his thin frame and the white hair on his chest. His stomach had shrunk. He was smeared with dust and mud, the white hair on his head was dishevelled, there was blood oozing out of his lower lip and from above his right eye. Expressing sorrow and regret, Satnam Singh said, 'How was I to know that this was a simple, straightforward, respectable man and that a twist of fate had reduced him to this condition?' Hari, the servant who washed the cups and plates in the dhaba, said that in between Pitaji would hurl incoherent words of abuse at the crowd and begin throwing stones. 'Come you wretches... come...I will kill each one of you bhosdiwaalon...tumhari ma ki....' But I doubt whether Pitaji would have cursed in this way. We never heard him abusing ever.

I can say with complete confidence, because I knew Pitaji very well, that up to this moment, he must have thought again and again that everything that was happening to him was not real, it was a dream. Pitaji would have found these incidents absurd and meaningless. He wouldn't have believed them. He would have thought: what is all this nonsense? He has not come to the city from the village, no tirich has bitten him. In fact, there's no such thing as a tirich, it is a fabrication, a superstition... and all this talk of drinking a medicinal extract made from datura is laughable, that too after hunting for the plant in an oil merchant's field. He would have given the matter some thought and then discovered that, after all, why would anyone file a legal case against him? What was the need for him to go to the court?

I know that Pitaji too must have dreamt the dream that I did, a dream like a tunnel, long, hypnotic but scary. We had so many things in common. I believe that by now Pitaji would have been totally convinced that all that was happening was untrue and unreal. That's why he must have kept trying to come out of the dream. If he had started talking loudly, or perhaps shouting abuse, it was out of a desperate attempt to come out of the nightmare with the help of his voice. From what the employees of National Restaurant and its owner Sardar Satnam Singh said, it seems Pitaji sustained several injuries at this spot. Many stones and bricks hit his temple, forehead, back, and other parts of his body. Sanju, the twenty, twenty-two-year-old-son of Arora, the contractor who had the contract for that road, even hit him two or three times with an iron rod. Satte said that anyone would have died after receiving so many injuries.

I feel a strange kind of relief and my ragged breaths become normal when I think that at that point Pitaji would have felt no pain; because he would have become fully, deeply aware, with complete logic, that this was a dream and, as soon as he got up, everything would be all right. As soon as he opened his eyes he would see Ma sweeping the courtyard or see me and my younger sister sleeping on the floor...or a bunch of sparrows... maybe he would have, in the middle of it, even felt like laughing at this strange dream of his.

If, in his anger, Pitaji had started throwing stones at the boys, the number one reason was that he knew very well that these stones were being thrown in a dream and no one would be hurt. It could even be that after throwing a stone with all his might he would have waited eagerly and uneasily, thinking that the moment the stone struck some boy's head and broke his forehead, this nightmare would, with one jolt, scatter into little pieces and the light of the real world would come flooding in. Even his screaming was not out of anger. He was, in fact, calling out to me, my younger sister, Ma, or anyone else that if he was unsuccessful in waking up from this dream, then someone should come and wake him up.

A most distressing thing happened at this point. Pandit Kandhai Ram Tiwari, the sarpanch of our village panchayat, and Pitaji's childhood friend, went past the street in front of National Restaurant at about three-thirty. He was in a rickshaw. He was to take a bus from the next crossing to go back to the village. He saw the crowd that had gathered outside the dhaba and came to know that some man was being beaten up. He wanted to find out exactly what was happening. He even asked the rickshaw to stop. But when he made enquiries, he was told that a Pakistani spy had been caught trying to poison the water tank, and he was the one being beaten. Exactly at this time Pandit Kandhai Ram spotted the bus to the village and he asked the rickshawallah to hurry up and take him to the next crossing. This was the last bus to the village. If that bus had come three or four minutes later, he would have definitely gone and seen Pitaji and recognized him. The state roadways bus was always late by thirty to forty-five minutes, but that day, by chance, it was bang on time.

Satnam Singh said that the crowd in front of National Restaurant started drifting away and people began dispersing when Pitaji didn't get up from the ground for a long time. A big piece of a brick had struck him on his temple. Blood had started coming out of his mouth. There were injuries on his head. Satnam said that when Pitaji didn't move for quite a while, one of the boys in the crowd said that it looked like he was dead. When Pitaji didn't move even ten or fifteen minutes after the crowd had dispersed, Satnam Singh asked Satte to sprinkle some water on his face to ascertain if he had just fainted, in which case he would get up. But Satte was scared at the thought of the police. Afterwards Satnam Singh himself emptied a bucket of water on him. Because the water was thrown from afar, the mud on the ground got wet and stuck to Pitaji's body.

Sardar Satnam Singh and Satte both said that Pitaji lay there till about five o'clock. The police hadn't come by then. Then Satnam Singh thought that he could get stuck as a witness or become involved in the police panchnama so he shut his dhaba and went to see the film *Aan Milo Sajna* in Delite Talkies.

It was around six o'clock when Pitaji poked his head into the kiosk of a cobbler, Ganeshva, in a row of cobblers' shops on the pavement of the Civil Lines Road. By this point, he wasn't even wearing his underwear, he was crawling on his hands and knees, like some four-legged creature. He was covered with mud and black smudges and there were injuries on different parts of his body.

Ganeshva is a cobbler from our village, from the quarter beyond the pond. He said he got very scared and couldn't recognize Master Sahib. His face had become very frightening and you couldn't make out any distinguishing features. Terrified, he came out of the shop and began shouting. Apart from the cobblers, some other people also gathered there. When they peered inside the shop, they saw Pitaji crouching in the far corner amidst the broken shoes, scraps of leather, rubber, and other bits and pieces of junk. His breath was coming faintly. He was pulled out from there on to the pavement. That's when Ganeshva recognized him. Ganeshva said that he spoke into Pitaji's ear but he didn't respond. After a long time Pitaji said something like 'Ramsvarth Prasad...' and 'Bakeli'. Then he was silent.

Pitaji's death occurred at around quarter past six. The date was 17 May 1972. The tirich had bitten him in the jungle twenty-four hours ago, around the same time. Could Pitaji have predicted these events and this death twenty-four hours earlier?

The police kept Pitaji's body in the morgue in the city. The post-mortem revealed that he had many fractures, his right eye had been completely smashed, his collar bone was broken. His death occurred because of mental trauma and excessive blood loss. According to the report, his gut was empty, there was nothing in his stomach. This meant that the extract made from the datura seeds had already come out when he had vomited.

But Thanu says that it is clear now that no one can escape the venom of the tirich. It revealed its extraordinary magic exactly twenty-four hours later and Pitaji died. Pandit Ram Avatar also says the same thing. It could be that Pandit Ram Avatar says this because he wants to convince himself that the datura extract had nothing to do with Pitaji's death.

I think, I try and speculate that perhaps, at the end, when Ganeshva spoke in Pitaji's ear outside his shop, he would have woken up from his dream. He would have seen me, Ma, and my little sister—and then he would have taken his neem twig for cleaning his teeth and gone towards the river. He would have washed his face in the cold water, rinsed his mouth, and forgotten this prolonged nightmare. He would have thought about going to the court. He would have been anxious about our house.

But I want to talk about my dream, which I get quite often. It is this—I have reached the jungle after crossing the mounds marking the boundaries of fields, and the rough, narrow paths of the village. I look at the stream of water, the keekar trees. The brown rock is in the same place, where it gets submerged in the stream during the rains. I see the body of the tirich lying on top of it. I am filled with joy. In the end, it was killed. I take a stone and start pounding the tirich with it, I keep hitting it with great force. Thanu is standing next to me holding kerosene and matches. Then, suddenly, I find I am not on that rock any longer. Thanu isn't there either, there's no jungle, instead I am actually in the city. My clothes are badly soiled, torn, and have turned into rags. The bones of my cheeks stick out. My hair is in a mess. I am thirsty and I try to speak. Perhaps I'm trying to ask the way to my home, in Bakeli, and that's when abruptly, a clamour rises from all around...bells start ringing...thousands and thousands of bells...I start running.

I run...my entire body is fighting for breath, my lungs start ballooning. I take short steps, and then suddenly long jumps, try to fly. But the crowd is closing in. A peculiar, hot, heavy wind makes me numb. The gusts of my own murder start touching me...and finally that moment arrives when my life is about to come to an end....

I cry...try to run. My entire body is drenched in sweat in my sleep. I talk loudly in an attempt to wake up...I want to believe that all this is a dream...and as soon as I open my eyes everything will be all right.... In my sleep I open my eyes wide and see...far away in the distance...but that moment does arrive in the end....

Ma is looking at me from the outside. Stroking my forehead gently, she covers me with a quilt and I am left alone. Struggling and fighting to escape my death, I become breathless, cry, scream, and run.

Ma says I still have the habit of mumbling and screaming in my sleep. But the question that constantly bothers me is—why don't I dream of the tirich any more?

THE SMELL OF BAMBOO BLOSSOMS

YESHE DORJEE THONGCHI

Translated from the Assamese by Aruni Kashyap

INSTEAD OF FISH, RATS ARE SWARMING THE KAMENG RIVER—AN unprecedented phenomenon! These days, as soon as the sun sets behind the Rang Hills, lakhs of rats come out from the thick bamboo forests that sprawl on both banks of the river. The rats are not only destroying crops and marching around inside houses, chewing everything they encounter, but they are also swimming across the Kameng River despite its strong currents. Maybe they are trying to breed or are searching for food.

Along with the rats, people hunting rats has become a regular sight. As soon as the hundreds and thousands of rats run towards the river at dusk to swim across it, the riverbanks are flooded with people trying to hunt them. Every rat hunter holds two lathis and a torch—it's all they will need for the hunting expedition. The Kameng is a broad and deep river with such a strong current that it is impossible for people to swim across it even during winter when the water level is lower. But these little rats are so strong! They swim across the surging monsoon river from one bank to another, and then back again, so easily. When they are about to reach the bank, the wet and exhausted rats require some kind of support to crawl up. The people waiting on the banks hold their lathis out. The rats crawl onto those lathis. The hunters hold their torches between their teeth, and with another lathi, they hit the rats hard on their little heads. In this way, they create a hillock of rat carcasses on the bank by dawn. In a single night, they gather several bags of rats and that's how the villagers living near the Kameng River and in Seppa town earn some quick money. They skewer four rats with a small piece of bamboo after cleaning them, and hollowing out the intestines, smoke them for three-four days, and process them into tasty meat. Four cleaned and smoked rats fetch them twenty rupees in cities such as Itanagar or in the markets of Naharlagun. In places like Along in West Siang district and Pasighat in East Siang district, they can sell them at even higher prices. That's why the people living on the banks of the Kameng are happy with the bamboo blossoms.

Tarak Dadao went to the riverbank every day to kill rats. Saddled with debt incurred to pay for his wedding, this was a golden opportunity for him to earn some money. He was the one who discovered the bamboo blossoms deep inside the forest one day. He had carefully chosen the bamboo plants before felling them. With great effort, he had dragged them out, heaped them together with their leaves and twigs on the ground and it was then, when he had started to clean the twigs and leaves and branchlets, that he noticed bunches of round seeds hanging from the bamboo. Dark-green, thick-skinned seeds. He was surprised. Bamboo had been an intimate part of his life since his birth, but he had never known bamboo to produce seeds. This was a nabhuta nashruta incident—never before-seen, never-before-heard. He plucked a seed and smelled it. It smelled exactly like raw bamboo, no different. Inside the thick green skin of the seed, there was something that looked like wheat grain. He chewed one grain and it tasted like bamboo shoot. He thought it could be used for food. He fished out his cane naara and filled it to the brim with bamboo seeds and, after that, he cleaned the bamboo plants, made a raft out of them, floated the raft on the Kameng and started travelling towards Seppa. From the raft, he saw that the bamboo on both banks of the river were bearing flowers and those seeds, like soft, green, new paddy.

A few suns later, as they say here, on the same day, Tarak reached Seppa. He brought the raft to the bank, tethered it to a tree trunk with a rope and walked home. Though he was tired, he was happy. He would be able to give Medak a gift today. She loved to eat bamboo shoots and he was sure she would love bamboo seeds as well.

When he reached his tin-roofed house, everything was silent. He pushed open the door made of broken tins, and entered the house, making a ker-ker-ker sound. When Medak realized her husband was home, she climbed down from the bamboo bed.

'What happened, why is it so dark?' He felt a bit annoyed.

'There's no light today,' Medak replied.

'That doesn't mean you should sleep in the dark. Please light the fire.' Medak said nothing. She walked towards the hearth in a corner of the room and started to make a fire.

What had happened to Medak, who on other days would wait for him impatiently at the gate of the compound? Something must be wrong, he thought.

Though he was exhausted and hungry and, despite her odd behaviour, he found himself overflowing with love for her. After all, she was still with him after overcoming so many hurdles, so many fights with her parents, brothers, and the community. He still felt as if the life he led with Medak was a dream from which, one day, he might wake up.

'I am starving, is there anything to eat?'

'There's some rice, but no curry. That old man Matung Burha ate everything before leaving. What would you like to have it with?' She started to cough.

'Is your cough worse?' He came closer to Medak and put his hand on her forehead. 'I think you have a fever.'

'I haven't been feeling well. The cough is getting worse, I think. Tomorrow I will go to the doctor again,' Medak said.

'I will come along. I will talk to the doctor properly.'

'There's no need. How long can we continue living like this in Matung Burha's house? We need to finish building our own house soon. Should I make some warm fried rice for you?'

'Okay. But tell the doctor everything, make sure he gives you a proper check-up. One more thing, look at what I've brought home for you from the forest.' Tarak fished out a bunch of bamboo flowers from his naara.

What are these?' Medak said, feeling the seeds with her fingers after she put the rice into the heated oil.

'These are bamboo seeds. I think they will be very tasty. We should peel off the green skin and try boiling them.'

'How can bamboo bear seeds like paddy?' Medak laughed.

'I don't know, but I plucked these myself.'

'Before we boil them, we should show these to Grandpa Matung. I have never heard about bamboo-bearing seeds. What if something goes wrong after we eat them?'

Tarak thought it was a good suggestion. He finished his hot fried rice that was cooked with methun chilli powder, before setting off to Matung Burha's house

Matung Burha owned the house in which Tarak and Medak were living. Burha was a lonely, single man, with no one to call his own. People said he was around a hundred years old but he didn't look like it. There weren't any contemporaries of the old man alive in the region. But though he was old, he was quite strong. He lived in a modest house of cane and bamboo, did odd jobs, and depended on the generosity of others for his meals. When Medak eloped with Tarak from Chingi village and came to Seppa town, Matung Burha had provided them shelter in his small house, which was just right for one person. After Tarak and Medak moved in, Burha went to live in Chama's house.

According to the customs of the Nyishi tribe, Medak was married to Tero Chingi, the man who paid the costly bride price. But as soon as she had reached her new husband's house, while the guests were busy dancing and singing, she ran away to Tarak's village, Jejudada. It was only after Medak was dressed in her bride clothes and sent to Chingi that she realized who she really wanted to spend her life with. On her way to Chingi, she had imagined Tarak beckoning to her. By the time the people of Chingi realized that she had gone, she was already far away. They didn't know where to look. The villagers asked people in the neighbouring villages, and when no one offered any leads, they concluded that she had been kidnapped by ghosts.

When Tarak heard about Medak's mysterious disappearance from Tero Chingi's house, he was surprised. Though Medak had never loved him, he had been in love with her for a long time. So, when she married someone else he was heartbroken and then when he heard that she had vanished from her groom's house he was worried.

When Medak arrived in Jejudada she couldn't gather the courage to go to Tarak. She knew he loved her but she had never given him any encouragement. She had left Chingi and her husband on an impulse. Now she took shelter in the forest near Tarak's village and lived off wild fruits for several days. She would watch the village people come and go. One day, she saw Tarak entering the forest to cut bamboo. They travelled to Seppa together and hid in Matung Burha's house for many days. When people learnt about this, it led to a fierce argument between the people of the Chingi and Dada tribes. But since the Dadas—Tarak's tribe—had the larger numbers, the minority Chingis were forced to settle for double the bride price from Tarak and to leave Medak alone.

When Yaro saw Medak and Tarak, he offered them two wooden stools from the hearth to sit on.

'We are here to show Grandpa Matung something. Only he will be able to tell us whether it is edible or not.'

Tarak took out the seeds from his naara and placed them on Matung Burha's palms. 'Grandpa, please tell us what these are.'

The old man picked one seed up and examined it, held it close to his eyes, smelled it, chewed it. Suddenly, the old man looked horrified. He screamed, 'Where did you get these seeds?'

He interrupted Tarak, 'The bamboos are flowering again! These seeds are a bad omen! Now rats will rule over people. They will devour the paddy, the maize, the wheat, everything! People will die without food. Village after village will be destroyed. Oh, Doni Polo, did you keep me alive this long just to show me this? Just kill me, please kill me.'

'Why are you so upset? Please tell us what happens when bamboos flower,' Yaro said, trying to calm the old man.

'I haven't spoken about those times to anyone. One day I will tell you.'

Soon, all the bamboo started to flower on both banks of the Kameng, from Siyang Taju to Bhalukpung. Well, not exactly flowers—they were large, green seeds that sprouted in bunches. Rats fed on the seeds and that led to an exponential increase in their ability to breed. As soon as dusk fell, thousands of rats would emerge from every corner and swim across the river. The rats didn't let the paddy ripen—they attacked the fields and destroyed the entire crop. They didn't differentiate between forest and crop: wherever they saw any fruit or seeds, they ate them all. But still, there was no famine or any signs of the plague as Matung Burha had predicted. The government was quite quick. To prevent people from starving, they distributed large quantities of food.

Tarak was happy that the rodent population had increased. Medak had developed a chest pain and chronic cough in the forest. The doctor said she had tuberculosis. To raise the money for the medicine and the injections, they processed and sold rat meat. At dusk, Tarak would go with Chomar to the riverbank to kill rats and they would return at dawn with a large bunch. Medak and Yaro would sit down together, hollow the rats by pulling out their intestines, and smoke them after piercing four cleaned rats with a slim bamboo stick. At first, this made Medak queasy. Burning rat fur produced a terrible smell that nearly choked her. After the fur was burned off, the naked rats would swell up, looking like little roasted piglets. The fat would melt and then drip from the rats' bodies into the fire, making a serek-serek sound, and smelling like rotten potatoes.

'Chi! What a dirty job!' Medak had said.

'Why don't you eat a little, it's so tasty!' Tarak had exclaimed.

'I can't eat rat meat! I will throw up!'

Amidst all this strife, the good news was that Tarak and Medak finally built a house for themselves. They had expanded Matung Burha's house, building rooms for themselves and for him. They had noticed a change in Matung Burha after the bamboos flowered. Fear, anxiety, and hatred oozed from his face. He would keep scolding Tarak. 'How many more rats are you going to kill? Stop this! These are inauspicious rats that have eaten bamboo blossoms!'

'What is so inauspicious? I have earned about nine thousand rupees just by selling rat meat. That's the price of a mithun! Why should I stop killing rats? You should join me.'

'I don't need money! If you kill too many rats I won't let you stay with me. I will throw you out of my house!'

Matung Burha didn't have much to do except leave the house in the morning and return with a bundle of firewood for the day. Then he would just roam around Seppa for the rest of the day or he would sit and sharpen his machete by rubbing it against a stone, a machete that was already quite sharp. As he sharpened it, he would say to Medak, 'You are suffering from the Rat Disease! You will not survive! No one survives this Rat Disease!'

'I am not suffering from Rat Disease. The doctor says I have TB.'

'Your doctor is lying to you. I know you have contracted the Rat Disease. Cough, fever—these are all symptoms of the Rat Disease.'

'It was you who said that the bamboo blossoms would lead to a famine, people would starve to death, hundreds of people would die of disease, but see, nothing has happened.' She would make fun of the old man.

'It will happen! People will die, entire villages will perish. It hasn't been long since the bamboo started to flower. You wait and see, it will happen.'

'No, Grandpa, no. Nothing like that will happen. This is the age of the harangs. The age of bangni simpletons from the hills are over. That's why, when the bamboos bloom famines and epidemics don't take place. On the contrary, this is the age to become rich!' The old man would grumble, unable to win the argument. But Medak would usually steer clear of Matung Burha. Sometimes, she was afraid of the old man. Since she had no idea about his past life, she was suspicious of him. Who knows, he might have been a killer in his past! On other days, she would placate him by cooking beef or pork with rice, strain him a mug of apong beer whenever he wanted one.

⸺

A year passed since the blossoming of the bamboo. As soon as the bamboo seeds started to ripen, the bamboo leaves turned yellow and started to fall. After the leaves fell off, the naked trees would remain standing for a few days, turn red and then slowly black, before drying up completely to the roots. Both banks of the Kameng River, usually full of fresh, green forests, now looked ugly with dying, blackened bamboo.

As soon as the bamboo started to die, the rats also started to die. In the forests and thickets, on the riverbanks, there were now only rat carcasses. The air had become heavy with the smell of rotting rats. The same rats that used to quickly cross the speedy river drowned or were carried away by the current.

Once the Kameng enters Assam, it is called Jiya Bhoroli, and when they saw the bodies of hundreds and thousands of rats on both banks of the Jiya Bhoroli, the people in Tezpur and Balipara were horrified. At the same time, in faraway Gujarat, in a city called Surat, the plague became an epidemic. The government took quick measures to prevent the plague in Arunachal and Assam. They first banned the consumption of rat meat. After the announcement was made through a loudspeaker, Matung Burha lit a large fire and burnt all the skewered and smoked rats.

On the second day, the government officials made announcements again over the loudspeaker: anyone suffering from fever and cough, please avoid contact with other people and report to the nearest Plague Prevention Committee without delay.

On the evening this announcement was made, the three of them were eating dinner. When Matung Burha heard it, he went into the house swiftly, and brought out his gleaming machete. Medak was so frightened that she felt as if her soul was about to leave her body through her head. She thought he was about to kill her, that he had been looking for a pretext to kill her, and that was why he had been sharpening his machete so meticulously. Matung Burha held the machete up in the air and started to sing and perform the traditional Boyo dance. When people in the neighbourhood heard the old man's song, they came out of their houses and Chama, Yaro, and others joined him in the dance. They made a circle.

Matung Burha danced and sang: this beautiful girl, Medak, is a fool. The chorus agreed, yes, what a fool. I sheltered her in my house, he sang, yet she couldn't fathom who I am. The chorus supported him: hun, hun, couldn't fathom who you are! He sang again, today, through this Boyo dance, I will tell her who I am, will tell my life story. All of you now listen, with full attention.

He continued singing, while others either repeated parts of his lines or just hummed along. 'Medak's father, Rakap, was my son—a secret that Rakap's mother, Yani, and I kept until today. Yani was my lover. Old Tali seized her from me by paying a large number of mithuns as bride price. When she was married to Tali, as his seventh wife, she carried my child in her womb. Rakap should have inherited my title, Jomoh, but he was known as Kinoo. In my mind, the flower of sadness had bloomed but in the forests the talamdarak had blossomed from the bamboo. Rats devoured entire crops and people started to starve to death. Listen, listen, during those days, there were no harang people from the plains like today. The entire hills only had bangni people. When the famine ended, there came the Rat Disease. To get rid of it, we started to burn houses. With these hands, I burnt many people to death, many houses, and many villages. Villages became empty. The hills were empty. The disease was conquered and only I lived to this old age. I didn't marry. I didn't raise a family. Rakap's daughter, Medak, doesn't know that I am her grandfather. Tarak didn't even give me one piece of meat as her bride price. Now, she has the Rat Disease and I will have to burn her alive with the house to prevent it spreading. This thought burns my heart. This is my Boyo song.'

The old man stopped dancing and singing. When they heard that Medak was suffering from the Rat Disease, the people fled.

Medak started to cry and Tarak hugged her close to his chest and rubbed his hands against her head. She wept, 'I think it is true that I have the Rat Disease. I will not survive. I will leave you alone in this world and die.'

Tarak wanted to comfort her but he couldn't stop crying. 'The old man is lying. If you die, I won't be able to live. Let the old man burn us alive together.'

Matung Burha watched the couple. They were drowning in a sea of sorrow. Finally, he entered his own room and locked the door.

The next morning, Chama told Tarak that the Plague Prevention Committee's office was hiring. They needed people to burn down the dead and dry bamboo as well as collect the rat carcasses to set them on fire. But Tarak didn't go looking for work. Instead, he took Medak to the doctors again. By then, several well-known doctors had gathered in Seppa. They examined Medak carefully and confirmed that she had nothing but tuberculosis and that she was doing much better.

On their way back, they decided that they wouldn't stay with Matung Burha any more. They would leave their house to him and, while Medak was still unwell, they would rent a place in Seppa to carry on her treatment and return to Tarak's village, Jejudada, eventually.

When they reached home, they saw that all their belongings were heaped up far from the house. The old man had put their clothes and kitchenware outside the house and had locked himself in. Everything they owned was in the heap. Along with their stuff, the old man had also put out his own large tin trunk. Medak tried to pick it up. It was impossibly heavy, as if weighed down by a large stone.

'Medak!' Medak was startled.

'Open that trunk!'

She looked around to locate the source of the old man's voice.

'Open that trunk!' The old man ordered once again.

Scared, she did as he asked. She was shocked to see that it was filled with precious gems, with tadak and chongre. Matung Burha spoke again, 'These jewels have been preserved for you. They belonged to your great-grandmother, my mother. She died of the Rat Disease, and along with her, my sisters too. When I heard that Rakap had a daughter, I was happy to know that a rightful heir had been born. Even though I have been terribly hungry, I never sold a single gem from this trunk. I am now giving these to you. Take them and go away from here.'

'Grandpa, I am not suffering from the Rat Disease. All those big big doctors have examined me and assured me I'm not,' Medak said.

'I know, I know everything. People who have the Rat Disease die after four or five days. You don't have that disease but I have it. I have had a fever since morning and have been coughing too. Don't come near me! Now go away from here, go away, there's no time, go away!'

'We will go and get a doctor. You will be fine,' Tarak shouted.

By then, a group of people had gathered around the house.

The old man screamed from inside, 'There is no point going to the doctor! When someone gets this disease, they have to be burnt alive inside the house. Otherwise, it spreads. I have killed many such patients along with their houses! I have burnt my mother, father, brothers, and sisters alive because they had the Rat Disease! Let this house burn down completely, otherwise, this disease will spread to others and the hills will be empty of people once again.'

The house started to burn.

Matung Burha had set it on fire. Within seconds, flames engulfed the house. On both the banks of the Kameng River too, massive flames were spreading. It was the fire that would overpower the smell of bamboo blossoms to welcome orchids. It was the fire of creation.

BOKHA

CYRUS MISTRY

I

BOKHA. IT MEANS TOOTHLESS. THAT'S WHAT EVERYONE CALLED HIM. THE name was a slight exaggeration. Only four of his front teeth were missing—two upper canines, two lower incisors—but the ones that remained were long, misshapen, and tar-stained. And one corner of the ungainly assortment sported an inordinately large gold pre-molar, installed not many years ago, when Bokha had had a lucky streak at the cotton figures—glinting dully every time his face spread itself in that ugly, leering grin that had earned him his nickname.

Bokha was known to be a deceitful, spiteful, untrustworthy, ridiculous sort of fellow. A petty swindler and, when occasion allowed, usually only with children, a wicked bully. His real name was Rutton Ollia, though few knew him by it. Short and rather puny, Bokha was getting on in years. His unshaven stubble and sparse hair were liberally sprinkled with grey, his clothes were old and baggy, and he had a comical manner of walking—especially, if he was in a hurry—when all his limbs appeared to be whirling about him in two or three tangential directions like the blades of a complex propeller. He was never seen without the greasy, black skullcap poised at the slightly pointed end of a large cranium. Most people were abominably rude to him, and pushed him around.

Worst of all, he was himself completely craven and obsequious. There were no limits to the amount of self-humiliation he could undertake just to bum a cigarette or a drink off someone. He clowned, spat, cursed foully, made obscene gestures and gross noises while grovelling before his tormentors, merely to earn their derisive laughter, or their blows. People despised Bokha; but the truth was, he despised them a hundred times more. He derived a queer satisfaction from having his long nose tweaked, or from slurping up a spilt drink like a cat from the sunmica-topped tables in the bar at the instigation of his enemies and his patrons. It was proof to him that they were animals of the worst sort, beasts, lower than himself.

Usually, for a few hours every morning, Bokha worked as a delivery boy at the local fire temple. That is to say, balancing the big, round, silver-plated trays of sanctified fruit knotted together in a white sheet, he carried them on his head to the homes of those who had ordered prayers for their dead that day. Eruchsaa, the head priest at the temple, was a burly, bearded old man who, though otherwise gentle and soft-spoken, became extraordinarily infuriated by the mere sight of Bokha, whom he considered sly and lazy.

'Donkey! Ghelo! Gadhero!' the old priest's deep voice would bellow in the vault-like back chambers of the fire temple, if some trays were lying uncleared or, simply, for no apparent reason. 'Where are your brains? In your arse? You lazy, good-for-nothing, bloody Bokha!' Frequently, the priest would give Bokha a hard rap with the flat of his palm and send his cap flying. On perceiving Bokha bareheaded, Eruchsaa would become even more incensed.

'Put it on! Put it on! Shameless! You naked, toothless beggar!' he'd splutter, and start pummelling him with blows. (For it was forbidden to be without a cap in the temple precincts.)

Though there would appear not to be anything so offensive or demeaning about a nickname like 'toothless', there was something in the way it was spat out by people—by everyone who addressed him—'Aae Bokha!'—that stung him deeply and made his hackles rise. But his anger was a strange, dislocated thing which had no bearing on the world of people; when shouted at, Bokha's own voice turned shrill and his knees trembled with an inexplicable fear too powerful to control.

'No, no, Eruchsaa! What did I do?' he would cry, dancing around the old priest, avoiding his fists. 'Beat me! Beat me more! I am yours. I have eaten your salt, now I'll eat your blows as well....'

Then Bokha would suddenly pretend to be frantically busy, rushing this way and that, stomping his feet as though impatient of his own slowness, make motions in the air, polish a table here for a brief second, shift a vase there, stop to kiss the feet of the Prophet every time he passed the large, heavily-garlanded painting on glass that reflected the flickering of oil-lamps lit by devotees in the temple's main hall. Oddly enough, this furious activity would placate Eruchsaa, who would leave him alone for the rest of the morning.

In the evening, Bokha could always be found in the crowded country liquor bar at the end of Forjett Road. Here, he earned his drinks working as bar help for the one-eyed Irani, Gustasp, mopping tables, collecting and rinsing out empty glasses, and providing general entertainment to the sadistic impulses of the regulars.

Regulars, who knew him well. He stayed till closing time, then trudged home, drunk, swaying reluctantly in the direction of his small, dark apartment. What if I don't go home? thought Bokha one night. Couldn't I just stretch out here beside that one.... Forget I have a bed and mattress, never enter that lane again, or see that house...? Bokha gazed at the row of pavement sleepers with envy. Supine in the warmth of the night, some embracing, limbs entangled in a daze of sleep, he longed to be one of them. Sometimes, during the day, when he glimpsed one of the old chaps from school, smartly decked out with tie and shoes and briefcase, he felt the same kind of longing. Mostly, those schoolmates never recognized him.... But no, here he was already. Too late to change anything now. In her bed, upstairs, his mother was lying awake waiting for him to return, so she could piss.

Those who had seen Bokha grow up placed the blame for his wretchedness squarely on his mother, the savage and formidable Khorshedmai. His father had died when he was only nine. Apoplexy, the doctor said. Something burst in his brain. And then she came into her own, this Khorshedmai. How she bloated! Lay in bed and ate and ate, while the boy ran completely wild. She showed more concern for stray alley cats, whom she fed saucersful of milk, people said, than she ever did for her own son. Yet, every now and then, she would rouse from her apathy, as from a dream, and brutally punish the boy for some reported misdemeanour. Then, late in the night, the tortured child's screams of pain would rack the neighbourhood. No one dared interfere. They remembered these things, some of the neighbours, and were moved to pity for that spineless, unhappy loafer without an iota of self-respect, that Bokha.

She was definitely a bad sort. On the very morning after her husband's funeral, Khorshedmai quarrelled violently with other tenants in her building over a small matter of uncleared garbage. Some of her neighbours had the careless habit of tipping their refuse in a back lot behind the building. But that wasn't all. She turned away Jimmy's relations and friends at the door when they came to condole. She even physically assaulted his best friend, Behram, nearly knocking him down the stairs when he showed a little persistence in trying to gain entry into his dead friend's flat.

On the fifth day, after services for the dead man were done, Khorshedmai came out onto the balcony of her third floor flat and began to beat her breast, beseeching God to bear witness to her sorrows. It was an extraordinary performance. She raised her head high, howled and shrieked, cursing her deceased husband to high heaven for abandoning her so thoughtlessly, without a paisa to her name, and a little one to tend for....

'O you cowardly wretch! Spendthrift, villainous rake! How could you trick me so, going off and dying like that, weakling...!'

Jimmy Ollia was respected in the neighbourhood, not least for the dignity with which he had borne his wife's shenanigans.

His friends knew of a handsome insurance policy he had made out in Khorshedmai's name, on which he had regularly paid the premiums. Nevertheless, Khorshedmai began to live in extreme poverty, like a miser. She pulled her son out of school and let him take to the streets.

It was then people began to say that though Jimmy Ollia had probably died in a fit of rage against his wife's laziness and gluttony, who was to say she hadn't slipped something into his food? They would lower their voices when they spoke of Khorshedmai—if they spoke at all. It was rumoured that she had more than just a smattering of knowledge of the black arts. Someone remembered an apocryphal story about a good-looking young servant boy from a nearby building whom Khorshedmai took a fancy to even while Jimmy was still alive. That boy had been caught by the watchman of the cemetery behind the hill one night, just as he was digging up a freshly buried corpse!

That was years ago. But it was commonly assumed that the servant had been a mere pawn in some evil design of hers. Overnight, the boy's hair had turned white and he had become completely deranged.

For three years, Khorshedmai let her son loaf. Then one day she spoke to a priest at the fire temple and arranged a job for him as a chasniwallah, a delivery boy. As for herself, she put on enormous amounts of weight. Day by day, week by week, she grew more obese until her ungainly masses of fat made her a sight to behold. Which was rare. She never left the house and was only glimpsed sometimes sitting at her window, impassive as a monument—a swollen old woman who was practically bedridden because her own corpulence had become too much. For her to carry about. Otherwise, even at seventy, she was strong as a horse.

Bokha turned his key in the night-latch and entered silently. The gross silhouette of his mother's mound-like figure stretched out in bed on the other side of his own narrow cot by the window was etched into the darkness. She was snoring. Probably pretending to be asleep, thought Bokha. Waiting for me to lie down. Sure enough, as soon as he had crept into bed, he heard her powerful bass croak, 'Bedpan aap.'

She raised her body a few inches, and he shoved the bedpan under her. He turned his face away; the long, metallic ringing that followed, like the sustained peal of an electric buzzer, filled his ears with disgust.

'So much wakefulness,' Khorshedmai mumbled. 'I lie in bed and wait and wait. Where were you? So late?' Her voice had a taunt hidden in it somewhere, like a splinter in a block of wood. He knew better than to answer.

Khorshedmai kept vigil for him not merely to relieve her distended bladder, but also to engage in nocturnal altercation. 'With her I suppose... your ayah.... Yes? Yes or no?' she pursued, as the ringing trickled to a halt. 'Take it out. Carefully now!'

Bokha did not need to be warned. Two nights ago he had come back tipsy and the bedpan, just as he had finished extricating it from under her, somehow tilted. Her thigh and mattress were splashed by urine. The suddenness of it all had caught Bokha off guard. He'd giggled. As soon as he had laid the pan on the floor, she had grabbed him by the arm and given him a sound thrashing. His ears still felt tender from the slaps she had showered on him. Once she had a grip on you, it was impossible to break loose. But so long as you remembered to stay outside her reach, you were all right because it was laughable to think of her pursuing anyone. The thought of his mother's restricted mobility amused Bokha, although it did not decrease the terror he held her in.

'Empty it out first,' his mother ordered.

But Bokha covered it with an old newspaper and hurriedly collapsed into bed.

'Tomorrow, in the morning,' he yawned and pretended to fall asleep instantly.

She cursed under her breath. For a few moments there was silence, punctuated by his mother's heavy breathing. Then she spoke again: 'Well, what do you do when you meet that ayah of yours...? Behind the bushes in the park? Do you stick your little finger in her? Or does she make you lick her black arse?' Khorshedmai laughed contemptuously. 'Poor boy, thirty-five and he's met his first girlfriend...a Catholic ayah, half-crazed like himself. I know everything that goes on, son. Sitting here, I get all the news....

'Well, take her at least, if you can,' her teasing flared and became a choking contempt. 'Can you? Eunuch! Or is your father's strain too strong in you, Bokha? My teeth are still good for cracking walnuts. Aae Bokha, why don't you answer?'

Bokha feigned a snore or two and lay very still. The moon had risen high, and its cold pallor bathed the room. He waited. At last he recognized a soft purring sound which told him his mother was really asleep. But Bokha was uncomfortable. An attack of gas was stirring biliously inside him. He had had nothing to eat all evening except peanuts and papad and stuff like that which people passed around while drinking.

Oh Lord, my ayah.... Bokha smiled, despite himself. Seraphina.... What a beautiful name. Not half so beautiful to look at, is she? And I don't know her quite so well as my jealous mother thinks I do. But I'll get to.... I'll get to, you can be sure....

It pleased Bokha to realize that his mother's contemptuous raving only thinly disguised her anger, her fear.... Fear of what? They had met two or three times in the municipal park where neighbourhood ayahs brought their little rich wards to while away the evening hours before it grew dark. Like a child she was herself, that Seraphina. Quite stupid, in fact.... People said that once, many years ago, she had been possessed by an evil spirit who had ravished her every night; then, perhaps, tiring of her body, he had vacated it, but not without leaving his claw-marks on her soul. She was a duffer really, his Seraphina.... But no matter what anyone said, she was kind to him.

She had been kind to him, to Bokha. Maybe he should just take over the evil spirit's place now. Bokha chuckled silently with lustful longing. But he would be a good spirit, of course. He would give her good times. He would do to her all those things his mad mother imagined he was doing. Seraphina. O Seraphina.... Her name reminded him of the shape of a swan's back.

The swan floated in his mind on a lake of alcohol. Its undulating sibilants soothed his besotted brain. Now he was caressing the swan. In the last moment before he reached his ecstasy, a cunning and triumphant thought reared its head and gloated: what if I really marry her, thought Bokha. Quite an ugly thing she is; but maybe I will.

II

My father has left us and gone to a better world. That is how they put it. But I know he is dead. I felt the ice of his cheek on my lips when I kissed him. I held his hand and even shook it, but he would not respond. When they carried him up the hill to the Tower of Silence, I knew I would never see him again. What's more, Mummy knows it too. But when I'm around she still tries to hide her tears and speaks of my father as if he had left us for only a few days. Where is that better world? I believe Uncle Framroze knows something about it, because he has been trying to make contact with the dead. But first I must tell you how I came to be living with him.

A few days after my father passed on, his ex-employer offered my mother a job. Mother explained to me that she would have to start working, that she would be busy all day. Since my summer holidays had just begun, it was decided that I would spend them with Uncle Framroze. Even so, when the day came for me to go, I made a terrific fuss. Until Uncle said, 'Oh come now, I thought you were a grown-up boy. Why, I've even brought my car along, just to let you drive it.' That put things in a different light. I climbed into the funny-looking old car, called a Hillman. The suitcase Mummy had packed for me was in the back seat. I was in front, driving. Well, almost. Uncle allowed me to hold the wheel, and I'd honk loudly every time someone got in our way.

We drove slowly, carefully, up the steep road right to its farthest extreme where an oddly shaped, two-storeyed bungalow nestled against the side of Forjett Hill. A sheer rock face rose dark behind the house and loomed over it. 'Happy Home'. That's what it was called. It was to be my home for the next three months.

I grew to love the place. I loved it for its many rooms, so still and cool and dark, its dusty, secluded corners which had not been disturbed in years. For the long central corridor curling into the back of the house where a purplish-blue night lamp glowed day and night. For Pestonjee, who hung in this passage, my uncle's grey, red-cheeked, white-crested cockatoo who was eighty-three years old, but still whistling as merrily as a schoolboy. During the day, he would leave his cage and walk around the outside of its bars and climb the chain by which it was suspended. But in the evening he would return inside and sit gloomily on his perch, in a kind of huff of puffed-up feathers. I loved feeding Pestonjee. Green chillies, guavas, nuts. But what I loved most about that house were the high beams of its sloping, tiled roof which met in my room, directly above my bed. At the highest point, in a cavity created by the conjunction of two beams, sparrows had built and abandoned a nest. I stared at the roof every night for what must have been hours before I fell asleep.

Uncle was much older than my mother. He was a retired civil engineer who had remained a bachelor all his life. A kind, shy man who was often embarrassed for not knowing what to say to me. Most of the time he would stay shut up in his room with his books and pamphlets and come out only for meals. His study-cum-prayer room fascinated me greatly. An entire wall had been converted into an altar and was covered with picture-frames of saints and sages, mystics, prophets, and miracle-workers before whom he burnt large amounts of incense. My greatest pleasure during those days was to get him to tell me each one's story.

Every Sunday morning, at ten o'clock sharp, my uncle would be visited by his three friends. They would drive up in an old DeSoto, honking loudly while they parked to announce their arrival. Bapsymai, Fardoon, and Ghauswalla. These were their names, or at least how Uncle addressed them. They were delighted to make my acquaintance, and all three shook hands with me.

Every Sunday they would first have a quick cup of tea; then Uncle would say to me, 'Okay dear, now you go and play'; and all four would lock themselves in his study. Sometimes I would put my ear to the door and listen, sniffing at the fragrance of the incense they were burning inside. I was utterly mystified by what I heard. Peculiar thumping noises, strange voices I was at a loss to recognize, loud exhortations to various people ('Jimmy Dorabji', 'Gool Palsetia', 'Ardesar Irani') to grace their table and make themselves available for questioning. I heard many amazing things. But mostly I heard only silence, and I was soon bored by this game of eavesdropping.

One day, I heard my father's name called out. Then I realized what they were doing—trying to make contact with that other world, the better world, to which the dead passed away. I heard Bapsymai repeat her invitation three times:

'Bomi Marker! Will you agree to answer our questions?'

As you can imagine, I was waiting eagerly for his reply. In my head, I could hear my father's voice. He was asking me to squeeze his legs and toes, which were aching after a long day at the office. But from the room behind the door, there was only silence. Later on, when I questioned him about these Sunday meetings, my uncle admitted, rather reluctantly, that they were trying to communicate with those of their friends who had passed into the world of the dead. 'We know that nothing ever dies. And if we could share their experience....' He explained that what they were doing was called 'holding a séance'. But he absolutely refused to allow me to be present at one.

When the séance was over, Uncle and his three friends emerged from his study looking very thirsty and tired. Bapsymai, heaving and walking very slowly on very high stiletto heels (she was only slightly taller than me even with them on); Fardoon Umrigar drenched in sweat, and Ghauswalla's round, shiny face beaming like a full moon. Then we sat down to the traditional Sunday meal of dhansak, fried fish, and kachumber. Pheena served us, her large eyes turned downwards as she handled dishes and spoons with extreme caution as though she could not trust herself not to drop them. At Sunday lunch she was always anxious. She was not like that when we were alone. Then she would chat with me for hours on end in her plaintive, sing-song version of the Parsi Gujarati my uncle and I spoke. She knew the language because she had grown up there, working for my uncle. Her mother had worked there before her and died in that same back room which was Pheena's room now. A small cubicle of a room with a window overlooking the backyard where the neighbours chucked their garbage. There was no furniture in this room; only her bedding rolled up in a corner and a large rusted trunk which contained most of her belongings. A mildewed calendar with pictures of the saints hung on the wall beside a Sacred Heart encased in glass; beneath it was a tray on which she lit small, slim candles every evening.

Here we sat in the evenings, after returning from our walk in the municipal playground, while my uncle said his prayers in the front hall in a loud, rasping voice, spectacles low on his nose, straining to read the words in a tattered prayer book. Sometimes I would sit on her trunk and she would sit on the floor between my knees and let me comb her hair which was shiny and slippery with coconut oil. Sometimes, while I plaited her hair, she would sing for me soft songs in Konkani. Her room, her hair, her brown body carried an odour I had never smelt before. I recognized it as alien, a smell that had no connection with my universe, the world of Parsis that I was familiar with. Did it come from the oil in her hair, the half-dried linen hanging for days on the clothesline in her room, or the patched sheets rolled up in a corner which had soaked in the sweat of every nightmare, perhaps a mixture of all these? Undeniably, it was a smell I associated with sadness, and I longed to know what made her such a strange, unhappy creature.

Pheena and I were friends. There was a bald patch just over her forehead on one side, which was thinly covered by the hair from above. We shared a private joke about it. I would ask her, 'Pheena what happen to your hair? Hey baldy, where it went?' And she would pull a long face and groan, 'What happen? Rat came at night. Eats up my hairs. Rat hungry, ouch, ouch, ouch, rat wants to eats up all my hairs.... Ouch, ouch....' And start tickling my ribs. My giggling was infectious and delighted her.

But one day, while sitting with Uncle in the hall after he had finished his prayers, on an impulse I asked him how Pheena had lost a patch of hair like that. He frowned and waited to see if I really wanted him to reply. Then he told me, 'Well, you see, many years ago.... Pheena was very sick. Poor girl, she was in great pain. She could not bear it.... She pulled it out herself.... Many years ago that was.... Not something to talk about. She's probably forgotten.... Here,' he said, pulling out half a dozen chicken soup cubes from the pocket of his dressing gown, which usually contained toffees, 'tell her to boil some soup for you.' He paused, then said: 'And look here, Soli, shut your door at night, if you want.... Sometimes in her sleep, Pheena gets up and walks around the house. You might get a scare if you wake up in the middle of the night and see her wandering about like that....'

That night, after dinner, I made my way to Pheena's room down the long corridor. There was no light on. A candle flickered beneath the Sacred Heart. For a moment, I thought she might be out. Then I saw her small figure kneeling, her elbows resting on the trunk, her hands clasped together. She may have been praying, but she was shaking with sobs. I went up to her and touched her hair.

'Pheena....'

She raised her face to me, streaming with tears, looking like the pictures of the saints in her calendar. Her look disturbed me; I thought, why is she looking at me like that, so pleadingly, as if she were asking my forgiveness for something?

'Why do you cry, Pheena?'

Her lips trembled and she said in the voice of a frightened child, 'I don't know.... I don't know why I cry....'

∽

One evening, during my third month at Happy Home, Pheena left me alone at the park to play with the other children. Rather, for them to play around me. I was pretty much older than all the rest. I would be eleven quite soon. In fact, that's why Pheena had left me and gone to the market, because Uncle Framroze had given her a long shopping list, even though my birthday was still a whole week away. Mummy was invited for the occasion, and Uncle's three friends. Maybe some others, too. He was planning a grand lunch.

When I tired of the swings and of balancing myself against the combined weight of three babies on the see-saw, I sat down on a bench. A man approached and stood rather aggressively before me. I had seen him before in the park. Pheena had pointed him out to me. He was the one they called Bokha.

'So you are Framroze's nephew,' he demanded angrily of me.

I nodded.

'What's your name?' he barked.

'Soli.'

'Who gave you permission to sit on the swing? How dare you sit on the see-saw! Don't you know they are meant for the children? You're a grown-up fellow, man. What if you break them?'

He had pushed back his shoulders and was glaring at me. Then, he grabbed my wrist in a most menacing way. I uttered a laugh and twisted my hand free. It was a shrill laugh, only half-afraid. He was such a comical, gnome-like figure, all skin and bones, he couldn't frighten anyone; yet he did manage to look rather dangerous.

'Well, I don't think they would break so easily,' I replied caustically. 'And if I'm grown-up, then what about you? I saw you on the see-saw day before yesterday.'

Bokha started laughing and squeezing my arm in a most friendly way, 'That's good. That's a good boy, Soli,' he said, congratulating me. 'I was only testing you. Honest. Honest to God. Don't be angry with me. I was only trying to find out if you have some guts, or you're just a namby-pamby. That's all, believe me....' He paused for breath and perched himself on the edge of the bench. 'Courage is the greatest thing in the world. If you have it, you can go anywhere, do anything, nothing and no one can stop you. A boy like you has to learn to be brave. That's what. You don't know me, but I know you. I'm Bokha,' he said, extending his hand. I was getting to rather like him.

'People say all kinds of things about me,' he continued. 'Let them say. You ask Seraphina about me. She knows me very well, your Seraphina. I have courage, too. I have real courage.... People can say anything. But if I'm pushed too far, watch it.

'There is nothing I cannot do. Don't push me, that's all. If it comes to that, then just watch me. I am capable of anything. Anything!' He tried to look menacing again. 'I can even slit your throat!'

And he did just that, drawing his thumbnail across my throat with a snarl. Then, with a straight face, he folded shut the imaginary knife and slipped it into his pocket. And further, as if letting me in on a secret of utmost importance, he whispered, 'My bark is worse than my bite, though.'

Drawing back his lips and contorting his features, he exhibited to me a rather depleted and misshapen set of teeth, while making a low, growling noise from the base of his throat. I giggled, and he continued to pull the funniest faces showing me his teeth from all possible angles. Until I could not hold back my laughter any more and he joined in with a curious, hiccupy kind of gurgling.

Suddenly, he challenged me: 'Let's have a bout of panja!' He threw himself on the ground on his stomach, and stuck out his elbow, placing it firmly on the ground. He wanted to hand-wrestle. I stretched myself out, too, and willingly fell to the challenge. We were in the throes of an intense, well-matched battle when Pheena returned.

'Chi, chi, chi! Rolling on the ground!' she exclaimed and gave Bokha a good dressing-down. Apparently she had asked him to keep an eye on me. She dusted my clothes with her hand, then looked at her wristwatch.

'Why don't you go play with the other children? It's still early....' she said. I wandered away. When it grew dark, and most of the other ayahs were getting ready to return home with the children, I saw Bokha move up close and link his hand with Pheena's.

Not until my penultimate week at Happy Home did I realize how close to Uncle's place Bokha and his mother lived. It was a Sunday afternoon. When Pheena had finished laying out all the dishes for us on the table, Uncle asked her to go and eat. The morning's séance had been a great success but had run on too late. It was already two o'clock, and everyone at the table was ravenous. After a certain amount had been tucked away in silence, Bapsymai initiated the conversation.

'How is she, then, these days?' she asked my uncle in an undertone.

Uncle hurriedly finished chewing a morsel and declared, 'You've seen the rings under her eyes. She won't sleep. She wanders from room to room, like a ghost. I had pills prescribed, but they don't work.'

Umrigar piped up: 'These pills are very bad for you. On the contrary, two spoons of honey, some brandy, hot water....'

'Pills won't work, Framroze,' said Bapsymai meaningfully, ignoring Umrigar's interjection. 'I've given you my opinion more than once. In the first place, hers was not a genuine case of possession at all. It was her mischief. You know who I'm referring to. We won't mention her name at the dinner table. If we hadn't realized it soon enough and taken precautions....'

'But what would be the reason for her continued interest in her?' enquired Ghauswalla learnedly. He seemed to be speaking for my uncle, who nodded and asked, 'Why should she prey on the poor girl?'

'Do you know how often she is with him?' Bapsymai continued. 'They're always together in the evening. Ask him,' she pointed to me, 'he must see them together in the park. She wants her to be his plaything—so he can be hers!'

All this was too confusing for me. But upon reference being made to my presence, Uncle was reminded of it and he brought the conversation to a halt. But not before Fardoon Umrigar piped up again in his peculiarly thin voice: 'Her days are numbered. But even on her deathbed she hatches her plots and mumbles her foul mantras....'

After the meal, my uncle's friends left and he settled down to his usual Sunday nap. The house was quiet again. From the kitchen came the faintly reassuring clatter of dishes. Pheena was washing up. Then she too went off to her room to rest.

The afternoon was hot and still. Outside my window the street was completely dead. Not even a crow or a stray mongrel in sight. The heat bounced off the asphalt paving around Happy Home and hung in the air. On the hillside nothing stirred except a few wisps of smoke, where a family of construction workers had built a fire and cooked a meal. The sky was unbearably bright.

The stillness became so oppressive I could not lie in bed any more. I wandered out into the front living room and, for a while, messed around with Uncle's Chinese Puzzle which was really just an intricate game of checkers, boring to play alone. I leaned out of the balcony and gazed at the deserted road tapering down the hill. A curious sensation crept into me that something wasn't quite as it should be. In the low wooden house diagonally across the street at the corner of Sorabji Lane, first among the series of lanes that converged on Forjett Hill—it couldn't be seen from my bedroom, but I'd always believed it to be unoccupied—one window was open, and the curtain raised. At the window sat the fattest, ugliest old woman I had ever seen in my life. She was staring directly at me. I felt uncomfortable, but only for a moment. That was how long it took me to realize that she could not see me. Because this must be the purblind Khorshedmai, whom Pheena had told me about, and that dark, hunched figure, the shape of his head unmistakable, was her only son, Bokha.

His skinny figure had entered the room and was tip-toeing behind Khorshedmai, very stealthily. She must have heard him because she turned suddenly and shouted something at him. This had the effect of turning a spring loose in him somewhere, activating him, like a clockwork toy: he began to dance around her in a circle, lunging at her, but only from a distance, as if some invisible barrier prevented him from coming closer. He was shaking his fists at her. She sat quite still. Then the curtain was pulled down.

That night I dreamt of my father. He was eating potatoes, wolfishly swallowing them whole. He must have been famished. I saw my mother's tearful face as she served him more and more potatoes, trying to keep pace with the peeling, singeing her fingers because they were steaming hot. I heard voices shouting in the corridor outside my door. I saw the purplish-blue night lamp glowing silently, mysteriously watchful, intense in its brief circumference of light. When I woke up in the morning, I found my bedroom door shut and bolted from inside, as I had left it the night before. But as if in vindication of my troubled sleep, there was a terrific row that morning and Uncle Framroze became hysterical and excessive in the rebukes he directed at Pheena.

When Uncle had opened the front door that morning and bent down to pick up his newspapers, he found instead a coconut split in half, its kernel black and rotten. Around the two halves was a ring of red chilli powder. Within the ring was a sour lime that had been quartered and stuffed with more powders, yellow and vermilion in colour. The sight of this unholy concoction had filled Framroze with terror, and he screamed for Pheena and called her names for a quarter of an hour. She began to cry. He warned her that if she was ever seen with that Bokha again, he would pack her off to the home run by the nuns. When the sweeper had come and cleared those things—for he dared not touch them himself or let Pheena touch them—Framroze sprinkled the doorway and the four corners of every room with holy bull's urine, of which he maintained a small bottle in his personal wardrobe. Then he began telephoning Bapsymai, Fardoon, and Ghauswalla to inform them of the new development.

III

Bokha's desperation grew with every hour that passed. He had to do something; he had to save her.... But what? How? A whole week had gone by. With inexorable certainty, the night of the full moon was approaching. Just six days ago, it had seemed infinitely distant, possibly altogether avoidable. Why that Sunday afternoon, six days ago, Bokha had lost his temper with Khorshedmai. He had grown fiercely out of control. It had frightened him later on, but also charged him with the elation of recklessness. Now see what had come of it....

She had insulted him. His mother. Her abuse was no more vicious than usual. But Bokha had lost his temper and spat on her. He had performed his dance of rage before her, lunging at her, always keeping outside the range of her wild snatches in the air. She was too slow, her arms were short and heavy. He had told her he was going. Packing up his things and leaving forever. She would have to pick up her own bedpan from now on. Or she could piss in her drawers for all he cared. Because he was going. He was going away to marry his ayah. He had found a room for them. They would live together happily there, his ayah and he, and he would never come back to see her, not even when she was dead. And she could keep her money which she had hidden away under her arse for so many years.

His anger expended, Bokha realized with a shock that Khorshedmai had believed every word he had said. The outburst was so unlike him; he hadn't known himself capable of it. She had sat in her chair, panting heavily; her face was pale. The blind white flecks in her eyes were expressionless as ever.

'Very well,' her voice had grated hoarsely. 'So she has given you the courage to defy me. At last this Bokha has become a man. Or has he? We'll see....'

Her voice had broken but she had never lost her cool.

'So you're challenging me? Very well. I take up your challenge.'

Get out! Empty-handed, be sure. Get out. And don't come back, tonight or any other night. The door will be locked to you from now on. As for the girl, I'll see to her.'

Bokha's voice had cracked with incredulity.

'You'll see to her? You? You, who can't even walk to the toilet for a piss? What can you do? Don't give us any more of your empty threats.'

Something like a smile had flickered on his mother's rubbery lips. 'The night of the full moon is only a few days away,' she had muttered to herself.

Her voice was low. But her words had made Bokha break out in a cold sweat.

'When the moon is at its height, I will do such a thing as will completely turn her brain. She won't know what happened. But her mind will go. Then she'll make you a good wife, the slut.'

Bokha had left the house white as a sheet, without saying another word. Had he imagined those tears, the wetness on those cheeks? He would have thought those eyes had hardened to marble long ago.

In the evening, he had returned and quietly inserted his key in the latch. It wouldn't turn. He had clicked it in the slot a few times, then hammered on the door, shouting, 'Mumma! Mumma! Open up!'

There was no sound from inside. He had spent the night on a bench in the garden behind the fire temple.

In the morning, it had been the same thing. She would not answer. He had spoken to her for ten minutes through the closed door, pleading, making wild promises, confessing it had all been a lie; begging for her mercy. Then he had kicked the door twice and walked away. When he returned to the fire temple, he had found Framroze waiting for him on the porch.

Framroze had caught hold of his collar, shaken him violently, and warned him that he would go to the police and asked him to warn his mother as well. Bokha had recoiled in horror when he heard what Framroze had found on his doorstep the previous morning. He had bent and clutched Framroze's feet and sworn that he knew nothing about it. But he was trembling. There was no doubt now that she meant to carry out her threat.

And yet, how cunningly the human mind defends itself against eventualities it cannot bear to acknowledge. Bokha had always believed implicitly in stories he had heard about his mother's maleficent powers. Now he made light of them. What can she do with her coconuts, her chillies, her lemons? The whole thing was laughable. Let her try her worst, he would see her in hell before he let her bend a single hair on Seraphina's head.

Bokha had just received his month's salary. He began to spend a lot of time in Gustasp's bar. He bought drinks for strangers and beleaguered them with stories about black magic, spells, wax dolls with needles stuck in them, and such like, in order to prove that the whole thing was hogwash. Not everyone gave him the confirmation he sought. One elderly man, a quiet, hard drinker told him a story of a spell that had been cast on his niece, which made her refuse to eat or sleep. She would have died, if the mischief had not been countered by a tantric sorcerer whose services the family employed. A most remarkable man.... Bokha had stopped listening. He was feeling sick in the tummy. He left his drink and went out into the sunlight.

As a child, Bokha had rarely seen doctors. His mother ascribed all forms of illness—from diarrhoea to the common cold—to the workings of an evil eye which had latched on to her son like a hook. She took her own measures to repel the envy at the root of his sickness. After sunset, a brazier of hot coals was prepared in which a mixture of alum, camphor, and rock salt was cooked. When it had boiled to a certain temperature, the ingredients of this mixture would begin to permute, and acquire strange shapes and colours, and a sharp, unnameable odour would overwhelm their rooms. Bokha would stand beside his mother transfixed, staring at the curious shapes the alum would begin to take; shapes suggestive of distorted human or animal figures, heads, faces, noses, eyeballs, lips—the grotesquerie of an entire evil universe condensing in a brazier of hot coals before his very eyes.

One of the few memories of his father that Bokha still retained was of him holding a handkerchief to his nose, eyes streaming behind glasses in the smoke-filled room as he stood obediently beside his son, muttering a private prayer. Bokha tried to remember if her magic had worked. He wasn't sure.

Often, his illness seemed to subside the day after the coals were finally quenched. His father at least had never questioned the validity of this procedure. But right through the ceremony, his face would remain puckered in a grimace of distaste.

The remembrance of hot coals lit up another memory in him, of another night. This was later, after his father died. One evening, his mother had returned home unexpectedly early and found him with his pants down, masturbating. She had prepared the brazier then, and branded him on his right arm with a red-hot iron. The crinkled patch of burnt skin still itched every time Bokha had a premonition of some disaster. It was itching now. Unbearably.

God help me. What a wretch I am. Sitting here all day getting drunk. Coward. Do something. What? Well, you tried to act too smart, inventing all those lies about yourself and Seraphina. On the spur of the moment too. And now...? Ah, come off it. Nothing's going to happen. The night of the full moon will pass like any other. Mumma will cool down and let you in again. Meanwhile, enjoy this little spell of freedom.... Bokha went back into the bar and ordered himself a quarter of naarangi.

∽

At the end of four days, Bokha had run through his salary. He was no longer very welcome at Gustasp's, especially during peak hours. He hadn't bathed or changed his clothes in all that time and people complained about the pungent odour emanating from him. On the morning of the fifth day, Bokha was climbing up the stairs of Jer Mansion, going up to his mother's flat to routinely bang at the door, when he heard it open and shut quickly, and the latch turn. Someone was coming down the stairs. It was Soma! He should have known. What was that rascal doing here? Bokha waited for him to come down.

'E-he-he-he-he,' the boy burst out laughing on seeing Bokha. 'Aae Bokha, how does it feel to be a real tramp? Without a roof over your head?'

'What are you doing here?' demanded Bokha. Soma was the local toughie among the neighbourhood servants. He worked for the Karanjias, and was known to have a special rapport with Khorshedmai for whom he did odd jobs.

'What's the matter, don't I do chores for her?' asked Soma insolently.

'What does she want now?' asked Bokha.

'Why, a whole list of things for a new recipe she's trying out,' the boy replied. 'What's it to you?'

'Soma, I'm warning you. She's up to some mischief.'

'Mischief? Your ma's just living it up, Bokha. She's turned you out and now she's planning to have a feast. Celebrating. Who would want to live with a Bokha like you? E-he-he-hehe,' the boy giggled. 'She's even asked me to buy a cock for her from the market for tonight. A live one. The live ones are always more tasty. E-he-hehe-he....'

'A cock!' gasped Bokha. He grabbed Soma by the shoulders and tried to shake him, his own body trembling as he screamed, 'Don't you dare, don't you dare!' The younger, muscular boy knocked Bokha's hands off his body with one upward swat of his arm and gave him a slight push. 'Aae Bokha! What's the matter with you? Can't bear to see your ma eat cock?'

Then a funny thing happened. Bokha started crying. He dissolved into tears of helplessness. Soma chuckled and patted his shoulder.

'O Bokha, come on. You're crying, she's crying. Only a minute ago your mother was sobbing away to me,' he said. 'She's afraid you'll leave her. Who'll look after her then? She's an old woman, after all. Go on, make up with her. She'll forgive you.'

'She was crying?' Bokha ceased snivelling when he heard this. 'Swear on God. You think she's happy without you?'

Bokha ran up the stairs like a madman and hammered at the door for a while. Then he pleaded with his mother with renewed earnestness, begging her to let bygones be bygones, he even started to say that if she wanted, he would never again—but there he stopped himself: he didn't say it. And from behind the door, there was nothing: silence.

'Mumma!' he screamed. He kicked the door. Then he spat on it. And walked downstairs again.

All those restless hours he had spent in the past four days came rushing at him again. He had wasted precious hours. Something had to be done, quickly. He had to save Seraphina. He couldn't trust his mother to be kind. Seraphina loved and cared for him. He loved her, too, decided Bokha. If this night passes without event, I will marry her.

Should he go and fall at Framroze's feet, tell him what was going on in the house across the road? But Framroze had warned him never to show his face again. He might not even give him a chance to speak. Besides, what could the old man do to stop Khorshedmai? Call in the cops? Maybe he should just explain everything to Eruchsaa, ask him to pray for Seraphina and protect her soul. But would Parsi prayers work for a Christian ayah? Eruchsaa would probably not believe a single word and give him a thrashing in the bargain.

Then, for a second, Bokha's mind was illumined by a small filament of hope. It hung on the slender thread of the memory of a bar room conversation. That man, the other day. Who was he? He had spoken of a sorcerer, a tantric who had the power to repel spells. Where was he? How could he be contacted? Why hadn't he been listening more carefully?.... Virar. Yes, that's what he had said. Somewhere in Virar, the farthest suburb of Bombay, lived this sorcerer. What was his name? He couldn't remember it now, though the man had mentioned it.... But he could go there and ask. A person like that would surely be well-known in his neighbourhood. He decided to set out at once.

As he caught the north-bound train from Grant Road station, he remembered: 'Motilal.... Ah, yes....' That was the name he had overheard.

⁂

The train was jam-packed. Bokha found himself stranded fairly close to the exit, at a loss to prevent himself from being flung out by anxious commuters who charged the exit every time the train halted at a station. Every new wave of passengers boarding the train pushed him back inside once again, crushing him against a solid wall of people. His cap was knocked off and trampled underfoot. Finally, Bokha managed to wedge himself between two men standing to one side, against the handrail. After a while, the one in front of him glared into his eyes from a distance of about four inches and said rudely, 'Stand straight, can't you?'

Bokha, whose fingers had just been crushed under the hard sole of a shoe while trying to retrieve his cap, lost his temper.

'What d'you mean stand straight! *You* stand straight! '

Just then, the man behind him gave him a shove and moved out. The other man, curiously, seemed to lose interest in the argument and looked away, muttering, 'A mad Bawaji from somewhere....'

At the next station, he too got off. Virar. The name hooted in his ears, while the train raced to its terminus. What was he to do, he wondered, when he finally arrived? He wandered for a few minutes on the platform looking for the exit. He chose a road that led away from the shops and residential areas, in the direction of vast stretches of marsh. He walked briskly, like a man who knew his business.

It was still early in the evening, but there were few people on the road. Every few minutes, a crowded public transport bus would speed past him, raising dust. For a long while, there were no more buses. Then the street lamps came to life. How do I find Motilal, how do I find the sorcerer? The question kept jogging his brain, but while he had been nearer the station among people, he hadn't known whom to ask, how to ask, and had kept walking, as if he knew exactly where he was headed. Now there was no one around to ask.

By the side of the road, an old destitute woman in rags had made a small bonfire, over which she was warming her hands. This seemed quite strange to Bokha since it was not a cold night at all. He stopped before the fire and waited till the old crone looked up.

Bokha said, 'Motilal.... Do you know Motilal?'

The old woman made no reply and lowered her head again.

Bokha repeated his question. She shook her head and gestured to him to move on. Bokha walked for another half hour. Then he saw a colony of makeshift huts by the side of the road; in one of them a Petromax lantern glowed brightly. It turned out to be a paan-and-cigarette shop. The vendor was an old man with white hair. A bright full moon had risen in the sky. Bokha stood before his kiosk, speechless.

'What do you want?' asked the old man, abruptly.

'Motilal....' he muttered, half under his breath.

'Who? Motilal? Motilal who?'

Bokha shook his head. The man understood.

'Motilal Jadoogar?'

'Yes, him,' cried Bokha, much too loudly.

'What do you want with him?' the man asked Bokha, narrowing his eyes a little.

'I.... I want to meet him.' What else could he say?

'You have a problem?' the old man enquired.

'Yes....'

'I'm sorry, he's not here any more.'

'Where can I find him?' Bokha cried urgently.

'Not in this world.... Motilal disappeared three years ago. A body was found chopped to pieces among the gravestones of the cemetery next to the dargah. Some said it was Motilal, that he had met an adversary more powerful than he.... I knew Motilal. He owed me some money. He owed everybody. But he was a good man. He helped a lot of people too.... I don't expect we'll ever see him again.'

The old man wanted to talk, find out more about Bokha's particular difficulty. But Bokha's mind had turned vacant. He didn't know any more why he was standing in front of that paan shop in the wilderness, asking after a man called Motilal, whom he had never met before and now never would. Bokha turned away without thanking the old man. He began walking back towards the station, the way he had come.

Only when he arrived at the station and reached for his wallet to buy a ticket (because he knew ticket collectors lurked at Grant Road station at this hour to nab the ticketless) only then did Bokha start crying. It was not there. His wallet. He felt for it a dozen times, but it was gone. Those two on the train. Stand straight indeed, you bastards! Bokha choked with frustration and his body shook with sobs. Anyway, there had only been five rupees in it.

When he reached Grant Road by the last train, he felt defeated but much calmer. He remembered to leave the station through the siding along the tracks, where the fence was broken. He walked homewards up the incline of Forjett Hill, though what sense it made going there he could not say.

Gustasp's bar had shut. It was too late, even for a Saturday night. Bokha trudged slowly, dragging his feet. God in heaven, what was that? A light on in the flat at this hour? What could that mean? Bokha didn't want to know. He wanted to flee. Something warned him to get out. But he forced himself to climb the stairs, as noiselessly as he could.

Bokha stood outside the door quietly and listened. There was dead silence. He fumbled for the key in his pocket. His hands were trembling so much he had difficulty inserting it in the latch-hole. The key turned. He pushed the door open a few inches.

'Come in. I was waiting for you.'

His mother was sitting up in bed, eating. There was nothing alarming or unusual about the scene that presented itself as he stepped into the room. Everything was as before. What was more, she had spoken to him kindly. A great flood of gratitude and relief drenched his fraught, embattled nerves. He could have cried.

'Mumma....'

'Come. You haven't eaten, have you?' said Khorshedmai. 'Have some of this.' Bokha tried to make out what was on her plate.

'What's that you're eating?' asked Bokha, suddenly tense.

'Cock.'

'Oh....' Bokha was silent.

'Eat some.'

'I'm not hungry.'

His mother continued to eat, chomping heartily at a bone. Bokha sat down on the bed near her feet.

'Mumma....' He began, contritely.

'Yes, Bokha,' said Khorshedmai. 'I've decided to forgive you. You can come back home now.'

'Oh Mumma, I'll never speak to you again like that. I'm so sorry,' Bokha genuinely was. 'I was so worried....'

Khorshedmai continued to chomp.

'I was so worried something would happen.... That you would....' muttered Bokha.

'Worried-burried, forget,' said Khorshedmai, putting her plate aside, looking satiated. 'Come and eat something now. Here. Wipe up what's left in the pot.'

Bokha was overwhelmed. He did something he had not done in many years. He hugged his mother. He threw his arms around her and kissed her.

'Mumma, you're so nice....'

'Yes, yes. Now watch—my hands are dirty,' said Khorshedmai, pleased. He buried his head in her vast bosom and let it rest there. Until she rumbled, 'Enough now.'

Bokha helped himself to a leg piece from the blackened pot on the table beside her bed. He bit into it.

'Mmm. Nice. Bit tough....' He chewed at the meat slowly.

'I was really worried. Thank God, she's safe.'

'What did you say?' asked Khorshedmai coldly.

'That girl, you know.... I thought something would happen.... Oh Mumma, I don't know what to say. You should meet her.... I'm so sorry I caused you all this pain.... But she's really quite a nice girl....'

Bokha didn't see her hand move. Thack! The slap nearly knocked him off the bed.

'What kind of fool do you take me for?' screeched Khorshedmai, hoarsely. 'Ungrateful wretch! I said I was willing to forgive you.'

Bokha stood up, trembling.

'Go. Go in there,' she said. 'Take a look....'

'What.... What have you been doing...?'

In an instant, Bokha was in the kitchen. On the floor, a circle had been inscribed with red and yellow powders. In it, a large kitchen knife, and the severed head of a rooster lying in a half-dried patch of blood. He became aware of her coarse laughter from the next room, grating on his senses.

'So you saw?' she called out. 'I always keep my word....'

The ocular mists in her eyes seemed to gleam with perverse delight. Through their haze, though, she saw Bokha re-enter the room.

Then the room turned red.

∽

It was my birthday, and the morning of my last day at Happy Home. Mother was coming over for lunch in the afternoon and then she would take me home with her. School would resume in just two days.

My uncle and I had finished breakfast and were still at the table when the doorbell rang thunderously. Someone had held his finger to it. Framroze and I stared at each other, paralysed.

Both of us had a premonition of disaster. But it was Pheena who ran to the door and flung it open. Bokha entered and collapsed in her arms. He was a ghastly sight. The front of his shirt was stiff with blood.

She sat him on a chair in the passage and caressed his head.

He was blubbering,

'I got her. I got her first.... She tried to make me eat it. In the end, I made her...eat cock!'

He giggled and said something even more incoherent.

Then he laughed again, and within a few moments it became clear to all of us that Bokha was far away in another world.

Seraphina continued to caress his hair, a remote sadness in her eyes. After a while, she began humming softly, some meaningless plaintive drone of mourning which seemed to soothe Bokha.

Framroze was on the phone to the police when we heard a loud tramping on the stairs. It was Bapsymai, Fardoon, and Ghauswalla, come early today for their morning's séance since guests were expected for lunch. In all the shock and commotion, no one had heard the honking of the car. My uncle had never been so glad to see his friends as he was that Sunday morning.

All this happened a very long time ago. When I was in my last year at school, Uncle Framroze suffered a massive stroke which left him paralysed. A few days later, he was dead. He had provided generously for Pheena, but she donated her entire pension to the Holy Mother's Convent which she joined as a lay kitchen worker. As for Bokha, try as I did, I was never able to find out what became of him, and whether he was still alive. The police hadn't maintained proper records of the case of an old Parsi woman on Forjett Hill Road who was stabbed with a kitchen knife fifty-two times.

THE LABYRINTH

SARA RAI

Translated from the Hindi by Poonam Saxena

THIS IS BANARAS CITY, KASHI NAGRI. IT STANDS ON SHIVJI'S TRISHUL. Incomparable among the ancient cities of the world. From the beginning of time, the business of life and death has gone on here. Banaras is alive; it gives shelter to the dead and the dying. Crowds of people throng the maze of alleys. In Banaras, there is a sea of people living with the desire to die. They who die here will go to heaven, to paradise. This belief is as old as truth itself. Living in this place, I too have come to believe it. Belief is the ultimate truth.

City of ghosts. Women who died centuries ago silently spread their thick hair across the sky. The air is heavy with the breathing of shadows. In the glow from the setting sun, these shadows bend over spire, minaret, and dome. Steps of worn-out stone lead down to the tank, where the water turns from muddy to dark green; the stench of moss and sludge has been hanging in the air for hundreds of years. The boy flying a kite in the lane cuts his finger on its sharp string and the blood that flows from it is thousands of years old. Crumbling monuments stand in this century but their windows open to another sky. The spread of the ancient city, crowded with the people living in it, can be read like a history book. People drift across it with their own rhythm. The city has been written upon by time. And in the clamour of life stretching from one century to the other there are cracks in which ghosts dwell.

Amidst the crowd of ghosts, in my quiet corner, I am still alive and well. Perhaps I've been here from the beginning of time. I, Kulsum Bano, resident of Noor Manzil, 18/20 Ausaanganj, behind Kabir Chaura Hospital, in a straight line from the old peepul tree. Kulsum Bano, the eldest daughter of Sayyid Naseem Haider. Look, there's Abba Huzoor's picture on the wall, clinging gently to a piece of decaying yellow paper. A Kashmiri fur cap, a jamawar shawl. Shoulders like the walls of a fortress, grand moustaches. His forty villages and dozen kothis are not in the picture but the air of command on Sayyid Naseem Haider's face comes from them. The relic of a family that has lived in this ancient city for generations, captured in a solitary moment long gone. After him, the last fruit left on this old tree—me. No one after me. Because this tree bore no other fruit.

Yesterday, that girl came to meet me, wearing men's clothes, slim, short-haired, bespectacled, her face exactly like a sparrow's! She looked closely at my face, at the deep hollows on its old, yellow, papery skin and at the lustreless valleys of my eyes. As if I belonged to an extinct species. Then she asked: 'How are you, Apa Begum?'—in a familiar manner, as if she was an acquaintance of many years.

Like an animal who'd lived shut up in its den, I growled nastily, 'I am very bad, worse than bad, I'm dissatisfied with everything, rude, extremely ill-mannered, an infinitely troublesome old woman, continuing to live shamelessly, a burden on everyone, worth even less than dust, absolutely good for nothing, unendurable....'

I would have continued talking in this vein but seeing her look so taken aback I stopped. She looked out of her depth. Her mouth was open, but not a sound came from it. She was speechless.

Then she tried again, look at her nerve! She extended a hand towards me, and said, 'If you'll allow me, I'd like to talk to you for a bit....'

I asked, 'What do you mean by a bit? A quarter of a kilo, half a kilo, one kilo?'

Poor thing! Again, she stared at me, at a loss for words. I had slain her with just two sentences! My wrinkled face broke into a smile at the thought. Looking reassured, she too laughed a little. Just like a twittering sparrow!

'Actually, I'm writing an article on old houses and the people who live in them, for a newspaper. I wanted to ask you a few questions....'

It would not be easy to put her off. All right then, ask. Ask whatever you want, then go your way so that I too may breathe a sigh of relief. No one's coming here after that, and I'm certainly not going anywhere. End of story. No sooner had I spoken than she fished out a black box-like object from the bag slung on her shoulder and said, 'If you permit this imposition, may I record the conversation?'

So now this girl will trap my voice and take it away.

Haan bhai, I'm the last of my family. No, no one else is left. Can you see a crowd of people milling around me? My father had four children. Five, if you count Ali Mian. He was just this high, three years old when he was struck down by cholera. I too fell prey to cholera. But I was tough, cholera didn't happen to me, it was I who happened to cholera. It ran away, tail between its legs! So, there were four of us left. I was the eldest, then Iqbal Mian, then Tahira, then Sakina. They've all gone now, each one of them. Come, let's move on. You want to know what my father did? What a question! What indeed did he do? Well, he didn't go about selling curds, that much I can tell you! He was an aristocrat, do aristocrats have any profession? He walked with his head held high. Yes, there was a lot of coming and going in this haveli. It became an abode of ghosts much later. On festivals, relatives would turn up from everywhere. The house was always full. People like bunches of grapes in every room. Food being cooked in enormous quantities and the size of the tablecloth growing ever larger. There'd be twenty-two to twenty-five people at a time. Those secret meetings, the laughter, the whispers. The singers would come in the evening and the place would turn joyful with their music and dance. That's how I got obsessed with dancing, just by watching them. I'd dance all over the house, but despite my nagging, Abba didn't get me the ghungroos I needed. I was not one to give up. I got Yaqub to buy them for me from the bazaar. Such a passion for dancing! I'd dance all day but my feet never tired. It was these same feet that are now twisted like a witch's. Those days have turned to dust. Many are the flowers the garden brings forth, countless the changing colours of the sky!

Where was I in 1947? When the country was broken up into pieces? In hell! I was here, in my home, my own country, where else would I be? How could I leave my neem tree and go away? We heard that Pakistan was coming up across the border, but which border, where was this border? No, nobody went to Pakistan from our house, except for Iqbal Mian. He was always faint-hearted and the riots scared him; he got taken in by what people said. And look what became of him. He left his heart on this madhumalati vine, yes, this vine that you see in front of you, with pink and white flowers. That didn't go with him. He died on alien soil, yearning for this madhumalati, for these wretched sparrows that live in it. After me? How do I know what will happen to this haveli after me? I don't waste my time thinking of such unnecessary things. The same that has been happening for centuries. The water drop is fated to be lost in the sea! The rooms on one side have already started caving in, the walls and the roof have long decayed. Getting them repaired is beyond me. Last month the fortified wall of the porch collapsed. And do you know what Halima brought for me from the rubble? Those wretched ghungroos that I'd asked Yaqub to get me almost eighty years ago, which had vanished.

Anyway, forget it, this story is very old and really long, like the entrails of a snake. End it here, just write down whatever you've heard till now. I'll say nothing more. The tale is over and done with, khuda hafiz.

What a relief that she's gone at last. With her black box and phone. Nowadays everyone you see has a phone in their hands, what do you call it? Mobile. The other day, Bittan Mehtarani's niece, Jhallo, came and stood in front of me with a mobile in her hand. She asked me, 'Apa Begum, do you know what this is?'

For God's sake! This is the twenty-first century. It's no joke. Not that I care! I live in my own time. My time creeps slowly alongside the swift current of that girl's time.

Whatever has happened in the past is not over, it grows and blossoms forever in my imagination. The shadows and the lights are still there. This journey, from noise to silence, life that starts suddenly and then pauses. The same labyrinth. Noor Manzil, lost in the fog of time, this is the same Noor Manzil. But Noor Manzil is not merely made of bricks and walls, beyond the reality of geography, it is spread out in the world of my mind, in my memories, where its likeness is set as though frozen in ice. So much time has passed. But I've got it wrong. Time doesn't pass, it's a constantly flowing river. Does it have a shore? No, I'm the one who's passing by. This monsoon, my bones will become ninety-three years old. By the grace of God, my hands and feet still function. I can walk without difficulty. If I live a little longer, I'll have been an eyewitness to an entire century. A whole century fallen from the tree of eternity!

That girl did her job and left but there is a clutter of images within me, a whole stack of them. And the pictures keep unspooling like a tape.

Abba's deep voice was heard in the porch, far away in the waiting hall. The buggy had just come and stopped in front of the house. The creaking of his leather shoes. The thak-thak of his ivory cane on the floor. Jerking my head away from Anna who was combing my hair, I swept aside the heavy curtains of the inner courtyard and ran out. The sunshine outside was blinding. In the distance, the well and along its edge a row of tall wild banana trees. Even taller was the silk cotton that stood alone like a sentry, in its full glory. Its bright red flowers stung my eyes. I ran like the wind. My long hair streamed behind me like the tail of a horse. I jumped up and swung on my abba's shoulders.

'Abba, I've been looking out for you for so long. Where were you? Did you get my ghungroos?'

He didn't say anything. There was a small frown on his face. Gently he disengaged me from his shoulder and turned his gaze to the syce, who was watching us attentively and listening to everything that was being said.

'Allahrakhe, go and put the gaadi in the stables.'

Then he addressed me, 'Come along child, come inside. What was the need to come out in this wild manner?'

Holding my arm, he took me inside.

Abbajaan, the most handsome, smartest, strongest man in the whole world.

And I was madly in love with him. There could be no other person like him in the whole world. When I was younger, I used to say, 'If I get married it will only be to Abba!' How they would laugh at that! Abba loved all three of us very much. He loved Iqbal Mian too but not as much as the girls. Intoxicated by his pampering, we were constantly preening, very pleased with ourselves. Who could put a stop to this strutting around? Anna would grumble to herself, 'I've never seen such attitude. These girls are really getting out of hand, they're up to some mischief or the other every day.'

Anna wasn't wrong. We were extremely naughty. When Maulvi Sahib came to teach us, we would study decorously for a while. Maulvi Sahib used to consume opium. As the opium started affecting him, we would quietly tiptoe out of the room. We'd come out on the nearby veranda where the gong hung and we would bang it hard. Maulvi Sahib would jump up, saying 'Hai hai!' and sit upright again. Then one of us would say, 'Maulvi Sahib, you had dozed off. We've been revising our lessons for an hour.'

'So, is the revision done?' Maulvi Sahib asked hesitantly.

'Yes, Maulvi Sahib,' we would chant together.

'All right, learn the lesson for tomorrow then,' he would say, as he slipped his feet into his shoes, and adjusting his cap, he'd step out into the alley. The entire study period would be over in just half an hour! And what after that! There would be mimicry of all the venerable elderly members of the household and general merriment on our part. We'd hide Anna's false teeth and go into splits at her toothless mutterings or, under cover of burqas in the afternoon, we'd frighten Anna's daughter, Suggan, by pretending to be ghosts. At other times we'd lock up Chachamian's younger son, Attu, in the hen coop and then run away. The sun never set on our mischief and devilry.

Even when complaints came in, Abba paid no attention. Secure in the circle of his love, we grew up wild. We'd do the mischief, and poor Iqbal Mian would get the scolding. He kept a strict eye on Iqbal, to see he didn't get spoiled. But he wasn't prepared to hear a word against his daughters. When the topic of our weddings arose, he thought no boy in the world worthy of us. If one of them had a pedigree not quite up to the mark, the other was too short or too dark, else he was too arrogant or talked more than he should. Taking a cue from his attitude, we'd give the would-be grooms all sorts of nicknames. 'Shorty', 'Monkey-nut', 'Black face', 'Arab horse', and so on. In short, he would reject any proposal that came on some pretext or the other. So we stayed on at Noor Manzil, at the height of our exalted family's fortunes, our impeccable pedigree, our beauty, and elegance. We didn't leave all of that to go anywhere. Look, Abba, I'm still at Noor Manzil. You won't have to ask for my address.

The sprawling grounds of Noor Manzil, where in the rains plants seem to grow at an incredible speed, and slugs and millipedes, red velvet-insects and newly born frogs celebrate joyously. Snakes that were imprisoned below the ground all year long slide out of their holes and welcome the monsoon, their supple bodies flexing, and tall grass spreads everywhere like green fire. Yes, these grounds are still there in the midst of all the hustle and bustle of Banaras city. You can still come here, slicing through the crowds.

Noor Manzil. Walls at least three feet thick of lakhori bricks, high doors, two massive gates studded with iron nails, a long curving entrance and in from the door you go down three steps to reach an enormous, open courtyard. In the middle of it, a water tank, from which a fountain leaps up ceaselessly, restless to touch the light. On both sides of the courtyard, two verandas with arches that had thick, heavy curtains in those days. In the winter the curtains would be drawn, ensuring that not a hint of cold entered, and in the summer they would be swept aside so that a rustling breeze could come in and cool down the place. Four madhumalati creepers climbed alongside the arches, whose stalks had grown so thick they'd have put any vine in a dense African jungle to shame.

Hundreds of sparrows lived in the vine.... At dawn and dusk their chirping created such a din you could hear nothing else.

In the rooms inside hung farshi punkahs whose cord, wound on the toe, was pulled by a servant sitting on the floor. Now that we have electricity those fans are of no use. But one of them still hangs in the hall. I remember the long summer afternoons when Suggan would grip the cord with her toe and pull it for hours on end. She'd doze off sometimes but her toe kept moving.

In one corner of the inner courtyard is a spiral staircase with wide steps that winds its way up to the room on the roof. Noor Manzil's sweeping, open roof. We would put out our cots on this roof on summer nights. The gleaming white sheets and pillows on the beds and the bela and chameli flowers placed at the head of the cots gave off such a heady fragrance! When it was suffocatingly humid and fire seemed to rain down from the sky, we would sprinkle water or rose and kewda on the charpais. If it rained we would drag the cots inside the room on the roof. And above the courtyard, in the eaves, were the pigeon cotes. Anna used to say that illness doesn't visit a house that has pigeons. Laqqa and Shirazi and Kabuli and that valuable Anardana, with eyes like those of Emperor Akbar.

Now more than half of the rooms are shut. One part of the haveli is open for my use. At the far end of the veranda four steps lead down to the basement which stays cool even in the summer; next to it the small courtyard in which I spend the winters and attached to it the little room that serves as my kitchen. Halima sleeps in front of it, with her daughter-in-law and grandchildren, while her good-for-nothing alcoholic son wanders aimlessly around the alleyways of Banaras. At night, when everyone spreads out their bedding, the stale smell of fatigue and sweat that rises from there makes my heart sink. But what can be done? I am the one who told them to sleep here. I have no choice but to endure it. Were I to fall at an odd hour and break my leg, there should be somebody around to pick me up.

In fact, Halima leaves no stone unturned in looking after me. She nags me all the time, 'Will Apa Begum have some tea?' or 'Apa Begum, shall I bring the water for your bath?'

May God save me from this witch's attempts to bathe me. Do I roll in mud all night that I need a bath? But small mercies, it's a blessing that she's around. It's not as if I'm showering her with riches. Just a couple of rotis and dal to keep body and soul together. She's seen misfortune and that's why she's here, otherwise where do you get servants these days?

The rest of the house is shut. The curving stairway to the roof leads to a long veranda. Martyr's veranda is the name it has acquired over the years. When silence falls late at night, the Martyr comes down the stairs in his sandals made of wood. I can hear the knocking sound they make. But he never does finish coming down the stairs; he's been doing that for the past two hundred years. In fact, his coming down the stairs has become part of family lore. If you open the window of the room on the roof, you can see his grave right there. There's a difference of opinion on whether he's a good ghost or a bad one that's out to create trouble. You can't really tell, can you, with ghosts. Every Friday I send Halima to the veranda to light a lamp and incense sticks. Though what can the spirit do to me now? I am well on the way to becoming one myself!

I have said farewell to everyone. Abba, Ammi, Chachamian, Chachijaan. Then both my sisters and brother. All three were younger than me. In the left wing of the haveli, the four children of Chachamian. All gone. They sleep blissfully beneath the neem tree. Yellow leaves float and fall on the graves. Again and again, I sweep them aside, clear the surface. I scrape away with my nails the soil that has settled on the graves and come upon the names inscribed on the marble epitaph. Just the names, no other sign of the illustrious ones now gone. There's just me, with one leg in this world, the second leg in the other—straddling them both. I, Kulsum Bano. There is no one left to call me by this name. I've beaten everyone hollow; I just don't die! But I do tread carefully now. I saw what happened to Ammi, I learnt my lesson. I want to keep living; the desire to live is in every pore of my being.

Standing on the parapet of the roof blackened with moss, I'd flap my arms as though they were wings. A large moon, like a yellow plate, would be out in the sky. Making a loud flapping sound I'd rise in a cloud of dust. Bright moonlit monuments, trees, pillars, all would be left behind. Carving the air with my wings, I'd turn around and look back on Noor Manzil that kept receding into the distance. And the sense of freedom. Happiness, like a sparkler, would light up my heart. For years, this dream danced in my eyes. I'd go and tell Ammi about it. Ammi would be lying in bed. Forget flying, she couldn't even walk.

My Ammi. Even a wicked person like me once had an ammi. Nusrat Bano. She fell down on this very porch. She broke her hip bone and could never stand again. She'd lie all day on a large teak bed in the small courtyard. The seasons changed from summer to monsoon, monsoon to winter, then spring and fall and then summer again. There would be no change in her condition. The bed sagged because she was always lying on it. She was fading away. That fearless beauty of hers. Her eyes, like rivers of fire, the passion on her face. I've seen the light go out of those eyes. Ya khuda! Why did you give her that passion, only for it to be vanquished?

I'm saying this today, when her image is before me as I wander in the labyrinth of days gone by. Those days we had little awareness of how helpless she was. She would lie in a corner of the haveli all day while we rushed about creating a ruckus, like the still point of a constantly spinning world. She'd call out if she saw someone go by; they'd listen sometimes and at others ignore her and move on. What energy was it that swept us ever forward so that her voice never reached us?

Sometimes in the afternoons, when I heard her calling and went to her, she would gesture with her hand that I should come and sit down next to her. Then she would draw my attention to the sunlight filtering through the henna bush in a corner of the courtyard.

The gently swaying, tightly entwined twigs created a fine maze of shadows on the wall in front of us. Both of us would look at it, she lying down, I seated, till the light lasted. These continuously forming, changing, dissolving shadows would barely last a moment but in this play of light and shadow we would see islands, or grass and trees rustling in the wind, smoke rising from burning leaves, a caravan of camels that had been crossing the desert for many days. A finite world that would slowly vanish. She would whisper and ask me, 'Look, can you see that cluster of coconut trees swaying in the breeze? Those huge ships, the cactus trees in the desert?' There was the rustle of a moth's broken wings in her raspy voice.

But more often than not, I too would pretend I hadn't heard her, preoccupied as I was with myself. I was very busy those days.

Tahira Bibi came running up to me.

'Apa! Apa! Come quickly. The kite has come again!'

Tahira, my sister, four years younger than me, my follower. The chicks had been released into the courtyard from under the bamboo basket which was their temporary home. They belonged to my Minorca hen, Kallo. For two days the kite had been circling over them; it carried off a chick yesterday and now it was back. A curse be upon this kite!

I leapt after Tahira like a streak of lightning, barefoot, without even the presence of mind to put on my jootis. The sky was stretched tight like a blue tent over the courtyard, on the tent were white clouds, like flags. No sign of a kite. But looking carefully, one could discern, high up in the distance, a miniscule black dot that kept growing. The kite was swooping down at great speed. My gaze went to the two little chicks, like balls of yellow wool, full of the innocence of their two-week-old life. Watching the kite filled me with rage. Suddenly the kite's shadow fell on the ground as she swooped down on the chicks. Then, in the blink of an eye I pounced on the kite, pressing down on it with my full weight. Its warm wings fluttered under my chest. They smelled of dust and heights.

'Suggan, Suggan!' I screamed. 'Quickly, get the big scissors.'

In a fit of rage, with the help of Suggan and Tahira, I cut off the kite's wings. My bloodlust cooled only when I saw it walking with the chicks.

It is the same courtyard. I sit there till late every evening, watching the light change from muddy to grey to inky. All around me, solitude spreads like dense black smoke. Halima's goat is tied on one side of the courtyard, it is also black. It gazes at me with its blank eyes and I stare back at it like a fool. A curse be on this Halima. She could find no other place to tie the goat. One day it got free and chewed up all the gul-e-abbasi flowers. After being eaten by a goat, a plant doesn't thrive. And I get enraged if I see goat droppings. Tiny, disgusting black pellets strewn all over. The witch doesn't have the good sense to clean up after, just knows how to spread dung. But how many things can I yell about; I just sit in this garbage dump doing nothing.

Today, when I was sitting in the courtyard, I heard Sakina Bibi's voice coming from the hall. Sakina, my youngest sister. Her rounded voice, as though her throat was slick with a smooth string of mellifluous notes. Sakina's delicate face appeared in front of me. In her ears, dangling emerald earrings. Her turquoise dupatta fluttered in the hall, in the air that had hung still for ages. She used to put her head inside a copper pot and sing. Captured inside the pot, trying to find a way out, her voice would echo even more deeply. That pot would turn up in different places in the house, in the grain-store or in a pile of broken utensils. Then it too disappeared, like my ghungroos. Because of the good-for-nothing servants of this house, no household object ever stayed in its appointed place. I could hear Sakina's voice clearly. She was singing her favourite song—

Jhuki aayi re badariya sawan ki
Sawan ki manbhawan ki...

The rainclouds of Saawan hang low
O so pleasing to the heart...

Sakina and I would remain closeted in the hall for hours on end.

Her singing and my dancing! I swear, it never ended. What madness had me in its grip those days. I don't know where I got this craze for dancing from. Was it the gift of the singers who used to come to the haveli in the evenings, or did the roots of this passion go back to some other deeper hidden place? Could it be in my blood, passed on to me from a beautiful dancing girl who, by her art of offering fragrant paan had stolen into the heart of one of my ancestors? This boiling intensity in my blood must have come from somewhere, this intensity that cooled down only with the movement of my feet and the motion of my body.

Eyes closed, a smile on my face, my heart and mind in some other world, I would keep dancing. My feet got bruised but I never tired. Round and round I would go, twirling in perfect circles on the stone floor of the hall. Then, a hand holding on to the voluminous folds of my gharara, I'd stand completely still, like a top that stopped spinning. The whole time that I danced, I would be in some other place; it was as if I was another person. Finally when I stopped, out of breath, that other world continued to dance within me!

Far away, in some corner of the world, Sakina Bibi is singing, her head inside that copper pot. Evening has fallen. Sakina's voice seems to echo from the rosy, golden sky. What a miracle that last month my ghungroos were found, lost for eighty years, hidden behind a wall. I take them in my hands and fiddle with them, turning them around. They were the same ghungroos; time and the humid atmosphere had imbued them with a green patina. With difficulty I bent my stiff back, and tied the ghungroos on my wooden feet. Then, like an ungainly bird moving clumsily, standing right there, I executed a shuffling, stumbling twirl. Something echoed in my heart, perhaps an old memory. A muted sound came from the rusty ghungroos, as though from far away.

CHARLIS AND I

SHASHI THAROOR

I WAS ABOUT EIGHT OR NINE WHEN I FIRST CAME ACROSS CHARLIS. A few of us children were kicking a ball around the dusty courtyard of my grandmother's house in rural Kerala, where my parents took me annually on what they called a holiday and I regarded as a cross between a penance and a pilgrimage. (Their pilgrimage, my penance.) Balettan, my oldest cousin, who was all of thirteen and had a bobbing Adam's apple to prove it, had just streaked across me and kicked the ball with more force than he realized he possessed. It soared upwards like a startled bird, curved perversely away from us, and disappeared over our high brick wall into the rubbish heap at the back of the neighbour's house.

'Damn,' I said. I had grown up in Bombay where one said things like that.

'Go and get it, da,' Balettan commanded one of the younger cousins. Da was a term of great familiarity, used especially when ordering young boys around.

A couple of the kids, stifling groans, dutifully set off towards the wall. But before they could reach it the ball came sailing back over their heads towards us, soon followed over the wall by a skinny, sallow youth with a pockmarked face and an anxious grin. He seemed vaguely familiar, someone I'd seen in the background on previous holidays but not really noticed, though I wasn't sure why.

'Charlis!' a couple of the kids called out. 'Charlis got the ball!'

Charlis sat on the wall, managing to look both unsure and pleased with himself. Bits of muck from the rubbish heap clung to his shirt and skin. 'Can I play?' he asked diffidently.

Balettan gave him a look that would have desiccated a coconut. 'No, you can't, Charlis,' he said shortly, kicking the ball towards me, away from the interloper who'd rescued it.

Charlis's face lost its grin, leaving only the look of anxiety across it like a shadow. He remained seated on the wall, his legs—bare and thin below the grubby mundu he tied around his waist—dangling nervously. The game resumed, and Charlis watched, his eyes liquid with wistfulness.

He would kick the brick wall aimlessly with his foot, then catch himself doing it and stop, looking furtively at us to see whether anyone had noticed. But no one paid any attention to him, except me, and I was the curious outsider.

'Why can't he play?' I finally found the courage to ask Balettan.

'Because he can't, that's all,' replied my eldest cousin.

'But why? We can always use another player,' I protested.

'We can't use him,' Balettan said curtly. 'Don't you understand anything, stupid?'

That was enough to silence me, because I had learned early on that there was a great deal about the village I didn't understand. A city upbringing didn't prepare you for your parents' annual return to their roots, to the world they'd left behind and failed to equip you for. Everything, pretty much, was different in my grandmother's house: there were hurricane lamps instead of electric lights, breezes instead of ceiling fans, a cow in the barn rather than a car in the garage. Water didn't come out of taps but from a well, in buckets laboriously raised by rope pulleys; you poured it over yourself out of metal vessels, hoping the maidservant who'd heated the bathwater over a charcoal fire had not made it so hot you'd scald yourself. There were the obscure indignities of having to be accompanied to the outhouse by an adult with a gleaming stainless-steel flashlight and of needing to hold his hand while you squatted in the privy, because the chair-like commodes of the city had made you unfit to discharge your waste as an Indian should, on his haunches. But it wasn't just a question of these inconveniences; there was the sense of being in a different world. Bombay was busy, bustling, unpredictable; there were children of every imaginable appearance, colour, language, and religion in my school; it was a city of strangers jostling one another all the time. In my grandmother's village everyone I met seemed to know one another and be related. They dressed alike, did the same things day after day, shared the same concerns, celebrated the same festivals. Their lives were ordered, predictable; things were either done or not done, according to rules and assumptions I'd never been taught in the city.

Some of the rules were easier than others to grasp. There were, for instance, complicated hierarchies that everyone seemed to take for granted. The ones I first understood were those relating to age. This was absolute, like an unspoken commandment: everyone older had to be respected and obeyed, even if they sent you off on trivial errands they should really have done themselves. Then there was gender: the women existed to serve the men, fetching and carrying and stitching and hurrying for them, eating only after they had fed the men first. Even my mother, who could hold her own at a Bombay party with a cocktail in her hand, was transformed in Kerala into a dutiful drudge, blowing into the wood fire to make the endless stacks of thin, soft, crisp-edged dosas we all wolfed down. None of this had to be spelled out, no explicit orders given; people simply seemed to adjust naturally to an immutable pattern of expectations, where everyone knew his place and understood what he had to do. As someone who came from Bombay for a month's vacation every year, spoke the language badly, hated the bathrooms, and swelled up with insect bites, I adjusted less than most. I sensed dimly that the problem with Charlis, too, had something to do with hierarchy, but since he was neither female nor particularly young, I couldn't fit him into what I thought I already knew of Kerala village life.

We finished the game soon enough, and everyone began heading indoors. Charlis jumped off the wall. Instinctively, but acting with the casual hospitality I usually saw around me, I went up to him and said, 'My mother'll be making dosas for tea. Want some?'

I was puzzled by the look of near panic that flooded his face. 'No, no, that's all right,' he said, practically backing away from me. I could see Balettan advancing towards us. 'I've got to go,' Charlis added, casting me a strange look as he fled.

'What's the matter with him?' I asked Balettan.

'What's the matter with you?' he retorted. 'What were you saying to him?'

'I just asked him to join us for some dosas, that's all,' I replied. Seeing his expression, I added lamely, 'you know, with all the other kids.'

Balettan shook his head in a combination of disgust and dismay, as if he didn't know whether to be angry or sad. 'You know what this little foreigner did?' he announced loudly as soon as we entered the house. 'He asked Charlis to come and have dosas with us!'

This was greeted with guffaws by some and clucks of disapproval by others. 'Poor little boy, what does he know?' said my favourite aunt, the widowed Ranivaliamma, gathering me to her ample bosom to offer a consolation I hadn't realized I needed. 'It's not his fault.'

'What's not my fault?' I asked, struggling free of her embrace. The Cuticura talcum powder in her cleavage tickled my nose, and the effort not to sneeze made me sound even more incoherent than usual. 'Why shouldn't I invite him? He got our ball back for us. And you invite half the village anyway if they happen to pass by.'

'Yes, but which half?' chortled Kunjunnimama, a local layabout and distant relative who was a constant presence at our dining table and considered himself a great wit. 'Which half, I say?' He laughed heartily at his own question, his eyes rolling, a honking sound emerging from the back of his nose.

I couldn't see why anyone else found this funny, but I was soon sent off to wash my hands. I sat down to my dosas feeling as frustrated as a vegetarian at a kebab shop.

'Who is Charlis, anyway?' I asked as my mother served me the mild chutney she made specially since I couldn't handle the fiery, spiced version everyone else ate.

'I don't know, dear, just a boy from the village,' she responded. 'Now finish your dosas, the adults have to eat.'

'Charlis is the Prince of Wales, didn't you know?' honked Kunjunnimama, enjoying himself hugely. 'I thought you went to a convent school, Neel.'

'First of all, only girls go to convent schools,' I responded hotly. 'And, anyway, the Prince of Wales is called Charles, not Charlis.' I shot him a look of pure hatred, but he was completely unfazed. He soaked it in as a paddy field would a rainstorm, and honked some more.

'Charlis, Charles, what's the difference to an illiterate Untouchable with airs above his station? Anyway, that's how it sounded in Malayalam, and that's how he wrote it. Charlis. So, you see how the Prince of Wales was born in Vanganassery.' He exploded into self-satisfied mirth, his honks suggesting he was inhaling his own pencil-line moustache. I hadn't understood what he meant, but I vowed not to seek any further clarification from him.

My mother came to my rescue. I could see that her interest was piqued. 'But why Charles?' she paused in her serving and asked Kunjunnimama. 'Are they Christians?'

'Christians?' Kunjunnimama honked again. 'My dear chechi, what do these people know of religion? Do they have any culture, any traditions? One of them, that cobbler fellow, Mandan, named his sons Mahatma Gandhi and Jawaharlal Nehru. Can you imagine? The fellow didn't even know that Mahatma was a title and Nehru a family surname. His brats were actually registered in school as M. Mahatma Gandhi and M. Jawaharlal Nehru. So, of course, when this upstart scavenger shopkeeper had to name his offspring, he went one better. Forget nationalism, he turned to the British royal family. So what if they had Christian names? So what if he couldn't pronounce them? You think Charlis is bad enough? He has two sisters, Elizabeth and Anne. Of course, everyone in the village calls them Eli and Ana.'

This time even I joined in the laughter: I had enough Malayalam to know that Eli meant rat and Ana meant elephant. But a Bombayite sense of fairness asserted itself.

'It doesn't matter what his name is,' I said firmly. 'Charlis seems a nice boy. He went into the rubbish heap to get our ball. I liked him.'

'Nice boy!' Kunjunnimama's tone was dismissive, and this time there was no laughter in his honk. 'Rubbish heaps are where they belong. They're not clean. They don't wash. They have dirty habits.'

'What dirty habits?' I asked, shaking off my mother's restraining hand. 'Who's they?'

'Eat your food,' Kunjunnimama said to me, adding to no one in particular, 'and now this communist government wants to put them in our schools. With our children.' He snorted. 'They'll be drinking out of our wells next.'

A few days later, the kids at home all decided to go to the local stream for a dip. On earlier Kerala holidays, my mother had firmly denied me permission to go along, sure that if I didn't drown I'd catch a cold; but now I was older, I'd learned to swim, and I was capable of towelling myself dry, so I was allowed the choice. It seemed a fun idea, and, in any case, there was nothing better to do at home: I'd long since finished reading the couple of Biggles books I'd brought along. I set out with a sense of adventure.

We walked through dusty, narrow lanes, through the village, Balettan in the lead, half a dozen of the cousins following. For a while the houses we passed seemed to be those of relatives and friends; the kids waved cheerful greetings to women hanging up their washing, girls plaiting or picking lice out of each other's hair, bare-chested men in white mundus sitting magisterially in easy chairs, perusing the day's *Mathrubhumi*. Then the lane narrowed and the whitewashed, tile-roofed houses with verdant backyards gave way to thatched huts squeezed tightly together, their interiors shrouded in a darkness from which wizened crones emerged stooping through low-ceilinged doorways, the holes in their alarmingly stretched earlobes gaping like open mouths. The ground beneath our feet, uneven and stony, hurt to walk on, and a stale odour hung in the air, a compound of rotting vegetation and decaying flesh. Despair choked my breath like smoke. I began to wish I hadn't come along.

At last we left the village behind, and picked our way down a rocky, moss-covered slope to the stream. I didn't know what I'd expected, but it wasn't this, a meandering rivulet that flowed muddily through the fields. At the water's edge, on a large rock nearby, women were beating the dirt out of their saris; in the distance, a man squatted at a bend in the stream, picking his teeth and defecating. My cousins peeled off their shirts and ran into the water.

'Come on, Neel,' Balettan exhorted me with a peremptory wave of the hand. 'Don't be a sissy. It's not cold.'

'Just don't feel like it,' I mumbled. 'It's okay. You go ahead. I'll watch.'

They tried briefly to persuade me to change my mind, then left me to my own devices. I stood on the shore looking at them, heard their squeals of laughter, then looked away at the man who had completed his ablutions and was scooping water from the river to wash himself. Downstream from him, my cousins ducked their heads underwater. I quickly averted my gaze.

That was when I saw him. Charlis was sitting on a rocky overhang, a clean shirt over his mundu, a book in his hand. But his eyes weren't on it. He was looking down at the stream, where my cousins were playing.

I clambered over the rocks to him. When he spotted me, he seemed to smile in recognition, then look around anxiously. But there was no one else about, and he relaxed visibly. 'Neel,' he said, smiling. 'Aren't you swimming today?'

I shook my head. 'Water's dirty,' I said.

'Not dirty,' he replied in Malayalam. 'The stream comes from a sacred river. Removes all pollution.'

I started to retort, then changed my mind. 'So, why don't you swim?' I asked.

'Ah, I do,' he said. 'But not here.' His eyes avoided mine, but seemed to take in the stream, the washerwomen, my cousins. 'Not now.'

Bits of the half-understood conversation from the dining table floated awkwardly back into my mind. I changed the subject. 'It was nice of you to get our ball back for us that day,' I said.

'Ah, it was nothing.' He smiled unexpectedly, his pockmarks creasing across his face. 'My father beat me for it when I got home, though. I had ruined a clean shirt. Just after my bath.'

'But I thought you people didn't—' I found myself saying. 'I'm sorry,' I finished lamely.

'Didn't what?' he asked evenly, but without looking at me. He was clearly some years older than me, but not much bigger. I wondered whether he was scared of me, and why.

'Nothing,' I replied. 'I'm really sorry your father beat you.'

'Ah, that's all right. He does it all the time. It's for my own good.'

'What does your father do?'

Charlis became animated by my interest. 'He has a shop,' he said, a light in his eyes. 'In our part of the village. The Nair families don't come there, but he sells all sorts of nice things. Provisions and things. And on Thursdays, you know what he has? The best halwa in Vanganassery.'

'Really? I like halwa.' It was, in fact, the only Indian dessert I liked; Bombay had given me a taste for ice cream and chocolate rather than the deep-fried laddoos and brick-like Mysore paak that were the Kerala favourites.

'You like halwa?' Charlis clambered to his feet. 'Come on, I'll get you some.'

This time it was my turn to hesitate. 'No, thanks,' I said, looking at my cousins cavorting in the water. 'I don't think I should. They'll worry about me. And besides, I don't know my way about the village.'

'That's okay,' Charlis said. 'I'll take you home. Come on.' He saw the expression on my face. 'It's really good halwa,' he added.

That was enough for a nine-year-old. 'Wait for me,' I said, and ran down to the water's edge. 'See you at home!' I called out to the others.

Balettan was the only one who noticed me. 'Sure you can find your way back?' he asked, as my cousins splashed around him, one leaping onto his shoulders.

'I'll be okay,' I replied, and ran back up the slope as Balettan went under.

~

Charlis left me at the bend in our lane, where all I had to do was to walk through a relative's yard to reach my grandmother's house. He would not come any farther, and I knew better than to insist. I walked slowly to the house, my mind full of the astonishment with which his father had greeted my presence in his shop, the taste of his sugary, milky tea still lingering on my palate, my hands full of the wobbling, orange-coloured slabs of halwa he had thrust upon me.

'Neel, my darling!' my mother exclaimed as I walked in. 'Where have you been? I've been so worried about you.'

'Look what I've got!' I said proudly, holding out the halwa. 'And there's enough for everyone.'

'Where did you get that?' Balettan asked, a white thorthumundu, a thin Kerala towel, in his hand, his hair still wet from his recent swim.

'Charlis gave it to me,' I said. 'I went to his father's shop. They—'

'You did what?' Balettan's rage was frightening. He advanced towards me.

'I—I—'

'Went to Charlis's shop?' He loomed over me, the towel draped over his shoulder making him look even older and more threatening. 'Took food from Untouchables?' I began to shrink back from him. 'Give that to me!'

'I won't!' I snatched the halwa away from his hands, and as he lunged, I turned and ran, the precious sweet sticky in my grasp. But he was too fast for me; I had barely reached the yard when he caught up, seized me roughly by the shoulders, and turned me around to face him.

'We don't do this here, understand?' he breathed fiercely. 'This isn't Bombay.' He pried my hands apart. The halwa gleamed in my palms. 'Drop it,' he commanded.

'No,' I wanted to say, but the word would not emerge. I wanted to cry out for my mother, but she did not come out of the house.

'Drop it,' Balettan repeated, his voice a whiplash across what remained of my resistance.

Slowly, I opened my hands outwards in a gesture of submission. The orange slabs slid reluctantly off them. It seemed to me they took an age to fall, their gelatinous surfaces clinging to the soft skin of my palms until the last possible moment. Then they were gone, fallen into the dust.

Balettan looked at them on the ground for a moment, then at me, and spat upon them where they lay. 'The dogs can have them,' he barked. He kicked more dust over them, then pulled me by the arm back towards the house. 'Don't you ever do this again.'

I burst into tears then, and at last the words came, tripping over themselves as I stumbled back into the house. 'I hate you! All of you! You're horrible and mean and cruel and I'll never come back here as long as I live!'

But, of course, I was back the next year; I hardly had any choice in the matter. For my parents, first-generation migrants to the big city, this was the vital visit home, to their own parents and siblings, to the friends and family they had left behind; it renewed them, it returned them to a sense of themselves, it maintained their connection to the past. I just came along because I was too young to be left behind, indeed too young to be allowed the choice.

In the year that had passed since my last visit, there had been much ferment in Kerala. Education was now universal and compulsory and free, so all sorts of children were flocking to school who had never been able to go before. There was talk of land reform, and giving title to tenant farmers; I understood nothing of this, but saw the throngs around men with microphones on the roadside, declaiming angry harangues I could not comprehend. None of this seemed, however, to have much to do with us, or to affect the unchanging rhythms of life at my grandmother's house.

My cousins were numerous and varied, the children of my mother's brothers and sisters, and also of her cousins, who lived in the neighbouring houses; sometimes, the relationship was less clear than that, but as they all ran about together and slept side by side like a camping army on mats on the floor of my grandmother's thalam, it was difficult to tell who was a first cousin and who an uncle's father-in-law's sister's grandson. After all, it was also their holiday season, and my parents' return was an occasion for everyone to congregate in the big house. On any given day, with my cousins joined by other children from the village, there could be as many as a dozen kids playing in the courtyard or going to the stream or breaking up for cards on the back porch. Sometimes I joined them, but sometimes, taking advantage of the general confusion, I would slip away unnoticed, declining to make the effort to scale the barriers of language and education and attitude that separated us, and sit alone with a book. Occasionally, someone would come and look for me. Most often, that someone was my aunt Ranivaliamma.

As a young widow, she didn't have much of a life. Deprived of the status that a husband would have given her, she seemed to walk on the fringes of the house; it had been whispered by her late husband's family that only the bad luck her stars had brought into his life could account for his fatal heart attack at the age of thirty-six, and a whiff of stigma clung to her like a cloying perfume she could never quite wash off. Remarriage was out of the question, nor could the family allow her to make her own way in the world; so, she returned to the village house she had left as a bride, and tried to lose herself in the routines of my grandmother's household. She sublimated her misfortune in random and frequent acts of kindness, of which I was a favoured beneficiary. She would bring me well-sugared lime and water from the kitchen without being asked, and whenever one of us brought down a green mango from the ancient tree with a lucky throw of a stone, she could be counted upon to return with it chopped up and marinated in just the right combination of salt and red chilli powder to drive my taste buds to ecstasy.

One day, Ranivaliamma and I were upstairs, eating devilled raw mango and looking out on the kids playing soccer below, when I saw something and nearly choked. 'Isn't that Charlis?' I asked, pointing to the skinny boy who had just failed to save a goal.

'Could be,' she replied indifferently. 'Let me see—yes, that's Charlis.'

'But he's playing in our yard! I remember last year—'

'That was last year,' Rani-valiamma said, and I knew that change had come to the village.

But not enough of it. When the game was over, the Nair kids trooped in as usual to eat, without Charlis. When I asked innocently where he was, it was Balettan, inevitably, who replied. 'We play with him at school, and we play with him outside,' he said. 'But playing stops at the front door.'

I didn't pursue the matter. I had learned that whenever any of the Untouchable tradespeople came to the house, they were dealt with outside.

With each passing vacation, though, the changes became more and more apparent. For years, my grandmother, continuing a tradition handed down over generations, had dispensed free medication (mainly aspirins and cough syrup) once a week to the poor villagers who queued for it; then, a real clinic was established in the village by the government, and her amateur charity was no longer needed. Electricity came to Vanganassery; my uncle strung up a brilliant neon light above the dining table, and the hurricane lamps began to disappear, along with the tin cans of kerosene from which they were fuelled. The metal vessels in the bathroom were replaced by shiny red plastic mugs. A toilet was installed in the outhouse for my father's, and my, convenience. And one year, one day, quite naturally, Charlis stepped into the house with the other kids after a game.

No one skipped a beat; it was as if everyone had agreed to pretend there was nothing unusual. Charlis stood around casually, laughing and chatting; some of the kids sat to eat, others awaited their turn. No one invited Charlis to sit or to eat, and he made no move himself to do either. Then those who had eaten rose and washed their hands and joined the chatter, while those who had been with Charlis took their places at the table. Still, Charlis stood and talked, his manner modest and respectful, until everyone but he had finished eating, and then they all strolled out again to continue their game.

'Charlis hasn't eaten,' I pointed out to the womenfolk.

'I know, child, but what can we do?' Ranivaliamma asked. 'He can't sit at our table or be fed on our plates. Even you know that.'

'It isn't fair,' I said, but without belligerence. What she had stated was, I knew, like a law of nature. Even the servants would not wash a plate off which an Untouchable had eaten.

'You know,' honked Kunjunnimama, tucking into his third helping, 'they say that boy is doing quite well at school. Very well, in fact.'

'He stood first in class last term,' a younger cousin chimed in.

'First!' I exclaimed. 'And Balettan failed the year, didn't he?'

'Now, why would you be asking that?' chortled Kunjunnimama meaningfully, slapping his thigh with his free hand.

I ignored the question and turned to my aunt. 'He's smarter than all of us, and we can't even give him something to eat?'

Ranivaliamma saw the expression on my face and squeezed my hand.

'Don't worry,' she whispered. 'I'll think of something.'

She did; and the next time Charlis walked in, he was served food on a plantain leaf on the floor, near the back door. I was too embarrassed to hover near him as I had intended to, but he seemed to eat willingly enough on his own.

'It's just not right!' I whispered to her as we watched him from a discreet distance.

'He doesn't mind,' she whispered back. 'Why should you?'

And it was true that Charlis probably ate on the floor in his own home. When he had finished, a mug of water was given to him on the back porch, so that he could wash his hands without stepping into our bathroom. And the plantain leaf was thrown away: no plate to wash.

We returned to the game, and now it was my turn to miskick. The ball cleared the low wall at one end of the courtyard, hit the side of the well, teetered briefly on the edge, and fell in with a splash.

It had happened before. 'Go and get it, da,' Balettan languidly commanded one of the kids. The well was designed to be climbed into: bricks jutted out from the inside wall at regular intervals, and others had been removed to provide strategic footholds. But this was a slippery business: since the water levels in the well rose and fell, the inside surface was pretty slimy, and many of those who'd gone in to retrieve a floating object, or a bucket that had slipped its rope, had ended up taking an unplanned dip. The young cousin who had received Balettan's instruction hesitated, staring apprehensively into the depths of the well.

'Don't worry,' Charlis said quietly. 'I'll get it.' He moved towards the edge of the well.

'No!' There was nothing languid now about Balettan's tone; we could all hear the alarm in his voice. 'I'll do it myself.' And Charlis, one half-raised foot poised to climb onto the well, looked at him, his face drained of expression, comprehension slowly burning into his cheeks. Balettan ran forward, roughly pushing aside the boy who had been afraid to go, and vaulted into the well.

I looked at Ranivaliamma, who had been watching the game.

'Balettan's right,' she said. 'Do you think anyone would have drunk water at our house again if Charlis had gone into our well?'

Years passed; school holidays, and trips to Kerala, came and went. Governments fell and were replaced in Kerala, farm labourers were earning the highest daily wage in the country, and my almost toothless grandmother was sporting a chalk-white set of new dentures under her smile. Yet, the house seemed much the same as before. A pair of ceiling fans had been installed, in the two rooms where family members congregated; a radio crackled with the news from Delhi; a tap made its appearance in the bathroom, though the pipe attached to it led from the same old well. These improvements, and the familiarity that came from repeated visits, made the old privations bearable. Kerala seemed less of a penance with each passing year.

Charlis was a regular member of the group now, admitted to our card-playing sessions on the porch outside, joining us on our expeditions to the cinema in the nearest town. But fun and games seemed to hold a decreasing attraction for Charlis. He was developing a reputation as something of an intellectual. He would ask me, in painstaking textbook English, about something he had read about the great wide world outside, and listen attentively to my reply. I was, in the quaint vocabulary of the villagers, 'convent-educated', a label they applied to anyone who emerged from the elite schools in which Christian missionaries served their foreign Lord by teaching the children of the Indian lordly. It was assumed that I knew more about practically everything than anyone in the village; but all I knew was what I had been taught from books, whereas they had learned from life. Even as I wallowed in their admiration, I couldn't help feeling their lessons were the more difficult, and the more valuable.

Balettan dropped out of school and began turning his attention to what remained of the family lands. It seemed to me that his rough edges became rougher as the calluses grew hard on his hands and feet. He had less time for us now; in his late teens, he was already a full-fledged farmer, sitting sucking a straw between his teeth and watching the boys kick a ball around. If he disapproved of Charlis's growing familiarity with all of us, though, he did not show it—not even when Charlis asked me one day to go into town with him to see the latest Bombay blockbuster.

I thought Charlis might have hoped I could explain the Hindi dialogues to him, since Keralites learned Hindi only as a third language from teachers who knew it, at best, as a second. But when we got to the movie theatre, Charlis was not disappointed to discover the next two screenings were fully sold out. 'I am really wanting to talk,' he said in English, leading me to an eatery across the street.

The Star of India, as the board outside proclaimed, was a 'military hotel'; in other words, it served meat, which my grandmother did not. 'I am thinking you might be missing it,' Charlis said, ushering me to a chair. It was only when the main dish arrived that I realized that I was actually sitting and eating at the same table with Charlis for the first time.

If he was conscious of this, Charlis didn't show it. He began talking, hesitantly at first, then with growing fluency and determination, about his life and his ambitions. His face shone when he talked of his father, who beat him with a belt whenever he showed signs of neglecting his books. 'You can do better than I did,' he would say, before bringing the whip down on Charlis. 'You will do better.'

And now Charlis was aiming higher than anyone in his family, in his entire community, had ever done before. He was planning to go to university.

'Listen, Charlis,' I said gently, not wanting to discourage him. 'You know it's not going to be easy. I know you're first in class and everything, but that's in the village. Don't forget you'll be competing for places with kids from the big cities. From the—convents.'

'I am knowing that,' Charlis replied simply. Then, from the front pocket of his shirt, he drew out a battered notebook filled with small, tightly packed curlicues of Malayalam lettering in blue ink, interspersed with phrases and sentences in English in the same precise hand. 'Look,' he said, jabbing at a page. 'The miserable hath no other medicine / But only hope.—Shakespeare, *Measure for Measure*, III.i.2,' I read. And a little lower down, 'Men at some time are masters of their fates; / The fault, dear Brutus, is not in our stars, / But in ourselves, that we are underlings.' Charlis had underlined these words.

'Whenever I am reading something that inspires me, I am writing it down in this book,' Charlis said proudly. 'Shakespeare is great man, isn't it?'

His Malayalam was, of course, much better, but in English Charlis seemed to cast off an invisible burden that had less to do with the language than with its social assumptions. In speaking it, in quoting it, Charlis seemed to be entering another world, a heady place of foreign ideas and unfamiliar expressions, a strange land in which the old rules no longer applied.

'For the Colonel's Lady an' Judy O'Grady,' he declaimed at one point, "are sisters under their skins!"—Rudyard Kipling,' he added. 'Is that how you are pronouncing it?'

'Rudyard, Roodyard, I haven't a clue,' I confessed. 'But who cares, Charlis? He's just an old imperialist fart. What does anything he ever wrote have to do with any of us today, in independent India?'

Charlis looked surprised, then slightly averted his eyes. 'But are we not,' he asked softly, 'are we not brothers under our skins?'

'Of course,' I replied, too quickly. And it was I who couldn't meet his gaze.

∽

The following summer, I was sitting down to my first meal of the holiday at my grandmother's dining table when Ranivaliamma said, 'Charlis was looking for you.'

'Really?' I was genuinely pleased, as much by Charlis's effort as by the fact that it could be mentioned so casually. 'What did he want?'

'He came to give you the news personally,' Ranivaliamma said. 'He's been admitted to Trivandrum University.'

'Wow!' I exclaimed. 'That's something, isn't it?'

'Untouchable quota,' honked the ever-present Kunjunnimama, whose pencil-line moustache had gone from bold black to sleek silver without his ever having done a stroke of work in his life.

'Reserved seats for the Children of God. Why, Chandrasekhara Menon's son couldn't get in after all the money they spent on sending him to boarding school, and here Charlis is on his way to university.'

'The village panchayat council is organizing a felicitation for him tomorrow,' Ranivaliamma said. 'Charlis wanted you to come, Neel.'

'Of course, I will,' I responded. 'We must all go.'

'All?' snorted Kunjunnimama, who was incapable of any action that could be called affirmative. 'To felicitate Charlis? Speak for yourself, boy. If you want to attend an Untouchable love-in organized by the communists who claim to represent our village, more's the pity. But don't expect to drag any members of the Nair community with you.'

'I'll come with you, Neel,' said a quiet voice by my side. It was Ranivaliamma, her ever-obliging manner transformed into something approaching determination.

'And me,' chirped a younger cousin, emboldened. 'May I go too, Amma?' asked another. And, by the next evening, I had assembled a sizeable delegation from our extended family to attend the celebration for Charlis.

Kunjunnimama and Balettan sat at the table, nursing their cups of tea, and watched us all troop out. Balettan was silent, his manner distant rather than disapproving. As I passed them, I heard the familiar honk: 'Felicitation, my foot.'

The speeches had begun when we arrived, and our entry sparked something of a commotion in the meeting hall, as Charlis's relatives and the throng of well-wishers from his community made way for us, whispers of excitement and consternation rippling like a current through the room. I thought I saw a look of sheer delight shine like a sunburst on Charlis's face, but that may merely have been a reaction to hearing the panchayat president say, 'The presence of all of you here today proves that Charlis's achievement is one of which the entire village is proud.' We applauded that, knowing our arrival had given some meaning to that trite declaration.

After the speeches, and the garlanding, and Charlis's modest reply, the meeting broke up. I wanted to congratulate Charlis myself, but he was surrounded by his own people, all proud and happy and laughing. We made our way towards the door, and then I heard his voice.

'Neel! Wait!' he called out. I turned to see him pulling himself away from the crush and advancing towards me with a packet in his hands. 'You mustn't leave without this.'

He stretched out the packet towards me, beaming. I opened it and peered in. Orange slabs of halwa quivered inside.

'It's the last bag,' Charlis said, the smile never fading from his face. 'My father sold the shop to pay for me to go to university. We're all moving to Trivandrum.' I looked at him, finding no words. He pushed the halwa at me. 'I wanted you to have it.'

I took the bag from him without a word. We finished the halwa before we got home.

Years passed. Men landed on the moon, a woman became prime minister, wars were fought; in other countries, coups and revolutions brought change (or attempted to), while in India elections were won and lost and things changed (or didn't). I couldn't go down to Kerala every time my parents did; my college holidays didn't always coincide with Dad's leave from the office. When I did manage a visit, it wasn't the same as before. I would come for a few days, be indulged by Ranivaliamma, and move on. There was not that much to do. Ranivaliamma had started studying for a teacher's training diploma. My grandmother spent most of her time reading the scriptures and chewing areca, usually simultaneously. Balettan, tough and taciturn, was the man of the house; now that agriculture was his entire life, we had even less to say to each other than ever. My cousins were scattered in several directions; a new generation of kids played football in the yard. No one had news of Charlis.

I began working in an advertising agency in Bombay, circulating in a brittle, showy world that could not have had less in common with Vanganassery. When I went to the village the talk was of pesticides and irrigation, of the old rice levy and the new government-subsidized fertilizer, and, inevitably, of the relentless pace of land reform, which was taking away the holdings of traditional landlords and giving them to their tenants. It was clear that Balettan did not understand much of this, and that he had not paid a great deal of attention to what was happening.

'Haven't you received any notification from the authorities, Balettan?' I asked him one day, when his usual reticence seemed only to mask ineffectually the mounting level of anxiety in his eyes.

'Some papers came,' he said in a tone the aggressiveness of which betrayed his deep shame at his own inadequacy. 'But do I have time to read them? I'm a busy man. Do I run a farm or push papers like a clerk?'

'Show them to Neel,' Kunjunnimama suggested, and as soon as I opened the first envelope I realized Balettan, high-school dropout and traditionalist, had left it too late.

'What are these lands here, near Kollengode?'

'They're ours, of course.'

'Not any more, Balettan. Who's T. Krishnan Nair, son of Kandath Narayananunni Nair?'

'He farms them for us, ever since Grandfather died. I farm here at Vanganassery, and Krishnan Nair takes care of Kollengode, giving us his dues after each harvest. It's the only way. I can't be at both places at the same time, can I?'

'Well, it says here he's just been registered as the owner of those lands. You were given fourteen days to show cause as to why his claim should not have been admitted. Why didn't you file an objection, Balettan?'

We were all looking at him.

'How can they say Krishnan Nair owns our land? Why, everybody knows it's our land. It's been ours ever since anyone can remember. It was ours before Grandmother was born.'

'It's not ours any more, Balettan. The government has just taken it away.'

Balettan shifted uneasily in his chair, a haunted, uncomprehending look on his face. 'But they can't do that,' he said. 'Can they?'

'They can, Balettan,' I told him sadly. 'You know they can.'

'We've got to do something,' honked Kunjunnimama with uncharacteristic urgency. 'Neel, you've got to do something.'

'Me? What can I do? I'm a Bombaywallah. I know less about all this than any of you.'

'Perhaps,' admitted Kunjunnimama, 'but you're an educated man. You can read and understand these documents. You can speak to the Collector. He's the top IAS man in the district, probably another city type like you, convent educated. You can speak to him in English and explain what has happened. Come on, Neel. You've got to do it.'

'I don't know,' I said dubiously. The advertising life had not brought me into contact with any senior Indian Administrative Service officers. I hadn't the slightest idea what I would say to the Collector when I met him.

And then I saw the look in Balettan's eyes. He had grown up knowing instinctively the rules and rituals of village society, the cycles of the harvest, how to do the right thing and what was never done. He could, without a second thought, climb trees that would make most of us dizzy, descend into wells, stand knee-deep in the slushy water of a paddy field to sprout grain into the world. But all these were skills he was born with, rhythms that sang in his blood like the whisper of his mother's breath. He wore a mundu around his waist, coaxed his buffalo across the fields, and treated his labourers and his family as his ancestors had done for thousands of years. He was good at the timeless realities of village India; but India, even village India, was no longer a timeless place. 'Don't you understand anything, stupid?' he had asked me all those years ago; and in his eyes I saw what I imagined he must have seen, at that time, in mine.

'I'll go,' I said, as Balettan averted his eyes. In relief, perhaps, or in gratitude. It didn't matter which.

The Collector's office in Palghat, the district capital, was already besieged by supplicants when I arrived. Two greasy clerks presided over his antechamber, their desks overflowing with papers loosely bound in crumbling files held together with string. Three phones rang intermittently, and were answered in a wide variety of tones, ranging from the uncooperative to the unctuous, depending on who was calling. People crowded around the desks, seeking attention, thrusting slips of paper forward, folding hands in entreaty, shouting to be heard. Occasionally a paper was dealt with, and a khaki-uniformed peon sent for to carry it somewhere; sometimes, people were sent away, though most seemed to be waved towards the walls where dozens were already waiting, weary resignation on their faces, for their problems to be dealt with. All eyes were on the closed teak door at the corner, bearing the brass nameplate M. C. THEKKOTE, IAS., behind which their destinies were no doubt being determined.

'It's hopeless,' I said to Balettan, who had accompanied me. 'I told you we should have tried to get an appointment. We'll be here all day.'

'How would we have got an appointment?' Balettan asked, reasonably, since we did not yet have a phone in the village. 'No, this is the only way. You go and give them your card.'

I did not share Balettan's faith in the magical properties of this small rectangular advertisement of my status, but I battled my way to the front of one of the desks and thrust it at an indifferent clerk.

'Please take this to the Collector-saare,' I said, trying to look both important and imploring. 'I must see him.'

The clerk seemed unimpressed by the colourful swirls and curlicues that proclaimed my employment by AdAge, Bombay's smartest new agency. 'You and everyone else,' he said sceptically, putting the card aside. 'Collector-saare very busy today. You come back tomorrow, we will see.'

At this point Balettan's native wisdom asserted itself. He insinuated a five-rupee note into the clerk's palm. 'Send the card in,' he said. 'It's important.'

The clerk was instantly responsive. 'I am doing as you wish,' he said grudgingly, 'but you will still have to wait. Collector-saare is so so very busy today.'

'You've told us that already,' I replied. 'We'll wait.'

A peon wandered in, bearing tea for the clerks. Once the man at the desk had satisfied himself that his tea was sugared to his taste, he added my card to the pile of papers he gave the peon to take in to the Collector. 'It will take some time,' he added curtly.

It didn't. Soon after the door had closed behind the peon, the black phone on the clerk's desk jangled peremptorily. 'Yes, saar. Yes, saar,' he said, perspiring. 'No, saar. Not long. Yes, saar. At once, saar.' He had stood up to attention during this exchange, and when he replaced the receiver there was a new look of respect in his eyes. 'Collector-saare will be seeing you now, saar,' he said, with a salaam. 'You didn't explain who you were, saar.' The five-rupee note re-emerged in his hand. 'You seem to have dropped this by mistake, saar,' he said shamefacedly, handing it to Balettan.

'Keep it,' Balettan said, as mystified as I by the transformation in the man's attitude. But the clerk begged him to take it back, and bowed and scraped us towards the imposing doorway.

'Obviously Bombay's ad world counts for more than I thought with these governmentwallahs,' I whispered to Balettan.

'He's just happy to be able to speak English with someone,' Balettan suggested.

The clerk opened the door into a high-ceilinged office. The Collector rose from behind a mahogany desk the size of a ping-pong table, and stretched out a hand. 'It's so good to see you again, Neel,' he said.

It was Charlis.

'Charlis!' I exclaimed, astonishment overcoming delight. 'B—but—the name—the IAS'

'You never did know my family name, did you? After all these years.' Charlis spoke without reproach. 'And, yes, I've been in the IAS for some time now.' The Administrative Service, too, I found myself thinking unworthily, offered one more of the quotas Kunjunnimama liked to complain about. 'But this is the first time I've been posted so close to Vanganassery. I've barely got here, but once I've settled in, I'm planning to visit the village again soon.' He added casually, 'It's part of my district, after all. That'd make it an official visit, you see.'

He seemed to enjoy the thought, and I found myself looking at Balettan. I didn't know what I expected to find in his expression, but it certainly wasn't the combination of hope, respect, and, yes, admiration with which he now regarded the man across the desk.

Charlis seemed to catch it, too. 'But what is this? We haven't even asked Balettan to sit down.' He waved us to chairs, as tea appeared. 'Tell me, what can I do for you?'

We explained the problem, and Charlis was sympathetic but grave.

The law was the law; it was also just, undoing centuries of absentee landlordism. In our case, though, thanks to Balettan's inattention (though Charlis didn't even imply that), it had been applied unfairly, leaving Balettan with less land than his former tenant. Some of this could be undone, and Charlis would help, but we would not be able to get back all the land that had been confiscated. Charlis explained all this carefully, patiently, speaking principally to Balettan rather than to me. 'Some changes are good, some are bad,' he concluded, 'but very few changes can be reversed.'

'Shakespeare or Rudyard Kipling?' I asked, only half in jest, remembering his little notebook.

'Neither,' he replied quite seriously. 'Charlis Thekkote. But you can quote me if you like.'

Charlis was as good as his word. He helped Balettan file the necessary papers to reclaim some of his land, and made sure the files were not lost in the bureaucratic maze. And the week after our visit, knowing I would not be staying in Vanganassery long, Charlis came to the village.

I will never forget the sight of Charlis seated at our dining table with the entire family bustling attentively around him: Ranivaliamma, on leave from the school where she was now vice principal, serving him her soft, crisp-edged dosas on Grandmother's best stainless steel thali; Kunjunnimama, honking gregariously, pouring him more tea; and half the neighbours, standing at a respectful distance, gawking at the dignitary.

But the image that will linger longest in my memory is from even before that, from the moment of Charlis's arrival at the village. His official car cannot drive the last half-mile to our house, on the narrow paths across the paddy fields, so Charlis steps down, in his off-white safari suit and open-toed sandals, and walks to our front door, through the dust. We greet him there and begin to usher him into the house, but Balettan stops us outside. For a minute, all the old fears come flooding back into my mind and Charlis's, but it is only for a minute, because Balettan is shouting out to the servant, 'Can't you see the Collector-saare is waiting? Hurry up!'

I catch Charlis's eye; he smiles. The servant pulls a bucketful of water out of the well to wash Charlis's feet.

PONNUTHAYI

BAMA

Translated from the Tamil by C. T. Indra

PONNUTHAYI WAS AROUND THIRTY YEARS OLD. A VERY ROBUSTLY BUILT woman, in the seven or eight years that she had been married, she had borne four sons. Ponnuthayi was incredibly dark-skinned and very good looking, with lovely features. If you were to look at her sons, roaming the streets like beggars on their spindly legs, they outdid ravens—the complexions they had, every one of them, inherited from their mother, were so dark that if one could dip one's finger and take a little of that inky colour, one could use it as a bindi.

Ponnuthayi was quite tall and had a build to match her height. When she walked along the street the earth would shake with her every step.

'Who could say she is a woman, looking at her stomping?' the other women would gossip. Even when she spoke it had the same effect. When she went to fetch water from the street tap, her voice could be heard till the end of the street, ringing like a bronze bell. Her tone was nothing if not brusque. It was for this reason that most people could not take to her.

Very few people knew her as Ponnuthayi. But everyone would know who the 'leathery lipped' one was—her lips were somewhat oversized.

'Are just her lips oversized?' they would remark.

'Her mouth is even bigger.'

Many did not at all like the fact that, unlike other women who were earning their wages working for a big landowner, she was running a business on her own.

Although illiterate, Ponnuthayi managed to take a bus to the neighbouring town, buy vegetables and fruits, and earn her livelihood as a vendor. No other woman was earning her living quite like this. Unmindful of all the comments made about her, Ponnuthayi carried on with her trade.

One day, Ponnuthayi brought a basketful of coconuts and went about on the street hawking them, calling out, 'Coconuts...coconuts...three for ten rupees. Come along and take a look.' One of the women, unable to restrain herself, asked for trouble when she remarked, 'If we buy coconuts at the grove we can get one for two rupees. Look how shamelessly she comes here, she thinks she is a big merchant.'

'I am not the one to pick a quarrel; but mind you if it comes my way, I will not leave it be. If you feel like buying, buy them, or else keep mum. Who are you to advise me about running a business?' Ponnuthayi retorted before moving away towards South Street.

The exchange rankled in her mind even after she reached South Street. Instead of hawking the coconuts, Ponnuthayi walked along shouting at the top of her voice, leaving the street in a state of terror. 'I will work or not, as I please. It's my sweet will and pleasure. Who's this whore of a woman to talk like that to me? How the hell does it matter to these women what business I do? If any woman dares to talk about me flippantly I will cut her tongue clean off.' Looking at the way Ponnuthayi was shouting, no one ventured to go anywhere near her to buy her wares. Only after she was out of earshot did the women dare to talk. 'Look how her speech smacks of arrogance! Can't she work in the fields like the rest of us to earn her living? Imagines herself to be one of those big shots from Melakalakudi... venturing to engage in trade! I tell you she is quite domineering....' As Muniyamma was running on like this, Ponnuthayi who had headed west again happened to turn east. Muniyamma promptly held her tongue.

When Ponnuthayi again approached the spot where the women had gathered she started yelling. 'Even the other day...just because I squeezed paste on to a brush and brushed my teeth, these women were shocked out of their wits and spoke in whispers among themselves. It's my money, I buy and I spend it as I please. I don't see how it is any of their business....'

Once Ponnuthayi had moved away, the woman from Akaasampatti said, 'Did you listen to what Leathery Lips said? Because she is so great she won't deign to brush her teeth with her finger! What vanity! As the saying goes, "You live on gruel but wash your backside with soap."'

Aathiamma cautioned, 'Don't ever say anything within her hearing, sister, if she hears it she'll tear you to pieces. Don't take her lightly. Remember once she made the police beat her own wedded husband black and blue, she is such a bully.'

There was hardly anyone in the village who didn't have a comment on this matter involving the police. For the past two years, Ponnuthayi had been living alone, having walked out on her husband. She lived with her mother and with the money she earned from her trade she managed to make ends meet.

When she got married to Mookkandi she set up house with him, hoping to lead a happy life like any other couple. Mookkandi was pitch-dark and his moustache stood out sharply. He was in the habit of twisting his moustache all the time. Being constantly twisted in this manner, the two ends of the moustache stood out belligerently like two pointed horns waiting to gore someone.

He went to work for two days in the week and stayed at home the rest of the week. But not a day would pass without his eating out at the 'club'. Visiting these eateries in the evening, he would stuff himself with idli, dosai, vadai, and what not; returning home he would not forego his rice in the night either. His day wouldn't be made if he didn't eat out at one of those 'otels'. The little that he earned he would spend on himself. On days when he didn't go for work he would bully Ponnuthayi and snatch away her wages. Come Sunday he had to have beef and then arrack from Mariappa Thevar to wash it down, or else he would make life hell for Ponnuthayi.

Ponnuthayi tried her best to carry on with him, holding her feelings in with great restraint. In the early days of their married life she somehow ran the household with her earnings. Later, when four sons were born, one after another, even gruel became a luxury at times. She went on trying to survive as she led a hand-to-mouth existence. She eventually managed to get a milch cow, but with the job of maintaining it, looking after the children, slogging both in the field and at home, her vitality was sapped.

One day, to cap it all, not only did Mookkandi sell the milch cow, he also pocketed all the money from the sale without giving Ponnuthayi a single rupee. It was because of the quarrel over this matter that she finally ran away from him, after being beaten and battered.

When she left her husband, she was still suckling the last child. She brought away only this child with her. After about four or five months, when he was weaned from the breast, she left him also at her husband's house and came away.

'Call her a woman? Not even a touch of maternal attachment in her! She struts around like a man, doesn't she? When did we ever see a woman leaving her children in her husband's care and go off gallivanting like this?'

Though in the village all sorts of people indulged in all kinds of gossip, Ponnuthayi went her own way.

'So what? Are they not his kids too? It was just for his own gratification that he made me bear children year after year. When I was going in for a tubectomy after two sons, he prevented it forcibly and brought me back.' Ponnuthayi would thus justify her decision to herself.

Mookkandi struggled with his four sons, all of them skinny and scrawny, and reached the verge of despair. Having waited quite some time for her to return on her own, he intercepted Ponnuthayi on the street one day, saying, 'You woman! Come home.'

'You and I have no relationship; whatever there was, it was done with two years ago. I don't want to live with you any more.' Ponnuthayi walked on.

'You wretched woman, how dare you tell your husband that you don't want to live with him? You bitch...are you a woman at all? You roam about like a whore dog leaving your own children uncared for,' Mookkandi shouted at her.

'I roam as I please. Who the hell are you to question me? Do you mean to say that I had those children without you? Try bringing them up. You will know then,' Ponnuthayi retorted in anger.

Mookkandi's fury knew no bounds. He yelled back angrily.

'You bitch! Shut up...look at those leathery lips, that body of yours! If it had been any other man, he wouldn't have married you at all looking at your lips. I took pity on you, and married you; serves me right. I deserve to be beaten with slippers.'

'Go ahead,' she shot back, 'not only with your slippers but also with a broomstick. Thoo! Good for nothing fellow...even then you will not come to your senses.' Spitting at him, she walked away. Mookkandi pulled her back by her hair and hit her on her face and arms. He dragged her along, raining blows all the way. Ponnuthayi kept writhing and struggling. She wriggled away from him and bit his hand. Stung by the bite, he kicked her hard in the abdomen. Unable to bear the pain she screamed aloud and fell down, her head colliding with the hard ground. Blood poured from her injured head, drenching her clothes. After that she did not shout, nor did she let out a single abusive term. Dripping blood, she ran towards the south.

Someone in the crowd shouted, 'Go, stop her. She is running through the fields. She might jump into a well and take her own life. Look at how fast she's running...she might do some such thing.'

'Let her go to hell! Wretched woman! I'll bury her and marry again. As if there's no other woman in the world if this one goes away!' Mookkandi retorted haughtily.

With her hair dishevelled, Ponnuthayi's mother ran screaming after her. By this time the whole village had gathered. Men and women ran behind Ponnuthayi. A few, after running some distance, gave up.

But Ponnuthayi did not jump into any well as they had thought she would do; instead she cut across the field ridges and ran straight to the police station in the next town. A huge crowd gathered in front of the police station at the sight of Ponnuthayi standing there, dripping blood. The police took her into the station and made enquiries.

'Sir, for the past two years I have been living by myself, minding my own business, having left my husband because he was torturing me. Today he comes, picks up a quarrel with me, and beats me till my head splits open. Sir! You must put him in his place.' As she spoke, Ponnuthayi wiped blood off her face with her sari. There was blood on the floor where she was standing. They enquired about her village, street, and other details, then asked her to go to the government hospital. By then her mother too had arrived, and took Ponnuthayi to the hospital with her. Surely it was God's grace that the policeman was capable of human consideration. He immediately sent two constables to fetch Mookkandi. Ponnuthayi came back after having her wound bandaged. In the station Mookkandi was beaten mercilessly. Then the policeman locked him up and turned to Ponnuthayi, 'What do you say? I will keep him inside for a couple of days, advise him, and send him back. Will you live with him? If he again starts giving you trouble, inform me at once.'

'Sir! You do whatever you want with him; as for me I won't live with him. I've had enough. Let me live by myself for the rest of my life.' Having said this, she left with her mother.

Mookkandi was released the next day after a severe warning. By this time the whole village had come to know that Ponnuthayi had gone to the police station, lodged a complaint, and got her husband soundly beaten up. There arose as many versions of the story as there were people in the village.

Aathiamma said, 'Whatever may have happened, is it wise to have complained to the police about her husband and had him beaten up? Stupid woman!'

Kuruvamma said, 'Don't say that. How long could that woman put up with this? Didn't she take all his beatings? One must hand over such heartless fellows to the police. Surely then other fellows will think twice before bossing over their wives.'

Aathiamma asked, 'Going by what you say if the husband beats the wife, she should have him beaten? Nice logic, isn't it? How long do you think this policeman will support her? One cannot trust policemen these days, you know? All said and done you must ultimately come back to the husband, and he'll put you in your place then, won't he?'

Kanniyamma, who had been listening to their exchange said, 'Of course, you know, for the past two years she has been living by herself after leaving him. He should have kept quiet; instead he called her back home, she said no. Now it is he who made trouble for her. If she does not want to go back to him, can't he just leave her alone?'

'Do you think he has called her back because he wants to live with her? Fact is, he is not able to bring up four children. That is why he somehow wants to pick up a quarrel so that he may leave the kids in her care.' When Kuruvamma said this, Kanniyamma retorted, 'How long will he remain single? It is possible for a woman, but certainly not for a man.'

Even as the womenfolk were talking among themselves the men too gathered in small groups and gossiped. 'Call him a man? No better than a woman. The wife who dared to go to the police station and had him beaten up—he has let such a woman go scot-free. What a shame! Useless fellow! If I were in his place, I would have strangled her to death right there in the police station,' Kuppusamy said hotly.

'You are a fool. It's no big deal killing a woman. He failed to keep her in her place, right from the beginning. Now he is paying for it. If a man can't control a woman what kind of a man is he? Why should he sport a moustache?' Govindan laughed as he said this.

When the men started deriding Mookkandi thus, it stung him to the quick. Grinding his teeth in a fury, Mookkandi paced about restlessly. Then, with his mind firmly made up, he went to Ponnuthayi's house. He spoke to her father. 'I shall never call your daughter back to live with me. Let her also keep the children here with her. I will marry another woman and go my way. Thanks to her I've faced many insults.'

Ponnuthayi's father patiently replied, 'Please bear with her, Maaple. Woman's wit, as the saying goes, is given to folly. Like a fool she went to the police station the other day. Give me time. I will put good sense into her and bring her around.'

'That won't work, I don't need her any more. I will come and leave the children. That's it.' Mookkandi turned to leave. Ponnuthayi, who had so far silently listened to the conversation, said, 'Why leave the children here? You take care of your children. I don't want to have anything to do with you or your children. What law says that only a mother should bring up the children? Don't bring them here or show your face anywhere here, I warn you.'

Mookkandi left with his pride injured. It was Ponnuthayi's mother who cried aloud saying. 'He might bring another woman as he threatened. That woman will harass the children. Listen to me. A husband is a husband, be he a stone or a blade of grass. Whether he kicks you or beats you, you should still be with him; instead what have you done coming over here like this, you sinner! Let us at least keep the children here.'

'Stop wailing and keep quiet, Mother. As if a father doesn't know how to bring up his children. Let him try that; I've had enough of stones and blades of grass.' Ponnuthayi stepped into the house, only to emerge with a razor blade. Sitting on the chicken coop railing in front of the house, she cut the thaali thread around her neck and pulled it off.

Seeing this, her mother shouted, 'You foolish woman! What are you doing? Why do you imagine that what has befallen you is something exceptional? Does anyone cut away the sacred thaali tied by her husband? It would have been better if I had borne a grindstone instead of you.' Her mother wept as she picked up the thaali.

Hearing her wailing, a few women gathered around and hurled abuse at Ponnuthayi. Ponnuthayi could not care less. She scolded her mother, 'Amma, will you stop this lament now? What has happened here for you to cry loud enough for the whole village to hear? I'll go to the town and be back. You fetch some tender leaves from the tank bund for the goat, poor dumb creature, it is starving.' She took the gold thaali and tucked it in a fold of her sari, picked up a basket, and left for town. The next morning, she set up a petty shop in the village centre and started her business. The thaali which had hung around her neck for ten years had filled her shop with many things for her to sell.

WINTER EVENINGS

NAVTEJ SARNA

Dr Anand unlocked the door and stepped into his house. The dark rooms were very cold. He switched on the light in the small living room. The window had been left open and the cold breeze had blown magazines and newspapers all over the room. Leaving his doctor's bag on the carved low table, he picked them up, folded them, and put them back on the table. Then he went to the window to shut it.

Though it was only six in the evening, the cold, brittle darkness was crowded with stars. The Milky Way was a faint and distant smudge of white smoke overhead. The mountains were strong, dark silhouettes but he couldn't see the moon. It must be there, somewhere, he thought, for he could see the glistening sheen of the river in the wide valley. An icy wind rushed to his face, and with a sudden, cold shudder he shut the window and drew the curtains.

Keeping his coat on, he went to the backyard to choose some firewood. Back in the living room, he set three neatly chopped pieces in the metal sheet drum known in those areas as the bukhari. Unfolding the newspapers, he pulled out the advertisement pages, crumpled these into balls, and stuffed them under the wood. Then he opened the vent on top of the bukhari, poured in a few drops of kerosene oil, and dropped in a match. In just a few minutes the paper had given its fire to the wood. It sent the smoke rushing up the pipe that led out through the chimney into the crystal night.

And from his window, higher up on the same hill, Rao saw the smoke rising. He was glad. Dr Anand was back and that meant that he could go over. The bank branch shut at two and the afternoons hung heavy on Rao. Sometimes he would go for a long walk to the monastery and back, to tire himself. But all of last week, the fierce afternoon wind had discouraged him. He had stayed in, reading disinterestedly, and writing letters to people halfway across the world whom he hadn't seen in ten years.

So he felt good when the doctor was back. He tied a woollen scarf around his neck, folding the ends into his coat, raised his coat collar, pulled on his leather gloves, and picked up a short, rounded stick. Ready, he stepped out into the cold.

It would be a long winter, and, inevitably, he looked up to the pass where the snow glistened in the night. Already the snow had been there for two months, cutting off the valley from the rest of the world. It would stay there at least another month, and then, if they were lucky, it would begin to melt.

The bank was crazy, sending him here. 'Baptism by blood,' he had been told! He had been a sucker to accept the offer. As if anybody cared what he did to disburse miserly loans to the handful of farmers here. It wouldn't make any difference. At least not in the winter and not if they couldn't keep that wretched pass open. His face flushed against the cold and his teeth set, he knocked on Dr Anand's door and quickly stepped inside.

'Come along, come along,' called out the doctor.

'Bloody cold.'

'Always cold, unless the sun is out.'

'When is the sun ever out?'

'Actually you are right, haven't seen it this week.'

Rao loosened his scarf and sat down, extending both hands towards the bukhari. He took out his pipe, and turning it around, tapped it vigorously on the palm of his hand. Dr Anand watched him do it but restrained himself from saying anything. He couldn't stand the sweet smell of tobacco that would hang in the room long after Rao left. He would have to open the window again at night.

Rao knew that the doctor would soon ask him what he would like to drink though he knew that the doctor only had whisky in the house, and that the doctor also knew that Rao preferred his whisky neat.

'What will you drink?'

'Whisky, neat, please.'

The doctor went to the little closet and took out the bottle of whisky. He had bought six glasses when he had gone down in the summer. Two had cracked during the journey but he still had four. 'Will never need more than two,' thought Dr Anand as he fixed the drinks. 'There's nobody in this village except Rao, blast him, that I can have a drink with.'

But when he turned back, he was smiling.

'Cheers.'

'Cheers.'

Rao took a small sip of his whisky and a few quick puffs from his pipe. Dr Anand pointedly moved his chair away before sitting down and then threw himself into it.

'What news?' asked Rao.

The doctor ran his fingers through his hair.

'A woman nearly died today.'

'What happened?'

'Allergy to anaesthesia. But she came out finally.'

'Good work.'

'Good luck, rather. How about you?'

'Dull day today.'

And usually, thought the doctor, your hole of a bank is a veritable hub of activity.

But aloud, he said: 'How come?'

'No mail, no work. Not one potential borrower.'

'They are all frozen, or sick. We really need that new hospital.'

Back to the new hospital, thought Rao, can't we ever talk of anything else?

And aloud: 'How's the work going?'

'The contractor says another four months, four months after the road opens, that is.'

'I'll be gone by then.'

'You'll get a good posting after this, you deserve it.' The doctor's smile was very pleasant, very friendly. But he was wondering what this city slicker had done to deserve anything.

Rao knew that the doctor would reach for the pack of cards secretly, mysteriously, as if he was going to come up with a great surprise, some marvellous Christmas present.

Dr Anand bent down and picked up the cards, hiding them in his cupped hands and then revealing them suddenly, in the manner of an oriental magician. Rao could have screamed.

'Rummy?' asked the doctor.

You don't know any other game, in any case, thought Rao.

'Okay, rummy.'

Rao placed his pipe on the table. The smoke curled up gently to the doctor's nostrils and into his head.

Throw away that wretched pipe, he wanted to say.

The cards were dealt and the game began. The room had warmed up with the fire and a comfortable glow had spread gradually over the room. Each of them was alone with his glass, his ten cards, and his thoughts.

A few weeks more of this, thought Rao. Then he would have better company in the evenings than a stuffy, small-town, self-centred doctor. He would be back in the thick of things, back in circulation. It was a pleasant thought. He took a large sip of the whisky. It seared his throat and he coughed.

My resident film star, thought Dr Anand. He must smoke a pipe and drink neat whisky even though he can't take it. Suffer him for a couple of months more and let's hope his replacement will be a more intelligent chap. Someone genuine and not an upstart.

Lost in thought, the doctor got up and put a small log in the bukhari. Then he blew at the dying flames and saw the blue licks rise again. He came back to the table and threw down a king of spades. Almost instantly, he realized that he had made a mistake. What a fool he was. He picked up the card quickly.

'Sorry, that was a mistake.'

Rao had seen this before. Tonight he would not let it pass. In his agitation he puffed at his pipe quickly and sent the smoke straight into the doctor's face.

'You can't pick it up, I say.'

'It's only a friendly game.'

'Friendly, my foot,' Rao was shouting now. 'It's cheating.'

'You call me a cheat, you...you pipe-smoking bank clerk.'

'I'm not a clerk. I'm the manager, you village doc, you vet!'

Dr Anand wouldn't be called a vet by anybody. With a short swift movement of his forearm, he slapped Rao across the face. Smarting from the blow, Rao slapped him back. Then he got up and walked out, leaving the door open to the chilly wind.

Dr Anand sat quietly for a long time. Then, slowly, he got up and put another log in the bukhari. When he washed the glasses and put them near the drinks closet, he was already hoping that he would need to use them the next evening.

Rao walked home and the chilly wind quickly blew away his anger. Perhaps he had been hasty to walk away like that. Perhaps he should go back and apologize, or at least he must do it tomorrow. He looked involuntarily at the snow on the pass. It looked so heavy, so permanent.

AND THEN LAUGHED THE HYENA

SYED MUHAMMAD ASHRAF

Translated from the Urdu by M. Asaduddin

THE EARLY HOURS OF THE MORNING. A COLD WIND WAS GUSTING against the darkened windows. Inside, the room was stuffy. The dim glow from a light bulb cast blue shadows everywhere, making the atmosphere mysterious and threatening. Apart from Munnu Bhaiya, everyone else lay awake. Even though everyone was aware of this, nobody spoke about it because of an unknown fear that gripped them. They felt very alone despite the presence of others.

Their hearts were drumming in their chests as though some creature was crawling over them.

Just then, Badi Appi asked in a breathless voice. 'Is it necessary to take Munnu Bhaiya to the zoo to show him a hyena?'

Everyone listening shivered. Badi Appi's voice died away in the bluish gloom. In the silence, you could almost hear the pounding of the hearts of the family who were her audience.

Ammi turned on her side and looked in Badi Appi's direction. She felt that the stuffiness in the room had intensified. The wind outside was blowing harder. She fixed her gaze on Badi Appi's frightened eyes and said in a strange, unnatural tone: 'So what are you suggesting I do? Take him to the jungle....'

'Oh, no. Who's talking about the jungle? Are you awake? Did you hear what I said?' Badi Appi asked tearfully.

'Go to sleep, girl. You must only be half awake to ask such a question. Go to sleep. It's very late.'

Papa, Bhaijan, and Chhoti Appi who were silent and awake knew that Chhoti Appi had not asked that question in her sleep. Ammi herself knew that such questions are only asked when one is wide awake. But no one was going to give Badi Appi's question the seriousness it deserved for fear that Ammi might come up with the right answer. None of them wanted to hear the right answer. Badi Appi herself, having asked the question, prayed fervently for Ammi to stay silent.

Outside, the wind blew fiercely. Everyone seemed to hear a frightening noise, chat-chat...chat-chat...chat-chat....

Hearing the noise their hearts began to beat even harder. They felt the presence of a shadow in the half-dark room. It became difficult to breathe; they cringed under their blankets and fervently hoped that dawn would break soon. Ammi turned and clasped Munnu Bhaiya to her chest in an effort to lessen her own fear. She felt that all this was happening because of Munnu Bhaiya.

For the past ten to fifteen days a hyena had created panic in the villages beyond the railway lines. Every second or third day would bring with it news of some incident involving the animal. When Munnu Bhaiya was told that hyenas like the flesh of small children, he was stricken with terror. He had never seen a live hyena or even its picture, having just heard its name. Whenever he heard its name he also heard that it was responsible for the death of children. That is why he was terrified.

That evening he again heard that the hyena had carried off a child from the area beyond the railway lines. His face had turned ashen when he had heard the news. He didn't go out of the house in the evening and, instead, kept silently pacing up and down. At night, Akhtar Bhai, Bhaijan's friend, tried to calm him down by saying that he would talk to the hyena and ask him not to come to the area. Munnu Bhaiya, who was only eleven or twelve years old, did not have the courage to ask whether a hyena could talk like human beings. He grew even more afraid when he heard that hyenas could. He felt that a hyena was a unique creature, although he had no idea what it looked like. His friends had told him that a hyena was as tall as a high brick wall, and that was how he could cross over walls to carry away children.

Papa and Ammi had told him that a hyena was about the size of a dog but ferocious and wild. Bhaijan, Badi Appi, and Chhoti Appi did not say much about the size of hyenas because they had never seen one.

Before going to bed Munnu Bhaiya secretly put a cricket bat and matchbox under the mattress. He had studied in the fourth standard that wild animals are afraid of fire.

Throughout the evening the hyena appeared in his imagination in different shapes and sizes. When he was going to bed these shapes and sizes took on frightening proportions.

Bhaijan got up and checked the bolts of all the doors, closed the windows and called out to the neighbours to warn them. He reassured us saying that there was no need to worry as the hyena would be captured or killed in a day or two. Nevertheless, there was panic in the neighbourhood. People locked themselves into their houses and made sure to keep an eye on their children at all times. The panic was at its height in the houses that were situated near the railway lines. Munnu Bhaiya's house was close to the railway lines.

Munnu Bhaiya, scared, huddled close to Ammi. Papa, once again, went over to the door and checked the bolt and then lay down.

Outside, a hard wind blew through the cold December night.

Suddenly, Munnu Bhaiya screamed and the entire house woke up. After that, no one was able to go back to sleep.

'What's it, Munnu Bhaiya...? Why did you scream?' Ammi asked nervously.

'Ammi Ammi....' Munnu Bhaiya hid his face in her body.

'Tell me, beta. Tell me quickly, what happened?' Papa asked.

'Ammi, the hyena...he was standing by me, he bent down and sniffed me.'

'No, Munnu Bhaiya, you must've had a dream.'

Papa, Bhaijan, Badi Appi, and Chhoti Appi gathered around Ammi's bed. It seemed that all the blood had drained from Munnu Bhaiya's face. His eyes were bulging with fear and his lips were dry.

'No, Ammi... I saw him, tall as a brick wall. He bent his long neck, sniffed me and thrust his long horns into my body.'

Everyone gazed at him, excitedly.

Papa said, 'Munnu beta, a hyena is not tall like a brick wall but like a dog in size, and it doesn't have horns. You've just had a terrible dream. Say the Kalma prayer before going to sleep.'

'I did, Papa. I said the Al-Hamd prayer, too.' Munnu Bhaiya put his head in Ammi's lap and began to cry.

Everyone felt ill at ease. They didn't know how to tell him that it was not the hyena that had frightened him but his fear of it, his imagining of it as a figure of terror.

At that moment Ammi said, 'Munnu beta, let me tell you what a hyena looks like so you are no longer afraid of it.'

Everyone dispersed to their beds, and said hoon or haan in response to what Ammi was saying. This was intended to let Munnu Bhaiya know that everyone was awake and listening to what was being said. The doors and windows rattled in the gusts of wind, adding to the scary atmosphere that had filled the room. They shivered in their beds. Munnu Bhaiya's muffled sobbing heightened their fear. In the mysterious blue light that fell on their frightened faces, Ammi began to talk of the hyena: 'Munnu Bhaiya, a hyena...are you listening to me? A hyena is an animal that looks like a dog. But in a pack of dogs you can identify it easily. It is a mean and violent animal.... You can't call it courageous.'

Bhaijan indicated that he understood all this with a long-drawn-out exclamation—hoon. Everyone was listening to Ammi with rapt attention.

'It always attacks innocent young children. It follows people stealthily. Hearing footsteps if you look back, you'd think that a faithful dog is following you...slowly, with his head lowered. But the moment he gets an opportunity...you look away and he pounces on you.'

Having proceeded this far, Ammi herself realized that her voice was beginning to sound strange. Munnu Bhaiya could feel the silent presence of the others, awake and listening.

'Ammi, is there any way to escape his clutches?' Munnu Bhaiya murmured.

'You have to take the right precautions if you want to escape. You shouldn't stay out late. Whenever you are passing a patch of jungle or shrubbery, always carry a sharp weapon. Most of all...if it's dark or foggy, never make the assumption that an animal which looks like a dog is a dog.'

Lying tense and watchful in their beds everyone listened and reflected on what Ammi had just said.

'When night begins to fall, be suspicious of any animal that appears to be a dog.... You want to fight it with a cricket bat and a matchbox? How stupid! Once an innocent child thought he could do exactly that. But when the hyena came, he froze, he couldn't do anything. The hyena pounced on him, locked his jaws on the child's throat, and drank his blood.... Then he opened up his stomach, pulled out his entrails...and tore off large mouthfuls of his flesh and swallowed it.'

'Ammi, Ammi....' Munnu Bhaiya cried out in terror and held his mother tightly.

'Don't be scared. I want to alert you to all the dangers, so you aren't taken by surprise.' Ammi said seriously.

Outside, a thick mist had descended. The wind roared, it seemed to be having a conversation with the darkness. Inside the stuffy room everyone lay listening to Ammi.

'Beta, I'm giving you so much detail about the hyena so you are able to take every precaution necessary. It's not courageous like the tiger which attacks from the front. It's a vile animal which pounces on you from behind. He knows that people mistake him for a dog and allow him to come close. Then he waits for an opportunity and when you aren't alert... the moment you become careless....'

There wasn't a sound in the room, it was so tense. Again you could fancy you could hear the pounding everyone's hearts.

'There's just one way you can identify it. When it walks, its claws make a clicking chat-chat sound. But people, sunk in their own thoughts, often do not hear it. That's why it's important that when you see an animal looking like a dog following you and pretending to be as innocent and loyal, then...stop in your tracks and listen carefully whether you can hear the chat-chat sound. But, my dear son, people cannot hear it unless they pay attention.'

Papa, Bhaijan, Badi Appi, Chhoti Appi—all of them felt as if their breathing would stop. All of them thought they could hear the chat-chat sound outside the house.

'Ammi, will you show me a hyena?' Munnu Bhaiya asked. Exhausted by all the tension, and the lateness of the hour, he was falling asleep. 'Of course, this time when we go to Lucknow, you can see it in the zoo. Now go to sleep. It's quite late.'

Ammi fell silent. Munnu Bhaiya was asleep. But Ammi's voice still reverberated in everyone's ears: 'When it's windy or dark, it looks exactly like a dog...pretends to be trustworthy but is very tricky...slinks up to you before you know it and the moment it gets an opportunity...pounces on you. It's very mean and cunning...never makes a frontal attack.'

All those who were awake in that darkened room, faintly lit with the mysterious blue light, were wondering why they had forgotten to utter hoon-haan when Ammi was speaking. They were still wondering about it when it seemed that the light in the room had brightened. Then, an idea struck Badi Appi. She suddenly seemed to get why everyone in the house was so frightened. She realized that everyone except Munnu Bhaiya was awake although they gave no indication that they weren't asleep. The blue light made the room mysterious. The windows rattled in the wind.

Badi Appi asked hesitantly. 'Ammi, is it necessary to take Munnu Bhaiya to the zoo to show him a hyena?'

Everyone else had the same question on their minds.

Why were they thinking that?

They felt that it was only natural that such a question would occur to them. Ammi asked Badi Appi to go to sleep...and then everyone heard the chat-chat sound resound in their heads. It wasn't coming from outside but from within their subconscious.

The long night finally came to an end and their daily routine began. But even as they went about their tasks they realized that the events of the night were still occupying their minds. No matter what it was they were doing, they could feel a mysterious...chat-chat...chat-chat...rising from somewhere—as though a hyena were close by. When Papa and Bhaijan went to work they heard the same sound at various places. The events of the night came to them. When they heard this sound while they were working, they would stop whatever they were doing and look around, scared. But it would be nothing, just a friend standing there. They would try and shrug it off, put the sound out of their heads.

He follows you like a trustworthy dog... The moment he gets the opportunity...pounces on you...doesn't make a frontal attack...vile and deceptive animal....

Badi Appi and Chhoti Appi went to their school. After class, when their friends were chatting and laughing, they heard the mysterious and frightening sound. Chat-chat...chat-chat. Agitated, they looked at each other but didn't say anything. What could they say?

In the evening when everybody came home, although everything seemed normal, all of them felt bonded together in a strange sort of way. The way to describe it would be the sort of connection that develops between patients in a hospital ward. A sense of dependence and helplessness binds them. But none of them gave any indication to the others of what they had been feeling all day.

All of them concealed the roiling tension within and pretended everything was normal. But every couple of minutes they seemed to hear the chat-chat sound reverberating in their heads.

Khaja Sahib, Papa's friend, was leaving the house after advising him on a very important business matter. It was dark outside the drawing room. Papa felt that the chat-chat sound was coming from Khaja Sahib's feet as he walked. When Khaja Sahib turned back and told Papa that he would gain immensely if he followed his advice, Papa felt that Khaja Sahib's eyes had turned red and ferocious just like...just like....

Papa threw himself on the bed as soon as his friend left.

A short time later Bhaijan's friend, Akhtar Bhai, arrived. Munnu Bhaiya discussed with him at length how much a big knife would cost. Then Bhaijan asked Munnu Bhaiya to go to the inner room and Akhtar Bhai and he began discussing something.

Chhoti Appi, who was passing, carrying water, paused when she heard what they were saying. Suddenly Bhaijan whispered into Akhtar Bhai's ear, 'You'll profit greatly if you begin this work. I'll assist you wholeheartedly. Friends must help one another. Don't you agree?'

It was a good thing Akhtar Bhai couldn't see Bhaijan's face because had he done so he would have seen that Bhaijan's eyes had become fierce and sharp teeth jutted from his jaw.

When Akhtar Bhai left, Bhaijan saw him out. As he was returning to the house, Chhoti Appi cried out, 'Hyena...the hyena!'

'Where is it?' Bhaijan cried as he entered the house. He stared at her.

'I don't know.... Were you coming in from the drawing room? I just heard the sound, chat-chat. Were your feet making that sound?'

'I've no idea', answered Bhaijan. His mind seemed somewhere else.

'I don't know what's happening...' he said. 'God knows, today I've heard this sound coming from the feet of several friends. Just now, when Akhtar Bhai left, I heard.... Don't know whether I'm imagining it...or probably....'

'Bhaijan...do you also...do you...' Chhoti Appi sounded scared.

'Shut up...please shut up. Don't talk about it.'

Papa and Bhaijan checked the doors several times at Munnu Bhaiya's insistence. And when they lay down to sleep all of them had something to think about. All except Munnu Bhaiya. They thought about their world, about their friends...about thousands of people they knew...and then... they thought about themselves.

Outside, the cold wind picked up. The people in the house were lost in an unpleasant reverie. They began thinking about things in the remote past that had been buried deep down, hidden. They felt something was crawling down their gullets. In their trance-like state they saw a jungle spreading deep into the gloom, in which many dog-like creatures were roaming. Munnu Bhaiya, who was asleep, turned on his side violently, and the sound drew everyone back to the room.

Their hearts began to flutter. It seemed to them that the clock hanging from the wall had just come alive...tick tick...tick tick....

The ticking of the clock, the hissing of the wind, and the beating of their hearts blended together to form the frightening sound—chat-chat. Everyone felt that just as there was a jungle outside the windows so also was there one inside. Lying in the jungle enclosed by walls, everyone remembered the previous night...follows silently like a dog.... Ammi had remarked.

Everyone kept thinking...reflected on their own lives...kept on reflecting.... Everyone was awake and they knew that the others, too, were awake.

The whistle of the nightwatchman could be heard from a distance. The terrifying darkness of the night slithered outside the window.... In the morning, when Papa got up before everyone else, a strange thing happened. He felt as though his feet were making the sound, chat-chat. Startled, he stopped in his tracks. As he took a step forward he heard the same noise. He stopped and looked at Ammi who was standing and looking down at her own feet.

'You, too....' Papa said...

'Yes,' Ammi replied in a tearful voice.

Both of them stared at each other. After a little while Badi Appi came over to Ammi and said in a hesitant, scared voice that she was hearing the chat-chat sound coming from her feet. Ammi looked at Papa helplessly and tried to comfort Badi Appi: 'Beti, don't worry, it's a delusion. Because of Munnu Bhaiya, since yesterday we have been able to think of nothing but the hyena. But there's no truth to it. Really.'

'Are you sure, Ammi?' Chhoti Appi, who was standing near Ammi, asked.

'Yes, beti. There's no truth to this.... Not at all....' Papa said.

Chhoti Appi had just opened her mouth to say something when Bhaijan got up from his bed, took one or two steps forward, and then stopped. He was looking at his feet in such a way that it seemed he was listening for something. Then he walked a few steps more and stopped again and paused to listen. Everyone looked at him, then looked at each other. Everything grew quiet.

Just then, the family servant came running. Panting for breath, he said that a hyena had been caught in the neighbouring village the previous night.... The villagers were planning to take him to the town. They would pass our house in a little while.

If he had expected his announcement to come as a surprise or create a ruckus he was disappointed. None of us seemed in the least bit surprised by his news. Disappointed, he left.

The family just kept standing there silently. It was as though they were waiting for something to happen even though they were scared. Finally, when Munnu Bhaiya woke up, their wait was over. Munnu Bhaiya jumped up and asked in a groggy but restless voice, 'Why are you all standing around like this? Has the hyena come?'

'No, beta. The hyena has been caught. Now you needn't be afraid of it.'

Saying this Papa took Munnu Bhaiya to the inner room. He gave him some toffees and asked Munnu Bhaiya, 'When you walk, do you hear the sound chat-chat coming from your feet?'

Munnu Bhaiya seemed stunned by the question.

'Beta, tell me quickly.... Do you hear the sound coming from your feet?'

'No, Papa. Why do you ask? Am I a hyena?' Munnu Bhaiya said.

Right at that moment they heard a noise outside. Everyone rushed to the window. A hyena was walking down the path, surrounded by hundreds of villagers. A muzzle was clamped over his powerful jaws, and there were chains on his feet. His eyes were red and he was trying to rip the muzzle off. Wounds striped his hide and his front paws were soaked in blood.

Papa, Ammi, Bhaijan, Badi Appi, Chhoti Appi—all looked at their own hands stealthily and kept on looking at them for a long while—it wasn't clear why. Now the hyena was passing by the window. The chat-chat sound of his feet could be heard clearly. Behind him were the villagers, armed with lathis and spears. Suddenly the beast stopped right outside our window. The chat-chat sound stopped. The people following him stopped. The dust slowly settled. The members of the family found it difficult to breathe as they peeped out of the window. Munnu Bhaiya clutched Ammi's feet. The crowd outside fell silent. The hyena looked at the window for a long moment. Then he broke into frenzied, maniacal laughter. His captors thought the sound meant he was making a determined effort to get rid of the muzzle. A villager struck him hard with a stick from behind and said in a voice filled with hate... '*Bastard, he steals up to people pretending to be a dog and then pounces the moment he gets a chance....*'

The savage blow brought tears to the hyena's eyes.... He took a long, hard look at the villager. Then his moist eyes took in the members of the family, one by one. That terrifying laugh burst forth once more and he moved on, surrounded by the crowd, the chat-chat sound marking their passage.

Papa stood at the window looking out. The crowd accompanying the hyena had not yet disappeared entirely. The dust kicked up by them still filled the air. Through it, he could see Munnu Bhaiya talking to his friends as they set off for school.

Papa felt that Munnu Bhaiya had suddenly stopped and was looking at his feet. It was as though he was trying to listen for something. Papa closed his eyes and prayed to God that the chat-chat sound might never rise from the feet of Munnu Bhaiya and those of his friends.

When Munnu Bhaiya and his friends disappeared from view, Papa clutched the iron bars of the window and gazed out at the world that spread beyond the railway lines, silently reflecting on everything that had taken place. When he finally turned around, he saw the members of the family sitting silently. They looked sad and disappointed with themselves. It was as though they had heard about the outbreak of an epidemic. They looked at each other shamefacedly. Ammi sighed deeply. Then everyone stood up and went about their work....

THE MURMUROUS DEAD
A VERY BRIEF EXCHANGE WITH A SPIRIT

DAVID DAVIDAR

Not so long ago, after a fall, I was laid up in bed. As a result of bruised ribs, and stitches in my jaw, sleep was often elusive. One restless night, in the predawn hours, just as grey began filtering through the kachnar trees outside my bedroom window, I had an unexpected visitor. My visitor had neither form nor substance but was simply a consciousness outside my own—its voice was nevertheless clear and unmistakable.

'Sir,' my visitor began, respectfully, 'I have a question for you'.

'Who are you?' I asked.

The voice belonged to the spirit of a fourteen-year-old girl who had died in a communal riot in a small town a few years ago.

'And what is this question you have for me?' I asked.

'Why,' she asked, 'are there no memorials for us? Rightfully, there are memorials to the brave men and women who gave their lives protecting our country, their sacrifice should never be forgotten, but how come there are no memorials for us, all of us innocents whom the country failed to protect?'

Nonplussed, I did not reply immediately and she spoke up again.

'There are hundreds of thousands of us who have paid with our lives in this glorious nation of ours because of the acts of commission or omission of our leaders, the least we deserve are memorials so we will be remembered.'

'But surely,' I said weakly, 'There must be plaques or memorial stones....'

She interrupted me. 'Private markers by our families and those who mourn us don't count. We died because the state did not look out for us, so it's the state which should erect memorials for us.'

She had piqued my interest, so I said, 'And what form should these memorials take?'

She said, 'The form doesn't really matter, though I would love it if my memorial were to be a garden by the main street of the town where I was killed. A haven of soft grass so green, each blade could have been carved from an emerald, with a stream running through it, and bulbuls and dragonflies flitting through the shrubbery. This would be a shelter for all the rejects and strays from the living and spirit world, homeless street children and dogs and cats and the unsung dead. My favourite flowering trees, kachnars and gulmohars and amaltases, would bend over the stream, raining petals and leaves into the murmuring waters, the play of colour and sound and movement and light creating a memorial that no human hand could better. Imagine if all us were honoured thus our ugly cities and towns would be transformed into paradisiacal places of shimmering green and pink and red and violet.'

I was momentarily lost in the vision she had conjured up, until she spoke again. 'No matter what form each memorial takes, every single one of them has to have an essential component.'

'And what is that?' I asked.

'Each of them must have a plaque listing the names of the leaders who failed us, those who were responsible for our deaths. Our leaders love to flaunt their faces on billboards and posters that are prominently displayed in public places, so their portraits should be engraved on these plaques for all eternity. That way the part they played in our deaths will never be forgotten.'

And with that she was gone, as abruptly as she had appeared, just as the morning light came flooding into the room.

PREDATORS

SYED SALEEM

Translated from the Telugu by Dasu Krishnamoorty and Tamraparni Dasu

KOTESU PARKED HIMSELF NEAR THE RYVES CANAL LOCK, WITH HIS NECK outstretched like a vulture eyeing carrion. His eyes travelled down the stream to study the shadows playing on the water not far from him. 'There is something odd about the blend of colours,' he thought. The red object moving seductively in his direction looked at first sight like a wet, unfurled sari. Shielding his eyes against the sun, he squinted into the waters and saw that it really was a red sari.

He stood on the high embankment of the canal, his humble frame filled with hope. His hawkish eyes glowed with expectation. He was sure his two-hour wait had paid off. Kotesu watched his reward approach the gates. An answer to his prayers. His eyes combed the surroundings anxiously for spoilsports who could cheat him of his catch. The couple of people he spotted moping around hardly noticed him. Others that passed by mistook him, with his tatters, emaciated cheeks, and gaunt face, for a beggar. They filed past unconcerned.

'Is begging heinous?' he wondered. Is rifling through the garments of dead strangers a crime? How can you call it stealing, when the corpses neither forbade nor approved such a crime? He'd never used force. Some loathsome human dregs he knew exhumed bodies, rid them of clothes and jewellery, and then sold the items. In his view, he was better than such guttersnipes. The poor wretches that jumped into the river to kill themselves did so of their free will. He had not driven them to suicide. He always waited for the bodies to float down from the Krishna River and get to the locks near the Ryves Canal masonry bridge. Only then did he rob them of gold ornaments. 'It is a wretched life nevertheless,' he conceded.

It had been like this, despicable, since he could remember: hunger, penury, indignity, disease, and hell. Images of his father coming home drunk and battering his mother daily had made him resolve to never touch alcohol. That resolve had melted away even before he'd shed adolescence. He loafed about the streets, watched blue films in Leela Mahal, and smoked bidis.

His happiness at the death of a feral father was short-lived. It had heaped additional misery on him. His mother, who had, until now, turned a blind eye to his vagrant ways, began badgering him to go out and bring home some money. After one such maternal dressing-down, he'd repaired to the canal to sulk. The sulk ended when he saw the body of a woman bobbing up near the canal gates. His eyes lit up when he saw the glittering mangalasutram, the sacred wedding chain, around her neck. A second look revealed an additional slender gold chain. Kotesu had realized in an instant that if he wavered, someone else, perhaps a policeman, would do it. Without a second thought he'd jumped into the water and briskly gathered the gold on the body.

He had sold off the loot to a pawnbroker, soaked himself in liquor, eaten chicken biryani in Srinivasa Hotel, and then gone home to sleep. His rest was disturbed—he'd been plagued by nightmares of the dead woman coming back to life and laughing at him viciously. She'd opened her eyes just as he snatched away the ornaments, sailed into his hut, and demanded her things back.

For a whole month, the nightmare had held him back from the locks. But the hardships of life had preyed upon him like a blood-sucking vampire and driven him back to his scavenging ways. After a month of restraint, Kotesu had reappeared at the canal site.

Now, he had learned to concentrate his five senses on the gold, like Arjuna, the legendary archer from the Mahabharata, fixing his aim on the bird's eye. His nose no longer flinched at the stench of the passing cadavers. Their touch no more sent a shudder through his body. For him, to lift the gold off the bodies became child's play, as easy as pulling it off a peg. He braced himself as he saw the bloated red sari sailing towards him. 'No hurry, the body will stop at the gates anyway,' he calculated. He would dive in and finish the job as adroitly as he could catch fish.

He was afraid that fucker Narigadu might be lurking somewhere close by to swoop down on the treasure. His eyes surveyed the scene for Narigadu who, in his eyes, was a menace. Kotesu had ruled the roost for eight months. Ever since Narigadu appeared, he'd literally snatched the food off his plate. The guy was older and stronger. Kotesu knew he could never win if it came down to a fight. Narigadu had already bested him four or five times.

He looked around once again and was convinced that it was not prudent to wait for the body to reach him. Yet, Kotesu had to abandon the dive because Narigadu had appeared out of nowhere and leapt into the water, and was now rapidly closing the distance between him and the woman's body.

Kotesu raged impotently at Narigadu. Like hunger, his anger singed his innards. His feeble heart beat weakly, eager to clobber his rival. 'Don't get in my way, just this once. I promise, you won't see me here for another month. Let it be my turn this time. Spare me for the sake of my sister. Her husband has deserted her for failing to bring in the five hundred rupees we owe him. I can't bear to see sorrow darken her eyes. Just five hundred rupees will do, not to drink or visit brothels but to make my sister happy once again. Her marriage, worth a mere five hundred rupees, must be saved,' he beseeched Narigadu in his mind.

Narigadu was within reach of his prize now. It was then that Kotesu's eyes lit up once again, after he'd despondently gazed at the red sari that had slipped from his hand. He took a second look. After walking a few steps along the embankment, he paused and gazed at what was happening.

Kotesu saw the red sari trapped in Narigadu's hands—but where was the corpse? Narigadu must have thought the sari had disengaged itself from the body. He had swum back and was searching for the corpse. He went under the water and surfaced three times, his head covered with flotsam. Not a hint of the body.

Narigadu's discomfiture set Kotesu laughing wildly. Kotesu told Narigadu, who was glaring at him, 'Keep all the gold to yourself,' and continued to laugh.

'Stay there if you have guts...you're destined to die by my hands today,' snarled Narigadu, swimming back to the embankment. Ready to flee before Narigadu reached the shore, Kotesu said from the embankment, 'Okay, come up. We will see who lives and who dies.'

Narigadu climbed up the embankment but whirled back in terror. Kotesu was baffled. What scared him? As if in answer, a heavy hand fell on his shoulder with a thud. It belonged to a policeman guffawing like an apparition. Kotesu knew the punk. 'This fellow is worse. If I feed off cadavers, this guy swipes commissions from the likes of us,' he muttered under his breath.

'Rascal, what are you up to?' the policeman asked.

'Nothing, sir. Just passing time.'

'Shut up, you son of a whore. You think I can't see through your games? You think I'm a fool to believe you're here to appreciate nature or breathe in the fresh air? I'll skin you alive. Take out whatever you have, you parasite,' the policeman said, hitting Kotesu on the knees with his baton.

'I beseech you, sir. I swear I didn't even get into the water. That fellow saw the body first. See, how dry my shirt is?' Kotesu pulled his shirt out for the policeman to see.

'You, clod, you think you're very smart. Don't play games with me. I'm sure the two of you are in league. Don't think you can cheat me out of my share.'

Clenching Kotesu's shirt with his left hand, the cop reached for Narigadu and shouted, 'Do you need a special invitation? Will you come out of the water or wait until you get a taste of this baton?'

Narigadu crawled up to the cop trembling with fear and wringing the water from his clothes.

'Where is the loot? Shell it out,' the policeman barked.

'I haven't taken anything, sir,' said Narigadu meekly, like a tiger morphed into a cat.

'You think the corpse is your mother's property? Take it out! I have other things to do.'

'What corpse, sir? Do you see it here? It's just the sari. I swear on my mother, sir.'

The policeman took a sharp look at the sari.

'Rascal! Tell me, what happened to the body?'

'No body, sir. Only the sari.'

The policeman landed one good whack on Narigadu's back.

'I'll charge you with murder. Put you in the cooler. Tell me, where's the body and what happened to the gold jewels?' the policeman said, shifting his hand from Kotesu's shirt to Narigadu's collar.

Kotesu thought it might be a good time to wriggle out. He said, 'Sir, may I go now?'

'Where are you going, bastard? Aren't you both in cahoots? First, empty your pockets!'

The policeman shoved his hand into Kotesu's pocket and searched. He found a bidi stub, two one-rupee coins, a half-rupee coin, and a soiled five-rupee note. He stuffed the loot into his pocket and said, 'You may go now. I'll settle this fellow's account.'

He turned to Narigadu and asked, 'Now tell me, where is the corpse and where are the things you took from it?' He then used the baton on him.

The policeman saw Kotesu still hanging about and asked him, 'What are you waiting around for? Do you want me to use the baton on you?'

'Sir, I haven't had a drop of water since morning. I'm hungry, please give me some money.'

'What money? You mean your hard-earned cash? Bloody thief, get lost without making a fuss.'

'Sir, true, it is a wretched way to make money. But hunger is no less wretched. I've nothing to buy tea with, sir. Please return my money,' Kotesu begged.

'Chee, useless fellow. You're all parasites. Take this and perish,' the policeman flung two and a half rupees at him.

Kotesu wanted to stand around and enjoy what awaited Narigadu but was afraid that if he stayed on too long the policeman might change his mind and take his money back. He left the scene at a brisk pace.

When he was out of the policeman's sight he slowed down. Two one-rupee coins and a half-rupee coin. 'Shit, what a miserable life...a policeman calls me a parasite,' Kotesu hated himself and spat in disgust. 'I'm not just a parasite but the vermin that thrive on shit. But what about the policemen who suck the blood of vermin like us? What about the officials who open the locks and push the bodies into the jurisdiction of the Guntur police to avoid the bother of conducting an investigation, and the expense of performing the last rites for these unclaimed bodies?'

To escape the pain of these questions, he reignited the bidi stub and filled his lungs with smoke. Ah, some relief! The sky was overcast. A gentle breeze hinted at rain. It was a disappointing day. He would have to go home and listen to his mother's curses, look at the piteous face of his sister waiting to see if he'd brought the money for her dowry. How was he to console her?

Kotesu's melancholy abruptly lifted when he remembered his defeat from last month and today's avenging humiliation of Narigadu, blow for blow, insult for insult, and sneer for sneer.

That day, a month ago, it was Narigadu who had first seen the body floating down. When he ran to jump into the canal Kotesu had tripped him and felled him to the ground. Narigadu rose to his feet and landed a couple of blows on Kotesu's face. Kotesu was dazed and his nose began to bleed. He kicked Narigadu hard in the stomach. As Kotesu tried to flee towards the canal, Narigadu stood in the way. Kotesu dug his teeth into Narigadu's right hand. In pain, Narigadu pushed Kotesu just as he neared the water.

'I can make it if I leap into the canal, swim like mad, and rip the mangalasutram and earrings off the body, then race to the other embankment,' Kotesu had thought. He dove into the water but, in a blink, Narigadu had jumped in too. Kotesu swam faster than him and reached the body, its face turned towards the gates. It had a string with a pendant of turmeric root around its neck. Hoping to find a gold mangalasutram, he turned the body towards him. It was the madwoman that begged for money on their street. He had turned to look behind him and seen Narigadu laughing wildly.

'The body is full of gold. Take it all. I won't ask for a share,' Narigadu had been in stitches.

Today, after one month, Kotesu was happy that Narigadu had finally got his due. How should he celebrate? Radhabai or booze? Which would give him a high—the nectar that burns the throat or sex that exhilarates the body? He chose Radhabai.

He found her sitting on her haunches in front of her hut, barbequing kebabs. Her shining thighs and taut body were a treat. She took time off from barbequing to get into bed with the client waiting inside her hut for five rupees. Once the client left, she returned and spoke to Kotesu.

'You want some kebabs?'

'Let's go to your shack,' he stammered, unable to look into her intoxicating eyes.

'The rate is ten rupees.'

'It was five rupees four days ago?'

'I hiked the rates. Haven't the others done it? You pay others without a murmur but you want to haggle with me. Get out of my sight,' she said.

'That is too much. I'm an old client. Give me a concession, Radhabai,' Kotesu pleaded.

'Do you get a concession at the liquor store? Nothing less than ten rupees will do,' Radhabai said stubbornly.

'Okay, let's walk in.'

'Pay first.'

Kotesu grumbled and took out the two and half rupees from his pocket and pressed it into the hooker's palm.

'The rest on credit,' he said.

Radhabai considered the stuff in her hand with disdain.

'You wretched bum, put this money on your pyre! You want to roll in my bed like a pig without a dime in your pocket? Go to hell,' she said and threw the money in his face.

He picked up the money from the floor and muttered, 'You fatty... sleeping with you is like mating with a hog.'

The liquor shop gave him credit. He drank with a vengeance. Drank because the policeman had called him a parasite. Drank because Radhabai had said he was a pig. Drank because it was a day when nobody jumped into the Krishna to die. Drank because he remembered his mother. Drank because his sister waited with her big black eyes to get the money to pay the needed dowry and reunite with her husband.

He awoke to the sound of his mother's voice unfolding a catalogue of his misdeeds.

'Is there anything that you do other than drink and loll in bed? It's been more than three months since that rascal ditched your sister. She cries every day. I'm able to feed her with what little I get working in four homes. You don't have the sense to send the girl to her husband's place. Lazing in bed is all you do....'

'I'll somehow get the money today. Please stop, Ma,' he said.

'You've been saying that for three months now. It's our mistake not to have paid the dowry. No, it's my fault that I bore a son like you. Will you send her back or keep her at home like a widow?' his mother asked.

Hurt, he hurried outside to head for the canal embankment, with a parting assurance to his mother who continued her tirade.

Outside the hut, Kotesu saw his sister crouching in a corner, a picture of sorrow personified. When she raised her head and looked at him, her big eyes brimmed with tears and contempt at his inability to stop them. 'Maybe, I'm imagining things,' he thought. He was familiar with the contemptuous looks of his mother; perhaps his sister was taking a page from her book.

She knew of his addiction to liquor, of his trips to brothels, but not what he did for a living. He wondered what his mother and sister would do if they knew he robbed corpses. Would they shun him like a leper?

Kotesu reached the locks. At least once a week, some unfortunate person jumped into the Krishna in an attempt at suicide. This week not a single corpse floated downstream. He hoped that at least one would show up and gift five hundred rupees to him.

Kotesu tried to figure out reasons why people killed themselves. Some did it because they were unable to bear the torture inflicted by their husbands, some killed themselves because they scored poor marks in their exams, and some did it for lost loves. Desperate women jumped into the dark waters of the Krishna with no thought for the ornaments on their body. That, of course, suited the likes of Kotesu and Narigadu.

He stopped his philosophizing and screwed up his eyes to look into the water gleaming like a mirror. He'd been keeping a sharp vigil for a couple of hours now. From the changing colours of the water he knew that some object was afloat. Definitely, it had to be a corpse. Corpse of a woman, he hoped. His eyes shone in anticipation. There will be gold on the body if it is a woman, or at least a mangalasutram, he thought.

He needed a mere five hundred. It would bring the light back into his sister's life. She would look at him with love and gratitude in her big shining eyes. He was determined to get her the five hundred rupees even if it meant kissing a rotting corpse.

Five hundred rupees—the price of his sister's happiness! Five hundred to save her marriage, to bring the sunshine back into her life!

The corpse drifted down close to him, wrapped in a dark blue sari, the face sunk in water. The hair was dishevelled and fanned out.

He looked around for a possible competitor. Narigadu was nowhere to be seen. Perhaps he was in police lock-up. He must be groaning in bed after the policeman had given him the works. The thought cheered him up.

The corpse ended its drift at the gates.

'This is mine. I need not struggle with Narigadu like dogs fighting over leftovers. All the gold and the money are mine. Radhabai must get a taste of my manhood for the insults she hurled at me. I'll hurl ten ten-rupee notes at her and make her pick them up like a beggar. That's how I'll avenge my humiliation,' he thought.

Kotesu waded slowly into the water. The water was cold. He got to the corpse and saw a turmeric string around its neck. The mangalasutram must be there too, he thought with glee as he overturned it.

His sister's face shone up at him, so peaceful, her dark eyes finally free of tears, resting behind the closed lids.

SHARAVANA SERVICES

VIVEK SHANBHAG

Translated from the Kannada by Jayanth Kodkani

I

WHEN SHARAVANA TOLD ME, 'NOT TODAY, SIR.... TODAY IS TUESDAY', I agreed because it was convenient for me. I had a lot of work to do by evening and it wouldn't have been possible to go with him and check out a plot. Since the Tuesday factor came in as a handy pretext, I agreed at once. And to sound as if I had indeed meant it, said: 'Arre, it is Tuesday! I had forgotten too amidst all the work.'

Even after two days, Sharavana didn't talk about going to see the site. Otherwise, his business would start with office hours in the morning—from the moment he came in and placed a cup of tea on the table. He had joined this office as a peon some years ago, but of late had managed to retain his job by handling additional chores such as running errands to the bank as well as helping with office upkeep. Everyone in the office has had some personal dealing with him. For any service you wanted—be it buying a second-hand fridge, disposing of an old fan, getting the dented rear of your car fixed for a low price, looking for a carpenter to drill holes in the walls of your house for nails and hang pictures at five rupees per nail—you could get in touch with him and the work was done. If you wanted a site in Bangalore and a lawyer to scrutinize the property papers, a contractor to build the house and a priest for the Bhoomi Puja, he was at your disposal. If you wanted pandits of Nadi Shastra or Vastu Shastra, wished to go for a darshan of the baba, wanted a priest of your own sub-caste for puja as laid down in the scriptures, you could tell him and he would readily arrange it. He could speak Kannada, Telugu, Tamil, and Hindi so fluently that one couldn't figure out what his mother tongue was. And his English, though faltering and faulty, could be understood.

After two days when my work pressure had eased a bit, I said, 'Let us go and check out the site today, Sharavana.'

'Just wait for one more day, sir.... Let's go on Friday.'

'Why? Are you looking for an auspicious time?' I said in jest.

'Take it that way. You'll see how smoothly the work gets done....'

That Friday, we went and saw the site. Hardly had we taken a look, when he got a bit restive and said, 'Ayyo, had I known that it faces the south, I wouldn't have brought you here at all.' I quite liked the plot. But Sharavana said, 'This is certainly not for you, sir. If you wish, I can find you another site in the same layout.'

'I don't care which direction it faces. Tell me if there is any other problem....' My tone suggested, 'Do what you're told. Don't act smart!'

But Sharavana wouldn't be cowed down. 'As you say, sir. Your belief alone matters....' he said.

'Are you doing business or are you in the job of reading people's horoscopes?'

'If those who buy through me don't thrive, it is my business that will suffer, right? If everything goes smoothly, they will bring me half a dozen other customers. Otherwise, they'll say, we bought it from him and look what we've had to face.'

'If you wish, I can give it in writing that I won't complain. Even if we had come here on Tuesday, this site would be facing the south, wouldn't it?'

'Sir, I don't say this for the sake of argument. It isn't that easy to remove the tangled knot between thought, belief, and experience. Even if we don't believe in astrology, don't our eyes pause for a moment at the horoscope column while flipping through a newspaper? Even a pseudo-palmist's words about our private lives stay in our mind, no, sir? I'll tell you a secret. Your views make me feel like sharing it. It's to do with our Shahane Saheb....'

I hadn't expected such skilful language from him. Yet, I composed myself and said, 'Let me hear what you have to say. What about Shahane Saheb? Isn't he enjoying a happy retired life?'

'He bought a site and built a house too. I myself found a Maharashtrian priest for his house-warming ceremony. When I met him after two months, he told me, "What do I do, Sharavana? My wife, who never raised her voice against me, has begun to pick quarrels with me every day for no reason." And, with a lump in his throat, he said he couldn't bear to see her grind her teeth during the fights. He had also secretly seen some doctors about this.

'....I felt this must be the handiwork of bad Vastu. I knew a person called Chennappa, who is well-versed in Vastu. I took him to Shahane's house. Chennappa said the direction of the water inflow into the house was not in order. Shahane didn't heed the advice. Just two days later, another mishap occurred. Leaving the front door wide open, his wife went out to buy vegetables. He was sitting on the sofa engrossed in the balance sheet of some company and thinking about the stock market. All of a sudden, a strong wind pushed the open door. To stop the door from slamming the frame, he rose swiftly, one hand still clutching the papers and the other stretched out. At that instant, he felt as if the devil had possessed him. The evil Vastu was acting again. Something strange happened as he forcefully bent his sixty-year-old body forward like a bow. He managed to prevent the door from banging but leaned on it and collapsed, unable to bear a shooting pain in his back. He was rushed to the hospital. They said it was a case of a slipped disc. And then, one after another, he suffered a series of aches.

'....I visited him at the hospital. "You needn't get anything done, I'll set everything right," I said. He told me, "I leave it all to you." That very day I got the nozzle of the water pipe in his house turned towards another side. Just that, sir. That was all. As if it was some miracle, peace returned to the household. Then onwards, I bet, the woman didn't quarrel at all.'

After listening to his story, I had no intention of devaluing its entertainment bit. Still, unable to stomach it all, I said, 'Haven't you heard of the proverb: the crow sat on the branch and the tree snapped?'

'Take it as coincidence if you want. For a big tree to crash, even the weight of a crow can suffice. You see, the world is said to hang in balance. But a piece of straw is enough to disturb the equilibrium. Or, a flutter of a butterfly's wings. Call it a Vastu defect or simply bad fortune, a slight change in the time you wake up in the morning might ruin your day.'

I did not argue with him further. The site was lost. 'Nothing to worry. Good riddance, in fact,' Sharavana told me after two days.

II

'I've seen a house. It belongs to some people in the movie business. The owner needs money urgently and wants to sell it. All it needs are some minor changes. It's a first-class house!' Sharavana continued to badger me.

I wasn't sure whether I wanted a site or a house. And then, I wasn't confident of taking a big leap in life by buying a house. When I told him that I would think it over for a day or two, he said: 'Ayyo, sir, it'll be sold by then. These matters are such—if you keep pondering over them, you'll lose the one you have in hand. You can't get a house so dirt cheap,' Sharavana persuaded me.

We decided to see the house that evening. Sharavana told me that we would have to start at two minutes before five o'clock, suggesting that the time after five would be inauspicious. I didn't respond.

We stepped out of the office. Crossing the scooters and motorcycles parked outside, we reached the edge of the road and stood there waiting to hail an autorickshaw. Sharavana, who stood facing me, had launched into a detailed description of the house we were going to see and the excessive vanity and opulence of film folk. He spoke of one who fell from the heights of prosperity to the depths of destitution and another—names that I had never heard of—who rose like a meteor.

That very moment....

A speeding bus lost control and hurtled towards us. Sharavana was standing with his back to the road, engrossed in his talk. All that was recorded in my memory was that the bus turned towards us. My dragging him aside, both of us falling on to the pavement after losing balance, and because of the fall, escaping the wheels of the bus by inches—all had happened outside of my will and intent. Like in a film sequence, the bus crashed into the parking lot, smashing the scooters and motorcycles much like a sickle scything through a cornfield. Earlier, it had mowed down a drowsy dog even before it could finish howling. Sharavana was terrified, having glimpsed his death amidst the piles of wrecked vehicles. As if he had imagined his own body in the heaps of mangled metal, Sharavana held my hand and squatted on the ground without uttering a word. His hands were trembling. So were mine. I sat down too. Our clothes were dusty and people who had gathered around us within no time were talking of our providential escape. The sight of the motionless corpse of the dog, which only a while ago had crossed us, reminded me for the first time of the transience of life. I too was horrified. And I didn't realize that I had kept his hand pressed in my palms. As we sat there comforting each other like brothers, our colleagues who had rushed there on hearing the noise, gathered around us.

From that day, Sharavana began to regard me as God. And with utmost trust, like confessing before God, recounted to me some providential and jinxed happenings in his life. He didn't unburden himself in one sitting. The incidents were unravelled in the span of a month, as different situations arose, in bits and snatches. All told in the ups and downs of his moods. When incidents are narrated by one person to another, many details pass through a sieve. If I tell them in his words, at least the emotional intensity might remain.

III

Sir, my name is Shravana. I come from a small village near Srirangapatna. When I started my business, I ironed out the consonant conjuncts in my name so that my customers could roll out the letters easily on their tongues. Since it sounded like a Tamil name, I didn't lose anything in terms of business. My father kept accounts in the temple. He also read horoscopes and could tell one's lakshana or characteristics. Lakshana was the word he used, he preferred not to say fortune-telling. After he quarrelled with the temple management committee, lakshana-reading became the only source of the family's income. But then, in such a small place, how many people come every day to know about their future? What could they do even if they knew? At least in this city, one sees ups and downs every day. A slight change in the price of oil or in the percentage of tax can lead to such ebbs and flows. As the day breaks, either there is a windfall or one goes stone broke. Fortune-telling or knowing may be a useful occupation in this city where uncertainty rules. But why would people of our village want to rack their brains about tomorrow? Their questions revolve around a daughter's marriage or a son gone astray. And if they heard the answers to that once, it was enough. They didn't feel the need to visit my father ever again. Managing a square meal at home became difficult at times.

I completed my pre-university commuting to and from Mysore every day. Left with no option, I later took a job with the cooperative society in our village. I was required to do all kinds of work. Although the pay was low, I carried out every task diligently because the president of the society was genial. Years later, when life seemed to be getting into a groove, and believing that the job was there to stay, I contemplated marriage.

Lavanya was born and brought up in Bangalore; she is a distant relative of ours. Her family was of modest means. Yet, she is said to have balked at the thought of shifting to a smaller place. The elders had to convince her to agree to the marriage. All this, we learnt later. When she wept bitterly on the day of the marriage, we presumed it was because of the sorrow of leaving her parents' home. Later, I suspected the grief might also have been about moving to a village. She had done her pre-university course. And in her talk, demeanour, and likes and dislikes, she tended to go the extra mile. In the beginning I liked that. But as days passed, the attitude annoyed me. I felt the show of her refinement was an expression of disgust towards our household. It would begin with what brand of tea leaves we must use. Even if she found fault with the cinema theatre in our village, I would take offence and get agitated. In the face of all this, when I recollect the first happy year of our life, all the romance seemed to belong to somebody else. It slowly dawned upon her that even if I toiled for my entire life, there wouldn't be any change in my job or in my status. Perhaps she had resigned herself to it. But I, who hadn't questioned it for so long, started to behave as though I was determined to transform everything.

One day my aunt's son came to our house from Bangalore. Shrikant was of my age, gaunt, and a dud at studies. We had nicknamed him Buddi because he wore spectacles as thick as that of a soda bottle. When he came this time, Buddi started talking about grandiose things in the share market. That was when the winds of change were blowing across the country, and wherever you went, people were talking of business and money. That night, after dinner, Buddi began to tell me thrilling stories of how people who bought stocks were making money. I am unable to say even now what happened in the room that night when this grand narration was on. But the heady sense of success and affluence gripped everybody there, at least a wee bit. The glance that Buddi threw at Lavanya as he spoke is still fresh in my mind. I wondered from where he had suddenly gathered that self-confidence. Almost the next instant, Lavanya looked at me. His glance followed by her look at me might seem casual to you. But it shot a message through me and I feel that it was then that my life forked in two directions. Sir, isn't it after such ordinary instances that the devil or spirit enters your life? My father, who had been listening to him in silence, said at last: 'Take care, son. Beware of this wealth that grows only on paper and doesn't come after hard work.'

I felt that unless I left my village, my life wouldn't change one bit. Before hitting the bed at night, I started dreaming about going abroad and returning with immense prosperity. Look at history, or consider the tales in *Chandamama*: the man chasing success goes away to a far-off land, doesn't he, sir? I felt Lavanya had spurred this dream indirectly. I told myself that her glance that day suggested that. I felt she was convinced that

I had it in me to pursue the dream. But I didn't know where to go after leaving the village. I pestered Buddi and got myself a job in Bangalore. My parents were frightened. They sobbed and kicked up a ruckus. They taunted me saying that I was looking after them too well for having named me Sharavana Kumar. They called their daughter-in-law a sorceress and hurled abuse. Not heeding anybody, I left.

Only two months after I came to Bangalore I lost my first job. For about six months after that I struggled a lot. Nobody came forward to help me. With the market scam exposed, the share prices had nosedived, putting even Buddi to great hardship. Helpless, I took up any job I could get. The person who got me my present job used to be my client. His name was Kannan. Along with this, I took up real estate and other miscellaneous services. Gradually I started Sharavana Services. What is it about, you may ask. This is a business I conceived and set up. As you know, sir, Bangalore has grown in the last ten years. People have come here from different places. They can't handle things as they did in their places. They can't find priests for auspicious events. They are all at sea when they have to organize a house-warming ceremony. In a place where they have no acquaintances at all, if the mother, who had come to live with her son, dies all of a sudden, who is to perform the rites? How do they find support and succour in times of mental agony? Who do they look to for solace? They are tormented by the guilt that they haven't done anything right. Worse, they can't spare time to go in search of all these. And they feel they can buy anything for a price. More importantly, they are ready to accept new-fangled rituals. What do smokers do if they can't find their brand? They settle for some other. Likewise, the addiction of faith and rituals. I provide them such beliefs.

I don't regret having disclosed to you the secrets of my business. A broker ought to have faith in everything, sir. But then he shouldn't have excessive faith in anything. If he does, his job is ruined. It would smack of prejudice. My clients don't have deep faith in caste and such matters. Nor can they renounce it. Their faith isn't deep-rooted but they would like to believe it is. Sharavana Services provides such people a crutch, you may say. I have converted a man from Uttar Pradesh into a devotee of Goddess Banashankari. I have turned Seth—who is in the lorry business—into a devotee of Auto Maramma, initiated Chatterjee into Nadi Shastra and driven the Vastu addiction into IIT engineer Singh. Don't laugh, sir.... That's a kind of intoxication. Those who are too intelligent don't relish simple things. The more complex life gets, the happier they are. Nothing better than Vastu for that. It gets more intricate as you involve yourself. My job is to provide those with what they need. Baba for those who want him, UG for some, and so on. Call my vocation selling contentment, if you may.

The man who climbs trees for a job must be wide-hipped, no? So, my language too had to change. I don't use any word that hurts one's belief. Hence, my language became dignified. I didn't learn astrology from my father. But from him, I learnt the art of expression. I haven't forgotten some of his words: 'People don't like it if you say "quarrel between husband and wife". They'll be satisfied if you say conflict in a marital relationship. They must feel the problem belongs to someone else but the solution is ours. In this profession, if you talk any other language, nobody will trust you....'

As I continued to engage in this business, my earnings rose. Even the real estate business may not fetch you the kind of money that this profession gets. Nobody hesitates to pay even if he is in trouble. Vastu, Nadi Shastra, Astrology, Yoga, Unani, Baba, Ayurveda, Kanaka Yajna—I offered what people needed. People began to tell me their problems. Then I became aware of this massive populace in Bangalore's belly, a community which belonged nowhere. They are prepared to accept anything. All they want is a foothold in this city. Even if roots can't be struck, the customary watering must be done so that hope doesn't dry up. You'll be surprised to know, sir, not just outsiders but this is the fate of people from our Malnad region. Sir, there is hardly any soil left to plant our feet in this city. There's nothing which we can call ours. How does a place that doesn't have a single unwritten code find its identity? I work magic, sir, magic. If I can't find flowers, I'll conduct the shastras with plastic flowers. All this calls for faith. Even frequenting pubs to drink and dance is related to faith; the belief there is that they are enjoying life. When I was a student, going to the cinema on the very day we finished our examinations was a way of rejoicing. Of course, it didn't offer me any great joy. Still, I used to believe that I was enjoying life. What was more significant was that others believed that to be so.

Within three years, money began to flow. But I didn't find time to spend with Lavanya. My relationship with her changed altogether. You may find this amusing: back in our village, every morning when my father went out to pick flowers for the puja, Amma would go for her bath. The privacy obtained then with Lavanya, used to turn me on. Although we shared the bed through the night, I couldn't imagine the kind of titillation those moments in the morning offered. Sir, that's how lovely our relationship was. I won't lie to you, sir. What was critical was that I sensed that my love for her had diminished. For her sake, I had left my village and my parents. There was a time when I would do anything to please her. But now my mind was fixed on something else. Nothing seemed more joyful than making money. She sensed this. She began to say we should go back to our village. I shut my ears to those requests.

One summer vacation, I left my daughter at my father's house and returned to the city. Two days later Lavanya told me, 'I'm running a fever. Don't go to work today.' I didn't even touch her to check the body temperature. I had to attend to some urgent work. So I left home. But the thought that she had never pleaded with me like that before tormented me all through the day. When I returned that night, she was sleeping as though she was unconscious. Her body was burning hot. Beside her bed was a bowl of porridge. The neighbour had brought it to her, made her drink some of it, and left. When I sat on the bed, my hand felt a few dried, hardened rice grains from the porridge. Parts of the sheets where some porridge had spilled had dried stiff. As my fingers ran up the marks left on the sheets, I felt something between us had snapped. And I decided then that there was no point in returning to our village. I cannot forget those moments I spent by her side, sir, never.... The message was as strong as the one carried by her glance the day Buddi had visited us one day.

Without informing anybody, she left behind a note and went away. At times I feel sad wondering whether she did not feel any remorse about leaving behind her daughter.

From that day my daughter has adopted a strange silence. She speaks only when it is absolutely necessary. Otherwise she stays mum. None of us can muster the courage to persuade her to speak.

IV

After Sharavana's narrow escape from the accident, his mother insisted upon performing Shanthi, Mrityunjaya, and other japas. He pressed me to attend the ceremony. I joked, 'I don't believe that I staked my life to save you. That happened beyond my will. Don't be obliged to me for the rest of your life for having dragged you to the side on seeing the bus.'

'Why do you say so, sir? Because you had it in you, you could save my life. You must come to this poor man's house at least today....' And he persuaded me to agree saying that I would be the only guest.

That Sunday I went to his house. It wasn't difficult locating the address. In the same street, two houses away, a crowd had gathered. Sharavana was waiting for me at the door of his house. He drew open the gate to welcome me and said, 'Sir, do you know why so many people have gathered there? UG is here.'

I was curious. 'Can anybody go and see him?' I said.

'Oh-ho.... I know the household very well. We can go see him right now if you want.' I was eager. 'Yes, let's go,' I said and we set out.

I met Prabha, my colleague, in front of that house. She is from Hyderabad. She was professionally very ambitious. She would do nothing without any definite purpose. 'What brings you here?' I asked. She said, 'I am a UG follower. As soon as he arrives in town, Mr Sharavana informs me. And I land here.' Then, as if she had noticed my surprise, added: 'He has been able to look at life without the help of any filter. In that lies his greatness.' Those words remained in my mind.

When we entered the house, it was eleven o'clock. By then many persons had gathered there. A heap of chappals was lying outside. Inside, people were leaning on a divan on the floor. Some others stood where they could find space. Everyone was listening to him in deep silence.

I found a corner for myself. All was still. Then my arm touched the TV there. Though it was me alone who felt the touch, UG suddenly turned towards me as if there was a big noise. He looked at the TV and my arm. Only then did I sense his power and the burden of carrying it, and felt a bit strange. I recollected what Prabha told me about the filter. How much can one person see without the medium of a filter? If one begins to seek the intricacies of the world in this manner, wouldn't the mind explode into thousands of pieces?

All kinds of people were asking questions. And UG would reply to them. It seemed as if he would have replied even without the questions, he was so fluent and relentless in his response. I stood listening. Terms like a son of a bitch, bastard, motherfucker, sister's paramour were pouring out incessantly. My presence there must have embarrassed Prabha. After a while I left that place. Prabha came out with me and tried to offer some sort of an explanation. She was opposed to such language, she told me.

'You like UG because he seeks his experiences without a mediating filter, isn't it? Now, while receiving his words, too, see them without the screen in the middle,' I tried to reason.

Hearing a roar of laughter from inside the house, Prabha took leave of us and went inside again.

I went to Sharavana's place with him. He said he had bought this house. It had a big, long hall. A glass showcase lined a part of it. In it were school photos of his daughter, some toys, and some glass articles. His aged mother was seated in a broad chair, observing the rituals closely as the priest conducted the homa, raising a lot of smoke. His daughter's name was Revathi. When her father called out, she emerged from an inner room, greeted me with folded hands, and went back in.

'I thought you arranged these rituals only for others,' I said in jest.

'Even the cook has to eat, doesn't he, sir?' he laughed. Then, for the first time, I observed wrinkles on his cheek at the corner of his eyes.

Though his mother appeared to be too old to walk, her vision, hearing, and speech were quite sound. She sat me next to her and recollected the days when they were in the village.

The question arose in my mind whether this was the house Sharavana's wife had run away from and immediately cursed my wretched curiosity.

After the meal, as I rose to leave, Sharavana walked in and told me, 'Please wait for a minute.' His mother got up from her seat with an effort, came to me and holding my arm, said: 'Ask him to forget that slut and marry again. He attends to a hundred tasks for other people. But there is no one to look after him. I am too old to venture out. Please don't think that I'm entrusting to you the work of a marriage broker. You have saved his life. He has survived a certain death. Let him consider this as a new life, and erase the old memories....' And then she walked back slowly to her seat.

Knowing that I was about to leave, his daughter came and stretched out an autograph book towards me. I told her I was no big name to put my signature in the book. Still, she stood in front of me without uttering a word.

AN IDEAL MAN

ADDEPALLI PRABHU

Translated from the Telugu by Dasu Krishnamoorty and Tamraparni Dasu

His friend Mahesh had always dreamt of living in an enchanting place that beckoned him like a beautiful girl with windswept hair, wearing hip-hugging jeans. Venkatesh too shared such a fantasy. Today, however, was not the kind of day one would run into such a vision in real life. It began to rain as soon as he had taken off in an auto from Amalapuram. He arrived at his destination, Bodasakurru port, and the rain was still in no mood to relent. On the contrary, it had picked up speed and strength along the way.

He climbed out of the auto and was completely drenched before he could pay the auto driver. He walked down to the launch bay. The mighty Godavari roared angrily before him, helped by the downpour that mercilessly thrashed the earth, in an unrivalled spectacle. The rain continued, noisily. He rushed to shelter under the awning of a nearby cigarette shop.

'Is there a launch that will take me to the other side?' he asked the owner of the shop.

'It is impossible in this rain,' the man said. After a minute he asked, 'Where do you want to go?'

'Adurru,' Venkatesh said.

'Forget it,' the man scoffed.

It was just four in the afternoon but the sky was already dark due to the rain and the clouds. The rain raged, threatening to hold the place hostage for days. Soon, the distinction between the river and the horizon disappeared, uniting the land with the sky. Several boats, small and big, were anchored to their pegs in the bay.

This was no time to panic, Venkatesh thought. He covered his head with his tote and walked into the rain. And not too far away, he found a small hut perched inches above the ground. He was sure to find help, he thought, and sprinted to the hut.

'Hello, hello,' he called.

Inside the hut, a person sitting by a mud stove turned his head and looked at the two feet visible under the door.

'Who's that?' the man shouted above the din of the rain.

Venkatesh replied, 'I need a boat.'

'Please come in, sir, you're soaking,' the man said.

Venkatesh ducked through the low entrance and walked into the hut.

A string cot in a corner was in such bad shape that its middle sagged and kissed the ground.

'You're completely drenched, sir, please sit on the cot; I assure you it won't crumble,' the man said.

Venkatesh dropped the bag and hauled himself onto the cot. Water was streaming down his head. Water from inside his boots spilt on the floor and formed a puddle.

'I want a boat to cross the river and someone to ferry me,' he said. His body shuddered from the cold and his teeth chattered when he spoke.

'You're so wet. Please dry your hair with this towel,' the man in the hut said and proffered a piece of cloth.

'No, no, thank you, I have one in my bag,' Venkatesh said and opened his bag. Though the tote was wet, the towel was dry and he sponged his head vigorously with it.

The man stoked the coal fire inside the stove, put a dented aluminium vessel on top and poured water into it.

Seeing Venkatesh still shivering, the hut man retrieved a few embers from the stove, put them in a pan and pushed it under the cot.

'Sir, please keep sitting here, you will get warmer,' the man said and brought two glasses of thick tea. The fragrance of the tea revived the traveller who downed it in two greedy gulps. The tea tasted good despite the jaggery used to sweeten it.

The man then pulled out a bidi from the folds of his lungi and lit it with an ember he picked out from the fire with his bare fingers.

'I must go to Adurru urgently. There is no launch available now. Could you take me in your boat to the other side? I will pay whatever you want,' Venkatesh said.

He had stopped shivering but his soggy clothes clung to him uncomfortably.

The man exhaled a long, leisurely breath and asked, 'Where are you from?'

'What business is that of yours?' Venkatesh said, trying to hide his irritation.

The man smiled and said, 'Don't be cross with me, sir. Do you have any idea how heavy the rain is? It's a cyclone. Look, how merciless it is.'

'I don't care if I'm drenched. I must go. Urgently. That's all there is to it,' Venkatesh said.

'No sir, not possible at all.'

'Didn't I say that money is no issue?' Venkatesh said.

'This is not something money can buy, sir. River Godavari is like a goddess possessed. We can do nothing except sit here in safety and witness the river's fury.'

Venkatesh was stunned. The fierce thunder and rain outside were deafening.

'You can go to Amalapuram when the rain relents a bit and take a bus from there to Rajole, get off at Jaggannapet, and take an auto to Adurru,' the man said.

Venkatesh sighed. He'd chosen this route because he wanted to get to Adurru early.

'Are there any lodges around here?' he asked.

'Only in Amalapuram, sir. But how will you get there?' the man asked. He got up, lit a lantern, and hung it on a rafter near the roof of the hut. He poked his head out of the hut and shouted, 'Ore Sovudu, Sovudu!'

A seven-year-old boy shot into the hut with a makeshift plastic poncho over his head. He was naked except for a piece of cloth tucked between his legs and around his waist like underwear. His shiny black body merged with the darkness that the lantern couldn't chase away. The boy held a palm reed basket in his hands.

'What heavy rain!' the boy exclaimed. He threw the plastic bag out of the door, hung the basket on the eaves, and sat by the fire. A woman entered the hut next, and seeing a stranger sitting on the cot, bolted into the kitchen.

The man took out a towel and began to wipe down the boy. 'Where did you go?' he asked.

The voice of the woman sailed towards them from inside the kitchen. 'Does he ever listen to me? He sloshed through the Godavari. It was so frightening.'

'You stupid brat, did you wade into the river in this rain?' his father asked.

The boy stood up and, pretending to raise an imaginary collar, said, 'What do you think? I am Siranjeevi—what can River Godavari do to me?'

The father laughed and told Venkatesh, 'He is a Chiranjeevi devotee, sir,' referring to the ruling movie star of the moment.

The woman had changed into dry clothes and now began to make noisy preparations for dinner. She set the stove roaring and began to cook the meal. The man raised the lantern's glass shutter and lit another bidi and sat in a corner hugging himself. The boy leapt on his mother's back and started rocking to and fro.

Venkatesh rose from the cot and pushed his bag aside. The embers under the cot had died. He tried to look outside. But where was the outside? It was lost in an impenetrable darkness. The orange light of the lantern travelled out of the hut only to vanish in the shadow of the gloom. The dull patter of the rain persisted. Overhead, coconut fronds danced in response to an occasional breeze.

'The rain may not abate now,' Venkatesh said to the man.

'Yes, when was the last time it rained like this?' the man wondered aloud, staring into the inky void. Venkatesh checked his watch in the light of the lantern. It was not yet seven.

'Where can I go in this rain?' Venkatesh asked.

The man gazed fixedly at the rain, his face bathed in the saffron luminescence of the lantern.

'Where can you go? Nowhere,' he said.

'Then what should I do?' Venkatesh asked irritably.

'Stay here tonight and think of your next step after the rain subsides,' the man said.

The boy came skipping out of the kitchen and vaulted on to the man's back.

'Go put on a shirt. You're running around half naked in this cold,' his father said.

The boy dove inside the adjacent room and returned wearing an outsized shirt and proudly cried, 'Aiyya!' The shirt tails brushed his knees and the half sleeves came up to his wrists. In the shadows cast by the lantern and the kitchen fire, the boy looked like an alien from another planet. The boy's father laughed and signalled for the boy to sit on his lap.

Venkatesh was confused and unable to figure out his role in this unfamiliar script. How could he spend the night in this hovel with a family of strangers? But the family, far from feeling awkward, treated him with all the comfort and ease they would a relative who was a frequent visitor to their home. His professional crisis management skills had left him. All he could do now was watch the raindrops unfurl as they descended into the orange orb of the lantern.

Meanwhile, his appetite grew ferocious as the fragrance of fish soup seeped out of the kitchen. He looked at his watch. Half past seven.

'Sovudu,' the boy's mother called from the kitchen. The boy went into the kitchen and returned with a bowl full of steaming rice mixed with fish soup. He sat by his father and began to eat with unabashed relish.

The man's wife brought out two plates of rice and two bowls of fish soup. The man said to Venkatesh, 'Please eat and rest, sir. God will take care of everything in the morning.'

Venkatesh was surprised at his own hunger. He sat down in front of a plate heaped with rice in the shape of a huge pyramid.

'This much rice?' he asked.

'I'm sorry, it is not much, really,' his hostess replied.

'It's hardly anything,' the man said.

'No, no. Please remove some,' Venkatesh said.

She brought a big dish containing fragrant, steaming, white rice from the kitchen and put back some from his plate into the vessel.

He mixed the rice with soup and even before he could transfer some to his mouth, there was a flood of saliva and he began drooling. He couldn't remember losing control like this since he was very little. He accepted several more helpings and wondered if he had ever experienced such indescribable joy.

After dinner, he checked the time again and took out his mobile. There was no signal. There was nothing he could do now except to lie down and go to sleep.

The boy dozed off almost immediately after he'd finished his meal. His mother carried him inside and went to bed.

The man cleared the dishes, lit a bidi, and sat down. Venkatesh was embarrassed that he had been drawn into an awkward situation and left with no choice.

Venkatesh took out a pair of shorts from his bag, and changed out of his wet clothes behind the cover of his towel. He pulled on a fresh shirt and hung out the wet clothes to dry on a palm rafter.

His head buzzed with thoughts: look at this small hut, their near-naked boy, a shack without electricity, without TV, a dining table, or sofa, or refrigerator. What kind of a life did these people lead? No goals, no ambition, no killer instinct to climb the social ladder. Like animals, they eat to live and live to eat. Is that all there was to their life? Had they ever heard of Einstein, or Newton, George Bush, Bill Gates, or at least Satyam Computers? Ignorance and poverty!

Meanwhile, the man went inside and brought out a fraying mat and a quilt of unknown vintage. He placed them beside the cot and said to Venkatesh, 'Please sleep. We'll worry about the rest in the morning.' He spread a jute mat for himself on the floor and lay down on it.

The lantern's dim light shone warmly on Venkatesh like a friend. He unrolled the mat and moved it to a dry patch on the floor and decided to do without the quilt. There was a bed sheet in his bag which he retrieved and spread on the mat. He used his rolled-up towel as a pillow.

The darkness outside was total. He checked the time on his mobile and chuckled—he'd never gone to bed this early.

When he opened his eyes it was light outside. But there was no change in the mood of the rain or in the force of the intimidating wind.

The boy was perched like a bird where his father had sat the night before, peering out.

'Where are your parents?' asked Venkatesh. The boy held up two fingers, the universal sign for going to the bathroom.

Venkatesh got up and looked out through the doorway. The river was lapping at its bank. The other bank was invisible. The river seemed to flow directly into the sky. He stretched out his hand and his heart skipped a beat. The rain was fierce and piercing, and came down in sheets, cutting off visibility beyond a few feet. Curtains of water shrouded everything including the vegetation. From behind the watery cascade emerged his host, covered in a plastic sheet from head to toe.

'It's not going to stop now, not for a while. Mad, mad rain. The orchard by the ridge and the harbour have gone under water. Look at the river. If it rises any more, we'll have to abandon the hut and flee. If you want to leave, cover yourself with this bag and take that route,' the man said, and shivering, he pointed the way to the visitor.

'Where's your mother?' he asked his son.

With the bag on his head Venkatesh stepped into the knee-deep water. He sloshed through the muddy water for a short distance and came back, partly drenched. His feet were encased in mud. He saw the man sitting on the floor of the hut with his wife and son. When she saw Venkatesh coming back, she moved the child into her lap to make place for him. Venkatesh spread the mat he'd slept on earlier and sat down.

'Make some tea, woman', the man ordered his wife.

She hugged the boy close and, sneaking a look at Venkatesh from the corner of her eye, said, 'But there is no jaggery.'

'Make it without jaggery, then!'

'But I can't kindle the stove in this wet weather. Do it yourself,' she said.

The man went to the kitchen and after persistently blowing at the wet fuel managed to start a fire. The boy abandoned his mother's lap and rushed to sit by his father near the fire.

A few minutes later, the man brought two tall glasses filled with boiling black water and passed one to Venkatesh. He sipped it cautiously. At first it had no taste, as though it was just hot water, but as he continued to drink there were hints of an agreeable bittersweet taste.

He asked, 'What's your son's name?'

'Somaraju. I gave him my father's name.'

'The boy looks sharp. Does he go to school?'

'What school?' he scoffed. 'Idling time away in a school won't feed us.'

Thinking that he meant that only idle guys went to school, Venkatesh said, 'No, no. You can get a good job if you study. The boy will earn a lot and prosper.'

'You're right. But how can he make a living without learning to fish?'

Venkatesh was amused. The man had no clue what a job was. That's why these people never get ahead in life, he thought.

'No, my dear man. Education teaches you many things. You can become famous. There is a boy I know, a slip of a brat. Ask him the names of countries anywhere in the world and the presidents of these countries... he'll tell you the correct answers in a snap. He was on TV too. It's all because of education,' Venkatesh said.

The man threw the bidi away and said, 'True, sir. My boy is very sharp too. He can tell you everything about the fish in the Godavari and the sea. Ask him, he'll tell you about all the types of fish that swim in the waters. Nobody in the entire neighbourhood knows the names of so many fish. Ore, Sovudu, tell this sir the names of the fish we catch,' he said to his son.

The boy looked at his dad and the visitor and rattled off, 'Catla, lobeo rohita, air-breathing fish, channa punctatus, mystus singhala, hill stream fish, garra kempi, ornamental fish, anchovy, giant moray, pacific sergeant, sea goldie....'

Initially, Venkatesh felt annoyed at this fish nonsense. However, soon the condescending smile on his face disappeared.

True, the boy did know all there was to know about fish. He could swim the Godavari in spate, even in the dark. His own son could recite the names of twenty countries and their presidents. It was possible only because it was all study and no play for him from the time he was five years old. But what use were these facts to his son at his age? The teachers were just cramming useless information into the little brains of their students as 'general knowledge'. Who was better off, his son or this boy who understood every nuance of his environment? Wasn't this education? Wasn't this 'knowledge'?

Venkatesh was beset with doubts. 'This boy Sovudu will never earn much,' he told himself, 'neither money nor fame. All his knowledge about rivers, the sea, and fish will perish in the market. Some good-for-nothing fellow will study marine biology and technology spending lakhs of rupees, scour the seas on a computer, and earn millions. This boy, with all his knowledge and skill, will be dredging some muddy pond for fish.' Comforted by such thoughts, Venkatesh fell into a deep sleep.

He woke up to the smell of cooking. He looked out of the hut and saw that it had stopped raining—only a few halting drops fell now and then.

'I think I can leave now,' he said to the man.

'Yes sir, you can reach Amalapuram if you leave early,' said the man and nodded.

'Cook some rice for our visitor,' he told his wife.

Venkatesh was hungry but said, 'Please don't bother. I'm going to Amalapuram anyway.' He squeezed his bed linen and wet clothes into the tote bag and was all set to leave in his shorts and shirt.

The woman brought a bowl of rice and soup and placed it near the cot. The visitor ate it greedily in his haste and, once done, pulled on his shoes over his bare feet and flung the bag over his shoulder, ready to leave. He looked around to make sure he hadn't left anything behind.

The woman and the boy holding on to her sari stood at the doorway to see him off. The man got ready to accompany him. Involuntarily, Venkatesh pressed his palms together in gratitude. He said to his hostess, 'You've treated me with more affection than my own sister. Thank you.'

Her dark face was overcome with embarrassment. She averted her gaze and drew the boy closer to her.

'We can't go that way. The harbour is under water.' The man said to Venkatesh as soon as they came out of the hut.

Venkatesh looked in the direction of the harbour and saw only the tip of the ridge. Godavari was dizzying and scary, eddying furiously like a mythical force. It was beautiful and frightening at once.

The man was wading through knee-deep water in front of the hut. Venkatesh took every step cautiously. The force of the rain had abated but a thin drizzle fell obstinately. Half an hour later they came upon a narrow strip of road. The man stopped and told the visitor, 'This is your route. Go straight; you'll see the centre there.' He narrowed his eyes and saw an auto coming towards them.

'Come, let us ask him if he'll take you.'

The auto stopped. The man went to him and returned quickly, 'The auto has a problem.'

Venkatesh stood there soaking in the rain. The man said, 'If we walk further we'll reach Peruru agraharam. From there you could take an auto and reach Amalapuram. If the roads are kind to you, you can go to Adurru from there.'

'How?' asked Venkatesh.

The man laughed and said, 'You can walk.'

Venkatesh was surprised—how could he have forgotten that he had two feet to walk with?

'Okay, sir. I'll take leave. If the Godavari rises any further, our hut will disappear,' said the man.

'You're right,' said Venkatesh and pulled out a purse from his bag and took out two hundred-rupee notes from it.

'Please keep this,' he told the man and held out the money to him.

'No, sir, that's not right,' the man said dropping his bidi on the road.

'It's all right. I shudder at the thought of what would have happened to me if you hadn't taken me in. You looked after me as if I were your own flesh and blood. That's why it's all right,' said Venkatesh.

The man laughed. He said, 'Sir, it's all right and fair to make money when the other person is in a position to bargain. It is not proper to exploit a person in distress. You are a human being. I'm one too. The tree shelters all birds from the rain. Same principle applies here.'

Venkatesh put the money back in his wallet and adjusted the bag over his shoulder.

The man continued, 'If we don't help one another how can we call ourselves human beings? If I were to stand outside your door, stranded, would you let me in or throw me out? Anyway, sir. Please get going; I have to go now. Goodbye.' He bowed and turned around to retrace his path home.

Venkatesh stood staring in the direction of the receding figure. He was afraid to consider his answer to the man's question because he knew it would shame him.

THE COST OF HUNGER

ABDUS SAMAD

Translated from the Assamese by Aruni Kashyap

Often branded foreigners or 'illegal immigrants', or forced to prove their nationality, Muslim families of Bengali origin are among the worst victims of the volatile floods in the plains of Assam. In the last few decades, thousands of villages have been eroded permanently by almost all of Assam's fifty-five rivers, creating a huge population of internally displaced people, who are often lower-caste, tribals, and migrant Muslims.

HE HAS BEEN HESITATING TO TAKE THE DECISION FOR A LONG TIME, BUT today, after Sultan leaves for work, Romzan Ali caresses the long beard that reaches his chest, sighs, and takes the final decision.

Romzan stands up slowly. As he gets up, to support himself, he places his hands on both his knees and then puts pressure on them. Then he takes slow steps towards the barber's shop, with some sadness. He has the expression of a man who is about to lose something he loves greatly.

'Ahok, bohok,' Sibpujan starts bustling about as soon as Romzan enters the hair-cutting saloon. The first customer of the day after all! His face brightens. 'You want a haircut?'

Romzan doesn't answer Sibpujan's questions. He sits down hesitantly on a chair. He doesn't want to be here. There is a large mirror in front of him.... He is startled. Is this really his reflection in the mirror? Romzan Ali's? Is this the image of Sikandar Maulavi's eldest son, Romzan Ali?

He can't believe what he is seeing. This is a man with a broken body.

His hair stands up on his head, branching in all directions like calendula herbs, and most of his beard is grey. His hair is also quite dirty, messy; and his eyes are that of a person who has been suffering from a prolonged illness. Is this really his reflection in the mirror?

For a moment, he is terrified. But still he accepts that the image he is looking at belongs to him, the man in the mirror is him. Right, the man in the mirror is him.

He was sad before coming here, but he is even sadder now.

When was the last time he stood in front of such a huge mirror? How many years ago? Three years?

Right, about that much.

It has been three years since he has visited a barber. Until around three years ago, he used to visit a barber's shop like this and have a haircut, trim his beard, watch himself in the mirror transfixed. A young man. Deep, dark, black hair, and beard.

'Are you going to get a haircut?' Sibpujan repeats. He has taken out the large white silk barber-cape to wrap around his customer. He takes out the scissors and combs, touches his forehead with them. He prays silently for good business for the day, and, with great enthusiasm, stands next to Romzan's chair.

'No.'

'Then?'

'Beard. I want to shave off my beard.'

'Ha!' Sibpujan is surprised. What is this man saying! Does he want to shave off his beard?

He shouldn't have been surprised. This is his profession. Every day he shaves and trims the facial hair of numerous people, Hindus and Muslims alike. But now when Romzan asks him to shave off his beard, Sibpujan feels sad. He doesn't feel the way he feels when other customers ask him to complete a similar task. He realizes that no one has come to his saloon to shave off such a long beard, that reaches down to the chest.

Whenever Sibpujan thinks about the beard of a Muslim man, he starts to think about his own tuft of hair, at the back of his head. He doesn't really know the religious or cultural significance of the beard. What he knows for sure is this: the way his religious sentiments are attached to his own little tuft of hair, the beard too has some religious connotation. He hasn't tried to figure it out.

Now, he touches his tuft and tells himself: wouldn't it be awkward to shave it off, and wouldn't it feel the same to shave off the beard of this man? He tries to understand what is Romzan thinking. Perhaps this person won't feel awkward. Perhaps this man is really comfortable with the idea of shaving his beard off. Otherwise, why would he come here?

Sibpujan leaves Romzan and goes to the drawer on the other side of the room. He puts aside the barber-cape and takes out a towel that he spreads across the chest of the customers when shaving their beards. When he wraps it around Romzan's neck, he notices the length of the beard. Really, it's a long beard! This beard has been grown and taken care of for a long time—it actually falls to his chest and lower.

Sibpujan, who can hold a strand of hair on a person's head and predict how long ago it was trimmed, tells himself: this beard is from this man's youth.

Why does he want to shave it off? And it is quite healthy. The man also looks handsome with a long beard. Yes, it hasn't been oiled and combed regularly, but still, it looks naturally healthy. At his age, a long beard enhances the man's personality and looks. But why should Sibpujan bother? He should just do his job. Still, he can't stop himself from giving a compliment, 'Your beard was beautiful once upon a time, dei.'

'Era!' Romzan sighs silently. This isn't the first time someone has complimented him on his beard. He has heard it from numerous people but from today, no more such compliments.

∽

'Don't shave your beard any more, o'. You look good with it and not everyone is lucky to have such a rich growth of beard, you know?' his friend Kadir says.

His beard is new. He has shaved only a few times in his life so far. They are both young men. New blades, new facial hair. He shaves in the morning, and by late afternoon, a thin shadow covers his face just like the ahu paddy that grows quickly after the weeds around its stems are shaved. Romzan's skin is bright, light. The thick, black facial hair against his light, clear, bright skin, creates a beautiful contrast.

Kadir is the first one to compliment him on his beard, but he won't be the last.

Idris supports him, 'Hoy de, you should keep it. You will look good.'

That night, Romzan admires his face in a small, round, hand-held mirror. The flame of the kerosene lamp barely lights up the room. He observes his face, his beard, and agrees with Idris and Kadir. He decides to grow a beard. To make his resolve stronger, he pulls out the shaving blade stored in the cracks of the wall constructed of fermented jute and throws it into the garbage dump. What if he feels like shaving off his beard if the blade is readily available?

In a few days, the beard covers his face beautifully, and then, slowly, like the tip of the flowers of kans grass, it continues to grow, going past his chest. His father, a maulvi, watches him closely. Perhaps he likes it because one day he encourages Romzan, 'Son, don't shave your beard any more. It looks good on you. It is a good deed to grow a long beard.'

Just the way gold starts to glitter after a polish, beauty is now accompanied by free blessings. Romzan doesn't think about shaving his beard any more.

But it is not that his beard is universally loved. One day, not so long after their wedding, when Rohima's body still smells of fresh turmeric and lentils paste—ingredients that a bride is bathed with—she tells him, 'You are a young man, why would you choose this appearance? Looks like an old man! Shave it off!'

He wriggles out of their embrace in an instant, jumps out of bed, and looks at her with fire in his eyes. 'Khobordar! Don't you say such a thing ever again. Things will get worse at home, I am warning you!'

Rohima is startled. Perhaps she isn't prepared for so much anger. She hadn't thought this would make him so angry. As the years go by, Romzan's beard becomes part of his identity, part of his body, like his legs and hands and other organs. There ceases to be any difference between shaving his beard and chopping off one of his legs.

When Sibpujan presses his razor on the corner of his cheeks and pulls downwards, Romzan is shocked. He shuts his eyes.

No, Romzan Ali, who shuts his eyes even when the mullah presses the sharp knife on the neck of a cow during Eid-ul-Zuha, is today unable to watch the razor work on his face.

No, he can't watch such heartbreaking scenes.

Three years ago, in the month of Shaon, when the Brahmaputra River had suddenly lost its sanity and eroded away the entire village of Birinabari, he wasn't able to watch that scene too.

It was an unbelievable sight.

In front of the insane river, the riverbank, and the massive village where they had lived for generations, seemed to be made of dry straw! As the water crashed against the riverbank, huge chunks of soil fell into the river—finally the land on which the village stood was swept away. The inhabitants of Birinabari were watching this horrifying scene. People from neighbouring villages were watching too as the village was consumed by the river.

Kadir's father, Jabar Burha, began to slap his forehead before crying out in a loud voice. Pointing to the unstable, vanishing riverbank on which the village stood, he shouted, 'Look, look all of you, how the village is being destroyed! This is not the current of the river Brahmaputra! This is like a sharp knife! A sharp knife that's slicing away the land, the entire village, the way a sharp knife works on a juicy bottle gourd!'

Nine days. In just nine days the village was swallowed by the river forever; the village that belonged to Jabar Burha, Kadir, Idris, Romzan. After losing everything, the people in the village moved to the top of the long embankment.

Now, when Romzan recalls those nine harrowing days, the sorrow in his heart is so intense that his chest feels like a balloon that is about to burst due to excess air. Those nine days changed the world of Romzan and the other villagers. They had so much in that past life: fourteen bighas of land, two pairs of cows; on one and a half bighas of land they had four houses made of bamboo and straw and soil; he lived there with his father who worked as a maulvi, his wife Rohima, and his three children.

On those one and a half bighas of land, and four houses made of locally available material, they also had happiness and peace, and sometimes, a bit of hardship. His mother had died when he was young. Now all of those are just memories.

Romzan sighs.

He is sitting next to the entrance of a hut made of torn polythene and old gunny bags. The hut is built on the embankment. Previously, when the village was still standing on the riverbank, there was occasional hardship, but now all he can see is absence, sorrow, and hunger. Inside the hut, his toddler son cries. The day is about to end but he hasn't found a job today and the child is hungry because he doesn't have money to buy rations.

What if he can't find something to do and earn some money tomorrow, too? How will he buy food for the kids? No, he is not able to think any further. He doesn't want to go there because two months ago, his father died of starvation in this hut built on the embankment. No, actually he had consumed some wild yams after staying hungry for two whole days and they didn't go down well. The stomach and the wild yams immediately got into a war. A whole night of gurum-garam sounds from the stomach. With pot in his hand, he had climbed down the embankment towards the river waters. After that, everything was over.

The boy is weeping again, asking for food.

From a little further down the path, a song floats towards him, *Mukkala muqabala laila ho laila*! This is Sultan's voice. He is the one who imports these terrible, uncultured songs from Guwahati. He came the day before yesterday and he is leaving for Guwahati again the day after. It has been a year or so, he works with a mason as a helper. His family is doing all right.

'Khura,' Sultan asked him the night before, 'would you like to go with me to Guwahati? I will make sure you get a job.'

'No, bopa, I am not going anywhere. I would rather die here of starvation,' Romzan says.

But...that was last night.

Now Romzan stands up, and like a person in a spell, follows the source of the song, Sultan. *Muqabala subhanallah laila ho laila.*

It has been six days since Romzan has come to Guwahati. He lives in Sijubari, along with Sultan and his friends. Every morning he eats some food and walks out with them to Hatigaon Chariali. At around seven-thirty or eight, thousands of people like Sultan and Romzan crowd the location. In the way in which cows are sold and bought in a trading market, bargains and deals are made here, at this spot, for the rest of the day.

Romzan gets work on the day he arrives. The contractor Bora asked him to get up on the truck along with Sultan but another contractor looks at him with disrespect and mockery before announcing, 'Hey, don't take this guy—will he work or manage his beard?'

Romzan, who is about to climb onto the truck with the help of Sultan who is holding his hand, steps back.

Hurt, he goes back to Sultan's room. In that small room, the child's voice bothers him and makes him sadder. For the first time, he feels disquiet about the long, beautiful beard he has been so proud of.

Romzan doesn't find work the next day either. When Sultan is about to leave with the contractor Saikia, he takes Sultan aside and speaks in a low voice, but Romzan hears it clearly.

'Don't ask this person to come to work with us. It doesn't feel good to make someone who has such a long beard work with us.'

When Sibpujan's razor slows down, Romzan opens his eyes and is surprised: who is this person in front of him?

Is this his reflection?

When he is able to recognize the reflection, he lets out another sigh.

TALE OF A TOILET

RAMNATH GAJANAN GAWADE

Translated from the Konkani by Vidya Pai

'ARRE, WHAT'S GOING ON HERE?' THE SARPANCH DEMANDED AS SOON AS he set foot in the panchayat office. Many of those who were just milling around drew back, while the ones who were seated sprang to their feet respectfully for he was not only the sarpanch of the village but also a man with immense clout, one whose word carried weight.

'What's happening here? Who is making such a noise?'

'Bhau, I've made at least ten trips to the panchayat office, why haven't I been allotted a toilet even now?'

'What? You don't have a toilet? What do you do, then?'

'What can I do? Nothing.'

'Nothing? You just hold it in?'

A ripple of laughter spread through the room and the man who was demanding a toilet was confused. 'No, no, I go like all the others go....' he stammered.

'So...you go. Every day. What do you need a toilet for, in that case?'

'Others have been given a toilet. I want one too.'

'All right. Others have been given a toilet, so you want one too. You don't really need one, do you?'

'Of course I do! That's why I'm making the request.'

'You are making a request. Then why are you raising your voice and fighting with people?'

'I'm not fighting. I just asked the Secretary why my application was rejected and he started giving me a lecture.'

'My God! He started lecturing you, did he? Arre, Secretary, why don't you see what he wants, don't make the poor fellow hold it all in!'

The Sarpanch walked into his room and sat down. The Secretary smiled his crooked smile and followed him into the room carrying a file. He showed the Sarpanch some papers and began to explain something which must have been of serious import because the Sarpanch asked the peon to shut the door of the room.

The Sarpanch and the Secretary were closeted in there for a long while and those who had come to meet the Sarpanch had to cool their heels in the outer room. The man who wanted the toilet kept telling everyone about the problems he was facing and instead of listening to him, people told him how they had gone about the process.

'We didn't want a toilet, even then they gave us one. How can you use that tiny space? We keep our hens there at night. At least they are safe now, the foxes would have made off with them otherwise.'

When he couldn't bear to listen to their stories any longer, the man sidled up to the Gram Sevak whose job it was to look after the welfare of the villagers.

'The government makes these schemes for the poor, but these officials give them to people who have no use for such schemes. The whole purpose is ruined. The hungry man gets nothing. But they heap food on the plates of those whose bellies are full. Do you think we don't know why all this is being done?' he spluttered.

'Now wait a minute, will anyone come to your house and build a toilet just because you make a ruckus here?' the Gram Sevak asked mildly. 'There is a procedure that must be followed. Your income must be within the prescribed limit, only then can you avail of this scheme.'

'Saiba, we have no income. I have no job, but we don't get a toilet. And those who roam around in motor cars get toilets under this scheme.'

'Didn't you apply to the panch who is in charge of your area?'

'The Sarpanch is the panch in our part of the village. Doesn't he know that there is no toilet in my house?'

'That's not how it works. There is a fixed quota of toilets. And those have to be distributed in the whole village.'

Just then the Secretary emerged from the Sarpanch's room. Two or three people pushed their way in and the man tried to follow them, but the Sarpanch sent him back. 'Why are you in such a hurry, you don't have to come here to meet me. You go past my house three or four times a day. Come and see me some time,' he said.

The man couldn't say anything to this, so he waited outside till everyone finished their work. He had decided that he would get the toilet allotted to his name today, come what may. He was tired of making these endless trips to the panchayat office and listening to excuses; his patience was wearing thin. People who didn't apply for a toilet were granted one under the scheme. Officials went to their homes and made them sign the forms. And people like us, who submitted the application forms more than once, got nothing. They don't say yes or no. How is it that only our application forms go missing? Do these people remove them from the list? He would get to the bottom of this matter today, he decided, standing with his arms crossed across his chest, waiting to meet the Sarpanch. It was a long while before the Sarpanch finished all his work and emerged from the room. The man rushed up to him, 'Bhau, you are the panch in our area, you should allot a toilet to us under the scheme,' he said.

'Panch? I am the sarpanch. I have to look after the interest of the whole ward.'

'But you are the panch in our section. So you must get it allotted in my name.'

'Now, who told you that?'

The Sarpanch cast an eye around the room and the Gram Sevak bent his head over his work, writing busily while the others remained silent as though to show that they were not responsible.

'Don't listen to what people say. You want a toilet? You'll get one. Don't walk away from us. I know you think you don't need us now as you have latched on to important people. Tell me, do they give you beer and mutton?'

'Bhau, many of them came to my house, but I didn't follow any of them. I didn't accept anything either.'

'I don't know if you followed them or took what they gave, but I know that you let us down.'

'No Bhau, I'm telling the truth…I voted for you!'

'Sheee shee! Don't say that. It's a crime to disclose who you voted for. You'll get me in trouble too.'

'How can I assure you, Bhau?'

'I'd summoned you the other day to repair the broken fence in my field. But you said you had other work.'

'How could I leave that work half done, Bhau?'

'So, how can we rely on you? What happens to the cows that graze in the field with the broken fence?'

'I'll come, Bhau, I'll come.'

'And look here, there's no need to come and shit on the embankment by our house just because you haven't been allotted a toilet. We have to pass that way every day and the stench is overpowering. I'll throw stones at you if I see you squatting there again.'

'No, no, Bhau. I don't go there. I take my tin can and go up the hill.'

'Don't tell lies.'

'It's the truth, Bhau. And even if I do go that side I don't squat on the embankment. I go down to the area by the stream.'

'No, no. Don't go down there. That stream waters our fields.'

'But there's no water in that stream now. It's dry.'

'I know. But it's full of water in the rainy season. You people only know how to dirty your surroundings. God knows when you'll learn something better.' The Sarpanch strode off briskly, muttering to himself.

The man felt as though he had been slapped publicly. The others in the room were immersed in their own work but he felt that they were laughing at his boorishness. Why did I ask the Sarpanch for a toilet, the man rued as he made his way home.

His mother was groaning loudly and calling his name aloud when he got home.

'What's the matter, why are you yelling like that?' he snapped.

'What else can I do? Come, come. Take me out at once. I can't hold on any longer, my son!'

'I've told you so many times. Lean on your stick and make your way slowly behind the house but no! You insist on waiting for me!'

'Look at my swollen fingers and my knees. Why would I wait for you if I could manage on my own?'

'Get up now. Quick. Or you'll mess up the whole place, right here.'

'Yes, yes. Give me that stick.'

'What do you need that stick for now?' He picked her up like a bundle of clothes and strode towards the hill.

'Set me down. I'll walk slowly, just give me some support,' she insisted but his patience had worn thin. Anger and frustration had set off a variety of thoughts loose in his brain and his body surged with strength as he strode up the hill.

He would usually make her squat close to the house but his neighbour Aku's words resounded in his ears. 'Our children play here. Take her somewhere that side,' Aku had said in front of the others, so he had moved ahead.

'Arre, why are you taking me so far?' the old woman protested.

'I'll take you up the hill and toss you down!'

'Do that. Do what you want. At least I'll be free of this fate worse than death!'

'The neighbours can't bear the stink, they say.'

'But I can't hold on any longer,' she whined, and the man dumped her on the ground.

'Why do you go and shit near his house?' he burst out angrily as she made her way behind a clump of bushes. He didn't wait there any longer and on his way down the hill, he saw the large number of toilets that had been built beside people's houses under the government scheme. His eyes fell on the toilet next to Molu's house and he was filled with hope. Molu was close to them, almost like a family member, maybe he would let the old woman use their toilet for a few days until they could get one for themselves. He hoped Molu would agree and wanted to ask him at once, but he remembered his mother would be waiting on the hill, so he filled a tin can with water and began the climb again. He was surprised to see that he was growing short of breath. How heavy this little can is, he thought.

He didn't have the confidence to carry his mother down the slope, so he held her hand and helped her down. He told her of his plan to approach Molu but she didn't think Molu would agree.

'You know what they are like. Why will they listen to you?' she said.

'Let's see. If he says yes, things will be easier for you and for me too. You'll just have to pour water when you are done.'

'I don't think....'

'Why won't he agree? He was like Baba's brother, wasn't he?'

His mother didn't say anything after that. She merely plonked herself down on the veranda when they got home, as though she had accomplished some huge task. The man, however, rushed to Molu's house. 'Kaka, Kaka!' he called.

'What's the matter, Somlya?' Molu's wife, who was working in the garden, asked.

'Isn't he home?'

'He was here just a while ago.'

Suddenly the door of the toilet in the yard opened and Molu emerged. 'What's the matter, Somlya? Why are you here?'

'I was wondering if Aai could use your toilet for a few days....'

'Of course. Whenever she wants. Just see that she pours a bucketful of water once she's done.'

'No, no! We'll have to keep it shut for some time. The rains will start soon, we'll store firewood in there,' Molu's wife said, all of a sudden.

'Aggo, is the toilet meant for storing firewood?' Molu asked.

'Fix a place for the firewood then.'

'What about the shack behind the house?'

'That shack is full of junk. And I'm scared that it will collapse with the first showers.'

'But it's just for a few days....'

'No, no. The septic tank is very small. It'll get filled quickly.'

'Bu—but....'

'Somlya, our toilet is new, we haven't started using it regularly. The children will get upset if we let others use it. Ask someone else. I'm sure they won't refuse if they know it's your mother who needs it.'

Somlo realized that there was no point in continuing the discussion, so he returned home. There were a couple of toilets outside some of the other houses in the neighbourhood but he didn't think the owners would agree to his request.

Instead, he asked his mother, 'Avai, when will Dada come? It's been a while since he came home.'

'Why? Let him come when he wants to.'

'I've been thinking, we don't want anyone's toilet. Let us build a small one for ourselves. I spoke to a mason who said it would cost about thirty thousand rupees. But if we build a simple structure close to the house, it could be done in twenty.'

'What about the money?'

'If Dada can give ten thousand, I'll dig the pit for the septic tank. We'll have to buy stone slabs and cement.'

A scooter came to a halt outside the house.

'Avai, Dada will live for a hundred years! I just took his name and here he is!'

The old woman seemed to forget her ill health as she pulled herself up eagerly, delighted to also see her daughter-in-law and granddaughter.

'What have you been up to, Avai, have you been well?' her elder son asked, and at once she lay back as though she was very ill. 'We were just talking about you,' she said.

'Me? Why?'

She remained silent and it was left to Somlo to explain the circumstances.

'Dada, Avai can't move about very easily these days. We need a small toilet near the house.'

His sister-in-law chimed in all of a sudden, 'Yes, yes. I was thinking of that, too. The government has built toilets for the whole world, why not for us? We find it very difficult when we come to the village. Bai isn't used to squatting in the open.'

'So, get one allotted to us then.'

'That's not happening. That's why I'm saying let's build one ourselves.'

'Not happening? Why? The big houses have toilets allotted to them, but we don't. Why don't you ask Bhau?'

'How many times will I ask him? I went there again today and the Secretary gave me a big lecture.'

'You must have tried to act smart.'

'All right, I act smart. Why don't you go and ask him right now? I'm telling you, I've submitted not one, but three application forms in Avai's name.'

'Weren't you talking of building a toilet just now?'

'Yes. Instead of begging this one and that one for favours, let's build a small toilet ourselves. You give ten thousand rupees and I'll manage the rest.'

'Ten thousand rupees! Do you think I earn in lakhs just because I have a regular job? There are instalments to be paid for the scooter and other things. Life in the village is simple and cheap, you can cook and eat anything. And Bai has to be admitted to kindergarten this year. The fees for this KG class are twelve thousand rupees. Maybe it is you who can give me ten thousand now....'

Somlo, who was staring at his sister-in-law while listening to his brother's litany of woes, noticed the new gold bangles on her wrists. She grew aware of his scrutiny and quickly drew the end of her sari about herself and walked into the house.

This wretched toilet has ruined my whole day, Somlya fumed, as he lay down for a while after lunch. He had missed out on being hired for work that morning and had done nothing productive all day. He suddenly remembered the broken fence in the field and made his way to the Sarpanch's house. The Sarpanch, who was lying on the porch, opened his eyes to see who was approaching and quickly shut them again.

'Bhau, the fence....'

'Yes, yes. The fence!' The Sarpanch sat up hurriedly and called out to someone.

'Aggo, Paru, show him the broken fence.'

'The fence can wait. What about the problem with our toilet?' Paru asked.

'Yes, yes. Someone was supposed to come and check that. He hasn't come yet. I'm glad you're here, Somlya. The water in the toilet just doesn't recede. I don't know if the septic tank is full.'

'But Bhau....'

'Don't pull a long face. I'm not asking you to empty the septic tank. Just open the cover and see if it's full. Paru, show him where the pickaxe and crowbar are kept. This must be done right now. The stench is overpowering.'

'Bhau, let your man come, I can help him....'

'He'll come, he'll come. But you take a look right now. I can't bear the stink. The Secretary was supposed to bring him but God knows where he's gone. And yes, Somlya, I've included you in the list for the new set of toilets that will be sanctioned. Get an application form from the Secretary and make it out in your name.'

'Not in my name. In my mother's. The house stands in her name.'

'That doesn't matter. I'll take care of all that. You should have been allotted one from the last set but they sanctioned only two hundred toilets while there were four hundred applicants. What could we do? But this time we have asked for eight hundred toilets. Now we know that everyone needs a toilet, the MLA has said that everyone should have a toilet by their home. You go to the Secretary tomorrow and fill the application form.'

'All right, Bhau.' He followed Paru as she led the way to the toilet and the septic tank.

He went to the panchayat office early the next morning, but the office was closed. It was a long while before someone at a nearby kiosk told him that the office would remain shut because it was the second Saturday of the month. It was past eleven, well past the time when he could be hired for any work that day. He had lost out on another day's wages, he thought angrily, as he made his way home.

Baburao, the panch from the Opposition party, who was riding past on his scooter, drew up by his side.

'Arre Somlya, where are you off to? Are you free today?' he asked.

'Yes...I mean no....'

'Forget what you were going to do. Come with me. There are two wells that need to be emptied and cleaned. You'll get double the usual wages.'

Somlo thought it was a good idea, he could make up for the wages he had lost on both days.

'Arre, say something. If you want to come, come at once. You'll get lunch there,' Baburao said.

Somlo knew that Baburao was the Sarpanch's sworn enemy and anyone caught hobnobbing with him was considered an enemy too. Perhaps it would be better to steer clear of this man, he thought.

'You people don't want to work, just to loaf around all day. You can earn something instead of wasting time. Now, hop on if you want to come or I'm going alone,' Baburao snapped.

Somlo felt his resolve crumble as he perched on the pillion behind

Baburao, but his mind was filled with misgivings. What he had feared soon came to pass as he saw the car that belonged to the Sarpanch approach in their direction. Somlo shrank into himself, trying to seem inconsequential. The car hurtled past and he was relieved to think that he hadn't been seen.

The labourers ate and drank and worked till sundown cleaning the two wells. The others in the team were also from the village, but they belonged to Baburao's party, so he learnt a lot from the gossip that was exchanged.

The panchayat had been sanctioned two hundred toilets on two occasions in recent times, he was told. The Sarpanch had kept the major share for himself and the panchs in his party, allotting a few toilets to those in the Opposition who were favourably disposed towards him. The application forms of the people in the Opposition who were in dire need of this facility went missing, they said. Somlo began to suspect that the Sarpanch had deliberately misplaced his application form too, but there was nothing to be gained in ranting against the powers that be.

The next day was a Sunday and there was a host of work that had to be done before the rains, but he couldn't concentrate on anything. He visited some friends who had been allotted toilets in the past and asked them what they had done. Some of them told him about the procedure, but many said they had only signed the application form, while the Panch and the Sarpanch had handled everything else, forcibly erecting the kiosks in their yards despite their protests.

Early on Monday, Somlo gathered all the necessary information and went to the panchayat office but the Secretary had not arrived. The Sarpanch showed up after a while and assured Somlo that he remembered his case, even before the man could open his mouth.

'Somlya, you looked very grand riding that scooter that day,' he added.

'Scooter? No Bhau, who will let me ride their scooter?'

'I don't know about that. But you were sitting on a blue scooter....'

'Blue? Oh! I was on the pillion on Baburao's scooter. He took me across the river to clean two wells.'

'Don't tell lies. I saw you partying there.'

'No, Bhau. They gave us lunch that day.'

'So who was that guzzling beer?'

'No, no, Bhau. That's not true.'

'All right, then. Did you people remove all the debris and clean the wells properly? Or did you just waste panchayat funds?' The Sarpanch asked as he cast an eye over the others gathered there.

Somlo's anger and frustration grew as thoughts of the toilet hovered like an immense weight on his head. His body seemed on fire and he wanted nothing more than to move away from all this and immerse himself in silence.

The Secretary arrived and those who were seated got up and those who had moved away crowded around his desk again. Everyone wanted him to attend to their needs at once. Someone wanted a signature, another wanted a receipt. Someone wanted this, someone else wanted to submit something. Each man had a different set of needs.

Many of those who surged forward managed to get their work done. Those who were well connected to the powers that be got their needs attended to quickly. Those who held back out of deference or because they wanted to avoid the jostling crowd, like Somlo did, had to wait.

'Sahib....'

'Arre, you were the one making a big fuss the other day. Did you get the toilet?'

'Sahib, I've come for that only...the Sarpanch has sent me.'

'Arre baba, getting a toilet allotted to someone is not in my hands. The Sarpanch has to do that. Go and speak to him.'

'I did. He told me to collect the application form from you.'

'All right. Let me tell you the old process has changed. There are new application forms which require an income certificate, land-holding proof, and an affidavit to be attached.'

'All right, sahib. Where will I get that done?'

'I'll explain all that later. I have just received this letter, I must see what it says.'

'But, sahib, we need to get the toilet this time.'

'Look, I don't provide toilets. The government does that and the panchayat allots them to people.'

'Panchayat? Isn't this our panchayat office?'

'Yes. But the Sarpanch and the other panchs have to pass the application.'

'The Sarpanch said he had passed the application.'

'All right. Get the documents I asked for, then we'll see.'

'But, sahib, I submitted all those documents. Twice.'

'Those forms have been cancelled.'

'No. The Sarpanch said he had passed them.'

'All right. You can go, now. It's half past one. I must have lunch.'

'All right. I'll come in the evening.'

He hesitated for a long while but he was hungry too. The desire to get the toilet allotted in his name made the hunger pangs seem unimportant, so he debated whether he should go home and have lunch or wait there for the Secretary to finish.

The Gram Sevak, who had gone to a nearby restaurant for lunch, was returning to the panchayat office. 'What's the matter? Isn't your job done?' he asked.

'No. It seems we must fill some new forms.'

'Yes. What happens now is that anyone can erect a toilet anywhere once it has been sanctioned. The Sarpanch issues a certificate saying someone he favours is a needy person, even if he is wealthy. So, the poor people are sidelined while the wealthy ones get the allotments. According to the new rules, the Secretary has to first issue a certificate of income.'

'But we had submitted the forms earlier.'

'Those would have been valid if they had been passed at that time. Now they have been cancelled. If you want a toilet now you must follow the new procedure.'

There was a rush for the new application forms soon and Somlo managed to get a copy too. He got the application and affidavit ready and returned to the panchayat office in four or five days.

'In whose name is the house registered?' the Secretary asked.

'In my mother's name.'

'Then get the application done in her name.'

'But the Sarpanch told me to apply in my name.'

'All right. Just don't blame me if this application is rejected and you don't get a toilet.'

Somlo didn't say another word. He felt that the Gram Sevak was the one he could trust, so he made his way to his room. The Gram Sevak echoed the Secretary's words, but if Somlo could take his mother to the taluka revenue office and get an affidavit issued by the mamlatdar, the other matters could be handled in the panchayat office.

Somlo dragged his ailing mother to the revenue office and rushed to the panchayat with the mamlatdar's affidavit but the Secretary was going out somewhere. He asked Somlo to deposit the documents with the clerk, he would look at them later, but Somlo wanted him to take a look right then, so he didn't budge. Suddenly a man rushed in with a file and the Secretary returned to his desk. He spent a long time going through the file's contents, handed the man a signed receipt, and told him to come the next day.

He was getting up to go when Somlo shoved his application before him. 'Sahib, take a look at this also,' he pleaded.

'Don't you understand anything that you're told? Give it to the clerk. I have to go. It's getting late.'

'It's not late, sahib. It's not even four.'

'So you're keeping a tab on the time, are you? Go...complain to whomever you want.'

'No, no, sahib. Just give me five minutes...please.'

'Do you think I'm your servant, you're going on and on like this! No. I won't do your work. Go, complain if you want.' The Secretary picked up his bag and stomped out of the room.

Somlo stared after him for a long time. His body seemed drained of strength as he stood rooted to the spot. He walked with leaden footsteps to the clerk's desk and placed all the papers before him with a woebegone expression.

'Arre Somlya, why do you get so excited? Why do you irritate sahib? He's not very efficient,' the clerk said.

Somlo wanted to say that it was not he who was excitable, it was the Secretary who was bad-tempered, but the clerk's comment made him hold his tongue.

'Bhau, please see if all the papers are in order. I must get the toilet this time,' he said.

'Everything seems to be in order. Come tomorrow, meet the Secretary and give him an estimate of your annual income. I will draw up an income certificate which will have to be signed by the Secretary and the Sarpanch. Then you must get it signed by the block development officer.'

'All right, I'll come tomorrow.'

'Be careful this time. We'll get only a hundred toilets and there will be at least two hundred applications.'

'Only a hundred! I must latch on to the Sarpanch then!'

Somlo arrived at the panchayat office early the next morning but there was no sign of the Secretary till the afternoon. He must have bunked duty since it's a Saturday, someone said, and Somlo was left tearing his hair in frustration. He arrived at the panchayat office early on Monday morning and the Secretary walked in at the usual time but Somlo didn't want to irritate him, so he stood at a distance and watched while he did his work. Then, when there was no one around, Somlo walked in and stood before his desk but the Secretary seemed immersed in the documents before him, and didn't raise his head.

'Sahib....'

'Wait. Let me finish this.' The Secretary remained immersed in the file for a long time. Somlo was about to address him again when the Sarpanch swept in with four or five men in tow.

'Arre Secretary, these men want toilets. Fill up the forms for them and see what they need. And you, Somlya! Hasn't your problem been solved? Secretary, give him what he wants, he's Baburao's man. This time Baburao has demanded fifteen toilets. Give Somlo one from that quota.'

'But Bhau, you said you would give me one.'

'Did I? Then we'll see if one is left over.'

'No, no, Bhau. I must get a toilet this time.'

'I said we'd see. Just make sure that your papers are in order.' The Sarpanch escorted the group of men to the clerk's desk.

Somlo was overcome by anxiety. 'Sahib...' he said.

'What? Are you getting late now?'

'Sahib, I have to serve lunch to my mother....'

'All right. What have you brought?'

'Income certi....'

The Secretary took a close look at the papers and began to question him.

'What does this Somnath do?'

'I'm Somnath, sahib. I do whatever work I get.'

'And Shivnath?'

'He's my elder brother. He drives vehicles belonging to the electricity department.'

'Oh, so he is a government servant. But you haven't shown his income.'

'He doesn't live here. He is in Margao.'

'He can live wherever he wants. His name is on this ration card, so his income must be listed in the total family income.'

'But sahib....'

'How much does he earn?'

'I don't know, sahib.'

'A driver must be earning twenty thousand or so...that would be two lakhs annually. Shall I write that?'

'But the toilet will be allotted only if the annual income is less than twenty-five thousand rupees, sahib.'

'Yes. Your family income exceeds that limit. So you can't get a toilet.'

'How do the others get toilets, sahib? They earn much more than us.'

'You can get one too. Just remove your brother's name from the ration card.'

Somlo turned away, disappointed. An official told him what he had to do to get a new ration card. He returned home and told his mother all that had happened but she was furious.

'You pay for my needs, but that doesn't mean you can break up the family like this. Your brother has as much of a right to this house as you do. His job makes him stay far away, but he takes part in all religious and family functions,' she ranted.

'Why doesn't he help build a toilet then?'

'Only he can answer that. But don't let people lead you astray, don't break up the family....'

'No, Avai....'

'I don't want your toilet. I'll do my best to control the urge. I'll lie down in a corner and die. But as long as I live, I won't let you remove his name from the ration card!' His mother worked herself up into a frenzy drawing on random incidents from the past to buttress her claim till Somlo walked out of the house in frustration.

He knew that many government servants had already built toilets in their backyards and irregularities such as these would continue. The husband had a government job, but the toilet was allotted in the wife's name. An unmarried son, living with his parents, cannot have a separate ration card. How does an unmarried young man with a government job manage to get a toilet allotted in his name, then?

Somlo thought long and hard and decided that it was the Secretary who would ultimately decide his fate, so he hurried back to the panchayat office, but the Secretary brushed him off. Someone told him that the Secretary would be more accommodating if he received a gift, but Somlo had nothing to offer. Suddenly, his eyes fell on the bunch of plantains dangling from the tree in the garden. He brought down the bunch, packed it neatly and set off for the nearby village where the Secretary had recently built a house.

The Secretary hadn't reached home, but his wife ushered him in urgently. 'Sahib has sent you, hasn't he? Come in, come in,' she said. She took him to the toilet 'This flush isn't working, we are having so much trouble. Set it right at once,' she said.

'I'm not the plumber, I can't repair toilets. I've come to meet sahib.'

'I saw the bag in your hand and thought you were the plumber.'

The Secretary arrived at this moment with the plumber in tow. 'What are you doing here?' he asked angrily on catching sight of Somlo.

'Sahib, I came to request you to please do something....'

'You must come to the panchayat office. Not here.'

'Sahib, I have some bananas for you....'

'We have plenty of bananas. Take a look at the garden behind the house.'

'Sahib, please....'

'Not another word. Meet me at the panchayat office.'

Somlo realized that it was pointless saying anything further, so he quietly slunk away. His eyes strayed to the garden behind the house and he stopped in his tracks. Two government-allotted toilets stood side by side for the exclusive use of the Secretary's tenants. Controlling his anger with great effort, Somlo returned home.

Many of those who had submitted the application forms were wealthy persons with considerable influence in the village. Yet Somlo, who lived in a mud-walled house, couldn't get a toilet sanctioned in his name. The time for submitting forms was running out, so Somlo phoned his brother, informed him about the situation and met the official who issued new ration cards. His head seemed to spin in dismay when the official told him that nothing could be done now as new ration cards were only issued in February and August.

The Secretary was nowhere to be seen, so Somlo rushed to the clerk, 'Bhau, what can I do now?' he asked.

'What can I say? I have one hundred and thirty applications here. I shall take them to the public works department tomorrow morning. Do whatever you can today.'

A cloud of darkness seemed to settle before Somlo's eyes and he began to tremble in rage. If the Secretary had appeared before him at that moment, Somlo would have hacked the man to pieces, but he had gone home for lunch and no one knew when he would be back. Somlo could feel his patience wearing thin, so he sprang to his feet and rushed to the Secretary's house.

The front door was shut and no one responded to his call. Somlo began to bang on it in a frenzied manner till the Secretary emerged angrily. 'What's wrong with you, you son of a dog?' he cried.

'Don't abuse me. Who do you think you are? Will you sanction that toilet or not?'

'Let go of my shirt. Or I'll call the police and have you locked up.'

'Call the police. I'll tell them everything too.'

'What will you tell the police? Tell me, what will you say?'

'We poor people don't get a toilet sanctioned, but you get to build two toilets in your yard.'

'I'll build two toilets or I'll build four. It's none of your father's business!'

'Don't drag my father into this. I tell you, I'll bury you right here!' Somlo grabbed the man by his collar and the two came to blows. The Secretary's wife rushed out of the house screaming loudly and threw herself into the fray forcing them apart. Some more women and children rushed to the scene on hearing the ruckus and the Secretary's wife, realizing that Somlo was more than a match for her husband, began to plead with him, 'Baba, don't fight. I beg of you, don't fight!'

'Tell your husband not to mess with me. I don't care if I die, but I won't die without finishing him off. We poor people don't get a toilet, but you get to build two in your backyard. Who does he think he is, the son-in-law of the ruling powers? I'll raise this in the village council...I'll file a case...!'

'Calm down, brother...don't do this. I'll see that you get a toilet sanctioned,' the woman pleaded.

'Do that. Or I'll finish him off.'

'I will, I will....' The woman turned to her husband frantically. 'Why do you behave so childishly? Give him a toilet and get this over with.'

'Do you want me to get suspended from my job?'

'No, but what if he does something terrible? For the children's sake, don't mess with him!'

A large crowd had gathered by this time and there was a lot of discussion. Some people found fault with Somlo, others thought the Secretary was in the wrong. The Secretary finally asked him to come to the office the next day and take the income certificate.

The Secretary had finished the paperwork and the certificate was ready by the time Somlo got to the panchayat office the next morning. But a new problem had arisen overnight. Only a hundred toilets had been sanctioned this time but the list of applications was continuing to swell, so the Sarpanch had taken whatever forms had been submitted already and deposited them in the PWD office the previous day. The forms that were being submitted now were languishing on his desk.

The Secretary was filled with fear on hearing of this development. He hastened to explain what had happened to Somlo and assured him that he would personally deliver his application to the PWD office at once.

A few days passed and masons employed by the government began to erect toilet sheds by the houses of the first hundred names on the list. Somlo rushed back to the panchayat office on seeing that his name was not on the list.

'Somlya, the government is introducing a new toilet allotment scheme only for Scheduled Castes and Scheduled Tribes. You don't have to submit any income certificate or anything. That's why all SC and ST names were withdrawn from the last list. You will automatically be allotted a toilet now,' the Secretary assured him.

Somlo turned away without another word. His mother passed away soon after that and Somlo's need for a government-allotted toilet began to wane. He has been waiting for news about this new scheme for the last five or six years. The Sarpanch looks away when he sees him and avoids eye contact but Somlo has become very resolute these days. The little stream and its banks are government property, so he takes his tin can and squats on the embankment in front of the Sarpanch's house every morning. The Sarpanch doesn't have the nerve to shoo him off. So the messy patches continue to spread and a foul stench hangs over the embankment in front of the Sarpanch's house all day.

ON SERNABATIM BEACH

JESSICA FALEIRO

I'VE REACHED HALFWAY BACK TO SHORE WHEN I SEE HER STANDING BY the water's edge.

She's pulling at her pigtail and chewing her lip. I lift my body out of the saltwater and wipe the sting from my eyes. I avoid her stare, sit down hard on the sand, and wrap my arms loosely around my knees. I need to steady my breath and rest for a moment before I go in again.

I angle my chin to feel the splintering sunlight beat down on my face. To my left, a green Kingfisher pint bottle catches the sunlight and winks at me. Next to it is an empty bottle of Teacher's whisky, half-buried in the sand. The sea has its addictions too. My fingernails automatically go to the edges of my teeth. I don't even mind the taste of salt and grit. I spit, stare at the bitten-down nubs, and then at my sister's straight, small back. She lifts her tiny, plump hands to her forehead to shade her unflinching stare out to sea, even in the noon heat. She's afraid to look at me as much as I'm afraid to look at her, even though she's too young to know for a fact what I already know.

It's been two whole days since Mama left us tucked in our bed in Furtado's guest house and went for a night walk on the beach. I knew about Mama's fondness for the sea and after that last episode, it didn't surprise me when she told my sister and I that we were going to Sernabatim beach for a short stay.

The guest house was basic but clean, with faded bed linen that smelt of detergent, bright yellow curtains that had seen better days, and fresh naphthalene balls placed on the bathroom drain. My sister and I tired ourselves out building sandcastle empires that first day we arrived. But I knew that Mama was distracted as I watched her from a distance, walking towards Benaulim, until she was a fine polka-dotted speck blending in with the other beachgoers. She kept looking out to sea, mumbling something to herself and then listening intently, as if in conversation with the waves. Even from a distance, I could feel her body wanting to merge with their endless drum roll. She didn't flinch from the silver-edged swell that rushed in suddenly, wetting the hem of her dress.

My sister and I were raised on bedtime stories filled with vast oceans, meandering rivers, and damp jungles smothered in mist. She'd read us stories full of secret waterfalls and bloodthirsty pirates, of King Neptune and sultry sirens. Her life was immersed in water. Once, she said that her ancestors must have been seafaring captains or fishermen because the Indian Ocean thrummed in her blood.

If my mother was about water, then my father was of fire. He had always been a hard man. But after I turned twelve, things seemed to get more difficult around the house. Mama started to wear bright, halter neck dresses instead of long-sleeved ones, showing off the purple patches on her arms, as if on a dare. I'd only seen her wear those showy outfits in old photographs, from before when I was born. I'd never actually seen him hit her, but maybe that was his gift: controlled violence. He always seemed to hold himself in check around us, even after he came home stinking of beer and cigarette smoke. He had, what Mama called, a respectable job in a government office, managing a team of staff under him. But respect wasn't a word I associated with him.

I can recall the names they called each other that morning we left. I was afraid the neighbours could hear them shouting but didn't dare venture out of my room. When Anna stirred, I brought her to her 'Hello Kitty' themed dressing table, brushed her hair, and sang loudly to her, hoping to drown out the sounds of our parents' verbal bullets fired at each other, all the time wishing someone would sing to me instead.

Papa drove off to work, slamming doors on his way out, and Mama locked herself in the bedroom for an hour. I listened outside the door and then, when Anna was hungry, sat her down at our dining table and poured cold milk over her Kellogg's cornflakes. I'd just finished washing our plastic breakfast bowls when I heard the bedroom door open. Mama was wearing a flowery sundress and had a wide grin on her face that didn't travel to her eyes. I couldn't spot any signs of new weals on her arms.

'We're going to the beach,' she said brightly in a voice that she reserved only for Anna and me.

She helped us pack a few clothes into her small, slightly worn American Tourister suitcase, and added two sundresses I hadn't seen before, except in photographs of her on her honeymoon. One had polka dots, the other had bright red flowers on it. I had stolen one of those photos from an overburdened, tattered photo album nobody looked at any more, and occasionally took the photo out of my secret hidey-hole to stare at the two of them together. They had fixed smiles on their faces, but I could see that their eyes were full of laughter, maybe even love. They looked like strangers to me.

We'd had a whole day together at the beach, the three of us. The June monsoon had kicked off, but downpours were still coming in extended stops and starts. We played for hours before we saw the clouds rushing in from the horizon. Mama stared out into the distance and said, 'We have thirty seconds. Get ready, set, go!' She raced us towards the nearest beach restaurant where we took shelter and had lunch as we watched the sky's extravagant deluge drown everything in a wall of water. Mama picked at my plate of fries and sipped her pint of Kingfisher. I'd never seen her drink alcohol before.

When I asked her once why she didn't like alcohol, she told me that she used to enjoy a glass of beer now and then with my father but stopped when she was pregnant with me. 'Afterwards, I just lost the taste for it,' she said.

After sunset we had an early dinner and Mama tucked us into bed, making sure the bulb of liquid mosquito repellent she'd packed was switched on in a corner of the room and that the fan wasn't running too fast for us. She'd even asked for a spare room key and left the main one with me. She stroked my sister's head until she was a peaceful comma on the large double bed, sound asleep.

'I'm just going for a walk on the beach. I'll be back soon. Keep the door locked,' she whispered in my ear.

I was sound asleep before I could hear her shut the door behind her.

The next morning, I couldn't tell whether Mama had been to bed and woken up early, or not. I helped Anna with her morning wash and we went to the beach shack next to the guest house for breakfast. I charged the meal to the room, just like Mama had before. No one blinked an eye. I was pleased that I seemed mature enough to do something like that.

We went to the beach to play. But even as I chiselled upturned pails of sand into castles for my sister to stomp on, my eyes scoured the beach looking for any sign of Mama. Whenever a grown-up asked where she was, I managed to keep the lie going that she'd gone to pick up something she'd forgotten from home and would be back that night. After feeding my sister and tucking her into bed, I went for a walk on the beach. I stayed close to the edge where the street lights along the walkway threw the curdling waves into relief. The water gave me nothing. I didn't know yet that the sea kept its secrets locked deep in its chest.

The day after, the hotel manager asked me where my mother was and I fibbed again. By the time Anna turned to me mid-play in the afternoon, against the backdrop of dark clouds threatening to bear down on us, and asked me where Mama was, I was done with lying. The fear in me snapped and I pointed out to sea. In her innocence, she looked out to where I was pointing and squinted her eyes. 'I don't see her,' she said in response.

Those four words broke my heart. I couldn't tell anyone, not yet. I waited another night and a day. My sister was used to me taking care of her. She trusted me, so it was easy to lie to her.

When the hot afternoon melts into a humid evening, I check quietly, not wanting to draw attention to ourselves. Nobody has found a body washed ashore. No one has come asking for us. I go for another swim while keeping an eye on my sister as she plays on the beach. I am thankful that she's forgotten to miss her Mama for a moment, as I dive and dive.

I avoid the places that are flagged red, just the way Mama taught me to, and course-correct when I see the lifeguard watching me nervously and motioning with his arms for me to move further away from a dangerous spot. He doesn't know how strong my upper body has become since I hit puberty or that I'm the gold medallist in this year's all-state swimming championships—junior boys division.

I dive down deep and swim further away from the continental shelf in search of my mother. There's a place inside me that tells me she's here, somewhere, loitering in the murky depths of the Arabian Sea, but I need to know for sure. I stop swimming and stay in one spot, eyes wide open, waiting, scanning the dim depths around me in a 360-degree angle. I shut my eyes for a moment, and imagine what it would be like to stay here forever; to never return to shore. My breathing slows in my ears. I feel a little more like myself here. Finally, just before I know I won't be able to resist the immensity of the sea entering my body a moment longer, I open my eyes and a dolphin nose, out of nowhere, prods my bare tummy. I kick wildly, propelling myself upwards, taken aback by the shock of the unexpected sight of the dolphin. I gasp for air as I break through the waterline, knowing I'm too far out for the lifeguard to spot me. I glance around. There's no sight of the dolphin as I start swimming to shore.

Just before I reach shallow water, I stop to rest and let my tears blend in with the drops of seawater on my face. I can't let my sister see me crying. Even from a distance, I can feel panic starting to build up inside her as I see her standing alone on the beach, staring at me. Oddly, that feeling reminds me of my father. I push it aside, just as I push aside the thought of his rage when I will try to tell him what has happened. She watches me anxiously as I break in and out of the water's surface. The sea is rougher than usual. I can sense huge grey clouds building up in the distance, even as the setting sun breaks through for long periods to watch over us.

When I come out of the water for the last time, I rub the sea out of my eyes and, for a moment, half expect Mama to be there at the water's edge, looking back at me with her arms folded and that honeymoon picture smile on her face. I see my baby sister tearing up instead.

I walk up to her and pull her taut, five-year-old body towards mine. I'm her only protector now.

'Where's Mama?' she sobs.

I practise saying the words in my mind first, as if preparing my tongue to pronounce something new.

As I sound out the words, I realize that they are true.

'The sea has her,' I say, knowing that whatever has happened, my mother doesn't want to be found.

THE GRAVESTONE

SHAHNAZ BASHIR

As soon as the mist lifts, which happens in the evenings these days, he'll dash straight to the graveyard. It promises to be a really chilly evening in the wake of the April rain. He is sure the drug-addicted gamblers, for whom the graveyard is a favourite place to play whist, won't be around today.

He's scared of the idea of doing it in the night. He can't sneak out in the presence of his vigilant family members. He usually goes to get his cheap Panama cigarettes from the village market in the evening. That's the time he can do it.

He lights a filterless cigarette and paces the short, narrow, flaking cement pathway outside his small mud-and-brick house. Cacti and dead geraniums, potted in discarded paint cans, and small, empty Fevicol buckets, are arrayed against the walls of the house. He finishes his cigarette, then slips back into the house, ascends the creaky wooden flight of stairs, and reaches for his old cobwebbed toolkit under the tin roof where the gable makes it difficult for a person to stand upright. His workman's fingers are calloused, the fingertips bristle with cracks, the fingernails are deformed. He rummages through the dusty tools, panting with the effort of climbing the stairs.

Shortly afterwards, he finds himself running towards the graveyard, a kilometre away from the house. The pale light of dusk falls on the drenched asphalt road riddled with muddy, water-filled puddles. The roofs and leaves still drip.

The mist is all gone and the snow-shrouded mountains opposite him appear closer than they actually are. A gust breathes through the village and shakes the groves, orchards, mustard crops, and grass. Scattered plastic bags balloon into the air.

Each wrinkle and crease on his pale and weathered face with its sunken cheeks tightens as he rushes on. Each strand of his grey hair stands on end.

The pits in the road make him watch where he places his plastic-shod feet. His left hand, almost dysfunctional, trembles badly. He grabs the underside of his pheran to keep the hand steady.

His worn-out pheran smells of rain and stale smoke. He scurries on. The sound of dull clanking comes from under his pheran as the rusty hammer comes into contact with the blunt chisel. Plumes of smoke-stained breath burst from his nostrils. Occasionally, a bus or a scooter passes, tooting its horn.

Today he is welcomed again by the same stubborn clumps of nettle and thistle that are sprinkled throughout the graveyard. And beyond—there, near the graves—are assorted irises, their stamens powdering the white petals with yellow pollen dust on the insides. He traces the path to a grave whose epitaph in Urdu reads: Shaheed Mushtaq Ahmad Najar.

⁂

Muhammad Sultan was a talented carpenter before he fell from a roof while working and permanently injured his left arm. And just when the injured arm had begun to heal, against the doctor's advice, he went back to work. He had to take care of three daughters and an adolescent son, which is why he couldn't afford to rest the injured arm. The internal soft tissue injury worsened to a haematoma. After a failed surgery, his arm was declared unfit for carpentry or any manual work.

He was a master khatamband, or lattice designer. Before cutting wood for use, he would smell it to gauge its quality. He specialized in mixing the classical with the modern, producing something that both old and new generations of Kashmiris liked. None in the entire village could rival his truss work. He was an expert in doors and windows—the thick part of work in carpentry. With each drag on the hookah, he came up with a new idea.

But Sultan had a shortcoming, too: he was not a diligent worker. He took on projects on a whim. He would hardly ever take on partners or apprentices. He liked to work alone. He normally worked for two days a week and took the rest of the days off. Sometimes, he would disappear for days and later compensate for his absence by working overtime. His second romance, after carpentry, was accompanying the local militants around the village. He'd help them with anything, fetch them cigarettes, and even lavish money on them.

Carpentry was not only work or a source of livelihood for him, but an art form too. Art through which he expressed himself. Once at work, he would passionately sink into it. Sometimes he worked through the night. He would even work on Fridays, against custom, when all the carpenters and masons took the day off. He never cared for money until he really needed it. He was more of a dissolute artist than a mere time-bound carpenter. His hands are worth their weight in gold, that is what almost all his customers would say after marvelling at his work. It was because of his talent that people tolerated his truancies and wild habits.

The situation with his arm depressed him. It became impossible to work, or hold tools in his left hand. Then he started taking on projects on a contract basis, employing other carpenters and directing them. But their designs and work neither impressed nor satisfied his customers. Though his employees took all his directions, they never really followed them to the letter. They even cheated him of his share of the commission. And eventually his financial situation deteriorated.

His fate grew worse—his eldest daughter was returned by her in-laws, for the sixth time in four years of her marriage, for not fulfilling the demands of dowry. The last time she had returned with a swollen wrist and her snivelling, sick one-year-old baby daughter. Her husband, the driver of a bus that somebody else owned, had wrung her wrist during an argument and thrown her out of his house. But, in her father's house, the eldest daughter behaved as though she was just on an occasional visit. She even waffled on about her in-laws to her sisters, praising them as if they were good people and as if nothing had happened. She talked about the 'generosity' of her in-laws' neighbours. She described her brother-in-law, his tastes in food. These details bored and irritated her sisters.

Without work, and with his broken arm, Sultan was struggling to deal with his two other daughters at home. His middle daughter was in her late thirties, a spinster, an almost illiterate woman, who, after her father's injury, had been supporting the household with her needlework skills. She worked well into the nights, tortured her eyes, strained and overburdened herself, and gained weight and premature wrinkles on her face. She was the most beautiful among her sisters, but there was an unattended fuzz of hair on her upper lip that made her look ugly at the same time. Lately, she was running short of work, and had taken to secretly begging at the shrine of Makhdoom Sahib on Fridays. She would slip on a long, dirty black burqa and leave home saying that she was visiting the shrine to pray to God to take away their hardships and grievances. But Muhammad Sultan had begun to suspect that her veiled expeditions were for another reason altogether—that she was out hustling to earn some money. He was furious about this but tried not to show it, especially as he never wanted to follow her to confirm his suspicions.

His youngest daughter had left school at the secondary level when Sultan's wife died of a colon haemorrhage. Since her mother's death, it was she who looked after the household, cooked and cleaned. Her presence in the house was the only presence Muhammad Sultan didn't feel. She almost didn't exist for him. She was just like the family cow she fed, washed, milked, and cleaned. Whenever she cried, she didn't make a sound, not a single snivel or sob, just tears, which quietly streamed down her cheeks like melting pearls. She was born just before Mushtaq, her brother, Muhammad Sultan's only son, who died in adolescence.

Mushtaq distanced himself from school and books and instead followed a group of local militants like his father did. One day Mushtaq stayed behind with an armed group in a hideout—a posh house in Nishat. In the middle of the night, the hideout was raided, and he was the only one who was unable to escape. He was killed in the kitchen of the house. Next morning, Muhammad Sultan managed to go to the spot and see his dead son for the last time. After looking at the bullet-riddled body lying face down on the kitchen floor, he fainted. When he regained consciousness, he found that Mushtaq was being placed on a bier. The funeral was attended by the militants with whom the boy had fallen in. Wearing masks, they mixed with the funeral procession, and later also directed the graveyard management committee to get a quality marmoreal headstone chiselled for their friend. They wanted to have the headstone inscribed with an Urdu epitaph with the title 'Shaheed' before the boy's full name, which would signify that he was a full-fledged militant and had died for the cause of Kashmir's freedom. The outfit will be proud to bear all the costs, the area commander of the militants assured the graveyard management committee.

After the burial, some days later, a shiny black granite gravestone was erected at the grave, with a beautifully calligraphed Urdu epitaph in sparkling golden paint.

It was some months after his son's death that Muhammad Sultan suffered the accident in which he damaged his left arm. Soon after the accident, his elder daughter was returned and the middle one lost her work. All possible sources of income disappeared. Vexed, he ate away at himself between sips from endless cups of salty nuun tea and puffs from filterless cigarettes.

He had often heard people mention how Sataar Wagay, one of his neighbours, whose son the army had tortured to death and dumped in the river, managed to get an ex-gratia compensation of one lakh rupees sanctioned by the government. In the beginning, when he was not burdened by his own tragedies, Muhammad Sultan hated Sataar Wagay for accepting the compensation. He even called him a traitor for 'selling his son's sacrifice to the government'. But then Muhammad Sultan became confused when Rahman Parray, another neighbour of his, who had even been an active member of a separatist organization, distorted the facts surrounding his younger brother's killing by the army and accepted compensation of one lakh rupees.

Who was right, Wagay or Parray or himself? Baffled, Muhammad Sultan remained indecisive until his own condition forced him to think about applying for compensation too. Initially he hated himself for even thinking about asking the government for money. He wrestled with himself day and night.

He was already heavily in debt. Each morning the local grocer had begun to come to the house and threaten to take away Sultan's cow to settle his account. He even owed the neighbourhood baker and barber. He had stopped passing by their shops and now took longer routes, back and side paths, whenever he had to leave the village. But when his baby granddaughter was diagnosed with acute pneumonia, he gave up. Finally, he threw off the guise of commitment to the cause of freedom, ignored his guilt, and applied for compensation. He tried as much as possible to hide this from Gul Baghwaan, one of his close childhood friends, who had vehemently rejected an offer of compensation from the government after his son was killed in a crossfire incident.

Now, the only hurdle that came between Muhammad Sultan and his compensation was the word Shaheed conspicuously engraved on his son's gravestone. If discovered anytime later, the word could ruin his chances.

⁓

The graveyard is a plateau studded with gravestones and clumps of irises. It is away from the village houses and nestled on the edge of a vast expanse of paddy fields. As Muhammad Sultan sees the irises in the cloud-dimmed evening, the first stray thought that crosses his mind is how much better it would be to replace the cacti at his home with the irises.

He waits for the darkness to grow thicker. With the darkness comes a drizzle. Soon the voice of the muezzin from a nearby mosque floats into the air and mingles with the hissing rain. The wet mud of the graveyard sticks to the soles of his shoes, exposing patches of ochre under the upper layer of earth.

A few minutes later, when the rain stops, he holds the blunt chisel with his trembling left hand against the word Shaheed. He repeatedly strikes the head of the chisel. The sounds of metal clanking and the hammer's whumping travel through the earth and reach down to Mushtaq Ahmad Najar. At one strike the pointed end of the chisel slips, misses its mark, and scrapes off Mushtaq instead.

CRIPPLED WORLD

VEMPALLE SHAREEF

Translated from the Telugu by N. S. Murty and R. S. Krishna Moorthy

SAYING THE DUA, AND RUBBING MY FACE WITH CUPPED HANDS, WAS MY daily ritual when I got up in the morning. But today I could not feel my right hand. When I looked for it, I found it severed from my body and lying cold and lifeless in one corner of the bed. I could not make out how this had happened. There wasn't a trace of blood around. It was as cleanly sawn off from my person as a neem branch sundered from a tree with a sharp saw.

'Oh no! My hand has been cut off,' I shrieked in fright.

My wife hurried into the bedroom. 'Oh, my! Was it because of this that you were making such a racket? I was frightened to death thinking it was about something else. Good riddance! Keep it safely in the almirah. We'll go to the doctor when we are able to find the time and get it reattached. Why are you so scared for every small, silly thing?' She left as quickly as she had arrived.

Only then did I notice something about her appearance that made me even more scared than before. Her left hand was missing. She was a southpaw. Whether to serve food, pick up a glass of water, scribble something in a notebook, dust a room, or even beat our seven-year-old child, Chandu, she would use only her left hand. And now, that all-important hand was missing. Forget about my severed hand, how and when had she lost hers? I wanted to call her back to ask her, but refrained from doing so. I knew she would snap at me again, and I would get no worthwhile explanation for her missing hand.

So, I said my prayers with the left hand, rubbed my face with it, and got up. I placed my severed right hand carefully next to my wife's left hand in the almirah.

Finishing my ablutions quickly with my left hand, I got dressed, ate my breakfast and, with the lunch box dangling from the stump of my right arm, I hurried to where my scooter was parked so I could head off to work. On the way, I saw the owner of the house that we were renting approaching me. To my surprise, both his hands were missing.

I cursed to myself, 'There is something terribly wrong with the world today!'

I wanted to ask the man about his two missing hands but didn't know what to say if he asked about my missing right hand in turn. So I said nothing, and simply gestured that I was going to the office and started the scooter. To my astonishment, I discovered that I was able to drive the scooter with a single hand. It wasn't because of any great skill on my part, it appeared that the scooter itself was designed to be driven single-handed. In fact, all the people on the road were driving single-handed. Some of them drove right-handed, others drove left-handed—that was the only difference.

How did the world get crippled overnight?

There was a famous hospital on the way to the office. People were lined up before it holding their amputated hands. Ignoring a 'No Parking' sign I parked my vehicle and asked bystanders nearby what the queue was for? Their answer blew me away. Apparently, the people who were queuing up had lost their hands almost a year back. When they had applied to have them reattached, the waiting period was so long that it was only today that they had received the appointment they had sought for the requisite surgical procedure.

My goodness! At this rate, I would have to wait a year for my turn! What's the alternative? So many crippled people in this country! I was under the impression that this had begun only last night. If everyone was to wait a year for treatment, they might as well get used to living with just one hand. In fact, they would probably find it difficult to adapt to living with two hands once the missing hand was reattached. 'No, that shouldn't happen to me,' I thought. I must apply and get an appointment to get my hand reattached as soon as possible.

Leaving the scooter in the no parking zone, I hurried towards the application counter. The queue there was even longer than the pilgrims' queue in front of the Tirupati temple. At least there, it was rumoured that the temple authorities were making arrangements for more areas to queue in, but here there seemed to be no such plan. It might take a week before my turn came. I saw that some people were attending to their personal hygiene while waiting in line. Others were besieged by hawkers and other vendors who were harassing people to buy something; if they didn't oblige, the aggressive hawkers would swear at them. Sometimes, they would even thrust goods into the hands of the unwilling buyers and forcibly try to take money out of their pockets. If they continued to resist, they were being pulled out of the queue to be shouted at and humiliated in front of everyone else.

I was only missing one hand. If I were to stand in this queue, I was not sure how many other limbs I would lose. I was already late to the office. It would require enormous stamina, pockets full of cash, and a week's leave to fight one's way through this queue. I left for the office.

The security guard greeted me with his lone hand. Greeting him in return I took the lift and reached my office floor. Everybody was effortlessly working at their computers with one hand.

'Can I do it as expertly as they?' I wondered.

Keeping my lunch box aside, I eased into my chair and switched on the computer. Hurrah! I did not feel any handicap working with just one hand. My left hand was able to negotiate the keyboard and mouse simultaneously. Everything seemed fine. The only thing I regretted was that nobody seemed to notice that I had lost a hand. That really hurt me.

I said to the colleague next to me: 'Till yesterday, every one of us had two hands. What happened to one of them all of a sudden?'

He laughed rather laconically.

'You are an inattentive fool! It's been a long time since all of us lost one of our hands. It was only because you continued to have two hands that you didn't notice that our hands were missing.'

He was right. That was the way of the world. Only when we miss something do we notice it in others. All these years I had taken little notice of him because he was a colleague, and it was only when there was a crisis that he had caught my attention. What a startling insight he had presented to me! Even as I was mulling this over, I felt proud that I had been able to hang on to both my hands for so long!

Suddenly, remembering the leave I had to take to submit the application at the hospital, I entered the office of my boss. He was operating his computer with his feet. I did not notice when he had lost them, but both his hands were missing!

For a second, I felt it was not proper for me to ask for leave. But then, realizing I had no other choice, I said: 'Sir! I need leave for a week. I need to submit my application at the hospital to get my hand reattached.'

He looked at me as though I were an idiot. Then he said: 'If I'd been able to find the time, I would have had my hands reattached long ago. I simply couldn't get away to submit my application. If every one of you goes on leave to get your hands reattached, I will have to shut down my business. Tell me, how is that bloody hand going to serve you? Get lost and get on with your work!'

That's what corporate culture is all about. Nobody cares about their fellows, nobody is considerate, all that matters is the work. Employees need to go about their routines as though there is nothing is wrong, even as their limbs fall off one after another. Because I lost my hand, I had begun noticing that people were missing their hands. If I were to lose my head, perhaps, I would see how many people around me were headless.

I sank into my seat after that dressing-down from my boss. When I looked at my watch, it was already one o'clock. My stomach was growling. A crazy thought passed through my mind…if only hunger were also short a hand and a leg then this need to appease it would be reduced by half. I walked across to the canteen, found an empty table, and settled down to eat my lunch. However, before I could open my lunch box, Sarayu, my HR friend, came running over to me with a box of sweets. Announcing 'good news', and without waiting for my response, she pushed a laddu into my mouth. I began munching on it, while enquiring with a raised eyebrow what the good news was.

'Yesterday, my baby, my darling, the apple of my eye...forgave me whole-heartedly,' she declared happily.

'Forgave you? Come on, how can you be so sure?'

She paid no attention to my cynical response. She deposited the box of sweets on a nearby table and hummed happily as she waved both her hands at me. I examined them keenly to see if they had been reattached. But, no, they were perfectly natural...like the plumes of a royal swan. They were a treat to watch. She excused herself to offer sweets to somebody else. Suddenly it struck me why I had lost my hand the previous night. Unable to overcome my grief, I broke down and sobbed, 'Chandu, my darling! Can you please forgive me for raising my hand against you?'

THE ADIVASI WILL NOT DANCE

HANSDA SOWVENDRA SHEKHAR

THEY PINNED ME TO THE GROUND. THEY DID NOT LET ME SPEAK, THEY did not let me protest, they did not even let me raise my head and look at my fellow musicians and dancers as they were being beaten up by the police. All I could hear were their cries for mercy. I felt sorry for them. I had failed them. Because what I did, I did on my own. Yet, did I have a choice? Had I only spoken to them about my plan, I am sure they would have stood by me. For they too suffer, the same as I. They would have stood by me, they would have spoken up with me and, together, our voices would have rung out loud. They would have travelled out of our Santhal Pargana, out of our Jharkhand, all the way to Dilli and all of Bharot-disom; the world itself would have come to know of our suffering. Then, perhaps, something would have been done for us. Then, perhaps, our President would have agreed with what I said to him.

But I did not share my plan with anyone. I went ahead alone, like a fool. They grabbed me, beat me to the ground, put their hands on my mouth, and gagged me. I felt so helpless and so foolish.

But we Santhals are fools, aren't we? All of us Adivasis are fools. Down the years, down generations, the Diku have taken advantage of our foolishness. Tell me if I am wrong.

I only said, 'We Adivasis will not dance any more'—what is wrong with that? We are like toys—someone presses our ON button, or turns a key in our backsides, and we Santhals start beating rhythms on our tamak and tumdak, or start blowing tunes on our tiriyo while someone snatches away our very dancing grounds. Tell me, am I wrong?

I had not expected things to go so wrong. I thought I was speaking to the best man in India, our President. I had thought he would listen to my words. Isn't he our neighbour? His forefathers were all from Birbhum district next door. His ancestral house still stands in Birbhum, where Rabi Haram lived in harmony with Santhals. I have been to that place Rabin Haram set up. What is it called? Yes, Santiniketan. I went there a long time ago, to perform with my troupe. I saw that we Santhals are held in high regard in Santiniketan. Santiniketan is in Birbhum and our President is also from Birbhum. He should have heard me speak, no? But he didn't.

Such a fool I am! A foolish Santhal. A foolish Adivasi.

My name is Mangal Murmu. I am a musician. No, wait...I am a farmer. Perhaps it should be: was a farmer. Was a farmer is right. Because I don't farm any more. In my village of Matiajore, in Amrapara block of the Pakur district, not many Santhals farm any more. Only a few of us still have farmland; most of it has been acquired by a mining company. It is a rich company. It is not that we didn't fight the acquisition. We did. While we were fighting, this political leader came, that political leader came, this Kiristan sister came, that Kiristan father came. Apparently to support us. But we lost. And after we lost, everyone left. The leaders went back to Ranchi and Dilli or wherever they had to go. The Kiristans returned to their missions. But our land did not come back to us. On the other hand, a Kiristan sister was killed and our boys were implicated in her murder. The papers, the media, everyone blamed our boys. They reported that the Kiristan sister was fighting for our rights and yet our boys killed her. No one bothered to see that our boys had been fighting for our land and rights even before that Kiristan sister came. Why would they kill her? Just because our boys did not have reporter friends, their fight went unseen; while the Kiristan sister, with her network of missionaries and their friends, got all the attention. Now that our boys are in jail on false charges of murder, who will fight for us? Where are the missionaries and their friends now? If the missionaries are our well-wishers and were fighting for us, why did they run away? Kill a well-known Kiristan sister, accuse a few unknown Santhal boys fighting for their lands of her murder, move both obstacles—the Kiristan sister and the Santhal boys—out of the way, grab as much land as possible, dig as many mines as possible, and extract all the coal. This is how this coal company works. Is this scenario so difficult to understand that the media does not get it?

If coal merchants have taken a part of our lands, the other part has been taken over by stone merchants, all Diku—Marwari, Sindhi, Mandal, Bhagat, Muslim. They turn our land upside down, inside out, with their heavy machines. They sell the stones they mine from our earth in faraway places—Dilli, Noida, Panjab. This coal company and these quarry owners, they earn so much money from our land. They have built big houses for themselves in town; they wear nice clothes; they send their children to good schools in faraway places; when sick, they get themselves treated by the best doctors in Ranchi, Patna, Bhagalpur, Malda, Bardhaman, Kolkata. What do we Santhals get in return? Tatters to wear. Barely enough food. Such diseases that we can't breathe properly, we cough up blood, and forever remain bare bones.

For education, our children are at the mercy of either those free government schools where teachers come only to cook the midday meal, or those Kiristan missionary schools where our children are constantly asked to stop worshipping our Bonga-Buru and start revering Jisu and Mariam. If our children refuse, the sisters and the fathers tell our boys that their Santhal names—Hopna, Som, Singrai—are not good enough. They are renamed David and Mikail and Kiristofer and whatnot. And as if that were not enough, Muslims barge into our homes, sleep with our women, and we Santhal men can't do a thing.

But what can we do? They outnumber us. Village after village in our Santhal Pargana—which should have been a home for us Santhals—are turning into Muslim villages. Hindus live around Pakur town or in other places. Those few Hindus here, who live in Santhal villages, belong to the lower castes. They, too, are powerless and outnumbered. But why would the Hindus help us? The rich Hindus living in Pakur town are only interested in our land. They are only interested in making us sing and dance at their weddings. If they come to help us, they will say that we Santhals need to stop eating cow meat and pig meat, that we need to stop drinking haandi. They, too, want to make us forget our traditional religion, convert us into Safa-Hor, and swell their numbers to become more valuable vote banks. Safa-Hor, the pure people, the clean people, but certainly not as clean and pure as themselves, that's for sure. Always a little less than they are. In the eyes of the Hindus, we Santhals can only either be Kiristan or the almost Safa-Hor. We are losing our traditional faith, our identities, and our roots. We are becoming people from nowhere.

It's the coal and the stone, sir; they are making us lazy. The Koyla Road runs through our village. When the monstrous Hyvas ferry coal on the Koyla Road, there is no space for any other vehicle. They are so rough, these truck drivers, they can run down any vehicle that comes in their way. They can't help it, it's their job. The more rounds they make, the more money they earn. And what if they kill? The coal company can't afford to have its business slowed down by a few deaths. They give money to the family of the dead, the matter remains unreported, and the driver goes scot-free, ferrying another load for the company.

And we Santhals? Well, we wait for when there is NO ENTRY on the Koyla Road, the stipulated time when heavy trucks are not allowed to ply on the road so they have to stop somewhere. For that is when all our men, women and children come out on to the road and swarm up these Hyvas. Then, using nails, fingers, hands, and whatever tools we can manage, we steal coal. The drivers can't stop us, nor can those pot-bellied Bihari security guards posted along the Koyla Road by the company. For they know that if they do not allow us to steal the coal, we will gherao the road and not let their trucks move.

But a few stolen quintals, when the company is mining tonnes and tonnes, hardly matters. They know that if we—the descendants of the great rebels Sido and Kanhu—make up our minds, we can stop all business in the area. So they behave sensibly, practically. After all, they already have our land, they are already stealing our coal, they don't want to snatch away from us our right to re-steal it.

It is this coal, sir, which is gobbling us up bit by bit. There is a blackness—deep, indelible—all along the Koyla Road. The trees and shrubs in our village bear black leaves. Our ochre earth has become black. The stones, the rocks, the sand, all black. The tiles on the roofs of our huts have lost their fire-burnt red. The vines and flowers and peacocks we

Santhals draw on the outer walls of our houses are black. Our children—dark-skinned as they are—are forever covered with fine black dust. When they cry, and tears stream down their faces, it seems as if a river is cutting across a drought-stricken land. Only our eyes burn red, like embers. Our children hardly go to school. But everyone—whether they attend school or not—remains on the alert, day and night, for ways to steal coal and for ways to sell it.

Santhals don't understand business. We get the coal easy yet we don't charge much for it; only enough for food, clothes, and drink. But these Jolha—you call them Muslim, we, Jolha—they know the value of coal, they know the value of money. They charge the price that is best for them. And the farther coal travels from Matiajore, the higher its price becomes.

A decade earlier, when the Santhals of Matiajore were beginning their annual journey to sharecrop in the farms of Namal, four Jolha families turned up from nowhere and asked us for shelter. A poor lot, they looked as impoverished as us. Perhaps worse. In return, they offered us their services. They told us that they would look after our fields in our absence and farm them for a share of the produce. We trusted them. They started working on our fields and built four huts in a distant corner of Matiajore. Today, that small cluster of four huts has grown into a tola of more than a hundred houses. Houses, not huts. While we Santhals, in our own village, still live in our mud houses, each Jolha house has at least one brick wall and a cemented yard. This tola is now called the Jolha tola of Matiajore.

Once, Matiajore used to be an exclusively Santhal village. Today, it has a Santhal tola and a Jolha tola, with the latter being bigger. Sometimes I wonder who the olposonkhyok is here. These Jolha are hard-working, and they are always united. They may fight among themselves, they may break each other's scalps for petty matters, they may file FIRs against each other at the thana, they may drag each other to court; but if any non-Jolha says even one offensive word to a Jolha, the entire Jolha tola gets together against that person. Jolha leaders from Pakur and Sahebganj and elsewhere come down to express solidarity. And we Santhals? Our men are beaten up, thrown into police lock-ups, into jails, for flimsy reasons, and on false charges. Our women are raped, some sell their bodies on Koyla Road. Most of us are fleeing our places of birth. How united are we? Where are *our* Santhal leaders? Those chor-chuhad leaders, where are they?

Forgive me. What can I do? I cannot help it. I am sixty years old and, sitting in this lock-up after being beaten black and blue, I have no patience any more. Only anger. So, what was I saying? Yes, there are no shouters, no powerful voice among us Santhals. And we Santhals have no money—though we are born on lands under which are buried riches. We Santhals do not know how to protect our riches. We only know how to escape.

That is probably why thousands of Santhals from distant corners of Pakur district and elsewhere in the Santhal Pargana board trains to Namal every farming season. They are escaping.

Did I tell you I was once a farmer? Once. My sons farm now. The eldest stays back to work our fields while the other two migrate seasonally to Namal, along with their families. I used to compose songs. I still do. And I still maintain a dance troupe. Though it is not a regular one, the kind I had earlier, some fifteen-twenty years ago, when I was younger and full of energy, enthusiasm, and hope. Matiajore, Patharkola, Amrapara—I had singers and dancers and musicians from all these villages. I used to compose songs and set them to music. And my troupe, young men and women, they used to bring my songs to life through their dances, through their voices, through the rhythms of the tamale and the tumdak, and the trilling of the tiriyo and the banam.

At that time, our Santhal Pargana was not broken up into so many districts. Today, the Diku have broken up our Santhal Pargana for their own benefit. If it suits them, they can go on breaking down districts and create a district measuring just ten feet by ten feet. At that time, when I was younger, even Jharkhand had not been broken off from Bihar. There used to be so much hope. We used to perform in our village, in neighbouring villages, in Pakur, in Dumka, in Sahebganj, in Deoghar, in Jamtara, in Patna, in Ranchi, even in Kolkata, and in Bhubaneswar, where we were taken to see the sea at Puri. What a sight it was! We performed in Godda, too. Godda, where my daughter, Mugli, was married. We used to be paid money. We used to be given good food, awarded medals, and shields, and certificates. We used to be written about in the papers.

All that has changed now. First, all the members of my troupe are old. Some have even died. Many have migrated, or migrate seasonally. The ones who remain hum songs, sing to each other, but a stage performance? No, not again. Like me, even they are tired, disillusioned. All our certificates and shields, what did they give us? Diku children go to schools and colleges, get education, jobs. What do we Santhals get? We Santhals can sing and dance, and we are good at our art. Yet, what has our art given us? Displacement, tuberculosis.

I have turned sixty. Perhaps more. I am called Haram now. Haram, respectfully. I have started wearing thick glasses. Even my hearing has weakened. Though my voice is still quite good. People in my village say that my voice still impresses them. Sometimes they ask me to sing. I sing some of my old compositions. It makes them happy. I still compose songs. Not many. Maybe one song every six or eight months. One song of just six to eight lines. And because I had some fame in the past, I am still invited to perform at public functions in Pakur and Dumka and Ranchi.

I keep putting together new troupes, though the members constantly change. I have a dancer today, tomorrow he is growing potatoes for some Bangali zamindar in Bardhaman. So I have to replace him with some other dancer. Two days later, the original dancer returns. So I have to replace the substitute. This is how my troupes work nowadays. But I keep it going because it brings us some money. And when we are hosted in towns, we are usually fed good food. So we perform.

Our music, our dance, our songs are sacred to us Santhals. But hunger and poverty have driven us to sell what is sacred to us. When my boys perform at a Diku wedding, I am so foolish, I expect everyone to pay attention. Which Diku pays attention to our music? Even at those high-profile functions, most Diku just wait for our performance to end. Yet, be it an athletic meet, some inauguration, or any function organized by someone high and mighty—in the name of Adivasi culture and Jharkhandi culture, it is necessary to make Adivasis dance. Even Bihari and Bangali and Odia people say that Jharkhand is theirs. They call their culture and music and dance superior to those of us Adivasi. Why don't they get their women to sing and dance in open grounds in the name of Jharkhandi culture? For every benefit, in jobs, in education, in whatever, the Diku are quick to call Jharkhand their own—let the Adivasi go to hell. But when it comes to displaying Jharkhandi culture, the onus of singing and dancing is upon the Adivasi alone.

So how did I land up in front of the President, you ask. Some three months ago, an official letter came to my house in Matiajore: a thick white envelope bearing the emblem of the government of Jharkhand. The paper on which the letter was typed in Hindi was equally thick and crisp. In fewer than five sentences I was told that the government of Jharkhand sought the pleasure of my musical performance at some event, the identity and venue of which would be communicated to me later, and that I should gather a troupe for a fifteen to twenty-minute performance, and that all participants would be paid well. The letter was signed by some high-ranking IAS officer in Ranchi.

What does a hungry man need? Food. What does a poor man need? Money. So, here I was, needing both. And recognition, too. We artistes are greedy people. We are hungry for acceptance, some acknowledgement, something to be remembered by. So, without thinking, I sent back a reply the very next day saying that, yes, I would be happy to perform. I was so happy, I went to the big post office in Pakur, more than twenty kilometres away, all by myself, to register that letter. I went in a Vikram, packed with many other Santhals like me, all going to Pakur. Nearly all of us travellers were blackened by the dust from the Koyla Road. Yet I was so happy that I did not notice it at all.

Around the time that I was preparing for our performance, selecting young men and women for my troupe, digging up old songs from memory, I was faced with a strange situation. I told you that Mugli, my daughter, is married into a family in the Godda district, didn't I? Well, she began calling me regularly on my mobile phone. I couldn't understand the situation clearly at first but it seemed to me that it had something to do with their land. Her husband was a farmer—they are a family of farmers—as are all the Santhal families in that village. There are more villages nearby, populated by Santhals, Paharias, and low-caste Hindus.

What had happened was that the district administration had asked the inhabitants of all the villages to vacate their land—their village, farms, everything. Eleven villages! Can you imagine? The first question everyone asked was: what will the sarkar do with so much land?

Initially, I thought they were all rumours. And, I thought, how can anyone force Santhals to vacate their land in the Santhal Pargana? Didn't we have the Tenancy Act to protect us?

Still, when the rumours started floating about, I went to Godda. We all marched to the block office in a huge group. The officers there assured us that they were all just rumours. The lands were safe. The villages were safe. Yet, later, police were sent to the villages. They came with written orders from the district administration. The villages would have to be vacated to make room for a thermal power plant. The villagers refused outright. Santhals, low-caste Hindus, Paharias, everyone began fighting for their land.

The district administration fought back. The agitators were all beaten up and thrown into police lock-ups. I called my daughter and her small children to Matiajore after her husband was taken away. Mugli arrived, her children and in-laws in tow. It was strange: a village which annually empties itself every few months was suddenly providing shelter to immigrants.

How would I manage to provide for all these people who were dependent on me now? How could the members of my troupe feed all those who had come to seek refuge in their houses? We needed money.

And our current—mysterious—assignment was our only hope. Despite our troubles, we kept practising.

In the meantime, some people arrived to help the villagers facing displacement in Godda. They wrote letters to the government, to people in Ranchi and Dilli. They even wrote letters to the businessman who was planning to build that thermal power plant in Godda. We heard that he was a very rich and very shrewd man. He was also a MP. We also heard that he liked polo—some game played with horses—and that his horses were far better off than all the Santhals of the whole of the Santhal Pargana.

News about the displacements taking place in Godda began to appear in newspapers and on TV after a few days. All of us tried to concentrate on our practice, but how could we sing and dance with such a storm looming ahead? In between, I received phone calls from several officers in Ranchi and Dumka and Pakur. They asked me to keep working for the show. They never forgot to remind me that this show was of the utmost importance, that we were going to perform before some very important people. Some officers from Dumka and Pakur even came to Matiajore to see if we were really practising or not. When they saw that we were really working hard, they were happy. They smiled and encouraged us, they talked to us very sweetly. So sweetly that we all wondered if they could really not see how troubled we were feeling. Many times, I felt like asking them: 'How can all of you be so indifferent? How can you expect us to sing and dance when our families are being uprooted from their villages?' At other times, I felt like asking: 'Which VIP is coming? The president of India? The president of America? You are making us Santhals dance in Pakur and you are displacing Santhals from their villages in Godda? Isn't your VIP going to see that? Doesn't your VIP read the papers or watch news on TV? We foolish Santhals can see what damage is happening around us. Doesn't your VIP see all that?'

But I stayed silent.

Reality started dawning on us three weeks before the date of our performance. First as floating rumours which were gradually confirmed by newspaper reports.

The reality was that the businessman was certainly going to set up a thermal power plant in Godda. That plant would run on coal from the mines in Pakur and Sahebganj. If needed, coal would be brought from other places. That businessman, in fact, needed electricity for the iron and steel plants he was planning to set up in Jharkhand. The plant was to be set up for his own selfish needs; but if he were to be believed, the whole of Jharkhand would receive electricity from his plant. Whole towns would be lit up non-stop, factories would never stop working for lack of power. There would be development and jobs and happiness all over. And, finally, news also reached us that the foundation stone of the plant would be laid by the president of India. We would be performing for him.

Yes, I was shocked. All of us were. Shocked and sad, but also surprised and delighted. We couldn't believe our luck. We had performed before ministers, chief ministers, and governors. But never before the president of the country!

Then we heard more news. People demonstrating and agitating against the forcible acquisition of land were being beaten up by the police, they were being thrown into lock-ups. Paramilitary forces, the CRPF, had been called in to control the situation. Four villages out of the eleven had already been razed to the ground by bulldozers to make room for the foundation stone laying ceremony.

But the papers carried glowing reports, along with pictures, of the roads which were being repaired or rebuilt in Ranchi and Dumka. Breathlessly, they reported that the President would stay in Jharkhand for three days. He would spend day one in Ranchi. On day two, he would preside over a university convocation in Dumka. On day three, he would visit Godda, lay the foundation stone, and fly out of Jharkhand.

We received official intimation of the event a week before it was to take place. One day before the event, we were taken to Godda by bus. The entire district, the district headquarters, was unrecognizable. A football ground had been converted into a massive helipad. There were hundreds of policemen and CRPF jawans. And everywhere we turned our heads, all we could see was a sea of people. I knew they had come to see the helicopter. Tucked away in the papers had been reports that all protestors had been detained and were being held somewhere. Perhaps my son-in-law, too, was among them.

From where I stood, the stage looked massive, but still not big enough for all the people who had climbed upon it. Ministers from Dilli and Ranchi, all dressed in their best neta clothes, laughing and chatting among themselves. All very happy with the progress, the development of the area. The Santhal Pargana would now fly to the moon. The Santhal Pargana would now turn into Dilli and Bombay. The businessman was grinning widely. Patriotic songs in Hindi were playing from the loudspeakers placed at all corners of the field. 'Bharat mahaan,' someone was shouting from the stage, trying to rouse the audience, his voice amplified by numerous loudspeakers. What mahaan? I wondered. Which great nation displaces thousands of its people from their homes and livelihoods to produce electricity for cities and factories? And jobs? What jobs? An Adivasi farmer's job is to farm. Which other job should he be made to do? Become a servant in some billionaire's factory built on land that used to belong to that very Adivasi just a week earlier?

Reporters with cameras swarmed all over the place. Three vans with huge dish antennas on their roofs were parked near the venue. I identified the logo of a popular TV channel painted on the sides of one of those vans. I wondered if any of its reporters had visited the place where the villagers were being detained by the police.

My troupe was waiting in an enclosure built specially for the performers at that event. All the women were wearing red blouses, blue lungis, and green panchhi, and huge, colourful plastic flowers in their buns. They were carrying steel lotas with flowers and leaves put inside them. All the men were wearing red football jerseys and green panchhi and had tied green gamchas around their heads. We all looked very good.

The helicopter arrived…thud thud thud thud…. Its rotors swirled up dust from the playing field. The crowd was excited and a slow roar began.

The President was accompanied by his security staff to the stage. He was a short, thoughtful man. All Bangalis look learned and thoughtful. Why should this Bangali president be any different?

The festivities began. The man who had been shouting 'Bharat mahaan' announced how fortunate the land of Jharkhand was that the iconic billionaire had deemed it suitable to set up a thermal power plant here. He didn't mention how fortunate the billionaire was that he got to come to Jharkhand, a place rich with mineral deposits beneath its earth; a naive population upon it; and a bunch of shrewd, greedy thief-leaders, officers, and businessmen who ran the state and controlled its land, people, and resources.

The 'Bharat mahaan' man announced the welcome dance and my troupe was ushered into the open space before the stage. We entered with our tamak, tumdak, tiriyo, and banam. The President seemed impressed. The businessman looked bored.

When we had taken our places before the stage, I took the mic in my hand and bowed to the President. Then I tapped the mic to check if it was working and began in Hindi, as good Hindi as I could muster at the height of my emotions. Actually, it was a miracle that I did not weep and choke up.

'Johar, Rashtrapati Babu. We are very proud and happy that you have come to our Santhal Pargana and we are also very proud that we have been asked to sing and dance before you and welcome you to our place. We will sing and dance before you, but tell us, do we have a reason to sing and dance? Do we have a reason to be happy? You will now start building the power plant, but this plant will be the end of us all, the end of all the Adivasis. These men sitting beside you have told you that this power plant will change our fortunes, but these same men have forced us out of our homes and villages. We have nowhere to go, nowhere to grow our crops. How can this power plant be good for us? And how can we Adivasis dance and be happy? Unless we are given back our homes and land, we will not sing and dance. We Adivasis will not dance. The Adivasi will not—'

FOR THE GREATER COMMON GOOD

ARUNI KASHYAP

NEERUMONI WAS THE FIRST ONE IN THE FAMILY TO SUSPECT THE BARK manuscripts. Anil had stared at her in silence. Where on earth had she heard of books being haunted? She said firmly that it wasn't the soul of her dead husband, his father Horokanto, who was troubling them, but the souls trapped in the manuscripts. She stood up and went out to the one-acre pond behind her house, bamboo creel in hand. She would spend some time there. Washing the rice, vegetables, clothes, and vessels from the afternoon's meal wouldn't take long. Chores done, she liked to change into a petticoat, tied just above her breasts, and swim for at least an hour.

Winters aren't harsh in Teteliguri, not like the villages at the foot of the Jaintia Hills on the Meghalaya border. The wind from the hills enters every nook and cranny there. Meghalaya is the abode of clouds. The white clouds descend as quiet as cats' paws, and soon people are in the middle of a fog, even before the cat's tongue can scrape their bones. No, here, in Teteliguri village, things are better. There are huge paddy fields. There are many houses, many people in these houses. Here, the climate remains warm and comfortable. Of course, when the trees in the stunted hills that guard the village start to sway, there is a storm. But the chill reigns only on nights when the winds freeze the stones, and then carry the bite of it into the houses of the village, an uninvited guest.

That's why, when Neerumoni first said she was hearing things, Anil had suggested it was the wind. It was usual for the wind to knock at the door, hover over the straw roof of their thatched hut. They had never finished reinforcing the walls with mud. Back then, she was confident that it was the soul of her spiteful husband, Horokanto, who had many unfulfilled desires when he died in an accident. He wanted to return to the mortal world, she thought. In the process, he would rob them of all peace.

Eventually, Anil took her seriously, as did most other women in the village. They prayed. They left a meal with Horokanto's favourite dishes on the western side of the house. But the manuscripts still opened and shut in the middle of the night (mainly on Saturdays and Tuesdays) all by themselves.

Nor did strange souls stop troubling Neerumoni: they left earthworm mounds on the food she cooked, and strange handprints on the bedsheets she washed with khar. And one day, when she had cooked duck meat with banana flower, they dropped a ball of curly hair in the pot.

Gradually, those murmurs, faint songs, the rustle of bark as the manuscripts turned their own pages, invaded the dreams of Neerumoni, and Anil too. On lonely afternoons, when everything was quiet, those sounds were louder, quicker, restless. One night, Neerumoni woke up, disturbed by the choric melody of the singing crickets. She saw four lanky men standing over the small wooden box where the manuscripts were kept. They were trying to open the lock with a knife that had a blue plastic handle.

When she shouted at them, they turned towards her, grew black wings and flew off through the ceiling, leaving it undisturbed. Her screams woke up the rest of the family, and she told them one of the figures had worn a long green dress, the other three white turbans and dhotis. They looked as if they were from a royal family. They didn't wear ornaments though.

No one believed her. Her suspicions were fortified when she saw one of the manuscripts take the shape of an old man in her dreams. He was crying, asking her to set him free, telling her that he was trapped there by mistake, unlike the other souls who had committed sins. He promised never to disturb her if she freed him from the fetters of the spells in the bark manuscripts. When she said that she hadn't trapped him, she wasn't holding him there, he got angry and screamed, called her a liar. Anil laughed it away. But Anju, who would have said many sarcastic things about her mother's superstitions, who would have fought with her even a month ago, was quiet.

Anil looked at Anju and felt again that, after she was raped, he required inhuman strength just to look at her face, let alone her eyes. She was sitting in a corner when her brother and mother were speaking about the old man trapped in the manuscripts, fingering the criss-cross of welts on her wrists, the result of being tied to a bed with steel threads ordinarily used to tie bamboo.

Everyone was away. It was the death anniversary of the village headman's mother. Neerumoni had asked her to come along, tried to tempt her by saying that she'd get to eat porridge at the function, but Anju said that Biren would come to leave his baby son with her. His wife was away and the little one wouldn't sleep until Anju sang him a lullaby. Even that day, Neerumoni reminded Anju that she shouldn't forget that Biren was after all a man. Though he was her first cousin, the sudden intimacy between them over the last two years was the talk among certain sections of the village.

But Anju was a popular girl. Everyone loved her. Almost every household in the village was indebted to her in some way or the other. 'Anju, would you please weave this mekhela for me? I won't pay you the full price, but I will give you something as a token of love.' Anju turned into Mother Teresa when phrases such as 'token of love' were mentioned. 'Anju, could you come to our house tomorrow morning? I have asked everyone in the village, but you know how the girls in our village have become after the cinema hall opened in Sonapur, they are afraid their hands will melt away like a leper's if they so much as touch the mix of cow dung and loamy soil.

Who else will I ask?' Anju nodded vigorously, agreeing with the old woman. 'Anju, don't you dare forget to come a week before the wedding. You know there is no one else I can trust with keys to the money, the ornaments, with supervising.... Oh, you are such an angel, what would I do without you?!'

So while some tongues were wagging, others remained quiet. Why should anyone suspect the relationship between first cousins? Those tongue-waggers said 'first cousins' in a dismissive, mocking tone, and suggested that Biren was 'woman-hungry'.

Thus, the day after Neerumoni found an unconscious Anju lying on the bed with bleeding wrists, the whole village blamed Biren and accompanied a near-crazy Anil to the police station to lodge a complaint. Biren was in jail now for raping Anju. And inside that haunted house, where books with souls created strange noises, a new Anju lived with a constantly growing belly. This new Anju didn't speak, and often cried silently.

Slopp-slopp-slopp! The sound brought him back to the present. His mother had rushed in and was now standing in front of him, her adult son, in wet clothes that had become translucent. She hadn't brought her bamboo creel back and looked terrified. When he asked what was wrong, she told him that a rough, hairy hand had pulled her down by the leg while she was bathing in the pond. 'I didn't see it, Anil, but it was a man's hand. Hairy. It's the manuscripts, I am telling you.'

⁓

Anil's father Horokanto learnt sorcery from Neerumoni's father Doityo Burha long before the Indian Army camp in this village became an integral part of the lives of people here. As the result of a small disagreement with his own father, Horokanto left home for good. He took shelter in the house of his closest friend, Neerumoni's brother Nilambor. The next day, when they were having breakfast in the kitchen, her father had asked him what he was interested in. Horokanto replied that he would like to learn the art of sorcery from Doityo Burha. It wasn't an easy art, said the man who was known across seven villages as a great magician, the man who controlled the souls of many rowdy ghosts, forced snakes to come crawling back to suck poison out from the wound of a dying man. Doityo Burha sipped his hot milk and looked at the younger man. But Horokanto was determined to learn. He promised to follow all the rules and regulations. The old man with the long white beard warned him again: if he neglected the rituals for even one day, the bark manuscripts that held the trapped spirits of wild but dead men would strike him dead.

In fact, when he was finally a master of the art, Horokanto managed to imprison a bidaa, a ghost who would be under his command like a genie in a bottle. But the only way to keep the bidaa under control was to give him more and more work. In the next room, Neerumoni, who was a seventeen-year-old girl then, laughed and told her elder sister that it wasn't difficult at all—one could just send the bidaa to a desert and ask him to dig as many wells as possible.

Neerumoni saw Horokanto for the first time three days later. He was swimming in the pond wearing a white gamosa around his waist. It clung to his buttocks. She remembered a long-forgotten feeling. The strange and disturbing pleasure she had felt when her pot-bellied thirty-year-old cousin, who had come to invite them to the rice ceremony for his second son, had pushed up her petticoat, taken out his penis, rubbed it against her inner thighs, asked her to hold it and move her hand slowly up and down. When he started to moan strangely, she got suddenly scared and fled, but not before he had kissed her lips, pushed his tongue inside her mouth and sucked her upper lip. That was her first time with a man. After a long time, seeing Horokanto, she wanted to lie down beside him.

They had sex for the first time on a rainy winter afternoon, just after the grains were harvested. It wasn't the sort of sudden winter rain that farmers worry will blacken the leaves of the potato. The day had been windy since morning. Clouds gathered little by little in the sky, leisurely, like people trickling into a wedding reception. Her grandmother had advised everyone not to spread out the new grains for drying in the courtyard that day because it might rain. Though it was winter, the sun was strong—you had to drink at least two glasses of water after a half-hour walk. When it finally rained, everyone was ready for it, and had taken to their beds, or settled down near the hearth with a drink of tea.

The cold, the fresh smell of water on earth, the wind: it was ideal. When she reached her house, the quietness of it and the empty veranda seemed to instruct her to go straight to the room that Horokanto shared with Nilambor. Inside, he was lying on his stomach. She latched the door. He looked at her, startled, and tried to smile, but she knew he found her sudden entry odd. She started taking off her clothes. When she was finished, she moved to Horokanto who was staring at her with rapid breaths. Later, lying naked beside her, he had pulled her closer and said he had never seen a more beautiful woman in his life. They smelled like coconut water.

After four months of random, wild lovemaking, behind the house at midnight, beside the pond early in the morning, in the mud of the Tamulidobha River, behind cowsheds, on hay stored to serve as fodder, they eloped. They knew her father would rather kill her than let her marry him. He stole most of the manuscripts. Her father died ten years later; by then, Nilambor had died unmarried and Neerumoni had given birth to three daughters and a son. Anju was her firstborn. Anil her second. On his deathbed, her father had met Horokanto finally, had given him the rest of the manuscripts, cautioned him to use them carefully and for the good of humanity. Doityo Burha also mentioned that since he had eloped with Neerumoni against her father's wishes, he would not be able to use the spells when he most needed them. 'It's not my curse. I have seen that Fate has decided this punishment for you. These manuscripts are powerful but they are unforgiving if you disrespect them.' Horokanto died in an accident about thirty years later. That morning, he had fought with Neerumoni and hadn't worshipped the ancient books for the first time in his life.

After the army crackdown, everybody in the family began believing Neerumoni's claims about the bark manuscripts. The previous day, rebels had blown up a bridge that connected the village with the National Highway and Guwahati. In the explosion, three Indian soldiers from the battalion stationed in the village were killed. The tall, long-haired Punjabi soldier, who always wore a red turban and was respectful towards women (unlike the others), lost his hand. The intensity of the explosion caused it to fly and land on the roof of the village fisherman's house. His wife was sitting in the courtyard having her lunch at the time. A stream of blood fell on her shoulders (some say most of it fell on her rice and face). At first, she thought a bird had shat on her clothes, but the shit was red and the bird looked like a hand. For a while, she stood staring at her roof where the hand was, and then fainted. When her neighbours found her an hour later, sprinkled water on her eyes, and brought her back to her senses, she vomited and started to wail hysterically. Everyone in the village went to see the wailing woman and the clenched fist, with five golden rings on its fingers—stones meant to ward off the evil influence of powerful planets. They sucked in sharp breaths through clenched teeth and wished Horokanto was still alive. When Dilipram came, they fell quiet. He was the only sorcerer left in the village now to take care of spirits and snakebites and barrenness in married women. They were convinced that the soul of the Punjabi man was refusing to leave. The army crackdown happened the next day. Scores of soldiers came in jeeps and surrounded the village. Their boots were loud as they ran towards the hamlets. Someone had started to play the drum in the village prayer hall, and it boomed like the announcement of a war. Neerumoni's neighbour Bibha came running to tell her to flee. 'Save yourself and your family members, forget the belongings.'

Neerumoni stood frozen for a moment, not knowing how Anju would run with that bulging stomach. Then the two of them hurried along as fast as Anju could manage, hoping it was just a false alarm, hoping that, in the village's central meeting ground, everyone would say, go back, nothing is wrong.

But Neerumoni saw that all the young men were running towards the forests. She saw women, children, girls, and old men running across the fields to get to the next village. They would cross the Tamulidobha River, dry in winter. She too ran that way with a heavily pregnant Anju, thinking how Horokanto and she had made love on the banks of this river, in the mud, like two buffaloes, one morning. It was the monsoon, and the river that ran beside the passionately love-making couple flowed with force, creating whirlpools, voluptuous with desire and laughter. Neerumoni heard gunshots. She turned back. Someone said it was Hiren and someone else said, no, no, no one has been shot. They started to run again.

They returned the next morning, after spending a worried night in Maloybari village across the river. Each and every house had been ransacked. There were boot prints on clothes, white bedsheets were soiled brown and black. Food was strewn around. Beds upturned. Tables broken. Chairs piled up in front of the courtyard and burnt, both plastic and wooden. Mattresses left out in the rain or set on fire and still smoking. Mud walls broken down. Earthen pots lay shattered in courtyards. As they were putting their houses back together somehow, the village folk could hear the cries of Prodhan Mahatu, the village milkman. He had forgotten to untie his twenty cows, and the army had shot and killed all of them. Their corpses were lying in the cowshed, stinking of blood and the greenish dung that had come out along with their intestines.

In the haunted house, Neerumoni asked Anil, 'Every single object in this house has been thrown around, but look, the bark manuscripts are where we had left them. They have even thrown away the mustard oil lamp that we lit in front of the manuscripts, so why didn't they try to open this locked wooden chest?' All of them believed that the chest would have been broken and the manuscripts removed, but those were haunted manuscripts, they didn't need legs to return to their original place. They imagined that the soldier who disrespected the manuscripts was dying slowly of some strange disease. For the first time, Neerumoni and her family felt safe because of the presence of the bark manuscripts. All these weeks after Horokanto's death, they were petrified, unable to solve the mystery of the sounds. That night, Prodhan Mahatu went to the army camp, stabbed one soldier and set one of the camps on fire. They shot him dead.

⁂

Dilipram wasn't a great sorcerer. Now middle-aged, he had learnt most of his charms from Horokanto even though he was apprenticed to an old sorcerer in Hatimura village, Mayong, for about five years. He lived in the old man's house and worked in his fields in lieu of fees. The sorcerer had given Dilipram the teeth of a male crocodile, the dried hands of a pregnant female monkey, severed legs of mating lizards, snakeskins, and many other indispensable things required in the art of serious sorcery for the greater common good. When Horokanto was alive, Dilipram would occasionally come to him with questions:

'Do we use a pregnant bitch's morning urine to make this potion?'

'I made the potion for cobra bite with khar, but I'm worried about whether the concentration is strong enough.'

The people in the village had thought Dilipram would inherit the bark manuscripts. In fact, Neerumoni had offered him the books, but he refused. She must know, he said, that those manuscripts had a soul and they always chose their owner, just as her father was once chosen.

So was Horokanto—or why would he fight with his father and come to stay in their house to learn sorcery when he had belonged to such a rich family? It's all decided 'above' he had told her with conviction, pointing to the sky. 'You will get signs.' One day she would have to let go of the manuscripts so that they reached the rightful owner. That person could even be Anil, or one of her future sons-in-law.

Now, when Anil told him about the strange sounds that shook their house and robbed them of their sleep, Dilipram suggested that they take out the manuscripts every Tuesday and Saturday, spread them under the sun (if there was no sun, the veranda would suffice), and light a mustard-oil lamp, offer some white or red flowers, and pray to the gods of the ancient books, requesting them not to trouble the family. 'Try it,' he said calmly. When Anil stood up to leave, Dilipram told him that, if it didn't work, he should return on the night of the twenty-second Saturday with a new steel plate. They would go to the cremation ground.

Anil started to walk away. The breeze lifted the light cotton cloth that covered Dilipram's flabby body. He turned and told Anil that he had this strange feeling that one of the trapped souls had become very powerful since they hadn't been controlled by spells for nearly a year now, since Horokanto's death; that soul might be trying to take corporeal form to fulfil its worldly wishes. In the deathly silence that followed, Anil felt he could hear ants moving across the courtyard. He broke out in a cold sweat. Dilipram added that the soul could be trying to take birth through Anju, so they would have to kill the child as soon as it was born if the first remedy didn't work. Anil decided that he wouldn't tell his mother about this last part. She would worry unnecessarily.

On the way home, Anil passed Prodhan's house. A strong stench of rotten animals rose from it. He rushed to get ahead of the smell and vomited. Tearing off some leaves from a eucalyptus tree nearby, he inhaled the scent of it until he felt better. The village would have to do something as soon as possible, he thought, wiping his face with the cotton handkerchief that Anju had woven on the waist loom before she was raped. After Prodhan was shot dead, his wife and two daughters vanished mysteriously. They must have fled to a relative's home. They didn't even wait to receive the body. But that was wise—the army would have killed them too had they gone to ask for his body. It was the villagers who received Prodhan's decomposing body. Before that, young men and women from the city had come with pens and tiny notebooks and cameras that made loud sounds. The army flew them in a helicopter, and took them on a tour of select localities. They would then report that no villagers were harmed during the operation. Some of them came by car, and the army helped them cross the river on boats.

Anil stopped by the grocery shop to buy some red lentils that his mother had asked for. The shopkeeper wrapped it in an old newspaper. Anil didn't notice the bloody picture that was printed on it.

On reaching home, he apologized to his mother. They should have believed her. He conveyed what Dilipram had told him, except the part about Anju's unborn baby. Neerumoni said, 'Let's wait and see what happens.' They would worship the manuscripts for twenty-one Saturdays and Tuesdays.

She went in to ask Anju if she needed something. But the girl just wept soundlessly, which she did a lot these days. Neerumoni knew why. After she was raped, for a long time, Neerumoni had blamed her for the incident: didn't I tell you not to roam around with Biren too much? Wasn't I cautioning you for a long time until it finally happened? You destroyed your life, and ours too.

After talking to Anil, Neerumoni shivered. She didn't know if she would raise Anju's child or kill it with the help of other women. Two more months left! It was already February. What would happen if she gave birth to twins? No, no, as if one child isn't enough trouble.... Would she be able to stuff a handful of salt into the infant's mouth and take his life? Wouldn't this child be her first grandchild?

When she went to the kitchen and unwrapped the lentils, Neerumoni saw the bloodied face of the slain man printed on the newspaper. She trembled, and imagined the blood being mixed with the lentils. Should she wash the lentils again to remove that blood? She felt queasy looking at the blood, the rose-pink lentils. Then she realized it was Prodhan's face: distorted with anger, full of the pain of losing twenty cows that he had reared like his own children: cows that came running to him whenever they saw him, red and brown and white cows that liked to rub their heads on his back; cows that licked their calves' balls and ears; cows that he rebuked if they chewed the clothes hung on the line to dry; cows that had the most beautiful eyes in the world.

She called out to Anil to ask if it was really Prodhan in the photograph. He looked at it and said, yes, that's him. He read the headline out to her.

TOP MILITANT GUNNED DOWN IN TETELIGURI VILLAGE

She threw away the lentils. They didn't have lunch that day. The day Anju spoke a full sentence, that too in her normal tone, Neerumoni couldn't believe her ears. In the nine months since the assault, she'd only heard her daughter cry in agony and impotent rage. Anju was whispering something. At first Neerumoni thought it was the sigh of the rain-bearing wind from the hills. It had been raining hard for a few weeks, an early monsoon. The previous morning, Neerumoni had noticed that the edges of the veranda had disintegrated. Probably the first wave of floods would arrive soon too.

Neerumoni went to Anju's room and asked what she was saying. Anju said she had seen a child with eyes that shone like flames in her dreams last night. When her mother heard this, she was sure the manuscripts were now troubling her daughter. She looked worried and promised that she would send Anil to Dilipram's house again as soon as he returned. Neerumoni sat beside her daughter. Anju extended her hands and pressed her mother's, wept, and said she didn't want the child. As soon as it was born, she would shove a handful of salt into his mouth.

It was dark outside. As if the sky had covered itself with a black shawl to keep away the chill. Even though it was still early in the day, a soft blanket of darkness settled on the wet roofs, over the rain-drenched trees, paths, stones, and red soil. Neerumoni held her daughter's hands. Through the window, she looked at their dog who was shivering in the sudden chill, curled up on hay in a corner of the cowshed. She noticed that the small wooden suitcase shook mildly—was it throbbing? Moving?—as if someone were trying to escape. She could feel her breaths become heavy, shallow.

Anil didn't return until late afternoon. After serving him lunch, Neerumoni mentioned Anju's dream, and Anil was too stunned to speak for a while. Then, slowly, he told her what Dilipram had cautioned him about—that one of the souls might have become too powerful and could be trying to attain physical shape by possessing Anju's child. Neerumoni thought about Anju's dream and whispered: he must have already taken possession of the unborn.

By the time Anil left for Dilipram's house, it was raining harder. He passed the Tamulidobha, suddenly becoming aware of its noisy waters. The hilly tributaries had given her a new life, youthful blood. It was as if she were mocking the village, or perhaps trying to wake people from their stupor, warning them of something. He also crossed Prodhan Mahatu's house. Last month, the villagers had cleaned up the mess. They didn't know what to do with his land and property, and left everything the way they found it. Even the clothes. One of the men had entered the house and told the villagers that, on the hearth, there was still a container of cooked rice and huge steel pots of milk that had curdled, grown fungi, turned green and yellow and brown, and were releasing another smell that was difficult to describe. Now, Anil noticed, wild creepers had completely covered the house, the huge cowshed and even the bamboo gate. There was not a glimpse to be had of the mud walls or the wood in the windows.

When he returned home, it was evening. When he told his mother that Dilipram had advised him to relinquish the manuscripts, she asked him if he was hiding something from her again. He lit a fire, and as he warmed his hands at it, Anil told her that he wasn't. In fact, he should have told her everything the last time too. A storm had broken out, running through the village like a madwoman. Their thatched hut started to vibrate.

Neerumoni wondered aloud if they would be able to go out. Anju's abdomen was hurting. Anil said that that was even more reason to go, because Dilipram had told them they had to act immediately, even if lightning strikes down the whole village and the hills. They would have to do it on their own, before Anju gave birth, otherwise the soul would be born in their own house, and no one could predict what it might do.

As they were leaving the house, Anju's water broke. She screamed, but in the wild roar of the dusk thunderstorm, they didn't hear her cries. Anju crawled down from her bed, breathless, and lay down on the green mattress on the ground, spread her legs, and waited, wondering if she would be able to do it all alone. At first, she lost consciousness.

Anil looked at the betel nut trees moving like drunken men weaving their way down a village street. He wondered if one of them would fall, killing them both. He held the wooden suitcase firmly with one hand and the umbrella over his mother's head. But they didn't have the umbrella for long. The wind was strong, like the spring storm Bordoisila. People believed the storm was the soul of a newly married woman rushing back to her mother's house with her long hair open, destroying everything in her way: huts, trees, cowsheds, and crops. The storm that evening was as mighty as the impatient Bordoisila. So, when they finally heard the wicked laughter of the youthful river, they were relieved.

The riverbank was slippery, and below, the water flowed furiously. Anil saw a wooden chair being carried away. Will they go really? The souls? It had to be done by Anil's hand, since he was the heir to his father who died without choosing the rightful owner of the bark manuscripts, who couldn't train someone, who did not give away the knowledge of those books before dying. After they had emptied the box into the tempestuous waters, Neerumoni told him that someone breathed on her cheeks, and she heard a sigh. Anil didn't say anything, but she stressed that it was warm, as warm as it could be that chilly evening. Then he said, it was just the wind, just the sound of the wind moving across the leaves and over the waters.

On their way back, they didn't worry about Anju, but only thought about Horokanto—the husband, the lover, the father. Before opening the gate to their compound, Neerumoni said, 'You know, even my father found most of these manuscripts in a wooden box. Things just get repeated.'

'What will happen now?'

'They will travel, maybe even to the sea, in search of another owner.' Inside the house, Anju was lying unconscious, a newborn between her legs, slick with blood. Neerumoni took a sharp knife and cut the cord. There was absolute silence. She waited; she patted the boy's back. It didn't cry.

Anil wanted to say that it'd be too soon, too good to be true, but he kept quiet. He looked at his sister's face, called to her. He wanted to show her the baby before he buried him.

The soil at the back of their house would be soft like mud now. Digging a deep hole would be easy. Neerumoni sniffed. The air smelled of fresh mud. She wondered why the baby's face reminded her of her dead father who was hurt because she had eloped with Horokanto.

SWIMMER AMONG THE STARS

KANISHK THAROOR

As A RULE, THE LAST SPEAKER OF A LANGUAGE NO LONGER USES IT. Ethnographers show up at the door with digital recorders, ready to archive every declension, each instance of the genitive, the idiosyncratic function of verbal suffixes. But this display hardly counts as normal speech. It simply confirms reality to the last speaker, that the old world of her mind is cut adrift from humans and can only be pulped into a computer. She finds it strange to listen to the sounds of her mouth. Inevitably, she mingles a more common language with her own. That common language, after all, is the speech that now keeps her company, that leads her through the market, that sits with her in the evenings by the television, that gives her the terminal diagnosis at the clinic, that pours through her letterbox, that comes in a crisp nurse's outfit to wash her feet. Her own language does nothing of the sort. It is nowhere to be found. She pauses, silent now, staring incredulously at the microphone. How am I the last speaker of my language? How can I be its keeper? My language left me.

She apologizes to the ethnographers. You must understand, she says, that though my memory is preserved better than a lemon, it is still difficult to remember which words are my own and which words are not.

Please speak as it comes naturally to you, the ethnographers say.

Thank you, I will try.

In any case, we can help you remember.

The last speaker looks up, puzzled. But if you know already, then why do you want to hear it from me?

It means something more if it comes from you.

Do you speak my language, then? Do you understand me when I say this, when I say that, and even now, when I am singing this song that my father sang every day as he disappeared down the valley? She sings and her alien words crackle about the room.

No, we do not understand, the ethnographers say. Or if we do, it is only distantly, as if we were reading shapes in a raincloud.

Oh, that is a shame, it would be nice to sing that song for someone.

Please, madam, sing it for the microphone.

She grins. So the microphone understands, does it?

Yes, it understands.

If only you could get microphones to talk! She laughs and then feels a little sorry for herself. She does not mean to sound sardonic, no one could accuse her of being indifferent to her plight. Some years before, it had occurred to her that she was no longer in the habit of hearing her own tongue. Everybody in the town seemed to be speaking the common language. She did not mind using their language since she had dwelled in it for a long time, almost as long as she could remember, and had kept it clean and given it a good airing, rearranged the furniture so it suited her just right. It was the language of her husband and her children, and she had made it hers. But always, in the darker corners, she placed mementos of her own, a proverb, a snatch of a rhyme, some light daily expressions the glimpse of which would startle her family. With nobody to speak her language to, she began talking with objects, the pots and pans, a creaking door, the sharp corner of a table. She never spoke it with animals because—and here, a foreign kind of pride sparked within her—it was never a language to waste on goats. Once, on a rare visit, her son came upon her in the living room, speaking in tongues with a teacup. He told her she was going mad. No, she sighed, you don't understand, this is what a conversation sounds like.

Would you like a cup of tea? the last speaker asks the ethnographers. They would. Let's have some tea and then I'll sing for you. She rises from her seat and waits as they shift their equipment, the light-stand and camera, the microphones, the attendant knots of wires. Brushing away their offers to assist her, she lights the stove with a match and stares out through the kitchen window. Poplars nod in the breeze over the mustard field. Someone's boy is loitering at the front gate, his hands in the pockets of his jeans. At each half step, his sneakers light up red. She thinks he must be here to look at the visitors, but she is wrong. He follows her movements with open and unblinking curiosity, as if there were something surprising about the way a kettle boils. She smiles: that's the matter with strange guests, they turn you into a stranger as well.

The tea warms her voice. When she sings, her eyes close and her chin, with its gentle down of hair, thrusts forward into the lamplight. The ethnographers cannot help but admire her strong set of teeth, a rare sight in so much of their fieldwork. They are used to thinking that there is half a relationship between dental health and endangered languages; languages, like people, become toothless. In her case, of course, a full mouth of teeth won't make any difference. She is the last, the very last. After her, the language has only a ghostly future. Its memory will haunt scholars and graduate students. Nobody misses it in the places where it was once spoken. Few even remember the time when its clambering rhythms united the valley and the uplands. Clinically speaking, it is already dead. A language cannot be alive if it exists alone in the mind of an old woman, no matter how fine her teeth.

The song is about a wedding. At the end of the festivities, the bride leads the groom out from the town, through the fields, and up the slope of a mountain. Where will it happen? the groom asks. The bride kisses him and beckons him to follow. He does. She allows him another kiss after a hundred steps, and another after another hundred, and so on until they can walk no further and are forced to start climbing. Perturbed, the groom grabs her wrist: why not here? She shakes her head and slips out of his grasp, removing a scarf and draping it over his shoulder. She hoists herself up the face of the mountain. The groom can see the stars shining through the black of her hair. As they climb, she leaves bits of clothing and jewellery for him to gather: bangles, her belt, a necklace, a vest, socks. When he reaches the top, he finds her naked and motionless. Only when he touches her does he realize that she has turned to stone.

The last speaker stops. She apologizes again. Our songs are sad songs. Nobody ever gets to have sex.

The ethnographers smile vaguely. Even the most capable among them can understand at most a handful of her words, an occasional phrase. The full meaning of the song awaits its patient digestion in a computer lab. For now, their responsibility is only to the collection of raw material and the husbanding of its source, a happy task. They are growing fond of the last speaker, softened by her unabashed, tuneless singing. Privately, they all feel the stirrings of great affection, the sort that civilians might call sympathy but they know to be truer still, the love of the student for the studied.

Can I sing it again? the last speaker asks. I would like to change the ending.

By all means, they say, whenever you are ready. The ethnographers, after all, are modern enough to know that nothing can be totally genuine. Traditions are invented to be reinvented. If the last speaker wants to sex up a folk song, so be it. In any case, it's the form of the words that matter, the syntax and structure of her speech. Everything else is just pleasant air.

This song departs entirely from the previous version, but the ethnographers cannot sense the fullness of the difference, nor can they tell that she is improvising fresh phrases. The bride eludes the groom and disappears from the wedding festivities. She journeys to the mountain. At its summit, she finds a rocket (here, the last speaker pauses to construct a suitable compound for the noun 'rocket', which she renders with verbal suffixes as 'fiery flight in void into void'). The bride enters and sets off up to the heavens. Everything recedes beneath her. The bride has never wanted to be a bride, but rather an astronaut ('swimmer among the stars'), and fair enough, why should brides be brides when they can be astronauts? In space, the astronaut dances between satellites ('invisible lightning moths') and befriends the moon. They drink wine and watch TV ('chaos of shadows in stillness') together. The sun grows jealous, since the moon is its bride. It asks mankind to fetch the astronaut back: why do you let her be up there? If your women become astronauts, who will be your brides? Mankind agrees: this is a worrying situation. The prime minister ('temporary rent-collector') is sent to the moon to reason with her. He sets up a table on the surface and waits for her to appear for negotiations. He waits and waits, not knowing that the moon has whisked the astronaut to its dark side. The vastness of space inspires only a deep tedium in him. But he has a mission to fulfil, so he remains seated on the surface of the moon, facing an empty chair, expecting a woman who will never come.

Look what I've done, the last speaker says after finishing, I'm such an old fool, I haven't changed the ending at all.

The ethnographers chuckle. There's no sex this time either?

Not a drop, she shakes her head, not a drop. She falls silent, her jowls sinking. The ethnographers think she must be tired—it is always a little unfair to bustle into the homes of lonely pensioners and force them to talk. Indeed, the last speaker is tired, but not from the physical exertion of speech. If anything, inventing within her language is invigorating. Why haven't I done this before? she wonders, why haven't I played with my language?

But another realization exhausts her: there is no simple direct way in her language to express the idea of a 'tractor'. Perhaps there was a time long ago, before she was born, when her language could tackle all concepts of the fields and towns, when it was savvy enough to run its world. In her life, it has only ever been in retreat. She grew up hearing it at home, in the living room and around the stoves and in the whispering dark of the bedroom she shared with her sisters. At school, they made her speak the common language. The teachers slapped her wrists if she ever misspoke and emitted the unwelcome sounds of her own tongue. As she grew older, the living room was overtaken by the radio, then the TV. She lost her bedroom and gained her husband's. The language survived a little while longer in the kitchen, nourished by the memory of food. Then her sisters passed away. For most of her life, funerals were the only occasions she would hear her language outside the home. Now there is no one else left to die.

When it comes time for her funeral, she will be remembered by common people, in common words, with common ideas.

One way to represent 'tractor', she thinks, could be 'making absence of presence', but surely that is a bit vague. 'Tilling with power of many men' seems too literal and inelegant for her liking. Piling on the suffixes to a verb, she settles on an image, 'smoke mowing through grass'. That might do for 'tractor', but this is an impossible task. She looks at all the equipment brought by the ethnographers. Her language has no natural way of referring to a camera, a microphone, a digital recorder. It has been in exile from this world, and so it is no longer of this world. She could come up with phrases for all of these objects, but what would be the point? No matter how innovative she is with her language, it does not have the force to take possession of an idea. In later years, they will say that her term 'swimmer among the stars' means 'astronaut'. They will never say that 'astronaut' means 'swimmer among the stars'.

Have you done this before? she asks the ethnographers. Have you listened to other old women sing?

Yes, they say, but none sing as magically as you.

You shouldn't flatter me. The ancient know their weaknesses better than anybody else.

When you are rested, we'd be happy to record more of your songs.

I don't need to rest. What do you do with these recordings? Where do they go? Who listens to them?

We'll take them to our university, the ethnographers say, we'll study them, we'll write about them, we'll archive them. We'll organize them such that all future generations can learn about you and your language.

It must get noisy over there, with all those voices of old people trying to make themselves heard. She laughs. She knows how computers work, how she can be skimmed into light, vanished into the whirring darkness of a hard drive. That's what will happen to me, she thinks, what a drab afterlife. Technology has so little romance.

She chooses instead to imagine a cavernous exhibition hall, its walls lined with screens. Old women and men stare out of each one, speaking their lonely languages in an unending loop. During the day, visitors come to marvel at the spectacle of so many lost tongues. Inevitably, they feel sad and perhaps light candles or leave flowers, as if they were at a mausoleum. The figures in the screens wait patiently for the visitors to leave. At night, after hours, they interrupt their own digitized soliloquies, listen to one another, and laugh at all the jokes.

Where is your university? she asks.

In our country, very far away from here.

She squints at them—though the creases around her eyes make it hard to tell when she is not squinting—and makes no attempt to veil her disappointment. Why didn't you take me there? It would be much easier. When you do this again, fetch the next old woman to your university. All of you wouldn't have had to go through this hassle or had to bring your van into our narrow streets. I would have got to see your country. Maybe I would have even recorded the way your people speak. Then, I could return home with your words and study you!

The ethnographers look at each other. In our work, they say a little hesitantly, it's best to talk to our informants in their native surroundings. In any case, we were worried about your health, we weren't sure if you would cope with the rigours of travel.

She straightens. I'm well aware that I'm on my way. It makes no difference to me where I die, in this chair, or on a plane, or in your university.

Why don't we let you rest for a bit? The ethnographers feel wretched for making her morose.

No, no, she waves them away. You're not tiring me. It's just...until you came, I never thought of my language as a burden, but that's what it is, isn't it? You want to take it from me so I no longer have to carry this weight.

It should not be just yours to bear.

Will you do me this favour? Whatever recordings you make of me speaking my language in the coming days, please put together a little package and have it played at my funeral ceremony.

The ethnographers melt a little. Their words seem to come through a mist. We can do that, they say.

I'm much obliged to you, she says, I'm very grateful that you have come here to see me and let me feel old in my language. She means it, too—to whom else can she pass this inheritance? Her children may have known a handful of words when they were young, but their mother's tongue was always too much of a responsibility. They shed what little of the language she gave them. Her son now farms in his wife's town on the other side of the valley, not far, but far away enough that he does not see his mother often. Her daughter was always the cleverer of the two, destined for the city and its indispensable comforts: air conditioning, good coffee, the admiring glances of strangers. Every month, her daughter sends her some money. They speak often on the phone, and their conversations are loving and repetitive as all loving conversations should be. She is proud that neither of her children are vulnerable to false nostalgia, that they find full satisfaction in the present of their lives. She would not have them bound to her relic. She would never wish that loneliness upon them.

In my language, she tells the ethnographers, words for gratitude are much different than in the common speech. We have many kinds. This, for instance, is used to express a very dark kind of gratitude, to be thankful for the loss of something. This means to be grateful despite yourself, with a hint of bitterness. This is used to describe a sudden, overwhelming feeling of gratitude. This is the feeling children have when they receive small treats, like sweets, or when they are lifted by an adult and spun and spun: a child's thanks.

The ethnographers take notes. Nobody ever compiled a complete grammar of the language, so part of their mission is to attempt to reconstruct the language in its fullness. They will never know that in her language there were more than a dozen ways of indicating and describing gratitude. Here are a few more: the gratitude of natural things for one another, like the hive for the branch, the tree for the bees, the cloud for the sun; collective gratitude, the thanks of a family or a town or a people; gratitude—directed to the cosmos—for superiority, for knowing that one is better than everybody else; the gratitude of one saved from death by starvation.

Her language boasted many verbs for which no simple equivalents exist in the common language. For example, this means to be afraid of seeing time pass. This means to tell bedtime stories in the depths of winter. This is the action of stirring a kind of gravy in a pot; this also denotes the motion of a pig rooting around in the mud. This refers to the way light splinters against a range of mountains at dusk. This describes in one word how mountains gain mass and shape at dawn. This means to feel strange in an unfamiliar place. This means to be patient for spring. As does this. And this.

If she remembered all or some of these words, the last speaker's testimony would be a little more elegant. Unfortunately, she doesn't remember them. Some she never knew in the first place. It's not her fault, no measure of her intelligence or sophistication. When the number of speakers of a language shrinks, so does the language itself. She grew up with an impoverished vocabulary, a skulking tongue, never with the means to recover those lost words. The ethnographers, despite their best efforts, won't be able to restore her language. How can anybody learn that which has never been written down, that which nobody knows any longer? It is sad, but sad in an unremarkable way. Humans always lose more history than they ever possess.

Speech, however, can be enriched, no matter its condition. When she cannot find the word she wants in her language, she builds compounds with the words she does have. Occasionally, she imports one from the common language. In this way she sketches her life for the ethnographers, narrates in her language the sequence of events and relationships that brought her to this chair before their camera and its severe lamp. Our father raised us in my mother's absence, which means that we raised ourselves, because he was away during the days, and often for many nights. My favourite thing to do in the summers was to wade into the irrigation channels and feel the chill of the mountain water on my ankles. I don't remember anything from my wedding night, you see, I got very drunk. Neither of my children likes eating cake, which is a real pity; life isn't complete without confectionery. The army installed solar ('fed by sun') street lamps—look, they just came on!—in the village so now it's never dark at night-time in the way our nights were once so totally dark. I miss that darkness, I miss angling lanterns and torches around corners. I only recently learned that I was the last. I had assumed there were others elsewhere, just not where I was, not here.

A neighbour interrupts the recording with a platter of pastries, a generous pretence with which to inspect the visitors. The ethnographers are ravenous. For a few moments, the sounds of grateful munching overwhelm all conversation. The neighbour studies the ethnographers and their equipment, and then, for a long while, her. How quickly something familiar becomes strange when it takes shape in another language. He makes his excuses and leaves. At the door, he passes the loitering boy, who is still poking about at the threshold. The last speaker beckons to the boy. Why don't you come in? The boy shakes his head, backs a few steps away, and stares.

It is getting late. Stray dogs growl in the dust. Bicycles rustle down paths. The most popular soap operas blare from the televisions in nearby houses where families assemble for dinner in the glow. My nurse will be coming soon, the last speaker reminds the ethnographers, and she will want to settle me for my bedtime. She won't be happy that I've strained myself like this.

Oh no! they protest. You should have allowed us to give you a break.

That's all right, I'm beginning to enjoy myself. It's coming back to me. Tomorrow, I hope I'll be able to tell you even more.

We'll return after breakfast. In fact, we'll return *with* breakfast.

How sweet, but don't go just yet. I'll sing you one more song today. Make certain your recorders are working, are they properly plugged in? Are you sure? I want an example of my singing played at my funeral, too.

Eager to please her, the ethnographers vigorously double-check all the controls and settings before signalling for her to begin. She sings, tuneless and a bit rasping, but a voice still captivating to men who have heard so many others.

On their wedding night, the bride and the groom retreat to the chamber prepared for them. He undresses and rushes to get under the covers. Awaiting her arrival in the pregnant darkness (a rough translation of one of many kinds of darkness in the last speaker's language), he realizes that he has not heard her talk at any point during the day. She must be shy, he thinks, she must be as nervous as I am about this moment. Is she? He feels her weight on the bed, her fingers now on his shoulder, her knee in the space between his knees. Her face looms above him, all light concentrated in the teeth. He moves to bring her mouth to his, but she pushes away and raises her torso, her hands firmly on his neck and chest, straddling him.

The last speaker stops. Thinking that she is done, the ethnographers start to commend her singing and to turn their thoughts towards dinner. She has not finished. Her eyes search the camera lens. She sings again, not quite song, more like an incantation, urgent in its rhythm, her feet tapping a measure on the floor. The ethnographers strain to discern the sequence in the flow of words. Weeks later, in the computer lab, they will discover that there is no order at all in this passage. It is merely a list of unconnected phrases, shards of speech, jagged and inscrutable, the debris of a language swept clean. But in the moment, in her living room, it rises in pitch and volume and dissolves the ethnographers' scholarly attention. They surrender to the unlikely beauty of it. She looks up when she finishes. Was the song racier this time? The ethnographers grin. Was there sex? She smiles, exhausted.

Her nurse enters and looks balefully upon the scene. I'm afraid your interviews are over for the day, the nurse says, it's time for me to take care of her. The ethnographers pack up their things. They linger at the door, watching the last speaker as she settles into an armchair, puts up her feet, and turns on the TV.

Until tomorrow, they say.

Until tomorrow, she replies, staring closely at the buttons on the remote. The ethnographers sputter away in their van. While the last speaker watches TV, her nurse does all the required nursely duties, checking blood pressure and temperature, feeding her the nightly quota of pills, talking to her about the antics of celebrities she only pretends to recognize. Restless, she eventually goes to the kitchen and insists on preparing dinner for both of them. What is the point of living if I can't exert myself? The nurse, who knows this routine well, protests and then acquiesces, expressing her earnest, simple gratitude. While the last speaker cooks, she sinks into the armchair and starts to channel surf on the TV.

The last speaker turns to the stove. The pots begin to murmur. She whispers in her language to a smattering of onions and garlic and greens and lentils: soon you'll become delicious and then, I'm afraid, I'm going to eat you...don't worry, there's much more of you where you came from. Through her kitchen window, the wheezing solar lamps cast a light gloom over the village. She is surprised to see a hunched form sitting on her courtyard wall. It is the boy from earlier. He's been here the entire time, she thinks. Whose son is he? At her gaze, he drops from the wall and runs down the village path, red flashes in the dark, leaving her wondering if there was ever a time when she knew his name.

MAKING

AISHWARYA SUBRAMANIAN

Months from now a god will casually touch a squirrel. A deceptively human gesture of thanks, his touch will burn through it and alter its very squirrelhood; searing the marks of his fingers on to the backs of all squirrels forever.

Mythili has been touched by a god. He has given her no ornaments, but has traced lines around her neck that glow like chains of gold, anklets for her feet, a line of light that sweeps up into her hair. He has drawn bracelets around her wrists (his hands gripping them tightly, thumb and forefinger just about meeting at the point where she can feel her pulse). These are the marks he has made deliberately but everywhere he has touched her she is radiant. His lightest touches have dappled her skin with brightness. Wherever she stands she will always look as she does now in this forest under these trees patterned with leaf and sun.

Yet it is she who looks at him. Her husband's long eyes are shaped like lotus petals. His skin is so much finer than her own that the blue tracery of his veins shows through. He is leaning against the wall of the shelter he coaxed the trees to form in this glade where it is always breezy and mild. When he hums to himself, tiny flowers spring up out of the earth in response. He smells of earth and herbs and the very trees yearn towards him, bending their heads closer to the ground to be as near him as possible. Mythili recognizes that feeling better than anybody.

They are being watched. Brother and sister hide in the bushes. When they leave, the grass where they stood is brown and dead.

∫

Meenakshi in her workshop crafts a body fit for a god. Limbs long and smooth, skin petal-soft. The feet are long and narrow, the hands small but with long nails. The hair is copper (they must stay true to their roots) and as it captures the light of the forges it glows. She cannot help but wonder what it will look like when the man in the forest has laid his light-giving hands upon it. Underneath the hair a perfect face—straight nose, wide mouth, lovely, fish-shaped eyes that slant. She lines the eyes with coal dust.

'It won't work,' her brother Vishravan sounds almost sorry.

She plays with the hair (her hair) and runs a finger down the lovely profile that will soon be hers.

'It will.'

His own workshop is as far away from hers as possible. Meenakshi can do a thousand things that he cannot. She can imitate the waxy texture of the surface of a leaf. She can make small birds that fly, look, and sound exactly like the real thing. Only Meenakshi could make herself a body fit for a god. If he asked her to, she could fill the city's gardens with trees and flowers and birds, make of it the place he dreamt of when he begged for ten years for a kingdom of his own. He does not ask.

Vishravan thinks too often about the frenzied sea turned white and the huge, pliant, living rope so strange under his hands. He has brooded for so long on that ancient story of a contract that was broken that sometimes he believes he was there himself. He knows how proud the Daityas were at being approached, how strange it was to be around these beings with whom they were now equals. The twinge of triumph at being needed, even if only to make up the numbers. And then, when it came time to divide the fruits of that great labour, finding out that the decision had been made without them. He doesn't remember how the gods looked at him, but he remembers that they lied.

They were promised nectar and given poison. It seeped into them and leached away what powers they had. They crept into the dark corners of the world (often forests, out of some perverse need for revenge) and nursed their wounds. Where they lived nothing would grow. Daityas turn the grass brown when they stand for too long in one place, and animals flee from them as if their breath is toxic. But they can still make things.

Meenakshi's greatest creations are the ones that look the most real. Vishravan will have no truck with the real. He will let her have her workshop but everything on the surface of the city he prayed for must look *made*.

He watches as Meenakshi leaves her workshop and brings back the broken body. Even now it is so lifelike that he can barely look at it. There is a gaping hole where the nose was; one ear still dangles on a tag of flesh and her skin is melted and corroded as if someone had thrown acid at her. His sister is shaken and hurt and also furious. As he comforts her he plays with her beautiful hair and notices how the light falls upon it. The god in the forest must have touched it. He prefers not to think about this.

⁂

Mythili's husband sits under a tree. When he returned from his hunting he wore smears of demon blood and an expression of distaste. Asked where he had been, all he would say was 'protecting you' before cleaning himself in the river and sitting down to meditate.

The low, rumbling note that comes from his throat is the oldest thing in the universe. Every living thing in the forest feels it stirring within them when they hear it. What must it be like to be at variance with that sound, as is the creature he has defended her against today? What must it be like to be forever, fundamentally discordant?

The thing the demon has built in his forge bears little resemblance to an actual deer. It is unashamedly fabricated (as if anyone could be taken in by a gold deer)—all polished gears and gleaming metals. But its gait is rather lovely and the bowing of its neck as graceful as that of any real animal. It is very beautiful.

'Capture it for me.'

Mythili has never ordered her husband to do anything before. She is prepared to argue her case (it is the most beautiful thing she's ever seen) but he is already off chasing it through the trees.

⁓

Her captor seems strangely uninterested in her. He is a huge man dressed entirely in bronze armour. She cannot see his face. She thinks that he must be blisteringly hot in there. He speaks to her just twice on the journey south, both apologies. Once for the kidnapping, and once for the 'barrenness' of his city. They arrive at night and all she can see of his home are the lights in the houses and the gleam of the domes.

Her servants (she has had none since her marriage) are automata, and her home is pink marble. She spends most of her time in the garden outside. There is no grass in Vishravan's city, but the ground is paved with coloured stones. There are trees of dead wood and dull iron, and the leaves and flowers (she will learn that they were made for her by her captor's wife) are tinted glass. The strange deer-like thing she saw in the forest is also here, though she doesn't ask how.

Of necessity she spends a lot of time in the palace. Everyone is wary of her, all but Vishravan's wife, Mandodari. From her she learns that her captor has many brothers (she never sees them while she's there and all that registers is that one is particularly pious and one particularly sleepy), and that the quiet, middle-aged lady who sits next to him on a throne is his sister, a widow and a clever craftswoman. She senses that Meenakshi avoids her on purpose, but even her new mentor doesn't know why.

She learns that this palace (a wonder in crystal and coloured stone) was made by her protector's father. In years to come he will make other celebrated palaces but this one, for his daughter, is his masterpiece.

So thoroughly has she been taken under Mandodari's wing that she is safer in this city than anywhere else in the world. They even hear a story about how her new protector dramatically stepped in to save her from rape by a besotted kidnapper.

In Vishravan's city, the physically strong are called upon to build. They make bridges and monuments and roads from strong blocks of grey and pink stone. The king himself works alongside them, carrying massive quantities of rock effortlessly. His sister is there too, as strong as he. Mythili has grown up among farmer kings and the first sight of the vast engineering works of Vishravan's city fills her with awe. The great turbines are constantly in motion on the shore. Water and steam power the city, and massive machines powered by systems of toothed wheels. She will learn that Vishravan has war machines as well.

Those who do not build apply their skills elsewhere. Mandodari is teaching Mythili how to weave cloth from the thin metallic wires that she herself draws from her forge. They are so thin as to be as soft and pliant as thread. Mythili learns to make elaborate pictures in the resulting cloth, and hangs her home with tapestries that gleam where the light touches them and make tiny chink-chink noises when the wind shifts them against the walls. As she becomes more proficient she weaves a cloth for herself in the rich copper of Meenakshi's beautiful hair.

She does not like the forges themselves. But the one time she enters Mandodari's workshop she does make something—a thick ring of pure gold. She presses her fingers into it to decorate it; the metal is still hot and it blisters her fingers but she is pleased with the result. Even when she learns (Mandodari laughs at her) that pure gold is so soft that she could have let it cool. She has had no ornaments since her marriage either.

She will give the gold ring to the first of her husband's ambassadors along with a message: 'Can he not rescue me himself?' By himself, for her, a personal act. Not some sort of cosmic war.

Word comes that her husband's army has reached the mainland shore.

Ridiculous to imagine that it is outraged pride that propelled the long chase southward. He is hardly a jealous local king. Yet, for some reason she has never quite understood, he must act out these petty human performances, as if he could not merely think different circumstances into existence. So he performs rage, and standing on the edge of a sea he could part with the mere flick of a hand, sends mortal creatures to do his work instead. A vanar is crushed to death when he strays into the path of a boulder that is being rolled into the sea. He reaches out a hand to stroke a passing squirrel whose only contribution to this huge enterprise is a handful of pebbles.

Everybody knows the war is coming.

It is while her husband and his motley army are throwing stones into the sea that Mandodari leads her into the forges for a second time. Around them everyone who can be spared from their regular duties has been drafted into making more weapons of iron and bronze; Mandodari is the only one to use gold. Mythili watches as her friend crafts first a necklace and then a thick belt of linked panels of gold.

'To remember us by,' she says, and Mythili realizes that she knows how this is going to end. This is the worst moment of all.

The belt is a story. She sees the birth of Vishravan in one panel, and she sees him praying for ten years for his city. And she learns what everyone in the city knows, no matter how hard Vishravan tries to escape it. And she learns that when he crouched in the bushes with his sister, he wasn't looking at her.

When the city catches fire, molten bronze flows through the cracks in the paving into the forges below. She does not know if her friend has escaped. On the day that she is to be tested Mythili arms herself in metals as an act of defiance. She wears the copper cloth that she wove for herself as a sari, and covers her head. She wears Mandodari's necklace and belt and covers her arms in bangles.

When she moves forward, the heat blisters her skin. She can feel molten copper and gold running down her arms and legs. The ground has begun to rumble even before she steps into the fire.

THE POWER TO FORGIVE

AVINUO KIRE

On bended knees, she riffled through pages of old documents and other papers, some of which would remain forever necessary and others which had long fulfilled their purpose. She had never been a particularly organized person. Marksheets, old Christmas and birthday cards, and various outdated church programmes were all jammed inside a single brown cardboard file with the words 'Government of Nagaland' on the cover. A piece of paper made a crackling sound of protest as she crumpled it into a ball and threw it towards the waste bin.

She was getting married soon. Sorting out her meagre belongings was the first phase of preparation for the new life she would soon embark upon. He had proposed a few nights ago and she had shyly accepted, as they both knew she would. She was twenty-eight and still retained youth's fresh-faced sweetness. He, on the other hand, was an unattractive man already well into his mid-forties, but she had no complaints. If anything, she was grateful that he had asked to marry her at all. She had long resigned herself to the likelihood that marriage was not to be part of her destiny. Therefore, it did not matter to her that he was unemployed or that he could seldom hold his liquor. He had asked her to be his and that excused all his weaknesses. A feeling of affection overcame her as she recalled his uncharacteristic solemnity while discussing plans for their impending nuptials. 'I shall ask my elder brother and grand-aunt to ask for your hand in marriage. You can tell your parents to expect a visit from my relatives this Saturday,' he had promised. To be treated so sensitively, as if she were as pure and untouched as any other sheltered young woman, moved her, endeared him to her. In the past she had been suspicious when other men had treated her similarly. 'Don't you know?' she would want to ask them.

Shaking free from her habit of ruminating endlessly, she gathered the papers together and tapped them against the floor to align them. As she did so, a newspaper clipping slipped from the pile and fell to the floor. FATHER FORGIVES MAN WHO RAPED DAUGHTER, read the headline in bold capital letters. 'In a supreme act of Christian forgiveness....' But she did not have to read the words, did not need to, she had felt their weight even before the clipping hit the smooth mud floor. She had been acutely aware of the clipping while sorting out her papers, and had been very careful to ignore it. Yet there it was, forcing her to confront once again a single devastating memory that clung to her entire past like an overpowering rotten smell, effectively erasing all else. It seemed to her that memory was partial to pain and loss. A torrent of emotions—the old familiar wave of anger, shame, and betrayal, a mind-numbing tornado of resentment that always left her with disastrous headaches—all these threatened to destroy her happy mood.

She picked up the tattered newspaper clipping with distaste and tucked it beneath the mattress on the bed. She no longer wanted to preserve it in her file. At the same time, she could not bring herself to destroy it. A thought struck her as she resisted her immediate impulse to consign the clipping to the waste bin. Perhaps it was quite natural for a person to form an attachment to anything—one simply had to live with it long enough.

⁂

It had happened sixteen years ago, when she was only twelve. Her rapist had been her paternal uncle. To this day, though other details had become vague with the passing of time, she distinctly remembered the nauseating smell of him—a mixture of sweat and a faint eggy sourness—and the wave of hot, heavy panting. She was alone in the house and her uncle had left hurriedly after committing the crime. He had murmured something to her before leaving but she could not remember what it was. A curious and kindly neighbour had come into their neat three-roomed bamboo house and found her curled up in a corner, dazed and crying. Upon the woman's concerned questioning, she had told her what had happened.

The little Naga village rose up in righteous rage when the incident came to light. The story was reported in the local newspapers and various organizations voiced their strong condemnation of the incident. Never had her little village received so much attention. She remembered her mother comforting her in the hospital while some police personnel recorded her statement. She also remembered a group of women from some women's rights organization who had come to visit her all the way from Kohima, the capital town. Her mother had described the horrific incident in dramatic detail to the visiting delegation, as though she had been a witness to everything. All this had happened a long time ago. There had been life before the incident and life after it as well. So it frustrated her that the incident alone often seemed to sum up the story of her existence.

Over the years, she had learned to accept what had happened to her. There were moments she even forgot—happy times while gathering water, or washing clothes beside the village river with other girls, when she imagined she was as carefree as any one of them. But such light-heartedness was always short-lived. 'People will think you have no shame!' her mother was always quick to remind her. Mother never failed to lament the stigma that had become attached to their family because of her; at the same time, she never encouraged anyone, her least of all, to put the incident behind them. She realized that Mother had changed irrevocably after the incident, maintaining a detached relationship with her own daughter, fearful that any intimacy would lead to unpleasant, hurtful emotional exchanges between them. Although nothing was ever said, she sometimes felt that her mother blamed her for what had happened. She sensed judgement in her mother's furtive glances, her pursed lips, her grimaces, her narrowed eyes. She thought no one understood the meaning of the silences between them better than her mother; in time, she too had learned that language well.

She would endlessly brood over the events that had unfolded that fateful day—should she have been more alert, more wary, fought harder? But above all, her most agonizing thought was whether life would have been simpler if she had kept that one day of her life a secret. She often wondered whether things would have been different had her mother discovered her first. Somehow, she believed she would have got over the violation of her body; found a way to bear her shame if it had all remained private. It only became intolerable when society 'shared' the shame.

She had been belatedly informed of her father's decision to forgive her uncle. It was a few weeks after the uproar had died down that her father came to her room and sat down beside her at the edge of her bed. He had said many things about forgiveness, justice, and family honour. He said so much in such a grave voice. But nothing had prepared her for what he announced at the end. He stood up slowly as he spoke, indicating to her that his speech was winding up. With an air of parental authority, her father had concluded: 'I have decided to forgive your uncle. But you need never worry about him; you will never see or hear from that man again.'

At his words, a strange and alien emotion stirred deep within her; feelings much too complicated for a child of twelve to grasp. Frustrated at being unable to express what she felt, she burst into helpless tears. Her father, a good but undemonstrative man, looked at her uneasily and said in a heavy voice, 'One day you will realize that this is the right thing to do. Hatred will only destroy us.' He said something about her uncle being in jail and also being excommunicated from their village. But, at that moment, nothing mattered more than her feeling of anger and resentment towards her own father as well as the unfamiliar emotion she had been unable to interpret. She did not realize then that the alien emotion she felt was betrayal. 'As if *he* had been the victim,' she would wonder aloud to herself many times in the years to come.

That night, she had an especially vivid nightmare. In her dream, her uncle's giant face seemed pressed to her and she could not escape. She tried to scream, but her voice died as the face of the enemy slowly morphed into her beloved father's worn features.

Sixteen years had passed since. Once a happy and cheerful child, she had now become withdrawn and reserved after the incident. She was still a dutiful daughter to her parents but it ended there. Her relationships with other people could be described as cordial at best. Though always polite, she was unable to forge close friendships. She had heard that her rapist uncle was now a free man. He had served seven years behind bars. Seven years in exchange for devastating her life. He had actually gone on to marry, have children, and was now living with his family in Dimapur district. She wondered bitterly who had married him. She often broke out in a cold sweat whenever she encountered anyone who resembled her uncle. Her biggest fear was the thought of meeting her uncle now, after all these years. This constant anxiety resulted in recurring nightmares. She knew it was illogical but she actually felt ashamed, even of what he might think of her—as if she had played a role in her own disgrace.

Except for the youngest, all her other siblings—three sisters and two brothers—had married and relocated elsewhere. She was not particularly close to any of them. The one person in the world she truly held dear was her youngest brother, Pele. He was the only one who saw her as she was; without sympathy or judgement, without the shadow of what had happened to her hanging over her head. It seemed incredible to her that her sixteen-year-old brother actually looked up to her as any sibling would to an older sister in normal circumstances, and she loved him all the more for it.

And now, here she was, finally getting married and about to move out of the house she thought she was destined to live out her life in. A wry smile touched her face as she realized that she was not much different from other women after all. Shifting required a sizeable amount of baggage, although in her case, the bulk of it remained unseen. It had become a part of her; she could not leave it behind.

'Your father will need a new suit,' her mother remarked. She looked at her mother, contentedly picking stones out of the rice while helping her make plans for the wedding. It had been a long time since she had seen her mother look so serene. She realized with sadness that she was not the only one who had changed. Her mother, once a warm and somewhat boisterous woman, had become timid and developed a pessimism about life; she was so unlike the fearless woman she had once been. Her mother, she decided, had developed three dominant personality traits—she was fierce towards her husband, long-suffering towards her children, and timorous towards society in general. A long time ago, she had witnessed her parents quarrelling after a visit to her paternal grandmother. Eavesdropping through bamboo walls, she gathered that her grandmother had blamed her mother for what had happened to her. 'You stood there without defending me while your mother accused me of being a bad mother! How dare she blame me for our daughter's...?' Her mother broke down before she could finish what she was saying. Her father had replied, 'You are overreacting! She does not blame you, how could she? All she said was that mothers should be careful not to leave young daughters unattended!' Her younger self had not wished to listen any more. She had put her hands over her ears and faked sleep until it finally came.

Mother poured the cleaned rice into an empty barrel, humming a soft lullaby while doing so. Her mother did not gossip. Perhaps she used to, but not any more: there was too much at stake. 'We each have our cross to bear,' was her mother's ambiguous response to everything and anything unsavoury she heard about anyone. She sometimes pitied her mother's naivety in hoping that by not judging others, she would escape being judged herself.

Her silent reverie was broken by her mother's quizzical glance.

'Girl! Where is your mind, did you hear what I just said? Your father will need a proper suit to walk you down the aisle.'

She braced herself; she had been prepared for this conversation.

'Yes, of course. Actually, I am planning to ask Pele to walk me down the aisle,' she replied tentatively.

'Nonsense! Your father should have that honour.'

'No, I want Pele to give me away, it's my wedding after all,' she said firmly.

Her mother gave her a pained look but did not argue. She simply said, 'Think about it, your father will be very hurt.'

She felt a savage satisfaction at Mother's words.

Her brother's reaction was predictable. 'Dear sister! Of course, I would be honoured, but don't you think it should be Father?'

'I'd rather you did it,' she insisted.

'It's your wedding,' he said.

She did not feel the same satisfaction at his reaction.

Traditional wisdom discouraged long engagements—delays gave rise to second thoughts and gossip. And so, a date was fixed quickly and before long the wedding preparations began in earnest. The villagers arrived in droves to help; different groups for different work. The menfolk came together to construct a makeshift bamboo pavilion for the reception, and later helped to butcher two cows and a pig for the wedding feast. The women arrived to decorate the reception area and helped with the cooking and cleaning. The villagers felt good about being kind and generous to her; she was their tragic child. As for the bride-to-be, for all her cynicism, she experienced a renewed faith in human goodness. She found it overwhelming that all the fuss and hectic preparations were for her benefit. Also, the strained relationship she'd had with her mother all these years had silently begun to heal of its own accord; the two women had never been as close as they were now. It was as if the prospect of her becoming a bride had finally released her mother from her unhappiness.

The brief period of her engagement was the happiest time in her life, so much so that she felt a sense of loss as the wedding date drew closer. The only thing that marred her happiness was the niggling unease that persisted whenever she thought of her father. He had calmly accepted that her brother would be walking her down the aisle but she knew he was disappointed. She knew that he was a good father, and in other circumstances she would have adored him. However aloof, he was an honest, hardworking man and provided for his family the best way he could. However, an invisible barrier had come up between father and daughter the night her father informed her of his decision. It was the last time they discussed what had happened. She had been angry and had resolutely avoided speaking to him the first few months, and he had let her be. After she entered adolescence, she became too ashamed to ever broach the painful topic. In vain she waited for him to take the initiative; considering her father's retiring nature now, she knew it had been foolish to expect that of him. So then, words that should have been spoken were bottled up instead, feeding the resentment within her. Denying her father his right to give her away was her manner of punishing him for taking away her right to forgive a crime committed against her. However, when she saw how calmly he had accepted her decision, she wondered whether he was all that affected by it. Had she managed to hurt him as deeply as he had her? It tormented her, this unfinished business. Finally, she resolved that she would tell him how she felt, how he had let her down. She would let it all out, only then would she find the peace that had constantly eluded her.

She found an opportunity to have it out with him the evening before her wedding. She had been sent home early to rest and prepare for her big day. Her mother, brother, and the rest of her married siblings who had arrived for the wedding with their respective families were still at the reception venue, making some final arrangements. She knew her father was alone at home. She carefully rehearsed her speech, the precise words she would say, and how she would begin. When she reached the house, she was so flustered and jittery that she lingered outside on the doorstep, willing her heart to slow down and stop beating so violently. She took a deep breath to steady her frazzled nerves. As she did so, a raw guttural sound from inside the house startled her. She quietly pushed opened the door and stepped inside. She heard unintelligible sounds broken by tormented sobs coming from inside her parents' bedroom. Her heart hammering against her chest, she looked inside the room. What she saw devastated her. Her father sat weeping awkwardly on a chair, his head in his hands, his prematurely greying hair in disarray; on the bed next to the chair was his new suit for her wedding and a rumpled copy of the church solemnization programme. She had never in her life seen her father show any strong emotion, let alone cry. It embarrassed and distressed her all at once. She was not sure what to do.

Her father was unaware of her presence, and so she quietly stepped back and retreated to her room. Feeling numb, she sat on her bed and tried to collect herself. She looked around the bare room, stripped of all its belongings but for three pieces of luggage neatly stacked beside her bed. All the worldly evidence of her twenty-eight years was packed inside those three pieces of luggage: a worn-out VIP suitcase, which had once belonged to her father, and two colourful bags. One she had owned for some time, and the other was a wedding gift from her parents. She made a mental checklist of the things she wanted to take to her new life. Her soon-to-be husband had revealed a surprisingly kind and thoughtful nature during their time together. Despite his shortcomings, she knew that he could make her happy if she allowed him to. Her thoughts turned towards the tragic figure a couple of rooms away. Instinct told her that she was the cause of his profound grief. She closed her eyes and her body trembled. She knew then what she must do. For the first time, she felt like doing what should have been done a long time ago. Her right hand reached under the mattress and pulled out the newspaper clipping, cosseted and kept for too long. For the first time, she felt no dread of the words staring back at her. She had allowed herself to play the victim for too long. It was now time to let go. She walked to the kitchen and threw the incriminating paper into the fireplace. She did not bother to look as the flames consumed it in seconds.

With every brisk, purposeful step she took, the carefully constructed wall around her heart began to break; each brick loosened and crumbled, one by one. Emboldened, and with a confidence she had never felt before, she pushed open the final door. Her stricken father looked up, and on seeing her, stood up clumsily. He faced her, all his defences down, a grown man unashamed about the tears and snot streaking his cheeks. It did not matter who closed the distance; they embraced and he kissed her forehead. That unadorned, loving act dispensed with the need for words or anything else.

Tomorrow would bring new challenges with it. Yet, somehow, she knew she was going to be all right. She even thought about the fear that had dogged her—the prospect of accidently running into her uncle. This possibility no longer filled her with dread. In fact, she hoped that she would meet him one day. She would hold her head high and look him in the eye so he would know that he had not 'ruined' her, that his evil had not tainted her. She revelled in the liberating absence of the bitterness that had long plagued her. For the first time since forever, she felt free.

THE DEVOURING SEA

AMAL

Translated from the Malayalam by A. J. Thomas

TAKING A LONG DRAG AT HIS CIGARETTE, ANDREWS CAST IT ASIDE AND looked impatiently into the darkness for signs of Ambrose's van. It was quarter past two in the morning. From where he sat on a rock, he could see his motorized boat, *Thomaasleehaa* or St Thomas, rocking gently on the small waves of the harbour. He eyed the boat with a kind of loving fondness. Andrews had purchased it from his former employer, Rappai Muthalaali, a wealthy man. The boat had been named *Saagarakanyaka* or The Maiden of the Sea, when he had acquired it; Andrews had converted 'her' into a 'him' by christening the vessel *Thomaasleehaa*. He had first begun to covet the boat when he had been driving it for Rappai. Over the years, he had grown so enamoured of the vessel that he was desperate to possess it despite having no money; he had taken loans from numerous friends and the Service Cooperative Bank and pleaded with Rappai to sell it to him. His employer had balked at the idea of a minion becoming the owner of a boat and rising in status to equal his own, but in the end he'd had no option but to sell, because in the long years Andrews had worked for him, he had been privy to many of the dark and unsavoury deeds Rappai had committed so he couldn't afford to alienate him. Still, being the lowlife that he was, Rappai tried to discourage Andrews from buying the boat by quoting an astronomical price for it. But Andrews wouldn't be denied. He had developed such an intimate bond with the vessel that he raised the money that was required and virtually flung it at Rappai, thinking as he did so, 'You are really mean, you wretched black money dealer, I am glad I am not like you.'

After the boat became his, and he had changed its name and gender, Andrews revelled in the joy of taking it out to sea, making it walk on water. But the occasional storms he encountered on his voyages were nothing compared to the storm of debt he had to overcome after he had purchased the boat. Its gigantic waves threatened to swallow the *Thomaasleehaa*. He had borrowed so much money to buy the vessel that the income generated from fishing alone could not repay what he owed to all his creditors. That was when the drunkard Lazar told him how he could make extra money, a lot of it, by transporting waste and garbage from various establishments in the town in his boat and illegally dumping it in the deep. It was a low-risk operation, and the money was welcome, but he felt guilty at the thought of polluting his beloved mother, the sea, even though he wasn't doing anything particularly unholy or illegal such as smuggling or human trafficking. When he voiced his discomfort, Lazar had laughed and said: 'There's nothing to worry about. Think of it as something you are doing for the betterment of this locality and its people. What you are doing is a virtuous act, elder!' And so it was that every second night, at a time when the sea and the light of the moon were fast asleep in each other's arms, Andrews's boat with its foul-smelling cargo would crawl across the sea without disturbing its sleep. He would get two hundred rupees per load. There were only six customers when he began, but their numbers had increased to ten, twelve, and now, fourteen.

There was still no sign of Ambrose or his tadpole-like van. Andrews picked up a bottle of liquor that he had planned to drink earlier that night, before he had been distracted by other things, and began swigging from it. A while later, he lay back on the sand and looked up at the face of the sky on which the stars were stuck like bindis and began counting them. He began to nod off. Just then Ambrose's ungainly looking vehicle came crawling along the sand, its headlights blinking on and off. Stopping next to where Andrews lay sprawled out on the sand, Ambrose got out of the vehicle and began shaking the boatman awake. Waking up with a start, Andrews yelled: 'Why are you so late? Who the hell do you think I am? If you think that I signed on for this so I could spend the night sleeping on the beach drenched in dew, then you had better look for other boats to do this job.'

'Not my fault, Syrang. When I was ready to move from the market with the cargo, I found two vehicles full of policemen blocking the way. We had to wait for them to move on before we could roll.' Andrews looked into the van; he could see it piled high with the reeking sacks of waste that he would have to get rid of. Ambrose wasn't finished. He said, 'And that wasn't all. When we took a shortcut around the Church of Our Lady of Lourdes we found even more police there.' Ambrose was so excited by the story he was telling that he was bobbing up and down like a Chakyar Koothu performer, his arms and legs flying about.

Ambrose continued melodramatically: 'O, my Syrang! In the middle of all this mayhem, that Lazar fellow who was supposed to be helping me downed two full bottles! Just as we finished loading the consignment that swine passed out. He lay on the ground as if he were dead; I left him behind the church.'

'O, my Jesus! What happened then?'

'What happened? The police had been lying in wait for some car thieves who had been coming down from Delhi to lift luxury cars. Somehow, I managed to give them the slip and drove into Peethaambaran's garage and lay low there. Only after the police had cleared off could I take a detour around the cemetery. And that's why I got delayed, struggling and taking a lot of trouble on the way, O, my Syrang!'

Andrews could see what Ambrose was leading up to; the fellow was going to bleed him of more than the agreed payment.

'For you this is a hugely profitable business, Syrang!' Ambrose said slyly. 'It looks like you might even have to take one more trip out to sea as the Honeymoon Residency hotel people are interested in getting rid of the loads of waste that pile up in their storage every day. They don't mind paying more.' Ambrose was jumping around in his excitement like children do when they have won a game they have been playing, 'Just say the word! We can turn millionaires in no time through this business with so many hoteliers around here!'

Andrews who was already in a bad mood because of the delay and the nerves that overcame him whenever he had to go out to sea on these illegal expeditions had been getting more and more angry and bothered as Ambrose had continued to babble on. Now he flew into a rage and knocked the delivery man down.

'Do you want to get me locked up, you son of a bitch? Haven't I told you a hundred times to do all this quietly, keep your mouth shut, and here you are, going around town, making a big noise about our operation.

'Once the cops get wind of this, that's the end. They catch you just for transporting garbage around town, imagine what they'll do if they found it on my boat to be taken out to sea to be dumped! Why don't you gulp everything down yourself, you avaricious pig...!'

As Andrews continued to abuse him, Ambrose staggered back to his feet, wiping the sand from his face, and yelled back: 'Don't play the saint, you hypocrite! You are the greedy bastard, doing roaring business with this filth.'

Andrews launched himself at Ambrose and the two men began grappling with each other. Just then the front door of the van opened and an apparition leapt out. Startled, Andrews broke free of Ambrose and retreated from this new threat. Ambrose burst out laughing and said: 'O, Syrang! This is our Claudia!'

Embarrassed now, Andrews tried to cover up his discomfiture and laughed. 'O, is it you, Claudi...? I thought it was some cop!'

'Ha! Why are you panicking like little kids? Don't you know that for me, Claudi, cops are nothing? Don't you also know that our Inspector Ananthan Sir has four restaurants in the city? Chicken Corners, no less. I will make him fall at your feet and beg you to take away a load of the chicken waste and help him out. Do you want me to do it?'

Andrews looked at her in astonishment. Claudia was the widow of Laban, the oarsman. Laban had been an alcoholic, always floating on a sea of liquor. Whenever he was drunk, which was pretty much all the time, he would grow mad at Claudia and begin abusing and beating her. He needed little or no provocation to get mad at her. He would drag her out of the miserable hut they lived in and beat her until she collapsed. During one particularly brutal beating, he started hitting her with an oar. One of her cheeks was torn open before she made her escape, weeping. That was the day the story changed.

Claudia's approach to Laban changed faster than the time it took for her torn-open and sewn-up cheek to heal. One day, the neighbours heard Laban wailing; they ignored his cries, it was something they had heard often. But, on this occasion, he was in real agony for Claudia had smashed his kneecap with an oar when he had tried to beat her up. When the vicar of the parish had tried to intervene, he was unceremoniously turfed out of the house by the furious Claudia. Enraged beyond belief, Laban had limped out of the hut, found an aruval, a machete, from somewhere, and returned to the hut, determined to hack his wife to death. But, stone drunk as he was, he was no match for his wife who bashed his head in with the oar that she hadn't let go off once that night. A fisherman returning from a night's fishing spotted Laban, dead and bloated like a sardine, floating on the waves and brought him ashore.

Following her arrest and time in prison, Claudia disappeared from the fishing village for about six years. When she returned, she dropped anchor at the seafront, surviving by doing odd jobs. Her cousin, Lazar the drunkard, who had first suggested that Andrews get involved with the illegal dumping of waste, introduced her to the boat owner and asked him to give her a job. She was taken on and had helped out on a couple of trips. And now here she was again, dressed in a checked lungi and full-sleeved shirt, her disfigured cheek visible in the dim light of the kerosene lamp. A large towel was wrapped around her head. Looking at the ropy muscles of her forearms that had smashed Laban's skull in, Andrews could only feel awe.

'O, Syrang, Lazar will raise his head only by tomorrow evening. So, I brought Claudi along. Boss, I will not send you to the deep sea all alone, so much is this Ambrose's love for you.' He snickered, brushing away some of the sand that was still stuck to his face. Andrews waited for him to demand more money, but Ambrose didn't say anything else and got to work, unloading the malodorous sacks from his van. The three of them began to feed them into the belly of the *Thomaasleehaa*, filling it up. The remaining sacks went on the deck. Ambrose and Andrews took a break but Claudia continued to work, taking the towel off her head and winding it tight over her nose and mouth to shut out the foul smell and taking great care not to let the putrid, sticky sacks touch her body. Finally, after dragging the last sack to the deck of the boat, the three of them dropped to the sand, panting with the effort of moving the fetid, noxious cargo. A foul-smelling fluid had leaked out from the sacks and the deck was covered with it.

'It's three in the morning, fellows,' Claudia said, and Andrews sat up quickly, it was time to get moving. Ambrose did not move. Remaining prone on the sand, he said: 'Launch the ship, O, captain! Let me slumber awhile, in the time you take to go and return.' Too exhausted to get up, he rolled over and over until he fetched up by one of the wheels of his van. He fell asleep.

Andrews and Claudia walked across to the boat. He could see her eyes shining in the moonlight. He thought about the day her cousin Lazar had told him that Claudia wanted to be employed as a deckhand on his boat.

For a handsome wage, of course. There was no way he could say no because he regarded Lazar as his saviour—without him he would not be making all this extra money and would have been sucked under by a whirlpool of debt. And that was how Claudia became a deckhand on Andrews's boat. And so here they were again, going out to the deep, clandestinely, while Lazar lay passed out behind the Church of Our Lady Lourdes.

There wasn't much for Claudia to do once the boat was loaded. All she had to do was cling to the boat's gunwale in rough seas so she wasn't washed overboard. When they reached the spot where the sacks were to be dumped, her job was to keep a lookout for fishing boats and dump the sacks one by one into the black water while Andrews steered the boat. As they approached the dumping spot, Andrews noticed Claudia had taken the towel she had wrapped around her nose and mouth and tied it around her head. As the boat puttered along on the gently heaving sea, Andrews was amazed to see a smile lift her disfigured cheek. This was the first sign of any emotion she had shown during the entire journey except once when she had vomited, with an expression of extreme haughtiness on her face. Noting him looking at her, she said, pointing to some ghostly phosphorescence on the waves, 'Don't know whether that's there because some white man's ship has just passed through here. If that's the case, we will be shot today.' Seeing that Andrews wasn't amused by her joke, which rose out of a recent incident in which some local fishermen had been shot dead by a couple of Italian navy men, she glared at him and said grumpily: 'Why are you so afraid? It's not as if we are smuggling gold biscuits!'

'Still....'

'What, still...?'

'That fellow Ambrose has told many people that we are doing this. Apparently, the Honeymoon Residency hotel people are prepared to give a full boatload....'

'Oh, that's great! You've struck it rich....'

'Forget it, Claudi! I am not going to do this job any more. Mother sea feeds me. The sea is my be-all and end-all. Should I do something like this to her? Is it right?'

He remembered Lazar mocking him when he had said something similar to him. He dismissed his contrite thoughts outright, 'The problem is that you know nothing of this world, O, Syrang!' Lazar continued. 'Not just here; it happens everywhere in the world. Do you think that people around the world eat their waste? White people are not like us. They are intelligent. They are the ones who eat the greatest number of chickens, goats, sheep, and pigs. Do they take all the waste that's generated by their consumption to the moon, and not to the sea? And the fish in the sea love to eat up this waste! Isn't that right, O, Syrang? What kind of a fisherman are you? Look! Don't you see that the sea is sooooo vast! We dump twelve sacks, the white men dump two thousand! Does the sea mind? No, not at all! Isn't the sea strong! Double strong!! You know, the sea is like fire. It will eat up almost anything...!'

Claudia looked at him curiously. 'Do you know what I was thinking the first time I travelled in the boat for such a long distance, sitting among these stinking sacks?' Without knowing how to respond to her, Andrews looked away from her to the hideous, oozing sacks piled high on the deck.

'I was thinking about jumping into the sea along with the sacks as I was throwing them overboard.'

Seeing that torn-up cheek trembling with emotion, the good-natured Andrews felt very sorry for her. But he found himself unable to think of a single thing to say to her. Fixing him with her gaze, Claudia continued: 'Just a single whack with the oar! I smashed his skull with a single blow. Weird are the ways in which humans act if you really think about it.... I remember thinking: what is the difference between the filth-filled sacks to be thrown into the sea and me? So, when those sacks went overboard, shouldn't I too have followed them?'

Andrews didn't know what to say. Irrationally, he started feeling afraid. He looked at her muscled arm, thought about it wielding an oar. Unwinding the towel from her head, and wiping her face with it, Claudia continued: 'There's only you and I here, all alone on these waters. Have you thought about what could happen now, Andrews?'

He felt his throat turning dry. What the hell was she going on about?

'Tell me....' she lisped coyly like a child.

He still couldn't bring himself to say anything. It was as though his tongue was crucified to his mouth.

'When you sit like this without uttering a word, terror-stricken, suspicious, looking at me as if I am another stinking sackful of filth, I think about many things so that I won't die of boredom. In one way, it was this shit-scared expression of yours that made me fantasize about those things. Do you want to hear about them?'

He nodded. Even in his fearful state, he didn't forget to take a sidelong glance at the sea to ascertain whether they had reached the spot where they could start dumping the waste.

Claudia continued: 'In the first fantasy the boat was caught in a tsunami. The storm was gigantic. The gargantuan waves hauled our boat up and hurled it down to the bottom of the sea. You and *Thomaasleehaa* sank like lead. But I noticed one of the sacks of garbage floating on the stormy sea. Without paying attention to the stench, I clung to it and was saved. I rode out the storm and somehow reached the shore. As they say in the scriptures, the sack worked like the stone the mason discarded, which eventually became the cornerstone of a mansion. On my first trip along with you and this filthy load, that was what I fantasized about....'

Has she gone completely crazy? Andrews thought. What did she think she was doing? But there was nothing to say, so he sat listening, the boat rocking on the surface of the deep, deep sea.

'On the next trip, you did not even look at me once. I turned into something more worthless than these filth-filled sacks that day. During my fantasy on that occasion, I wreaked vengeance on you in full measure. There came another cataclysmic tsunami. At that time, you were saved, clinging on to one of those sacks we brought to throw into the sea. But you were tossed hither and thither on the waves, clutching that stinking sack for days on end, without an iota of an idea as to where you were heading. You were feeling hellish agony from hunger and thirst. Sharks surrounded you, scaring the hell out of you, but they didn't attack you. Finally, driven mad by hunger, you bit open the sack, devoured the rotting entrails and skin, licking, chewing, chomping, guzzling up the putrid contents....'

Within Andrews's eyes, shipwrecks occurred and chaos ruled the waves. Claudia was laughing close-mouthed. 'At the same time, I swam and swam, and reached the shores of another land. The inhabitants were good-natured, but naive, tribespeople. Thinking that I was a deity of the sea, they honoured and worshipped me, offered me delicacies, and anointed me their princess....'

He began to summon to his mind Rappai Muthalaali, Lazar, Laban, Ambrose...and began to lash them with whips. His expression said it all, though he didn't utter a word. 'Are you done with your craziness? It's not for nothing that Laban beat you with an oar.... He should have split open not just your cheek....'

He switched off the engine and got up and began to walk towards her. From the experience of her several trips with him, Claudia realized that they had reached the spot at which they could begin dumping the cargo overboard. As he swayed across the heaving deck of the *Thomaasleehaa*, towards the heaps of stinking, oozing sacks, Claudia, a menacing frown on her face, stayed put, showing no sign of rising or beginning to dump the sacks, remaining like another one of them. She muttered to herself: 'You stinking Syrang! Years before you had even dreamed of slinking away at midnight into the sea in your motorboat with these sacks, this Claudi had come all alone in a rowboat out to the deep sea...in that sack was Laban whose skull she had spilt open with one blow.' Then, she twined the fingers of both hands together, and using them as a pillow, lay down supine on the sacks, and grimaced at Andrews who was standing over her musing to himself, 'Only I know what Rappai Muthalaali used to do to such women, bringing them out to the deep sea in this boat, while I was with him as his employee.'

Neither of them said a word to each other. The *Thomaasleehaa* rolled and skittered on the vastness of the sea. On its heaving deck, the silence of the dark blue sky had fallen between Claudia and Andrews.

THE SEARCH

DHEEBA NAZIR

Translated from the Kashmiri by Neerja Mattoo

DUSK WAS FALLING AS I ARRIVED AT THE SRTC STAND IN SRINAGAR. I WAS a stranger to the city. I saw an auto and asked its driver whether there was a hotel nearby. Asking me to get into his auto, he drove me to what was called the Jahangir Hotel.

I had two jobs to do in this city.

The next morning, I rose early. The hotel being in the middle of the city, the loud noise of traffic was inevitable. I lifted a corner of the curtain and looked out—big vehicles, a flyover, children in uniform being dragged along by their mothers carrying their satchels. I was reminded of my own childhood. Every day I used to....

I walked out of the hotel and asked a passer-by to guide me to a bus that would take me to the Safakadal and Habbakadal—that is where I was going. He pointed to a crossing in the distance, and said that was where I would find the right bus.

I found a seat on the bus. The passenger next to me was speaking on his mobile phone, telling somebody that he was going to 'downtown'... maybe it was the name of a locality in the city.

The conductor called out 'Safakadal' and I got down. There was a bridge in front of me. Crossing it, I looked over the side and thought it must be the Vyeth flowing underneath. 'Yes...it is the Vyeth,' I said aloud. 'What is it that you said?' a man dressed in a suit and tie was asking me. 'It is the Jhelum, my son,' he corrected me. I smiled and said, 'Jhelum it may be to you, but for us it is the Vyeth.'

I looked at the banks of the Vyeth, at the shrines and temples dotting them. My eyes travelled to other bridges on the river in the distance. I spotted a temple close by and a thought occurred to me—why not pay my obeisance to the deity? Maybe that will help me in accomplishing my job. After crossing the bridge, I turned right and kept walking. There was a house in front of me built of bricks with projecting balconies, a veritable mansion. There was a huge mulberry tree in the yard and I froze in my tracks staring at it. But the people living in that house now were different.

I found myself standing in front of the temple, bowed my head down, and suddenly felt like I had lost my bearings. Who was I? Where was I going? Nothing was familiar, everything had changed. Something seemed to push me along on my feet. Next to the temple stood another house, with gaping spaces in place of doors and windows, and a collapsed fencing wall.

A double door faced a veranda occupied by stray dogs. A huge walnut tree still stood in the compound. The dilapidated house seemed to tell its own story. Who had reduced it to this hollow shell I could not say, my tongue would not dare.

On my right were steps going down to the river. Perhaps the people used the boats moored alongside the banks to ferry themselves across. I saw more houses in ruins, some with broken doors and windows, others mere burnt-out shells covered in layers of grime and dust and festooned with cobwebs, the yards choked with weeds and nettles, the chinars and fruit trees in their compounds all struck by an unseasonal autumn. I stood, irresolute, having quite forgotten the purpose of my visit to this place. Where was I going? Where had I come from?

Suddenly, I recalled that it was Friday. She and I had also been born on a Friday. I had heard from my grandfather that Muslims make yellow rice on Fridays. At a turning, I saw a woman come out of her house with a platter of yellow rice. All the children around rushed to her, holding out their bowls. She beckoned me and I too went forward and took the yellow rice in my spread-out palms. It somewhat appeased my hunger. But I remained hungry, starving for everything in this place. I took a few more steps and found myself before a shrine of Sharifuddin Abdul Rehman alias Bulbul Shah. It also stood on the Vyeth riverbank.

It was as if these lanes, welcoming me with festive arches, had been waiting just for me all these long years. A small group of people, dressed in pherans, were sitting in a shop, smoking a hookah. Women walked by, their heads covered with long veils. Suddenly, a whiff of an aroma hit my nose. It was the smell of freshly baked unleavened bread from a baker's shop. Ah, the stacks of lavasas and girdas! I looked up and heard the cooing of pigeons perched on the wires of an electric pole. I stopped at every step, as though I wanted to drink in all the sights, relishing them with all my senses, everything that had been lost to us. Hence, the anguish in my heart.

Now, I was truly lost. What place was this, I wondered. Just then, I spotted a milkman's shop. I asked him what this locality was called. He answered this place was mockingly named 'downtown', but actually it was the Shehr-i-Khas. I recalled the words of that passenger on the bus. The milkman continued, 'You are standing at the door of Shah-i-Hamadan.' I looked ahead and saw the shrine before me. 'Where are you headed to, son?' he asked me. I replied that I wanted to go to Safakadal and Habbakadal, but seemed to have lost my way. He asked me not to worry and to take a seat in his shop and rest for a while. I took my seat and he placed a blob of thick yogurt from his pot on my palm. I was somewhat bewildered, but then thought, 'This must be a custom, perhaps.' He said, 'You are quite close to Habbakadal. Take this road in front of the shop and you will come to a crossroads. There you must go straight ahead and you will find yourself in Habbakadal.' I felt a wave of relief wash over me.

I took the road he had pointed me to and did reach Habbakadal. My father had told me that I should look out for a lane with a public water tap at its entrance and that the house to the left in that lane was once our home. I saw a house exactly where he had suggested. I moved forward but my legs turned to lead—I just could not walk any further. Somehow, I dragged myself towards it. The house had a double door in the front, with a large iron ring hanging from it. In the yard full of irises in bloom, there were a couple of pomegranate trees. The outer wall had fallen in and the windows hung loose on their hinges. The walls of the house closed in on me, to hold me in a deadly embrace. The din and clamour of my family as they fled this place, their home, in the middle of that fateful night, seemed to resound all around me. The house held out an appeal, 'Come back, all of you. Don't you see my plight? I totter, barely able to stand, hiding my face, as though ashamed of my existence.'

The veranda was made of divri stone. I saw my grandmother sitting on it, a pile of greens before her, picking out and discarding the yellowed leaves, preparing them for dinner. And there was my mother, holding me in her arms, singing a lullaby. And my brother hiding under the pomegranate tree, ignoring my grandmother's call. And Rahti calling out, peering over the wall, 'Tulsi! Is the cooking done?'

All of a sudden, I felt somebody's hand on my shoulder and came out of my reverie. A voice was asking me, 'Who are you? What are you looking for?' And I answered, 'I am Motilal's grandson—he was my mother's father.' His eyes filled with tears as he held out his arms and hugged me tight. 'The whole of Habbakadal has been bereft since you all left. It has not been the same....' Saying this, he took me home. He told his family that I was Sunil's son. They all crowded around me, some crying, others wanting to know everything about my family.

They brought salt tea for me, made rice flour rotis and saw to it that I ate at least two of them. They begged me to stay. I told them that I had to go to Safakadal. They insisted that I stay with them for a couple of days and then I could go wherever I wanted to. I said, 'I have seen what I had come to see. If I linger on and see more, I shall no longer be who I am.' Their son took out his scooter from the garage and asked me where exactly in Safakadal I had to go. I told him that it was a place known as Dyers' Lane. My mother had told me that it was the third house on the left. I stood before it and knocked at the door. A woman came out and I asked her, 'Does Masterji live here?'

'They left this place fourteen years ago. We are the owners of this house now,' she announced, and my hopes crumbled like a house of cards. She asked me to step inside, but I stood frozen in my tracks—where was I to look for her now?

I asked her whether they had left an address with her. She said if they had, she would certainly have given it to me. Then she asked what my purpose in looking for them was. I replied, 'I have a very strong connection with them.'

'What might that be?' she asked.

'It was the February of 1986 when a relationship was formed in ward number 12 of the Lal Ded Hospital. My mother's bed was number 201, while Masterji's wife occupied the adjacent bed, 202. My mother had just given birth to me and then fallen seriously ill. Masterji's wife had delivered a baby girl. My mother, because of her illness, could not suckle me, but, for two whole days, Masterji's wife fed me at her breast. I am told when a pen was put between the fingers according to the custom in our community, and a mantra was whispered in my ear, the same was done to her too, for my sister. She was born at half past eight in the evening while I had been born at two o'clock in the afternoon. Today, I am in desperate need of my sister. I am getting married next month. A sister's presence is essential at her brother's wedding. It is she who performs the ritual of welcoming the new bride and the ceremony is incomplete without her receiving the gifts due to her on the occasion. My blood yearns to meet my foster mother and sister.'

'Why did it take you so long to remember their existence? Did you think of them all these years...? Why didn't you come earlier?' she wanted to know.

'We have lost so much—our very identity is lost. Houses and mansions may be rebuilt, but the loss of one's near and dear ones is tough to bear. I do remember my sister, and miss her on every Raksha Bandhan day.... Whether she remembers me or not is something I do not know. But I do know that she will remember me, particularly on the day when they deck her hands with henna.'

My final words to her were, 'If you ever happen to see her, tell her that her brother is searching for her, and yearning to meet her.'

GUL

SHREYA ILA ANASUYA

for Saleem Kidwai

'A woman in the shape of a monster
a monster in the shape of a woman
the skies are full of them.'

—Adrienne Rich

THE HALLS OF THIS VAST HOUSE ARE WINDY. THERE ARE DOMED LAMPS and carpets woven to dizzying intricacy covering every inch of the floor. Honoured guests recline on bolsters, the scent of jasmine wafting on their expensive wrists, fragrant blossoms that are theirs for the taking. But take it from this old courtesan. There are unseen women everywhere, though you will not know them even if I tell you their true names. Step into the shadows, and there they are, filling the halls.

Women who knew how to arch an eyebrow or make a bawdy remark at just the right moment, or laugh wildly, just as they pleased. Expert musicians of their time, breathtaking poets, dancers who could put any master of yours to shame. I know these women, I knew them.

Of them, only very few survived the bloody tides of the Mutiny and its aftermath. The old order, in which they had had a place, perhaps sometimes a precarious and strange one, but a place nonetheless, collapsed entirely. Begum Hazrat Mahal's unending war ended. Lucknow fell and the pale ghosts who arrived to plunder this land bit down on its jugular. All our patrons and paramours scattered; many were hanged, many more exiled. That was the moment the axis of our world shifted—and precisely because it was pivotal and bloody, it is the moment they recount the most.

Lucknow of 1858.

But what is far more brutal is the slow passing of time—what the pale ghosts started, the good people of this land made sure to finish. People of high standing, wearing crisp cotton woven by hand, lovers of music and culture all—people who couldn't move a finger without walking on the backs of those who washed their fine clothes and scrubbed their inherited mansions clean. They wrung our necks; they smiled as they did it. Over the next few decades, those of us who would not, or could not, afford to hide our origins were pushed, pushed, pushed—whirling away from the centre of the mehfil to the corners, where most of us lingered, where our daughters linger, where their daughters will linger until the last one perishes.

Some of us survived it. Some through marriage, some by hiding our true names, some by becoming safe embodiments of the very world that had been destroyed. I, Munni Begum, survived by doing all of this. This is how you still hear my voice, echoing at you from the years that stretch between us. This is the plain truth—I am among a handful who were lucky.

And then there was Gulbadan.

She arrived one morning at Zeenat Bai's establishment. I was nineteen then, and had been performing for a few years. She wouldn't tell us where she came from, but that was par for the course for us. She was no girl, but time had not left its mark on her face in the way it criss-crosses most faces. It only became a kind of knowing that never left her eyes, even when her moon-face was twisted in peals of laughter.

She had exquisite, long fingers, and a perfectly straight back. She held her body with the ease and grace of a dancer. Her voice was low—honeyed when it needed to be and rumbling when the situation demanded, breaking and circling and echoing through our usual repertoire of songs that were either about love or worship, or often about both at the same time. Ghazal, thumri, qawwali—she could sing it all with ease, locking eyes with each person in the audience so that, for a moment, they felt like the only person in the world.

It was this quality that quickly made her one of the most feted tawaifs in Chowk. It was not simply that she was considered beautiful or that she could be perfectly charming; there was something else about Gul that made people of all kinds throw themselves in her path.

I saw nawabs blush when she winked at them during a performance, sigh when she seemed to consider them lovingly for a minute and then turn away, her eyes flashing like the diamond in her nose. In a matter of three months she was adding more to Zeenat Bai's coffers than could have been expected of any new entrant to the house.

There, I have told you the public version. It is no secret. Anyone who was alive then, and knew her, will tell you as much. That she was skilful. That she was magnetic. That she was a mistress of her arts.

But what nobody knows about her is that she was my Gul.

I was besotted with her. She could tilt her head at me and I would trace the arch of her eyebrows in my head for nights afterwards. She made me feel impossibly tender. If we were simply lounging together early in the evening, the sound of her smoke-filled voice would have me tracing circles on my thigh.

She knew it, of course, though she feigned not knowing at first. I could not have hidden it from her for all my trying. I tried hard, embarrassed at the force of my own passion, confused by the heavy presence of her in my breath, in all my days. She had reached out and taken my heart in her fist, simply, easily, just by standing before me one morning.

I suppose I should not have been surprised that she crushed it just as easily when she fled in the suffocating days following the end of the

Mutiny. This is after she had lifted my chin one evening in the middle of me reciting a foolish ghazal I had written in her honour and made my heart leap to my throat when she kissed me softly. I could not believe she loved me back, and never fully trusted that she did, although she insisted as much to me in hushed whispers when we awoke entwined some mornings, or by way of thrilling notes that she passed to me even as we hurried to change our finery in the middle of crowded performances.

Her love was lush, it is true, but it was entirely on her terms.

She chose the nights I could spend in her chambers, and this I did not mind. What I did mind was the way she dismissed our relationship in front of the other girls in the house. This was by no means the first time in Zeenat Bai's house that two women had fallen in love. But because of Gul's magnetism, her popularity, the way so many of the men who came to our salons were as besotted with her as I, the household's acceptance of our relationship was hesitant. About this she did absolutely nothing; there was no sign in front of them of the ardour she displayed when we were alone together.

She remained icily silent when my eyes filled with tears if she took a lover from among our patrons. But when I tried to rebel by taking up with Samina, my age-mate and equal in the household, Gul's retaliation was swift and unforgiving. Her anger was always reserved solely for me, and only behind the closed doors of her room. There she became something else, my moon-faced Gul, when she showed her teeth to me in a way that had nothing to do with smiling. The dark spot high on one bronzed cheek, her eyes the colour of burning coal, her waist-length raven hair, her full, dark lips—all this seemed to melt away in that moment, and the enchantment of her face turned fiercer, wilder. I was in love with her; I was terrified of her. Fear and love became locked in a fierce embrace, and fed each other like air feeds fire.

But then a different, more menacing fear gripped our entire household. The pale ghosts introduced a rifle that used ammunition encased in paper greased with the fat of both cows and pigs. In order to load their rifles before firing, Indian soldiers would need to tear open the cartridges with their teeth. An entire regiment refused to do so and was punished mercilessly for disobeying. That is when, you can say, our troubles began, for many of the plans for the long months of rebellion that followed were hatched in our very salons.

Those months were subdued; the air itself felt oppressive. We had fewer performances, and when we did, the mehfils were not as joyful as they had once been. With more time on our hands, Gul and I started shopping for the household ourselves. Sometimes we took Zeenat Bai's only son, Karim, with us to help us haul our bags home. Karim's birth, unlike his sisters', had not been celebrated, nor had he been as extensively educated as them, so he earned his keep by running errands for the house and making sure our books were kept in order.

On the day before I was to turn twenty, Gul insisted she wanted to make me some kheer, and we went to buy the ingredients—thick, fresh milk, fragrant saffron, and raisins. Karim came along and the three of us were in good humour after what felt like aeons. Gul was wearing a simple embroidered kurta of white, and as usual her diamond pin flashed on her face. To this day when I think of her, it is this image of this Gul that comes to me—fresh-faced, light, laughing easily.

Perhaps this was the final moment of my innocence, the final blossoming of the years in which I had spent so much time immersed in reading and writing, understanding music and dance, learning how to converse and compose. It was a light that a darkening world cannot bear, especially on the faces of women, especially on the faces of women such as I. Perhaps someone cast an evil eye upon us. Perhaps I was too happy, despite the fact that things were crumbling around us, and I had no right to be. Perhaps I loved her too much.

For at that very next moment Gul caught the eye of a Lal Kurti. The officer stopped us with a glint in his eye, which travelled to his mouth and became a smirk as he looked long and lasciviously at Gul. My blood curdled. I wanted to tear his eyes off her and I was about to say something. She knew me so well that she sensed it and put a steadying hand on me. Karim, beside me, seemed struck silent with fear. I had never felt so humiliated.

Then he spoke, in the kind of accent we had mocked hundreds of times. 'How much for a turn with you, girl?'

I started forward, but Gul pushed me back. I whirled to look at her. In the entire year I had spent with her, I had never seen the kind of cold fury that washed over her face then.

'What did you say to me?' She spoke in a voice I did not know. It boomed with the power of a thousand more, echoes within echoes. My stomach felt cold as ice. For a few seconds, the market seemed to cease its jostling around us. Then, as suddenly as it had seemed to be sucked out of the world, the clamour came back. I saw the soldier's face tighten, but he didn't seem to be startled, like I was. 'Don't waste my time, girl. I know you are one of those nautch girls. Don't make me haul you off.'

She had arranged her face into a too-radiant smile. I knew this face well, she used it with particularly cloying patrons, who wanted to hang around too long after the mehfil was officially over. 'Come with me, sahib, my rooms are just around the corner.'

I stared at her, but they were off already. I watched them for a few seconds before I ran after them. She glanced back and shot me a look. *Stand back*, it said. *I know what I am doing.*

When she emerged from the alley she had led him into a mere handful of minutes later, it was by herself. She refused to say a word to me all the way home, while I cried silent tears of rage and confusion. The fear had returned, so intense I was virtually incapacitated, though she said nothing, and scarcely even looked at me—and it was here to stay, for the next morning she had disappeared.

We had spent the night together, but she had said she would much rather speak the next morning. I usually awoke if she did, but that night I had felt unusually laden with sleep—when we finally slept—and did not stir. When I woke up to the first rays of the sun filtering through her gauze curtains, I noticed that I was alone. The cream bed sheets—usually tied in place—were rumpled, her satin-wrapped pillow abandoned. I thought she had gone to wash her face, and stretched while I waited for her, anxious to discuss what had passed the day before.

Some strands of her impossibly thick hair lay scattered upon her lightly embroidered pillow. They made me think of our love-making the night before, how forceful we both had been, different from the languorous nights I had come to expect from our time together, nights I savoured. But the night before had left a tight knot of desire in me still, I wanted more of her—and the unanswered questions from the market only made me more restless. As the light outside intensified, I grew more and more nervous, and still she did not return.

By midday, the household began to hum with questions. By then, I had searched everywhere, every room, every balcony, every terrace. I had run out of the gates, madly, tears streaming down my face, and Zeenat Bai had to restrain me. I had punched Karim when he tried to placate me, and I had refused to stop screaming her name until they shut me up in her room. They did not do it unkindly, nor was I left alone—Samina was there with me, but nothing would console me.

I was sure she was in danger. Perhaps the soldier had returned under cover of night and taken her. Perhaps even now she lay dead in an alley somewhere. My moon-faced Gul would never have left me on purpose, I knew. She had been taken, and had I been allowed to leave the house I would have scoured the city for her, looked in every street and corner until I found her and brought her back to me.

And then, in the afternoon, just as I had fallen into an exhausted stupor, the doors of her rooms were flung open and I came face to face with three Lal Kurtis. 'Where is she? Gulbadan?'

Before they could stop me I ran out to the main halls, where more Lal Kurtis were stationed. Zeenat Bai was sitting on the floor, coolly gurgling at her hookah. The man Plowden, their captain and our sometime patron, was questioning her. Strange to see him here after so many months—he had attended many of our mujras and his wife, Lucy, had had a special fondness for Gul. She had even asked Gul for lessons. Zeenat Bai wore a tight smile on her face. 'I do not know where she is, sahib, she has abandoned the hearth that fed her for a year. She is as faithless as a wildcat.' Zeenat Bai was nothing if not astute. I knew that most of her valuables and our money had already been spirited away, just enough remained in the house that they could take. I was hopeful then, thinking she herself had stowed Gul away somewhere. But in a second, she said something that dashed my hopes. 'And I'm well rid of her, for I will have no murderer in my house.'

I shrieked then, and she started. 'Shut up, you foolish, lovesick girl. Your precious Gul seems to have killed a soldier that she was seen talking to in the market yesterday. They found him in an alley this morning, not a single mark on him, dead as a block of wood. Lord knows in what dark arts she dealt, to be able to do this.... She has left all of us here to rot, you included. Pull yourself together, or get out of my sight.'

I do not know how I spent the next weeks, months, year. At first I refused to perform, and they let me be. I kept vigil by her windows, by sunlight, moonlight, and candlelight. I scarcely ate or slept. I cried until the tears ran dry, and when I could no longer cry I read poetry she had written through swollen eyes. In my head I heard her sing, a monsoon dadra about dark clouds gathering, a woman tormented by the absence of her lover. I felt myself floating out of my body, and from my vantage point near the ceiling I saw the thing I had become: hollow-eyed, my hair unwashed and in knots, my lips dry. I had become the absence of Gul.

After a few months, Zeenat Bai herself started coming to feed me. She called the munshi to read me poetry, she dragged me to see the other girls rehearse for mehfils. Soon, she began pestering me to sing again, lamenting, screaming that all that education had been wasted on me, that I was not the first girl to be betrayed by a lover, that my name would forever be lost if I did not come to my senses.

I had begun to feel other sensations slowly, and this included a considerable degree of guilt, for I had contributed nothing to the household income for over six months. I began to sing again, though I still could not bring myself to dance. I sang with lowered eyes. But my voice, when it emerged again after a few days of careful riyaz, surprised me. I had been a competent enough singer before, my training substantial enough and my delight in poetry genuine, so that I could sing convincingly. This voice, though, was different—richer, deeper, unwavering, and immense, as though it was coming from somewhere else. Had I always had this ability and, obsessed with my love for Gul, never noticed it? Or had she, by leaving me—for I knew by then that she had deliberately left me—made me into the singer I had become? I do not know, except that now when I sang about longing I felt it in my bones, when I sang about the fecklessness of a lover I understood the words, and the bylanes and alleyways of the music itself, like I never had before. Betrayal had enriched my voice, and anger, when it gathered, fuelled my riyaz, so that I began to sing more and more, better and better, each raag I learned and each thumri I mastered an answer to Gul's desertion.

And that is the voice you now know, if you know your music. The voice that took me in the decades of my life that followed to the Delhi Durbar to sing before King George, the voice by which I made a fortune for myself, setting up my own establishment at the passing of Zeenat Bai, and eventually buying property all over the city even as many of the women I had grown up surrounded by faded into obscurity. As they retreated to the shadows, pursued by lectures on morality and demonized as being unclean, I took my spot in the light. Yet, even as I prospered, my heart crumbled.

I met and married a devastatingly beautiful businessman, Irfan Ali Khan, and became Munni Begum. His family disdained me, and threatened to disown him. For a time, I was forced to give up music, but through that time he loved me truly, and could not bear to see me with my face tightened in agony as I watched others, always others, perform. Much quarrelling and cajoling later, his family decided that I could sing anywhere in the country, as long as I sang nowhere I could sully their good name. And so I took off to Banaras, to Rampur, to Calcutta, with Karim acting as my manager, and a handful of young pupils in tow.

It is not that I did not love again. I was very fond of my husband, I enjoyed his gentleness, his fine mind. I liked making love to him. But I never loved him like I had loved Gul, and if our partnership lacked the inconsistency and ultimate cruelty of the one I had shared with her, it also never matched its life-giving fire. Now, what set my pulse dancing was singing, and teaching the young girls whose training I had been entrusted with. To them I was everything, they called me their mother, and followed me where I went. The older ones, in some years, started accompanying me onstage.

Eventually, long after my body died, they would be celebrated, honours conferred upon them by famous men. But even as their greatness would be lauded, they would always be known as pupils of the great Munni Begum. Some would write books about their years with me, and one or two would sing forever like me, never finding that precious and irreplaceable thing—the power of their own voices. The more successful ones would train many pupils of their own, and one would start a school in my name, established in my honour. For I would become what only a handful of humans become through what they leave in their wake—immortal.

But you've read this script. Greatness, true greatness, is only conferred upon the crone. As maiden and grown woman, whispers followed me, and even as my career arced upward like a meteor, it would be years before my considerable donations to the freedom movement would even be acknowledged. I was old when they came to love me simply for my music, for by that time my origins and my story became two different things.

In one's sixth decade, it is difficult to stay angry. What fire I had in my belly I reserved for music, for the push and pull of the taan, for the trick and love affair of singing two exquisite lines of poetry in three different and expansive ways. I had outlived my husband by ten years already, and had immersed myself in caring for my pupils. Still, what artist with some ambition remaining can resist the lure of the capital? Younger women than I were thronging to Calcutta, playing parts on the stage at the big theatres—Star, Minerva, Classic. Some of them had been dancers, some could sing.

The capital called to me, the same pale ghosts who had so tormented us during the Mutiny were soliciting women of my talents to sing for a new contraption that had been created, for which a man called Gaisberg was meeting with gaanewalis both young and experienced.

It was called the gramophone player, a golden creature with a gaping flower for a head and a box at its tail. This is how you sang for it—you not only had to scream into the blasted cylinder that snatched at your voice, you had to hurry it up. A lingering thumri would not do—you had to squeeze the song, with all of its pathos and play, into less than one-third of the time you would otherwise have had with it. And, when you were done, you had to tell the machine your name, or they would not know who on earth you were.

We had taken some rooms in the Great Eastern Hotel, and it was there that Gaisberg had set up his little studio. Every day I spied the young girls going in and emerging. Gaisberg's assistant, a reedy Bengali man named Sen, had approached us—but even though we were there, Karim remained sceptical.

'I don't know, Muniya...I have heard some strange things about this machine.... Let's wait and see,' he told me.

'Like what? Don't tell me this is like that time those men came to photograph me?' I teased. All these years of working and living with me, and my poor Karim was still so naive! It went back to our upbringing—so differently were we brought up in the same house and by the same woman. My affection for him strengthened rather than waned because of this.

'Muniya, I am serious. Someone from Janki Bai's party told me that the machine...it traps bits of your soul into it every time it catches your voice. It may be best to stay away.' I began to laugh and he knew he had already lost the fight. After this, I decided to not push the gramophone issue too much with him; I knew I could make him come around in a few days. I could do what I pleased, but he was my oldest friend, and I did not like to frighten him.

The Bengalee had a review of a show in town, played by a tremendous new actress called Elokeshi. Zoha, my oldest pupil, had cajoled Karim to take us to the Star that evening to see her play Janabai.

The theatre that evening was absolutely packed. I had dressed in one of my favourite saris, and put my hair up carefully into a bun, but in the quiet hush of the theatre just before the show, everyone's eyes, including my own, were turned towards the stage. I heard the soft creak of one of the doors being opened and turned around in some irritation. I should not have paid it much mind but something kept my eyes on the figure that slid quietly inside. She was simply dressed, almost nondescript, but when she passed me, I recognized her with a start, with a pain in my heart that is impossible to capture in words.

The only person I had known my entire life who could have captured it with her song was now looking directly at me, as surely as she had looked at me when I was only nineteen: Gulbadan.

And she looked exactly as she did then—how was this possible? And how was it possible that no one else noticed her, not even Karim, seated beside me? As though she was putting on a private performance meant only for me, the woman I had known as Gulbadan transformed before my very eyes. Her limbs looked somehow more supple, her hair grew longer and more lustrous, her face suddenly—terrifyingly—sharper. Her clothes changed, became a mendicant's, her forehead suddenly marked with a little ash. And, almost as though she had always been there, she was onstage, and everyone around me broke into applause.

That evening Gul—Elokeshi—gave the best performance I had seen her give. It would be a surprise if audiences forever after did not call her Jana. There was a standing ovation at the end, and she was called back onstage by the audience's cheers. She returned, bowed, disappeared.

My heart hammering, I turned to Karim, who had not recognized her at all. How could he? He had only been allowed to see her terrible beauty, the face of Elokeshi.

I did not say a word to him. I spent the night awake as I had once lain awake thinking about her after she had left decades before. But now I began to see how she could have been so clairvoyant. Her little tricks. Her great skills. Her overwhelming fame. Her ability to slip away at will. Her face, teeth bared, monstrous in anger.

She was not just a keeper of lore. She was part of its very fabric.

The next day I told Karim I had an evening appointment with Gaisberg and went back to the theatre. I watched her again. I was certain she knew I was there. And, acting upon my certainty, I went backstage. I told an attendant to let her know Muniya was here to see her. In a matter of minutes, I was inside her dressing room.

Her hair was long, loose. Her moon-face full, not a day older than she had looked when I was so much younger. Her eyebrows arched darkly on her forehead. She smiled; her face shifted, she made herself, again, the Gul of old.

'How are you, my love?' She was smiling as she once had, in the way that had wrenched my heart when I first met her...a way that she knew, I could see, still worked.

'Gul.'

'I owe you an apology, my darling, and an explanation. But I am afraid I am only able to give you one of these things. Please accept my sincerest apologies. I should not have left you like that.' She was calm, perfectly calm, calm in a way that frightened me even more.

'What I saw last night...that was you? What were you doing? What....'

'What am I? Only cloud and water, my love. I am Elokeshi on the

Bengali stage. I was Mah Laqa in Hyderabad, and a long time ago, I was called Amrapali. In the coming years I will have more names and faces. The calamities are not over for our kind, my darling one. I am so glad you made a name for yourself. It will carry you far.'

'I have so much to ask you. So much to tell. Come with me, spend some time with me.'

'I wish I could have stayed, Muniya....'

I knew then she meant to leave me again. For the first time in many years, I felt an old resentment swell up inside me.

'Why do you do this?' I asked. 'Play with a little human life?'

She turned to me then, eyes flashing. If she was capable of being hurt, I had managed to hurt her. I felt a tiny whiff of satisfaction. 'I never played with you. Never. It gets exhausting, watching people die. It is better to go when you get too close.... My love, it was good to see you again.'

With that, she opened the dressing room door, and was almost borne away by the crowd that thronged outside. It called her name, 'Elokeshi!', and wanted to swallow her up. She paused, turned. Her face was different again—tinged with softness. I saw an old fire in her eyes, older than me, older than time, a fire at which I had warmed myself in the time we had had together, and without knowing it, for years after.

We looked at one another for a long moment. Then she spoke again, this time with a new urgency. 'Listen, there is something called the gramophone now, it can copy your beautiful voice for people in another time. You must record as soon as you can.'

What was this? I could not fathom why she wanted to now focus on something so inconsequential. 'I intend to, Karim doesn't trust the machine, says he hears strange things about it.'

'What, that it captures a little bit of your soul and keeps it trapped inside it forever?' She laughed then, the same wolfish laugh that undid me as though I were still a waif of nineteen, the same fear gripping my insides as though it had never gone away. 'It's true, my love. It's all true. And that is why you must do it. Do it.' She opened the door, stepped away.

I stood there alone, blinking in the sudden light.

∽

BOMBAY, 1995

Amol is hooked, he can't help it. He's at Sagar Bar every night with his buddies, after a day of running around collecting dues for their bosses, occasionally beating up the shopkeepers and business owners who won't pay up. The work is exciting and the money is easy, and how better to spend it than see moon-faced Rosy every night?

Raju and Guru are in the mood to heckle him tonight. 'What, took your girl to Apsara Theatre again yesterday? What were you doing? Watching the picture, or something else?'

Bastards. They love their dancers too. Raju is even seeing one of the girls, Meena. Besides, Rosy doesn't let him touch her. He doesn't much care. Being with her every evening—being the man who gets to do that—this is somehow enough. He isn't used to this...this feeling. Is this what all the film songs are about?

Just look at her. The most famous dancer in the joint, men throw thousands and thousands of rupees at her in the course of one night. And why shouldn't they? Look at her whirling, her skirts aglow, the silver moons embroidered on them gleaming. She is dancing to an old ghazal, something about thousands of men driven mad by her eyes. When she dances like that, when she smiles like that and looks at him, he feels like the only man in the room.

Afterwards, he is impatient to go home. She is not one to be pushed, so he waits—what else is he going to do? He watches even as Raju and Guru leave with their girlfriends. Finally, she emerges, dressed in a simple white kurta.

'Rosy jaan, I've got something for you. Come, let's go to your rooms, na.'

She is indulgent today. The season's first rains have begun. She had once told him the monsoon was her favourite season.

In her rooms with the gauzy curtains and the old-fashioned lamps he proudly pulls the disc out of a slim bag. It has the flat, round face of an old singer on it—it looks impossibly old, like it belongs to a different world. '*Munni Begum—Classic Hits*! See, huh?' He is delighted, nervous. He doesn't quite understand this music himself, but he knows she likes it.

The rain starts to fall gently outside, and inside they let the little needle fall on the black disc which turns and turns. The song is about dark clouds gathering, a woman looking for her lover. Rosy closes her eyes and throws her head back. He feels a rush of love overcome him. When she opens her dark eyes he thinks he can see pinpricks of tears in them. She smiles. 'It's gorgeous,' she whispers.

In the flickering light, the diamond in her nose glints, and you could be forgiven for thinking that her face changes ever so slightly.

THE ACCOUNTS OFFICER'S WIFE

LAKSHMIKANTH K. AYYAGARI

MANY YEARS AGO, IN A VILLAGE CALLED UTTARAPURAM, THERE WAS A Brahmin settlement. Houses with red potsherd roofs, common walls, and wide verandas stretched for about half a kilometre. At one end stood a peepul tree, and at the other a wall, with red and white stripes, enclosing a temple dedicated to Sri Venkateswara Swamy. Dhanalakshmi came here after her marriage to Kutumba Rao. She was sixteen. She had spent most of her childhood skipping stones across the pond and chasing puppies in the coconut plantations. Her education comprised a few poems her mother taught her, and she sang them aloud as she walked along the goat trail by the pond, stopping wherever she found a pebble promising enough to trump nine bounces, her unbeaten record.

One day, her father announced that she would marry Kutumba Rao, the accounts officer from Uttarapuram, and she didn't quite understand what it meant. Leaving her mother and her village, and moving to Uttarapuram with Kutumba Rao, was too much to wrap her head around at once. Her mother-in-law, Ramayamma, was a stout woman, five feet tall, with a large face and probing eyes. She wore a spot of dense vermilion between her thick eyebrows, which Dhanalakshmi found unsettling. Ramayamma had waited a long time for a daughter-in-law; when she got one, she declared that she would relinquish her responsibilities and dedicate the rest of her life to serve her gods: her husband and Sri Venkateswara Swamy.

Dhanalakshmi's lessons began from her first day at Uttarapuram. Ramayamma expounded the ways of a married woman, both as a daughter-in-law, and as a wife. Dhanalakshmi imbibed her new life by degrees. At first, she was silent and contemplative, often staring at objects with a vacant expression that belied the train of thought that chugged on in her head.

With time, the clamour subsided. She perfected the routine of waking up before sunrise, fetching two pails of water from the community well, bathing, cooking while her clothes were still damp, and maintaining all the rules she was expected to. She learnt what spices were allowed on what days. She noted how many spoons of sugar her husband and her father-in-law preferred in their coffees. There were precise timings for serving breakfast, lunch, and dinner, and all were met with impeccable punctuality. She learnt the required propriety when conversing with the men in her family.

'Never ask men where they are going. It will jinx their purpose.' Ramayamma told her when she stopped Kutumba Rao at the door one day.

Many mornings, when they sat in front of bronze and silver idols, long lists were committed to memory: what offerings for what gods, which flowers for which goddesses, what rituals for male children, which days to fast on for a husband's longevity.

But dawn after dawn, the crowing of roosters brought days that felt longer, more tiresome. Chores multiplied and appeared out of nowhere. She began feeling hauled through the hours of the day by an invisible force. As the sun sank below the horizon, a strange weariness descended upon her. Was it exhaustion? Was it her mother-in-law? Was it because she wasn't able to befriend her neighbours? She didn't know.

Sometimes, after serving lunch, she would croon, her mother's poems on her lips, under the cool of the guava tree in the backyard. Sometimes, she spent a while longer at the well and skipped stones, although the well limited the bounces to two. When she missed her mother, she suppressed her tears by grasping tighter the handle of the pail, or the wood of the millstone, or the strip of husk she was peeling off a coconut. Some evenings, a mixture of confusion, fear, and gloom stirred her stomach. She was someone else in a place she couldn't recognize no matter how hard she tried.

One such evening, Ramayamma found her in the backyard, gazing at the horizon, lost in its dim hues. When she turned, Ramayamma saw her misty eyes. She went to her and held her by her shoulders.

'What is this? Are you crying?' she asked.

Dhanalakshmi lowered her head and remained silent.

'You are not your mother's little girl any more. Do you know who you are now?'

Ramayamma placed two fingers under Dhanalakshmi's chin and lifted her face. 'You are the wife of Kutumba Rao! You are the accounts officer's wife! You understand?'

Ramayamma's vermilion appeared more menacing from this close. But a hint of a smile that for the first time lingered on the otherwise stern face lightened Dhanalakshmi's heart.

'Do you know how many accounts officers there are in this district?'

Dhanalakshmi shook her head. A faint 'no' slipped past her quivering lips.

'Only one! And that one is your husband!'

'Now, say it aloud.... I am the accounts officer's wife!'

Dhanalakshmi hesitated.

'Come on!'

'I am the accounts officer's wife,' she said, trembling.

'Louder now!'

'I am the accounts officer's wife!' she said, her voice still faint.

'That's right. Now go. No more crying like a little girl.'

These words calmed her. Like in one of the poems she recited that extolled the luminous image of Sri Ram, she imagined her soul take the form of a warm flame and travel across the sky to fuse with a luminous image of her husband, Kutumba Rao. Albeit inchoate, a new determination took root in her, and she refused to be a young girl in a strange place. She accepted, at that moment, that she belonged to a different family and welcomed with new-found confidence her responsibility to this family.

Kutumba Rao was kind to Dhanalakshmi. Like many women in Uttarapuram, she too was struck by his handsomeness. With perfectly combed hair, thick-rimmed spectacles, a golden pen in the front pocket of his crisply starched shirt, and a stark white dhoti, he exuded an officer's dignity and grandeur. Every day, after returning from his office, he would ask Dhanalakshmi about her day, and whether she'd had lunch. Although that was almost the extent of his conversation with her, we must note that a certain aloofness and reserve in husbands were common those days and often was what was expected of them.

For a while, Dhanalakshmi felt better. The disquietude that had once been a constant feature of her evenings dwindled to mild yearnings for her life before marriage. But soon, a new concern distressed her. It was the end of the first year of her marriage, and she was still without child.

Her visits to the temple along with Ramayamma increased in number and duration. She could discern the disappointment in Ramayamma. She felt stifled, shunned. Wives and grandmothers whispered in her ears and gave her powders. She stacked their little bottles in her trunk. Some of these could have been useful, but her problem was different, and she couldn't tell anyone about it.

The act itself was, to her, painful. Kutumba Rao was gentle, still she couldn't help but protest when her skin felt lacerated. Some nights, when he gave up, she was relieved. Other nights, when he persisted, the subsequent mornings were so painful that she wished she could go back in time. She often wondered how other women felt, how her mother felt, if something was wrong with her. These questions remained unasked. With each of these nights, she built endurance, but it didn't help enough.

As she despaired, a letter from her mother arrived, bringing relief. It requested Kutumba Rao to send Dhanalakshmi back to her natal village for her father's sixtieth birthday. Kutumba Rao and his parents agreed, and Dhanalakshmi packed her trunk with much excitement. A bullock-cart ride to the nearby bus station, and a three-hour journey in a state transport bus, took her to her village.

After the celebrations were over, she spent time with her mother in the kitchen. Besides flaunting her newly honed culinary skills, she managed a few whispered conversations. With a pleasant smile and tender words, her mother assured her that nothing was wrong with her and that everything would get better with time. Vague and heavy guilt lifted off her bosom. Her gait took on the cheerful bounce that was once hers. A day before her scheduled departure, a smooth flat pebble bounced nine times and fell on the other side of the pond. After all these months, she was still the same girl she used to be. She smiled a childish smile, but immediately replaced it with a collected expression befitting an accounts officer's wife.

That evening, when she returned from the pond, a telegram arrived from Kutumba Rao's father. It assured the good health of everyone, yet urged Dhanalakshmi's father to visit Uttarapuram at once. It said nothing about Dhanalakshmi.

The next day, Dhanalakshmi and her father journeyed to Uttarapuram. As they entered the house, Ramayamma asked Dhanalakshmi to go into the kitchen and wait till called. Dhanalakshmi obliged, although her eyes questioned the silence that engulfed the hall and the presence of strange persons there. Kutumba Rao stood straight, with his hands crossed. An old man with a freckled face and two other elderly men stood opposite him. Beckoned by Kutumba Rao's father, the elders sat in their chairs.

Dhanalakshmi tarried in the kitchen, sliding her palm over the steel jars lined up on the shelf. Questions flooded her mind, and the silence unnerved her. Sunlight streamed in through the window and reflected off the jars, blinding her. When she heard her father shout, a shiver traversed her spine. She had never heard her father speak above a whisper. Ramayamma appeared and asked Dhanalakshmi to make coffee as if to distract her from what was transpiring in the hall.

The milk began to boil and the firewood burnt with a heavy smoke. She was blowing air through a sooty iron pipe when, through the window, she saw a young woman in the backyard with someone who looked like her mother. They stood next to the guava tree. The mother had covered her head with her sari, and her daughter stood with one hand resting on the lower branch of the tree. She was remarkably fair with a beautiful face, elegant, almond-shaped eyes, and a finely shaped nose that sported a glittering, ruby-studded nose ring. Her hair was jet-black and braided into one long plait that hung below her trim waist. She stood there with apparent breathlessness and a tremble which, though visible, did not betray the grace she seemed to possess. Dhanalakshmi stared at her for more than a minute, wondering if she was indeed as delicate as she looked.

The milk spilled over. Dhanalakshmi took the pot down with her bare hands and her fingers turned a deep pink. As she dipped them in a pail of water, Ramayamma appeared again and asked her to join her father in the hall. She also called in the mother and her daughter from the backyard. Everyone assembled, and, for a moment, everyone was silent.

In the next few minutes, truth, like an executioner's whip, lashed Dhanalakshmi. Her husband had slept with the young woman in the backyard, and she was pregnant with Kutumba Rao's child. And, after all the deliberations that had happened without her in the hall, it was agreed by all, including her father, that Kutumba Rao would marry this woman, and they, that is, Kutumba Rao, this woman, and Dhanalakshmi would enter into this arrangement under the blessings of Sri Venkateswara Swamy, who was wed to both Goddess Sridevi and Goddess Padmavati. It was also announced that the wedding ceremony would take place the coming Thursday in the very same Sri Venkateswara Swamy temple. Dhanalakshmi looked at her father. On hearing nothing from him, she wobbled a bit, regained her balance, and ran out of the house towards the well and jumped into the water with a heavy splash.

And that is when, some said, Dhanalakshmi became a little odd. What went on inside her head is something we, of course, cannot be sure of. It is indeed true that ever since that day the local doctors visited her house frequently. Then again, the causes behind these visits, to the extent we can adduce, were more to do with the frailty of her body than of her mind, for both the doctors were physicians and not psychiatrists.

After she was brought home, Dhanalakshmi slept all day. Her father, who had not yet left, tried to persuade her to eat, but she refused. He sat by her side throughout the day and throughout the night, and at some point during the night, he fell asleep in the armchair he had been sitting in. Next morning, before the roosters crowed, when Ramayamma entered the room, Dhanalakshmi wasn't there. Ramayamma woke Kutumba Rao up. He ran to the well, dived into the cold water, and searched for long, but nothing indicated her having drowned. A search party consisting of Kutumba Rao and a few able men went out with their torchlights. They split into two groups and searched in different directions, one along the track leading to the bus station by the highway eight kilometres away, and the other along the muddy road that went through Uttarapuram to the adjacent village twelve kilometres away. At noon both parties returned without success despite enquiring with everyone they met on their way.

They assembled in front of Kutumba Rao's house. Dhanalakshmi's father grew frantic by the minute. Ramayamma tried a few pacifying words but was quickly silenced by her husband, who stood stiff and straight on the veranda, tapping his knuckles with his fingers. Dhanalakshmi's disappearance caused much stir in the settlement. It couldn't be contained, unlike the news of her jumping into the well. Consumed by guilt and standing in the presence of his wife's father, whom he felt answerable to, Kutumba Rao explained to the men why Dhanalakshmi had disappeared. Everyone had questions. Could she have boarded the bus to her village? Are there any morning buses to her village? Did she carry any money on her? Kutumba Rao replied patiently to all. When the questions petered out, he sat down on the veranda step, his head in his hands.

About half past noon, Dhanalakshmi appeared, coming out of the Sri Venkateswara Swamy temple merely yards away. After the initial shriek from a young man who first spotted her, everyone remained silent and stared at her as she neared, carrying a baby turtle from the temple tank in her hand. It had never occurred to any of them to search the temple. Regular temple-goers wouldn't have spotted her, for the pillars limited their view. Only a thorough search could have revealed someone sheltering there, but no one, even once, suggested searching for her in the temple. And when they saw her walk out of the gate, they gaped in silence. Some said that, as she came out, she was talking to the turtle with much animation. Some claimed that she was sweating profusely, and that her countenance showed wild excitement interspersed with ghastly frowns. Both could have been right. But what everyone remembered clearly was the answer she gave her father near the porch.

As she approached, she appeared utterly oblivious to everything around her. Kutumba Rao was relieved. He kept looking at her, hoping for some sort of acknowledgement. His parents stared at her like the rest of the crowd. Her appearance appeased her father's pounding heart and dissolved the stone that was stuck in his parched throat. He was angry with her but didn't know how to rebuke her. She walked up to the house unconcernedly.

'WHAT were you doing in the temple since daybreak?'

'Oh,' she replied, 'I was sleeping with the pandit.'

⁘

Dhanalakshmi went to her room and slept. Kutumba remained at the door and didn't step in as if thwarted by an invisible line that would burst into flames were he to cross it. For a long while, he watched her sleep. Later, he returned to his room and tallied his accounts. Her father sat by her side, like the previous day, in an armchair. As his fatigued nerves relaxed, he descended into a deep slumber. Ramayamma went into the room the following morning, and again, Dhanalakshmi wasn't there.

Ramayamma was furious. The sympathy she'd had for her daughter-in-law vanished. She decided that she wouldn't care any more. It was better her son slept. There was no point searching for this woman in the chilly morning. It was her karma; there was nothing one could do about it. Half an hour later, Dhanalakshmi's father woke up. He stormed out of the room, saw Ramayamma sweeping the backyard, and enquired about his daughter. At her reply, he slapped his forehead, rushed to Kutumba Rao's room, and woke him up.

Kutumba Rao went to the well first. He walked at a measured pace, and was less agitated than the day before. From the well, he went to the temple and searched behind every pillar, and enquired with the pandits. She was not there. Walking back to his house, he wondered if the neighbours would be willing to assist him again. Choosing not to take their help, he walked eight kilometres to the bus station, making enquiries along the way. Unsuccessful in finding her whereabouts, he returned at about quarter past seven in the morning. His mother served breakfast. He was hungry, but when Dhanalakshmi's father refused to eat, he followed suit.

This enraged Ramayamma further. Muttering inaudibly, she took both plates back into the kitchen.

Kutumba Rao was leaving the house to search in another direction when, at the end of the street, below the peepul tree, he saw Dhanalakshmi. She was carrying a stray puppy and was swaying sideways as if drunk. The street dogs were barking, jumping, and howling. They were so riotous that everyone rushed out to see what was happening. Kutumba Rao stood on the porch steps as motionless as the day before.

Ramayamma was thoroughly scandalized. She dropped a copper bowl, and it tumbled down the porch steps. Her face contorted. Cursing loudly, she went back into the house with heavy, resounding steps.

Dhanalakshmi's father looked resignedly at his daughter as she approached him. This time, it was clear that she was talking to the puppy. She staggered, stumbled, and zigzagged up to the porch. The stench of palm toddy was pungent, and everyone took a step back involuntarily. She almost fell when, with a swift manoeuvre, she regained her balance and stood, puppy in arms, in front of her father, smiling a broad smile. Neighbours stood on their verandas, their mouths betraying their inner excitement. The dogs followed her, barking incessantly. Ramayamma paced about in the kitchen, vexed by the intolerable growls that now echoed from the hall. She threw a steel plate from the kitchen into the hall, expecting it to silence the dogs. The dogs didn't stop.

Dhanalakshmi fell forward and her father caught her in time. She stood erect again and pushed the puppy towards him. He took the puppy with a downcast face and was about to put it down, but it looked like the dogs would tear it apart. Confounded by everything around him, he went to place the puppy on the veranda when she stopped him, saying, 'No, Appa...take him to the backyard. I am marrying him tomorrow in the temple.'

Kutumba Rao's father postponed his son's second marriage by a month. Did he expect Dhanalakshmi to become normal by then? Dhanalakshmi left every day before dawn and no one could do anything to stop her. Her father wrote to his wife asking her to come immediately. However, she was sick and took two weeks to visit Uttarapuram. Meanwhile, Kutumba Rao resumed office work, the two old men read newspapers in their armchairs, and Ramayamma grew more and more furious by the day.

One day, Dhanalakshmi prepared a variety of delicacies: spiced dal with spinach, tender purple brinjals incised with precision and stuffed with a paste of fenugreek seeds, rasam, fried pumpkin crisps, thick curd, rice steamed to perfection, and a payasam made of rice, lentils, jaggery, cardamom, cashews, and thin wedges of copra. She made these the way Ramayamma had taught her, but at three in the morning. She feasted all alone and left for the toddy stalls, having exhausted quite a share of the monthly rations, and leaving behind many used utensils.

Another day, she returned with a stiff roll of tobacco sticking out of the corner of her mouth, and seemed to have mastered the art of smoking tobacco the rustic way. Another morning, she took away both the water pails and brought them back filled with toddy. Ramayamma hurled abuse at her to no effect.

After two weeks, when her mother arrived, Dhanalakshmi wasn't at home. Ramayamma complained at length about all the scandalous behaviour she'd had to witness. Her mother listened silently, nodding at intervals. That day too, both the pails were missing. Dhanalakshmi returned after an hour, swaying more than usual, holding the toddy-filled buckets, and puffing at her tobacco roll. She looked at her mother and paused. Her mother surveyed her with wide eyes and, for a moment, smiled—a gentle, cautious expansion of the cheeks, a soft inhale, an indiscernible parting of the lips, and a dimple of tempered surprise. Dhanalakshmi stood still, blinking.

A brief silence ensued, and then the frenzied voice of Ramayamma shattered the quiet: 'Look at her! This is her routine. What a disgrace! This is unacceptable, madam, no matter the cause. Unacceptable by any standard! She must be thrown out of the house, but my son won't allow it! God help us with this abomination! Knock some sense into her. You are her mother; it's your....'

Dhanalakshmi dropped the pails. They fell with a heavy thud, shook, and lay still on the floor. Toddy splashed on Kutumba Rao's father's newspaper, and on his clean-shaven face. He folded the soiled paper and went into the yard, wiping his face. Dhanalakshmi stepped up, stood in front of Ramayamma, peered into her face, and blew a wisp of smoke at her.

'What effrontery! Nasty woman!' Ramayamma screamed.

Dhanalakshmi's mother stood up in an effort to defuse the situation, but before she could take one step, Dhanalakshmi, with loud retching, vomited all over Ramayamma and collapsed.

Kutumba Rao came home with the local doctor. Dhanalakshmi was on her bed and her parents sat by her side. Her father-in-law was in the armchair, troubled by the smell of toddy that persisted despite his meticulous scrubbing of his face and body. Ramayamma was still bathing. Kutumba Rao stood by the doctor who was checking Dhanalakshmi's pulse. His mother-in-law's presence renewed his sense of guilt. The doctor unplugged the stethoscope from his ears and replaced it in his briefcase.

'Nothing to worry about...is she your wife?'

'Yes.'

'Congratulations! She is pregnant.'

THE DEMON SAGE'S DAUGHTER

VARSHA DINESH

In one version of the story, nobody dies, and you get to keep the princess as your maid.

She chafes against this, longing for her silks and jewels. You scoff, tugging her after you, a tangle of jasmine wound around her arms. She's tried to break free many times, plaintively singing to the deer and the birds and the sky for help, but everything in your ashram bows to your father, even the quilt of sky above, and he is the one who bound her. And so, your princess just weeps.

But for all her faults, in that version of the story, the princess at least is a pious girl beloved of the gods. So much so that all her tears turn into sapphires and rubies, collecting in little piles by her feet. And although she protests when you sweep them into the folds of your sari, she knows that you are her mistress and she cannot stop you from doing what you want.

What you want, in that version of the story, is to take the riches from your princess's tears, buy all the weapons of Patala, and then march into Amaravati, the great celestial city, where you will kill all the gods.

Every single one of the 330 million.

And when their slithering godblood runs down the diamond facade of Mount Meru, you will bathe your hair in it, soaking in it until your scalp is drenched and your sari drips crimson, and then—only then—will your revenge be complete.

In that version of the story.

In another version of the story, which is still not the real story, you are on your knees in your ashram, trying to put your father back together. You have already tried this with frantic hands and magic, with careful hands and needles, with sticky paste from deodar trees, and the decanted salts of your own tears, and the drip drip of your blood churned black with incantation. Now, hours later, you are appealing to his logic: telling him how stupid you are, what an idiot-child, can't even put your father back together.

Your father is saying nothing back at all, having burst open some time ago like a ripe fruit.

In the version of the story you choose to be true, you are kneeling in your father's blood, silent. His godly killer has just fled the scene, hoisted on to a heavenly chariot, fading into a distant astral blip in seconds. In his wake, at this scene of crime, there is no revenge, no confrontation, no loud lamentation. Only silence.

Lotuses bloom vividly everywhere a piece of your father has landed. They're beneath your feet, climbing the walls. Great lotus leaves brush your face when you move, enfolding you in shadow over and over. Your princess sits slumped on the floor, blowing her nose into one.

'Did you hear it?' you ask, hushed. 'The spell. Do you know it?'

Beneath the mountain of lotus blooms, your princess is naked as the day she was born. There is no blood on her skin, clean and new, but gore drips from her hair and coats her shoulders like a grim cape.

'Answer me.'

Your princess's nod is minuscule, just a quick jerk of her head before she resumes staring pallidly at the violence.

'I'll free you.'

Your princess's eyes snap wide open.

'I'll free you from your curse, and in return, you'll tell me what you heard. Do we have a deal?'

You wonder what you will do if she says no. If she leaves you alone to deal with the shattered bone and adipose florets and stringy grey matter that is all that is left of your father. But the princess is too crafty to pass up this opportunity.

'You'll free me,' she echoes. 'No tricks.'

'None.'

'And after I'm freed?' she asks. 'What will you do?'

That is none of her business. You wring your father's blood from your hands. You crush a flower under your foot. You wait until your princess stops waiting for an answer, blood-stained face shuttering over.

When you put your arm out in partnership, your princess takes it.

There are two threads of stories here woven together into a loose braid, one bloodier than the other. Your princess is the strongest strand in the first thread. Your father is the bloodiest one in the other. Between the two, linking force, are you and Kacha.

Maybe you should have started the story with Kacha.

In a more traditional story, he is the hero after all. Kacha, in his blue silks and gold earrings. Kacha, with his silver tongue. Kacha, who even the goats liked, the traitorous bastards.

Some months ago, when his big celestial retinue arrived, all flappy-winged vimanas and heralds blowing conch shells, some of your handmaidens crowded the dance hall. They jostled each other, ankle bells tinkling, a murmuration of gentle creatures hiding vicious teeth. Each one called out a new, juicy bit of information. He wears a diamond on his chest the size of a mango! His body is strong and robust like a peach! Oh, my lady, my lady, his servants carry bowls of fruit, gold-stringed veenas, and such heavenly flowers!

You tossed your braid over your shoulder. 'If he adorns his chest with such sizeable jewels, girls, should we worry that he is lacking elsewhere?'

'He's come to study with your father, my lady,' Maniprabha said. 'What he lacks in physical prowess, he must possess in spirit.'

'Spirit,' Samyukta laughed. 'Are the gods' spirits not destroyed after centuries of losing wars against us? Are they not tired of their little sons dying like pitiful worms on the battlefields? Do they not seek peace by sending their own to study here at the ashram of the demon sage?'

'It's not peace they want,' you said. 'It's something else.'

The girls all exchanged glances at that, swooning with curiosity, but you were the mistress. You decided if you wanted to include them in your secret. You decided if you wanted to leave them hanging, spinning their theories as intricately as they worked the ashram's looms.

'The gods have sent him to sniff out a secret,' you said. 'He's a spy.'

'A spy? A secret? What secret?'

But a queen without secrets is no queen at all, and you only smiled. 'Father will need me. I must go now to welcome our new guest.'

Outside, in the seething emerald fields of your father's ashram, Kacha stood bent in half, hands clasped, all his attendants singing harmonious praises of your father's might. Your new guest's face was neither stunning nor memorable. His voice, however, boomed in messianic thunder when he spoke: 'Oh, Saint of Saints! Most Knowledgeable One in Patala! I thank you for accepting me as your most humble student.'

He kneeled, bejewelled forehead pressed to your father's feet. Flowers tumbled from the centre of his palms: jasmine and marigold, rose mallow and calotrope, oleander and parijat.

Your father cast a bemused smile on the kneeling god. Lightning flickered in his coiled beard. Raw cosmic power thrummed from him in tympanic waves, flattening the grass, buffeting the crown off Kacha's head. 'Rise, student,' he boomed, motioning you forward. You performed the welcoming rituals: washing Kacha's feet with rose water, smearing sandalwood and turmeric paste on his forehead, garlanding him with marigolds so bright the bees swarmed in droves.

'This is my daughter, Devayani,' your father said. 'It's her job to make sure that your stay with us is most pleasurable.'

Most pleasurable! Ha! You knew your father. You knew he expected you to sidle up to Kacha and seduce him, lure his secrets from his mouth, feed him lies and flirtations just like you fed milk and ghee to the snakes in the ashram's groves every morning.

Kacha was already assessing the curve of your mouth, your hip where you had shifted your sari to offer a glimpse of your skin. 'Lady Devayani,' he murmured. 'They whisper rumours in Amaravati that the demon sage's daughter is more beautiful than all of heaven's apsaras. I see now that there was no hyperbole.'

'You flatter me, my lord.'

'I look forward to studying under your father,' Kacha said. 'But I fear now, after meeting you, that I will have to work very hard indeed to stay focused.'

His shoulders blocked out the sun. The diamond on his chest, set amidst repeating lotus patterns of embroidery, made you suddenly dizzy. You stumbled, momentarily blinded, dropping your tray of rose and turmeric. He caught your neatly, long fingers folding around your wrist.

'Lady Devayani,' he said. 'I'm sure you will have much to teach me, as well.'

Your fingers rubbed unconsciously the welts his touch left on your wrists, an effect of his godblood. Each one was reddened, raised; alphabets in a harsh language carved into your skin. Your father's future murderer saw them and only smiled: a whetted thing, sharp and profane.

That was the beginning.

This is the circuitous route you take to an ending.

You and your princess leave your dead father in the ashram and descend into the realms of Patala.

This is where the demons live, in their underground cities of gold and gemstone trees. At the gates, your princess pulls weakly against her flower-chains, unwilling to go any further.

'They won't eat you,' you say. 'There are better things to eat in Patala. The exquisite glair of Naga eggs. Black-skinned fish from the river Hataki. Sweets from the tables of the demon king Bali, wrapped in sugar-soaked silver. They have no need for bland princess-flesh.'

She stares at you, aghast. You wonder how she will tell this story to the future princes lining up for her attention. You: demoness, daughter of the Dark Sage, leading her into the realms of ghosts and goblins. She: victim, hostage, held captive by a beautiful monster.

What a repugnant fable.

Your mouth turns in a curdled grimace. 'Stay with me and maybe they won't rip the meat off your bones.'

The vimana you summon to travel into the underworld is elegant, with swan wings that ruffle at every breeze, and seats of blue and gold. A glittering green snake adorns its side, fat diamonds for eyes.

'O Pious Daughter!' it hisses when you board. 'How is your father?'

Your princess opens her mouth, surely to blab about how your father is currently a formless flesh-splatter, but you hum the opening words of an incantation, the syllables slippery as eels. Your princess clicks her mouth shut, pop, hands jumping in surprise to her throat. It is not until you're descending into the first level of Patala that you let her speak again.

'You're not my mistress any more,' she spits. 'Don't do that again.'

'If the demons know their sage is dead, they will march against the gods. The gods will call the sun and moon to arms, and the earth will be plunged into eons of icy nights and monstrous tides. Do you want that?'

'Don't you? It's your father who's dead—'

'Another word and I'll stitch your mouth shut. With iron.'

Your princess believes you. She looks out instead, eyes wide, at the winding streets and drinking parlours.

The first city of Patala is resplendently beautiful. The demon architect Maya's miraculous palaces glisten like beetle carapaces, all stained glass and coruscating light beams. Canopies of ivory filigree and statues of bronze adorn the wide avenues. A vista of gemstones spills slanted light across an artificial sky, illuminating the city in strange, twinkling light.

Your father always called it excess. When the demons came to him for advice, he told them not to test the gods. Build just enough marvels. Keep your palaces just a bit smaller than theirs. Do not tempt celestial wrath, and maybe the demons could keep their cities, their sorcery, their strange and darkling denizens.

'It's beautiful,' your princess says. 'I didn't think it would be beautiful.'

'Did you think it would all be vermin and filth?'

'No. I've heard the stories....'

'Women that lie with any man for a drink. Nagas that live in holes like animals. Are those the stories you've heard?'

In the gemlight, your princess looks like she wants to put her fist through your face. 'They won't come back, you know,' she says. 'Kacha's gone. Your father never loved you. So, you can snap at me all you wish, but they won't come back for you. Nobody wants you.'

But this is where she misunderstands you. This is not a story about your father, or Kacha. This is a story about you.

You are Devayani, daughter of the demon sage, mistress of his ashram now that he is gone. Your father taught you how to meditate for as long as it took to bottle thunderstorms and weaponize blood. In your grottos of horns and teeth, he instructed you on dance mantras that brought about droughts or floods. Your feet became a palimpsest of scars, layered and sliced by hours of dancing. Your very bones are carved with treatises on the importance of illusions and hypnosis, the mysteries of augury, the secretive, coded stratagems of celestial warfare.

Kacha and your father are in your past.

Your present is about you.

'Where are we going?' your princess asks.

'To the night markets. To find a locksmith who knows sorcery. Your shackles are demon-made and answer only to the one who put them on you.'

'But your father is dead.'

'Someone there will know how to free you.'

'And after that?'

You turn your head away, pressing your lips together, pretending to feast your eyes on the sights. It doesn't take your princess too long to stop asking.

In any version of your universe, this is heaven's most coveted secret, your father's greatest legacy: he can raise the dead.

After the day's battle climaxed, when the battlefields smoked and dozed uneasy at night, your father would walk through mounds of corpses and broken chariots, chanting the incantations. As he walked, demonic corpse-soldiers rose in his wake, shambling after him into the ashram.

You and your handmaidens would sit at the looms, weaving the soldiers' new skins. The dead could not live in the skin they'd died in; their souls hung out of it, untucked, and they flopped about like fish. When the new skins were finished, you and your father stitched them on to the demons, dusted off their thick clubs, and sent them back to war.

The gods and demons have been at war for centuries. The gods were forever dying, being sucked into the karmic pipeline, cycling through reincarnation like leaves buffeting helplessly in a gale. The demons died and simply came back, as if dying was nothing but a mild inconvenience.

It ruffled some big heavenly feathers. Bruised some tall celestial egos.

You and your father were prepared for spies. Many from heaven's ranks had come here before, pretending to seek tutelage, burrowing instead for information on the resurrection spell. But none were as subtle and determined as Kacha.

He was a good student. He studied deep into the night, poring over palm-leaf texts while your father meditated. He took diligent notes and debated for hours with your father on complex cosmic paradoxes. When he was not taking lessons, Kacha whittled wood into fantastic creatures that followed you around. There was a parrot with a green glass eye, and a rabbit so small it would fit in the cup of your palm. A monkey swung from the folds of your sari, bringing you flowers and oddly patterned stones.

Or he would write you: today I watched you dance. I have seen celestial apsaras dance in Indra's palace above Mount Meru. They are not as skilled as you are, Devayani. Or: I wish these treatises on conjuring spirits and calculating cumulative karmic scores were as arresting as your singing, Devayani.

You pretended to be charmed, blushing whenever he sent you a new message. His overtures of love cloyed in your mouth like oversweet rose jam.

At Kacha's request, you took him on tours of the ashram. You showed him the looms and the dance hall. You let him row the two of you out to the middle of the lotus pond, far enough in dawn's fog that there was nothing in either direction but mist-shrouded blooms.

'This is where apsaras are born,' he told you, plucking a plush pink blossom. 'In the hearts of flowers, soft as morning dew. Have you seen an apsara?'

You shook your head.

'I'll show you one day,' he said. 'Oh, Devayani, don't you chafe at being locked up here in your ashram? Such a clever girl should see the world. I could take you.'

Kacha came to see you after his lessons, coaxing you to feed the deer with him or augur the shapes of clouds in the sky. He tucked flowers behind your ear and told you stories of Amaravati, his home in the skies. He made you a model of it with clay and silk and precious things, laying out wide boulevards and golden gates, sparkling indoor waterways, food halls where celestial cooks prepared the loveliest of dishes for the gods' banquets.

'What does an ascetic's daughter know of sweets?' he lamented. 'When I take you to Amaravati, I will bring you to the halls and let you have your pick of the sweets. Sugar wafers drizzled with honey so light it melts on your tongue. Milk and khoya confections with surprise berry hearts. Frosted, sugar-soaked cucumber garnished with candied petals.'

A coy grin parted your lips. 'You seem to have a sweet tongue, my lord.'

Tangerine flowers rinsed through the trees like flotsam. Butterflies spun in spiralling drifts. Kacha's smile sharpened. 'Would you like a taste, my lady?'

His touch made you burn and bubble, a beautiful firework held too close to skin. Pain bloomed, white and scalding, and you cried out again and again. Still he, feigning oblivion, pressed his mouth to yours, seeking the heat of your tongue.

He did not taste sweet. He tasted like iron, and salt, and the acid tang of godblood. You clenched your fists tight enough to carve bloody moons into your palms but did not pull away.

This was what your father expected from you, after all.

That you would dance close enough to serpents that they showed you their venom. That you would sit through the heat of a hundred scorpion stings. That you would bathe in godblood, if required, let it slough your skin off, if only it meant you could catch your father his godly spy.

'Oh, Devayani, my love,' Kacha cried, when you parted at last. 'I fear our happiness will be short-lived. The demons suspect me of being a spy. I fear they are plotting to harm me. I am terrified that if I die, our love will break your heart. How could I bear leaving you? How could my soul rest, knowing you will be in pain?'

And here, well-rehearsed, you assured Kacha with syrup-thick words that he need not fear. You would speak to your father on his behalf. You were the demon sage's daughter after all. You promised: your love would always protect him.

The very next day, you found Kacha dead for the first time.

The night markets occupy the riverside of the third level of Patala.

The river here runs aureate, casting a glow over the ghosts and goblins that call the city its home. Boats full of men row across it, blowing long plumes of fire. When the fire fans the surface of the water, it spits and hisses, turning into ropes of gleaming gold which adorn the chests of the vendors at the market.

The market is a dizzying tangle of wares, sourced from all seven of Patala's realms. Foggy glass tanks, teeming with bathypelagic creatures from the primordial ocean of the lowest level. Spines of gods, crackling with power, battle-won, and encased in silver by Maya's craftsmen. Fangs of panthers and elephant hair, sold by all manner of strange netherworld folk: mottled-blue vetalas, living upside-down in trees; grey-skinned pisachas, feeding on corpse-flesh; dark-eyed rakshasas, shifting shape into whoever you desire the most.

You once purchased your dancing bells from here, from a pisacha woman whose breath was thick with death and sorcery. It is to her you go now, tugging your princess behind you.

She blanches at the sight of the shop. 'This doesn't look like the house of a locksmith.'

Rows of skulls line the shelves, and bones hang from the rafters, tinkling grotesquely. Vertiginous drifts of corpse-ash execute strange calligraphy in the still air. The pisacha woman shuffles to you, bells decorating the hollows of her desiccated ribcage, jangling with each step she takes.

'Pious Daughter,' she rasps, her flickering tongue dusty grey. 'You smell of death and blood. What can I do for you?'

Your princess quivers. 'No tricks,' she whispers. 'You promised.'

Your promises are not worth much. Still: 'My father made these bonds,' you tell the pisacha. 'Can you break them?'

'Upala can do all sorcery,' the pisacha says, glassy eyes focused intently on your princess. 'Snip, snip with the magic knife. Cuts through even Indra's armour.'

While Upala goes to get her magic knife, your princess gives you a suspicious look. 'If it's that easy, why couldn't you just do it yourself?'

'I have other business here.'

When Upala comes back, you ask the price of her magic knife. Your princess's brows furrow. A piece of bone from your father is still stuck in her hastily washed hair. You think of saying something but then turn away, deciding to let her have the pleasure of discovering this ghoulish accessory all to herself.

⁂

In some versions of your story, which you do not want to be the story, you are nothing but the querulous daughter of a powerful man, spending your days conversing with twee forest creatures. You learn dance and music, but never the spells and incantations that make them your weapons. Your father never thinks to teach you because what use is teaching a daughter?

In those versions, you are simply a distraction in the tales of conflicts between powerful men. A girl living in the margins of her own story.

Those versions of you are not ambitious. Those versions of you do not go exploring Patala, or demand things from your father. Things like: tell me how to brew elixirs, or teach me how to enter another's consciousness, or give me the secret of resurrection.

In every version of you that exists, your father chastises you for demanding the resurrection spell.

He banishes you from his hut when you persist, corralling you to your dance hall for weeks. In your rage, you break every pane of glass adorning the latticed walls. You kick at pots of saffron and turmeric and indigo. You dance in the mess, painting the hall vivid in your anger, casting spells to turn all your handmaidens into brightly dyed rabbits.

Your father lets you.

'The only obstacle to the victory of the gods is the resurrection spell,' he tells you while you sulk on the floor, boneless. 'It's a secret I must guard closely.'

'I'm your daughter,' you spit. 'Why can't you teach me everything?'

Your father's eyes flash, miniature suns. 'You act like a spoiled child, Devayani,' he says, dispassionate. 'What if I teach you the resurrection spell today and you, fickle as you are, teach it to any simple paramour the gods might send to trick you? What if I teach you my greatest secret and you use it on birds to look mighty in front of your handmaidens?'

In every version of your story, you try to show him that you are more than that. That you have bled and scarred yourself to be worthy of him. You siphon secrets. You feed men sweet poison. You press shlokas into silk and bone and metal, turning them into potent weapons. You are a blade: a bejewelled one, but a blade, nevertheless. You can be equals.

Your father only laughs. Your role is set, he says. You are the demon sage's daughter, using your beauty and middling magic to set snares for his enemies.

But you want to be more than that.

You want to be his heir.

When he hears this, your father laughs so long and so loud that all hell and heaven reverberates with the sound. So long and loud that the blades of grass seem to shake with it, trees all joining in, your handmaidens hiding their faces with rabbit paws while they try not to gloat at your shame.

(Nobody's laughing in the end, when Kacha rips your father apart. But that part comes later.)

This is the story of how you find your princess: after your father laughs at you, you leave the dance hall a mess of pigments and tears. Your sari is dirty from days of tantrums. Your handmaidens are still rabbits, so you go alone to the river, where you stare in loathing at your reflection for what feels like eons.

When you enter the water, the river swirls about you in icy, varicoloured eddies. Red for ambition. Blue for humiliation.

You stay for hours, sobbing, breathing a fortitude prayer.

At dusk, you are disturbed by a fit of laughter.

'Do you think she thinks she can wash away the embarrassment?' a voice whispers. Your spiritual cognition identifies the speakers: the king's daughter and her favoured handmaiden. 'Look,' the princess continues, and you know she's pressing her feet against your discarded sari. 'She's the daughter of the demon sage, yet all she wears are rags.'

'She's a demoness,' her handmaiden says. 'This is what they know, princess.

Corpse-ash and charnel house raiment. Filthy things that smell like death.'

'Neither a dutiful daughter nor a talented sage. No wonder her father has been so displeased.'

It is frivolously cruel. You think of cursing the princess, something inventive and alienating: all her lovers will turn into frogs, or everything she touches will turn to slimy snails.

The princess is beautiful, after all. Delicate face and dark gaze rimmed with rings of kohl. Her fingers are red from the dye of the henna plant, elegant when she reaches down to pick up your sari.

'Come and get it, hut dweller,' she laughs. 'Come out of the water.'

It is silly, childish cruelty. But you are a child yourself, hurting because of a father you can never please. And so it is that you clothe yourself in the foam of the river, skimming the crests of small waves to weave yourself a sari. So it is that you rush out of the water, sputtering in your anger. So it is that you fall right into their trap: a muddy hole in the ground.

They must have dug it hours ago.

You twist your ankles, scrape your elbows, lose your illusory river-garb. Naked, wet mud slicks and slithers over you, weighing you down with its stickiness. Something else is in there, foul-smelling, squishing underfoot as you try to stand. You cry out when you see it: fish guts, at least a day old, likely gathered from the palace kitchens. The smell sears your nostrils. You retch, and your tormentors' faces glisten with mirth far above you, bright from the sun.

'There, there,' your princess says, satisfied. 'Isn't that hole much more befitting for a demoness?'

You ready yourself to curse her, but she surprises you once again. Something small falls on to your lap from the surface. You scramble for it, panic squeezing your throat, and lift up a rabbit.

Its hue is unnaturally pink. Its neck is broken.

The next one is grey, still warm and twitching. As you hold it—her, her, one of your girls, which one?—your spine turns to ice. Your tongue goes slack in your mouth. The horror of it mutes you, blinds you, stoppers your blood in your veins.

'Can't bring them back to life?' the princess asks. 'Maybe your father will show them mercy?'

Later, burying the small bodies of your handmaidens, you will wonder if the princess had known. If she had understood the weight of her cruelty.

If she had even had reason, save that she was a princess of something, and you were the disagreeable daughter of the demon sage.

You will never ask her this. Not when you are finally rescued, and your father—apoplectic at the loss of perfectly good servants—curses your princess to be your handmaiden. Not when you set her to impossible tasks, picking up stray leaves in the garden with her teeth, or polishing the dance hall floor with arms bound behind her back. Not even after your father is dead, and his blood is all over her, and you barter with her for her freedom.

Your princess killed six of your handmaidens that day. You do not know how to weigh cruelties on a grand karmic scale, but you think the balance is still tipped in your favour.

You make one more stop before you leave the night markets.

Your princess, newly freed, continues to trail after you, terrified of goblins and ghosts. Her fingers are laced tightly in yours, the scent of her fear sharp and distinctly peppery.

'What will you do?' she keeps asking. Devayani, whose father is dead. Devayani, whose Kacha has fled. What will you do now?

'You're free,' you snap, hiding Upala's knife in the folds of your sari. 'What will you do?'

'If I go back to my father, he'll just make me marry a prince.'

'How terrible for you.'

'I don't want to marry a prince,' she sneers. 'I want to learn the things you know. I always have.'

You give her your most contemptuous look. 'Is that why you murdered my handmaidens? Because you were jealous?'

Your princess's face briefly crumples. 'I didn't know,' she says. 'They were rabbits, how was I supposed to know?'

'As character traits go, a rabbit-killer isn't much better.'

'I was angry. All this knowledge you have, all this potential, and you waste it all on Kacha.'

'You said it yourself. He's not coming back.'

'True,' your princess says, restlessly. 'So, what now?'

You settle your face into its grimmest expression. 'The demon sage is dead,' you drone, bored. 'Killed by his own treacherous student. It's time for retribution.'

You swivel right, dipping into the dim liquor shop of a Naga distiller.

Gold scales dapple his hood, and a ruby glistens atop it. He is surprised to see you, enquiring in his sibilant tongue as to your father's whereabouts. You wait until after you have made your purchases to tell him: 'He's dead.'

The Naga's hood rises in shock. His lidless eyes travel over you, trying to discern if you are joking. His coils shift closer.

'He's dead,' you repeat. 'Tell everyone in Patala. Their demon sage is dead. Killed by the traitorous gods!'

And then you leave, turning around and racing down the market, feet slipping against mottled glass and gleaming stone. Your princess trails behind you, hand in yours, gasping.

'This is why you came!' she pants. 'This is what you wanted. For them to know, to panic. This is what you wanted, isn't it?'

You hide your smile. As your vimana rises, you can hear the whispers begin, rising to screams by the time you are in the sky.

In the version of the story you tell the demons later, you will give inventory of all the different ways Kacha died in his pursuit of the spell.

The first time you let him go cold, godblood congealing against singed grass, while you tried to understand. He was sprawled just outside the dance hall, a great swathe of his flesh ripped out, ribs cracked open, his insides glinting like a ruby geode. The expression on his face was that of a man trying awfully hard to look dignified while something tore him open like an orange being peeled.

You stood staring, mind racing, silent in the afternoon's blood-rich breeze. The proximity of his body to your favourite haunt meant that he had expected you to find him. But why? Simply because he guessed your love for him would propel you to accelerate his resurrection?

You paced for a bit, shooing away the flies and the birds. It was only after you held his heart in your fist that you made your decision.

You tore at your hair and burned your fingers taking his heart to your father, screaming, wailing, begging until your father cried out that you had become exactly what he predicted: a weak-hearted, foolish girl, giving her heart away to sweet-talking paramours.

'I love Kacha,' you wept, disconsolate. 'He is no spy, Father, only my beloved. And now the demons have killed him for no crime but his love for me!'

You were adept at acting. Your father had demanded you be. Now you were putting on a show, playing a part, and he stormed and blustered at you, betrayed.

'You will not take me as your heir,' you spat, your throat raw, eyes stinging. 'At least give me my lover.'

'Be quiet!' roared your father. His lightning whip cracked across your shoulder: searing, splintering your collarbone. 'I will raise him from the dead because he is my student. Only because of that. End this stupidity, Devayani. He does not love you.'

While your father resurrected Kacha, stitching him into a skin you had woven so lovingly, you hid behind a wall, craning to listen. But your father did not need words for the spell any more, only the power of his mind. And so, thwarted, you ignored Kacha for two days, sulking in your hut while your shoulder healed.

A little before the second time, Kacha lamented repeatedly that he was afraid the demons would kill him again. You wept into his chest. He sighed: 'Oh, Devayani, why does fate test our love so?'

The two of you were lying in a boat, buoyed gently by the waves of the lotus pond. You pretended not to notice a lowly demigod creeping towards you. Sunlight glimmered on the assassin's golden crown, throwing shards of brightness in your eye. Kacha motioned with his fingers, as if telling him to hurry up.

You ignored them, playing the part of an idiot, sighing, and pressing your lips to Kacha's neck. When the hitman struck, arterial godblood splashed all over you. It slithered down your throat, liquefying your lungs. You spat out a glob of blood contemplatively, and then collapsed against Kacha. When you woke next, both you and he had new skins, and neither of you were any closer to figuring out the spell.

The third and final time, you followed a secretive Kacha into the forest without his knowledge. There he met with his co-conspirators, other demigods, all dressed unobtrusively in the fashions of demon folk. 'The gods are growing tired of waiting,' they said. 'How long until you have the spell?'

For all his dying, Kacha had managed to glean only a few words of the incantation. He caught them each time his soul was yanked from the astral plane, an echo of a whisper that was not enough. The gods needed all of it, the whole spell, and they needed it fast.

It was time to do something drastic.

This time, you watched as the gods cut Kacha's throat on his instructions and burned his body. You watched them mix his ashes into a chalice of your father's favourite wine. It flummoxed you, this new trick. How was this different from the other times?

But then, as you paced your dance hall, and your princess swept the floor, realization crept up on you. 'Come with me,' you said, tugging at her chains. 'I need you.'

You took her to a glade, far from the ashram. She huffed and spat on the floor, demanding to know what you were going to do. Throw her in a hole of fish guts? Ask her to pluck fruits with her teeth?

'You'll see in a moment,' you promised. Then you bit your lip against the unpleasantness, took out a knife, and got to work.

Later, when your father requested his favourite wine, it was you who took it to him.

You, dutiful daughter of sweet comportment, had poured him just the quantity he liked. He, pleased with you for once, downed the first cup in a single swallow.

'I am tired of fighting you, Devayani,' he said, a deep sigh fluttering his beard. 'Must we bicker with each other because of an outsider?'

You kneeled, folding your hands in your lap. 'Forgive me, Father, but Kacha is not an outsider to me any more. He has promised to marry me and take me to Amaravati.'

Your father's face twisted in ugly displeasure, but he hid it under a smile. You poured him more of the wine. He swilled it, and said: 'If you want him so much, perhaps I can consult the celestial astrologers. But if you intend to marry, Kacha must leave the ashram this instant. It is not appropriate, the two of you living in such close proximity.'

You nodded, contrite. You had seen this coming. 'You will not regret this, Father,' you trilled, hands clasped to your chest. 'Kacha is wonderful.'

'If you believe in his intentions, I believe you,' your father said, sly.

He drained the last of the wine. 'Where is Kacha? I have not seen him today. We must find him, instruct him to leave.'

'I've seen neither Kacha nor the princess all day,' you lied, wringing the hem of your sari to appear concerned. 'But there were some strangers in the forest today. And a strange smell of fire in the afternoon.'

A flickering in the air, like ghosts convening.

Your father's expression began to change. A storm descended upon his face, dark and tempestuous, and he snatched the wine glass off the floor.

He peered into it, swirling it this way and that, face twisting in a horrific grimace when he spotted the flecks of ash.

'What is it?' you asked. 'What is it, Father?'

'Daughter,' he said, eyes wide and thunderstruck. 'I have been tricked.'

Varying expressions of disgust crossed your father's face. Someone, he raged, had tricked him. Mixing Kacha's ashes into the wine! Knowingly feeding him his own student! What wicked treachery! If the gods came to know, they would destroy the cities of Patala. They would plunge both sides into a catastrophic war. And how was your father to explain, great sage that he was, that he had not been cognizant of Kacha swimming around in his wine?

You wailed, crumpled on the floor, 'Oh, Father! Father, what will we do?'

'There is no other way,' your father said, through violent retching. 'I must resurrect him.'

'But he's within you! If you resurrect Kacha now, it will kill you! Won't you be ripped open? Torn apart?'

A long, querulous moan escaped your father. He clutched his stomach. 'Go, make us both new skins,' he said. 'I have no choice. I will need to teach the resurrection spell to the part of Kacha within me. Once I resurrect him, he can tear himself out of me, you can stitch him up, and he will revive me. Kacha knows the situation. He wouldn't want to start another war.'

'Or,' you ventured, quietly, 'you can teach it to me. And I can revive you, Father, after you resurrect Kacha.'

The simpler solution. The safest, most obvious one. But even then, your father's gaze for you was stinging. 'You don't have Kacha's aptitude for spell and sorcery,' he scoffed. 'You concern yourself with middling spells and think too highly of your own talents. Your place is at the looms, and later, at your husband's side. Understood?'

Your face stiffens into a rictus. 'Yes, Father.'

'Go now. No time to waste.'

You worked the warp and the weft at the looms, possessed by a strange calm. The weave slithered and moved, enlivened by the sorcery of its production, quickly taking shape under your skilled hands. Just as they were done, two skins perfectly woven, you heard your father scream: a wretched sound. It went on—bones cracking like fireworks, spine splitting with a wet crunch—for a long while. Only when it stopped did you move, skins thrown over your shoulder, bare feet crushing the grass beneath your feet as you ran.

The scene in the hut was a nightmare. On the floor lay Kacha: bloody, stirring, watching you with empty eyes. He strained weakly in your direction. You threw the new skin atop him, careless. He keened, tugging uselessly at it, fingers grazing your thigh. You simply stepped past him, towards where your father's blood splattered the hut floor, crying out: 'Princess!'

A loop of jasmine, pristine, unspooled from the rapidly blooming lotus-field of your father's ribcage. You took it in your hands and pulled. It took you a few tries before you could see her, head and neck crowning blind terror in her face as you yanked her free of your father's torso.

You had made two skins, just like your father instructed.

One for Kacha. One for your princess, whom you had murdered earlier in the glade, mixing her remains with that of Kacha's in the wine.

As you slipped the skin over her, stitching her up tight, you could hear Kacha slithering about. He shuffled and croaked, half-alive, struggling to slip into the skin. His technique was poor, having never practised it himself. Did he wonder why you were not weeping at his side? What was he thinking, in his untucked mind, that his eyes were starting to cloud with terror?

You began to scream. Loud, deliberate, rending your throat. The scream ripped itself out of you even as you worked fastidiously at fixing up your princess.

Help, he's killed my father!

Help, the gods have murdered him!

Kacha belly-flopped, new skin fluttering like that of a half-sloughed snake. Footsteps sounded, running into the hut. You smelled godblood and stayed kneeling, clutching your head in despair, pretending to splutter and choke on your own grief.

Just a poor, helpless woman, bereft of both father and lover.

Behind you, there was gasping and grunting as Kacha's people carried him away. In front of you, your princess panted and mewled, stretching out her new skin, gaping at you with the sick terror of something faced with both its destroyer and creator.

You could hear the gods' chariot outside, wheels aflame, taking to the sky with Kacha still flailing uselessly at the back. When Kacha was nothing but a spark in the sky, you straightened up, taking in the scene.

Your father dead. Kacha indisposed. Your princess the sole, accidental keeper of the resurrection spell's secret.

There was silence now, hazy and friable, broken only by your princess's fitful crying. Into that stillness you spoke, hoarse and hushed, the question that would both begin and end your story: 'Did you hear it? The spell. Do you know it?'

And in your princess's affirmation, her awed terror, her perfect new skin and the bloody crown of her head, you glimpsed a strange new future:

dark, malleable, free for you to shape.

An hour after you return from Patala, you have at last finished collecting your father's skin, piled neatly what is left of his ribs and hips, and placed fragments of his spine in wraps of golden silk.

Your ashram is starting to fill with scores of demons. There are kings and queens, pisachas and vetalas, rakshasas and Nagas. There are demonic maidens so fragile they waver in the wind. Their loud lamenting rises like song, thrilling your blood, raising the hair on your skin.

You do not know where your princess is. Her absence makes you strangely lonely, but you have let her go. She kept her bargain by teaching you the resurrection spell and deserves her freedom. This is all she owes you, after you cut her throat to outsmart Kacha. Now, the two of you are even.

Briefly, you wonder what your father will think. That in the end it was not Kacha who betrayed him, but you. You wonder if he will be disappointed. But: oh Father, what did you expect? He had never seen you for what you really are: a weapon, gluttonous for power.

You will suck the marrow of it, for as long as you please, and the sweetness of it will linger on your tongue far longer than any memory of love.

Upala's knife cuts easily through bone. You put away the last sliver of your father's skull, collecting all the remains in a wide-rimmed container. The lotus blooms have all withered away. Outside, the demons wait: for explanation, lamentation, confrontation. You can taste their hunger for vengeance and blood in the very air.

You have rehearsed the version of the story you will tell them. The one where you screamed, and wept, and fantasized revenge on Amaravati. The one where you promise you will help them annihilate the gods—all 330 million of them—and bathe in their blood at the top of Mount Meru.

There is no version of the story branching from here where the demons do not follow you to the ends of the universe. You are the holder of the resurrection spell, the avenger of your father, the saviour of demonkind.

You are no longer the demon sage's daughter. You are the demon sage herself.

But before you speak to them, you will pour them all liquor. A sip to remember your father, to honour and celebrate his great life.

In each glass, you will place a tiny piece of him, obscuring the taste with the strength of freshly purchased Naga wine. No piece of him will go to waste. You will make sure of it.

In this way, distributed bit by bit amongst the demonic army, you will scatter your father's remains, that he may never be brought back whole.

One last safeguard to make sure that this is the deterministic version of your story: the final draft, the inevitable conclusion.

You drink your cup of wine, forcing it all down in one gulp.

Then you go out to start your war.

EGGS KEEP FALLING FROM THE FOURTH FLOOR

BHAVIKA GOVIL

On the fourth floor, an auntie lives. She calls out to the kids passing by, and whistles at us, and shouts, Hellooo, get me a shikanji, will you? But all the parents, the good ones, the bad ones, have told us to look away when she's shouting. She doesn't really need anything, don't go to her when she asks for things. And when she's crying or wailing, they say, it's fake. But it's hard not to look, because when she shouts, it sounds almost like she's singing. She has a voice like that—a little like imli—khatta-meetha. Or like honey with lemon when you pour it into a scratchy throat and it feels bad at first and then goes down smooth like plonk! and you fall asleep. Auntie's voice is like that.

When Papa started hitting Amma more often, they made so much noise that they couldn't even hear it when a gunshot went off on TV or when some boys set off firecrackers outside the house or when the watchman's mad wife was so angry with him for looking at another woman that she shrieked like she had seen a huge spider, for days and days and days. So, I started slipping out of our flat and going to Auntie's house. Her door was always open which was funny because most people in our building keep their doors shut, then double-shut with locks and bolts and all sorts of things like that as though they are rich and have plenty of things to lose.

When I complained to Auntie about my parents, she fixed me with her gaze and grinned widely and said: there are three ways to get their attention. You know, na, what to do. When you think they're not listening to you, you can jump out of a window.

I said, But I'll break my head.

She continued, scratching her hair which was a little grey and a little brown in places, That's right, the problem is that you'll break your head.

Yes.

When you go falling down down down.

Like an egg? I asked.

Like an egg, she confirmed.

So we dropped the idea.

The next time I was at her house, Auntie said, Let's move on to option number two. She said, I can run away from home and run faster than everyone and go to a place where everybody listens to me.

I said, You mean *I* can?

She looked at me blankly and nodded. Yes, of course. You can.

But my legs are shorter than Papa's, I said.

She scratched her head and said: Ah.

Then her eyes, which before this were sleepy and weepy, and even a little bit crusty, became big and brilliant, and she said, But this one will work. Then she whispered in my ear and grinned. Yes, this one *will* work.

⁓

Misi at school still can't believe I had the guts to go to Auntie's house all alone but that's because Misi gets scared easily. I told her that Auntie looks like a monster from way way way below—with scraggy hair and big, bulbous eyes and a little goop that always hangs from the side of her mouth. But she isn't really like that.

No one thought Misi and I would ever become friends either. We are so different. For one thing, she has many siblings and I have none. She has parents that don't hit each other, in fact, they don't really talk at all, and I have ones that bash and beat each other up like they are villains in a movie. Misi lives in a big house with one whole floor all to herself and many big windows to look out of. I don't. I have to climb on top of the cupboard in our one-room flat and then peer out the tiny, dirty window that we never clean because Amma always says, What's the point? There's nothing outside to look at anyway.

Plus, Misi has long hair that never get lice. Mine get lice. Mine have got lice twice. But we still became friends.

Whenever I go to school after a whole night of drama in our house, I have big, puffy eyes. I try to keep quiet and not say anything even when the teacher asks us to because if I do, I'll cry. So I keep my feet tap-tapping and roll my head into my top like a turtle and put my head on the desk. And whenever I feel like I need to see people I just pop my face out and there I am. And although Misi is rich and Amma and Papa and Auntie and everyone says that rich people don't understand much and can't think outside of themselves, Misi still does. When I'm in my turtle home, she knocks on my shell and comes sits next to me and holds my hand. And if there's nothing to say, she braids my hair and says it doesn't matter if I have lice or not. That's Misi for you.

⁓

Amma and Papa didn't always hit each other. When I was four, maybe five, they told each other things like I love you and No, I love you more. When they hugged, they took me into the centre of their hug and wrapped themselves around me until I couldn't see or smell anything but them. And when they thought I couldn't tell, they held hands under the blanket but we shared a bed and, of course, I could tell what they were doing by the lump. But when Papa stopped going to the factory and Amma started coming home late from the building she works in, they began spending more time fighting and hating everything: our house, each other. Even me.

⁓

When Auntie whispered the third idea to me, I didn't understand at first what she was talking about.

Get me the pills, the pills, she said, and began rubbing her eyes fast.

I looked at her blankly, wondering if she had a tummy ache and wanted the pink Digene medicine which tasted horrible but always worked.

No, no, Auntie said, irritated. The pills that make your mouth foam up like someone washed it out with soap. They make your body act as though an earthquake is taking place inside you.

You can get the pills from the man in the striped shirt behind the market. Then she added, If you ask nicely enough.

I stared at her.

She continued, Eat enough of the pills and everyone will notice you.

Everyone? I asked. I was thinking of Amma and Papa.

Everyone. And you'll share them with me, won't you?

People in the building say a lot of things about Auntie. That she used to be married to a woman. That she's a witch. That she was rich. That she drinks her face off. Drink what? I once asked, but they just laughed. That she came here from Pakistan. That she secretly owns a big van. They say a lot of things, but they don't say one thing for sure—she's smart as hell.

∫

Misi is not coming to school nowadays. The girls are saying lots of things—that Misi has moved schools, which can't be true because she'd never do that without telling me; that she has fallen down and broken her neck and legs and teeth all at once; and, worst of all, that her parents died, which is a very bad thing to say when it's false but even more so when it's true.

The teacher shushed them all and said, not die, they got *divorced*. Everyone sniggered. Later, I told Auntie the die-divorce thing, and she muttered that sometimes it means the same thing. Then, she roared with laughter. I asked her if she was married once and she said, Yes, perhaps. Perhaps, I was.

∫

The guy behind the market exploded with laughter when I went to him. He looked at me like I was joking. And even though my legs were shivering and I wanted to escape into my turtle home, I asked again loudly, pointing vaguely towards Auntie's flat. The man creased his eyebrows, and said, So, she's sent you this time, has she?

Then, he asked, Got the money?

When I said no, he said, There are other ways to pay, you know. Surely, your auntie must have told you that. He looked at me in my school uniform from top to bottom, slowly, licking his lips as he did. I ran away to my house as quickly as I could, thinking the whole time that Misi would *never* believe I had the guts to do this.

∽

Today, after ages, Misi came to school. I asked her what happened. Why was she gone for so long without telling me? But this time she was the one who was shivering, not me, so I took her to a corner in the girls' bathroom. She said that her mother didn't love her father any more. It was true, what the girls said, they were getting divorced. In fact...Misi began, But you can't tell anyone this. She paused, her words hanging in the air. So, I nodded violently and promised.

I don't know if it's true or not but Misi says that she saw her mother kissing her best friend.

Kissing? I asked, opening my eyes wide.

She nodded. Apparently, her mother never loved her father very much at all, and now she goes around kissing her best friend who's a woman.

At least that's what Misi says.

∽

Auntie with the imli voice fell from her balcony two days ago. She fell falling splat and made such a mess that people around complained that they had to pay money to get the courtyard scrubbed. Her head broke and cracked like an eggshell, but instead of yellow, red blood spilled out, and kept on flowing and flowing and flowing. I thought a lot of police people with their big cars and red rotating lights would come like they do in the movies to see a body crumpled on the ground. But only one man came and he was wearing loose brown trousers and honestly, I swear, he looked like he also didn't want to be there.

Misi at school says that it's not possible that Auntie just fell. People don't simply fall out of balconies. Sometimes, I think maybe Misi's right. But other times, I think that maybe what people said *is* true. Maybe Misi doesn't understand these things because she is too rich. And even if I'm not, I think, at least I'm better than Misi. At least my amma only kisses my Papa when she does and not strange women, and at least lice like me enough to come stay in my hair. And at least my building has four floors, not two, even if people fall out of it like eggs sometimes. At least.

TWENTY-FIRST TIFFIN

RAAM MORI

Translated from the Gujarati by Rita Kothari

'Neetu....' Mummy's shrill voice interrupted my chat. I left the drawing room and went into the kitchen.

'Mummy, please stop calling me Neetu. You know my name is Neetal. You seem to conveniently forget things. And then you make a point of repeating the same mistake. When my friend visited me recently and heard you yelling, "Neetu...Neetu..." it turned into a joke in college. People have been calling me R. K.'s mom since then.'

I stood there, seething with anger. Unruffled and calm, Mummy briskly filled up tiffin boxes.

'Who's R. K.?' she asked, as she counted the rotis.

'Oh, God. R. K. stands for Ranbir Kapoor. Neetu Kapoor's son. Now, for heaven's sake, don't tell me you don't know who he is. This is not some random boy from my college, by the way. In any case, why am I even bothering to recite an epic to an ignoramus? Listen, Mummy, it's time you shed all your orthodox nonsense. It's as stale as the leftovers in your tiffin boxes. And, please get a hold on your suspicious nature. All right, tell me now, why did you need me?' I asked, twirling my dry locks with a finger.

'It's past eleven, you see, it's time to quickly send off the lunch boxes. You know I can't prepare twenty tiffin boxes by myself. Obviously, I need some help from you.' She kept working as she talked to me.

'Mummy, you managed perfectly all this while. I have only been home for the past ten days or so. How is it that you suddenly can't manage now and you feel tired? You know what, just stop all this tiffin-shiffin business. Please.'

'And tell twenty boys, "Sorry, I cannot supply you food from tomorrow?" Like that, abruptly?' She glared at me, leaving me perplexed. 'Your father has not felt the need to provide money for running this house; it's thanks to these tiffin boxes that he is able to invest and move money around in stocks and shares without worrying about household expenses. You are able to study in a fancy college because of these tiffin boxes.'

'Oh stop it, Mummy. Are you saying that Papa is running away from his responsibilities? Or that he has not bothered to care for you? He loves you very much. He gave us this house, provides food to eat, clothes to wear, and his presence makes us feel safe.'

'Even a prison does all that,' she retorted. I looked at her, wide-eyed. Was her frustration with Papa peering out of her large, shapely eyes? I couldn't read them. I have come to realize that Mummy's eyes express nothing: they are simply flat and empty. And the lines on her expressionless face don't speak to me either. They always stay the same. My mother has been like this from the beginning: unkempt, unmoved, busy, and yet, a puzzle. On the other hand, I know Papa so well that I can almost predict his next sentence.

I have seen a certain kind of routine at home ever since I was a child. Papa would be constantly occupied. What comes to mind are his phone conversations, half-smoked cigarettes, white vest, and blue lungi. He would make calculations based on the financial projections he saw on TV, and buy and sell stocks and shares throughout the day, even at mealtimes, and go to sleep a tired man at night. As for my mother, she prepared tiffin boxes for twenty people day and night. She became the pressure cooker she cooked in. Her day began and ended in the kitchen. I often feel that Mummy has tied herself to this routine. When I picture her, what comes to mind is a woman indifferent to everything, clad in a dull sari, hair coiled up in a tight, stern-looking bun on her head, locks of grey hair around her face, an expanding waistline, and always reeking of perspiration. I remember that in the early days she used to prepare lunch for five people, later it became ten, and now it's twenty. I put aside the tablet I was holding and began to pack tiffin boxes in cloth bags. When all twenty were ready, I retreated to the drawing room and resumed chatting. Mummy joined me in a few minutes. She switched on the television and began to flip through the channels.

'Mummy, don't you think you should dye your hair?' I asked, my eyes on the tablet on which I was texting my friends.

'It's fine just the way it is. In fact, it's more than fine.' As she changed channels, a Ranbir Kapoor song appeared on the screen.

'Wow! Mummy, let it be. Don't change.'

She stood up and went towards the door to look for Bhanu Dada, who ferried her lunch boxes to different locations.

'Neetu, it's very exhausting now. I can't cook more than this,' she said, as she tucked her grey locks behind her ears. I threw a cursory glance at her, only to be lured back to the song on the TV. Silence hung heavy for a while. I felt that she wanted to say something to me, but was perhaps waiting for the right moment.

'Neetu, will you open the window? It's so dark in here.' I pushed down the window latch and nudged the window open to let the light in. Just then I heard the sound of the main gate being opened. I didn't bother getting up, assuming that it was Bhanu Dada who had arrived to pick up the tiffin boxes. But he usually rang his bicycle bell when he arrived. In which case....

'Namaste. May I come in, ma'am?'

Wow! What a voice, exactly like Ranbir's. I put aside the tablet and peered out of the window.

A young man was standing outside our house. He seemed to be around twenty years old. Mummy looked at me and said softly, 'Neetu, you go inside....' Before I knew what was happening, the man had already entered the house. He sat down on the sofa. I kept staring at him. He was dressed in a formal, body-hugging purple shirt that seemed more appropriate for a party, and black trousers. He had a pleasant and neat hairstyle and wore an elegant wristwatch. His eyes were light in colour. He had a large forehead, chiselled features, and glistening, white, symmetrical teeth—the kind you see in the commercials for toothpaste. His skin looked as though he had just come out of a spa. In short, he was a veritable five-foot-six-inch-tall package for marriage. My eyes were riveted on him.

As if he knew, he smiled at me and my mother, and said, 'Hello, my name is Dhruv Majumdar. I am an engineer. I arrived yesterday in this city for six months of training in a company.'

My mother must have realized that I hadn't taken my eyes off him. I was about to say, 'Hi, I'm Neetal,' but Mummy spoke up, 'Neetu, go and bring a glass of water.'

I muttered under my breath as I went into the kitchen. Mummy followed me. Before I could say anything she pounced upon me, 'At least keep a dupatta with you. We do a tiffin service from home; you never know when some boy will drop by to make a payment. Ever since you have come on vacation, they all seem to visit quite frequently.'

'Don't say anything more, Mummy. Please finish your job and go.' I was really irritated with her. All she could do was criticize me. If she wasn't yelling some four hundred times a day, she wouldn't know what else to do. While cooking, if she banged utensils or broke cups and saucers, it was a message to me to go to the kitchen. And this kitchen of hers was like a battlefield, everything was strewn all over the place.

I stood by a window looking at that fellow in the living room. My mother was sizing him up like he were a potential match on shaadi.com; I was feeling uncomfortable. I was hardly of marriageable age, and what was my mother trying to do but....

When we returned to the living room, the young man said: 'By the way, ma'am, my roommate uses your tiffin service. When I arrived yesterday, he was out, so I ate the meal you had prepared. I really enjoyed it. It was so tasty. And I am particularly fond of potatoes. Even the toor dal was delicious. The seasoning of the kadhi was also great. You know, I was really happy to eat such a meal. My sister-in-law used to make such food. Really wonderful.'

When I looked at Mummy's face, I was surprised to see a smile. What's more, her cheeks had turned crimson and her earlobes looked flushed! Was I imagining all this when I heard my pleased mother say, 'Thank you.' The expression on my mother's face made me feel dizzy. Of course, this guy was not merely flattering her. Her cooking had to be good, otherwise why would Bhanu Dada have increased the number of deliveries from five to twenty tiffins? I immediately thought of Papa. I wondered if my father had ever said something like, 'Wah, such good food....' Or if I had seen

Mummy laugh or blush before....

I was lost in my thoughts when this fellow said, 'Ma'am, if you don't mind, would you prepare lunch for me as well? It's only a matter of six months. I really like your cooking.'

'Oh, a twenty-first tiffin?' In my head I could visualize the vexations, cacophony, and stress that accompanied the preparation of twenty tiffins: utensils clashing, cups and saucers breaking, the sweat on her body, the mess in the kitchen, and everything ending with her plonking herself down on the sofa in exhaustion and muttering: 'Neetu, I can't handle more... not more than twenty, this much is enough.'

I was about to decline the request at once, but before I could do that my smiling mother said, 'Not a problem. I anyway make twenty. One more it is. I will give Bhanu Dada your tiffin from tonight.'

I frowned. The boy paid for a month and left. Without counting the cash, Mummy went to put it in a drawer. I stood between her and the drawer.

'Mummy, what is going on? What is this?' I asked with exasperation.

She began to dust the drawing room. 'How does it matter? One more tiffin is not going to kill me, child.'

'Oh. Now you better stop yelling for me from the kitchen. And stop breaking crockery. You are a fine one to complain to me, "Neetu, I can't manage." You have added more work for yourself now.' I knew I was overreacting. I took the keys of the scooty and left the house. When I came back home, I saw my mother smiling at me. Something nagged at me, the smile perhaps—I wasn't used to it.

From that day on, Mummy changed in small ways. Papa had no time to notice, but the changes didn't escape me. She stopped shouting altogether. She even started to hum while she was working. At every mealtime, her enthusiasm to prepare the tiffins was different now. I would pack the tiffin boxes and put them away, but the moment I reached the twenty-first tiffin, she would say, 'One minute, Neetal, don't shut that one.' I would watch in silence as she dragged a stool from the drawing room and climbed on to it. She would take out the pickle jar from the top shelf, and after filling up a small container with slivers of mango pickle, she would close the tiffin box and gaze at it with contentment. These days, potato sabzi appeared more frequently on the menu, and the other day, I saw generous amounts of it in the twenty-first tiffin. Even the rotis that went into that tiffin had more ghee on them. I found all this really childish. I watched it all and felt it was all stupid.

As soon as the month ended, Dhruv would come home to make his payment. Without planning to, I had begun to ignore him. Mummy would make special ginger tea for him, accompanied by some snacks. He would sit for an hour or so, chatting with her. From my room, I would peep out at them talking and laughing together. Their friendliness made me uncomfortable.

One day, he came up with a new thing. He said to my mother,

'Ma'am, since you cook with such commitment, why don't you start a small restaurant at home? I am sure it'll do very well.'

'I won't be able to sustain it even for six months,' my mother quipped, and the two of them laughed. It was a shock for me to see my mother making these smart comebacks.

I was beginning to feel impatient with myself as well as my father. An outsider had been able to change my mother so fundamentally, to make her laugh while we, the people who had lived with her for years, had failed to do so. On one occasion, sick and tired of Mummy and Papa's quarrels, I remember saying to her, 'Mummy what is the matter with you? You seem to pick a fight with Papa all the time.'

'Do I initiate the fights, Neetu?' she replied, with her usual flat tone and unemotional demeanour.

'It doesn't make a difference, Mummy. Why don't you just learn to let go a little? He's really perfect.'

She had put her hand on my head, and said with an emptiness in her eyes, 'Beta, he's your papa, that's why he is perfect for you. He's a husband to me, and the way I look at him is bound to be different.' I remember how pale her face was then. But today, where has that pallor gone? At times, when I start thinking about Mummy and Dhruv...my thoughts hit the blades of the fan and scatter throughout the room, wounded. I don't know what I'm supposed to think any more.

The biggest shock was when my mother began to dye her hair. She looked at herself in the mirror, and asked me, 'Neetu, how do I look?' What had not been possible through all my efforts had been achieved by that fellow's visits. While it was true that all the boys Mummy cooked for came home to make payment, Dhruv stayed the longest. Mummy would seldom chat with the other boys.

Dhruv is a really special case! Now Mummy wears her hair in a loose, low bun. Her sari is draped carefully, every fold in place, held together by a safety pin. And no matter how little time she has, she makes sure to wear a matching bindi on her forehead. She would steal a moment to check her reflection on the gleaming surface of a utensil as she cooked. And gone were the sounds of vessels banging and clashing about; a mellifluous humming had taken their place. I would often scream, 'Mummy, what are you doing? Where's your mind? The roti is going to burn.'

'Neetal, why are you shouting? I am paying attention....' she would reply.

'To what?' I would ask with a meaningful glance, but this would be lost on her and she would happily go back to being lost in her own world. She would drag out the stool, reach for the sweet-sour gorkeri pickle on the top shelf, and fill up the twenty-first tiffin.

I have noticed these days, that on the last Sunday of the month, namely, Dhruv Day, Mummy takes longer than usual in the shower, and lingers over her reflection in the mirror. Although she would sit on the sofa watching television, she would be waiting for the sound of the doorbell. She would run to the door the moment it rang. I was beginning to find all this quite intolerable. All these lights had begun to singe me...and that fellow constantly came up with new gimmicks:

'Ma'am, why don't you participate in MasterChef? We can put your cuisine on the international map.'

'Ma'am, you should also learn some foreign dishes, you know, progress....'

'Ma'am, do you use Tarla Dalal's cookbooks?'

Now I was the one screaming. I would knock down tiffins, break crockery, and bang utensils down but Mummy seemed oblivious to all this.

One day, Dhruv did not come on a Dhruv Day but in the middle of the week. He held a present in his hand. He sat with Mummy and they sipped tea and talked.

'Ma'am, today my training is over. Six months went by so fast, eating food prepared by you. I didn't even realize how quickly time has passed.... This is a small token of my appreciation for you.' My heart began to thud vigorously. So we will not see Dhruv any more, then? Mummy unwrapped the present. It was a recipe book of cuisines from different parts of the world. Mummy thanked him. The two of them sat quietly for a while. He drank the rest of the tea and stood up to leave. I felt as though I ought to see him off to the gate, but I asked myself the very next moment why I wanted to do so considering the fact that I didn't even like him coming to the house. As he left, he turned around, smiled at me, and left, closing the gate. Numerous cups and saucers broke inside me. I felt worried about Mummy. She stood in the drawing room, unmoving, for God knows how long. I could sense a funereal silence around me. The sun had set and darkness was upon us.

At night, Mummy was filling up tiffins in the kitchen while I was folding clothes in my room. 'Neetu...where the hell are you now?' I heard Mummy shout. I rushed to the kitchen. A saucer had slipped from Mummy's hand. I noticed that Mummy's hair was tied up in a stern, tight bun. Her back was drenched with sweat and she was panting from her exertions. Loose strands of hair clung to her sweat-drenched face. I immediately filled up dal and sabzi in different tiffins. Mummy counted the rotis and began putting them in each box. When all the tiffins were filled up, Mummy went to the shelf on which the pickle jar was, dragging the stool with her. My eyes were downcast but I knew what she was doing. She brought the pickle jar down. With pursed lips, and downcast eyes, I struggled to speak, 'Mummy, you...but...he....'

My mother looked at me. Our eyes met, mother's and daughter's, and I could not bear her gaze. I looked away, out the window. Mummy also turned her gaze away. But I had noticed three lines on her flat forehead and a hazy mist clouding her eyes. Dark shadows had descended upon and between us—between mother and daughter.

GOBYAER[*]

SADAF WANI

WHILE I EXIST AS A SPIRIT IN THIS COLD GREY VALLEY, SOMETIMES I GET tired of not being seen and perceived, not being heard, and not being able to leave my footprints on the snow as I pass by mountains, towns, and villages. However, in this valley marred by grief, complaining about these little inconveniences seems a bit absurd and, at times, quite selfish. Selfish, even for someone like me, whose entire sense of self is unresolved and perpetually in doubt. This valley that I have grown to call my home, I don't call it by its name, for it makes me uneasy. Every time I hear its name being said out loud, I fear something bad might happen. The thought of leaving this place and its disquiet crosses my mind often. In the past, I have acted upon this impulse, but every time I left, I found myself making the arduous journey back.

I leave this valley, which is my home, because I get tired of being invisible here. Sometimes, I long to participate in the events that are taking place in the streets, rivers, and markets. However, people pass through me as I reach out for them. I am ridiculed by other spirits for these frivolous desires. They mock my longing for home by saying that spirits do not have homes. I disagree. I say home is only a place, and a place is its people. So, doesn't that make these people my people, and this valley my home?

I speak about these people in the valley as 'my people' like I know them or like they know me. I speak of them as if I like them and as if they like me. In fact, I do not know them, and they do not know me. We are mutually oblivious of each other's existence for the most part. However, something cuts through this relationship of oblivion and ties us to each other. There is a gobyaer on our being. It is amusing that a phenomenon as physical as weight and heaviness connects me, who is supposed to have transcended the physical realm, to these people and this place.

At first, I did not understand how a word representing something so physical could describe what I was feeling. So I started paying attention to how humans across the valley were using this word. Once, I was passing through a cluster of villages by a small hill near the south of Jhelum. There, I saw that a crowd had gathered around a young boy who had fainted, just as he had reached his village, after spending a long day in the deep forest. The boy was speaking gibberish and appeared to have

---

[*]Heaviness or weight in Kashmiri. In the everyday vernacular, gobyaer is also used to refer to the state of being possessed by djinns or other supernatural forces.

a concussion. It was intriguing, for I knew at first sight that it was the work of my distant cousins. The older djinns are known to take offence at humans disturbing the quiet of the deep forest. They get enraged when humans shamelessly relieve themselves under the old chinar trees that they've made their home. To teach them a lesson, and dissuade the rest of the villagers from venturing into the forest, they possess the bodies of people who've invoked their wrath. Having seen that it was just another young boy possessed by the djinns, I lost interest and started moving away from the crowd where the imam was inspecting the boy. However, as I started moving away, the imam suddenly got up, walking quickly in my direction. He stopped right before he could pass through me. It's the closest I've come to being perceived. I swear I thought he was talking to me when he said, 'Ye chu gobyaer (It's the heaviness).'

After this incident, I started getting drawn to this word, to every conversation where it was mentioned. One night I was passing by an old street towards the south of the valley, and I saw a grim-looking young man smoking cigarettes, standing outside the house of his lover from long ago. The sound of the tumbaknari, the Kashmiri drum, from the house filled up the street, where he stood for a while. There was nothing he could do and nothing he wanted to do to stop the event, but the loss he experienced throughout that night of anticipation he also called gobyaer. Similarly, towards the east of the valley, I was once roaming through an apple orchard enjoying the blossoms when I noticed an older woman in the middle of the orchard. She looked up at the May sky, overcast with dark clouds, and knew they were the clouds of misfortune and hailstones. She looked around her apple trees, knowing very well that in a few hours the blossoms and the promise of a good harvest would be gone. The heavy footsteps she took towards her home, as she waited for the rains to intensify, she called gobyaer too.

However, this gobyaer prompted by personal grievances is not what connects me to these people. Since I don't have loved ones who I yearn for, or land that I cultivate, or a future to prepare for, I cannot relate to these emotions. There is an overarching feeling of impending loss and terror that goes far beyond the everyday affairs of my people, something that everyone here is always waiting for. Sometimes it is realized sooner than at other times, but each cycle of loss confirms that our fears are not unfounded. The fear grows in hearts, as does the gobyaer. I cannot tell exactly what this gobyaer does to humans, for they don't seem to hear me, so I cannot ask them anything. I am only telling you what I have overheard in open markets and closed rooms.

Having heard about it from so many people over decades, I have started seeing it as well, even though I don't experience it like humans do. I have started seeing that gobyaer has a personhood as abstract as mine. I say this because I have seen how gobyaer surrounds and seeps into people and what it does to them. When I look at my people, I see that this strange presence has engulfed their lives, the gobyaer has attached itself to their skin, sedimented in their bones, and it feeds off the hope in their hearts. It lives in their homes now, sits in their hammams, and shares their rice with them. And when they are watching TV late at night, it occupies the cosiest spot in the room, and my people pretend not to see it.

The old people in the valley seem to have found a dedicated corner in their lives for this gobyaer. They put it in the deepest pocket of their baend, which they always wear under their pherans, carrying it around with them wherever they go. The younger ones, however, are more ambitious. 'Why should we carry this burden with us all our lives? Why should we give in like you cowards did?' they ask the old ones, who do not smile, and only smoke their jijeers. Spurred on by their ambitions, some young ones travel to far-off lands, hoping they could leave this gobyaer behind. Some go to the tallest mountains, some to distant deserts, and others towards seas because it was rumoured that seawater could melt it.

One time, when I ran away from the valley to travel the world and find a new home, I was surprised at how easily I could spot my people wherever I went. I had thought everybody carried this gobyaer with them until I met people who are not my people. It was then that I realized that it is something that only people of the valley have, and I also found the answer to what differentiated my people from the crowds in cities, riversides, and deserts. Naturally, I followed some of my people when I saw them outside the valley. I found some of them running through iced alleyways. Some were plodding through desert towns, and others were hiding in muddy lanes by the sea. I found a few walking briskly on the wide roads and dingy streets of big cities visiting pirs, faqirs, and shamans seeking foreign remedies for their very indigenous disease. Some of them kept running for years and years, and when they thought enough time had passed, they came back home. However, to their horror, they found this gobyaer waiting on their dastarkhwan to share their razma-dal with them.

Some people who have got tired of running have now realized that the gobyaer always finds a way home. So, they have started building houses with a spare room. They make it big and cosy so that they can scream and wail in it. Men who have only one room and not enough razma-dal to share cannot find a quiet place to sit with their fears. The children are always crying, and the creditors are always knocking on their doors. They deal with the gobyaer by bringing it up all the time and to everyone they can find. In the fields, in the bus, at the shop, on their verandas. They repeat the same stories every day with minor additions and deletions, of how they first encountered this feeling, how they tried to run away from it, and how there is no place like home, so they come back. 'Gari wandihai gari saasah, bari nyerihai ni zanh (There is no place like home)', they keep repeating all day. I often see women peeling vegetables on the verandas of their houses sigh in exasperation and put their hands on both their ears as they run inside. They seem to be sick of hearing the same stories every day. Women have their versions of how they encountered gobyaer and how they live with it. But the men never stop talking, and so the women always leave the room in frustration.

One of the reasons I keep coming back to this valley from faraway places is my belief that the cure of this indigenous disease cannot be found outside the valley. So, I pass through the valley looking for comfort, if not the ultimate answer. There is a small, lonesome house in an apricot orchard in the valley's northern end, where an old woman puts her granddaughter and daughter to sleep every night. In this house, there are no men, so women talk out loud without interruptions. But that's not the only reason I come back here. Every night, before putting them to sleep, the grandmother whispers a six-letter word into their ears as they fall asleep. A six-letter charm that gets you in trouble if you say it out loud in the valley, but the only known charm that puts the gobyaer to rest, at least for some time. The old woman tells them stories of the day when the charm will manifest itself, cutting through the grey cloudy sky, falling softly on the valley like morning sunlight on all its living and non-living things. It will slowly melt away what occupies the heart and weighs it down. It is said that after that day the spare rooms in the houses will be filled with the aroma of sun-dried tomatoes, the young ones will not need to run off to deserts, mountains, seas, and cities, and men will finally let the women narrate their own stories.

After the lights in the entire valley are dimmed, the last batch of soldiers and rebels have gone off to sleep, and the placards and flags have been locked in for the night, I come back to hear the same story night after night. I feel comforted watching the little girl fall asleep to this reassurance. Last night, as she fell asleep, her little fist unclenched at some point to reveal the charm she had just learned to write: azaadi.

THE ALLIGATOR OF ALIGARH

A. M. GAUTAM

KALUA LISTENED TO HIS BELLY GROAN WITH HUNGER. He mopped at the beads of sweat on his forehead with a gamcha and peeked over his wife's shoulder into a pot in which she was cooking some nameless concoction the colour of mucus, with a few pieces of onion here and there trying to drown themselves. The sight of it was enough to dull his appetite a little. To make things worse, there wasn't nearly enough of it to sneak some off to Safeda. His friend would just have to go hungry again.

He looked at Gudiya, his little sister, reading a scrap of a newspaper in a corner, and felt guilty about thinking of Safeda when he was failing to provide enough even for his family. Only last month, Gudiya had fallen sick and the doctor had advised Kalua to include meat in her diet at least once a week to make up for protein deficiency.

Despite this guilt, however, Safeda was also important to Kalua. Like many other people in the world, Kalua had found his best friend at his workplace. Only, the workplace happened to be a gutter, and the best friend happened to be an alligator.

Kalua didn't know how Safeda came to be there, only that the creature was hurt and starving when they first met. Kalua fed it his own lunch and applied cool mud to its bruises. Because of the whitish grey colour of its skin, which Kalua thought unusual, he named the alligator Safeda. The absence of sunlight in the creature's life might have had something to do with its unusual pigmentation. Or maybe it was just an anomaly. Whatever the cause, the contrast between the alligator's pale hide and his own had amused Kalua no end.

A few days later, Kalua heard someone in the nearby market talking about a man arrested for smuggling exotic reptiles to Indian connoisseurs. The police were forced to release him from custody soon afterwards; apparently he had flushed his specimens down the toilet to remove all incriminating evidence. Kalua knew now where a part of that evidence had ended up, but not intending to get mixed up with the police, he kept his suspicions to himself.

That was twelve years ago.

Kalua had not been married then and Gudiya hadn't even been born. In those days, he used to go into the sewers only when his father's cough was exceptionally bad. He hated every second of it and swore daily to himself that he would become anything but a jamadaar.

That, of course, was before the world had explained the inescapability of his caste to him, and before his parents had died of tuberculosis, leaving him to bring up his baby sister all alone.

'Ae, Gudiya, what are you doing reading in this bad evening light? You'll ruin your eyes,' he called out to the girl whom he had managed to keep away from the sewers, and had even sent to school.

Up until now, at least.

Gudiya was now almost ten years old, but looked like she was only six or seven. This wasn't unusual in their neighbourhood, though—malnutrition made the kids all look younger than they actually were, and the adults older.

Gudiya looked at him and threw aside the newspaper scrap she was reading. 'Went to the butcher in the afternoon, but he had already gutted and skinned everything. He asked me to come only when my cut had healed completely.'

After school, Gudiya often went to help the neighbourhood butcher in his shop, and he tossed her a few coins for her labour every now and then. Two days ago, she had cut her hand while slicing a piece of meat.

It was an ugly gash, and Kalua had tied a clean piece of cloth around it, hoping that it would not get infected. The butcher, Kalua knew, had sent Gudiya away not out of concern for her but because he did not want to risk her blood making the meat impure for his customers.

'It's okay, beta, don't worry about it. This is just a temporary situation. Things will go back to normal soon,' Kalua told her with a conviction he did not possess himself. His wife joined them and put the cooking pot between them, holding it carefully with rags in her hands. She rotated it a few times, as though trying to pull off some magic trick that would turn that mixture of water, flour, and salt into real food. There were only two spoons in the pot.

'Aren't you eating, Bhabhi?' Gudiya asked.

'I'll eat later. You two eat now, and please make sure you wipe the pot clean.'

But, there was nothing to be had later, Kalua knew that well enough. Tomorrow it would be a week since either of them had gone to work. This muck in the pot, this was the last of their rations.

He got up so quickly that his head swam a little and his stomach growled in protest.

'I am sorry, I remembered just now—Varshneyji had asked me to visit his house today. He wants me to help unload some stuff from his terrace. I'll just go there and come back in a while, okay?'

'But your dinner?' his wife asked, not meeting his eyes.

'You two finish it off. I'll have some chai–nashta with Varshneyji.'

Kalua did not wait for her response, but at the door he paused for just a moment to look at her moving slowly to sit beside Gudiya. After he emerged from the hut, he took a few steps to the right so that they wouldn't see him standing there. Then, he let out a long, heavy sigh, the sort that can crush those who hear it and must, therefore, only be released once you are at a safe distance from the people you love.

His wife must have seen through his lie. She knew full well that he wouldn't even be allowed to sit on the curb outside a baniya's house, let alone be invited inside and asked to handle his possessions. Not in a million years—a pamphlet of Swachh Bharat Abhiyan fluttered near his feet and Kalua spat at it in disgust—not after a thousand more Swachh Bharat Abhiyans had come and gone could that happen in their world.

The only place Kalua, or anyone from his caste, could go to in the house of someone from an upper caste, like Varshneyji, was the latrine. Straight in, straight out, and a few coins dropped on their palms at the door without a word exchanged. Kalua and his kin were like elves. Shit-scooping, latrine-scraping elves. Invisible and inaudible to everyone.

Still, even while wading through all the literal and figurative shit in their lives, they had kept going, one way or another. Until a fortnight ago, when a saffron-robed rally had snaked its way through the jamadaar basti where they lived, holding up bright posters that most of the residents couldn't read.

Fat government men with sweat-shined faces, saccharine smiles, and noses scrunched up against the smell of Kalua and his people. They declared proudly through their loudspeakers that no one would be required to lower themselves into a sewer any more. If anybody asked them to do so, the government would penalize that person.

They were told that the credit for all this went to their chief minister and the prime minister, both of whom cared deeply for all Hindus, including Dalits like Kalua and his neighbours.

Once they had finished making their speeches, the fat men got in their vehicles and waved to Kalua and the other shanty dwellers; they were careful not to shake hands with them or touch them in any way. Amidst much fanfare, with satisfied smiles, they departed the same way they had arrived and breathed freely once more in the clean air outside the slum.

It was only a couple of hours later that Kalua, his wife, and their friends realized that the government men had forgotten to mention what jobs they would be doing now that their present employment had been declared illegal.

And so it was that the slum had begun to crawl towards starvation.

They had held up until now by dipping into their meagre savings. A few of them had managed to get odd jobs here and there, but no one really wanted to employ a jamadaar in their shop or house, or anywhere that there would be a chance of being touched by them.

Kalua wondered where he could go to pass the time while his family had their dinner and decided upon the only place that felt a little like home.

A horrible home, true, but still a home, with the comfort of an old friend.

Maybe he would also be able to catch a few rats down there and feed them to Safeda.

'Do you think Bhaiya will be able to get some work today?' Gudiya asked her bhabhi, back in the house.

'Yes, yes, of course, he'll find some work. Don't you worry about it.'

But Gudiya did worry about it.

She worried that her brother had not been able to feed his pet for the past two weeks and it was making him even sadder than usual. Gudiya had never met this pet, but she knew its name was Safeda; it had slipped out of Kalua once, though he had not noticed it.

Gudiya liked to imagine that Safeda was a fluffy white dog like the pet one of her classmates had. Only, her bhaiya kept his pet in a sewer instead of at home. This didn't seem strange to her ten-year-old mind because she knew that Bhabhi would never have allowed Bhaiya to keep the dog in the house, not when they never had enough food or money for the three of them.

Like most kids in the neighbourhood, Gudiya knew that the last couple of weeks had been especially bad for everyone. It was evident in the way that people she had known all her life to wake up at dawn and go to work now spent their days sitting despondently in front of their shacks, waiting for something to happen. The desperate wait reminded Gudiya of the days when she was a toddler and would keep looking out anxiously for the ice cream man, who never came to their gully. The worst of it was the change that had come over her bhaiya. No matter how bad things had got in the past, he would always have a joke tucked away somewhere in his head, ready to be summoned and released to laughter all around when things began to look too grim. He was a doer who liked to make things happen, rather than wait passively for situations to resolve themselves for better or for worse. Like when Gudiya had waited, and waited, and waited, for the ice cream man day after day, one day Bhaiya had just brought back three orange-flavoured ice creams from God knew where. These past few days, however, he hardly talked to her at all.

Some days, while taking a bath, Gudiya would move her fingers slowly underwater in the bucket and watch them for minutes on end. That's how her brother looked these days. Like a man living underwater in his head; walking around in a bubble of empty space where no one could really reach him. Except for his pet, maybe. It might cheer him up if Gudiya brought it to the house and surprised him. Anyway, she was sure that it would cheer her up!

So, after her bhabhi had put her to bed, and gone to sleep herself, Gudiya put on the robe that Kalua wore when he went into the sewers. He had made it by stitching together discarded polythene bags. It was too large for her, of course, and fluttered behind her like a superhero's cape. In the weak light leaking into the hut from a street light, the multicoloured robe of polythene bags shimmered like an undisciplined rainbow. She then put on Kalua's yellow safety helmet and his brown leather boots.

Quietly, Gudiya stole out of the hut and closed the door behind her.

She walked up to the open manhole down which she had seen her bhaiya disappear many times. Then, with a look at the moon overhead, she lowered herself down into the darkness, down the iron rungs of the sewer.

⌇

This manhole into which Gudiya had lowered herself was connected to other manholes in the city through large pipes constituting Aligarh's sewage network. As Gudiya descended further down the hole, she could hear the water splashing at the bottom and her guts contracted a little with the inherent fear of invisible, damp things.

The stench of sewage was overwhelming and made her feel a little faint.

To steel herself, she looked up at the circle of the night sky through the open manhole, but it looked so far away suddenly that she thought it better to concentrate on her descent.

Finally, after a few moments, or minutes, or millennia, her boots found mushy ground.

A small part of her mind wondered how a dog could live in a place where the water came up to her ankles. But before she could give it a thought, there was a sound of water splashing nearby.

It sounded like she wasn't alone. Someone else was also taking a night walk here. Or maybe it was just the sound of her heart tumbling out of her mouth and falling into the sewer.

Gudiya moved forward, putting one foot in front of the other, like a little soldier in large boots. Her polythene robe made an almost-but-not-quite-silent slithering sound behind her.

A few more steps and the darkness would be absolute. Gudiya pressed a little wire in the helmet and the bulb–battery combination that Kalua had taped together came to life. The feeble light threw long shadows on the sewer's walls and Gudiya saw that the pipe turned sharply to the left a little way off in the distance.

Again, she heard the sound of water splashing. Despite an instinctive urge to run back, she kept walking in the direction of the sound. And then, as she stood at the bend in the pipe she saw in front of her a man tossing something into the water at his feet.

No, not into the water. Tossing something to a creature on the ground.

A creature that definitely was not the fluffy white dog that she imagined Pinky's pet looked like. Sharp white teeth glinted in an evil grin at her.

A pair of dull green eyes with black slits for pupils measured the flesh on her bones. In the wavering light of Gudiya's helmet-bulb, she thought she saw a ripple of excitement pass through the monster's dirty rubbery-white body.

The man standing beside it, startled by the light, turned to face Gudiya. It was her bhaiya, of course, and how shocked he looked! Dead rats dangled by their tails in his hand like the balls of the neighbourhood butcher, who had shown them to Gudiya last week and had given her twenty rupees just for touching them.

She looked from her brother to the monster at his feet and opened her mouth to scream but found the sound missing. She closed her fists so tightly at her sides that the cloth Kalua had tied as a bandage came off and two tiny drops of blood dropped down from the open cut into the water. The starving alligator, half-blind, but no less a predator for it, caught the whiff of fresh blood and lunged towards it.

Kalua's mind tried to make sense of the situation and failed irrevocably. His thoughts came to him only as snatches of the self-evident truth. Must do something. Quickly. His friend, whose primary trait in the last twelve years had been laziness, was now paddling furiously towards his sister, who stood rooted to the spot.

A large piece of stone, dislodged long ago from the sewer's wall, was lying near where Safeda's tail was thrashing around in the water, and Kalua picked it up.

'Gudiya! GUDIYA! Run. NOW!'

But Gudiya's eyes were locked on Safeda, as though hypnotized, and she looked like she could not even hear Kalua.

Kalua moved towards Safeda, stumbling in the water and almost falling down. He righted himself and was near the alligator's head in a couple of strides. Safeda turned to look at him and, for a moment, Kalua thought he could see a trace of human intelligence in the green eyes, a hesitation in moving towards Gudiya.

But hunger is hunger.

It turned again towards Gudiya and with a flick of its tail almost hit Kalua, as if warning him not to meddle with its dinner.

Kalua raised the stone high above his head, stepped forward, and brought down its jagged corner into Safeda's left eye. He wanted only to buy enough time to send Gudiya away, but it was as if the violence had unleashed something inside him which he did not know existed.

Before Safeda could turn towards him, he straddled the creature, and brought the stone down once again with all his strength. And then again, and again, until there was no movement left in the body and the light had gone out of Safeda's eyes. It felt a little like the final cleaning away of the shit that other people had flushed his way. Regular work, nothing odd. A frightened little giggle escaped Kalua's mouth at this thought.

He did not know what made him stop finally. Maybe it happened when Gudiya managed to find her voice again.

'Bhaiya, please. Enough.'

Her face looked so small, so fragile, in the half-light-half-shadow of the bulb in her helmet. It reminded him, strangely enough, of how little Safeda had been when he had found it starving in the sewer.

'Come, let's go.'

Kalua got off Safeda's lifeless body and took Gudiya by her hand.

He took one last look at his friend before turning away. An eyeball, dislodged from its socket, dangled from the destroyed face by a thin string of flesh. Even as he watched, the eyeball fell into the sewer water...Plop!

Kalua bent down for Gudiya to climb on to his back and like that they walked to the manhole's ladder. Slowly, Kalua climbed out.

In her cot, tucked in by her brother, the monster in the sewer seemed little more than one of her regular nightmares to Gudiya.

With half-closed eyes she watched Kalua put on the polythene robe she had taken off—he had thrown his own on the street, blood-stained and grimy as it was—and pick something up from the kitchen shelf before going out again.

Fear crept back into her heart. 'Where are you going, Bhaiya? Come to sleep, please?'

As he put the thing that he had picked up from the shelf into his pocket, Gudiya saw that it was the knife she took with her when she went to work at the butcher's shop.

'Don't you worry, I'll be back up in no time at all,' he said with a tired little smile. Then, with a little hesitation, he added, 'And maybe tomorrow, we will have meat again for lunch. It'll be good for you, the doctor said.'

THE CURRENT CLIMATE

ARAVIND JAYAN

THE NEW BRANCH MANAGER, MR CHANDRU, NOTICED THE IDOL AS SOON as he entered the bank. It stood on a white pedestal in the centre of the foyer, was about two feet tall, and depicted Shiva, Parvati, and Ganesha sitting together. It looked heavy—and might have been made out of brass—though he couldn't be sure. Mr Chandru introduced himself to the staff and learned their names. On his second day at work he asked to have the idol moved into the storeroom.

The bank branch was a shoebox with around twenty-five staff. Apart from one Muslim loan officer named Asif, and two Christian tellers, they were all Hindu like him. Anyway, it wasn't the denomination of the staff that mattered to Mr Chandru. What mattered was that they were a national establishment, and the nation was secular. Religious artefacts had no place being displayed so prominently in the bank.

Mr Chandru's order was received with some reluctance. He'd expected this, given the general climate, and he'd looked forward to explaining himself. During his college days—a long time ago now—he had been involved in some local politics. In his final year, he had even published not one but two revolutionary poems in a magazine run by the student body. Such experiences had little to do with banking, but as they'd said at one of his management seminars, when you take charge of an office, you're in charge not only of the staff but also of the culture.

Amit Agarwal, the assistant manager, was the first to react. He'd listened to Mr Chandru's explanation and nodded with a sullen expression. Having to explain in Hindi, Mr Chandru, a South Indian, felt he had been less eloquent than he'd hoped.

'But you're a Hindu, sir?' Agarwal said.

'Yes, but that's beside the point.'

'It's just that the idol gives us a feeling of protection. Nothing political, sir.'

'I'd like to have it removed, nonetheless. That's all.'

After some hesitation, Agarwal left his cabin. Later, almost as an afterthought, he popped his head around the door to extend a dinner invitation to Mr Chandru for the following night.

Mr Chandru was not only new to the branch but also to the town where he'd been posted. The bank had provided him with a one-storey, two-bedroom house that wasn't too far from work. The house was small, but it came with a dining table, a double bed, a stove, a velvet sofa, a fridge, a television, and a small alcove on the wall that was supposed to be used to set up a puja unit. The dusty floor was tiled in a mosaic pattern and the windows were dirty. In fact, everything needed a thorough cleaning. Mr Chandru had planned to do just that, but by the time he got back from work, the temperature had dropped to a single digit. The sky had turned grey, and a sharp wind had picked up.

Unused to this sort of cold, Mr Chandru felt tired and lazy. He boiled some rice in a cooker, made dal, and ate it by the small red heater he'd borrowed from his office. Afterwards, he washed up and sat wrapped in a blanket, watching the news and thinking about the day's events. Something about the cold and the bland food made him uncomfortable. It was homesickness, he decided—that's all.

When the power went, Mr Chandru pulled the blanket even closer around himself, and wished the stray dogs outside would stop howling. If he felt spooked, it was only for a moment. Soon, his wife and his son would join him. Things would start to fall into place, and he would feel better about everything.

The idol was still there when Mr Chandru reached work the next day. Now the whole thing had become a matter of insubordination or at least laziness. Either way, it wasn't good. Most of the staff members had already arrived. Those who were walking in wished him a good morning.

Mr Chandru went around looking for a peon, then failing to find anyone, he decided to move the idol himself. This would not only make the peons feel bad but would also establish that he was a hands-on manager who wasn't afraid to sweat a little, if need be.

The idol was heavier than he had anticipated. Having picked it up, though, there was no way he could put it back down without looking foolish. Even though he felt several eyes on him, no one stepped forward to help. Perhaps they were unsure of his exact intentions or didn't want to seem overfamiliar.

Wobbly on his feet, and thinking he probably looked comical, Mr Chandru carried the idol some twenty-five feet, pushed open the storeroom door with his shoulders, and placed it on a metal table that was covered with dust. Among the broken computers and racks of dumped files, he found a piece of white cloth, shook it twice, and covered the idol with it. That done, he closed the door with an officious air and went to his cabin, sneezing so hard he felt some of his hair come loose. That morning, as Mr Chandru was doing his rounds, he wondered if Asif didn't look somewhat happier. He even sensed some admiration in the man's smile.

When Asst. Manager Agarwal came to his cabin later that day, Mr Chandru said, 'By the way, I moved the idol to the storeroom myself.'

In between licking his finger and turning a page of the file he was checking, Agarwal looked up and nodded. 'Okay, sir.'

That was all he said, though something in his tone didn't feel quite right—so much so that in the evening, Mr Chandru wondered if the dinner invitation that had been extended to him the day before was still valid. It wasn't that he pined for friendship; just that he hated the thought of going back and eating yesterday's food.

Thankfully, at precisely six, Agarwal came in and asked him if he was done with work. Mr Chandru packed stuff away in his briefcase, got in his old Maruti car—freshly shipped—and followed the other man's bike. Agarwal's house was farther from the bank than the house Mr Chandru had been allotted, and when they arrived, he saw that it was noticeably smaller too.

Agarwal's wife was a thin woman who looked much more dignified than the man she had married. She wore a plain housecoat—clearly not dressed to receive a guest, especially her husband's boss.

'So good to have you here,' she said.

'Thank you for having me,' Mr Chandru said.

Dinner was served as soon as they entered the house. Nothing fancy: white rice, chickpeas, a few tough rotis, aloo jeera, and spiced curd. Agarwal's wife was quiet throughout the meal and, at one point, apologized for not cooking non-veg.

'We are not used to that kind of food here,' she said.

Maybe he was reading too much into it, but the statement felt like a barb.

'I hardly eat any non-vegetarian food myself,' Mr Chandru said. This was a lie, though he didn't know why he had bothered to say so considering that he didn't care about sparing the woman's feelings.

After dinner, there was no dessert and no apology for this omission. Maybe it wasn't customary. What did he know?

In all, by the time Mr Chandru was done, he was tired and a little bit offended.

'Do you know the way back, sir?' Agarwal asked him.

'I can manage, yes.'

The town was small, and most of the roads were an unpaved mess. Several of the shop signs were written only in Hindi, and there were hardly any vehicles on the road. Most shops had been shuttered already. The streetlights were few and far between. Every now and then, he would pass a pool of construction workers huddled around a tyre fire. Broken bottles, garbage bags, and, at one junction, a burned bus lay on the side of the road. The windshield of his car began to fog up, and he had to wipe it clean every so often so he could see where he was going.

No sooner had Mr Chandru reached home than he latched his door.

He looked out of the peephole at the compound. For some reason, he had the feeling that he was being followed. It was nonsense, but still, a feeling was a feeling. He switched on the heater and squatted in front of it, wiping his wet nose. He had marked the date of his wife's arrival on the calendar pinned to the living room wall. He looked at it for reassurance and thought, almost there.

Later, Mr Chandru noticed through his front window several figures carrying flashlights and walking about on the road outside his house. They were only there for a few minutes.

When the idol reappeared in the office foyer the following day, Mr Chandru stood in front of it, baffled. He summoned the peon who was supposed to remove it in the first place, before he had done so himself.

'Why is this back here?' Mr Chandru hissed.

The peon scratched his head and mumbled that he had no idea.

Then his finger shot up. 'It's the other fellow!' he said. 'The other peon, sir. He was on leave till now. He must have thought we put it aside for cleaning. But I'll take care of it, sir. I'll remove it. Maybe I should find another place for it besides the storeroom?'

'Not in the foyer, and not on display.' With that, Mr Chandru went into his cabin and closed the door.

He was unaware of the confabulations that went on in the background, but when he returned from lunch that afternoon, Mr Chandru was told that a priest from the local temple was waiting in his office.

'Why is he here?'

'No idea, sir,' the peon said.

Mr Chandru grew nervous but told himself that perhaps the man was there to ask about a loan or introduce himself to the new manager.

The priest did not get up when Mr Chandru walked in. Instead, he gestured towards the foyer.

'It's not a good idea to have something like this gathering dust in the building,' he said. 'In fact, it's a bad omen. If it's okay with you, I'll have the idol placed in the temple. I'm sure we can find a spot for it.'

Mr Chandru tried to project the same manner of seriousness that the priest was putting on.

'If you think that works, you have my blessing,' he said.

'Then we'll send someone next week to get the idol.'

'Great.'

After the priest left, Mr Chandru wondered if his use of the word 'blessing' had been too mocking, even though he hadn't intended it to be.

He found himself thinking about this all evening. Maybe once his wife arrived, they could visit the temple together and be properly introduced to the priest.

That night, there was another power cut in his lane. Mr Chandru would not have noticed had the dead heater not made it impossible for him to stay asleep. He had a scratchy throat, so he decided to make himself a glass of hot tea. As soon as he opened the bedroom door, he heard the dogs. And closer than the dogs, he heard voices. He parted the curtains and saw people holding flashlights. They were standing in front of his house, deep in conversation. He waited for them to pass, then tried to reassure himself that, in all likelihood, these were no more than labourers unloading goods late at night to avoid union trouble.

Mr Chandru couldn't sleep well the entire week. His ears kept tuning into whatever was going on outside. Everything bothered him: the creatures scuttling across the terrace, the tumble and drag of dry leaves that had begun to accumulate in his compound. Even when there was no sound out there, his brain would conjure it up.

The following Monday, Mr Chandru stepped on dog shit. It was on his porch, right outside his door. He lifted his foot and frowned at the floor. The main gate had abnormally wide slats. It was entirely possible, extremely plausible even, that a dog could have wandered in and done the deed on his doorstep. Still, Mr Chandru stood there, staring at his soiled shoe for a long time. He took it off, inspected the underside, and retched as the smell met his nose. Then he took a short walk around the compound, looking for signs of human activity in the mud: footprints, a paan masala wrapper, anything....

By the time he had washed up and left for work, he was late. A few employees tittered, probably making fun of the big speech he'd given about punctuality just last week.

Mr Chandru checked the date on his watch. Three days till his family got here. It made him nervous.

'Excuse me, sir,' the peon said, pressing his face against the glass wall of his cabin. 'The men from the temple called. They want to know if they can come get the idol today.'

Mr Chandru was in a meeting with a local seth, a jewel merchant who owned a two-storey building in the centre of town—one of the few that showed a recent coat of paint. The interruption annoyed Mr Chandru. What annoyed him even more was the fact he'd been put on the spot.

'Tell them to check with me later,' Mr Chandru said quickly.

'Okay, sir.'

When the peon left, the seth said, 'I was wondering where the idol went. It used to be the first thing you saw walking in. Are you getting it cleaned?'

Mr Chandru said it was in the storeroom for the day, then started discussing a new credit scheme.

Mr Chandru's wife and son were arriving on the last train into town. He drove up to the two-platform station and waited for them in the cold. It was past eleven at night, and as he had come to expect, the train was late. From the car, Mr Chandru grabbed a shawl, wrapped it around himself, and began pacing the length of the platform. The only other person there was a homeless man sleeping against a large sack of cement. Mr Chandru avoided looking in his direction.

Occasionally, sharp sounds of clashing metal came from further down the tracks. It startled Mr Chandru each time he heard it. His breath came out as heavy puffs of mist.

Finally, just as he was thinking about calling up the bigger station a few kilometres north to find out why there had been a delay, the train crept up to the platform and came to a stop. The only passengers who got off were his wife and, asleep on her shoulder, their six-year-old son. Mr Chandru took their bags and hurried them into the car. Even when they got inside, they were too cold to talk. Mr Chandru asked if the journey was okay, then without listening to the muttered answer, started the car. The engine revved but after that went silent.

'What's the matter?' his wife asked.

'Must be the cold,' Mr Chandru said, trying to keep his voice calm. 'Everything was fine when I got here.'

Could someone have snipped a wire or loosened a screw?

Mr Chandru turned the key in the ignition again—so hard, he feared it might break off. The car spluttered and went silent.

'I told you, we should have bought a new car a long time ago,' his wife said, trying to sound playful.

Mr Chandru didn't respond. In his rear-view mirror, he noticed two men approaching. By now the fog had picked up, and it felt like they were in a slowly sinking boat.

'Lock your door,' Mr Chandru said.

'What?'

'Lock your door.'

In the back seat, his son woke up and rubbed his eyes.

The men approached Mr Chandru's side of the car.

The fatter of the two asked, 'Brother, is everything okay?'

'Yes,' Mr Chandru said. 'All good.'

'Engine trouble?'

'No, no; I'm sure it'll start in a second.'

'We'll give you a push if you want.'

'That's okay. It's all good.'

The other man asked, 'You have fuel in the tank?'

'Yes.'

'You sure?'

'Yes. Full tank.'

'Then all you need is a push. You'll have to come out and help, though.

My hand is sprained.'

'It really is all right,' Mr Chandru said. 'We'll manage.'

Then he turned the key one more time. Suddenly, the engine came to life. Mumbling a quick thank you, he accelerated out of the station yard faster than was safe on such bumpy roads.

That night too, Mr Chandru heard people outside his front gate. With his wife and son asleep, he came out to the living room to check the windows. Again, there were those flashlights and soft-footed scurrying. He watched the figures through his curtains, then once they were gone, lay down on the couch, unable to fall asleep.

The next day, Mr Chandru called the peon to his cabin and asked him to return the idol to the pedestal in the foyer.

The peon stood there for a few seconds, his mouth half-open.

'Just move it from the storeroom to the foyer,' he said, slowly, as though the peon were an idiot. 'Then leave it there till someone from the temple picks it up. Understood?'

'Yes, sir. I'll do so right away.'

Later that evening, when the temple called, Mr Chandru declined to talk to them. They called the following day, and then again, later in the week. Both times, he pretended to be busy. Finally, they stopped calling altogether.

NOTES AND ACKNOWLEDGEMENTS

The editor would like to thank Aienla Ozukum, publishing director, Aleph Book Company, for her help in putting this book together. Thanks are also due to Vidisha Ghosh and Aayushi Gupta for assisting with the clearing of permissions and tracking down publication dates of the stories and biographical details of the authors and translators.

The text of the stories has been standardized and copy-edited according to Aleph's house style. However, where appropriate, the text has been left unaltered in keeping with the style and intent of individual authors and translators or to be faithful to regional and linguistic variants of pan-Indian words and phrases.

Grateful acknowledgement is made to the following copyright holders for permission to reprint copyrighted material in this volume. While every effort has been made to locate and contact copyright holders and obtain permission, this has not always been possible; any inadvertent omissions brought to our notice will be remedied in future editions.

'Rebati' by Fakir Mohan Senapati, translated by Leelawati Mohapatra, Paul St-Pierre, and K. K. Mohapatra is reprinted by permission of the translators. The story was first published in 1898.

'The Kabuliwallah' by Rabindranath Tagore, translated by Arunava Sinha, was published in *The Greatest Bengali Stories Ever Told*, 2016, by Aleph Book Company. Reprinted by permission of the translator and the publisher. The story was first published in 1892.

'The Offering' by Pramatha Chaudhuri, translated by Arunava Sinha, was published in *The Greatest Bengali Stories Ever Told*, 2016, by Aleph Book Company. Reprinted by permission of the translator and the publisher.

'Mahesh' by Sarat Chandra Chattopadhyay, translated by Arunava Sinha, was published in *The Greatest Bengali Stories Ever Told*, 2016, by Aleph Book Company. Reprinted by permission of the translator and the publisher.

'The Shroud' by Munshi Premchand, translated by Muhammad Umar Memon is reprinted by permission of Nakako Memon. This story is believed to have been first published in 1935 as 'Kafan' in *Chaand*.

'The Story of a Crow Learning Prosody' by Subramania Bharati, translated by P. Raja is reprinted by permission of the translator.

'A Letter' by K. M. Munshi, translated by Rita Kothari is reprinted by the permission of Bharatiya Vidya Bhavan, Mumbai, and the translator.

'The Acharya's Wife' by Masti Venkatesha Iyengar, translated by Ramachandra Sharma is reprinted by the permission of the author's estate and Katha Books.

'Einstein and Indubala' by Bibhutibhushan Bandyopadhyay, translated by Arunava Sinha, was published in *The Greatest Bengali Stories Ever Told*, 2016, by Aleph Book Company. Reprinted by permission of the translator and the publisher. The story was first featured in *Upalkhanda* by Bibhutibhushan Bandyopadhyay, published by Mitra & Ghosh, Kolkata, on 16 April 1945.

'The Madiga Girl' by Chalam, translated by Dasu Krishnamoorty and Tamraparni Dasu is reprinted by permission of the translators.

'The Governor's Visit' by Kalki, translated by Gowri Ramnarayan is reprinted by permission of the translator. This story appeared in 1925 in the magazine *Navashakti*.

'Dhanavantri's Healing' by Kuvempu, translated by Chandan Gowda is reprinted by permission of the author's estate and the translator.

'The Gold Coin' by Laxmanrao Sardessai, translated by Paul Melo e Castro is reprinted by permission of the translator. The story was first published in 1966.

'The Discovery of Telenapota' by Premendra Mitra, translated by Arunava Sinha, was published in *The Greatest Bengali Stories Ever Told*, 2016, by Aleph Book Company. Reprinted by permission of Mrinmoy Mitra, the translator, and the publisher.

'An Astrologer's Day' by R. K. Narayan is reprinted by permission of Indian Thought Publications. The story was first published in 1947 in an eponymous collection of stories by the author.

'A Life' by Buddhadeva Bose, translated by Arunava Sinha, was published in *The Greatest Bengali Stories Ever Told*, 2016, by Aleph Book Company. Reprinted by permission of the translator and the publisher.

'The Blue Light' by Vaikom Muhammad Basheer, translated by O. V. Usha is reprinted by permission of the translator. It was originally published as 'Neela Velichcham' in a short story collection, *Paavappettavarude Veshya*, in 1952.

'The Flood' by Thakazhi Sivasankara Pillai, translated by O. V. Usha is reprinted by permission of the author's estate and the translator.

'On the Riverbank' by S. K. Pottekkatt, translated by A. J. Thomas is reprinted by permission of DC Books and the translator.

'The Solution' by Gopinath Mohanty, translated by Leelawati Mohapatra, Paul St-Pierre, and K. K. Mohapatra is reprinted by permission of Omkar Nath Mohanty and the translators.

'The Holy Banyan' by Bamacharan Mitra, translated by Leelawati Mohapatra, Paul St-Pierre, and K. K. Mohapatra is reprinted by permission of Sanghamitra Ghosh and the translators.

'A Feast for the Boss' by Bhisham Sahni, translated by Poonam Saxena, was published in *The Greatest Hindi Stories Ever Told*, 2020, by Aleph Book Company. Reprinted by permission of Rajkamal Prakashan, the translator, and the publisher.

'Of Fists and Rubs' by Ismat Chughtai, translated by Muhammad Umar Memon, was published in *The Greatest Urdu Stories Ever Told*, 2017, by Aleph Book Company. Reprinted by permission of Ashish Sawhny, Nakako Memon, and the publisher.

'Portrait of a Lady' by Khushwant Singh is reprinted by permission of Mala Dayal.

'Laajwanti' by Rajinder Singh Bedi, translated by Muhammad Umar Memon is reprinted by permission of Penguin Random House, India, and Nakako Memon.

'Reply-paid Card' by Dinanath Nadim, translated by Neerja Mattoo is reprinted by permission of the translator. This story is believed to have been first published in 1955 as 'Jawabi Kaard' in *Kong Posh*.

'The Night of the Full Moon' by K. S. Duggal, translated by Khushwant Singh is reprinted by permission of Suhel Duggal and Mala Dayal.

'Gold from the Graves' by Anna Bhau Sathe, translated by Vernon Gonsalves is reprinted by permission of the author's estate and the translator.

'Two Magicians' by Satyajit Ray, translated by Arunava Sinha is reprinted by permission of Sandip Ray and the translator. The story was first published in *Sandesh*, in 1962.

'Savage Harvest' by Mohinder Singh Sarna, translated by Navtej Sarna is reprinted by permission of the translator.

'Inspector Matadeen on the Moon' by Harishankar Parsai, translated by C. M. Naim is reprinted by permission of Katha Books. The story was first published in Hindi as 'Inspector Matadeen Chand Par' in 1968.

'The Times Have Changed' by Krishna Sobti, translated by Poonam Saxena, was published in *The Greatest Hindi Stories Ever Told*, 2020, by Aleph Book Company. Reprinted by permission of Rajkamal Prakashan, the translator, and the publisher. It was originally published as 'Sikka Badal Gaya' in 1948.

'Lord of the Rubble' by Mohan Rakesh, translated by Poonam Saxena, was published in *The Greatest Hindi Stories Ever Told*, 2020, by Aleph Book Company. Reprinted by permission of Rajkamal Prakashan, the translator, and the publisher.

'Urvashi and Johnny' by Mahasweta Devi, translated by Arunava Sinha, was first published in *The Greatest Bengali Stories Ever Told*, 2016, by Aleph Book Company. Reprinted by permission of Seagull Books, the translator, and the publisher.

'Countless Hitlers' by Vijaydan Detha, translated by Christi A. Merrill and Kailash Kabir is reprinted by permission of Kailash Kabir.

'Beyond the Fog' by Qurratulain Hyder, translated by Muhammad Umar Memon, was published in *The Greatest Urdu Stories Ever Told*, 2017, by Aleph Book Company. Reprinted by permission of Nakako Memon and the publisher. The original story, 'Kohr ke Peeche', was published in *Qurratulain Hyder Ki Muntakhab Kahaaniyan* in 1995.

'King Maruti' by Vyankatesh Madgulkar, translated by Shanta Gokhale is reprinted by permission of Mehta Publishing House and the translator.

'Mirror of Illusion' by Nirmal Verma, translated by Geeta Kapur is reprinted by permission of Gagan Gill and the translator.

'The Hanging' by O. V. Vijayan, translated by A. J. Thomas is reprinted by permission of DC Books and the translator.

'Trishanku' by Mannu Bhandari, translated by Poonam Saxena, was published in *The Greatest Hindi Stories Ever Told*, 2020, by Aleph Book Company. Reprinted by permission of Rachana Yadav, the translator, and the publisher.

'Naadar Sir' by Sundara Ramaswamy, translated by Malini Seshadri is reprinted by permission of Kalachuvadu Publications and the translator. The story was first published in a collection entitled *Kagankal* in 2000.

'The Beggars at Dargah' by Taj Begum Renzu, translated by Neerja Mattoo is reprinted by permission of Zarina Hamid and the translator.

'Rats' by Bhabendra Nath Saikia, translated by Gayatri Bhattacharyya is reprinted by permission of Preeti Saikia and the translator.

'A Death in Delhi' by Kamleshwar, translated by Poonam Saxena, was published in *The Greatest Hindi Stories Ever Told*, 2020, by Aleph Book Company. Reprinted by permission of Penguin Random House, India, the translator, and the publisher.

'Mouni' by U. R. Ananthamurthy, translated by H. Y. Sharada Prasad is reprinted by permission of the author's estate and Katha Books. The story was first published in 1966.

'Job's Children' by Vimala Devi, translated by Paul Melo e Castro is reprinted by permission of the translator. The story was originally published in a collection entitled *Monção*, published in 1963.

'Vision' by M. T. Vasudevan Nair, translated by A. J. Thomas is reprinted by permission of the author and the translator.

'Green Sparrows' by Ajeet Cour, translated by Ajeet Cour is reprinted by permission of the author. The story first appeared in a collection entitled *Dead End*, published in 1997.

'Mrs Crocodile' by Manoj Das, translated by Leelawati Mohapatra, Paul St-Pierre, and K. K. Mohapatra is reprinted by permission of the translators.

'The Prospect of Flowers' by Ruskin Bond is reprinted by permission of the author.

'Yaatra' by Turaga Janaki Rani, translated by Dasu Krishnamoorty and Tamraparni Dasu is reprinted by permission of Usha Turaga-Revelli and the translators.

'A Black Hole' by Jayant Vishnu Narlikar, translated by Anil Zankar is reprinted by permission of the author and the translator.

'House Number' by Kavana Sarma, translated by Dasu Krishnamoorty and Tamraparni Dasu is reprinted by permission of Vijayalakshmi Kandula and the translators.

'Labour' by R. R. Borade, translated by Anjali Nerlekar is reprinted by permission of the author and the translator. This story was originally published in the anthology of short stories by R. R. Borade entitled *Vaalvan* in 1970.

'A Sheet' by Salam Bin Razzaq, translated by Muhammad Umar Memon is reprinted by permission of Nakako Memon.

'And Then It Poured' by Gauri Deshpande, translated by Anjali Nerlekar is reprinted by permission of Surindar Singh and the translator.

'Values' by Mamoni Raisom Goswami, translated by Gayatri Bhattacharyya is reprinted by permission of South East Asia Ramayana Research Centre and the translator.

'A Revolt of the Gods' by Vilas Sarang, translated by Vilas Sarang is reprinted by permission of Penguin Random House, India.

'Journey 4' by Ambai, translated by Lakshmi Holmström is reprinted by permission of Radhika Holmström and Penguin Random House, India.

'Coinsanv's Cattle' by Damodar Mauzo, translated by Xavier Cota is reprinted by permission of the author and the translator.

'Salvation' by Pratibha Ray, translated by Leelawati Mohapatra, Paul St-Pierre, and K. K. Mohapatra is reprinted by permission of the author and the translators.

'Reflections of a Hen in Her Last Hour' by Paul Zacharia, translated by A. J. Thomas is reprinted by permission of the author and the translator. The original Malayalam story entitled 'Oru Pidakkozhiyude Aasannamaranachintakal' was first published on 12 April 1981 in *Kalakaumudi Weekly*.

'Laburnum for my Head' by Temsula Ao is reprinted by permission of Penguin Random House, India. The story was first published in *Laburnum for My Head: Stories*, in 2009.

'The Fourth Direction' by Waryam Singh Sandhu, translated by Nirupama Dutt is reprinted by permission of the author and the translator. The story was originally published as 'Chauthi Koot', in *Samdarshi* in 1988.

'The Spirits of Shah Alam Camp' by Asghar Wajahat, translated by Poonam Saxena, was published in *The Greatest Hindi Stories Ever Told*, 2020, by Aleph Book Company.

Reprinted by permission of the author, the publisher, and the translator.

'Air and Water' by Amar Mitra, translated by Arunava Sinha, was published in *The Greatest Bengali Stories Ever Told*, 2016, by Aleph Book Company. Reprinted by permission of the author, the publisher, and the translator.

'The Witch' by Kamalakanta Mohapatra, translated by Leelawati Mohapatra and Paul St-Pierre is reprinted by permission of the author and the translators.

'Two Old Kippers' by Siddiq Aalam, translated by Muhammad Umar Memon, was published in *The Greatest Urdu Stories Ever Told*, 2017, by Aleph Book Company. Reprinted by permission of Nakako Memon and the publisher. The story was originally published as 'Kabhi Do Peer-e Fartoot' in *Aaj 59*, 2008.

'Tirich' by Uday Prakash, translated by Poonam Saxena, was published in *The Greatest Hindi Stories Ever Told*, 2020, by Aleph Book Company. Reprinted by permission of the author, translator, and the publisher.

'The Smell of Bamboo Blossoms' by Yeshe Dorjee Thongchi, translated by Aruni Kashyap is reprinted by permission of the author and the translator.

'Bokha' by Cyrus Mistry is reprinted by permission of the author. The story was first published in *Vox 2* (*Gentleman Magazine's Anthology of New Fiction* edited by Jeet Thayil), in 1997.

'The Labyrinth' by Sara Rai, translated by Poonam Saxena, was published in *The Greatest Hindi Stories Ever Told*, 2020, by Aleph Book Company. Reprinted by permission of the author, the translator, and the publisher.

'Charlis and I' by Shashi Tharoor is reprinted by permission of Penguin Random House, India. The story was first published in *India: From Midnight to the Millennium* in 1997.

'Ponnuthayi' by Bama, translated by C. T. Indra is reprinted by permission of the author and the translator.

'Winter Evenings' by Navtej Sarna is reprinted by permission of the author.

'And then Laughed the Hyena' by Syed Muhammad Ashraf, translated by M. Asaduddin is reprinted by permission of the author and the translator. The story was first published as 'Lakar Bagha Hansa' in Syed Muhammad Ashraf's *Daar se Bichhre* in 1994.

'The Murmurous Dead: A Very Brief Exchange with a Spirit' by David Davidar is reprinted by permission of the author. It first appeared in an online anthology published by PEN America in 2022.

'Predators' by Syed Saleem, translated by Dasu Krishnamoorty and Tamraparni Dasu is reprinted by permission of the author and the translators.

'Sharavana Services' by Vivek Shanbhag, translated by Jayanth Kodkani is reprinted by permission of the author and the translator.

'An Ideal Man' by Addepalli Prabhu, translated by Dasu Krishnamoorty and Tamraparni Dasu is reprinted by permission of the author and the translators.

'The Cost of Hunger' by Abdus Samad, translated by Aruni Kashyap is reprinted by permission of the author and the translator.

'Tale of a Toilet' by Ramnath Gajanan Gawade, translated by Vidya Pai is reprinted by permission of the author and the translator.

'On Sernabatim Beach' by Jessica Faleiro is reprinted by permission of the author.

NOTES AND ACKNOWLEDGEMENTS

'The Gravestone' by Shahnaz Bashir is reprinted by permission of the author.

'Crippled World' by Vempalle Shareef, translated by N. S. Murty and the late R. S. Krishna Moorthy is reprinted by permission of the author and N. S. Murty. The story was first published first published as 'Arm Stump' in *Indian Literature* (Volume 59, Number 5) by the Sahitya Akademi in September/October 2015.

'The Adivasi Will Not Dance' by Hansda Sowvendra Shekhar is reprinted by permission of Speaking Tiger Books. The story was first published in the anthology *The Adivasi Will Not Dance* (Speaking Tiger Books, 2017).

'For the Greater Common Good' by Aruni Kashyap is reprinted by permission of the author.

'Swimmer Among the Stars' by Kanishk Tharoor is reprinted by permission of the author. The story first appeared in a collection of short stories entitled *Swimmer Among the Stars* (Aleph Book Company, 2016).

'Making' by Aishwarya Subramanian is reprinted by permission of the author. The story first appeared in *Breaking the Bow* edited by Anil Menon and Vandana Singh (Zubaan, 2014).

'The Power to Forgive' by Avinuo Kire is reprinted by permission of Zubaan. The story first appeared in *The Power to Forgive* (Zubaan, 2015).

'The Devouring Sea' by Amal, translated by A. J. Thomas is reprinted by permission of the author and the translator.

'The Search' by Dheeba Nazir, translated by Neerja Mattoo is reprinted by permission of the author and the translator.

'Gul' by Shreya Ila Anasuya is reprinted by permission of the author. The story was first published in *Magical Women* edited by Sukanya Venkatraghavan (Hachette India, 2019).

'The Accounts Officer's Wife' by Lakshmikanth K. Ayyagari is reprinted by permission of the author. The story was first published in *Out of Print* in September 2021.

'The Demon Sage's Daughter' by Varsha Dinesh is reprinted by permission of the author. The story was first published in *Strange Horizons* in February 2021.

'Eggs Keep Falling from the Fourth Floor' by Bhavika Govil is reprinted by permission of the author. The story was shortlisted for the 2021 Queen Mary Wasafiri New Writing Prize and first published on wasafiri.org.

'Twenty-first Tiffin' by Raam Mori, translated by Rita Kothari is reprinted by permission of the author and the translator.

'Gobyaer' by Sadaf Wani is reprinted by permission of the author. The story was first published in *Himal Southasian* in July 2021.

'The Alligator of Aligarh' by A. M. Gautam is reprinted by permission of the author. The story was first published in the *Bombay Review* in May 2020.

'The Current Climate' by Aravind Jayan is reprinted by permission of the author. The story was first published in *adda* in October 2021 by the Commonwealth Foundation.

NOTES ON THE AUTHORS

Fakir Mohan Senapati (1843–1918) is widely acknowledged as the father of modern Odia prose. He wrote four novels, including the iconic *Chha Mana Atha Guntha*, considered a foundational text of Indian literature, two collections of short stories, an autobiography, and several essays, besides textbooks, and a book of verse. He translated the Ramayana and the Mahabharata into Odia.

Rabindranath Tagore (1861–1941) was the fourteenth son of Debendranath Tagore and Sarada Devi, and started writing early in his life. He joined the Swadeshi Movement against the British in the 1900s. He won the Nobel Prize for Literature in 1913 and used his earnings to partly fund his school and university, Visva-Bharati, in Santiniketan. His influence on Bengali culture extends beyond his highly regarded poetry and prose, into music, visual art, and theatre.

Pramatha Chaudhuri (1868–1946) was born in Jessore (now in Bangladesh), and educated in Calcutta. He was the founder and editor of the literary journal *Sabujpatra*, and influenced many young Bengali intellectuals. He wrote essays and short stories under the pseudonym Birbal, and was also a poet, critic, and satirist. He is celebrated for his championing of a colloquial style over more formal forms of writing.

Sarat Chandra Chattopadhyay (1876–1938) was a novelist and short story writer. He was born into poverty in Debanandapur and received very little formal education. He began to write in his teens and went on to become an extremely prolific writer producing many novels, novellas, short stories, essays, and plays, including *Parineeta* (1914), *Palli Samaj* (1916), *Charitraheen* (1917), *Devdas* (1917), and *Griha Daha* (1920). His works have been adapted into numerous films in many Indian languages.

Munshi Premchand (1880–1936) was a pioneer of modern Hindi and Urdu fiction. He wrote nearly 300 stories and novels. Among his best-known novels are *Sevasadan*, *Rangmanch*, *Gaban*, *Nirmala*, and *Godan*. Much of Premchand's best work is found in his 250 short stories, collected in Hindi entitled *Manasarovar*.

Subramania Bharati (1882–1921) was a freedom fighter, social reformer, translator, editor, and, above all, a great poet. His timeless expressions indelibly mark Tamil phraseology. His prodigious output included poems, songs, essays, articles, translations, and children's writings.

K. M. Munshi (1887–1971) is synonymous with regional pride in Gujarat, for he popularized the idea of asmita. His trilogy of Patan novels (*The Glory of Patan*; *The Lord and Master of Gujarat*; and *The King of Kings*) has recently been translated by Rita and Abhijit Kothari. Munshi contributed to every genre of Gujarati literature. He established numerous institutions including the Bharatiya Vidya Bhawan. He also participated in the Gandhian movement for independence and served as a member of the Rajya Sabha as well as the Constitution Assembly of India.

Masti Venkatesha Iyengar (1891–1986) was a prominent figure in Kannada literature, often called 'Maasti Kannadada Aasti', meaning 'Masti is Kannada's Treasure'. Born in Karnataka, he earned a master's degree in English from Madras University and later joined the Indian Civil Service. Writing under the pen name Srinivasa, he was known for his short stories, novels, poems, and plays. His novel *Chikkavira Rajendra* earned him the Jnanpith Award in 1983. Masti's works remain influential in Kannada literature for their simplicity and depth of social and philosophical themes.

Bibhutibhushan Bandyopadhyay (1894–1950) was born in the village of Muratipur to an impoverished family. He took up a string of jobs before he wrote his first novel, *Pather Panchali*, for which he became very well known. He led a peripatetic life and was fond of taking long walks in the woods, where he would write. *Aparajito, Aranyak, Ichchamoti*, and *Chander Pahar* are among his most well-known works. His novels, *Pather Panchali* and *Aparajito*, were famously adapted by Satyajit Ray into the Apu Trilogy.

Chalam (1894–1979), as Gudipati Venkata Chalam was popularly known, typically wrote on themes related to the unconsummated passions of women, the social consequences of the repression of women's desires, and their real and fantasy lives. His novels include *Maidanam, Sasirekha, Dyvamicchina Bharya, Jeevitadarsam, Brahmanikam*, and *Bujjigadu*. Prominent among his fifteen short story collections are *Jealousy, Aa Raathri, Prema Paryavasanam*, and *Satyam Sivam Sundaram*.

Kalki (1899–1954) was the pen name of R. Krishnamurthy, a writer known for his humorous and satirical articles and nationalist and historical novels, serialized in popular magazines and cherished by generations of readers. A nationalist and freedom fighter, he was jailed thrice during the freedom struggle. He launched and edited the magazine *Kalki* after having worked in *Ananda Vikatan*, another weekly, for several years.

Kuvempu (1904–94), born Kuppali Venkatappa Puttappa, is one of the most revered figures in Kannada literature. Known for his profound contributions to modern Kannada poetry and literature, he was also a fierce advocate for the use of Kannada in education. His magnum opus, *Sri Ramayana Darshanam*, a reimagined take on the Ramayana, earned him the Jnanpith Award in 1967, making him the first Kannada author to receive it. Kuvempu's other celebrated works include *Kanooru Heggaditi* and *Malegalalli Madumagalu*. He is widely regarded as the greatest Kannada poet of the twentieth century.

Laxmanrao Sardessai (1904–86) was born in Savoi-Verem in Ponda. Considered one of the territory's finest writers in the Marathi language, he also wrote prose and verse in Konkani and Portuguese. His first short story, 'Sasurvani', was published in *Yeshwant* magazine. He wrote about 700 short stories in Marathi; these deal with a spectrum of Goan life over the twentieth century. Towards the end of his life, he began writing in Portuguese and Konkani. His book of essays, *Khabri*, won the Sahitya Akademi Award in Konkani in 1982.

Premendra Mitra (1904–88) was a novelist, short story writer, poet, scriptwriter, and film director of the 'Kallol' era in Bengali literature. He also wrote thrillers, fairy tales, ghost stories, and science fiction, and was associated with the journal *Kalikalam*. Born in Varanasi and brought up in Uttar Pradesh, he later lived in Dhaka and Calcutta. He created the beloved children's book character, Ghanada. He was awarded the Sahitya Akademi Award, the Rabindra Puraskar, and the Padma Shri, among many other honours.

R. K. Narayan (1906–2001) is one of the most prominent Indian novelists of the twentieth century. Born in 1906, Narayan was a recipient of the Sahitya Akademi Award in 1958, the A. C. Benson Medal by the (British) Royal Society of Literature in 1982, and the Padma Vibhushan—India's second-highest civilian honour—in 2000. His numerous works include *Malgudi Days, Swami and Friends, The Man-Eater of Malgudi, The Vendor of Sweets, The Guide, A Horse and Two Goats*, and *Waiting for the Mahatma*.

Buddhadeva Bose (1908–74), one of the most celebrated Bengali writers of the twentieth century, was a central figure in the Bengali modernist movement and was widely considered to be the successor to Rabindranath Tagore. Bose wrote numerous novels, short story collections, plays, essays, memoirs, and volumes of poetry. He started and edited the renowned poetry magazine *Kavita*. He was also the acclaimed translator into Bengali of Baudelaire, Hölderlin, and Rilke. Bose was awarded the Padma Bhushan in 1970.

Vaikom Muhammad Basheer (1908–94) was a humanist, freedom fighter, novelist, and short story writer who revolutionized Malayalam literature through sarcasm, satire, and black humour. His notable works include *Balyakalasakhi, Shabdangal, Pathummayude Aadu, Mathilukal, Ntuppuppakkoranendarnnu, Janmadinam,* and *Anargha Nimisham*. He was awarded the Padma Shri in 1982.

Thakazhi Sivasankara Pillai (1912–99) was a Malayalam novelist and short story writer, popularly known as Thakazhi, after his place of birth. He wrote several novels and over 600 short stories. His most famous works are the epic novel *Kayar* (Coir, 1978), for which he won the Jnanpith; and *Chemmeen* (Prawns, 1956).

S. K. Pottekkatt (1913–82) is often considered to be the pioneer of travel writing in India. A seasoned globetrotter, he emerged as the most distinguished practitioner of the travelogue genre in Malayalam literature. Pottekkatt's works have been extensively translated into English, Italian, Russian, Czech, German, and other Indian languages. His short story, 'Kadathuthoni', was adapted into an award-winning short film by M. T. Vasudevan Nair. He is the winner of the Sahitya Akademi Award and the Jnanpith Award.

Gopinath Mohanty (1914–91) was one of the greatest Odia writers of the mid-twentieth century. His first novel, *Mana Gahirara Chasa*, was published in 1940, which was followed by *Dadi Budha* (1944), *Paraja* (1945), and *Amrutara Santan* (1947). He published twenty-four novels and ten collections of short stories in addition to three plays, two biographies, two volumes of critical essays, and five books on the languages of the Kandh, Gadaba, and Saora tribes. He also translated Tolstoy's *War and Peace* and Tagore's *Jogajog* into Odia.

Bamacharan Mitra (1915–75) was lauded by critics for his extraordinary depth and perception, and his diverse interests ranging from classical music to swimming to football and detective fiction. He published three novels and more than a hundred short stories, which have been collected in eight volumes.

Bhisham Sahni (1915–2003) was one of Hindi's most iconic writers. Fluent in several languages, his body of work includes plays, short stories, novels, and essays. He received the Sahitya Akademi Award for *Tamas* in 1975. He was the editor of *Nayi Kahaniyan* from 1965–67 and the general secretary of the All-India Progressive Writers' Association from 1975–87. He was awarded the Padma Bhushan in 1998 and the Shalaka Samman, in 1999.

Ismat Chughtai (1915–91), counted among the earliest and foremost women Urdu writers, was born in Badayun, UP, in 1915 and was educated at Agra, Aligarh, and Lucknow. Her published work includes several collections of short stories, three novellas, and two novels, including *Terhi Lakir* (The Crooked Line). 'Lihaf' (The Quilt) is considered her most controversial short story, as it deals with the plight of a married woman thirsting for her husband's love which, when denied, drives her to the affections of another woman.

Khushwant Singh (1915–2014) was, arguably, India's best-known and most widely read author, columnist, and journalist. He was the founder-editor of *Yojana*, and editor of the *Illustrated Weekly of India*, *National Herald*, and the *Hindustan Times*. He wrote several books, including the novels *Train to Pakistan*, *I Shall Not Hear the Nightingale*, and *Delhi*; his autobiography, *Truth, Love & a Little Malice*; and the two-volume *A History of the Sikhs*. He also translated from Hindi, Urdu, and Punjabi. Khushwant Singh was a member of the Rajya Sabha from 1980 to 1986. In 2007, he was awarded, the Padma Vibhushan.

Rajinder Singh Bedi (1915–84) was born in Lahore. He first worked as a clerk in the postal department; later he joined the Lahore office of All India Radio and wrote many successful plays, having meanwhile established himself as a highly nuanced fiction writer, with the publication of *Daanao-Daam*, his first collection of short stories. After Partition, he moved to India. After working briefly as Station Director, Radio Kashmir, he joined the Bombay film industry, producing and writing scripts for several successful films. His Urdu novel, *Ek Chaadar Maili Si*, translated into English by Khushwant Singh as *I Take This Woman*, received the Sahitya Akademi Award in 1965. Bedi is regarded as the second most prominent Urdu fiction writer after Saadat Hasan Manto. He received the Filmfare Best Dialogue Award for *Madhumati* (1958) and *Satyakam* (1969).

Dinanath Nadim (1916–88) was a celebrated poet and wrote the first Kashmiri short story. Poetry, however, was his chosen medium and he experimented with different forms, including operas, with great success. He was the recipient of many awards, including the Sahitya Akademi Award for his opera *Shihul Kul* in 1986.

K. S. Duggal (1917–2012) wrote in both Urdu and Punjabi and published over fifty books in his lifetime. He won several major awards including the Sahitya Akademi Award and the Padma Bhushan.

Anna Bhau Sathe (1920–69) was a writer and social reformer. Despite a lack of formal education, he wrote thirty-five novels in Marathi, of which the most famous—*Fakira*—is in its nineteenth edition. He also wrote numerous collections of short stories, screenplays, ballads, and a travelogue on Russia. Much like his life, his stories embody the human struggle against immense odds.

Satyajit Ray (1921–92) was born in Calcutta, and educated in the city and later at Visva-Bharati in Santiniketan. He then joined an advertising firm and started illustrating books and designing their covers. He made his first film, *Pather Panchali*, in 1955, and it won several international prizes, including at the Cannes Festival. It is the first part of Ray's famed Apu trilogy. He was also a well-known writer and created the popular characters Feluda and Professor Shonku. He revived *Sandesh*, a magazine that had been founded by his grandfather. In 1992, he won an honorary Oscar and was awarded the Bharat Ratna.

Mohinder Singh Sarna (1923–2001) moved to Delhi from Rawalpindi after Partition and joined the Indian Audit and Accounts Service in 1950. In a writing career spanning six decades, Sarna produced several volumes of poetry, short stories, and novels, many of which have been widely translated into other Indian languages and made into telefilms. Sarna's work has received critical acclaim and is prescribed in university syllabi in India and abroad. He was the recipient of the Sahitya Akademi Award, the Sahitya Kala Parishad Award, the Balraj Sahni Trust Award, the Nanak Singh Fiction Award on four occasions, the Katha Award, the Bhai Santokh Singh Poetry Award, the Giani Gurmukh Singh Poetry Award, the Sewa Sifti International Award, the Zehne Jadid Award, the Bawa Balwant Trust Award, and the Waris Shah Samman. He was recognized as the Shiromani Punjabi Sahitkar by the Government of Punjab in 1989.

Harishankar Parsai (1924–95) was a noted satirist and humorist of modern Hindi literature, a writer who was almost completely defined by his chosen genre: satire. He wrote a number of short story collections, among them *Premchand ke Phattey Joote* and *Viklang Sharaddha ka Daur* for which he won the Sahitya Akademi Award in 1982.

Krishna Sobti (1925–2019) is regarded as the grande dame of Hindi literature. Her novels *E Ladaki* and *Mitro Marjani* are cult classics and are known for their inventive formal approach and strong female characters. Her first short story, 'Sikka Badal Gaya', was notably published without a single change in the prestigious Hindi magazine, *Pratap*, edited by Agyeya. In her last novel, *Gujarat Pakistan Se Gujarat Hindustan* (A Gujarat Here, A Gujarat There), she wrote about her painful memories of Partition. She won the Sahitya Akademi Award in 1980 for *Zindaginama* (1979) and the Jnanpith Award in 2017.

Mohan Rakesh (1925–72) was an acclaimed novelist, translator, travel writer, and playwright. He played a significant role in the revival of Hindi theatre in the 1960s. His literary work includes novels like *Andhere Band Kamare* (1961) and plays like *Aashad Ka Ek Din* (1958) and *Adhe Adhure* (1968). His story 'Uski Roti' was made into an eponymous Hindi film in 1971. He won the Sangeet Natak Akademi Award in 1968 for *Adhe Adhure*.

Mahasweta Devi (1926–2016) was born in Dhaka. She was educated at Vishva-Bharati and Calcutta University. She then became a writer, journalist, and professor. Her first book, *Jhansir Rani*, was published in 1956. She retired from her professorship in 1984 and became a full-time writer of fiction and a champion of Adivasi rights. For her achievements as a writer and human rights worker, she has been given several awards and honours, among them the Ramon Magsaysay Award and the Jnanpith Award. Her works *Rudaali* and *Hajar Churashir Maa* have been adapted into films.

Vijaydan Detha (1926–2013), also known as Bijji and 'the Shakespeare of Rajasthan', has more than 800 short stories to his credit, including *Bataan ri Phulwadi* (A Garden of Tales), a fourteen-volume collection of stories that draws on folklore and the spoken dialects of Rajasthan. His stories and novels have been adapted into many plays and movies including Habib Tanvir's *Charandas Chor*, Amol Palekar's *Paheli*, and *Duvidha* by Mani Kaul. He was the co-founder of Rupayan Sansthan, an institute that documents Rajasthani folklore, arts, and music; he was a recipient of the Padma Shri and Sahitya Akademi awards.

Qurratulain Hyder (1927–2007) ranked among the foremost women writers of Urdu fiction, produced seven novels, several collections of short stories, and translations into Urdu of writers such as Henry James, T. S. Eliot, and Truman Capote. Her critically acclaimed, but no less controversial, novel *Aag kaa Daryaa* has been translated into fifteen Indian languages, and was published in 1999 as *River of Fire*, transcreated by the author herself. She worked as one of the editors of *Imprint* magazine (Bombay) and later as a member of the editorial staff of the *Illustrated Weekly of India*. She spent a year as a writer-in-residence in the International Writers Program at the University of Iowa. She was the recipient of many honours and awards, among them the Sahitya Akademi Award for her collection of short stories *Patjhar ki Aavaaz*, and the Jnanpith Award. She was conferred the Padma Shri in 1984 and the Padma Bhushan in 2005 by the Government of India for her contribution to Urdu literature and education.

Vyankatesh Madgulkar (1927–2001) was a Marathi storyteller, playwright, screenplay writer, and novelist born in Madgul in Sangli district. Despite not having finished school, he studied literature. He participated in the struggle for Independence in 1942. After a short stint as a journalist, he came to Mumbai around 1950 and started writing Marathi screenplays, prior to which his collection of short stories *Mandeshi Manase* (1949) was published. Some of his other short story collections are *Gavakadchya Goshti* (1951), *Hastacha Paus* (1953), *Sitaram Eknath* (1951), *Kaali Aai* (1951), and *Jambhlache Diwas* (1957). His novels are *Bangarwadi* (1955), *Vavtal* (1964), *Pudhach Paul* (1950), *Kovale Divas* (1979), *Karunashtak* (1982), and *Sattantar* (1982). Madgulkar also wrote plays, folk dramas, film stories, screenplays, and essays. He was known as a nature lover, hunter, and painter, without having received any formal education in painting. Many of his books won Maharashtra state awards, and he received several other awards for his writing—including the Sahitya Akademi Award for the novel *Sattantar* in 1983. His stories have been translated into Danish, German, Japanese, Russian, and other languages.

Nirmal Verma (1929–2005) was a pioneer of the Nayi Kahani movement in Hindi literature. He wrote five novels, eight collections of short stories, and nine volumes of essays and travelogues. Following his work at the Oriental Institute in Prague in the 1960s, he undertook translations of contemporary Czech writers such as Milan Kundera, Bohumil

Hrabal, and Vaclav Havel in Hindi, much before their work became popular internationally. He won the Sahitya Akademi Lifetime Achievement Award (1985), the Jnanpith Award (1999), and was awarded the Padma Bhushan in 2002.

O. V. Vijayan (1931–2005) was an Indian author and cartoonist, and an important figure in modern Malayalam language literature. Best known for his first novel *Khasakkinte Itihasam* (1969), Vijayan was the author of six novels, nine short story collections, and nine collections of essays, memoirs, and reflections.

Mannu Bhandari (1931–2021) was an eminent Hindi novelist. She was one of the founders of the Nayi Kahani movement alongside Nirmal Verma, Rajendra Yadav, and others, and wrote extensively on the realities of urban life. Her major works include *Aap ka Bunty* (1971) and *Mahabhoj* (1976).

Sundara Ramaswamy (1931–2005) was an influential Tamil writer. As a native of Nagercoil in Tamil Nadu, which lies in close proximity to Kerala, he represented the bilingual felicity of Tamil and Malayalam. His literary career, spanning over five decades, included short stories, novels, translations, poetry, and criticism. He published poetry under the name Pasuvayya. His novel, *Oru Puliya Maraththin Kathai*, was a classic, presenting contemporary life in the dialect of the region. The University of Toronto conferred on him the inaugural Iyal Award in 2001.

Taj Begum Renzu (1931–2006) was one of the very few women short story writers to come out of Kashmir. She was an acclaimed writer, broadcaster, and activist. Her published book of short stories is entitled *Alaav*.

Bhabendra Nath Saikia (1932–2003), filmmaker, playwright, and writer, was a recipient of the Sahitya Akademi Award for fiction. He was also a Padma Shri awardee, as well as a recipient of seven Rajat Kamal awards for his films, several of which are based on his own stories. He was also a recipient of the Srimanta Sankardeva Award and the Assam Valley Literary Award. A teacher of Physics at Gauhati University, he was also a member of the Sangeet Natak Akademi, New Delhi. Among his works are three novels, eleven short story collections, twenty-eight plays, several books for children, and collections of essays. His short stories are known for their delineation of character and their psychological motivations, as well as their powers of observation and plotting.

Kamleshwar (1932–2007) was one of post-Independence India's most prominent Hindi writers, having published over thirty novels and several short story collections. He won the Sahitya Akademi Award in 2003 for his book *Kitney Pakistani* and the Padma Bhushan in 2005. He was also editor of *Dainik Jagran*, *Dainik Bhaskar*, the now-defunct *Sarika*, and worked as a scriptwriter for Hindi movies and TV serials.

U. R. Ananthamurthy (1932–2014) was a Gandhian socialist and one of the pioneers of the Navya (new) movement in Kannada literature. He published five novels, one play, eight short story collections, as well as anthologies of poetry and essays—his work has been translated into several languages. His best-known work is his *novel Samskara*, which was a finalist for the Man Booker International Prize in 2013. Another of his novels, *Bharatipura*, was shortlisted for the 2011 Hindu Literary Prize and the DSC Prize for South Asian Literature.

Vimala Devi (b. 1932) is the pseudonym of Teresa da Piedade de Baptista Almeida, a well-known Goan poet, writer, and translator. She was born in a landowning family in Penha de França and spent her adult years in Lisbon and London before finally settling down in Barcelona. Her works include *Monsoon*, a collection of short stories, several collections of poetry including *Súria*, and a memoir. She co-authored the two-volume *A Literatura IndoPortuguesa*, which won the Prémio Abílio Lopes do Rego of the Academia das Ciências de Lisboa in 1972.

M. T. Vasudevan Nair (b. 1933) is an author, screenplay writer, and film director. He has won many prestigious literary awards including the Kerala Sahitya Akademi Award for his novel *Naalukettu* in 1958, Kerala Sahitya Akademi Award for his short story 'Swargam Thurakkunna Samayan' in 1986, and the Jnanpith Award in 1995 for his contribution to Malayalam literature.

Ajeet Cour (b. 1934) is a recipient of the Sahitya Akademi Award and the Padma Shri. Born in Lahore to Sardar Makhan Singh, she completed her early education from there, where she was also taught by Kartar Singh Hitkari (the father of Amrita Pritam). After Partition, her family came to Delhi, where she earned an MA degree. She has written novels and short stories in Punjabi on social realist themes such as the experiences of women in relationships and their position in society. She received the Kuvempu Rashtriya Puraskar Award in 2019. Her works include nineteen short story anthologies, novellas, and novels, as well as nine translations. She has also edited over twenty works.

Manoj Das (1934–2021) was a bilingual novelist, short-story writer, essayist, and columnist, and a hugely popular public speaker. Das was a left-wing student leader in college and led a delegation to the first Afro-Asian Students Conference at Bandung, Indonesia, in 1956. He received several literary awards, among them, the Sahitya Akademi Award in 1972, the Sarala Award in 1980, and the Saraswati Samman in 2000. He was awarded the Padma Shri in 2001 and the Sahitya Akademi Fellowship in 2006. He published ten novels, nineteen collections of short stories, six travelogues, five books of essays and commentaries on history and culture, a memoir, and two volumes of poetry.

Ruskin Bond (b. 1934) is the author of several bestselling novels and collections of short stories, essays and poems. These include: *The Room on the Roof* (winner of the John Llewellyn Rhys Prize); *A Flight of Pigeons; The Night Train at Deoli; Time Stops at Shamli; Our Trees Still Grow in Dehra* (winner of the Sahitya Akademi Award); *Angry River; The Blue Umbrella; Delhi is Not Far; Rain in the Mountains; Tigers for Dinner; Tales of Fosterganj; A Gathering of Friends; Upon an Old Wall Dreaming; Small Towns, Big Stories; Unhurried Tales; A Gallery of Rascals; Rhododendrons in the Mist; Miracle at Happy Bazaar* (winner of the Kalinga Literary Festival Children's Book of the Year 2021); and *It's a Wonderful Life*. He was awarded the Padma Shri in 1999, a Lifetime Achievement Award by the Delhi government in 2012, and the Padma Bhushan in 2014. He was awarded the Sahitya Akademi Fellowship in 2021, and the Ramnath Goenka Sahithya Samman Lifetime Achievement Award in 2024.

Turaga Janaki Rani (1936–2014) was a playwright, short story writer, poet, biographer, and broadcaster with a writing career that spanned more than a half century. Her works include the short story collections *Janaki Rani Kathalu, Erra Gulabilu,* and *Navvani Puvvu,* and the novels *Veyyabovani Talupu, Sangharshana,* and *Eee Desam Oka Himalayam*. She was honoured with many awards including the Grihalakshmi Swarnakankanam and Telugu University Sahitya Award.

Jayant Vishnu Narlikar (b. 1938) is a renowned astrophysicist. For his accomplishments, Narlikar was conferred the Padma Bhushan by the Government of India at the age of twenty-six. He set up the renowned Inter University Centre for Astronomy and Astrophysics (IUCAA) in 1989 in Pune. Since his retirement in 2008, Narlikar has continued to live in Pune. His first book of science fiction stories, *Yakshanchi Denagi*, was published in 1979. He has also edited encyclopaedias and anthologies and written non-fiction books, which present the history and poetry of science in an engaging way. His books have been translated into many Asian and European languages.

Kavana Sarma (1939–2018) is known to Telugu readers both as a storyteller and as a man of science. A former professor at the Indian Institute of Science, Bangalore, he taught and lectured at universities in the US, the UK, Iraq, Australia, and the West Indies. *Vyangya Kavanalu*, *Kavana Sarma Kathalu*, *America Majili Kathalu*, and *Sangha Puranam* are prominent among his short story collections. He won the Jyeshta Award and Telugu University Award.

R. R. Borade (b. 1940) started his career as a writer through a story published in the Marathi newspaper *Sakal*. He has written over fifteen novels, seven short story collections, and thirteen plays. He has been the recipient of numerous awards for his work: the Bhairu Ratan Award (1989); the Marathwada Gaurav Award (2001), the Jayawant Dalwi Award (2003), and the Sadashiv Kulli Memorial Award (2011).

Salam Bin Razzaq (1941–2024) was the pen name of Shaikh Abdussalam Abdurrazzaq who was born in Panwil in Maharashtra. He finished high school in 1960 and published his first short story two years later in the literary magazine *Shaa'ir*. He was the author of three collections of short stories, two in Urdu and one in Hindi; he had also translated Marathi fiction into Urdu.

Gauri Deshpande (1942–2003) was born in Pune. She was a writer of stories, novels, essays, columns, and poems and a professor of English at the Savitribai Phule Pune University and Fergusson College. She wrote in Marathi as well as English. She translated Richard Burton's *Arabian Nights* into Marathi. Some of her popular works in Marathi include fiction like *Ahe He Ase Ahe* (1986), *Ekek Pan Galawaya* (1985), *Niragathi Ani Chandrike Ga Sarike Ga* (1987), *Goph* (1999), and *Utkhanan* (2002). One of her most well-known works in English is the short story collection *The Lackadaisical Sweeper: Short Stories* (1970). She also translated remarkable writings from Marathi into English, including works like ... *And Pine for What Is Not* (a translation of Sunita Deshpande's *Ahe Manohar Tari...*). Her published work also includes three volumes of poetry in English—*Between Births* (1968), *Lost Love* (1970), and *Beyond the Slaughterhouse* (1972).

Mamoni Raisom Goswami (1942–2011), also known as Indira Goswami, is a Jnanpith awardee, a Sahitya Akademi awardee, and a noted Ramayan scholar whose work was recognized and lauded worldwide. Though awarded a Padma Shri, she declined the award. She was also the recipient of the Principal Prince Claus Laureate Award of the Netherlands, the monetary component of which she donated to charitable causes. Among the numerous other awards she received were the Kamal Kumari Award, the Mahiyoshi Joymoti Award, the Katha National Award, a honorary DLitt degree from Rabindra Bharati University, West Bengal, The International Tulsi Award, and the highest civilian award of the Government of Assam, the Assam Ratna. Her popular novels are *Chenabor Srot*, *Neelkanthi Braja*, *Mamore Dhora Torowal*, *Dontal Hatir Uiyey Khowa Howdah*, *Tej aru Dhulirey Dhuxorito Prishtha*, *Thengphakhri Tehsildaror Tamor Tarowal* as also several collections of short stories and autobiographical works.

Vilas Sarang (1942–2015) was born in Karwar, a coastal town in Karnataka. He secured a doctorate in English literature from Bombay University and then went on to secure a second doctorate in comparative literature from Bloomington, Indiana. He spent five years in Iraq (1974–79), where he taught English at the University of Basrah. Sarang was head of the English Department at Bombay University from 1988 to 1991, during which time he also edited the *Bombay Literary Review*. From 1991 to 2002, he taught at Kuwait University. As a bilingual writer, Sarang wrote stories, novels, and poetry in both languages. His Marathi short story collections were *Soledad* (1975) and *Atank* (1999) and translations of his stories in English were collected in *A Fair Tree of the Void* (1990) and more recently *The Women in the Cages* (2006). His other works included the English novel *The Dinosaur Ship* (2005) and the Marathi novel *Enkichya Rajyat* (1983), and *Kavita* (1969–84), a collection of Marathi poems. His collection of English poems was published as *A Kind of Silence* (1978).

Ambai (b. 1944) is the nom de plume of C. S. Lakshmi, a historian, researcher, and creative writer, who has published short stories, novels, and articles. In 2006, she (along with Lakshmi Holmström) won the Vodafone Crossword Book Award. She received the Iyal Virudhu (Lifetime Achievement Award) in 2008, awarded by the Tamil Literary Garden. A PhD from Jawaharlal Nehru University, she has been an independent researcher in Women's Studies for the last thirty-five years. In 1988, she founded SPARROW (Sound and Picture Archives for Research on Women), an NGO for documenting and archiving the work of female writers and artists.

Damodar Mauzo (b. 1944) is a short story writer, novelist, critic, and scriptwriter who lives in Goa and writes in Konkani. He received the Jnanpith Award, in 2022. His most recent published book is *The Wait: And Other Stories*. He was awarded the Sahitya Akademi Award in 1983 for his novel *Karmelin*, and the Vimala V. Pai Vishwa Konkani Sahitya Puraskar in 2011 for his novel *Tsunami Simon*. His collection of short stories, *Teresa's Man and Other Stories from Goa*, was nominated for the Frank O'Connor International Short Story Award in 2015. He has served as a member of the executive board of the Sahitya Akademi.

Pratibha Ray (b. 1944) is a short story writer and novelist. Her prodigious output includes twenty-one novels, among them *Yajnaseni* (also available in an eponymous English translation), which has had one hundred editions since its publication in 1984, twenty-two collections of stories, ten travelogues, two books of essays, and an autobiography. She has received many literary awards, like the Sarala Award in 1990, the Moorti Devi Award in 1991, the Sahitya Akademi Award in 2000, and the Jnanpith Award in 2011.

Paul Zacharia (b. 1945) is an eminent Malayalam fiction writer and essayist. He was awarded the Kendra Sahitya Akademi Award in 2005 for his short story collection, *Zachariyayute Kathakal*. His works that have been translated into English include *Bhaskara Pattelar and Other Stories*, *Reflections of a Hen in Her Last Hour and Other Stories*, and *Paul Zacharia: Two Novellas*.

Temsula Ao (1945–2022) was a celebrated poet, short story writer, and ethnographer from Nagaland. She was a key figure in the literature of Northeast India, often highlighting themes of tribal identity, displacement, and the resilience of the Naga people. Her works, such as the short story collection *These Hills Called Home* and the poetry collection *Songs That Tell*, deeply reflect the oral traditions and folklore of her Ao Naga community. Beyond literature, she was an advocate for indigenous cultures and women's rights, contributing significantly to preserving Naga heritage. Ao was awarded the Padma Shri and the Sahitya Akademi Award for her contributions to literature and advocacy.

Waryam Singh Sandhu (b. 1945) is a celebrated Punjabi short story writer. He received a Sahitya Akademi Award for his short story collection, *Chauthi Koot*, which was also made into a national award-winning film of the same name by Gurvinder Singh. He has published five collections of short stories. He holds a Doctorate in Philosophy from Panjab University and taught Punjabi at Lyallpur Khalsa College in Jalandhar. He now lives with his family in Canada.

Asghar Wajahat (b. 1946) is a Hindi scholar, novelist, documentary filmmaker, and a playwright, best known for his novel, *Saat Aasman* (1996), and his acclaimed play, *Jis Lahore Nai Dekhya, O Jamyai Nai*. He has published twenty books including five novels, six full-length plays, five collections of short stories, a travelogue, a collection of street plays, and a book of literary criticism. Along with film scripts and short stories, he regularly writes for various newspapers and magazines. He received the Katha Best Novel of the Year Award in 2006 for his novel, *Kaisi Aagi Lalaee*.

NOTES ON THE AUTHORS

Amar Mitra (b. 1951) lives in Kolkata, and had published thirty novels, four books for children, and ten collections of short stories. He was awarded the Sahitya Akademi Award in 2006 for his novel *Dhrubaputra*, and the Bankim Puraskar from the West Bengal government for his novel *Aswacharit* in 2001.

Kamalakanta Mohapatra (b. 1951) is a writer and translator who has published a novel, two collections of short stories, and a book of essays in Odia. He has translated selected works of Isaac Bashevis Singer, Jean-Paul Sartre, and Gabriel García Márquez in Odia. He has collaborated with Leelawati Mohapatra and Paul St. Pierre on several translations into English, notable among them are *The HarperCollins Book of Oriya Short Stories, Ants, Ghosts and Whispering Trees: An Anthology of Oriya Short Stories, JP Das: Sundardas, Bijay Mishra: The Gravediggers*, and Gopinath Mohanty's *Dark Loneliness: Selected Poems*.

Siddiq Aalam (b. 1952) was born in a small town, Purulia, in West Bengal. Since 1983, he has lived in Calcutta, a city that is the background of his first novel, *Charnock ki Kashti*. He holds an M. A. in English and a degree in law. He has published three collections of short stories, *Aakhri Chhaa'on, Lamp Jaalaney Vaaley*, and *Bain*.

Uday Prakash (b. 1952) is a Hindi poet, scholar, writer, journalist, teacher, and translator. Some of his best-known works include *Suno Kariger, Darayayee Ghoda, Abutar-Kabootar, Tirichh*, and *Palgomra ka scootar*. His major works of translation are *Romyo Rola Ki Diary* and *Lal Ghaas Par Neele Ghode*. He received the Omprakash Sahitya Sammaan in 1982, the Shri Kant Verma Smriti Sammaan in 1990 and, most recently, the SAARC Literary Award in 2009.

Yeshe Dorjee Thongchi (b. 1952) is an acclaimed writer from Arunachal Pradesh, known for his contributions to Assamese literature. Born in a Serdukpen tribal family, he began his literary journey by writing poetry, later shifting to short stories and novels. Thongchi's works vividly depict the customs and traditions of various tribal communities in Arunachal Pradesh, reflecting their struggles with modernity. A retired civil servant, Thongchi has been honored with prestigious awards like the Padma Shri and the Sahitya Akademi Award.

Cyrus Mistry (b. 1956) began his writing career as a playwright, freelance journalist, and short story writer. His play, *Doongaji House*, written in 1977 when he was twenty-one, has acquired classic status in contemporary Indian theatre in English. One of his short stories was made into a Gujarati feature film. His plays and screenplays have won several awards. His novel, *Chronicle of a Corpse Bearer* (2012), won the DSC Prize for South Asian Literature, 2014.

Sara Rai (b. 1956) is a writer, editor, and translator of Hindi and Urdu fiction. Born into an illustrious literary family, she published her first collection of short stories, *Ababeel ki Udaan*, in 1997. In her fiction, she explores the inner world and complexities of ordinary lives in modern-day India. She has won many awards for writing and translation, including the Katha Translation Prize in 1993 and again in 1997, the A. K. Ramanujan Prize for Translation in 2000, and the Coburg Rückert Prize in 2019.

Shashi Tharoor (b. 1956) is the bestselling author of twenty-seven books, both fiction and non-fiction, besides being a noted critic and columnist, a former Under Secretary-General of the United Nations and a former Minister of State for Human Resource Development and Minister of State for External Affairs in the Government of India. In his third term, he is the longest-serving member of the Lok Sabha from Thiruvananthapuram and has chaired Parliament's Standing Committees on External Affairs and Information Technology. He has won numerous literary awards, including the Sahitya Akademi Award, the Ramnath Goenka Award for Excellence in Books (non-fiction), the Commonwealth Writers' Prize, and the Crossword Lifetime Achievement Award. He was honoured as New Age Politician of the

Year by NDTV in 2010 and won the Pravasi Bharatiya Samman, India's highest honour for overseas Indians, in 2004.

Bama (b. 1957), as Bama Faustina is known, is a celebrated Dalit woman writer. She has been at the forefront of Dalit literary activism and has given Dalit aesthetics the visibility it had previously lacked. Besides *Karukku* (1992), her autobiography, she has published *Sangati* (1994), *Kisumbukkaran* (1996), *Vanmam* (2002), *Oru Thathauvm Erumayum* (2004), *Kondattam* (2009), and *Manushi* (2011) in Tamil. Her works have been widely translated. In 2000, the English translation of *Karukku*, translated by Lakshmi Holmström, won the Crossword Award, establishing her as a distinct voice in Dalit literature.

Navtej Sarna (b. 1957) was India's Ambassador to the United States, High Commissioner to the United Kingdom, and Ambassador to Israel. He has also served as Secretary to the Government of India and as the Foreign Office Spokesperson. His earlier diplomatic assignments were in Moscow, Warsaw, Thimphu, Tehran, Geneva, and Washington DC. His literary work includes the novels *The Exile* and *We Weren't Lovers Like That*, the short story collection *Winter Evenings*, non-fiction works *The Book of Nanak*, *Second Thoughts*, and *Indians at Herod's Gate*, as well as two translations, *Zafarnama* and *Savage Harvest*. He is a prolific columnist and commentator on foreign policy and literary matters, contributing regularly to media platforms in India and abroad.

Syed Muhammad Ashraf (b. 1957) is an Urdu novelist and short story writer of great distinction. He has written two novels and several collections of short stories. Some of his stories have been translated into English and other languages. He has received the Sahitya Akademi Award and several other awards.

David Davidar (b. 1958) is the author of three novels, *The House of Blue Mangoes* (2002), which was published in sixteen languages in an equal number of countries and was a *New York Times* Notable Book; *The Solitude of Emperors* (2007), which was shortlisted for a Commonwealth Writers' Prize; and *Ithaca* (2011). He is the editor of two anthologies of Indian short stories, *A Clutch of Indian Masterpieces* and *A Case of Indian Marvels*. He co-founded Aleph Book Company, a literary publishing firm based in New Delhi, in 2011.

Syed Saleem (b. 1959) won the Sahitya Akademi Award for his novel *Kaaluthunna Poolathota* in 2010. Many of his short stories have appeared in four collections, *Swati Chinukulu*, *Nissabda Sangeetham*, *Roopayi Chettu*, and *Chadarapu Enugu*. Several of them have been translated into Hindi, Kannada, Marathi, Odia, and English. He also won the National Human Rights Commission Award for the English translation of *Kaaluthunna Poolathota*. Saleem has written four novels, and two poetry collections. His other awards include the Bhasha Puraskar from the Andhra Pradesh government, Madabhushi Rangacharyulu award, and Sahitya award from Telugu University.

Vivek Shanbhag (b. 1962) is a novelist, playwright, short story writer, and editor who writes in Kannada. He has published thirteen works of fiction and edited two anthologies. He is the founding editor of the literary journal *Desha Kaala*. His critically acclaimed novel *Ghachar Ghochar* has been translated into nineteen languages worldwide. Shanbhag is the co-translator of U. R. Ananthamurthy's book *Hindutva or Hind Swaraj* into English. He is a Visiting Professor at Ashoka University teaching Creative Writing. An engineer by training, Shanbhag lives in Bengaluru.

Addepalli Prabhu (b. 1963) was born in Kakinada as Addepalli Prabhakara Rao. He has authored three poetry collections, *Aavaahana*, *Paaripolem*, and *Pittaleni Lokam*. He has written more than seventeen novels, three short story collections, and several poetry collections. He is the recipient of the Vummadisetty Literary Trust Award.

NOTES ON THE AUTHORS

Abdus Samad (b. 1969) is the author of six novels and two fiction collections, including *Boi Jai Chompaboti, Kurukhetrar Akhora*, and *Bonkukurar Daak*. Widely loved and read in Assam, his subversive fiction critiques Assamese nationalism and religious divides and often depicts the life of the immigrant Muslim community of Bengal origin in Assam. He is the winner of some of the highest literary awards in Assam, such as the Munin Borkotoky Award (2006) and the President's Centenary Literary Award (2017) from Asom Sahitya Sabha.

Ramnath Gajanan Gawade (b. 1969) is a short story writer, novelist, and playwright writing in Konkani. His works include six short story collections, seven novels (including three for children), and two plays. He has been felicitated with many awards during his career such as the Bal Sahitya Puraskar in 2015 for *Sadu Ani Jadugar Mhadu*, two state awards from Goa Konkani Academy (in 2009 and 2011), and a state award from Goa Kala Academy in 2010.

Jessica Faleiro (b. 1976) was born in Goa and has lived abroad for longer than she has lived in India. She is a member of the Goan diaspora and an adult Third Culture Kid. Faleiro's fiction, poetry, essays, and travel pieces have been published in *Asia Literary Review, Forbes, Indian Quarterly, Himal Southasian, IndiaCurrents, Coldnoon, Joao-Roque Literary Journal, Mascara Literary Review, Muse India*, and the *Times of India* as well as in various anthologies. She is the author of the novel *Afterlife: Ghost Stories from Goa* (2012) and *The Delicate Balance of Little Lives* (2018), a collection of interlinked stories. She has an M. A. in Creative Writing from Kingston University, UK. Jessica currently lives in Goa and teaches creative writing workshops.

Shahnaz Bashir (b. 1980) teaches creative journalism and literary reportage at the Central University of Kashmir, where he is the coordinator of the media studies programme. His debut novel, *The Half Mother*, was published in 2014.

Vempalle Shareef (b. 1980) won the Sahitya Akademi's Yuva Puraskar in 2011. Born in Vempalle in Kadapa district, his story collections include *Katha Minar* and *Topi Jabbar*, and a collection of children's stories, *Thiyyani Chaduvu*. A TV journalist, he began his literary career by writing children's stories. His stories have appeared in many anthologies; some have been translated into English and Maithili. His story 'Jumma' received a special mention in the nationwide competition held by *Muse India* for regional stories. He has won numerous awards including the Chaso Award, Karnataka Sahitya Parishad Award, and the Andhra Pradesh Ugadi Puraskaram.

Hansda Sowvendra Shekhar (b. 1983) is a doctor from Jharkhand. He received the Sahitya Akademi Yuva Puraskar in 2015. His critically acclaimed books include *The Mysterious Ailment of Rupi Baskey* (shortlisted for the Hindu Prize and Crossword Award), *My Father's Garden* (shortlisted for the JCB Prize), and *The Adivasi Will Not Dance* (shortlisted for The Hindu Prize). Sowvendra translates writings from Santhali, Hindi, and Bengali into English.

Aruni Kashyap (b. 1984) is the author of the novels *How to Date a Fanatic, The House With a Thousand Stories, Noikhon Etia Duroit*, and the story collection *His Father's Disease*. Along with editing a collection of stories called *How to Tell the Story of an Insurgency*, he has translated three novels from Assamese to English. Recipient of a Harvard Radcliffe Fellowship, the National Endowment for the Arts Fellowship, the Faculty Research Grant in the Humanities and Arts Program, the Arts Lab Faculty Fellowship, and the Charles Wallace India Trust Scholarship for Creative Writing to the University of Edinburgh, his poetry collection, *There is No Good Time for Bad News*, was nominated for several prestigious awards. He is an Associate Professor of English & Creative Writing and the Director of the Creative Writing Program at the University of Georgia, Athens.

Kanishk Tharoor (b. 1984) is the author of *Swimmer Among the Stars*, an award-winning collection of short stories. His writing has appeared in publications around the world, including the *New York Times*, *The Guardian*, *The Caravan*, and the *Times of India*. He is the presenter of the BBC radio series *Museum of Lost Objects*. He is a senior editor of *Foreign Affairs* magazine. He grew up in and currently lives in New York City with his wife and two children.

Aishwarya Subramanian (b. 1985) is an assistant professor of English at O. P. Jindal Global University. She has previously worked as an editor, book reviewer, and columnist. She holds a PhD in English literature from the University of Newcastle. She's also a reviews editor at *Strange Horizons*, an award-winning magazine of speculative fiction.

Avinuo Kire (b. 1985) is a writer and teacher. She is the author of *The Power to Forgive and Other Stories*, *The Last Light of Glory Days and Other Stories*, *Where the Cobbled Path Leads*, and a collection of poetry, *Where Wildflowers Grow*, and has co-authored an anthology of oral narratives entitled *Naga Heritage Centre, People Stories: Volume One*. Kire lives in Kohima where she teaches English at Kohima College.

Amal (b. 1987) is a Malayalam novelist, short story writer, graphic novelist, illustrator, and cartoonist from Kerala. He is a graduate in painting from the Raja Ravi Varma College of Fine Arts and a postgraduate in Art History from VisvaBharati. His first novel, *Kalhanan*, was shortlisted for the Kerala Sahitya Akademi Award and later won the Sidhardha Award and K. Sarasvathi Amma Award. His second novel, *Vyasanasamuchayam*, won the 2018 Kendra Sahitya Akademi Yuva Puraskar and Basheer Yuva Prathibha Award. He has received several other awards including the Kerala Sahitya Akademi Geetha Hiranyan Endowment for best short story collection in 2019. He lives between Thiruvananthapuram and Tokyo.

Dheeba Nazir (b. 1988) is a research scholar and teacher. She has translated three books from Kashmiri into Urdu: *Gul Bakawali Dastan*, *Kuliyaat Abdul Ahad Azad*, and *Kuliyaat Ropi Bhawani*. In 2008, she received the Sahitya Akademi Yuva Puraskar for her collection of Kashmiri short stories, *Zareen Zakham*.

Shreya Ila Anasuya (b. 1989) is a writer from Kolkata. Anasuya's fiction has appeared in *Strange Horizons* and the *Magazine of Fantasy & Science Fiction*, among others, and has been recognized by the Toto Award for Creative Writing in English, the Otherwise Fellowship, and the Sangam House Residency. Her story 'Gul' was originally published in the anthology *Magical Women* (ed. Sukanya Venkatraghavan) and was adapted into a stage show.

Lakshmikanth K. Ayyagari (b. 1990) is from Visakhapatnam but now lives in Rajahmundry, a city on the banks of the river Godavari. His day job involves data, predictions, s-shaped curves, and loan defaults. On most nights, he finds warmth and comfort in literature.

Varsha Dinesh (b. 1992) is a writer and marketing professional from myth-haunted Kerala. She is a member of the Clarion West Workshop class of 2022. Her work has previously appeared in *Strange Horizons* and *Podcastle*. She is an avid enthusiast of folklore, theatre, and pop music. She is currently working on her first novel.

Bhavika Govil (b. 1993) was born in New Delhi yet dreams of the sea. Her debut novel, *Hot Water*, is forthcoming with HarperCollins India in 2025. A portion of the manuscript won the 2021 Pontas & JJ Bola Emerging Writers Prize and was a finalist for the DHA New Writers' Open Week. Her short fiction won the Bound Short Story Prize, was shortlisted for the Queen Mary Wasafiri New Writing Prize, longlisted for the Toto Award for Creative Writing (English), and was a notable contender for the Bristol Short Story Prize. She has performed at the Edinburgh International Book Festival, Paisley Book Festival, and Push the Boat Out Festival. She has a Master's in Creative Writing from the University of Edinburgh.

NOTES ON THE AUTHORS

Raam Mori (b. 1993) was one of the youngest recipients of the Sahitya Akademi Award in 2017. His short story collections in Gujarati, *Mahotu*, *Coffee Stories*, and *Confession Box* have received great acclaim in Gujarat. He also writes columns, plays, and scripts for television and films.

Sadaf Wani (b. 1993) is a Kashmiri writer and a senior communications professional. Her writings, both fiction and non-fiction, have been published extensively, including in *Himal Southasian*, *Scroll.in*, and *Inverse Journal*, among others. Her short stories have been featured in two critically acclaimed anthologies—*The Greatest Indian Stories Ever Told* (2023) and *A Case of Indian Marvels: Dazzling Stories from the Country's Finest New Writers* (2022). *City as Memory: A Short Biography of Srinagar* is her first book.

A. M. Gautam (b. 1994) is an internationally published author whose work explores and examines India's sociopolitical curiosities through the lenses of speculative fiction and magical realism. One of his stories was included in the Best Asian Fiction Anthology by *Kitaab*, Singapore, in 2018, and most recently his work has appeared in the April 2022 issue of the literary journal *Orca*. His debut book is *Indian Millennials: Who Are They, Really?* (2024).

Aravind Jayan (b. 1994) is a writer from Thiruvananthapuram. He's the winner of the 2017 Toto Award for Creative Writing (English) and was shortlisted for the Commonwealth Short Story Prize in 2021. His first novel, *Teen Couple Have Fun Outdoors*, was published in July 2022.

NOTES ON THE TRANSLATORS

Leelawati Mohapatra published her debut novel, *Hanging by a Tail*, in 2008. She has co-translated (with K. K. Mohapatra and Paul St-Pierre) extensively from Odia into English. Her books of translation include, among others, *The HarperCollins Book of Oriya Short Stories, Ants, Ghosts and Whispering Trees: An Anthology of Oriya Short Stories, J P Das: Sundardas, Fakir Mohan Senapati: The Brideprice and Other Stories,* and *Laxmikanta Mahapatra: Uncle One Eye*.

Paul St-Pierre is a former professor of Translation Studies at Montreal University. He has co-edited several books on translation theory and practice and has spent nearly a quarter-century collaborating with, apart from the Mohapatras, several Odia translators such as Ganeswar Mishra, Basant Kumar Tripathy, Himansu Sekhar Mohapatra, Rabindra Swain, and Dipti Ranjan Patnaik. With the Mohapatras he has also recently finished a new translation of Fakir Mohan Senapati's iconic novel, *Chha Mana Atha Guntha*.

K. K. Mohapatra has written three collections of short stories, a novel, a book of non-fiction, and an autobiography. He has also translated into Odia selected stories by Isaac Bashevis Singer, Jean-Paul Sartre, Franz Kafka, as well as William Shakespeare's *King Lear*, and collaborated with Leelawati Mohapatra and Paul St-Pierre on numerous works of translation from Odia into English.

Arunava Sinha translates classic, modern, and contemporary Bengali fiction and non-fiction from Bangladesh and India into English. He also translates fiction from English into Bengali. Over seventy of his translations have been published so far in India, the UK, and the US. He is the editor and translator of *The Greatest Bengali Stories Ever Told*. He has won India's top translation prize, the Crossword Award for translated books, twice. He teaches at Ashoka University, where he is also the co-director of the Ashoka Centre for Translation, and is the Books Editor at *Scroll.in*.

Muhammad Umar Memon was professor emeritus of Urdu literature and Islamic studies at the University of Wisconsin, Madison. He was a critic, short story writer, and translated numerous works of Urdu fiction. He was editor of the *Annual of Urdu Studies* (1993–2014). He passed away in June 2018 in Madison, Wisconsin.

P. Raja, formerly a professor of English, Kanchi Mamunivar Centre for Postgraduate Studies, Pondicherry, is a bilingual author. Raja has published more than 5,000 articles, short stories, poems, interviews, plays, reviews, skits, translations, and features in no less than 350 newspapers and magazines, both in India and abroad. He has authored thirty-two books in English and fourteen books in Tamil.

Rita Kothari is the Vani Foundation Distinguished Translator and has translated widely from Gujarati and Sindhi. A multilingual scholar, Kothari speaks and writes on language politics, translation theory, Partition, and border studies. She is the author of *Translating India*, *The Burden of Refuge*, and numerous other publications. She teaches at Ashoka University.

Ramachandra Sharma was a writer, critic, translator, and educationist. He wrote several anthologies of poems and short stories, as well as plays. Apart from Masti Venkatesha Iyengar, he translated the works of distinguished Kannada writers like Kuvempu and Yashwant Chittal. He received the Sahitya Akademi Award in 1998 for his poetry collection, *Saptapadi*. Other notable awards include the Karnataka Sahithya Academy award, the Karnataka Rajyotsava award, and the Shivaram Karanth Award. He passed away in Bengaluru in 2005.

Dasu Krishnamoorty is an anthologist, translator, and storyteller based in New Jersey. He was educated at Andhra University, the University of Bombay (LLB), and Osmania University (Journalism), before becoming an influential Indian print media journalist. He has worked in an editorial capacity at the *Indian Express, Times of India,* and *Patriot*. He was a senior political commentator with All India Radio and taught mass communications at Osmania University, the Indian Institute of Mass Communications in New Delhi, and the University of Hyderabad. His works include *1947 Santoshabad Passenger and Other Stories,* and *The Seaside Bride and Other Stories*.

Tamraparni Dasu, along with her father, Dasu Krishnamoorty, founded the literary non-profit organization IndiaWrites Publishers Inc. to support high quality translation and the dissemination of short fiction written in Indian languages. The non-profit supported *Literary Voices of India* (2006–12), an online magazine, culminating in the anthology *1947 Santoshabad Passenger and Other Stories*. Dasu publishes genre fiction under the name T. Dasu. Her works include *Spy, Interrupted: The Waiting Wife* and *Spy, Interrupted: The Perfect Candidate*. She has a PhD in Statistics from the University of Rochester and specializes in computational statistics, machine learning, data quality, and stream analytics. She was a Lead Inventive Scientist at AT&T and has numerous patents and academic publications to her credit.

Gowri Ramnarayan is a playwright, theatre director, journalist (formerly deputy editor, *The Hindu,* now freelance writer), and was a vocal accompanist to legendary musician M. S. Subbulakshmi. Dr Ramnarayan's *Dark Horse & Other Plays* anthologizes her original plays. She has authored children's books and a biography of M. S. Subbulakshmi (*MS & Radha*), and translated two plays by Marathi playwright Vijay Tendulkar, and the Tamil short stories of Kalki Krishnamurthy.

Chandan Gowda is a writer, translator, and academic. He is the Ramakrishna Hegde Chair Professor of Decentralization and Development at the Institute for Social and Economic Change, Bengaluru. He is the author of *Another India: Events, Memories, People*. Currently, he is working on translating and editing several anthologies.

Paul Melo e Castro teaches comparative literature and Portuguese at the University of Glasgow. He is a regular translator of short stories from across the Portuguese-speaking world.

O. V. Usha is a Malayalam poet and novelist. She has published four volumes of poems and a novel. Her articles have appeared in various journals. She served the Mahatma Gandhi University, Kottayam, as its director of publications. She won the Kerala State Film Award for Best Lyrics for *Mazha,* a Malayalam film released in 2000.

A. J. Thomas is a poet, editor, and translator who writes in English. He has more than twenty books to his credit and is the former editor of *Indian Literature,* the Sahitya Akademi's bi-monthly journal. Thomas taught English at Benghazi University, Libya, and worked as a Senior Consultant at IGNOU. He is a recipient of the Katha Award, AKMG Prize, and the Vodafone Crossword Award for Translation. Thomas holds a Senior Fellowship, Government of India, and was an Honorary Fellow, Department of Culture, Government of South Korea.

Poonam Saxena is a journalist, writer, and translator. She worked with the *Hindustan Times* for several years, first as editor of *Brunch* and then of the weekend section. She has translated Dharamvir Bharati's *Gunahon ka Devta* from Hindi to English (*Chander & Sudha*), Rahi Masoom Raza's *Scene: 75*, and co-authored filmmaker Karan Johar's memoir, *An Unsuitable Boy*. She lives in Delhi.

Neerja Mattoo is an eminent writer, teacher, and translator who has taught in Kashmir for over three decades. She has published five books, the most recent being the critically acclaimed *The Mystic and the Lyric: Four Women Poets from Kashmir*. Her works have been published by the Sahitya Akademi, and she has been awarded a Fellowship and a Visitorship to Oxford, by the Ministry of Education and the British Council respectively. She lives in Srinagar.

Khushwant Singh was, arguably, India's best-known and most widely read author, columnist, and journalist. He was the founder-editor of *Yojana*, and editor of the *Illustrated Weekly of India*, *National Herald* and the *Hindustan Times*. He wrote several books, including the novels *Train to Pakistan*, *I Shall Not Hear the Nightingale* and *Delhi*; his autobiography, *Truth, Love & a Little Malice*; and the two-volume *A History of the Sikhs*. He also translated from Hindi, Urdu, and Punjabi. Khushwant Singh was a member of the Rajya Sabha from 1980 to 1986. In 2007, he was awarded India's second highest civilian honour, the Padma Vibhushan. He passed away in 2014.

Vernon Gonsalves is a social and political activist. He was on the editorial board of *Thingi Kamgar Masik*, a Marathi-language monthly magazine for workers, from 1981 to 1986. He has been associated with the Marathi magazine *Jahirnama* since the 1980s; until his arrest in August 2007 (on charges of being a Naxalite), he was also involved with a bilingual Hindi-Marathi magazine, *Kamgar*. He was released from prison in 2013.

Navtej Sarna was India's Ambassador to the United States, High Commissioner to the United Kingdom, and Ambassador to Israel. He has also served as Secretary to the Government of India and as the Foreign Office Spokesperson. His earlier diplomatic assignments were in Moscow, Warsaw, Thimphu, Tehran, Geneva, and Washington DC. His literary work includes the novels *Crimson Spring*, *The Exile*, and *We Weren't Lovers Like That*, the short story collection *Winter Evenings*, non-fiction works *The Book of Nanak*, *Second Thoughts*, and *Indians at Herod's Gate*, as well as two translations, *Zafarnama* and *Savage Harvest*. He is a prolific columnist and commentator on foreign policy and literary matters, contributing regularly to media platforms in India and abroad.

C. M. Naim is an American scholar of Urdu language and literature. He is currently Professor Emeritus at the University of Chicago. Naim is the founding editor of both *Annual of Urdu Studies* and *Mahfil* (now *Journal of South Asian Literature*), as well as the author of the definitive textbook for Urdu pedagogy in English.

Christi A. Merrill is an assistant professor of South Asian Literature and postcolonial studies at the University of Michigan. Her translations from Hindi, French, and Rajasthani and essays on translation have appeared in journals such as *Genre*, *Studies in Twentieth Century Literature*, *The Iowa Review*, *Modern Poetry in Translation*, and *Indian Literature*, the Sahitya Akademi's bi-monthly journal.

Kailash Kabir is an award-winning translator and poet of Hindi and Rajasthani who makes his home in Jodhpur.

NOTES ON THE TRANSLATORS

Shanta Gokhale is an accomplished translator and writer of novels, plays, short stories, film scripts, and innumerable newspaper articles. She has translated essays, short fiction, novels, autobiographies, and plays from Marathi into English and a play and a novel from English into Marathi. Gokhale has published a volume on the history of Marathi theatre and edited books on the works of theatre directors Satyadev Dubey, Veenapani Chawla, and oral history experimental theatre in Mumbai.

Geeta Kapur is a noted art critic, art historian, and curator. One of the pioneers of art criticism in India, she taught in the Humanities and Social Sciences department of IIT, Delhi, from 1967 to 1973. She has held fellowships at the Indian Institute of Advanced Study, Shimla, and Nehru Memorial Museum and Library, New Delhi.

Malini Seshadri is a freelance writer, editor, and translator based in Chennai. She has over three decades of experience writing newspaper columns and magazine articles on a wide variety of themes. Recently, she co-authored a series of value education books for schools titled *Living in Harmony*. She has translated Bama's novel *Vanmam*, and ten Tamil short stories by various authors as part of an anthology. She has also written a work of fiction for children, and co-edited a textbook for an undergraduate programme.

Gayatri Bhattacharyya worked in St. Edmund's College, Shillong, before joining Gauhati University. After retirement, she took up translation as a hobby, and has since translated many anthologies of short stories and novels written by eminent Assamese writers, into English, including works by Sarat Chandra Goswami, Bhabendra Nath Saikia, Mamoni Raisom Goswami, Anuradha Sarma Pujari, Dipak Barkakati, and Birinchi Kumar Barua. She has written fifteen books, and has published short stories and articles in anthologies and newspapers.

H. Y. Sharada Prasad began his professional life as a journalist. He went on to edit the Planning Commission's journal, *Yojana*, and then became Indira Gandhi's media adviser and speech writer. He was the Joint Editor of the *Selected Works of Jawaharlal Nehru* and authored several books, the last of which was *The Book I Won't Be Writing*. He passed away in 2008.

Anil Zankar is a film-maker and a winner of two national awards for writing. He has taught scriptwriting, direction, and film history. He has written extensively on films and film history in Marathi and English. His recent work includes a documentary on Dr Jayant Narlikar for the Sahitya Akademi. He is currently working on a book on Mumbai.

Anjali Nerlekar is an associate professor at Rutgers University, New Brunswick, in New Jersey, USA. Her first book is *Bombay Modern: Arun Kolatkar and Bilingual Literary Culture* (2017). She has also co-edited (with Laetitia Zecchini) a special double issue of the *Journal of Postcolonial Writing* ('The Worlds of Bombay Poetry', 2017). Her other publications include translations of Arun Kolatkar's poetry and texts of Marathi short fiction, essays on modern Indian poets, and on Indo-Caribbean writing. Her ongoing project (in collaboration with Bronwen Bledsoe at Cornell University South Asia collections) is the building of an archive of multilingual post-1960 Bombay poetry at Cornell University entitled 'The Bombay Poets Archive'.

Lakshmi Holmström was a British-Indian writer, translator, and literary critic. She is known for her translations of Tamil novels and short stories by important modern writers such as Sundara Ramaswamy, Ambai, Ashokamitran, Imayam, and Bama. Her translation of *Karukku* by Bama won the Crossword Book Award 2000. She was awarded an MBE in 2011 for her contributions to the field of literature. She passed away in 2016.

Xavier Cota has worked as a teacher, banker, and sports administrator, and translates fiction from Konkani to English and non-fiction from Portuguese to English. His translated fiction and other articles have appeared in publications like *The Week*, *Man's World*, *Katha Prize Stories*, and the Sahitya Akademi's journal. He won the 2005 Katha Award for Translation. His Konkani-to-English translations of Damodar Mauzo's works include the short story collections *The Wait: And Other Stories*, *These Are My Children*, and *Teresa's Man and Other Stories from Goa*, and the novel *Tsunami Simon*. He lives in Betalbatim, Goa.

Nirupama Dutt is a poet, translator, journalist, and literary critic. She writes in Punjabi and English. She has published an anthology of poetry, *Ik Nadi Sanwali Jahi*, for which she received the Punjabi Akademi Award. She has translated *Poet of the Revolution: The Memoirs of Lal Singh Dil*, Punjabi short stories in a volume called *Stories of the Soil*, and Gulzar's anthology of poetry, *Pluto*. She wrote the biography of a Dalit icon of Punjab, *The Ballad of Bant Singh*.

Aruni Kashyap is the author of the novels, *The House With a Thousand Stories* and *Noikhon Etia Duroit*, the story collection, *His Father's Disease*, and the poetry collection, *There is No Good Time for Bad News*. Along with editing a collection of stories called *How to Tell the Story of an Insurgency*, he has translated three novels from Assamese to English. He has received a Harvard Radcliffe Fellowship, the National Endowment for the Arts Fellowship, the Faculty Research Grant in the Humanities and Arts Program, the Arts Lab Faculty Fellowship, and the Charles Wallace India Trust Scholarship for Creative Writing to the University of Edinburgh. Currently, he is an Associate Professor of English & Creative Writing and the Director of the Creative Writing Program at the University of Georgia, Athens.

M. Asaduddin is an author, critic, and translator. Currently, he is Dean, Faculty of Humanities and Languages, Jamia Millia Islamia, New Delhi. His books include *Premchand: The Complete Short Stories* in four volumes (editor and translator); *Premchand in World Languages: Translation, Reception and Cinematic Representations*; and *Filming Fiction: Tagore, Premchand and Ray*, among others. He is the recipient of the Katha Award, the Dr A. K. Ramanujan Award, the Sahitya Akademi Award, and the Crossword Book Award.

C. T. Indra is the former Head of English, Madras University. She has translated short stories, plays, novellas, and critical writings from Tamil into English. Indra's translations include *The Legend of Nandan*, *Cross Section* with Prema Jagannathan, *Internal Colloquies*, *Indira Parthasarathy: Three Plays* with T. Sriraman, and *The Solitary Sprout: Selected stories of R. Chudamani* with T. Sriraman. She won the Katha–British Council Special Mention Award for translation (1994) and the Katha Award for Tamil (1995).

Jayanth Kodkani is a writer and journalist based in Bengaluru. He has written extensively on social and cultural topics, besides trying his hand at fiction and translation. His stories and essays have been part of anthologies like the *Puffin Book of Funny Stories*, *Where the Rain is Born*, *Dots and Lines*, and *Playback: Sports Legends of Bangalore*. He has co-edited an anthology entitled *Beantown Boomtown: Bangalore* *in the World of Words*. Among his English translations of Kannada are K. V. Akshara's *Two Plays*.

Vidya Pai stumbled on to the field of translation after winning the Konkani Award at the Katha-British Council Translation Contest in 1993. Her translated stories have appeared in several anthologies published by Penguin, Katha, the Sahitya Akademi, *Govapuri*, *Goa Today*, and *Navhind Times*. She has translated seven Konkani novels; the most recent of them are Mahableshwar Sail's *Forest Saga* (2014) and *Age of Frenzy* (2017), and Meena Kakodkar's *Abode of Joy* (2020). She has also translated and published *Kaleidoscope*, a collection of Ravindra Kelekar's essays, and *Mirage and Other Stories*, a collection of short stories by Damodar Mauzo.

N. S. Murty has an M.Sc. in Applied Mathematics and an MA in English Literature from Andhra University. Murty was also a graduate student of English Literature at the University of Houston, Texas, in Spring 2011. He has published two collections of his poetry, *Incidental Muses* and *PenChants*; two collections of Telugu poems translated into English, *The Wakes on the Horizon* and *The Voices of the Surf*; a collection of the 100 best poems from world literature rendered into Telugu with a brief introduction for each poem, *Kavitvamto Edadugulu*; and a collection of the best short stories from world literature rendered into Telugu, *Katha Lekhini*.

R. S. Krishna Moorthy was born and brought up in Vizianagaram. Krishna Moorthy was friends with the famous Telugu short story writers Bhamidipati Rama Gopalam (Bharago) and Avasarala Ramakrishna Rao. Starting his career as stenographer in Bhilai Steel Plant, he retired as OSD in Ferro Scrap Nigam Ltd. His short story collection, *Chayachitralu*, won the Jyeshtha Literary Trust Prize in 1997. He also won the Katha-British Council South Asian Translation Award 2000 for his translation of Allam Seshagiri Rao's story 'Mrigatrishna'.